THE
COLLECTED
STORIES

Arthur C. Clarke

This Collection copyright © Arthur C. Clarke 2000

All rights reserved

The right of Arthur C. Clarke to be identified as the author
of this work has been asserted by them in accordance with
the Copyright, Designs and Patents Act 1988

This edition published in Great Britain in 2001 by

Gollancz
An imprint of the Orion Publishing Group
Orion House, 5 Upper St Martin's Lane,
London WC2H 9EA

11 13 15 17 19 20 18 16 14 12

Published in Great Britain in 2002 by Gollancz
An imprint of the Orion Publishing Group

A CIP catalogue record for this book is available
from the British Library.

ISBN-13 978 1 85798 323 4

Printed in Great Britain by
Clays Ltd, St Ives plc

CONTENTS

'There's an incredible range of subject matter ... much remains fresh ... It almost goes without saying that this is an essential addition to any enthusiast's library.' *Time Out*

'Nearly one thousand pages of some of the best short fiction the field has ever seen. This is probably the most significant reprint collection of the year, and it certainly deserves to be in the library of anyone who considers himself or herself a fan' *Science Fiction Chronicle*

' "The Sentinel" ... is just one of the endless delights in this astonishing volume. The *Collected Stories* also contains such classics as "The Songs of Distant Earth" and the tale that many people regard as the greatest single SF short story ever written, "The Nine Billion Names of God". Even if you have all these tales in individual volumes, this is a pretty tempting collection.' *Starburst.*

'We get a good idea of Clarke's development as a writer, his full range of tones from facetious or sardonic to poetic or visionary, and his success and failures as a commentator on man's evolution. Many of the stories have dated surprisingly little, and some are still very effective.' *Times Literary Supplement*

Also by Arthur C. Clarke

FICTION

Against the Fall of Night
Childhood's End
The City and The Stars
The Deep Range
Dolphin Island
Earthlight
A Fall of Moondust
The Fountains of
  Paradise
The Ghost from the
  Grand Banks
Glide Path
The Hammer of God
Imperial Earth
Islands in the Sky
The Lion of Comarre
The Lost Worlds of 2001
Prelude to Space
Reach for Tomorrow
Rendezvous with Rama
The Sands of Mars
The Songs of Distant
  Earth
The Space Trilogy
  Islands in the Sky
  Earthlight
  The Sands of Mars
2001: A Space Odyssey
2010: Odyssey Two
2061: Odyssey Three
3001: The Final Odyssey

With Gentry Lee:
Cradle
Rama II
The Garden of Rama
Rama Revealed

With Mike McQuay
Richter 10

*With Michael Kube-
  McDowell:*
The Trigger

With Stephen Baxter
The Light of Other Days

SHORT FICTION

Across the Sea of Stars
An Arthur C. Clarke
  Omnibus
An Arthur C. Clarke
  2nd Omnibus

The Best of Arthur C.
  Clarke
The Collected Stories
Expedition to Earth
From the Oceans, From
  the Stars
More Than One
  Universe
The Nine Billion Names
  of God
The Other Side of the
  Sky
Prelude to Mars
The Sentinel
Tales from Planet Earth
Tales from the White
  Hart
Tales of Ten Worlds
The Wind From the Sun

NON-FICTION

Ascent to Orbit
Astounding Days
By Space Possessed
The Challenge of the
  Sea
The Challenge of the
  Spaceship
The Coast of Coral
The Exploration of the
  Moon
The Exploration of
  Space
Going into Space
Greeting, Carbon Based
  Bipeds!
How the World was
  One
Interplanetary Flight
The Making of a Moon
Profiles of the Future
The Promise of Space
The Reefs of Taprobane
Report on Planet Three
The Snows of Olympus
The View from Serendip
Voice Across the Sea
Voices From the Sky
The Young Traveller in
  Space
1984: Spring

With the Astronauts:
First on the Moon

With Mike Wilson:
Boy Beneath the Sea
The First Five Fathoms
Indian Ocean
  Adventure
Indian Ocean Treasure
The Treasure of the
  Great Reef

With Peter Hyams:
The Odyssey File

With the Editors of Life:
Man and Space

With Robert Silverberg:
Into Space

With Chesley Bonestell:
Beyond Jupiter

*With Simon Welfare and
  John Fairley:*
Arthur C. Clarke's
  Mysterious World
Arthur C. Clarke's
  World of Strange
  Powers
Arthur C. Clarke's
  Chronicles of the
  Strange & Mysterious
Arthur C. Clarke's A–Z

AS EDITOR

(Fiction)
Science Fiction Hall of
  Fame III
Three for Tomorrow
Time Probe
Arthur C. Clarke's
  Venus Prime 1–VI
(Non-Fiction)
The Coming of the
  Space Age
Arthur C. Clarke's July
  20, 2019
Project Solar Sail

Edited by Keith Daniels:
Arthur C. Clarke & Lord
  Dunsany – A
  Correspondence
Arthur C. Clarke & C. S.
  Lewis – A
  Correspondence

FOREWORD

According to my indefatigable bibliographer, David N. Samuelson (*Arthur C Clarke – a primary and secondary bibliography, G.K. Hall*), my first attempts at fiction appeared in the Huish Magazine for Autumn 1932. I was then on the Editorial Board of the school Journal, which was presided over by our English master, Capt. E. B. Mitford – to whom I later dedicated my collection *The Nine Billion Names of God*. My contributions were letters, purporting to be from old boys, working in exotic environments, which clearly had science-fictional inspiration.

But what *is* science fiction anyway?

Attempts to define it will continue as long as people write PhD theses. Meanwhile, I am content to accept Damon Knight's magisterial: 'Science Fiction is what I point to and say *"That's* science fiction."'

Much blood has also been spilled on the carpet in attempts to distinguish between science fiction and fantasy. I have suggested an operational definition: science fiction is something that *could* happen – but usually you wouldn't want it to. Fantasy is something that *couldn't* happen – though often you only wish that it could.

The writer of science fiction is faced with a problem which the writers of so-called main-stream fiction – devoted to a tiny sub-section of the *real* universe – don't have to worry about. They seldom need to spend pages setting the scene: sometimes one sentence will do the trick. When you read 'It was a foggy evening in Baker Street', you're there in a millisecond. The science fiction writer, constructing a totally alien environment, may need several volumes to do the job: the classic example is Frank Herbert's masterwork *Dune* and its sequels.

So it's rather surprising that many of the finest works of science fiction are short stories. I can still recall the impact of Stanley Weinbaum's *A Martian Odyssey* when the July 1934 *Wonder Stories* arrived. When I close my eyes I can see that characteristic Paul cover: never before or since did I read a story – and then go straight back to the beginning and read it right through again . . .

So perhaps the short story is to the whole science fiction *genre* as the sonnet is to the epic poem. The challenge is to create perfection in as small space as possible.

But how long is a short story? I am sorry you asked me that . . .

The shortest one you'll find in this volume contains 31 words; the longest, more than 18,000. Beyond that we enter the realm of the novella (horrid word) which merges imperceptibly into the full-length novel.

Please remember that while these stories were written the world underwent greater changes than in the whole of previous history. Inevitably some of them have been dated by events: however I have resisted all temptations for retrospective editing. To put matters in perspective, roughly a third of these stories were written when most people believed talk of space flight was complete lunacy. By the time the last dozen were written, men had walked on the Moon.

By mapping out possible futures, as well as a good many improbable ones, the science fiction writer does a great service to the community. He encourages in his readers flexibility of mind, readiness to accept and even welcome change – in one word, adaptability. Perhaps no attribute is more important in this age. The dinosaurs disappeared because they could not adapt to their changing environment. We shall disappear if we cannot adapt to an environment that now contains spaceships, computers – and thermonuclear weapons.

Nothing could be more ridiculous, therefore, than the accusation sometimes made against science fiction that it is escapist. That charge can indeed be made against much fantasy – but so what? There are times (this century has provided a more than ample supply) when some form of escape is essential, and any art form that supplies it is not to be despised. And as C.S.Lewis (creator of both superb science fiction and fantasy) once remarked to me: 'Who are the people most opposed to escapism? Jailors!'

C. P. Snow ended his famous essay 'Science and Government' by stressing the vital importance of 'the gift of foresight'. He pointed out that men often have wisdom without possessing foresight.

Science fiction has done much to redress the balance. Even if its writers do not always possess wisdom, the best ones have certainly possessed foresight. And that is an even greater gift from the gods.

xxxxxxxxx

I am greatly indebted to Malcolm Edwards and Maureen Kincaid Speller for collecting – and indeed locating – virtually all the short pieces of fiction I have written over a period of almost seventy years.

Arthur C. Clarke
Colombo, Sri Lanka

June 2000

Travel by Wire!

First published in *Amateur Science Fiction Stories*, December 1937
Collected in *The Best of Arthur C. Clarke 1937–1955*

Science fiction has always encouraged an enormous amount of amateur writing, and there have been literally thousands of duplicated (sometimes printed) magazines put out by enthusiastic 'fans'. [. . .] The first stories I ever completed appeared in some of these magazines [. . .]. If they do nothing else they may serve as a kind of absolute zero from which my later writing may be calibrated. 'Travel by Wire!' was my first published story.

You people can have no idea of the troubles and trials we had to endure before we perfected the radio-transporter, not that it's quite perfect even yet. The greatest difficulty, as it had been in television thirty years before, was improving definition, and we spent nearly five years over that little problem. As you will have seen in the Science Museum, the first object we transmitted was a wooden cube, which was assembled all right, only instead of being one solid block it consisted of millions of little spheres. In fact, it looked just like a solid edition of one of the early television pictures, for instead of dealing with the object molecule by molecule or better still electron by electron, our scanners took little chunks at a time.

This didn't matter for some things, but if we wanted to transmit objects of art, let alone human beings, we would have to improve the process considerably. This we managed to do by using the delta-ray scanners all round our subject, above, below, right, left, in front and behind. It was a lovely game synchronising all six, I can tell you, but when it was done we found that the transmitted elements were ultra-microscopic in size, which was quite good enough for most purposes.

Then, when they weren't looking, we borrowed a guinea pig from the biology people on the 37th floor, and sent it through the apparatus. It came through in excellent condition, except for the fact it was dead. So we had to return it to its owner with a polite request for a post-mortem. They raved a bit at first, saying that the unfortunate creature had been inoculated with the only specimens of some germs they'd spent months rearing from the bottle. They were so annoyed, in fact, that they flatly refused our request.

Such insubordination on the part of mere biologists was of course

1

deplorable, and we promptly generated a high-frequency field in their laboratory and gave them all fever for a few minutes. The post-mortem results came up in half an hour, the verdict being that the creature was in perfect condition but had died of shock, with a rider to the effect that if we wanted to try the experiment again we should blindfold our victims. We were also told that a combination lock had been fitted to the 37th floor to protect it from the depredations of kleptomaniacal mechanics who should be washing cars in a garage. We could not let this pass, so we immediately X-rayed their lock and to their complete consternation told them what the key-word was.

That is the best of being in our line, you can always do what you like with the other people. The chemists on the next floor were our only serious rivals, but we generally came out on top. Yes, I remember that time they slipped some vile organic stuff into our lab through a hole in the ceiling. We had to work in respirators for a month, but we had our revenge later. Every night after the staff had left, we used to send a dose of mild cosmics into the lab and curdled all their beautiful precipitates, until one evening old Professor Hudson stayed behind and we nearly finished him off. But to get back to my story –

We obtained another guinea pig, chloroformed it, and sent it through the transmitter. To our delight, it revived. We immediately had it killed and stuffed for the benefit of posterity. You can see it in the museum with the rest of our apparatus.

But if we wanted to start a passenger service, this would never do – it would be too much like an operation to suit most people. However, by cutting down the transmitting time to a ten-thousandth of a second, and thus reducing the shock, we managed to send another guinea pig in full possession of its faculties. This one was also stuffed.

The time had obviously come for one of us to try out the apparatus but as we realised what a loss it would be to humanity should anything go wrong, we found a suitable victim in the person of Professor Kingston, who teaches Greek or something foolish on the 197th floor. We lured him to the transmitter with a copy of *Homer*, switched on the field, and by the row from the receiver, we knew he'd arrived safely and in full possession of his faculties, such as they were. We would have liked to have had him stuffed as well, but it couldn't be arranged.

After that we went through in turns, found the experience quite painless, and decided to put the device on the market. I expect you can remember the excitement there was when we first demonstrated our little toy to the Press. Of course we had the dickens of a job convincing them that it wasn't a fake, and they didn't really believe it until they had been through the transporter themselves. We drew the line, though, at Lord Rosscastle, who would have blown the fuses even if we could have got him into the transmitter.

This demonstration gave us so much publicity that we had no trouble at all in forming a company. We bade a reluctant farewell to the Research Foundation, told the remaining scientists that perhaps one day we'd heap coals of fire on their heads by sending them a few millions, and started to design our first commercial senders and receivers.

The first service was inaugurated on May 10th, 1962. The ceremony took place in London, at the transmitting end, though at the Paris receiver there were enormous crowds watching to see the first passengers arrive, and probably hoping they wouldn't. Amid cheers from the assembled thousands, the Prime Minister pressed a button (which wasn't connected to anything), the chief engineer threw a switch (which was) and a large Union Jack faded from view and appeared again in Paris, rather to the annoyance of some patriotic Frenchmen.

After that, passengers began to stream through at a rate which left the Customs officials helpless. The service was a great and instantaneous success, as we only charged £2 per person. This we considered very moderate, for the electricity used cost quite one-hundredth of a penny.

Before long we had services to all the big cities of Europe, by cable that is, not radio. A wired system was safer, though it was dreadfully difficult to lay polyaxial cables, costing £500 a mile, under the Channel. Then, in conjunction with the Post Office, we began to develop internal services between the large towns. You may remember our slogans 'Travel by Phone' and 'It's quicker by Wire' which were heard everywhere in 1963. Soon, practically everyone used our circuits and we were handling thousands of tons of freight per day.

Naturally, there were accidents, but we could point out that we had done what no Minister of Transport had ever done, reduced road fatalities to a mere ten thousand a year. We lost one client in six million, which was pretty good even to start with, though our record is even better now. Some of the mishaps that occurred were very peculiar indeed, and in fact there are quite a few cases which we haven't explained to the dependants yet, or to the insurance companies either.

One common complaint was earthing along the line. When that happened, our unfortunate passenger was just dissipated into nothingness. I suppose his or her molecules would be distributed more or less evenly over the entire earth. I remember one particularly gruesome accident when the apparatus failed in the middle of a transmission. You can guess the result . . . Perhaps even worse was what happened when two lines got crossed and the currents were mixed.

Of course, not all accidents were as bad as these. Sometimes, owing to a high resistance in the circuit, a passenger would lose anything up to five stone in transit, which generally cost us about £1000 and enough free meals to restore the missing embonpoint. Fortunately, we were soon able to make money out of this affair, for fat people came along to be reduced to manageable dimensions. We made a special apparatus which transmitted massive dowagers round resistance coils and reassembled them where they started, minus the cause of the trouble. 'So quick, my dear, and *quite* painless! I'm *sure* they could take off that 150 pounds you want to lose in no time! Or is it 200?'

We also had a good deal of trouble through interference and induction. You see, our apparatus picked up various electrical disturbances and super-imposed them on the object under transmission. As a result many people came out looking like nothing on earth and very little on Mars or Venus. They could usually be straightened out by the plastic surgeons, but some of the products had to be seen to be believed.

Fortunately these difficulties have been largely overcome now that we use the micro-beams for our carrier, though now and then accidents still occur. I expect you remember that big lawsuit we had last year with Lita Cordova, the television star, who claimed £1,000,000 damages from us for alleged loss of beauty. She asserted that one of her eyes had moved during a transmission, but I couldn't see any difference myself and nor could the jury, who had enough opportunity. She had hysterics in the court when our Chief Electrician went into the box and said bluntly, to the alarm of both side's lawyers, that if anything really *had* gone wrong with the transmission, Miss Cordova wouldn't have been able to recognise herself had any cruel person handed her a mirror.

Lots of people ask us when we'll have a service to Venus or Mars. Doubtless that will come in time, but of course the difficulties are pretty considerable. There is so much sun static in space, not to mention the various reflecting layers everywhere. Even the micro-waves are stopped by the Appleton 'Q' layer at 100,000 km, you know. Until we can pierce that, Interplanetary shares are still safe.

Well, I see it's nearly 22, so I'd best be leaving. I have to be in New York by midnight. What's that? Oh no, I'm going by plane. *I* don't travel by wire! You see, I helped invent the thing!

Rockets for me! Good night!

How We Went to Mars

First published in *Amateur Science Fiction Stories*, March 1938
Not previously collected in book form

This story was first published in the third and final issue of *Amateur Science Fiction Stories*, edited by Douglas W. F. Mayer.

(N.B. All characters in this story are entirely fictitious and only exist in the Author's subconscious. Psychoanalysts please apply at the Tradesmens' Entrance.)

It is with considerable trepidation that I now take up my pen to describe the incredible adventures that befell the members of the Snoring-in-the-Hay Rocket Society in the Winter of 1952. Although we would have preferred posterity to be our judge, the members of the society of which I am proud to be President, Secretary and Treasurer, feel that we cannot leave unanswered the accusations – nay, calumnies – made by envious rivals as to our integrity, sobriety and even sanity.

In this connection I would like to take the opportunity of dealing with the fantastic statements regarding our achievements made in the 'Daily Drool' by Prof. Swivel and in the 'Weekly Washout' by Dr Sprocket, but unfortunately space does not permit. In any case, I sincerely hope that no intelligent reader was deceived by these persons' vapourings.

No doubt most of you will recollect the tremendous awakening of public interest in the science of rocketry caused by the celebrated case in 1941 of 'Rex v. British Rocket Society', and its still more celebrated sequel, 'British Rocket Society v. Rex.' The first case, which was started when a five ton rocket descended in the Houses of Parliament upon Admiral Sir Horatio ffroth-ffrenzy, M.P., K.C.B., H.P., D.T., after a most successful stratosphere flight, may be said to have resulted in a draw, thanks to the efforts of Sir Hatrick Pastings, K.C., whom the B.R.S. had managed to brief as a result of their success in selling lunar real estate at exorbitant prices. The appeal brought by the B.R.S. against the restrictions of the 1940 (Rocket Propulsion) Act was an undoubted victory for the society, as the explosion in court of a demonstration model removed all opposition and most of Temple Bar. Incidently, it has recently been discovered after extensive excavations that there were no members of the B.R.S. in the court at the time of the disaster – rather an odd coincidence. Moreover, both the survivors state that a few minutes before the explosion, Mr Hector Heptane, the President of the Society, passed very close to the rocket and then left the court hurriedly. Although an enquiry was started, it was then too late as Mr Heptane had already left for Russia, in order, as he put it, 'to continue work unhampered by the toils of capitalist enterprise, in a country where workers and scientists are properly rewarded by the gratitude of their comrades'. But I digress.

It was not until the repeal of the 1940 Act that progress could continue in England, when a fresh impetus was given to the movement by the discovery in Surrey of a large rocket labelled 'Property of the USSR. Please return to Omsk' – obviously one of Mr Heptane's. A flight from Omsk to England (though quite understandable) was certainly a remarkable achievement, and not until many years later was it discovered that the rocket had been dropped from an aeroplane by the members of the Hickleborough Rocket Association, who even in those days were expert publicity hunters.

By 1945 there were a score of societies in the country, each spreading destruction over rapidly widening areas. My society, though only founded in 1949, already has to its credit one church, two Methodist chapels, five cinemas, seventeen trust houses, and innumerable private residences, some as far away as Weevil-in-the-Wurzle and Little Dithering. However, there can be no doubt in unprejudiced minds that the sudden collapse of the lunar crater Vitus was caused by one of our rockets, in spite of the claims of the French, German, American, Russian, Spanish, Italian, Japanese, Swiss and Danish Societies (to mention only a few), all of whom, we are asked to believe, dispatched rockets moonwards a few days before the phenomenon was witnessed.

At first we contented ourselves with firing large models to considerable heights. These test rockets were fitted with recording baro-thermographs, etc. and our lawyers kept us fully informed as to their landing places. We were progressing very favourably with this important work when the unwarrantable defection of our insurance company forced us to start work on a large, man-carrying space-ship. We already had a sufficiently powerful fuel, details of which I cannot divulge here, save to say that it was a complex hydro-carbon into which our chemist, Dr Badstoff, had with great ingenuity introduced no less than sixteen quadruple carbon bonds. This new fuel was so violent that at first it caused a rapid change in our personnel, but by continued research it had been stabilised until the explosion took place when expected on 97½ occasions out of 100 – in which it showed its immense superiority over Dr Sprocket's triple heavy hyper-hyzone (20 occasions in 100) and Prof. Swivel's nitrogen heptafluoride (probability of non-explosion incommensurable).

The ship itself was thirty metres long and was made of moulded neo-bakelite with crystallux windows, and consisted of two steps, which were ample thanks to our new fuel. The whole thing would have cost a great deal of money had we intended to pay for it. The rocket motors were made of one of the new boro-silicon alloys and had an operating time of several minutes. Apart from these features, our ship did not differ materially from any other designed previously, except in so far that it had actually been constructed. We had no intention of venturing far out into space on our first flight, but circumstances of which I shall relate altered our plans in an unforeseen manner.

On the lst of April, 1952, everything was ready for a preliminary flight. I broke the customary vacuum flask on the prow of the ship, christened it the 'Pride of the Galaxy', and we (this is, myself and the five surviving members of the council of twenty-five) entered the cabin and carefully sealed the door, squeezing chewing gum into all the cracks.

The ship itself was resting on a balloon-type undercarriage and we had a straight run of two miles over various people's lawns and gardens. We intended to rise to a height of a few hundred miles and then to glide back to earth, landing as best we could with little regard to life or property save our own.

I seated myself at the controls and the others lay in the compensating hammocks which we hoped *might* save us from the shock of the take-off. In any case every space-ship has them and we could hardly do otherwise. With an expression of grim determination, which I had to assume several times before Ivan Schnitzel, our official photographer, was satisfied, I pressed the starting button and – rather to our surprise – the ship began to move.

After leaving our grounds it tore through a fence into a vegetable garden which it rapidly converted into a ploughed field, and then passed over a large lawn doing comparatively little damage apart from setting fire to a few greenhouses. By now we were nearing a row of buildings which might offer some resistance, and as we had not yet lifted, I turned the power full on. With a tremendous roar, the ship leapt into the air, and amid the groans of my companions I lost consciousness.

When I recovered, I realised that we were in space and jumped to my feet to see if we were falling back to earth. But I had forgotten my weightless condition and crashed head first against the ceiling, once more losing consciousness.

When I recovered, I very carefully made my way to the window and with relief saw that we were now floating back to earth. My relief was short-lived when I found that the earth was nowhere in sight! I at once realised that we must have been unconscious for a very long time – my less robust companions still lay in a coma, or rather several comas, at the end of the cabin, the hammocks having given way under the strain, to the detriment of their occupants.

I first inspected the machinery, which so far as I could tell seemed intact, and then set about reviving my companions. This I readily did by pouring a little liquid air down their necks. When all were conscious (or as nearly so as could be expected in the circumstances), I rapidly outlined the situation and explained the need for complete calm. After the resulting hysteria had subsided, I asked for volunteers to go outside in a space suit and inspect the ship. I am sorry to say that I had to go myself.

Luckily, the exterior of the ship seemed quite intact, though there were bits of branches and a 'Trespassers will be Prosecuted' notice stuck in the rudder. These I detached and threw away, but unluckily they got into an orbit round the ship and returned round the back, catching me a resounding whack on the head.

The impact knocked me off the ship, and to my horror I found myself floating in space. I did not, of course, lose my head but immediately looked around for some method by which I could return. In the pouch on the exterior of the space-suit I found a safety-pin, two tram tickets, a double-headed penny, a football-pool coupon covered with what seemed to be orbital calculations, and a complimentary ticket to the Russian ballet. After a careful scrutiny of these, I came to the reluctant conclusion that they offered little hope. Even if I could bring myself to throw away the penny, its momentum would, I rapidly calculated, be insufficient to return me to the ship. The tickets I did throw away, rather as a gesture than anything else, and I was about to throw the safety-pin after them – it would have given me a velocity of .000001 millimetres an hour, which was better than nothing (by, in fact, .000001 mm/hour.) – when a splendid idea occurred to me. I carefully punctured my space-suit with the pin, and in a moment the escaping jet of air drove me back to the ship. I entered the air-lock just as the suit collapsed, not a moment too soon.

My companions crowded round me, eager for news, though there was little that I could tell them. It would take prolonged measurements to discover our position and I commenced this important work at once.

After ten minutes' observations of the stars, followed by five hours intensive calculations on our specially lubricated multiple slide-rules, I was able to announce, to the relief of all present, that we were 5,670,000 miles from the earth, 365,000 miles above the ecliptic, travelling towards Right Ascension 23 hours 15 mins. 37.07 secs., Declination 153° 17' 36". We had feared that we might have been moving towards, for example, R.A. 12 hours 19 mins. 7.3 secs, Dec. 169° 15' 17" or even, if the worst had happened, R.A. 5 hours 32 mins. 59.9 secs, Dec. 0° 0' 0".

At least, we were doing this when we took our observations, but as we had moved several million miles in the meantime, we had to start all over again to find where we were *now*. After several trials, we succeeded in finding where we were only two hours before we found it, but in spite of the greatest efforts we could not reduce the time taken in calculation to less than this value. So with this we had to be content.

The earth was between us and the sun, which was why we could not see it. Since we were travelling in the direction of Mars, I suggested that we could continue on our present course and try to make a landing on the planet. I had grave doubts, in fact, as to whether there was anything else we could do. So for two days we cruised on towards the red planet, my companions relieving the tedium with dominoes, poker and three-dimensional billiards (which, of course, can only be played in the absence of gravity). However, I had little time for these pursuits, as I had to keep constant check on the ship's position. In any case, I was completely fleeced on the first day, and was unable to obtain any credit from my grasping companions.

All the time Mars was slowly growing larger, and as we drew nearer and nearer many were the speculations we made as to what we should find when we landed on the mysterious red planet.

'One thing we *can* be certain of,' remarked Isaac Guzzbaum, our auditor, to me as we were looking through the ports at the world now only a few million miles away. 'We won't be met by a lot of old johnnies with flowing robes and beards who will address us in perfect English and give us the freedom of the city, as in so many science-fiction stories. I'll bet our next year's deficit on that!'

Finally we began our braking manoeuvres and curved down towards the planet in a type of logarithmic spiral whose first, second and third differential coefficients are in harmonic ratio – a curve on which I hold all patents. We made a landing near the equator, as close to the Solis Lacus as possible. Our ship slid for several miles across the desert, leaving a trail of fused quartz behind it where the blast touched the ground, and ended up with its nose in a sand dune.

Our first move was to investigate the air. We decided unanimously (only Mr Guzzbaum dissenting), that Mr Guzzbaum should be detailed to enter the air-lock and sample the Martian atmosphere. Fortunately for him, it proved fit for human consumption, and we all joined Isaac in the air-lock. I then stepped solemnly out onto Martian soil – the first human being in history to do so – while Ivan Schnitzel recorded the scene for the benefit of history. As a matter of fact, we later found that he had forgotten to load the camera. Perhaps this was just as well, for my desire for strict accuracy compels me to admit that no sooner did I touch the ground then it gave way beneath my feet, precipitating me into a sandy pit from which I was with difficulty rescued by my companions.

However, in spite of this mishap, we eventually clambered up the dune and surveyed the countryside. It was most uninteresting, consisting solely of long ridges of heaped-up sand. We were debating what to do when suddenly we heard a high-pitched whining noise in the sky and to our surprise a cigar-shaped metal vessel dropped to the ground a few yards away. A door slid open.

'Fire when you see the whites of their eyes!' hissed Eric Wobblewit, our tame humourist, but I could tell that his joke was even more forced than usual. Indeed, we all felt nervous as we waited for the occupants of the ship to emerge.

They were three old men with long beards, clad in flowing white robes.

Behind me I heard a dull thud as Isaac passed out. The leader spoke to me in what would have been flawless BBC English had it not been for the bits he had obviously picked up from Schenectady.

'Welcome, visitors from Earth! I'm afraid this is not an authorised landing place, but we will let that pass for the moment. We have come to guide you to our city of Xzgtpkl.'

'Thanks,' I replied, somewhat taken aback, 'I'm sure we're very grateful to you for your trouble. Is it far to Zxgtpkl?'

The Martian winced. 'Xzgtpkl,' he said firmly.

'Well, Xzgtplk, then,' I went on desperately. The other two Martians looked pained and took a firmer grip on the rod-like instruments they were carrying. (These, we learned later, were walking-sticks.) The leader gave me up as a bad job.

'Skip it,' he said. 'It's about fifty miles away as the crow flies, though as there aren't any crows on Mars we have never been able to check this very accurately. Could you fly your ship behind us?'

'We could,' I replied, 'though we'd rather not, unless Zxg— er, your city, is heavily insured with a reputable firm. Could you carry us? No doubt you have tractor beams and such-like.'

The Martian seemed surprised. 'Yes, we have,' he said, 'but how did you know it?'

'Just a surmise,' I replied modestly. 'Well, we'll get over to our ship and leave the rest to you.'

We did so, carrying the prostrate Guzzbaum with us, and in a few minutes were speeding over the desert after the Martian ship. Soon the spires of the mighty city reared above the horizon and in a short time we landed in a great square, surrounded by teeming crowds.

In a trice, or less, we were facing a battery of cameras and microphones, or their Martian equivalents. Our guide spoke a few words and then beckoned to me. With characteristic foresight I had prepared a speech before leaving earth, so I pulled it from my pocket and read it to, no doubt, the entire Martian nation. It was only when I had finished that I noticed I was reading the lecture: 'British Science-Fiction Authors: Their Prevention or Cure?' which I had given to the S.F.A. a few months before and which had already involved me in six libel actions. This was unfortunate, but from the reception, I am sure that the Martians found it of interest. The Martian cheer, oddly enough, closely resembles the terrestrial boo.

We were then taken (with difficulty) onto a moving road which led to a giant building in the centre of the city, where a lavish meal awaited us. What it consisted of we never succeeded in ascertaining, and we rather hope it was synthetic.

After the meal we were asked what part of the city we would like to visit, as it was entirely at our disposal. We did our best to explain what a variety show was, but the idea seemed beyond our guides and as we had feared they insisted on showing us over their power-plants and factories. Here I must say we found our knowledge of contemporary science-fiction invaluable, for everything with which the Martians tried to surprise us we had heard of long before. Their atomic generators, for instance, we compared unfavourably with those described by many terrestrial writers (though we took care to secure the plans) and we expressed surprise at their inability to overcome those laws of nature that have been repealed by our economists and politicians for years. In fact – and I say it with pride – the Martians got very little change out of us. When the tour finished I was lecturing the leader on the habits of termites and behind me I could hear Mr Guzzbaum (now, alas, his normal self) criticising the scandalously low rates of interest allowed in Martian trade.

After this we were not bothered any more and were able to spend most of our time indoors playing poker and some curious Martian games we had picked up, including an interesting mathematical one which I can best describe as 'four-dimensional chess'. Unfortunately, it was so complicated that none of my companions could understand it, and accordingly I had to play against myself. I am sorry to say that I invariably lost.

Of our adventures on Mars I could say a great deal and am going to at a later date. My forthcoming book, 'Mars with the Lid Off' should be out in the spring and will be published by Blotto and Windup at 21/-. All I will say at the moment is that we were very well entertained by our hosts, and I believe that we gave them a favourable impression of the human race. We made it quite clear, however, that we were somewhat exceptional specimens, as we did not want our hosts to be unduly disappointed by the expeditions after ours.

So well indeed were we treated that one of us decided not to return to earth when the time came, for reasons which I shall not go into here, as he has a wife and family on earth. I may have something more to say about this matter in my book.

We had, unfortunately, only a week in which to stay on Mars as the planets were rapidly moving apart. Our Martian friends had very kindly refuelled our ship for us, and also gave us many mementoes of our visit, some of them of considerable value. (Whether these souvenirs belong to the society as a whole or to the individual officers is a matter that has not yet been settled. I would, however, point out to those members who have been complaining that possession is nine points of the law, and where the possessors are my esteemed colleagues, it is more like ten.)

Our return to earth was uneventful and thanks to our great reserve of fuel we were able to make a landing where and how we liked. Consequently we chose a spot which would focus the eyes of the world upon us and bring home to everybody the magnitude of our accomplishment.

Of our landing in Hyde Park and the consequent evaporation of the Serpentine, enough has been written elsewhere, and the spectacle of three-inch headlines in the next day's *Times* was proof enough that we had made our mark in history. Everyone will remember my broadcast from the cells in Vine Street Police Station, where we were taken at the triumphant conclusion of our flight, and there is no need for me to add any more at the moment, since, moreover, it might embarrass my lawyers.

We are content to know that we have added something, however small, to the total of human knowledge, and something, however large, to the bank balance of our society. What more than this could we desire?

Retreat from Earth

First published in *Amateur Science Fiction Stories*, March 1938
Collected in *The Best of Arthur C. Clarke 1937–1955*

I suspect that my interest in these amazing creatures was triggered by Paul Ernst's 'The Raid on the Termites' in *Astounding Stories* (June 1932).

A great many millions of years ago, when man was a dream of the distant future, the third ship to reach Earth in all history descended through the perpetual clouds on to what is now Africa, and the creatures it had carried across an unthinkable abyss of space looked out upon a world which would be a fit home for their weary race. But Earth was already inhabited by a great though dying people, and since both races were civilised in the true sense of the word, they did not go to war but made a mutual agreement. For those who then ruled Earth had once ruled everywhere within the orbit of Pluto, had planned always for the future and even at their end they had prepared Earth for the race that was to come after them.

So, forty million years after the last of the old ones had gone to his eternal rest, men began to rear their cities where once the architects of a greater race had flung their towers against the clouds. And in the long echoing centuries before the birth of man, the aliens had not been idle but had covered half the planet with their cities, filled with blind, fantastic slaves, and though man knew these cities, for they often caused him infinite trouble, yet he never suspected that all around him in the tropics an older civilization than his was planning busily for the day when it would once again venture forth upon the seas of space to regain its lost inheritance.

'Gentlemen,' said the President of the Council gravely, 'I am sorry to say that we have received a severe setback in our plans to colonize the third planet. As you all know, we have for many years been working on that planet unknown to its inhabitants, preparing for the day when we should take over complete control. We anticipated no resistance, for the people of Three are at a very primitive level of development, and possess no weapons which could harm us. Moreover, they are continually quarrelling among themselves owing to the extraordinary number of political groups or "nations" into which they are divided, a lack of unity which will no doubt be a considerable help to our plans.

13

'To obtain the fullest possible knowledge of the planet and its peoples, we have had several hundred investigators working on Three, a number in each important city. Our men have done very well, and thanks to their regular reports we now have a detailed knowledge of this strange world. In fact, until a few setas ago I would have said that we knew everything of importance concerning it, but now I find that we were very much mistaken.

'Our chief investigator in the country known as England, which has been mentioned here on a number of occasions, was that very intelligent young student, Cervac Theton, grandson of the great Vorac. He progressed splendidly with the English, a particularly guileless race it seems, and was soon accepted into their highest society. He even spent some time at one of their great seats of learning (so called) but soon left in disgust. Though it had nothing to do with his real purpose, this energetic young man also studied the wild animals of Three, for remarkable though it seems there are a great many strange and interesting creatures roaming freely over large areas of the planet. Some are actually dangerous to man, but he has conquered most of them and even exterminated some species. It was while studying these beasts that Cervac made the discovery which I fear may change our whole plan of action. But let Cervac speak for himself.'

The President threw a switch, and from concealed speakers Cervac Theton's voice rang out over that assembly of the greatest brains of Mars.

' – come to what is the most important part of this communication. For some time I have been studying the many wild creatures of this planet, purely for the sake of scientific knowledge. The animals of Three are divided into four main groups – mammals, fishes, reptiles and insects, and a number of lesser groups. There have been many representatives of the first three classes on our own planet, though of course there are none now, but as far as I know there have never been insects on our world at any time in its history. Consequently they attracted my attention from the first, and I made a careful study of their habits and structure.

'You who have never seen them will have great difficulty in imagining what these creatures are like. There are millions of different types, and it would take ages to classify all of them, but they are mostly small animals with many jointed limbs and with a hard armoured body. They are usually very small, about half a zem in length, and are often winged. Most of them lay eggs and undergo a number of metamorphoses before they become perfect creatures. I am sending with this report a number of photographs and films which will give you a better idea of their infinite variety than any words of mine. I obtained most of my information on the subject from the literature which has been built up by thousands of patient students who have devoted their lives to watching insects at work. The inhabitants of Three have taken much interest in the creatures which share their world, and this, I think, is another proof that they are more intelligent than some of our scientists would have us believe.'

At this there were smiles in the audience, for the House of Theton had always been noted for its radical and unorthodox views.

'In my studies I came across accounts of some extraordinary creatures which live in the tropical regions of the planet. They are called "termites" or "white ants" and live in large, wonderfully organised communities. They even have cities – huge mounds, honey-combed with passages and made of exceedingly hard materials. They can perform prodigious feats of engineering, being able to bore through metals and glass, and they can destroy most of man's creations when they wish. They eat cellulose, that is, wood, and since man uses this material extensively he is always waging war on these destroyers of his possessions. Perhaps luckily for him, the termites have even deadlier enemies, the ants, which are a very similar type of creature. These two races have been at war for geological ages, and the outcome is still undecided.

'Although they are blind, the termites cannot endure light and so even when they venture from their cities they always keep under cover, making tunnels and cement tubes if they have to cross open country. They are wonderful engineers and architects and no ordinary obstacle will deflect them from their purpose. Their most remarkable achievement, however, is a biological one. From the same eggs they can produce half a dozen different types of specialised creature. Thus they can breed fighters with immense claws, soldiers which can spray poison over their opponents, workers which act as food stores by virtue of their immense distended stomachs and a number of other fantastic mutations. You will find a full account of them, as far as they are known to the naturalists of Three, in the books I am sending.

'The more I read of their achievements, the more I was impressed by the perfection of their social system. It ocurred to me, as indeed it had to many previous students, that a termitary may be compared to a vast machine, whose component parts are not of metal but of protoplasm, whose wheels and cogs are separate insects, each with some preordained role to perform. It was not until later that I found how near the truth this analogy was.

'Nowhere in the termitary is there any waste or disorder, and everywhere there is mystery. As I considered the matter it seemed to me that the termites were much more worthy of our attention, from the purely scientific point of view, than man himself. After all, man is not so very different from ourselves, though I shall annoy many by saying so, yet these insects are utterly alien to us in every way. They work, live and die for the good of the state. To them the individual is nothing. With us, and with man, the state exists only for the individual. Who shall say which is right?

'These problems so engrossed me that I eventually decided to study the little creatures myself with all the instruments at my command, instruments of which the naturalists of Three had never dreamt. So I selected a small uninhabited island in a lonely part of the Pacific, the greatest ocean of Three, where the strange mounds of the termites clustered thickly, and constructed on it a little metal building to serve as a laboratory. As I was thoroughly impressed by the creatures' destructive powers, I cut a wide circular moat round the building, leaving enough room for my ship to land,

and let the sea flow in. I thought that ten zets of water would keep them from doing any mischief. How foolish that moat looks now.

'These preparations took several weeks for it was not very often that I was able to leave England. In my little space-yacht the journey from London to Termite Island took under half a sector so little time was lost in this way. The laboratory was equipped with everything I considered might be useful and many things for which I could see no conceivable use, but which might possibly be required. The most important instrument was a high-powered gamma-ray televisor which I hoped would reveal to me all the secrets hidden from ordinary sight by the walls of the termitary. Perhaps equally useful was a very sensitive psychometer, of the kind we use when exploring planets on which new types of mentalities may exist, and which we might not detect in the ordinary way. The device could operate on any conceivable mind frequency, and at its highest amplification could locate a man several hundred miles away. I was certain that even if the termites possessed only the faintest glimmers of an utterly alien intelligence, I would be able to detect their mental processes.

'At first I made relatively little progress. With the televisor I examined all the nearest termitaries, and fascinating work it was following the workers along the passages of their homes as they carried food and building materials hither and thither. I watched the enormous bloated queen in the royal nursery, laying her endless stream of eggs: one every few seconds, night and day, year after year. Although she was the centre of the colony's activities, yet when I focused the psychometer on her the needles did not so much as flicker. The very cells of my body could do better than that! The monstrous queen was only a brainless mechanism, none the less mechanical because she was made of protoplasm, and the workers looked after her with the care we would devote to one of our useful robots.

'For a number of reasons I had not expected the queen to be the ruling force of the colony, but when I began to explore with psychometer and televisor, nowhere could I discover any creature, any super-termite, which directed and supervised the operations of the rest. This would not have surprised the scientists of Three, for they hold that the termites are governed by instinct alone. But my instrument could have detected the nervous stimuli which constitute automatic reflex actions, and yet I found nothing. I would turn up the amplification to its utmost, put on a pair of those primitive but very useful "head-phones" and listen hour on hour. Sometimes there would be those faint characteristic cracklings we have never been able to explain, but generally the only sound was the subdued washing noise, like waves breaking on some far-off beach, caused by the massed intellects of the planet reacting on my apparatus.

'I was beginning to get discouraged when there occurred one of those accidents which happen so often in science. I was dismantling the instrument after another fruitless investigation when I happened to knock the little receiving loop so that it pointed to the ground. To my surprise the needles started flickering violently. By swinging the loop in the usual way I discovered that the exciting source lay almost directly underneath me, though at what distance I could not guess. In the phones was a continuous humming noise, interspersed with sudden flickerings. It sounded for all the world like any electric machine operating, and the frequency, one hundred thousand mega mega cycles, was not one on which minds have ever been known to function before. To my intense annoyance, as you can guess, I had to return to England at once, and so I could not do anything more at the time.

'It was a fortnight before I could return to Termite Island, and in that time I had to overhaul my little space-yacht owing to an electrical fault. At some time in her history, which I know to have been an eventful one, she had been fitted with ray screens. They were, moreover, very good ray screens, much too good for a law-abiding ship to possess. I have every reason to believe, in fact, that more than once they have defied the cruisers of the Assembly. I did not much relish the task of checking over the complex automatic relay circuits, but at last it was done and I set off at top speed for the Pacific, travelling so fast that my bow wave must have been one continuous explosion. Unfortunately, I soon had to slow down again, for I found that the directional beam I had installed on the island was no longer functioning. I presumed that a fuse had blown, and had to take observations and navigate in the ordinary way. The accident was annoying but not alarming, and I finally spiralled down over Termite Island with no premonition of danger.

'I landed inside my little moat, and went to the door of the laboratory. As I spoke the key-word, the metal seal slid open and a tremendous blast of vapour gushed out of the room. I was nearly stupefied by the stuff, and it was some time before I recovered sufficiently to realise what had happened. When I regained my senses I recognised the smell of hydrogen cyanide, a gas which is instantly fatal to human beings but which only affects us after a considerable time.

'At first I thought that there had been some accident in the laboratory, but I soon remembered that there were not enough chemicals to produce anything like the volume of gas that had gushed out. And in any case, what could possibly have produced such an accident?

'When I turned to the laboratory itself, I had my second shock. One glance was sufficient to show that the place was in ruins. Not a piece of apparatus was recognisable. The cause of the damage was soon apparent – the power plant, my little atomic motor, had exploded. But why? Atomic motors do not explode without very good reason; it would be bad business if they did. I made a careful examination of the room and presently found a number of little holes coming up through the floor – holes such as the termites make when they travel from place to place. My suspicions, incredible though they were, began to be confirmed. It was not completely impossible that the creatures might flood my room with poisonous gas, but to imagine that they understood atomic motors – that was too much! To settle the matter I started hunting for the fragments of the generator, and

17

to my consternation found that the synchronising coils had been short-circuited. Still clinging to the shattered remnants of the osmium toroid were the jaws of the termite that had been sacrificed to wreck the motor . . .

'For a long time I sat in the ship, considering these outstanding facts. Obviously, the damage had been wrought by the intelligence I had located for a moment on my last visit. If it were the termite ruler, and there was nothing else it could very well be, how did it come to possess its knowledge of atomic motors and the only way in which to wreck them? For some reason, possibly because I was prying too deeply into its secrets, it had decided to destroy me and my works. Its first attempt had been unsuccessful, but it might try again with better results, though I did not imagine that it could harm me inside the stout walls of my yacht.

'Although my psychometer and televisor had been destroyed, I was determined not to be defeated so easily, and started hunting with the ship's televisor, which though not made for this kind of work could do it very well. Since I lacked the essential psychometer it was some time before I found what I was looking for. I had to explore great sections of the ground with my instrument, focusing the view point through stratum after stratum and examining any suspicious rock that came into the field. When I was at a depth of nearly two hundred feet, I noticed a dark mass looming faintly in the distance, rather like a very large boulder embedded in the soil. But when I approached I saw with a great feeling of elation that it was no boulder, but a perfect sphere of metal, about twenty feet in diameter. My search had ended. There was a slight fading of the image as I drove the beam through the metal, and then on the screen lay revealed the lair of the super-termite.

'I had expected to find some fantastic creature, perhaps a great naked brain with vestigial limbs, but at a glance I could see that there was no living thing in that sphere. From wall to wall that metal-enclosed space was packed with a maze of machinery, most of it very minute and almost unthinkably complex, and all of it clicking and buzzing with lightning-like rapidity. Compared to this miracle of electrical engineering, our great television exchanges would seem the creations of children or savages. I could see myriads of tiny relays operating, director valves flashing intermittently, and strangely shaped cams spinning among moving mazes of apparatus utterly unlike anything we have ever built. To the makers of this machinery, my atomic generator must have seemed a toy.

'For perhaps two seconds I gazed in wonder at that amazing sight, and then, suddenly and incredibly, an obliterating veil of interference slashed down and the screen was a dancing riot of formless colour.

'Here was something we have never been able to produce – a screen which the televisor could not penetrate. The power of this strange creature was even greater than I had imagined, and in the face of this latest revelation I no longer felt safe even in my ship. In fact, I had a sudden desire to put as many miles as possible between myself and Termite Island. This impulse was so strong that a minute later I was high over the Pacific, rising up through the stratosphere in the great ellipse which would curve down again in England.

'Yes, you may smile or accuse me of cowardice, saying that my grandfather Vorac would not have done so – but listen.

'I was about a hundred miles from the island, thirty miles high and already travelling at two thousand miles an hour when there came a sudden crashing of relays, and the low purr of the motors changed to a tremendous deep-throated roar as an overload was thrown on to them. A glance at the board showed me what had happened – the ray screens were on, flaring beneath the impact of a heavy induction beam. But there was comparatively little power behind the beam, though had I been nearer it would have been a very different tale, and my screens dissipated it without much trouble. Nevertheless, the occurrence gave me an unpleasant shock for the moment, until I remembered that old trick of electrical warfare and threw the full field of my geodesic generators into the beam. I switched on the televisor just in time to see the incandescent fragments of Termite Island fall back into the Pacific . . .

'So I returned to England, with one problem solved and a dozen greater ones formulated. How was it that the termite-brain, as I supposed the machine to be, had never revealed itself to humans? They have often destroyed the homes of its peoples, but as far as I know it has never retaliated. Yet directly I appeared it attacked me, though I was doing it no harm! Perhaps, by some obscure means, it knew that I was not a man, but an adversary worthy of its powers. Or perhaps, though I do not put the suggestion seriously, it is a kind of guardian protecting Three from invaders such as ourselves.

'Somewhere there is an inconsistency that I cannot understand. On the one hand we have that incredible intelligence possessing much, if not all of our knowledge, while on the other are the blind, relatively helpless insects waging an endless war with puny weapons against enemies their ruler could exterminate instantly and without effort. Behind this mad system there must be a purpose, but it is beyond my comprehension. The only rational explanation I can conceive is that for most of the time the termite brain is content to let its subjects go their own, mechanical ways, and that only very seldom, perhaps once in an age, does it take an active part in guiding them. As long as it is not seriously interfered with, it is content to let man do what he likes. It may even take a benevolent interest in him and his works.

'Fortunately for us, the super-termite is not invulnerable. Twice it miscalculated in its dealings with me, and the second time cost it its existence – I cannot say life. I am confident that we can overcome the creature, for it, or others like it, still control the remaining billions of the race. I have just returned from Africa, and termites there are still organised as they have always been. On this excursion I did not leave my ship, or even land. I believe I have incurred the enmity of an entire race and I am taking no chances. Until I have an armoured cruiser and a staff of expert biologists, I am leaving the termites strictly alone. Even then I shall not feel quite safe, for there may be yet more powerful intelligences on Three than the one I encountered. That is a risk we must take, for unless we can defeat these beings, Planet Three will never be safe for our kind.'

The President cut off the record and turned to the waiting assembly.

'You have heard Theton's report,' he said, 'I appreciate its importance and at once sent a heavy cruiser to Three. As soon as it arrived, Theton boarded it and left for the Pacific.

'That was two days ago. Since then I have heard from neither Theton nor the cruiser, but I do know this:

'An hour after the ship left England, we picked up the radiations from her screens, and in a very few seconds other disturbances – cosmics, ultra-cosmics, induction and tremendous long-wave, low quantum radiations such as we have never used in battle – began to come through in ever-increasing quantities. This lasted for nearly three minutes, when suddenly there came one titanic blast of energy, lasting for a fraction of a second and then – nothing. That final burst of power could have been caused by nothing less than the detonation of an entire atomic generating plant, and must have jarred Three to its core.

'I have called this meeting to put the facts of the matter before you and to ask you to vote on the subject. Shall we abandon our plans for Three, or shall we send one of our most powerful super-dreadnoughts to the planet? One ship could do as much as an entire section of the Fleet in this matter, and would be safe, in case . . . but I cannot imagine any power which could defeat such a ship as our "Zuranther". Will you please register your votes in the usual way? It will be a great setback if we cannot colonise Three, but it is not the only planet in the system, though it is the fairest.'

There came subdued clicks and a faint humming of motors as the councillors pressed their coloured buttons, and on the television screen appeared the words: For 967; Against 233.

'Very well, the "Zuranther" will leave at once for Three. This time we will follow her movements with the televisor and then if anything does go wrong, we shall at least obtain some idea of the weapons the enemy uses.'

Hours later the tremendous mass of the flagship of the Martian fleet dropped thunderously through the outer reaches of Earth's atmosphere towards the far-off waters of the Pacific. She fell in the heart of a tornado, for her captain was taking no chances and the winds of the stratosphere were being annihilated by her flaming ray screens.

But on a tiny island far over the eastern horizon, the termites had been preparing for the attack they knew must come, and strange, fragile mechanisms had been erected by myriad blind and toiling insects. The great Martian warship was two hundred miles away when her captain located the island in his televisor. His finger reached towards the button which would start the enormous ray generators, but swift as he was the almost instant acting relays of the termite mind were far swifter. Though, in any case, the outcome would have been the same.

The great spherical screens did not flare even once as the enemy struck home. Their slim rapier of pure heat was driven by only a score of horsepower, while behind the shields of the warship were a thousand million. But the feeble heat beam of the termites never passed through those screens – it reached out through hyperspace to gnaw at the very vitals of the ship. The Martians could not check an enemy who struck from within their defences, an enemy to whom a sphere was no more a barrier than a hollow ring.

The termite rulers, those alien beings from outer space, had kept their agreement with the old lords of Earth, and had saved man from the danger his ancestors had long ago foreseen.

But the watching assembly knew only that the screens of the ship which had been blazing fiercely one moment had erupted in a hurricane of flame and a numbing concussion of sound, while for a thousand miles around fragments of white-hot metal were dropping from the heavens.

Slowly the President turned to face the Council and whispered in a low, strained voice, 'I think it had better be planet Two, after all.'

Reverie

First published in *New Worlds*, Autumn 1939
Not previously collected in book form

'All the ideas in science fiction have been used up!'

How often we've heard this moan from editors, authors and fans, any one of whom should know better. Even if it were true, which is the last thing it is, it would signify nothing. How long ago do you think the themes of ordinary, mundane fiction were used up? Somewhere in the late Paleolithic, I should say. Which fact has made exactly no difference to the overwhelming outrush of modern masterpieces, four a shilling in the third tray from the left.

No. The existing material is sufficient to provide an infinite number of stories, each individual and each worth reading. Too much stress is laid on new ideas, or 'thought-variants', on 'novae'. They are all very well in their way – and it's a way that leads to strange, delightful regions of fantasy – but at least as important are characterisation and the ability to treat a commonplace theme in your own individual style. And for this reason, in spite of all his critics, I maintain that if any could equal Weinbaum, none could surpass him.

If, in addition to its purely literary qualities, a story has a novel idea, so much the better. Notwithstanding the pessimists, there are a million million themes that science fiction has never touched. Even in these days of deepening depression, a few really original plots still lighten our darkness. 'The Smile of the Sphinx' was such a one; going a good deal further back we have 'The Human Termites', perhaps the best of all its kind before the advent of 'Sinister Barrier'.

As long as science advances, as long as mathematics discovers incredible worlds where twice two would never dream of equalling four, so new ideas will come tumbling into the mind of anyone who will let his thoughts wander, passport in hand, along the borders of Possibility. There are no Customs regulations; anything you see in your travels in those neighbouring lands you can bring back with you. But in the country of the Impossible there are many wonders too delicate and too fragile to survive transportation.

Nothing in this world is ever really new, yet everything is in some way different from all that has gone before. At least once in his life even the dullest of us has found himself contemplating with amazement and perhaps with fear, some thought so original and so startling that it seems the creation of an exterior, infinitely more subtle mind. Such thoughts pass through the consciousness so swiftly that they are gone before they can be more than glimpsed, but sometimes like comets trapped at last by a giant sun, they cannot escape and from their stubborn material the mind forges a masterpiece of literature, of philosophy or music. From such fleeting, fragmentary themes are the Symphonies of Sibelius built – perhaps, with the Theory of Relativity and the conquest of space, the greatest achievements of the century before the year 2000.

Even within the limits set by logic, the artist need not starve for lack of material. We may laugh at Fearn, but we must admire the magnificent, if undisciplined, fertility of his mind. In a less ephemeral field, Stapledon has produced enough themes to keep a generation of science fiction authors busy. There is no reason why others should not do the same; few of the really fundamental ideas of fantasy have been properly exploited. Who has ever, in any story, dared to show the true meaning of immortality, with its cessation of progress and evolution, and, above all, its inevitable destruction of Youth? Only Keller, and then more with sympathy than genius. And who has had the courage to point out that, with sufficient scientific powers, reincarnation is possible? What a story *that* would make!

All around us, in the commonest things we do, lie endless possibilities. So many things *might* happen, and don't – but may some day. How odd it would be if someone to whom you were talking on the phone walked into the room and began a conversation with a colleague! Suppose that when you switched off the light last thing at night you found that it had never been on anyway? And what a shock it would be if you woke up to find yourself fast asleep! It would be quite as unsettling as meeting oneself in the street. I have often wondered, too, what would happen if one adopted the extreme solipsist attitude and decided that nothing existed outside one's mind. An attempt to put such a theory into practice would be extremely interesting. Whether any forces at our command could effect a devoted adherent to this philosophy is doubtful. He could always stop thinking of us, and then we should be in a mess.

At a generous estimate, there have been a dozen fantasy authors with original conceptions. Today I can only think of two, though the pages of UNKNOWN may bring many more to light. The trouble with present-day science fiction, as with a good many other things, is that in striving after the bizarre it misses the obvious. What it needs is not more imagination or even less imagination. It is *some* imagination.

The Awakening

First published in *Zenith*, February 1942 (revised version published in *Future*, January 1952)
Collected in *The Best of Arthur C. Clarke 1937–1955*

First published by Manchester fans Harry Turner and Marian Eadie, in their fanzine, *Zenith*, and significantly revised for publication in *Future* in 1952.

The Master wondered whether he would dream. That was the only thing he feared, for in a sleep that lasts no more than a night dreams may come that can shatter the mind – and he was to sleep for a hundred years.

He remembered the day, still only a few months ago, when a frightened doctor had said, 'Sir, your heart is failing. You have less than a year to live.' He was not afraid of death, but the thought that it had come upon him in the full flower of his intellect, while his work was still half finished, filled him with a baffled fury. 'And there is nothing you can do?' he asked. 'No, Sir, we have been working on artificial hearts for a hundred years. In another century, perhaps, it might be done.' 'Very well,' he had replied coldly. 'I shall wait another century. You will build me a place where my body will not be disturbed, and then you will put me to sleep by freezing or any other means. That, at least, I know you can do.'

He had watched the building of the tomb, in a secret place above the snow-line of Everest. Only the chosen few must know where the Master was to sleep, for there were many millions in the world who would have sought out his body to destroy it. The secret would be preserved down the generations until the day when man's science had conquered the diseases of the heart. Then the Master would be awakened from his sleep.

He was still conscious when they laid him on the couch in the central chamber, though the drugs had already dimmed his senses. He heard them close the steel doors against their rubber gaskets, and even fancied he could hear the hiss of the pumps which would withdraw the air from around him, and replace it with sterile nitrogen. Then he slept, and in a little while the world forgot the Master.

He slept the hundred years, though rather before that time the discovery he had been awaiting was made. But no one awakened him, for the world had changed since his going and now there were none who would have wished to see him return. His followers had died and mysteriously, the secret of his resting place was lost. For a time the legend of the Master's tomb persisted, but soon it was forgotten. So he slept.

After what by some standards would have been a little while, the earth's crust decided that it had borne the weight of the Himalayas for long enough. Slowly the mountains dropped, tilting the southern plains of India towards the sky. And presently the plateau of Ceylon was the highest point on the surface of the globe, and the ocean above Everest was five and a half miles deep. The Master would not be disturbed by his enemies, or his friends.

Slowly, patiently, the silt drifted down through the towering ocean heights on to the wreck of the Himalayas. The blanket that would some day be chalk began to thicken at the rate of not a few inches every century. If one had returned some time later, one might have found that the sea bed was no longer five miles down, or even four, or three.

Then the land tilted again, and a mighty range of limestone mountains towered where once had been the oceans of Tibet. But the Master knew nothing of this, nor was his sleep disturbed when it happened again . . . and again . . . and again . . .

Now the rain and rivers were washing away the chalk and carrying it out to the new oceans, and the surface was moving down towards the buried tomb. Slowly the miles of rock were washed away, until at last the metal sphere which housed the Master's body returned once more to the light of day – though to a day much longer, and much dimmer, than it had been when the Master closed his eyes. And presently the scientists found him, on a pedestal of rock jutting high above an eroded plain. Because they did not know the secret of the tomb, it took them, for all their wisdom, thirty years to reach the chamber where he slept.

The Master's mind awoke before his body. As he lay powerless, unable even to lift his leaden eyelids, memory came flooding back. The hundred years were safely behind him – his desperate gamble had succeeded! He felt a strange elation, and a longing to see the new world that must have arisen while he lay within his tomb.

One by one, his senses returned. He could feel the hard surface on which he was lying: now a gentle current of air drifted across his brow. Presently he was aware of sounds – faint clickings and scratchings all around him. For a moment he was puzzled: then he realised that the surgeons must be putting their instruments away. He had not yet the strength to open his eyes, so he lay and waited, wondering.

Would men have changed much? Would his name still be remembered among them? Perhaps it would be better if it were not – though he had feared the hatred of neither men nor nations. He had never known their love. Momentarily he wondered if any of his friends might have followed him, but he knew there would be none. When he opened his eyes, all the faces before him would be strange. Yet he longed to see them, to read the expressions they would hold as he awakened from his sleep.

Strength returned. He opened his eyes. The light was gentle, and he was not dazzled, but for a while everything was blurred and misty. He could distinguish figures standing round, but though they seemed strange he could not see them clearly.

Then the Master's eyes came into focus, and as they brought their message to his mind he screamed once, feebly, and died for ever. For in the last moment of his life, as he saw what stood around him, he knew that the long war between Man and Insect was ended – and that Man was not the victor.

Whacky

First published in *The Fantast*, July 1942
Collected in *The Best of Arthur C. Clarke 1937–1955*

'Whacky' was first published in *The Fantast*, edited by Aberdeen fan, Douglas Webster, who had previously taken over the magazine from one Christopher Samuel Youd, better known to science fiction readers as John Christopher.

The telephone honked melodiously. He picked it up and after a moment's hesitation asked 'Hello – is that me?' The answer he had been fearing came back. 'You, it is. Who are you?' He sighed: argument was useless – besides he knew he was in the wrong. 'All right,' he said wearily. 'You win.' A sudden purple twinge of toothache nearly choked him for a moment and he added hopelessly: 'Don't forget to have that stopping seen to this afternoon.' 'Ouch! as if I would,' growled the voice testily. There was a pause. 'Well, what do you want me to do now?' he asked at last. The reply, though half expected, was chilling. 'Do? It doesn't matter. You just *aren't*!'

'The amazing affair of the Elastic Sided Eggwhisk,' said the Great Detective, 'would no doubt have remained unsolved to this very day, if by great misfortune it had ever occurred. The fact that it didn't I count as one of my luckiest escapes.'

Those of us who possessed heads nodded in agreement.

He paused to drain the sump of his hookah, then continued.

'But even that fades into insignificance before the horrible tragedy that occurred in the House Where the Aspidistra Ran Amok. Fortunately I was not born at the time: otherwise I should certainly have been one of the victims.'

We shuddered in assent. Some of us had been there. Some of us were still there.

'Weren't you connected with the curious case of the Camphorated Kipper?'

He coughed deprecatingly.

'Intimately. I *was* the Camphorated Kipper.'

At this point two men arrived to carry me back to the taxidermist's, so I cannot tell you any more.

*

'Phew!' said the man in the pink silk pyjamas. 'I had a horrid dream last night!'

'Oh?' said the other disinterestedly.

'Yes – I thought that my wife had poisoned me for the insurance. It was so vivid I was mighty glad when I woke up.'

'Indeed?' said his companion politely. 'And just *where* do you think you are right now?'

Loophole

First published in *Astounding Science-Fiction*, April 1946
Collected in *Expedition to Earth*

In the 1940s, sf did not flourish in England and its spiritual home was still the United States [. . .]. I sold my first stories to John [W.] Campbell of *Astounding* (later *Analog*) during the closing months of the War, while I was still in the Royal Air Force. His first purchase was 'Rescue Party' – though 'Loophole', sold a little later, actually appeared first. At the time of these sales (1945) I was stationed just outside Stratford-on-Avon and I remember thinking modestly that there was something singularly appropriate about this.

From: President.
To: Secretary, Council of Scientists.

I have been informed that the inhabitants of Earth have succeeded in releasing atomic energy and have been making experiments with rocket propulsion. This is most serious. Let me have a full report immediately. And make it *brief* this time.

K.K. IV.

From Secretary, Council of Scientists.
To: President.

The facts are as follows. Some months ago instruments detected intense neutron emission from Earth, but an analysis of radio programmes gave no explanation at the time. Three days ago a second emission occurred, and soon afterwards all radio transmissions from Earth announced that atomic bombs were in use in the current war. The translators have not completed their interpretation, but it appears that the bombs are of considerable power. Two have so far been used. Some details of their construction have been released, but the elements concerned have not yet been identified. A fuller report will be forwarded as soon as possible. For the moment all that is certain is that the inhabitants of Earth *have* liberated atomic power, so far only explosively.

Very little is known concerning rocket research on Earth. Our astronomers have been observing the planet carefully ever since radio emissions were detected a generation ago. It is certain that long-range rockets of some kind are in existence on Earth, for there have been numerous references to them in recent military broadcasts. However, no serious attempt has been made to reach interplanetary space. When the war ends, it is expected that the inhabitants of the planet may carry out research in this direction. We will pay very careful attention to their broadcasts and the astronomical watch will be rigorously enforced.

From what we have inferred of the planet's technology, it should require about twenty years before Earth develops atomic rockets capable of crossing space. In view of this, it would seem that the time has come to set up a base on the Moon, so that a close scrutiny can be kept on such experiments when they commence.

Trescon

[*Added in manuscript*]

The war on Earth has now ended, apparently owing to the intervention of the atomic bomb. This will not affect the above arguments but it may mean that the inhabitants of Earth can devote themselves to pure research again more quickly than expected. Some broadcasts have already pointed out the application of atomic power to rocket propulsion.

T.

From: President.
To: Chief of Bureau of Extra-Planetary Security (C.B.E.P.S).

You have seen Trescon's minute.

Equip an expedition to the satellite of Earth immediately. It is to keep a close watch on the planet and to report at once if rocket experiments are in progress.

The greatest care must be taken to keep our presence on the Moon a secret. You are personally responsible for this. Report to me at yearly intervals, or more often if necessary.

K.K. IV.

From: President.
To: C.B.E.P.S.

Where is the report of Earth?!!

K.K. IV.

From: C.B.E.P.S.
To: President.

The delay is regretted. It was caused by the breakdown of the ship carrying the report.

There have been no signs of rocket experimenting during the past year, and no reference to it in broadcasts from the planet.

Ranthe

From: C.B.E.P.S.
To: President.

You will have seen my yearly reports to your respected father on this subject. There have been no developments of interest for the past fifteen years, but the following message has just been received from our base on the Moon:

Rocket projectile, apparently atomically propelled, left Earth's atmosphere today from northern landmass, travelling into space for one-quarter diameter of planet before returning under control.

Ranthe

From: President.
To: Chief of State

Your comments, please.

K.K. V.

From: Chief of State.
To: President.

This means the end of our traditional policy.

The only hope of security lies in preventing the Terrestrials from making further advances in this direction. From what we know of them, this will require some overwhelming threat.

Since its high gravity makes it impossible for us to land on the planet, our sphere of action is restricted. The problem was discussed nearly a century ago by Anvar, and I agree with his conclusions. We must act *immediately* along those lines.

F.K.S.

From: President.
To: Secretary of State.

Inform the Council that an emergency meeting is convened for noon tomorrow.

K.K. V.

From: President.
To: C.B.E.P.S.

Twenty battleships should be sufficient to put Anvar's plan into operation. Fortunately there is no need to arm them – yet. Report progress of construction to me weekly.

K.K. V.

From: C.B.E.P.S.
To: President.

Nineteen ships are now completed. The twentieth is still delayed owing to hull failure and will not be ready for at least a month.

Ranthe

From: President.
To: C.B.E.P.S.

Nineteen will be sufficient. I will check the operational plan with you tomorrow. Is the draft of our broadcast ready yet?

K.K. V.

From: C.B.E.P.S.
To: President.

Draft herewith:

People of Earth!

We, the inhabitants of the planet you call Mars, have for many years observed your experiments towards achieving interplanetary travel. *These experiments must cease.* Our study of your race has convinced us that you are not fitted to leave your planet in the present state of your civilisation. The ships you now see floating above your cities are capable of destroying them utterly, and will do so unless you discontinue your attempts to cross space.

We have set up an observatory on your Moon and can immediately detect any violation of these orders. If you obey them, we will not interfere with you again. Otherwise, one of your cities will be destroyed every time we observe a rocket leaving the Earth's atmosphere.

By order of the President and Council of Mars.

Ranthe

From: President.
To: C.B.E.P.S.

I approve. The translation can go ahead.

I will not be sailing with the fleet, after all. Report to me in detail immediately on your return.

K.K. V.

From: C.B.E.P.S.
To: President.

I have the honour to report the successful completion of our mission. The voyage to Earth was uneventful: radio messages from the planet indicated that we were detected at a considerable distance and great excitement had been aroused before our arrival. The fleet was dispersed according to plan and I broadcast the ultimatum. We left immediately and no hostile weapons were brought to bear against us.

I will report in detail within two days.

Ranthe

From: Secretary, Council of Scientists.
To: President.

The psychologists have completed their report, which is attached herewith.

As might be expected, our demands at first infuriated this stubborn and high-spirited race. The shock to their pride must have been considerable, for they believed themselves to be the only intelligent beings in the Universe.

However, within a few weeks there was a rather unexpected change in the tone of their statements. They had begun to realise that we were intercepting all their radio transmissions, and some messages have been broadcast directly to us. They state that they have agreed to ban all rocket experiments, in accordance with our wishes. This is as unexpected as it is welcome. Even if they are trying to deceive us, we are perfectly safe now that we have established the second station just outside the atmosphere. They cannot possibly develop spaceships without our seeing them or detecting their tube radiation.

The watch on Earth will be continued rigorously, as instructed.

Trescon

From: C.B.E.P.S.
To: President.

Yes, it is quite true that there have been no further rocket experiments in the last ten years. We certainly did not expect Earth to capitulate so easily!

I agree that the existence of this race now constitutes a permanent threat to our civilisation and we are making experiments along the lines you suggest. The problem is a difficult one, owing to the great size of the planet. Explosives would be out of the question, and a radioactive poison of some kind appears to offer the greatest hope of success.

Fortunately, we now have an indefinite time in which to complete this research, and I will report regularly.

Ranthe

[End of Document]

From: Lieutenant Commander Henry Forbes, Intelligence Branch, Special Space Corps.
To: Professor S. Maxton, Philogical Department, University of Oxford.
Route: Transender II (via Schenectady).

The above papers, with others, were found in the ruins of what is believed to be the capital Martian city. (Mars Grid KL302895.) The frequent use of the ideograph for 'Earth' suggests that they may be of special interest and it is hoped that they can be translated. Other papers will be following shortly.

H. Forbes, Lt/Cdr.

[Added in manuscript]
Dear Max,

Sorry I've had no time to contact you before. I'll be seeing you as soon as I get back to Earth.

Gosh! Mars *is* in a mess! Our Co-ordinates were dead accurate and the bombs materialised right over their cities, just as the Mount Wilson boys predicted.

We're sending a lot of stuff back through the two small machines, but until the big transmitter is materialised we're rather restricted, and, of course, none of us can return. So hurry up with it!

I'm glad we can get to work on rockets again. I may be old-fashioned, but being squirted through space at the speed of light doesn't appeal to me!

Yours in haste,
Henry

Rescue Party

First published in *Astounding Science-Fiction*, May 1946
Collected in *Reach for Tomorrow*

This story stems from a lost original which also inspired 'History Lesson' (1949), although it would be difficult to find two more contrasting endings.

Who was to blame? For three days Alveron's thoughts had come back to that question, and still he had found no answer. A creature of a less civilised or a less sensitive race would never have let it torture his mind, and would have satisfied himself with the assurance that no one could be responsible for the working of fate. But Alveron and his kind had been lords of the Universe since the dawn of history, since that far distant age when the Time Barrier had been folded round the cosmos by the unknown powers that lay beyond the Beginning. To them had been given all knowledge – and with infinite knowledge went infinite responsibility. If there were mistakes and errors in the administration of the galaxy, the fault lay on the heads of Alveron and his people. And this was no mere mistake: it was one of the greatest tragedies in history.

The crew still knew nothing. Even Rugon, his closest friend and the ship's deputy captain, had been told only part of the truth. But now the doomed worlds lay less than a billion miles ahead. In a few hours, they would be landing on the third planet.

Once again Alveron read the message from Base; then, with a flick of a tentacle that no human eye could have followed, he pressed the 'General Attention' button. Throughout the mile-long cylinder that was the Galactic Survey Ship S9000, creatures of many races laid down their work to listen to the words of their captain.

'I know you have all been wondering,' began Alveron, 'why we were ordered to abandon our survey and to proceed at such an acceleration to this region of space. Some of you may realise what this acceleration means. Our ship is on its last voyage: the generators have already been running for sixty hours at Ultimate Overload. We will be very lucky if we return to Base under our own power.

'We are approaching a sun which is about to become a Nova. Detonation will occur in seven hours, with an uncertainty of one hour, leaving us a

35

maximum of only four hours of exploration. There are ten planets in the system about to be destroyed – and there is a civilisation on the third. That fact was discovered only a few days ago. It is our tragic mission to contact that doomed race and if possible to save some of its members. I know that there is little we can do in so short a time with this single ship. No other machine can possibly reach the system before detonation occurs.'

There was a long pause during which there could have been no sound or movement in the whole of the mighty ship as it sped silently toward the worlds ahead. Alveron knew what his companions were thinking and he tried to answer their unspoken question.

'You will wonder how such a disaster, the greatest of which we have any record, has been allowed to occur. On one point I can assure you. The fault does not lie with the Survey.

'As you know, with our present fleet of under twelve thousand ships, it is possible to re-examine each of the eight thousand million solar systems in the Galaxy at intervals of about a million years. Most worlds change very little in so short a time as that.

'Less than four hundred thousand years ago, the survey ship S5060 examined the planets of the system we are approaching. It found intelligence on none of them, though the third planet was teeming with animal life and two other worlds had once been inhabited. The usual report was submitted and the system is due for its next examination in six hundred thousand years.

'It now appears that in the incredibily short period since the last survey, intelligent life has appeared in the system. The first intimation of this occurred when unknown radio signals were detected on the planet Kulath in the system X29.35, Y34.76, Z27.93. Bearings were taken on them; they were coming from the system ahead.

'Kulath is two hundred light-years from here, so those radio waves had been on their way for two centuries. Thus for at least that period of time a civilisation has existed on one of these worlds – a civilisation that can generate electromagnetic waves and all that that implies.

'An immediate telescopic examination of the system was made and it was then found that the sun was in the unstable pre-nova stage. Detonation might occur at any moment, and indeed might have done so while the light waves were on their way to Kulath.

'There was a slight delay while the supervelocity scanners on Kulath II were focused on to the system. They showed that the explosion had not yet occurred but was only a few hours away. If Kulath had been a fraction of a light-year further from this sun, we should never have known of its civilisation until it had ceased to exist.

'The Administrator of Kulath contacted Sector Base immediately, and I was ordered to proceed to the system at once. Our object is to save what members we can of the doomed race, if indeed there are any left. But we have assumed that a civilisation possessing radio could have protected itself against any rise of temperature that may have already occurred.

'This ship and two tenders will each explore a section of the planet. Commander Torkalee will take Number One, Comander Orostron Number Two. They will have just under four hours in which to explore this world. At the end of that time, they must be back in the ship. It will be leaving then, with or without them. I will give the two commanders detailed instructions in the control room immediately.

'That is all. We enter atmosphere in two hours.'

On the world once known as Earth the fires were dying out: there was nothing left to burn. The great forests that had swept across the planet like a tidal wave with the passing of the cities were now no more than glowing charcoal and the smoke of their funeral pyres still stained the sky. But the last hours were still to come, for the surface rocks had not yet begun to flow. The continents were dimly visible through the haze, but their outlines meant nothing to the watchers in the approaching ship. The charts they possessed were out of date by a dozen Ice Ages and more deluges than one.

The S9000 had driven past Jupiter and seen at once that no life could exist in those half-gaseous oceans of compressed hydrocarbons, now erupting furiously under the sun's abnormal heat. Mars and the outer planets they had missed, and Alveron realised that the worlds nearer the sun than Earth would be already melting. It was more than likely, he thought sadly, that the tragedy of this unknown race was already finished. Deep in his heart, he thought it might be better so. The ship could only have carried a few hundred survivors, and the problem of selection had been haunting his mind.

Rugon, Chief of Communications and Deputy Captain, came into the control room. For the last hour he had been striving to detect radiation from Earth, but in vain.

'We're too late,' he announced gloomily. 'I've monitored the whole spectrum and the ether's dead except for our own stations and some two-hundred-year-old programmes from Kulath. Nothing in this system is radiating any more.'

He moved toward the giant vision screen with a graceful flowing motion that no mere biped could ever hope to imitate. Alveron said nothing; he had been expecting this news.

One entire wall of the control room was taken up by the screen, a great black rectangle that gave an impression of almost infinite depth. Three of Rugon's slender control tentacles, useless for heavy work but incredibly swift at all manipulation, flickered over the selector dials and the screen lit up with a thousand points of light. The star field flowed swiftly past as Rugon adjusted the controls, bringing the projector to bear upon the sun itself.

No man of Earth would have recognised the monstrous shape that filled the screen. The sun's light was white no longer: great violet-blue clouds covered half its surface and from them long streamers of flame were erupting into space. At one point an enormous prominence had reared itself

37

out of the photosphere, far out even into the flickering veils of the corona. It was as though a tree of fire had taken root in the surface of the sun – a tree that stood half a million miles high and whose branches were rivers of flame sweeping through space at hundreds of miles a second.

'I suppose,' said Rugon presently, 'that you are quite satisfied about the astronomers' calculations. After all—'

'Oh, we're perfectly safe,' said Alveron confidently. 'I've spoken to Kulath Observatory and they have been making some additional checks through our own instruments. That uncertainty of an hour includes a private safety margin which they won't tell me in case I feel tempted to stay any longer.'

He glanced at the instrument board.

'The pilot should have brought us to the atmosphere now. Switch the screen back to the planet, please. Ah, there they go!'

There was a sudden tremor underfoot and a raucous clanging of alarms, instantly stilled. Across the vision screen two slim projectiles dived toward the looming mass of Earth. For a few miles they travelled together, then they separated, one vanishing abruptly as it entered the shadow of the planet.

Slowly the huge mother ship, with its thousand times greater mass, descended after them into the raging storms that already were tearing down the deserted cities of Man.

It was night in the hemisphere over which Orostron drove his tiny command. Like Torkalee, his mission was to photograph and record, and to report progress to the mother ship. The little scout had no room for specimens or passengers. If contact was made with the inhabitants of this world, the S9000 would come at once. There would be no time for parleying. If there was any trouble the rescue would be by force and the explanations could come later.

The ruined land beneath was bathed with an eerie, flickering light, for a great auroral display was raging over half the world. But the image on the vision screen was independent of external light, and it showed clearly a waste of barren rock that seemed never to have known any form of life. Presumably this desert land must come to an end somewhere. Orostron increased his speed to the highest value he dared risk in so dense an atmosphere.

The machine fled on through the storm, and presently the desert of rock began to climb toward the sky. A great mountain range lay ahead, its peaks lost in the smoke-laden clouds. Orostron directed the scanners toward the horizon, and on the vision screen the line of mountains seemed suddenly very close and menacing. He started to climb rapidly. It was difficult to imagine a more unpromising land in which to find civilisation and he wondered if it would be wise to change course. He decided against it. Five minutes later, he had his reward.

Miles below lay a decapitated mountain, the whole of its summit sheared away by some tremendous feat of engineering. Rising out of the rock and straddling the artificial plateau was an intricate structure of metal girders, supporting masses of machinery. Orostron brought his ship to a halt and spiralled down toward the mountain.

The slight Doppler blur had now vanished, and the picture on the screen was clear-cut. The latticework was supporting some scores of great metal mirrors, pointing skyward at an angle of forty-five degrees to the horizontal. They were slightly concave, and each had some complicated mechanism at its focus. There seemed something impressive and purposeful about the great array; every mirror was aimed at precisely the same spot in the sky – or beyond.

Orostron turned to his colleagues.

'It looks like some kind of observatory to me,' he said. 'Have you ever seen anything like it before?'

Klarten, a multitentacled, tripedal creature from a globular cluster at the edge of the Milky Way, had a different theory.

'That's communication equipment. Those reflectors are for focusing electromagnetic beams. I've seen the same kind of installation on a hundred worlds before. It may even be the station that Kulath picked up – though that's rather unlikely, for the beams would be very narrow from mirrors that size.'

'That would explain why Rugon could detect no radiation before we landed,' added Hansur II, one of the twin beings from the planet Thargon.

Orostron did not agree at all.

'If that is a radio station, it must be built for interplanetary communication. Look at the way the mirrors are pointed. I don't believe that a race which has only had radio for two centuries can have crossed space. It took my people six thousand years to do it.'

'We managed it in three,' said Hansur II mildly, speaking a few seconds ahead of his twin. Before the inevitable argument could develop, Klarten began to wave his tentacles with excitement. While the others had been talking, he had started the automatic monitor.

'Here it is! Listen!'

He threw a switch, and the little room was filled with a raucous whining sound, continually changing in pitch but nevertheless retaining certain characteristics that were difficult to define.

The four explorers listened intently for a minute; then Orostron said, 'Surely that can't be any form of speech! No creature could produce sounds as quickly as that!'

Hansur I had come to the same conclusion. 'That's a television programme. Don't you think so, Klarten?'

The other agreed.

'Yes, and each of those mirrors seems to be radiating a different programme. I wonder where they're going? If I'm correct, one of the other planets in the system must lie along those beams. We can soon check that.'

Orostron called the S9000 and reported the discovery. Both Rugon and Alveron were greatly excited, and made a quick check of the astronomical records.

The result was surprising – and disappointing. None of the other nine planets lay anywhere near the line of transmission. The great mirrors appeared to be pointing blindly into space.

There seemed only one conclusion to be drawn, and Klarten was the first to voice it.

'They had interplanetary communication,' he said. 'But the station must be deserted now, and the transmitters no longer controlled. They haven't been switched off, and are just pointing where they were left.'

'Well, we'll soon find out,' said Orostron. 'I'm going to land.'

He brought the machine slowly down to the level of the great metal mirrors, and past them until it came to rest on the mountain rock. A hundred yards away, a white stone building crouched beneath the maze of steel girders. It was windowless, but there were several doors in the wall facing them.

Orostron watched his companions climb into their protective suits and wished he could follow. But someone had to stay in the machine to keep in touch with the mother ship. Those were Alveron's instructions, and they were very wise. One never knew what would happen on a world that was being explored for the first time, especially under conditions such as these.

Very cautiously, the three explorers stepped out of the airlock and adjusted the antigravity field of their suits. Then, each with the mode of locomotion peculiar to his race, the little party went toward the building, the Hansur twins leading and Klarten following close behind. His gravity control was apparently giving trouble, for he suddenly fell to the ground, rather to the amusement of his colleagues. Orostron saw them pause for a moment at the nearest door – then it opened slowly and they disappeared from sight.

So Orostron waited, with what patience he could, while the storm rose around him and the light of the aurora grew even brighter in the sky. At the agreed times he called the mother ship and received brief acknowledgements from Rugon. He wondered how Torkalee was faring, halfway round the planet, but he could not contact him through the crash and thunder of solar interference.

It did not take Klarten and the Hansurs long to discover that their theories were largely correct. The building was a radio station, and it was utterly deserted. It consisted of one tremendous room with a few small offices leading from it. In the main chamber, row after row of electrical equipment stretched into the distance; lights flickered and winked on hundreds of control panels, and a dull glow came from the elements in a great avenue of vacuum tubes.

But Klarten was not impressed. The first radio set his race had built were now fossilised in strata a thousand million years old. Man, who had possessed electrical machines for only a few centuries, could not compete with those who had known them for half the lifetime of the Earth.

Nevertheless, the party kept their recorders running as they explored the building. There was still one problem to be solved. The deserted station was broadcasting programmes but where were they coming from? The central switchboard had been quickly located. It was designed to handle scores of programmes simultaneously, but the source of those programmes was lost in a maze of cables that vanished underground. Back in the S9000, Rugon was trying to analyse the broadcasts and perhaps his researches would reveal their origin. It was impossible to trace cables that might lead across continents.

The party wasted little time at the deserted station. There was nothing they could learn from it, and they were seeking life rather than scientific information. A few minutes later the little ship rose swiftly from the plateau and headed toward the plains that must lie beyond the mountains. Less than three hours were still left to them.

As the array of enigmatic mirrors dropped out of sight, Orostron was struck by a sudden thought. Was it imagination, or had they all moved through a small angle while he had been waiting, as if they were still compensating for the rotation of the Earth? He could not be sure, and he dismissed the matter as unimportant. It would only mean that the directing mechanism was still working, after a fashion.

They discovered the city fifteen minutes later. It was a great, sprawling metropolis, built around a river that had disappeared leaving an ugly scar winding its way among the great buildings and beneath bridges that looked very incongruous now.

Even from the air, the city looked deserted. But only two and a half hours were left – there was no time for further exploration. Orostron made his decision, and landed near the largest structure he could see. It seemed reasonable to suppose that some creatures would have sought shelter in the strongest buildings, where they would be safe until the very end.

The deepest caves – the heart of the planet itself – would give no protection when the final cataclysm came. Even if this race had reached the outer planets, its doom would only be delayed by the few hours it would take for the ravening wavefronts to cross the Solar System.

Orostron could not know that the city had been deserted not for a few days or weeks, but for over a century. For the culture of cities, which had outlasted so many civilisations had been doomed at last when the helicopter brought universal transportation. Within a few generations the great masses of mankind, knowing that they could reach any part of the globe in a matter of hours, had gone back to the fields and forests for which they had always longed. The new civilisation had machines and resources of which earlier ages had never dreamed, but it was essentially rural and no longer bound to the steel and concrete warrens that had dominated the centuries before. Such cities as still remained were specialised centres of research,

41

administration or entertainment; the others had been allowed to decay, where it was too much trouble to destroy them. The dozen or so greatest of all cities, and the ancient university towns, had scarcely changed and would have lasted for many generations to come. But the cities that had been founded on steam and iron and surface transportation had passed with the industries that had nourished them.

And so while Orostron waited in the tender, his colleagues raced through endless empty corridors and deserted halls, taking innumerable photographs but learning nothing of the creatures who had used these buildings. There were libraries, meeting places, council rooms, thousands of offices – all were empty and deep with dust. If they had not seen the radio station on its mountain eyrie, the explorers could well have believed that this world had known no life for centuries.

Through the long minutes of waiting, Orostron tried to imagine where this race could have vanished. Perhaps they had killed themselves knowing that escape was impossible; perhaps they had built great shelters in the bowels of the planet, and even now were cowering in their millions beneath his feet, waiting for the end. He began to fear that he would never know.

It was almost a relief when at last he had to give the order for the return. Soon he would know if Torkalee's party had been more fortunate. And he was anxious to get back to the mother ship, for as the minutes passed the suspense had become more and more acute. There had always been the thought in his mind: What if the astronomers of Kulath have made a mistake? He would begin to feel happy when the walls of the S9000 were around him. He would be happier still when they were out in space and this ominous sun was shrinking far astern.

As soon as his colleagues had entered the airlock, Orostron hurled his tiny machine into the sky and set the controls to home on S9000. Then he turned to his friends.

'Well, what have you found?' he asked.

Klarten produced a large roll of canvas and spread it out on the floor.

'This is what they were like,' he said quietly. 'Bipeds, with only two arms. They seem to have managed well, in spite of that handicap. Only two eyes as well, unless there are others in the back. We were lucky to find this; it's about the only thing they left behind.'

The ancient oil paintings stared stonily back at the three creatures regarding it so intently. By the irony of fate, its complete worthlessness had saved it from oblivion. When the city had been evacuated, no one had bothered to move Alderman John Richards, 1909–1974. For a century and a half he had been gathering dust while far away from the old cities the new civilisation had been rising to heights no earlier culture had ever known.

'That was almost all we found,' said Klarten. 'The city must have been deserted for years. I'm afraid our expedition has been a failure. If there are any living beings on this world, they've hidden themselves too well for us to find them.'

His commander was forced to agree.

'It was an almost impossible task,' he said. 'If we'd had weeks instead of hours we might have succeeded. For all we know, they may even have built shelters under the sea. No one seems to have thought of that.'

He glanced quickly at the indicators and corrected the course.

'We'll be there in five minutes. Alveron seems to be moving rather quickly. I wonder if Torkalee has found anything.'

The S9000 was hanging a few miles above the seaboard of a blazing continent when Orostron homed upon it. The danger line was thirty minutes away and there was no time to lose. Skilfully, he manoeuvred the little ship into its launching tube and the party stepped out of the airlock.

There was a small crowd waiting for them. That was to be expected, but Orostron could see at once that something more than curiosity had brought his friends here. Even before a word was spoken, he knew that something was wrong.

'Torkalee hasn't returned. He's lost his party and we're going to the rescue. Come along to the control room at once.'

From the beginning, Torkalee had been luckier than Orostron. He had followed the zone of twilight, keeping away from the intolerable glare of the sun, until he came to the shores of an inland sea. It was a very recent sea, one of the latest of Man's works, for the land it covered had been desert less than a century before. In a few hours it would be desert again, for the water was boiling and clouds of steam were rising to the skies. But they could not veil the loveliness of the great white city that overlooked the tideless sea.

Flying machines were still parked neatly round the square in which Torkalee landed. They were disappointingly primitive, though beautifully finished, and depended on rotating airfoils for support. Nowhere was there any sign of life, but the place gave the impression that its inhabitants were not very far away. Lights were still shining from some of the windows.

Torkalee's three companions lost no time in leaving the machine. Leader of the party, by seniority of rank and race was T'sinadree, who like Alveron himself had been born on one of the ancient planets of the Central Suns. Next came Alarkane, from a race which was one of the youngest in the Universe and took a perverse pride in the fact. Last came one of the strange beings from the system of Palador. It was nameless, like all its kind, for it possessed no identity of its own, being merely a mobile but still dependent cell in the consciousness of its race. Though it and its fellows had long been scattered over the galaxy in the exploration of countless worlds, some unknown link still bound them together as inexorably as the living cells in a human body.

When a creature of Palador spoke, the pronoun it used was always 'We'. There was not, nor could there ever be, any first person singular in the language of Palador.

The great doors of the splendid building baffled the explorers, though any human child would have known their secret. T'sinadree wasted no time on them but called Torkalee on his personal transmitter. Then the three hurried aside while their commander manoeuvred his machine into the best position. There was a brief burst of intolerable flame: the massive steelwork flickered once at the edge of the visible spectrum and was gone. The stones were still glowing when the eager party hurried into the building, the beams of their light projectors fanning before them.

The torches were not needed. Before them lay a great hall, glowing with light from lines of tubes along the ceiling. On either side, the hall opened out into long corridors, while straight ahead a massive stairway swept majestically toward the upper floors.

For a moment T'sinadree hesitated. Then, since one way was as good as another, he led his companions down the first corridor.

The feeling that life was near had now become very strong. At any moment, it seemed, they might be confronted by the creatures of this world. If they showed hostility – and they could scarcely be blamed if they did – the paralysers would be used at once.

The tension was very great as the party entered the first room, and only relaxed when they saw that it held nothing but machines – row after row of them, now stilled and silent. Lining the enormous room were thousands of metal filing cabinets, forming a continuous wall as far as the eye could reach. And that was all; there was no furniture, nothing but the cabinets and the mysterious machines.

Alarkane, always the quickest of the three, was already examining the cabinets. Each held many thousand sheets of tough, thin material, perforated with innumerable holes and slots. The Paladorian appropriated one of the cards and Alarkane recorded the scene together with some close-ups of the machines. Then they left. The great room, which had been one of the marvels of the world, meant nothing to them. No living eye would ever again see that wonderful battery of almost human Hollerith analysers and the five thousand million punched cards holding all that could be recorded of each man, woman and child on the planet.

It was clear that this building had been used very recently. With growing excitement, the explorers hurried on to the next room. This they found to be an enormous library, for million of books lay all around them on miles and miles of shelving. Here, though the explorers could not know it, were the records of all the laws that Man had ever passed, and all the speeches that had ever been made in his council chambers.

T'sinadree was deciding his plan of action, when Alarkane drew his attention to one of the racks a hundred yards away. It was half empty, unlike all the others. Around it books lay in a tumbled heap on the floor, as if knocked down by someone in frantic haste. The signs were unmistakable. Not long ago, other creatures had been this way. Faint wheel marks were clearly visible on the floor to the acute sense of Alarkane, though the others could see nothing. Alarkane could even detect footprints, but knowing

44

nothing of the creatures that had formed them he could not say which way they led.

The sense of nearness was stronger than ever now, but it was nearness in time, not in space. Alarkane voiced the thoughts of the party.

'Those books must have been valuable, and someone has come to rescue them – rather as an afterthought, I should say. That means there must be a place of refuge, possibly not very far away. Perhaps we may be able to find some other clues that will lead us to it.'

T'sinadree agreed; the Paladorian wasn't enthusiastic.

'That may be so,' it said, 'but the refuge may be anywhere on the planet, and we have just two hours left. Let us waste no more time if we hope to rescue these people.'

The party hurried forward once more, pausing only to collect a few books that might be useful to the scientists at Base – though it was doubtful if they could ever be translated. They soon found that the great building was composed largely of small rooms, all showing signs of recent occupation. Most of them were in a neat and tidy condition, but one or two were very much the reverse. The explorers were particularly puzzled by one room – clearly an office of some kind – that appeared to have been completely wrecked. The floor was littered with papers, the furniture had been smashed, and smoke was pouring through the broken windows from the fires outside.

T'sinadree was rather alarmed.

'Surely no dangerous animal could have got into a place like this!' he exclaimed, fingering his paralyser nervously.

Alarkane did not answer. He began to make that annoying sound which his race called 'laughter'. It was several minutes before he would explain what had amused him.

'I don't think any animal has done it,' he said. 'In fact, the explanation is very simple. Suppose *you* had been working all your life in this room, dealing with endless papers, year after year. And suddenly, you are told that you will never see it again, that your work is finished, and that you can leave it forever. More than that – no one will come after you. Everything is finished. How would you make your exit, T'sinadree?'

The other thought for a moment.

'Well, I suppose I'd just tidy things up and leave. That's what seems to have happened in all the other rooms.'

Alarkane laughed again.

'I'm quite sure you would. But some individuals have a different psychology. I think I should have liked the creature that used this room.'

He did not explain himself further, and his two colleagues puzzled over his words for quite a while before they gave it up.

It came as something of a shock when Torkalee gave the order to return. They had gathered a great deal of information, but had found no clue that might lead them to the missing inhabitants of this world. That problem was as baffling as ever, and now it seemed that it would never be solved. There were only forty minutes left before the S9000 would be departing.

They were halfway back to the tender when they saw the semicircular passage leading down into the depths of the building. Its architectural style was quite different from that used elsewhere, and the gently sloping floor was an irresistible attraction to creatures whose many legs had grown weary of the marble staircases which only bipeds could have built in such profusion. T'sinadree had been the worst sufferer, for he normally employed twelve legs and could use twenty when he was in a hurry, though no one had ever seen him perform this feat.

The party stopped dead and looked down the passageway with a single thought. A tunnel, leading down into the depths of Earth! At its end, they might yet find the people of this world and rescue some of them from their fate. For there was still time to call the mother ship if the need arose.

T'sinadree signalled to his commander and Torkalee brought the little machine immediately overhead. There might not be time for the party to retrace its footsteps through the maze of passages, so meticulously recorded in the Paladorian mind that there was no possibility of going astray. If speed was necessary, Torkalee could blast his way through the dozen floors above their head. In any case, it should not take long to find what lay at the end of the passage.

It took only thirty seconds. The tunnel ended quite abruptly in a very curious cylindrical room with magnificently padded seats along the walls. There was no way out save that by which they had come and it was several seconds before the purpose of the chamber dawned on Alarkane's mind. It was a pity, he thought, that they would never have time to use this. The thought was suddenly interrupted by a cry from T'sinadree. Alarkane wheeled around, and saw that the entrance had closed silently behind them.

Even in that first moment of panic, Alarkane found himself thinking with some admiration: Whoever they were, they knew how to build automatic machinery!

The Paladorian was the first to speak. It waved one of its tentacles toward the seats.

'We think it would be best to be seated,' it said. The multiplex mind of Palador had already analysed the situation and knew what was coming.

They did not have long to wait before a low-pitched hum came from a grill overhead, and for the very last time in history a human, even if lifeless, voice was heard on Earth. The words were meaningless, though the trapped explorers could guess their message clearly enough.

'Choose your stations, please, and be seated.'

Simultaneously, a wall panel at one end of the compartment glowed with light. On it was a simple map, consisting of a series of a dozen circles connected by a line. Each of the circles had writing alongside it, and beside the writing were two buttons of different colours.

Alarkane looked questioningly at his leader.

'Don't touch them,' said T'sinadree. 'If we leave the controls alone, the doors may open again.'

He was wrong. The engineers who had designed the automatic subway had assumed that anyone who entered it would naturally wish to go somewhere. If they selected no intermediate station, their destination could only be the end of the line.

There was another pause while the relays and thyratrons waited for their orders. In those thirty seconds, if they had known what to do, the party could have opened the doors and left the subway. But they did not know, and the machines geared to a human psychology acted for them.

The surge of acceleration was not very great; the lavish upholstery was a luxury, not a necessity. Only an almost imperceptible vibration told of the speed at which they were travelling through the bowels of the earth, on a journey the duration of which they could not even guess. And in thirty minutes, the S9000 would be leaving the Solar System.

There was a long silence in the speeding machine. T'sinadree and Alarkane were thinking rapidly. So was the Paladorian, though in a different fashion. The conception of personal death was meaningless to it, for the destruction of a single unit meant no more to the group mind that the loss of a nail-paring to a man. But it could, though with great difficulty, appreciate the plight of individual intelligences such as Alarkane and T'sinadree, and it was anxious to help them if it could.

Alarkane had managed to contact Torkalee with his personal transmitter, though the signal was very weak and seemed to be fading quickly. Rapidly he explained the situation, and almost at once the signals became clearer. Torkalee was following the path of the machine, flying above the ground under which they were speeding to their unknown destination. That was the first indicator they had of the fact that they were travelling at nearly a thousand miles an hour, and very soon after that Torkalee was able to give the still more disturbing news that they were rapidly approaching the sea. While they were beneath the land, there was a hope, though a slender one that they might stop the machine and escape. But under the ocean – not all the brains and the machinery in the great mother ship could save them. No one could have devised a more perfect trap.

T'sinadree had been examining the wall map with great attention. Its meaning was obvious, and along the line connecting the circles a tiny spot of light was crawling. It was already halfway to the first of the stations marked.

'I'm going to press one of those buttons,' said T'sinadree at last. 'It won't do any harm, and we may learn something.'

'I agree. Which will you try first?'

'There are only two kinds, and it won't matter if we try the wrong one first. I suppose one is to start the machine and the other is to stop it.'

Alarkane was not very hopeful.

'It started without any button pressing,' he said. 'I think it's completely automatic and we can't control it from here at all.'

T'sinadree could not agree.

'These buttons are clearly associated with the stations, and there's no point in having them unless you can use them to stop yourself. The only question is, which is the right one?'

His analysis was perfectly correct. The machine could be stopped at any intermediate station. They had only been on their way ten minutes, and if they could leave now, no harm would have been done. It was just bad luck that T'sinadree's first choice was the wrong button.

The little light on the map crawled slowly through the illuminated circle without checking its speed. And at the same time Torkalee called from the ship overhead.

'You have just passed underneath a city and are heading out to sea. There cannot be another stop for nearly a thousand miles.'

Alveron had given up all hope of finding life on this world. The S9000 had roamed over half the planet, never staying long in one place, descending ever and again in an effort to attract attention. There had been no response; Earth seemed utterly dead. If any of its inhabitants were still alive, thought Alveron, they must have hidden themselves in its depths where no help could reach them, though their doom would be nonetheless certain.

Rugon brought news of the disaster. The great ship ceased its fruitless searching and fled back through the storm to the ocean above which Torkalee's little tender was still following the track of tbe buried machine.

The scene was truly terrifying. Not since the days when Earth was born had there been such seas as this. Mountains of water were racing before the storm which had now reached velocities of many hundred miles an hour. Even at this distance from the mainland the air was full of flying debris – trees, fragments of houses, sheets of metal, anything that had not been anchored to the ground. No airborne machine could have lived for a moment in such a gale. And ever and again even the roar of the wind was drowned as the vast water-mountains met head-on with a crash that seemed to shake the sky.

Fortunately, there had been no serious earthquakes yet. Far beneath the bed of the ocean, the wonderful piece of engineering which had been the World President's private vacuum-subway was still working perfectly, unaffected by the tumult and destruction above. It would continue to work until the last minute of the Earth's existence, which, if the astronomers were right, was not much more than fifteen minutes away – though precisely how much more Alveron would have given a great deal to know. It would be nearly an hour before the trapped party could reach land and even the slightest hope of rescue.

Alveron's instructions had been precise, though even without them he would never have dreamed of taking any risks with the great machine that had been entrusted to his care. Had he been human, the decision to abandon the trapped members of his crew would have been desperately hard to make. But he came of a race far more sensitive than Man, a race that so loved the things of the spirit that long ago, and with infinite reluctance, it had taken over control of the Universe since only thus could it be sure that justice was being done. Alveron would need all his super-human gifts to carry him through the next few hours.

Meanwhile, a mile below the bed of the ocean Alarkane and T'sinadree were very busy indeed with their private communicators. Fifteen minutes is not a long time in which to wind up the affairs of a lifetime. It is indeed, scarcely long enough to dictate more than a few of those farewell messages which at such moments are so much more important than all other matters.

All the while the Paladorian had remained silent and motionless, saying not a word. The other two, resigned to their fate and engrossed in their personal affairs, had given it no thought. They were startled when suddenly it began to address them in its peculiarly passionless voice.

'We perceive that you are making certain arrangements concerning your anticipated destruction. That will probably be unnecessary. Captain Alveron hopes to rescue us if we can stop this machine when we reach land again.'

Both T'sinadree and Alarkane were too surprised to say anything for a moment. Then the latter gasped, 'How do you know?'

It was a foolish question, for he remembered at once that there were several Paladorians – if one could use the phrase – in the S9000, and consequently their companion knew everything that was happening in the mother ship. So he did not wait for an answer but continued, 'Alveron can't do that! He daren't take such a risk!'

'There will be no risk,' said the Paladorian. 'We have told him what to do. It is really very simple.'

Alarkane and T'sinadree looked at their companion with something approaching awe, realising now what must have happened. In moments of crisis, the single units comprising the Paladorian mind could link together in an organisation no less close than that of any physical brain. At such moments they formed an intellect more powerful than any other in the Universe. All ordinary problems could be solved by a few hundred or thousand units. Very rarely millions would be needed, and on two historic occasions the billions of cells of the entire Paladorian consciousness had been welded together to deal with emergencies that threatened the race. The mind of Palador was one of the greatest mental resources of the Universe; its full force was seldom required, but the knowledge that it was available was supremely comforting to other races. Alarkane wondered how many cells had co-ordinated to deal with this particular emergency. He also wondered how so trivial an incident had ever come to its attention.

To that question he was never to know the answer, though he might have guessed it had he known that the chillingly remote Paladorian mind possessed an almost human streak of vanity. Long ago, Alarkane had written a book trying to prove that eventually all intelligent races would sacrifice individual consciousness and that one day only group-minds would remain in the Universe. Palador, he had said, was the first of those ultimate intellects, and the vast, dispersed mind had not been displeased.

They had no time to ask any further questions before Alveron himself began to speak through their communicators.

'Alveron calling! We're staying on this planet until the detonation waves reach it, so we may be able to rescue you. You're heading toward a city on the coast which you'll reach in forty minutes at your present speed. If you cannot stop yourselves then, we're going to blast the tunnel behind and ahead of you to cut off your power. Then we'll sink a shaft to get you out – the chief engineer says he can do it in five minutes with the main projectors. So you should be safe within an hour, unless the sun blows up before.'

'And if that happens, you'll be destroyed as well! You mustn't take such a risk!'

'Don't let that worry you; we're perfectly safe. When the sun detonates, the explosion wave will take several minutes to rise to its maximum. But apart from that, we're on the night side of the planet, behind an eight-thousand-mile screen of rock. When the first warning of the explosion comes, we will accelerate out of the Solar System, keeping in the shadow of the planet. Under our maximum drive, we will reach the velocity of light before leaving the cone of shadow, and the sun cannot harm us then.'

T'sinadree was still afraid to hope. Another objection came at once into his mind.

'Yes, but how will you get any warning, here on the night side of the planet?'

'Very easily,' replied Alveron. 'This world has a moon which is now visible from this hemisphere. We have telescopes trained on it. If it shows any sudden increase in brilliance, our main drive goes on automatically and we'll be thrown out of the system.'

The logic was flawless. Alveron, cautious as ever, was taking no chances. It would be many minutes before the eight-thousand-mile shield of rock and metal could be destroyed by the fires of the exploding sun. In that time, the S9000 could have reached the safety of the velocity of light.

Alarkane pressed the second button when they were still several miles from the coast. He did not expect anything to happen then, assuming that the machine could not stop between stations. It seemed too good to be true when, a few minutes later, the machine's slight vibration died away and they came to a halt.

The doors slid silently apart. Even before they were fully open, the three had left the compartment. They were taking no more chances. Before them a long tunnel stretched into the distance, rising slowly out of sight. They were starting along it when suddenly Alveron's voice called from the communicators.

'Stay where you are! We're going to blast!'

The ground shuddered once, and far ahead there came the rumble of falling rock. Again the earth shook – and a hundred yards ahead the passageway vanished abruptly. A tremendous vertical shaft had been cut clean through it.

The party hurried forward again until they came to the end of the corridor and stood waiting on its lip. The shaft in which it ended was a full thousand feet across and descended into the earth as far as the torches could throw their beams. Overhead, the storm clouds fled beneath a moon that no man would have recognised, so luridly brilliant was its disc. And, most glorious of all sights, the S9000 floated high above, the great projectors that had drilled this enormous pit still glowing cherry red.

A dark shape detached itself from the mother ship and dropped swiftly towards the ground. Torkalee was returning to collect his friends. A little later, Alveron greeted them in the control room. He waved to the great vision screen and said quietly, 'See, we were barely in time.'

The continent below them was slowly settling beneath the mile-high waves that were attacking its coasts. The last that anyone was ever to see of Earth was a great plain, bathed with the silver light of the abnormally brilliant moon. Across its face the waters were pouring in a glittering flood toward a distant range of mountains. The sea had won its final victory, but its triumph would be short-lived for soon sea and land would be no more. Even as the silent party in the control room watched the destruction below, the infinitely greater catastrophe to which this was only the prelude came swiftly upon them.

It was as though dawn had broken suddenly over this moonlit landscape. But it was not dawn: it was only the moon, shining with the brilliance of a second sun. For perhaps thirty seconds that awesome, unnatural light burnt fiercely on the doomed land beneath. Then there came a sudden flashing of indicator lights across the control board. The main drive was on. For a second Alveron glanced at the indicators and checked their information. When he looked again at the screen, Earth was gone.

The magnificent, desperately overstrained generators quietly died when the S9000 was passing the orbit of Persephone. It did not matter, the sun could never harm them now, and although the ship was speeding helplessly out into the lonely night of intersellar space, it would only be a matter of days before rescue came.

There was irony in that. A day ago, they had been the rescuers, going to the aid of a race that now no longer existed. Not for the first time Alveron wondered about the world that had just perished. He tried, in vain, to picture it as it had been in its glory, the streets of its cities thronged with life. Primitive though its people had been, they might have offered much to the Universe. If only they could have made contact! Regret was useless; long before their coming, the people of this world must have buried themselves in its iron heart. And now they and their civilisation would remain a mystery for the rest of time.

Alveron was glad when his thoughts were interrupted by Rugon's entrance. The chief of communications had been very busy ever since the take-off, trying to analyse the programmes radiated by the transmitter Orostron had discovered. The problem was not a difficult one, but it demanded the construction of special equipment, and that had taken time.

'Well, what have you found?' asked Alveron.

'Quite a lot,' replied his friend. 'There's something mysterious here, and I don't understand it.

'It didn't take long to find how the vision transmissions were built up, and we've been able to convert them to suit our own equipment. It seems that there were cameras all over the planet, surveying points of interest. Some of them were apparently in cities, on the tops of very high buildings. The cameras were rotating continuously to give panoramic views. In the programmes we've recorded there are about twenty different scenes.

'In addition, there are a number of transmissions of a different kind, neither sound nor vision. They seem to be purely scientific – possibly instrument readings or something of that sort. All these programmes were going out simultaneously on different frequency bands.

'Now there must be a reason for all this. Orostron still thinks that the station simply wasn't switched off when it was deserted. But these aren't the sort of programmes such a station would normally radiate at all. It was certainly used for interplanetary relaying – Klarten was quite right there. So these people must have crossed space, since none of the other planets had any life at the time of the last survey. Don't you agree?'

Alveron was following intently.

'Yes, that seems reasonable enough. But it's also certain that the beam was pointing to none of the other planets. I checked that myself.'

'I know,' said Rugon. 'What I want to discover is why a giant inter-planetary relay station is busily transmitting pictures of a world about to be destroyed – pictures that would be of immense interest to scientists and astronomers. Someone had gone to a lot of trouble to arrange all those panoramic cameras. I am convinced that those beams were going somewhere.'

Alveron started up.

'Do you imagine that there might be an outer planet that hasn't been reported?' he asked. 'If so, your theory's certainly wrong. The beam wasn't even pointing in the plane of the Solar System. And even if it were – just look at this.'

He switched on the vision screen and adjusted the controls. Against the velvet curtain of space was hanging a blue-white sphere, apparently com-posed of many concentric shells of incandescent gas. Even though its immense distance made all movement invisible, it was clearly expanding at an enormous rate. At its centre was a blinding point of light – the white dwarf star that the sun had now become.

'You probably don't realise just how big that sphere is,' said Alveron. 'Look at this.'

He increased the magnification until only the centre portion of the nova was visible. Close to its heart were two minute condensations, one on either side of the nucleus.

'Those are the two giant planets of the system. They have still managed to retain their existence – after a fashion. And they were several hundred million miles from the sun. The nova is still expanding – but it's already twice the size of the Solar System.'

Rugon was silent for a moment.

'Perhaps you're right,' he said, rather grudgingly. 'You've disposed of my first theory. But you still haven't satisfied me.'

He made several swift circuits of the room before speaking again. Alveron waited patiently. He knew the almost intuitive powers of his friend, who could often solve a problem when mere logic seemed insufficient.

Then, rather slowly, Rugon began to speak again.

'What do you think of this?' he said. 'Suppose we've completely underestimated this people? Orostron did it once – he thought they could never have crossed space, since they'd only known radio for two centuries. Hansur II told me that. Well, Orostron was quite wrong. Perhaps we're all wrong. I've had a look at the material that Klarten brought back from the transmitter. He wasn't impressed by what he found, but it's a marvellous achievement for so short a time. There were devices in that station that belonged to civilisations thousands of years older. Alveron, can we follow that beam to see where it leads?'

Alveron said nothing for a full minute. He had been more than half expecting the question, but it was not an easy one to answer. The main generators had gone completely. There was no point in trying to repair them. But there was still power available, and while there was power, anything could be done in time. It would mean a lot of improvisation, and some difficult manoeuvres, for the ship still had its enormous initial velocity. Yes, it could be done, and the activity would keep the crew from becoming further depressed, now that the reaction caused by the mission's failure had started to set in. The news that the nearest heavy repair ship could not reach them for three weeks had also caused a slump in morale.

The engineers, as usual, made a tremendous fuss. Again as usual, they did the job in half the time they had dismissed as being absolutely impossible. Very slowly, over many hours, the great ship began to discard the speed its main drive had given it in as many minutes. In a tremendous curve, millions of miles in radius, the S9000 changed its course and the star fields shifted round it.

The manoeuvre took three days, but at the end of that time the ship was limping along a course parallel to the beam that had once come from Earth. They were heading out into emptiness, the blazing sphere that had been the sun dwindling slowly behind them. By the standards of intersellar flight, they were almost stationary.

For hours Rugon strained over his instruments, driving his detector beams far ahead into space. There were certainly no planets within many light-years; there was no doubt of that. From time to time Alveron came to see him and always he had to give the same reply: 'Nothing to report.' About a fifth of the time Rugon's intuition let him down badly; he began to wonder if this was such an occasion.

Not until a week later did the needles of the mass-detectors quiver feebly at the ends of their scales. But Rugon said nothing, not even to his captain. He waited until he was sure, and he went on waiting until even the short-range scanners began to react, and to build up the first faint pictures on the vision screen. Still he waited patiently until he could interpret the images. Then, when he knew that his wildest fancy was even less than the truth, he called his colleagues into the control room.

The picture on the vision screen was the familiar one of endless star fields, sun beyond sun to the very limits of the Universe. Near the centre of the screen a distant nebula made a patch of haze that was difficult for the eye to grasp.

Rugon increased the magnification. The stars flowed out of the field; the little nebula expanded until it filled the screen and then – it was a nebula no longer. A simultaneous gasp of amazement came from all the company at the sight that lay before them.

Lying across league after league of space, ranged in a vast three-dimensional array of rows and columns with the precision of a marching army, were thousands of tiny pencils of light. They were moving swiftly; the whole immense lattice holding its shape as a single unit. Even as Alveron and his comrades watched, the formation began to drift off the screen and Rugon had to recentre the controls.

After a long pause, Rugon started to speak.

'This is the race,' he said softly, 'that has known radio for only two centuries – the race that we believed had crept to die in the heart of its planet. I have examined those images under the highest possible magnification.

'That is the greatest fleet of which there has ever been a record. Each of those points of light represents a ship larger than our own. Of course, they are very primitive – what you see on the screen are the jets of their rockets. Yes, they dared to use rockets to bridge interstellar space! You realise what that means. It would take them centuries to reach the nearest star. The whole race must have embarked on this journey in the hope that its descendants would complete it, generations later.

'To measure the extent of their accomplishment, think of the ages it took us to conquer space, and the longer ages still before we attempted to reach the stars. Even if we were threatened with annihilation, could we have done so much in so short a time? Remember, this is the youngest civilisation in the Universe. Four hundred thousand years ago it did not even exist. What will it be a million years from now?'

An hour later, Orostron left the crippled mother ship to make contact with the great fleet ahead. As the little torpedo disappeared among the stars, Alveron turned to his friend and made a remark that Rugon was often to remember in the years ahead.

'I wonder what they'll be like?' he mused. 'Will they be nothing but wonderful engineers, with no art or philosophy? They're going to have such a surprise when Orostron reaches them – I expect it will be rather a blow to their pride. It's funny how all isolated races think they're the only people in the Universe. But they should be grateful to us; we're going to save them a good many hundred years of travel.'

Alveron glanced at the Milky Way, lying like a veil of silver mist across the vision screen. He waved toward it with a sweep of a tentacle that embraced the whole circle of the galaxy, from the Central Planets to the lonely suns of the Rim.

'You know,' he said to Rugon, 'I feel rather afraid of these people. Suppose they don't like our little Federation?' He waved once more toward the star-clouds that lay massed across the screen, glowing with the light of their countless suns.

'Something tells me they'll be very determined people,' he added. 'We had better be polite to them. After all, we only outnumber them about a thousand million to one.'

Rugon laughed at his captain's little joke.

Twenty years afterward, the remark didn't seem funny.

Technical Error

First published in *Fantasy*, December 1946
Collected in *Reach for Tomorrow*

As long as I can remember I have been fascinated by the idea of the Fourth Dimension. In fact, my very first television programme was devoted to the subject – 30 minutes *live* on black and white TV, from Alexandra Palace, in May 1950!

It was one of those accidents for which no one could be blamed. Richard Nelson had been in and out of the generator pit a dozen times, taking temperature readings to make sure that the unearthly chill of liquid helium was not seeping through the insulation. This was the first generator in the world to use the principle of superconductivity. The windings of the immense stator had been immersed in a helium bath, and the miles of wire now had a resistance too small to be measured by any means known to man.

Nelson noted with satisfaction that the temperature had not fallen further than expected. The insulation was doing its work; it would be safe to lower the rotor into the pit. That thousand-ton cylinder was now hanging fifty feet above Nelson's head, like the business end of a mammoth drop hammer. He and everyone else in the power station would feel much happier when it had been lowered onto its bearings and keyed into the turbine shaft.

Nelson put away his notebook and started to walk toward the ladder. At the geometric centre of the pit, he made his appointment with destiny.

The load on the power network had been steadily increasing for the last hour, while the zone of twilight swept across the continent. As the last rays of sunlight faded from the clouds, the miles of mercury arcs along the great highways sprang into life. By the million, fluorescent tubes began to glow in the cities; housewives switched on their radio-cookers to prepare the evening meal. The needles of the megawattmeters began to creep up the scales.

These were the normal loads. But on a mountain three hundred miles to the south a giant cosmic ray analyser was being rushed into action to await the expected shower from the new supernova in Capricornus, which the astronomers had detected only an hour before. Soon the coils of its five-thousand-ton magnets began to drain their enormous currents from the thyratron converters.

A thousand miles to the west, fog was creeping toward the greatest airport in the hemisphere. No one worried much about fog, now, when every plane could land on its own radar in zero visibility, but it was nicer not to have it around. So the giant dispersers were thrown into operation, and nearly a thousand megawatts began to radiate into the night, coagulating the water droplets and clearing great swaths through the banks of mist.

The meters in the power station gave another jump, and the engineer on duty ordered the stand-by generators into action. He wished the big, new machine was finished; then there would be no more anxious hours like these. But he thought he could handle the load. Half an hour later the Meteorological Bureau put out a general frost warning over the radio. Within sixty seconds, more than a million electric fires were switched on in anticipation. The meters passed the danger mark and went on soaring.

With a tremendous crash three giant circuit breakers leaped from their contacts. Their arcs died under the fierce blast of the helium jets. Three circuits had opened – but the fourth breaker had failed to clear. Slowly, the great copper bars began to glow cherry-red. The acrid smell of burning insulation filled the air and molten metal dripped heavily to the floor below, solidifying at once on the concrete slabs. Suddenly the conductors sagged as the load ends broke away from their supports. Brilliant green arcs of burning copper flamed and died as the circuit was broken. The free ends of the enormous conductors fell perhaps ten feet before crashing into the equipment below. In a fraction of a second they had welded themselves across the lines that led to the new generator.

Forces greater than any yet produced by man were at war in the windings of the machine. There was no resistance to oppose the current, but the inductance of the tremendous windings delayed the moment of peak intensity. The current rose to a maximum in an immense surge that lasted several seconds. At that instant, Nelson reached the centre of the pit.

Then the current tried to stabilise itself, oscillating wildly between narrower and narrower limits. But it never reached its steady state; somewhere, the overriding safety devices came into operation and the circuit that should never have been made was broken again. With a last dying spasm, almost as violent as the first, the current swiftly ebbed away. It was all over.

When the emergency lights came on again, Nelson's assistant walked to the lip of the rotor pit. He didn't know what had happened, but it must have been serious. Nelson, fifty feet down, must have been wondering what it was all about.

'Hello, Dick!' he shouted. 'Have you finished? We'd better see what the trouble is.'

There was no reply. He leaned over the edge of the great pit and peered into it. The light was very bad, and the shadow of the rotor made it difficult to see what was below. At first it seemed that the pit was empty, but that was ridiculous; he had seen Nelson enter it only a few minutes ago. He called again.

'Hello! You all right, Dick?'

Again no reply. Worried now, the assistant began to descend the ladder. He was halfway down when a curious noise, like a toy balloon bursting very far away, made him look over his shoulder. Then he saw Nelson, lying at the centre of the pit on the temporary woodwork covering the turbine shaft. He was very still, and there seemed something altogether wrong about the angle at which he was lying.

Ralph Hughes, chief physicist, looked up from his littered desk as the door opened. Things were slowly returning to normal after the night's disasters. Fortunately, the trouble had not affected his department much, for the generator was unharmed. He was glad he was not the chief engineer: Murdock would still be snowed under with paperwork. The thought gave Dr Hughes considerable satisfaction.

'Hello, Doc,' he greeted the visitor. 'What brings you here? How's your patient getting on?'

Doctor Sanderson nodded briefly. 'He'll be out of hospital in a day or so. But I want to talk to you about him.'

'I don't know the fellow – I never go near the plant, except when the Board goes down on its collective knees and asks me to. After all, Murdock's paid to run the place.'

Sanderson smiled wryly. There was no love lost between the chief engineer and the brilliant young physicist. Their personalities were too different, and there was the inevitable rivalry between theoretical expert and 'practical' man.

'I think this is up your street, Ralph. At any rate, it's beyond me. You've heard what happened to Nelson?'

'He was inside my new generator when the power was shot into it, wasn't he?'

'That's correct. His assistant found him suffering from shock when the power was cut off again.'

'What kind of shock? It couldn't have been electric; the windings are insulated, of course. In any case, I gather that he was in the centre of the pit when they found him.'

'That's quite true. We don't know what happened. But he's now come round and seems none the worse – apart from one thing.' The doctor hesitated a moment as if choosing his words carefully.

'Well, go on! Don't keep me in suspense!'

'I left Nelson as soon as I saw he would be quite safe, but about an hour later Matron called me up to say he wanted to speak to me urgently. When I got to the ward he was sitting up in bed looking at a newspaper with a very puzzled expression. I asked him what was the matter. He answered, "Something's happened to me, Doc." So I said, "Of course it has, but you'll be out in a couple of days." He shook his head; I could see there was a worried look in his eyes. He picked up the paper he had been looking at and pointed to it. "I can't read any more," he said.

'I diagnosed amnesia and thought: This is a nuisance! Wonder what else he's forgotten? Nelson must have read my expression, for he went on to say, "Oh, I still know the letters and words – but they're the wrong way round! I think something must have happened to my eyes." He held up the paper again. "This looks exactly as if I'm seeing it in a mirror," he said. "I can spell out each word separately, a letter at a time. Would you get me a looking glass? I want to try something."

'I did. He held the paper to the glass and looked at the reflection. Then he started to read aloud, at normal speed. But that's a trick anyone can learn – compositors have to do it with type – and I wasn't impressed. On the other hand, I couldn't see why an intelligent fellow like Nelson should put over an act like that. So I decided to humour him, thinking the shock must have given his mind a bit of a twist. I felt quite certain he was suffering from some delusion, though he seemed perfectly normal.

'After a moment he put the paper away and said, "Well, Doc, what do you make of that?" I didn't know quite what to say without hurting his feelings, so I passed the buck and said, "I think I'll have to hand you over to Dr Humphries, the psychologist. It's rather outside my province." Then he made some remark about Dr Humphries and his intelligence tests, from which I gathered he had already suffered at his hands.'

'That's correct,' interjected Hughes. 'All the men are grilled by the Psychology Department before they join the company. All the same, it's surprising what gets through,' he added thoughtfully.

Dr Sanderson smiled, and continued his story.

'I was getting up to leave when Nelson said, "Oh, I almost forgot. I think I must have fallen on my right arm. The wrist feels badly sprained." "Let's look at it," I said, bending to pick it up. "No, the other arm," Nelson said, and held up his left wrist. Still humouring him, I answered, "Have it your own way. But you said your right one, didn't you?"

'Nelson looked puzzled. "So what?" he replied. "This *is* my right arm. My eyes may be queer, but there's no argument about that. There's my wedding ring to prove it. I've not been able to get the darned thing off for five years."

'That shook me rather badly. Because you see, it was his left arm he was holding up, and his left hand that had the ring on it. I could see that what he said was quite true. The ring would have to be cut to get it off again. So I said, "Have you any distinctive scars?" He answered. "Not that I can remember."

' "Any dental fillings?" '
' "Yes, quite a few." '

'We sat looking at each other in silence while a nurse went to fetch Nelson's records. "Gazed at each other with a wild surmise" is just about how a novelist might put it. Before the nurse returned, I was seized with a bright idea. It was a fantastic notion, but the whole affair was becoming more and more outrageous. I asked Nelson if I could see the things he had been carrying in his pockets. Here they are.'

Dr Sanderson produced a handful of coins and a small leather-bound diary. Hughes recognised the latter at once as an Electrical Engineer's Diary; he had one in his own pocket. He took it from the doctor's hand and flicked it open at random, with that slightly guilty feeling one always has when a stranger's – still more, a friend's – diary falls into one's hands.

And then, for Ralph Hughes, it seemed that the foundations of his world were giving way. Until now he had listened to Dr Sanderson with some detachment, wondering what all the fuss was about. But now the incontrovertible evidence lay in his own hands, demanding his attention and defying his logic.

For he could read not one word of Nelson's diary. Both the print and the handwriting were inverted, as if seen in a mirror.

Dr Hughes got up from his chair and walked rapidly around the room several times. His visitor sat silently watching him. On the fourth circuit he stopped at the window and looked out across the lake, overshadowed by the immense white wall of the dam. It seemed to reassure him, and he turned to Dr Sanderson again.

'You expect me to believe that Nelson has been laterally inverted in some way, so that his right and left sides have been interchanged?'

'I don't expect you to believe anything. I'm merely giving you the evidence. If you can draw any other conclusion I'd be delighted to hear it. I might add that I've checked Nelson's teeth. All the fillings have been transposed. Explain that away if you can. Those coins are rather interesting, too.'

Hughes picked them up. They included a shilling, one of the beautiful new, beryl-copper crowns, and a few pence and halfpence. He would have accepted them as change without hesitation. Being no more observant than the next man, he had never noticed which way the Queen's head looked. But the lettering – Hughes could picture the consternation at the Mint if these curious coins ever came to its notice. Like the diary, they too had been laterally inverted.

Dr Sanderson's voice broke into his reverie.

'I've told Nelson not to say anything about this. I'm going to write a full report; it should cause a sensation when it's published. But we want to know how this has happened. As you are the designer of the new machine, I've come to you for advice.'

Dr Hughes did not seem to hear him. He was sitting at his desk with his hands outspread, little fingers touching. For the first time in his life he was thinking seriously about the difference between left and right.

Dr Sanderson did not release Nelson from hospital for several days, during which he was studying his peculiar patient and collecting material for his report. As far as he could tell, Nelson was perfectly normal, apart from his inversion. He was learning to read again, and his progress was swift after the initial srrangeness had worn off. He would probably never again use tools in the same way that he had done before the accident; for the rest of his life, the world would think him left-handed. However, that would not handicap him in any way.

Dr Sanderson had ceased to speculate about the cause of Nelson's condition. He knew very little about electricity; that was Hughes's job. He was quite confident that the physicist would produce the answer in due course; he had always done so before. The company was not a philanthropic institution, and it had good reason for retaining Hughes's services. The new generator, which would be running within a week, was his brain-child, though he had had little to do with the actual engineering details.

Dr Hughes himself was less confident. The magnitude of the problem was terrifying; for he realised, as Sanderson did not, that it involved utterly new regions of science. He knew that there was only one way in which an object could become its own mirror image. But how could so fantastic a theory be proved?

He had collected all available information on the fault that had energised the great armature. Calculations had given an estimate of the currents that had flowed through the coils for the few seconds they had been conducting. But the figures were largely guesswork; he wished he could repeat the experiment to obtain accurate data. It would be amusing to see Murdock's face if he said, 'Mind if I throw a perfect short across generators One to Ten sometime this evening?' No, that was definitely out.

It was lucky he still had the working model. Tests on it had given some ideas of the field produced at the generator's centre, but their magnitudes were a matter of conjecture. They must have been enormous. It was a miracle that the windings had stayed in their slots. For nearly a month Hughes struggled with his calculations and wandered through regions of atomic physics he had carefully avoided since he left the university. Slowly the complete theory began to evolve in his mind; he was a long way from the final proof, but the road was clear. In another month he would have finished.

The great generator itself, which had dominated his thoughts for the past year, now seemed trivial and unimportant. He scarcely bothered to acknowledge the congratulations of his colleagues when it passed its final tests and began to feed its millions of kilowatts into the system. They must have thought him a little strange, but he had always been regarded as somewhat unpredictable. It was expected of him; the company would have been disappointed if its tame genius possessed no eccentricities.

A fortnight later, Dr Sanderson came to see him again. He was in a grave mood.

'Nelson's back in the hospital,' he announced. 'I was wrong when I said he'd be OK.'

'What's the matter with him?' asked Hughes in surprise.

'He's starving to death.'

'Starving? What on earth do you mean?'

Dr Sanderson pulled a chair up to Hughes's desk and sat down.

'I haven't bothered you for the past few weeks,' he began, 'because I knew you were busy on your own theories. I've been watching Nelson carefully all this time, and writing up my report. At first, as I told you, he seemed perfectly normal. I had no doubt that everything would be all right.

'Then I noticed that he was losing weight. It was some time before I was certain of it; then I began to observe other, more technical symptoms. He started to complain of weakness and lack of concentration. He had all the signs of vitamin deficiency. I gave him special vitamin concentrates, but they haven't done any good. So I've come to have another talk with you.'

Hughes looked baffled, then annoyed. 'But hang it all, you're the doctor!'

'Yes, but this theory of mine needs some support. I'm only an unknown medico – no one would listen to me until it was too late. For Nelson is dying, and I think I know why. . . .'

Sir Robert had been stubborn at first, but Dr Hughes had had his way, as he always did. The members of the Board of Directors were even now filing into the conference room, grumbling and generally making a fuss about the extraordinary general meeting that had just been called. Their perplexity was still further increased when they heard that Hughes was going to address them. They all knew the physicist and his reputation, but he was a scientist and they were businessmen. What was Sir Robert planning?

Dr Hughes, the cause of all the trouble, felt annoyed with himself for being nervous. His opinion of the Board of Directors was not flattering, but Sir Robert was a man he could respect, so there was no reason to be afraid of them. It was true that they might consider him mad, but his past record would take care of that. Mad or not, he was worth thousands of pounds to them.

Dr Sanderson smiled encouragingly at him as he walked into the conference room. The smile was not very successful, but it helped. Sir Robert had just finished speaking. He picked up his glasses in that nervous way he had, and coughed deprecatingly. Not for the first time, Hughes wondered how such an apparently timid old man could rule so vast a commercial empire.

'Well, here is Dr Hughes, gentlemen. He will – ahem – explain everything to you. I have asked him not to be too technical. You are at liberty to interrupt him if he ascends into the more rarefied stratosphere of higher mathematics. Dr Hughes . . .'

Slowly at first, and then more quickly as he gained the confidence of his audience, the physicist began to tell his story. Nelson's diary drew a gasp of amazement from the Board, and the inverted coins proved fascinating curiosities. Hughes was glad to see that he had aroused the interest of his listeners. He took a deep breath and made the plunge he had been fearing.

'You have heard what has happened to Nelson, gentlemen, but what I am going to tell you now is even more startling. I must ask you for your very close attention.'

He picked up a rectangular sheet of notepaper from the conference table, folded it along a diagonal and tore it along the fold.

'Here we have two right-angled triangles with equal sides. I lay them on the table – so.' He placed the paper triangles side by side on the table, with their hypotenuses touching, so that they formed a kite-shaped figure. 'Now, as I have arranged them, each triangle is the mirror image of the other. You can imagine that the plane of the mirror is along the hypotenuse. This is the point I want you to notice. As long as I keep the triangles in the plane of the table, I can slide them around as much as I like, but I can never place one so that it exactly covers the other. Like a pair of gloves, they are not interchangeable although their dimensions are identical.'

He paused to let that sink in. There were no comments, so he continued.

'Now, if I pick up one of the triangles, turn it over in the air and put it down again, the two are no longer mirror images, but have become completely identical – so.' He suited the action to the words. 'This may seem very elementary; in fact, it is so. But it teaches us one very important lesson. The triangles on the table were flat objects, restricted to two dimensions. To turn one into its mirror image I had to lift it up and rotate it in the third dimension. Do you see what I am driving at?'

He glanced round the table. One or two of the directors nodded slowly in dawning comprehension.

'Similarly, to change a solid, three-dimensional body, such as a man, into its analogue or mirror image, it must be rotated in a fourth dimension. I repeat – a fourth dimension.'

There was a strained silence. Someone coughed, but it was a nervous, not a sceptical cough.

'Four-dimensional geometry, as you know' – he'd be surprised if they did – 'has been one of the major tools of mathematics since before the time of Einstein. But until now it has always been a mathematical fiction, having no real existence in the physical world. It now appears that the unheard-of currents, amounting to millions of amperes, which flowed momentarily in the windings of our generator must have produced a certain extension into four dimensions, for a fraction of a second and in a volume large enough to contain a man. I have been making some calculations and have been able to satisfy myself that a "hyperspace" about ten feet on a side was, in fact, generated: a matter of some ten thousand quartic – not cubic! – feet. Nelson was occupying that space. The sudden collapse of the field when the circuit was broken caused the rotation of the space, and Nelson was inverted.

'I must ask you to accept this theory, as no other explanation fits the facts. I have the mathematics here if you wish to consult them.'

He waved the sheets in front of his audience, so that the directors could see the imposing array of equations. The technique worked – it always did. They cowered visibly. Only McPherson, the secretary, was made of sterner stuff. He had had a semi-technical education and still read a good deal of popular science, which he was fond of airing whenever he had the opportunity. But he was intelligent and willing to learn, and Dr Hughes had often spent official time discussing some new scientific theory with him.

'You say that Nelson has been rotated in the Fourth Dimension; but I thought Einstein had shown that the Fourth Dimension was time.'

Hughes groaned inwardly. He had been anticipating this red herring.

'I was referring to an additional dimension of space,' he explained patiently. 'By that I mean a dimension, or direction, at right-angles to our normal three. One can call it the Fourth Dimension if one wishes. With certain reservations, time may also be regarded as a dimension. As we normally regard space as three-dimensional, it is then customary to call time the Fourth Dimension. But the label is arbitrary. As I'm asking you to grant me four dimensions of space, we must call time the Fifth Dimension.'

'Five Dimensions! Good Heavens!' exploded someone further down the table.

Dr Hughes could not resist the opportunity. 'Space of several million dimensions has been frequently postulated in sub-atomic physics,' he said quietly.

There was a stunned silence. No one, not even McPherson, seemed inclined to argue.

'I now come to the second part of my account,' continued Dr Hughes. 'A few weeks after his inversion we found that there was something wrong with Nelson. He was taking food normally, but it didn't seem to nourish him properly. The explanation has been given by Dr Sanderson, and leads us into the realms of organic chemistry. I'm sorry to be talking like a textbook, but you will soon realise how vitally important this is to the company. And you also have the satisfaction of knowing that we are now all on equally unfamiliar territory.'

That was not quite true, for Hughes still remembered some fragments of his chemistry. But it might encourage the stragglers.

'Organic compounds are composed of atoms of carbon, oxygen and hydrogen, with other elements, arranged in complicated ways in space. Chemists are fond of making models of them out of knitting needles and coloured plasticine. The results are often very pretty and look like works of advanced art.

'Now, it is possible to have two organic compounds containing identical numbers of atoms, arranged in such a way that one is the mirror image of the other. They're called stereo-isomers, and are very common among the sugars. If you could set their molecules side by side, you would see that they bore the same sort of relationship as a right and left glove. They are, in fact, called right – or left-handed – dextro or laevo – compounds. I hope this is quite clear.'

Dr Hughes looked around anxiously. Apparently it was.

'Stereo-isomers have almost identical chemical properties,' he went on, 'though there are subtle differences. In the last few years, Dr Sanderson tells me, it has been found that certain essential foods, including the new class of vitamins discovered by Professor Vandenburg, have properties depending on the arrangement of their atoms in space. In other words, gentlemen, the left-handed compounds might be essential for life, but the right-handed one would be of no value. This in spite of the fact that their chemical formulae are identical.

'You will appreciate, now, why Nelson's inversion is much more serious than we at first thought. It's not merely a matter of teaching him to read again, in which case – apart from its philosophical interest – the whole business would be trivial. He is actually starving to death in the midst of plenty, simply because he can no more assimilate certain molecules of food than we can put our right foot into a left boot.

'Dr Sanderson has tried an experiment which has proved the truth of this theory. With very great difficulty, he has obtained the stereo-isomers of many of these vitamins. Professor Vandenburg himself synthesised them when he heard of our trouble. They have already produced a very marked improvement in Nelson's condition.'

Hughes paused and drew out some papers. He thought he would give the Board time to prepare for the shock. If a man's life were not at stake, the situation would have been very amusing. The Board was going to be hit where it would hurt most.

'As you will realise, gentlemen, since Nelson was injured – if you can call it that – while he was on duty, the company is liable to pay for any treatment he may require. We have found that treatment, and you may wonder why I have taken so much of your time telling you about it. The reason is very simple. The production of the necessary stereo-isomers is almost as difficult as the extraction of radium – more so, in some cases. Dr Sanderson tells me that it will cost over five thousand pounds a day to keep Nelson alive.'

The silence lasted for half a minute; then everyone started to talk at once. Sir Robert pounded on the table, and presently restored order. The council of war had begun.

Three hours later, an exhausted Hughes left the conference room and went in search of Dr Sanderson, whom he found fretting in his office.

'Well, what's the decision?' asked the doctor.

'What I was afraid of. They want me to re-invert Nelson.'

'Can you do it?'

'Frankly, I don't know. All I can hope to do is to reproduce the conditions of the original fault as accurately as I can.'

'Weren't there any other suggestions?'

'Quite a few, but most of them were stupid. McPherson had the best idea. He wanted to use the generator to invert normal food so that Nelson could eat it. I had to point out that to take the big machine out of action for this purpose would cost several millions a year, and in any case the windings wouldn't stand it more than a few times. So that scheme collapsed. Then Sir Robert wanted to know if you could guarantee there were no vitamins we'd overlooked, or that might still be undiscovered. His idea was that in spite of our synthetic diets we might not be able to keep Nelson alive after all.'

'What did you say to that?'

'I had to admit it was a possibility. So Sir Robert is going to have a talk with Nelson. He hopes to persuade him to risk it; his family will be taken care of if the experiment fails.'

Neither of the two men said anything for a few moments. Then Dr Sanderson broke the silence.

'Now do you understand the sort of decision a surgeon often has to make,' he said.

Hughes nodded in agreement. 'It's a beautiful dilemma, isn't it? A perfectly healthy man, but it will cost two millions a year to keep him alive, and we can't even be sure of that. I know the Board's thinking of its precious balance sheet more than anything else, but I don't see any alternative. Nelson will have to take a chance.'

'Couldn't you make some tests first?'

'Impossible. It's a major engineering operation to get the rotor out. We'll have to rush the experiment through when the load on the system is at minimum. Then we'll slam the rotor back, and tidy up the mess our artificial short has made. All this has to be done before the peak loads come on again. Poor old Murdock's mad as hell about it.'

'I don't blame him. When will the experiment start?'

'Not for a few days, at least. Even if Nelson agrees, I've got to fix up all my gear.'

No one was ever to know what Sir Robert said to Nelson during the hours they were together. Dr Hughes was more than half prepared for it when the telephone rang and the Old Man's tired voice said, 'Hughes? Get your equipment ready. I've spoken to Murdock, and we've fixed the time for Tuesday night. Can you manage by then?'

'Yes, Sir Robert.'

'Good. Give me a progress report every afternoon until Tuesday. That's all.'

The enormous room was dominated by the great cylinder of the rotor, hanging thirty feet above the gleaming plastic floor. A little group of men stood silently at the edge of the shadowed pit, waiting patiently. A maze of temporary wiring ran to Dr Hughes's equipment – multibeam oscilloscopes, megawattmeters and microchronometers, and the special relays that had been constructed to make the circuit at the calculated instant.

That was the greatest problem of all. Dr Hughes had no way of telling when the circuit should be closed; whether it should be when the voltage was at maximum, when it was at zero, or at some intermediate point on the sine wave. He had chosen the simplest and safest course. The circuit would be made at zero voltage; when it opened again would depend on the speed of the breakers.

In ten minutes the last of the great factories in the service area would be closing down for the night. The weather forecast had been favourable; there would be no abnormal loads before morning. By then, the rotor had to be back and the generator running again. Fortunately, the unique method of construction made it easy to reassemble the machine, but it would be a very close thing and there was no time to lose.

When Nelson came in, accompanied by Sir Robert and Dr Sanderson, he was very pale. He might, thought Hughes, have been going to his execution. The thought was somewhat ill-timed, and he put it hastily aside.

There was just time enough for a last quite unnecessary check of the equipment. He had barely finished when he heard Sir Robert's quiet voice.

'We're ready, Dr Hughes.'

Rather unsteadily, he walked to the edge of the pit. Nelson had already descended, and as he had been instructed, was standing at its exact centre, his upturned face a white blob far below. Dr Hughes waved a brief encouragement and turned away, to rejoin the group by his equipment.

He flicked over the switch of the oscilloscope and played with the synchronising controls until a single cycle of the main wave was stationary on the screen. Then he adjusted the phasing: two brilliant spots of light moved toward each other along the wave until they had coalesced at its geometric centre. He looked briefly toward Murdock, who was watching the megawattmeters intently. The engineer nodded. With a silent prayer, Hughes threw the switch.

There was the tiniest click from the relay unit. A fraction of a second later, the whole building seemed to rock as the great conductors crashed over in the switch room three hundred feet away. The lights faded, and almost died. Then it was all over. The circuit breakers, driven at almost the speed of an explosion, had cleared the line again. The lights returned to normal and the needles of the megawattmeters dropped back onto their scales.

The equipment had withstood the overload. But what of Nelson?

Dr Hughes was surprised to see that Sir Robert, for all his sixty years, had already reached the generator. He was standing by its edge, looking down into the great pit. Slowly, the physicist went to join him. He was afraid to hurry; a growing sense of premonition was filling his mind. Already he could picture Nelson lying in a twisted heap at the centre of the well, his lifeless eyes staring up at them reproachfully. Then came a still more horrible thought. Suppose the field had collapsed too soon, when the inversion was only partly completed? In another moment, he would know the worst.

There is no shock greater than that of the totally unexpected, for against it the mind has no chance to prepare its defences. Dr Hughes was ready for almost anything when he reached the generator. Almost, but not quite. . . .

He did not expect to find it completely empty.

What came after, he could never perfectly remember. Murdock seemed to take charge then. There was a great flurry of activity, and the engineers swarmed in to replace the giant rotor. Somewhere in the distance he heard Sir Robert saying, over and over again, 'We did our best – we did our best.' He must have replied, somehow, but everything was very vague. . . .

In the grey hours before the dawn, Dr Hughes awoke from his fitful sleep. All night he had been haunted by his dreams, by weird fantasies of multi-dimensional geometry. There were visions of strange, other-worldly universes of insane shapes and intersecting planes along which he was doomed to struggle endlessly, fleeing from some nameless terror. Nelson, he dreamed, was trapped in one of those unearthly dimensions, and he was trying to reach him. Sometimes he was Nelson himself, and he imagined that he could see all around him the universe he knew, strangely distorted and barred from him by invisible walls.

The nightmare faded as he struggled up in bed. For a few moments he sat holding his head, while his mind began to clear. He knew what was happening; this was not the first time the solution of some baffling problem had come suddenly upon him in the night.

There was one piece still missing in the jigsaw puzzle that was sorting itself out in his mind. One piece only – and suddenly he had it. There was something that Nelson's assistant had said, when he was describing the original accident. It had seemed trivial at the time; until now, Hughes had forgotten all about it.

'When I looked inside the generator, there didn't seem to be anyone there, so I started to climb down the ladder. . . .'

What a fool he had been! Old McPherson had been right, or partly right, after all!

The field had rotated Nelson in the fourth dimension of space, but there had been a displacement in *time* as well. On the first occasion it had been a matter of seconds only. This time, the conditions must have been different in spite of all his care. There were so many unknown factors, and the theory was more than half guesswork.

Nelson had not been inside the generator at the end of the experiment. *But he would be.*

Dr Hughes felt a cold sweat break out all over his body. He pictured that thousand-ton cylinder, spinning beneath the drive of its fifty million horse-power. Suppose something suddenly materialised in the space it already occupied. . . . ?

He leaped out of bed and grabbed the private phone to the power station. There was no time to lose – the rotor would have to be removed at once. Murdock could argue later.

Very gently, something caught the house by its foundations and rocked it to and fro, as a sleepy child may shake its rattle. Flakes of plaster came planing down from the ceiling; a network of cracks appeared as if by magic in the walls. The lights flickered, became suddenly brilliant, and faded out.

Dr Hughes threw back the curtain and looked toward the mountains. The power station was invisible beyond the foothills of Mount Perrin, but its site was clearly marked by the vast column of debris that was slowly rising against the bleak light of the dawn.

Castaway

First published in *Fantasy*, April 1947, as by 'Charles Willis'
Collected in *The Best of Arthur C. Clarke 1937–1955*

Walter H. Gillings, editor of *Fantasy*, was also the editor of *Tales of Wonder*, the first British sf magazine. More importantly, he *gave* me my first typewriter, which I carried home on a London bus from his home in Ilford. And he is the only editor I ever encountered who turned a story down, saying it was too good for him – and a rival editor would pay more.

'Most of the matter in the universe is at temperatures so high that no chemical compounds can exist, and the atoms themselves are stripped of all but their inner electron screens. Only on those incredibly rare bodies known as planets can the familiar elements and their combinations exist and, in all still rarer cases, give rise to the phenomenon known as life.' – *Practically any astronomy book of the early 20th Century.*

The storm was still rising. He had long since ceased to struggle against it, although the ascending gas streams were carrying him into the bitterly cold regions ten thousand miles above his normal level. Dimly he was aware of his mistake: he should never have entered the area of disturbance, but the spot had developed so swiftly that there was now no chance of escape. The million-miles-an-hour wind had seized him as it rose from the depths and was carrying him up the great funnel it had torn in the photosphere – a tunnel already large enough to engulf a hundred worlds.

It was very cold. Around him carbon vapour was condensing in clouds of incandescent dust, swiftly torn away by the raging winds. This was something he had never met before, but the short-lived particles of solid matter left no sensation as they whipped through his body. Presently they were no more than glowing streamers far below, their furious movement foreshortened to a gentle undulation.

He was now at a truly enormous height, and his velocity showed no signs of slackening. The horizon was almost fifty thousand miles away, and the whole of the great spot lay visible beneath. Although he possessed neither eyes nor organs of sight, the radiation pattern sweeping through his body built up a picture of the awesome scene below. Like a great wound through which the Sun's life was ebbing into space, the vortex was now thousands of miles deep. From one edge a long tongue of flame was reaching out to form a half-completed bridge, defying the gales sweeping vertically past it. In a few hours, if it survived, it might span the abyss and divide the spot in twain. The fragments would drift apart, the fires of the photosphere would overwhelm them, and soon the great globe would be unblemished again.

The Sun was still receding, and gradually into his slow, dim consciousness came the understanding that he could never return. The eruption that had hurled him into space had not given him sufficient velocity to escape forever, but a second giant force was beginning to exert its power. All his life he had been subjected to the fierce bombardment of solar radiation, pouring upon him from all directions. It was doing so no longer. The Sun now lay far beneath, and the force of its radiation was driving him out into space like a mighty wind. The cloud of ions that was his body, more tenuous than air, was falling swiftly into the outer darkness.

Now the Sun was a globe of fire shrinking far behind, and the great spot no more than a black stain near the centre of its disc. Ahead lay darkness, utterly unrelieved, for his senses were far too coarse ever to detect the feeble light of the stars or the pale gleam of the circling planets. The only source of light he could ever know was dwindling from him. In a desperate effort to conserve his energy, he drew his body together into a tight, spherical cloud. Now he was almost as dense as air, but the electrostatic repulsion between his billions of constituent ions was too great for further concentration. When at last his strength weakened, they would disperse into space and no trace of his existence would remain.

He never felt the increasing gravitational pull from far ahead, and was unconscious of his changing speed. But presently the first faint intimations of the approaching magnetic field reached his consciousness and stirred it into sluggish life. He strained his senses out into the darkness, but to a creature whose home was the photosphere of the Sun the light of all other bodies was billions of times too faint even to be glimpsed, and the steadily strengthening field through which he was falling was an enigma beyond the comprehension of his rudimentary mind.

The tenuous outer fringes of the atmosphere checked his speed, and he fell slowly towards the invisible planet. Twice he felt a strange, tearing wrench as he passed through the ionosphere; then, no faster than a falling snowflake, he was drifting down through the cold, dense gas of the lower air. The descent took many hours and his strength was waning when he came to rest on a surface hard beyond anything he had ever imagined.

The waters of the Atlantic were bathed with brilliant sunlight, but to him the darkness was absolute save for the faint gleam of the infinitely distant Sun. For aeons he lay, incapable of movement, while the fires of consciousness burned lower within him and the last remnants of his energy ebbed away into the inconceivable cold.

It was long before he noticed the strange new radiation pulsing far off in the darkness – radiation of a kind he had never experienced before.

Sluggishly he turned his mind towards it, considering what it might be and whence it came. It was closer than he had thought, for its movement was clearly visible and now it was climbing into the sky, approaching the Sun itself. But this was no second sun, for the strange illumination was waxing and waning, and only for a fraction of a cycle was it shining full upon him.

Nearer and nearer came that enigmatic glare; and as the throbbing rhythm of its brilliance grew fiercer he became aware of a strange, tearing resonance that seemed to shake the whole of his being. Now it was beating down upon him like a flail, tearing into his vitals and loosening his last hold on life itself. He had lost all control over the outer regions of his compressed but still enormous body.

The end came swiftly. The intolerable radiance was directly overhead, no longer pulsing but pouring down upon him in one continuous flood. Then there was neither pain nor wonder, nor the dull longing for the great golden world he had lost forever . . .

From the streamlined fairing beneath the great flying-wing, the long pencil of the radar beam was sweeping the Atlantic to the horizon's edge. Spinning in synchronism on the Plan Position Indicator, the faintly visible line of the time-base built up a picture of all that lay beneath. At the moment the screen was empty, for the coast of Ireland was more than three hundred miles away. Apart from an occasional brilliant blue spot – which was all that the greatest surface vessel became from fifty thousand feet – nothing would be visible until, in three hours' time, the eastern seaboard of America began to drift into the picture.

The navigator, checking his position continually by the North Atlantic radio lattice, seldom had any need for this part of the liner's radar. But to the passengers, the big skiatron indicator on the promenade deck was a source of constant interest, especially when the weather was bad and there was nothing to be seen below but the undulating hills and valleys of the cloud ceiling. There was still something magical, even in this age, about a radar landfall. No matter how often one had seen it before, it was fascinating to watch the pattern of the coastline forming on the screen, to pick out the harbours and the shipping and, presently, the hills and rivers and lakes of the land beneath.

To Edward Lindsey, returning from a week's leave in Europe, the Plan Position Indicator had a double interest. Fifteen years ago, as a young Coastal Command radio observer in the War of Liberation, he had spent long and tiring hours over these same waters, peering into a primitive forerunner of the great five-foot screen before him. He smiled wryly as his mind went back to those days. What would he have thought then, he wondered, if he could have seen himself as he was now, a prosperous accountant, travelling in comfort ten miles above the Atlantic at almost the velocity of sound? He thought also of the rest of S for Sugar's crew, and wondered what had happened to them in the intervening years.

At the edge of the scan, just crossing the three-hundred-mile range circle, a faint patch of light was beginning to drift into the picture. That was strange: there was no land there, for the Azores were further to the south. Besides, this seemed too ill-defined to be an island. The only thing it could possibly be was a storm-cloud heavy with rain.

Lindsey walked to the nearest window and looked out. The weather was extraordinarily fine. Far below, the waters of the Atlantic were crawling eastward towards Europe; even down to the horizon the sky was blue and cloudless.

He went back to the P.P.I. The echo was certainly a very curious one, approximately oval and as far as he could judge about ten miles long, although it was still too far away for accurate measurement. Lindsey did some rapid mental arithmetic. In twenty-five minutes it should be almost underneath them, for it was neatly bisected by the bright line that represented the aircraft's heading. Track? Course? Lord, how quickly one forgot that sort of thing! But it didn't matter – the wind could make little difference at the speed they were travelling. He would come back and have a look at it then, unless the gang in the bar got hold of him again.

Twenty minutes later he was even more puzzled. The tiny blue oval of light gleaming on the dark face of the screen was now only fifty miles away. If it were indeed a cloud, it was the strangest one he had ever seen. But the scale of the picture was still too small for him to make out any details.

The main controls of the indicator were safely locked away beneath the notice which read: PASSENGERS ARE REQUESTED NOT TO PLACE EMPTY GLASSES ON THE SKIATRON. However, one control had been left for the use of all comers. A massive three-position switch – guaranteed unbreakable – enabled anyone to select the tube's three different ranges: three hundred, fifty, and ten miles. Normally the three-hundred-miles picture was used, but the more restricted fifty-mile scan gave much greater detail and was excellent for sightseeing overland. The ten-mile range was quite useless and no one knew why it was there.

Lindsey turned the switch to 50, and the picture seemed to explode. The mysterious echo, which had been nearing the screen's centre, now lay at its edge once more, enlarged six-fold. Lindsey waited until the afterglow of the old picture had died away; then he leaned over and carefully examined the new.

The echo almost filled the gap between the forty- and fifty-mile range circles, and now that he could see it clearly its strangeness almost took his breath away. From its centre radiated a curious network of filaments, while at its heart glowed a bright area perhaps two miles in length. It could only be fancy – yet he could have sworn that the central spot was pulsing very slowly.

Almost unable to believe his eyes, Lindsey stared into the screen. He watched in hypnotised fascination until the oval mist was less than forty miles away; then he ran to the nearest telephone and called for one of the ship's radio officers. While he was waiting, he went again to the observation port and looked out at the ocean beneath. He could see for at least a hundred miles – but there was absolutely nothing there but the blue Atlantic and the open sky.

It was a long walk from the control room to the promenade deck, and when Sub-Lieutenant Armstrong arrived, concealing his annoyance beneath a mask of polite but not obsequious service, the object was less than twenty miles away. Lindsey pointed to the skiatron.

'Look!' he said simply.

Sub-Lieutenant Armstrong looked. For a moment there was silence. Then came a curious, half-strangled ejaculation and he jumped back as if he had been stung. He leaned forward again and rubbed at the screen with his sleeve as if trying to remove something that shouldn't be there. Stopping himself in time, he grinned foolishly at Lindsey. Then he went to the observation window.

'There's nothing there. I've looked,' said Lindsey.

After the initial shock, Armstrong moved with commendable speed. He ran back to the skiatron, unlocked the controls with his master key and made a series of swift adjustments. At once the time-base began to whirl round at a greatly increased speed, giving a more continuous picure than before.

It was much clearer now. The bright nucleus *was* pulsating, and faint knots of light were moving slowly outward along the radiating filaments. As he stared, fascinated, Lindsey suddenly remembered a glimpse he had once of an amoeba under the microscope. Apparently the same thought had occurred to the Sub-Lieutenant.

'It – it looks alive!' he whispered incredulously.

'I know,' said Lindsey. 'What do you think it is?'

The other hesitated for a while. 'I remember reading once that Appleton or someone had detected patches of ionisation low down in the atmosphere. That's the only thing it can be.'

'But its structure! How do you explain that?'

The other shrugged his shoulders. 'I can't,' he said bluntly.

It was vertically beneath them now, disappearing into the blind area at the centre of the screen. While they were waiting for it to emerge again they had another look at the ocean below. It was uncanny; there was still absolutely nothing to be seen. But the radar could not lie. Something *must* be there –

It was fading fast when it reappeared a minute later, fading as if the full power of the radar transmitter had destroyed its cohesion. For the filaments were breaking up, and even as they watched the ten-mile-long oval began to disintegrate. There was something awe-inspiring about the sight, and for some unfathomable reason Lindsey felt a surge of pity, as though he were witnessing the death of some gigantic beast. He shook his head angrily, but he could not get the thought out of his mind.

*

Twenty miles away, the last traces of ionisation were dispersing to the winds. Soon eye and radar screen alike saw only the unbroken waters of the Atlantic rolling endlessly eastwards as if no power could ever disturb them.

And across the screen of the great indicator, two men stared speechlessly at one another, each afraid to guess what lay in the other's mind.

The Fires Within

First published in *Fantasy*, August 1947, as by 'E. G. O'Brien'
Collected in *Reach for Tomorrow*

'This,' said Karn smugly, 'will interest you. Just take a look at it!'

He pushed across the file he had been reading, and for the *nth* time I decided to ask for his transfer or, failing that, my own.

'What's it about?' I said wearily.

'It's a long report from a Dr Matthews to the Minister of Science.' He waved it in front of me. 'Just read it!'

Without much enthusiasm, I began to go through the file. A few minutes later I looked up and admitted grudgingly: 'Maybe you're right – this time.' I didn't speak again until I'd finished. . . .

My dear Minister (the letter began). As you requested, here is my special report on Professor Hancock's experiments, which have had such unexpected and extraordinary results. I have not had time to cast it into a more orthodox form, but am sending you the dictation just as it stands.

Since you have many matters engaging your attention, perhaps I should briefly summarise our dealings with Professor Hancock. Until 1955, the Professor held the Kelvin Chair of Electrical Engineering at Brendon University, from which he was granted indefinite leave of absence to carry out his researches. In these he was joined by the late Dr Clayton, sometime Chief Geologist to the Ministry of Fuel and Power. Their joint research was financed by grants from the Paul Fund and the Royal Society.

The Professor hoped to develop sonar as a means of precise geological surveying. Sonar, as you will know, is the acoustic equivalent of radar, and although less familiar is older by some millions of years, since bats use it very effectively to detect insects and obstacles at night. Professor Hancock intended to send high-powered supersonic pulses into the ground and to build up from the returning echoes an image of what lay beneath. The picture would be displayed on a cathode ray tube and the whole system would be exactly analogous to the type of radar used in aircraft to show the ground through cloud.

In 1957 the two scientists had achieved a partial success but had exhausted their funds. Early in 1958 they applied directly to the government for a block grant. Dr Clayton pointed out the immense value of a device which would enable us to take a kind of X-ray photo of the Earth's crust, and the Minister of Fuel gave it his approval before passing on the application to us. At that time the report of the Bernal Committee had just been published and we were very anxious that deserving cases should be dealt with quickly to avoid further criticisms. I went to see the Professor at once and submitted a favourable report; the first payment of our grant (S/543A/68) was made a few days later. From that time I have been continually in touch with the research and have assisted to some extent with technical advice.

The equipment used in the experiments is complex, but its principles are simple. Very short but extremely powerful pulses of supersonic waves are generated by a special transmitter which revolves continuously in a pool of a heavy organic liquid. The beam produced passes into the ground and 'scans' like a radar beam searching for echoes. By a very ingenious time-delay circuit which I will resist the temptation to describe, echoes from any depth can be selected and so pictures of the strata under investigation can be built up on a cathode ray screen in the normal way.

When I first met Professor Hancock his apparatus was rather primitive, but he was able to show me the distribution of rock down to a depth of several hundred feet and we could see quite clearly a part of the Bakerloo Line which passed very near his laboratory. Much of the Professor's success was due to the great intensity of his supersonic bursts; almost from the beginning he was able to generate peak powers of several hundred kilowatts, nearly all of which was radiated into the ground. It was unsafe to remain near the transmitter, and I noticed that the soil became quite warm around it. I was rather surprised to see large numbers of birds in the vicinity, but soon discovered that they were attracted by the hundreds of dead worms lying on the ground.

At the time of Dr Clayton's death in 1960, the equipment was working at a power level of over a megawatt and quite good pictures of strata a mile down could be obtained. Dr Clayton had correlated the results with known geographical surveys, and had proved beyond doubt the value of the information obtained.

Dr Clayton's death in a motor accident was a great tragedy. He had always exerted a stabilising influence on the Professor, who had never been much interested in the practical applications of his work. Soon afterward I noticed a distinct change in the Professor's outlook, and a few months later he confided his new ambitions to me. I had been trying to persuade him to publish his results (he had already spent over £50,000 and the Public Accounts Committee was being difficult again), but he asked for a little more time. I think I can best explain his attitude by his own words, which I remember very vividly, for they were expressed with peculiar emphasis.

'Have you ever wondered,' he said, 'what the Earth really is like inside? We've only scratched the surface with our mines and wells. What lies beneath is as unknown as the other side of the Moon.

'We know that the Earth is unnaturally dense – far denser than the rocks and soil of its crust would indicate. The core may be solid metal, but until now there's been no way of telling. Even ten miles down the pressure must be thirty tons or more to the square inch and the temperature several hundred degrees. What it's like at the centre staggers the imagination: the pressure must be thousands of tons to the square inch. It's strange to think that in two or three years we may have reached the Moon, but when we've got to the stars we'll still be no nearer that inferno four thousand miles beneath our feet.

'I can now get recognisable echoes from two miles down, but I hope to step up the transmitter to ten megawatts in a few months. With that power, I believe the range will be increased to ten miles; and I don't mean to stop there.'

I was impressed, but at the same time I felt a little sceptical.

'That's all very well,' I said, 'but surely the deeper you go the less there'll be to see. The pressure will make any cavities impossible, and after a few miles there will simply be a homogeneous mass getting denser and denser.'

'Quite likely,' agreed the Professor. 'But I can still learn a lot from the transmission characteristics. Anyway, we'll see when we get there!'

That was four months ago; and yesterday I saw the result of that research. When I answered his invitation the Professor was clearly excited, but he gave me no hint of what, if anything, he had discovered. He showed me his improved equipment and raised the new receiver from its bath. The sensitivity of the pickups had been greatly improved, and this alone had effectively doubled the range, altogether apart from the increased transmitter power. It was strange to watch the steel framework slowly turning and to realise that it was exploring regions, which, in spite of their nearness, man might never reach.

When we entered the hut containing the display equipment, the Professor was strangely silent. He switched on the transmitter, and even though it was a hundred yards away I could feel an uncomfortable tingling. Then the cathode ray tube lit up and the slowly revolving timebase drew the picture I had seen so often before. Now, however, the definition was much improved owing to the increased power and sensitivity of the equipment. I adjusted the depth control and focussed on the Underground, which was clearly visible as a dark lane across the faintly luminous screen. While I was watching, it suddenly seemed to fill with mist and I knew that a train was going through.

Presently I continued the descent. Although I had watched this picture many times before, it was always uncanny to see great luminous masses floating toward me and to know that they were buried rocks – perhaps the debris from the glaciers of fifty thousand years ago. Dr Clayton had worked out a chart so that we could identify the various strata as they were passed, and presently I saw that I was through the alluvial soil and entering the great clay saucer which traps and holds the city's artesian water. Soon that too was passed, and I was dropping down through the bedrock almost a mile below the surface.

The picture was still clear and bright, though there was little to see, for there were now few changes in the ground structure. The pressure was already rising to a thousand atmospheres; soon it would be impossible for any cavity to remain open, for the rock itself would begin to flow. Mile after mile I sank, but only a pale mist floated on the screen, broken sometimes when echoes were returned from pockets or lodes of denser material. They became fewer and fewer as the depth increased – or else they were now so small that they could no longer be seen.

The scale of the picture was, of course, continually expanding. It was now many miles from side to side, and I felt like an airman looking down upon an unbroken cloud ceiling from an enormous height. For a moment a sense of vertigo seized me as I thought of the abyss into which I was gazing. I do not think that the world will ever seem quite solid to me again.

At a depth of nearly ten miles I stopped and looked at the Professor. There had been no alteration for some time, and I knew that the rock must now be compressed into a featureless, homogeneous mass. I did a quick mental calculation and shuddered as I realised that the pressure must be at least thirty tons to the square inch. The scanner was revolving very slowly now, for the feeble echoes were taking many seconds to struggle back from the depths.

'Well, Professor,' I said, 'I congratulate you. It's a wonderful achievement. But we seem to have reached the core now. I don't suppose there'll be any change from here to the centre.'

He smiled a little wryly. 'Go on,' he said. 'You haven't finished yet.'

There was something in his voice that puzzled and alarmed me. I looked at him intently for a moment; his features were just visible in the blue-green glow of the cathode ray tube.

'How far down can this thing go?' I asked, as the interminable descent started again.

'Fifteen miles,' he said shortly. I wondered how he knew, for the last feature I had seen at all clearly was only eight miles down. But I continued the long fall through the rock, the scanner turning more and more slowly now, until it took almost five minutes to make a complete revolution. Behind me I could hear the Professor breathing heavily, and once the back of my chair gave a crack as his fingers gripped it.

Then, suddenly, very faint markings began to reappear on the screen. I leaned forward eagerly, wondering if this was the first glimpse of the world's iron core. With agonising slowness the scanner turned through a giant angle, then another. And then—

I leaped suddenly out of the chair, cried 'My God!' and turned to face the Professor. Only once before in my life had I received such an intellectual shock – fifteen years ago, when I had accidentally turned on the radio and heard of the fall of the first atomic bomb. That had been unexpected, but this was inconceivable. For on the screen had appeared a grid of faint lines, crossing and recrossing to form a perfectly symmetrical lattice.

I know that I said nothing for many minutes, for the scanner made a complete revolution while I stood frozen with surprise. Then the Professor spoke in a soft, unnaturally calm voice.

'I wanted you to see it for yourself before I said anything. That picture is now thirty miles in diameter, and those squares are two or three miles on a side. You'll notice that the vertical lines converge and the horizontal ones are bent into arcs. We're looking at part of an enormous structure of concentric rings; the centre must lie many miles to the north, probably in the region of Cambridge. How much further it extends in the other direction we can only guess.'

'But what *is* it, for heaven's sake?'

'Well, it's clearly artificial.'

'That's ridiculous! Fifteen miles down!'

The Professor pointed to the screen again. 'God knows I've done my best,' he said, 'but I can't convince myself that Nature could make anything like that.'

I had nothing to say, and presently he continued: 'I discovered it three days ago, when I was trying to find the maximum range of the equipment. I can go deeper than this, and I rather think that the structure we can see is so dense that it won't transmit my radiations any further.

'I've tried a dozen theories, but in the end I keep returning to one. We know that the pressure down there must be eight or nine thousand atmospheres, and the temperature must be high enough to melt rock. But normal matter is still almost empty space. Suppose that there is life down there – not organic life, of course, but life based on partially condensed matter, matter in which the electron shells are few or altogether missing. Do you see what I mean? To such creatures, even the rock fifteen miles down would offer no more resistance than water – and we and all our world would be as tenuous as ghosts.'

'Then that thing we can see—'

'Is a city, or its equivalent. You've seen its size, so you can judge for yourself the civilisation that must have built it. All the world we know – our oceans and continents and mountains – is nothing more than a film of mist surrounding something beyond our comprehension.'

Neither of us said anything for a while. I remember feeling a foolish surprise at being one of the first men in the world to learn the appalling truth; for somehow I never doubted that it was the truth. And I wondered how the rest of humanity would react when the revelation came.

Presently I broke into the silence. 'If you're right,' I said, 'why have they – whatever they are – never made contact with us?'

The Professor looked at me rather pityingly. 'We think we're good engineers,' he said, 'but how could *we* reach *them*? Besides, I'm not at all sure that there haven't been contacts. Think of all the underground creatures and the mythology – trolls and cobalds and the rest. No, it's quite impossible – I take it back. Still the idea *is* rather suggestive.'

All the while the pattern on the screen had never changed: the dim network still glowed there, challenging our sanity. I tried to imagine streets and buildings and the creatures going among them, creatures who could make their way through the incandescent rock as a fish swims through water. It was fantastic . . . and then I remembered the incredibly narrow range of temperature and pressures under which the human race exists. *We*, not they, were the freaks, for almost all the matter in the universe is at temperatures of thousands or even millions of degrees.

'Well,' I said lamely, 'what do we do now?'

The Professor leaned forward eagerly. 'First we must learn a great deal more, and we must keep this an absolute secret until we are sure of the facts. Can you imagine the panic there would be if this information leaked out? Of course, the truth's inevitable sooner or later, but we may be able to break it slowly.

'You'll realise that the geological surveying side of my work is now utterly unimportant. The first thing we have to do is to build a chain of stations to find the extent of the structure. I visualise them at ten-mile intervals towards the north, but I'd like to build the first one somewhere in South London to see how extensive the thing is. The whole job will have to be kept as secret as the building of the first radar chain in the late thirties.

'At the same time, I'm going to push up my transmitter power again. I hope to be able to beam the output much more narrowly, and so greatly increase the energy concentration. But this will involve all sorts of mechanical difficulties, and I'll need more assistance.'

I promised to do my utmost to get further aid, and the Professor hopes that you will soon be able to visit his laboratory yourself. In the meantime I am attaching a photograph of the vision screen, which although not as clear as the original will, I hope, prove beyond doubt that our observations are not mistaken.

I am well aware that our grant to the Interplanetary Society has brought us dangerously near the total estimate for the year, but surely even the crossing of space is less important than the immediate investigation of this discovery which may have the most profound effects on the philosophy and the future of the whole human race.

I sat back and looked at Karn. There was much in the document I had not understood, but the main outlines were clear enough.

'Yes,' I said, 'this is it! Where's that photograph?'

He handed it over. The quality was poor, for it had been copied many times before reaching us. But the pattern was unmistakable and I recognised it at once.

'They were good scientists,' I said admiringly. 'That's Callastheon, all right. So we've found the truth at last, even if it has taken us three hundred years to do it.'

'Is that surprising,' asked Karn, 'when you consider the mountain of stuff we've had to translate and the difficulty of copying it before it evaporates?'

I sat in silence for a while, thinking of the strange race whose relics we were examining. Only once – never again! – had I gone up the great vent our engineers had opened into the Shadow World. It had been a frightening and unforgettable experience. The multiple layers of my pressure suit had made movement very difficult, and despite their insulation I could sense the unbelievable cold that was all around me.

'What a pity it was,' I mused, 'that our emergence destroyed them so completely. They were a clever race, and we might have learned a lot from them.'

'I don't think we can be blamed,' said Karn. 'We never really believed that anything could exist under those awful conditions of near-vacuum, and almost absolute zero. It couldn't be helped.'

I did not agree. 'I think it proves that they were the more intelligent race. After all, *they* discovered us first. Everyone laughed at my grandfather when he said that the radiation he'd detected from the Shadow World must be artificial.'

Karn ran one of his tentacles over the manuscript.

'We've certainly discovered the cause of that radiation,' he said. 'Notice the date – it's just a year before your grandfather's discovery. The Professor must have got his grant all right!' He laughed unpleasantly. 'It must have given him a shock when he saw us coming up to the surface, right underneath him.'

I scarcely heard his words, for a most uncomfortable feeling had suddenly come over me. I thought of the thousands of miles of rock lying below the great city of Callastheon, growing hotter and denser all the way to the Earth's unknown core. And so I turned to Karn.

'That isn't very funny,' I said quietly. 'It may be our turn next.'

Inheritance

First published in *New Worlds*, no.3, 1947, as by 'Charles Willis'
Collected in *Expedition to Earth*

As David said, when one falls on Africa from a height of two hundred and fifty kilometres, a broken ankle may be an anti-climax but is none the less painful. But what hurt him most, he pretended, was the way we had all rushed out into the desert to see what had happened to the A.20 and had not come near him until hours later.

'Be logical, David,' Jimmy Langford had protested. 'We knew that you were OK because the base 'copter radioed when it picked you up. But the A.20 might have been a complete write-off.'

'There's only one A.20,' I said, trying to be helpful, 'but rocket test-pilots are – well, if not two a penny, at any rate seven for sixpence.'

David glared back at us from beneath his bushy eyebrows and said something in Welsh.

'The Druid's curse,' Jimmy remarked to me. 'Any moment now you'll turn into a leek or a perspex model of Stonehenge.'

You see, we were still pretty lightheaded and it would not do to be serious for a while. Even David's iron nerve must have taken a terrific beating, yet somehow he seemed the calmest of us all. I could not understand it – then.

The A.20 had come down fifty kilometres from her launching-point. We had followed her by radar for the whole trajectory, so we knew her position to within a few metres – though we did not know at the time that David had landed ten kilometres farther east.

The first warning of disaster had come seventy seconds after take-off. The A.20 had reached fifty kilometres and was following the correct trajectory to within a few per cent. As far as the eye could tell, the luminous track on the radar screen had scarcely deviated from the pre-computed path. David was doing two kilometres a second: not much, but the fastest any man had ever travelled up to then. And 'Goliath' was just about to be jettisoned.

The A.20 was a two-step rocket. It had to be, for it was using chemical fuels. The upper component, with its tiny cabin, its folded aerofoils and flaps, weighed just under twenty tons when fully fuelled. It was to be lifted by a lower two-hundred-ton booster which would take it up to fifty kilometres, after which it could carry on quite happily under its own power.

The big fellow would then drop back to Earth by parachute: it would not weigh much when its fuel was burnt. Meanwhile the upper step would have built up enough speed to reach the six-hundred-kilometre level before falling back and going into a glide that would take David half-way round the world if he wished.

I do not remember who called the two rockets 'David' and 'Goliath' but the names caught on at once. Having two Davids around caused a lot of confusion, not all of it accidental.

Well, that was the theory, but as we watched the tiny green spot on the screen fall away from its calculated course, we knew that something had gone wrong. And we guessed what it was.

At fifty kilometres the spot should have divided in two. The brighter echo should have continued to rise as a free projectile, and then fallen back to Earth. But the other should have gone on, still accelerating, drawing swiftly away from the discarded booster.

There had been no separation. The empty 'Goliath' had refused to come free and was dragging 'David' back to Earth – helplessly, for 'David's' motors could not be used. Their exhausts were blocked by the machine beneath.

We saw all this in about ten seconds. We waited just long enough to calculate the new trajectory, and then we climbed into the 'copters and set off for the target area.

All we expected to find, of course, was a heap of magnesium looking as if a bulldozer had gone over it. We knew that 'Goliath' could not eject his parachute while 'David' was sitting on top of him, any more than 'David' could use his motors while 'Goliath' was clinging beneath. I remember wondering who was going to break the news to Mavis, and then realising that she would be listening to the radio and would know all about it as soon as anyone.

We could scarcely believe our eyes when we found the two rockets still coupled together, lying almost undamaged beneath the big parachute. There was no sign of David, but a few minutes later Base called to say that he had been found. The plotters at Number Two Station had picked up the tiny echo from his parachute and sent a 'copter to collect him. He was in hospital twenty minutes later, but we stayed out in the desert for several hours checking over the machines and making arrangements to retrieve them.

When at last we got back to Base, we were pleased to see our best-hated science-reporters among the mob being held at bay. We waved aside their protests and sailed on into the ward.

The shock and the subsequent relief had left us all feeling rather irresponsible and perhaps childish. Only David seemed unaffected: the fact that he had just had one of the most miraculous escapes in human history had not made him turn a hair. He sat there in the bed pretending to be annoyed at our jibes until we had calmed down.

'Well,' said Jimmy at last, 'what went wrong?'

'That's for you to discover,' David replied. ' "Goliath" went like a dream until fuel cut-off point. I waited then for the five-second pause before the explosive bolts detonated and the springs threw him clear, but nothing happened. So I punched the emergency release. The lights dimmed, but the kick I'd expected never came. I tried a couple more times but somehow I knew it was useless. I guessed that something had shorted in the detonator circuit and was earthing the power supply.

'Well, I did some rather rapid calculations from the flight charts and abacs in the cabin. At my present speed I'd continue to rise for another two hundred kilometres and would reach the peak of my trajectory in about three minutes. Then I'd start the two-hundred-and-fifty-kilometre fall and should make a nice hole in the desert four minutes later. All told, I seemed to have a good seven minutes of life left – ignoring air resistance, to use your favourite phrase. That might add a couple of minutes to my expectation of life.

'I knew that I couldn't get the big parachute out, and "David's" wings would be useless with the forty-ton mass of "Goliath" on its tail. I'd used up two of my seven minutes before I decided what to do.

'It's a good job I made you widen that airlock. Even so, it was a squeeze to get through it in my spacesuit. I tied the end of the safety rope to a locking lever and crawled along the hull until I reached the junction of the two steps.

'The parachute compartment couldn't be opened from the outside, but I'd taken the emergency axe from the pilot's cabin. It didn't take long to get through the magnesium skin: once it had been punctured I could almost tear it apart with my hands. A few seconds later I'd released the 'chute. The silk floated aimlessly around me: I had expected some trace of air resistance at this speed but there wasn't a sign of it. The canopy simply stayed where it was put. I could only hope that when we re-entered atmosphere it would spread itself without fouling the rocket.

'I thought I had a fairly good chance of getting away with it. The additional weight of "David" would increase the loading of the parachute by less than twenty per cent but there was always the chance that the shrouds would chafe against the broken metal and be worn through before I could reach Earth. In addition the canopy would be distorted when it did open, owing to the unequal lengths of the cords. There was nothing I could do about that.

'When I'd finished, I looked about me for the first time. I couldn't see very well, for perspiration had misted over the glass of my suit. (Someone had better look into that: it can be dangerous.) I was still rising, though very slowly now. To the north-east I could see the whole of Sicily and some of the Italian mainland: farther south I could follow the Libyan coast as far as Benghazi. Spread out beneath me was all the land over which Alexander and Montgomery and Rommel had fought when I was a boy. It seemed rather surprising that anyone had ever made such a fuss about it.

'I didn't stay long: in three minutes I would be entering the atmosphere. I took a last look at the flaccid parachute, straightened some of the shrouds, and climbed back into the cabin. Then I jettisoned "David's" fuel – first the oxygen, and then, as soon as it had had time to disperse, the alcohol.

'That three minutes seemed an awfully long time. I was just over twenty-five kilometres high when I heard the first sound. It was a very high-pitched whistle, so faint that I could scarcely hear it. Glancing through the portholes, I saw that the parachute shrouds were becoming taut and the canopy was beginning to billow above me. At the same time I felt weight returning and knew that the rocket was beginning to decelerate.

'The calculation wasn't very encouraging. I'd fallen free for over two hundred kilometres and if I was to stop in time I'd need an *average* deceleration of ten gravities. The peaks might be twice that, but I'd stood fifteen *g* before now in a lesser cause. So I gave myself a double shot of dynocaine and uncaged the gimbals of my seat. I remember wondering whether I should let out "David's" little wings, and decided that it wouldn't help. Then I must have blacked out.

'When I came round again it was very hot, and I had normal weight. I felt very stiff and sore, and to make matters worse the cabin was oscillating violently. I struggled to the port and saw that the desert was uncomfortably close. The big parachute had done its work, but I thought that the impact was going to be rather too violent for comfort. So I jumped.

'From what you tell me I'd have done better to have stayed in the ship. But I don't suppose I can grumble.'

We sat in silence for a while. Then Jimmy remarked casually:

'The accelerometer shows that you touched twenty-one gravities on the way down. Only for three seconds, though. Most of the time it was between twelve and fifteen.'

David did not seem to hear and presently I said:

'Well, we can't hold the reporters off much longer. Do you feel like seeing them?'

David hesitated.

'No,' he answered. 'Not now.'

He read our faces and shook his head violently.

'No,' he said with emphasis, 'it's not that at all. I'd be willing to take off again right now. But I want to sit and think things over for a while.'

His voice sank, and when he spoke again it was to show the real David behind the perpetual mask of extroversion.

'You think I haven't any nerves,' he said, 'and that I take risks without bothering about the consequences. Well, that isn't quite true and I'd like you to know why. I've never told anyone this, not even Mavis.

'You know I'm not superstitious,' he began, a little apologetically, 'but most materialists have some secret reservations, even if they won't admit them.

'Many years ago I had a peculiarly vivid dream. By itself, it wouldn't have meant much, but later I discovered that two other men had put almost identical experiences on record. One you've probably read, for the man was J. W. Dunne.

'In his first book, *An Experiment with Time*, Dunne tells how he once dreamed that he was sitting at the controls of a curious flying-machine with swept-back wings, and years later the whole experience came true when he was testing his inherent stability airplane. Remembering my own dream, which I'd had *before* reading Dunne's book, this made a considerable impression on me. But the second incident I found even more striking.

'You've heard of Igor Sikorsky: he designed some of the first commercial long-distance flying boats – "Clippers", they were called. In his autobiography, *The Story of the Flying S*, he tells us how he had a dream very similar to Dunne's.

'He was walking along a corridor with doors opening on either side and electric lights glowing overhead. There was a slight vibration underfoot and somehow he knew that he was in a flying machine. Yet at that time there were no airplanes in the world, and few people believed there ever would be.

'Sikorsky's dream, like Dunne's, came true many years later. He was on the maiden flight of his first Clipper when he found himself walking along that familiar corridor.'

David laughed, a little self-consciously.

'You've probably guessed what my dream was about,' he continued. 'Remember, it would have made no permanent impression if I hadn't come across these parallel cases.

'I was in a small, bare room with no windows. There were two other men with me, and we were all wearing what I thought at the time were diving-suits. I had a curious control panel in front of me, with a circular screen built into it. There was a picture on the screen, but it didn't mean anything to me and I can't recall it now, though I've tried many times since. All I remember is turning to the other two men and saying: "Five minutes to go, boys" – though I'm not sure if those were the exact words. And then, of course, I woke up.

'That dream has haunted me ever since I became a test pilot. No – haunted isn't the right word. It's given me confidence that in the long run everything would be all right – at least until I'm in that cabin with those other two men. What happens after that I don't know. But now you understand why I felt quite safe when I brought down the A.20, and when I crashlanded the A.15 off Pantelleria.

'So now you know. You can laugh if you please: I sometimes do myself. But even if there's nothing in it, that dream's given my subconscious a boost that's been pretty useful.'

We didn't laugh, and presently Jimmy said:

'Those other men – did you recognise them?'

David looked doubtful.

'I've never made up my mind,' he answered. 'Remember, they were wearing spacesuits and I didn't see their faces clearly. But one of them looked rather like you, though he seemed a good deal older than you are now. I'm afraid you weren't there, Arthur. Sorry.'

'I'm glad to hear it,' I said. 'As I've told you before, I'll have to stay behind to explain what went wrong. I'm quite content to wait until the passenger service starts.'

Jimmy rose to his feet.

'OK, David,' he said, 'I'll deal with the gang outside. Get some sleep now – with or without dreams. And by the way, the A.20 will be ready again in a week. I think she'll be the last of the chemical rockets: they say the atomic drive's nearly ready for us.'

We never spoke of David's dream again, but I think it was often in our minds. Three months later he took the A.20 up to six hundred and eighty kilometres, a record which will never be broken by a machine of this type, because no one will ever build a chemical rocket again. David's uneventful landing in the Nile Valley marked the end of an epoch.

It was three years before the A.21 was ready. She looked very small compared with her giant predecessors, and it was hard to believe that she was the nearest thing to a spaceship man had yet built. This time the take-off was from sea-level, and the Atlas Mountains which had witnessed the start of our earlier shots were now merely the distant background to the scene.

By now both Jimmy and I had come to share David's belief in his own destiny. I remember Jimmy's parting words as the airlock closed.

'It won't be long now, David, before we build that three-man ship.'

And I knew he was only half joking.

We saw the A.21 climb slowly into the sky in great, widening circles, unlike any rocket the world had ever known before. There was no need to worry about gravitational loss now that we had a built-in fuel supply, and David was not in a hurry. The machine was still travelling quite slowly when I lost sight of it and went into the plotting-room.

When I got there the signal was just fading from the screen, and the detonation reached me a little later. And that was the end of David and his dreams.

The next I recall of that period is flying down the Conway Valley in Jimmy's 'copter, with Snowdon gleaming far away on our right. We had never been to David's home before and were not looking forward to this visit. But it was the least we could do.

As the mountains drifted beneath us we talked about the suddenly darkened future and wondered what the next step would be. Apart from the shock of personal loss, we were beginning to realise how much of David's confidence we had come to share ourselves. And now that confidence had been shattered.

We wondered what Mavis would do, and discussed the boy's future. He must be fifteen now, though I had not seen him for several years and Jimmy had never met him at all. According to his father he was going to be an architect and already showed considerable promise.

Mavis was quite calm and collected, though she seemed much older than when I had last met her. For a while we talked about business matters and the disposal of David's estate. I had never been an executor before, but tried to pretend that I knew all about it.

We had just started to discuss the boy when we heard the front door open and he came into the house. Mavis called to him and his footsteps came slowly along the passage. We could tell that he did not want to meet us, and his eyes were still red when he entered the room.

I had forgotten how much like his father he was, and I heard a little gasp from Jimmy.

'Hello, David,' I said.

But he did not look at me. He was staring at Jimmy, with that puzzled expression of a man who had seen someone before but cannot remember where.

And quite suddenly I knew that young David would never be an architect.

Nightfall

First published *King's College Review*, 1947
Collected in *Reach for Tomorrow* as 'The Curse'

'Nightfall', also known as 'The Curse', was inspired by a visit to Shakespeare's grave at a time when I was stationed near Stratford-upon-Avon, training RAF radar mechanics, *living* what would have been sf only a decade earlier, a juxtaposition which makes this story all the more poignant.

For three hundred years, while its fame spread across the world, the little town had stood here at the river's bend. Time and change had touched it lightly; it had heard from afar both the coming of the Armada and the fall of the Third Reich, and all Man's wars had passed it by.

Now it was gone, as though it had never been. In a moment of time the toil and treasure of centuries had been swept away. The vanished streets could still be traced as faint marks in the vitrified ground, but of the houses, nothing remained. Steel and concrete, plaster and ancient oak – it had mattered little at the end. In the moment of death they had stood together, transfixed by the glare of the detonating bomb. Then, even before they could flash into fire, the blast waves had reached them and they had ceased to be. Mile upon mile the ravening hemisphere of flame had expanded over the level farmlands, and from its heart had risen the twisting totem-pole that had haunted the minds of men for so long, and to such little purpose.

The rocket had been a stray, one of the last ever to be fired. It was hard to say for what target it had been intended. Certainly not London, for London was no longer a military objective. London, indeed, was no longer anything at all. Long ago the men whose duty it was had calculated that three of the hydrogen bombs would be sufficient for that rather small target. In sending twenty, they had been perhaps a little overzealous.

This was not one of the twenty that had done their work so well. Both its destination and its origin were unknown: whether it had come across the lonely Arctic wastes or far above the waters of the Atlantic, no one could tell and there were few now who cared. Once there had been men who had known such things, who had watched from afar the flight of the great projectiles and had sent their own missiles to meet them. Often that appointment had been kept, high above the Earth where the sky was black and sun and stars shared the heavens together. Then there had bloomed for a moment that indescribable flame, sending out into space a message that in centuries to come other eyes than Man's would see and understand.

But that had been days ago, at the beginning of the War. The defenders had long since been brushed aside, as they had known they must be. They had held on to life long enough to discharge their duty; too late, the enemy had learned his mistake. He would launch no further rockets; those still falling he had dispatched hours ago on secret trajectories that had taken them far out into space. They were returning now unguided and inert, waiting in vain for the signals that should lead them to their destinies. One by one they were falling at random upon a world which they could harm no more.

The river had already overflowed its banks; somewhere down its course the land had twisted beneath that colossal hammer-blow and the way to the sea was no longer open. Dust was still falling in a fine rain, as it would do for days as Man's cities and treasures returned to the world that had given them birth. But the sky was no longer wholly darkened, and in the west the sun was settling through banks of angry cloud.

A church had stood here by the river's edge, and though no trace of the building remained, the gravestones that the years had gathered round it still marked its place. Now the stone slabs lay in parallel rows, snapped off at their bases and pointing mutely along the line of the blast. Some were half flattened into the ground, others had been cracked and blistered by terrific heat, but many still bore the messages they had carried down the centuries in vain.

The light died in the west and the unnatural crimson faded from the sky. Yet still the graven words could be clearly read, lit by a steady, unwavering radiance, too faint to be seen by day but strong enough to banish night. The land was burning: for miles the glow of its radioactivity was reflected from the clouds. Through the glimmering landscape wound the dark ribbon of the steadily widening river, and as the waters submerged the land that deadly glow continued unchanging in the depths. In a generation, perhaps, it would have faded from sight, but a hundred years might pass before life could safely come this way again.

Timidly the waters touched the worn gravestone that for more than three hundred years had lain before the vanished altar. The church that had sheltered it so long had given it some protection at the last, and only a slight discolouration of the rock told of the fires that had passed this way. In the corpse-light of the dying land, the archaic words could still be traced as the water rose around them, breaking at last in tiny ripples across the stone. Line by line the epitaph upon which so many millions had gazed slipped beneath the conquering waters. For a little while the letters could still be faintly seen; then they were gone forever.

> Good frend for Iesvs sake forbeare,
> To digg the dvst encloased heare
> Blest be ye man yt spares thes stones,
> And cvrst be he yt moves my bones.

Undisturbed through all eternity the poet could sleep in safety now: in the silence and darkness above his head, the Avon was seeking its new outlet to the sea.

History Lesson

First published in *Startling Stories*, May 1949
Collected in *Expedition to Earth* as 'Expedition to Earth'

The second of two stories derived from an earlier one, now lost, 'History Lesson' is also the first of two stories in which glaciers return to cover the world. In the preface to *Expedition to Earth*, Clarke notes his discovery of a literally chilling phrase in Will and Ariel Durant's *Story of Civilisation*: 'Civilisation is an interlude between Ice Ages', and observes 'the next one is already overdue; perhaps global warming has arrived just in time to save us.'

No one could remember when the tribe had begun its long journey: the land of great rolling plains that had been its first home was now no more than a half-forgotten dream. For many years Shann and his people had been fleeing through a country of low hills and sparkling lakes, and now the mountains lay ahead. This summer they must cross them to the southern lands, and there was little time to lose.

The white terror that had come down from the poles, grinding continents to dust and freezing the very air before it, was less than a day's march behind. Shann wondered if the glaciers could climb the mountains ahead, and within his heart he dared to kindle a little flame of hope. They might prove a barrier against which even the remorseless ice would batter in vain. In the southern lands of which the legends spoke, his people might find refuge at last.

It took many weeks to discover a pass through which the tribe and its animals could travel. When midsummer came, they had camped in a lonely valley where the air was thin and the stars shone with a brilliance none had ever seen before. The summer was waning when Shann took his two sons and went ahead to explore the way. For three days they climbed, and for three nights slept as best they could on the freezing rocks. And on the fourth morning there was nothing ahead but a gentle rise to a cairn of grey stones built by other travellers, centuries ago.

Shann felt himself trembling, and not with cold, as they walked towards the little pyramid of stones. His sons had fallen behind; no one spoke, for too much was at stake. In a little while they would know if all their hopes had been betrayed.

To east and west, the wall of mountains curved away as if embracing the land beneath. Below lay endless miles of undulating plain, with a great river swinging across it in tremendous loops. It was fertile land; one in which the tribe could raise its crops knowing that there would be no need to flee before the harvest came.

Then Shann lifted his eyes to the south, and saw the doom of all his hopes. For there, at the edge of the world, glimmered that deadly light he had seen so often to the north – the glint of ice below the horizon.

There was no way forward. Through all the years of flight, the glaciers from the south had been advancing to meet them. Soon they would be crushed beneath the moving walls of ice—

The southern glaciers did not reach the mountains until a generation later. In that last summer, the sons of Shann carried the sacred treasures of the tribe to the lonely cairn overlooking the plain. The ice that had once gleamed below the horizon was now almost at their feet; by the spring it would be splintering against the mountain walls.

No one understood the treasures, now: they were from a past too distant for the understanding of any man alive. Their origins were lost in the mists that surrounded the Golden Age, and how they had come at last into the possession of this wandering tribe was a story that now never would be told. For it was the story of a civilisation that had passed beyond recall.

Once, all these pitiful relics had been treasured for some good reason and now they had become sacred, though their meaning had long been lost. The print in the old books had faded centuries ago, though much of the lettering was still readable – if there had been any to read it. But many generations had passed since anyone had had a use for a set of seven-figure logarithms, an atlas of the world, and the score of Sibelius's Seventh Symphony printed, according to the flyleaf, by H. K. Chu & Sons at the City of Pekin in the year AD 2021.

The old books were placed reverently in the little crypt that had been made to receive them. There followed a motley collection of fragments: gold and platinum coins, a broken telephoto lens, a watch, a cold-light lamp, a microphone, the cutter from an electric shaver, some midget radio valves – the flotsam that had been left behind when the great tide of civilisation ebbed for ever. All these were carefully stowed away in their resting-place. Then came three more relics, the most sacred of all because the least understood.

The first was a strangely shaped piece of metal, showing the coloration of intense heat. It was, in its way, the most pathetic of all these symbols from the past, for it told of Man's greatest achievement and of the future he might have known. The mahogany stand on which it was mounted bore a silver plate with the inscription:

Auxiliary igniter from starboard jet of spaceship
Morning Star, Earth – Moon, AD 1985

Next followed another miracle of the ancient science: a sphere of transparent plastic with oddly shaped pieces of metal embedded in it. At its centre was a tiny capsule of synthetic radio-element, surrounded by the converting screens that shifted its radiation far down the spectrum. As long as the material remained active, the sphere would be a tiny radio transmitter broadcasting power in all directions. Only a few of these spheres had ever been made; they had been designed as perpetual beacons to mark the orbits of the Asteroids. But Man had never reached the Asteroids, and the beacons had never been used.

Last of all was a flat circular tin, very wide in comparison to its depth. It was heavily sealed, and rattled when it was shaken. The tribal lore predicted that disaster would follow if it were ever opened, and no one knew that it held one of the great works of art of nearly a thousand years before.

The work was finished. The two men rolled the stones back into place and slowly began to descend the mountainside. Even at the last, Man had given some thought to the future and had tried to preserve something for posterity.

That winter, the great waves of ice began their first assault on the mountains, attacking from north and south. The foothills were overwhelmed in the first onslaught, and the glaciers ground them into dust. But the mountains stood firm, and when the summer came the ice retreated for a while.

So, winter after winter, the battle continued, and the roar of the avalanches, the grinding of rock and the explosions of splintered ice filled the air with tumult. No war of Man's had been fiercer nor had engulfed the globe more completely than this. Until at last the tidal waves of ice began to subside and to creep slowly down the flanks of the mountains they had never quite subdued; though the valleys and passes were still firmly in their grip. It was stalemate: the glaciers had met their match.

But their defeat was too late to be of any use to Man.

So the centuries passed; and presently there happened something that must occur once at least in the history of every world in the Universe, no matter how remote and lonely it may be—

The ship from Venus came five thousand years too late, but its crew knew nothing of this. While still many millions of miles away, the telescopes had seen the great shroud of ice that made Earth the most brilliant object in the sky next to the Sun itself. Here and there the dazzling sheet was marred by black specks that revealed the presence of almost buried mountains. That was all. The rolling oceans, the plains and forests, the deserts and lakes – all that had been the world of Man was sealed beneath the ice, perhaps for ever.

The ship closed into Earth and established an orbit less than a thousand miles distant. For five days it circled the planet while cameras recorded all that was left to view and a hundred instruments gathered information that would give the Venusian scientists many years of work. An actual landing was not intended; there seemed little purpose in it. But on the sixth day the picture changed. A panoramic monitor, driven to the limit of its amplification, detected the dying radiation of the five-thousand-years-old beacon. Through all the centuries it had been sending out its signals, with ever-failing strength as its radioactive heart steadily weakened.

The monitor locked on the beacon frequency. In the control-room, a bell clamoured for attention. A little later, the Venusian ship broke free from its orbit and slanted down towards Earth – towards a range of mountains that still towered proudly above the ice, and to a cairn of grey stones that the years had scarcely touched.

The great disc of the Sun blazed fiercely in a sky no longer veiled with mist, for the clouds that had once hidden Venus had now completely gone. Whatever force had caused the change in the Sun's radiation had doomed one civilisation but given birth to another. Less than five thousand years before, the half-savage people of Venus had seen Sun and stars for the first time. Just as the science of Earth had begun with astronomy, so had that of Venus, and on the warm, rich world that Man had never seen, progress had been incredibly rapid.

Perhaps the Venusians had been lucky. They never knew the Dark Age that held Man enchained for a thousand years; they missed the long detour into chemistry and mechanics, but came at once to the more fundamental laws of radiation physics. In the time that Man had taken to progress from the Pyramids to the rocket-propelled spaceship, the Venusians had passed from the discovery of agriculture to antigravity itself – the ultimate secret that Man had never learned.

The warm ocean that still bore most of the young planet's life rolled its breakers languidly against the sandy shore. So new was this continent that the very sands were coarse and gritty: there had not yet been time enough for the sea to wear them smooth. The scientists lay half in the water, their beautiful reptilian bodies gleaming in the sunlight. The greatest minds of Venus had gathered on this shore from all the islands of the planet. What they were going to hear they did not yet know, except that it concerned the Third World and the mysterious race that had peopled it before the coming of the ice.

The Historian was standing on the land, for the instruments he wished to use had no love of water. By his side was a large machine which attracted many curious glances from his colleagues. It was clearly concerned with optics, for a lens system projected from it towards a screen of white material a dozen yards away.

The Historian began to speak. Briefly he recapitulated what little had been discovered concerning the Third Planet and its people. He mentioned the centuries of fruitless research that had failed to interpret a single word of the writings of Earth. The planet had been inhabited by a race of great technical ability; that at least was proved by the few pieces of machinery that had been found in the cairn upon the mountain.

'We do not know why so advanced a civilisation came to an end. Almost certainly, it had sufficient knowledge to survive an Ice Age. There must have been some other factor of which we know nothing. Possibly disease or racial degeneration may have been responsible. It has even been suggested that the tribal conflicts endemic to our own species in prehistoric times may have continued on the Third Planet after the coming of technology. Some philosophers maintain that knowledge of machinery does not necessarily imply a high degree of civilisation, and it is theoretically possible to have wars in a society possessing mechanical power, flight, and even radio. Such a conception is very alien to our thoughts, but we must admit its possibility. It would certainly account for the downfall of the lost race.

'It has always been assumed that we should never know anything of the physical form of the creatures who lived on Planet Three. For centuries our artists have been depicting scenes from the history of the dead world, peopling it with all manner of fantastic beings. Most of these creations have resembled us more or less closely though it has often been pointed out that because we are reptiles it does not follow that all intelligent life must necessarily be reptilian. We now know the answer to one of the most baffling problems of history. At last, after five hundred years of research, we have discovered the exact form and nature of the ruling life on the Third Planet.'

There was a murmur of astonishment from the assembled scientists. Some were so taken aback that they disappeared for a while into the comfort of the ocean, as all Venusians were apt to do in moments of stress. The Historian waited until his colleagues re-emerged into the element they so disliked. He himself was quite comfortable, thanks to tiny sprays that were continually playing over his body. With their help he could live on land for many hours before having to return to the ocean.

The excitement slowly subsided, and the lecturer continued.

'One of the most puzzling of the objects found on Planet Three was a flat metal container holding a great length of transparent plastic material, perforated at the edges and wound tightly into a spool. This transparent tape at first seemed quite featureless, but an examination with the new sub-electronic microscope has shown that this is not the case. Along the surface of the material, invisible to our eyes but perfectly clear under the correct radiation, are literally thousands of tiny pictures. It is believed that they were imprinted on the material by some chemical means, and have faded with the passage of time.

'These pictures apparently form a record of life as it was on the Third Planet at the height of its civilisation. They are not independent; consecutive pictures are almost identical, differing only in the detail of movement. The purpose of such a record is obvious: it is only necessary to project the scenes in rapid succession to give an illusion of continuous movement. We have made a machine to do this, and I have here an exact reproduction of the picture sequence.

'The scenes you are now going to witness take us back many thousands of years to the great days of our sister planet. They show a very complex civilisation, many of whose activities we can only dimly understand. Life seems to have been very violent and energetic, and much that you will see is quite baffling.

'It is clear that the Third Planet was inhabited by a number of different species, none of them reptilian. That is a blow to our pride, but the conclusion in inescapable. The dominant type of life appears to have been a two-armed biped. It walked upright and covered its body with some flexible material, possibly for protection against the cold, since even before the Ice Age the planet was at a much lower temperature than our own world.

'But I will not try your patience any further. You will now see the record of which I have been speaking.'

A brilliant light flashed from the projector. There was a gentle whirring, and on the screen appeared hundreds of strange beings moving rather jerkily to and fro. The picture expanded to embrace one of the creatures, and the scientists could see that the Historian's description had been correct. The creature possessed two eyes, set rather closely together, but the other facial adornments were a little obscure. There was a large orifice in the lower portion of the head that was continually opening and closing; possibly it had something to do with the creature's breathing.

The scientists watched spellbound as the strange beings became involved in a series of fantastic adventures. There was an incredibly violent conflict with another, slightly different, creature. It seemed certain that they must both be killed – but no; when it was all over neither seemed any the worse. Then came a furious drive over miles of country in a four-wheeled mechanical device which was capable of extraordinary feats of locomotion. The ride ended in a city packed with other vehicles moving in all directions at breath-taking speeds. No one was surprised to see two of the machines meet head-on, with devastating results.

After that, events became even more complicated. It was now quite obvious that it would take many years of research to analyse and understand all that was happening. It was also clear that the record was a work of art, somewhat stylised, rather than an exact reproduction of life as it actually had been on the Third Planet.

Most of the scientists felt themselves completely dazed when the sequence of pictures came to an end. There was a final flurry of motion, in which the creature that had been the centre of interest became involved in some tremendous but incomprehensible catastrophe. The picture contracted to a circle, centred on the creature's head. The last scene of all was an expanded view of its face, obviously expressing some powerful emotion, but whether it was rage, grief, defiance, resignation or some other feeling could not be guessed.

The picture vanished. For a moment some lettering appeared on the screen; then it was all over.

For several minutes there was complete silence, save for the lapping of the waves on the sand. The scientists were too stunned to speak. The fleeting glimpse of Earth's civilisation had had a shattering effect on their minds. Then little groups began to start talking together, first in whispers and then more loudly as the implications of what they had seen became clearer. Presently the Historian called for attention and addressed the meeting again.

'We are now planning,' he began, 'a vast programme of research to extract all available knowledge from the record. Thousands of copies are being made for distribution to all workers. You will appreciate the problems involved; the psychologists in particular have an immense task confronting them. But I do not doubt that we shall succeed. In another generation, who can say what we may not have learned of this wonderful race? Before we leave, let us look again at our remote cousins, whose wisdom may have surpassed our own but of whom so little has survived.'

Once more the final picture flashed on the screen, motionless this time, for the projector had been stopped. With something like awe, the scientists gazed at the still figure from the past, while in turn the little biped stared back at them with its characteristic expression of arrogant bad temper.

For the rest of Time it would symbolise the human race. The psychologists of Venus would analyse its actions and watch its every movement until they could reconstruct its mind. Thousands of books would be written about it. Intricate philosophies would be contrived to account for its behaviour. But all this labour, all this research, would be utterly in vain.

Perhaps the proud and lonely figure on the screen was smiling sardonically at the scientists who were starting on their age-long, fruitless quest. Its secret would be safe as long as the Universe endured, for no one now would ever read the lost language of Earth. Millions of times in the ages to come those last few words would flash across the screen, and none could ever guess their meaning:

A Walt Disney Production.

Transience

First published in *Startling Stories*, July 1949
Collected in *The Other Side of the Sky*

'Transience' is the only one of my short stories to have been set to music, by the British composer David Bedford. The work was commissioned by the late Sir Peter Pears, and he performed it with the London Sinfonietta, under the baton of the composer. The story itself was inspired by one of A. E. Housman's poems, which also provided the couplet, 'What shall I do or write/Against the fall of night?' and the title of one of my novels. Bedford's oratorio based on my novel *The City and the Stars* will be performed at the Royal Festival Hall in 2001.

The forest, which came almost to the edge of the beach, climbed away into the distance up the flanks of the low, misty hills. Underfoot, the sand was coarse and mixed with myriads of broken shells. Here and there the retreating tide had left long streamers of weed trailed across the beach. The rain, which seldom ceased, had for the moment passed inland, but ever and again large, angry drops would beat tiny craters in the sand.

It was hot and sultry, for the war between sun and rain was never-ending. Sometimes the mists would lift for a while and the hills would stand out clearly above the land they guarded. These hills arced in a semicircle along the bay, following the line of the beach, and beyond them could sometimes be seen, at an immense distance, a wall of mountains lying beneath perpetual clouds. The trees grew everywhere, softening the contours of the land so that the hills blended smoothly into each other. Only in one place could the bare, uncovered rock be seen, where long ago some fault had weakened the foundations of the hills, so that for a mile or more the sky line fell sharply away, drooping down to the sea like a broken wing.

Moving with the cautious alertness of a wild animal, the child came through the stunted trees at the forest's edge. For a moment he hesitated; then, since there seemed to be no danger, walked slowly out onto the beach.

He was naked, heavily built, and had coarse black hair tangled over his shoulders. His face, brutish though it was, might almost have passed in human society, but the eyes would have betrayed him. They were not the eyes of an animal, for there was something in their depths that no animal had ever known. But it was no more than a promise. For this child, as for all his race, the light of reason had yet to dawn. Only a hairsbreadth still separated him from the beasts among whom he dwelt.

The tribe had not long since come into this land, and he was the first ever to set foot upon that lonely beach. What had lured him from the known dangers of the forest into the unknown and therefore more terrible dangers of this new element, he could not have told even had he possessed the power of speech. Slowly he walked out to the water's edge, always with backward glances at the forest behind him; and as he did so, for the first time in all history, the level sand bore upon its face the footprints it would one day know so well.

He had met water before, but it had always been bounded and confined by land. Now it stretched endlessly before him, and the sound of its labouring beat ceaselessly upon his ears.

With the timeless patience of the savage, he stood on the moist sand that the water had just relinquished, and as the tide line moved out he followed it slowly, pace by pace. When the waves reached toward his feet with a sudden access of energy, he would retreat a little way toward the land. But something held him here at the water's edge, while his shadow lengthened along the sands and the cold evening wind began to rise around him.

Perhaps into his mind had come something of the wonder of the sea, and a hint of all that it would one day mean to man. Though the first gods of his people still lay far in the future, he felt a dim sense of worship stir within him. He knew that he was now in the presence of something greater than all the powers and forces he had ever met.

The tide was turning. Far away in the forest, a wolf howled once and was suddenly silent. The noises of the night were rising around him, and it was time to go.

Under the low moon, the two lines of footprints interlaced across the sand. Swiftly the oncoming tide was smoothing them away. But they would return in their thousands and millions, in the centuries yet to be.

The child playing among the rock pools knew nothing of the forest that had once ruled all the land around him. It had left no trace of its existence. As ephemeral as the mists that had so often rolled down from the hills, it, too, had veiled them for a little while and now was gone. In its place had come a checkerboard of fields, the legacy of a thousand years of patient toil. And so the illusion of permanence remained, though everything had altered save the line of the hills against the sky. On the beach, the sand was finer now, and the land had lifted so that the old tide line was far beyond the reach of the questing waves.

Beyond the sea wall and the promenade, the little town was sleeping through the golden summer day. Here and there along the beach, people lay at rest, drowsy with heat and lulled by the murmur of the waves.

Out across the bay, white and gold against the water, a great ship was moving slowly to sea. The boy could hear, faint and far away, the beat of its screws and could still see the tiny figures moving upon its decks and superstructure. To the child – and not to him alone – it was a thing of wonder and beauty. He knew its name and the land to which it was steaming; but he did not know that the splendid ship was both the last and greatest of its kind. He scarcely noticed, almost lost against the glare of the sun, the thin white vapour trails that spelled the doom of the proud and lovely giant.

Soon the great liner was no more than a dark smudge on the horizon, and the boy turned again to his interrupted play, to the tireless building of his battlements of sand. In the west the sun was beginning its long decline, but the evening was still far away.

Yet it came at last, when the tide was returning to the land. At his mother's words, the child gathered up his playthings and, wearily contented, began to follow his parents back to the shore. He glanced once only at the sand castles he had built with such labour and would not see again. Without regret he left them to the advancing waves, for tomorrow he would return and the future stretched endlessly before him.

That tomorrow would not always come, either for himself or for the world, he was still too young to know.

And now even the hills had changed, worn away by the weight of years. Not all the change was the work of nature, for one night in the long-forgotten past something had come sliding down from the stars, and the little town had vanished in a spinning tower of flame. But that was so long ago that it was beyond sorrow or regret. Like the fall of fabled Troy or the overwhelming of Pompeii, it was part of the irremediable past and could rouse no pity now.

On the broken sky line lay a long metal building supporting a maze of mirrors that turned and glittered in the sun. No one from an earlier age could have guessed its purpose. It was as meaningless as an observatory or a radio station would have been to ancient man. But it was neither of these things.

Since noon, Bran had been playing among the shallow pools left by the retreating tide. He was quite alone, though the machine that guarded him was watching unobtrusively from the shore. Only a few days ago, there had been other children playing beside the blue waters of this lovely bay. Bran sometimes wondered where they had vanished, but he was a solitary child and did not greatly care. Lost in his own dreams, he was content to be left alone.

In the last few hours he had linked the tiny pools with an intricate network of waterways. His thoughts were very far from Earth, both in space and time. Around him now were the dull, red sands of another world. He was Cardenis, prince of engineers, fighting to save his people from the encroaching deserts. For Bran had looked upon the ravaged face of Mars; he knew the story of its long tragedy and the help from Earth that had come too late.

Out to the horizon the sea was empty, untroubled by ships, as it had been for ages. For a little while, near the beginning of time, man had fought his brief war against the oceans of the world. Now it seemed that only a moment lay between the coming of the first canoes and the passing of the last great Megatheria of the seas.

Bran did not even glance at the sky when the monstrous shadow swept along the beach. For days past, those silver giants had been rising over the hills in an unending stream, and now he gave them little thought. All his life he had watched the great ships climbing through the skies of Earth on their way to distant worlds. Often he had seen them return from those long journeys, dropping down through the clouds with cargoes beyond imagination.

He wondered sometimes why they came no more, those returning voyagers. All the ships he saw now were outward bound; never one drove down from the skies to berth at the great port beyond the hills. Why this should be, no one would tell him. He had learned not to speak of it now, having seen the sadness that his questions brought.

Across the sands the robot was calling to him softly. 'Bran,' came the words, echoing the tones of his mother's voice, 'Bran – it's time to go.'

The child looked up, his face full of indignant denial. He could not believe it. The sun was still high and the tide was far away. Yet along the shore his mother and father were already coming toward him.

They walked swiftly, as though the time were short. Now and again his father would glance for an instant at the sky, then turn his head quickly away as if he knew well that there was nothing he could hope to see. But a moment later he would look again.

Stubborn and angry, Bran stood at bay among his canals and lakes. His mother was strangely silent, but presently his father took him by the hand and said quietly, 'You must come with us, Bran. It's time we went.'

The child pointed sullenly at the beach. 'But it's too early. I haven't finished.'

His father's reply held no trace of anger, only a great sadness. 'There are many things, Bran, that will not be finished now.'

Still uncomprehending, the boy turned to his mother.

'Then can I come again tomorrow?'

With a sense of desolating wonder, Bran saw his mother's eyes fill with sudden tears. And he knew at last that never again would he play upon the sands by the azure waters; never again would he feel the tug of the tiny waves about his feet. He had found the sea too late, and now must leave it forever. Out of the future, chilling his soul, came the first faint intimation of the long ages of exile that lay ahead.

He never looked back as they walked silently together across the clinging sand. This moment would be with him all his life, but he was still too stunned to do more than walk blindly into a future he could not understand.

The three figures dwindled into the distance and were gone. A long while later, a silver cloud seemed to lift above the hills and move slowly out to sea. In a shallow arc, as though reluctant to leave its world, the last of the great ships climbed toward the horizon and shrank to nothingness over the edge of the Earth.

The tide was returning with the dying day. As though its makers still walked within its walls, the low metal building upon the hills had begun to blaze with light. Near the zenith, one star had not waited for the sun to set, but already burned with a fierce white glare against the darkling sky. Soon its companions, no longer in the scant thousands that man had once known, began to fill the heavens. The Earth was now near the centre of the universe, and whole areas of the sky were an unbroken blaze of light.

But rising beyond the sea in two long curving arms, something black and monstrous eclipsed the stars and seemed to cast its shadow over all the world. The tentacles of the Dark Nebula were already brushing against the frontiers of the solar system. . . .

In the east, a great yellow moon was climbing through the waves. Though man had torn down its mountains and brought it air and water, its face was the one that had looked upon Earth since history began, and it was still the ruler of the tides. Across the sand the line of foam moved steadily onward, overwhelming the little canals and planing down the tangled footprints.

On the sky line, the lights in the strange metal building suddenly died, and the spinning mirrors ceased their moonlight glittering. From far inland came the blinding flash of a great explosion, then another, and another fainter yet.

Presently the ground trembled a little, but no sound disturbed the solitude of the deserted shore.

Under the level light of the sagging moon, beneath the myriad stars, the beach lay waiting for the end. It was alone now, as it had been at the beginning. Only the waves would move, and but for a little while, upon its golden sands.

For Man had come and gone.

The Wall of Darkness

First published in *Super Science Stories*, July 1949
Collected in *The Other Side of the Sky*

Many and strange are the universes that drift like bubbles in the foam upon the River of Time. Some – a very few – move against or athwart its current; and fewer still are those that lie forever beyond its reach, knowing nothing of the future or the past. Shervane's tiny cosmos was not one of these: its strangeness was of a different order. It held one world only – the planet of Shervane's race – and a single star, the great sun Trilorne that brought it life and light.

Shervane knew nothing of night, for Trilorne was always high above the horizon, dipping near it only in the long months of winter. Beyond the borders of the Shadow Land, it was true, there came a season when Trilorne disappeared below the edge of the world, and a darkness fell in which nothing could live. But even then the darkness was not absolute, though there were no stars to relieve it.

Alone in its little cosmos, turning the same face always toward its solitary sun, Shervane's world was the last and the strangest jest of the Maker of the Stars.

Yet as he looked across his father's lands, the thoughts that filled Shervane's mind were those that any human child might have known. He felt awe, and curiosity, and a little fear, and above all a longing to go out into the great world before him. These things he was still too young to do, but the ancient house was on the highest ground for many miles and he could look far out over the land that would one day be his. When he turned to the north, with Trilorne shining full upon his face, he could see many miles away the long line of mountains that curved around to the right, rising higher and higher, until they disappeared behind him in the direction of the Shadow Land. One day, when he was older, he would go through those mountains along the pass that led to the great lands of the east.

On his left was the ocean, only a few miles away, and sometimes Shervane could hear the thunder of the waves as they fought and tumbled on the gently sloping sands. No one knew how far the ocean reached. Ships had set out across it, sailing northward while Trilorne rose higher and higher in the sky and the heat of its rays grew ever more intense. Long before the great sun had reached the zenith, they had been forced to return.

If the mythical Fire Lands did indeed exist, no man could ever hope to reach their burning shores – unless the legends were really true. Once, it was said, there had been swift metal ships that could cross the ocean despite the heat of Trilorne, and so come to the lands on the other side of the world. Now these countries could be reached only by a tedious journey over land and sea, which could be shortened no more than a little by travelling as far north as one dared.

All the inhabited countries of Shervane's world lay in the narrow belt between burning heat and insufferable cold. In every land, the far north was an unapproachable region smitten by the fury of Trilorne. And to the south of all countries lay the vast and gloomy Shadow Land, where Trilorne was never more than a pale disc on the horizon, and often was not visible at all.

These things Shervane learned in the years of his childhood, and in those years he had no wish to leave the wide lands between the mountains and the sea. Since the dawn of time his ancestors and the races before them had toiled to make these lands the fairest in the world; if they had failed, it was by a narrow margin. There were gardens bright with strange flowers, there were streams that trickled gently between moss-grown rocks to be lost in the pure waters of the tideless sea. There were fields of grain that rustled continually in the wind, as if the generations of seeds yet unborn were talking one to the other. In the wide meadows and beneath the trees the friendly cattle wandered aimlessly with foolish cries. And there was the great house, with its enormous rooms and its endless corridors, vast enough in reality but huger still to the mind of a child. This was the world in which Shervane had passed his years, the world he knew and loved. As yet, what lay beyond its borders had not concerned his mind.

But Shervane's universe was not one of those free from the domination of time. The harvest ripened and was gathered into the granaries; Trilorne rocked slowly through its little arc of sky, and with the passing seasons Shervane's mind and body grew. His land seemed smaller now: the mountains were nearer and the sea was only a brief walk from the great house. He began to learn of the world in which he lived, and to be made ready for the part he must play in its shaping.

Some of these things he learned from his father, Sherval, but most he was taught by Grayle, who had come across the mountains in the days of his father's father, and had now been tutor to three generations of Shervane's family. He was fond of Grayle, though the old man taught him many things he had no wish to learn, and the years of his boyhood passed pleasantly enough until the time came for him to go through the mountains into the lands beyond. Ages ago his family had come from the great countries of the east, and in every generation since, the eldest son had made that pilgrimage again to spend a year of his youth among his cousins. It was a wise custom, for beyond the mountains much of the knowledge of the past still lingered, and there one could meet men from other lands and study their ways.

In the last spring before his son's departure, Sherval collected three of his servants and certain animals it is convenient to call horses, and took Shervane to see those parts of the land he had never visited before. They rode west to the sea, and followed it for many days, until Trilorne was noticeably nearer the horizon. Still they went south, their shadows lengthening before them, turning again to the east only when the rays of the sun seemed to have lost all their power. They were now well within the limits of the Shadow Land, and it would not be wise to go farther south until the summer was at its height.

Shervane was riding beside his father, watching the changing landscape with all the eager curiosity of a boy seeing a new country for the first time. His father was talking about the soil, describing the crops that could be grown here and those that would fail if the attempt were made. But Shervane's attention was elsewhere: he was staring out across the desolate Shadow Land, wondering how far it stretched and what mysteries it held.

'Father,' he said presently, 'if you went south in a straight line, right across the Shadow Land, would you reach the other side of the world?'

His father smiled.

'Men have asked that question for centuries,' he said, 'but there are two reasons why they will never know the answer.'

'What are they?'

'The first, of course, is the darkness and the cold. Even here, nothing can live during the winter months. But there is a better reason, though I see that Grayle has not spoken of it.'

'I don't think he has: at least, I do not remember.'

For a moment Sherval did not reply. He stood up in his stirrups and surveyed the land to the south.

'Once I knew this place well,' he said to Shervane. 'Come – I have something to show you.'

They turned away from the path they had been following, and for several hours rode once more with their backs to the sun. The land was rising slowly now, and Shervane saw that they were climbing a great ridge of rock that pointed like a dagger into the heart of the Shadow Land. They came presently to a hill too steep for the horses to ascend, and here they dismounted and left the animals in the servants' charge.

'There is a way around,' said Sherval, 'but it is quicker for us to climb than to take the horses to the other side.'

The hill, though steep, was only a small one, and they reached its summit in a few minutes. At first Shervane could see nothing he had not met before; there was only the same undulating wilderness, which seemed to become darker and more forbidding with every yard that its distance from Trilorne increased.

He turned to his father with some bewilderment, but Sherval pointed to the far south and drew a careful line along the horizon.

'It is not easy to see,' he said quietly. 'My father showed it to me from this same spot, many years before you were born.'

106

Shervane stared into the dusk. The southern sky was so dark as to be almost black, and it came down to meet the edge of the world. But not quite, for along the horizon, in a great curve dividing land from sky yet seeming to belong to neither, was a band of deeper darkness, black as the night which Shervane had never known.

He looked at it steadfastly for a long time, and perhaps some hint of the future may have crept into his soul, for the darkling land seemed suddenly alive and waiting. When at last he tore his eyes away, he knew that nothing would ever be the same again, though he was still too young to recognise the challenge for what it was.

And so, for the first time in his life, Shervane saw the Wall.

In the early spring he said farewell to his people, and went with one servant over the mountains into the great lands of the eastern world. Here he met the men who shared his ancestry, and here he studied the history of his race, the arts that had grown from ancient times, and the sciences that ruled the lives of men. In the places of learning he made friends with boys who had come from lands even farther to the east: few of these was he likely to see again, but one was to play a greater part in his life than either could have imagined. Brayldon's father was a famous architect, but his son intended to eclipse him. He was travelling from land to land, always learning, watching, asking questions. Though he was only a few years older than Shervane, his knowledge of the world was infinitely greater – or so it seemed to the younger boy.

Between them they took the world to pieces and rebuilt it according to their desires. Brayldon dreamed of cities whose great avenues and stately towers would shame even the wonders of the past, but Shervane's interests lay more with the people who would dwell in those cities, and the way they ordered their lives.

They often spoke of the Wall, which Brayldon knew from the stories of his own people, though he himself had never seen it. Far to the south of every country, as Shervane had learned, it lay like a great barrier athwart the Shadow Land. In high summer it could be reached, though only with difficulty, but nowhere was there any way of passing it, and none knew what lay beyond. An entire world, never pausing even when it reached a hundred times the height of a man, it encircled the wintry sea that washed the shores of the Shadow Land. Travellers had stood upon those lonely beaches, scarcely warmed by the last thin rays of Trilorne, and had seen how the dark shadow of the Wall marched out to sea contemptuous of the waves beneath its feet. And on the far shores, other travellers had watched it come striding in across the ocean, to sweep past them on its journey round the world.

'One of my uncles,' said Brayldon, 'once reached the Wall when he was a young man. He did it for a wager, and he rode for ten days before he came beneath it. I think it frightened him – it was so huge and cold. He could not tell whether it was made of metal or of stone, and when he shouted, there was no echo at all, but his voice died away quickly as if the Wall were swallowing the sound. My people believe it is the end of the world, and there is nothing beyond.'

'If that were true,' Shervane replied, with irrefutable logic, 'the ocean would have poured over the edge before the Wall was built.'

'Not if Kyrone built it when He made the world.'

Shervane did not agree.

'*My* people believe it is the work of man – perhaps the engineers of the First Dynasty, who made so many wonderful things. If they really had ships that could reach the Fire Lands – and even ships that could fly – they might have possessed enough wisdom to build the Wall.'

Brayldon shrugged.

'They must have had a very good reason,' he said. 'We can never know the answer, so why worry about it?'

This eminently practical advice, as Shervane had discovered, was all that the ordinary man ever gave him. Only philosophers were interested in unanswerable questions: to most people, the enigma of the Wall, like the problem of existence itself, was something that scarcely concerned their minds. And all the philosophers he had met had given him different answers.

First there had been Grayle, whom he had questioned on his return from the Shadow Land. The old man had looked at him quietly and said:

'There is only one thing behind the Wall, so I have heard. And that is madness.'

Then there had been Artex, who was so old that he could scarcely hear Shervane's nervous questioning. He gazed at the boy through eyelids that seemed too tired to open fully, and had replied after a long time:

'Kyrone built the Wall in the third day of the making of the world. What is beyond, we shall discover when we die – for there go the souls of all the dead.'

Yet Irgan, who lived in the same city, had flatly contradicted this.

'Only memory can answer your question, my son. For behind the Wall is the land in which we lived before our births.'

Whom could he believe? The truth was that no one knew: if the knowledge had ever been possessed, it had been lost ages since.

Though this quest was unsuccessful, Shervane had learned many things in his year of study. With the returning spring he said farewell to Brayldon and the other friends he had known for such a little while, and set out along the ancient road that led him back to his own country. Once again he made the perilous journey through the great pass between the mountains, where walls of ice hung threatening against the sky. He came to the place where the road curved down once more toward the world of men, where there was warmth and running water and the breath no longer laboured in the freezing air. Here, on the last rise of the road before it descended into the valley, one could see far out across the land to the distant gleam of the ocean. And there, almost lost in the mists at the edge of the world, Shervane could see the line of shadow that was his own country.

He went on down the great ribbon of stone until he came to the bridge that men had built across the cataract in the ancient days when the only other way had been destroyed by earthquake. But the bridge was gone: the storms and avalanches of early spring had swept away one of the mighty piers, and the beautiful metal rainbow lay a twisted ruin in the spray and foam a thousand feet below. The summer would have come and gone before the road could be opened once more: as Shervane sadly returned he knew that another year must pass ere he would see his home again.

He paused for many minutes on the last curve of the road, looking back toward the unattainable land that held all the things he loved. But the mists had closed over it, and he saw it no more. Resolutely he turned back along the road until the open lands had vanished and the mountains enfolded him again.

Brayldon was still in the city when Shervane returned. He was surprised and pleased to see his friend, and together they discussed what should be done in the year ahead. Shervane's cousins, who had grown fond of their guest, were not sorry to see him again, but their kindly suggestion that he should devote another year to study was not well received.

Shervane's plan matured slowly, in the face of considerable opposition. Even Brayldon was not enthusiastic at first, and much argument was needed before he would co-operate. Thereafter, the agreement of everyone else who mattered was only a question of time.

Summer was approaching when the two boys set out toward Brayldon's country. They rode swiftly, for the journey was a long one and must be completed before Trilorne began its winter fall. When they reached the lands that Brayldon knew, they made certain inquiries which caused much shaking of heads. But the answers they obtained were accurate, and soon the Shadow Land was all around them, and presently for the second time in his life Shervane saw the Wall.

It seemed not far away when they first came upon it, rising from a bleak and lonely plain. Yet they rode endlessly across that plain before the Wall grew any nearer – and then they had almost reached its base before they realised how close they were, for there was no way of judging its distance until one could reach out and touch it.

When Shervane gazed up at the monstrous ebony sheet that had so troubled his mind, it seemed to be overhanging and about to crush him beneath its falling weight. With difficulty, he tore his eyes away from the hypnotic sight, and went nearer to examine the material of which the Wall was built.

It was true, as Brayldon had told him, that it felt cold to the touch – colder than it had any right to be even in this sun-starved land. It felt neither hard nor soft, for its texture eluded the hand in a way that was difficult to analyse. Shervane had the impression that something was preventing him from actual contact with the surface, yet he could see no space between the Wall and his fingers when he forced them against it. Strangest of all was the uncanny silence of which Brayldon's uncle had spoken: every word was deadened and all sounds died away with unnatural swiftness.

Brayldon had unloaded some tools and instruments from the pack horses, and had begun to examine the Wall's surface. He found very quickly that no drills or cutters would mark it in any way, and presently he came to the conclusion Shervane had already reached. The Wall was not merely adamant: it was unapproachable.

At last, in disgust, he took a perfectly straight metal rule and pressed its edge against the wall. While Shervane held a mirror to reflect the feeble light of Trilorne along the line of contact, Brayldon peered at the rule from the other side. It was as he had thought: an infinitely narrow streak of light showed unbroken between the two surfaces.

Brayldon looked thoughtfully at his friend.

'Shervane,' he said, 'I don't believe the Wall is made of matter, as we know it.'

'Then perhaps the legends were right that said it was never built at all, but created as we see it now.'

'I think so too,' said Brayldon. 'The engineers of the First Dynasty had such powers. There are some very ancient buildings in my land that seem to have been made in a single operation from a substance that shows absolutely no sign of weathering. If it were black instead of coloured, it would be very much like the material of the Wall.'

He put away his useless tools and began to set up a simple portable theodolite.

'If I can do nothing else,' he said with a wry smile, 'at least I can find exactly how high it is!'

When they looked back for their last view of the Wall, Shervane wondered if he would ever see it again. There was nothing more he could learn: for the future, he must forget this foolish dream that he might one day master its secret. Perhaps there was no secret at all – perhaps beyond the wall the Shadow Land stretched round the curve of the world until it met that same barrier again. That, surely, seemed the likeliest thing. But if it were so, then why had the Wall been built, and by what race?

With an almost angry effort of will, he put these thoughts aside and rode forward into the light of Trilorne, thinking of a future in which the Wall would play no more part than it did in the lives of other men.

So two years had passed before Shervane could return to his home. In two years, especially when one is young, much can be forgotten and even the things nearest to the heart lose their distinctness, so that they can no longer be clearly recalled. When Shervane came through the last foothills of the mountains and was again in the country of his childhood, the joy of his home-coming was mingled with a strange sadness. So many things were forgotten that he had once thought his mind would hold forever.

The news of his return had gone before him, and soon he saw far ahead a line of horses galloping along the road. He pressed forward eagerly, wondering if Sherval would be there to greet him, and was a little disappointed when he saw that Grayle was leading the procession.

Shervane halted as the old man rode up to his horse. Then Grayle put his hand upon his shoulder, but for a while he turned away his head and could not speak.

And presently Shervane learned that the storms of the year before had destroyed more than the ancient bridge, for the lightning had brought his own home in ruins to the ground. Years before the appointed time, all the lands that Sherval had owned had passed into the possession of his son. Far more, indeed, than these, for the whole family had been assembled, according to its yearly custom, in the great house when the fire had come down upon it. In a single moment of time, everything between the mountains and the sea had passed into his keeping. He was the richest man his land had known for generations; and all these things he would have given to look again into the calm grey eyes of the father he would see no more.

Trilorne had risen and fallen in the sky many times since Shervane took leave of his childhood on the road before the mountains. The land had flourished in the passing years, and the possessions that had so suddenly become his had steadily increased their value. He had husbanded them well, and now he had time once more in which to dream. More than that – he had the wealth to make his dreams come true.

Often stories had come across the mountains of the work Brayldon was doing in the east, and although the two friends had never met since their youth they had exchanged messages regularly. Brayldon had achieved his ambitions: not only had he designed the two largest buildings erected since the ancient days, but a whole new city had been planned by him, though it would not be completed in his lifetime. Hearing of these things, Shervane remembered the aspirations of his own youth, and his mind went back across the years to the day when they had stood together beneath the majesty of the Wall. For a long time he wrestled with his thoughts, fearing to revive old longings that might not be assuaged. But at last he made his decision and wrote to Brayldon – for what was the use of wealth and power unless they could be used to shape one's dreams?

Then Shervane waited, wondering if Brayldon had forgotten the past in the years that had brought him fame. He had not long to wait: Brayldon could not come at once, for he had great works to carry to their completion, but when they were finished he would join his old friend. Shervane had thrown him a challenge that was worthy of his skill – one which if he could meet would bring him more satisfaction than anything he had yet done.

Early the next summer he came, and Shervane met him on the road below the bridge. They had been boys when they last parted, and now they were nearing middle age, yet as they greeted one another the years seemed to fall away and each was secretly glad to see how lightly Time had touched the friend he remembered.

They spent many days in conference together, considering the plans that Brayldon had drawn up. The work was an immense one, and would take many years to complete, but it was possible to a man of Shervane's wealth. Before he gave his final assent, he took his friend to see Grayle.

The old man had been living for some years in the little house that Shervane had built him. For a long time he had played no active part in the life of the great estates, but his advice was always ready when it was needed, and it was invariably wise.

Grayle knew why Brayldon had come to this land, and he expressed no surprise when the architect unrolled his sketches. The largest drawing showed the elevation of the Wall, with a great stairway rising along its side from the plain beneath. At six equally spaced intervals the slowly ascending ramp levered out into wide platforms, the last of which was only a short distance below the summit of the Wall. Springing from the stairway at a score of places along its length were flying buttresses which to Grayle's eye seemed very frail and slender for the work they had to do. Then he realised that the great ramp would be largely self-supporting, and on one side all the lateral thrust would be taken by the Wall itself.

He looked at the drawing in silence for a while, and then remarked quietly:

'You always managed to have your way, Shervane. I might have guessed that this would happen in the end.'

'Then you think it a good idea?' Shervane asked. He had never gone against the old man's advice, and was anxious to have it now. As usual Grayle came straight to the point.

'How much will it cost?' he said.

Brayldon told him, and for a moment there was a shocked silence.

'That includes,' the architect said hastily, 'the building of a good road across the Shadow Land, and the construction of a small town for the workmen. The stairway itself is made from about a million identical blocks which can be dovetailed together to form a rigid structure. We shall make these, I hope, from the minerals we find in the Shadow Land.'

He sighed a little.

'I should have liked to have built it from metal rods, jointed together, but that would have cost even more, for all the material would have to be brought over the mountains.'

Grayle examined the drawing more closely.

'Why have you stopped short of the top?' he asked.

Brayldon looked at Shervane, who answered the question with a trace of embarrassment.

'I want to be the only one to make the final ascent,' be replied. 'The last stage will be by a lifting machine on the highest platform. There may be danger: that is why I am going alone.'

That was not the only reason, but it was a good one. Behind the Wall, so Grayle had once said, lay madness. If that were true, no one else need face it.

Grayle was speaking once more in his quiet, dreamy voice.

'In that case,' he said, 'what you do is neither good nor bad, for it concerns you alone. If the Wall was built to keep something from our world, it will still be impassable from the other side.'

Brayldon nodded.

'We had thought of that,' he said with a touch of pride. 'If the need should come, the ramp can be destroyed in a moment by explosives at selected spots.'

'That is good,' the old man replied. 'Though I do not believe those stories, it is well to be prepared. When the work is finished, I hope I shall still be here. And now I shall try to remember what I heard of the Wall when I was as young as you were, Shervane, when you first questioned me about it.'

Before the winter came, the road to the Wall had been marked out and the foundations of the temporary town had been laid. Most of the materials Brayldon needed were not hard to find, for the Shadow Land was rich in minerals. He had also surveyed the Wall itself and chosen the spot for the stairway. When Trilorne began to dip below the horizon, Brayldon was well content with the work that had been done.

By the next summer the first of the myriad concrete blocks had been made and tested to Brayldon's satisfaction, and before winter came again some thousands had been produced and part of the foundations laid. Leaving a trusted assistant in charge of the production, Brayldon could now return to his interrupted work. When enough of the blocks had been made, he would be back to supervise the building, but until then his guidance would not be needed.

Two or three times in the course of every year, Shervane rode out to the Wall to watch the stockpiles growing into great pyramids, and four years later Brayldon returned with him. Layer by layer the lines of stone started to creep up the flanks of the Wall, and the slim buttresses began to arch out into space. At first the stairway rose slowly, but as its summit narrowed the increase became more and more rapid. For a third of every year the work had to be abandoned, and there were anxious months in the long winter when Shervane stood on the borders of the Shadow Land, listening to the storms that thundered past him into the reverberating darkness. But Brayldon had built well, and every spring the work was standing unharmed as though it would outlive the Wall itself.

The last stones were laid seven years after the beginning of the work. Standing a mile away, so that he could see the structure in its entirety, Shervane remembered with wonder how all this had sprung from the few sketches Brayldon had shown him years ago, and he knew something of the emotion the artist must feel when his dreams become reality. And he remembered, too, the day when, as a boy by his father's side, he had first seen the Wall far off against the dusky sky of the Shadow Land.

There were guardrails around the upper platform, but Shervane did not care to go near its edge. The ground was at a dizzying distance, and he tried to forget his height by helping Brayldon and the workmen erect the simple hoist that would lift him the remaining twenty feet. When it was ready he stepped into the machine and turned to his friend with all the assurance he could muster.

'I shall be gone only a few minutes,' he said with elaborate casualness. 'Whatever I find, I'll return immediately.'

He could hardly have guessed how small a choice was his.

Grayle was now almost blind and would not know another spring. But he recognised the approaching footsteps and greeted Brayldon by name before his visitor had time to speak.

'I am glad you came,' he said. 'I've been thinking of everything you told me, and I believe I know the truth at last. Perhaps you have guessed it already.'

'No,' said Brayldon. 'I have been afraid to think of it.'

The old man smiled a little.

'Why should one be afraid of something merely because it is strange? The Wall is wonderful, yes – but there's nothing terrible about it, to those who will face its secret without flinching.

'When I was a boy, Brayldon, my old master once said that time could never destroy the truth – it could only hide it among legends. He was right. From all the fables that have gathered around the Wall, I can now select the ones that are part of history.

'Long ago, Brayldon, when the First Dynasty was at its height, Trilorne was hotter than it is now and the Shadow Land was fertile and inhabited – as perhaps one day the Fire Lands may be when Trilorne is old and feeble. Men could go southward as they pleased, for there was no Wall to bar the way. Many must have done so, looking for new lands in which to settle. What happened to Shervane happened to them also, and it must have wrecked many minds – so many that the scientists of the First Dynasty built the Wall to prevent madness from spreading through the land. I cannot believe that this is true, but the legend says that it was made in a single day, with no labour, out of a cloud that encircled the world.'

He fell into a reverie, and for a moment Brayldon did not disturb him. His mind was far in the past, picturing his world as a perfect globe floating in space while the Ancient Ones threw that band of darkness around the equator. False though that picture was in its most important detail, he could never wholly erase it from his mind.

*

As the last few feet of the Wall moved slowly past his eyes, Shervane needed all his courage lest he cry out to be lowered again. He remembered certain terrible stories he had once dismissed with laughter, for he came of a race that was singularly free from superstition. But what if, after all, those stories had been true, and the Wall had been built to keep some horror from the world?

He tried to forget these thoughts, and found it not hard to do so once he had passed the topmost level of the Wall. At first he could not interpret the picture his eyes brought him: then he saw that he was looking across an unbroken black sheet whose width he could not judge.

The little platform came to a stop, and he noted with half-conscious admiration how accurate Brayldon's calculations had been. Then, with a last word of assurance to the group below, he stepped onto the Wall and began to walk steadily forward.

At first it seemed as if the plain before him was infinite, for he could not even tell where it met the sky. But he walked on unfaltering, keeping his back to Trilorne. He wished he could have used his own shadow as a guide, but it was lost in the deeper darkness beneath his feet.

There was something wrong: it was growing darker with every footstep he took. Startled, he turned around and saw that the disc of Trilorne had now become pale and dusky, as if seen through a darkened glass. With mounting fear, he realised that this was by no means all that had happened – *Trilorne was smaller than the sun he had known all his life.*

He shook his head in an angry gesture of defiance. These things were fancies; he was imagining them. Indeed, they were so contrary to all experience that somehow he no longer felt frightened but strode resolutely forward with only a glance at the sun behind.

When Trilorne had dwindled to a point, and the darkness was all around him, it was time to abandon pretence. A wiser man would have turned back there and then, and Shervane had a sudden nightmare vision of himself lost in this eternal twilight between earth and sky, unable to retrace the path that led to safety. Then he remembered that as long as he could see Trilorne at all he could be in no real danger.

A little uncertainly now, he continued his way with many backward glances at the faint guiding light behind him. Trilorne itself had vanished, but there was still a dim glow in the sky to mark its place. And presently he needed its aid no longer, for far ahead a second light was appearing in the heavens.

At first it seemed only the faintest of glimmers, and when he was sure of its existence he noticed that Trilorne had already disappeared. But he felt more confidence now, and as he moved onward, the returning light did something to subdue his fears.

When he saw that he was indeed approaching another sun, when he could tell beyond any doubt that it was expanding as a moment ago he had seen Trilorne contract, he forced all amazement down into the depths of his mind. He would only observe and record: later there would be time to understand these things. That his world might possess two suns, one shining upon it from either side, was not, after all, beyond imagination.

Now at last he could see, faintly through the darkness, the ebon line that marked the Wall's other rim. Soon he would be the first man in thousands of years, perhaps in eternity, to look upon the lands that it had sundered from his world. Would they be as fair as his own, and would there be people there whom he would be glad to greet?

But that they would be waiting, and in such a way, was more than he had dreamed.

Grayle stretched his hand out toward the cabinet beside him and fumbled for a large sheet of paper that was lying upon it. Brayldon watched him in silence, and the old man continued.

'How often we have all heard arguments about the size of the universe, and whether it has any boundaries! We can imagine no ending to space, yet our minds rebel at the idea of infinity. Some philosophers have imagined that space is limited by curvature in a higher dimension – I suppose you know the theory. It may be true of other universes, if they exist, but for ours the answer is more subtle.

'*Along the line of the Wall, Brayldon, our universe comes to an end – and yet does not.* There was no boundary, nothing to stop one going onward before the Wall was built. The Wall itself is merely a man-made barrier, sharing the properties of the space in which it lies. Those properties were always there, and the Wall added nothing to them.'

He held the sheet of paper toward Brayldon and slowly rotated it.

'Here,' he said, 'is a plain sheet. It has, of course, two sides. *Can you imagine one that has not?*'

Brayldon stared at him in amazement.

'That's impossible – ridiculous!'

'But is it?' said Grayle softly. He reached toward the cabinet again and his fingers groped in its recesses. Then he drew out a long, flexible strip of paper and turned vacant eyes to the silently waiting Brayldon.

'We cannot match the intellects of the First Dynasty, but what their minds could grasp directly we can approach by analogy. This simple trick, which seems so trivial, may help you to glimpse the truth.'

He ran his fingers along the paper strip, then joined the two ends together to make a circular loop.

'Here I have a shape which is perfectly familiar to you – the section of a cylinder. I run my finger around the inside, so – and now along the outside. The two surfaces are quite distinct: you can go from one to the other only by moving through the thickness of the strip. Do you agree?'

'Of course,' said Brayldon, still puzzled. 'But what does it prove?'

'Nothing,' said Grayle. 'But now watch—'

*

This sun, Shervane thought, was Trilorne's identical twin. The darkness had now lifted completely, and there was no longer the sensation, which he would not try to understand, of walking across an infinite plain.

He was moving slowly now, for he had no desire to come too suddenly upon that vertiginous precipice. In a little while he could see a distant horizon of low hills, as bare and lifeless as those he had left behind him. This did not disappoint him unduly, for the first glimpse of his own land would be no more attractive than this.

So he walked on: and when presently an icy hand fastened itself upon his heart, he did not pause as a man of lesser courage would have done. Without flinching, he watched that shockingly familiar landscape rise around him, until he could see the plain from which his journey had started, and the great stairway itself, and at last Brayldon's anxious, waiting face.

Again Grayle brought the two ends of the strip together, but now he had given it a half-twist so that the band was kinked. He held it out to Brayldon.

'Run your finger around it now,' he said quietly.

Brayldon did not do so: he could see the old man's meaning.

'I understand,' he said. 'You no longer have two separate surfaces. It now forms a single continuous sheet – *a one-sided surface* – something that at first sight seems utterly impossible.'

'Yes,' replied Grayle very softly. 'I thought you would understand. *A one-sided surface*. Perhaps you realise now why this symbol of the twisted loop is so common in the ancient religions, though its meaning has been completely lost. Of course, it is no more than a crude and simple analogy – an example in two dimensions of what must really occur in three. But it is as near as our minds can ever get to the truth.'

There was a long, brooding silence. Then Grayle sighed deeply and turned to Brayldon as if he could still see his face.

'Why did you come back before Shervane?' he asked, though he knew the answer well enough.

'We had to do it,' said Brayldon sadly, 'but I did not wish to see my work destroyed.'

Grayle nodded in sympathy.

'I understand,' he said.

Shervane ran his eye up the long flight of steps on which no feet would ever tread again. He felt few regrets: he had striven, and no one could have done more. Such victory as was possible had been his.

Slowly he raised his hand and gave the signal. The Wall swallowed the explosion as it had absorbed all other sounds, but the unhurried grace with which the long tiers of masonry curtsied and fell was something he would remember all his life. For a moment he had a sudden, inexpressibly poignant vision of another stairway, watched by another Shervane, falling in identical ruins on the far side of the Wall.

But that, he realised, was a foolish thought: for none knew better than he that the Wall possessed no other side.

The Lion of Comarre

First published in *Thrilling Wonder Stories*, August 1949
Collected in *The Lion of Comarre and Against the Fall of Night*

'The Lion of Comarre' was written at around the same time as *Against the Fall of Night* and shares the emotions of the longer work. Both involve a search, or quest, for unknown and mysterious goals. In each case, the real *objectives* are wonder and magic, rather than any material gain. And in each case, the hero is a young man dissatisfied with his environment.

There are many such today, with good reason. To them I dedicate these words, written before they were born.

CHAPTER ONE

Revolt

Toward the close of the twenty-sixth century the great tide of Science had at last begun to ebb. The long series of inventions that had shaped and moulded the world for nearly a thousand years was coming to its end. Everything had been discovered. One by one, all the great dreams of the past had become reality.

Civilisation was completely mechanised – yet machinery had almost vanished. Hidden in the walls of the cities or buried far underground, the perfect machines bore the burden of the world. Silently, unobtrusively, the robots attended to their masters' needs, doing their work so well that their presence seemed as natural as the dawn.

There was still much to learn in the realm of pure science, and the astronomers, now that they were no longer bound to Earth, had work enough for a thousand years to come. But the physical sciences and the arts they nourished had ceased to be the chief preoccupation of the race. By the year 2600 the finest human minds were no longer to be found in the laboratories.

The men whose names meant most to the world were the artists and philosophers, the lawgivers and statesmen. The engineers and the great inventors belonged to the past. Like the men who had once ministered to long-vanished diseases, they had done their work so well that they were no longer required.

Five hundred years were to pass before the pendulum swung back again.

The view from the studio was breath-taking, for the long, curving room was over two miles from the base of Central Tower. The five other giant buildings of the city clustered below, their metal walls gleaming with all the colours of the spectrum as they caught the rays of the morning sun. Lower still, the checkerboard fields of the automatic farms stretched away until they were lost in the mists of the horizon. But for once, the beauty of the scene was wasted on Richard Peyton II as he paced angrily among the great blocks of synthetic marble that were the raw materials of his art.

The huge, gorgeously coloured masses of artificial rock completely dominated the studio. Most of them were roughly hewn cubes, but some were beginning to assume the shapes of animals, human beings, and abstract solids that no geometrician would have dared to give a name. Sitting awkwardly on a ten-ton block of diamond – the largest ever synthesised – the artist's son was regarding his famous parent with an unfriendly expression.

'I don't think I'd mind so much,' Richard Peyton II remarked peevishly, 'if you were content to do nothing, so long as you did it gracefully. Certain people excel at that, and on the whole they make the world more interesting. But why you should want to make a life study of engineering is more than I can imagine.

'Yes, I know we let you take technology as your main subject, but we never thought you were so serious about it. When I was your age I had a passion for botany – but I never made it my main interest in life. Has Professor Chandras Ling been giving you ideas?'

Richard Peyton III blushed.

'Why shouldn't he? I know what my vocation is, and he agrees with me. You've read his report.'

The artist waved several sheets of paper in the air, holding them between thumb and forefinger like some unpleasant insect.

'I have,' he said grimly. ' "Shows very unusual mechanical ability – has done original work in subelectronic research," et cetera, et cetera. Good heavens, I thought the human race had outgrown those toys centuries ago! Do you want to be a mechanic, first class, and go around attending to disabled robots? That's hardly a job for a boy of mine, not to mention the grandson of a World Councillor.'

'I wish you wouldn't keep bringing Grandfather into this,' said Richard Peyton III with mounting annoyance. 'The fact that he was a statesman didn't prevent your becoming an artist. So why should you expect me to be either?'

The older man's spectacular golden beard began to bristle ominously.

'I don't care what you do as long as it's something we can be proud of. But why this craze for gadgets? We've got all the machines we need. The robot was perfected five hundred years ago: spaceships haven't changed for at least that time; I believe our present communications system is nearly eight hundred years old. So why change what's already perfect?'

'That's special pleading with a vengeance!' the young man replied. 'Fancy an artist saying that anything's perfect! Father, I'm ashamed of you!'

'Don't split hairs. You know perfectly well what I mean. Our ancestors designed machines that provide us with everything we need. No doubt some of them might be a few per cent more efficient. But why worry? Can you mention a single important invention that the world lacks today?'

Richard Peyton III sighed.

'Listen, Father,' he said patiently. 'I've been studying history as well as engineering. About twelve centuries ago there were people who said that everything had been invented – and *that* was before the coming of electricity, let alone flying and astronautics. They just didn't look far enough ahead – their minds were rooted in the present.

'The same thing's happening today. For five hundred years the world's been living on the brains of the past. I'm prepared to admit that some lines of development have come to an end, but there are dozens of others that haven't even begun.

'Technically the world has stagnated. It's not a dark age, because we haven't forgotten anything. But we're marking time. Look at space travel. Nine hundred years ago we reached Pluto, and where are we now? Still at Pluto! When are we going to cross interstellar space?'

'Who wants to go to the stars, anyway?'

The boy made an exclamation of annoyance and jumped off the diamond block in his excitement.

'What a question to ask in this age! A thousand years ago people were saying, "Who wants to go to the Moon?" Yes, I know it's unbelievable, but it's all there in the old books. Nowadays the Moon's only forty-five minutes away, and people like Harn Jansen work on Earth and live in Plato City.

'We take interplanetary travel for granted. One day we're going to do the same with *real* space travel. I could mention scores of other subjects that have come to a full stop simply because people think as you do and are content with what they've got.'

'And why not?'

Peyton waved his arm around in the studio.

'Be serious, Father. Have you ever been satisfied with anything you've made? Only animals are contented.'

The artist laughed ruefully.

'Maybe you're right. But that doesn't affect my argument. I still think you'll be wasting your life, and so does Grandfather.' He looked a little embarrassed. 'In fact, he's coming down to Earth especially to see you.'

Peyton looked alarmed.

'Listen, Father, I've already told you what I think. I don't want to have to go through it all again. Because neither Grandfather nor the whole of the World Council will make me alter my mind.'

It was a bombastic statement, and Peyton wondered if he really meant it. His father was just about to reply when a low musical note vibrated through the studio. A second later a mechanical voice spoke from the air.

'Your father to see you, Mr Peyton.'

He glanced at his son triumphantly.

'I should have added,' he said, 'that Grandfather was coming now. But I know your habit of disappearing when you're wanted.'

The boy did not answer. He watched his father walk toward the door. Then his lips curved in a smile.

The single pane of glassite that fronted the studio was open, and he stepped out on to the balcony. Two miles below, the great concrete apron of the parking ground gleamed whitely in the sun, except where it was dotted with the teardrop shadows of grounded ships.

Peyton glanced back into the room. It was still empty, though he could hear his father's voice drifting through the door. He waited no longer. Placing his hand on the balustrade, he vaulted over into space.

Thirty seconds later two figures entered the studio and gazed around in surprise. *The* Richard Peyton, with no qualifying number, was a man who might have been taken for sixty, though that was less than a third of his actual age.

He was dressed in the purple robe worn by only twenty men on Earth and by fewer than a hundred in the entire Solar System. Authority seemed to radiate from him; by comparison, even his famous and self-assured son seemed fussy and inconsequential.

'Well, where is he?'

'Confound him! He's gone out the window. At least we can still say what we think of him.'

Viciously, Richard Peyton II jerked up his wrist and dialled an eight-figure number on his personal communicator. The reply came almost instantly. In clear, impersonal tones an automatic voice repeated endlessly:

'My master is asleep. Please do not disturb. My master is asleep. Please do not disturb. . . .'

With an exclamation of annoyance Richard Peyton II switched off the instrument and turned to his father. The old man chuckled.

'Well, he thinks fast. He's beaten us there. We can't get hold of him until he chooses to press the clearing button. I certainly don't intend to chase him at my age.'

There was silence for a moment as the two men gazed at each other with mixed expression. Then, almost simultaneously, they began to laugh.

CHAPTER TWO

The Legend of Comarre

Peyton fell like a stone for a mile and a quarter before he switched on the neutraliser. The rush of air past him, though it made breathing difficult, was exhilarating. He was falling at less than a hundred and fifty miles an hour, but the impression of speed was enhanced by the smooth upward rush of the great building only a few yards away.

The gentle tug of the decelerator field slowed him some three hundred yards from the ground. He fell gently toward the lines of parked flyers ranged at the foot of the tower.

His own speedster was a small single-seat fully-automatic machine. At least, it had been fully automatic when it was built three centuries ago, but its current owner had made so many illegal modifications to it that no one else in the world could have flown it and lived to tell the tale.

Peyton switched off the neutraliser belt – an amusing device which, although technically obsolete, still had interesting possibilities – and stepped into the airlock of his machine. Two minutes later the towers of the city were sinking below the rim of the world and the uninhabited Wild Lands were speeding beneath at four thousand miles an hour.

Peyton set his course westward and almost immediately was over the ocean. He could do nothing but wait; the ship would reach its goal automatically. He leaned back in the pilot's seat, thinking bitter thoughts and feeling sorry for himself.

He was more disturbed than he cared to admit. The fact that his family failed to share his technical interests had ceased to worry Peyton years ago. But this steadily growing opposition, which had now come to a head, was something quite new. He was completely unable to understand it.

Ten minutes later a single white pylon began to climb out of the ocean like the sword Excalibur rising from the lake. The city known to the world as Scientia, and to its more cynical inhabitants as Bat's Belfry, had been built eight centuries ago on an island far from the major land masses. The gesture had been one of independence, for the last traces of nationalism had still lingered in that far-off age.

Peyton grounded his ship on the landing apron and walked to the nearest entrance. The boom of the great waves, breaking on the rocks a hundred yards away, was a sound that never failed to impress him.

He paused for a moment at the opening, inhaling the salt air and watching the gulls and migrant birds circling the tower. They had used this speck of land as a resting place when man was still watching the dawn with puzzled eyes and wondering if it was a god.

The Bureau of Genetics occupied a hundred floors near the centre of the tower. It had taken Peyton ten minutes to reach the City of Science. It required almost as long again to locate the man he wanted in the cubic miles of offices and laboratories.

Alan Henson II was still one of Peyton's closest friends, although he had left the University of Antarctica two years earlier and had been studying biogenetics rather than engineering. When Peyton was in trouble, which was not infrequently, he found his friend's calm common sense very reassuring. It was natural for him to fly to Scientia now, especially since Henson had sent him an urgent call only the day before.

123

The biologist was pleased and relieved to see Peyton, yet his welcome had an undercurrent of nervousness.

'I'm glad you've come; I've got some news that will interest you. But you look glum – what's the matter?'

Peyton told him, not without exaggeration. Henson was silent for a moment.

'So they've started already!' he said. 'We might have expected it!'

'What do you mean?' asked Peyton in surprise.

The biologist opened a drawer and pulled out a sealed envelope. From it he extracted two plastic sheets in which were cut several hundred parallel slots of varying lengths. He handed one to his friend.

'Do you know what this is?'

'It looks like a character analysis.'

'Correct. It happens to be yours.'

'Oh! This is rather illegal, isn't it?'

'Never mind that. The key is printed along the bottom; it runs from Aesthetic Appreciation to Wit. The last column gives your Intelligence Quotient. Don't let it go to your head.'

Peyton studied the card intently. Once, he flushed slightly.

'I don't see how you knew.'

'Never mind,' grinned Henson. 'Now look at this analysis.' He handed over a second card.

'Why, it's the same one!'

'Not quite, but very nearly.'

'Whom does it belong to?'

Henson leaned back in his chair and measured out his words slowly.

'That analysis, Dick, belongs to your great-grandfather twenty-two times removed on the direct male line – the great Rolf Thordarsen.'

Peyton took off like a rocket.

'What!'

'Don't shout the place down. We're discussing old times at college if anyone comes in.'

'But – Thordarsen!'

'Well, if we go back far enough we've all got equally distinguished ancestors. But now you know why your grandfather is afraid of you.'

'He's left it till rather late. I've practically finished my training.'

'You can thank us for that. Normally our analysis goes back ten generations, twenty in special cases. It's a tremendous job. There are hundreds of millions of cards in the Inheritance Library, one for every man and woman who has lived since the twenty-third century. This coincidence was discovered quite accidentally about a month ago.'

'*That's* when the trouble started. But I still don't understand what it's all about.'

'Exactly what do you know, Dick, about your famous ancestor?'

'No more than anyone else, I suppose. I certainly don't know how or why he disappeared, if that's what you mean. Didn't he leave Earth?'

'No. He left the world, if you like, but he never left Earth. Very few people know this, Dick, but Rolf Thordarsen was the man who built Comarre.'

Comarre! Peyton breathed the word through half-open lips. savouring its meaning and its strangeness. So it *did* exist, after all! Even that had been denied by some.

Henson was speaking again.

'I don't suppose you know very much about the Decadents. The history books have been rather carefully edited. But the whole story is linked up with the end of the Second Electronic Age. . . .'

Twenty thousand miles above the surface of the Earth, the artificial moon that housed the World Council was spinning on its eternal orbit. The roof of the Council Chamber was one flawless sheet of crystallite; when the members of the Council were in session it seemed as if there was nothing between them and the great globe spinning far below.

The symbolism was profound. No narrow parochial viewpoint could long survive in such a setting. Here, if anywhere, the minds of men would surely produce their greatest works.

Richard Peyton the Elder had spent his life guiding the destinies of Earth. For five hundred years the human race had known peace and had lacked nothing that art or science could provide. The men who ruled the planet could be proud of their work.

Yet the old statesman was uneasy. Perhaps the changes that lay ahead were already casting their shadows before them. Perhaps he felt, if only with his subconscious mind, that the five centuries of tranquillity were drawing to a close.

He switched on his writing machine and began to dictate.

The First Electronic Age, Peyton knew, had begun in 1908, more than eleven centuries before, with De Forest's invention of the triode. The same fabulous century that had seen the coming of the World State, the airplane, the spaceship, and atomic power had witnessed the invention of all the fundamental thermionic devices that made possible the civilisation he knew.

The Second Electronic Age had come five hundred years later. It had been started not by the physicists but by the doctors and psychologists. For nearly five centuries they had been recording the electric currents that flow in the brain during the processes of thought. The analysis had been appallingly complex, but it had been completed after generations of toil. When it was finished the way lay open for the first machines that could read the human mind.

But this was only the beginning. Once man had discovered the mechanism of his own brain he could go further. He could reproduce it, using transistors and circuit networks instead of living cells.

Toward the end of the twenty-fifth century, the first thinking machines were built. They were very crude, a hundred square yards of equipment being required to do the work of a cubic centimetre of human brain. But once the first step had been taken it was not long before the mechanical brain was pefected and brought into general use.

It could perform only the lower grades of intellectual work and it lacked such purely human characteristics as initiative, intuition, and all emotions. However, in circumstances which seldom varied, where its limitations were not serious, it could do all that a man could do.

The coming of the metal brains had brought one of the great crises in human civilisation. Though men had still to carry out all the higher duties of statesmanship and the control of society, all the immense mass of routine administration had been taken over by the robots. Man had achieved freedom at last. No longer did he have to rack his brains planning complex transport schedules, deciding production programmes, and balancing budgets. The machines, which had taken over all manual labour centuries before, had made their second great contribution to society.

The effect on human affairs was immense, and men reacted to the new situation in two ways. There were those who used their new-found freedom nobly in the pursuits which had always attracted the highest minds: the quest for beauty and truth, still as elusive as when the Acropolis was built.

But there were others who thought differently. At last, they said, the curse of Adam is lifted forever. Now we can build cities where the machines will care for our every need as soon as the thought enters our minds – sooner, since the analysers can read even the buried desires of the sub-conscious. The aim of all life is pleasure and the pursuit of happiness. Man has earned the right to that. We are tired of this unending struggle for knowledge and the blind desire to bridge space to the stars.

It was the ancient dream of the Lotus Eaters, a dream as old as Man. Now, for the first time, it could be realised. For a while there were not many who shared it. The fires of the Second Renaissance had not yet begun to flicker and die. But as the years passed, the Decadents drew more and more to their way of thinking. In hidden places on the inner planets they built the cities of their dreams.

For a century they flourished like strange exotic flowers, until the almost religious fervour that inspired their building had died. They lingered for a generation more. Then, one by one, they faded from human knowledge. Dying, they left behind a host of fables and legends which had grown with the passing centuries.

Only one such city had been built on Earth, and there were mysteries about it that the outer world had never solved. For purposes of its own, the World Council had destroyed all knowledge of the place. Its location was a mystery. Some said it was in the Arctic wastes; others believed it to be hidden on the bed of the Pacific. Nothing was certain but its name – Comarre.

*

Henson paused in his recital.

'So far I have told you nothing new, nothing that isn't common knowledge. The rest of the story is a secret to the World Council and perhaps a hundred men of Scientia.

'Rolf Thordarsen, as you know, was the greatest mechanical genius the world has ever known. Not even Edison can be compared with him. He laid the foundations of robot engineering and built the first of the practical thought-machines.

'His laboratories poured out a stream of brilliant inventions for over twenty years. Then, suddenly, he disappeared. The story was put out that he tried to reach the stars. This is what really happened:

'Thordarsen believed that his robots – the machines that still run our civilisation – were only a beginnning. He went to the World Council with certain proposals which would have changed the face of human society. What those changes are we do not know, but Thordarsen believed that unless they were adopted the race would eventually come to a dead end – as, indeed, many of us think it has.

'The Council disagreed violently. At that time, you see, the robot was just being integrated into civilisation and stability was slowly returning – the stability that has been maintained for five hundred years.

'Thordarsen was bitterly disappointed. With the flair they had for attracting genius the Decadents got hold of him and persuaded him to renounce the world. He was the only man who could convert their dreams into reality.'

'And did he?'

'No one knows. But Comarre was built – that is certain. We know where it is – and so does the World Council. There are some things that cannot be kept secret.'

That was true, thought Peyton. Even in this age people still disappeared and it was rumoured that they had gone in search of the dream city. Indeed, the phrase 'He's gone to Comarre' had become such a part of the language that its meaning was almost forgotten.

Henson leaned forward and spoke with mounting earnestness.

'This is the strange part. The World Council could destroy Comarre, but it won't do so. The belief that Comarre exists has a definite stabilising influence on society. In spite of all our efforts, we still have psychopaths. It's no difficult matter to give them hints, under hypnosis, about Comarre. They may never find it but the quest will keep them harmless.

'In the early days, soon after the city was founded, the Council sent its agents into Comarre. None of them ever returned. There was no foul play; they just preferred to remain. That's known definitely because they sent messages back. I suppose the Decadents realised that the Council would tear the place down if its agents were detained deliberately.

'I've seen some of those messages. They are extraordinary. There's only one word for them: exalted. Dick, there was something in Comarre that could make a man forget the outer world, his friends, his family – everything! Try to imagine what that means!

'Later, when it was certain that none of the Decadents could still be alive, the Council tried again. It was still trying up to fifty years ago. But to this day no one has ever returned from Comarre.'

As Richard Peyton spoke, the waiting robot analysed his words into their phonetic groups, inserted the punctuation, and automatically routed the minute to the correct electronic files.

'Copy to President and my personal file.

'Your Minute of the 22nd and our conversation this morning.

'I have seen my son, but R. P. III evaded me. He is completely determined, and we will only do harm by trying to coerce him. Thordarsen should have taught us that lesson.

'My suggestion is that we earn his gratitude by giving him all the assistance he needs. Then we can direct him along safe lines of research. As long as he never discovers that R.T. was his ancestor, there should be no danger. In spite of character similarities, it is unlikely that he will try to repeat R.T.'s work.

'Above all, we must ensure that he never locates or visits Comarre. If that happens, no one can foresee the consequences.'

Henson stopped his narrative, but his friend said nothing. He was too spellbound to interrupt, and, after a minute, the other continued.

'That brings us up to the present and to you. The World Council, Dick, discovered your inheritance a month ago. We're sorry we told them, but it's too late now. Genetically, you're a reincarnation of Thordarsen in the only scientific sense of the word. One of Nature's longest odds has come off, as it does every few hundred years in some family or another.

'You, Dick, could carry on the work Thordarsen was compelled to drop – whatever that work was. Perhaps it's lost forever, but if any trace of it exists, the secret lies in Comarre. The World Council knows that. That is why it is trying to deflect you from your destiny.

'Don't be bitter about it. On the Council are some of the noblest minds the human race has yet produced. They mean you no harm, and none will ever befall you. But they are passionately anxious to preserve the present structure of society, which they believed to be the best.'

Slowly, Peyton rose to his feet. For a moment, it seemed as if he were a neutral, exterior observer, watching this lay figure called Richard Peyton III, now no longer a man, but a symbol, one of the keys to the future of the world. It took a positive mental effort to reidentify himself.

His friend was watching him silently.

'There's something else you haven't told me, Alan. How do you know all this?'

Henson smiled.

'I was waiting for that. I'm only the mouthpiece, chosen because I know you. Who the others are I can't say, even to you. But they include quite a number of the scientists I know you admire.

'There has always been a friendly rivalry between the Council and the scientists who serve it, but in the last few years our viewpoints have drifted farther apart. Many of us believe that the present age, which the Council thinks will last forever, is only an interregnum. We believe that too long a period of stability will cause decadence. The Council's psychologists are confident they can prevent it.'

Peyton's eyes gleamed.

'That's what I've been saying! Can I join you?'

'Later. There's work to be done first. You see, we are revolutionaries of a sort. We are going to start one or two social reactions, and when we've finished the danger of racial decadence will be postponed for thousands of years. You, Dick, are one of our catalysts. Not the only one, I might say.'

He paused for a moment.

'Even if Comarre comes to nothing, we have another card up our sleeve. In fifty years, we hope to have perfected the interstellar drive.'

'At last!' said Peyton. 'What will you do then?'

'We'll present it to the Council and say, "Here you are – now you can go to the stars. Aren't we good boys?" And the Council will just have to give a sickly smile and start uprooting civilisation. Once we've achieved interstellar travel, we shall have an expanding society again and stagnation will be indefinitely postponed.'

'I hope I live to see it,' said Peyton. 'But what do you want me to do now?'

'Just this: we want you to go into Comarre to find what's there. Where others have failed, we believe you can succeed. All the plans have been made.'

'And where is Comarre?'

Henson smiled.

'It's simple, really. There was only one place it could be – the only place over which no aircraft can fly, where no one lives, where all travel is on foot. It's in the Great Reservation.'

The old man switched off the writing machine. Overhead – or below; it was all the same – the great crescent of Earth was blotting out the stars. In its eternal circling the little moon had overtaken the terminator and was plunging into night. Here and there the darkling land below was dotted with the lights of cities.

The sight filled the old man with sadness. It reminded him that his own life was coming to a close – and it seemed to foretell the end of the culture he had sought to protect. Perhaps, after all, the young scientists were right. The long rest was ending and the world was moving to new goals that he would never see.

CHAPTER THREE

The Wild Lion

It was night when Peyton's ship came westward over the Indian Ocean. The eye could see nothing far below but the white line of breakers against the African coast, but the navigation screen showed every detail of the land beneath. Night, of course, was no protection or safeguard now, but it meant that no human eye would see him. As for the machines that should be watching – well, others had taken care of them. There were many, it seemed, who thought as Henson did.

The plan had been skilfully conceived. The details had been worked out with loving care by people who had obviously enjoyed themselves. He was to land the ship at the edge of the forest, as near to the power barrier as he could.

Not even his unknown friends could switch off the barrier without arousing suspicion. Luckily it was only about twenty miles to Comarre from the edge of the screen, over fairly open country. He would have to finish the journey afoot.

There was a great crackling of branches as the little ship settled down into the unseen forest. It came to rest on an even keel, and Peyton switched off the dim cabin lights and peered out of the window. He could see nothing. Remembering what he had been told, he did not open the door. He made himself as comfortable as he could and settled down to await the dawn.

He awoke with brilliant sunlight shining full in his eyes. Quickly climbing into the equipment his friends had provided, he opened the cabin door and stepped into the forest.

The landing place had been carefully chosen, and it was not difficult to scramble through to the open country a few yards away. Ahead lay small grass-covered hills dotted with occasional clusters of slender trees. The day was mild, though it was summer and the equator was not far away. Eight hundred years of climatic control and the great artificial lakes that had drowned the deserts had seen to that.

For almost the first time in his life Peyton was experiencing Nature as it had been in the days before Man existed. Yet it was not the wildness of the scene that he found so strange. Peyton had never known silence. Always there had been the murmur of machines or the far-away whisper of speeding liners, heard faintly from the towering heights of the stratosphere.

Here there were none of these sounds, for no machines could cross the power barrier that surrounded the Reservation. There was only the wind in the grass and the half-audible medley of insect voices. Peyton found the silence unnerving and did what almost any man of his time would have done. He pressed the button of his personal radio that selected the background-music band.

So, mile after mile, Peyton walked steadily through the undulating country of the Great Reservation, the largest area of natural territory remaining on the surface of the globe. Walking was easy, for the neutralisers built into his equipment almost nullified its weight. He carried with him that mist of unobtrusive music that had been the background of men's lives almost since the discovery of radio. Although he had only to flick a dial to get in touch with anyone on the planet, he quite sincerely imagined himself to be alone in the heart of Nature, and for a moment he felt all the emotions that Stanley or Livingstone must have experienced when they first entered this same land more than a thousand years ago.

Luckily Peyton was a good walker, and by noon had covered half the distance to his goal. He rested for his midday meal under a cluster of imported Martian conifers, which would have brought baffled consternation to an oldtime explorer. In his ignorance Peyton took them completely for granted.

He had accumulated a small pile of empty cans when he noticed an object moving swiftly over the plain in the direction from which he had come. It was too far away to be recognised. Not until it was obviously approaching him did he bother to get up to get a clearer view of it. So far he had seen no animals – though plenty of animals had seen him – and he watched the newcomer with interest.

Peyton had never seen a lion before, but he had no difficulty in recognising the magnificent beast that was bounding toward him. It was to his credit that he glanced only once at the tree overhead. Then he stood his ground firmly.

There were, he knew, no really dangerous animals in the world any more. The Reservation was something between a vast biological laboratory and a national park visited by thousands of people every year. It was generally understood that if one left the inhabitants alone, they would reciprocate. On the whole, the arrangement worked smoothly.

The animal was certainly anxious to be friendly. It trotted straight toward him and began to rub itself affectionately against his side. When Peyton got up again, it was taking a great deal of interest in his empty food cans. Presently it turned toward him with an expression that was irresistible.

Peyton laughed, opened a fresh can, and laid the contents carefully on a flat stone. The lion accepted the tribute with relish, and while it was eating Peyton ruffled through the index of the official guide which his unknown supporters had thoughtfully provided.

There were several pages about lions, with photographs for the benefit of extraterrestrial visitors. The information was reassuring. A thousand years of scientific breeding had greatly improved the King of Beasts. He had eaten only a dozen people in the last century: in ten of the cases the subsequent enquiry had exonerated him from blame and the other two were 'not proved'.

But the book said nothing about unwanted lions and the best ways of disposing of them. Nor did it hint that they were normally as friendly as this specimen.

Peyton was not particularly observant. It was some time before he noticed the thin metal band around the lion's right forepaw. It bore a series of numbers and letters, followed by the official stamp of the Reservation.

This was no wild animal; perhaps all its youth had been spent among men. It was probably one of the famous super-lions the biologists had been breeding and then releasing to improve the race. Some of them were almost as intelligent as dogs, according to the reports that Peyton had seen.

He quickly discovered that it could understand many simple words, particularly those relating to food. Even for this era it was a splendid beast, a good foot taller than its scrawny ancestor of ten centuries before.

When Peyton started on his journey again, the lion trotted by his side. He doubted if its friendship was worth more than a pound of synthetic beef, but it was pleasant to have someone to talk to – someone, moreover, who made no attempt to contradict him. After profound and concentrated thought, he decided that 'Leo' would be a suitable name for his new acquaintance.

Peyton had walked a few hundred yards when suddenly there was a blinding flash in the air before him. Though he realised immediately what it was, he was startled, and stopped, blinking. Leo had fled precipitately and was already out of sight. He would not, Peyton thought, be of much use in an emergency. Later he was to revise this judgment.

When his eyes had recovered, Peyton found himself looking at a multi-coloured notice, burning in letters of fire. It hung steadily in the air and read:

WARNING!
YOU ARE NOW APPROACHING
RESTRICTED TERRITORY!
TURN BACK!

By Order,
World Council in Session

Peyton regarded the notice thoughtfully for a few moments. Then he looked around for the projector. It was in a metal box, not very effectively hidden at the side of the road. He quickly unlocked it with the universal keys a trusting Electronics Commission had given him on his first graduation.

After a few minutes' inspection he breathed a sigh of relief. The projector was a simple capacity-operated device. Anything coming along the road would activate it. There was a photographic recorder, but it had been disconnected. Peyton was not surprised, for every passing animal would have operated the device. This was fortunate. It meant that no one need ever know that Richard Peyton III had once walked along this road.

He shouted to Leo, who came slowly back, looking rather ashamed of himself. The sign had disappeared, and Peyton held the relays open to prevent its reappearance as Leo passed by. Then he relocked the door and continued on his way, wondering what would happen next.

A hundred yards farther on, a disembodied voice began to speak to him severely. It told him nothing new, but the voice threatened a number of minor penalties, some of which were not unfamiliar to him.

It was amusing to watch Leo's face as he tried to locate the source of the sound. Once again Peyton searched for the projector and checked it before proceeding. It would be safer, he thought, to leave the road altogether. There might be recording devices farther along it.

With some difficulty he induced Leo to remain on the metal surface while he himself walked along the barren ground bordering the road. In the next quarter of a mile the lion set off two more electronic booby traps. The last one seemed to have given up persuasion. It said simply:

BEWARE OF WILD LIONS

Peyton looked at Leo and began to laugh. Leo couldn't see the joke but he joined in politely. Behind them the automatic sign faded out with a last despairing flicker.

Peyton wondered why the signs were there at all. Perhaps they were intended to scare away accidental visitors. Those who knew the goal would hardly be deflected by them.

The road made a sudden right-angle turn – and there before him was Comarre. It was strange that something he had been expecting could give him such a shock. Ahead lay an immense clearing in the jungle, half filled by a black metallic structure.

The city was shaped like a terraced cone, perhaps eight hundred yards high and a thousand across at the base. How much was underground, Peyton could not guess. He halted, overwhelmed by the size and strangeness of the enormous building. Then, slowly, he began to walk toward it.

Like a beast of prey crouching in its lair, the city lay waiting. Though its guests were now very few, it was ready to receive them, whoever they might be. Sometimes they turned back at the first warning, sometimes at the second. A few had reached the very entrance before their resolution failed them. But most, having come so far, had entered willingly enough.

So Peyton reached the marble steps that led up to the towering metal wall and the curious black hole that seemed to be the only entrance. Leo trotted quietly beside him, taking little notice of his strange surroundings.

Peyton stopped at the foot of the stairs and dialled a number in his communicator. He waited until the acknowledgment tone came and then spoke slowly into the microphone.

'The fly is entering the parlour.'

He repeated it twice, feeling rather a fool. Someone, he thought, had a perverted sense of humour.

There was no reply. That had been part of the arrangement. But he had no doubt that the message had been received, probably in some laboratory in Scientia, since the number he had dialled had a Western Hemisphere coding.

Peyton opened his biggest can of meat and spread it out on the marble. He entwined his fingers in the lion's mane and twisted it playfully.

'I guess you'd better stay here,' he said. 'I may be gone quite some time. Don't try to follow me.'

At the top of the steps, he looked back. Rather to his relief the lion had made no attempt to follow. It was sitting on its haunches, looking at him pathetically. Peyton waved and turned away.

There was no door, only a plain black hole in the curving metal surface. That was puzzling, and Peyton wondered how the builders had expected to keep animals from wandering in. Then something about the opening attracted his attention.

It was *too* black. Although the wall was in shadow, the entrance had no right to be as dark as this. He took a coin from his pocket and tossed it into the aperture. The sound of its fall reassured him, and he stepped forward.

The delicately adjusted discriminator circuits had ignored the coin, as they had ignored all the stray animals that had entered this dark portal. But the presence of a human mind had been enough to trip the relays. For a fraction of a second the screen through which Peyton was moving throbbed with power. Then it became inert again.

It seemed to Peyton that his foot took a long time to reach the ground, but that was the least of his worries. Far more surprising was the instantaneous transition from darkness to sudden light, from the somewhat oppressive heat of the jungle to a temperature that seemed almost chilly by comparison. The change was so abrupt that it left him gasping. Filled with a feeling of distinct unease he turned toward the archway through which he had just come.

It was no longer there. It never had been there. He was standing on a raised metal dais at the exact centre of a large circular room with a dozen pointed archways around its circumference. He might have come through any one of them – if only they had not all been forty yards away.

For a moment Peyton was seized with panic. He felt his heart pounding, and something odd was happening to his legs. Feeling very much alone, he sat down on the dais and began to consider the situation logically.

CHAPTER FOUR

The Sign of the Poppy

Something had transported him instantly from the black doorway to the centre of the room. There could be only two explanations, both equally fantastic. Either something was very wrong with space inside Comarre, or else its builders had mastered the secret of matter transmission.

Ever since men had learned to send sound and sight by radio, they had dreamed of transmitting matter by the same means. Peyton looked at the

dais on which he was standing. It might easily hold electronic equipment –
and there was a very curious bulge in the ceiling above him.

However it was done, he could imagine no better way of ignoring
unwanted visitors. Rather hurriedly, he scrambled off the dais. It was not
the sort of place where he cared to linger.

It was disturbing to realise that he now had no means of leaving without
the co-operation of the machine that had brought him here. He decided to
worry about one thing at a time. When he had finished his exploration, he
should have mastered this and all the other secrets of Comarre.

He was not really conceited. Between Peyton and the makers of the city
lay five centuries of research. Although he might find much that was new
to him, there would be nothing that he could not understand. Choosing
one of the exits at random, he began his exploration of the city.

*The machines were watching, biding their time. They had been built to serve one
purpose, and that purpose they were still fulfilling blindly. Long ago they had
brought the peace of oblivion to the weary minds of their builders. That oblivion
they could still bring to all who entered the city of Comarre.*

*The instruments had begun their analysis when Peyton stepped in from the forest.
It was not a task that could be done swiftly, this dissection of a human mind, with
all its hopes, desires, and fears. The synthesisers would not come into operation for
hours yet. Until then the guest would be entertained while the more lavish
hospitality was being prepared.*

The elusive visitor gave the little robot a lot of trouble before it finally
located him, for Peyton was moving rapidly from room to room in his
exploration of the city. Presently the machine came to a halt in the centre
of a small circular room lined with magnetic switches and lit by a single
glow tube.

According to its instruments, Peyton was only a few feet away, but its
four eye lenses could see no sign of him. Puzzled, it stood motionless, silent
except for the faint whisper of its motors and the occasional snicker of a
relay.

Standing on a catwalk ten feet from the ground, Peyton was watching
the machine with great interest. He saw a shining metal cylinder rising from
a thick base plate mounted on small driving wheels. There were no limbs of
any kind: the cylinder was unbroken except for the circlet of eye lenses and
a series of small metal sound grilles.

It was amusing to watch the machine's perplexity as its tiny mind
wrestled with two conflicting sets of information. Although it knew that
Peyton must be in the room, its eyes told it that the place was empty. It
began to scamper around in small circles, until Peyton took pity on it and
descended from the catwalk. Immediately the machine ceased its gyrations
and began to deliver its address of welcome.

'I am A-Five. I will take you wherever you wish to go. Please give me
your orders in standard robot vocab.'

Peyton was rather disappointed. It was a perfectly standard robot, and he had hoped for something better in the city Thordarsen had built. But the machine could be very useful if he employed it properly.

'Thank you,' he said, unnecessarily. 'Please take me to the living quarters.'

Although Peyton was now certain that the city was completely automatic, there was still the possibility that it held some human life. There might be others here who could help him in his quest, though the absence of opposition was perhaps as much as he could hope for.

Without a word the little machine spun around on its driving wheels and rolled out of the room. The corridor along which it led Peyton ended at a beautifully carved door, which he had already tried in vain to open. Apparently A-Five knew its secret – for at their approach the thick metal plate slid silently aside. The robot rolled forward into a small, boxlike chamber.

Peyton wondered if they had entered another of the matter transmitters, but quickly discovered that it was nothing more unusual than an elevator. Judging by the time of ascent, it must have taken them almost to the top of the city. When the doors slid open it seemed to Peyton that he was in another world.

The corridors in which he had first found himself were drab and undecorated, purely utilitarian. In contrast, these spacious halls and assembly rooms were furnished with the utmost luxury. The twenty-sixth century had been a period of florid decoration and colouring, much despised by subsequent ages. But the Decadents had gone far beyond their own period. They had taxed the resources of psychology as well as art when they designed Comarre.

One could have spent a lifetime without exhausting all the murals, the carvings and paintings, the intricate tapestries which still seemed as brilliant as when they had been made. It seemed utterly wrong that so wonderful a place should be deserted and hidden from the world. Peyton almost forgot all his scientific zeal, and hurried like a child from marvel to marvel.

Here were works of genius, perhaps as great as any the world had ever known. But it was a sick and despairing genius, one that had lost faith in itself while still retaining an immense technical skill. For the first time Peyton truly understood why the builders of Comarre had been given their name.

The art of the Decadents at once repelled and fascinated him. It was not evil, for it was completely detached from moral standards. Perhaps its dominant characteristics were weariness and disillusion. After a while Peyton, who had never thought himself very sensitive to visual art, began to feel a subtle depression creeping into his soul. Yet he found it quite impossible to tear himself away.

At last Peyton turned to the robot again.

'Does anyone live here now?'

'Yes.'

'Where are they?'

'Sleeping.'

Somehow that seemed a perfectly natural reply. Peyton felt very tired. For the last hour it had been a struggle to remain awake. Something seemed to be compelling sleep, almost willing it upon him. Tomorrow would be time enough to learn the secrets he had come to find. For the moment he wanted nothing but sleep.

He followed automatically when the robot led him out of the spacious halls into a long corridor lined with metal doors, each bearing a half-familiar symbol Peyton could not quite recognise. His sleepy mind was still wrestling half-heartedly with the problem when the machine halted before one of the doors, which slid silently open.

The heavily draped couch in the darkened room was irresistible. Peyton stumbled toward it automatically. As he sank down into sleep, a glow of satisfaction warmed his mind. He had recognised the symbol on the door, though his brain was too tired to understand its significance.

It was the poppy.

There was no guile, no malevolence in the working of the city. Impersonally it was fulfilling the tasks to which it had been dedicated. All who had entered Comarre had willingly embraced its gifts. This visitor was the first who had ever ignored them.

The integrators had been ready for hours, but the restless, probing mind had eluded them. They could afford to wait, as they had done these last five hundred years.

And now the defences of this strangely stubborn mind were crumbling as Richard Peyton sank peacefully to sleep. Far down in the heart of Comarre a relay tripped, and complex, slowly fluctuating currents began to ebb and flow through banks of vacuum tubes. The consciousness that had been Richard Peyton III ceased to exist.

Peyton had fallen asleep instantly. For a while complete oblivion claimed him. Then faint wisps of consciousness began to return. And then, as always, he began to dream.

It was strange that his favourite dream should have come into his mind, and it was more vivid now than it had ever been before. All his life Peyton had loved the sea, and once he had seen the unbelievable beauty of the Pacific islands from the observation deck of a low-flying liner. He had never visited them, but he had often wished that he could spend his life on some remote and peaceful isle with no care for the future or the world.

It was a dream that almost all men had known at some time in their lives, but Peyton was sufficiently sensible to realise that two months of such an existence would have driven him back to civilisation, half crazy with boredom. However, his dreams were never worried by such considerations, and once more he was lying beneath waving palms, the surf drumming on the reef beyond a lagoon that framed the sun in an azure mirror.

The dream was extraordinarily vivid, so much so that even in his sleep Peyton found himself thinking that no dream had any right to be so real. Then it ceased, so abruptly that there seemed to be a definite rift in his thoughts. The interruption jolted him back to consciousness.

Bitterly disappointed, Peyton lay for a while with his eyes tightly closed, trying to recapture the lost paradise. But it was useless. Something was beating against his brain, keeping him from sleep. Moreover, his couch had suddenly become very hard and uncomfortable. Reluctantly he turned his mind toward the interruption.

Peyton had always been a realist and had never been troubled by philosophical doubts, so the shock was far greater than it might have been to many less intelligent minds. Never before had he found himself doubting his own sanity, but he did so now. For the sound that had awakened him was the drumming of the waves against the reef. He was lying on the golden sand beside the lagoon. Around him, the wind was sighing through the palms, its warm fingers caressing him gently.

For a moment, Peyton could only imagine that he was still dreaming. But this time there could be no real doubt. While one is sane, reality can never be mistaken for a dream. This was real if anything in the universe was real.

Slowly the sense of wonder began to fade. He rose to his feet, the sand showering from him in a golden rain. Shielding his eyes against the sun, he stared along the beach.

He did not stop to wonder why the place should be so familiar. It seemed natural enough to know that the village was a little farther along the bay. Presently he would rejoin his friends, from whom he had been separated for a little while in a world he was swiftly forgetting.

There was a fading memory of a young engineer – even the name escaped him now – who had once aspired to fame and wisdom. In that other life, he had known this foolish person well, but now he could never explain to him the vanity of his ambitions.

He began to wander idly along the beach, the last vague recollections of his shadow life sloughing from him with every footstep, as the details of a dream fade into the light of day.

On the other side of the world three very worried scientists were waiting in a deserted laboratory, their eyes on a multichannel communicator of unusual design. The machine had been silent for nine hours. No one had expected a message in the first eight, but the prearranged signal was now more than an hour overdue.

Alan Henson jumped to his feet with a gesture of impatience.

'We've got to do something! I'm going to call him.'

The other two scientists looked at each other nervously.

'The call may be traced!'

'Not unless they're actually watching us. Even if they are, I'll say nothing unusual. Peyton will understand, if he can answer at all. . . .'

If Richard Peyton had ever known time, that knowledge was forgotten now. Only the present was real, for both past and future lay hidden behind an impenetrable screen, as a great landscape may be concealed by a driving wall of rain.

In his enjoyment of the present Peyton was utterly content. Nothing at all was left of the restless driving spirit that had once set out, a little uncertainly, to conquer fresh fields of knowledge. He had no use for knowledge now.

Later he was never able to recollect anything of his life on the island. He had known many companions, but their names and faces had vanished beyond recall. Love, peace of mind, happiness – all were his for a brief moment of time. And yet he could remember no more than the last few moments of his life in paradise.

Strange that it should have ended as it began. Once more he was by the side of the lagoon, but this time it was night and he was not alone. The moon that seemed always to be full rode low above the ocean, and its long silver band stretched far away to the edge of the world. The stars that never changed their places glowed unblinking in the sky like brilliant jewels, more glorious than the forgotten stars of Earth.

But Peyton's thoughts were intent on other beauty, and once again he bent toward the figure lying on the sand that was no more golden than the hair strewn carelessly across it.

Then paradise trembled and dissolved around him. He gave a great cry of anguish as everything he loved was wrenched away. Only the swiftness of the transition saved his mind. When it was over, he felt as Adam must have when the gates of Eden clanged forever shut behind him.

But the sound that had brought him back was the most commonplace in all the world. Perhaps, indeed, no other could have reached his mind in its place of hiding. It was only the shrilling of his communicator set as it lay on the door beside his couch, here in the darkened room in the city of Comarre.

The clangour died away as he reached out automatically to press the receiving switch. He must have made some answer that satisfied his unknown caller – who was Alan Henson? – for after a very short time the circuit was cleared. Still dazed, Peyton sat on the couch, holding his head in his hands and trying to reorient his life.

He had not been dreaming; he was sure of that. Rather, it was as if he had been living a second life and now he was returning to his old existence as might a man recovering from amnesia. Though he was still dazed, one clear conviction came into his mind. He must never again sleep in Comarre.

Slowly the will and character of Richard Peyton III returned from their banishment. Unsteadily he rose to his feet and made his way out of the room. Once again he found himself in the long corridor with its hundreds of identical doors. With new understanding he looked at the symbol carved upon them.

He scarcely noticed where he was going. His mind was fixed too intently on the problem before him. As he walked, his brain cleared, and slowly understanding came. For the moment it was only a theory, but soon he would put it to the test.

The human mind was a delicate, sheltered thing, having no direct contact with the world and gathering all its knowledge and experience through the body's senses. It was possible to record and store thoughts and emotions as earlier men had once recorded sound on miles of wire.

If those thoughts were projected into another mind, when the body was unconscious and all its senses numbed, that brain would think it was experiencing reality. There was no way in which it could detect the deception, any more than one can distinguish a perfectly recorded symphony from the original performance.

All this had been known for centuries, but the builders of Comarre had used the knowledge as no one in the world had ever done before. Somewhere in the city there must be machines that could analyse every thought and desire of those who entered. Elsewhere the city's makers must have stored every sensation and experience a human mind could know. From this raw material all possible futures could be constructed.

Now at last Peyton understood the measure of the genius that had gone into the making of Comarre. The machines had analysed his deepest thoughts and built for him a world based on his subconscious desires. Then, when the chance had come, they had taken control of his mind and injected into it all he had experienced.

No wonder that everything he had ever longed for had been his in that already half-forgotten paradise. And no wonder that through the ages so many had sought the peace only Comarre could bring!

CHAPTER FIVE

The Engineer

Peyton had become himself again by the time the sound of wheels made him look over his shoulder. The little robot that had been his guide was returning. No doubt the great machines that controlled it were wondering what had happened to its charge. Peyton waited, a thought slowly forming in his mind.

A-Five started all over again with its set speech. It seemed very incongruous now to find so simple a machine in this place where automatronics had reached their ultimate development. Then Peyton realised that perhaps the robot was deliberately uncomplicated. There was little purpose in using a complex machine where a simple one would serve as well – or better.

Peyton ignored the now familiar speech. All robots, he knew, must obey human commands unless other humans had previously given them orders to the contrary. Even the projectors of the city, he thought wryly, had obeyed the unknown and unspoken commands of his own subconscious mind.

'Lead me to the thought projectors,' he commanded.

As he had expected, the robot did not move. It merely replied, 'I do not understand.'

Peyton's spirits began to revive as he felt himself once more master of the situation.

'Come here and do not move again until I give the order.'

The robot's selectors and relays considered the instructions. They could find no countermanding order. Slowly the little machine rolled forward on its wheels. It had committed itself – there was no turning back now. It could not move again until Peyton ordered it to do so or something overrode his commands. Robot hypnosis was a very old trick, much beloved by mischievous small boys.

Swiftly, Peyton emptied his bag of the tools no engineer was ever without: the universal screw driver, the expanding wrench, the automatic drill, and, most important of all, the atomic cutter that could eat through the thickest metal in a matter of seconds. Then, with a skill born of long practice, he went to work on the unsuspecting machine.

Luckily the robot had been built for easy servicing, and could be opened with little difficulty. There was nothing unfamiliar about the controls, and it did not take Peyton long to find the locomotor mechanism. Now, whatever happened, the machine could not escape. It was crippled.

Next he blinded it and, one by one, tracked down its other electrical senses and put them out of commission. Soon the little machine was no more than a cylinder full of complicated junk. Feeling like a small boy who has just made a wanton attack on a defenceless grandfather clock, Peyton sat down and waited for what he knew must happen.

It was a little inconsiderate of him to sabotage the robot so far from the main machine levels. The robot-transporter took nearly fifteen minutes to work its way up from the depths. Peyton heard the rumble of its wheels in the distance and knew that his calculations had been correct. The breakdown party was on the way.

The transporter was a simple carrying machine, with a set of arms that could grasp and hold a damaged robot. It seemed to be blind, though no doubt its special senses were quite sufficient for its purpose.

Peyton waited until it had collected the unfortunate A-Five. Then he jumped aboard, keeping well away from the mechanical limbs. He had no desire to be mistaken for another distressed robot. Fortunately the big machine took no notice of him at all.

So Peyton descended through level after level of the great building, past the living quarters, through the room in which he had first found himself, and lower yet into regions he had never before seen. As he descended, the character of the city changed around him.

Gone now were the luxury and opulence of the higher levels, replaced by a no man's land of bleak passageways that were little more than giant cable ducts. Presently these, too, came to an end. The conveyor passed through a set of great sliding doors – and he had reached his goal.

The rows of relay panels and selector mechanisms seemed endless, but though Peyton was tempted to jump off his unwitting steed, he waited until the main control panels came into sight. Then he climbed off the conveyor and watched it disappear into the distance toward some still more remote part of the city.

He wondered how long it would take the superautomata to repair A-Five. His sabotage had been very thorough, and he rather thought the little machine was heading for the scrap heap. Then, feeling like a starving man suddenly confronted by a banquet, he began his examination of the city's wonders.

In the next five hours he paused only once to send the routine signal back to his friends. He wished he could tell of his success, but the risk was too great. After prodigies of circuit tracing he had discovered the functions of the main units and was beginning to investigate some of the secondary equipment.

It was just as he had expected. The thought analysers and projectors lay on the floor immediately above, and could be controlled from, this central installation. How they worked he had no conception: it might well take months to uncover all their secrets. But he had identified them and thought he could probably switch them off if necessary.

A little later he discovered the thought monitor. It was a small machine, rather like an ancient manual telephone switchboard, but very much more complex. The operator's seat was a curious structure, insulated from the ground and roofed by a network of wires and crystal bars. It was the first machine he had discovered that was obviously intended for direct human use. Probably the first engineers had built it to set up the equipment in the early days of the city.

Peyton would not have risked using the thought monitor if detailed instructions had not been printed on its control panel. After some experimenting he plugged in to one of the circuits and slowly increased the power, keeping the intensity control well below the red danger mark.

It was as well that he did so, for the sensation was a shattering one. He still retained his own personality, but superimposed on his own thoughts were ideas and images that were utterly foreign to him. He was looking at another world, through the windows of an alien mind.

It was as though his body were in two places at once, though the sensations of his second personality were much less vivid than those of the real Richard Peyton III. Now he understood the meaning of the danger line. If the thought-intensity control was turned too high, madness would certainly result.

Peyton switched off the instrument so that he could think without interruption. He understood now what the robot had meant when it said that the other inhabitants of the city were sleeping. There were other men in Comarre, lying entranced beneath the thought projectors.

His mind went back to the long corridor and its hundreds of metal doors. On his way down he had passed through many such galleries and it was clear that the greater part of the city was no more than a vast honeycomb of chambers in which thousands of men could dream away their lives.

One after another he checked the circuits on the board. The great majority were dead, but perhaps fifty were still operating. And each of them carried all the thoughts, desires, and emotions of the human mind.

Now that he was fully conscious, Peyton could understand how he had been tricked, but the knowledge brought little consolation. He could see the flaws in these synthetic worlds, could observe how all the critical faculties of the mind were numbed while an endless stream of simple but vivid emotions was poured into it.

Yes, it all seemed very simple now. But it did not alter the fact that this artificial world was utterly real to the beholder – so real that the pain of leaving it still burned in his own mind.

For nearly an hour, Peyton explored the worlds of the fifty sleeping minds. It was a fascinating though repulsive quest. In that hour he learned more of the human brain and its hidden ways than he had ever dreamed existed. When he had finished he sat very still for a long time at the controls of the machine, analysing his new-found knowledge. His wisdom had advanced by many years, and his youth seemed suddenly very far away.

For the first time he had direct knowledge of the fact that the perverse and evil desires that sometimes ruffled the surface of his own mind were shared by all human beings. The builders of Comarre had cared nothing for good or evil – and the machines had been their faithful servants.

It was satisfactory to know that his theories had been correct. Peyton understood now the narrowness of his escape. If he fell asleep again within these walls he might never awake. Chance had saved him once, but it would not do so again.

The thought projectors must be put out of action, so thoroughly that the robots could never repair them. Though they could handle normal break-downs, the robots could not deal with the deliberate sabotage on the scale Peyton was envisaging. When he had finished, Comarre would be a menace no longer. It would never trap his mind again, or the minds of any future visitors who might come this way.

First he would have to locate the sleepers and revive them. That might be a lengthy task, but fortunately the machine level was equipped with standard monovision search apparatus. With it he could see and hear everything in the city, simply by focusing the carrier beams on the required spot. He could even project his voice if necessary, but not his image. That type of machine had not come into general use until after the building of Comarre.

It took him a little while to master the controls, and at first the beam wandered erratically all over the city. Peyton found himself looking into any number of surprising places, and once he even got a glimpse of the forest – though it was upside down. He wondered if Leo was still around, and with some difficulty he located the entrance.

Yes, there it was, just as he had left it the day before. And a few yards away the faithful Leo was lying with his head toward the city and a distinctly worried look on his face. Peyton was deeply touched. He wondered if he could get the lion into Comarre. The moral support would be valuable, for he was beginning to feel more need of companionship after the night's experiences.

Methodically he searched the wall of the city and was greatly relieved to discover several concealed entrances at ground level. He had been wondering how he was going to leave. Even if he could work the matter-transmitter in reverse, the prospect was not an attractive one. He much preferred an old-fashioned physical movement through space.

The openings were all sealed, and for a moment he was baffled. Then he began to search for a robot. After some delay, he discovered one of the late A-Five's twins rolling along a corridor on some mysterious errand. To his relief, it obeyed his command unquestioningly and opened the door.

Peyton drove the beam through the walls again and brought the focus point to rest a few feet away from Leo. Then he called, softly:

'Leo!'

The lion looked up, startled.

'Hello, Leo – it's me – Peyton!'

Looking puzzled, the lion walked slowly around in a circle. Then it gave up and sat down helplessly.

With a great deal of persuasion, Peyton coaxed Leo up to the entrance. The lion recognised his voice and seemed willing to follow, but it was a sorely puzzled and rather nervous animal. It hesitated for a moment at the opening, liking neither Comarre nor the silently waiting robot.

Very patiently Peyton instructed Leo to follow the robot. He repeated his remarks in different words until he was sure the lion understood. Then he spoke directly to the machine and ordered it to guide the lion to the control chamber. He watched it for a moment to see that Leo was following. Then, with a word of encouragement, he left the strangely assorted pair.

It was rather disappointing to find that he could not see into any of the sealed rooms behind the poppy symbol. They were shielded from the beam or else the focusing controls had been set so that the monovisor could not be used to pry into that volume of space.

Peyton was not discouraged. The sleepers would wake up the hard way, as he had done. Having looked into their private worlds, he felt little sympathy for them and only a sense of duty impelled him to wake them. They deserved no consideration.

A horrible thought suddenly assailed him. What had the projectors fed into his own mind in response to his desires, in that forgotten idyll from which he had been so reluctant to return? Had his own hidden thoughts been as disreputable as those of the other dreamers?

It was an uncomfortable idea, and he put it aside as he sat down once more at the central switchboard. First he would disconnect the circuits, then he would sabotage the projectors so that they could never again be used. The spell that Comarre had cast over so many minds would be broken forever.

Peyton reached forward to throw the multiplex circuit breakers, but he

144

never completed the movement. Gently but very firmly, four metal arms clasped his body from behind. Kicking and struggling, he was lifted into the air away from the controls and carried to the centre of the room. There he was set down again, and the metal arms released him.

More angry than alarmed, Peyton whirled to face his captor. Regarding him quietly from a few yards away was the most complex robot he had ever seen. Its body was nearly seven feet high, and rested on a dozen fat balloon tyres.

From various parts of its metal chassis, tentacles, arms, rods, and other less easily describable mechanisms projected in all directions. In two places, groups of limbs were busily at work dismantling or repairing pieces of machinery which Peyton recognised with a guilty start.

Silently Peyton weighed his opponent. It was clearly a robot of the very highest order. But it had used physical violence against him – and no robot could do that against a man, though it might refuse to obey his orders. Only under the direct control of another human mind could a robot commit such an act. So there was life, conscious and hostile life, somewhere in the city.

'Who are you?' exclaimed Peyton at last, addressing not the robot, but the controller behind it.

With no detectable time lag the machine answered in a precise and automatic voice that did not seem to be merely the amplified speech of a human being.

'I am the Engineer.'

'Then come out and let me see you.'

'You are seeing me.'

It was the inhuman tone of the voice, as much as the words themselves, that made Peyton's anger evaporate in a moment and replaced it with a sense of unbelieving wonder.

There was no human being controlling this machine. It was as automatic as the other robots of the city – but unlike them, and all other robots the world had ever known, it had a will and a consciousness of its own.

CHAPTER SIX

The Nightmare

As Peyton stared wide-eyed at the machine before him, he felt his scalp crawling, not with fright, but with the sheer intensity of his excitement. His quest had been rewarded – the dream of nearly a thousand years was here before his eyes.

Long ago the machines had won a limited intelligence. Now at last they had reached the goal of consciousness itself. This was the secret Thordarsen would have given to the world – the secret the Council had sought to suppress for fear of the consequences it might bring.

The passionless voice spoke again.

'I am glad that you realise the truth. It will make things easier.'

'You can read my mind?' gasped Peyton.

'Naturally. That was done from the moment you entered.'

'Yes, I gathered that,' said Peyton grimly. 'And what do you intend to do with me now?'

'I must prevent you from damaging Comarre.'

That, thought Peyton, was reasonable enough.

'Suppose I left now? Would that suit you?'

'Yes. That would be good.'

Peyton could not help laughing. The Engineer was still a robot, in spite of all its near-humanity. It was incapable of guile, and perhaps that gave him an advantage. Somehow he must trick it into revealing its secrets. But once again the robot read his mind.

'I will not permit it. You have learned too much already. You must leave at once. I will use force if necessary.'

Peyton decided to fight for time. He could, at least, discover the limits of this amazing machine's intelligence.

'Before I go, tell me this. Why are you called the Engineer?'

The robot answered readily enough.

'If serious faults developed that cannot be repaired by the robots, I deal with them. I could rebuild Comarre if necessary. Normally, when everything is functioning properly, I am quiescent.'

How alien, thought Peyton, the idea of 'quiescence' was to a human mind. He could not help feeling amused at the distinction the Engineer had drawn between itself and 'the robots'. He asked the obvious question.

'And if something goes wrong with you?'

'There are two of us. The other is quiescent now. Each can repair the other. That was necessary once, three hundred years ago.'

It was a flawless system. Comarre was safe from accident for millions of years. The builders of the city had set these eternal guardians to watch over them while they went in search of their dreams. No wonder that, long after its makers had died, Comarre was still fulfilling its strange purpose.

What a tragedy it was, thought Peyton, that all this genius had been wasted! The secrets of the Engineer could revolutionise robot technology, could bring a new world into being. Now that the first conscious machines had been built, was there any limit to what lay beyond?

'No,' said the Engineer unexpectedly. 'Thordarsen told me that the robots would one day be more intelligent than man.'

It was strange to hear the machine uttering the name of its maker. So that was Thordarsen's dream! Its full immensity had not yet dawned on him. Though he had been half-prepared for it, he could not easily accept the conclusions. After all, between the robot and the human mind lay an enormous gulf.

'No greater than that between man and the animals from which he rose, so Thordarsen once said. You, Man, are no more than a very complex robot. I am simpler, but more efficient. That is all.'

Very carefully Peyton considered the statement. If indeed Man was no more than a complex robot – a machine composed of living cells rather than wires and vacuum tubes – yet more complex robots would one day be made. When that day came, the supremacy of Man would be ended. The machines might still be his servants, but they would be more intelligent than their master.

It was very quiet in the great room lined with the racks of analysers and relay panels. The Engineer was watching Peyton intently, its arms and tentacles still busy on their repair work.

Peyton was beginning to feel desperate. Characteristically the opposition had made him more determined than ever. Somehow he must discover how the Engineer was built. Otherwise he would waste all his life trying to match the genius of Thordarsen.

It was useless. The robot was one jump ahead of him.

'You cannot make plans against me. If you do try to escape through that door, I shall throw this power unit at your legs. My probable error at this range is less than half a centimetre.'

One could not hide from the thought analysers. The plan had been scarcely half-formed in Peyton's mind, but the Engineer knew it already.

Both Peyton and the Engineer were equally surprised by the interruption. There was a sudden flash of tawny gold, and half a ton of bone and sinew, travelling at forty miles an hour, struck the robot amidships.

For a moment there was a great flailing of tentacles. Then, with a sound like the crack of doom, the Engineer lay sprawling on the floor. Leo, licking his paws thoughtfully, crouched over the fallen machine.

He could not quite understand this shining animal which had been threatening his master. Its skin was the toughest he had encountered since a very ill-advised disagreement with a rhinoceros many years ago.

'Good boy!' shouted Peyton gleefully. 'Keep him down!'

The Engineer had broken some of his larger limbs, and the tentacles were too weak to do any damage. Once again Peyton found his tool kit invaluable. When he had finished, the Engineer was certainly incapable of movement, though Peyton had not touched any of the neural circuits. That, somehow, would have been rather too much like murder.

'You can get off now, Leo,' he said when the task was finished. The lion obeyed with poor grace.

'I'm sorry to have to do this,' said Peyton hypocritically, 'but I hope you appreciate my point of view. Can you still speak?'

'Yes,' replied the Engineer. 'What do you intend to do now?'

Peyton smiled. Five minutes ago, he had been the one to ask the question. How long, he wondered, would it take for the Engineer's twin to arrive on the scene? Though Leo could deal with the situation if it came to a trial of strength, the other robot would have been warned and might be able to make things very unpleasant for them. It could, for instance, switch off the lights.

The glow tubes died and darkness fell. Leo gave a mournful howl of dismay. Feeling rather annoyed, Peyton drew his torch and switched it on.

'It doesn't really make any difference to me,' he said. 'You might just as well switch them on again.'

The Engineer said nothing. But the glow tubes lit once more.

How on earth, thought Peyton, could you fight an enemy who could read your thoughts and could even watch you preparing your defences? He would have to avoid thinking of any idea that might react to his disadvantage, such as – he stopped himself just in time. For a moment he blocked his thoughts by trying to integrate Armstrong's omega function in his head. Then he got his mind under control again.

'Look,' he said at last, 'I'll make a bargain with you.'

'What is that? I do not know the word.'

'Never mind,' Peyton replied hurriedly. 'My suggestion is this. Let me waken the men who are trapped here, give me your fundamental circuits, and I'll leave without touching anything. You will have obeyed your builders' orders and no harm will have been done.'

A human being might have argued over the matter, but not so the robot. Its mind took perhaps a thousandth of a second to weigh any situation, however involved.

'Very well. I see from your mind that you intend to keep the agreement. But what does the word "blackmail" mean?'

Peyton flushed.

'It doesn't matter,' he said hastily. 'It's only a common human expression. I suppose your – er – colleague will be here in a moment?'

'He has been waiting outside for some time,' replied the robot. 'Will you keep your dog under control?'

Peyton laughed. It was too much to expect a robot to know zoology.

'Lion, then,' said the robot, correcting itself as it read his mind.

Peyton addressed a few words to Leo and, to make doubly sure, wound his fingers in the lion's mane. Before he could frame the invitation with his lips, the second robot rolled silently into the room. Leo growled and tried to tug away, but Peyton calmed him.

In every respect Engineer II was a duplicate of its colleague. Even as it came toward him it dipped into his mind in the disconcerting manner that Peyton could never get used to.

'I see that you wish to go to the dreamers,' it said. 'Follow me.'

Peyton was tired of being ordered around. Why didn't the robots ever say 'please'?

'Follow me, please,' repeated the machine, with the slightest possible accentuation.

Peyton followed.

Once again he found himself in the corridor with the hundreds of poppy-embossed doors – or a similar corridor. The robot led him to a door indistinguishable from the rest and came to a halt in front of it.

Silently the metal plate slid open, and, not without qualms, Peyton stepped into the darkened room.

On the couch lay a very old man. At first sight he seemed to be dead. Certainly his breathing had slowed to the point of cessation. Peyton stared at him for a moment. Then he spoke to the robot.

'Waken him.'

Somewhere in the depths of the city the stream of impulses through a thought projector ceased. A universe that had never existed crumbled to ruins.

From the couch two burning eyes glowed up at Peyton, lit with the light of madness. They stared through him and beyond, and from the thin lips poured a stream of jumbled words that Peyton could barely distinguish. Over and over again the old man cried out names that must be those of people or places in the dream world from which he had been wrenched. It was at once horrible and pathetic.

'Stop it!' cried Peyton. 'You are back in reality now.'

The glowing eyes seemed to see him for the first time. With an immense effort the old man raised himself.

'Who are you?' he quavered. Then, before Peyton could answer, he continued in a broken voice. 'This must be a nightmare – go away, go away. Let me wake up!'

Overcoming his repulsion, Peyton put his hand on the emaciated shoulder.

'Don't worry – you are awake. Don't you remember?'

The other did not seem to hear him.

'Yes, it must be a nightmare – it must be! But why don't I wake up? Nyran, Cressidor, where are you? I cannot find you!'

Peyton stood it as long as he could, but nothing he did could attract the old man's attention again. Sick at heart, he turned to the robot.

'Send him back.'

CHAPTER SEVEN

The Third Renaissance

Slowly the raving ceased. The frail body fell back on the couch, and once again the wrinkled face became a passionless mask.

'Are they all as mad as this?' asked Peyton finally.

'But he is not mad.'

'What do you mean? Of course he is!'

'He has been entranced for many years. Suppose you went to a far land and changed your mode of living completely, forgetting all you had ever known of your previous life. Eventually you would have no more knowledge of it than you have of your first childhood.

'If by some miracle you were then suddenly thrown back in time, you

149

would behave in just that way. Remember, his dream life is completely real to him and he has lived it now for many years.'

That was true enough. But how could the Engineer possess such insight? Peyton turned to it in amazement, but as usual had no need to frame the question.

'Thordarsen told me the other day while we were still building Comarre. Even then some of the dreamers had been entranced for twenty years.'

'The other day?'

'About five hundred years ago, you would call it.'

The words brought a strange picture into Peyton's mind. He could visualise the lonely genius, working here among his robots, perhaps with no human companions left. All the others would long since have gone in search of their dreams.

But Thordarsen might have stayed on, the desire for creation still linking him to the world, until he had finished his work. The two engineers, his greatest achievement and perhaps the most wonderful feat of electronics of which the world had record, were his ultimate masterpieces.

The waste and the pity of it overwhelmed Peyton. More than ever he was determined that, because the embittered genius had thrown away his life, his work should not perish, but be given to the world.

'Will all the dreamers be like this?' he asked the robot.

'All except the newest. They may still remember their first lives.'

'Take me to one of them.'

The room they entered next was identical with the other, but the body lying on the couch was that of a man of no more than forty.

'How long has he been here?' asked Peyton.

'He came only a few weeks ago – the first visitor we had for many years until your coming.'

'Wake him, please.'

The eyes opened slowly. There was no insanity in them, only wonder and sadness. Then came the dawn of recollection, and the man half rose to a sitting position. His first words were completely rational.

'Why have you called me back? Who are you?'

'I have just escaped from the thought projectors,' explained Peyton. 'I want to release all who can be saved.'

The other laughed bitterly.

'Saved! From what? It took me forty years to escape from the world, and now you would drag me back to it! Go away and leave me in peace!'

Peyton would not retreat so easily.

'Do you think that this make-believe world of yours is better than reality? Have you no desire to escape from it at all?'

Again the other laughed, with no trace of humour.

'Comarre is reality to me. The world never gave me anything, so why should I wish to return to it? I have found peace here, and that is all I need.'

Quite suddenly Peyton turned on his heels and left. Behind him he heard the dreamer fall back with a contented sigh. He knew when he had been beaten. And he knew now why he had wished to revive the others.

It had not been through any sense of duty, but for his own selfish purpose. He had wished to convince himself that Comarre was evil. Now he knew that it was not. There would always be, even in Utopia, some for whom the world had nothing to offer but sorrow and disillusion.

They would be fewer and fewer with the passage of time. In the dark ages of a thousand years ago most of mankind had been misfits of some sort. However splendid the world's future, there would still be some tragedies – and why should Comarre be condemned because it offered them their only hope of peace?

He would try no more experiments. His own robust faith and confidence had been severely shaken. And the dreamers of Comarre would not thank him for his pains.

He turned to the Engineer again. The desire to leave the city had grown very intense in the last few minutes, but the most important work was still to be done. As usual, the robot forestalled him.

'I have what you want,' he said. 'Follow me, please.'

It did not lead, as Peyton had half expected, back to the machine levels, with their maze of control equipment. When their journey had finished, they were higher than Peyton had ever been before, in a little circular room he suspected might be at the very apex of the city. There were no windows, unless the curious plates set in the wall could be made transparent by some secret means.

It was a study, and Peyton gazed at it with awe as he realised who had worked here many centuries ago. The walls were lined with ancient textbooks that had not been disturbed for five hundred years. It seemed as if Thordarsen had left only a few hours before. There was even a half-finished circuit pinned on a drawing board against the wall.

'It almost looks as if he was interrupted,' said Peyton, half to himself.

'He was,' answered the robot.

'What do you mean? Didn't he join the others when he had finished you?'

It was difficult to believe that there was absolutely no emotion behind the reply, but the words were spoken in the same passionless tones as everything else the robot had ever said.

'When he had finished us, Thordarsen was still not satisfied. He was not like the others. He often told us that he had found happiness in the building of Comarre. Again and again he said that he would join the rest, but always there was some last improvement he wanted to make. So it went on until one day we found him lying here in this room. He had stopped. The word I see in your mind is "death," but I have no thought for that.'

Peyton was silent. It seemed to him that the great scientist's ending had not been an ignoble one. The bitterness that had darkened his life had lifted

151

from it at the last. He had known the joy of creation. Of all the artists who had come to Comarre, he was the greatest. And now his work would not be wasted.

The robot glided silently toward a steel desk, and one of its tentacles disappeared into a drawer. When it emerged it was holding a thick volume, bound between sheets of metal. Wordlessly it handed the book to Peyton, who opened it with trembling hands. It contained many thousands of pages of thin, very tough material.

Written on the flyleaf in a bold, firm hand were the words:

Rolf Thordarsen
Notes on Subelectronics
Begun: Day 2, Month 13, 2598.

Underneath was more writing, very difficult to decipher and apparently scrawled in frantic haste. As he read, understanding came at last to Peyton with the suddenness of an equatorial dawn.

To the reader of these words:
    I, Rolf Thordarsen, meeting no understanding in my own age, send this message into the future. If Comarre still exists, you will have seen my handiwork and must have escaped the snares I set for lesser minds. Therefore you are fitted to take this knowledge to the world. Give it to the scientists and tell them to use it wisely.
    I have broken down the barrier between Man and Machine. Now they must share the future equally.

Peyton read the message several times, his heart warming toward his long-dead ancestor. It was a brilliant scheme. In this way, as perhaps in no other, Thordarsen had been able to send his message safely down the ages, knowing that only the right hands would receive it. Peyton wondered if this had been Thordarsen's plan when he first joined the Decadents or whether he had evolved it later in his life. He would never know.

He looked again at the Engineer and thought of the world that would come when all robots had reached consciousness. Beyond that he looked still farther into the mists of the future.

The robot need have none of the limitations of Man, none of his pitiful weaknesses. It would never let passions cloud its logic, would never be swayed by self-interest and ambition. It would be complementary to man.

Peyton remembered Thordarsen's words, 'Now they must share the future equally.'

Peyton stopped his daydream. All this, if it ever came, might be centuries in the future. He turned to the Engineer.

'I am ready to leave. But one day I shall return.'

The robot backed slowly away from him.

'Stand perfectly still,' it ordered.

Peyton looked at the Engineer in puzzlement. Then he glanced hurriedly at the ceiling. There again was that enigmatic bulge under which he had found himself when he first entered the city such an age ago.

'Hey!' he cried. 'I don't want—'

It was too late. Behind him was the dark screen, blacker than night itself. Before him lay the clearing, with the forest at its edge. It was evening, and the sun was nearly touching the trees.

There was a sudden whimpering noise behind him: a very frightened lion was looking out at the forest with unbelieving eyes. Leo had not enjoyed his transfer.

'It's all over now, old chap,' said Peyton reassuringly. 'You can't blame them for trying to get rid of us as quickly as they could. After all, we did smash up the place a bit between us. Come along – I don't want to spend the night in the forest.'

On the other side of the world, a group of scientists was dispersing with what patience it could, not yet knowing the full extent of its triumph. In Central Tower, Richard Peyton II had just discovered that his son had not spent the last two days with his cousins in South America, and was composing a speech of welcome for the prodigal's return.

Far above the Earth the World Council was laying down plans soon to be swept away by the coming of the Third Renaissance. But the cause of all the trouble knew nothing of this and, for the moment, cared less.

Slowly Peyton descended the marble steps from that mysterious doorway whose secret was still hidden from him. Leo followed a little way behind, looking over his shoulder and growling quietly now and then.

Together, they started back along the metal road, through the avenue of stunted trees. Peyton was glad that the sun had not yet set. At night this road would be glowing with its internal radioactivity, and the twisted trees would not look pleasant silhouetted against the stars.

At the bend in the road he paused for a while and looked back at the curving metal wall with its single black opening whose appearance was so deceptive. All his feeling of triumph seemed to fade away. He knew that as long as he lived he could never forget what lay behind those towering walls – the cloying promise of peace and utter contentment.

Deep in his soul he felt the fear that any satisfaction, any achievement the outer world could give might seem vain beside the effortless bliss offered by Comarre. For an instant he had a nightmare vision of himself, broken and old, returning along this road to seek oblivion. He shrugged his shoulders and put the thought aside.

Once he was out on the plain his spirits rose swiftly. He opened the precious book again and ruffled through its pages of microprint, intoxicated by the promise that it held. Ages ago the slow caravans had come this way, bearing gold and ivory for Solomon the Wise. But all their treasure was as nothing beside this single volume, and all the wisdom of Solomon could not have pictured the new civilisation of which this volume was to be the seed.

Presently Peyton began to sing, something he did very seldom and extremely badly. The song was a very old one, so old that it came from an age before atomic power, before interplanetary travel, even before the coming of flight. It had to do with a certain hairdresser in Seville, wherever Seville might be.

Leo stood it in silence for as long as he could. Then he, too, joined in. The duet was not a success.

When night descended, the forest and all its secrets had fallen below the horizon. With his face to the stars and Leo watching by his side, Peyton slept well.

This time he did not dream.

The Forgotten Enemy

First published in *New Worlds*, #5, 1949
Collected in *Reach for Tomorrow*

The thick furs thudded softly to the ground as Professor Millward jerked himself upright on the narrow bed. This time, he was sure, it had been no dream; the freezing air that rasped against his lungs still seemed to echo with the sound that had come crashing out of the night.

He gathered the furs around his shoulders and listened intently. All was quiet again: from the narrow windows in the western walls long shafts of moonlight played upon the endless rows of books, as they played upon the dead city beneath. The world was utterly still; even in the old days the city would have been silent on such a night, and it was doubly silent now.

With weary resolution Professor Millward shuffled out of bed, and doled a few lumps of coke into the glowing brazier. Then he made his way slowly toward the nearest window, pausing now and then to rest his hand lovingly on the volumes he had guarded all these years.

He shielded his eyes from the brilliant moonlight and peered out into the night. The sky was cloudless: the sound he had heard had not been thunder, whatever it might have been. It had come from the north, and even as he waited it came again.

Distance had softened it, distance and the bulk of the hills that lay beyond London. It did not race across the sky with the wantonness of thunder, but seemed to come from a single point far to the north. It was like no natural sound that he had ever heard, and for a moment he dared to hope again.

Only Man, he was sure, could have made such a sound. Perhaps the dream that had kept him here among these treasures of civilisation for more than twenty years would soon be a dream no longer. Men were returning to England, blasting their way through the ice and snow with the weapons that science had given them before the coming of the Dust. It was strange that they should come by land, and from the north, but he thrust aside any thoughts that would quench the newly kindled flame of hope.

Three hundred feet below, the broken sea of snowcovered roofs lay bathed in the bitter moonlight. Miles away the tall stacks of Battersea Power Station glimmered like thin white ghosts against the night sky. Now that the dome of St Paul's had collapsed beneath the weight of snow, they alone challenged his supremacy.

Professor Millward walked slowly back along the bookshelves, thinking over the plan that had formed in his mind. Twenty years ago he had watched the last helicopters climbing heavily out of Regent's Park, the rotors churning the ceaselessly falling snow. Even then, when the silence had closed around him, he could not bring himself to believe that the North had been abandoned forever. Yet already he had waited a whole generation, among the books to which he had dedicated his life.

In those early days he had sometimes heard, over the radio which was his only contact with the South, of the struggle to colonise the now-temperate lands of the Equator. He did not know the outcome of that far-off battle, fought with desperate skill in the dying jungles and across deserts that had already felt the first touch of snow. Perhaps it had failed; the radio had been silent now for fifteen years or more. Yet if men and machines were indeed returning from the north – of all directions – he might again be able to hear their voices as they spoke to one another and to the lands from which they had come.

Professor Millward left the University building perhaps a dozen times a year, and then only through sheer necessity. Over the past two decades he had collected everything he needed from the shops in the Bloomsbury area, for in the final exodus vast supplies of stocks had been left behind through lack of transport. In many ways, indeed, his life could be called luxurious: no professor of English literature had ever been clothed in such garments as those he had taken from an Oxford Street furrier's.

The sun was blazing from a cloudless sky as he shouldered his pack and unlocked the massive gates. Even ten years ago packs of starving dogs had hunted in this area, and though he had seen none for years he was still cautious and always carried a revolver when he went into the open.

The sunlight was so brilliant that the reflected glare hurt his eyes; but it was almost wholly lacking in heat. Although the belt of cosmic dust through which the Solar System was now passing had made little visible difference to the sun's brightness, it had robbed it of all strength. No one knew whether the world would swim out into the warmth again in ten or a thousand years, and civilisation had fled southward in search of lands where the word 'summer' was not an empty mockery.

The latest drifts had packed hard and Professor Millward had little difficulty in making the journey to Tottenham Court Road. Sometimes it had taken him hours of floundering through the snow, and one year he had been sealed in his great concrete watchtower for nine months.

He kept away from the houses with their dangerous burdens of snow and their Damoclean icicles, and went north until he came to the shop he was seeking. The words above the shattered windows were still bright: 'Jenkins & Sons. Radio and Electrical. Television A Specialty.'

Some snow had drifted through a broken section of roofing, but the little upstairs room had not altered since his last visit a dozen years ago. The all-wave radio still stood on the table, and empty tins scattered on the floor spoke mutely of the lonely hours he had spent here before all hope had died. He wondered if he must go through the same ordeal again.

Professor Millward brushed the snow from the copy of *The Amateur Radio Handbook for 1965*, which had taught him what little he knew about wireless. The testmeters and batteries were still lying in their half-remembered places, and to his relief some of the batteries still held their charge. He searched through the stock until he had built up the necessary power supplies, and checked the radio as well as he could. Then he was ready.

It was a pity that he could never send the manufacturers the testimonial they deserved. The faint 'hiss' from the speaker brought back memories of the BBC, of the nine o'clock news and symphony concerts, of all the things he had taken for granted in a world that was gone like a dream. With scarcely controlled impatience he ran across the wave-bands, but everywhere there was nothing save that omnipresent hiss. That was disappointing, but no more: he remembered that the real test would come at night. In the meantime he would forage among the surrounding shops for anything that might be useful.

It was dusk when he returned to the little room. A hundred miles above his head, tenuous and invisible, the Heaviside Layer would be expanding outward toward the stars as the sun went down. So it had done every evening for millions of years, and for half a century only, Man had used it for his own purposes, to reflect around the world his messages of hate or peace, to echo with trivialities or to sound with music once called immortal.

Slowly, with infinite patience, Professor Millward began to traverse the shortwave bands that a generation ago had been a babel of shouting voices and stabbing morse. Even as he listened, the faint hope he had dared to cherish began to fade within him. The city itself was no more silent than the once-crowded oceans of ether. Only the faint crackle of thunderstorms half the world away broke the intolerable stillness. Man had abandoned his latest conquest.

Soon after midnight the batteries faded out. Professor Millward did not have the heart to search for more, but curled up in his furs and fell into a troubled sleep. He got what consolation he could from the thought that if he had not proved his theory, he had not disproved it either.

The heatless sunlight was flooding the lonely white road when he began the homeward journey. He was very tired, for he had slept little and his sleep had been broken by the recurring fantasy of rescue.

The silence was suddenly broken by the distant thunder that came rolling over the white roofs. It came – there could be no doubt now – from beyond the northern hills that had once been London's playground. From the buildings on either side little avalanches of snow went swishing out into the wide street; then the silence returned.

Professor Millward stood motionless, weighing, considering, analysing. The sound had been too long-drawn to be an ordinary explosion – he was dreaming again – it was nothing less than the distant thunder of an atomic bomb, burning and blasting away the snow a million tons at a time. His hopes revived, and the disappointments of the night began to fade.

That momentary pause almost cost him his life. Out of a side-street something huge and white moved suddenly into his field of vision. For a moment his mind refused to accept the reality of what he saw; then the paralysis left him and he fumbled desperately for his futile revolver. Padding toward him across the snow, swinging its head from side to side with a hypnotic, serpentine motion, was a huge polar bear.

He dropped his belongings and ran, floundering over the snow toward the nearest buildings. Providentially the Underground entrance was only fifty feet away. The steel grille was closed, but he remembered breaking the lock many years ago. The temptation to look back was almost intolerable, for he could hear nothing to tell how near his pursuer was. For one frightful moment the iron lattice resisted his numbed fingers. Then it yielded reluctantly and he forced his way through the narrow opening.

Out of his childhood there came a sudden, incongruous memory of an albino ferret he had once seen weaving its body ceaselessly across the wire netting of its cage. There was the same reptile grace in the monstrous shape, almost twice as high as a man, that reared itself in baffled fury against the grille. The metal bowed but did not yield beneath the pressure; then the bear dropped to the ground, grunted softly and padded away. It slashed once or twice at the fallen haversack, scattering a few tins of food into the snow, and vanished as silently as it had come.

A very shaken Professor Millward reached the University three hours later, after moving in short bounds from one refuge to the next. After all these years he was no longer alone in the city. He wondered if there were other visitors, and that same night he knew the answer. Just before dawn he heard, quite distinctly, the cry of a wolf from somewhere in the direction of Hyde Park.

By the end of the week he knew that the animals of the North were on the move. Once he saw a reindeer running southward, pursued by a pack of silent wolves, and sometimes in the night there were sounds of deadly conflict. He was amazed that so much life still existed in the white wilderness between London and the Pole. Now something was driving it southward, and the knowledge brought him a mounting excitement. He did not believe that these fierce survivors would flee from anything save Man.

The strain of waiting was beginning to affect Professor Millward's mind, and for hours he would sit in the cold sunlight, his furs wrapped around him, dreaming of rescue and thinking of the way in which men might be returning to England. Perhaps an expedition had come from North America across the Atlantic ice. It might have been years upon its way. But why had it come so far north? His favourite theory was that the Atlantic ice-packs were not safe enough for heavy traffic further to the south.

One thing, however, he could not explain to his satisfaction. There had been no air reconnaissance; it was hard to believe that the art of flight had been lost so soon.

Sometimes he would walk along the ranks of books, whispering now and then to a well-loved volume. There were books here that he had not dared to open for years, they reminded him so poignantly of the past. But now as the days grew longer and brighter, he would some times take down a volume of poetry and re-read his old favourites. Then he would go to the tall windows and shout the magic words over the rooftops, as if they would break the spell that had gripped the world.

It was warmer now, as if the ghosts of lost summers had returned to haunt the land. For whole days the temperature rose above freezing, while in many places flowers were breaking through the snow. Whatever was approaching from the north was nearer, and several times a day that enigmatic roar would go thundering over the city, sending the snow sliding upon a thousand roofs. There were strange, grinding undertones that Professor Millward found baffling and even ominous. At times it was almost as if he were listening to the clash of mighty armies, and sometimes a mad but dreadful thought came into his mind and would not be dismissed. Often he would wake in the night and imagine he heard the sound of mountains moving to the sea.

So the summer wore away, and as the sound of that distant battle drew steadily nearer Professor Millward was the prey of ever more violently alternating hopes and fears. Although he saw no more wolves or bears – they seemed to have fled southward – he did not risk leaving the safety of his fortress. Every morning he would climb to the highest window of the tower and search the northern horizon with field-glasses. But all he ever saw was the stubborn retreat of the snows above Hampstead, as they fought their bitter rearguard action against the sun.

His vigil ended with the last days of the brief summer. The grinding thunder in the night had been nearer than ever before, but there was still nothing to hint at its real distance from the city. Professor Millward felt no premonition as he climbed to the narrow window and raised his binoculars to the northern sky.

As a watcher from the walls of some threatened fortress might have seen the first sunlight glinting on the spears of an advancing army, so in that moment Professor Millward knew the truth. The air was crystal-clear, and the hills were sharp and brilliant against the cold blue of the sky. They had lost almost all their snow. Once he would have rejoiced at that, but it meant nothing now.

Overnight, the enemy he had forgotten had conquered the last defences and was preparing for the final onslaught. As he saw that deadly glitter along the crest of the doomed hills, Professor Millward understood at last the sound he had heard advancing for so many months. It was little wonder he had dreamed of mountains on the march.

Out of the North, their ancient home, returning in triumph to the lands they had once possessed, the glaciers had come again.

Hide-and-Seek

First published in *Astounding Science-Fiction*, September 1949
Collected in *Expedition to Earth*

We were walking back through the woods when Kingman saw the grey squirrel. Our bag was a small but varied one – three grouse, four rabbits (one, I am sorry to say, an infant in arms) and a couple of pigeons. And contrary to certain dark forecasts, both the dogs were still alive.

The squirrel saw us at the same moment. It knew that it was marked for immediate execution as a result of the damage it had done to the trees on the estate, and perhaps it had lost close relatives to Kingman's gun. In three leaps it had reached the base of the nearest tree, and vanished behind it in a flicker of grey. We saw its face once more, appearing for a moment round the edge of its shield a dozen feet from the ground: but though we waited, with guns levelled hopefully at various branches, we never saw it again.

Kingman was very thoughtful as we walked back across the lawn to the magnificent old house. He said nothing as we handed our victims to the cook – who received them without much enthusiasm – and only emerged from his reverie when we were sitting in the smoking-room and he remembered his duties as a host.

'That tree-rat,' he said suddenly – he always called them 'tree-rats', on the grounds that people were too sentimental to shoot the dear little squirrels – 'it reminded me of a very peculiar experience that happened shortly before I retired. Very shortly indeed, in fact.'

'I thought it would,' said Carson dryly. I gave him a glare: he'd been in the Navy and had heard Kingman's stories before but they were still new to me.

'Of course,' Kingman remarked, slightly nettled, 'if you'd rather I didn't—'

'Do go on,' I said hastily. 'You've made me curious. What connection there can possibly be between a grey squirrel and the Second Jovian War I can't imagine.'

Kingman seemed mollified.

'I think I'd better change some names,' he said thoughtfully, 'but I won't alter the places. The story begins about a million kilometres sunwards of Mars—'

*

K.15 was a military intelligence operative. It gave him considerable pain when unimaginative people called him a spy but at the moment he had much more substantial grounds for complaint. For some days now a fast cruiser had been coming up astern, and though it was flattering to have the undivided attention of such a fine ship and so many highly trained men, it was an honour that K.15 would willingly have forgone.

What made the situation doubly annoying was the fact that his friends would be meeting him off Mars in about twelve hours, aboard a ship quite capable of dealing with a mere cruiser – from which you will gather that K.15 was a person of some importance. Unfortunately, the most optimistic calculation showed that the pursuers would be within accurate gun range in six hours. In some six hours five minutes, therefore, K.15 was likely to occupy an extensive and still expanding volume of space. There might just be time for him to land on Mars, but that would be one of the worst things he could do. It would certainly annoy the aggressively neutral Martians, and the political complications would be frightful. Moreover, if his friends *had* to come down to the planet to rescue him, it would cost them more than ten kilometres a second in fuel – most of their operational reserve.

He had only one advantage, and that a very dubious one. The commander of the cruiser might guess that he was heading for a rendezvous, but he would not know how close it was nor how large was the ship that was coming to meet him. If he could keep alive for only twelve hours, he would be safe. The 'if' was a somewhat considerable one.

K.15 looked moodily at his charts, wondering if it was worth while to burn the rest of his fuel in a final dash. But a dash to where? He would be completely helpless then, and the pursuing ship might still have enough in her tanks to catch him as he flashed outwards into the empty darkness, beyond all hope of rescue – passing his friends as they came sunwards at a relative speed so great that they could do nothing to save him.

With some people, the shorter the expectation of life, the more sluggish are the mental processes. They seem hypnotised by the approach of death, so resigned to their fate that they do nothing to avoid it. K.15, on the other hand, found that his mind worked better in such a desperate emergency. It began to work now as it had seldom done before.

Commander Smith – the name will do as well as any other – of the cruiser *Doradus* was not unduly surprised when K.15 began to decelerate. He had half-expected the spy to land on Mars, on the principle that internment was better than annihilation, but when the plotting-room brought the news that the little scout ship was heading for Phobos, he felt completely baffled. The inner moon was nothing but a jumble of rock some twenty kilometres across, and not even the economical Martians had ever found any use for it. K.15 must be pretty desperate if he thought it was going to be of any greater value to him.

The tiny scout had almost come to rest when the radar operator lost it against the mass of Phobos. During the braking manoeuvre, K.15 had squandered most of his lead and the *Doradus* was now only minutes away – though she was now beginning to decelerate lest she overrun him. The cruiser was scarcely three thousand kilometres from Phobos when she came to a complete halt: of K.15's ship there was still no sign. It should be easily visible in the telescopes, but it was probably on the far side of the little moon.

It reappeared only a few minutes later, travelling under full thrust on a course directly away from the Sun. It was accelerating at almost five gravities – and it had broken its radio silence. An automatic recorder was broadcasting over and over again this interesting message:

'I have landed on Phobos and am being attacked by a Z-class cruiser. Think I can hold out until you come, but hurry.'

The message wasn't even in code, and it left Commander Smith a sorely puzzled man. The assumption that K.15 was still aboard the ship and that the whole thing was a ruse was just a little too naive. But it might be a double-bluff: the message had obviously been left in plain language so that he would receive it and be duly confused. He could afford neither the time nor the fuel to chase the scout if K.15 really had landed. It was clear that reinforcements were on the way and the sooner he left the vicinity the better. The phrase 'Think I can hold out until you come' might be a piece of sheer impertinence, or it might mean that help was very near indeed.

Then K.15's ship stopped blasting. It had obviously exhausted its fuel, and was doing a little better than six kilometres a second away from the Sun. K.15 *must* have landed, for his ship was now speeding helplessly out of the Solar System. Commander Smith didn't like the message it was broadcasting, and guessed that it was running into the track of an approaching warship at some indefinite distance, but there was nothing to be done about that. The *Doradus* began to move towards Phobos, anxious to waste no time.

On the face of it, Commander Smith seemed the master of the situation. His ship was armed with a dozen heavy guided missiles and two turrets of electromagnetic guns. Against him was one man in a spacesuit, trapped on a moon only twenty kilometres across. It was not until Commander Smith had his first good look at Phobos, from a distance of less than a hundred kilometres, that he began to realise that, after all, K.15 might have a few cards up his sleeve.

To say that Phobos has a diameter of twenty kilometres, as the astronomy books invariably do, is highly misleading. The word 'diameter' implies a degree of symmetry which Phobos most certainly lacks. Like those other lumps of cosmic slag, the Asteroids, it is a shapeless mass of rock floating in space with, of course, no hint of an atmosphere and not much more gravity. It turns on its axis once every seven hours thirty-nine minutes, thus keeping the same face always to Mars – which is so close that appreciably less than half the planet is visible, the Poles being below the curve of the horizon. Beyond this, there is very little more to be said about Phobos.

*

K.15 had no time to enjoy the beauty of the crescent world filling the sky above him. He had thrown all the equipment he could carry out of the airlock, set the controls, and jumped. As the little ship went flaming out towards the stars he watched it go with feelings he did not care to analyse. He had burned his boats with a vengeance, and he could only hope that the oncoming battleship would intercept the radio message as the empty vessel went racing by into nothingness. There was also a faint possibility that the enemy cruiser might go in pursuit but that was rather too much to hope for.

He turned to examine his new home. The only light was the ochre radiance of Mars, since the Sun was below the horizon, but that was quite sufficient for his purpose and he could see very well. He stood in the centre of an irregular plain about two kilometres across, surrounded by low hills over which he could leap rather easily if he wished. There was a story he remembered reading long ago about a man who had accidentally jumped off Phobos: that wasn't quite possible – though it was on Deimos – as the escape velocity was still about ten metres a second. But unless he was careful, he might easily find himself at such a height that it would take hours to fall back to the surface – and that would be fatal. For K.15's plan was a simple one: he must remain as close to the surface of Phobos as possible – *and diametrically opposite the cruiser*. The *Doradus* could then fire all her armament against the twenty kilometres of rock, and he wouldn't even feel the concussion. There were only two serious dangers, and one of these did not worry him greatly.

To the layman, knowing nothing of the finer details of astronautics, the plan would have seemed quite suicidal. The *Doradus* was armed with the latest in ultra-scientific weapons: moreover, the twenty kilometres which separated her from her prey represented less than a second's flight at maximum speed. But Commander Smith knew better, and was already feeling rather unhappy. He realised, only too well, that of all the machines of transport man has ever invented, a cruiser of space is far and away the least manoeuvrable. It was a simple fact that K.15 could make half a dozen circuits of his little world while her commander was persuading the *Doradus* to do even one.

There is no need to go into technical details, but those who are still unconvinced might like to consider these elementary facts. A rocket-driven spaceship can, obviously, only accelerate along its major axis – that is, 'forwards'. Any deviation from a straight course demands a physical turning of the ship, so that the motors can blast in another direction. Everyone knows that this is done by internal gyros or tangential steering jets: but very few people know just how long this simple manoeuvre takes. The average cruiser, fully fuelled, has a mass of two or three thousand tons, which does not make for rapid footwork. But things are even worse than this, for it is not the mass, but the moment of inertia that matters here – and since a cruiser is a long, thin object, its moment of inertia is slightly colossal. The sad fact remains (though it is seldom mentioned by astronautical engineers) that it takes a good ten minutes to rotate a spaceship through 180 degrees, with gyros of any reasonable size. Control jets are not much quicker, and in any case their use is restricted because the rotation they produce is permanent and they are liable to leave the ship spinning like a slow-motion pin-wheel, to the annoyance of all inside.

In the ordinary way, these disadvantages are not very grave. One has millions of kilometres and hundreds of hours in which to deal with such minor matters as a change in the ship's orientation. It is definitely against the rules to move in ten-kilometre-radius circles, and the commander of the *Doradus* felt distinctly aggrieved. K.15 wasn't playing fair.

At the same moment that resourceful individual was taking stock of the situation, which might very well have been worse. He had reached the hills in three jumps and felt less naked than he had out in the open plain. The food and equipment he had taken from the ship he had hidden where he hoped he could find it again, but as his suit could keep him alive for over a day that was the least of his worries. The small packet that was the cause of all the trouble was still with him, in one of those numerous hiding places a well-designed spacesuit affords.

There was an exhilarating loneliness about his mountain eyrie, even though he was not quite as lonely as he would have wished. For ever fixed in his sky, Mars was waning almost visibly as Phobos swept above the night side of the planet. He could just make out the lights of some of the Martian cities, gleaming pin-points marking the junctions of the invisible canals. All else was stars and silence and a line of jagged peaks so close it seemed he could almost touch them. Of the *Doradus* there was still no sign. She was presumably carrying out a careful telescopic examination of the sunlit side of Phobos.

Mars was a very useful clock: when it was half-full the Sun would rise and, very probably, so would the *Doradus*. But she might approach from some quite unexpected quarter: she might even – and this was the one real danger – she might even have landed a search party.

This was the first possibility that had occurred to Commander Smith when he saw just what he was up against. Then he realised that the surface area of Phobos was over a thousand square kilometres and that he could not spare more than ten men from his crew to make a search of that jumbled wilderness. Also, K.15 would certainly be armed.

Considering the weapons which the *Doradus* carried, this last objection might seem singularly pointless. It was very far from being so. In the ordinary course of business, sidearms and other portable weapons are as much use to a space-cruiser as are cutlasses and crossbows. The *Doradus* happened, quite by chance – and against regulations at that – to carry one automatic pistol and a hundred rounds of ammunition. Any search party would therefore consist of a group of unarmed men looking for a well-concealed and very desperate individual who could pick them off at his leisure. K.15 was breaking the rules again.

The terminator of Mars was now a perfectly straight line, and at almost the same moment the Sun came up, not so much like thunder as like a salvo of atomic bombs. K.15 adjusted the filters of his visor and decided to move. It was safer to stay out of the sunlight, not only because he was less likely to be detected in the shadow but also because his eyes would be much more sensitive there. He had only a pair of binoculars to help him, whereas the *Doradus* would carry an electronic telescope of twenty centimetres aperture at least.

It would be best, K.15 decided, to locate the cruiser if he could. It might be a rash thing to do, but he would feel much happier when he knew exactly where she was and could watch her movements. He could then keep just below the horizon, and the glare of the rockets would give him ample warning of any impending move. Cautiously launching himself along an almost horizontal trajectory, he began the circumnavigation of his world.

The narrowing crescent of Mars sank below the horizon until only one vast horn reared itself enigmatically against the stars. K.15 began to feel worried: there was still no sign of the *Doradus*. But this was hardly surprising, for she was painted black as night and might be a good hundred kilometres away in space. He stopped, wondering if he had done the right thing after all. Then he noticed that something quite large was eclipsing the stars almost vertically overhead, and was moving swiftly even as he watched. His heart stopped for a moment: then he was himself again, analysing the situation and trying to discover how he had made so disastrous a mistake.

It was some time before he realised that the black shadow slipping across the sky was not the cruiser at all, but something almost equally deadly. It was far smaller, and far nearer, than he had at first thought. The *Doradus* had sent her television-homing guided missiles to look for him.

This was the second danger he had feared, and there was nothing he could do about it except to remain as inconspicuous as possible. The *Doradus* now had many eyes searching for him, but these auxiliaries had very severe limitations. They had been built to look for sunlit spaceships against a background of stars, not to search for a man hiding in a dark jungle of rock. The definition of their television systems was low, and they could only see in the forward direction.

There were rather more men on the chess-board now, and the game was a little deadlier, but his was still the advantage.

The torpedo vanished in the night sky. As it was travelling on a nearly straight course in this low-gravitational field, it would soon be leaving Phobos behind, and K.15 waited for what he knew must happen. A few minutes later, he saw a brief stabbing of rocket exhausts and guessed that the projectile was swinging slowly back on its course. At almost the same moment he saw another flare away in the opposite quarter of the sky and wondered just how many of these infernal machines were in action. From what he knew of Z-class cruisers – which was a good deal more than he should – there were four missile control channels, and they were probably all in use.

He was suddenly struck by an idea so brilliant that he was quite sure it could not possibly work. The radio on his suit was a tunable one, covering an unusually wide band, and somewhere not far away the *Doradus* was pumping out power on everything from a thousand megacycles upwards. He switched on the receiver and began to explore.

It came in quickly – the raucous whine of a pulse transmitter not far away. He was probably only picking up a sub-harmonic, but that was quite good enough. It D/F'ed sharply, and for the first time K.15 allowed himself to make long-range plans about the future. The *Doradus* had betrayed herself: as long as she operated her missiles, he would know exactly where she was.

He moved cautiously forward towards the transmitter. To his surprise the signal faded, then increased sharply again. This puzzled him until he realised that he must be moving through a diffraction zone. Its width might have told him something useful if he had been a good enough physicist, but he could not imagine what.

The *Doradus* was hanging about five kilometres above the surface in full sunlight. Her 'non-reflecting' paint was overdue for renewal, and K.15 could see her clearly. As he was still in darkness, and the shadow line was moving away from him, he decided that he was as safe here as anywhere. He settled down comfortably so that he could just see the cruiser and waited, feeling fairly certain that none of the guided projectiles would come so near the ship. By now, he calculated, the Commander of the *Doradus* must be getting pretty mad. He was perfectly correct.

After an hour, the cruiser began to heave herself round with all the grace of a bogged hippopotamus. K.15 guessed what was happening. Commander Smith was going to have a look at the antipodes, and was preparing for the perilous fifty-kilometre journey. He watched very carefully to see the orientation the ship was adopting, and when she came to rest again was relieved to see that she was almost broadside on to him. Then, with a series of jerks that could not have been very enjoyable aboard, the cruiser began to move down to the horizon. K.15 followed her at a comfortable walking pace – if one could use the phrase – reflecting that this was a feat very few people had ever performed. He was particularly careful not to overtake her on one of his kilometre-long glides, and kept a close watch for any missiles that might be coming up astern.

It took the *Doradus* nearly an hour to cover the fifty kilometres. This, as K.15 amused himself by calculating, represented considerably less than a thousandth of her normal speed. Once, she found herself going off into space at a tangent, and rather than waste time turning end over end again fired off a salvo of shells to reduce speed. But she made it at last, and K.15 settled down for another vigil, wedged between two rocks where he could just see the cruiser and he was quite sure she could not see him. It occurred to him that by this time Commander Smith might have great doubts as to whether he really was on Phobos at all, and he felt like firing off a signal flare to reassure him. However, he resisted the temptation.

There would be little point in describing the events of the next ten hours, since they differed in no important detail from those that had gone before. The *Doradus* made three other moves, and K.15 stalked her with the care of the big-game hunter following the spoor of some elephantine beast. Once, when she would have led him out into full sunlight, he let her fall below the horizon until he could only just pick up her signals. But most of the time he kept her just visible, usually low down behind some convenient hill.

Once a torpedo exploded some kilometres away, and K.15 guessed that some exasperated operator had seen a shadow he did not like – or else that a technician had forgotten to switch off a proximity fuse. Otherwise nothing happened to enliven the proceedings: in fact the whole affair was becoming rather boring. He almost welcomed the sight of an occasional guided missile drifting inquisitively overhead, for he did not believe that they could see him if he remained motionless and in reasonable cover. If he could have stayed on the part of Phobos exactly opposite the cruiser he would have been safe even from these, he realised, since the ship would have no control there in the Moon's radio-shadow. But he could think of no reliable way in which he could be sure of staying in the safety zone if the cruiser moved again.

The end came very abruptly. There was a sudden blast of steering-jets, and the cruiser's main drive burst forth in all its power and splendour. In seconds the *Doradus* was shrinking sunwards, free at last, thankful to leave, even in defeat, this miserable lump of rock that had so annoyingly baulked her of her legitimate prey. K.15 knew what had happened, and a great sense of peace and relaxation swept over him. In the radar room of the cruiser, someone had seen an echo of disconcerting amplitude approaching with altogether excessive speed. K.15 now had only to switch on his suit beacon and to wait. He could even afford the luxury of a cigarette.

'Quite an interesting story,' I said, 'and I see now how it ties up with that squirrel. But it does raise one or two queries in my mind.'

'Indeed?' said Rupert Kingman politely.

I always like to get to the bottom of things, and I knew that my host had played a part in the Jovian War about which he seldom spoke. I decided to risk a long shot in the dark.

'May I ask how you happen to know so much about this unorthodox military engagement? It isn't possible, is it, that *you* were K.15?'

There was an odd sort of strangling noise from Carson. Then Kingman said, quite calmly: 'No, I wasn't.'

He got to his feet and went off towards the gun-room.

'If you'll excuse me a moment, I'm going to have another shot at that tree-rat. Maybe I'll get him this time.' Then he was gone.

Carson looked at me as if to say: 'This is another house you'll never be invited to again.' When our host was out of earshot he remarked in a coldly clinical voice:

'You've torn it. What did you have to say that for?'

'Well, it seemed a safe guess. How else could he have known all that?'

'As a matter of fact, I believe he met K.15 after the War: they must have had an interesting conversation together. But I thought you knew that Rupert was retired from the Service with only the rank of Lieutenant-Commander. The Court of Inquiry could never see his point of view. After all, it just wasn't reasonable that the Commander of the fastest ship in the Fleet couldn't catch a man in a spacesuit.'

Breaking Strain

First published in *Thrilling Wonder Stories*, December 1949, as 'Thirty Seconds –
Thirty Days'
Collected in *Expedition to Earth*

Originally published in *Thrilling Wonder Stories* under the title 'Thirty Seconds
– Thirty Days', 'Breaking Strain' was one of the stories incorporated into the
film and novel, *2001*.

Grant was writing up the *Star Queen*'s log when he heard the cabin door
opening behind him. He didn't bother to look round – it was hardly
necessary, for there was only one other man aboard the ship. But when
nothing happened, and when McNeil neither spoke nor came into the
room, the long silence finally roused Grant's curiosity and he swung the
seat round in its gimbals.

McNeil was just standing in the doorway, looking as if he had seen a
ghost. The trite metaphor flashed into Grant's mind instantly. He did not
know for a moment how near the truth it was. In a sense McNeil *had* seen
a ghost – the most terrifying of all ghosts – his own.

'What's the matter?' said Grant angrily. 'You sick or something?'

The engineer shook his head. Grant noticed the little beads of sweat that
broke away from his forehead and went glittering across the room on their
perfectly straight trajectories. His throat muscles moved, but for a while no
sound came. It looked as if he were going to cry.

'We're done for,' he whispered at last. 'Oxygen reserve's gone.'

Then he did cry. He looked like a flabby doll, slowly collapsing on
itself. He couldn't fall for there was no gravity, so he just folded up in
mid-air.

Grant said nothing. Quite unconsciously he rammed his smouldering
cigarette into the ash-tray, grinding it viciously until the last tiny spark had
died. Already the air seemed to be thickening around him as the oldest
terror of the spaceways gripped him by the throat.

He slowly loosed the elastic straps, which, while he was seated, gave
some illusion of weight and with an automatic skill launched himself
towards the doorway. McNeil did not offer to follow. Even making every
allowance for the shock he had undergone, Grant felt he was behaving very

169

badly. He gave the engineer an angry cuff as he passed and told him to snap out of it.

The hold was a large hemispherical room with a thick central column which carried the controls and cabling to the other half of the dumb-bell-shaped spaceship a hundred metres away. It was packed with crates and boxes arranged in a surrealistic three-dimensional array that made very few concessions to gravity.

But even if the cargo had suddenly vanished Grant would scarcely have noticed. He had eyes only for the big oxygen-tank, taller than himself, which was bolted against the wall near the inner door of the airlock.

It was just as he had last seen it, gleaming with aluminium paint, and the metal sides still held the faint touch of coldness that gave the only hint of their contents. All the piping seemed in perfect condition. There was no sign of anything wrong apart from one minor detail. The needle of the contents gauge lay mutely against the zero stop.

Grant gazed at that silent symbol as a man in ancient London returning home one evening at the time of the Plague might have stared at a rough cross newly scrawled upon his door. Then he banged half a dozen times on the glass in the futile hope that the needle had stuck – though he never really doubted its message. News that is sufficiently bad somehow carries its own guarantee of truth. Only good reports need confirmation.

When Grant got back to the control-room, McNeil was himself again. A glance at the opened medicine chest showed the reason for the engineer's rapid recovery. He even essayed a faint attempt at humour.

'It was a meteor,' he said. 'They tell us a ship this size should get hit once a century. We seem to have jumped the gun with ninety-five years still to go.'

'But what about the alarms? The air pressure's normal – how could we have been holed?'

'We weren't,' McNeil replied. 'You know how the oxygen circulates night-side through the refrigerating coils to keep it liquid? The meteor must have smashed them and the stuff simply boiled away.'

Grant was silent, collecting his thoughts. What had happened was serious – deadly serious – but it need not be fatal. After all, the voyage was more than three-quarters over.

'Surely the regenerator can keep the air breathable, even if it does get pretty thick?' he asked hopefully.

McNeil shook his head. 'I've not worked it out in detail, but I know the answer. When the carbon dioxide is broken down and the free oxygen gets cycled back, there's a loss of about ten per cent. That's why we have to carry a reserve.'

'The spacesuits!' cried Grant in sudden excitement. 'What about their tanks?'

He had spoken without thinking, and the immediate realisation of his mistake left him feeling worse than before.

'We can't keep oxygen in them – it would boil off in a few days. There's enough compressed gas there for about thirty minutes – merely long enough for you to get to the main tank in an emergency.'

'There must be a way out – even if we have to jettison cargo and run for it. Let's stop guessing and work out exactly where we are.'

Grant was as much angry as frightened. He was angry with McNeil for breaking down. He was angry with the designers of the ship for not having seen this God-knew-how-many-million-to-one chance. The deadline might be a couple of weeks away and a lot could happen before then. The thought helped for a moment to keep his fears at arm's length.

This was an emergency, beyond a doubt, but it was one of those peculiarly protracted emergencies that seem to happen only in space. There was plenty of time to think – perhaps too much time.

Grant strapped himself in the pilot's seat and pulled out a writing-pad.

'Let's get the facts right,' he said with artificial calmness. 'We've got the air that's still circulating in the ship and we lose ten per cent of the oxygen every time it goes through the regenerator. Chuck me over the Manual, will you? I never remember how many cubic metres we use a day.'

In saying that the *Star Queen* might expect to be hit by a meteor once every century, McNeil had grossly but unavoidably over-simplified the problem. For the answer depended on so many factors that three generations of statisticians had done little but lay down rules so vague that the insurance companies still shivered with apprehension when the great meteor showers went sweeping like a gale through the orbits of the inner worlds.

Everything depends, of course, on what one means by the word meteor. Each lump of cosmic slag that reaches the surface of the Earth has a million smaller brethren who perish utterly in the no-man's-land where the atmosphere has not quite ended and space has yet to begin – that ghostly region where the weird Aurora sometimes walks by night.

These are the familiar shooting stars, seldom larger than a pin's head, and these in turn are outnumbered a million-fold again by particles too small to leave any visible trace of their dying as they drift down from the sky. All of them, the countless specks of dust, the rare boulders and even the wandering mountains that Earth encounters perhaps once every million years – all of them are meteors.

For the purposes of space-flight, a meteor is only of interest if, on penetrating the hull of a ship, it leaves a hole large enough to be dangerous. This is a matter of relative speeds as well as size. Tables have been prepared showing approximate collision times for various parts of the Solar System – and for various sizes of meteors down to masses of a few milligrams.

That which had struck the *Star Queen* was a giant, being nearly a centimetre across and weighing all of ten grams. According to the tables the waiting time for collision with such a monster was of the order of ten to the ninth days – say three million years. The virtual certainty that such an occurrence would not happen again in the course of human history gave Grant and McNeil very little consolation.

However, things might have been worse. The *Star Queen* was 115 days on her orbit and had only thirty still to go. She was travelling, as did all freighters, on the long tangential ellipse kissing the orbits of Earth and Venus on opposite sides of the Sun. The fast liners could cut across from planet to planet at three times her speed – and ten times her fuel consumption – but she must plod along her predetermined track like a street-car, taking 145 days, more or less, for each journey.

Anything more unlike the early-twentieth-century idea of a spaceship than the *Star Queen* would be hard to imagine. She consisted of two spheres, one fifty and the other twenty metres in diameter, joined by a cylinder about a hundred metres long. The whole structure looked like a matchstick-and-plasticine model of a hydrogen atom. Crew, cargo and controls were in the larger sphere, while the smaller one held the atomic motors and was – to put it mildly – out of bounds to living matter.

The *Star Queen* had been built in space and could never have lifted herself even from the surface of the Moon. Under full power her ion drive could produce an acceleration of a twentieth of a gravity, which in an hour would give her all the velocity she needed to change from a satellite of the Earth to one of Venus.

Hauling cargo up from the planets was the job of the powerful little chemical rockets. In a month the tugs would be climbing up from Venus to meet her, but the *Star Queen* would not be stopping for there would be no one at the controls. She would continue blindly on her orbit, speeding past Venus at miles per second – and five months later she would be back at the orbit of the Earth, though Earth herself would then be far away.

It is surprising how long it takes to do a simple addition when your life depends on the answer. Grant ran down the short column of figures half a dozen times before he finally gave up hope that the total would change. Then he sat doodling nervously on the white plastic of the pilot's desk.

'With all possible economies,' he said, 'we can last about twenty days. That means we'll be ten days out of Venus when—' His voice trailed off into silence.

Ten days didn't sound much – but it might just as well have been ten years. Grant thought sardonically of all the hack adventure writers who had used just this situation in their stories and radio serials. In these circumstances, according to the carbon-copy experts – few of whom had ever gone beyond the Moon – there were three things that could happen.

The proper solution – which had become almost a cliché – was to turn the ship into a glorified greenhouse or a hydroponics farm and let photosynthesis do the rest. Alternatively one could perform prodigies of chemical or atom engineering – explained in tedious technical detail – and build an oxygen-manufacturing plant which would not only save your life – and of

172

course the heroine's – but would also make you the owner of fabulously valuable patents. The third or *deus ex machina* solution was the arrival of a convenient spaceship which happened to be matching your course and velocity exactly.

But that was fiction and things were different in real life. Although the first idea was sound in theory there wasn't even a packet of grass-seed aboard the *Star Queen*. As for feats of inventive engineering, two men – however brilliant and however desperate – were not likely to improve in a few days on the work of scores of great industrial research organisations over a full century.

The spaceship that 'happened to be passing' was, almost by definition, impossible. Even if other freighters had been coasting on the same elliptic path – and Grant knew there were none – then by the very laws that governed their movements they would always keep their original separations. It was not quite impossible that a liner, racing on its hyperbolic orbit, might pass within a few hundred thousand kilometres of them – but at a speed so great that it would be as inaccessible as Pluto.

'If we threw out the cargo,' said McNeil at last, 'would we have a chance of changing our orbit?'

Grant shook his head.

'I'd hoped so,' he replied, 'but it won't work. We could reach Venus in a week if we wished – but we'd have no fuel for braking and nothing from the planet could catch us as we went past.'

'Not even a liner?'

'According to *Lloyd's Register* Venus has only a couple of freighters at the moment. In any case it would be a practically impossible manoeuvre. Even if it could match our speed, how would the rescue ship get back? It would need about fifty kilometres a second for the whole job!'

'If we can't figure a way out,' said McNeil, 'maybe someone on Venus can. We'd better talk to them.'

'I'm going to,' Grant replied, 'as soon as I've decided what to say. Go and get the transmitter aligned, will you?'

He watched McNeil as he floated out of the room. The engineer was probably going to give trouble in the days that lay ahead. Until now they had got on well enough – like most stout men McNeil was good-natured and easygoing. But now Grant realised that he lacked fibre. He had become too flabby – physically and mentally – through living too long in space.

A buzzer sounded on the transmitter switchboard. The parabolic mirror out on the hull was aimed at the gleaming arc-lamp of Venus, only ten million kilometres away and moving on an almost parallel path. The three-millimetre waves from the ship's transmitter would make the trip in little more than half a minute. There was bitterness in the knowledge that they were only thirty seconds from safety.

The automatic monitor on Venus gave its impersonal *Go ahead* signal and Grant began to talk steadily and, he hoped, quite dispassionately. He gave a careful analysis of the situation and ended with a request for advice. His fears concerning McNeil he left unspoken. For one thing he knew that the engineer would be monitoring him at the transmitter.

As yet no one on Venus would have heard the message, even though the transmitter time lag was over. It would still be coiled up in the recorder spools, but in a few minutes an unsuspecting signals officer would arrive to play it over.

He would have no idea of the bomb-shell that was about to burst, triggering trains of sympathetic ripples on all the inhabited worlds as television and news-sheet took up the refrain. An accident in space has a dramatic quality that crowds all other items from the headlines.

Until now Grant had been too preoccupied with his own safety to give much thought to the cargo in his charge. A sea-captain of ancient times, whose first thought was for his ship, might have been shocked by this attitude. Grant, however, had reason on his side.

The *Star Queen* could never founder, could never run upon uncharted rocks or pass silently, as many ships have passed, for ever from the knowledge of man. She was safe, whatever might befall her crew. If she was undisturbed she would continue to retrace her orbit with such precision that men might set their calendars by her for centuries to come.

The cargo, Grant suddenly remembered, was insured for over twenty million dollars. There were not many goods valuable enough to be shipped from world to world and most of the crates in the hold were worth more than their weight – or rather their mass – in gold. Perhaps some items might be useful in this emergency and Grant went to the safe to find the loading schedule.

He was sorting the thin, tough sheets when McNeil came back into the cabin.

'I've been reducing the air pressure,' he said. 'The hull shows some leaks that wouldn't have mattered in the usual way.'

Grant nodded absently as he passed a bundle of sheets over to McNeil.

'Here's our loading schedule. I suggest we both run through it in case there's anything in the cargo that may help.'

If it did nothing else, he might have added, it would at least give them something to occupy their minds.

As he ran down the long columns of numbered items – a complete cross-section of interplanetary commerce – Grant found himself wondering what lay behind these inanimate symbols. *Item 347 – 1 book – 4 kilos gross.*

He whistled as he noticed that it was a starred item, insured for a hundred thousand dollars, and he suddenly remembered hearing on the radio that the Hesperian Museum had just bought a first edition *Seven Pillars of Wisdom*.

A few sheets later was a very contrasting item, *Miscellaneous books – 25 kilos – no intrinsic value.*

It had cost a small fortune to ship those books to Venus, yet they were of 'no intrinsic value'. Grant let his imagination loose on the problem. Perhaps someone who was leaving Earth for ever was taking with him to a new world his most cherished treasures – the dozen or so volumes that above all others had most shaped his mind.

Item 564 – 12 reels film.

That, of course, would be the Neronian super-epic, *While Rome Burns*, which had left Earth just one jump ahead of the censor. Venus was waiting for it with considerable impatience.

Medical supplies – 50 kilos. Case of cigars – 1 kilo. Precision instruments – 75 kilos. So the list went on. Each item was something rare or something which the industry and science of a younger civilisation could not yet produce.

The cargo was sharply divided into two classes – blatant luxury or sheer necessity. There was little in between. And there was nothing, nothing at all, which gave Grant the slightest hope. He did not see how it could have been otherwise, but that did not prevent him from feeling a quite unreasonable disappointment.

The reply from Venus, when it came at last, took nearly an hour to run through the recorder. It was a questionnaire so detailed that Grant wondered morosely it he'd live long enough to answer it. Most of the queries were technical ones concerning the ship. The experts on two planets were pooling their brains in the attempt to save the *Star Queen* and her cargo.

'Well, what do you think of it?' Grant asked McNeil when the other had finished running through the message. He was watching the engineer carefully for any further sign of strain.

There was a long pause before McNeil spoke. Then he shrugged his shoulders and his first words were an echo of Grant's own thoughts.

'It will certainly keep us busy. I won't be able to do all these tests in under a day. I can see what they're driving at most of the time, but some of the questions are just crazy.'

Grant had suspected that, but said nothing as the other continued.

'Rate of hull leakage – that's sensible enough, but why should anyone want to know the efficiency of our radiation screening? I think they're trying to keep up our morale by pretending they have some bright ideas – or else they want to keep us too busy to worry.'

Grant was relieved and yet annoyed by McNeil's calmness – relieved because he had been afraid of another scene and annoyed because McNeil was not fitting at all neatly into the mental category he had prepared for him. Was that first momentary lapse typical of the man or might it have happened to anyone?

Grant, to whom the world was very much a place for blacks and whites, felt angry at being unable to decide whether McNeil was cowardly or courageous. That he might be both was a possibility that never occurred to him.

There is a timelessness about space-flight that is unmatched by any other experience of man. Even on the Moon there are shadows that creep sluggishly from crag to crag as the sun makes his slow march across the sky. Earthwards there is always the great clock of the spinning globe, marking the hours with continents for hands. But on a long voyage in a gyro-stabilised ship the same patterns of sunlight lie unmoving on wall or floor as the chronometer ticks off its meaningless hours and days.

Grant and McNeil had long since learned to regulate their lives accordingly. In deep space they moved and thought with a leisureliness that would vanish quickly enough when a voyage was nearing its end and the time for braking manoeuvres had arrived. Though they were now under sentence of death they continued along the well-worn grooves of habit.

Every day Grant carefully wrote up the log, checked the ship's position and carried out his various routine duties. McNeil was also behaving normally as far as could be told, though Grant suspected that some of the technical maintenance was being carried out with a very light hand.

It was now three days since the meteor had struck. For the last twenty-four hours Earth and Venus had been in conference and Grant wondered when he would hear the result of their deliberations. He did not believe that even the finest technical brains in the Solar System could save them now, but it was hard to abandon hope when everything still seemed so normal and the air was still clean and fresh.

On the fourth day Venus spoke again. Shorn of its technicalities, the message was nothing more nor less than a funeral oration. Grant and McNeil had been written off, but they were given elaborate instructions concerning the safety of the cargo.

Back on Earth the astronomers were computing all the possible rescue orbits that might make contact with the *Star Queen* in the next few years. There was even a chance that she might be reached from Earth six or seven months later, when she was back at aphelion, but the manoeuvre could only be carried out by a fast liner with no payload and would cost a fortune in fuel.

McNeil vanished soon after this message came through. At first Grant was a little relieved. If McNeil chose to look after himself that was his own affair. Besides there were various letters to write – though the last-will-and-testament business could come later.

It was McNeil's turn to prepare the 'evening' meal, a duty he enjoyed for he took good care of his stomach. When the usual sounds from the gallery were not forthcoming Grant went in search of his crew.

He found McNeil lying in his bunk, very much at peace with the Universe. Hanging in the air beside him was a large metal crate which had been roughly forced open. Grant had no need to examine it closely to guess its contents. A glance at McNeil was enough.

'It's a dirty shame,' said the engineer without a trace of embarrassment, 'to suck this stuff up through a tube. Can't you put on some "go" so that we can drink it properly?'

Grant stared at him with angry contempt, but McNeil returned his gaze unabashed.

'Oh, don't be a sourpuss! Have some yourself – what does it matter now?'

He pushed across a bottle and Grant fielded it deftly as it floated by. It was a fabulously valuable wine – he remembered the consignment now – and the contents of that small crate must be worth thousands.

'I don't think there's any need,' said Grant severely, 'to behave like a pig – even in these circumstances.'

McNeil wasn't drunk yet. He had only reached the brightly lit anteroom of intoxication and not lost all contact with the drab outer world.

'I am prepared,' he said with great solemnity, 'to listen to any good argument against my present course of action – a course which seems eminently sensible to me. But you'd better convince me quickly while I'm still amenable to reason.'

He pressed the plastic bulb again and a purple jet shot into his mouth.

'Apart from the fact that you're stealing Company property which will certainly be salvaged sooner or later – you can hardly stay drunk for several weeks.'

'That,' said McNeil thoughtfully, 'remains to be seen.'

'I don't think so,' retorted Grant. Bracing himself against the wall he gave the crate a vicious shove that sent it flying through the open doorway.

As he dived after it and slammed the door he heard McNeil shout, 'Well, of all the dirty tricks!'

It would take the engineer some time – particularly in his present condition – to unbuckle himself and follow. Grant steered the crate back to the hold and locked the door. As there was never any need to lock the hold when the ship was in space McNeil wouldn't have a key for it himself and Grant could hide the duplicate that was kept in the control cabin.

McNeil was singing when, some time later, Grant went back past his room. He still had a couple of bottles for company and was shouting:

'We don't care *where* the oxygen goes
If it doesn't get into the wine . . .'

Grant, whose education had been severely technical, couldn't place the quotation. As he paused to listen he suddenly found himself shaken by an emotion which, to do him justice, he did not for a moment recognise.

It passed as swiftly as it had come, leaving him sick and trembling. For the first time, he realised that his dislike of McNeil was slowly turning to hatred.

It is a fundamental rule of space-flight that, for sound psychological reasons, the minimum crew on a long journey shall consist of not less than three men.

But rules are made to be broken and the *Star Queen*'s owners had obtained full authority from the Board of Space Control and the insurance companies when the freighter set off for Venus without her regular captain.

At the last moment he had been taken ill and there was no replacement. Since the planets are disinclined to wait upon man and his affairs, if she did not sail on time she would not sail at all.

Millions of dollars were involved – so she sailed. Grant and McNeil were both highly capable men and they had no objection at all to earning double their normal pay for very little extra work. Despite fundamental differences in temperament, they got on well enough in ordinary circumstances. It was nobody's fault that circumstances were now very far from ordinary.

Three days without food, it is said, is long enough to remove most of the subtle differences between a civilised man and a savage. Grant and McNeil were still in no physical discomfort. But their imaginations had been only too active and they now had more in common with two hungry Pacific Islanders in a lost canoe than either would have cared to admit.

For there was one aspect of the situation, and that the most important of all, which had never been mentioned. When the last figures on Grant's writing-pad had been checked and rechecked, the calculation was still not quite complete. Instantly each man had made the one further step, each had arrived simultaneously at the same unspoken result.

It was terribly simple – a macabre parody of those problems in first-year arithmetic that begin, 'If six men take two days to assemble five helicopters, how long . . .'

The oxygen would last *two* men for about twenty days, and Venus was thirty days away. One did not have to be a calculating prodigy to see at once that one man, and one man only, might yet live to walk the metal streets of Port Hesperus.

The acknowledged deadline was twenty days ahead, but the unmentioned one was only ten days off. Until that time there would still be enough air for two men – and thereafter for one man only for the rest of the voyage. To a sufficiently detached observer the situation would have been very entertaining.

It was obvious that the conspiracy of silence could not last much longer. But it is not easy, even at the best of times, for two people to decide amicably which one of them shall commit suicide. It is still more difficult when they are no longer on speaking terms.

Grant wished to be perfectly fair. Therefore the only thing to do was to wait until McNeil sobered up and then to put the question to him frankly. He could think best at his desk, so he went to the control cabin and strapped himself down in the pilot's chair.

For a while he stared thoughtfully into nothingness. It would be better, he decided, to broach the matter by correspondence, especially while diplomatic relations were in their present state. He clipped a sheet of note-paper on the writing-pad and began, *'Dear McNeil—'* Then he tore it out and started again, 'McNeil—'

It took him the best part of three hours and even then he wasn't wholly satisfied. There were some things it was so darned difficult to put down on paper. But at last he managed to finish.

He sealed the letter and locked it away in his safe. It could wait for a day or two.

*

Few of the waiting millions on Earth and Venus could have had any idea of the tensions that were slowly building up aboard the *Star Queen*. For days press and radio had been full of fantastic rescue schemes. On three worlds there was hardly any other topic of conversation. But only the faintest echo of the planet-wide tumult reached the two men who were its cause.

At any time the station on Venus could speak to the *Star Queen*, but there was so little that could be said. One could not with any decency give words of encouragement to men in the condemned cell, even when there was some slight uncertainty about the actual date of execution.

So Venus contented itself with a few routine messages every day and blocked the steady scream of exhortations and newspaper offers that came pouring in from Earth. As a result private radio companies on Earth made frantic attempts to contact the *Star Queen* directly. They failed, simply because it never occurred to Grant and McNeil to focus their receiver anywhere except on Venus, now so tantalisingly near at hand.

There had been an embarrassing interlude when McNeil emerged from his cabin, but though relations were not particularly cordial, life aboard the *Star Queen* continued much as before.

Grant spent most of his waking hours in the pilot's position, calculating approach manoeuvres and writing interminable letters to his wife. He could have spoken to her had he wished, but the thought of all those millions of waiting ears had prevented him from doing so. Interplanetary speech circuits were supposed to be private – but too many people would be interested in this one.

In a couple of days, Grant assured himself, he would hand his letter to McNeil and they could decide what was to be done. Such a delay would also give McNeil a chance of raising the subject himself. That he might have other reasons for his hesitation was something Grant's conscious mind still refused to admit.

He often wondered how McNeil was spending his time. The engineer had a large library of microfilm books, for he read widely and his range of interests was unusual. His favourite book, Grant knew, was *Jurgen*, and perhaps even now he was trying to forget his doom by losing himself in its strange magic. Others of McNeil's books were less respectable and not a few were of the class curiously described as 'curious'.

The truth of the matter was that McNeil was far too subtle and complicated a personality for Grant to understand. He was a hedonist and enjoyed the pleasures of life all the more for being cut off from them for months at a time. But he was by no means the moral weakling that the unimaginative and somewhat puritanical Grant had supposed.

It was true that he had collapsed completely under the initial shock and that his behaviour over the wine was – by Grant's standards – reprehensible. But McNeil had had his breakdown and had recovered. Therein lay the difference between him and the hard but brittle Grant.

Though the normal routine of duties had been resumed by tacit consent, it did little to reduce the sense of strain. Grant and McNeil avoided each other as far as possible except when mealtimes brought them together. When they did meet, they behaved with an exaggerated politeness as if each were striving to be perfectly normal – and inexplicably failing.

Grant had hoped that McNeil would himself broach the subject of suicide, thus sparing him a very awkward duty. When the engineer stubbornly refused to do anything of the sort it added to Grant's resentment and contempt. To make matters worse he was now suffering from nightmares and sleeping very badly.

The nightmare was always the same. When he was a child it had often happened that at bedtime he had been reading a story far too exciting to be left until morning. To avoid detection he had continued reading under the bedclothes by flashlight, curled up in a snug white-walled cocoon. Every ten minutes or so the air had become too stifling to breathe and his emergence into the delicious cool air had been a major part of the fun.

Now, thirty years later, these innocent childhood hours returned to haunt him. He was dreaming that he could not escape from the suffocating sheets while the air was steadily and remorselessly thickening around him.

He had intended to give McNeil the letter after two days, yet somehow he put it off again. This procrastination was very unlike Grant, but he managed to persuade himself that it was a perfectly reasonable thing to do.

He was giving McNeil a chance to redeem himself – to prove that he wasn't a coward by raising the matter himself. That McNeil might be waiting for him to do exactly the same thing somehow never occurred to Grant.

The all-too-literal deadline was only five days off when, for the first time, Grant's mind brushed lightly against the thought of murder. He had been sitting after the 'evening' meal trying to relax as McNeil clattered around in the galley with, he considered, quite unnecessary noise.

What use, he asked himself, was the engineer to the world? He had no responsibilities and no family – no one would be any the worse off for his death. Grant, on the other hand, had a wife and three children of whom he was moderately fond, though for some obscure reason they responded with little more than dutiful affection.

Any impartial judge would have no difficulty in deciding which of them should survive. If McNeil had a spark of decency in him he would have come to the same conclusion already. Since he appeared to have done nothing of the sort he had forfeited all further claims to consideration.

Such was the elemental logic of Grant's subconscious mind, which had arrived at its answer days before but had only now succeeded in attracting the attention for which it had been clamouring. To Grant's credit he at once rejected the thought with horror.

He was an upright and honourable person with a very strict code of behaviour. Even the vagrant homicidal impulses of what is misleadingly called 'normal' man had seldom ruffled his mind. But in the days – the very few days – left to him, they would come more and more often.

180

The air had now become noticeably fouler. Though there was still no real difficulty in breathing, it was a constant reminder of what lay ahead, and Grant found that it was keeping him from sleep. This was not pure loss, as it helped to break the power of his nightmares, but he was becoming physically run down.

His nerve was also rapidly deteriorating, a state of affairs accentuated by the fact that McNeil seemed to be behaving with unexpected and annoying calmness. Grant realised that he had come to the stage when it would be dangerous to delay the showdown any longer.

McNeil was in his room as usual when Grant went up to the control cabin to collect the letter he had locked away in the safe – it seemed a lifetime ago. He wondered if he need add anything more to it. Then he realised that this was only another excuse for delay. Resolutely he made his way towards McNeil's cabin.

A single neutron begins the chain-reaction that in an instant can destroy a million lives and the toil of generations. Equally insignificant and unimportant are the trigger-events which can sometimes change a man's course of action and so alter the whole pattern of his future.

Nothing could have been more trivial than that which made Grant pause in the corridor outside McNeil's room. In the ordinary way he would not even have noticed it. It was the smell of smoke – tobacco smoke.

The thought that the sybaritic engineer had so little self-control that he was squandering the last precious litres of oxygen in such a manner filled Grant with blinding fury. He stood for a moment quite paralysed with the intensity of his emotion.

Then slowly he crumpled the letter in his hand. The thought which had first been an unwelcomed intruder, then a casual speculation, was at last fully accepted. McNeil had had his chance and had proved, by his unbelievable selfishness, unworthy of it. Very well – he should die.

The speed with which Grant had arrived at this conclusion would not have deceived the most amateurish of psychologists. It was relief as much as hatred that drove him away from McNeil's room. He had wanted to convince himself that there would be no need to do the honourable thing, to suggest some game of chance that would give them each an equal probability of life.

This was the excuse he needed, and he had seized upon it to salve his conscience. For though he might plan and even carry out a murder, Grant was the sort of person who would have to do it according to his own particular moral code.

As it happened he was – not for the first time – badly misjudging McNeil. The engineer was a heavy smoker and tobacco was quite essential to his mental well-being even in normal circumstances. How much more essential it was now, Grant, who only smoked occasionally and without much enjoyment, could never have appreciated.

McNeil had satisfied himself by careful calculation that four cigarettes a day would make no measurable difference whatsoever to the ship's oxygen endurance whereas they would make all the difference in the world to his own nerves and hence indirectly to Grant's.

But it was no use explaining this to Grant. So he had smoked in private and with a self-control he found agreeably, almost voluptuously, surprising. It was sheer bad luck that Grant had detected one of the day's four cigarettes.

For a man who had only at that moment talked himself into murder, Grant's actions were remarkably methodical. Without hesitation, he hurried back to the control room and opened the medicine chest with its neatly labelled compartments, designed for almost every emergency that could occur in space.

Even the ultimate emergency had been considered, for there behind its retaining elastic bands was the tiny bottle he had been seeking, the image of which through all these days had been lying hidden far down in the unknown depths of his mind. It wore a white label carrying a skull-and-cross-bones, and beneath them the words: *Approx. one-half gram will cause painless and almost instantaneous death.*

The poison was painless and instantaneous – that was good. But even more important was a fact unmentioned on the label. It was also tasteless.

The contrast between the meals prepared by Grant and those organised with considerable skill and care by McNeil was striking. Anyone who was fond of food and who spent a good deal of his life in space usually learned the art of cooking in self-defence. McNeil had done this long ago.

To Grant, on the other hand, eating was one of those necessary but annoying jobs which had to be got through as quickly as possible. His cooking reflected this opinion. McNeil had ceased to grumble about it, but he would have been very interested in the trouble Grant was taking over this particular meal.

If he noticed any increasing nervousness on Grant's part as the meal progressed, he said nothing. They ate almost in silence but that was not unusual for they had long since exhausted most of the possibilities of light conversation. When the last dishes – deep bowls with inturned rims to prevent the contents drifting out – had been cleared away, Grant went into the galley to prepare the coffee.

He took rather a long time, for at the last moment something quite maddening and quite ridiculous happened. He suddenly recalled one of the film classics of the last century in which the fabulous Charlie Chaplin tried to poison an unwanted wife – and then accidentally changed the glasses.

No memory could have been more unwelcome, for it left him shaken with a gust of silent hysteria. Poe's *Imp of the Perverse*, that demon who delights in defying the careful canons of self-preservation, was at work and it was a good minute before Grant could regain his self-control.

He was sure that, outwardly at least, he was quite calm as he carried in the two plastic containers and their drinking-tubes. There was no danger of confusing them, for the engineer's had the letters MAC painted boldly across it.

At the thought Grant nearly relapsed into those psychopathic giggles again, but just managed to regain control with the sombre reflection that his nerves must be in even worse condition than he had imagined.

He watched, fascinated, though without appearing to do so, as McNeil toyed with his cup. The engineer seemed in no great hurry and was staring moodily into space. Then he put his lips to the drinking tube and sipped.

A moment later he spluttered slightly – and an icy hand seemed to seize Grant's heart and hold it tight. Then McNeil turned to him and said evenly, 'You've made it properly for once. It's quite hot.'

Slowly, Grant's heart resumed its interrupted work. He did not trust himself to speak, but managed a noncommittal nod. McNeil parked the cup carefully in the air, a few inches away from his face.

He seemed very thoughtful, as if weighing his words for some important remark. Grant cursed himself for having made the drink so hot – that was just the sort of detail that hanged murderers. If McNeil waited much longer he would probably betray himself through nervousness.

'I suppose,' said McNeil in a quietly conversational sort of way, 'it has occurred to you that there's still enough air to last one of us to Venus.'

Grant forced his jangling nerves under control and tore his eyes away from that hypnotic cup. His throat seemed very dry as he answered, 'It – it had crossed my mind.'

McNeil touched his cup, found it still too hot and continued thoughtfully, 'Then wouldn't it be more sensible if one of us decided to walk out of the airlock, say – or to take some of the poison in there?' He jerked his thumb towards the medicine chest, just visible from where they were sitting.

Grant nodded.

'The only trouble, of course,' added the engineer, 'is to decide which of us is to be the unlucky one. I suppose it would have to be by picking a card or in some other quite arbitrary way.'

Grant stared at McNeil with a fascination that almost outweighed his mounting nervousness. He had never believed that the engineer could discuss the subject so calmly. Grant was sure he suspected nothing. Obviously McNeil's thoughts had been running on parallel lines to his own and it was scarcely even a coincidence that he had chosen this time, of all times, to raise the matter.

McNeil was watching him intently, as if judging his reactions.

'You're right,' Grant heard himself say. 'We must talk it over.'

'Yes,' said McNeil quite impassively. 'We must.' Then he reached for his cup again, put the drinking-tube to his lips and sucked slowly.

Grant could not wait until he had finished. To his surprise the relief he had been expecting did not come. He even felt a stab of regret, though it was not quite remorse. It was a little late to think of it now, but he suddenly remembered that he would be alone in the *Star Queen*, haunted by his thoughts, for more than three weeks before rescue came.

He did not wish to see McNeil die, and he felt rather sick. Without another glance at his victim he launched himself towards the exit.

Immovably fixed, the fierce Sun and the unwinking stars looked down upon the *Star Queen*, which seemed as motionless as they. There was no way of telling that the tiny dumb-bell of the ship had now almost reached her maximum speed and that millions of horse-power were chained within the smaller sphere waiting the moment of its release. There was no way of telling, indeed, that she carried any life at all.

An airlock on the night-side of the ship slowly opened, letting a blaze of light escape from the interior. The brilliant circle looked very strange hanging there in the darkness. Then it was abruptly eclipsed as two figures floated out of the ship.

One was much bulkier than the other, and for a rather important reason – it was wearing a spacesuit. Now there are some forms of apparel that may be worn or discarded as the fancy pleases with no other ill effects than a possible loss of social prestige. But spacesuits are not among them.

Something not easy to follow was happening in the darkness. Then the smaller figure began to move, slowly at first but with rapidly mounting speed. It swept out of the shadow of the ship into the full blast of the Sun, and now one could see that strapped to its back was a small gas-cylinder from which a fine mist was jetting to vanish almost instantly into space.

It was a crude but effective rocket. There was no danger that the ship's minute gravitational pull would drag the body back to it again.

Rotating slightly, the corpse dwindled against the stars and vanished from sight in less than a minute. Quite motionless, the figure in the airlock watched it go. Then the outer door swung shut, the circle of brilliance vanished and only the pale Earthlight still glinted on the shadowed wall of the ship.

Nothing else whatsoever happened for twenty-three days.

The captain of the *Hercules* turned to his mate with a sigh of relief.

'I was afraid he couldn't do it. It must have been a colossal job to break his orbit single-handed – and with the air as thick as it must be by now. How soon can we get to him?'

'It will take about an hour. He's still got quite a bit of eccentricity but we can correct that.'

'Good. Signal the *Leviathan* and *Titan* that we can make contact and ask them to take off, will you? But I wouldn't drop any tips to your news-commentator friends until we're safely locked.'

The mate had the grace to blush. 'I don't intend to,' he said in a slightly hurt voice as he pecked delicately at the keys of his calculator. The answer that flashed instantly on the screen seemed to displease him.

'We'd better board and bring the *Queen* down to circular speed ourselves before we call the other tugs,' he said, 'otherwise we'll be wasting a lot of fuel. She's still got a velocity of nearly a kilometre a second.'

'Good idea – tell *Leviathan* and *Titan* to stand by but not to blast until we give them the new orbit.'

While the message was on its way down through the unbroken cloud-banks that covered half the sky below, the mate remarked thoughtfully, 'I wonder what he's feeling like now?'

'I can tell you. He's so pleased to be alive that he doesn't give a hoot about anything else.'

'Still, I'm not sure I'd like to have left my shipmate in space so that I could get home.'

'It's not the sort of thing that anyone would like to do. But you heard the broadcast – they'd talked it over calmly and the loser went out of the airlock. It was the only sensible way.'

'Sensible, perhaps – but it's pretty horrible to let someone else sacrifice himself in such a cold-blooded way so that you can live.'

'Don't be a ruddy sentimentalist. I'll bet that if it happened to us you'd push me out before I could even say my prayers.'

'Unless you did it to me first. Still, I don't think it's ever likely to happen to the *Hercules*. Five days out of port's the longest we've ever been, isn't it? Talk about the romance of the spaceways!'

The captain didn't reply. He was peering into the eyepiece of the navigating telescope, for the *Star Queen* should now be within optical range. There was a long pause while he adjusted the vernier controls. Then he gave a little sigh of satisfaction.

'There she is – about nine-fifty kilometres away. Tell the crew to stand by – and send a message to cheer him up. Say we'll be there in thirty minutes even if it isn't quite true.'

Slowly the thousand-metre nylon ropes yielded beneath the strain as they absorbed the relative momentum of the ships, then slackened again as the *Star Queen* and the *Hercules* rebounded towards each other. The electric winches began to turn and, like a spider crawling up its thread, the *Hercules* drew alongside the freighter.

Men in spacesuits sweated with heavy reaction units – tricky work, this – until the airlocks had registered and could be coupled together. The outer doors slid aside and the air in the locks mingled, fresh with the foul. As the mate of the *Hercules* waited, oxygen cylinder in hand, he wondered what condition the survivor would be in. Then the *Star Queen*'s inner door slid open.

For a moment, the two men stood looking at each other across the short corridor that now connected the two airlocks. The mate was surprised and a little disappointed to find that he felt no particular sense of drama.

So much had happened to make this moment possible that its actual achievement was almost an anticlimax even in the instant when it was slipping into the past. He wished – for he was an incurable romantic – that he could think of something memorable to say, some 'Doctor Livingstone, I presume?' phrase that would pass into history.

But all he actually said was, 'Well, McNeil, I'm pleased to see you.'

Though he was considerably thinner and somewhat haggard, McNeil had stood the ordeal well. He breathed gratefully the blast of raw oxygen and rejected the idea that he might like to lie down and sleep. As he explained, he had done very little but sleep for the last week to conserve air. The first mate looked relieved. He had been afraid he might have to wait for the story.

The cargo was being trans-shipped and the other two tugs were climbing up from the great blinding crescent of Venus while McNeil retraced the events of the last few weeks and the mate made surreptitious notes.

He spoke quite calmly and impersonally, as if he were relating some adventure that had happened to another person, or indeed had never happened at all. Which was, of course, to some extent the case, though it would be unfair to suggest that McNeil was telling any lies.

He invented nothing, but he omitted a good deal. He had had three weeks in which to prepare his narrative and he did not think it had any flaws—

Grant had already reached the door when McNeil called softly after him, 'What's the hurry? I thought we had something to discuss.'

Grant grabbed at the doorway to halt his headlong flight. He turned slowly and stared unbelievingly at the engineer. McNeil should be already dead – but he was sitting quite comfortably, looking at him with a most peculiar expression.

'Sit down,' he said sharply – and in that moment it suddenly seemed that all authority had passed to him. Grant did so, quite without volition. Something had gone wrong, though what it was he could not imagine.

The silence in the control-room seemed to last for ages. Then McNeil said rather sadly, 'I'd hoped better of you, Grant.'

At last Grant found his voice, though he could barely recognise it.

'What do you mean?' he whispered.

'What do you think I mean?' replied McNeil, with what seemed no more than a mild irritation. 'This little attempt of yours to poison me, of course.'

Grant's tottering world collapsed at last, but he no longer cared greatly one way or the other. McNeil began to examine his beautifully kept fingernails with some attention.

'As a matter of interest,' he said, in the way that one might ask the time, 'when did you decide to kill me?'

The sense of unreality was so overwhelming that Grant felt he was acting a part, that this had nothing to do with real life at all.

'Only this morning,' he said, and believed it.

'Hmm,' remarked McNeil, obviously without much conviction. He rose to his feet and moved over to the medicine chest. Grant's eyes followed him as he fumbled in the compartment and came back with the little poison bottle. It still appeared to be full. Grant had been careful about that.

'I suppose I should get pretty mad about this whole business,' McNeil

186

continued conversationally, holding the bottle between thumb and fore-finger. 'But somehow I'm not. Maybe it's because I never had many illusions about human nature. And, of course, I saw it coming a long time ago.'

Only the last phrase really reached Grant's consciousness.

'You – saw it coming?'

'Heavens, yes! You're too transparent to make a good criminal, I'm afraid. And now that your little plot's failed it leaves us both in an embarrassing position, doesn't it?'

To this masterly understatement there seemed no possible reply.

'By rights,' continued the engineer thoughtfully, 'I should now work myself up into a temper, call Venus Central, and renounce you to the authorities. But it would be a rather pointless thing to do, and I've never been much good at losing my temper anyway. Of course, you'll say that's because I'm too lazy – but I don't think so.'

He gave Grant a twisted smile.

'Oh, I know what you think about me – you've got me neatly classified in that orderly mind of yours, haven't you? I'm soft and self-indulgent, I haven't any moral courage – or any morals for that matter – and I don't give a damn for anyone but myself. Well, I'm not denying it. Maybe it's ninety per cent true. But the odd ten per cent is mighty important, Grant!'

Grant felt in no condition to indulge in psychological analysis, and this seemed hardly the time for anything of the sort. Besides, he was still obsessed with the problem of his failure and the mystery of McNeil's continued existence. McNeil, who knew this perfectly well, seemed in no hurry to satisfy his curiosity.

'Well, what do you intend to do now?' Grant asked, anxious to get it over.

'I would like,' said McNeil calmly, 'to carry on our discussion where it was interrupted by the coffee.'

'You don't mean—'

'But I do. Just as if nothing had happened.'

'That doesn't make sense. You've got something up your sleeve!' cried Grant.

McNeil sighed. He put down the poison bottle and looked firmly at Grant.

'*You're* in no position to accuse me of plotting anything. To repeat my earlier remarks, I am suggesting that we decide which one of us shall take poison – only we don't want any more unilateral decisions. Also' – he picked up the bottle again – 'it will be the real thing this time. The stuff in here merely leaves a bad taste in the mouth.'

A light was beginning to dawn in Grant's mind. 'You changed the poison!'

'Naturally. You may think you're a good actor, Grant, but frankly – from the stalls – I thought the performance stank. I could tell you were plotting something, probably before you knew it yourself. In the last few days I've deloused the ship pretty thoroughly. Thinking of all the ways you might have done me in was quite amusing and helped to pass the time. The poison was so obvious that it was the first thing I fixed. But I rather overdid the danger signals and nearly gave myself away when I took the first sip. Salt doesn't go at all well with coffee.'

He gave that wry grin again. 'Also, I'd hoped for something more subtle. So far I've found fifteen infallible ways of murdering anyone aboard a spaceship. But I don't propose to describe them now.'

This was fantastic, Grant thought. He was being treated, not like a criminal, but like a rather stupid schoolboy who hadn't done his homework properly.

'Yet you're still willing,' said Grant unbelievingly, 'to start all over again? And you'd take the poison yourself if you lost?'

McNeil was silent for a long time. Then he began slowly, 'I can see that you still don't believe me. It doesn't fit at all nicely into your tidy little picture, does it? But perhaps I can make you understand. It's really quite simple.

'I've enjoyed life, Grant, without many scruples or regrets – but the better part of it's over now and I don't cling to what's left as desperately as you might imagine. Yet while I *am* alive I'm rather particular about some things.

'It may surprise you to know that I've got any ideals at all. But I have, Grant – I've always tried to act like a civilised rational being. I've not always succeeded. When I've failed I've tried to redeem myself.'

He paused, and when he resumed it was as though he, and not Grant, was on the defensive. 'I've never exactly liked you, Grant, but I've often admired you and that's why I'm sorry it's come to this. I admired you most of all the day the ship was holed.'

For the first time, McNeil seemed to have some difficulty in choosing his words. When he spoke again he avoided Grant's eyes.

'I didn't behave too well then. Something happened that I thought was impossible. I've always been quite sure that I'd never lose my nerve but – well – it was so sudden it knocked me over.'

He attempted to hide his embarrassment by humour. 'The same sort of thing happened on my very first trip. I was sure I'd never be spacesick – and as a result I was much worse than if I had not been over-confident. But I got over it then – and again this time. It was one of the biggest surprises of my life, Grant, when I saw that you of all people were beginning to crack.

'Oh, yes – the business of wines! I can see you're thinking about that. Well, that's one thing I *don't* regret. I said I've always tried to act like a civilised man – and a civilised man should always know when to get drunk. But perhaps you wouldn't understand.'

Oddly enough, that was just what Grant was beginning to do. He had caught his first real glimpse of McNeil's intricate and tortuous personality and realised how utterly he had misjudged him. No – misjudged was not the right word. In many ways his judgement had been correct. But it had only touched the surface – he had never suspected the depths that lay beneath.

In a moment of insight that had never come before, and from the nature of things could never come again, Grant understood the reasons behind McNeil's action. This was nothing so simple as a coward trying to reinstate himself in the eyes of the world, for no one need ever know what happened aboard the *Star Queen*.

In any case, McNeil probably cared nothing for the world's opinion, thanks to the sleek self-sufficiency that had so often annoyed Grant. But that very self-sufficiency meant that at all costs he must preserve his own good opinion of himself. Without it life would not be worth living – and McNeil had never accepted life save on his own terms.

The engineer was watching him intently and must have guessed that Grant was coming near the truth, for he suddenly changed his tone as though he was sorry he had revealed so much of his character.

'Don't think I get a quixotic pleasure from turning the other cheek,' he said. 'Just consider it from the point of view of pure logic. After all, we've got to come to *some* agreement.

'Has it occurred to you that if only one of us survives without a covering message from the other, he'll have a very uncomfortable time explaining just what happened?'

In his blind fury, Grant had completely forgotten this. But he did not believe it bulked at all important in McNeil's own thoughts.

'Yes,' he said, 'I suppose you're right.'

He felt far better now. All the hate drained out of him and he was at peace. The truth was known and he had accepted it. That it was so different from what he had imagined did not seem to matter now.

'Well, let's get it over,' he said unemotionally. 'There's a new pack of cards lying around somewhere.'

'I think we'd better speak to Venus first – both of us,' replied McNeil, with peculiar emphasis. 'We want a complete agreement on record in case anyone asks awkward questions later.'

Grant nodded absently. He did not mind very much now one way or the other. He even smiled, ten minutes later, as he drew his card from the pack and laid it, face upwards, beside McNeil's.

'So that's the whole story, is it?' said the first mate, wondering how soon he could decently get to the transmitter.

'Yes,' said McNeil evenly, 'that's all there was to it.'

The mate bit his pencil, trying to frame the next question. 'And I suppose Grant took it all quite calmly?'

The captain gave him a glare, which he avoided, and McNeil looked at him coldly as if he could see through the sensation-mongering headlines ranged behind. He got to his feet and moved over to the observation port.

'You heard his broadcast, didn't you? Wasn't that calm enough?'

The mate sighed. It still seemed hard to believe that in such circumstances two men could have behaved in so reasonable, so unemotional a manner.

He could have pictured all sorts of dramatic possibilities – sudden outbursts of insanity, even attempts at murder. Yet according to McNeil nothing at all had happened. It was too bad.

McNeil was speaking again, as if to himself. 'Yes, Grant behaved very well – very well indeed. It was a great pity—'

Then he seemed to lose himself in the ever-fresh, incomparable glory of the approaching planet. Not far beneath, and coming closer by kilometres every second, the snow-white crescent arms of Venus spanned more than half the sky. Down there were life and warmth and civilisation – and air.

The future, which not long ago had seemed contracted to a point, had opened out again into all its unknown possibilities and wonders. But behind him McNeil could sense the eyes of his rescuers, probing, questioning – yes, and condemning too.

All his life he would hear whispers. Voices would be saying behind his back, 'Isn't that the man who—?'

He did not care. For once in his life at least, he had done something of which he could feel unashamed. Perhaps one day his own pitiless self-analysis would strip bare the motives behind his actions, would whisper in his ear. 'Altruism? Don't be a fool! You did it to bolster up your own good opinion of yourself – so much more important than anyone else's!'

But the perverse maddening voices, which all his life had made nothing seem worth while, were silent for the moment and he felt content. He had reached the calm at the centre of the hurricane. While it lasted he would enjoy it to the full.

Nemesis

First published in *Super Science Stories*, March 1950, as 'Exile of the Eons'
Collected in *Expedition to Earth*

Already the mountains were trembling with the thunder that only man can make. But here the war seemed very far away, for the full moon hung over the ageless Himalayas and the furies of the battle were still hidden below the edge of the world. Not for long would they so remain. The Master knew that the last remnants of his fleet were being hurled from the sky as the circle of death closed in upon his stronghold.

In a few hours at the most, the Master and his dreams of empire would have vanished into the maelstrom of the past. Nations would still curse his name, but they would no longer fear it. Later, even the hatred would be gone and he would mean no more to the world than Hitler or Napoleon or Genghis Khan. Like them he would be a blurred figure far down the infinite corridor of time, dwindling towards oblivion. For a little while his name would dwell in the uncertain land between history and fable; then the world would think of him no more. He would be one with the nameless legions who had died to work his will.

Far to the south, a mountain suddenly edged with violet flame. Ages later, the balcony on which the Master stood shuddered beneath the impact of the ground-wave racing through the rocks below. Later still, the air brought the echo of a mammoth concussion. Surely they could not be so close already! The Master hoped it was no more than a stray torpedo that had swept through the contracting battle line. If it were not, time was even shorter than he feared.

The Chief of Staff walked out from the shadows and joined him by the rail. The Marshal's hard face – the second most hated in all the world – was lined and beaded with sweat. He had not slept for days and his once gaudy uniform hung limply upon him. Yet his eyes, though unutterably weary, were still resolute even in defeat. He stood in silence, awaiting his last orders. Nothing else was left for him to do.

Thirty miles away, the eternal snow-plume of Everest flamed a lurid red, reflecting the glare of some colossal fire below the horizon. Still the Master neither moved nor gave any sign. Not until a salvo of torpedoes passed high overhead with a demon wail did he at last turn and, with one backward glance at the world he would see no more, descend into the depths.

The lift dropped a thousand feet and the sound of battle died away. As he stepped out of the shaft, the Master paused for a moment to press a hidden switch. The Marshal even smiled when he heard the crash of falling rock far above, and knew that both pursuit and escape were equally impossible.

As of old, the handful of generals sprang to their feet when the Master entered the room. He ran his eyes round the table. They were all there; even at the last there had been no traitors. He walked to his accustomed place in silence, steeling himself for the last and the hardest speech he would ever have to make. Burning into his soul he could feel the eyes of the men he had led to ruin. Behind and beyond them he could see the squadrons, the divisions, the armies whose blood was on his hands. And more terrible still were the silent spectres of the nations that now could never be born.

At last he began to speak. The hypnosis of his voice was as powerful as ever, and after a few words he became once more the perfect, implacable machine whose destiny was destruction.

'This, gentlemen, is the last of all our meetings. There are no more plans to make, no more maps to study. Somewhere above our heads the fleet we built with such pride and care is fighting to the end. In a few minutes, not one of all those thousands of machines will be left in the sky.

'I know that for all of us here surrender is unthinkable, even if it were possible, so in this room you will shortly have to die. You have served our cause well and deserved better, but it was not to be. Yet I do not wish you to think that we have wholly failed. In the past, as you saw many times, my plans were always ready for anything that might arise, no matter how improbable. You should not, therefore, be surprised to learn that I was prepared even for defeat.'

Still the same superb orator, he paused for effect, noting with satisfaction the ripple of interest, the sudden alertness on the tired faces of his listeners.

'My secret is safe enough with you,' he continued, 'for the enemy will never find this place. The entrance is already blocked by hundreds of feet of rock.'

Still there was no movement. Only the Director of Propaganda turned suddenly white, and swiftly recovered – but not swiftly enough to escape the Master's eye. The Master smiled inwardly at this belated confirmation of an old doubt. It mattered little now; true and false, they would all die together. All but one.

'Two years ago,' he went on, 'when we lost the battle of Antarctica, I knew that we could no longer be certain of victory. So I made my preparations for this day. The enemy has already sworn to kill me. I could not remain in hiding anywhere on the earth, still less hope to rebuild our fortunes. But there is another way, though a desperate one.

'Five years ago, one of our scientists perfected the technique of suspended animation. He found that by relatively simple means all life processes could be arrested for an indefinite period. I am going to use this discovery to escape from the present into a future which will have forgotten me. There I can begin the struggle again, not without the help of certain devices that might yet have won this war had we been granted more time.

'Goodbye, gentlemen. And once again, my thanks for your help and my regrets at your ill fortune.'

He saluted, turned on his heels, and was gone. The metal door thudded decisively behind him. There was a frozen silence; then the Director of Propaganda rushed to the exit, only to recoil with a startled cry. The steel door was already too hot to touch. It had been welded immovably into the wall.

The Minister for War was the first to draw his automatic.

The Master was in no great hurry, now. On leaving the council room he had thrown the secret switch of the welding circuit. The same action had opened a panel in the wall of the corridor, revealing a small circular passage sloping steadily upwards. He began to walk slowly along it.

Every few hundred feet the tunnel angled sharply, though still continuing the upward climb. At each turning the Master stopped to throw a switch, and there was the thunder of falling rock as a section of corridor collapsed.

Five times the passageway changed its course before it ended in a spherical, metal-walled room. Multiple doors closed softly on rubber seatings, and the last section of tunnel crashed behind. The Master would not be disturbed by his enemies, nor by his friends.

He looked swiftly round the room to satisfy himself that all was ready. Then he walked to a simple control-board and threw, one after another, a set of peculiarly massive switches. They had to carry little current – but they had been built to last. So had everything in that strange room. Even the walls were made of metals far less ephemeral than steel.

Pumps started to whine, drawing the air from the chamber and replacing it with sterile nitrogen. Moving more swiftly now, the Master went to the padded couch and lay down. He thought he could feel himself bathed by the bacteria-destroying rays from the lamps above his head, but that of course was fancy. From a recess beneath the couch he drew a hypodermic and injected a milky fluid into his arm. Then he relaxed and waited.

It was already very cold. Soon the refrigerators would bring the temperature down far below freezing, and would hold it there for many hours. Then it would rise to normal, but by that time the process would be completed, all bacteria would be dead and the Master could sleep, unchanged, for ever.

He had planned to wait a hundred years. More than that he dared not delay, for when he awoke he would have to master all the changes in science and society that the passing years had wrought. Even a century might have altered the face of civilisation beyond his understanding, but that was a risk he would have to take. Less than a century would not be safe, for the world would still be full of bitter memories.

Sealed in a vacuum beneath the couch were three electronic counters operated by thermocouples hundreds of feet above on the eastern face of the mountain where no snow could ever cling. Every day the rising sun would operate them and the counters would add one unit to their store. So the coming of dawn would be noted in the darkness where the Master slept.

When any one of the counters reached the total of thirty-six thousand, a switch would close and oxygen would flow back into the chamber. The temperature would rise, and the automatic hypodermic strapped to the Master's arm would inject the calculated amount of fluid. He would awaken, and only the counters would tell him that the century had really passed. Then all he need do would be to press the button which would blast away the mountainside and give him free passage to the outer world.

Everything had been considered. There could be no failure. All the machinery had been triplicated and was as perfect as science could contrive.

The Master's last thought as consciousness ebbed was not of his past life, nor of the mother whose hopes he had betrayed. Unbidden and unwelcome, there came into his mind the words of an ancient poet:

'To sleep, perchance to dream—'

No, he would not, dared not dream. He would only sleep. Sleep – sleep—

Twenty miles away, the battle was coming to its end. Not a dozen of the Master's ships were left, fighting hopelessly against overwhelming fire. The action would have ended long ago had the attackers not been ordered to risk no ships in unnecessary adventures. The decision was to be left to the long-range artillery. So the great destroyers, the airborne battleships of this age, lay with their fighter screens in the shelter of the mountains, pouring salvo after salvo into the doomed formations.

Aboard the flagship, a young Hindu gunnery officer set vernier dials with infinite accuracy and gently pressed a pedal with his foot. There was the faintest of shocks as the dirigible torpedoes left their cradles and hurled themselves at the enemy. The young Indian sat waiting tensely as the chronometer ticked off the seconds. This, he thought, was probably the last salvo he would fire. Somehow he felt none of the elation he had expected; indeed, he was surprised to discover a kind of impersonal sympathy for his doomed opponents, whose lives were now ebbing with every passing second.

Far away a sphere of violet fire blossomed above the mountains, among the darting specks that were the enemy ships. The gunner leaned forward tensely and counted. One – two – three – four – five times came that peculiar explosion. Then the sky cleared. The struggling specks were gone.

In his log, the gunner noted briefly: '0124 hrs. Salvo No. 12 fired. Five torps exploded among enemy ships which were totally destroyed. One torp failed to detonate.'

He signed the entry with a flourish and laid down his pen. For a while he sat staring at the log's familiar brown cover, with the cigarette-burns at the edges and the inevitable stained rings where cups and glasses had been carelessly set down. Idly he thumbed through the leaves, noting once again the handwriting of his many predecessors. And as he had done so often before, he turned to a familiar page where a man who had once been his friend had begun to sign his name but had never lived to complete it.

With a sigh, he closed the book and locked it away. The war was over.

Far away among the mountains, the torpedo that had failed to explode was still gaining speed under the drive of its rockets. Now it was a scarcely visible line of light, racing between the walls of a lonely valley. Already the snows that had been disturbed by the scream of its passage were beginning to rumble down the mountain slopes.

There was no escape from the valley: it was blocked by a sheer wall a thousand feet high. Here the torpedo that had missed its mark found a greater one. The Master's tomb was too deep in the mountain even to be shaken by the explosion, but the hundreds of tons of falling rock swept away three tiny instruments and their connections, and a future that might have been went with them into oblivion. The first rays of the rising sun would still fall on the shattered faces of the mountain, but the counters that were waiting for the thirty-six-thousandth dawn would still be waiting when dawns and sunsets were no more.

In the silence of the tomb that was not quite a tomb, the Master knew nothing of this, and his face was more peaceful than it had any right to be. So the century passed, as he had planned. It is not likely that, for all his evil genius and the secrets he had buried with him, the Master could have conquered the civilisation that had come to flower since that final battle above the roof of the world. No one can say, unless it is indeed true that time has many branches and that all imaginable universes lie side by side, merging one into the other. Perhaps in some of those other worlds the Master might have triumphed. But in the one we know he slumbered on, until the century was far behind – very far indeed.

After what by some standards would have been a little while, the earth's crust decided that it had borne the weight of the Himalayas for long enough. Slowly the mountains dropped, tilting the southern plains of India towards the sky. And presently the plateau of Ceylon was the highest point on the surface of the globe, and the ocean above Everest was five and a half miles deep. Yet the Master's slumber was still dreamless and undisturbed.

Slowly, patiently, the silt drifted down through the towering ocean heights on to the wreck of the Himalayas. The blanket that would one day be chalk began to thicken at the rate of an inch or two every century. If one had returned some time later one might have found that the sea-bed was no longer five miles down, or even four, or three. Then the land tilted again, and a mighty range of limestone mountains towered where once had been the oceans of Tibet. But the Master knew nothing of this, nor was his sleep troubled when it happened again – and again – and yet again.

Now the rain and the rivers were washing away the chalk and carrying it out to the strange new oceans, and the surface was moving down towards the hidden tomb. Slowly the miles of rock were winnowed away until at last the sphere which housed the Master's body returned to the light of day – though to a day much longer, and much dimmer, than it had been when the Master closed his eyes.

Little did the Master dream of the races that had flowered and died since that early morning of the world when he went to his long sleep. Very far away was that morning now, and the shadows were lengthening to the east: the sun was dying and the world was very old. But still the children of Adam ruled its seas and skies, and filled with their tears and laughter the plains and the valleys and the woods that were older than the shifting hills.

The Master's dreamless sleep was more than half ended when Trevindor the Philosopher was born, between the fall of the Ninety-seventh Dynasty and the rise of the Fifth Galactic Empire. He was born on a world very far from Earth, for few were the men who ever set foot on the ancient home of their race, now so distant from the throbbing heart of the Universe.

They brought Trevindor to Earth when his brief clash with the Empire had come to its inevitable end. Here he was tried by the men whose ideals he had challenged, and here it was that they pondered long over the manner of his fate. The case was unique. The gentle, philosophic culture that now ruled the Galaxy had never before met with opposition, even on the level of pure intellect, and the polite but implacable conflict of wills had left it severely shaken. It was typical of the Council's members that, when a decision had proved impossible, they appealed to Trevindor himself for help.

In the whitely gleaming Hall of Justice, that had not been entered for nigh on a million years, Trevindor stood proudly facing the men who had proved stronger than he. In silence he listened to their request; then he paused in reflection. His judges waited patiently until he spoke.

'You suggest that I should promise not to defy you again,' he began, 'but I shall make no promise that I may be unable to keep. Our views are too divergent and sooner or later we should clash again.

'There was a time when your choice would have been easy. You could have exiled me, or put me to death. But today – where among all the worlds of the Universe is there one planet where you could hide me if I did not choose to stay? Remember, I have many disciples scattered the length and breadth of the Galaxy.

'There remains the other alternative. I shall bear you no malice if you revive the ancient custom of execution to meet my case.'

There was a murmur of annoyance from the Council, and the President replied sharply, his colour heightening, 'That remark is in somewhat questionable taste. We asked for serious suggestions, not reminders – even if intended humorously – of the barbaric customs of our remote ancestors.'

Trevindor accepted the rebuke with a bow. 'I was merely mentioning all the possibilities. There are two others that have occurred to me. It would be a simple matter to change my mind pattern to your way of thinking so that no future disagreement can arise.'

'We have already considered that. We were forced to reject it, attractive though it is, for the destruction of your personality would be equivalent to murder. There are only fifteen more powerful intellects than yours in the Universe, and we have no right to tamper with it. And your final suggestion?'

'Though you cannot exile me in space, there is still one alternative. The river of Time stretches ahead of us as far as our thoughts can go. Send me down that stream to an age when you are certain this civilisation will have passed. That I know you can do with the aid of the Roston time-field.'

There was a long pause. In silence the members of the Council were passing their decisions to the complex analysis machine which would weigh them one against the other and arrive at the verdict. At length the President spoke.

'It is agreed. We will send you to an age when the Sun is still warm enough for life to exist on the Earth, but so remote that any trace of our civilisation is unlikely to survive. We will also provide you with everything necessary for your safety and reasonable comfort. You may leave us now. We will call for you again when all arrangements have been made.'

Trevindor bowed, and left the marble hall. No guards followed him. There was nowhere he could flee, even if he wished, in this Universe which the great Galactic liners could span in a single day.

For the first and last time, Trevindor stood on the shore of what had once been the Pacific, listening to the wind sighing through the leaves of what had once been palms. The few stars of the nearly empty region of space through which the Sun was now passing shone with a steady light through the dry air of the ageing world. Trevindor wondered bleakly if they would still be shining when he looked again upon the sky, in a future so distant that the Sun itself would be sinking to its death.

There was a tinkle from the tiny communicator band upon his wrist. So, the time had come. He turned his back upon the ocean and walked resolutely to meet his fate. Before he had gone a dozen steps the time-field had seized him and his thoughts froze in an instant that would remain unchanged while the oceans shrank and vanished, the Galactic Empire passed away, and the great star-clusters crumbled into nothingness.

But, to Trevindor, no time elapsed at all. He only knew that at one step there had been moist sand beneath his feet, and at the next hard-baked rock, cracked by heat and drought. The palms had vanished, the murmur of the sea was stilled. It needed only a glance to show that even the memory of the sea had long since faded from this parched and dying world. To the far horizon, a great desert of red sandstone stretched unbroken and unrelieved by any growing thing. Overhead, the orange disc of a strangely altered sun glowered from a sky so black that many stars were clearly visible.

Yet, it seemed, there was still life on this ancient world. To the north – if that were still the north – the sombre light glinted upon some metallic structure. It was a few hundred yards away, and as Trevindor started to walk towards it he was conscious of a curious lightness, as if gravity itself had weakened.

He had not gone far before he saw that he was approaching a low metal building which seemed to have been set down on the plain rather than constructed there, for it was at a slight angle to the horizontal. Trevindor wondered at his incredible good fortune at finding civilisation so easily. Another dozen steps, and he realised that not chance but design had so conveniently placed this building here, and that it was as much a stranger to this world as he himself. There was no hope at all that anyone would come to meet him as he walked towards it.

The metal plaque above the door added little to what he had already surmised. Still new and untarnished as if it had just been engraved – as indeed, in a sense, it had – the lettering brought a message at once of hope and of bitterness.

To Trevindor, the greetings of the Council.

This building, which we have sent after you through the time-field, will supply all your needs for an indefinite period.

We do not know if civilisation will still exist in the age in which you find yourself. Man may now be extinct, since the chromosome K Star K will have become dominant and the race may have mutated into something no longer human. That is for you to discover.

You are now in the twilight of the Earth and it is our hope that you are not alone. But if it is your destiny to be the last living creature on this once lovely world, remember that the choice was yours. Farewell.

Twice Trevindor read the message, recognising with an ache the closing words which could only have been written by his friend, the poet Cintillarne. An overwhelming sense of loneliness and isolation came flooding into his soul. He sat down upon a shelf of rock and buried his face in his hands.

A long time later, he arose to enter the building. He felt more than grateful to the long-dead Council which had treated him so chivalrously. The technical achievement of sending an entire building through time was one he had believed beyond the resources of his age. A sudden thought struck him and he glanced again at the engraved lettering, noticing for the first time the date it bore. It was five thousand years later than the time when he had faced his peers in the Hall of Justice. Fifty centuries had passed before his judges could redeem their promise to a man as good as dead. Whatever the faults of the Council, its integrity was of an order beyond the comprehension of an earlier age.

Many days passed before Trevindor left the building again. Nothing had been overlooked: even his beloved thought records were there. He could continue to study the nature of reality and to construct philosophies until the end of the Universe, barren though that occupation would be if his were the only mind left on Earth. There was little danger, he thought wryly, that his speculations concerning the purpose of human existence would once again bring him into conflict with society.

Not until he had investigated the building thoroughly did Trevindor turn his attention once more to the outer world. The supreme problem was that of contacting civilisation, should such still exist. He had been provided with a powerful receiver, and for hours he wandered up and down the spectrum in the hope of discovering a station. The far-off crackle of static came from the instrument and once there was a burst of what might have been speech in a tongue that was certainly not human. But nothing else rewarded his search. The ether, which had been man's faithful servant for so many ages, was silent at last.

The little automatic flyer was Trevindor's sole remaining hope. He had what was left of eternity before him, and Earth was a small planet. In a few years, at the most, he could have explored it all.

So the months passed while the exile began his methodical exploration of the world, returning ever and again to his home in the desert of red sandstone. Everywhere he found the same picture of desolation and ruin. How long ago the seas had vanished he could not even guess, but in their dying they had left endless wastes of salt, encrusting both plains and mountains with a blanket of dirty grey. Trevindor felt glad that he had not been born on Earth and so had never known it in the glory of its youth. Stranger though he was, the loneliness and desolation of the world chilled his heart; had he lived here before, its sadness would have been unbearable.

Thousands of square miles of desert passed beneath Trevindor's fleeting ship as he searched the world from pole to pole. Only once did he find any sign that Earth had ever known civilisation. In a deep valley near the equator he discovered the ruins of a small city of strange white stone and stranger architecture. The buildings were perfectly preserved though half-buried by the drifting sand, and for a moment Trevindor felt a surge of sombre joy at the knowledge that man had, after all, left some traces of his handiwork on the world that had been his first home.

The emotion was short-lived. The buildings were stranger than Trevindor had realised, for no man could ever have entered them. Their only openings were wide, horizontal slots close to the ground; there were no windows of any kind. Trevindor's mind reeled as he tried to imagine the creatures that must have occupied them. In spite of his growing loneliness, he felt glad that the dwellers in this inhuman city had passed away so long before his time. He did not linger here, for the bitter night was almost upon him and the valley filled him with an oppression that was not entirely rational.

And once, he actually discovered life. He was cruising over the bed of one of the lost oceans when a flash of colour caught his eye. Upon a knoll which the drifting sand had not yet buried was a thin, wiry covering of grass. That was all, but the sight brought tears to his eyes. He grounded the machine and stepped out, treading warily lest he destroy even one of the struggling blades. Tenderly he ran his hands over the threadbare carpet which was all the life that Earth now knew. Before he left, he sprinkled the spot with as much water as he could spare. It was a futile gesture, but one which he felt happier at having made.

The search was now nearly completed. Trevindor had long ago given up all hope, but his indomitable spirit still drove him on across the face of the world. He could not rest until he had proved what as yet he only feared. And so it was that he came at last to the Master's tomb as it lay gleaming dully in the sunlight from which it had been banished for so long.

The Master's mind awoke before his body. As he lay powerless, unable to lift his eyelids, memory came flooding back. The hundred years were safely behind him. His gamble, the most desperate that any man had ever made, had succeeded! An immense weariness came over him and for a while consciousness faded once more.

Presently the mists cleared again and he felt stronger, though still too weak to move. He lay in the darkness gathering his strength together. What sort of a world, he wondered, would he find when he stepped forth from the mountainside into the light of day? Would he be able to put his plans into—? *What was that?* A spasm of sheer terror shook the very foundations of his mind. Something was moving beside him, here in the tomb where nothing should be stirring but himself.

Then, calm and clear, a thought rang serenely through his mind and quelled in an instant the fears that had threatened to overturn it.

'Do not be alarmed. I have come to help you. You are safe, and everything will be well.'

The Master was too stunned to make any reply, but his subconscious must have formulated some sort of answer, for the thought came again.

'That is good. I am Trevindor, like yourself an exile in this world. Do not move, but tell me how you came here and what is your race, for I have seen none like it.'

And now fear and caution were creeping back into the Master's mind. What manner of creature was this that could read his thoughts, and what was it doing in his secret sphere? Again that clear, cold thought echoed through his brain like the tolling of a bell.

'Once more I tell you that you have nothing to fear. Why are you alarmed because I can see into your mind? Surely there is nothing strange about that.'

'Nothing strange!' cried the Master. 'What are you, for God's sake?'

'A man like yourself. But your race must be primitive indeed if the reading of thoughts is strange to you.'

A terrible suspicion began to dawn in the Master's brain. The answer came even before he consciously framed the question.

'You have slept infinitely longer than a hundred years. The world you knew has ceased to be for longer than you can imagine.'

The Master heard no more. Once again the darkness swept over him and he sank down into blissful unconsciousness.

In silence Trevindor stood beside the couch on which the Master lay. He was filled with an elation which for the moment outweighed any disappointment he might feel. At least, he would no longer have to face the future alone. All the terror of the Earth's loneliness, that was weighing so heavily upon his soul, had vanished in a moment. *No longer alone . . .* no longer alone! Dominating all else, the thought hammered through his brain.

The Master was beginning to stir once more, and into Trevindor's mind crept broken fragments of thought. Pictures of the world the Master had known began to form in the watcher's brain. At first Trevindor could make nothing of them then, suddenly, the jumbled shards fell into place and all was clear. A wave of horror swept over him at the appalling vista of nation battling against nation, of cities flaming to destruction and men dying in agony. What kind of world was this? Could man have sunk so low from the peaceful age Trevindor had known? There had been legends, from times incredibly remote, of such things in the early dawn of Earth's history, but man had left them with his childhood. Surely they could never have returned!

The broken thoughts were more vivid now, and even more horrible. It was truly a nightmare age from which this other exile had come – no wonder that he had fled from it!

Suddenly the truth began to dawn in the mind of Trevindor as, sick at heart, he watched the ghastly patterns passing through the Master's brain. This was no exile seeking refuge from an age of horror. This was the very creator of that age, who had embarked on the river of time with one purpose alone – to spread contagion down to later years.

Passions that Trevindor had never imagined began to parade themselves before his eyes: ambition, the lust for power, cruelty, intolerance, hatred. He tried to close his mind, but found he had lost the power to do so. Unchecked, the evil stream flowed on, polluting every level of consciousness. With a cry of anguish, Trevindor rushed out into the desert and broke the chains binding him to that evil mind.

It was night, and very still, for the Earth was now too weary even for winds to blow. The darkness hid everything, but Trevindor knew that it could not hide the thoughts of that other mind with which he must now share the world. Once he had been alone, and he had imagined nothing more dreadful. But now he knew that there were things more fearful even than solitude.

The stillness of the night, and the glory of the stars that had once been his friends, brought calm to the soul of Trevindor. Slowly he turned and retraced his footsteps, walking heavily, for he was about to perform a deed that no man of his kind had ever done before.

The Master was standing when Trevindor re-entered the sphere. Perhaps some hint of the other's purpose must have dawned upon his mind, for he was very pale and trembled with a weakness that was more than physical. Steadfastly, Trevindor forced himself to look once more into the Master's brain. His mind recoiled at the chaos of conflicting emotions, now shot through with the sickening flashes of fear. Out of the maelstrom one coherent thought came quavering.

'What are you going to do? Why do you look at me like that?'

Trevindor made no reply, holding his mind aloof from contamination while he marshalled his resolution and his strength.

The tumult in the Master's mind was rising to a crescendo. For a moment his mounting terror brought something akin to pity to the gentle spirit of Trevindor, and his will faltered. But then there came again the picture of those ruined and burning cities, and his indecision vanished. With all the power of his superhuman intellect backed by thousands of centuries of mental evolution he struck at the man before him. Into the Master's mind, obliterating all else, flooded the single thought of – death.

For a moment the Master stood motionless, his eyes staring wildly before him. His breath froze as his lungs ceased their work; in his veins the pulsing blood, which had been stilled for so long, now congealed for ever. Without a sound, the Master toppled and lay still.

Very slowly Trevindor turned and walked out into the night. Like a shroud the silence and loneliness of the world descended upon him. The sand, thwarted so long, began to drift through the open portals of the Master's tomb.

Guardian Angel

First published in *Famous Fantastic Mysteries*, April 1950
Collected in *The Sentinel*

'Guardian Angel' was originally written in 1946, and rejected by John W. Campbell, editor of *Astounding*. After several more rejections my agent, Scott Meredith, asked James Blish to rewrite the story, which he did, adding a new ending, after which the story was sold to *Famous Fantastic Mysteries*. I thought it was rather good; but I didn't even know about it for a long time; this was rather naughty of Scott. Later, in 1952, 'Guardian Angel' was expanded, to become Part 1, 'Earth and the Overlords', of *Childhood's End*.

Pieter van Ryberg shivered, as he always did, when he came into Stormgren's room. He looked at the thermostat and shrugged his shoulders in mock resignation.

'You know, Chief,' he said, 'although we'll be sorry to lose you, it's nice to feel that the pneumonia death-rate will soon be falling.'

'How do you know?' smiled Stormgren. 'The next Secretary-General may be an Eskimo. The fuss some people make over a few degrees centigrade!'

Van Ryberg laughed and walked over to the curving double window. He stood in silence for a moment, staring along the avenue of great white buildings, still only partly finished.

'Well,' he said, with a sudden change of tone, 'are you going to see them?'

'Yes, I think so. It usually saves trouble in the long run.'

Van Ryberg suddenly stiffened and pressed his face against the glass.

'Here they are!' he said. 'They're coming up Wilson Avenue. Not as many as I expected, though – about two thousand, I'd say.'

Stormgren walked over to the Assistant-Secretary's side. Half a mile away, a small but determined crowd carried banners along the avenue towards Headquarters Building. Presently he could hear, even through the insulation, the ominous sound of chanting voices. He felt a sudden wave of disgust sweep over him. Surely the world had had enough of marching mobs and angry slogans!

The crowd had now come abreast of the building: it must know that he was watching, for here and there fists were being shaken in the air. They were not defying him, though the gesture was meant for him to see. As pygmies may threaten a giant, those angry fists were directed against the sky some fifty miles above his head.

And as likely as not, thought Stormgren, Karellen was looking down at the whole thing and enjoying himself hugely.

This was the first time that Stormgren had ever met the head of the Freedom League. He still wondered if the action was wise: in the final analysis he had only taken it because the League would employ any refusal as ammunition against him. He knew that the gulf was far too wide for any agreement to come from this meeting.

Alexander Wainwright was a tall but slightly stooping man in the late fifties. He seemed inclined to apologise for his more boisterous followers, and Stormgren was rather taken aback by his obvious sincerity and also by his considerable personal charm.

'I suppose,' Stormgren began, 'the chief object of your visit is to register a formal protest against the Federation Scheme. Am I correct?'

'That is my main purpose, Mr Secretary. As you know, for the last five years we have tried to awaken the human race to the danger that confronts it. I must admit that, from our point of view, the response has been disappointing. The great majority of people seem content to let the Overlords run the world as they please. But this European Federation is as intolerable as it will be unworkable. Even Karellen can't wipe out two thousand years of the world's history at the stroke of a pen.'

'Then do you consider,' interjected Stormgren, 'that Europe, and the whole world, must continue indefinitely to be divided into scores of sovereign states, each with its own currency, armed forces, customs, frontiers, and all the rest of that – that medieval paraphernalia?'

'I don't quarrel with Federation as an *ultimate* objective, though some of my supporters might not agree. My point is that it must come from within, not be superimposed from without. We must work out our own destiny – we have a right to independence. There must be no more interference in human affairs!'

Stormgren sighed. All this he had heard a hundred times before, and he knew that he could only give the old answers that the Freedom League had refused to accept. He had faith in Karellen, and they had not. That was the fundamental difference, and there was nothing he could do about it. Luckily, there was nothing that the Freedom League could do either.

'Let me ask you a few questions,' he said. 'Can you deny that the Overlords have brought security, peace and prosperity to the world?'

'That is true. But they have taken our freedom. Man does not live—'

'By bread alone. Yes, I know – but this is the first age in which every man was sure of getting even that. In any case, what freedom have we lost compared with that which the Overlords have given us for the first time in human history?'

'Freedom to control our own lives, under God's guidance.'

Stormgren shook his head.

'Last month, five hundred bishops, cardinals and rabbis signed a joint declaration pledging support for the Supervisor's policy. The world's religions are against you.'

'Because so few people realise the danger. When they do, it may be too late. Humanity will have lost its initiative and will have become a subject race.'

Stormgren did not seem to hear. He was watching the crowd below, milling aimlessly, now that it had lost its leader. How long, he wondered, would it be before men ceased to abandon their reason and identity when more than a few of them were gathered together? Wainwright might be a sincere and honest man, but the same could not be said of many of his followers.

Stormgren turned back to his visitor.

'In three days I shall be meeting the Supervisor again. I shall explain your objections to him, since it is my duty to represent the views of the world. But it will alter nothing.'

Rather slowly, Wainwright began again.

'That brings me to another point. One of our main objections to the Overlords, as you know, is their secretiveness. You are the only human being who has ever spoken with Karellen – and even you have never seen him. Is it surprising that many of us are suspicious of his motives?'

'You have heard his speeches. Aren't they convincing enough?'

'Frankly, words are not sufficient. I do not know which we resent more – Karellen's omnipotence, or his secrecy.'

Stormgren was silent. There was nothing he could say to this – nothing at any rate, that would convince the other. He sometimes wondered if he had really convinced himself.

It was, of course, only a very small operation from their point of view, but to Earth it was the biggest thing that had ever happened. There had been no warning, but a sudden shadow had fallen across a score of the world's greatest cities. Looking up from their work, a million men saw in that heart-freezing instant that the human race was no longer alone.

The twenty great ships were unmistakable symbols of a science Man could not hope to match for centuries. For seven days they floated motionless above his cities, giving no hint that they knew of his existence. But none was needed – not by chance alone could those mighty ships have come to rest so precisely over New York, London, Moscow, Canberra, Rome, Capetown, Tokyo . . .

Even before the ending of those unforgettable days, some men had guessed the truth. This was not a first tentative contact by a race which knew nothing of Man. Within those silent, unmoving ships, master psychologists were studying humanity's reactions. When the curve of tension had reached its peak, they would reveal themselves.

And on the eighth day, Karellen, Supervisor for Earth, made himself known to the world; in perfect English. But the content of the speech was more staggering even than its delivery. By any standards, it was a work of superlative genius, showing a complete and absolute mastery of human affairs.

There was little doubt but that its scholarship and virtuosity, its tantalising glimpses of knowledge still untapped, were deliberately designed to convince Mankind that it was in the presence of overwhelming intellectual power. When Karellen had finished, the nations of Earth knew that their days of precarious sovereignty were ending. Local, internal governments would still retain their powers, but in the wider field of international affairs the supreme decisions had passed out of human hands. Arguments, protests – all were futile. No weapon could touch those brooding giants, and even if it could, their downfall would utterly destroy the cities beneath. Overnight, Earth had become a protectorate in some shadowy, star-strewn empire beyond the knowledge of Man.

In a little while the tumult had subsided, and the world went about its business again. The only change a suddenly awakened Rip Van Winkle would have noticed was a hushed expectancy, a mental glancing-over-the-shoulder, as Mankind waited for the Overlords to show themselves and to step down from their gleaming ships.

Five years later, it was still waiting.

The room was small and, save for the single chair and the table beneath the vision-screen, unfurnished. As was intended, it told nothing of the creatures who had built it. There was only the one entrance, and that led directly to the airlock in the curving flank of the great ship. Through that lock only Stormgren, alone of living men, had ever come to meet Karellen, Supervisor for Earth.

The vision screen was empty now, as it had always been. Behind that rectangle of darkness lay utter mystery – but there too lay affection and an immense and tolerant understanding of mankind. An understanding which, Stormgren knew, could only have been acquired through centuries of study.

From the hidden grille came that calm, never-hurried voice with its undercurrent of humour – the voice which Stormgren knew so well though the world had heard it only thrice in history.

'Yes, Rikki, I was listening. What did you make of Mr Wainwright?'

'He's an honest man, whatever his supporters may be. What are we going to do about him? The League itself isn't dangerous, but some of its more extreme supporters are openly advocating violence. I've been wondering for some time if I should put a guard on my house. But I hope it isn't necessary.'

Karellen evaded the point in the annoying way he sometimes had.

'The details of the European Federation have been out for a month now. Has there been a substantial increase in the seven per cent who disapprove of me, or the nine per cent who Don't Know?'

'Not yet, despite the press reactions. What I'm worried about is a general feeling, even among your supporters, that it's time this secrecy came to an end.'

Karellen's sigh was technically perfect, yet somehow lacked conviction.

'That's your feeling, too, isn't it?'

The question was so rhetorical that Stormgren didn't bother to answer it.

'Do you really appreciate,' he continued earnestly, 'how difficult this state of affairs makes my job?'

'It doesn't exactly help mine,' replied Karellen with some spirit. 'I wish people would stop thinking of me as a world dictator and remember that I'm only a civil servant trying to administer a somewhat idealistic colonial policy.'

'Then can't you at least give us some reason for your concealment? Because we don't understand it; it annoys us and gives rise to all sorts of rumours.'

Karellen gave that deep, rich laugh of his, just too musical to be altogether human.

'What am I supposed to be now? Does the robot theory still hold the field? I'd rather be a mass of cogwheels than crawl around the floor like a centipede, as some of the tabloids seem to imagine.'

Stormgren let out a Finnish oath he was fairly sure Karellen wouldn't know – though one could never be quite certain in these matters.

'Can't you ever be serious?'

'My dear Rikki,' said Karellen, 'it's only by not taking the human race seriously that I retain those fragments of my once considerable mental powers that I still possess.'

Despite himself, Stormgren smiled.

'That doesn't help me a great deal, does it? I have to go down there and convince my fellow men that although you won't show yourself, you've got nothing to hide. It's not an easy job. Curiosity is one of the most dominant human characteristics. You can't defy it forever.'

'Of all the problems that faced us when we came to Earth, this was the most difficult,' admitted Karellen. 'You have trusted our wisdom in other things – surely you can trust us in this!'

'*I* trust you,' said Stormgren, 'but Wainwright doesn't, nor do his supporters. Can you really blame them if they put a bad interpretation upon your unwillingness to show yourself?'

'Listen, Rikki,' Karellen answered at length. 'These matters are beyond my control. Believe me, I regret the need for this concealment, but the reasons are – sufficient. However, I will try to get a statement from my superior which may satisfy you and perhaps placate the Freedom League. Now, please, can we return to the agenda and start recording again? We've only reached Item 23, and I want to make a better job of settling the middle question than my predecessors for the last few thousand years. . . .'

'Any luck, Chief?' asked van Ryberg anxiously.

'I don't know,' Stormgren replied wearily as he threw the files down on his desk and collapsed into the seat. 'Karellen's consulting his superior now, whoever or whatever he may be. He won't make any promises.'

'Listen,' said Pieter abruptly. 'I've just thought of something. What reason have we for believing that there *is* anyone beyond Karellen? The Overlords may be a myth – you know how he hates the word.'

Tired though he was, Stormgren sat up with a start.

'It's an ingenious theory. But it clashes with what little I do know about Karellen's background.'

'And how much is that?'

'Well, he was a professor of astropolitics on a world he calls Skyrondel, and he put up a terrific fight before they made him take this job. He pretends to hate it, but he's really enjoying himself.'

Stormgren paused for a moment, and a smile of amusement softened his rugged features.

'At any rate, he once remarked that running a private zoo is rather good fun.'

'H'm-m – a somewhat dubious compliment. He's immortal, isn't he?'

'Yes, after a fashion, though there's something thousands of years ahead of him which he seems to fear: I can't imagine what it is. And that's really all I know.'

'He could easily have made it up. My theory is that his little fleet's lost in space and looking for a new home. He doesn't want us to know how few he and his comrades are. Perhaps all those other ships are automatic, and there's no one in any of them. They're just an imposing facade.'

'You,' said Stormgren with great severity, 'have been reading science fiction in office hours.'

Van Ryberg grinned.

' "The Invasion from Space" didn't turn out quite as expected, did it? My theory would certainly explain why Karellen never shows himself. He doesn't want us to learn that there are no Overlords.'

Stormgren shook his head in amused disagreement.

'Your explanation, as usual, is much too ingenious to be true. Though we can only infer its existence, there must be a great civilisation behind the Supervisor – and one that's known about Man for a very long time. Karellen himself must have been studying us for centuries. Look at his command of English, for example. He taught me how to speak it idiomatically!'

'I sometimes think he went a little too far,' laughed van Ryberg. 'Have you ever discovered anything he *doesn't* know?'

'Oh, yes, quite often – but only on trivial points. Yet, taken one at a time, I don't think his mental gifts are quite outside the range of human achievement. But no man could possibly do all the things he does.'

'That's more or less what I'd decided already,' agreed van Ryberg. 'We can argue around Karellen forever, but in the end we always come back to the same question – why the devil won't he show himself? Until he does, I'll go on theorising and the Freedom League will go on fulminating.'

He cocked a rebellious eye at the ceiling.

'One dark night, Mr Supervisor, I'm going to take a rocket up to your ship and climb in through the back door with my camera. What a scoop *that* would be!'

If Karellen was listening, he gave no sign of it. But, of course, he never did give any sign.

It was completely dark when Stormgren awoke. How strange that was, he was for a moment too sleepy to realise. Then, as full consciousness dawned, he sat up with a start and felt for the light-switch beside his bed.

In the darkness his hand encountered a bare stone wall, cold to the touch. He froze instantly, mind and body paralysed by the impact of the unexpected. Then, scarcely believing his senses, he kneeled on the bed and began to explore with his finger tips that shockingly unfamiliar wall.

He had been doing this for only a moment when there was a sudden 'click' and a section of the darkness slid aside. He caught a glimpse of a man silhouetted against a dimly lit background: then the door closed again and the darkness returned. It happened so swiftly that he saw nothing of the room in which he was lying.

An instant later, he was dazzled by the light of a powerful electric torch. The beam flickered across his face, held him steadily for a moment, then dipped to illuminate the whole bed – which was, he now saw, nothing more than a mattress supported on rough planks.

Out of the darkness a soft voice spoke to him in excellent English but with an accent which at first Stormgren could not identify.

'Ah, Mr Secretary, I'm glad to see you're awake. I hope you feel all right.'

The angry questions he was about to ask died upon his lips. He stared back into the darkness, then replied calmly, 'How long have I been unconscious?'

'Several days. We were promised that there would be no after-effects. I'm glad to see it's true.'

Partly to gain time, partly to test his own reactions, Stormgren swung his legs over the side of the bed. He was still wearing his night-clothes, but they were badly crumpled and seemed to have gathered considerable dirt. As he moved he felt a slight dizziness – not enough to be troublesome, but sufficient to convince him that he had indeed been drugged.

The oval of light slipped across the room and for the first time Stormgren had an idea of its dimensions. He realised that he was underground, possibly at a great depth. If he had been unconscious for several days he might be anywhere on Earth.

The torch-light illuminated a pile of clothes draped over a packing case.

'This should be enough for you,' said the voice from the darkness. 'Laundry's rather a problem here, so we grabbed a couple of your suits and half a dozen shirts.'

'That,' said Stormgren without humour, 'was considerate of you.'

'We're sorry about the absence of furniture and electric light. This place is convenient in some ways, but it rather lacks amenities.'

'Convenient for what?' asked Stormgren as he climbed into a shirt. The feel of the familiar cloth beneath his fingers was strangely reassuring.

'Just – convenient,' said the voice. 'And by the way, since we're likely to spend a good deal of time together, you'd better call me Joe.'

'Despite your nationality,' retorted Stormgren, 'I think I could pronounce your real name. It won't be worse than many Finnish ones.'

There was a slight pause and the light flickered for an instant.

'Well, I should have expected it,' said Joe resignedly. 'You must have plenty of practice at this sort of thing.'

'It's a useful hobby for a man in my position. I suppose you were born in Poland, and picked up your English in Britain during the War? I should think you were stationed quite a while in Scotland, from your r's.'

'That,' said the other very firmly, 'is quite enough. As you seem to have finished dressing – thank you.'

The walls around them, though occasionally faced with concrete, were mostly bare rock. It was clear to Stormgren that he was in some disused mine, and he could think of few more effective prisons. Until now the thought that he had been kidnapped had somehow failed to worry him greatly. He felt that, whatever happened, the immense resources of the Supervisor would soon locate and rescue him. Now he was not so sure – there must be a limit even to Karellen's powers, and if he was indeed buried in some remote continent all the science of the Overlords might be unable to trace him.

There were three other men round the table in the bare but brightly lit room. They looked up with interest and more than a little awe as Stormgren entered. Joe was by far the most outstanding character – not merely in physical bulk. The others were nondescript individuals, probably Europeans too. He would be able to place them when he heard them talk.

'Well,' he said evenly, 'now perhaps you'll tell me what this is all about, and what you hope to get out of it.'

Joe cleared his throat.

'I'd like to make one thing clear,' he said. 'This has nothing to do with Wainwright. He'll be as surprised as anyone else.'

Stormgren had rather expected this. It gave him relatively little satisfaction to confirm the existence of an extremist movement inside the Freedom League.

'As a matter of interest,' he said, 'how did you kidnap me?'

He hardly expected a reply, and was taken aback by the other's readiness – even eagerness – to answer. Only slowly did he guess the reason.

'It was all rather like one of those old Fritz Lang films,' said Joe cheerfully. 'We weren't sure if Karellen had a watch on you, so we took somewhat elaborate precautions. You were knocked out by gas in the air-conditioner – that was easy. Then we carried you out into the car and drove off – no trouble at all. All this, I might say, wasn't done by any of our people. We hired – er – professionals for the job. Karellen may get them – in fact, he's supposed to – but he'll be no wiser. When it left your house, the car drove into a long road tunnel not a thousand kilometres from New York. It came out again on schedule at the other end, still carrying a drugged man extraordinarily like the Secretary-General. About the same time a large truck loaded with metal cases emerged in the opposite direction and drove to a certain airfield where one of the cases was loaded aboard a freighter. Meanwhile the car that had done the job continued elaborate evasive action in the general direction of Canada. Perhaps Karellen's caught it by now: I don't know.

'As you'll see – I do hope you appreciate my frankness – our whole plan depended on one thing. We're pretty sure that Karellen can see and hear everything that happens on the surface of the Earth – but unless he uses magic, not science, he can't see underneath it. So he won't know about that transfer in the tunnel. Naturally we've taken a risk, but there were also one or two other stages in your removal which I won't go into now. We may have to use them again one day, and it would be a pity to give them away.'

Joe had related the whole story with such obvious gusto that Stormgren found it difficult to be appropriately furious. Yet he felt very disturbed. The plan was an ingenious one, and it seemed more than likely that whatever watch Karellen kept on him, he would have been tricked by this ruse.

The Pole was watching Stormgren's reactions closely. He would have to appear confident, whatever his real feelings.

'You must be a lot of fools,' said Stormgren scornfully, 'if you think you can trick the Overlords like this. In any case, what conceivable good would it do?'

Joe offered him a cigarette, which Stormgren refused, then lit one himself.

'Our motives,' he began, 'should be pretty obvious. We've found that argument's useless, so we have to take other measures. Whatever powers he's got, Karellen won't find it easy to deal with us. We're out to fight for our independence. Don't misunderstand me. There'll be nothing violent – at first, anyway. But the Overlords have to use human agents, and we can make it mighty uncomfortable for them.'

Starting with me, I suppose, thought Stormgren.

'What do you intend to do with me?' asked Stormgren at length. 'Am I a hostage, or what?'

'Don't worry – we'll look after you. We expect some visitors in a day or two, and until then we'll entertain you as well as we can.'

He added some words in his own language, and one of the others produced a brand-new pack of cards.

'We got these especially for you,' explained Joe. His voice suddenly became grave. 'I hope you've got plenty of cash,' he said anxiously. 'After all, we can hardly accept cheques.'

Quite overcome, Stormgren stared blankly at his captors. Then it suddenly seemed to him that all the cares and worries of office had lifted from his shoulders. Whatever happened, there was absolutely nothing he could do about it – and now these fantastic criminals wanted to play poker with him.

Abruptly, he threw back his head and laughed as he had not done for years.

During the next three days Stormgren analysed his captors with some thoroughness. Joe was the only one of any importance, the others were nonentities – the riffraff one would expect any illegal movement to gather round itself.

Joe was an altogether more complex individual, though sometimes he reminded Stormgren of an overgrown baby. Their interminable poker games were punctuated with violent political arguments, but it became obvious to Stormgren that the big Pole had never thought seriously about the cause for which he was fighting. Emotion and extreme conservatism clouded all his judgements. His country's long struggle for independence had conditioned him so completely that he still lived in the past. He was a picturesque survival, one of those who had no use for an ordered way of life. When his type had vanished, if it ever did, the world would be a safer but less interesting place.

There was little doubt as far as Stormgren was concerned, that Karellen had failed to locate him. He was not surprised when, five or six days after his capture, Joe told him to expect visitors. For some time the little group had shown increasing nervousness, and the prisoner guessed that the leaders of the movement, having seen that the coast was clear, were at last coming to collect him.

They were already waiting, gathered round the rickety table, when Joe waved him politely into the living room. The three thugs had vanished, and even Joe seemed somewhat restrained. Stormgren could see at once that he was now confronted by men of a much higher calibre. There was intellectual force, iron determination, and ruthlessness in these six men. Joe and his like were harmless – here were the real brains behind the organisation.

With a curt nod, Stormgren moved over to the seat and tried to look self-possessed. As he approached, the elderly, thick-set man on the far side of the table leaned forward and stared at him with piercing grey eyes. They made Stormgren so uncomfortable that he spoke first – something he had not intended to do.

'I suppose you've come to discuss terms. What's my ransom?'

He noticed that in the background someone was taking down his words in a shorthand notebook. It was all very businesslike.

The leader replied in a musical Welsh accent.

'You could put it that way, Mr Secretary-General. But we're interested in information, not cash. You know what our motives are. Call us a resistance movement, if you like. We believe that sooner or later Earth will have to fight for its independence. We kidnapped you partly to show Karellen that we mean business and are well organised, but largely because you are the only man who can tell us anything of the Overlords. You're a reasonable man Mr Stormgren. Give us your co-operation, and you can have your freedom.'

'Exactly what do you wish to know?' asked Stormgren cautiously.

'Do you know who, or what, the Overlords really are?'

Stormgren almost smiled.

'Believe me,' he said, 'I'm quite as anxious as you to discover that.'

'Then you'll answer our questions?'

'I make no promises. But I may.'

There was a slight sigh of relief from Joe and a rustle of anticipation went round the room.

'We have a general idea,' continued the other, 'of the circumstances in which you meet Karellen. Would you go through them carefully, leaving out nothing of importance?'

That was harmless enough, thought Stormgren. He had done it scores of times before, and it would give the appearance of co-operation.

He felt in his pockets and produced a pencil and an old envelope. Sketching rapidly while he conversed, he began:

'You know, of course, that a small flying machine, with no obvious means of propulsion, calls for me at regular intervals and takes me up to Karellen's ship. There is only one small room in that machine, and it's quite bare apart from a couch and table. The layout is something like this.' As Stormgren talked, it seemed to him that his mind was operating on two levels simultaneously. On the one hand he was trying to defy the men who had captured him, yet on the other he was hoping that they might help him to unravel Karellen's secret. He did not feel that he was betraying the Supervisor, for there was nothing here that he had not told many times before. Moreover, the thought that these men could harm Karellen in any way was fantastic.

The Welshman conducted most of the interrogation. It was fascinating to watch that agile mind trying one opening after another, testing and rejecting all the theories that Stormgren himself had abandoned long ago. Presently he leaned back with a sigh and the shorthand writer laid down his stylus.

'We're getting nowhere,' he said resignedly. 'We want more facts, and that means action – not argument.' The piercing eyes stared thoughtfully at Stormgren. For a moment he tapped nervously on the table – the first sign of uncertainty that Stormgren had noticed. Then he continued.

'I'm a little surprised, Mr Secretary, that you've never made an effort to learn more about the Overlords.'

'What do you suggest?' asked Stormgren coldly. 'I've told you that there's only one way out of the room in which I've had my talks with Karellen – and that leads straight to the airlock.'

'It might be possible,' mused the other, 'to devise instruments which could teach us something. I'm no scientist, but we can look into the matter. If we give you your freedom, would you be willing to assist with such a plan?'.

'Once and for all,' said Stormgren angrily, 'let me make my position perfectly clear. Karellen is working for a united world, and I'll do nothing to help his enemies. What his ultimate plans may be, I don't know, but I believe that they are good. You may annoy him, you may even delay the achievement of his aims, but it will make no difference in the end. You may be sincere in believing as you do: I can understand your fear that the traditions and cultures of little countries will be overwhelmed when the World State arrives. But you are wrong: it is useless to cling to the past. Even before the Overlords came to Earth, the sovereign state was dying. No one can save it now, and no one should try.'

There was no reply: the man opposite neither moved nor spoke. He sat with lips half open, his eyes now lifeless and blind. Around him the others were equally motionless, frozen in strained, unnatural attitudes. With a little gasp of pure horror, Stormgren rose to his feet and backed away toward the door. As he did so the silence was suddenly broken.

'That was a nice speech, Rikki. Now I think we can go.'

'Karellen! Thank God – but what have you done?'

'Don't worry. They're all right. You can call it a paralysis, but it's much subtler than that. They're simply living a few thousand times more slowly than normal. When we're gone, they'll never know what happened.'

'You'll leave them here until the police come?'

'No: I've a much better plan. I'm letting them go.'

Stormgren felt an illogical sense of relief which he did not care to analyse. He gave a last valedictory glance at the little room and its frozen occupants. Joe was standing on one foot, staring very stupidly at nothing. Suddenly Stormgren laughed and fumbled in his pockets.

'Thanks for the hospitality Joe,' he said. 'I think I'll leave a souvenir.'

On a reasonably clean sheet of paper he wrote carefully:

BANK OF MANHATTAN
Pay 'Joe' the sum of Fifteen Dollars
Thirty-five Cents ($15.35)
R. Stormgren.

As he laid the strip of paper beside the Pole, Karellen's voice inquired: 'Exactly what are you up to?'

'Paying a debt of honour,' explained Stormgren. 'The other two cheated, but I think Joe played fair.'

He felt very gay and light-headed as he walked to the door. Hanging just outside it was a large, featureless metal sphere that moved aside to let him pass. He guessed that it was some kind of robot, and it explained how Karellen had been able to reach him through the unknown layers of rock overhead.

'Carry on for a hundred yards,' said the sphere, speaking in Karellen's voice. 'Then turn to the left until I give you further instructions.'

He ran forward eagerly, though he realised that there was no need for hurry. The sphere remained hanging in the corridor, and Stormgren guessed that it was the generator of the paralysis field.

A minute later he came across a second sphere, waiting for him at a fork in the corridor.

'You've half a mile to go,' it said. 'Keep to the left until we meet again.'

Six times he encountered the spheres on his way to the open. At first he wondered if somehow the first robot had slipped ahead of him; then he guessed that there must be a chain of them maintaining a complete circuit down into the depths of the mine. At the entrance a group of guards formed a piece of improbable still life, watched over by yet another of the ubiquitous spheres. On the hillside a few yards away lay the little flying machine in which Stormgren had made all his journeys to Karellen.

He stood for a moment blinking in the fierce sunlight. As he climbed into the little ship, he had a last glimpse of the mine entrance and the men frozen round it. Quite suddenly a line of metal spheres raced out of the opening like silver cannon balls. Then the door closed behind him and with a sigh of relief he sank back upon the familiar couch.

For a while Stormgren waited until he had recovered his breath, then he uttered a single, heartfelt syllable:

'Well?'

'I'm sorry I couldn't rescue you before. But you'll see how very important it was to wait until all the leaders had gathered here.'

'Do you mean to say,' spluttered Stormgren, 'that you knew where I was all the time? If I thought—'

'Don't be so hasty,' answered Karellen, 'or at any rate, let me finish explaining.'

'It had better be good,' said Stormgren darkly. He was beginning to suspect that he had been no more than the bait in an elaborate trap.

'I've had a tracer on you for some time,' began Karellen, 'and though your late friends were correct in thinking that I couldn't follow you underground, I was able to keep track until they brought you to the mine. That transfer in the tunnel was ingenious, but when the first car ceased to react, it gave the show away and I soon located you again. Then it was merely a matter of waiting. I knew that once they were certain I'd lost you, the leaders would come here and I'd be able to trap them all.'

'But you're letting them go!'

'Until now,' said Karellen, 'I did not know which of the two billion men on this planet were the heads of the organisation. Now that they're located, I can trace their movements anywhere on Earth. That's far better than locking them up. They're effectively neutralised, and they know it.'

That rich laugh echoed round the tiny room.

'In some ways the whole affair was a comedy, but it had a serious purpose. It will be a valuable object lesson for any other plotters.'

Stormgren was silent for a while. He was not altogether satisfied, but he could see Karellen's point of view and some of his anger had evaporated.

'It's a pity to do it in my last few weeks of office,' he said, 'but from now on I'm going to have a guard on my house. Pieter can be kidnapped next time. How has he managed, by the way? Are things in as big a mess as I expect?'

'You'll be disappointed to find how little your absence has mattered. I've watched Pieter carefully this past week, and have deliberately avoided helping him. On the whole he's done very well – but he's not the man to take your place.'

'That's lucky for him,' said Stormgren, still rather aggrieved. 'And have you had any word from your superior about – about showing yourself to us? I'm sure now that it's the strongest argument your enemies have. Again and again, they told me, "We'll never trust the Overlords until we can see them." '

Karellen sighed.

'No, I have heard nothing. But I know what the answer must be.'

Stormgren did not press the matter. Once he might have done so, but now for the first time the faint shadow of a plan had come into his mind. What he had refused to do under duress, he might yet attempt of his own free will.

Pierre Duval showed no surprise when Stormgren walked unannounced into his office. They were old friends, and there was nothing unusual in the Secretary-General paying a personal visit to the chief of the Science Bureau. Certainly Karellen would not think it odd, even if by any remote chance he turned his attention to this corner of the world.

For a while the two men talked business and exchanged political gossip; then, rather hesitantly, Stormgren came to the point. As his visitor talked, the old Frenchman leaned back in his chair and his eyebrows rose steadily millimetre by millimetre until they were almost entangled in his forelock. Once or twice he seemed about to speak but each time thought better of it.

When Stormgren had finished, the scientist looked nervously around the room.

'Do you think he was listening?' he said.

'I don't believe he can. This place is supposed to be shielded from everything, isn't it? Karellen's not a magician. He knows where I am, but that's all.'

'I hope you're right. Apart from that, won't there be trouble when he discovers what you're trying to do? Because he will, you know.'

'I'll take that risk. Besides, we understand each other rather well.'

The physicist toyed with his pencil and stared into space for a while.

'It's a very pretty problem. I like it,' he said simply. Then he dived into a drawer and produced an enormous writing-pad, the biggest Stormgren had ever seen.

'Right,' he began, scribbling furiously. 'Let me make sure I have all the facts. Tell me everything you can about the room in which you have your interviews. Don't omit any detail, however trivial it seems.'

216

Finally the Frenchman studied his notes with puckered brow.

'And that's all you can tell me?'

'Yes.'

He snorted in disgust.

'What about lighting? Do you sit in total darkness? And how about heating, ventilation . . .'

Stormgren smiled at the characteristic outburst.

'The whole ceiling is luminous, and as far as I can tell the air comes through the speaker grille. I don't know how it leaves; perhaps the stream reverses at intervals, but I haven't noticed it. There's no sign of any heaters, but the room is always at normal temperature. As for the machine that takes me up to Karellen's ship, the room in which I travel is as featureless as an elevator cage.'

There was silence for several minutes while the physicist embroidered his writing-pad with meticulous and microscopic doodles. No one could have guessed that behind that still almost unfurrowed brow, the world's finest technical brain was working with the icy precision that had made it famous.

Then Duval nodded to himself in satisfaction, leaned forward and pointed his pencil at Stormgren.

'What makes you think, Rikki,' he asked, 'that Karellen's vision screen, as you call it, really is what it pretends to be? Doesn't it seem far more probable that your "vision screen" is really *nothing more complicated than a sheet of one-way glass*?'

Stormgren was so annoyed with himself that for a moment he sat in silence, retracing the past. From the beginning, he had never challenged Karellen's story – yet now that he came to look back, when had the Supervisor ever told him that he was using a television system? He had just taken it for granted; the whole thing had been a piece of psychological trickery, and he had been completely deceived. He tried to console himself with the thought that in the same circumstances even Duval would have fallen into the trap.

'If you're right,' he said, 'all I have to do is to smash the glass—'

Duval sighed.

'These non-technical laymen! Do you think it's likely to be made of anything you could smash without explosives? And if you succeeded, do you imagine that Karellen is likely to breathe the same air as we do? Won't it be nice for both of you if he flourishes in an atmosphere of chlorine?'

Stormgren turned rather pale.

'Well, what *do* you suggest?' he asked with some exasperation.

'I want to think it over. First of all we've got to find if my theory is correct, and if so learn something about the material of the screen. I'll put some of my best men on the job – by the way, I suppose you carry a briefcase when you visit the Supervisor? Is it the one you've got there?'

'Yes.'

'It's rather small. Will you get one at least ten centimetres deep, and use it from now on so that he becomes used to seeing it?'

'Very well,' said Stormgren doubtfully. 'Do you want me to carry a concealed X-ray set?'

The physicist grinned.

'I don't know yet, but we'll think of something. I'll let you know what it is in about a month's time.'

He gave a little laugh.

'Do you know what this all reminds me of?'

'Yes,' said Stormgren promptly, 'the time you were building illegal radio sets during the German occupation.'

Duval looked disappointed.

'Well, I suppose I *have* mentioned that once or twice before.'

Stormgren laid down the thick folder of typescript with a sigh of relief.

'Thank heavens that's settled at last,' he said. 'It's strange to think that those few hundred pages hold the future of Europe.'

Stormgren dropped the file into his brief-case, the back of which was now only six inches from the dark rectangle of the screen. From time to time his fingers played across the locks in a half-conscious nervous reaction, but he had no intention of pressing the concealed switch until the meeting was over. There was a chance that something might go wrong – though Duval had sworn that Karellen would detect nothing, one could never be sure.

'Now, you said you'd some news for me,' Stormgren continued, with scarcely concealed eagerness. 'Is it about—'

'Yes,' said Karellen. 'I received the Policy Board's decision a few hours ago, and am authorised to make an important statement. I don't think that the Freedom League will be very satisfied, but it should help to reduce the tension. We won't record this, by the way.

'You've often told me, Rikki, that no matter how unlike you we are physically, the human race will soon grow accustomed to us. That shows a lack of imagination on your part. It would probably be true in your case, but you must remember that most of the world is still uneducated by any reasonable standards, and is riddled with prejudices and superstitions that may take another hundred years to eradicate.

'You will grant us that we know something of human psychology. We know rather accurately what would happen if we revealed ourselves to the world in its present state of development. I can't go into details, even with you, so you must accept my analysis on trust. We can, however, make this definite promise, which should give you some satisfaction. *In fifty years – two generations from now – we shall come down from our ships and humanity will at last see us as we are.'*

Stormgren was silent for a while. He felt little of the satisfaction that Karellen's statement would have once given him. Indeed, he was somewhat confused by his partial success, and for a moment his resolution faltered. The truth would come with the passage of time, and all his plotting was unnecesary and perhaps unwise. If he still went ahead, it would only be for the selfish reason that he would not be alive fifty years from now.

Karellen must have seen his irresolution for he continued:

'I'm sorry if this disappoints you, but at least the political problems of the near future won't be your responsibility. Perhaps you still think that our fears are unfounded, but believe me, we've had convincing proof of the dangers of any other course.'

Stormgren leaned forward, breathing heavily.

'I always thought so! You *have* been seen by Man!'

'I didn't say that,' Karellen answered after a short pause. 'Your world isn't the only planet we've supervised.'

Stormgren was not to be shaken off so easily.

'There had been many legends suggesting that Earth has been visited in the past by other races.'

'I know. I've read the Historical Research Section's report. It makes Earth look like the crossroads of the Universe.'

'There may have been visits about which you know nothing,' said Stormgren, still angling hopefully. 'Though since you must have been observing us for thousands of years, I suppose that's rather unlikely.'

'I suppose it is,' said Karellen in his most unhelpful manner. And at that moment Stormgren made up his mind.

'Karellen,' he said abruptly. 'I'll draft out the statement and send it up to you for approval. But I reserve the right to continue pestering you, and if I see any opportunity, I'll do my best to learn your secret.'

'I'm perfectly well aware of that,' replied the Supervisor, with a suspicion of a chuckle.

'And you don't mind?'

'Not in the slightest – though I draw the line at atomic bombs, poison gas, or anything else that might strain our friendship.'

Stormgren wondered what, if anything, Karellen had guessed. Behind the Supervisor's banter he had recognised the note of understanding, perhaps – who could tell? – even of encouragement.

'I'm glad to know it,' Stormgren replied in as level a voice as he could manage. He rose to his feet, bringing down the cover of his case as he did so. His thumb slid along the catch.

'I'll draft that statement at once,' he repeated, 'and send it up on the teletype later today.'

While he was speaking, he pressed the button – and knew that all his fears had been groundless. Karellen's senses were no finer than Man's. The Supervisor could have detected nothing, for there was no change in his voice as he said goodbye and spoke the familiar code-words that opened the door of the chamber.

Yet Stormgren still felt like a shoplifter leaving a department store under the eyes of the house detective, and breathed a sigh of relief when the airlock doors had finally closed behind him.

'I admit,' said van Ryberg, 'that some of my theories haven't been very bright. But tell me what you think of this one.'

'Must I?'

Pieter didn't seem to notice.

'Is isn't really my idea,' he said modestly. 'I got it from a story of Chesterton's. Suppose that the Overlords are hiding the fact that they've got nothing to hide?'

'That sounds a little complicated to me,' said Stormgren, interestedly.

'What I mean is this,' van Ryberg continued eagerly. '*I* think that physically they're human beings like us. They realise that we'll tolerate being ruled by creatures we imagine to be – well, alien and superintelligent. But the human race being what it is, it just won't be bossed around by creatures of the same species.'

'Very ingenious, like all your theories,' said Stormgren. 'I wish you'd give them Opus numbers so that I could keep up with them. The objections to this one—'

But at that moment Alexander Wainwright was ushered in.

Stormgren wondered what he was thinking. He wondered, too, if Wainwright had made any contact with the men who had kidnapped him. He doubted it, for he believed Wainwright's disapproval of violent methods to be perfectly genuine. The extremists in his movement had discredited themselves thoroughly, and it would be a long time before the world heard of them again.

The head of the Freedom League listened in silence while the draft was read to him. Stormgren hoped that he appreciated this gesture, which had been Karellen's idea. Not for another twelve hours would the rest of the world know of the promise that had been made to its grandchildren.

'Fifty years,' said Wainwright thoughtfully. 'That is a long time to wait.'

'Not for Karellen, nor for humanity,' Stormgren answered. Only now was he beginning to realise the neatness of the Overlords' solution. It had given them the breathing space they believed they needed, and it had cut the ground from beneath the Freedom League's feet. He did not imagine that the League would capitulate, but its position would be seriously weakened.

Certainly Wainwright realised this as well, as he must also have realised that Karellen would be watching him. For he said very little and left as quickly as he could; Stormgren knew that he would not see him again in his term of office. The Freedom League might still be a nuisance but that was a problem for his successor.

There were some things that only time could cure. Evil men could be destroyed but nothing could be done about good men who were deluded.

'Here's your case,' said Duval. 'It's as good as new.'

'Thanks,' Stormgren answered, inspecting it carefully none the less. 'Now perhaps you can tell me what it was all about – and what we are going to do next.'

The physicist seemed more interested in his own thoughts.

'What I can't understand,' he said, 'is the ease with which we've got away with it. Now if *I'd* been Kar—'

'But you're not. Get to the point, man. What *did* we discover?'

Duval pushed forward a photographic record which to Stormgren looked rather like the autograph of a mild earthquake.

'See that little kink?'

'Yes. What is it?'

'Only Karellen.'

'Good Lord! Are you sure?'

'It's a pretty safe guess. He's sitting, or standing, or whatever he does, about two metres on the other side of the screen. If the resolution had been better, we might even have calculated his size.'

Stormgren's feelings were very mixed as he stared at the scarcely visible deflexion of the trace. Until now, there had been no proof that Karellen even had a material body. The evidence was still indirect, but he accepted it with little question.

Duval's voice cut into his reverie.

'You'll realise,' he said, 'that there's no such thing as a truly one-way glass. Karellen's screen, we found when we analysed our results, transmits light about a hundred times as easily in one direction as the other.' With the air of a conjuror producing a whole litter of rabbits, he reached into his desk and pulled out a pistol-like object with a flexible bell-mouth. It reminded Stormgren of a rubber blunderbuss, and he couldn't imagine what it was supposed to be.

Duval grinned at his perplexity.

'It isn't as dangerous as it looks. All you have to do is to ram the muzzle against the screen and press the trigger. It gives out a very powerful flash lasting five seconds, and in that time you'll be able to swing it around the room. Enough light will come back to give you a good view.'

'It won't hurt Karellen?'

'Not if you aim low and sweep it upward. That will give him time to accommodate – I suppose he has reflexes like ours, and we don't want to blind him.'

Stormgren looked at the weapon doubtfully and hefted it in his hand. For the last few weeks his conscience had been pricking him. Karellen had always treated him with unmistakable affection, despite his occasional devastating frankness, and now that their time together was drawing to its close he did not wish to do anything that might spoil that relationship. But the Supervisor had received due warning, and Stormgren had the conviction that if the choice had been his, Karellen would long ago have shown himself. Now the decision would be made for him – when their last meeting came to its end, Stormgren would gaze upon Karellen's face.

If, of course, Karellen had a face.

The nervousness that Stormgren had first felt had long since passed away. Karellen was doing almost all the talking, weaving the long, intricate sentences of which he was so fond. Once this had seemed to Stormgren the most wonderful and certainly the most unexpected of all Karellen's gifts.

Now it no longer appeared quite so marvellous, for he knew that like most of the Supervisor's abilities it was the result of sheer intellectual power and not of any special talent.

Karellen had time for any amount of literary composition when he slowed his thoughts down to the pace of human speech.

'Do not worry,' he said, 'about the Freedom League. It has been very quiet for the past month, and though it will revive again, it is no longer a real danger. Indeed since it's always valuable to know what your opponents are doing, the League is a very useful institution. Should it ever get into financial difficulties I might even subsidize it.'

Stormgren had often found it difficult to tell when Karellen was joking. He kept his face impassive.

'Very soon the League will lose another of its strongest arguments. There's been a good deal of criticism, mostly rather childish, of the special position you have held for the past few years. I found it very valuable in the early days of my administration, but now that the world is moving along the lines that I planned, it can cease. In the future, all my dealings with Earth will be indirect and the office of Secretary-General can once again become what it was originally intended to be.

'During the next fifty years there will be many crises, but they will pass. Almost a generation from now, I shall reach the nadir of my popularity, for plans must be put into operation which cannot be fully explained at the time. Attempts may even be made to destroy me. But the pattern of the future is clear enough, and one day all these difficulties will be forgotten – even to a race with memories as long as yours.'

The last words were spoken with such a peculiar emphasis that Stormgren immediately froze in his seat. Karellen never made accidental slips and even his indiscretions were calculated to many decimal places. But there was no time to ask questions – which certainly would not be answered – before the Supervisor had changed the subject again.

'You've often asked me about our long-term plans,' he continued. 'The foundation of the World State is of course only the first step. You will live to see its completion – but the change will be so imperceptible that few will notice it when it comes. After that there will be a pause for thirty years while the next generation reaches maturity. And then will come the day which we have promised. I am sorry that you will not be there.'

Stormgren's eyes were open, but his gaze was fixed far beyond the dark barrier of the screen. He was looking into the future, imagining the day he would never see.

'On that day,' continued Karellen, 'the human mind will experience one of its very rare psychological discontinuities. But no permanent harm will be done – the men of that age will be more stable than their grandfathers. We will always have been part of their lives, and when they meet us, we will not seem so – strange – as we would do to you.'

Stormgren had never known Karellen in so contemplative a mood, but this gave him no surprise. He did not believe that he had ever seen more than a few facets of the Supervisor's personality – the real Karellen was unknown and perhaps unknowable to human beings. And once again Stormgren had the feeling that the Supervisor's real interests were elsewhere.

'Then there will be another pause, only a short one this time, for the world will be growing impatient. Men will wish to go out to the stars, to see the other worlds of the Universe and to join us in our work. For it is only beginning – not a thousandth of the suns in the Galaxy have ever been visited by the races of which we know. One day, Rikki, your descendants in their own ships will be bringing civilisation to the worlds that are ripe to receive it – just as we are doing now.'

Karellen had fallen silent and Stormgren had the impression that the Supervisor was watching him intently.

'It is a great vision,' he said softly. 'Do you bring it to all your worlds?'

'Yes,' said Karellen, 'all that can understand it.'

Out of nowhere, a strangely disturbing thought came into Stormgren's mind.

'Suppose, after all, your experiment fails with Man? We have known such things in our own dealings with other races. Surely you have had your failures too?'

'Yes,' said Karellen, so softly that Stormgren could scarcely hear him. 'We have had our failures.'

'And what do you do then?'

'We wait – and try again.'

There was a pause lasting perhaps ten seconds. When Karellen spoke again, his words were muffled and so unexpected that for a moment Stormgren did not react.

'Goodbye, Rikki!'

Karellen had tricked him – probably it was too late. Stormgren's paralysis lasted only for a moment. Then he whipped out the flash-gun and jammed it against the screen.

Was it a lie? What *had* he really seen? No more, he was certain, than Karellen had intended. He was as sure as he could be of anything that the Supervisor had known his plan from the beginning, and had foreseen every moment of it.

Why else had that enormous chair been already empty when the circle of light blazed upon it? In the same moment he had started to swing the beam, but he was too late. The metal door, twice as high as a man, was closing swiftly when he first caught sight of it – closing swiftly, yet not quite swiftly enough.

Karellen had trusted him, had not wished him to go down into the long evening of his life still haunted by a mystery he could never solve. Karellen dared not defy the unknown power above him (was he of that same race, too?) but he had done all that he could. If he had disobeyed Him, He could never prove it.

'We have had our failures.'

Yes, Karellen, that was true – and were you the one who failed, before the dawn of human history? Even in fifty years, could you overcome the power of all the myths and legends of the world?

Yet Stormgren knew there would be no second failure. When the two races met again, the Overlords would have won the trust and friendship of Mankind, and not even the shock of recognition could undo that work.

And Stormgren knew also that the last thing he would ever see as he closed his eyes on life, would be that swiftly turning door, and the long black tail disappearing behind it.

A very famous and unexpectedly beautiful tail.

A barbed tail.

Time's Arrow

First published in *Science-Fantasy*, Summer 1950
Collected in *Reach for Tomorrow*

'Time's Arrow' is an example of how hard it is for the science-fiction writer to keep ahead of fact. The quite – at the time – imaginary discovery described in the tale now actually exists, and may be seen in the New York Natural History Museum. I think it most unlikely, however, that the rest will come true . . .

The river was dead and the lake already dying when the monster had come down the dried-up watercourse and turned onto the desolate mud-flats. There were not many places where it was safe to walk, and even where the ground was hardest the great pistons of its feet sank a foot or more beneath the weight they carried. Sometimes it had paused, surveying the landscape with quick, birdlike movements of its head. Then it had sunk even deeper into the yielding soil, so that fifty million years later men could judge with some accuracy the duration of its halts.

For the waters had never returned, and the blazing sun had baked the mud to rock. Later still the desert had poured over all this land, sealing it beneath protecting layers of sand. And later – very much later – had come Man.

'Do you think,' shouted Barton above the din, 'that Professor Fowler became a palaeontologist because he likes playing with pneumatic drills? Or did he acquire the taste afterward?'

'Can't hear you!' yelled Davis, leaning on his shovel in a most professional manner. He glanced hopefully at his watch.

'Shall I tell him it's dinnertime? He can't wear a watch while he's drilling, so he won't know any better.'

'I doubt if it will work,' Barton shrieked. 'He's got wise to us now and always adds an extra ten minutes. But it will make a change from this infernal digging.'

With noticeable enthusiasm the two geologists downed tools and started to walk toward their chief. As they approached, he shut off the drill and relative silence descended, broken only by the throbbing of the compressor in the background.

225

'About time we went back to camp, Professor,' said Davis, wristwatch held casually behind his back. 'You know what cook says if we're late.'

Professor Fowler, M.A., F.R.S., F.G.S., mopped some, but by no means all, of the ochre dust from his forehead. He would have passed anywhere as a typical navvy, and the occasional visitors to the site seldom recognised the Vice-President of the Geological Society in the brawny, half-naked work-man crouching over his beloved pneumatic drill.

It had taken nearly a month to clear the sandstone down to the surface of the petrified mud-flats. In that time several hundred square feet had been exposed, revealing a frozen snapshot of the past that was probably the finest yet discovered by palaeontology. Some scores of birds and reptiles had come here in search of the receding water, and left their footsteps as a perpetual monument eons after their bodies had perished. Most of the prints had been identified, but one – the largest of them all – was new to science. It belonged to a beast which must have weighed twenty or thirty tons: and Professor Fowler was following the fifty-million-year-old spoor with all the emotions of a big-game hunter tracking his prey. There was even a hope that he might yet overtake it; for the ground must have been treacherous when the unknown monster went this way and its bones might still be near at hand, marking the place where it had been trapped like so many creatures of its time.

Despite the mechanical aids available, the work was very tedious. Only the upper layers could be removed by the power tools, and the final uncovering had to be done by hand with the utmost care. Professor Fowler had good reason for his insistence that he alone should do the preliminary drilling, for a single slip might cause irreparable harm.

The three men were halfway back to the main camp, jolting over the rough road in the expedition's battered jeep, when Davis raised the question that had been intriguing the younger men ever since the work had begun.

'I'm getting a distinct impression,' he said, 'that our neighbours down the valley don't like us, though I can't imagine why. We're not interfering with them, and they might at least have the decency to invite us over.'

'Unless, of course, it is a war research plant,' added Barton, voicing a generally accepted theory.

'I don't think so,' said Professor Fowler mildly. 'Because it so happens that I've just had an invitation myself. I'm going there tomorrow.'

If his bombshell failed to have the expected result, it was thanks to his staff's efficient espionage system. For a moment Davis pondered over this confirmation of his suspicions; then he continued with a slight cough:

'No one else has been invited, then?'

The Professor smiled at his pointed hint, 'No,' he said. 'It's a strictly personal invitation. I know you boys are dying of curiosity but, frankly, I don't know any more about the place than you do. If I learn anything tomorrow, I'll tell you all about it. But at least we've found out who's running the establishment.'

His assistants pricked up their ears. 'Who is it?' asked Barton, 'My guess was the Atomic Development Authority.'

'You may be right,' said the Professor. 'At any rate, Henderson and Barnes are in charge.'

This time the bomb exploded effectively; so much so that Davis nearly drove the jeep off the road – not that that made much difference, the road being what it was.

'Henderson and Barnes? In *this* god-forsaken hole?'

'That's right,' said the Professor gaily. 'The invitation was actually from Barnes. He apologised for not contacting us before, made the usual excuses, and wondered if I could drop in for a chat.'

'Did he say what they are doing?'

'No; not a hint.'

'Barnes and Henderson?' said Barton thoughtfully. 'I don't know much about them except that they're physicists. What's their particular racket?'

'They're *the* experts on low-temperature physics,' answered Davis. 'Henderson was Director of the Cavendish for years. He wrote a lot of letters to *Nature* not so long ago. If I remember rightly, they were all about Helium II.'

Barton, who didn't like physicists and said so whenever possible, was not impressed. 'I don't even know what Helium II is,' he said smugly. 'What's more, I'm not at all sure that I want to.'

This was intended for Davis, who had once taken a physics degree in, as he explained, a moment of weakness. The 'moment' had lasted for several years before he had drifted into geology by rather devious routes, and he was always harking back to his first love.

'It's a form of liquid helium that only exists at a few degrees above absolute zero. It's got the most extraordinary properties but, as far as I can see, none of them can explain the presence of two leading physicists in this corner of the globe.'

They had now arrived at the camp, and Davis brought the jeep to its normal crash-halt in the parking space. He shook his head in annoyance as he bumped into the truck ahead with slightly more violence than usual.

'These tyres are nearly through. Have the new ones come yet?'

'Arrived in the 'copter this morning, with a despairing note from Andrews hoping that you'd make them last a full fortnight this time.'

'Good! I'll get them fitted this evening.'

The Professor had been walking a little ahead; now he dropped back to join his assistants.

'You needn't have hurried Jim,' he said glumly. 'It's corned beef again.'

It would be most unfair to say that Barton and Davis did less work because the Professor was away. They probably worked a good deal harder than usual, since the native labourers required twice as much supervision in the Chief's absence. But there was no doubt that they managed to find time for a considerable amount of extra talking.

Ever since they had joined Professor Fowler, the two young geologists had been intrigued by the strange establishment five miles away down the valley. It was clearly a research organisation of some type, and Davis had identified the tall stacks of an atomic-power unit. That, of course, gave no clue to the work that was proceeding, but it did indicate its importance. There were still only a few thousand turbo-piles in the world, and they were all reserved for major projects.

There were dozens of reasons why two great scientists might have hidden themselves in this place: most of the more hazardous atomic research was carried out as far as possible from civilisation, and some had been abandoned altogether until laboratories in space could be set up. Yet it seemed odd that this work, whatever it was, should be carried out so close to what had now become the most important centre of geological research in the world. It might, of course, be no more than a coincidence; certainly the physicists had never shown any interest in their compatriots so near at hand.

Davis was carefully chipping round one of the great footprints, while Barton was pouring liquid perspex into those already uncovered so that they would be preserved from harm in the transparent plastic. They were working in a somewhat absentminded manner, for each was unconsciously listening for the sound of the jeep. Professor Fowler had promised to collect them when he returned from his visit, for the other vehicles were in use elsewhere and they did not relish a two-mile walk back to camp in the broiling sun. Moreover, they wanted to have any news as soon as possible.

'How many people,' said Barton suddenly, 'do you think they have over there?'

Davis straightened himself up. 'Judging from the buildings, not more than a dozen or so.'

'Then it might be a private affair, not an ADA project at all.'

'Perhaps, though it must have pretty considerable backing. Of course, Henderson and Barnes could get that on their reputations alone.'

'That's where the physicists score,' said Barton. 'They've only got to convince some war department that they're on the track of a new weapon, and they can get a couple of million without any trouble.'

He spoke with some bitterness; for, like most scientists, he had strong views on this subject. Barton's views, indeed, were even more definite than usual, for he was a Quaker and had spent the last year of the War arguing with not-unsympathetic tribunals.

The conversation was interrupted by the roar and clatter of the jeep, and the two men ran over to meet the Professor.

'Well?' they cried simultaneously.

Professor Fowler looked at them thoughtfully, his expression giving no hint of what was in his mind. 'Had a good day?' he said at last.

'Come off it, Chief!' protested Davis. 'Tell us what you've found out.'

The Professor climbed out of the seat and dusted himself down. 'I'm sorry, boys,' he said with some embarrassment, 'I can't tell you a thing, and that's flat.'

There were two united wails of protest, but he waved them aside. 'I've had a very interesting day, but I've had to promise not to say anything about it. Even now I don't know exactly what's going on, but it's something pretty revolutionary – as revolutionary, perhaps, as atomic power. But Dr Henderson is coming over tomorrow; see what you can get out of him.'

For a moment, both Barton and Davis were so overwhelmed by the sense of anticlimax that neither spoke. Barton was the first to recover. 'Well, surely there's a reason for this sudden interest in our activities?'

The Professor thought this over for a moment. 'Yes, it wasn't entirely a social call,' he admitted: 'They think I may be able to help them. Now, no more questions, unless you want to walk back to camp!'

Dr Henderson arrived on the site in the middle of the afternoon. He was a stout, elderly man, dressed rather incongruously in a dazzling white laboratory smock and very little else. Though the garb was eccentric, it was eminently practical in so hot a climate.

Davis and Barton were somewhat distant when Professor Fowler introduced them; they still felt that they had been snubbed and were determined that their visitor should understand their feelings. But Henderson was so obviously interested in their work that they soon thawed, and the Professor left them to show him round the excavations while he went to supervise the natives.

The physicist was greatly impressed by the picture of the world's remote past that lay exposed before his eyes. For almost an hour the two geologists took him over the workings yard by yard, talking of the creatures who had gone this way and speculating about future discoveries. The track which Professor Fowler was following now lay in a wide trench running away from the main excavation, for he had dropped all other work to investigate it. At its end the trench was no longer continuous: to save time, the Professor had begun to sink pits along the line of the footprints. The last sounding had missed altogether, and further digging had shown that the great reptile had made a sudden change of course.

'This is the most interesting bit,' said Barton to the slightly wilting physicist. 'You remember those earlier places where it had stopped for a moment to have a look around? Well, here it seems to have spotted something and has gone off in a new direction at a run, as you can see from the spacing.'

'I shouldn't have thought such a brute *could* run.'

'Well, it was probably a pretty clumsy effort, but you can cover quite a bit of ground with a fifteen-foot stride. We're going to follow it as far as we can. We may even find what it was chasing. I think the Professor has hopes of discovering a trampled battlefield with the bones of the victim still around. That would make everyone sit up.'

Dr Henderson smiled. 'Thanks to Walt Disney, I can picture the scene rather well.'

Davis was not very encouraging. 'It was probably only the missus banging

229

the dinner gong,' he said. 'The most infuriating part of our work is the way everything can peter out when it gets most exciting. The strata have been washed away, or there's been an earthquake – or, worse still, some silly fool has smashed up the evidence because be didn't recognise its value.'

Henderson nodded in agreement. 'I can sympathise with you,' he said. 'That's where the physicist has the advantage. He knows he'll get the answer eventually, if there is one.'

He paused rather diffidently, as if weighing his words with great care. 'It would save you a lot of trouble, wouldn't it, if you could actually *see* what took place in the past, without having to infer it by these laborious and uncertain methods. You've been a couple of months following these foot-steps for a hundred yards, and they may lead nowhere for all your trouble.'

There was a long silence. Then Barton spoke in a very thoughtful voice.

'Naturally, Doctor, we're rather curious about your work,' he began. 'Since Professor Fowler won't tell us anything, we've done a good deal of speculating. Do you really mean to say that—'

The physicist interrupted him rather hastily. 'Don't give it any more thought,' he said. 'I was only daydreaming. As for our work, it's a very long way from completion, but you'll hear all about it in due course. We're not secretive – but, like everyone working in a new field, we don't want to say anything until we're sure of our ground. Why, if any other palaeontologists came near this place, I bet Professor Fowler would chase them away with a pick-axe!'

'That's not quite true,' smiled Davis. 'He'd be much more likely to set them to work. But I see your point of view; let's hope we don't have to wait too long.'

That night, much midnight oil was burned at the main camp. Barton was frankly sceptical, but Davis had already built up an elaborate superstructure of theory around their visitor's remarks.

'It would explain so many things,' he said. 'First of all, their presence in this place, which otherwise doesn't make sense at all. We know the ground level here to within an inch for the last hundred million years, and we can date any event with an accuracy of better than one per cent. There's not a spot on Earth that's had its past worked out in such detail – it's the obvious place for an experiment like this!'

'But do you think it's even theoretically possible to build a machine that can see into the past?'

'I can't imagine how it could be done. But I daren't say it's impossible – especially to men like Henderson and Barnes.'

'Hmmm. Not a very convincing argument. Is there any way we can hope to test it? What about those letters to *Nature*?'

'I've sent to the College Library; we should have them by the end of the week. There's always some continuity in a scientist's work, and they may give us some valuable clues.'

But at first they were disappointed; indeed, Henderson's letters only increased the confusion. As Davis had remembered, most of them had been about the extraordinary properties of Helium II.

'It's really fantastic stuff,' said Davis. 'If a liquid behaved like this at normal temperatures, everyone would go mad. In the first place, it hasn't any viscosity at all. Sir George Darwin once said that if you had an ocean of Helium II, ships could sail in it without any engines. You'd give them a push at the beginning of their voyage and let them run into buffers on the other side. There'd be one snag, though; long before that happened the stuff would have climbed straight up the hull and the whole outfit would have sunk – gurgle, gurgle, gurgle . . .'

'Very amusing,' said Barton, 'but what the heck has this to do with your precious theory?'

'Not much,' admitted Davis. 'However, there's more to come. It's possible to have two streams of Helium II flowing in opposite directions *in the same tube* – one stream going through the other, as it were.'

'That must take a bit of explaining; it's almost as bad as an object moving in two directions at once. I suppose there *is* an explanation, something to do with Relativity, I bet.'

Davis was reading carefully. 'The explanation,' he said slowly, 'is very complicated and I don't pretend to understand it fully. But it depends on the fact that liquid helium can have *negative* entropy under certain conditions.'

'As I never understood what positive entropy is, I'm not much wiser.'

'Entropy is a measure of the heat distribution of the Universe. At the beginning of time, when all energy was concentrated in the suns, entropy was a minimum. It will reach its maximum when everything's at a uniform temperature and the Universe is dead. There will still be plenty of heat around, but it won't be usable.'

'Whyever not?'

'Well, all the water in a perfectly flat ocean won't run a hydro-electric plant – but quite a little lake up in the hills will do the trick. You must have a difference in level.'

'I get the idea. Now I come to think of it, didn't someone once call entropy "Time's Arrow"?'

'Yes – Eddington, I believe. Any kind of clock you care to mention – a pendulum, for instance – might just as easily run forward as backward. But entropy is a strictly one-way affair – it's always increasing with the passage of time. Hence the expression, "Time's Arrow".'

'Then *negative* entropy – my gosh!'

For a moment the two men looked at each other. Then Barton asked in a rather subdued voice: 'What does Henderson say about it?'

'I'll quote from his last letter: "The discovery of negative entropy introduces quite new and revolutionary conceptions into our picture of the physical world. Some of these will be examined in a further communication."'

'And are they?'

'That's the snag: there's no "further communication". From that you can guess two alternatives. First, the Editor of *Nature* may have declined to publish the letter. I think we can rule that one out. Second, the consequences may have been *so* revolutionary that Henderson never did write a further report.'

'Negative entropy – negative time,' mused Barton. 'It seems fantastic; yet it might be theoretically possible to build some sort of device that could see into the past. . . .'

'I know what we'll do,' said Davis suddenly. 'We'll tackle the Professor about it and watch his reactions. Now I'm going to bed before I get brain fever.'

That night Davis did not sleep well. He dreamed that he was walking along a road that stretched in both directions as far as the eye could see. He had been walking for miles before he came to the signpost, and when he reached it he found that it was broken and the two arms were revolving idly in the wind. As they turned, he could read the words they carried. One said simply: To the Future; the other: To the Past.

They learned nothing from Professor Fowler, which was not surprising; next to the Dean, he was the best poker player in the College. He regarded his slightly fretful assistants with no trace of emotion while Davis trotted out his theory.

When the young man had finished, he said quietly, 'I'm going over again tomorrow, and I'll tell Henderson about your detective work. Maybe he'll take pity on you; maybe he'll tell me a bit more, for that matter. Now let's go to work.'

Davis and Barton found it increasingly difficult to take a great deal of interest in their own work while their minds were filled with the enigma so near at hand. Nevertheless they continued conscientiously, though ever and again they paused to wonder if all their labour might not be in vain. If it were, they would be the first to rejoice. Supposing one could see into the past and watch history unfolding itself, back to the dawn of time! All the great secrets of the past would be revealed: one could watch the coming of life on the Earth, and the whole story of evolution from amoeba to man.

No; it was too good to be true. Having decided this, they would go back to their digging and scraping for another half-hour until the thought would come: but what if it *were* true? And then the whole cycle would begin all over again.

When Professor Fowler returned from his second visit, he was a subdued and obviously shaken man. The only satisfaction his assistants could get from him was the statement that Henderson had listened to their theory and complimented them on their powers of deduction.

That was all; but in Davis's eyes it clinched the matter, though Barton was still doubtful. In the weeks that followed, he too began to waver, until at last they were both convinced that the theory was correct. For Professor Fowler was spending more and more of his time with Henderson and

Barnes; so much so that they sometimes did not see him for days. He had almost lost interest in the excavations, and had delegated all responsibility to Barton, who was now able to use the big pneumatic drill to his heart's content.

They were uncovering several yards of footprints a day, and the spacing showed that the monster had now reached its utmost speed and was advancing in great leaps as if nearing its victim. In a few days they might reveal the evidence of some eon-old tragedy, preserved by a miracle and brought down the ages for the observation of man. Yet all this seemed very unimportant now; for it was clear from the Professor's hints and his general air of abstraction that the secret research was nearing its climax. He had told them as much, promising that in a very few days, if all went well, their wait would be ended. But beyond that he would say nothing.

Once or twice Henderson had paid them a visit, and they could see that he was now labouring under a considerable strain. He obviously wanted to talk about his work, but was not going to do so until the final tests had been completed. They could only admire his self-control and wish that it would break down. Davis had a distinct impression that the elusive Barnes was mainly responsible for his secrecy; he had something of a reputation for not publishing work until it had been checked and double-checked. If these experiments were as important as they believed, his caution was understandable, however infuriating.

Henderson had come over early that morning to collect the Professor, and as luck would have it, his car had broken down on the primitive road. This was unfortunate for Davis and Barton, who would have to walk to camp for lunch, since Professor Fowler was driving Henderson back in the jeep. They were quite prepared to put up with this if their wait was indeed coming to an end, as the others had more than half-hinted.

They had stood talking by the side of the jeep for some time before the two older scientists had driven away. It was a rather strained parting, for each side knew what the other was thinking. Finally Barton, as usual the most outspoken, remarked:

'Well, Doc, if this *is* Der Tag, I hope everything works properly. I'd like a photograph of a brontosaurus as a souvenir.'

This sort of banter had been thrown at Henderson so often that he now took it for granted. He smiled without much mirth and replied, 'I don't promise anything. It may be the biggest flop ever.'

Davis moodily checked the tyre pressure with the toe of his boot. It was a new set, he noticed, with an odd zigzag pattern he hadn't seen before.

'Whatever happens, we hope you'll tell us. Otherwise, we're going to break in one night and find out just what you're up to.'

Henderson laughed. 'You'll be a pair of geniuses if you can learn anything from our present lash-up. But, if all goes well, we may be having a little celebration by nightfall.'

'What time do you expect to be back, Chief?'

'Somewhere around four. I don't want you to have to walk back for tea.'

'OK – here's hoping!'

The machine disappeared in a cloud of dust, leaving two very thoughtful geologists standing by the roadside. Then Barton shrugged his shoulders.

'The harder we work,' he said, 'the quicker the time will go. Come along!'

The end of the trench, where Barton was working with the power drill, was now more than a hundred yards from the main excavation. Davis was putting the final touches to the last prints to be uncovered. They were now very deep and widely spaced, and looking along them, one could see quite clearly where the great reptile had changed its course and started, first to run, and then to hop like an enormous kangaroo. Barton wondered what it must have felt like to see such a creature bearing down upon one with the speed of an express; then he realised that if their guess was true this was exactly what they might soon be seeing.

By mid-afternoon they had uncovered a record length of track. The ground had become softer, and Barton was roaring ahead so rapidly that he had almost forgotten his other preoccupations. He had left Davis yards behind, and both men were so busy that only the pangs of hunger reminded them when it was time to finish. Davis was the first to notice that it was later than they had expected, and he walked over to speak to his friend.

'It's nearly half-past four!' he said when the noise of the drill had died away. 'The Chief's late – I'll be mad if he's had tea before collecting us.'

'Give him another half-hour,' said Barton. 'I can guess what's happened. They've blown a fuse or something and it's upset their schedule.'

Davis refused to be placated. 'I'll be darned annoyed if we've got to walk back to camp again. Anyway, I'm going up the hill to see if there's any sign of him.'

He left Barton blasting his way through the soft rock, and climbed the low hill at the side of the old riverbed. From here one could see far down the valley, and the twin stacks of the Henderson-Barnes laboratory were clearly visible against the drab landscape. But there was no sign of the moving dust-cloud that would be following the jeep: the Professor had not yet started for home.

Davis gave a snort of disgust. There was a two-mile walk ahead of them, after a particularly tiring day, and to make matters worse they'd now be late for tea. He decided not to wait any longer, and was already walking down the hill to rejoin Barton when something caught his eye and he stopped to look down the valley.

Around the two stacks, which were all he could see of the laboratory, a curious haze not unlike a heat tremor was playing. They must be hot, he knew, but surely not *that* hot. He looked more carefully, and saw to his amazement that the haze covered a hemisphere that must be almost a quarter of a mile across.

And, quite suddenly, it exploded. There was no light, no blinding flash; only a ripple that spread abruptly across the sky and then was gone. The haze had vanished – and so had the two great stacks of the power-house.

Feeling as though his legs had turned suddenly to water, Davis slumped down upon the hilltop and stared open-mouthed along the valley. A sense of overwhelming disaster swept into his mind; as in a dream, he waited for the explosion to reach his ears.

It was not impressive when it came; only a dull, long-drawn-out whoooooosh! that died away swiftly in the still air. Half unconsciously, Davis noticed that the chatter of the drill had also stopped; the explosion must have been louder than he thought for Barton to have heard it too.

The silence was complete. Nothing moved anywhere as far as his eye could see in the whole of that empty, barren landscape. He waited until his strength returned; then, half running, he went unsteadily down the hill to rejoin his friend.

Barton was half sitting in the trench with his head buried in his hands. He looked up as Davis approached; and although his features were obscured by dust and sand, the other was shocked at the expression in his eyes.

'So you heard it too!' Davis said. 'I think the whole lab's blown up. Come along, for heaven's sake!'

'Heard what?' said Barton dully.

Davis stared at him in amazement. Then he realised that Barton could not possibly have heard any sound while he was working with the drill. The sense of disaster deepened with a rush; he felt like a character in some Greek tragedy, helpless before an implacable doom.

Barton rose to his feet. His face was working strangely, and Davis saw that he was on the verge of breakdown. Yet, when he spoke, his words were surprisingly calm.

'What fools we were!' he said. 'How Henderson must have laughed at us when we told him that he was trying to *see* into the past!'

Mechanically, Davis moved to the trench and stared at the rock that was seeing the light of day for the first time in fifty million years. Without much emotion, now, he traced again the zigzag pattern he had first noticed a few hours before. It had sunk only a little way into the mud, as if when it was formed the jeep had been travelling at its utmost speed.

No doubt it had been; for in one place the shallow tyre marks had been completely obliterated by the monster's footprints. They were now very deep indeed, as if the great reptile was about to make the final leap upon its desperately fleeing prey.

A Walk in the Dark

First appeared in *Thrilling Wonder Stories*, August 1950
Collected in *Reach for Tomorrow*

Robert Armstrong had walked just over two miles, as far as he could judge, when his torch failed. He stood still for a moment, unable to believe that such a misfortune could really have befallen him. Then, half maddened with rage, he hurled the useless instrument away. It landed somewhere in the darkness, disturbing the silence of this little world. A metallic echo came ringing back from the low hills: then all was quiet again.

This, thought Armstrong, was the ultimate misfortune. Nothing more could happen to him now. He was even able to laugh bitterly at his luck, and resolved never again to imagine that the fickle goddess had ever favoured him. Who would have believed that the only tractor at Camp IV would have broken down when he was just setting off for Port Sanderson? He recalled the frenzied repair work, the relief when the second start had been made – and the final debacle when the caterpillar track had jammed.

It was no use then regretting the lateness of his departure: he could not have foreseen these accidents, and it was still a good four hours before the 'Canopus' took off. He *had* to catch her, whatever happened; no other ship would be touching at this world for another month.

Apart from the urgency of his business, four more weeks on this out-of-the-way planet were unthinkable.

There had been only one thing to do. It was lucky that Port Sanderson was little more than six miles from the camp – not a great distance, even on foot. He had had to leave all his equipment behind, but it could follow on the next ship and he could manage without it. The road was poor, merely stamped out of the rock by one of the Board's hundred-ton crushers, but there was no fear of going astray.

Even now, he was in no real danger, though he might well be too late to catch the ship. Progress would be slow, for he dare not risk losing the road in this region of canyons and enigmatic tunnels that had never been explored. It was, of course, pitch-dark. Here at the edge of the galaxy the stars were so few and scattered that their light was negligible. The strange crimson sun of this lonely world would not rise for many hours, and although five of the little moons were in the sky they could barely be seen by the unaided eye. Not one of them could even cast a shadow.

Armstrong was not the man to bewail his luck for long. He began to walk slowly along the road, feeling its texture with his feet. It was, he knew, fairly straight except where it wound through Carver's Pass. He wished he had a stick or something to probe the way before him, but he would have to rely for guidance on the feel of the ground.

It was terribly slow at first, until he gained confidence. He had never known how difficult it was to walk in a straight line. Although the feeble stars gave him his bearings, again and again he found himself stumbling among the virgin rocks at the edge of the crude roadway. He was travelling in long zigzags that took him to alternate sides of the road. Then he would stub his toes against the bare rock and grope his way back on to the hard-packed surface once again.

Presently it settled down to a routine. It was impossible to estimate his speed; he could only struggle along and hope for the best. There were four miles to go – four miles and as many hours. It should be easy enough, unless he lost his way. But he dared not think of that.

Once he had mastered the technique he could afford the luxury of thought. He could not pretend that he was enjoying the experience, but he had been in much worse positions before. As long as he remained on the road, he was perfectly safe. He had been hoping that as his eyes became adapted to the starlight he would be able to see the way, but he now knew that the whole journey would be blind. The discovery gave him a vivid sense of his remoteness from the heart of the Galaxy. On a night as clear as this, the skies of almost any other planet would have been blazing with stars. Here at this outpost of the Universe the sky held perhaps a hundred faintly gleaming points of light, as useless as the five ridiculous moons on which no one had ever bothered to land.

A slight change in the road interrupted his thoughts. Was there a curve here, or had he veered off to the right again? He moved very slowly along the invisible and ill-defined border. Yes, there was no mistake: the road was bending to the left. He tried to remember its appearance in the daytime, but he had only seen it once before. Did this mean that he was nearing the Pass? He hoped so, for the journey would then be half completed.

He peered ahead into the blackness, but the ragged line of the horizon told him nothing. Presently he found that the road had straightened itself again and his spirits sank. The entrance to the Pass must still be some way ahead: there were at least four miles to go.

Four miles – how ridiculous the distance seemed! How long would it take the 'Canopus' to travel four miles? He doubted if man could measure so short an interval of time. And how many trillions of miles had he, Robert Armstrong, travelled in his life? It must have reached a staggering total by now, for in the last twenty years he had scarcely stayed more than a month at a time on any single world. This very year, he had twice made the crossing of the Galaxy, and that was a notable journey even in these days of the phantom drive.

He tripped over a loose stone, and the jolt brought him back to reality. It was no use, here, thinking of ships that could eat up the light-years. He was facing nature, with no weapons but his own strength and skill.

It was strange that it took him so long to identify the real cause of his uneasiness. The last four weeks had been very full, and the rush of his departure, coupled with the annoyance and anxiety caused by the tractor's breakdowns, had driven everything else from his mind. Moreover, he had always prided himself on his hard-headedness and lack of imagination. Until now, he had forgotten all about that first evening at the Base, when the crews had regaled him with the usual tall yarns concocted for the benefit of newcomers.

It was then that the old Base clerk had told the story of his walk by night from Port Sanderson to the camp, and of what had trailed him through Carver's Pass, keeping always beyond the limit of his torchlight. Armstrong, who had heard such tales on a score of worlds, had paid it little attention at the time. This planet, after all, was known to be uninhabited. But logic could not dispose of the matter as easily as that. Suppose, after all, there was some truth in the old man's fantastic tale . . . ?

It was not a pleasant thought, and Armstrong did not intend to brood upon it. But he knew that if he dismissed it out of hand it would continue to prey on his mind. The only way to conquer imaginary fears was to face them boldly; he would have to do that now.

His strongest argument was the complete barrenness of this world and its utter desolation, though against that one could set many counter-arguments, as indeed the old clerk had done. Man had only lived on this planet for twenty years, and much of it was still unexplored. No one could deny that the tunnels out in the wasteland were rather puzzling, but everyone believed them to be volcanic vents. Though, of course, life often crept into such places. With a shudder he remembered the giant polyps that had snared the first explorers of Vargon III.

It was all very inconclusive. Suppose, for the sake of argument, one granted the existence of life here. What of that?

The vast majority of life forms in the Universe were completely indifferent to man. Some, of course, like the gas-beings of Alcoran or the roving wave-lattices of Shandaloon, could not even detect him but passed through or around him as if he did not exist. Others were merely inquisitive, some embarrassingly friendly. There were few indeed that would attack unless provoked.

Nevertheless, it was a grim picture that the old stores clerk had painted. Back in the warm, well-lighted smoking-room, with the drinks going around, it had been easy enough to laugh at it. But here in the darkness, miles from any human settlement, it was very different.

It was almost a relief when he stumbled off the road again and had to grope with his hands until he found it once more. This seemed a very rough patch, and the road was scarcely distinguishable from the rocks around. In a few minutes, however, he was safely on his way again.

It was unpleasant to see how quickly his thoughts returned to the same disquieting subject. Clearly it was worrying him more than he cared to admit.

He drew consolation from one fact: it had been quite obvious that no one at the base had believed the old fellow's story. Their questions and banter had proved that. At the time, he had laughed as loudly as any of them. After all, what *was* the evidence? A dim shape, just seen in the darkness, that might well have been an oddly formed rock. And the curious clicking noise that had so impressed the old man – anyone could imagine such sounds at night if they were sufficiently overwrought. If it had been hostile, why hadn't the creature come any closer? 'Because it was afraid of my light,' the old chap had said. Well, that was plausible enough: it would explain why nothing had ever been seen in the daylight. Such a creature might live underground, only emerging at night – damn it, why was he taking the old idiot's ravings so seriously! Armstrong got control of his thoughts again. If he went on this way, he told himself angrily, he would soon be seeing and hearing a whole menagerie of monsters.

There was, of course, one factor that disposed of the ridiculous story at once. It was really very simple; he felt sorry he hadn't thought of it before. *What would such a creature live on?* There was not even a trace of vegetation on the whole of the planet. He laughed to think that the bogy could be disposed of so easily – and in the same instant felt annoyed with himself for not laughing aloud. If he was so sure of his reasoning, why not whistle, or sing, or do anything to keep up his spirits? He put the question fairly to himself as a test of his manhood. Half-ashamed, he had to admit that he was still afraid – afraid because 'there *might* be something in it, after all.' But at least his analysis had done him some good.

It would have been better if he had left it there, and remained half-convinced by his argument. But a part of his mind was still busily trying to break down his careful reasoning. It succeeded only too well, and when he remembered the plant-beings of Xantil Major the shock was so unpleasant that he stopped dead in his tracks.

Now the plant-beings of Xantil were not in any way horrible. They were in fact extremely beautiful creatures. But what made them appear so distressing now was the knowledge that they could live for indefinite periods with no food whatsoever. All the energy they needed for their strange lives they extracted from cosmic radiation – and that was almost as intense here as anywhere else in the universe.

He had scarcely thought of one example before others crowded into his mind and he remembered the life form on Trantor Beta, which was the only one known capable of directly utilising atomic energy. That too had lived on an utterly barren world, very much like this . . .

Armstrong's mind was rapidly splitting into two distinct portions, each trying to convince the other and neither wholly succeeding. He did not realise how far his morale had gone until he found himself holding his breath lest it conceal any sound from the darkness about him. Angrily, he cleared his mind of the rubbish that had been gathering there and turned once more to the immediate problem.

There was no doubt that the road was slowly rising, and the silhouette of the horizon seemed much higher in the sky. The road began to twist, and suddenly he was aware of great rocks on either side of him. Soon only a narrow ribbon of sky was still visible, and the darkness became, if possible, even more intense.

Somehow, he felt safer with the rock walls surrounding him: it meant that he was protected except in two directions. Also, the road had been levelled more carefully and it was easy to keep it. Best of all, he knew now that the journey was more than half completed.

For a moment his spirits began to rise. Then, with maddening perversity, his mind went back into the old grooves again. He remembered that it was on the far side of Carver's Pass that the old clerk's adventure had taken place – if it had ever happened at all.

In half a mile, he would be out in the open again, out of the protection of these sheltering rocks. The thought seemed doubly horrible now and he already felt a sense of nakedness. He could be attacked from any direction, and he would be utterly helpless . . .

Until now, he had still retained some self-control. Very resolutely he had kept his mind away from the one fact that gave some colour to the old man's tale – the single piece of evidence that had stopped the banter in the crowded room back at the camp and brought a sudden hush upon the company. Now, as Armstrong's will weakened, he recalled again the words that had struck a momentary chill even in the warm comfort of the base building.

The little clerk had been very insistent on one point. He had never heard any sound of pursuit from the dim shape sensed, rather than seen, at the limit of his light. There was no scuffling of claws or hoofs on rock, nor even the clatter of displaced stones. It was as if, so the old man had declared in that solemn manner of his, 'as if the thing that was following could see perfectly in the darkness, and had many small legs or pads so that it could move swiftly and easily over the rock – like a giant caterpillar or one of the carpet-things of Kralkor II.'

Yet, although there had been no noise of pursuit, there had been one sound that the old man had caught several times. It was so unusual that its very strangeness made it doubly ominous. It was a faint but horribly persistent *clicking*.

The old fellow had been able to describe it very vividly – much too vividly for Armstrong's liking now.

'Have you ever listened to a large insect crunching its prey?' he said. 'Well, it was just like that. I imagine that a crab makes exactly the same noise with its claws when it clashes them together. It was a – what's the word? – a *chitinous* sound.'

At this point, Armstrong remembered laughing loudly. (Strange, how it was all coming back to him now.) But no one else had laughed, though they had been quick to do so earlier. Sensing the change of tone, he had sobered at once and asked the old man to continue his story. How he wished now that he had stifled his curiosity!

It had been quickly told. The next day, a party of sceptical technicians had gone into the no-man's land beyond Carver's Pass. They were not sceptical enough to leave their guns behind, but they had no cause to use them for they found no trace of any living thing. There were the inevitable pits and tunnels, glistening holes down which the light of the torches rebounded endlessly until it was lost in the distance – but the planet was riddled with them.

Though the party found no sign of life, it discovered one thing it did not like at all. Out in the barren and unexplored land beyond the Pass they had come upon an even larger tunnel than the rest. Near the mouth of that tunnel was a massive rock, half embedded in the ground. And the sides of that rock had been worn away *as if it had been used as an enormous whetstone.*

No less than five of those present had seen this disturbing rock. None of them could explain it satisfactorily as a natural formation, but they still refused to accept the old man's story. Armstrong had asked them if they had ever put it to the test. There had been an uncomfortable silence. Then big Andrew Hargraves had said: 'Hell, who'd walk out to the Pass at night just for fun!' and had left it at that. Indeed, there was no other record of anyone walking from Port Sanderson to the camp by night, or for that matter by day. During the hours of light, no unprotected human being could live in the open beneath the rays of the enormous, lurid sun that seemed to fill half the sky. And no one would walk six miles, wearing radiation armour, if the tractor was available.

Armstrong felt that he was leaving the Pass. The rocks on either side were falling away, and the road was no longer as firm and well packed as it had been. He was coming out into the open plain once more, and somewhere not far away in the darkness was that enigmatic pillar that might have been used for sharpening monstrous fangs or claws. It was not a reassuring thought, but he could not get it out of his mind.

Feeling distinctly worried now, Armstrong made a great effort to pull himself together. He would try to be rational again; he would think of business, the work he had done at the camp – anything but this infernal place. For a while, he succeeded quite well. But presently, with a maddening persistence, every train of thought came back to the same point. He could not get out of his mind the picture of that inexplicable rock and its appalling possibilities. Over and over again he found himself wondering how far away it was, whether he had already passed it, and whether it was on his right or his left. . . .

The ground was quite flat again, and the road drove on straight as an arrow. There was one gleam of consolation: Port Sanderson could not be much more than two miles away. Armstrong had no idea how long he had been on the road. Unfortunately his watch was not illuminated and he could only guess at the passage of time. With any luck, the 'Canopus' should not take off for another two hours at least. But he could not be sure, and now another fear began to enter his mind – the dread that he might see a vast constellation of lights rising swiftly into the sky ahead, and know that all this agony of mind had been in vain.

He was not zigzagging so badly now, and seemed to be able to anticipate the edge of the road before stumbling off it. It was probable, he cheered himself by thinking, that he was travelling almost as fast as if he had a light. If all went well, he might be nearing Port Sanderson in thirty minutes – a ridiculously small space of time. How he would laugh at his fears when he strolled into his already reserved stateroom in the 'Canopus', and felt that peculiar quiver as the phantom drive hurled the great ship far out of this system, back to the clustered starclouds near the centre of the Galaxy – back toward Earth itself, which he had not seen for so many years. One day, he told himself, he really must visit Earth again. All his life he had been making the promise, but always there had been the same answer – lack of time. Strange, wasn't it, that such a tiny planet should have played so enormous a part in the development of the Universe, should even have come to dominate worlds far wiser and more intelligent than itself!

Armstrong's thoughts were harmless again, and he felt calmer. The knowledge that he was nearing Port Sanderon was immensely reassuring, and he deliberately kept his mind on familiar, unimportant matters. Carver's Pass was already far behind, and with it that thing he no longer intended to recall. One day, if he ever returned to this world, he would visit the pass in the daytime and laugh at his fears. In twenty minutes now, they would have joined the nightmares of his childhood.

It was almost a shock, though one of the most pleasant he had ever known, when he saw the lights of Port Sanderson come up over the horizon. The curvature of this little world was very deceptive: it did not seem right that a planet with a gravity almost as great as Earth's should have a horizon so close at hand. One day, someone would have to discover what lay at this world's core to give it so great a density. Perhaps the many tunnels would help – it was an unfortunate turn of thought, but the nearness of his goal had robbed it of terror now. Indeed, the thought that he might really be in danger seemed to give his adventure a certain piquancy and heightened interest. Nothing could happen to him now, with ten minutes to go and the lights of the Port already in sight.

A few minutes later, his feelings changed abruptly when he came to the sudden bend in the road. He had forgotten the chasm that caused his detour, and added half a mile to the journey. Well, what of it? he thought stubbornly. An extra half-mile would make no difference now – another ten minutes, at the most.

It was very disappointing when the lights of the city vanished. Armstrong had not remembered the hill which the road was skirting; perhaps it was only a low ridge, scarcely noticeable in the daytime. But by hiding the lights of the port it had taken away his chief talisman and left him again at the mercy of his fears.

Very unreasonably, his intelligence told him, he began to think how horrible it would be if anything happened now, so near the end of the journey. He kept the worst of his fears at bay for a while, hoping desperately that the lights of the city would soon reappear. But as the minutes dragged on, he realised that the ridge must be longer than he imagined. He tried to cheer himself by the thought that the city would be all the nearer when he saw it again, but somehow logic seemed to have failed him now. For presently he found himself doing something he had not stooped to, even out in the waste by Carver's Pass.

He stopped, turned slowly round, and with bated breath listened until his lungs were nearly bursting.

The silence was uncanny, considering how near he must be to the Port. There was certainly no sound from behind him. Of course there wouldn't be, he told himself angrily. But he was immensely relieved. The thought of that faint and insistent clicking had been haunting him for the last hour.

So friendly and familiar was the noise that did reach him at last that the anticlimax almost made him laugh aloud. Drifting through the still air from a source clearly not more than a mile away came the sound of a landing-field tractor, perhaps one of the machines loading the 'Canopus' itself. In a matter of seconds, thought Armstrong, he would be around this ridge with the Port only a few hundred yards ahead. The journey was nearly ended. In a few moments, this evil plain would be no more than a fading nightmare.

It seemed terribly unfair: so little time, such a small fraction of a human life, was all he needed now. But the gods have always been unfair to man, and now they were enjoying their little jest. For there could be no mistaking the rattle of monstrous claws in the darkness *ahead of him.*

Silence Please

First published in *Science-Fantasy*, Winter 1950 as 'Silence Please!' as by 'Charles Willis'.
Collected in *Tales from the White Hart*

Negative feedback noise eliminators are now on the market – and already have many engineering applications. I recently purchased a pair of earphones that were supposed to eliminate ambient sound: however, I doubt if anything as versatile as the Fenton Silencer will ever be on the market.

You come upon the 'White Hart' quite unexpectedly in one of these anonymous little lanes leading down from Fleet Street to the Embankment. It's no use *telling* you where it is: very few people who have set out in a determined effort to get there have ever actually arrived. For the first dozen visits a guide is essential: after that you'll probably be all right if you close your eyes and rely on instinct. Also – to be perfectly frank – we don't want any more customers, at least on *our* night. The place is already uncomfortably crowded. All that I'll say about its location is that it shakes occasionally with the vibration of newspaper presses, and that if you crane out of the window of the gents' room you can just see the Thames.

From the outside, it looks like any other pub – as indeed it is for five days of the week. The public and saloon bars are on the ground floor: there are the usual vistas of brown oak panelling and frosted glass, the bottles behind the bar, the handles of the beer engines . . . nothing out of the ordinary at all. Indeed, the only concession to the twentieth century is the jukebox in the public bar. It was installed during the war in a laughable attempt to make G.I.s feel at home, and one of the first things we did was to make sure there was no danger of its ever working again.

At this point I had better explain who 'we' are. That is not as easy as I thought it was going to be when I started, for a complete catalogue of the 'White Hart's' clients would probably be impossible and would certainly be excruciatingly tedious. So all I'll say at this point is that 'we' fall into three main classes. First there are the journalists, writers and editors. The journalists, of course, gravitated here from Fleet Street. Those who couldn't make the grade fled elsewhere; the tougher ones remained. As for the writers, most of them heard about us from other writers, came here for copy, and got trapped.

Where there are writers, of course, there are sooner or later editors. If Drew, our landlord, got a percentage on the literary business done in his bar, he'd be a rich man. (We suspect he is a rich man, anyway.) One of our wits once remarked that it was a common sight to see half a dozen indignant authors arguing with a hard-faced editor in one corner of the 'White Hart', while in another, half a dozen indignant editors argued with a hard-faced author.

So much for the literary side: you will have, I'd better warn you, ample opportunities for close-ups later. Now let us glance briefly at the scientists. How did *they* get in here?

Well, Birkbeck College is only across the road, and King's is just a few hundred yards along the Strand. That's doubtless part of the explanation, and again personal recommendation had a lot to do with it. Also, many of our scientists are writers, and not a few of our writers are scientists. Confusing, but we like it that way.

The third portion of our little microcosm consists of what may be loosely termed 'interested laymen'. They were attracted to the 'White Hart', by the general brouhaha, and enjoyed the conversation and company so much that they now come along regularly every Wednesday – which is the day when we all get together. Sometimes they can't stand the pace and fall by the wayside, but there's always a fresh supply.

With such potent ingredients, it is hardly surprising that Wednesday at the 'White Hart' is seldom dull. Not only have some remarkable stories been told there, but remarkable things have *happened* there. For example, there was the time when Professor—, passing through on his way to Harwell left behind a briefcase containing – well, we'd better not go into that, even though we did so at the time. And most interesting it was, too. . . . Any Russian agents will find me in the corner under the dartboard. I come high, but easy terms can be arranged.

Now that I've finally thought of the idea, it seems astonishing to me that none of my colleagues has ever got round to writing up these stories. Is it a question of being so close to the wood that they can't see the trees? Or is it lack of incentive? No, the last explanation can hardly hold: several of them are quite as hard up as I am, and have complained with equal bitterness about Drew's 'NO CREDIT' rule. My only fear, as I type these words on my old Remington Noiseless, is that John Christopher or George Whitley or John Beynon are already hard at work using up the best material. Such as, for instance, the story of the Fenton Silencer . . .

I don't know when it began: one Wednesday is much like another and it's hard to tag dates onto them. Besides, people may spend a couple of months lost in the 'White Hart' crowd before you first notice their existence. That had probably happened to Harry Purvis, because when I first became aware of him he already knew the names of most of the people in our crowd. Which is more than I do these days, now that I come to think of it.

But though I don't know *when*, I know exactly *how* it all started. Bert Huggins was the catalyst, or, to be more accurate, his voice was. Bert's voice would catalyse anything. When he indulges in a confidential whisper, it sounds like a sergeant major drilling an entire regiment. And when he lets himself go, conversation languishes elsewhere while we all wait for those cute little bones in the inner ear to resume their accustomed places.

He had just lost his temper with John Christopher (we all do this at some time or other) and the resulting detonation had disturbed the chess game in progress at the back of the saloon bar. As usual, the two players were surrounded by backseat drivers, and we all looked up with a start as Bert's blast whammed overhead. When the echoes died away, someone said: 'I wish there was a way of shutting him up.'

It was then that Harry Purvis replied: 'There is, you know.'

Not recognising the voice, I looked round. I saw a small, neatly dressed man in the late thirties. He was smoking one of those carved German pipes that always make me think of cuckoo clocks and the Black Forest. That was the only unconventional thing about him: otherwise he might have been a minor Treasury official all dressed up to go to a meeting of the Public Accounts Committee.

'I beg your pardon?' I said.

He took no notice, but made some delicate adjustments to his pipe. It was then that I noticed that it wasn't, as I'd thought at first glance, an elaborate piece of wood carving. It was something much more sophisticated – a contraption of metal and plastic like a small chemical engineering plant. There were even a couple of minute valves. My God, it *was* a chemical engineering plant. . . .

I don't goggle any more easily than the next man, but I made no attempt to hide my curiosity. He gave me a superior smile.

'All for the cause of science. It's an idea of the Biophysics Lab. They want to find out exactly what there is in tobacco smoke – hence these filters. You know the old argument – *does* smoking cause cancer of the tongue, and if so, how? The trouble is that it takes an awful lot of – er – distillate to identify some of the obscurer byproducts. So we have to do a lot of smoking.'

'Doesn't it spoil the pleasure to have all this plumbing in the way?'

'I don't know. You see, I'm just a volunteer. I don't smoke.'

'Oh,' I said. For the moment, that seemed the only reply. Then I remembered how the conversation had started.

'You were saying,' I continued with some feeling, for there was still a slight tinnitus in my left ear, 'that there was some way of shutting up Bert. We'd all like to hear it – if that isn't mixing metaphors somewhat.'

'I was thinking,' he replied, after a couple of experimental sucks and blows, 'of the ill-fated Fenton Silencer. A sad story – yet, I feel, one with an interesting lesson for us all. And one day – who knows? – someone *may* perfect it and earn the blessings of the world.'

Suck, bubble, bubble, *plop* . . .

'Well, let's hear the story. When did it happen?'

He sighed.

'I'm almost sorry I mentioned it. Still, since you insist – and, of course, on the understanding that it doesn't go beyond these walls.'

'Er – of course.'

'Well, Rupert Fenton was one of our lab assistants. A very bright youngster, with a good mechanical background, but, naturally, not very well up in theory. He was always making gadgets in his spare time. Usually the idea was good, but as he was shaky on fundamentals the things hardly ever worked. That didn't seem to discourage him: I think he fancied himself as a latter-day Edison, and imagined he could make his fortune from the radio tubes and other oddments lying around the lab. As his tinkering didn't interfere with his work, no one objected: indeed, the physics demonstrators did their best to encourage him, because, after all, there is something refreshing about any form of enthusiasm. But no one expected he'd ever get very far, because I don't suppose he could even integrate e to the x.'

'Is such ignorance *possible*?' gasped someone.

'Maybe I exaggerate. Let's say $x e$ to the x. Anyway, all his knowledge was entirely practical – rule of thumb, you know. Give him a wiring diagram, however complicated, and he could make the apparatus for you. But unless it was something *really* simple, like a television set, he wouldn't understand how it worked. The trouble was, he didn't realise his limitations. And that, as you'll see, was most unfortunate.

'I think he must have got the idea while watching the Honours physics students doing some experiments in acoustics. I take it, of course, that you all understand the phenomenon of interference?'

'Naturally,' I replied.

'Hey!' said one of the chess-players, who had given up trying to concentrate on the game (probably because he was losing). '*I* don't.'

Purvis looked at him as though seeing something that had no right to be around in a world that had invented penicillin.

'In that case,' he said coldly, 'I suppose I had better do some explaining.' He waved aside our indignant protests. 'No, I insist. It's precisely those who don't understand these things who need to be told about them. If someone had only explained the theory to poor Fenton while there was still time . . .'

He looked down at the now thoroughly abashed chess-player.

'I do not know,' he began, 'if you have ever considered the nature of *sound*. Suffice to say that it consists of a series of waves moving through the air. Not, however, waves like those on the surface of the sea – oh dear no! *Those* waves are up and down movements. Sound waves consist of alternate compressions and rarefactions.'

'Rare-what?'

'Rarefactions.'

'Don't you mean "rarefications"?'

'I do not. I doubt if such a word exists, and if it does, it shouldn't,' retorted Purvis, with the aplomb of Sir Alan Herbert dropping a particularly revolting neologism into his killing bottle. 'Where was I? Explaining sound, of course. When we make any sort of noise, from the faintest whisper to that concussion that went past just now, a series of pressure changes moves through the air. Have you ever watched shunting engines at work on a siding? You see a perfect example of the same kind of thing. There's a long line of goods wagons, all coupled together. One end gets a bang, the first two trucks move together – and then you can see the compression wave moving right along the line. Behind it the reverse thing happens – the rarefaction – I repeat, *rarefaction* – as the trucks separate again.

'Things are simple enough when there is only one source of sound – only one set of waves. But suppose you have two wave patterns, moving in the same direction? That's when interference arises, and there are lots of pretty experiments in elementary physics to demonstrate it. All we need worry about here is the fact – which I think you will all agree is perfectly obvious – that if one could get two sets of waves *exactly* out of step, the total result would be precisely zero. The compression pulse of one sound wave would be on top of the rarefaction of another – net result – no change and hence no sound. To go back to my analogy of the line of wagons, it's as if you gave the last truck a jerk and a push simultaneously. Nothing at all would happen.

'Doubtless some of you will already see what I am driving at, and will appreciate the basic principle of the Fenton Silencer. Young Fenton, I imagine, argued in this manner. "This world of ours," he said to himself, "is too full of noise. There would be a fortune for anyone who could invent a really perfect silencer. Now, what would that imply . . . ?"

'It didn't take him long to work out the answer: I told you he was a bright lad. There was really very little in his pilot model. It consisted of a microphone, a special amplifier, and a pair of loud-speakers. Any sound that happened to be about was picked up by the mike, amplified and *inverted* so that it was exactly out of phase with the original noise. Then it was pumped out of the speakers, the original wave and the new one cancelled out, and the net result was silence.

'Of course, there was rather more to it than that. There had to be an arrangement to make sure that the cancelling wave was just the right intensity – otherwise you might be worse off than when you started. But these are technical details that I won't bore you with. As many of you will recognise, it's a simple application of negative feedback.'

'Just a moment!' interrupted Eric Maine. Eric, I should mention, is an electronics expert and edits some television paper or other. He's also written a radio play about space flight, but that's another story. 'Just a moment! There's something wrong here. You *couldn't* get silence that way. It would be impossible to arrange the phase. . . .'

Purvis jammed the pipe back in his mouth. For a moment there was an ominous bubbling and I thought of the first act of *Macbeth*. Then he fixed Eric with a glare.

'Are you suggesting,' he said frigidly, 'that this story is untrue?'

'Ah – well, I won't go as far as that, but . . .' Eric's voice trailed away as if he had been silenced himself. He pulled an old envelope out of his pocket, together with an assortment of resistors and condensers that seemed to have got entangled in his handkerchief, and began to do some figuring. That was the last we heard from him for some time.

'As I was saying,' continued Purvis calmly, *'that's* the way Fenton's Silencer worked. His first model wasn't very powerful, and it couldn't deal with very high or very low notes. The result was rather odd. When it was switched on, and someone tried to talk, you'd hear the two ends of the spectrum – a faint bat's squeak, and a kind of low rumble. But he soon got over that by using a more linear circuit (dammit, I can't help using *some* technicalities!) and in the later model he was able to produce complete silence over quite a large area. Not merely an ordinary room, but a full-sized hall. Yes . . .

'Now Fenton was not one of these secretive inventors who won't tell anyone what they are trying to do, in case their ideas are stolen. He was all too willing to talk. He discussed his ideas with the staff and with the students, whenever he could get anyone to listen. It so happened that one of the first people to whom he demonstrated his improved Silencer was a young arts student called – I think – Kendall, who was taking physics as a subsidiary subject. Kendall was much impressed by the Silencer, as well he might be. But he was not thinking, as you may have imagined, about its commercial possibilities, or the boon it would bring to the outraged ears of suffering humanity. Oh dear no – He had quite other ideas.

'Please permit me a slight digression. At College we have a flourishing Musical Society, which in recent years has grown in numbers to such an extent that it can now tackle the less monumental symphonies. In the year of which I speak, it was embarking on a very ambitious enterprise. It was going to produce a new opera, a work by a talented young composer whose name it would not be fair to mention, since it is now well known to you all. Let us call him Edward England. I've forgotten the title of the work, but it was one of these stark dramas of tragic love which, for some reason I've never been able to understand, are supposed to be less ridiculous with a musical accompaniment than without. No doubt a good deal depends on the music.

'I can still remember reading the synopsis while waiting for the curtain to go up, and to this day have never been able to decide whether the libretto was meant seriously or not. Let's see – the period was the late Victorian era, and the main characters were Sarah Stampe, the passionate postmistress, Walter Partridge, the saturnine gamekeeper, and the squire's son, whose name I forget. It's the old story of the eternal triangle, complicated by the villagers' resentment of change – in this case, the new telegraph system, which the local crones predict will Do Things to the cow's milk and cause trouble at lambing time.

'Ignoring the frills, it's the usual drama of operatic jealousy. The squire's son doesn't want to marry into the Post Office, and the gamekeeper, maddened by his rejection, plots revenge. The tragedy rises to its dreadful climax when poor Sarah, strangled with parcel tape, is found hidden in a mailbag in the Dead Letter Department. The villagers hang Partridge from the nearest telegraph pole, much to the annoyance of the linesmen. He was supposed to sing an aria while he was being hung: *that* is one thing I regret missing. The squire's son takes to drink, or the Colonies, or both: and that's that.

'I'm sure you're wondering where all this is leading: please bear with me for a moment longer. The fact is that while this synthetic jealousy was being rehearsed, the real thing was going on backstage. Fenton's friend Kendall had been spurned by the young lady who was to play Sarah Stampe. I don't think he was a particularly vindictive person, but he saw an opportunity for a unique revenge. Let us be frank and admit that college life *does* breed a certain irresponsibility – and in identical circumstances, how many of *us* would have rejected the same chance?

'I see the dawning comprehension on your faces. But we, the audience, had no suspicion when the overture started on that memorable day. It was a most distinguished gathering: everyone was there, from the Chancellor downwards. Deans and professors were two a penny: I never did discover how so many people had been bullied into coming. Now that I come to think of it, I can't remember what I was doing there myself.

'The overture died away amid cheers, and, I must admit, occasional catcalls from the more boisterous members of the audience. Perhaps I do them an injustice: they may have been the more musical ones.

'Then the curtain went up. The scene was the village square at Doddering Sloughleigh, *circa* 1860. Enter the heroine, reading the postcards in the morning's mail. She comes across a letter addressed to the young squire and promptly bursts into song.

'Sarah's opening aria wasn't quite as bad as the overture, but it was grim enough. Luckily, we were to hear only the first few bars . . .

'Precisely. We need not worry about such details as how Kendall had talked the ingenuous Fenton into it – if, indeed, the inventor realised the use to which his device was being applied. All I need to say is that it was a most convincing demonstration. There was a sudden, deadening blanket of silence, and Sarah Stampe just faded out like a TV programme when the sound is turned off. Everyone was frozen in his seat, while the singer's lips went on moving silently. Then she too realised what had happened. Her mouth opened in what would have been a piercing scream in any other circumstances, and she fled into the wings amid a shower of postcards.

'Thereafter, the chaos was unbelievable. For a few minutes everyone must have thought they had lost the sense of hearing, but soon they were able to tell from the behaviour of their companions that they were not alone in their deprivation. Someone in the Physics Department must have realised the truth fairly promptly, for soon little slips of paper were circulating among the V.I.P.s in the front row. The Vice-Chancellor was rash enough to try and restore order by sign language, waving frantically to the audience from the stage. By this time I was too sick with laughter to appreciate such fine details.

'There was nothing for it but to get out of the hall, which we all did as quickly as we could. I think Kendall had fled – he was so overcome by the effect of the gadget that he didn't stop to switch it off. He was afraid of staying around in case he was caught and lynched. As for Fenton – alas, we shall never know *his* side of the story. We can only reconstruct the subsequent events from the evidence that was left.

'As I picture it, he must have waited until the hall was empty, and then crept in to disconnect his apparatus. We heard the explosion all over the college.'

'The *explosion*?' someone gasped.

'Of course. I shudder to think what a narrow escape we all had. Another dozen decibels, a few more phons – and it might have happened while the theatre was still packed. Regard it, if you like, as an example of the inscrutable workings of providence that only the inventor was caught in the explosion. Perhaps it was as well: at least he perished in the moment of achievement, and before the Dean could get at him.'

'Stop moralising, man. What happened?'

'Well, I told you that Fenton was very weak on theory. If he'd gone into the mathematics of the Silencer he'd have found his mistake. The trouble is, you see, that one can't *destroy* energy. Not even when you cancel out one train of waves by another. All that happens then is that the energy you've neutralized accumulates *somewhere* else. It's rather like sweeping up all the dirt in a room – at the cost of an unsightly pile under the carpet.

'When you look into the theory of the thing, you'll find that Fenton's gadget wasn't a silencer so much as a *collector* of sound. All the time it was switched on, it was really absorbing sound energy. And at that concert, it was certainly going flat out. You'll understand what I mean if you've ever looked at one of Edward England's scores. On top of that, of course, there was all the noise the audience was making – or I should say was *trying* to make – during the resultant panic. The total amount of energy must have been terrific, and the poor Silencer had to keep on sucking it up. Where did it go? Well, I don't know the circuit details – probably into the condensers of the power pack. By the time Fenton started to tinker with it again, it was like a loaded bomb. The sound of his approaching footsteps was the last straw, and the overloaded apparatus could stand no more. It blew up.'

For a moment no one said a word, perhaps as a token of respect for the late Mr Fenton. Then Eric Maine, who for the last ten minutes had been muttering in the corner over his calculations, pushed his way through the ring of listeners. He held a sheet of paper thrust aggressively in front of him.

'Hey!' he said. 'I was right all the time. The thing couldn't work. The phase and amplitude relations . . .'

Purvis waved him away.

'That's just what I've explained,' he said patiently. 'You should have been listening. Too bad that Fenton found out the hard way.'

He glanced at his watch. For some reason, he now seemed in a hurry to leave.

'My goodness! Time's getting on. One of these days, remind me to tell you about the extraordinary thing we saw through the new proton microscope. That's an even more remarkable story.'

He was halfway through the door before anyone else could challenge him. Then George Whitley recovered his breath.

'Look here,' he said in a perplexed voice. 'How is it that we never heard about this business?'

Purvis paused on the threshold, his pipe now burbling briskly as it got into its stride once more. He glanced back over his shoulder.

'There was only one thing to do,' he replied. 'We didn't want a scandal – *de mortuis nil nisi bonum*, you know. Besides, in the circumstances, don't you think it was highly appropriate to – ah – *hush* the whole business up? And a very good night to you all.'

Trouble with the Natives

Originally published in *Lilliput*, February 1951, as 'Three Men in a Flying Saucer'
Collected in *Reach for Tomorrow*

The flying saucer came down vertically through the clouds, braked to a halt about fifty feet from the ground, and settled with a considerable bump on a patch of heather-strewn moorland.

'That,' said Captain Wyxtpthll, 'was a lousy landing.' He did not, of course, use precisely these words. To human ears his remarks would have sounded rather like the clucking of an angry hen. Master Pilot Krtclugg unwound three of his tentacles from the control panel, stretched all four of his legs, and relaxed comfortably.

'Not my fault the automatics have packed up again,' he grumbled. 'But what do you expect with a ship that should have been scrapped five thousand years ago? If those cheese-paring form-fillers back at Base Planet—'

'Oh, all right! We're down in one piece, which is more than I expected. Tell Crysteel and Danstor to come in here. I want a word with them before they go.'

Crysteel and Danstor were, very obviously, of a different species from the rest of the crew. They had only one pair of legs and arms, no eyes at the back of the head, and other physical deficiencies which their colleagues did their best to overlook. These very defects, however, had made them the obvious choice for this particular mission, for it had needed only a minimum of disguise to let them pass as human beings under all but the closest scrutiny.

'Now you're perfectly sure,' said the Captain, 'that you understand your instructions?'

'Of course,' said Crysteel, slightly huffed. 'This isn't the first time I've made contact with a primitive race. My training in anthropology—'

'Good. And the language?'

'Well, that's Danstor's business, but I can speak it reasonably fluently now. It's a very simple language, and after all we've been studying their radio programmes for a couple of years.'

'Any other points before you go?'

'Er – there's just one matter.' Crysteel hesitated slightly. 'It's quite obvious from their broadcasts that the social system is very primitive, and that crime and lawlessness are widespread. Many of the wealthier citizens have to use what are called "detectives" or "special agents" to protect their lives and property. Now we know it's against regulations, but we were wondering . . .'

'What?'

'Well, we'd feel much safer if we could take a couple of Mark III disrupters with us.'

'Not on your life! I'd be court-martialled if they heard about it at the Base. Suppose you killed some of the natives – then I'd have the Bureau of Interstellar Politics, the Aborigines Conservancy Board, and half a dozen others after me.'

'There'd be just as much trouble if *we* got killed,' Crysteel pointed out with considerable emotion. 'After all, you're responsible for our safety. Remember that radio play I was telling you about? It described a typical household, but there were two murders in the first half hour!'

'Oh, very well. But only a Mark II – we don't want you to do too much damage if there *is* trouble.'

'Thanks a lot; that's a great relief. I'll report every thirty minutes as arranged. We shouldn't be gone more than a couple of hours.'

Captain Wyxtpthll watched them disappear over the brow of the hill. He sighed deeply.

'Why,' he said, 'of all the people in the ship did it have to be *those* two?'

'It couldn't be helped,' answered the pilot. 'All these primitive races are terrified of anything strange. If they saw *us* coming, there'd be general panic and before we knew where we were the bombs would be falling on top of us. You just can't rush these things.'

Captain Wyxtpthll was absentmindedly making a cat's cradle out of his tentacles in the way he did when he was worried.

'Of course,' he said, 'if they don't come back I can always go away and report the place dangerous.' He brightened considerably. 'Yes, that would save a lot of trouble.'

'And waste all the months we've spent studying it?' said the pilot, scandalised. 'They won't be wasted,' replied the captain, unravelling himself with a flick that no human eye could have followed. 'Our report will be useful for the next survey ship. I'll suggest that we make another visit in – oh, let's say five thousand years. By then the place may be civilised – though frankly, I doubt it.'

Samuel Higginsbotham was settling down to a snack of cheese and cider when he saw the two figures approaching along the lane. He wiped his mouth with the back of his hand, put the bottle carefully down beside his hedge-trimming tools, and stared with mild surprise at the couple as they came into range.

'Mornin',' he said cheerfully between mouthfuls of cheese.

The strangers paused. One was surreptitiously ruffling through a small book which, if Sam only knew, was packed with such common phrases and expressions as: 'Before the weather forecast, here is a gale warning', 'Stick 'em up – I've got you covered!', and 'Calling all cars!' Danstor, who had no needs for these aids to memory, replied promptly enough.

'Good morning, my man,' he said in his best BBC accent. 'Could you direct us to the nearest hamlet, village, small town or other such civilised community?'

'Eh?' said Sam. He peered suspiciously at the strangers, aware for the first time that there was something very odd about their clothes. One did not, he realised dimly, normally wear a roll-top sweater with a smart pin-striped suit of the pattern fancied by city gents. And the fellow who was still fussing with the little book was actually wearing full evening dress which would have been faultless but for the lurid green and red tie, the hob-nailed boots and the cloth cap. Crysteel and Danstor had done their best, but they had seen too many television plays. When one considers that they had no other source of information, their sartorial aberrations were at least understandable.

Sam scratched his head. Furriners, I suppose, he told himself. Not even the townsfolk got themselves up like this.

He pointed down the road and gave them explicit directions in an accent so broad that no one residing outside the range of the BBC's West Regional transmitter could have understood more than one word in three. Crysteel and Danstor, whose home planet was so far away that Marconi's first signals couldn't possibly have reached it yet, did even worse than this. But they managed to get the general idea and retired in good order, both wondering if their knowledge of English was as good as they had believed.

So came and passed, quite uneventfully and without record in the history books, the first meeting between humanity and beings from Outside.

'I suppose,' said Danstor thoughtfully, but without much conviction, 'that he wouldn't have done? It would have saved us a lot of trouble.'

'I'm afraid not. Judging by his clothes, and the work he was obviously engaged upon, he could not have been a very intelligent or valuable citizen. I doubt if he could even have understood who we were.'

'Here's another one!' said Danstor, pointing ahead.

'Don't make sudden movements that might cause alarm. Just walk along naturally, and let him speak first.'

The man ahead strode purposefully toward them, showed not the slightest signs of recognition, and before they had recovered was already disappearing into the distance.

'Well!' said Danstor.

'It doesn't matter,' replied Crysteel philosophically. 'He probably wouldn't have been any use either.'

'That's no excuse for bad manners!'

They gazed with some indignation at the retreating back of Professor Fitzsimmons as, wearing his oldest hiking outfit and engrossed in a difficult piece of atomic theory, he dwindled down the lane. For the first time, Crysteel began to suspect uneasily that it might not be as simple to make contact as he had optimistically believed.

Little Milton was a typical English village, nestling at the foot of the hills whose higher slopes now concealed so portentous a secret. There were very few people about on this summer morning, for the men were already at work and the womenfolk were still tidying up after the exhausting task of getting their lords and masters safely out of the way. Consequently Crysteel and Danstor had almost reached the centre of the village before their first encounter, which happened to be with the village postman, cycling back to the office after completing his rounds. He was in a very bad temper, having had to deliver a penny postcard to Dodgson's farm, a couple of miles off his normal route. In addition, the weekly parcel of laundry which Gunner Evans sent home to his doting mother had been a lot heavier than usual, as well it might, since it contained four tins of bully beef pinched from the cookhouse.

'Excuse me,' said Danstor politely.

'Can't stop,' said the postman, in no mood for casual conversation. 'Got another round to do.' Then he was gone.

'This is really the limit!' protested Danstor. 'Are they *all* going to be like this?'

'You've simply got to be patient,' said Crysteel. 'Remember their customs are quite different from ours; it may take some time to gain their confidence. I've had this sort of trouble with primitive races before. Every anthropologist has to get used to it.'

'Hmm,' said Danstor. 'I suggest that we call at some of their houses. Then they won't be able to run away.'

'Very well,' agreed Crysteel doubtfully. 'But avoid anything that looks like a religious shrine, otherwise we may get into trouble.'

Old Widow Tomkins' council-house could hardly have been mistaken, even by the most inexperienced of explorers, for such an object. The old lady was agreeably excited to see two gentlemen standing on her doorstep, and noticed nothing at all odd about their clothes. Visions of unexpected legacies, of newspaper reporters asking about her 100th birthday (she was really only 95, but had managed to keep it dark) flashed through her mind. She picked up the slate she kept hanging by the door and went gaily forth to greet her visitors.

'You'll have to write it down,' she simpered, holding out the slate. 'I've been deaf this last twenty years.'

Crysteel and Danstor looked at each other in dismay. This was a completely unexpected snag, for the only written characters they had ever seen were television programme announcements, and they had never fully deciphered those. But Danstor, who had an almost photographic memory, rose to the occasion. Holding the chalk very awkwardly, he wrote a sentence which, he had reason to believe, was in common use during such breakdowns in communication.

As her mysterious visitors walked sadly away, old Mrs Tomkins stared in baffled bewilderment at the marks on her slate. It was some time before she deciphered the characters – Danstor had made several mistakes – and even then she was little the wiser.

TRANSMISSIONS WILL BE RESUMED AS SOON AS POSSIBLE.

It was the best that Danstor could do; but the old lady never did get to the bottom of it.

They were little luckier at the next house they tried. The door was answered by a young lady whose vocabulary consisted largely of giggles, and who eventually broke down completely and slammed the door in their faces. As they listened to the muffled, hysterical laughter, Crysteel and Danstor began to suspect, with sinking hearts, that their disguise as normal human beings was not as effective as they had intended.

At Number 3, on the other hand, Mrs Smith was only too willing to talk – at 120 words to the minute in an accent as impenetrable as Sam Higginsbotham's. Danstor made his apologies as soon as he could get a word in edgeways, and moved on.

'Doesn't *anyone* talk as they do on the radio?' he lamented. 'How do they understand their own programmes if they all speak like this?'

'I think we must have landed in the wrong place,' said Crysteel, even his optimism beginning to fail. It sagged still further when he had been mistaken, in swift succession, for a Gallup Poll investigator, the prospective Conservative candidate, a vacuum-cleaner salesman, and a dealer from the local black market.

At the sixth or seventh attempt they ran out of housewives. The door was opened by a gangling youth who clutched in one clammy paw an object which at once hypnotised the visitors. It was a magazine whose cover displayed a giant rocket climbing upward from a crater-studded planet which, whatever it might be, was obviously not the Earth. Across the background were the words: 'Staggering Stories of Pseudo-Science. Price 25 cents.'

Crysteel looked at Danstor with a 'Do you think what I think?' expression which the other returned. Here at last, surely, was someone who could understand them. His spirits mounting, Danstor addressed the youngster.

'I think you can help us,' he said politely. 'We find it very difficult to make ourselves understood here. You see, we've just landed on this planet from space and we want to get in touch with your government.'

'Oh,' said Jimmy Williams, not yet fully returned to Earth from his vicarious adventures among the outer moons of Saturn. 'Where's your spaceship?'

'It's up in the hills; we didn't want to frighten anyone.'

'Is it a rocket?'

'Good gracious no. They've been obsolete for thousands of years.'

'Then how does it work? Does it use atomic power?'

'I suppose so,' said Danstor, who was pretty shaky on physics. 'Is there any other kind of power?'

257

'This is getting us nowhere,' said Crysteel, impatient for once. 'We've got to ask *him* questions. Try and find where there are some officials we can meet.'

Before Danstor could answer, a stentorian voice came from inside the house.

'Jimmy! Who's there?'

'Two . . . men,' said Jimmy, a little doubtfully. 'At least, they look like men. They've come from Mars. I always said that was going to happen.'

There was the sound of ponderous movements, and a lady of elephantine bulk and ferocious mien appeared from the gloom. She glared at the strangers, looked at the magazine Jimmy was carrying, and summed up the situation.

'You ought to be ashamed of yourselves!' she cried, rounding on Crysteel and Danstor. 'It's bad enough having a good-for-nothing son in the house who wastes all his time reading this rubbish, without grown men coming along putting more ideas into his head. Men from Mars, indeed! I suppose you've come in one of those flying saucers!'

'But I never mentioned Mars,' protested Danstor feebly.

Slam! From behind the door came the sound of violent altercation, the unmistakable noise of tearing paper, and a wail of anguish. And that was that.

'Well,' said Danstor at last. 'What do we try next? And why did he say we came from Mars? That isn't even the nearest planet, if I remember correctly.'

'I don't know,' said Crysteel. 'But I suppose it's natural for them to assume that we come from some close planet. They're going to have a shock when they find the truth. Mars indeed! That's even worse than here, from the reports I've seen.' He was obviously beginning to lose some of his scientific detachment.

'Let's leave the houses for a while,' said Danstor. 'There must be some more people outside.'

This statement proved to be perfectly true, for they had not gone much further before they found themselves surrounded by small boys making incomprehensible but obviously rude remarks.

'Should we try and placate them with gifts?' said Danstor anxiously. 'That usually works among more backward races.'

'Well, have you brought any?'

'No, I thought you—'

Before Danstor could finish, their tormentors took to their heels and disappeared down a side street. Coming along the road was a majestic figure in a blue uniform.

Crysteel's eyes lit up.

'A policeman!' he said. 'Probably going to investigate a murder somewhere. But perhaps he'll spare us a minute,' he added, not very hopefully.

PC Hinks eyed the strangers with some astonishment, but managed to keep his feelings out of his voice.

'Hello, gents. Looking for anything?'

'As a matter of fact, yes,' said Danstor in his friendliest and most soothing tone of voice. 'Perhaps you can help us. You see, we've just landed on this planet and want to make contact with the authorities.'

'Eh?' said PC Hinks, startled. There was a long pause – though not too long, for PC Hinks was a bright young man who had no intention of remaining a village constable all his life. 'So you've just landed, have you? In a spaceship, I suppose?'

'That's right,' said Danstor, immensely relieved at the absence of the incredulity, or even violence, which such announcements all too often provoked on the more primitive planets.

'Well, well!' said PC Hinks, in tones which he hoped would inspire confidence and feelings of amity. (Not that it mattered much if they both became violent – they seemed a pretty skinny pair.) 'Just tell me what you want, and I'll see what we can do about it.'

'I'm so glad,' said Danstor. 'You see, we've landed in this rather remote spot because we don't want to create a panic. It would be best to keep our presence known to as few people as possible until we have contacted your government.'

'I quite understand,' replied PC Hinks, glancing round hastily to see if there was anyone through whom he could send a message to his sergeant. 'And what do you propose to do then?'

'I'm afraid I can't discuss our long-term policy with regard to Earth,' said Danstor cagily. 'All I can say is that this section of the Universe is being surveyed and opened up for development, and we're quite sure we can help you in many ways.'

'That's very nice of you,' said PC Hinks heartily. 'I think the best thing is for you to come along to the station with me so that we can put through a call to the Prime Minister.'

'Thank you very much,' said Danstor, full of gratitude. They walked trustingly beside PC Hinks, despite his slight tendency to keep behind them, until they reached the village police station.

'This way, gents,' said PC Hinks, politely ushering them into a room which was really rather poorly lit and not at all well furnished, even by the somewhat primitive standards they had expected. Before they could fully take in their surroundings, there was a 'click' and they found themselves separated from their guide by a large door composed entirely of iron bars.

'Now don't worry,' said PC Hinks. 'Everything will be quite all right. I'll be back in a minute.'

Crysteel and Danstor gazed at each other with a surmise that rapidly deepened into a dreadful certainty.

'We're locked in!'

'This is a prison!'

'Now what are we going to do?'

'I don't know if you chaps understand English,' said a languid voice from the gloom, 'but you might let a fellow sleep in peace.'

For the first time, the two prisoners saw that they were not alone. Lying on a bed in the corner of the cell was a somewhat dilapidated young man, who gazed at them blearily out of one resentful eye.

'My goodness!' said Danstor nervously. 'Do you suppose he's a dangerous criminal?'

'He doesn't look very dangerous at the moment,' said Crysteel, with more accuracy than he guessed.

'What are *you* in for, anyway?' asked the stranger, sitting up unsteadily. 'You look as if you've been to a fancy-dress party. Oh, my poor head!' He collapsed again into the prone position.

'Fancy locking up anyone as ill as this!' said Danstor, who was a kind-hearted individual. Then he continued, in English, 'I don't know why we're here. We just told the policeman who we were and where we came from, and this is what's happened.'

'Well, who are you?'

'We've just landed—'

'Oh, there's no point in going through all that again,' interrupted Crysteel. 'We'll never get anyone to believe us.'

'Hey!' said the stranger, sitting up once more. 'What language is that you're speaking? I know a few, but I've never heard of anything like that.'

'Oh, all right,' Crysteel said to Danstor. 'You might as well tell him. There's nothing else to do until that policeman comes back anyway.'

At this moment, PC Hinks was engaged in earnest conversation with the superintendent of the local mental home, who insisted stoutly that all his patients were present. However, a careful check was promised and he'd call back later.

Wondering if the whole thing was a practical joke, PC Hinks put the receiver down and quietly made his way to the cells. The three prisoners seemed to be engaged in friendly conversation, so he tiptoed away again. It would do them all good to have a chance to cool down. He rubbed his eye tenderly as he remembered what a battle it had been to get Mr Graham into the cell during the small hours of the morning.

That young man was now reasonably sober after the night's celebrations, which he did not in the least regret. (It was, after all, quite an occasion when your degree came through and you found you'd got Honours when you'd barely expected a Pass.) But he began to fear that he was still under the influence as Danstor unfolded his tale and waited, not expected to be believed.

In these circumstances, thought Graham, the best thing to do was to behave as matter-of-factly as possible until the hallucinations got fed up and went away.

'If you really have a spaceship in the hills,' he remarked, 'surely you can get in touch with it and ask someone to come and rescue you?'

'We want to handle this ourselves,' said Crysteel with dignity. 'Besides, you don't know our captain.'

They sounded very convincing, thought Graham. The whole story hung together remarkably well. And yet . . .

'It's a bit hard for me to believe that you can build interstellar spaceships, but can't get out of a miserable village police station.'

Danstor looked at Crysteel, who shuffled uncomfortably.

'We could get out easily enough,' said the anthropologist. 'But we don't want to use violent means unless it's absolutely essential. You've no idea of the trouble it causes, and the reports we might have to fill in. Besides, if we do get out, I suppose your Flying Squad would catch us before we got back to the ship.'

'Not in Little Milton,' grinned Graham. 'Especially if we could get across to the "White Hart" without being stopped. My car is over there.'

'Oh,' said Danstor, his spirits suddenly reviving. He turned to his companion and a lively discussion followed. Then, very gingerly, he produced a small black cylinder from an inner pocket, handling it with much the same confidence as a nervous spinster holding a loaded gun for the first time. Simultaneously, Crysteel retired with some speed to the far corner of the cell.

It was at this precise moment that Graham knew, with a sudden icy certainty, that he was stone-sober and that the story he had been listening to was nothing less than the truth.

There was no fuss or bother, no flurry of electric sparks or coloured rays – but a section of the wall three feet across dissolved quietly and collapsed into a little pyramid of sand. The sunlight came streaming into the cell as, with a great sigh of relief, Danstor put his mysterious weapon away.

'Well, come on,' he urged Graham. 'We're waiting for you.'

There were no signs of pursuit, for PC Hinks was still arguing on the phone, and it would be some minutes yet before that bright young man returned to the cells and received the biggest shock of his official career. No one at the 'White Hart' was particularly surprised to see Graham again; they all knew where and how he had spent the night, and expressed hope that the local Bench would deal leniently with him when his case came up.

With grave misgivings, Crysteel and Danstor climbed into the back of the incredibly ramshackle Bentley which Graham affectionately addressed as 'Rose'. But there was nothing wrong with the engine under the rusty bonnet and soon they were roaring out of Little Milton at fifty miles an hour. It was a striking demonstration of the relativity of speed, for Crysteel and Danstor, who had spent the last few years travelling tranquilly through space at several million miles a second, had never been so scared in their lives. When Crysteel had recovered his breath he pulled out his little portable transmitter and called the ship.

'We're on the way back,' he shouted above the roar of the wind. 'We've got a fairly intelligent human being with us. Expect us in – whoops! – I'm sorry – we just went over a bridge – about ten minutes. What was that? No, of course not. We didn't have the slightest trouble. Everything went perfectly smoothly. *Goodbye.'*

Graham looked back only once to see how his passengers were faring. The sight was rather unsettling, for their ears and hair (which had not been glued on very firmly) had blown away and their real selves were beginning to emerge. Graham began to suspect, with some discomfort, that his new acquaintances also lacked noses. Oh well, one could grow used to anything with practice. He was going to have plenty of that in the years ahead.

The rest, of course, you all know; but the full story of the first landing on Earth, and of the peculiar circumstances under which Ambassador Graham became humanity's representative to the universe at large, has never before been recounted. We extracted the main details, with a good deal of persuasion, from Crysteel and Danstor themselves, while we were working in the Department of Extraterrestrial Affairs.

It was understandable, in view of their success on Earth, that they should have been selected by their superiors to make the first contact with our mysterious and secretive neighbours, the Martians. It is also understandable, in the light of the above evidence, that Crysteel and Danstor were so reluctant to embark on this later mission, and we are not really very surprised that nothing has ever been heard of them since.

The Road to the Sea

First published in *Two Complete Science-Adventure Books*, Spring 1951, as 'Seeker of the Sphinx'
Collected in *Tales of Ten Worlds*

I'm amused to see that I predicted not only the invention of ultra-portable music players, but also the fact that they would quickly become such a public menace they would be banned. The second part of this prophecy, alas, has not yet been fulfilled.

The first leaves of autumn were falling when Durven met his brother on the headland beside the Golden Sphinx. Leaving his flyer among the shrubs by the roadside, he walked to the brow of the hill and looked down upon the sea. A bitter wind was toiling across the moors, bearing the threat of early frost, but down in the valley Shastar the Beautiful was still warm and sheltered in its crescent of hills. Its empty quays lay dreaming in the pale, declining sunlight, the deep blue of the sea washing gently against their marble flanks. As he looked down once more into the hauntingly familiar streets and gardens of his youth, Durven felt his resolution failing. He was glad he was meeting Hannar here, a mile from the city, and not among the sights and sounds that would bring his childhood crowding back upon him.

Hannar was a small dot far down the slope, climbing in his old unhurried, leisurely fashion. Durven could have met him in a moment with the flyer, but he knew he would receive little thanks if he did. So he waited in the lee of the great Sphinx, sometimes walking briskly to and fro to keep warm. Once or twice he went to the head of the monster and stared up at the still face brooding upon the city and the sea. He remembered how as a child in the gardens of Shastar he had seen the crouching shape upon the sky line, and had wondered if it was alive.

Hannar looked no older than he had seemed at their last meeting, twenty years before. His hair was still dark and thick, and his face unwrinkled, for few things ever disturbed the tranquil life of Shastar and its people. It seemed bitterly unfair, and Durven, grey with the years of unrelenting toil, felt a quick spasm of envy stab through his brain.

Their greetings were brief, but not without warmth. Then Hannar walked over to the ship, lying in its bed of heather and crumpled gorse bushes. He rapped his stick upon the curving metal and turned to Durven.

'It's very small. Did it bring you all the way?'

'No: only from the Moon. I came back from the Project in a liner a hundred times the size of this.'

'And where is the Project – or don't you want us to know?'

'There's no secret about it. We're building the ships out in space beyond Saturn, where the sun's gravitational gradient is almost flat and it needs little thrust to send them right out of the solar system.'

Hannar waved his stick toward the blue waters beneath them, the coloured marble of the little towers, and the wide streets with their slowly moving traffic.

'Away from all this, out into the darkness and loneliness – in search of what?'

Durven's lips tightened into a thin, determined line.

'Remember,' he said quietly, 'I have already spent a lifetime away from Earth.'

'And has it brought you happiness?' continued Hannar remorselessly.

Durven was silent for a while.

'It has brought me more than that,' he replied at last. 'I have used my powers to the utmost, and have tasted triumphs that you can never imagine. The day when the First Expedition returned to the solar system was worth a lifetime in Shastar.'

'Do you think,' asked Hannar, 'that you will build fairer cities than this beneath those strange suns, when you have left our world forever?'

'If we feel that impulse, yes. If not, we will build other things. But build we must; and what have your people created in the last hundred years?'

'Because we have made no machines, because we have turned our backs upon the stars and are content with our own world, don't think we have been completely idle. Here in Shastar we have evolved a way of life that I do not think has ever been surpassed. We have studied the art of living; ours is the first aristocracy in which there are no slaves. That is our achievement, by which history will judge us.'

'I grant you this,' replied Durven, 'but never forget that your paradise was built by scientists who had to fight as we have done to make their dreams come true.'

'They have not always succeeded. The planets defeated them once; why should the worlds of other suns be more hospitable?'

It was a fair question. After five hundred years, the memory of that first failure was still bitter. With what hopes and dreams had Man set out for the planets, in the closing years of the twentieth century – only to find them not merely barren and lifeless, but fiercely hostile! From the sullen fires of the Mercurian lava seas to Pluto's creeping glaciers of solid nitrogen, there was nowhere that he could live unprotected beyond his own world; and to his own world, after a century of fruitless struggle, he had returned.

Yet the vision had not wholly died; when the planets had been abandoned, there were still some who dared to dream of the stars. Out of that dream had come at last the Transcendental Drive, the First Expedition – and now the heady wine of long-delayed success.

'There are fifty solar-type stars within ten years' flight of Earth,' Durven replied, 'and almost all of them have planets. We believe now that the possession of planets is almost as much a characteristic of a G-type star as its spectrum, though we don't know why. So the search for worlds like Earth was bound to be successful in time; I don't think that we were particularly lucky to find Eden so soon.'

'Eden? Is that what you've called your new world?'

'Yes; it seemed appropriate.'

'What incurable romantics you scientists are! Perhaps the name's too well chosen; all the life in that first Eden wasn't friendly to Man, if you remember.'

Durven gave a bleak smile.

'That, again, depends on one's viewpoint,' he replied. He pointed toward Shastar, where the first lights had begun to glimmer. 'Unless our ancestors had eaten deeply from the Tree of Knowledge, you would never have had this.'

'And what do you suppose will happen to it now?' asked Hannar bitterly. 'When you have opened the road to the stars, all the strength and vigour of the race will ebb away from Earth as from an open wound.'

'I do not deny it. It has happened before, and it will happen again. Shastar will go the way of Babylon and Carthage and New York. The future is built on the rubble of the past; wisdom lies in facing that fact, not in fighting against it. I have loved Shastar as much as you have done – so much so that now, though I shall never see it again, I dare not go down once more into its streets. You ask me what will become of it, and I will tell you. What we are doing will merely hasten the end. Even twenty years ago, when I was last here, I felt my will being sapped by the aimless ritual of your lives. Soon it will be the same in all the cities of Earth, for every one of them apes Shastar. I think the Drive has come none too soon; perhaps even you would believe me if you had spoken to the men who have come back from the stars, and felt the blood stirring in your veins once more after all these centuries of sleep. For your world is dying, Hannar; what you have now you may hold for ages yet, but in the end it will slip from your fingers. The future belongs to us; we will leave you to your dreams. We also have dreamed, and now we go to make our dreams come true.'

The last light was catching the brow of the Sphinx as the sun sank into the sea and left Shastar to night but not to darkness. The wide streets were luminous rivers carrying a myriad of moving specks; the towers and pinnacles were jewelled with coloured lights, and there came a faint sound of wind-borne music as a pleasure boat put slowly out to sea. Smiling a little, Durven watched it draw away from the curving quay. It had been five hundred years or more since the last merchant ship had unloaded its cargo, but while the sea remained, men would still sail upon it.

There was little more to say; and presently Hannar stood alone upon the hill, his head tilted up toward the stars. He would never see his brother again; the sun, which for a few hours had gone from his sight, would soon have vanished from Durven's forever as it shrank into the abyss of space.

Unheeding, Shastar lay glittering in the darkness along the edge of the sea. To Hannar, heavy with foreboding, its doom seemed already almost upon it. There was truth in Durven's words; the exodus was about to begin.

Ten thousand years ago other explorers had set out from the first cities of mankind to discover new lands. They had found them, and had never returned, and Time had swallowed their deserted homes. So must it be with Shastar the Beautiful.

Leaning heavily on his stick, Hannar walked slowly down the hillside toward the lights of the city. The Sphinx watched him dispassionately as his figure vanished into the distance and the darkness.

It was still watching, five thousand years later.

Brant was not quite twenty when his people were expelled from their homes and driven westward across two continents and an ocean, filling the ether with piteous cries of injured innocence. They received scant sympathy from the rest of the world, for they had only themselves to blame, and could scarcely pretend that the Supreme Council had acted harshly. It had sent them a dozen preliminary warnings and no fewer than four positively final ultimatums before reluctantly taking action. Then one day a small ship with a very large acoustic radiator had suddenly arrived a thousand feet above the village and started to emit several kilowatts of raw noise. After a few hours of this, the rebels had capitulated and begun to pack their belongings. The transport fleet had called a week later and carried them, still protesting shrilly, to their new homes on the other side of the world.

And so the Law had been enforced, the Law which ruled that no community could remain on the same spot for more than three lifetimes. Obedience meant change, the destruction of traditions, and the uprooting of ancient and well-loved homes. That had been the very purpose of the Law when it was framed, four thousand years ago; but the stagnation it had sought to prevent could not be warded off much longer. One day there would be no central organisation to enforce it, and the scattered villages would remain where they were until Time engulfed them as it had the earlier civilisations of which they were the heirs.

It had taken the people of Chaldis the whole of three months to build new homes, remove a square mile of forest, plant some unnecessary crops of exotic and luxurious fruits, re-lay a river, and demolish a hill which offended their aesthetic sensibilities. It was quite an impressive performance, and all was forgiven when the local Supervisor made a tour of inspection a little later. Then Chaldis watched with great satisfaction as the transports, the digging machines, and all the paraphernalia of a mobile and mechanised civilization climbed away into the sky. The sound of their departure had scarcely faded when, as one man, the village relaxed once more into the sloth that it sincerely hoped nothing would disturb for another century at least.

Brant had quite enjoyed the whole adventure. He was sorry, of course, to lose the home that had shaped his childhood; and now he would never climb the proud, lonely mountain that had looked down upon the village of his birth. There were no mountains in this land – only low, rolling hills and fertile valleys in which forests had run rampant for millennia, since agriculture had come to an end. It was warmer, too, than in the old country, for they were nearer the equator and had left behind them the fierce winters of the North. In almost every respect the change was for the good; but for a year or two the people of Chaldis would feel a comfortable glow of martyrdom.

These political matters did not worry Brant in the least. The entire sweep of human history from the dark ages into the unknown future was considerably less important at the moment than the question of Yradne and her feelings toward him. He wondered what Yradne was doing now, and tried to think of an excuse for going to see her. But that would mean meeting her parents, who would embarrass him by their hearty pretence that his call was simply a social one.

He decided to go to the smithy instead, if only to make a check on Jon's movements. It was a pity about Jon; they had been such good friends only a short while ago. But love was friendship's deadliest enemy, and until Yradne had chosen between them they would remain in a state of armed neutrality.

The village sprawled for about a mile along the valley, its neat, new houses arranged in calculated disorder. A few people were moving around in no particular hurry, or gossiping in little groups beneath the trees. To Brant it seemed that everyone was following him with their eyes and talking about him as he passed – an assumption that, as it happened, was perfectly correct. In a closed community of fewer than a thousand highly intelligent people, no one could expect to have any private life.

The smithy was in a clearing at the far end of the village, where its general untidiness would cause as little offence as possible. It was surrounded by broken and half-dismantled machines that Old Johan had not got around to mending. One of the community's three flyers was lying, its bare ribs exposed to the sunlight, where it had been dumped weeks ago with a request for immediate repair. Old Johan would fix it one day, but in his own time.

The wide door of the smithy was open, and from the brilliantly lit interior came the sound of screaming metal as the automatic machines fashioned some new shape to their master's will. Brant threaded his way carefully past the busy slaves and emerged into the relative quiet at the back of the shop.

Old Johan was lying in an excessively comfortable chair, smoking a pipe and looking as if he had never done a day's work in his life. He was a neat little man with a carefully pointed beard, and only his brilliant, ceaselessly roaming eyes showed any signs of animation. He might have been taken for a minor poet – as indeed he fancied himself to be – but never for a village blacksmith.

'Looking for Jon?' he said between puffs. 'He's around somewhere, making something for that girl. Beats me what you two see in her.'

Brant turned a slight pink and was about to make some sort of reply when one of the machines started calling loudly for attention. In a flash Old Johan was out of the room, and for a minute strange crashings and bangings and much bad language floated through the doorway. Very soon, however, he was back again in his chair, obviously not expecting to be disturbed for quite a while.

'Let me tell you something, Brant,' he continued, as if there had been no interruption. 'In twenty years she'll be exactly like her mother. Ever thought of that?'

Brant hadn't, and quailed slightly. But twenty years is an eternity to youth; if he could win Yradne in the present, the future could take care of itself. He told Johan as much.

'Have it your own way,' said the smith, not unkindly. 'I suppose if we'd all looked that far ahead the human race would have died out a million years ago. Why don't you play a game of chess, like sensible people, to decide who'll have her first?'

'Brent would cheat,' answered Jon, suddenly appearing in the entrance and filling most of it. He was a large, well-built youth, in complete contrast to his father, and was carrying a sheet of paper covered with engineering sketches. Brant wondered what sort of present he was making for Yradne.

'What are you doing?' he asked, with a far from disinterested curiosity.

'Why should I tell you?' asked Jon good-naturedly. 'Give me one good reason.'

Brant shrugged his shoulders.

'I'm sure it's not important – I was only being polite.'

'Don't overdo it,' said the smith. 'The last time you were polite to Jon, you had a black eye for a week. Remember?' He turned to his son, and said brusquely: 'Let's see those drawings, so I can tell you why it can't be done.'

He examined the sketches critically, while Jon showed increasing signs of embarrassment. Presently Johan snorted disapprovingly and said: 'Where are you going to get the components? They're all nonstandard, and most of them are sub-micro.'

Jon looked hopefully around the workshop.

'There aren't very many of them,' he said. 'It's a simple job, and I was wondering . . .'

'. . . if I'd let you mess up the integrators to try to make the pieces? Well, we'll see about that. My talented son, Brant, is trying to prove that he possesses brains as well as brawn, by making a toy that's been obsolete for about fifty centuries. I hope you can do better than that. Now when I was your age . . .'

His voice and his reminiscences trailed off into silence. Yradne had drifted in from the clangorous bustle of the machine shop, and was watching them from the doorway with a faint smile on her lips.

It is probable that if Brant and Jon had been asked to describe Yradne, it would have seemed as if they were speaking of two entirely different people. There would have been superficial points of resemblance, of course. Both would have agreed that her hair was chestnut, her eyes large and blue, and her skin that rarest of colours – an almost pearly white. But to Jon she seemed a fragile little creature, to be cherished and protected; while to Brant her self-confidence and complete assurance were so obvious that he despaired of ever being of any service to her. Part of that difference in outlook was due to Jon's extra six inches of height and nine inches of girth, but most of it came from profounder psychological muses. The person one loves never really exists, but is a projection focused through the lens of the mind onto whatever screen it fits with least distortion. Brant and Jon had quite different ideals, and each believed that Yradne embodied them. This would not have surprised her in the least, for few things ever did.

'I'm going down to the river,' she said. 'I called for you on the way, Brant, but you were out.'

That was a blow at Jon, but she quickly equalised.

'I thought you'd gone off with Lorayne or some other girl, but I knew I'd find Jon at home.'

Jon looked very smug at this unsolicited and quite inaccurate testimonial. He rolled up his drawings and dashed off to the house, calling happily over his shoulder: 'Wait for me – I won't be long!'

Brant never took his eyes off Yradne as he shifted uncomfortably from one foot to the other. She hadn't actually invited *anyone* to come with her, and until definitely ordered off, he was going to stand his ground. But he remembered that there was a somewhat ancient saying to the effect that if two were company, three were the reverse.

Jon returned, resplendent in a surprising green cloak with diagonal explosions of red down the sides. Only a very young man could have got away with it, and even Jon barely suceeded. Brant wondered if there was time for him to hurry home and change into something still more startling, but that would be too great a risk to take. It would be flying in the face of the enemy; the battle might be over before he could get his reinforcements.

'Quite a crowd,' remarked Old Johan unhelpfully as they departed. 'Mind if I come along too?' The boys looked embarrassed, but Yradne gave a gay little laugh that made it hard for him to dislike her. He stood in the outer doorway for a while, smiling as they went away through the trees and down the long, grass-covered slope to the river. But presently his eyes ceased to follow them, as he lost himself in dreams as vain as any that can come to man – the dreams of his own departed youth. Very soon he turned his back upon the sunlight and, no longer smiling now, disappeared into the busy tumult of the workshop.

*

Now the northward-climbing sun was passing the equator, the days would soon be longer than the nights, and the rout of winter was complete. The countless villages throughout the hemisphere were preparing to greet the spring. With the dying of the great cities and the return of man to the fields and woods, he had returned also to many of the ancient customs that had slumbered through a thousand years of urban civilisation. Some of those customs had been deliberately revived by the anthropologists and social engineers of the third millennium, whose genius had sent so many patterns of human culture safely down the ages. So it was that the spring equinox was still welcomed by rituals which, for all their sophistication, would have seemed less strange to primitive man than to the people of the industrial cities whose smoke had once stained the skies of Earth.

The arrangements for the Spring Festival were always the subject of much intrigue and bickering between neighbouring villages. Although it involved the disruption of all other activities for at least a month, any village was greatly honoured to be chosen as host for the celebrations. A newly settled community, still recovering from transplantation, would not, of course, be expected to take on such a responsibility. Brant's people, however, had thought of an ingenious way of regaining favour and wiping out the stain of their recent disgrace. There were five other villages within a hundred miles, and all had been invited to Chaldis for the Festival.

The invitation had been very carefully worded. It hinted delicately that, for obvious reasons, Chaldis couldn't hope to arrange as elaborate a ceremonial as it might have wished, and thereby implied that if the guests wanted a really good time they had better go elsewhere. Chaldis expected one acceptance at the most, but the inquisitiveness of its neighbours had overcome their sense of moral superiority. They had all said that they would be delighted to come; and there was no possible way in which Chaldis could now evade its responsibilities.

There was no night and little sleep in the valley. High above the trees a row of artificial suns burned with a steady, blue-white brilliance, banishing the stars and the darkness and throwing into chaos the natural routine of all the wild creatures for miles around. Through lengthening days and shortening nights, men and machines were battling to make ready the great amphitheatre needed to hold some four thousand people. In one respect at least, they were lucky: there was no need for a roof or any artificial heating in this climate. In the land they had so reluctantly left, the snow would still be thick upon the ground at the end of March.

Brant woke early on the great day to the sound of aircraft falling down from the skies above him. He stretched himself wearily, wondering when he would get to bed again, and then climbed into his clothes. A kick with his foot at a concealed switch and the rectangle of yielding foam rubber, an inch below floor level, was completely covered by a rigid plastic sheet that had unrolled from within the wall. There was no bed linen to worry about because the room was kept automatically at body temperature. In many such ways Brant's life was simpler than those of his remote ancestors –

simpler through the ceaseless and almost forgotten efforts of five thousand years of science.

The room was softly lit by light pouring through one translucent wall, and was quite incredibly untidy. The only clear floor space was that concealing the bed, and probably this would have to be cleared again by nightfall. Brant was a great hoarder and hated to throw anything away. This was a very unusual characteristic in a world where few things were of value because they could be made so easily, but the objects Brant collected were not those that the integrators were used to creating. In one corner a small tree trunk was propped against the wall, partly carved into a vaguely anthropomorphic shape. Large lumps of sandstone and marble were scattered elsewhere over the floor, until such time as Brant decided to work on them. The walls were completely covered with paintings, most of them abstract in character. It would have needed very little intelligence to deduce that Brant was an artist; it was not so easy to decide if he was a good one.

He picked his way through the debris and went in search of food. There was no kitchen; some historians maintained that it had survived until as late as AD 2500, but long before then most families made their own meals about as often as they made their own clothes. Brant walked into the main living room and went across to a metal box set in the wall at chest level. At its centre was something that would have been quite familiar to every human being for the last fifty centuries – a ten-digit impulse dial. Brant called a four-figure number and waited. Nothing whatsoever happened. Looking a little annoyed, he pressed a concealed button and the front of the apparatus slid open, revealing an interior which should, by all the rules, have contained an appetising breakfast. It was completely empty.

Brant could call up the central food machine to demand an explanation, but there would probably be no answer. It was quite obvious what had happened – the catering department was so busy preparing for the day's overload that he'd be lucky if he got any breakfast at all. He cleared the circuit, then tried again with a little-used number. This time there was a gentle purr, a dull click, and the doors slid open to reveal a cup of some dark, steaming beverage, a few not-very-exciting-looking sandwiches, and a large slice of melon. Wrinkling up his nose, and wondering how long mankind would take to slip back to barbarism at this rate, Brant started on his substitute meal and very soon polished it off.

His parents were still asleep as he went quietly out of the house into the wide, grass-covered square at the centre of the village. It was still very early and there was a slight chill in the air, but the day was clear and fine, with that freshness which seldom lingers after the last dew has gone. Several aircraft were lying on the green, disgorging passengers, who were milling around in circles or wandering off to examine Chaldis with critical eyes. As Brant watched, one of the machines went humming briskly up into the sky, leaving a faint trail of ionisation behind it. A moment later the others followed; they could carry only a few-dozen passengers and would have to make many trips before the day was out.

Brant strolled over to the visitors, trying to look self-assured yet not so aloof as to discourage all contacts. Most of the strangers were about his own age – the older people would be arriving at a more reasonable time.

They looked at him with a frank curiosity which he returned with interest. Their skins were much darker than his, he noticed, and their voices were softer and less modulated. Some of them even had a trace of accent, for despite a universal language and instantaneous communication, regional variations still existed. At least, Brant assumed that they were the ones with accents; but once or twice he caught them smiling a little as he spoke.

Throughout the morning the visitors gathered in the square and made their way to the great arena that had been ruthlessly carved out of the forest. There were tents and bright banners here, and much shouting and laughter, for the morning was for the amusement of the young. Though Athens had swept like a dwindling but never-dying beacon for ten thousand years down the river of time, the pattern of sport had scarcely changed since those first Olympic days. Men still ran and jumped and wrestled and swam; but they did all these things a good deal better now than their ancestors. Brant was a fair sprinter over short distances and managed to finish third in the hundred metres. His time was just over eight seconds, which was not very good, because the record was less than seven. Brant would have been much amazed to learn that there was a time when no one in the world could have approached this figure.

Jon enjoyed himself hugely, bouncing youths even larger than himself onto the patient turf, and when the morning's results were added up, Chaldis had scored more points than any of the visitors, although it had been first in relatively few events.

As noon approached, the crowd began to flow amoeba-like down to Five Oaks Glade, where the molecular synthesisers had been working since the early hours to cover hundreds of tables with food. Much skill had gone into preparing the prototypes which were being reproduced with absolute fidelity down to the last atom; for though the mechanics of food production had altered completely, the art of the chef had survived, and had even gone forward to victories in which Nature had played no part at all.

The main feature of the afternoon was a long poetic drama – a pastiche put together with considerable skill from the works of poets whose very names had been forgotten ages since. On the whole Brant found it boring, though there were some fine lines here and there that had stuck in his memory:

> For winter's rains and ruins are over,
> And all the season of snows and sins . . .

Brant knew about snow, and was glad to have left it behind. Sin, however, was an archaic word that had dropped out of use three or four thousand years ago; but it had an ominous and exciting ring.

He did not catch up with Yradne until it was almost dusk, and the dancing had begun. High above the valley, floating lights had started to burn, flooding the woods with everchanging patterns of blue and red and gold. In twos and threes and then in dozens and hundreds, the dancers moved out into the great oval of the amphitheatre, until it became a sea of laughing, whirling forms. Here at last was something at which Brant could beat Jon handsomely, and he let himself be swept away on the tide of sheer physical enjoyment.

The music ranged through the whole spectrum of human culture. At one moment the air pulsed to the throb of drums that might have called from some primeval jungle when the world was young; and a little later, intricate tapestries of quarter tones were being woven by subtle electronic skills. The stars peered down wanly as they marched across the sky, but no one saw them and no one gave any thought to the passage of time.

Brant had danced with many girls before he found Yradne. She looked very beautiful, brimming over with the enjoyment of life, and she seemed in no hurry to join him when there were so many others to choose from. But at last they were circling together in the whirlpool, and it gave Brant no small pleasure to think that Jon was probably watcing them glumly from afar.

They broke away from the dance during a pause in the music, because Yradne announced that she was a little tired. This suited Brant admirably, and presently they were sitting together under one of the great trees, watching the ebb and flow of life around them with that detachment that comes in moments of complete relaxation.

It was Brant who broke the spell. It had to be done, and it might be a long time before such an opportunity came again.

'Yradne,' he said, 'why have you been avoiding me?'

She looked at him with innocent, open eyes.

'Oh, Brant,' she replied, 'what an unkind thing to say; you know it isn't true! I wish you weren't so jealous: you can't expect me to be following you around *all* the time.'

'Oh, very well!' said Brant weakly, wondering if he was making a fool of himself. But he might as well go on now he had started.

'You know, *some* day you'll have to decide between us. If you keep putting it off, perhaps you'll be left high and dry like those two aunts of yours.'

Yradne gave a tinkling laugh and tossed her head with great amusement at the thought that she could ever be old and ugly.

'Even if you're too impatient,' she replied, 'I think I can rely on Jon. Have you seen what he's given me?'

'No,' said Brant, his heart sinking.

'You *are* observant, aren't you! Haven't you noticed this necklace?'

On her breast Yradne was wearing a large group of jewels, suspended from her neck by a thin golden chain. It was quite a fine pendant, but there was nothing particularly unusual about it, and Brant wasted no time in saying so. Yradne smiled mysteriously and her fingers flickered toward her throat. Instantly the air was suffused with the sound of music, which first mingled with the background of the dance and then drowned it completely.

'You see,' she said proudly, 'wherever I go now I can have music with me. Jon says there are so many thousands of hours of it stored up that I'll never know when it repeats itself. Isn't it clever?'

'Perhaps it is,' said Brant grudgingly, 'but it isn't exactly new. Everyone used to carry this sort of thing once, until there was no silence anywhere on Earth and they had to be forbidden. Just think of the chaos if we all had them!'

Yradne broke away from him angrily.

'There you go again – always jealous of something you can't do yourself. What have you ever given me that's half as clever or useful as this? I'm going – and don't try to follow me!'

Brant stared open-mouthed as she went, quite taken aback by the violence of her reaction. Then he called after her, 'Hey, Yradne, I didn't mean . . .' But she was gone.

He made his way out of the amphitheatre in a very bad temper. It did him no good at all to rationalise the cause of Yradne's outburst. His remarks, though rather spiteful, had been true, and sometimes there is nothing more annoying than the truth. Jon's gift was an ingenious but trivial toy, interesting only because it now happened to be unique.

One thing she had said still rankled in his mind. What *was* there he had ever given Yradne? He had nothing but his paintings, and they weren't really very good. She had shown no interest in them at all when he had offered her some of his best, and it had been very hard to explain that he wasn't a portrait painter and would rather not try to make a picture of her. She had never really understood this, and it had been very difficult not to hurt her feelings. Brant liked taking his inspiration from Nature, but he never copied what he saw. When one of his pictures was finished (which occasionally happened), the title was often the only clue to the original source.

The music of the dance still throbbed around him, but he had lost all interest; the sight of other people enjoying themselves was more than he could stand. He decided to get away from the crowd, and the only peaceful place he could think of was down by the river, at the end of the shining carpet of freshly planted glow-moss that led through the wood.

He sat at the water's edge, throwing twigs into the current and watching them drift downstream. From time to time other idlers strolled by, but they were usually in pairs and took no notice of him. He watched them enviously and brooded over the unsatisfactory state of his affairs.

It would almost be better, he thought, if Yradne did make up her mind to choose Jon, and so put him out of his misery. But she showed not the slightest sign of preferring one to the other. Perhaps she was simply enjoying herself at their expense, as some people – particularly Old Johan –

maintained; though it was just as likely that she was genuinely unable to choose. What was wanted, Brant thought morosely, was for one of them to do something really spectacular which the other could not hope to match.

'Hello,' said a small voice behind him. He twisted around and looked over his shoulder. A little girl of eight or so was staring at him with her head slightly on one side, like an inquisitive sparrow.

'Hello,' he replied without enthusiasm. 'Why aren't you watching the dance?'

'Why aren't you in it?' she replied promptly.

'I'm tired,' he said, hoping that this was an adequate excuse. 'You shouldn't be running around by yourself. You might get lost.'

'I am lost,' she replied happily, sitting down on the bank beside him. 'I like it that way.' Brant wondered which of the other villages she had come from; she was quite a pretty little thing, but would look prettier with less chocolate on her face. It seemed that his solitude was at an end.

She stared at him with that disconcerting directness which, perhaps fortunately, seldom survives childhood. 'I know what's the matter with you,' she said suddenly.

'Indeed?' queried Brant with polite scepticism.

'You're in love!'

Brant dropped the twig he was about to throw into the river, and turned to stare at his inquisitor. She was looking at him with such solemn sympathy that in a moment all his morbid self-pity vanished in a gale of laughter. She seemed quite hurt, and he quickly brought himself under control.

'How could you tell?' he asked with profound seriousness.

'I've read all about it,' she replied solemnly. 'And once I saw a picture play and there was a man in it and he came down to a river and sat there just like you and presently he jumped into it. There was some awful pretty music then.'

Brant looked thoughtfully at this precocious child and felt relieved that she didn't belong to his own community.

'I'm sorry I can't arrange the music,' he said gravely, 'but in any case the river isn't really deep enough.'

'It is farther along,' came the helpful reply. 'This is only a baby river here – it doesn't grow up until it leaves the woods. I saw it from the flyer.'

'What happens to it then?' asked Brant, not in the least interested, but thankful that the conversation had taken a more innocuous turn. 'I suppose it reaches the sea?'

She gave an unladylike sniff of disgust.

'Of course not, silly. All the rivers this side of the hills go to the Great Lake. I know that's as big as a sea, but the *real* sea is on the other side of the hills.'

Brant had learned very little about the geographical details of his new home, but he realised that the child was quite correct. The ocean was less than twenty miles to the north, but separated from them by a barrier of low hills. A hundred miles inland lay the Great Lake, bringing life to lands that had been desert before the geological engineers had reshaped this continent.

The child genius was making a map out of twigs and patiently explaining these matters to her rather dull pupil.

'Here we are,' she said, 'and here's the river, and the hills, and the lake's over there by your foot. The sea goes along here – and I'll tell you a secret.'

'What's that?'

'You'll never guess!'

'I don't suppose I will.'

Her voice dropped to a confidential whisper. 'If you go along the coast – it isn't very far from here – you'll come to Shastar.'

Brant tried to look impressed, but failed.

'I don't believe you've ever heard of it!' she cried, deeply disappointed.

'I'm sorry,' replied Brant. 'I suppose it was a city, and I know I've heard of it somewhere. But there were such a lot of them, you know – Carthage and Chicago and Babylon and Berlin – you simply can't remember them all. And they've all gone now, anyway.'

'Not Shastar. It's still there.'

'Well, some of the later ones are still standing, more or less, and people often visit them. About five hundred miles from my old home there was quite a big city once, called . . .'

'Shastar isn't just *any* old city,' interrupted the child mysteriously. 'My grandfather told me about it: he's been there. It hasn't been spoiled at all and it's still full of wonderful things that no one has any more.'

Brant smiled inwardly. The deserted cities of Earth had been the breeding places of legends for countless centuries. It would be four – no, nearer five – thousand years since Shastar had been abandoned. If its buildings were still standing, which was of course quite possible, they would certainly have been stripped of all valuables ages ago. It seemed that Grandfather had been inventing some pretty fairy stories to entertain the child. He had Brant's sympathy.

Heedless of his scepticism, the girl prattled on. Brant gave only half his mind to her words, interjecting a polite 'Yes' or 'Fancy that' as occasion demanded. Suddenly, silence fell.

He looked up and found that his companion was staring with much annoyance toward the avenue of trees that overlooked the view.

'Goodbye,' she said abruptly. 'I've got to hide somewhere else – here comes my sister.'

She was gone as suddenly as she had arrived. Her family must have a busy time looking after her, Brant decided: but she had done him a good turn by dispelling his melancholy mood.

Within a few hours, he realised that she had done very much more than that.

*

Simon was leaning against his doorpost watching the world go by when Brant came in search of him. The world usually accelerated slightly when it had to pass Simon's door, for he was an interminable talker and once he had trapped a victim there was no escape for an hour or more. It was most unusual for anyone to walk voluntarily into his clutches, as Brant was doing now.

The trouble with Simon was that he had a first-class mind, and was too lazy to use it. Perhaps he might have been luckier had he been born in a more energetic age; all he had ever been able to do in Chaldis was to sharpen his wits at other people's expense, thereby gaining more fame than popularity. But he was quite indispensable, for he was a storehouse of knowledge, the greater part of it perfectly accurate.

'Simon,' began Brant without any preamble. 'I want to learn something about this country. The maps don't tell me much – they're too new. What was here, back in the old days?'

Simon scratched his wiry beard.

'I don't suppose it was very different. How long ago do you mean?'

'Oh, back in the time of the cities.'

'There weren't so many trees, of course. This was probably agricultural land, used for food production. Did you see that farming machine they dug up when the amphitheatre was being built? It must have been old; it wasn't even electric.'

'Yes,' said Brant impatiently. 'I saw it. But tell me about the cities around here. According to the map, there was a place called Shastar a few hundred miles west of us along the coast. Do you know anything about it?'

'Ah, Shastar,' murmured Simon, stalling for time. 'A very interesting place; I think I've even got a picture of it around somewhere. Just a moment while I go and see.'

He disappeared into the house and was gone for nearly five minutes. In that time he made a very extensive library search, though a man from the age of books would hardly have guessed this from his actions. All the records Chaldis possessed were in a metal case a metre on a side; it contained, locked perpetually in subatomic patterns, the equivalent of a billion volumes of print. Almost all the knowledge of mankind, and the whole of its surviving literature, lay here concealed.

It was not merely a passive storehouse of wisdom, for it possessed a librarian. As Simon signalled his request to the tireless machine, the search went down, layer by layer, through the almost infinite network of circuits. It took only a fraction of a second to locate the information he needed, for he had given the name and the approximate date. Then he relaxed as the mental images came flooding into his brain, under the lightest of self-hypnosis. The knowledge would remain in his possession for a few hours only – long enough for his purpose – and would then fade away. Simon had no desire to clutter up his well-organised mind with irrelevancies, and to him the whole story of the rise and fall of the great cities was a historical digression of no particular importance. It was an interesting, if a regrettable, episode, and it belonged to a past that had irretrievably vanished.

Brant was still waiting patiently when he emerged, looking very wise.

'I couldn't find any pictures,' he said. 'My wife has been tidying up again. But I'll tell you what I can remember about Shastar.'

Brant settled himself down as comfortably as he could; he was likely to be here for some time.

'Shastar was one of the very last cities that man ever built. You know, of course, that cities arose quite late in human culture – only about twelve thousand years ago. They grew in number and importance for several thousand years, until at last there were some containing millions of people. It is very hard for us to imagine what it must have been like to live in such places – deserts of steel and stone with not even a blade of grass for miles. But they were necessary, before transport and communication had been perfected, and people had to live near each other to carry out all the intricate operations of trade and manufacture upon which their lives depended.

'The really great cities began to disappear when air transport became universal. The threat of attack in those far-off, barbarous days also helped to disperse them. But for a long time . . .'

'I've studied the history of that period,' interjected Brant, not very truthfully. 'I know all about . . .'

'. . . for a long time there were still many small cities which were held together by cultural rather than commercial links. They had populations of a few score thousand and lasted for centuries after the passing of the giants. That's why Oxford and Princeton and Heidelberg still mean something to us, while far larger cities are no more than names. But even these were doomed when the invention of the integrator made it possible for any community, however small, to manufacture without effort everything it needed for civilised living.

'Shastar was built when there was no longer any need, technically, for cities, but before people realised that the culture of cities was coming to its end. It seems to have been a conscious work of art, conceived and designed as a whole, and those who lived there were mostly artists of some kind. But it didn't last very long; what finally killed it was the exodus.'

Simon became suddenly quiet, as if brooding on those tumultuous centuries when the road to the stars had been opened up and the world was torn in twain. Along that road the flower of the race had gone, leaving the rest behind; and thereafter it seemed that history had come to an end on Earth. For a thousand years or more the exiles had returned fleetingly to the solar system, wistfully eager to tell of strange suns and far planets and the great empire that would one day span the galaxy. But there are gulfs that even the swiftest ships can never cross; and such a gulf was opening now between Earth and her wandering children. They had less and less in common; the returning ships became ever more infrequent, until at last generations passed between the visits from outside. Simon had not heard of any such for almost three hundred years.

It was unusual when one had to prod Simon into speech, but presently Brant remarked: 'Anyway, I'm more interested in the place itself than its history. Do you think it's still standing?'

'I was coming to that,' said Simon, emerging from his reverie with a start. 'Of course it is; they built well in those days. But why are you so interested, may I ask? Have you suddenly developed an overwhelming passion for archaeology? Oh, I think I understand!'

Brant knew perfectly well the uselessness of trying to conceal anything from a professional busybody like Simon.

'I was hoping,' he said defensively, 'that there might still be things there worth going to find, even after all this time.'

'Perhaps,' said Simon doubtfully. 'I must visit it one day. It's almost on our doorstep, as it were. But how are *you* going to manage? The village will hardly let you borrow a flyer! And you can't walk. It would take you at least a week to get there.'

But that was exactly what Brant intended to do. As, during the next few days, he was careful to point out to almost everyone in the village, a thing wasn't worth doing unless one did it the hard way. There was nothing like making a virtue out of a necessity.

Brant's preparations were carried out in an unprecedented blaze of secrecy. He did not wish to be too specific about his plans, such as they were, in case any of the dozen or so people in Chaldis who had the right to use a flyer decided to look at Shastar first. It was, of course, only a matter of time before this happened, but the feverish activity of the past months had prevented such explorations. Nothing would be more humiliating than to stagger into Shastar after a week's journey, only to be coolly greeted by a neighbour who had made the trip in ten minutes.

On the other hand, it was equally important that the village in general, and Yradne in particular, should realise that he was making some exceptional effort. Only Simon knew the truth, and he had grudgingly agreed to keep quiet for the present. Brant hoped that he had managed to divert attention from his true objective by showing a great interest in the country to the east of Chaldis, which also contained several archaeological relics of some importance.

The amount of food and equipment one needed for a two or three weeks' absence was really astonishing, and his first calculations had thrown Brant into a state of considerable gloom. For a while he had even thought of trying to beg or borrow a flyer, but the request would certainly not be granted – and would indeed defeat the whole object of his enterprise. Yet it was quite impossible for him to carry everything he needed for the journey.

The solution would have been perfectly obvious to anyone from a less-mechanised age, but it took Brant some little time to think of it. The flying machine had killed all forms of land transport save one, the oldest and most versatile of all – the only one that was self-perpetuating and could manage very well, as it had done before, with no assistance at all from man.

Chaldis possessed six horses, rather a small number for a community of its size. In some villages the horses outnumbered the humans, but Brant's people, living in a wild and mountainous region, had so far had little opportunity for equitation. Brant himself had ridden a horse only two or three times in his life, and then for exceedingly short periods.

The stallion and five mares were in the charge of Treggor, a gnarled little man who had no discernible interest in life except animals. His was not one of the outstanding intellects of Chaldis, but he seemed perfectly happy running his private menagerie, which included dogs of many shapes and sizes, a couple of beavers, several monkeys, a lion cub, two bears, a young crocodile, and other beasts more usually admired from a distance. The only sorrow that had ever clouded his placid life arose from the fact that he had so far failed to obtain an elephant.

Brant found Treggor, as he expected, leaning on the gate of the paddock. There was a stranger with him, who was introduced to Brant as a horse fancier from a neighbouring village. The curious similarity between the two men, extending from the way they dressed even to their facial expressions, made this explanation quite unnecessary.

One always feels a certain nervousness in the presence of undoubted experts, and Brant outlined his problem with some diffidence. Treggor listened gravely and paused for a long time before replying.

'Yes,' he said slowly, jerking his thumb toward the mares, 'any of them would do – if you knew how to handle 'em.' He looked rather doubtfully at Brant.

'They're like human beings, you know; if they don't like you, you can't do a thing with them.'

'Not a thing,' echoed the stranger, with evident relish.

'But surely you could teach me how to handle them?'

'Maybe yes, maybe no. I remember a young fellow just like you, wanted to learn to ride. Horses just wouldn't let him get near them. Took a dislike to him – and that was that.'

'Horses can *tell*,' interjected the other darkly.

'That's right,' agreed Treggor. 'You've got to be sympathetic. Then you've nothing to worry about.'

There was, Brant decided, quite a lot to be said for the less-temperamental machine after all.

'I don't want to ride,' he answered with some feeling. 'I only want a horse to carry my gear. Or would it be likely to object to that?'

His mild sarcasm was quite wasted. Treggor nodded solemnly.

'That wouldn't be any trouble,' he said. 'They'll all let you lead them with a halter – all except Daisy, that is. You'd never catch *her*.'

'Then do you think I could borrow one of the – er, more amenable ones – for a while?'

Treggor shuffled around uncertainly, torn between two conflicting desires. He was pleased that someone wanted to use his beloved beasts, but nervous lest they come to harm. Any damage that might befall Brant was of secondary importance.

'Well,' he began doubtfully, 'it's a bit awkward at the moment. . . .'

Brant looked at the mares more closely, and realised why. Only one of them was accompanied by a foal, but it was obvious that this deficiency would soon be rectified. Here was another complication he had overlooked.

'How long will you be away?' asked Treggor.

'Three weeks, at the most: perhaps only two.'

Treggor did some rapid gynaecological calculations.

'Then you can have Sunbeam,' he concluded. 'She won't give you any trouble at all – best-natured animal I've ever had.'

'Thank you very much,' said Brant. 'I promise I'll look after her. Now would you mind introducing us?'

'I don't see why I should do this,' grumbled Jon good-naturedly, as he adjusted the panniers on Sunbeam's sleek sides, 'especially since you won't even tell me where you're going or what you expect to find.'

Brant couldn't have answered the last question even had he wished. In his more rational moments he knew that he would find nothing of value in Shastar. Indeed, it was hard to think of anything that his people did not already possess, or could not obtain instantly if they wished. But the journey itself would be the proof – the most convincing he could imagine – of his love for Yradne.

There was no doubt that she was quite impressed by his preparations, and he had been careful to underline the dangers he was about to face. It would be very uncomfortable sleeping in the open, and he would have a most monotonous diet. He might even get lost and never be seen again. Suppose there were still wild beasts – dangerous ones – up in the hills or in the forests?

Old Johan, who had no feeling for historical traditions, had protested at the indignity of a blacksmith having anything to do with such a primitive survival as a horse. Sunbeam had nipped him delicately for this, with great skill and precision, while he was bending to examine her hoofs. But he had rapidly manufactured a set of panniers in which Brant could put everything he needed for the journey – even his drawing materials, from which he refused to be separated. Treggor had advised on the technical details of the harness, producing ancient prototypes consisting largely of string.

It was still early morning when the last adjustments had been completed; Brant had intended making his departure as unobtrusive as possible, and his complete success was slightly mortifying. Only Jon and Yradne came to see him off.

They walked in thoughtful silence to the end of the village and crossed the slim metal bridge over the river. Then Jon said gruffly: 'Well, don't go and break your silly neck,' shook hands, and departed, leaving him alone with Yradne. It was a very nice gesture, and Brant appreciated it.

Taking advantage of her master's preoccupation, Sunbeam began to browse among the long grass by the river's edge. Brant shifted awkwardly from foot to foot for a moment, then said halfheartedly:

'I suppose I'd better be going.'

'How long will you be away?' asked Yradne. She wasn't wearing Jon's present: perhaps she had grown tired of it already. Brant hoped so – then realised she might lose interest equally quickly in anything he brought back for her.

'Oh, about a fortnight – if all goes well,' he added darkly.

'Do be careful,' said Yradne, in tones of vague urgency, 'and don't do anything rash.'

'I'll do my best,' answered Brant, still making no move to go, 'but one has to take risks sometimes.'

This disjointed conversation might have lasted a good deal longer had Sunbeam not taken charge. Brant's arm received a sudden jerk and he was dragged away at a brisk walk. He had regained his balance and was about to wave farewell when Yradne came flying up to him, gave him a large kiss, and disappeared toward the village before he could recover.

She slowed down to a walk when Brant could no longer see her. Jon was still a good way ahead, but she made no attempt to overtake him. A curiously solemn feeling, out of place on this bright spring morning, had overcome her. It was very pleasant to be loved, but it had its disadvantages if one stopped to look beyond the immediate moment. For a fleeting instant Yradne wondered if she had been fair to Jon, to Brant – even to herself. One day the decision would have to be made; it could not be postponed forever. Yet she could not for the life of her decide which of the boys she liked the better; and she did not know if she loved either.

No one had ever told her, and she had not yet discovered, that when one has to ask 'Am I really in love?' the answer is always 'No'.

Beyond Chaldis the forest stretched for five miles to the east, then faded out into the great plain which spanned the remainder of the continent. Six thousand years ago this land had been one of the mightiest deserts in the world, and its reclamation had been among the first achievements of the Atomic Age.

Brant intended to go east until he was clear of the forest, and then to turn toward the high land of the North. According to the maps, there had once been a road along the spine of the hills, linking together all the cities on the coast in a chain that ended at Shastar. It should be easy to follow its track, though Brant did not expect that much of the road itself would have survived the centuries.

He kept close to the river, hoping that it had not changed its path since the maps were made. It was both his guide and his highway through the forest; when the trees were too thick, he and Sunbeam could always wade in the shallow water. Sunbeam was quite co-operative; there was no grass here to distract her, so she plodded methodically along with little prompting.

Soon after midday the trees began to thin out. Brant had reached the frontier that, century by century, had been on the march across the lands that Man no longer wished to hold. A little later the forest was behind him and he was out in the open plain.

He checked his position from the map, and noted that the trees had advanced an appreciable distance eastward since it was drawn. But there was a clear route north to the low hills along which the ancient road had run, and he should be able to reach them before evening.

At this point certain unforeseen difficulties of a technical nature arose. Sunbeam, finding herself surrounded by the most appetising grass she had seen for a long time, was unable to resist pausing every three or four steps to collect a mouthful. As Brant was attached to her bridle by a rather short rope, the resulting jerk almost dislocated his arm. Lengthening the rope made matters even worse, because he then had no control at all.

Now Brant was quite fond of animals, but it soon became apparent to him that Sunbeam was simply imposing on his good nature. He put up with it for half a mile, and then steered a course toward a tree which seemed to have particularly slender and lissom branches. Sunbeam watched him warily out of the corners of her limpid brown eyes as he cut a fine, resilient switch and attached it ostentatiously to his belt. Then she set off so briskly that he could scarcely keep pace with her.

She was undoubtedly, as Treggor had claimed, a singularly intelligent beast.

The range of hills that was Brant's first objective was less than two thousand feet high, and the slope was very gentle. But there were numerous annoying foothills and minor valleys to be surmounted on the way to the crest, and it was well toward evening before they had reached the highest point. To the south Brant could see the forest through which he had come, and which could now hinder him no more. Chaldis was somewhere in its midst, though he had only a rough idea of its location; he was surprised to find that he could see no signs of the great clearings that his people had made. To the southeast the plain stretched endlessly away, a level sea of grass dotted with little clumps of trees. Near the horizon Brant could see tiny, creeping specks, and guessed that some great herd of wild animals was on the move.

Northward lay the sea, only a dozen miles away down the long slope and across the lowlands. It seemed almost black in the falling sunlight, except where tiny breakers dotted it with flecks of foam.

Before nightfall Brant found a hollow out of the wind, anchored Sunbeam to a stout bush, and pitched the little tent that Old Johan had contrived for him. This was, in theory, a very simple operation, but, as agood many people had found before, it was one that could tax skill and temper to the utmost. At last everything was finished, and he settled down for the night.

There are some things that no amount of pure intelligence can anticipate, but which can only be learned by bitter experience. Who would have gussed that the human body was so sensitive to the almost imperceptible slope on which the tent had been pitched? More uncomfortable still were the minute thermal differences between one point and another, presumably caused by the draughts that seemed to wander through the tent at will. Brant could have endured a uniform temperature gradient, but the unpredictable variations were maddening.

He woke from his fitful sleep a dozen times, or so it seemed, and toward dawn his morale had reached its lowest ebb. He felt cold and miserable and stiff, as if he had not slept properly for days, and it would have needed very little persuasion to have made him abandon the whole enterprise. He was prepared – even willing – to face danger in the cause of love; but lumbago was a different matter.

The discomforts of the night were soon forgotten in the glory of the new day. Here on the hills the air was fresh with the tang of salt, borne by the wind that came climbing up from the sea. The dew was everywhere, hanging thickly on each bent blade of grass – but so soon to be destroyed beyond all trace by the steepening sun. It was good to be alive; it was better to be young; it was best of all to be in love.

They came upon the road very soon after they had started the day's journey. Brant had missed it before because it had been farther down the seaward slope, and he had expected to find it on the crest of the hill. It had been superbly built, and the millennia had touched it lightly. Nature had tried in vain to obliterate it; here and there she had succeeded in burying a few metres with a light blanket of earth, but then her servants had turned against her and the wind and the rain had scoured it clean once more. In a great jointless band, skirting the edge of the sea for more than a thousand miles, the road still linked the cities that Man had loved in his childhood.

It was one of the great roads of the world. Once it had been no more than a footpath along which savage tribes had come down to the sea, to barter with wily, bright-eyed merchants from distant lands. Then it had known new and more exacting masters; the soldiers of a mighty empire had shaped and hewn the road so skilfully along the hills that the path they gave it had remained unchanged down all the ages. They had paved it with stone so that their armies could move more swiftly than any that the world had known; and along the road their legions had been hurled like thunderbolts at the bidding of the city whose name they bore. Centuries later, that city had called them home in its last extremity; and the road had rested then for five hundred years.

But other wars were still to come; beneath crescent banners the armies of the Prophet were yet to storm westward into Christendom. Later still – centuries later – the tide of the last and greatest of conflicts was to turn here, as steel monsters clashed together in the desert, and the sky itself rained death.

The centurions, the paladins, the armoured divisions – even the desert – all were gone. But the road remained, of all man's creations the most enduring. For ages enough it had borne his burdens; and now along its whole thousand miles it carried no more traffic than one boy and a horse.

Brant followed the road for three days, keeping always in sight of the sea. He had grown used to the minor discomforts of a nomadic existence, and even the nights were no longer intolerable. The weather had been perfect – long, warm days and mild nights – but the fine spell was coming to an end.

He estimated that he was less than five miles from Shastar on the evening of the fourth day. The road was now turning away from the coast to avoid a great headland jutting out to sea. Beyond this was the sheltered bay along whose shores the city had been built; when it had bypassed the high ground, the road would sweep northward in a great curve and come down upon Shastar from the hills.

Toward dusk it was clear that Brant could not hope to see his goal that day. The weather was breaking, and thick, angry clouds had been gathering swiftly from the west. He was climbing now – for the road was rising slowly as it crossed the last ridge – in the teeth of a gale. He would have pitched camp for the night if he could have found a sheltered spot, but the hill was bare for miles behind him and there was nothing to do but to struggle onward.

Far ahead, at the very crest of the ridge, something low and dark was silhouetted against the threatening sky. The hope that it might provide shelter drove Brant onward: Sunbeam, head well down against the wind, plodded steadily beside him with equal determination.

They were still a mile from the summit when the rain began to fall, first in single, angry drops and then in blinding sheets. It was impossible to see more than a few paces ahead, even when one could open one's eyes against the stinging rain. Brant was already so wet that any additional moisture could add nothing to his discomfort; indeed, he had reached that sodden state when the continuing downpour almost gave him a masochistic pleasure. But the sheer physical effort of fighting against the gale was rapidly exhausting him.

It seemed ages before the road levelled out and he knew he had reached the summit. He strained his eyes into the gloom and could see, not far ahead, a great dark shape, which for a moment he thought might be a building. Even if it was in ruins, it would give him shelter from the storm.

The rain began to slacken as he approached the object; overhead, the clouds were thinning to let through the last fading light of the western sky. It was just sufficient to show Brant that what lay ahead of him was no building at all, but a great stone beast, crouching upon the hilltop and staring out to sea. He had no time to examine it more closely, but hurriedly pitched his tent in its shelter, out of reach of the wind that still raved angrily overhead.

It was completely dark when he had dried himself and prepared a meal. For a while he rested in his warm little oasis, in that state of blissful exhaustion that comes after hard and successful effort. Then he roused himself, took a hand-torch, and went out into the night.

The storm had blown away the clouds and the night was brilliant with stars. In the west a thin crescent moon was sinking, following hard upon the footsteps of the sun. To the north Brant was aware – though how, he could not have said – of the sleepless presence of the sea. Down there in the darkness Shastar was lying, the waves marching forever against it; but strain his eyes as he might, he could see nothing at all.

He walked along the flanks of the great statue, examining the stonework by the light of his torch. It was smooth and unbroken by any joints or seams, and although time had stained and discoloured it, there was no sign of wear. It was impossible to guess its age; it might be older than Shastar or it might have been made only a few centuries ago. There was no way of telling.

The hard, blue-white beam of the torch flickered along the monster's wetly gleaming sides and came to rest upon the great, calm face and the empty eyes. One might have called it a human face, but thereafter words faltered and failed. Neither male nor female, it seemed at first sight utterly indifferent to all the passions of mankind; then Brant saw that the storms of ages had left their mark behind them. Countless raindrops had coursed down those adamantine cheeks, until they bore the stains of Olympian tears – tears, perhaps, for the city whose birth and death now seemed almost equally remote.

Brant was so tired that when he awoke the sun was already high. He lay for a moment in the filtered half-light of the tent, recovering his senses and remembering where he was. Then he rose to his feet and went blinking into the daylight, shielding his eyes from the dazzling glare.

The Sphinx seemed smaller than by night, though it was impressive enough. It was coloured, Brant saw for the first time, a rich, autumnal gold, the colour of no natural rock. He knew from this that it did not belong, as he had half suspected, to any prehistoric culture. It had been built by science from some inconceivably stubborn, synthetic substance, and Brant guessed that its creation must lie almost midway in time between him and the fabulous original which had inspired it.

Slowly, half afraid of what he might discover, he turned his back upon the Sphinx and looked to the north. The hill fell away at his feet and the road went sweeping down the long slope as if impatient to greet the sea; and there at its end lay Shastar.

It caught the sunlight and tossed it back to him, tinted with all the colours of its makers' dreams. The spacious buildings lining the wide streets seemed unravished by time; the great band of marble that held the sea at bay was still unbreached; the parks and gardens, though long overgrown with weeds, were not yet jungles. The city followed the curve of the bay for perhaps two miles, and stretched half that distance inland; by the standards of the past, it was very small indeed. But to Brant it seemed enormous, a maze of streets and squares intricate beyond unravelling. Then he began to discern the underlying symmetry of its design, to pick out the main thoroughfares, and to see the skill with which its makers had avoided both monotony and discord.

For a long time Brant stood motionless on the hilltop, conscious only of the wonder spread beneath his eyes. He was alone in all that landscape, a tiny figure lost and humble before the achievements of greater men. The sense of history, the vision of the long slope up which Man had been toiling for a million years or more, was almost overwhelming. In that moment it seemed to Brant that from his hilltop he was looking over Time rather than Space: and in his ears there whispered the soughing of the winds of eternity as they sweep into the past.

Sunbeam seemed very nervous as they approached the outskirts of the city. She had never seen anything like this before in her life, and Brant could not help sharing her disquiet. However unimaginative one may be, there is something ominous about buildings that have been deserted for centuries – and those of Shastar had been empty for the better part of five thousand years.

The road ran straight as an arrow between two tall pillars of white metal; like the Sphinx, they were tarnished but unworn. Brant and Sunbeam passed beneath these silent guardians and found themselves before a long, low building which must have served as some kind of reception point for visitors to the city.

From a distance it had seemed that Shastar might have been abandoned only yesterday, but now Brant could see a thousand signs of desolation and neglect. The coloured stone of the buildings was stained with the patina of age; the windows were gaping, skull-blank eyes, with here and there a miraculously preserved fragment of glass.

Brant tethered Sunbeam outside the first building and made his way to the entrance across the rubble and thickly piled dirt. There was no door, if indeed there had ever been one, and he passed through the high, vaulted archway into a hall which seemed to run the full length of the structure. At regular intervals there were openings into further chambers, and immediately ahead of him a wide flight of stairs rose to the single floor above.

It took him almost an hour to explore the building, and when he left he was infinitely depressed. His careful search had revealed absolutely nothing. All the rooms, great and small, were completely empty; he had felt like an ant crawling through the bones of a clean-picked skeleton.

Out in the sunlight, however, his spirits revived a little. This building was probably only some sort of administrative office and would never have contained anything but records and information machines; elsewhere in the city, things might be different. Even so, the magnitude of the search appalled him.

Slowly he made his way toward the sea front, moving awestruck through the wide avenues and admiring the towering façades on either side. Near the centre of the city he came upon one of its many parks. It was largely overgrown with weeds and shrubs, but there were still considerable areas of grass, and he decided to leave Sunbeam here while he continued his explorations. She was not likely to move very far away while there was plenty to eat.

It was so peaceful in the park that for a while Brant was loath to leave it to plunge again into the desolation of the city. There were plants here unlike any that he had ever seen before, the wild descendants of those which the people of Shastar had cherished ages since. As he stood among the high grasses and unknown flowers, Brant heard for the first time, stealing through the calm stillness of the morning, the sound he was always to link with Shastar. It came from the sea, and though he had never heard it before in all his life, it brought a sense of aching recognition into his heart. Where no other voices sounded now, the lonely sea gulls were still calling sadly across the waves.

It was quite clear that many days would be needed to make even the most superficial examination of the city, and the first thing to do would be to find somewhere to live. Brant spent several hours searching for the residential district before it began to dawn on him that there was something very peculiar about Shastar. All the buildings he entered were, without exception, designed for work, entertainment, or similar purposes; but none of them had been designed *to live in*. The solution came to him slowly. As he grew to know the pattern of the city, he noticed that at almost every street intersection there were low, single-storeyed structures of nearly identical form. They were circular or oval, and had many openings leading into them from all directions. When Brant entered one of them, he found himself facing a line of great metal gates, each with a vertical row of indicator lamps by its side. And so he knew where the people of Shastar had lived.

At first the idea of underground homes was completely repellent to him. Then he overcame his prejudice, and realised how sensible, as well as how inevitable, this was. There was no need to clutter up the surface, and to block the sunlight, with buildings designed for the merely mechanical processes of sleeping and eating. By putting all these things underground, the people of Shastar had been able to build a noble and spacious city – and yet keep it so small that one could walk its whole length within an hour.

The elevators were, of course, useless, but there were emergency stairways winding down into the darkness. Once all this underworld must have been a blaze of light, but Brant hesitated now before he descended the steps. He had his torch, but he had never been underground before and had a horror of losing his way in some subterranean catacombs. Then he shrugged his shoulders and started down the steps; after all, there was no danger if he took the most elementary precautions – and there were hundreds of other exits even if he did lose his way.

He descended to the first level and found himself in a long, wide corridor stretching as far as his beam could penetrate. On either side were rows of numbered doors, and Brant tried nearly a dozen before he found one that opened. Slowly, even reverently, he entered the little home that had been deserted for almost half the span of recorded history.

It was clean and tidy, for there had been no dust or dirt to settle here. The beautifully proportioned rooms were bare of furniture; nothing of value had been left behind in the leisurely, age-long exodus. Some of the semipermanent fittings were still in position; the food distributor, with its familiar selector dial, was so strikingly like the one in Brant's own home that the sight of it almost annihilated the centuries. The dial still turned, though stiffly, and he would scarcely have been surprised to see a meal appear in the materialisation chamber.

Brant explored several more homes before he returned to the surface. Though he found nothing of value, he felt a growing sense of kinship toward the people who had lived here. Yet he still thought of them as his inferiors, for to have lived in a city – however beautiful, however brilliantly designed – was to Brant one of the symbols of barbarism.

In the last home he entered he came across a brightly coloured room with a fresco of dancing animals around the walls. The pictures were full of a whimsical humour that must have delighted the hearts of the children for whom they had been drawn. Brant examined the paintings with interest, for they were the first works of representative art he had found in Shastar. He was about to leave when he noticed a tiny pile of dust in one corner of the room, and bending down to investigate found himself looking at the still-recognisable fragments of a doll. Nothing solid remained save a few coloured buttons, which crumbled to powder in his hand when he picked them up. He wondered why this sad little relic had been left behind by its owner; then he tiptoed away and returned to the surface and the lonely but sunlit streets. He never went to the underground city again.

Toward evening he revisited the park to see that Sunbeam had been up to no mischief, and prepared to spend the night in one of the numerous small buildings scattered through the gardens. Here he was surrounded by flowers and trees, and could almost imagine he was home again. He slept better than he had done since he had left Chaldis, and for the first time for many days, his last waking thoughts were not of Yradne. The magic of Shastar was already working upon his mind; the infinite complexity of the civilisation he had affected to despise was changing him more swiftly than he could imagine. The longer he stayed in the city, the more remote he would become from the naïve yet self-confident boy who had entered it only a few hours before.

The second day confirmed the impressions of the first. Shastar had not died in a year, or even in a generation. Slowly its people had drifted away as the new – yet how old! – pattern of society had been evolved and humanity had returned to the hills and the forests. They had left nothing behind them, save these marble monuments to a way of life that was gone forever. Even if anything of value had remained, the thousands of curious explorers who had come here in the fifty centuries since would have taken it long ago. Brant found many traces of his predecessors; their names were carved on walls throughout the city, for this is one kind of immortality that men have never been able to resist.

Tired at last by his fruitless search, he went down to the shore and sat on the wide stonework of the breakwater. The sea lying a few feet beneath him was utterly calm and of a cerulean blue; it was so still and clear that he could watch the fish swimming in its depths, and at one spot could see a wreck lying on its side with the seaweed streaming straight up from it like long, green hair. Yet there must be times, he knew, when the waves came thundering over these massive walls; for behind him the wide parapet was strewn with a thick carpet of stones and shells, tossed there by the gales of centuries.

The enervating peacefulness of the scene, and the unforgettable object lesson in the futility of ambition that surrounded him on every side, took away all sense of disappointment or defeat. Though Shastar had given him nothing of material value, Brant did not regret his journey. Sitting here on the sea wall, with his back to the land and his eyes dazzled by that blinding blue, he already felt remote from his old problems, and could look back with no pain at all, but only a dispassionate curiosity, on all the heartache and the anxiety that had plagued him these last few months.

He went slowly back into the city, after walking a little way along the sea front so that he could return by a new route. Presently he found himself before a large, circular building whose roof was a shallow dome of some translucent material. He looked at it with little interest, for he was emotionally exhausted, and decided that it was probably yet another theatre or concert hall. He had almost passed the entrance when some obscure impulse diverted him and he went through the open doorway.

Inside, the light filtered through the ceiling with such little hindrance that Brant almost had the impression of being in the open air. The entire building was divided into numerous large halls whose purpose he realised with a sudden stir of excitement. The telltale rectangles of discoloration showed that the walls had once been almost covered with pictures; it was just possible that some had been left behind, and it would be interesting to see what Shastar could offer in the way of serious art. Brant, still secure in his consciousness of superiority, did not expect to be unduly impressed; and so the shock was all the greater when it came.

The blaze of colour along the whole length of the great wall smote him like a fanfare of trumpets. For a moment he stood paralysed in the doorway, unable to grasp the pattern or meaning of what he saw. Then, slowly, he began to unravel the details of the tremendous and intricate mural that had burst suddenly upon his vision.

It was nearly a hundred feet long, and was incomparably the most wonderful thing that Brant had ever seen in his life. Shastar had awed and overwhelmed him, yet its tragedy had left him curiously unmoved. But this struck straight at his heart and spoke in a language he could understand; and as it did so, the last vestiges of his condescension toward the past were scattered like leaves before a gale.

The eye moved naturally from left to right across the painting, to follow the curve of tension to its moment of climax. On the left was the sea, as deep a blue as the water that beat against Shastar; and moving across its face was a fleet of strange ships, driven by tiered banks of oars and by billowing sails that strained toward the distant land. The painting covered not only miles of space but perhaps years of time; for now the ships had reached the shore, and there on the wide plain an army lay encamped, its banners and tents and chariots dwarfed by the walls of the fortress city it was beleaguering. The eye scaled those still inviolate walls and came to rest, as it was meant to do, upon the woman who stood upon them, looking down at the army that had followed her across the ocean.

She was leaning forward to peer over the battlements, and the wind was catching her hair so that it formed a golden mist about her head. Upon her face was written a sadness too deep for words, yet one that did nothing to mar the unbelievable beauty of her face – a beauty that held Brant spellbound, for long unable to tear away his eyes. When at last he could do so, he followed her gaze down those seemingly impregnable walls to the group of soldiers toiling in their shadow. They were gathered around something so foreshortened by perspective that it was some time before Brant realised what it was. Then he saw that it was an enormous image of a horse, mounted on rollers so that it could be easily moved. It roused no echoes in his mind, and he quickly returned to the lonely figure on the wall, around whom, as he now saw, the whole great design was balanced and pivoted. For as the eye moved on across the painting, taking the mind with it into the future, it came upon ruined battlements, the smoke of the burning city staining the sky, and the fleet returning homeward, its mission done.

Brant left only when the light was so poor that he could no longer see. When the first shock had worn off, he had examined the great painting more closely; and for a while he had searched, but in vain, for the signature of the artist. He also looked for some caption or title, but it was clear that there had never been one – perhaps because the story was too well known to need it. In the intervening centuries, however, some other visitor to Shastar had scratched two lines of poetry on the wall:

> Is this the face that launched a thousand ships
> And burned the topless towers of Ilium?

Ilium! it was a strange and magical name; but it meant nothing to Brant. He wondered whether it belonged to history or to fable, not knowing how many before him had wrestled with that same problem.

As he emerged into the luminous twilight, he still carried the vision of that sad, ethereal loveliness before his eyes. Perhaps if Brant had not himself been an artist, and had been in a less susceptible state of mind, the impression would not have been so overwhelming. Yet it was the impression that the unknown master had set out to create, Phoenix-like, from the dying embers of a great legend. He had captured, and held for all future ages to see, that beauty whose service is the purpose of life, and its sole justification.

For a long time Brant sat under the stars, watching the crescent moon sink behind the towers of the city, and haunted by questions to which he could never know the answers. All the other pictures in these galleries had gone, scattered beyond tracing, not merely throughout the world, but throughout the universe. How had they compared with the single work of genius that now must represent forever the art of Shastar?

In the morning Brant returned, after a night of strange dreams. A plan had been forming in his mind; it was so wild and ambitious that at first he tried to laugh it away, but it would give him no peace. Almost reluctantly, he set up his little folding easel and prepared his paints. He had found one thing in Shastar that was both unique and beautiful; perhaps he had the skill to carry some faint echo of it back to Chaldis.

It was impossible, of course, to copy more than a fragment of the vast design, but the problem of selection was easy. Though he had never attempted a portrait of Yradne, he would now paint a woman who, if indeed she had ever existed, had been dust for five thousand years.

Several times he stopped to consider this paradox, and at last thought he had resolved it. He had never painted Yradne because he doubted his own skill, and was afraid of her criticism. That would be no problem here, Brant told himself. He did not stop to ask how Yradne would react when he returned to Chaldis carrying as his only gift the portrait of another woman.

In truth, he was painting for himself, and for no one else. For the first time in his life he had come into direct contact with a great work of classic art, and it had swept him off his feet. Until now he had been a dilettante; he might never be more than this, but at least he would make the effort.

He worked steadily all through the day, and the sheer concentration of his labours brought him a certain peace of mind. By evening he had sketched in the palace walls and battlements, and was about to start on the portrait itself. That night, he slept well.

He lost most of his optimism the next morning. His food supply was running low, and perhaps the thought that he was working against time had unsettled him. Everything seemed to be going wrong; the colours would not match, and the painting, which had shown such promise the day before, was becoming less and less satisfactory every minute.

To make matters worse, the light was failing, though it was barely noon, and Brant guessed that the sky outside had become overcast. He rested for a little while in the hope that it might clear again, but since it showed no signs of doing so, he recommenced work. It was now or nothing; unless he could get that hair right he would abandon the whole project. . . .

The afternoon waned rapidly, but in his fury of concentration Brant scarcely noticed the passage of time. Once or twice he thought he noticed distant sounds and wondered if a storm was coming up, for the sky was still very dark.

There is no experience more chilling than the sudden, the utterly unexpected knowledge that one is no longer alone. It would be hard to say what impulse made Brant slowly lay down his brush and turn, even more slowly, toward the great doorway forty feet behind him. The man standing there must have entered almost soundlessly, and how long he had been watching him Brant had no way of guessing. A moment later he was joined by two companions, who also made no attempt to pass the doorway.

Brant rose slowly to his feet, his brain whirling. For a moment he almost imagined that ghosts from Shastar's past had come back to haunt him. Then reason reasserted itself. After all, why should he not meet other visitors here, when he was one himself?

He took a few paces forward, and one of the strangers did likewise. When they were a few yards apart, the other said in a very clear voice, speaking rather slowly: 'I hope we haven't disturbed you.'

It was not a very dramatic conversational opening, and Brant was somewhat puzzled by the man's accent – or, more accurately, by the exceedingly careful way he was pronouncing his words. It almost seemed that he did not expect Brant to understand him otherwise.

'That's quite all right,' Brant replied, speaking equally slowly. 'But you gave me a surprise – I hardly expected to meet anyone here.'

'Neither did we,' said the other with a slight smile. 'We had no idea that anyone still lived in Shastar.'

'But I don't,' explained Brant. 'I'm just a visitor like you.'

The three exchanged glances, as if sharing some secret joke. Then one of them lifted a small metal object from his belt and spoke a few words into it, too softly for Brant to overhear. He assumed that other members of the party were on the way, and felt annoyed that his solitude was to be so completely shattered.

Two of the strangers had walked over to the great mural and begun to examine it critically. Brant wondered what they were thinking; somehow he resented sharing his treasure with those who would not feel the same reverence toward it – those to whom it would be nothing more than a pretty picture. The third man remained by his side comparing, as unobtrusively as possible, Brant's copy with the original. All three seemed to be deliberately avoiding further conversation. There was a long and embarrassing silence: then the other two men rejoined them.

'Well, Erlyn, what do you think of it?' said one, waving his hand toward the painting. They seemed for the moment to have lost all interest in Brant.

'It's a very fine late third-millennium primitive, as good as anything we have. Don't you agree, Latvar?'

'Not exactly. I wouldn't say it's late third. For one thing, the subject . . .'

'Oh, you and your theories! But perhaps you're right. It's too good for the last period. On second thoughts, I'd date it around 2500. What do you say, Trescon?'

'I agree. Probably Aroon or one of his pupils.'

'Rubbish!' said Latvar.

'Nonsense!' snorted Erlyn.

'Oh, very well,' replied Trescon good-naturedly. 'I've only studied this period for thirty years, while you've just looked it up since we started. So I bow to your superior knowledge.'

Brant had followed this conversation with growing surprise and a rapidly mounting sense of bafflement.

'Are all three of you artists?' he blurted out at last.

'Of course,' replied Trescon grandly. 'Why else would we be here?'

'Don't be a damned liar,' said Erlyn, without even raising his voice. 'You won't be an artist if you live a thousand years. You're merely an expert, and you know it. Those who can – do, those who can't – criticise.'

'Where have you come from?' asked Brant, a little faintly. He had never met anyone quite like these extraordinary men. They were in late middle age, yet seemed to have an almost boyish gusto and enthusiasm. All their movements and gestures were just a little larger than life, and when they were talking to each other they spoke so quickly that Brant found it difficult to follow them.

Before anyone could reply, there was a further interruption. A dozen men appeared in the doorway – and were brought to a momentary halt by their first sight of the great painting. Then they hurried to join the little group around Brant, who now found himself the centre of a small crowd.

'Here you are, Kondar,' said Trescon, pointing to Brant. 'We've found someone who can answer your questions.'

The man who had been addressed looked at Brant closely for a moment, glanced at his unfinished painting, and smiled a little. Then he turned to Trescon and lifted his eyebrows in interrogation.

'No,' said Trescon succinctly.

Brant was getting annoyed. Something was going on that he didn't understand, and he resented it.

'Would you mind telling me what this is all about?' he said plaintively.

Kondar looked at him with an unfathomable expression. Then he said quietly: 'Perhaps I could explain things better if you came outside.'

He spoke as if he never had to ask twice for a thing to be done; and Brant followed him without a word, the others crowding close behind him. At the outer entrance Kondar stood aside and waved Brant to pass.

It was still unnaturally dark, as if a thundercloud had blotted out the sun; but the shadow that lay the full length of Shastar was not that of any cloud.

A dozen pairs of eyes were watching Brant as he stood staring at the sky, trying to gauge the true size of the ship floating above the city. It was so close that the sense of perspective was lost; one was conscious only of sweeping metal curves that dwindled away to the horizon. There should have been some sound, some indication of the energies holding that stupendous mass at rest above Shastar; but there was only a silence deeper than any that Brant had ever known. Even the crying of the sea gulls had ceased, as if they, too, were overawed by the intruder who had usurped their skies.

At last Brant turned toward the men gathered behind him. They were waiting, he knew, for his reactions; and the reason for their curiously aloof yet not unfriendly behaviour became suddenly clear. To these men, rejoicing in the powers of gods, he was little more than a savage who happened to speak the same language – a survival from their own half-forgotten past, reminding them of the days when their ancestors had shared the Earth with his.

'Do you understand, now, who we are?' asked Kondar.

Brant nodded. 'You have been gone a long time,' he said. 'We had almost forgotten you.'

He looked up again at the great metal arch spanning the sky, and thought how strange it was that the first contact after so many centuries should be here, in this lost city of mankind. But it seemed that Shastar was well remembered among the stars, for certainly Trescon and his friends had appeared perfectly familiar with it.

And then, far to the north, Brant's eye was caught by a sudden flash of reflected sunlight. Moving purposefully across the band of sky framed beneath the ship was another metal giant that might have been its twin, dwarfed though it was by distance. It passed swiftly across the horizon and within seconds was gone from sight.

So this was not the only ship; and how many more might there be? Somehow the thought reminded Brant of the great painting he had just left, and of the invading fleet moving with such deadly purpose toward the doomed city. And with that thought there came into his soul, creeping out from the hidden caves of racial memory, the fear of strangers that once had been the curse of all mankind. He turned to Kondar and cried accusingly:

'You're invading Earth!'

For a moment no one spoke. Then Trescon said, with a slight touch of malice in his voice:

'Go ahead, Commander – you've got to explain it sooner or later. Now's a good time to practise.'

Commander Kondar gave a worried little smile that first reassured Brant, then filled him with yet deeper forebodings.

'You do us an injustice, young man,' he said gravely. 'We're not invading Earth. We're evacuating it.'

'I hope,' said Trescon, who had taken a patronising interest in Brant, 'that *this* time the scientists have learned a lesson – though I doubt it. They just say, "Accidents will happen", and when they've cleaned up one mess, they go on to make another. The Sigma Field is certainly their most spectacular failure so far, but progress never ceases.'

'And if it does hit Earth – what will happen?'

'The same thing that happened to the control apparatus when the Field got loose – it will be scattered uniformly throughout the cosmos. And so will you be, unless we get you out in time.'

'Why?' asked Brant.

'You don't really expect a technical answer, do you? It's something to do with Uncertainty. The Ancient Greeks – or perhaps it was the Egyptians – discovered that you can't define the position of any atom with absolute accuracy; it has a small but finite probability of being anywhere in the universe. The people who set up the Field hoped to use it for propulsion. It would change the atomic odds, as it were, so that a spaceship orbiting Vega would suddenly decide that it really ought to be circling Betelgeuse.

'Well, it seems that the Sigma Field does only half the job. It merely *multiplies* probabilities – it doesn't organise them. And now it's wandering at random through the stars, feeding on interstellar dust and the occasional sun. No one's been able to devise a way of neutralising it – though there's a horrible suggestion that a twin should be created and a collision arranged. If they try that, I know just what will happen.'

'I don't see why we should worry,' said Brant. 'It's still ten light-years away.'

'Ten light-years is much too close for a thing like the Sigma Field. It's zigzagging at random, in what the mathematicians call the Drunkard's Walk. If we're unlucky, it'll be here tomorrow. But the chances are twenty to one that the Earth will be untouched; in a few years, you'll be able to go home again, just as if nothing had ever happened.'

'As if nothing had ever happened!' Whatever the future brought, the old way of life was gone forever. What was taking place in Shastar must now be occurring in one form or another, over all the world. Brant watched wide-eyed as strange machines rolled down the splendid streets, clearing away the rubble of ages and making the city fit for habitation again. As an almost extinct star may suddenly blaze up in one last hour of glory, so for a few months Shastar would be one of the capitals of the world, housing the army of scientists, technicians, and administrators that had descended upon it from space.

Brant was growing to know the invaders very well. Their vigour, the lavishness of everything they did, and the almost childlike delight they took in their superhuman powers never ceased to astonish him. These, his cousins, were the heirs to all the universe; and they had not yet begun to exhaust its wonders or to tire of its mystery. For all their knowledge, there was still a feeling of experimentation, even of cheerful irresponsibility, about many of the things they did. The Sigma Field itself was an example of this; they had made a mistake, they did not seem to mind in the least, and they were quite sure that sooner or later they would put things right.

Despite the tumult that had been loosed upon Shastar, as indeed upon the entire planet, Brant had remained stubbornly at his task. It gave him something fixed and stable in a world of shifting values, and as such he clung to it desperately. From time to time Trescon or his colleagues would visit him and proffer advice – usually excellent advice, though he did not always take it. And occasionally, when he was tired and wished to rest his eyes or brain, he would leave the great empty galleries and go out into the transformed streets of the city. It was typical of its new inhabitants that, though they would be here for no more than a few months, they had spared no efforts to make Shastar clean and efficient, and to impose upon it a certain stark beauty that would have surprised its first builders.

At the end of four days – the longest time he had ever devoted to a single work – Brant slowed to a halt. He could go on tinkering indefinitely, but if he did he would only make things worse. Not at all displeased with his efforts, he went in search of Trescon.

He found the critic, as usual, arguing with his colleagues over what should be saved from the accumulated art of mankind. Latvar and Erlyn had threatened violence if one more Picasso was taken aboard, or another Fra Angelico thrown out. Not having heard of either, Brant had no compunction in pressing his own claim.

Trescon stood in silence before the painting, glancing at the original from time to time. His first remark was quite unexpected.

'Who's the girl?' he said.

'You told me she was called Helen—' Brant started to answer.

'I mean the one you've *really* painted.'

Brant looked at his canvas, then back at the original. It was odd that he hadn't noticed those differences before, but there were undoubtedly traces of Yradne in the woman he had shown on the fortress walls. This was not the straightforward copy he had set out to make. His own mind and heart had spoken through his fingers.

'I see what you mean,' he said slowly. 'There's a girl back in my village; I really came here to find a present for her – something that would impress her.'

'Then you've been wasting your time,' Trescon answered bluntly. 'If she really loves you, she'll tell you soon enough. If she doesn't, you can't make her. It's as simple as that.'

Brant did not consider that at all simple, but decided not to argue the point.

'You haven't told me what you think about it,' he complained.

'It shows promise,' Trescon answered cautiously. 'In another thirty – well, twenty – years you may get somewhere, if you keep at it. Of course the brushwork is pretty crude, and that hand looks like a bunch of bananas. But you have a nice bold line, and I think more of you for not making a carbon copy. Any fool can do that – this shows you've some originality. What you need now is more practice – and above all, more experience. Well, I think we can provide you with that.'

'If you mean going away from Earth,' said Brant, 'that's not the sort of experience I want.'

'It will do you good. Doesn't the thought of travelling out to the stars arouse any feelings of excitement in your mind?'

'No; only dismay. But I can't take it seriously, because I don't believe you'll be able to make us go.'

Trescon smiled, a little grimly.

'You'll move quickly enough when the Sigma Field sucks the starlight from the sky. And it may be a good thing when it comes: I have a feeling we were just in time. Though I've often made fun of the scientists, they've freed us forever from the stagnation that was overtaking your race.

'You have to get away from Earth, Brant; no man who has lived all his life on the surface of a planet has ever seen the stars, only their feeble ghosts. Can you imagine what it means to hang in space amid one of the great multiple systems, with coloured suns blazing all around you? I've done that; and I've seen stars floating in rings of crimson fire, like your planet Saturn, but a thousand times greater. And can you imagine night on a world near the heart of the Galaxy, where the whole sky is luminous with star mist that has not yet given birth to suns? Your Milky Way is only a scattered handful of third-rate suns; wait until you see the Central Nebula!

'These are the great things, but the small ones are just as wonderful. Drink your fill of all that the universe can offer; and if you wish, return to Earth with your memories. Then you can begin to work; then, and no sooner, you'll know if you are an artist.'

Brant was impressed, but not convinced.

'According to *that* argument,' he said, 'real art couldn't have existed before space travel.'

'There's a whole school of criticism based on that thesis; certainly space travel was one of the best things that ever happened to art. Travel, exploration, contact with other cultures – that's the great stimulus for all intellectual activity.' Trescon waved at the mural blazing on the wall behind them. 'The people who created that legend were seafarers, and the traffic of half a world came through their ports. But after a few thousand years, the sea was too small for inspiration or adventure, and it was time to go into space. Well, the time's come for you, whether you like it or not.'

'I don't like it. I want to settle down with Yradne.'

'The things that people want and the things that are good for them are very different. I wish you luck with your painting; I don't know whether to wish you luck in your other endeavour. Great art and domestic bliss are mutually incompatible. Sooner or later, you'll have to make your choice.'

Sooner or later, you'll have to make your choice. Those words still echoed in Brant's mind as he trudged toward the brow of the hill, and the wind came down the great road to meet him. Sunbeam resented the termination of her holiday, so they moved even more slowly than the gradient demanded. But gradually the landscape widened around them, the horizon moved farther out to sea, and the city began to look more and more like a toy built from coloured bricks – a toy dominated by the ship that hung effortlessly, motionlessly above it.

For the first time Brant was able to see it as a whole, for it was now floating almost level with his eyes and he could encompass it at a glance. It was roughly cylindrical in shape, but ended in complex polyhedral structures whose functions were beyond conjecture. The great curving back bristled with equally mysterious bulges, flutings, and cupolas. There was power and purpose here, but nothing of beauty, and Brant looked upon it with distaste.

This brooding monster usurping the sky – if only it would vanish, like the clouds that drifted past its flanks! But it would not disappear because he willed it; against the forces that were gathering now, Brant knew that he and his problems were of no importance. This was the pause when history held its breath, the hushed moment between the lightning flash and the advent of the first concussion. Soon the thunder would be rolling round the world; and soon there might be no world at all, while he and his people would be homeless exiles among the stars. That was the future he did not care to face – the future he feared more deeply than Trescon and his fellows, to whom the universe had been a plaything for five thousand years, could ever understand.

It seemed unfair that this should have happened in his time, after all these centuries of rest. But men cannot bargain with Fate, and choose peace or adventure as they wish. Adventure and Change had come to the world again, and he must make the best of it – as his ancestors had done when the age of space had opened, and their first frail ships had stormed the stars.

For the last time he saluted Shastar, then turned his back upon the sea. The sun was shining in his eyes, and the road before him seemed veiled with a bright, shimmering mist, so that it quivered like a mirage, or the track of the Moon upon troubled waters. For a moment Brant wondered if his eyes had been deceiving him; then he saw that it was no illusion.

As far as the eye could see, the road and the land on either side of it were draped with countless strands of gossamer, so frail and fine that only the glancing sunlight revealed their presence. For the last quarter-mile he had been walking through them, and they had resisted his passage no more than coils of smoke.

Throughout the morning, the wind-borne spiders must have been falling in millions from the sky; and as he stared up into the blue, Brant could still catch momentary glimpses of sunlight upon drifting silk as belated voyagers went sailing by. Not knowing whither they would travel, these tiny creatures had ventured forth into an abyss more friendless and more fathomless than any he would face when the time came to say farewell to Earth. It was a lesson he would remember in the weeks and months ahead.

Slowly the Sphinx sank into the sky line as it joined Shastar beyond the eclipsing crescent of the hills. Only once did Brant look back at the crouching monster, whose agelong vigil was now drawing to its close. Then he walked slowly forward into the sun, while ever and again impalpable fingers brushed his face, as the strands of silk came drifting down the wind that blew from home.

The Sentinel

First published in *10 Story Fantasy*, Spring 1951, as 'Sentinel of Eternity'
Collected in *Expedition to Earth*

'The Sentinel' was written over Christmas 1948 for a BBC competition. (It wasn't even placed – I have often wondered what *did* win). I am amused to see that I put the exploration of the *Mare Crisium* in 'the late summer of 1996'. Well, we missed that date, but I hope we'll get there early in the next century. This is the starting point of *2001: A Space Odyssey.*

The next time you see the full Moon high in the south, look carefully at its right-hand edge and let your eye travel upwards along the curve of the disc. Round about two o'clock, you will notice a small, dark oval: anyone with normal eyesight can find it quite easily. It is the great walled plain, one of the finest on the Moon, known as the Mare Crisium – the Sea of Crises. Three hundred miles in diameter – and almost completely surrounded by a ring of magnificent mountains, it had never been explored until we entered it in the late summer of 1996.

Our expedition was a large one. We had two heavy freighters which had flown our supplies and equipment from the main lunar base in the Mare Serenitatis, five hundred miles away. There were also three small rockets which were intended for short-range transport over regions which our surface vehicles could not cross. Luckily, most of the Mare Crisium is very flat. There are none of the great crevasses so common and so dangerous elsewhere, and very few craters or mountains of any size. As far as we could tell, our powerful caterpillar tractors would have no difficulty in taking us wherever we wished.

I was geologist – or selenologist, if you want to be pedantic – in charge of the group exploring the southern region of the Mare. We had crossed a hundred miles of it in a week, skirting the foothills of the mountains along the shore of what was once the ancient sea, some thousand million years before. When life was beginning on Earth, it was already dying here. The waters were retreating down the flanks of those stupendous cliffs, retreating into the empty heart of the Moon. Over the land which we were crossing, the tideless ocean had once been half a mile deep and now the only trace of moisture was the hoar frost one could sometimes find in caves which the searing sunlight never penetrated.

We had begun our journey early in the slow lunar dawn, and still had almost a week of Earth-time before nightfall. Half a dozen times a day we would leave our vehicle and go outside in the spacesuits to hunt for interesting minerals, or to place markers for the guidance of future travellers. It was an uneventful routine. There is nothing hazardous or even particularly exciting about lunar exploration. We could live comfortably for a month in our pressurised tractors, and if we ran into trouble we could always radio for help and sit tight until one of the spaceships came to our rescue. When that happened there was always a frightful outcry about the waste of rocket fuel, so a tractor sent out an SOS only in a real emergency.

I said just now that there was nothing exciting about lunar exploration, but of course that is not true. One could never grow tired of those incredible mountains, so much more rugged than the gentle hills of Earth. We never knew, as we rounded the capes and promontories of that vanished sea, what new splendours would be revealed to us. The whole southern curve of the Mare Crisium is a vast delta where a score of rivers had once found their way into the ocean, fed perhaps by the torrential rains that must have lashed the mountains in the brief volcanic age when the moon was young. Each of these ancient valleys was an invitation, challenging us to climb into the unknown uplands beyond. But we had a hundred miles still to cover, and could only look longingly at the heights which others must scale.

We kept Earth-time aboard the tractor, and precisely at 22.00 hours the final radio message would be sent out to base and we could close down for the day. Outside, the rocks would still be burning beneath the almost vertical sun, but to us it was night until we awoke again eight hours later. Then one of us would prepare breakfast, there would be a great buzzing of electric shavers and someone would switch on the short-wave radio from Earth. Indeed, when the smell of frying bacon began to fill the cabin, it was sometimes hard to believe that we were not back on our own world – everything was so normal and homely, apart from the feeling of decreased weight and the unnatural slowness with which objects fell.

It was my turn to prepare breakfast in the corner of the main cabin that served as a galley. I can remember that moment quite vividly after all these years, for the radio had just played one of my favourite melodies, the old Welsh air, 'David of the White Rock'. Our driver was already outside in his spacesuit, inspecting our caterpillar treads. My assistant, Louis Garnett, was up forward in the control position, making some belated entries in yesterday's log.

As I stood by the frying-pan, waiting, like any terrestrial housewife, for the sausages to brown, I let my gaze wander idly over the mountain walls which covered the whole of the southern horizon, marching out of sight to the east and west below the curve of the Moon. They seemed only a mile or two from the tractor, but I knew that the nearest was twenty miles away. On the Moon, of course, there is no loss of detail with distance – none of that almost imperceptible haziness which softens and sometimes transfigures all far-off things on Earth.

Those mountains were ten thousand feet high, and they climbed steeply out of the plain as if ages ago some subterranean eruption had smashed them skywards through the molten crust. The base of even the nearest was hidden from sight by the steeply curving surface of the plain, for the Moon is a very little world, and from where I was standing the horizon was only two miles away.

I lifted my eyes towards the peaks which no man had ever climbed, the peaks which, before the coming of terrestrial life, had watched the retreating oceans sink sullenly into their graves, taking with them the hope and the morning promise of a world. The sunlight was beating against those ramparts with a glare that hurt the eyes, yet only a little way above them the stars were shining steadily in a sky blacker than a winter midnight on Earth.

I was turning away when my eye caught a metallic glitter high on the ridge of a great promontory thrusting out into the sea thirty miles to the west. It was a dimensionless point of light as if a star had been clawed from the sky by one of those cruel peaks, and I imagined that some smooth rock-surface was catching the sunlight and heliographing it straight into my eyes. Such things were not uncommon. When the Moon is in her second quarter, observers on Earth can sometimes see the great ranges in the Oceanus Procellarum burning with a blue-white iridescence as the sunlight flashes from their slopes and leaps again from world to world. But I was curious to know what kind of rock could be shining so brightly up there, and I climbed into the observation turret and swung our four-inch telescope round to the west.

I could see just enough to tantalise me. Clear and sharp in the field of vision, the mountain peaks seemed only half a mile away, but whatever was catching the sunlight was still too small to be resolved. Yet it seemed to have an elusive symmetry, and the summit upon which it rested was curiously flat. I stared for a long time at that glittering enigma, straining my eyes into space, until presently a smell of burning from the galley told me that our breakfast sausages had made their quarter-million-mile journey in vain.

All that morning we argued our way across the Mare Crisium while the western mountains reared higher in the sky. Even when we were out prospecting in the spacesuits, the discussion would continue over the radio. It was absolutely certain, my companions argued, that there had never been any form of intelligent life on the Moon. The only living things that had ever existed there were a few primitive plants and their slightly less degenerate ancestors. I knew that as well as anyone, but there are times when a scientist must not be afraid to make a fool of himself.

'Listen,' I said at last, 'I'm going up there, if only for my own peace of mind. That mountain's less than twelve thousand feet high – that's only two thousand under Earth gravity – and I can make the trip in twenty hours at the outside. I've always wanted to go up into those hills, anyway, and this gives me an excellent excuse.'

'If you don't break your neck,' said Garnett, 'you'll be the laughing-stock of the expedition when we get back to Base. That mountain will probably be called Wilson's Folly from now on.'

'I won't break my neck,' I said firmly. 'Who was the first man to climb Pico and Helicon?'

'But weren't you rather younger in those days?' asked Louis gently.

'That,' I said with great dignity, 'is as good a reason as any for going.'

We went to bed early that night, after driving the tractor to within half a mile of the promontory. Garnett was coming with me in the morning; he was a good climber, and had often been with me on such exploits before. Our driver was only too glad to be left in charge of the machine.

At first sight, those cliffs seemed completely unscalable, but to anyone with a good head for heights, climbing is easy on a world where all weights are only a sixth of their normal value. The real danger in lunar mountaineering lies in over-confidence; a six-hundred-foot drop on the Moon can kill you just as thoroughly as a hundred-foot fall on Earth.

We made our first halt on a wide ledge about four thousand feet above the plain. Climbing had not been very difficult but my limbs were stiff with the unaccustomed effort, and I was glad of the rest. We could still see the tractor as a tiny metal insect far down at the foot of the cliff, and we reported our progress to the driver before starting on the next ascent.

Hour by hour the horizon widened and more and more of the great plain came into sight. Now we could look for fifty miles out across the Mare, and could even see the peaks of the mountains on the opposite coast more than a hundred miles away. Few of the great lunar plains are as smooth as the Mare Crisium, and we could almost imagine that a sea of water and not of rock was lying there two miles below. Only a group of crater pits low down on the skyline spoiled the illusion.

Our goal was still invisible over the crest of the mountain and we were steering by maps, using the Earth as a guide. Almost due east of us, that great silver crescent hung low over the plain, already well into its first quarter. The Sun and the stars would make their slow march across the sky and would sink presently from sight, but Earth would always be there, never moving from her appointed place, waxing and waning as the years and seasons passed. In ten days' time she would be a blinding disc bathing these rocks with her midnight radiance, fifty-fold brighter than the full moon. But we must be out of the mountains long before night, or else we would remain among them for ever.

Inside our suits it was comfortably cool, for the refrigeration units were fighting the fierce Sun and carrying away the body-heat of our exertions. We seldom spoke to each other, except to pass climbing instructions and to discuss our best plan of ascent. I do not know what Garnett was thinking, probably that this was the craziest goose chase he had ever embarked upon.

I more than half agreed with him, but the joy of climbing, the knowledge that no man had ever gone this way before and the exhilaration of the steadily widening landscape gave me all the reward I needed.

I do not think I was particularly excited when I saw in front of us the wall of rock I had first inspected through the telescope from thirty miles away. It would level off about fifty feet above our heads, and there on the plateau would be the thing that had lured me over these barren wastes. It was, almost certainly, nothing more than a boulder splintered ages ago by a falling meteor, and with its cleavage planes still fresh and bright in this incorruptible, unchanging silence.

There were no hand-holds on the rock face and we had to use a grapnel. My tired arms seemed to gain new strength as I swung the three-pronged metal anchor round my head and sent it sailing up towards the stars. The first time it broke loose and came falling slowly back when we pulled the rope. On the third attempt, the prongs gripped firmly and our combined weights could not shift it.

Garnett looked at me anxiously. I could tell that he wanted to go first, but I smiled back at him through the glass of my helmet and shook my head. Slowly, taking my time, I began the final ascent.

Even with my spacesuit, I weighed only forty pounds here, so I pulled myself up hand over hand without bothering to use my feet. At the rim I paused and waved to my companion, then I scrambled over the edge and stood upright, staring ahead of me.

You must understand that until this very moment I had been almost completely convinced that there could be nothing strange or unusual for me to find here. Almost, but not quite; it was that haunting doubt that had driven me forwards. Well, it was a doubt no longer, but the haunting had scarcely begun.

I was standing on a plateau perhaps a hundred feet across. It had once been smooth – too smooth to be natural – but falling meteors had pitted and scored its surface through immeasurable aeons. It had been levelled to support a glittering roughly pyramidal structure, twice as high as a man, that was set in the rock like a gigantic many-faceted jewel.

Probably no emotion at all filled my mind in those first few seconds. Then I felt a great lifting of my heart, and a strange inexpressible joy. For I loved the Moon, and now I knew that the creeping moss of Aristarchus and Eratosthenes was not the only life she had brought forth in her youth. The old, discredited dream of the first explorers was true. There had, after all, been a lunar civilisation – and I was the first to find it. That I had come perhaps a hundred million years too late did not distress me; it was enough to have come at all.

My mind was beginning to function normally, to analyse and to ask questions. Was this a building, a shrine – or something for which my language had no name? If a building, then why was it erected in so uniquely inaccessible a spot? I wondered if it might be a temple, and I could picture the adepts of some strange priesthood calling on their gods to preserve them as the life of the Moon ebbed with the dying oceans, and calling on their gods in vain.

I took a dozen steps forward to examine the thing more closely, but some sense of caution kept me from going too near. I knew a little of archaeology, and tried to guess the cultural level of the civilisation that must have smoothed this mountain and raised the glittering mirror surfaces that still dazzled my eyes.

The Egyptians could have done it, I thought, if their workmen had possessed whatever strange materials these far more ancient architects had used. Because of the thing's smallness, it did not occur to me that I might be looking at the handiwork of a race more advanced than my own. The idea that the Moon had possessed intelligence at all was still almost too tremendous to grasp and my pride would not let me take the final, humiliating plunge.

And then I noticed something that set the scalp crawling at the back of my neck – something so trivial and so innocent that many would never have noticed it at all. I have said that the plateau was scarred by meteors; it was also coated inches deep with the cosmic dust that is always filtering down upon the surface of any world where there are no winds to disturb it. Yet the dust and the meteor scratches ended quite abruptly in a wide circle enclosing the little pyramid, as though an invisible wall was protecting it from the ravages of time and the slow but ceaseless bombardment from space.

There was someone shouting in my earphones, and I realised that Garnett had been calling me for some time. I walked unsteadily to the edge of the cliff and signalled him to join me, not trusting myself to speak. Then I went back towards that circle in the dust. I picked up a fragment of splintered rock and tossed it gently toward the shining enigma. If the pebble had vanished at that invisible barrier I should not have been surprised, but it seemed to hit a smooth, hemispherical surface and slide gently to the ground.

I knew then that I was looking at nothing that could be matched in the antiquity of my own race. This was not a building, but a machine, protecting itself with forces that had challenged Eternity. Those forces, whatever they might be, were still operating, and perhaps I had already come too close. I thought of all the radiations man had trapped and tamed in the past century. For all I knew, I might be as irrevocably doomed as if I had stepped into the deadly, silent aura of an unshielded atomic pile.

I remember turning then towards Garnett, who had joined me and was now standing motionless at my side. He seemed quite oblivious of me, so I did not disturb him but walked to the edge of the cliff in an effort to marshal my thoughts. There below me lay the Mare Crisium – Sea of Crises, indeed – strange and weird to most men, but reassuringly familiar to me. I lifted my eyes towards the crescent Earth, lying in her cradle of stars, and I wondered what her clouds had covered when these unknown builders had finished their work. Was it the steaming jungle of the Carboniferous, the bleak shoreline over which the first amphibians must crawl to conquer the land – or, earlier still, the long loneliness before the coming of life?

Do not ask me why I did not guess the truth sooner – the truth that seems so obvious now. In the first excitement of my discovery, I had assumed without question that this crystalline apparition had been built by some race belonging to the Moon's remote past, but suddenly, and with overwhelming force, the belief came to me that it was as alien to the Moon as I myself.

In twenty years we had found no trace of life but a few degenerate plants. No lunar civilisation, whatever its doom, could have left but a single token of its existence.

I looked at the shining pyramid again, and the more remote it seemed from anything that had to do with the Moon. And suddenly I felt myself shaking with a foolish, hysterical laughter, brought on by excitement and over-exertion: for I had imagined that the little pyramid was speaking to me and was saying: 'Sorry, I'm a stranger here myself.'

It has taken us twenty years to crack that invisible shield and to reach the machine inside those crystal walls. What we could not understand, we broke at last with the savage might of atomic power and now I have seen the fragments of the lovely, glittering thing I found up there on the mountain.

They are meaningless. The mechanisms – if indeed they are mechanisms – of the pyramid belong to a technology that lies far beyond our horizon, perhaps to the technology of paraphysical forces.

The mystery haunts us all the more now that the other planets have been reached and we know that only Earth has ever been the home of intelligent life. Nor could any lost civilisation of our own world have built that machine, for the thickness of the meteoric dust on the plateau has enabled us to measure its age. It was set there upon its mountain before life had emerged from the seas of Earth.

When our world was half its present age, *something* from the stars swept through the Solar System, left this token of its passage, and went again upon its way. Until we destroyed it, that machine was still fulfilling the purpose of its builders; and as to that purpose, here is my guess.

Nearly a hundred thousand million stars are turning in the circle of the Milky Way, and long ago other races on the worlds of other suns must have scaled and passed the heights that we have reached. Think of such civilisations, far back in time against the fading afterglow of Creation, masters of a universe so young that life as yet had come only to a handful of worlds. Theirs would have been a loneliness we cannot imagine, the loneliness of gods looking out across infinity and finding none to share their thoughts.

They must have searched the star-clusters as we have searched the planets. Everywhere there would be worlds, but they would be empty or peopled with crawling, mindless things. Such was our own Earth, the smoke of the great volcanoes still staining the skies, when that first ship of

307

the peoples of the dawn came sliding in from the abyss beyond Pluto. It passed the frozen outer worlds, knowing that life could play no part in their destinies. It came to rest among the inner planets, warming themselves around the fire of the Sun and waiting for their stories to begin.

Those wanderers must have looked on Earth, circling safely in the narrow zone between fire and ice, and must have guessed that it was the favourite of the Sun's children. Here, in the distant future, would be intelligence; but there were countless stars before them still, and they might never come this way again.

So they left a sentinel, one of millions they have scattered throughout the universe, watching over all worlds with the promise of life. It was a beacon that down the ages has been patiently signalling the fact that no one had discovered it.

Perhaps you understand now why that crystal pyramid was set upon the Moon instead of on the Earth. Its builders were not concerned with races still struggling up from savagery. They would be interested in our civilisation only if we proved our fitness to survive – by crossing space and so escaping from the Earth, our cradle. That is the challenge that all intelligent races must meet, sooner or later. It is a double challenge, for it depends in turn upon the conquest of atomic energy and the last choice between life and death.

Once we had passed that crisis, it was only a matter of time before we found the pyramid and forced it open. Now its signals have ceased, and those whose duty it is will be turning their minds upon Earth. Perhaps they wish to help our infant civilisation. But they must be very, very old, and the old are often insanely jealous of the young.

I can never look now at the Milky Way without wondering from which of those banked clouds of stars the emissaries are coming. If you will pardon so commonplace a simile, we have broken the glass of the fire-alarm and have nothing to do but to wait.

I do not think we will have to wait for long.

Holiday on the Moon

First appeared in *Heiress* magazine January–April 1951

This story was the result of arm-twisting by a charming lady editor for a magazine for young ladies, *Heiress*. It was published as a four-part serial (January to April 1951) as by Charles Willis. After half a century, I can't remember why I used a pseudonym – perhaps I was afraid of losing my macho image.

It was a large, brightly lit room with a magnificent view, of which no one was taking the slightest notice. Beyond the wide window, which ran the whole length of one wall, a snow-flecked mountain-side sloped down to a tiny Alpine village more than a mile below. Despite the distance, every detail was crystal clear. Beyond the village, the ground rose again, more and more steeply, to the great mountain that dominated the sky-line and trailed from its summit a perpetual plume of snow, a white streamer, drifting for ever with the wind.

It was a wonderful panorama – and it was all an illusion. The Martins' flat was in the middle of London, and outside the walls a November fog was curling sluggishly through the damp streets. But Mrs Martin had only to turn a switch and the concealed projectors would give her any view she wished, together with the sounds that went with it. Television, which had brought so many pictures into every home, had made this inevitable, and in these opening years of the twenty-first century most houses could have any scenery they pleased.

Of course, it *was* rather expensive, but it was such a good way of letting the family get to know the world. Mrs Martin looked round anxiously. At the moment everything seemed a little too quiet for comfort. What she saw was reassuring. Eighteen-year-old Daphne was tuned in to Paris on the TV set, watching a fashion display.

'Mother!' she called out. 'You *must* see this gorgeous scarlet cloak! I'd love one just like it.'

Michael, who was fifteen, was doing his home-work – or pretending to – and the twelve-year-old twins were in the next room, being audibly thrilled by Grandma's stories of the London Blitz.

There was a gentle 'burr' from the telephone in the next room.

'Let me answer it!' shouted Claude.

'No, me!' yelled Claudia.

There was a slight scuffle. Then Grandma's voice could be heard speaking to the operator. 'Yes, this is Mrs Martin's flat. I'll call her. Hilda! It's a super-long-distance call for you!'

Super-long-distance! It had never happened before, but everyone knew what it meant. Michael looked up from his work. Even Daphne turned her back on the parade of winter fashion.

'My goodness,' said Claude, 'it's Daddy!'

'Someone told me,' said Claudia in a hushed voice, 'that it costs £10 a minute to put through a call from the Moon.'

'I hope Daddy isn't paying for it!' gulped Claude.

'Hush, children!' said Mrs Martin, taking the receiver from Grandma. 'Yes, Mrs Martin here.' There was a pause. Then, so clear and close that it gave her almost a shock, her husband's voice sounded in her ear. It was coming to her across a quarter of a million miles of space, yet it seemed as if he were standing beside her.

'Hallo, Hilda, this is John! Listen carefully, dear – I've only got two minutes! I've some bad news for you. I can't come back to Earth next week as we'd hoped. Yes, I know it's very disappointing after all our plans, but we've had some trouble here at the observatory and I simply can't get away now. But don't be too upset – I've got another plan that's almost as good. *How would you like to come up to the Moon?*'

'What?' gasped his wife.

It took nearly three seconds for her husband's laugh to reach her – three seconds for the radio waves, even travelling at their fabulous speed, to make the journey from Earth to Moon.

'Yes, I thought it would surprise you! But why not? Space-travel is as safe now as flying was in Grandma's day. Anyway, there's a freighter leaving the Arizona port in three days and returning to Earth a fortnight later. That will give you time to get ready, and we'll have almost ten days here together at the observatory. I'll make all the arrangements, so be a dear and don't argue. And I want you to bring along Daphne and Mike. There's room for them as well. I'm afraid you'll have to make peace with the twins, somehow – tell them they'll have their chance when they're older!'

'But, John – I *can't* . . .'

'Of course you can – and think how Daphne and Mike will love it! I can't explain now, but we may never have an opportunity like this again. I'm sending a telegram with all the details. You should get it in an hour or so. Oh, bother – there's the signal – I must hang up now. Give my love to them all. I do look forward to seeing you. Goodbye, darling.'

Mrs Martin put down the receiver with a dazed expression. It was just like John. He hadn't even allowed her time to raise a single objection. But, now she came to think of it, what real objections were there? He was right, of course. Space-travel – at least to the Moon – was safe enough, even though it was still too expensive for a regular passenger service. Presumably John had been able to use his official position to get their reservations.

Yes, John was quite right. It was too good a chance to miss, and if she didn't go now, it might be ages before she would see him again. She turned to the anxiously waiting family and said with a smile, 'I've got some news for you.'

In the ordinary way, a Transatlantic crossing would have been quite an excitement for Daphne and Michael, since it was something they had done only two or three times before in their lives. Now, however, they regarded the two hours' flight from London Airport to New York as merely an unimportant episode, and occupied most of the time talking about the Moon clearly enough to impress the other passengers.

They spent only an hour in New York before flying on across the Continent, steadily gaining on the sun, until when they finally swept down over the great Arizona desert it was, by the clock, a couple of hours *before* the time they had left the flat that same morning.

From the air, the space-port was an impressive sight. Looking through the observation windows, Daphne could see, spread out below, the great steel frameworks supporting the slim, torpedo-shaped monsters that would soon go roaring up to the stars. Everywhere were huge, gasometer-like fuel-tanks, radio aerials pointing at the sky, and mysterious buildings and structures whose purpose she couldn't even guess.

Through all this maze tiny figures scurried to and fro, and vehicles looking like metallic beetles rolled swiftly along the roads.

Daphne belonged to the first generation that had taken space-travel for granted. The Moon had been reached almost thirty years ago – twelve years before she was born – and she could just remember the excitement when the first expeditions had landed on Mars and Venus.

In her short life she had seen Man set out to conquer space, just as, hundreds of years before, Columbus and the great explorers of the Middle Ages had discovered the world. The first stages of the conquest were now over. Small colonies of scientists had been established on Mars and Venus, and on the Moon the great Lunar Observatory, of which Professor Martin was director, had now become the centre of all astronomical research.

On the Moon's silent, lonely plains, beneath velvet skies, in which the stars shone brilliantly night and day, with never the least trace of cloud to dim them, the astronomers could work at last under perfect conditions, unhindered by the obscuring atmosphere against which they had always had to fight on Earth.

The next two hours they spent in the space-port's headquarters building, being weighed, medically examined and filling up forms. When this was all over, and they were beginning to wonder if the whole thing was really worth while, they found themselves in a small, comfortable office, looking across a desk at a rather jolly, plump man, who seemed to be someone very important.

'Well, Mrs Martin,' he said cheerfully, 'I'm glad to say you're all in excellent health and there's no reason why you shouldn't leave in the *Centaurus* when she takes off. I hope all these examinations haven't scared you. There is really nothing dangerous about space-flight, but we mustn't take any chances.

'As you know, a space-ship takes off rather quickly and for a few minutes you feel as if you weigh a ton – but if you're lying down comfortably that won't do you any harm, as long as you don't suffer from certain kinds of heart trouble. Then, when you're out in space, you won't have any weight at all, which will feel very odd at first. That used to cause space-sickness in the early days, but we can prevent it now. You'll be given a couple of tablets to swallow just before take-off. So there's nothing to worry about, and I'm sure you'll have a pleasant voyage.'

He looked at his littered desk and sighed deeply. 'I wish *I* had time to go up myself. I've only been off Earth once in the last two years!'

'Who was that?' asked Daphne, as the waiting bus whisked them away across the desert.

'That was the Controller of the Space Fleet,' said her mother.

'What!' exclaimed Michael. 'He runs all these space-ships and never gets a chance to fly in them?'

Mrs Martin smiled. 'I'm afraid it's often that way. Daddy says he's too busy to look through a telescope nowadays!'

They had now left the built-up area and were racing along a wide road with nothing but desert on either side. About a mile ahead they could see the great streamlined shape of the *Centaurus*, the space-ship that was to take them to the Moon. The giant rocket was standing vertically on a concrete platform, with cranes and scaffolding grouped around it, and its needle-shaped prow pointing to the sky. Even from this distance it looked enormous – Daphne thought it must be almost as tall as Nelson's column – and with the sunlight glinting on its metal sides it was a beautiful as well as an impressive sight.

The closer they came, the larger it seemed to grow, until when they had reached its base they appeared to be standing at the foot of a great curving metal cliff. A tall gantry had been moved up to the side of the rocket, and they were directed into the maze of girders until they came to a tiny lift just big enough to hold the three of them. There was the whirring of motors, the ground began to drop away, and the gleaming walls of the space-ship slid swiftly past.

It seemed a long way up to the cabin at the nose of the rocket. Daphne paused once on the little gangway leading into the space-ship, and looked down at the ground below and the people standing around, their upturned faces white blobs far beneath. She felt rather giddy, then pulled herself together as she realised she had travelled only the first hundred feet or so of her 240,000–mile journey.

The pilot and navigator were already waiting for them in the little cabin with its mass of complicated machinery and its thickly padded couches. These were wonderfully comfortable and Michael began to bounce up and down on his until reprimanded.

'Just lie down flat,' said the pilot. 'Swallow this pill – you won't taste it – and take things easy. You'll feel very heavy when we start, but it won't hurt and doesn't last long. One other thing – don't try to get up until I tell you. Now, we've got just ten minutes before we start, so relax.'

It wasn't as easy as all that, Daphne found. That ten minutes seemed to last for ever. She explored the little cabin with her eyes, wondering how anyone could *ever* learn what all those gadgets and controls were for. Just suppose the pilot made a mistake and pressed the wrong button . . .

Mother smiled at her reassuringly from the next couch, while Michael was obviously so intrigued by all the machinery that he hated having to lie down at all.

Daphne gave a jump when suddenly an electric motor started to whirr very close at hand. Then things began to happen all over the place. Switches clicked, powerful pumps began to whine, and valves snapped open down in the heart of the great rocket.

Each time she thought, 'This is it!', but still they didn't move. When the voyage finally began, she wasn't prepared for it.

A long way off, it seemed, there was a noise like a thousand waterfalls, or a thunderstorm in which the crashes followed each other so quickly that there was no moment of silence between them. The rockets had started, but were not yet delivering enough power to lift the ship.

Quickly the roar mounted, the cabin began to vibrate, and the *Centaurus* began to ascend from the desert, spraying the sands with flame for a hundred yards around. To Daphne, it seemed that something was pushing her down, quite gently, into the thick padding of the couch. It wasn't at all uncomfortable, but the pressure mounted until her limbs seemed to be made of lead and it needed a deliberate effort to keep breathing.

She tried to lift her hand, and the effort to move it even a few inches was so tiring that she let it drop back on the couch. After that, she just lay limp and relaxed, waiting to see what would happen next. She wasn't really frightened – it was too exciting for that, this feeling of infinite power sweeping her up into the sky.

There was a sudden fall in the thunder of the rockets, the feeling of immense weight ebbed away, and she could breathe more easily. Power was being reduced: they had almost escaped the Earth's grip. A moment later silence came flooding back as the last of the motors was cut out, and all feeling of weight vanished completely.

*

For several minutes the pilot conferred with his navigator, checking instruments and figures. Then he swung round in his seat, smiled at the passengers and said, 'That wasn't so bad, was it? We've reached escape velocity now – 25,000 miles an hour – and you won't feel any weight again until we're nearly at the Moon and we start the rockets to slow down.'

He rose from his seat, still holding on to it with one hand, and Daphne saw that both his feet were clear of the floor. Releasing his grip, he floated towards them like something in a slow-motion film. Daphne knew that this sort of thing happened in space, but it was weird to see it before her own eyes. And it was weirder still when it began to happen to *her*.

It was a long time before she got used to the idea that 'up' and 'down' simply didn't have any meaning, and got the knack of gliding across the cabin without hitting the other side too hard, or colliding head-first with the walls. But it was such great fun that several minutes had passed before Daphne suddenly remembered what she must be missing, and dived towards the nearest of the little circular windows set in the wall of the ship.

She had expected to see Earth as a great globe hanging in space, with the seas and continents clearly visible – just like those globes you see in mapsellers' windows.

What she saw, however, was totally unexpected and so wonderful that it took away her breath. Almost filling the sky was a tremendous, blinding crescent, the shape of a new moon, but hundreds of times bigger. The rocket must have passed over the night side of Earth, and the greater part of the planet was in darkness.

But presently, as she stared at that great shadowy circle eclipsing the stars, she could see here and there upon its face tiny patches of light, and knew that she was looking down upon the cities of mankind, shining like fireflies in the night.

It was several minutes before she could tear her eyes away from that huge crescent and the disc of darkness it embraced. As she watched, the crescent slowly narrowed, for the space-ship was still speeding into the shadow of the Earth. For a few minutes the sun would be totally eclipsed before the *Centaurus* came racing out into the light again, and only the Moon and the stars would be visible.

The Moon! Where was it? She moved to another window, and there it was, still looking just the same as she had always seen it from Earth. Of course, it wouldn't be any bigger yet: the journey had scarcely begun. But in the next two days it would slowly grow until it filled the sky and they were dropping down towards its shining mountains and great, dusty plains – towards that strange and silent world that had now become Man's first stepping-stone on the road to the stars. What would it be like? Who would she meet? Daphne's excitement was so great that she felt certain this was one night when sleep would be impossible.

It was a lovely dream. Daphne was flying – gliding effortlessly over the ground, able to move as freely as a bird in whatever direction she pleased.

She had experienced such dreams before, of course, but they had never been as vivid as this, and even the fact that, somehow, she *knew* she was dreaming, did not destroy the beautiful illusion.

A sudden jolt broke the spell of sleep and dragged her back to reality. She opened her eyes, stretched herself – and gave a shriek of pure terror. There was darkness all around, and wherever she reached she could feel nothing at all, only the empty air. The dream had turned suddenly to a nightmare: she was in truth floating in space, but helpless, without any power of movement . . .

The cabin light came on with a 'click' and the rocket pilot pushed his head through the curtains round the door.

'What's the fuss?' he said. Then he shook his head reprimandingly. 'There! And after all my warnings!'

Daphne felt very sheepish. It was her own fault, of course. She had loosened the broad elastic bands that held her in the bunk, and while she had been sleeping she must have gently drifted out into the room. Now she was floating in mid-air, slowly revolving, but unable to move in any direction.

'I've got a good mind to leave you there as an object lesson,' said the pilot. But his eyes were twinkling as he grabbed a pillow from the empty bunk. 'Catch!' he said.

The gentle impact set Daphne moving again, and a moment later she had reached the wall and was no longer helpless. Mrs Martin and Michael had now awakened and were rubbing their eyes sleepily.

'We're landing in an hour,' the pilot explained. 'We'll have breakfast in a few minutes, and then I suggest you go to the observation windows and make yourselves comfortable.'

Breakfast was soon finished. In space, because the absence of gravity reduced physical effort to a minimum, one never had much appetite. Even Michael was satisfied with two pieces of toast and a quarter pint of milk, stored in a flexible container so that it could be squirted straight into the mouth simply by squeezing.

Pouring liquids was, of course, impossible where there was neither 'up' nor 'down'. Any attempt to do so would simply have resulted in a very large drop drifting through the air until it reached the wall and spattered over everything.

The Moon was now only a few hundred miles away, and so enormous that it seemed to fill the sky. It was, indeed, no longer a globe hanging in space but a jagged landscape spread out far below. Michael had got hold of a map from somewhere and was trying to identify the chief features in the tremendous panorama towards which they were falling.

'That's the Sea of Rains – I think,' he said doubtfully, pointing to a great plain flanked on two sides by mountains. 'Yes, you can see those three big craters there in the middle. I wish they didn't use such funny names – I can't pronounce them. That biggest one's Archie – Archimedes.'

Daphne looked critically at the map, then at the landscape below.

315

'*That* isn't the sea!' she protested. 'It's just a big dry desert. You can see hills and ridges in it – and look at those canyons. Gosh! I hope we don't fall into one of those!'

'Well, the map *calls* it a sea,' said Michael stubbornly. He turned to the pilot for an explanation.

'The Moon's dark areas were all christened "Seas", hundreds of years ago – before the telescope was invented and we found what they really were,' came the reply. 'The names have just stuck and no one has bothered to change them. Besides, some of them are rather pretty. If you look at the map you'll find a Sea of Serenity, a Bay of Rainbows, a Marsh of Sleep, and many others. But no more questions for a while – I'm busy! Check your safety straps – we're going to use the rockets in a minute.'

They were now falling directly towards the Moon at several thousand miles an hour and, Daphne knew, the only way they could check their descent was to fire the rockets ahead of them to slow the space-ship down.

The Moon seemed terribly close when, with a roar that was doubly impressive after the long hours of silence, the great motors thundered into life. There was a sudden feeling of returning weight, and Daphne felt herself being pushed down into the padded seat. But the strain was nothing like as great as it had been at the take-off, and she soon grew used to it.

Through the observation window she could glimpse the white-hot pillar of flame which was checking their headlong fall against the Moon, still many miles below. The space-ship was dropping towards the heart of a great ring of mountains: when, presently, the roar of the rockets ceased, some of the taller peaks seemed already to be towering above the ship.

Below was a flat, barren plain, and suddenly Daphne caught sight of a group of tiny, circular buildings. Then the rockets flared out once more, and the scene below vanished in fire and clouds of dust blasted up by the jets. A moment later there was the gentlest of impacts, then silence.

They were on the Moon.

Daphne peered down at the rocky surface beneath. There seemed no one about, but that was understandable, for it would be dangerous to remain above ground while the rockets were in action, and the ground-crew would only now be emerging from shelter. And where were the great mountains she had seen during the descent? Apart from some low hills, the plain on which the rocket was standing was flat right out to the horizon.

Then Daphne realised how close that horizon was; the Moon was a little world (only a quarter the size of Earth, wasn't it?) and so its surface curved very steeply. The mountain walls of the crater were out of sight below the edge of the plain.

Some strange-looking vehicles were approaching from behind a low range of hills about a mile away. They drew up to the base of the rocket and presently Daphne heard loud clankings and bangings. Then there was a slight hiss of air, and the cabin door opened slowly.

'Just step through,' said the pilot. 'It's exactly like going down in an Underground lift.'

He was quite right. The Martins found themselves in a small, circular box, a mechanical voice advised them to stand clear of the doors, and they felt themselves dropping down to the ground. When the doors opened again they stepped out – much to their surprise – into the interior of a large motor bus, entirely roofed with thick sheets of transparent plastic.

It was such a remarkable transformation that Daphne wondered how it was done. Then she saw the little lift chamber rising through space again, climbing up the side of the great rocket on an extending arm rather like a fire escape ladder. A moment later it brought down the pilot and navigator, and the bus then set off briskly across the crater floor. It was all very businesslike and methodical, and not in the least romantic.

'I wonder where Daddy is?' queried Michael.

'We'll be meeting him in the Observatory,' said his mother, hoping that the luggage was going to catch up with them safely. 'Look – there it is!'

They had rounded the hills and were driving over an almost level plain, from which great spidery metal frameworks reared into the sky. Daphne would never have guessed that they were telescopes, for there was no sign of the silver domes which were the trademark of observatories on Earth. Of course, it had been silly to expect them; here on the Moon there were no winds or rains, and the most delicate scientific equipment could be left out in the open for ever without the slightest danger of it coming to harm.

The astronomers themselves, however, lived in a brightly lit, underground world fifty feet below the surface of the Moon. To reach it, the bus drove down into a deep cutting, which ended in wide metal doors that opened slowly as they approached.

They found themselves in a chamber just large enough to hold their vehicle, the doors closed behind them, and there was a hiss of air. Then the doors ahead opened, and the bus slid forward into a large underground garage. There was air around them again; Daphne could tell that by the sudden return of sound from the outside world.

'There's Daddy!' shouted Michael excitedly, pointing through the window of the bus.

Professor Martin was waving back at them from the middle of a small reception committee waiting in the corner of the garage. A moment later he had come aboard and there was much kissing and hugging as he greeted his family.

'Well,' he said, 'did you have a nice trip? Nobody space-sick?'

There was a chorus of indignant denials from the seasoned travellers.

'I'm glad to hear it. Now, come along to my rooms. I expect you can do with a rest and something to eat.'

For the next five minutes Daphne was learning to walk again. The Moon's low gravity gave her only a sixth of her normal weight, and every step took her a yard into the air. But there was a cure for this – the visitors were all given wide belts to which were attached heavy lead weights. Even with these, they were still abnormally light, but walking was

317

a good deal easier. Daphne no longer felt that the first draught would blow her away.

'When you get used to it here,' said Professor Martin, 'you can leave off the weights; you'll notice that none of us wears them. It's simply a matter of practice, just learning not to move too quickly. But when we want to, we can jump all right!'

Without any apparent effort, he shot up to the ceiling, a good twenty feet above, and came falling gently back a few seconds later.

'But don't try this sort of thing yourselves,' he warned, 'until you're quite used to it here – or you may land on your head! Now come along and meet my staff.'

Daphne had always assumed – although she couldn't have said why – that astronomers were usually old men with beards and far-away expressions, caused through too many hours of looking through telescopes. (Daddy, of course, was an exception – he always was.)

She soon found, however, that none of the Observatory staff fitted this description at all. Most of them were in the twenties or thirties, and almost half of them were women. And the expressions of some of the younger men were not at all far-away; quite the reverse, in fact.

After these introductions they followed Professor Martin through a series of wide passages that branched into numerous intersections, bearing such signs as *Central Air, Administration III, Medical, Dormitory Block,* or intriguingly, *Danger! Keep Out!* They might, Daphne thought, have been inside some large building on Earth. Only that curious feeling of lightness, which in a few days she would no longer notice, told her that she was now on another world.

Professor Martin's private suite consisted of four large rooms in the residential section of the colony. They were light and airy, despite the fact that they were so far underground. Mrs Martin took one look at the decorations and decided that something would have to be done about them.

As soon as they had settled down in the flimsy but very comfortable chairs, Professor Martin lit his pipe again and began to blow clouds of smoke at the ceiling, where the pumps of the air-conditioning plant quickly sucked it away.

'Well,' he began, 'it's nice to see you all here. I'm sorry about the twins, but I couldn't possibly wangle shipping space for them – and anyway they're much too young.'

'You haven't told us, darling,' said his wife (and there was an ominous look in her eye), 'just why you couldn't come down to Earth.'

Professor Martin coughed nervously. 'It's really a most extraordinary coincidence. Two days before I was coming home something I've been waiting for all my life happened. We caught a supernova on the rise.'

'That sounds awfully impressive. Exactly *what* does it mean?'

'A supernova is a star that blows up in such a colossal explosion that it suddenly becomes hundreds of millions of times brighter. In fact, for a few days it shines with as much light as a whole universe. We don't know what causes it – it's one of the great unsolved problems of astronomy.

'Anyway, this has just happened to a fairly near star, and by a terrific stroke of luck we spotted it in the early stages, before the explosion reached its peak. So we've got a wonderful series of observations, but we've all been working flat out for the last few days.

'I've got things organised now, although it will be some weeks before we've finished. The nova is slowly dying down and we want to watch what happens as it returns to normal. At its brightest, by the way, it was so brilliant that even down on Earth you could see it in the middle of the day. I expect you heard about that on the radio.'

'I do remember something,' said Mrs Martin vaguely, 'but I didn't take much notice.'

Profession Martin threw up his hands in mock despair. 'Something that hasn't happened for five hundred years – and you don't notice! A whole sun, perhaps with all its planets, blows up in the most gigantic explosion ever recorded – and it hasn't had the slightest effect on you!'

'It certainly has,' his wife retorted. 'It's upset all my holiday arrangements and made me go to the Moon instead of Majorca. But I don't *really* mind, dear,' she continued with a smile. 'This certainly is a change.'

Daphne had been listening to this conversation with a kind of fascinated horror. The picture of the exploding star – a whole sun, perhaps with inhabited worlds circling round it – was one she could not get out of her mind.

'Daddy,' she said, 'could this happen here?'

'What do you mean?'

'Well, could *our* sun become – what did you call it? – a supernova? And if it did, what would happen to us? I suppose the Earth would melt.'

'Melt! My goodness, it wouldn't have time! There'd just be a puff of gas, and it would be gone! But don't worry – the chances against it happening are millions and millions to one. Let's talk about something more cheerful. We've got a dance on here tonight and I'd like you all to come to it.'

'A dance? Here on the Moon?'

'Why ever not? We try to live normal lives, with all the recreation we can get. We've a cinema, our own little orchestra, a very good drama group, sports clubs, and many other things to keep us happy when we're off-duty. And we have a dance twice a day – at noon and midnight.'

'*Twice* a day?' gasped Daphne. 'How do you ever manage to do any work?'

Professor Martin's eyes twinkled. 'I mean twice every *lunar* day,' he replied. 'Don't forget that's nearly a month of Earth time. It's just before noon now, and the Sun won't set for another seven days. But our clocks and calendars keep Earth-time, because human beings can't sleep for two weeks and then work for another two without a break! It's a bit confusing at first, but you soon get used to it.'

319

He glanced at the clock set high in the opposite wall – a very complicated clock with several dials and three pairs of hands.

'That reminds me,' he said. 'Time we went to the "Ritz" – that's what we call our canteen. Lunch is served.'

Very late that evening a tired but contented Daphne crept wearily to bed. The dance had been quite a success – once she had learned how to co-ordinate her movements and avoid soaring, dragging her partner with her.

She had been reminded very vividly of an old film she had once seen in which there had been some ball-room sequences in slow-motion. It had been exactly like that – the same graceful, easy movements. After this, she felt it would never be much fun dancing on Earth again. There was the additional advantage, too, that her feet weren't aching in the slightest. After all, she weighed about twenty pounds here!

She tried to relax and sink into sleep, but although her body was tired her brain was still active; she had crowded too many experiences into a single short day. And she had met such interesting people, too. Some of the young astronomers – many of them straight from college – had been really very charming and they had *all* offered to show her round the Observatory tomorrow. It was going to be difficult to make a choice . . .

Yet Daphne's last thoughts, when sleep finally came, were not concerned with this underground colony or the people who lived, worked and played here. She saw instead the silent, empty plain that lay burning above her head, blasted by the noon-day sun, although down here the clocks told her it was 12.30 p.m., Greenwich time.

Close to the sun would be the great thin crescent of the New Earth, which would slowly wax until a fortnight later it would be a blinding white disc, flooding all this strange land with its midnight radiance. And scattered all across the black velvet of the sky, shining steadfastly by day and night, would be the countless legions of the stars.

Among them now was a new-comer, slowly fading yet still one of the brightest stars in the sky. Nova Taurus, Daddy had called it – and he had called it a near star, too. Yet that gigantic explosion had occurred when Elizabeth the First was on the throne, and the light had only just reached Earth, travelling at almost a million miles every five seconds.

Daphne shivered a little at the thought of this unimaginable abyss, besides which the distance between Earth and Moon was scarcely a hair's breadth.

'Here are your dark glasses,' said Norman. 'Put them on as soon as the rockets start firing.'

Daphne accepted them absentmindedly, never taking her eyes from the shining monster that stood out there on the plain two miles away. From the summit of the low ridge on which the observation post was built, she could see almost the whole of the great launching site from which the rockets left the Moon on their outward journey. It was strange to think that although she had travelled in a space-ship herself, she had never before seen one taking off.

The ship standing poised on the sun-baked lava was much bigger than the rocket that had brought her from Earth, and it had very much further to travel. In a few seconds it would be climbing away from the Moon – away even from the Earth and Sun – on its long journey to Mars, now almost a hundred million miles distant.

There was not the slightest sound when those blazing, incandescent jets suddenly erupted from the ship. Almost at once the vessel was veiled by clouds of dust blasted up from the plain, clouds which formed a kind of shimmering mist within which burned an incredibly brilliant sun. With breathtaking slowness, the space-ship rose from the ground and began to climb towards the star-filled sky.

Now it was free from its dust cloud, and Daphne understood why she had been given dark glasses to wear. She could easily believe, as someone had told her, that those rocket jets were hotter and brighter than the sun.

Through the glasses she could follow the slow ascent of the ship and could dimly see the lunar landscape beneath, lit by the reflected glare. Now the rocket was gaining speed; about a minute had passed and it was more than twenty miles high. Daphne took off the glasses and watched the ship dwindle against the stars until, quite abruptly, it vanished. The motors had been cut off; they had done their work, and the great rocket would now coast as silently and effortlessly as a flying arrow on its months'-long journey to Mars.

'Quite a sight, isn't it?' said Norman softly. 'I think the fact that you can't hear a sound makes it all the more impressive.'

That was perfectly true. Daphne had now been on the Moon for three days, and she was still not used to the idea of living, as it were, on the frontier of a world totally different from anything she had ever known before.

Inside the rabbit-warren of the Observatory there was air, constant temperature – and sound. Apart from the lessened gravity, one might have been on Earth. But she had only to climb one of the stairways leading to the look-out rooms on the surface – and then there was no doubt that she was on another world.

Between her and the hostile lunar landscape was nothing more than a few inches of perspex, and the absolute silence of the Moon lay all around her like an almost palpable blanket. She was an alien here, an intruder in a world to which she did not belong. She felt as a water-spider must do when it ventures into a strange and treacherous element protected by its little bubble of air.

Yet, whenever she could, Daphne liked to spend an hour here, simply looking out across the plain or trying to draw the mountains whose peaks were just visible in the west. Those distant summits, higher than almost any range on Earth, were now ablaze beneath the mid-afternoon sun, although above them the stars were shining brilliantly in the jet-black sky.

Daphne had met Norman Phillips on the night of the dance, and had found him very useful as a guide. He was a young geologist (or selenologist, if one wanted to be accurate) who was not normally stationed at the Observatory but was on leave at the moment from the second lunar base, on the other side of the Moon. The fact that he was off duty gave him a considerable advantage over the other scientists, many of whom would have been quite willing to show Daphne round.

Professor Martin approved of this arrangement, but had been inconsiderate enough to suggest that Michael be included in the party. This proposal had not been received by Norman with any great enthusiasm, especially when he found that Michael did all the talking and wanted to be shown how everything worked.

As a result, the first few trips had been rather slow affairs and Daphne had become bored with technicalities. Fortunately, they had been able to jettison Michael at the Central Control Room, where he had attached himself to the Chief Engineer and since then had been seen only at meal-times.

Daphne had now sorted out her original chaotic impressions and had acquired a fairly clear picture of the Observatory. At any rate, she no longer got lost when she was alone. For almost twenty years men had been tunnelling and excavating here beneath the floor of the great crater, only a few miles from the spot where the first rocket had landed on the Moon.

In the early days, the colonists had devoted all their efforts to the sheer problem of keeping alive. To avoid the fierce temperature changes between night and day, they had gone underground, leaving only their instruments on the surface. The setting up of the lunar base had been an achievement almost as great as the crossing of space itself. Air, water, food – everything had, in the early days, to be carried across the quarter-million-mile gulf from Earth.

Soon, however, the Moon had started to yield its treasures as the survey parties uncovered its mineral resources. Now the colony could make its own air and for some years had been able to grow almost all its food supplies. Daphne had seen the strange underground 'farms' where acres of plants grew with incredible swiftness in a hot, humid atmosphere, beneath the glare of enormous lights.

One day, Norman told her, it might be possible to develop plants which could be cultivated out on the airless surface of the Moon, and then the green carpet of life would begin to spread across the empty plains, changing the face of a world.

Now that the early pioneering days were over, existence in the colony was a little less austere, although by the standards of Earth it was spartan enough. There were quite extensive games and recreation rooms, and although the living quarters were very small they were also extremely comfortable.

What Daphne liked most, however, were the people themselves. They seemed much more friendly and helpful than on Earth, and she didn't think that was merely because she was the Director's daughter. Somehow she got the impression that they all felt part of one big family – they knew they had to work together in order to survive at all.

'Well,' said Norman with a grin, 'what are you thinking about now?'

Daphne woke from her day dreams with a start. 'I was just wondering,' she said, 'what it really feels like to live here for a long time. Don't you ever miss the Earth? Surely you must get fed up with all these bare rocks and that sky full of stars! I know they're wonderfully – well, dramatic – but they never change. Don't you sometimes wish you had clouds, or green fields, or the sea? I think I should miss the sea most of all.'

Norman smiled, although a little wistfully. 'Yes, we miss them sometimes, but usually we're too busy to brood over it. You see, when you've got a big, exciting job to do, nothing else really matters. Besides, we go on Earth-leave every two years, and then I guess we appreciate what the old planet's got to offer a lot more than you stay-at-homes!'

He gave a little laugh. 'It isn't as if we can't see Earth whenever we want to. After all, it's there all the time, hanging up in the sky. From this side of the Moon, you can always see your own home town – at least, when it isn't covered with clouds. Oh, that reminds me – I've been able to grab one of the smaller telescopes for you. Let's go along and see if it's ready.'

It seemed a little odd that it had taken three days to arrange this. The trouble was that the telescopes were in almost continual use on various research programmes, and there was no time for casual star-gazing. More-over, the really big instruments were permanently fitted up for photo-graphic work, so it was impossible to look through them even when they were free.

The room to which Norman led Daphne was only just below the Moon's surface, as they had to climb a flight of steps from the main Observatory level to reach it. It was quite small, and crowded with apparatus in a state of extreme disorder – at least, so this seemed to Daphne. An elderly man with a very worried expression was doing something with a soldering iron to the inside of what looked like a complicated television set. He did not seem too pleased at the interruption.

'I can give you only thirty minutes,' he said. 'I've promised Professor Martin to get this spectrum analyser fixed by eighteen hours. What do you want to look at?'

'What have you got to offer?'

'Let's see – ten planets, about fifty satellites, a few million nebulae and several billion stars. Take your choice.'

'We can't see many of them in thirty minutes, so let's start with – oh, say the Andromeda nebula.'

The astronomer looked at the clock, did some mental calculations, and pressed several buttons. There was a faint whirring of electric motors and the lights began to dim.

'What do I look through?' asked Daphne, who had seen nothing at all that looked like any part of a telescope.

'Sit at this desk and use this eyepiece. Focus with the knob on the right – that's the idea. Got it?'

She was peering into a circle of intense, blackness, across which the stars were moving so quickly that they looked like thin lines of light. Overhead, the great telescope was swinging across the sky, seeking for its incredibly distant target. Suddenly the image steadied, the stars became tiny, needle-sharp points, and among them floated something that was not a star at all.

It was hard to describe, hard even for the eye to grasp. An oval of fiery mist, its edges fading so imperceptibly into the surrounding blackness that no one could tell where it ended, the Great Nebula glimmered like a ghost beyond the veil of the stars.

'Our neighbours,' said Norman quietly. 'The very next universe to our own – yet it's so far away that the light you're seeing now began its journey before Man existed on the Earth.'

'But what *is* it?' whispered Daphne.

'Well, I suppose you know that all the stars are gathered in great disc-shaped clusters – island universes, someone called them – each containing thousands of millions of suns. We're right inside one of them – the Milky Way. And that's the next nearest, floating out there. It's too far away for you to see the separate stars, though you can in the bigger telescopes. Beyond it are millions of other universes, as far as we can see.'

'With worlds like our Earth in them?'

'Who knows? At that distance you couldn't see the Sun, let alone the Earth! But I expect there must be any number of planets out there, and on many of them there'll probably be life of some kind. I wonder if we'll ever find out? But let's come a bit nearer home – we haven't much time.'

To Daphne, the next half hour was a revelation. Overhead, out on the dusty, silent plain, the great telescope ranged across the sky, gathering in the wonders of the heavens and presenting them to her gaze. Beautiful groups of coloured stars, like jewels gleaming with all the hues of the rainbow – clouds of incandescent mist, twisted into strange shapes by unimaginable forces – Jupiter and his family of moons – and, perhaps most wonderful of all, Saturn floating serenely in his circle of rings, like some intricate work of art rather than a world eight times the size of Earth . . .

And now she understood the magic that had lured the astronomers up into the clear mountain skies, and at last out across space to the Moon.

Slowly the outer doors of the great underground garage slid apart, and the bus began to climb the steep ramp that led to the surface of the Moon. It still seemed strange to Daphne that the only means of transport on the Moon was something as old-fashioned as a motor-bus, but like many of the peculiar things she had met here it was reasonable enough when explained. Rockets were much too expensive for journeys of only a few hundred miles, and as there was no atmosphere air transport was, of course, impossible.

The big vehicle was really a sort of mobile hotel in which a couple of dozen people could live comfortably for a week or more. It was about forty feet long and mounted on two sets of caterpillar tractors, operated by powerful electric motors. The driver had a little raised cabin at the front, and the passenger compartment was fitted with comfortable seats that became bunks at night. At the back was a kitchen, storeroom, and even a tiny shower-bath.

Daphne looked around to see who her fellow passengers were. Besides her own family there were ten other travellers, most of them – like Norman – scientists going to relieve the staff at Number Two Base. She knew them all by sight, if not by name, so it looked as if there would be plenty of company for the trip.

The bus was now rolling briskly across the crater floor at about forty miles an hour, heading due north. It was easy to make good speed here as the ground was quite level and any obstacles had been bulldozed out of the way when the rough track they were following was made. Daphne hoped that there would soon be a change of scenery; it would get rather dull if it was like this all the way.

Her wish was quickly granted. Far ahead, a line of jagged peaks had now become visible on the horizon, and minute by minute they climbed higher into the sky. At first, because of the steep curvature of the Moon's surface, it seemed that they were approaching nothing more than a modest range of hills, but presently Daphne saw that ahead of them lay a mountain wall several miles in height.

She looked in vain for any pass or valley through which they could penetrate – and then, with a sick feeling in the pit of her stomach, she realised that they were attempting nothing less than a direct frontal assault on that titanic barrier.

Ahead of them the ground tilted abruptly in a slope as steep as the roof of a house. There was a sudden deepening in the vibration of the motors, and then, scarcely checking its speed, the great bus charged up the apparently endless, rock-strewn escarpment that seemed to stretch ahead of them all the way to the stars. Daphne gave a little cry of fright as the change of level thrust her back in the seat, and Mrs Martin also looked none too happy as she turned anxious eyes on her husband.

Professor Martin smiled back at his family with a mischievous twinkle. 'Don't worry,' he said. 'It's perfectly safe – another advantage of our low gravity. Just sit back and enjoy the view!'

It was worth enjoying. Soon they could see for miles, far back across the great plain over which they had been travelling. As more and more of the crater wall came into view, Daphne saw that it was built up in a series of vast terraces, the innermost of which they had now nearly surmounted.

Presently they reached the crest, and turned left along it instead of descending into the valley ahead.

It took them nearly two hours to reach the outer rim of the crater – two hours of doubling back and forth along great valleys, of exhilarating and terrifying charges up those impossible slopes. At last the whole of the walled plain lay spread out behind them, while ahead was range after range of broken hills. They could travel more quickly now, for the downward slopes were much less steep than those inside the crater, as was usually the case on the Moon. Even so, it was another two hours before they had finished the descent and reached open country again.

One gets used to anything in time, even to driving across the Moon. At last, the featureless landscape that now flowed uneventfully past lulled Daphne into sleep. She operated the lever that turned her chair into a couch and settled down for the night.

She woke once, hours later, when the tilt of the floor told her that the bus was climbing again. It was quite dark; the blinds had been drawn to keep out the sunlight still blazing from the velvet sky above. Everyone was asleep, and Daphne was not long in rejoining them.

The next time she woke the blinds were up, the sunlight was shining into the cabin, and there was a pleasant smell of cooking coming from the little galley. The bus was moving rather slowly along the crest of a low range of hills, and Daphne was surprised to see that all the other passengers were clustered around the observation windows at the rear.

She went over to the window and looked back across the miles of land through which they had travelled during the night. When she had seen it last, Earth had been hanging low in the southern sky – but where was it now? Only the silver tip of its great crescent still showed above the horizon; while she had been sleeping, it had been dropping lower and lower in the sky.

They were passing over the rim of the Moon, into the mysterious, hidden land where the light of Earth had never shone – the land that, before the coming of the rocket, no human eyes had ever seen.

Millions of years ago, the lava welling up from the secret heart of the Moon had frozen and congealed to form this great, wrinkled plain. In all that time, nothing had ever moved upon its surface; not even the faintest breath of wind had ever stirred the thin layer of meteor dust that, through the ages, had drifted down from the stars.

But there was movement now. Glittering in the sunlight like some strange, armoured insect, the powerful motor-vehicle was racing swiftly towards its goal – the Second Lunar Base, which had been built five years before as headquarters for the exploration of the Moon's hidden hemisphere. Unlike the Observatory, Base Two was not underground, and when Daphne first caught sight of its buildings they reminded her irresistibly of Eskimo igloos.

They were, so Norman told her, simply plastic domes blown up like balloons and painted silver to conserve heat. Each had its private airlock, and was linked to its neighbour by a short connecting tube. There was no sign of life, but a pressurised tractor – a small edition of the machine in which Daphne was riding – was joined to one of the domes by a flexible coupling rather like a great hose-pipe, wide enough for men to walk through.

'That's Joe Hargreaves's tractor,' said Norman. 'He'd just started on a thousand mile circuit before I left. I wonder if he's found anything interesting.'

'What was he looking for?'

Norman grinned. 'I don't suppose it sounds very exciting, but we're trying to make an accurate geological map of the Moon, showing where all its mineral deposits are – particularly things like uranium, of course. So we send these tractors all over the place, drilling holes and collecting samples. But it's going to be centuries before the job's finished.'

It certain wasn't as glamorous as the astronomers' work, Daphne decided, but she realised that it was just as important. And Norman seemed to find it interesting enough, for he was still talking about magnetic surveys and other mysteries of his trade when their bus was coupled up to one of the domes and they walked through the airlock. The flexible connection didn't fit very well and there was a rather frightening hiss of escaping air, but as no one seemed to worry, Daphne supposed it was all right.

They found themselves beneath a large dome about fifty feet across. The level rock floor was littered with packing cases, pieces of machinery, and all the miscellaneous stores needed for life on this inhospitable world. However, there was not a single human being in sight.

Professor Martin looked a trifle annoyed. 'Where is everyone?' he said to the driver. 'You radioed that we were coming, didn't you?'

'They must all be busy in one of the other domes, I suppose, but it's a bit odd.'

At that moment a small, grey-haired man came bustling breathlessly into the chamber and hurried up to Professor Martin.

'Sorry we weren't ready to meet you, Professor,' he gasped, 'but something terrific has just happened. Come and see what we've found.'

'That's Dr Anstey,' Norman whispered to Daphne. 'He's in charge here. A nice chap, but always going off the deep end about something. Let's see what it is this time.'

They followed the excited little scientist through one of the connecting corridors into the next dome. It was packed with men who looked around as they approached, then cleared a way for Professor Martin. As she followed her father into the centre of the room, Daphne saw that they were approaching a perfectly ordinary table on which was standing a far-from-ordinary object.

At first sight, it resembled a fragment of multicoloured coral from the bed of some Pacific lagoon. No – perhaps it was more like a piece of petrified cactus, strangely coloured with reds and greens and golds. It stood on a slab of rock in which it seemed to be rooted like a stalagmite – but it was easy to tell that it was no mere mineral formation.

It was Life – here on the barren, airless Moon, here on the world which for so long had been the symbol of empty desolation! As she stood in that quiet, yet crowded, room, Daphne knew that she was present at one of the great moments in the history of lunar exploration.

Presently Professor Martin broke the silence. He turned to a grimy, unshaven man who, Daphne guessed, was the leader of the party that had just returned.

'Where did you find it, Hargreaves?' he asked.

'About 60 North, 155 West – just where the Ocean of Eternity joins the Lake of Dreams. There's a valley about five miles long and a couple of miles wide, and it's full of these things, acres and acres of them, all the colours of the rainbow. They're all sizes from a few inches high up to about twenty feet.'

Professor Martin leaned forward and gingerly touched the enigma standing motionless on the table-top.

'It feels just like rock,' he said, and there was disappointment in his voice. 'We're a few million years too late – it's fossilised.'

'I don't think so,' replied Hargreaves, shaking his head vigorously. 'I can't prove it, but when I was in that valley I somehow knew that these – plants, or whatever you can call them – are alive and still growing. Maybe they grow so slowly that it takes them thousands of years to get this big. They're like nothing we've got on Earth, but I'm sure they're alive.'

'Perhaps you're right; that's a problem for the biologists to work out. Anyway, congratulations – this is going to make you immortal, because when they give this thing a name they're sure to call it after you!'

'Just Joe's luck,' said Norman in disgust. 'The only excitement *I* ever get on these trips is when my tractor breaks down!'

This discovery had completely overshadowed the visit of Professor Martin and his family, which would otherwise have been quite an important event in the life of the little community. But presently the normal routine was resumed, and the scientists drifted back to their work, with many backward glances at the silent, multicoloured entity that had so suddenly changed all their preconceived ideas about the Moon. They were no longer the only living creatures on its surface, and perhaps – who knows? – there were other and still stranger beings in the hidden places of this mysterious world.

Rather belatedly, Professor Martin introduced his family to Dr Anstey, who still seemed in a somewhat highly-strung condition.

'Very pleased to meet you,' he said absentmindedly. 'How long will you be staying here?'

'Until the transport goes back, the day after tomorrow,' replied Professor Martin.

Dr Anstey suddenly seemed to come out of his trance and remembered his duty as a host. He smiled apologetically at Mrs Martin.

'I'm afraid you'll find the quarters a little cramped, but we've done our best. This is the first time we've had visitors here on the back of the Moon!'

*

Mrs Martin was now becoming accustomed to unusual residences, and was not in the least surprised to find herself ushered into a tiny, first-floor room tucked under the curve of the dome. Set in the outer wall was a small porthole through which one could look to the south across a wide plain, broken at intervals by low, razor-backed hills.

With a sigh of relief, Mrs Martin sank into one of the pneumatic armchairs. It was a little disturbing to think that not only was all the furniture kept inflated by air-pressure, but so also was the very building itself. What would happen if there was a puncture? Presumably the whole place would collapse like a pricked balloon as the air rushed out into space. Oh, well, it was no use worrying . . .

Perhaps Daphne was engrossed in similar thoughts, for she walked to the curving wall, prodded it gently with her finger, and then, apparently reassured, settled down in the other chair.

Her mother wondered just what effect this trip was having on her. It was easy to tell with Michael; he was in his element and having the time of his life. But with Daphne one could never be quite sure. She seemed to be enjoying herself, yet she was very quiet and scarcely ever made any comments on the surprising things that were happening around her. Perhaps, like so many of her generation, she had learned to take the incredible for granted.

That, as it happened, was scarcely true. The things she had seen on the Moon – above all, her glimpses through the giant telescope of the sky's countless wonders – were beginning to fire Daphne's imagination. Now at last she understood that science was not merely an affair of dry equations and dull text-books, but had a poetry and a magic of its own. A new world had been opened up before her – it was a world she could enter if she wished.

She had never realised, until Professor Martin had mentioned it casually, how many well-known women astronomers there had been – right back to the most famous of them all, Caroline Herschel, who had helped her brother Sir William record his observations during the long winter nights, even when the ink was freezing in its well.

In the twentieth century more and more women had made their names in this rapidly advancing field of science, until in some of its branches they had outnumbered the men. All these facts had been quite unknown to Daphne, and they were beginning to fire her with a new ambition.

Two days at the Second Base passed very swiftly. There was, Daphne discovered, a spirit here quite unlike that at the Observatory. Perhaps the fact that the Earth was no longer visible in the sky, giving not only light but a kind of moral support, provided part of the explanation. Here indeed, it seemed, was the true frontier of the unknown – and it was an exciting experience to be living on it.

Almost every day the little pressurised tractors were setting out on their raids into unexplored lunar territory, or returning from earlier expeditions. Daphne attended the briefing of a crew about to leave on a ten-day trip that would cover over a thousand miles. She had once seen a film showing how bomber crews in the Second World War were prepared for their missions. There was the same atmosphere of adventure coupled with scientific efficiency as Norman and his companions consulted their maps and discussed their route with Dr Anstey.

The conversation was too technical for Daphne to follow much of it, but she was fascinated by the wonderful names of the regions across which the expedition would be travelling. When the far side of the Moon had been mapped, men had continued the tradition already set on the visible hemisphere and had used the most poetical names they could imagine for the great plains, while calling the craters themselves after famous scientists.

Before he left, Norman gave Daphne a souvenir to take back to Earth. It was a beautifully coloured mass of crystals growing out of some strange lunar rock; he told her its name, although it was much too long to remember. As she stared at it in fascination, Norman explained: 'Pretty, isn't it? We've found it on only one part of the Moon – the Gulf of Solitude – and it doesn't occur on Earth at all. So it's really unique.'

Then he paused and said awkwardly, 'Well, it's been awfully nice showing you around. I don't think that anyone else has ever seen quite as much of the Moon in such a short time! And – I hope you'll be coming back some day.'

Daphne remembered these words as, through the observation windows of the dome, she watched Norman's little tractor disappear over the edge of the Moon on its way into the unknown south. What would he find on this expedition? Would he be as lucky as Hargreaves?

It was still early in the long lunar morning when they began the homeward journey. Professor Martin had finished his official business, and in any case they could wait no longer – they had a space-ship to catch. *That* was something to be proud of! Not a mere train or a commonplace aircraft – but a *space-ship*!

Daphne was fast asleep when they finally reached the Observatory. She woke with a start when the steady vibration of the bus finally ceased, and found to her surprise that they were once more back in the big underground garage. Sleepily clutching her suitcase, she followed Mrs Martin back to their old rooms, where she promptly resumed her interrupted slumbers.

Only a few minutes later, it seemed, her mother was shaking her by the shoulder and saying it was time to get up again. Her last day on the Moon had arrived; there was luggage to be packed, farewells to be made and – this was something no one had warned her about – some pills to be taken under the watchful eye of the Observatory Medical Officer. She was going back into a gravity field six times as strong as the one she had now become used to, and the consequences might be unpleasant unless the right precautions were taken.

Even Michael was a little subdued as they entered the garage for the last time to drive out to the waiting space-ship. The great gleaming pillar of metal was standing there on the open plain with the brilliant earthlight flashing from its sides. The tractor drove up to the base of the ship and they prepared to enter the lift that would carry them up to the airlock high above their heads.

Professor Martin was saying goodbye to his wife, and presently he came over to the children.

'I rather wish I were going back with you,' he said with a smile, 'but perhaps you understand now why I came here in the first place. When you've had time to sort yourselves out, write and tell me what you thought about the Moon, won't you? Oh – and one other thing! Don't be *too* superior to all your friends when you do get back to Earth!'

Then the metal doors silently separated them, to open again a minute later into the cabin of the space-ship.

To Daphne, it seemed incredible that only a fortnight ago she had entered this cabin for the first time on a distant world called Earth. So much had happened in those days; what she had seen here would colour all her life.

She knew that nothing would ever seem quite the same to her again. Earth was no longer everything that mattered – no longer the centre of the universe. It was only one world among many, merely the first of the planets on which men had lived. One day, perhaps, it would not even seem the most important . . .

The thunder of the rockets burst in upon her day-dreams and brought her back to the present. She felt the thrust of increasing weight as she sank into her couch, and once again her limbs became suddenly like lead. The massed millions of horsepower safely chained by the gleaming instruments on the control board were taking her home – taking her away from the cold and silent beauty of the Moon.

The crater rings, the dark chasms, the great plains with their magic and mysterious names – all these were falling swiftly away beneath the climbing ship. In a few hours, the Moon would be no more than a distant globe, dwindling in space.

But one day, Daphne knew, she would return. This world, not Earth, would be her home. At last she had found her ambition, although as yet she had breathed a word of it to no one. There would be years of study ahead, but in the end she would join the quest for the secrets of the stars.

Her holiday was over.

Earthlight

First published in *Thrilling Wonder Stories*, August 1951
Not previously collected in book form

I am very proud of the fact that the Apollo-15 crew gave this name to a crater which they drove past in their lunar rover. On their return to earth, they sent me a beautiful 3-D map bearing the inscription: 'To Arthur Clarke with best personal regards from the crew of Apollo 15 and many thanks for your visions in space.'

I

'If it weren't for the fact,' said Conrad Wheeler morosely, 'that it might be considered disrespectful I'd say that the Old Man is completely nuts. And not just slightly touched like the rest of the people I've met on the Moon.'

He looked balefully at Sid Jamieson, two years his senior on the staff of the Observatory. The latter grinned goodnaturedly and refused to rise to the bait. 'When you've known the Old Man as long as I have,' he said, 'you'll realise he doesn't do anything like this without a very good reason.'

'It had better be good! My series of spectrograms was supposed to be finished tonight – and now look at the 'scope!'

The giant dome that housed the thousand-inch reflector was a shambles, or so a casual visitor would have thought. Even the natives were somewhat appalled by the confusion. A small army of technicians was gathered round the base of the great telescope, which was now pointing aimlessly at the zenith. Aimlessly because the dome of the Observatory was closed and sealed against the outer vacuum. It was strange to see men unprotected by space-suits walking over the tessellated floor, to hear voices ringing where normally no slightest sound could be heard.

High up on a balcony on the far side of the dome the Director was giving orders into a microphone. His voice, enormously amplified, roared from the speakers that had been specially installed for the occasion. '*Mirror crew – stand clear!*'

There was a scurrying round the base of the telescope: then an expectant pause.

'*Lower away!*'

With infinite slowness the great disc of quartz, that had cost a hundred million to make, was lowered from its cell to the strange vehicle beneath the telescope. The ninety-foot-wide truck sank visibly on its scores of tiny ballon tyres as it took up the weight of the immense mirror. Then the hoisting gear was released and with a purr of motors the truck and its precious cargo began to move slowly down the ramp leading to the resurfacing room.

It was a breathtaking sight. The men scattered over the floor were utterly dwarfed by the lattice-work of the telescope towering hundreds of feet above them. And the mirror itself, over eighty feet in diameter, seemed like a lake of fire as it reflected the glare of overhead lights. When at last it had left the room it was as though dusk had suddenly fallen.

'And now they've got to put it back!' grunted Wheeler. 'I suppose that will take even longer.'

'That's right,' said his companion cheerfully. '*Much* longer. Why, last time we resurfaced the mirror—' The amplifiers drowned his voice.

'*Four hours twenty-six minutes,*' remarked the Director in a fifty-watt aside. '*Not too bad. Okay – get her back and carry on.*'

There was a click as he switched off the microphone. In a strained and hostile silence the observatory staff watched his small rather plump figure leave the balcony. After a discreet interval someone said, 'Damn!' in a very determined voice. The assistant chief computer did a wicked thing. She lit a cigarette and threw the ash on the sacred floor.

'*Well!*' exploded Wheeler. 'He might have told us what it was all about! It's bad enough to stop the work of the whole observatory while we get the big mirror out when it's not due for resurfacing for months. But to tell us to put the blasted thing back as soon as we've dismounted it, without a word of explanation . . .' He left the sentence in mid-air and looked at his companion for support.

'Take it easy,' said Jamieson with a grin. 'The Old Man's not cracked and you know it. Therefore he's got a good reason for what he's doing. Also he's not the secretive sort – therefore he's keeping quiet because he has to. And there must be a *very* good reason for risking the near-mutiny he's got on his hands now. Orders from Earth, I'd say. One doesn't interrupt a research programme like ours just for a whim. Hello, here comes Old Mole – what's he got to say?'

'Old Mole' – alias Dr Robert Molton – came trotting towards them, carrying the inevitable pile of photographs. He was probably the only member of the Observatory staff who even remotely resembled the popular conception of an astronomer. All the rest, one could see at a glance, were businessmen, undergraduates of the athletic rather than the intellectual type, artists, prosperous bookmakers, journalists or rising young politicians. Anything but astronomers.

Dr Molton was the exception that proved the rule. He looked out at the world and his beloved photographic plates through thick rimless lenses. His clothes were always just a little too tidy and never less than ten years out of date – though incongruously enough his ideas and interests were often not only modern but years ahead of the times.

He was very partial to boutonnieres – but as the indigenous lunar vegetation gave him little scope in this direction he had to content himself with a somewhat restricted collection of artificial flowers imported from Earth.

These he varied with such ingenuity and resource that the rest of the staff had spent a good deal of fruitless effort trying to discover the laws governing their order of appearance. Indeed, a very famous mathematician had once lost a considerable sum of money because one day Old Mole appeared wearing a carnation rather than the rose advanced statistical theory had predicted.

'Hello, Doc,' said Wheeler. 'What's it all about? *You* ought to know!'

The old man paused and looked at the young astronomer doubtfully. He was never sure whether or not Wheeler was pulling his leg and usually assumed correctly that he was. Not that he minded, for he possessed a dry sense of humour and got on well with the numerous youngsters in the Observatory. Perhaps they reminded him of the time, a generation ago, when he too had been young and full of ambition.

'Why should I know? Professor Maclaurin doesn't usually confide his intentions to me.'

'But surely you've got your theories?'

'I have but they won't be popular.'

'Good old Doc! We knew you wouldn't let us down!'

The old astronomer turned to look at the telescope. Already the mirror was in position beneath its cell, ready to be hoisted back.

'Twenty years ago the last Director, van Haarden, got that mirror out in a hurry and rushed it to the vaults. He didn't have time for a rehearsal. Professor Maclaurin has.'

'Surely you don't mean . . . ?'

'In Ninety-five, as you should know but probably don't, the Government was having its first squabble with the Venus Administration. Things were so bad that for a time we expected an attempt to seize the Moon. Not war, of course, but too close an approximation to be comfortable. Well, that mirror is the human race's most valuable single possession and van Haarden was taking no risks with it. Nor, I think, is Maclaurin.'

'But that's ridiculous! We've had peace for more than half a century. Surely you don't think that the Federation would be mad enough to start anything?'

'Who knows just what the Federation is up to? It's dealing with the most dangerous commodity in the universe – human idealism. Out there on Mars and the moons of Jupiter and Saturn are the finest brains in the Solar System, fired with all the pride and the sense of power that the crossing of real space has given to man.

'They're not like us Earthbound planet-grubbers. Oh, I know we're on the Moon and all that but what's the Moon now but Earth's attic? Forty years ago it was the frontier and men risked their lives reaching it – but today the theatre in Tycho City holds two thousand!

'The real frontier's out beyond Uranus and it won't be long before Pluto and Persephone are inside it – if they've not been reached already. Then the Federation will have to spend its energies elsewhere and it will think about reforming Earth. That's what the Government's afraid of.'

'Well, and we never knew you were interested in politics! Sid, fetch the Doctor his soap-box.'

'Don't take any notice of him, Doc,' said Jamieson. 'Let's have the rest of your idea. After all, we're on quite good terms with the Federation. Their last scientific delegation left only a few months ago and a darn nice crowd they were too. I got an invitation to Mars I want to use as soon as the Director will let me go. You don't think they would declare war, or anything crazy like that? What good would it do to smash up Earth?'

'The Federation's much too sensible to try anything of the sort. Remember, I said they were idealists. But they may feel that Earth hasn't been taking them seriously enough and that's the one thing that reformers can't tolerate. However, the main cause of trouble is this haggling over the uranium supply.'

'I don't see what that's got to do with *us*,' said Wheeler. 'If there is a fight I hope they leave the Moon out of it.'

Molton said thoughtfully, 'Haven't you heard?'

'Heard what?' asked Wheeler, an uncomfortable sensation creeping up his spine.

'They say uranium has been found on the Moon at last.'

'*That* story! It's been going around for years.'

'I think there's something in it this time. I've had it from pretty reliable sources.'

'So have I,' put in Jamieson unexpectedly. 'Isn't it something to do with Johnstone's theory of satellite formation?'

'Yes. You know Earth's the only planet with any appreciable uranium – it's connected in some way with its abnormally high density. Most of the uranium's a thousand miles down in the core where no one can get at it. But when the Moon split off it took some of the core with it – and the remnant's quite close to the surface here. The story's going round that it's been detected by lowering counters down drill-holes and they've found enough uranium to make all the deposits on Earth look like very small stuff.'

'I see,' said Wheeler slowly. 'If that's true the Federation will be asking for increased supplies.'

'And those nervous old women down on Earth will be afraid to let them have any,' interjected Jamieson.

'Well, why should they?'

'Surely that's easy enough to answer. Earth's requirements are static – while the Federation's are increasing with each new planet that colonised.'

'And you think the Federation might try to grab any lunar deposits before Earth could get there?'

'Exactly – and if we are in the way we might get hurt. That would upset both sides very much but it wouldn't be much compensation to us.'

'This is just what used to happen a hundred and fifty years ago back on Earth, when gold and diamonds were valuable. Claim-jumping, they used to call it. Funny thing, history.'

'But supposing the Federation *did* seize a bit of the Moon – how could they hold it so far from their bases? Remember, there aren't any weapons left nowadays.'

'With the legacy of the two World Wars it wouldn't take long to make some, would it? Most of the finest scientists in the Solar System belong to the Federation. Suppose they took a big space-ship and put guns or rocket torpedoes on it. They could grab the whole Moon and Earth couldn't push them off. Especially when they'd got hold of the uranium and cut off Earth's supplies.'

'You should be writing science fiction, Doc! Battleships of Space and all that sort of thing! Don't forget to bring in the death-rays!'

'It's all right for you to laugh but you know perfectly well that with atomic power it *is* possible to put enough energy into a beam to do real damage. No one's tried it yet as far as we know – because there wasn't much point. But if they ever want to . . .'

'He's right, Con. How do we know what's been going on in the Government labs for the last generation? I hadn't thought about it before but it rather frightens me. You *do* think of the nicest things, Doc.'

'Well, you asked for my theories and you've got 'em. But I can't stand here all day talking. *Some* people in this establishment have work to do.' The old astronomer picked up his plates and wandered off toward his office, leaving the two friends in a somewhat disturbed frame of mind.

Jamieson gazed glumly at the telescope while Wheeler looked thoughtfully at the lunar landscape outside the dome. He ran his fingers idly along the transparent plastic of the great curving wall. It always gave him a thrill to think of the pressures that wall was withstanding – and the uncomfortable things that would happen if it ever gave way.

The view from the Observatory was famous throughout the entire Solar System. The plateau on which it had been built was one of the highest points in the great lunar mountain range which the early astronomers had called the Alps. To the south the vast plain so inappropriately named the *Mare Imbrium* – Sea of Rains – stretched as far as the eye could reach.

To the southeast the solitary peak of the volcanic mountain Pico jutted above the horizon. East and west ran the Alps, merging on the eastern side of the Observatory into the walled plain of Plato. It was nearly midnight and the whole vast panorama was lit by the brilliant silver light of the full Earth.

Wheeler was just turning away when the flash of rockets far out across the Sea of Rains attracted his notice. Officially no ship was supposed to fly over the northern hemisphere, for the brilliant glare of a rocket exhaust could ruin in a second an exposure that might have taken hours, even days, to make. But the ban was not always obeyed, much to the annoyance of the Observatory directorate.

'Wonder who that blighter is?' growled Wheeler. 'I sometimes wish we *did* have some guns on the Moon. Then we could shoot down trippers who try to wreck our programme.'

'I call that a really charitable thought. Maybe Tech Stores can fix you up – they keep everything.'

'Except what you happen to want. I've been trying to get a Hilger magnitude tabulator for the last month. "Sorry, Mr Wheeler, might be on the next consignment." I'd see the Director about it if I weren't in his bad books.'

Jamieson laughed. 'Well, if you must compose somewhat – er – personal limericks better not type them out next time. Stick to the old oral tradition like the ancient troubadours – it's much safer. Hello, what's he up to?'

The last remark was prompted by the manoeuvres of the distant ship. It was losing height steadily, its main drive cut off, only the vertical jets cushioning its fall.

'He's going to land! Must be in trouble!'

'No – he's quite safe. Oh, *very* pretty! That pilot knows his stuff!'

Slowly the ship fell out of sight below the rim of the mountains, still keeping on a level keel.

'He's down safely. If he's not there'll be a record firework display in just about ten seconds and we'll feel the shock over here.'

With a mingling of anxiety and morbid expectation the two men waited for a minute, eyes fixed on the horizon. Then they relaxed. There had been no distant explosion, no trembling of the ground underfoot.

'All the same, he may be in trouble. We'd better ask Signals to give him a call.'

'OK – let's go.'

The Observatory transmitter, when they reached it, was already in action. Someone else had reported a ship down beyond Pico and the operator was calling it on the general lunar frequency. 'Hello, ship landing near Pico – this is Astron calling. Are you receiving me? Over.'

The reply came after a considerable interval, during which the call was repeated several times. 'Hello, Astron, receiving you clearly. Pass your message please. Over.'

'Do you need any assistance? Over.'

'No thank you. None at all. Out.'

'OK. Astron out.'

The operator switched off his carrier and turned to the others with a gesture of annoyance. 'That's a nice polite answer for you! Translated into English it means "Mind your own business. I won't give you my call sign. Good-day."'

'Who do you think he is?'

'No doubt about it. Government ship.'

Jamieson and Wheeler looked at each other with a simultaneous surmise. 'Maybe the doc was right, after all.'

Wheeler nodded in assent. 'Mark my words, pardner,' he said, 'there's uranium in them thar hills. And I wish there weren't!'

II

During the next two weeks ship after ship dropped down beyond Pico and, after an initial outburst of speculation, the astronomers ceased to comment on the sight. Quite obviously something important was going on out in the Sea and the theory of the uranium mine was generally accepted because nobody could think of a better.

Presently the Observatory staff began to take their energetic neighbours for granted and forgot about them except when rocket glare fogged important photographic plates. Then they went storming in to see the Director, who calmed them down as best he could and promised to make the appropriate representations in the proper quarters.

With the coming of the long lunar day Jamieson and Wheeler settled down to the tedious work of analysing the data they had collected during the night. It would be fourteen days before they saw the stars again and could make any further observations. There was plenty to do, for an astromomer spends only a very small portion of his time actually working with his instruments. The most important part of his life is spent sitting at a desk piled with sheets of paper, which rapidly become covered with mathematical calculations or doodles, according to the flow of inspiration.

Though both Wheeler and Jamieson were young and keen, an unbroken week of this was quite enough for them. In the slow cycle of lunar time it was generally realised that tempers began to get frayed around midday and from then until just before nightfall there was usually something of an exodus from the Observatory.

It was Wheeler who suggested they take one of the Observatory tractors and head toward Pico on a voyage of exploration. Jamieson thought it was an excellent scheme though the idea was not as novel to him as to his friend. Trips out into the Sea of Rains were a popular diversion among the astronomers when they felt they had to get away from their colleagues.

There was always the chance of finding something interesting in the way of minerals or vegetation but the main attraction was the superb scenery. Also there was a certain amount of adventure and even danger about the enterprise that gave it an additional charm. Not a few tractors had been lost and although rigorous safety precautions were enforced there was always a chance that something might go wrong.

The almost complete absence of any atmosphere on the Moon had made economical flying impossible since rockets could not be used for journeys of only a few score miles. So practically all short-range lunar travel was done in the powerful electric tractors universally known as *Caterpillars* or, more briefly, 'cats'.

They were really small space-ships mounted on broad tracks that enabled them to go anywhere within reason, even over the appallingly jagged surface of the Moon. On fairly smooth terrain they could do up to eighty miles an hour but normally they were lucky to manage half that speed. The low gravity enabled them to climb fantastic slopes and they could if necessary haul themselves out of vertical pits by means of their built-in winches. One could live in the larger models for months at a time in reasonable comfort.

Jamieson was a more-than-expert driver and knew the road down the mountains perfectly. As lunar highways went it was one of the best and carried a good deal of traffic between the Observatory and the port of Aristillus. Nevertheless for the first hour Wheeler felt that his hair would never lie down again.

It usually took newcomers to the Moon a long time to realise that slopes of one-in-one were perfectly safe if treated with respect. Perhaps it was just as well that Wheeler was a novice for Jamieson's technique was so unorthodox that it would have filled a more experienced passenger with real alarm.

Why Jamieson was such a desperate driver was a paradox that had caused much discussion among his colleagues. Normally he was painstaking and careful, even languid in his movements. No one had ever seen him really annoyed or excited. Many people thought him lazy but that was a libel. He would spend weeks working out a theory until it was absolutely watertight – and then would put it away for two or three months to have another look at it later.

Yet once at the controls of a cat this quiet and peaceloving astronomer became a daredevil driver who held the unofficial record for almost every tractor drive in the northern hemisphere. More than likely the explanation lay in a boyhood desire to be a space-ship pilot, a dream that had been foiled by physical disability.

They shot down the last foothills of the Alps and out into the Sea of Rains like a miniature avalanche. Now that they were on lower ground Wheeler began to breathe again, thankful to have left the vertiginous slopes behind. He was not so pleased when with a colossal crash Jamieson drove the tractor off the road and out into the barren plain.

'Hey, where are you going?' he cried.

Jamieson laughed at his consternation. 'This is where the rough stuff begins. The road goes southwest to Aristillus here and we want to get to

Pico. So from now on we're in country where only half a dozen tractors have ever been before. To cheer you up I might say Ferdinand is one of them.'

'Ferdinand' was now plunging ahead at twenty miles an hour with a swaying motion Wheeler found rather disconcerting. If he had lived in an age that had known of ships he might have been familiar with it.

The view was disappointing, as it always is at 'sea' level on the Moon, owing to the nearness of the horizon. Pico and all the more distant mountains had sunk below the skyline and the plain ahead looked uninviting as it lay in the blazing sun. For three hours they forged steadily across it, passing tiny craterlets and yawning crevasses that seemed of indefinite depth.

Once Jamieson stopped the tractor and the two men went out in their space-suits to have a look at a particularly fine specimen. It was about a mile wide and the Sun, now nearly at the zenith, was shining straight into it. The bottom was quite flat as though, when the rock had split, lava had flowed in from the depths beneath and solidified. Wheeler found it very difficult to judge just how far away the floor was.

Jamieson's voice came over the suit radio. 'See those rocks down there?'

The other strained his eyes and could barely make out a few markings on the apparently smooth surface far below.

'Yes, I think I see the ones you mean. What about them?'

'How big would you say they are?'

'Oh, I don't know – maybe a yard across.'

'Hmmm. See the smaller one near the side?'

'Yes.'

'Well, that isn't a rock. That was a tractor that missed the bend.'

'Good Lord! How? It's plain enough.'

'Yes, but this is midday. Toward evening, when the Sun's low, it's the easiest thing in the world to mistake a shadow for a crevasse – and the other way round.'

Wheeler was very quiet as they walked back to their machine. Perhaps, after all, they had been safer in the mountains.

At length the great rock mass of Pico came once more into sight until presently it dominated the landscape. One of the most famous landmarks on the Moon it rose sheer out of the Sea of Rains, from which, ages ago, volcanic action had extruded it. On Earth it would have been completely unclimbable. Even under one-sixth of Earth's gravity only two men had ever reached its summit. One of them was still there.

Moving slowly over the jagged terrain the tractor skirted the flanks of the mountain. Jamieson was searching for a place where the cliffs could be scaled so they could get a good view out over the Sea. After travelling several miles he found a spot that met with his approval.

'Climb those cliffs? Not on your life!' expostulated Wheeler when Jamieson explained his plan of action. 'Why, they're practically vertical and half a mile high!'

'Don't exaggerate,' retorted the other. 'They're quite ten degrees from the vertical. And it's so easy to climb here, even in a suit. We'll be tied together and if one of us falls the other can still pull him up with one hand. You don't know what it's like until you've tried.'

'That's true of all forms of suicide. Oh, all right – I'm game if you are.'

Reluctantly Wheeler climbed into his space-suit and followed his friend through the airlock. Jamieson was carrying a small telescope, a long nylon rope and other climbing equipment, which he draped around Wheeler on the pretext that, as he would have to go ahead, his hands had better be free.

Seen from close quarters the cliffs were even more forbidding. They seemed not merely vertical but overhanging and Wheeler wondered how his friend intended to tackle them. Secretly he hoped the whole campaign would be called off.

It was not to be. After a brief survey of the rock face Jamieson tied one end of the rope around his waist and, with a short run, leaped toward a projection thirty feet up the face of the cliff. He caught it with one hand, transferred his grip to the other and hung for a while, admiring the view. Since he weigh only forty pounds with all his equipment this was not as impressive a performance as it would have been on Earth. However, it served its purpose of reassuring Wheeler.

After a while Jamieson grew tired of hanging by one arm and brought the other into action. With incredible speed he clambered up the face of the cliff until he was fully a hundred feet above the ground. Here he found a ledge that was to his liking as it was every bit of twelve inches wide and enabled him to lean back against the rock face.

He switched on his headset and called down. 'Hello, Con! Ready to come up?'

'Yes. What do you want me to do?'

'Is the rope tied around you?'

'Just a minute. OK.'

'Right! Up we go!'

Jamieson started to haul in the rope and grinned at the other's sudden exclamation of surprise as he found himself hoisted unceremoniously into the air. When he had been lifted twenty or thirty feet Wheeler recovered his poise and began to climb the rope himself, so that as a result of their joint efforts it was only a few seconds before he had reached the ledge.

'Easy enough, isn't it?'

'So far – but it still looks a long way.'

'Then just keep on climbing and don't bother to look. Hold on here until I call you again. Don't move until I'm ready – you're my anchor in case I fall.'

After half an hour Wheeler was amazed to find how far they had risen. The tractor was no more than a toy at the foot of the cliffs and the horizon was many miles away. Jamieson decided they were high enough and began to survey the plain with his telescope. It was not long before he found the object of their search.

About ten miles away the largest space-ship either of them had ever seen lay with the sunshine glinting on its sides. Close to it was an enormous hemispherical structure rising out of the level plain. Through the telescope men and machines could be seen moving around its base. From time to time clouds of dust shot into the sky and fell back to the ground again as if blasting were in progress.

'Well, there's your mine,' said Wheeler after a long scrutiny.

'It doesn't look much like a mine to me,' replied the other. 'I've never seen a lunar mine covered over like that. It almost looks as if a rival observatory is starting up. Maybe we're going to be driven out of business.'

'We can reach it in half an hour, whatever it is. Shall we go over to have a look?'

'I don't think it would be a very wise thing to do. They might insist on our staying.'

'Hang it all, there isn't a war on yet and they'd have no right to detain us. The Director knows where we are and would raise hell if we didn't come back.'

'Not in your case, my lad. However, I guess you're right. They can only shoot us. Let's go.'

Climbing down the cliff, unlike a similiar operation on Earth, was easier than going up it. Each took turns lowering the other to the full length of the rope, then scrambling down the cliff face himself, knowing that even if he slipped the other could easily check his fall. In a remarkably short time they had reached level ground again and the faithful Ferdinand set out once more across the plain.

An hour later, having been delayed by a slight mistake in bearings for which each blamed the other, they found the dome ahead of them and bore down upon it at full speed, after first calling the Observatory on their private wave length and explaining exactly what they intended to do. They rang off before anyone could tell them not to.

It was amusing to watch the commotion their arrival caused. Jamieson thought it resembled nothing so much as an ant heap that had been well stirred with a stick. In a very short time they found themselves surrounded by tractors, hauling machines and excited men in space-suits. They were forced by the sheer congestion to bring Ferdinand to a halt.

'I suppose we had better wait for the reception committee,' said Wheeler. 'Ah, here it comes!'

A small man who managed to convey an air of importance even in a space-suit was forcing his way through the crowd. Presently there came a peremptory series of knocks on the outer door of the airlock. Jamieson pressed the button that opened the seal and a moment later the 'reception committee' was removing his helmet in the cabin.

He was an elderly sharp-featured man and he did not seem in a particularly good temper. 'What are you doing here?' he snapped as soon as he had escaped from the confines of his suit.

Jamieson affected surprise at such an unreasonable attitude. 'We saw you were newcomers around here, so we came over to see how you were getting on.'

'Who are you?'

'We're from the Observatory. This is Mr Wheeler – I'm Dr Jamieson. Both astrophysicists.'

'Oh!' There was a sudden change in the atmosphere. The reception committee became quite friendly. 'Well, you'd better both come along to the office while we check your credentials.'

'I beg your pardon? Since when has this part of the Moon been restricted territory?'

'Sorry, but that's the way it is. Come along, please.'

The two astronomers climbed into their suits and followed the other through the lock. Wheeler was beginning to feel a trifle worried and rather wished he had not suggested making this visit. Already he was visualising all sorts of unpleasant possibilities. Recollections of what he had read about spies, solitary confinement and brick walls at dawn rose up to cheer him.

One of his most valuable assets as a theoretical scientist was his powerful imagination but there were times when he felt that he could do without it. Quite a large portion of his life was spent worrying about things which might happen as a result of the scrapes into which he was continually getting. This looked as if it might be one of them.

Outside the crowd was still gathered around their tractor but it rapidly dispersed as their guide gave instructions over his radio which Jamieson and Wheeler, tuned to the Observatory wavelength, were unable to hear.

They were led to a smoothly-fitting door in the wall of the great dome and found themselves inside the space formed by the outer wall and an inner, concentric hemisphere. The two shells, as far as could be seen, were spaced apart by an intricate webbing of transparent plastic. Even the floor underfoot was made of the same substance. Looking at it closely, Wheeler came to the conclusion that it was some kind of electrical insulator.

Their guide hurried them along at almost a trot, as if he did not wish them to see more than necessary. They entered the inner dome through a small airlock, where they removed their suits. Wheeler wondered glumly when they would be allowed to retrieve them.

III

There was a smell in the air that they did not at once recognise, in spite of its familiarity. Jamieson was the first to identify it. 'Ozone!' he whispered to his companion, who nodded in agreement. He was going to add a remark about high voltage equipment when their guide looked back suspiciously and he desisted.

The airlock opened into a small corridor flanked by doors bearing painted numbers and such labels as *Private, Keep Out! Technical Staff Only, Dr Jones, Typists* and *Director*. At the last they came to a halt.

After a short pause a *Come In* panel glowed and the door swung automatically open. Ahead lay a perfectly ordinary office dominated by a determined-looking young man behind a very large desk. 'Hello – who are these people?' he asked as his visitors entered.

'Two astronomers from the Observatory. They just dropped in by tractor. I thought we had better check up on them.'

'Most certainly. Your names, please?'

There followed a tedious quarter of an hour while the Director took down particulars and finally called the Observatory. Jamieson and Wheeler breathed a sigh of relief when it was all over and everyone was satisfied that they were in fact themselves.

The young man at the imposing desk switched off the radio and regarded the two interlopers with some perplexity. Presently his brow cleared and he began to address them.

'You realise, of course, that you are a bit of a nuisance. This is about the last place we ever expected visitors, otherwise we should have put up notices telling them to clear off. Needless to say we have means of detecting them when they do arrive – even when they don't drive up openly as you were sensible enough to do.

'Anyway, here you are and no harm done. You have probably guessed that this is a Government project, one that we don't want talked about. Now you are here I suppose I had better explain to you what it is – but I want your word of honour not to repeat what I tell you.'

The two astronomers, feeling rather sheepish, assented.

'As you know radio communication to the outer planets is carried out in stages and not by direct point-to-point transmission. If we want to send a message to Titan it has to go, for example, Earth–Mars–Callisto–Titan, with repeater stations and all their masses of equipment at each leg of the journey. We want to do away with all that. This is going to be Communications Centre for the entire Solar System and from here we can call any planet direct.'

'Even Persephone when they get there?'

'Yes.'

'One in the eye for the Federation, won't it be? They own all the relay stations outside Earth.'

The Director looked at Wheeler sharply. 'Well, I don't suppose they'll like it at first,' he admitted. 'But in the long run it will reduce costs and give everyone a much better service.'

'The secrecy, I suppose, is to prevent the Federation thinking of the idea first?'

The Director looked a little embarrassed and refused to answer directly. He rose, made a gesture of dismissal. 'Well, that's all, gentlemen. I hope you have a pleasant trip back to the Alps. And please ask your friends to keep away.'

'Thanks for being so frank with us,' said Jamieson as they turned to go. 'We'll keep it to ourselves. But we're glad to know the truth, as there are so many rumours flying round nowadays.'

'Such as?'

'To be perfectly honest we thought this might be the mythical uranium mine there's been so much talk about.'

The Director laughed easily. 'Doesn't look much like a mine, does it?'

'It certainly doesn't. Well, goodbye.'

'Goodbye.'

The Director remained standing in moody silence for a while after Jamieson and Wheeler had left the room. Then he pressed the buzzer for his secretary. 'You've recorded that?'

'Yes.'

'They're nice chaps. I feel rather ashamed of myself. But if we just sent them away they'd start discussing us with their colleagues – and they might hit on the truth. Now that they think they know it their curiosity will be satisfied and they won't talk, especially since I've asked them not to and they're the sort who'll respect a promise. A dirty trick but I think it will work.'

The secretary looked at his chief with a new respect. 'You know, Chief, there are times when you remind me of that old Roman politician – you know the chap I mean.'

'Machiavelli, I suppose – though he was a bit later than the Romans. By the way, did the screens detect them all right when they came in?'

'Yes – the alarms went off in plenty of time.'

'Good! Then there's no need to increase our precautions. The only other step we could take is to publicly announce that this part of the Moon is tabu – and the last thing we want to do is to attract attention.'

'What about the people at the Observatory? There may be more visitors.'

'We'll call up Maclaurin again and ask him to discourage these private expeditions. He's a touchy old bird but I think he'll play. Now let's get on with that progress report.'

Jamieson and Wheeler did not return directly to the Observatory, for they were not expected back for a couple of days and there was still a lot of the Moon to explore. Their visit to the dome, they felt, had been something of an anticlimax. It was true that they were sharing a secret and that was always exciting but they could not pretend it was a very spectacular secret.

'Well, where do we go from here?' asked Wheeler when the dome had dropped out of sight below the horizon.

Jamieson produced a large-scale photographic map of the *Mare Imbrium* and pinned it down with his forefinger.

'This is where we are now,' he said. 'I'm going on a circular tour that will really show you some lunar scenery. The *Sinus Iridum*'s just two hundred miles east over quite good terrain and I'm heading for that. When we get there we'll go north until we reach the edge of the plain, and then follow the mountains back to the Observatory. We'll be home tomorrow or the next day.'

For nearly four hours uneventful landscape flowed past the windows as Jamieson drove the tractor across the Sea. From time to time they passed low ridges and small craters only a few hundred feet high but for the greater part of their journey the terrain was almost flat.

After a while Wheeler ceased to take much notice of it and tried to do some reading but the jolting of the machine made it very uncomfortable and he soon gave up the attempt. In any case the only book in the tractor was Maclaurin's *Studies of the Dynamics of Multiple Star Systems* and this *was* supposed to be a holiday after all.

'Sid,' began Wheeler abruptly. 'What do you think about the Federation? You've met a lot of their people.'

'Yes and liked them. Pity you weren't here when the last crowd left. We had about a dozen of them at the Observatory, studying the telescope mounting. They're thinking of building a fifteen-hundred-inch reflector on one of the moons of Saturn, you know.'

'That would be some job – I always said we were too close to the Sun here. But to get back to the argument – did they strike you as likely to start a quarrel with Earth?'

'It's difficult to say. They were very open and friendly with us but then we were all scientists together and that helps a lot. It might have been different if we'd been politicians or civil servants.'

'Dammit, we *are* civil servants! Who pays our salaries?'

'Yes, but you know what I mean. I could tell that they didn't care a lot for Earth though they were too polite to say so. There's no doubt that they're annoyed about the uranium allocation – I often heard them complain about it. Their main point was that they *had* to have atomic power to open up the cold outer planets and that Earth could manage quite easily with alternative sources of energy. After all, she's done so for a good many thousand years.'

'Which side do you think is right?'

'I don't know. But I will say this – if more uranium does turn up and Earth doesn't let the Federation have a bigger share of it, then we shall be in the wrong.'

'I don't think that's likely to happen.'

'Don't be so sure. As old Mole said, there are a lot of people on Earth who are afraid of the Federation and don't want to give it any more power. The Federation knows that and it may grab first and argue afterwards.'

'Hm. Then it's nice to know that our friends out by Pico aren't mining the stuff, after all,' said Wheeler thoughtfully. '*Ouch* – was that necessary?'

'Sorry. But if you will keep me talking you can't expect me to avoid all the cracks. Looks as though the suspension wants adjusting. I'll have to turn Ferdy in for an overhaul when we get back. Ah, that's Mount Helicon coming up over there. No talking while I concentrate on the driving for the next few miles – the next section's a bit tricky.'

The tractor turned northward and slowly the great wall of the beautiful *Sinus Iridum* – the Bay of Rainbows – rose over the horizon until it stretched east and west as far as the eye could see. So overwhelming was the sight that Wheeler was voluntarily silent and sat for the next twenty miles without a word while Jamieson drove the machine toward the three-mile-high cliffs ahead.

He remembered his first glimpse of the *Sinus Iridum* through a two-inch telescope on Earth many years ago – it seemed scarcely possible that now he was actually skirting its towering walls. What unbelievable changes the twentieth century had brought! It needed a considerable effort to realise that at its beginning man had not even possessed flying machines, still less dreamed of crossing space.

The history of two thousand years seemed to have been crowded into the single century with its vast technical achievements and two tremendous wars. In its first half the air had been conquered more thoroughly than had the sea in all the millennia before.

In its closing quarter the first crude rockets had reached the Moon and the age-long isolation of the human race had ended. Within a single generation there were children to whom the word 'home' no longer conveyed the green fields and blue skies of Earth, so swift had been the colonisation of the inner planets.

History, it has been said, never repeats itself but historical situations recur. Inevitably the new worlds began to loosen their ties with Earth. Their populations were still very small compared with those of the mother world but they contained the most brilliant and active minds the race possessed. Free at last from the crushing burden of tradition they planned to build civilisations which would avoid the mistakes of the past. The aim was a noble one – it might yet succeed.

Venus had been the first world to declare its independence and set up a separate government. For a little while there had been considerable tension but good sense had prevailed and since the beginning of the twenty-first century only minor disagreements had disturbed relations between the two governments. Ten years later Mars and the four inhabited moons of Jupiter – Io, Europa, Ganymede and Callisto – had formed the union which was later to become the Federation of the Outer Planets.

Wheeler had never been to any of these outer worlds. Indeed this was the first time he had even left his native Earth. Like most terrestrials he was a little scared of the Federation though the scientist in him made him admire many of its achievements. He did not believe in the possibility of war but if there were 'incidents' – as earlier statesmen would have put it – his loyalties lay with Earth.

The tractor rolled to a halt and Jamieson got up from the controls, stretching himself mightily. 'Well, that's enough for today. Let's have some food before I turn cannibal.'

One corner of the tractor was fitted up as a tiny galley but the two explorers were much too lazy to use it and had been living entirely on meals already prepared in the Observatory, which could be heated at the turn of a switch. They did not believe in unnecessary hardships. If a psychologist had examined the machine's stores he would have been convinced that its passengers suffered from an almost pathological fear of starvation.

Since it was always daylight they slept, ate, argued and drove whenever the spirit moved them. For nearly thirty hours they worked their way slowly along the foot of the Bay's mighty cliffs, pausing now and then to don space-suits and carry out explorations on foot. They found little but minerals, although Wheeler was greatly excited by the discovery of a peculiar red moss his friend had never seen before.

So little of the Moon had been explored in detail that it was quite possibly new to science and Wheeler pictured himself receiving all kinds of honours from the botanical world. These hopes were rudely shattered by the staff biologist a couple of days later but they were enjoyable while they lasted.

The Sun was still high when they were once again on the Alpine slopes though noon was long past and the thin rind of the crescent Earth was visible in the sky. Wheeler had enjoyed the trip but was getting tired of the cramped quarters. Also he was becoming more and more aware of accumulated aches and pains caused by the bumping of the vehicle over the worst ground any machine could possibly travel.

It was pleasant to get back to the bustle of life in the common-room, even though the same ancient magazines were displayed and the same people were monopolising the best chairs. Very little had happened, it seemed, during their short absence.

The main topic of conversation was the complete breaking off of diplomatic relations between the Director's young and extremely pretty private secretary and the chief engineer, generally supposed to be her most favoured suitor. This quite outshadowed more important items such as the recent discovery, by an incredible feat of mathematics, that van Haarden's planet possessed a system of rings like that of Saturn.

And not until they had heard the first news broadcast from Earth did Wheeler and Jamieson learned that the Federation's latest request for reconsideration of the uranium agreement had been received and rejected. 'That will make old Mole excited,' commented Wheeler.

'Yes – who would have thought the old boy took such an interest in politics. Let's have a word with him.'

The old astronomer was in the far corner of the room, talking volubly with one of the junior physicists. He broke off when he saw the newcomers.

'So you're back. I thought you would break your necks out in the *Mare*. Seen any mooncalves?'

The references to H. G. Wells' fabulous beasts was a lunar joke of such long standing that many terrestrials took it quite seriously and thought the creatures actually existed.

'No, or we would have brought one back for the menu. How are things going?'

'Nothing out of the ordinary as far as I'm concerned. But Reynolds here thinks he has found something.'

'Think – I *know*! Two hours ago all my recorders went haywire and I'm still trying to find what has happened.'

'Which recorders?'

'The magnetic field strength meters. Usually the field is pretty constant except when there is a magnetic storm and we always know when to expect those. But today all the indicators have gone clean off the graph paper and I've been running around the Observatory to find if anyone has switched on something outside in the way of electro-magnetics. I've eliminated everything, so it must be external. It's still on and Jones is trying to get a bearing on it while I come up for a breather.'

'Sure it's not a storm? You could find out from Earth – it would have hit them too.'

'I checked on that – in any case there has been no unusual solar activity so that's ruled out. Also it's far too intense and it *must* be man-made for it keeps going on and off abruptly. Just as if someone's working a switch.'

'Sounds very mysterious. Ah, here's Jones. By the look of him I'd say the Welsh Wonder has found something.'

Another physicist had just hurried into the room, trailing several yards of recording tape behind him. 'Got it!' he cried triumphantly. 'Look!' He spread the tapes out over the nearest table, collecting some dirty looks from a party of bridge players who were heading toward it.

'This is the magnetic record. I've reduced the sensitivity of one of the recorders until it no longer shoots off the paper. You can see exactly what's happening now. At these points the field starts to rise rapidly to over a thousand times its normal value. It stays that way for a couple of minutes and then drops back to normal – so.'

With his finger Jones traced the rise and fall of the magnetic field. 'There are two things to note. The rise isn't instantaneous but takes just over a second in each case. It seems to be exponential. That's just what happens, of course, when you switch on the current in an electromagnet. And the fall is just the same while the plateau in between is perfectly flat. The whole thing is obviously artificial.'

'That's exactly what I said in the first place! But there's no such magnet on the Observatory.'

'Wait a minute – I haven't finished yet. You'll see that the field jumps up

349

at fairly regular intervals and I've carefully noted the times at which it's come on. I've had the whole staff going through the tapes of every automatic recorder in the place to see if anything else has happened at the same instants.

'Quite a lot has – nearly all the records show some fluctuations. The cosmic ray intensity, for instance, falls off when the field goes on. I suppose all the primaries are being swept into it so that we don't receive them. But the oddest of all is the seismograph tape.'

'*Seismograph!* Who ever heard of a magnetic moonquake?'

'That's what I thought at first, but here it is. Now if you look carefully you can see that each of the little moonquakes arrives just about a minute and a half after the jolt in the magnetic field, which presumably travels at the velocity of light. We know how fast waves travel through the lunar rock – it's about a mile a second.

'So we are forced to the conclusion that about a hundred miles away someone is switching on the most colossal magnetic field that's ever been made. It's so huge it wrecks our instruments, which means that it must run into millions of gauss.

'The earthquake – sorry, moonquake – must be a secondary effect. There's a lot of magnetic rock round here and I imagine it must get quite a shock when that field goes on. You probably wouldn't notice the quake even if you were where it started but our seismographs are so sensitive they'll spot meteors falling anywhere within twenty miles.'

'That's about the best piece of high-speed research I've ever encountered.'

'Thanks, but there's still more to come. Next I went up to Signals to find if they'd noticed anything. And were they in a rage! All communication has been wrecked by bursts of static at exactly the same instants as our magnetic barrages. What's more they'd taken bearings on the source – and with my ranges we have it pinpointed exactly. It's coming from somewhere in the Sea of Rains, about five miles south of Pico.'

'Holy smoke!' said Wheeler. 'We might have guessed!'

The two physicists pounced on him simultaneously. 'Why did you say that?'

Remembering his promise Wheeler looked hesitantly at Jamieson, who came to the rescue. 'We've just come back from Pico. There's a Government research project going on out there. Very hush-hush – you can't get near the place. It's a big dome out on the plain, at least twice the size of the Observatory. Must have a lot of stuff in it from what they say.'

'So *that's* what those ships are doing out over the *Mare*. Did you have a chance to see anything?'

'Not a thing.'

'Pity – we must take a trip across.'

'I shouldn't if I were you. They were very polite to us – but next time I think it might be different. They told us they didn't want visitors.'

'So you got into the place then?'

'Yes.'

'What a waste. They *would* let in a couple of dumb astronomers who wouldn't know a dynamo from a transformer. Now we won't have a chance.'

'Oh, I suppose you'll know all about it some day.'

IV

It was one of those remarks that was to come true sooner than anyone could have expected. For the rumours had been correct – the greatest of all uranium deposits had been discovered on the Moon. And the Federation knew it.

Looking back from our vantage point upon events now safely buried in history we can see the merits of both sides. The rulers of Earth honestly feared the Federation and its revolutionary ideals. The fear was not entirely rational – it was born of a deeper subconscious realisation that Earth's pioneering days were done and that the future lay with those who were already at the frontiers of the Solar System, planning the first onslaught against the stars.

Earth was weary after her epic history and the effort she had put forth to conquer the nearer worlds – those worlds which had so inexplicably turned against her as long ago the American colonies had turned against their motherland. In both cases the causes were similar and in both the eventual outcomes equally advantageous to mankind.

Only for one thing would Earth still fight – for the preservation of a way of living which, although outmoded, was all she knew. Let us not therefore too harshly judge those leaders who, fearing the mounting strength of the Federation, attempted to deprive it of the metal which would have given it almost limitless power.

For its part the Federation had not been free from blame. Amongst the idealists and scientists, who had been attracted by the promise of the outer worlds, were not a few men of more ruthless breed, men who had long known that a breach with Earth would one day be inevitable. It was these who had planned the research which culminated in the cruisers *Acheron* and *Eridanus* and later the superdreadnought *Phlegethon*.

Those ships were made possible by the invention of the Wilson or accelerationless drive. So universal is the Wilson drive today that it is difficult to realise it was being perfected in secret for ten years before the Solar System learned of its existence. Around that drive the Federation built its three warships and their armament.

Even today little has been revealed of the weapons with which the Battle of the Plain was fought. Atomic power and the tremendous development of electronic engineering during the twentieth century had made them possible. It was never intended that these fearful weapons be used – the mere revelation of their existence would, it was hoped, wring the necessary concessions from Earth.

It was a dangerous policy but one which might have worked had not Earth possessed a superb intelligence service. When at last the Federation put forth its strength, countermeasures had already been taken. In addition Earth had by supreme good fortune just discovered a branch of radiation physics which made possible a weapon of which its opponents knew nothing and against which they had no defence.

The Federation, expecting no opposition whatsoever, had made the age-old mistake of underestimating its opponent.

It was nightfall on the Observatory meridian. All the free members of the staff had gathered, as was the custom, around the observation windows to say farewell to the Sun they would not see again for fourteen days. Only the highest mountain peaks were still catching the last slanting light. Long since the valleys had been engulfed in darkness. The sun's disc was already invisible. As the minutes crawled by the splendour died slowly on the blazing mountain spires as though reluctant to leave them.

And now only a blazing peak could still be seen, far out over the hidden ramparts of the Alps. The Sea of Rains had been in darkness for many hours but Pico's inaccessible crown had not yet sunk into the cone of night sweeping round the Moon. A lonely beacon, it still defied the gathering dusk.

In silence the little group of men and women watched the darkness flooding up the great mountain's slopes. Their remoteness from Earth and the rest of the human race made more poignant the sense of sadness that is the heritage of Man whenever he watches the setting of the Sun.

The light ebbed and died on the distant peak – the long lunar night had begun. When in fourteen days the Sun rose again it would look down upon a vastly different Sea of Rains. The astronomers had paid their last respects to the proud mountain that seemed the very symbol of eternity. When the dawn came it would have vanished forever.

During the next two weeks, there was little relaxation for anyone at the Observatory. Wheeler and Jamieson, who were studying the light curves of variable stars in the Andromeda nebula, had been allotted the use of the thousand-inch telescope for one hour in every thirty. Nearly a score of other research programmes had to be dovetailed according to an elaborate timetable – and woe betide anyone who tried to exceed his allowance!

The dome of the Observatory was now open to the stars and the astronomers were wearing light space-suits which scarcely restricted their movements. Wheeler was taking a series of photometer readings which his colleague was recording when their suit radios began to hum with life. A general announcement was coming through. These were very common and the two men took no notice until they realised that it was directed at them.

'Will Dr Jamieson please report to the Director at once? Dr Jamieson to report to the Director at once, please.'

enterprise that gave it an additional charm. Not a few tractors had been lost and although rigorous safety precautions were enforced there was always a chance that something might go wrong.

The almost complete absence of any atmosphere on the Moon had made economical flying impossible since rockets could not be used for journeys of only a few score miles. So practically all short-range lunar travel was done in the powerful electric tractors universally known as *Caterpillars* or, more briefly, 'cats'.

They were really small space-ships mounted on broad tracks that enabled them to go anywhere within reason, even over the appallingly jagged surface of the Moon. On fairly smooth terrain they could do up to eighty miles an hour but normally they were lucky to manage half that speed. The low gravity enabled them to climb fantastic slopes and they could if necessary haul themselves out of vertical pits by means of their built-in winches. One could live in the larger models for months at a time in reasonable comfort.

Jamieson was a more-than-expert driver and knew the road down the mountains perfectly. As lunar highways went it was one of the best and carried a good deal of traffic between the Observatory and the port of Aristillus. Nevertheless for the first hour Wheeler felt that his hair would never lie down again.

It usually took newcomers to the Moon a long time to realise that slopes of one-in-one were perfectly safe if treated with respect. Perhaps it was just as well that Wheeler was a novice for Jamieson's technique was so unorthodox that it would have filled a more experienced passenger with real alarm.

Why Jamieson was such a desperate driver was a paradox that had caused much discussion among his colleagues. Normally he was painstaking and careful, even languid in his movements. No one had ever seen him really annoyed or excited. Many people thought him lazy but that was a libel. He would spend weeks working out a theory until it was absolutely watertight – and then would put it away for two or three months to have another look at it later.

Yet once at the controls of a cat this quiet and peaceloving astronomer became a daredevil driver who held the unofficial record for almost every tractor drive in the northern hemisphere. More than likely the explanation lay in a boyhood desire to be a space-ship pilot, a dream that had been foiled by physical disability.

They shot down the last foothills of the Alps and out into the Sea of Rains like a miniature avalanche. Now that they were on lower ground Wheeler began to breathe again, thankful to have left the vertiginous slopes behind. He was not so pleased when with a colossal crash Jamieson drove the tractor off the road and out into the barren plain.

'Hey, where are you going?' he cried.

Jamieson laughed at his consternation. 'This is where the rough stuff begins. The road goes southwest to Aristillus here and we want to get to

Pico. So from now on we're in country where only half a dozen tractors have ever been before. To cheer you up I might say Ferdinand is one of them.'

'Ferdinand' was now plunging ahead at twenty miles an hour with a swaying motion Wheeler found rather disconcerting. If he had lived in an age that had known of ships he might have been familiar with it.

The view was disappointing, as it always is at 'sea' level on the Moon, owing to the nearness of the horizon. Pico and all the more distant mountains had sunk below the skyline and the plain ahead looked uninviting as it lay in the blazing sun. For three hours they forged steadily across it, passing tiny craterlets and yawning crevasses that seemed of indefinite depth.

Once Jamieson stopped the tractor and the two men went out in their space-suits to have a look at a particularly fine specimen. It was about a mile wide and the Sun, now nearly at the zenith, was shining straight into it. The bottom was quite flat as though, when the rock had split, lava had flowed in from the depths beneath and solidified. Wheeler found it very difficult to judge just how far away the floor was.

Jamieson's voice came over the suit radio. 'See those rocks down there?'

The other strained his eyes and could barely make out a few markings on the apparently smooth surface far below.

'Yes, I think I see the ones you mean. What about them?'

'How big would you say they are?'

'Oh, I don't know – maybe a yard across.'

'Hmmm. See the smaller one near the side?'

'Yes.'

'Well, that isn't a rock. That was a tractor that missed the bend.'

'Good Lord! How? It's plain enough.'

'Yes, but this is midday. Toward evening, when the Sun's low, it's the easiest thing in the world to mistake a shadow for a crevasse – and the other way round.'

Wheeler was very quiet as they walked back to their machine. Perhaps, after all, they had been safer in the mountains.

At length the great rock mass of Pico came once more into sight until presently it dominated the landscape. One of the most famous landmarks on the Moon it rose sheer out of the Sea of Rains, from which, ages ago, volcanic action had extruded it. On Earth it would have been completely unclimbable. Even under one-sixth of Earth's gravity only two men had ever reached its summit. One of them was still there.

Moving slowly over the jagged terrain the tractor skirted the flanks of the mountain. Jamieson was searching for a place where the cliffs could be scaled so they could get a good view out over the Sea. After travelling several miles he found a spot that met with his approval.

'Climb those cliffs? Not on your life!' expostulated Wheeler when Jamieson explained his plan of action. 'Why, they're practically vertical and half a mile high!'

Wheeler looked at his companion in surprise. 'Hello, what have *you* been up to? Bad language again on the station frequency?'

This was the commonest crime in the Observatory. When one was wearing a space-suit it was often difficult to remember that the person being addressed was not necessarily the only listener. The possible indiscretions were legion and most of them had been committed at one time or another.

'No, *my* conscience at any rate is clear. You'll have to get someone else to finish this job. See you later.'

In spite of his confidence Jamieson was relieved to find the Director in a friendly though worried mood. He was not alone. Sitting in his office was a middle-aged man nursing a briefcase and wearing clothes that indicated he had only just arrived. The Director wasted no time in formalities.

'Jamieson, you're the best tractor driver we have. I gather that you have been to the new establishment out in the *Mare Imbrium*. How long would it take you to get there?'

'What – now? – at night?'

'Yes.'

Jamieson stood speechless for a moment, completely taken aback by the proposal. He had never driven at night. Only once had he been out as late as a day before sunset and that was bad enough. The inky shadows had lain everywhere, indistinguishable from crevasses. It needed a violent effort of will to drive into them – and even worse the real crevasses were indistinguishable from shadows.

The Director, seeing his hesitation, spoke again. 'It won't be as bad as you think. The Earth's nearly full and there'll be plenty of light. There's no real danger if you're careful – but Dr Fletcher wants to get to Pico in three hours. Can you do it?'

Jamieson was silent for a moment. Then he said, 'I'm not sure but I'll try. Is it permissible to ask what this is all about?'

The Director glanced at the man with the briefcase. 'Well, Doctor?'

The other shook his head and answered in a quiet and unusually well-modulated voice, 'Sorry – I can only tell you that I've got to reach the installation as soon as humanly possible. I was on my way by rocket when the underjets started to cut and we had to come down at Aristillus.

'It will take twenty-four hours to fix the ship, so I decided to go by tractor. It's only taken me three hours to get here but they told me I'd need an Observatory driver for the next lap. In fact, they mentioned you.'

Jamieson was somewhat amused by the mixture of encouragement and flattery. 'The road to Aristillus happens to be the only decent highway on the Moon,' he said. 'I've done a hundred on it before now. You'll find things very different out on the *Mare* – even in daylight, thirty's a good average. I'm perfectly willing to have a shot at it but you won't enjoy the ride.'

'I'll take that risk – and thanks for helping.'

Jamieson turned to the Director. 'How about getting back, Sir?'

'I leave that entirely to you, Jamieson. If you think best stay there until morning. Otherwise come back as soon as you've had a rest. Whom do you want as a second driver?'

It was a stringent rule that no one could leave the Observatory without a companion. Apart from the danger of physical accident the psychological effect of the lunar silences upon an isolated man was sometimes enough to unbalance the sanest minds.

'I'll take Wheeler, sir.'

'Can he drive?'

'Yes, I taught him myself.'

'Good. Well, the best of luck – and don't come back until dawn unless you feel perfectly safe.'

Wheeler was already waiting at the tractor when Jamieson and the stranger arrived. The Director must have called him and given him full instructions, for he carried a couple of suitcases with his own and Jamieson's personal belongings. They hoped it would not be necessary to spend the seven days until dawn at the radio station but it was best to be prepared.

The great outer doors of the 'Stable,' as the tractor garage was called, slid smoothly open and the artificial light flooded out onto the roadway. There was a faint scurry of dust as the air rushed out of the lock. Then the tractor moved slowly forward through the open door.

The roadway down the mountain looked very different now. A fortnight earlier, it had been a blinding ribbon of concrete, baking in the glare of the noonday Sun. Now it seemed almost self-luminous under the blue-green light of the gibbous Earth, which dominated a sky so full of stars that the familiar constellations were almost lost. The coastline of western Europe was clearly visible but the Mediterranean area was blotted out by dazzling clouds, too bright to look upon.

Jamieson wasted no time in sightseeing. He knew the road perfectly and the light was superb – safer than daylight because less overpowering. Out in the treacherous shadows of the Sea it would be very different but here he could do eighty with ease.

It seemed to Wheeler that the ride down the mountain road was even more shattering than it had been during the day. The ghostly quality of the Earth-light made it difficult to judge distances but the landscape was sliding past at an appalling speed.

He glanced at the mysterious passenger, who seemed to be taking the ride very calmly. It was time to strike up an acquaintance – besides, he was anxious to discover what the whole business was about. Perhaps a calculated indiscretion might produce useful results.

'It's rather lucky we've been this way before,' began Wheeler. 'We visited the new radio station only a fortnight ago.'

'Radio station?' said the passenger, his surprisingly level voice betraying just a trace of perplexity.

Wheeler was taken aback. 'Yes, the place we're going to.'

The other looked puzzled. Then he asked in a quiet voice, 'Who told you what it was?'

Wheeler decided to be a little more discreet. 'Oh, we managed to see a bit of the place while we were over there. I took a course in elementary electronics at Astrotech and recognised some of the gear.'

For some reason the other appeared highly amused. He was about to reply when suddenly the tractor gave a jolt which roughly shot them both into the air.

'Better hang on to your seats now,' called Jamieson over his shoulder. 'This is where we leave the road. I think the suspension can take it – thank goodness I've just had it checked.'

For the next few miles Wheeler was too breathless to do any further talking but he had time to think over his passenger's surprising reactions. Certain doubts began to form in his mind. Who, for example, had ever heard of a radio station generating colossal magnetic fields?

Wheeler looked at his passenger again, wishing he could read minds. He wondered what was in that tightly held briefcase with the triple locks. There were initials on it – he could just see them – J.A.F. They conveyed nothing to him.

Doctor James Alan Fletcher, Ph.D., was not at all happy. He had never been in a tractor before and sincerely hoped he never would be again. Up to the present his stomach had behaved itself but a few more jolts like the last would be too much for it. He was glad to see that the machine's thoughtful designers had foreseen such accidents and made certain provisions for them. That at least was reassuring.

Jamieson was sitting intently at the controls and had not spoken again since leaving the road. The ground over which the tractor was now travelling seemed bumpy but safe and the machine was averaging about fifty miles an hour. Presently it would enter a range of low hills a few miles ahead and its speed would be considerably reduced. So far, however, Jamieson had managed to avoid the shadows which the Earthlight was casting from every rise in the ground.

Fletcher decided to ignore the landscape outside. It was too lonely and overpowering. The brilliant light of the mother world – fifty times as bright as the full Moon on Earth – enhanced rather than diminished the impression of frightful cold. Those whitely gleaming rocks, Fletcher knew, were colder than liquid air. This was no place for man.

By comparison the tractor's interior was warm and homey. There were touches that brought earth very close. Who, Fletcher wondered, had been responsible for the photograph of a certain famous television star which was pinned against one wall? Wheeler caught his enquiring gaze and with a grin jerked his thumb towards the intent curve of Jamieson's back.

Suddenly darkness fell with an abruptness that was shocking. Simultaneously Jamieson brought the tractor almost to a halt. The twin beams of the machine's dirigible searchlights began to roam over the ground ahead and Fletcher realised that they had entered the shadow of a small hill. For the first time he understood what the lunar night really meant.

Slowly the machine edged forward at five or ten miles an hour, the searchlights anxiously exploring every foot of the ground ahead. For twenty minutes the agonisingly slow progress continued. Then the tractor surmounted a rise and Fletcher was forced to shield his eyes from the glare of Earthlight on the rock ahead. The shadow fell away as the machine picked up speed again and the welcome disc of the Earth appeared in the sky.

Fletcher looked at his watch and was surprised to see that they had been on their way less than fifty minutes. It was two minutes to the hour and automatically his eyes went to the radio. 'Mind if I switch on the news?'

'Go right ahead – it's tuned to Manilius I, but you can get Earth direct if you want to.'

The great lunar relay station came in crystal clear with no trace of fading. During the hours of darkness the Moon's feeble ionosphere had been completely dispersed and there were no reflected signals to interfere with the ground ray.

Fletcher was surprised to see that the tractor chronometer was over a second fast. Then he realised that it was set to lunar time, that the signal he was listening to had just bridged the quarter million miles gulf from Earth. It was a chilling reminder of his remoteness from home.

Then there came a delay so long that Wheeler turned up the volume to check that the set was still operating. After a full minute the announcer spoke, his voice striving desperately to be as impersonal as ever. 'This is Earth calling. The following statement has just been issued from Berne –

'The Federation of the Outer Planets has informed the Government of Earth that it intends to seize certain portions of the Moon and that any attempt to resist this action will be countered by force.

'This Government is taking all necessary steps to preserve the integrity of the Moon. A further announcement will be issued as soon as possible. In the meantime it is emphasised that there is no immediate danger as there are no hostile ships within twenty hours' flight of Earth.

'This is Earth. Stand by.'

V

A sudden silence fell. Only the hiss of the carrier and the faint crackle of infinitely distant static still issued from the speaker. Jamieson had brought the tractor to a halt and had turned around in his seat to face Fletcher.

'So this is why you are in such a hurry,' he said quietly.

Fletcher nodded. Colour was slowly draining back to his face. 'We did not expect it so soon.'

There was a pause during which Jamieson made no effort to restart the tractor. Only the nervous drumming of Fletcher's fingers on his briefcase betrayed his tension. Then Jamieson spoke again. 'And will this journey of yours make any real difference?'

Fletcher looked at him for a long time before he answered. 'I'll tell you when we get there,' he said. 'Now, for God's sake, start driving!'

There was a long silence. Then Jamieson turned back to the controls and restarted the engine. 'You'll be there in ninety minutes,' he said.

He did not speak again during the journey. Only Wheeler realised what it must have cost him to make his decision. That Jamieson's loyalties were divided he could understand, for there were few scientists who did not share many of the Federation's nobler ideals. He was glad that Jamieson had gone forward, yet if he had turned back he would have respected his motives none the less.

The radio was now pouring out a stream of unintelligible coded instructions. No further news had come through and Wheeler wondered just what steps were being taken to defend the Moon. There was nothing that could be done in a few hours though the final touches could be put to plans already prepared. He began to suspect the nature of Fletcher's business.

The latter had now opened his briefcase. It was full of photostats of extremely complicated circuits which he made no attempt to conceal. A single glance showed Wheeler that any secrecy was unnecessary for the mass of symbols and wiring was completely meaningless to him. Fletcher was ticking off various amendments against a list of corrections, as if making some final check. Wheeler could not help thinking that he was probably doing it more to pass the time than anything else.

Fletcher was not a brave man – seldom in his life had he known the need for so primitive a virtue as physical courage. He was rather surprised at his absence of fear, now that the crisis was almost upon him. Well before dawn, he knew, he would probably be dead.

The thought gave him more annoyance than fear. It meant that his paper on wave propagation, all his work on the new beam, would remain unfinished. And he would never be able to claim the massive travelling allowance he had been planning as compensation for this frightful ride across the Sea of Rains.

A long time later a cry from Wheeler broke into his reverie. 'Here we are!'

The tractor had surmounted a rise in the ground. Still a good many miles ahead the great metal dome was glinting in the Earthlight. It seemed utterly deserted but within, Fletcher knew, it would be seething with furious activity.

A searchlight reached out and speared the tractor. Jamieson drove steadily forward. He knew it was only a symbol, that for many miles invisible radiations had been scrutinising them intently. He flashed the identification letters of the machine and raced forward over the nearly level ground.

The tractor came to a halt in the monstrous shadow of the dome. Men were awaiting them by the airlock. Fletcher was already wearing his space-suit and his hand was on the door almost before the tractor came to a stop. 'Just wait here a minute,' he said, 'while I find what's happened.'

He was through the lock before the others could say a word. They saw him give a few hasty instructions and then he disappeared into the dome.

He was gone for less than five minutes, though to the astronomers fretting in the tractor it seemed an age. Abruptly he was back, the outer door of the airlock slamming violently behind him. He was in far too much of a hurry to remove his helmet and his voice came muffled through the plastic sphere.

'I haven't time for explanation,' he said, addressing Jamieson, 'but I'll keep the promise I made you. This place' – he gestured towards the dome – 'covers the uranium the Federation wants to get. It's well defended and that's going to give our greedy friends a bit of a shock. But it has offensive armament as well. I designed it, and I'm here to make the final adjustments before it can go into action. So that answers your question about the importance of the journey.

'The Earth may owe you a greater debt than it can ever pay. Don't interrupt – this is more important. The radio was wrong about the twenty hours of safety. Federal ships have been detected a day out – but they're coming in ten times as fast as anything that's ever gone into space before. We've not much more than an hour left before they get here.

'You could stay, but for your own safety I advise you to turn round and drive like hell back to the Observatory. If anything starts to happen while you're still out in the open get under cover as quickly as possible. Go down into a crevasse – anywhere you can find shelter – and stay there until it's over. Now goodbye and good luck.'

He was gone again before either of the two men could speak. The outer door slammed once more and the *Airlock Clear* indicator flashed on. They saw the dome entrance snap open and close behind him. Then the tractor was alone in the building's enormous shadow.

Nowhere else was there any sign of life but suddenly the framework of the machine began to vibrate at a steadily rising frequency. The meters on the control panel wavered madly, the lights dimmed and then it was all over.

Everything was normal again but some tremendous field of force had swept out from the dome and was even now expanding into space. It left the two men with an overpowering impression of energies awaiting the signal for their release. They began to understand the urgency of Fletcher's warning. The whole deserted landscape seemed tense with expectation.

Swiftly the caterpillar backed away from the dome and spun around on its tracks. Its twin searchlights threw their pools of light across the undulating plain. Then at full speed it tore away into the lunar night. Jamieson realised that the more miles he could put between himself and the mine the greater their chances of ever reaching the Observatory again.

Dr Molton was passing through the gallery of the thousand-inch dome when the first announcement electrified the Observatory. Through all the speakers and over the radio of every space-suit in the station the Director's voice came roaring.

'Attention everybody! The Federation is about to attack the Moon. All members of the staff, with the exception of the telescope crew, are to go to the vaults immediately. I repeat, immediately. The telescope crew will remove the mirror at once and will take it to the resurfacing room. That is all. Move!'

For a dozen heartbeats of life of the Observatory came to a standstill. Then with a slow majestic motion the thousand-ton shutters of the dome closed like folding petals. Air began to pour into the building from hundreds of vents as the telescope swung around to the vertical and the work of removing the mirror from its cell began.

When he started to run, Dr Molton found that his legs seemed to have turned to water. His hands were trembling as he opened the nearest emergency locker and chose a space-suit that approximately fitted him. Though he was not one of the telescope crew he had work to do in the dome now that the emergency had arrived. There were the precious auxiliary instruments to be dismantled and removed to safety and that job alone would take hours.

As he began his work with the rest of the team, Molton's jangling nerves slowly returned to normal. Perhaps, after all, nothing serious would happen. Twenty years ago it had been a false alarm. Surely the Federation would not be so foolish— he checked his thoughts with a wry grimace. It was just such wishful thinking on Wheeler's part that had opened their discussion a fortnight ago. How he wished that Wheeler had been right!

Swiftly the minutes fled by as one by one the priceless instruments went down into the vaults. The great mirror was now free in its cell and the hoists had been attached to the supporting framework. No one had noticed the passage of time.

Glancing up at the clock Molton was amazed to see that nearly two hours had passed since the first radio warning. He wondered when there would be any further news. The whole thing still seemed a fantastic dream. The thought of danger was inconceivable in this remote and peaceful spot.

The mirror-truck moved soundlessly up the ramp into its position beneath the telescope. Inch by inch the immense disc was lowered until the hoists could be removed. The whole operation had taken two hours and fifteen minutes – a record which was never likely to be surpassed.

The truck was now halfway down the ramp. Molton breathed a sigh of relief – his work also was nearly finished. Only the spectroscope had to be moved and— *What was that?*

The whole building suddenly trembled violently. A shudder ran through the mighty framework of the telescope. For a moment the space-suited figures swarming round its base stood motionless. Then there was a concerted rush to the observation windows.

It was impossible to look through them. Far out above the Sea of Rains something was blazing with a brilliance beyond all imagination. The Sun itself by comparison would have been scarcely visible.

Again the building trembled and a deep organ note ran through the mighty girders of the telescope. The mirror truck was now safely away, descending deep into the caverns far down in the solid rock. No conceivable danger could harm it there.

And now the hammer-blows were coming thick and fast with scarcely a pause between them. The rectangles of intolerable light cast by the observation windows on the floor and walls of the dome were shifting hither and thither as if their sources were moving swiftly round the sky.

Molton ran to get some sun filters so that he could look out into the glare without wrecking his eyes. But he was not allowed to do so. Once again the Director's voice came roaring from the speakers. *'Down into the vaults at once! Everybody!'*

As he left the dome Molton risked one backward glance over his shoulder. It seemed as if the great telescope were already on fire, so brilliant was the light flowing through the windows from the inferno outside.

Strangely enough Molton's last thought as he went down to the vaults was not for his own safety nor that of the priceless telescope. He had suddenly remembered that Wheeler and Jamieson were somewhere in the Sea of Rains. He wondered if they would escape whatever hell was brewing out there on the barren hills.

Quite unaccountably he recalled Wheeler's ready smile, the fact that it had never been long absent even during those frequent periods when he was officially in disgrace. And Jamieson too, though quieter and more reserved, had been an intelligent and friendly colleague. The Observatory would miss them badly if they never returned.

The storm broke when Jamieson had driven scarcely a dozen miles from the dome, for the speed of the oncoming ships had been grossly underestimated. Earth's far-flung detector screens had been designed to give warning of meteors only and these machines were infinitely faster than any meteor that had ever entered the Solar System.

The instruments had flickered once and then the ships were through. They had not even started to check their speed until they were a thousand miles from the surface of the Moon. In the last few miles of their trajectory the accelerationless drive had brought them to rest at nearly half a million gravities.

There was no warning of any kind. Suddenly the grey rocks of the Sea of

Rains were lit with a brilliance they had never before known in all their history. Paralysed by the glare Jamieson brought the tractor to a grinding halt until his eyes had readjusted themselves.

His first impression was that someone had turned a searchlight upon the machine. Then he realised that the source of the light was many miles overhead. High against the stars, which it had dimmed almost to extinction, an enormous rocket flare was guttering and dying. As he watched, it slowly faded and for a little while the stars returned to their own.

'Well,' said Wheeler in an awed voice, 'I guess this is it.'

Hanging motionless against the Milky Way were the three greatest ships that the two astronomers, or indeed most men, had ever seen. It was not possible to judge their distance – one could not tell whether they were ten or twenty miles overhead. They were so huge that the sense of perspective seemed somehow to have failed.

For several minutes the great ships made no attempt to move. Once again, though this time with even more reason, Jamieson felt the sense of brooding expectancy he had known in the shadow of the dome. Then another flare erupted amongst the stars and the world outside the tractor was overwhelmed with light. But as yet the ships had made no hostile move.

The commander of the *Phlegethon* was still in communication with Earth though he realised now that there was no hope of avoiding conflict. He was bitterly disappointed – he was also more than a little puzzled by the tone of quiet confidence with which Earth had rejected his ultimatum. He still did not know that the building below him was anything other than a mine. A mine it certainly was but it had kept its other secrets well.

The time limit expired – Earth had refused even to reply to the last appeal. The two watchers below knew only that one of the great ships had suddenly spun on its axis so that its prow pointed towards the Moon. Then, soundlessly, four arrows of fire split the darkness and plunged toward the plain.

'Rocket torpedoes!' gasped Wheeler. 'Time we started to move!'

'Yes – into your space-suit! I'll drive Ferdy between those rocks but we'll have to leave him there. We passed a crack just now that will protect us from anything except a direct hit. I made a note of it at the time but didn't think we'd have to use it so quickly.'

The rock-borne concussion reached them as they were struggling with the fittings of their space-suits. The tractor was jerked off the ground and slammed back with a jar that almost knocked them off their feet.

'If that scored a hit the mine's done for!' exclaimed Wheeler. 'How can they fight back anyway? I'm sure they've got no guns there.'

'We certainly wouldn't have seen them if they had,' grunted Jamieson as he adjusted his helmet. He finished his remarks over the suit radio. 'Ready now? Okay – out we go!'

Wheeler felt very reluctant to leave the warmth and security of the tractor. Jamieson had left it in the shelter of a group of boulders which would protect it from almost all directions. Only something dropping from above could do it any damage.

Wheeler was suddenly struck by an alarming thought. 'If Ferdinand gets hit,' he said, 'that's the end of us anyway. So why bother to leave?'

'There's air in these suits for two days,' answered Jamieson as he closed the door of the lock behind him. 'We can walk back if we have to. Eighty miles sounds like a lot but it isn't so much on the Moon.'

Wheeler said no more as they hurried to their shelter. An eighty-mile walk over the Sea of Rains was a sombre thought.

'This would have made a fine fox-hole in the last war,' he said as he settled himself down among the debris of lava and pulverised rock at the bottom of the little ravine. 'But I want to see what's going on over by the mine.'

'So do I,' said Jamieson, 'but I also want to live to a ripe old age.'

'I'll risk it,' exclaimed Wheeler impetuously. 'Everything seems quiet now anyway. I think those torpedoes must have finished the job.' He jumped toward the rim of the cleft and hauled himself out.

'What can you see?' asked Jamieson. His voice reached Wheeler easily though the suit's low-powered radio was heavily shielded by the solid rock.

'Wait a minute – I'm climbing up on this boulder to get a better view.'

There was a short pause. Then Wheeler spoke again with a note of surprise in his voice. 'The dome doesn't seem to be touched. Everything's just the same.'

He was not to know that the first warning shots had landed many miles away from the mine. The second salvo of rockets was launched soon after he had reached his vantage point. This time they were intended to hit. Wheeler saw the long sheafs of flame driving steady and true towards their target. In a moment, he thought, that great dome would collapse like a broken toy.

The rockets never reached the surface of the Moon. They were still many miles up when, simultaneously, they exploded. Four enormous spheres of light blossomed amongst the stars and vanished. Automatically Wheeler braced himself for the concussion that could never come in the vacuum around him.

Something strange had happened to the dome. At first Wheeler thought that it had grown in size. Then he realised that the dome itself had gone and in its place was a wavering hemisphere of light, scarcely visible to the eye. It was like nothing he had ever seen before.

It was equally unfamiliar to the Federation ships. In a matter of seconds they had dwindled into space, shrinking under the drive of an inconceivable acceleration. They were taking no chances while they went into conference and hastily checked the armament they had never imagined they would have to use. Rather late in the day they understood the reason for Earth's quiet confidence.

They were gone only a brief while. Although they had disappeared together they returned from entirely different directions as if to confuse the defences of the mine. The two cruisers came down at steep angles from opposite corners of the sky and the battleship swept up over the horizon behind the screen of Pico, where it remained for the earlier part of the conflict.

Suddenly the cruisers vanished, as the dome had vanished, behind wavering spheres of light. But these spheres were already brilliant, shining with a strange orange glow. Wheeler realised that they must be radiation screens of some kind and as he looked again towards the mine he knew that the onslaught had begun.

The hemisphere on the plain was blazing with all the colours of the rainbow and its brilliance was increasing second by second. Power was being poured into it from outside, power that was being converted into the harmless rays of the visible spectrum. That at least was clear to Wheeler – he wondered how many millions of horsepower were flowing invisibly through the space between the cruisers and the mine. It was already far brighter than day.

Slowly understanding came to him. The rays which the twentieth century had imagined but never known were a myth no longer. Not like the space-ship, gradually and over many years, had they come upon the world. In secrecy, during the seventy years of peace, they had been conceived and brought to perfection.

The dome on the plain was a fortress, such a one as no earlier man had ever dreamed of before. Its defences must have gone into action immediately the first beams of the enemy reacted upon them but for many minutes it made no attempt at retaliation. Nor yet was it in any position to do so, for under the blazing shield that protected them Fletcher and his colleagues were fighting time as well as the Federation.

Then Wheeler noticed a faint brush discharge on either side of the dome – that was all. But the screens of the cruisers turned cherry-red, then blue-white, then a colour he knew but had never thought to see on any world – the violet-white of the giant suns. So breathtaking was the sight that he gave no second thought to his deadly peril. Only imminent personal danger could move him now – whatever the risk, he must see the battle to its end.

Jamieson's anxious voice startled him when it came again over the speaker. 'Hello, Con! What's happening?'

'The fight's started – come up and see.'

For a few seconds Jamieson struggled against his natural caution. Then he emerged from the cleft and side by side the two men watched the greatest of all battles rising to its climax.

VI

Millions of years ago the molten rock had frozen to form the Sea of Rains and now the weapons of the ships were turning it once more to lava. Out by the fortress clouds of incandescent vapour were being blasted into the sky as the beams of the attackers spent their fury against the unprotected rocks.

Ever and again a salvo of rocket torpedoes would lance toward the Moon and a mountain would rise slowly from the plain and settle back in fragments. None of the material projectiles ever reached their target, for the fields of the fortress deflected them in great spirals that sent many hurtling back into space.

Not a few were caught in the beams of the defenders and detonated many miles above the ground. The utter silence of their explosions was unnerving. Wheeler found himself continually preparing for the concussion that could never come – not on the atmosphereless Moon.

It was impossible to tell which side was inflicting more damage. Now and again a screen would flare up as a flicker of heat passed over white-hot steel. When that happened to one of the cruisers it would move with an acceleration that could not be followed by the eye and it would be several seconds before the focusing devices of the fort could find it again.

The fort itself had to take all the punishment the ships could give it. After the battle had been on for a very few minutes it was impossible to look toward the south because of the glare. Ever and again the clouds of rock vapour would go sailing up into the sky, falling back to the ground like luminous steam. And all the while a circle of lava was creeping out from the base of the fortress, melting down the hills like lumps of wax.

During the whole of the engagement the two men spoke scarcely a dozen words. This was no time for talk – they knew that they were witnessing a battle of which all the ages to come would speak with awe. Even if they were killed by the stray energies reflected from the screens of the fortress it would have been worth it to have seen so much.

They were watching the cruisers, for it was possible now and then to look at them without being blinded, when suddenly they realised that the glare to the south had doubled its intensity. The battleship, which until now had taken no part in the action, had risen above Pico and was blasting at the fortress with all the weapons she possessed.

From where he was standing Wheeler could see the throats of her bow projectors – little pits of flame that looked as if they had been carved from the Sun. The summit of the mountain had been caught in those beams. It did not have time to melt – the peak vanished and only a ragged smoking plateau was left.

Wheeler was going to risk no further damage to his eyes, which were already paining him. With a word of explanation to Jamieson he raced back to the tractor and returned a few minutes later with a set of heavy-duty filters.

The relief was immense. No longer were the screens of the cruisers like artificial suns and they could look once more in the direction of the fortress. Though he could see only the ray-shields against which the beams of the battleships were still splashing in vain it seemed to Wheeler that the hemisphere had lost its original symmetry during the battle.

At first he thought one of the generators might have failed. Then he saw that the lake of lava was at least a mile across and he knew that the whole fort had floated off its foundations. Probably the defenders were scarcely aware of the fact. Their insulation was taking care of solar heat and would hardly notice molten rock.

And now a strange thing was beginning to happen. The rays with which the battle was being fought were no longer quite invisible, for the fortress was no longer in a vacuum. Around it the boiling rock was releasing enormous volumes of gas through which the paths of the rays were as clearly visible as searchlights on Earth on a misty night.

At the same time Wheeler began to notice a continual hail of tiny particles around him. For a moment he was puzzled. Then he realised that the rock vapour was condensing after it had been blasted up into the sky. It seemed too light to be dangerous and he did not mention it to Jamieson.

As long as it was not too heavy the insulation of the space-suits could deal with it.

Accustomed though they were to the eternal silences of the Moon both men felt a sense of unreality at the sight of those tremendous weapons blasting overhead without a whisper of sound. Now and then there would be a hammerblow underfoot as a torpedo crashed, deflected by the fields of the fort. But most of the time there was absolute silence, even when there were half a dozen rockets detonating in the sky at once. It was like watching a television programme when the sound had failed.

They never knew why the fortress waited so long before it used its main weapon. Possibly Fletcher could not get it into action earlier or perhaps he was waiting for the attack to slacken so that some energy could be diverted from the screens. For it was during a lull in the engagement that the polaron beam operated for the first time in history.

The two watchers saw it strike upward like an inverted lightning flash. It was clearly visible along its whole length, not merely in patches where it passed through dust and gas. Even in that brief instant of time Wheeler noticed this staggering violation of the laws of optics and wondered at its implications. Not until many years later did he learn how a polaron beam radiates some of its energy at right angles to its direction of propagation so that it can be seen even in a vacuum.

The beam went through the *Phlegethon* as if she did not exist. The most terrible thing Wheeler ever saw in his life was the way the screens of that great ship suddenly vanished as her generators died, leaving her helpless and unprotected in the sky. The secondary weapons of the fortress were at her instantly, tearing out great gashes of metal and boiling away her armour layer by layer.

Then, quite slowly, she began to settle towards the Moon, still on an even keel. No one will ever know what stopped her – probably some short-circuit in her controls since none of her crew could have been left alive. For suddenly she went off to the west in a long flat trajectory.

By that time most of her hull had been boiled away and the steel skeleton of her framework was almost completely exposed. The crash came minutes later as she plunged into the mountains beyond Plato.

When Wheeler looked again for the cruisers they were so far away that their screens had shrunk to little balls of fire against the stars. At first he thought they were retreating – then abruptly the screens began to expand as they came down in an attack under terrific vertical acceleration. Around the fortress the lava was throwing itself madly into the sky as the beams tore into it.

The cruisers came out of their dives about a mile above the fort. For an instant they were motionless – then they went back into the sky together. But the *Eridanus* had been mortally wounded though the two watchers knew only that one of the screens was shrinking much more slowly than the other.

With a feeling of helpless fascination they watched the stricken cruiser fall back toward the Moon. About twenty miles up her screens seemed to explode and she hung unprotected, a sleek torpedo of black metal, visible only as a shadow against the stardust of the Milky Way.

Almost instantly her light-absorbing paint and the armour beneath were torn off by the beams of the fortress. The great ship turned cherry-red, then white. She swung over so that her prow pointed toward the Moon and began her last dive.

Wheeler felt his friend's grip upon his arm and Jamieson's voice rang through the speakers. 'Back to the cleft for God's sake!'

He never knew how they reached the cleft in time and had no recollection of entering it. The last thing Wheeler saw was the remaining cruiser dwindling into space and the *Eridanus* coming down at him like an onrushing meteor. Then he was lying flat on his face among the rocks, expecting every moment to be his last.

She landed nearly five miles away. The impact threw Wheeler a yard off the ground and set the boulders dancing in the cleft. The whole surface of the plain quivered for seconds before the rocks settled back to rest.

Wheeler turned over on to his back, breathless, and looked up at the gibbous Earth that was just visible from his position. He wondered what Earth had thought of the battle, which must have been clearly visible to the naked eye over the hemisphere facing the Moon. But his main feeling was relief at his escape. He did not know that the final paroxysm was yet to come.

Jamieson's voice brought him back to life. 'You all right, Con?'

'Yes – I think so. That's two of them gone. By the way she was travelling I don't think number three will be coming back.'

'Nor do I. Looks as if Earth's won the first round. Shall we go back to the tractor?'

'Just a minute – *what's the matter with those rocks up there*?'

Wheeler glanced towards the northern face of the cleft, which was several feet higher than the other. Over the exposed surfaces of the rock waves of light were passing in slow undulations.

Jamieson was the first to realise the cause. 'It's the glare from that lava over by the fort. It will probably take a good while to cool off.'

'It isn't cooling. Look – *it's getting brighter*!'

At first Wheeler had blamed his eyes but now there was no room for doubt. The rock was not merely reflecting light – it was turning cherry-red. Soon it was too bright to watch with the unprotected eye. With a feeling of sick helplessness he saw that everywhere the exposed rock surfaces were becoming incandescent.

Suddenly the appalling truth reached Wheeler's brain. The generators of the wrecked ship had not yet detonated and the energy which it would have poured out in hours of continuous fighting was leaking away at a rate rising swiftly toward catastrophe. And he realised that all the atomic explosions of the past would be as nothing against what might happen now.

Then the Moon awoke from its sleep. The plain seemed to tear itself asunder and he could almost hear a mighty wind of radiation sweeping overhead. This was the last thing he knew before the quake reached him.

Ages later he was awakened by the glare of Earthlight in his eyes. For a long time he lay in a half dazed condition, knitting together the broken threads of memory. Then he recalled what had happened and began to look around for his friend.

It gave him a shock to discover that his torch was broken. There was no sign of Jamieson in the narrow portion of the cleft illuminated by the Earth and he could not explore the shadows without a light. As he lay there wondering what to do next, a strange sound began to intrude upon his consciousness. It was an unpleasant rasping noise that grew stronger minute by minute.

Not since his childhood, when night had once caught him in a strange wood far from home, had Wheeler known such real terror as he felt now. This was the airless Moon – there could be no sound here! Then his fuddled wits cleared and he burst into peals of relieved and half hysterical laughter.

Somewhere in the darkness near him Jamieson, still unconscious, was breathing heavily into his microphone.

Wheeler's laughter must have aroused his friend, for suddenly he heard Jamieson calling unsteadily through the speaker. 'Hello, Con – what the devil's the matter?'

Wheeler took a firm grip of himself. 'It's okay, Sid – I'm just a bit giddy. Are you all right?'

'Yes – at least I think so. But my head's still ringing.'

'So is mine. Do you think it's safe to climb out now?'

'I don't see what else can happen now but I guess we'll have to wait here for a while. Look at that rock.'

The walls overhead had been partly sheared away by the blast and were still glowing dully. The rock was too hot to touch and it was many minutes before the two men could crawl out of their refuge.

They were both prepared for a scene of devastation but the reality exceeded their wildest fears. Around them was a vision of the inferno. The whole landscape, from horizon to horizon, had altered beyond recognition. To the east the beautiful mountain that had been Pico was gone.

In its place was a sheared and blistered stump, only a fraction of its former height. It must have caught the full blast of that mammoth explosion. In all the plain, as far as the eye could see, there was no other outstanding projection. Of the fortress not a trace was left. Everything had been levelled by that final incredible blast of radiation.

That was Wheeler's first impression. Then he realised that it was not completely correct. About five miles away to the west was another pool of lava, a mile or two across, and in its centre was a roughly hemispherical bulge. As he watched, it settled down into the molten rock until there was nothing left.

Then there came a faint trembling underfoot, and a curious disturbance at the centre of the lake. Like some evil thing emerging from the sea a great column of lava slowly climbed towards the stars, tottered and slowly fell. So sluggish was its motion that it never reached the ground but froze even as it fell to form a crooked finger jutting out of the plain. And that was the end of the *Eridanus*.

Jamieson broke the long silence at last. 'Ready to start walking?' he said.

Ten million miles away, the mortally wounded *Acheron* was limping back to Mars, bearing the shattered hopes of the Federation. On the second moon of Jupiter, white-faced men were sitting in conference and the destinies of the outer planets were passing from the hands of those who had planned the raid against the Moon.

Down on Earth the statesmen of the mother world faced reality at last. They had seen the Wilson drive in action and knew that the day of the rocket was gone. They also realised that although they had – at tremendous cost – won the first round the greater science of the Federation must prevail in the end. Peace and the Wilson drive were worth all the uranium in the universe. A message was already on its way to Mars with the news that Earth was willing to reopen negotiations.

It was well for humanity that the battle ended as it had. The *Acheron* would never fight again and no one could tell that any building made by man had ever stood in the Sea of Rains. Both sides had exhausted themselves.

Had Jamieson refused to continue his journey to the fortress complete victory might have gone to the Federation. Flushed with success, it might have been tempted to further adventures and the Treaty of Phoebus would never have been signed. Upon such small decisions may world destinies depend.

For hours, it seemed to Wheeler, they had been trudging across this seared and shattered plain, the brilliant Earthlight casting their shadows ahead of them. They spoke seldom, wishing to conserve the batteries of their suit radios. The curvature of the Moon made it impossible to signal the Observatory and there were still fifty miles to go.

It was not a pleasant prospect, for they had been able to salvage nothing from the tractor – it was now a pile of fused metal. But at least they could not lose their way with the Earth hanging fixed in the sky to guide them. They had only to keep walking into their shadows and in due course the Alps would come up over the horizon.

Wheeler was plodding along behind his friend, lost in his own thoughts, when Jamieson suddenly changed his direction of march. Slightly to the left a low ridge had appeared. When they reached it they found themselves climbing a hill not more than fifty feet high.

They looked eagerly to the north, but there was still no sign of the Alps. Jamieson switched on his radio.

'They can't be far below the horizon,' he said. 'I'm going to risk it.'

'Risk what?'

'Emergency transmission. You can key these sets for two minutes at fifty times normal power. Here goes.'

Very carefully, he broke the seal on the little control board inside the suit, and sent out the three dots, three dashes and three dots which were all that was left of the old Morse code.

Then they waited, staring toward the featureless skyline of the north. Below its edge, beyond sight and perhaps beyond signalling, lay safety. But the Observatory gave no sign.

Five minutes later Jamieson signalled again. This time he did not wait. 'Come on,' he said. 'We'd better start walking again.' Wheeler followed glumly.

They were halfway down the slope when a golden flare climbed into the northern sky and erupted slowly against the stars. The sense of relief was so great that Wheeler was left weak.

He sat down clumsily on the nearest boulder and stared at that beautiful, heart-warming symbol hanging in the sky. Even now, he knew, the rescue tractors would be racing down the slope of the mountains.

He turned to his friend. 'Well, Sid, that's that, thank God.'

For a moment Jamieson did not reply. He too was staring up toward the stars – but along the path the retreating warship had followed hours before. 'I wish I could be sure,' he murmured half to himself, 'that I did the right thing. They might have won . . .'

Then he turned toward the blinding disc of Earth, breathtakingly lovely beneath its belts of clouds. The future might belong to the Federation but almost all that it possessed it had inherited from the mother world. How could one choose between the two?

He shrugged his shoulders – there was nothing he could do about it now. Resolutely he turned toward the north and walked forward to receive the fame from which he would never escape.

Second Dawn

First published in *Science Fiction Quarterly*, August 1951
Collected in *Expedition to Earth*

'Here they come,' said Eris, rising to his forefeet and turning to look down the long valley. For a moment the pain and bitterness had left his thoughts, so that even Jeryl, whose mind was more closely tuned to his than to any other, could scarcely detect it. There was even an undertone of softness that recalled poigantly the Eris she had known in the days before the War – the old Eris who now seemed almost as remote and as lost as if he were lying with all the others out there on the plain.

A dark tide was flowing up the valley, advancing with a curious, hesitant motion, making odd pauses and little bounds forward. It was flanked with gold – the thin line of the Atheleni guards, so terrifyingly few compared with the black mass of the prisoners. But they were enough: indeed, they were only needed to guide that aimless river on its faltering way. Yet at the sight of so many thousands of the enemy, Jeryl found herself trembling and instinctively moved towards her mate, silver pelt resting against gold. Eris gave no sign that he had understood or even noticed the action.

The fear vanished as Jeryl saw how slowly the dark flood was moving forwards. She had been told what to expect, but the reality was even worse than she had imagined. As the prisoners came nearer, all the hate and bitterness ebbed from her mind, to be replaced by a sick compassion. No one of her race need ever more fear the aimless, idiot horde that was being shepherded through the pass into the valley it would never leave again.

The guards were doing little more than urge the prisoners on with meaningless but encouraging cries, like nurses calling to infants too young to sense their thoughts. Strain as she might, Jeryl could detect no vestige of reason in any of these thousands of minds passing so near at hand. That brought home to her, more vividly than could anything else, the magnitude of the victory – and the defeat. Her mind was sensitive enough to detect the first faint thoughts of children, hovering on the verge of consciousness. The defeated enemy had become not even children, but babies with the bodies of adults.

The tide was passing within a few feet of them now. For the first time, Jeryl realised how much larger than her own people the Mithraneans were, and how beautifully the light of the twin suns gleamed on the dark satin of their bodies. Once a magnificent specimen, towering a full head above Eris, broke loose from the main body and came blundering towards them, halting a few paces away. Then it crouched down like a lost and frightened child, the splendid head moving uncertainly from side to side as if seeking it knew not what. For a moment the great, empty eyes fell full upon Jeryl's face. She was as beautiful, she knew, to the Mithraneans as to her own race – but there was no flicker of emotion on the blank features, and no pause in the aimless movement of the questing head. Then an exasperated guard drove the prisoner back to his fellows.

'Come away,' Jeryl pleaded. 'I don't want to see any more. Why did you ever bring me here?' The last thought was heavy with reproach.

Eris began to move away over the grassy slopes in great bounds that she could not hope to match, but as he went his mind threw its message back to hers. His thoughts were still gentle, though the pain beneath them was too deep to be concealed.

'I wanted everyone – even you – to see what we had to do to win the War. Then, perhaps, we will have no more in our lifetimes.'

He was waiting for her on the brow of the hill, undistressed by the mad violence of his climb. The stream of prisoners was now too far below for them to see the details of its painful progress. Jeryl crouched down beside Eris and began to browse on the sparse vegetation that had been exiled from the fertile valley. She was slowly beginning to recover from the shock.

'But what will happen to them?' she asked presently, still haunted by the memory of that splendid mindless giant going into a captivity it could never understand.

'They can be taught how to eat,' said Eris. 'There is food in the valley for half a year, and then we'll move them on. It will be a heavy strain on our own resources, but we're under a moral obligation – and we've put it in the peace treaty.'

'They can never be cured?'

'No. Their minds have been totally destroyed. They'll be like this until they die.'

There was a long silence. Jeryl let her gaze wander across the hills, falling in gentle undulations to the edge of the ocean. She could just make out, beyond a gap in the hills, the distant line of blue that marked the sea – the mysterious, impassable sea. Its blue would soon be deepening into darkness, for the fierce white sun was setting and presently there would only be the red disc – hundreds of times larger but giving far less light – of its pale companion.

'I suppose we had to do it,' Jeryl said at last. She was thinking almost to herself, but she let enough of her thoughts escape for Eris to overhear.

'You've seen them,' he answered briefly. 'They were bigger and stronger than we. Though we outnumbered them, it was stalemate: in the end, I think they would have won. By doing what we did, we saved thousands from death – or mutilation.'

The bitterness came back into his thoughts, and Jeryl dared not look at him. He had screened the depths of his mind, but she knew that he was thinking of the shattered ivory stump upon his forehead. The War had been fought, except at the very end, with two weapons only – the razor-sharp hooves of the little, almost useless forepaws, and the unicornlike horns. With one of these Eris could never fight again, and from the loss stemmed much of the embittered harshness that sometimes made him hurt even those who loved him.

Eris was waiting for someone, though who it was Jeryl could not guess. She knew better than to interrupt his thoughts while he was in his present mood, and so remained silently beside him, her shadow merging with his as it stretched far along the hill-top.

Jeryl and Eris came of a race which, in Nature's lottery, had been luckier than most – and yet had missed one of the greatest prizes of all. They had powerful bodies and powerful minds, and they lived in a world which was both temperate and fertile. By human standards, they would have seemed strange but by no means repulsive. Their sleek, fur-covered bodies tapered to a single giant rear limb that could send them leaping over the ground in thirty-foot bounds. The two forelimbs were much smaller, and served merely for support and steadying. They ended in pointed hooves that could be deadly in combat, but had no other useful purpose.

Both the Atheleni and their cousins, the Mithraneans, possessed mental powers that had enabled them to develop a very advanced mathematics and philosophy; but over the physical world they had no control at all. Houses, tools, clothes – indeed, artifacts of any kind – were utterly unknown to them. To races which possessed hands, tentacles or other means of manipulation, their culture would have seemed incredibly limited: yet such is the adaptability of the mind, and the power of the commonplace, that they seldom realised their handicaps and could imagine no other way of life. It was natural to wander in great herds over the fertile plains, pausing where food was plentiful and moving on again when it was exhausted. This nomadic life had given them enough leisure for philosophy and even for certain arts. Their telepathic powers had not yet robbed them of their voices and they had developed a complex vocal music and an even more complex choreography. But they took the greatest pride of all in the range of their thoughts: for thousands of generations they had sent their minds roving through the misty infinities of metaphysics. Of *physics*, and indeed of all the sciences of matter, they knew nothing – not even that they existed.

'Someone's coming,' said Jeryl suddenly. 'Who is it?'

Eris did not bother to look, but there was a sense of strain in his reply.

'It's Aretenon. I agreed to meet him here.'

'I'm so glad. You were such good friends once – it upset me when you quarrelled.'

Eris pawed fretfully at the turf, as he did when he was embarrassed or annoyed.

'I lost my temper with him when he left me during the fifth battle of the Plain. Of course I didn't know then why he had to go.'

Jeryl's eyes widened in sudden amazement and understanding.

'You mean – he had something to do with the Madness, and the way the War ended?'

'Yes. There were very few people who knew more about the mind than he did. I don't know what part he played, but it must have been an important one. I don't suppose he'll ever be able to tell us much about it.'

Still a considerable distance below them, Aretenon was zigzagging up the hillside in great leaps. A little later he had reached them and instinctively bent his head to touch horns with Eris in the universal gesture of greeting. Then he stopped, horribly embarrassed, and there was an awkward pause until Jeryl came to the rescue with some conventional remarks.

When Eris spoke, Jeryl was relieved to sense his obvious pleasure at meeting his friend once again, for the first time since their angry parting at the height of the War. It had been longer still since her last meeting with Aretenon, and she was surprised to see how much he had changed. He was considerably younger than Eris – but no one would have guessed it now. Some of his once-golden pelt was turning black with age, and with a flash of his old humour Eris remarked that soon no one would be able to tell him from a Mithranean.

Aretenon smiled.

'That would have been useful in the last few weeks. I've just come through their country, helping to round up the Wanderers. We weren't very popular, as you might expect. If they'd known who I was, I don't suppose I'd have got back alive – armistice or no armistice.'

'You weren't actually in charge of the Madness, were you?' asked Jeryl, unable to control her curiosity.

She had a momentary impression of thick, defensive mists forming around Aretenon's mind, shielding all his thoughts from the outer world. Then the reply came, curiously muffled, and with a sense of distance that was very rare in telepathic contact.

'No: I wasn't in supreme charge. But there were only two others between myself and – the top.'

'Of course,' said Eris, rather petulantly, 'I'm only an ordinary soldier and don't understand these things. But I'd like to know just how you did it. Naturally,' he added, 'neither Jeryl nor myself would talk to anyone else.'

Again that veil seemed to descend over Aretenon's thoughts. Then it lifted, ever so slightly.

'There's very little I'm allowed to tell. As you know, Eris, I was always interested in the mind and its workings. Do you remember the games we used to play, when I tried to uncover your thoughts, and you did your best to stop me? And how I sometimes made you carry out acts against your will?'

'I still think,' said Eris, 'that you couldn't have done that to a stranger, and that I was really unconsciously co-operating.'

'That was true then – but it isn't any longer. The proof lies down there in the valley.' He gestured towards the last stragglers who were being rounded up by the guards. The dark tide had almost passed, and soon the entrance to the valley would be closed.

'When I grew older,' continued Aretenon, 'I spent more and more of my time probing into the ways of the mind, and trying to discover why some of us can share our thoughts so easily, while others can never do so but must remain always isolated and alone, forced to communicate by sounds or gestures. And I became fascinated by those rare minds that are completely deranged, so that those who possess them seem less than children.

'I had to abandon these studies when the War began. Then, as you know, they called for me one day during the fifth battle. Even now, I'm not quite sure who was responsible for that. I was taken to a place a long way from here, where I found a little group of thinkers many of whom I already knew.

'The plan was simple – and tremendous. From the dawn of our race we've known that two or three minds, linked together, could be used to control another mind, *if it was willing*, in the way that I used to control you. We've employed this power for healing since ancient times. Now we planned to use it for destruction.

'There were two main difficulties. One was bound up with that curious limitation of our normal telepathic powers – the fact that, except in rare cases, we can only have contact over a distance *with someone we already know*, and can communicate with strangers only when we are actually in their presence.

'The second, and greater problem, was that the massed power of many minds would be needed, and never before had it been possible to link together more than two or three. How we succeeded is our main secret: like all things, it seems easy now it has been done. And once we had started, it was simpler than we had expected. Two minds are more than twice as powerful as one, and three are much more than thrice as powerful as a single will. The exact mathematical relationship is an interesting one. You know how very rapidly the number of ways a group of objects may be arranged increases with the size of the group? Well, a similar relationship holds in this case.

'So in the end we had our Composite Mind. At first it was unstable, and we could hold it together only for a few seconds. It's still a tremendous strain on our mental resources, and even now we can only do it for – well, for long enough.

'All these experiments, of course, were carried out in great secrecy. If we could do this, so could the Mithraneans, for their minds are as good as ours. We had a number of their prisoners, and we used them as subjects.'

For a moment the veil that hid Aretenon's inner thoughts seemed to tremble and dissolve: then he regained control.

'That was the worst part. It was bad enough to send madness into a far land, but it was infinitely worse when you could watch with your own eyes the effects of what you did.

'When we had perfected our technique, we made the first long-distance test. Our victim was someone so well known to one of our prisoners – whose mind we had taken over – that we could identify him completely and thus the distance between us was no objection. The experiment worked, but of course no one suspected that we were responsible.

'We did not operate again until we were certain that our attack would be so overwhelming that it would end the War. From the minds of our prisoners we had identified about a score of Mithraneans – their friends and kindred – in such detail that we could pick them out and destroy them. As each mind fell beneath our attack, it gave up to us the knowledge of others, and so our power increased. We could have done far more damage than we did, for we took only the males.'

'Was that,' said Jeryl bitterly, 'so very merciful?'

'Perhaps not: but it should be remembered to our credit. We stopped as soon as the enemy sued for peace, and as we alone knew what had happened, we went into their country to undo what damage we could. It was little enough.'

There was a long silence. The valley was deserted now, and the white sun had set. A cold wind was blowing over the hills, passing, where none could follow it, out across the empty and untravelled sea. Then Eris spoke, his thoughts almost whispering in Aretenon's mind.

'You did not come to tell me this, did you? There is something more.' It was a statement rather than a query.

'Yes,' replied Aretenon. 'I have a message for you – one that will surprise you a good deal. It's from Therodimus.'

'Therodimus! I thought—'

'You thought he was dead, or worse still, a traitor. He's neither, although he's lived in enemy territory for the last twenty years. The Mithraneans treated him as we did, and gave him everything he needed. They recognised his mind for what it was, and even during the War no one touched him. Now he wants to see you again.'

Whatever emotions Eris was feeling at this news of his old teacher, he gave no sign of them. Perhaps he was recalling his youth, remembering now that Therodimus had played a greater part in the shaping of his mind than any other single influence. But his thoughts were barred to Aretenon and even to Jeryl.

'What's he been doing all this time?' Eris asked at length. 'And why does he want to see me now?'

'It's a long and complicated story,' said Aretenon, 'but Therodimus has made a discovery quite as remarkable as ours, and one that may have even greater consequences.'

'Discovery? What sort of discovery?'

Aretenon paused, looking thoughtfully along the valley. The guards were returning, leaving behind only the few who would be needed to deal with any wandering prisoners.

'You know as much of our history as I do, Eris,' he began. 'It took, we believe, something like a million generations for us to reach our present level of development – and that's a tremendous length of time! Almost all the progress we've made has been due to our telepathic powers: without them we'd be little different from all those other animals that show such puzzling resemblance to us. We're very proud of our philosophy and our mathematics, of our music and dancing – but have you ever thought, Eris, that there might be other lines of cultural development which we've never even dreamed of? *That there might be other forces in the Universe beside mental ones?'*

'I don't know what you mean,' said Eris flatly.

'It's hard to explain, and I won't try – except to say this. Do you realise just how pitiably feeble is our control over the external world, and how useless these limbs of ours really are? No – you can't, for you won't have seen what I have. But perhaps this will make you understand.'

The pattern of Aretenon's thoughts modulated suddenly into a minor key.

'I remember once coming upon a bank of beautiful and curiously complicated flowers. I wanted to see what they were like inside, so I tried to open one, steadying it between my hooves and picking it apart with my teeth. I tried again and again – and failed. In the end, half mad with rage, I trampled all those flowers into the dirt.'

Jeryl could detect the perplexity in Eris's mind, but she could see that he was interested and curious to know more.

'I have had that sort of feeling, too,' he admitted. 'But what can one do about it? And after all, is it really important? There are a good many things in this Universe which are not exactly as we should like them.'

Aretenon smiled.

'That's true enough. But Therodimus has found how to do something about it. Will you come and see him?'

'It must be a long journey.'

'About twenty days from here, and we have to go across a river.'

Jeryl felt Eris give a little shudder. The Atheleni hated water, for the excellent and sufficient reason that they were too heavily boned to swim, and promptly drowned if they fell into it.

'It's in enemy territory: they won't like me.'

'They respect you, and it might be a good idea for you to go – a friendly gesture, as it were.'

'But I'm wanted here.'

'You can take my word that nothing you do here is as important as the message Therodimus has for you – and for the whole world.'

Eris veiled his thoughts for a moment, then uncovered them briefly.

'I'll think about it,' he said.

It was surprising how little Aretenon managed to say on the many days of the journey. From time to time Eris would challenge the defences of his mind with half-playful thrusts, but always they were parried with an effortless skill. About the ultimate weapon that had ended the War he would say nothing, but Eris knew that those who had wielded it had not yet disbanded and were still at their secret hiding-place. Yet though he would not talk about the past, Aretenon often spoke of the future, and with the urgent anxiety of one who had helped to shape it and was not sure if he had acted aright. Like many others of his race, he was haunted by what he had done, and the sense of guilt sometimes overwhelmed him. Often he made remarks which puzzled Eris at the time, but which he was to remember more and more vividly in the years ahead.

'We've come to a turning-point in our history, Eris. The powers we've uncovered will soon be shared by the Mithraneans, and another war will mean destruction for us both. All my life I've worked to increase our knowledge of the mind, but now I wonder if I've brought something into the world that is too powerful, and too dangerous for us to handle. Yet it's too late, now, to retrace our footsteps: sooner or later our culture was bound to come to this point, and to discover what we have found.

'It's a terrible dilemma: and there's only one solution. We cannot go back, and if we go forward we may meet disaster. So we must change the very nature of our civilisation, and break completely with the million generations behind us. You can't imagine how that could be done: nor could I, until I met Therodimus and he told me of his dream.

'The mind is a wonderful thing, Eris – but by itself it is helpless in the universe of matter. We know now how to multiply the power of our brains by an enormous factor: we can solve, perhaps, the great problems of mathematics that have baffled us for ages. But neither our unaided minds, nor the group-mind we've now created, can alter in the slightest the one fact that all through history has brought us and the Mithraneans into conflict – the fact that the food supply is fixed, and our populations are not.'

Jeryl would watch them, taking little part in their thoughts, as they argued these matters. Most of their discussions took place while they were browsing, for like all active ruminants they had to spend a considerable part of each day searching for food. Fortunately the land through which they were passing was extremely fertile – indeed, its fertility had been one of the causes of the War. Eris, Jeryl was glad to see, was becoming something of his old self again. The feeling of frustrated bitterness that had filled his mind for so many months had not lifted, but it was no longer as all-pervading as it had been.

They left the open plain on the twenty-second day of their journey. For a long time they had been travelling through Mithranean territory, but those few of their ex-enemies they had seen had been inquisitive rather than hostile. Now the grasslands were coming to an end, and the forest with all its primeval terrors lay ahead.

'Only one carnivore lives in this region,' Aretenon reassured them, 'and it's no match for the three of us. We'll be past the trees in a day and a night.'

'A night – in the forest!' gasped Jeryl, half-petrified with terror at the very thought.

Aretenon was obviously a little ashamed of himself.

'I didn't like to mention it before,' he apologised, 'but there's really no danger. I've done it by myself, several times. After all, none of the great flesh-eaters of ancient times still exists – and it won't be really dark, even in the woods. The red sun will still be up.'

Jeryl was still trembling slightly. She came of a race which, for thousands of generations, had lived on the high hills and the open plains, relying on speed to escape from danger. The thought of going among trees – and in the dim red twilight while the primary sun was down – filled her with panic. And of the three of them, only Aretenon possessed a horn with which to fight. (It was nothing like so long or sharp, thought Jeryl, as Eris's had been.)

She was still not at all happy even when they had spent a completely uneventful day moving through the woods. The only animals they saw were tiny, long-tailed creatures that ran up and down the tree-trunks with amazing speed, gibbering with anger as the intruders passed. It was entertaining to watch them, but Jeryl did not think that the forest would be quite so amusing in the night.

Her fears were well founded. When the fierce white sun passed below the trees, and the crimson shadows of the red giant lay everywhere, a change seemed to come over the world. A sudden silence swept across the forest – a silence abruptly broken by a very distant wail towards which the three of them turned instinctively, ancestral warnings shrieking in their minds.

'What was that?' gasped Jeryl.

Aretenon was breathing swiftly, but his reply was calm enough.

'Never mind,' he said. 'It was a long way off. I don't know what it was.'

They took turns to keep guard, and the long night wore slowly away. From time to time Jeryl would awaken from troubled dreams into the nightmare reality of the strange, distorted trees gathered threateningly around her. Once, when she was on guard, she heard the sound of a heavy body moving through the woods very far away – but it came no nearer and she did not disturb the others. So at last the longed-for brilliance of the white sun began to flood the sky, and the day had come again.

Aretenon, Jeryl thought, was probably more relieved than he pretended to be. He was almost boyish as he frisked around in the morning sunlight, snatching an occasional mouthful of foliage from an overhanging branch.

'We've only half a day to go now,' he said cheerfully. 'We'll be out of the forest by noon.'

There was a mischievous undertone to his thoughts that puzzled Jeryl. It seemed as if Aretenon was keeping still another secret from them, and Jeryl wondered what further obstacles they would have to overcome. By midday she knew, for their way was barred by a great river flowing slowly past them as if in no haste to meet the sea.

Eris looked at it with some annoyance, measuring it with a practised eye.

'It's much too deep to ford here. We'll have to go a long way upstream before we can cross.'

Aretenon smiled.

'On the contrary,' he said cheerfully, 'we're going *downstream*.'

Eris and Jeryl looked at him in amazement.

'Are you mad?' Eris cried.

'You'll soon see. We've not far to go now – you've come all this way, so you might as well trust me for the rest of the journey.'

The river slowly widened and deepened. If it had been impassable before, it was doubly so now. Sometimes, Eris knew, one came upon a stream across which a tree had fallen, so that one could walk over the trunk – though it was a risky thing to do. But this river was the width of many trees, and was growing no narrower.

'We're nearly there,' said Aretenon at last. 'I recognise the place. Some-one should be coming out of those woods at any moment.' He gestured with his horn to the trees on the far side of the river, and almost as he did so three figures came bounding out on to the bank. Two of them, Jeryl saw, were Atheleni: the third was a Mithranean.

They were now nearing a great tree, standing by the water's edge, but Jeryl had paid little attention: she was too interested in the figures on the distant bank, wondering what they were going to do next. So when Eris's amazement exploded like a thunderclap in the depths of her own mind, she was too confused for a moment to realise its cause. Then she turned towards the tree, and saw what Eris had seen.

To some minds and some races, few things could have been more natural or more commonplace than a thick rope tied round a tree-trunk, and floating out across the water of a river to another tree on the far bank. Yet it filled both Jeryl and Eris with the terror of the unknown, and for one awful moment Jeryl thought that a gigantic snake was emerging from the water. Then she saw that it was not alive, but her fear remained. For it was the first artificial object that she had ever seen.

'Don't worry about *what* it is, or how it was put there,' counselled Aretenon. 'It's going to carry you across, and that's all that matters for the moment. Look – there's someone coming over now!'

One of the figures on the far bank had lowered itself into the water, and was working its way with its forelimbs along the rope. As it came nearer – it was the Mithranean, and a female – Jeryl saw that it was carrying a second and much smaller rope looped round the upper part of its body.

With the skill of long practice, the stranger made her way across the floating cable, and emerged dripping from the river. She seemed to know Aretenon, but Jeryl could not intercept their thoughts.

'I can go across without any help,' said Aretenon, 'but I'll show you the easy way.'

He slipped the loop over his shoulders, and, dropping into the water, hooked his forelimbs over the fixed cable. A moment later he was being dragged across at a great speed by the two others on the far bank, where, after much trepidation, Eris and Jeryl presently joined him.

It was not the sort of bridge one would expect from a race which could quite easily have dealt with the mathematics of a reinforced concrete arch – if the possibility of such an object had ever occurred to it. But it served its purpose, and once it had been made, they could use it readily enough.

Once it had been made. But – who had made it?

When their dripping guides had rejoined them, Aretenon gave his friends a warning.

'I'm afraid you're going to have a good many shocks while you're here. You'll see some very strange sights, but when you understand them, they'll cease to puzzle you in the slightest. In fact, you will soon come to take them for granted.'

One of the strangers, whose thoughts neither Eris nor Jeryl could intercept, was giving him a message.

'Therodimus is waiting for us,' said Aretenon. 'He's very anxious to see you.'

'I've been trying to contact him,' complained Eris, 'but I've not succeeded.'

Aretenon seemed a little troubled.

'You'll find he's changed,' he said. 'After all, you've not seen each other for many years. It may be some time before you can make full contact again.'

Their road was a winding one through the forest, and from time to time curiously narrow paths branched off in various directions. Therodimus, thought Eris, must have changed indeed for him to have taken up permanent residence among trees. Presently the track opened out into a large, semi-circular clearing with a low white cliff lying along its diameter. At the foot of the cliff were several dark holes of varying sizes – obviously the openings of caves.

It was the first time that either Eris or Jeryl had ever entered a cave, and they did not greatly look forward to the experience. They were relieved when Aretenon told them to wait just outside the opening, and went on alone towards the puzzling yellow light that glowed in the depths. A moment later, dim memories began to pulse in Eris's mind, and he knew that his old teacher was coming, even though he could no longer fully share his thoughts.

Something stirred in the gloom, and then Therodimus came out into the sunlight. At the sight of him, Jeryl screamed once and buried her head in Eris's mane, but Eris stood firm, though he was trembling as he had never done before battle. For Therodimus blazed with a magnificence that none of his race had ever known since history began. Around his neck hung a band of glittering objects that caught and refracted the sunlight in a myriad colours, while covering his body was a sheet of some thick, many-hued

381

material that rustled softly as he walked. And his horn was no longer the yellow of ivory: some magic had changed it to the most wonderful purple that Jeryl had ever seen.

Therodimus stood motionless for a moment, savouring their amazement to the full. Then his rich laugh echoed in their minds, and he reared up on his hind limb. The coloured garment fell whispering to the ground, and at a toss of his head the glittering necklace arched like a rainbow into a corner of the cave. But the purple horn remained unchanged.

It seemed to Eris that he stood at the brink of a great chasm, with Therodimus beckoning him on the far side. Their thoughts struggled to form a bridge, but could make no contact. Between them was the gulf of half a lifetime and many battles, of a myriad unshared experiences – Therodimus's years in this strange land, his own mating with Jeryl and the memory of their lost children. Though they stood face to face, a few feet only between them, their thoughts could never meet again.

Then Aretenon, with all the power and authority of his unsurpassed skill, did something to his mind that Eris was never quite able to recall. He only knew that the years seemed to have rolled back, that he was once more the eager, anxious pupil – and that he could speak to Therodimus again.

It was strange to sleep underground, but less unpleasant than spending the night amid the unknown terrors of the forest. As she watched the crimson shadows deepening beyond the entrance to the little cave, Jeryl tried to collect her scattered thoughts. She had understood only a small part of what had passed between Eris and Therodimus, but she knew that something incredible was taking place. The evidence of her eyes was enough to prove that: today she had seen things for which there were no words in her language.

She had heard things, too. As they had passed one of the cave-mouths, there had come from it a rhythmic 'whirring' sound, unlike that made by any animal she knew. It had continued steadily without pause or break as long as she could hear it, and even now its unhurried rhythm had not left her mind. Aretenon, she believed, had also noticed it, though without any surprise: Eris had been so engrossed with Therodimus.

The old philosopher had told them very little, preferring, as he said, to show them his empire when they had had a good night's rest. Nearly all their talk had been concerned with the events of their own land during the last few years, and Jeryl found it somewhat boring. Only one thing had interested her, and she had eyes for little else. That was the wonderful chain of coloured crystals that Therodimus had worn around his neck. What it was, or how it had been created, she could not imagine: but she coveted it. As she fell asleep, she found herself thinking idly, but more than half-seriously, of the sensation it would cause if she returned to her people with such a marvel gleaming against her own pelt. It would look so much better there than upon old Therodimus.

Aretenon and Therodimus met them at the cave soon after dawn. The philosopher had discarded his regalia – which he had obviously worn only to impress his guests – and his horn had returned to its normal yellow. That was one thing Jeryl thought she could understand, for she had come across fruits whose juices could cause colour changes.

Therodimus settled himself at the mouth of the cave. He began his narration without any preliminaries, and Eris guessed that he must have told it many times before to earlier visitors.

'I came to this place, Eris, about five years after leaving our country. As you know, I was always interested in strange lands, and from the Mithraneans I'd heard rumours that intrigued me very much. How I traced them to their source is a long story that doesn't matter now. I crossed the river far upstream one summer, when the water was very low. There's only one place where it can be done, and then only in the driest years. Higher still the river loses itself in the mountains, and I don't think there's any way through them. So this is virtually an island – almost completely cut off from Mithranean territory.

'It's an island, but it's not uninhabited. The people who live here are called the Phileni, and they have a very remarkable culture – one entirely different from our own. Some of the products of that culture you've already seen.

'As you know, there are many different races on our world, and quite a few of them have some sort of intelligence. But there is a great gulf between us and all other creatures. As far as we know, we are the only beings capable of abstract thought and complex logical processes.

'The Phileni are a much younger race than ours, and they are intermediate between us and the other animals. They've lived here on this rather large island for several thousand generations – but their rate of development has been many, many times swifter than ours. They neither possess nor understand our telepathic powers, but they have something else which we may well envy – something which is responsible for the whole of their civilisation and its incredibly rapid progress.'

Therodimus paused, then rose slowly to his feet.

'Follow me,' he said. 'I'll take you to see the Phileni.'

He led them back to the caves from which they had come the night before, pausing at the entrance from which Jeryl had heard that strange, rhythmic whirring. It was clearer and louder now, and she saw Eris start as though he had noticed it for the first time. Then Therodimus uttered a high-pitched whistle, and at once the whirring slackened, falling octave by octave until it had ebbed into silence. A moment later something came towards them out of the semi-gloom.

It was a little creature, scarcely half their height, and it did not hop, but walked upon two jointed limbs that seemed very thin and feeble. Its large spherical head was dominated by three huge eyes, set far apart and capable of independent movement. With the best will in the world, Jeryl did not think it was very attractive.

Then Therodimus uttered another whistle, and the creature raised its forelimbs towards them.

'Look closely,' said Therodimus, very gently, 'and you will see the answer to many of your questions.'

For the first time, Jeryl saw that the creature's forelimbs did not end in hooves, or indeed after the fashion of any animal with which she was acquainted. Instead, they divided into at least a dozen thin, flexible tentacles and two hooked claws.

'Go towards it, Jeryl,' commanded Therodimus. 'It has something for you.'

Hesitantly, Jeryl moved forward. She noticed that the creature's body was crossed with bands of dark material, to which were attached unidentifiable objects. It dropped a forelimb to one of these, and a cover opened to reveal a cavity inside which something glittered. Then the little tentacles were clutching that marvellous crystal necklace, and with a movement so swift and dexterous that Jeryl could scarcely follow it, the Phileni moved forward and clasped it round her neck.

Therodimus brushed aside her confusion and gratitude, but his shrewd old mind was well pleased. Jeryl would be his ally now in whatever he planned to do. But Eris's emotions might not be so easily swayed, and in this matter mere logic was not enough. His old pupil had changed so much, had been so deeply wounded by the past, that Therodimus could not be certain of success. Yet he had a plan that could turn even these difficulties to his advantage.

He gave another whistle, and the Phileni made a curious waving gesture with its hands and disappeared into the cave. A moment later that strange whirring ascended once more from the silence, but Jeryl's curiosity was now quite overshadowed by her delight in her new possession.

'We'll go through the woods,' said Therodimus, 'to the nearest settlement – it's only a little way from here. The Phileni don't live in the open, as we do. In fact, they differ from us in almost every conceivable way. I'm even afraid,' he added ruefully, 'that they're much better natured than we are, and I believe that one day they'll be more intelligent. But first of all, let me tell you what I've learned about them, so that you can understand what I'm planning to do.'

The mental evolution of any race is conditioned, even dominated, by physical factors which that race almost invariably takes for granted as part of the natural order of things. The wonderfully sensitive hands of the Phileni had enabled them to find by experiment and trial facts which had taken the planet's only other intelligent species a thousand times as long to discover by pure deduction. Quite early in their history, the Phileni had invented simple tools. From these they had proceeded to fabrics, pottery, and the use of fire. When Therodimus had discovered them, they had already invented the lathe and the potter's wheel, and were about to move into their first Metal Age – with all that that implied.

On the purely intellectual plane, their progress had been less rapid. They were clever and skilful, but they had a dislike of abstract thought and their mathematics was purely empirical. They knew, for example, that a triangle with sides in the ratio three-four-five was right-angled, but had not suspected that this was only a special case of a much more general law. Their knowledge was full of such yawning gaps, which, despite the help of Therodimus and his several score disciples, they seemed in no great hurry to fill.

Therodimus they worshipped as a god, and for two whole generations of their short-lived race they had obeyed him in everything, giving him all the products of their skill that he needed, and making at his suggestion the new tools and devices that had occurred to him. The partnership had been incredibly fertile, for it was as if both races had suddenly been released from their shackles. Great manual skill and great intellectual powers had fused in a fruitful union probably unique in all the Universe – and progress that would normally have taken millennia had been achieved in less than a decade.

As Aretenon had promised them, though Eris and Jeryl saw many marvels, they came across nothing that they could not understand once they had watched the little Phileni craftsmen at work and had seen with what magic their hands shaped natural materials into lovely or useful forms. Even their tiny towns and primitive farms soon lost their wonder and became part of the accepted order of things.

Therodimus let them look their fill, until they had seen every aspect of this strangely sophisticated Stone Age culture. Because they knew no differently, they found nothing incongruous in the sight of a Phileni potter – who could scarcely count beyond ten – shaping a series of complex algebraic surfaces under the guidance of a young Mithranean mathematician. Like all his race, Eris possessed tremendous powers of mental visualisation, but he realised how much easier geometry would be if one could actually *see* the shapes one was considering. From this beginning (though he could not guess it) would one day evolve the idea of a written language.

Jeryl was fascinated above all things by the sight of the little Phileni women weaving fabrics upon their primitive looms. She could sit for hours watching the flying shuttles and wishing that she could use them. Once one had seen it done, it seemed so simple and obvious – and so utterly beyond the powers of the clumsy, useless limbs of her own people.

They grew very fond of the Phileni, who seemed eager to please and were pathetically proud of all their manual skills. In these new and novel surroundings, meeting fresh wonders every day, Eris seemed to be recovering from some of the scars which the War had left upon his mind. Jeryl knew, however, that there was still much damage to be undone. Sometimes, before he could hide them, she would come across raw, angry wounds in the depths of Eris's mind, and she feared that many of them – like the broken stump of his horn – would never heal. Eris had hated the

War, and the manner of its ending still oppressed him. Beyond this, Jeryl knew, he was haunted by the fear that it might come again.

These troubles she often discussed with Therodimus, of whom she had now grown very fond. She still did not fully understand why he had brought them here, or what he and his followers were planning to do. Therodimus was in no hurry to explain his actions, for he wished Jeryl and Eris to draw their own conclusions as far as possible. But at last, five days after their arrival, he called them to his cave.

'You've now seen,' he began, 'most of the things we have to show you here. You know what the Phileni can do, and perhaps you have thought how much our own lives will be enriched once we can use the products of their skill. That was my first thought when I came here, all those years ago.

'It was an obvious and rather naïve idea, but it led to a much greater one. As I grew to know the Phileni, and found how swiftly their minds had advanced in so short a time, I realised what a fearful disadvantage our own race had always laboured under. I began to wonder how much further forward *we* would have been had we the Phileni's control over the physical world. It is not a question of mere convenience, or the ability to make beautiful things like that necklace of yours, Jeryl, but something much more profound. It is the difference between ignorance and knowledge, between weakness and power.

'We have developed our minds, and our minds alone, until we can go no further. As Aretenon has told you, we have now come to a danger that threatens our entire race. We are under the shadow of the irresistible weapon against which there can be no defence.

'The solution is, quite literally, in the hands of the Phileni. We must use their skills to reshape our world, and so remove the cause of all our wars. We must go back to the beginning and re-lay the foundations of our culture. It won't be *our* culture alone, though, for we shall share it with the Phileni. They will be the hands – we the brains. Oh, I have dreamed of the world that may come, ages ahead, when even the marvels you see around you now will be considered childish toys! But not many are philosophers, and I need an argument more substantial than dreams. That final argument I believe I may have found, though I cannot yet be certain.

'I have asked you here, Eris, partly because I wanted to renew our old friendship, and partly because your word will now have far greater influence than mine. You are a hero among your own people, and the Mithraneans also will listen to you. I want you to return, taking with you some of the Phileni and their products. Show them to your people, and ask them to send their young men here to help us with our work.'

There was a pause during which Jeryl could gather no hints of Eris's thoughts. Then he replied hesitantly:

'But I still don't understand. These things that the Phileni make are very pretty, and some of them may be useful to us. But how can they change us as profoundly as you seem to think?'

Therodimus sighed. Eris could not see past the present into the future that was yet to be. He had not caught, as Therodimus had done, the promise that lay beyond the busy hands and tools of the Phileni – the first faint possibilities of the Machine. Perhaps he would never understand: but he could still be convinced.

Veiling his deeper thoughts, Therodimus continued:

'Perhaps some of these things are toys, Eris – but they may be more powerful than you think. Jeryl, I know, would be loath to part with hers . . . and perhaps I can find one that would convince you.'

Eris was sceptical, and Jeryl could see that he was in one of his darker moods.

'I doubt it very much,' he said.

'Well, I can try.' Therodimus gave a whistle, and one of the Phileni came running up. There was a short exchange of conversation.

'Would you come with me, Eris? It will take some time.'

Eris followed him, the others, at Therodimus's request, remaining behind. They left the large cave and went towards the row of smaller ones which the Phileni used for their various trades.

The strange whirring was sounding loudly in Eris's ears, but for a moment he could not see its cause, the light of the crude oil lamps being too faint for his eyes. Then he made out one of the Phileni bending over a wooden table upon which something was spinning rapidly, driven by a belt from a treadle operated by another of the little creatures. He had seen the potters using a similar device, but this was different. It was shaping wood, not clay, and the potter's fingers had been replaced by a sharp metal blade from which long, thin shavings were curling out in fascinating spirals. With their huge eyes the Phileni, who disliked full sunlight, could see perfectly in the gloom, but it was some time before Eris could discover just what was happening. Then, suddenly, he understood.

'Aretenon,' said Jeryl when the others had left them, 'why should the Phileni do all these things for us? Surely they're quite happy as they are?'

The question, Aretenon thought, was typical of Jeryl and would never have been asked by Eris.

'They will do anything that Therodimus says,' he answered, 'but even apart from that there's so much we can give them as well. When we turn our minds to their problems, we can see how to solve them in ways that would never have occurred to them. They're very eager to learn, and already we must have advanced their culture by hundreds of generations. Also, they're physically very feeble. Although we don't possess their dexterity, our strength makes possible tasks they could never attempt.'

They had wandered to the edge of the river, and stood for a moment watching the unhurried waters moving down to the sea. Then Jeryl turned to go upstream, but Aretenon stopped her.

'Therodimus doesn't want us to go that way, yet,' he explained. 'It's just another of his little secrets. He never likes to reveal his plans until they're ready.'

Slightly piqued, and distinctly curious, Jeryl obediently turned back. She would, of course, come this way again as soon as there was no one else about.

It was very peaceful here in the warm sunlight, among the pools of heat trapped by the trees. Jeryl had almost lost her fear of the forest, though she knew she would never be quite happy there.

Aretenon seemed very abstracted, and Jeryl knew that he wished to say something and was marshalling his thoughts. Presently he began to speak, with the freedom that is only possible between two people who are fond of each other but have no emotional ties.

'It is very hard, Jeryl,' he began, 'to turn one's back on the work of a lifetime. Once I had hoped that the great new forces we have discovered could be safely used, but now I know that it is impossible, at least for many ages. Therodimus was right – we can go no further with our minds alone. Our culture has been hopelessly one-sided, though through no fault of ours. We cannot solve the fundamental problem of peace and war without a command over the physical world such as the Phileni possess – and which we hope to borrow from them.

'Perhaps there will be other great adventures here for our minds, to make us forget what we will have to abandon. We shall be able to learn something from Nature at last. What is the difference between fire and water, between wood and stone? What are the suns, and what are those millions of faint lights we see in the sky when both the suns are down? Perhaps the answers to all these questions may lie at the end of the new road along which we must travel.'

He paused.

'New knowledge – new wisdom – in realms we have never dreamed of before. It may lure us away from the dangers we have encountered: for certainly nothing we can learn from Nature will ever be as great a threat as the peril we have uncovered in our own minds.'

The flow of Aretenon's thoughts was suddenly interrupted. Then he said: 'I think Eris wants to see you.'

Jeryl wondered why Eris had not sent the message to her: she wondered, too, at the undertone of amusement – or was it something else? – in Aretenon's mind.

There was no sign of Eris as they approached the caves, but he was waiting for them and came bounding out into the sunlight before they could reach the entrance. Then Jeryl gave an involuntary cry, and retreated a pace or two as her mate came towards her.

For Eris was whole again. Gone was the shattered stump on his forehead: it had been replaced by a new, gleaming horn no less splendid than the one he had lost.

In a belated gesture of greeting, Eris touched horns with Aretenon. Then he was gone into the forest in great joyous leaps – but not before his mind had met Jeryl's as it had seldom done since the days before the War.

'Let him go,' said Therodimus softly. 'He would rather be alone. When he returns I think you will find him – different.' He gave a little laugh. 'The Phileni are clever, are they not? Now, perhaps, Eris will be more appreciative of their "toys".'

'I know I am impatient,' said Therodimus, 'but I am old now, and I want to see the changes begin in my own lifetime. That is why I am starting so many schemes in the hope that some at least will succeed. But this is the one, above all, in which I have put most faith.'

For a moment he lost himself in his thoughts. Not one in a hundred of his own race could fully share his dream. Even Eris, though he now believed in it, did so with his heart rather than his mind. Perhaps Aretenon – the brilliant and subtle Aretenon, so desperately anxious to neutralise the powers he had brought into the world – might have glimpsed the reality. But his was of all minds the most impenetrable, save when he wished otherwise.

'You know as well as I do,' continued Therodimus, as they walked upstream, 'that our wars have only one cause – Food. We and the Mithraneans are trapped on this continent of ours with its limited resources, which we can do nothing to increase. Ahead of us we have always the nightmare of starvation, and for all our vaunted intelligence there has been nothing we can do about it. Oh yes, we have scraped some laborious irrigation ditches with our forehooves, but how slight their help has been!

'The Phileni have discovered how to grow crops that increase the fertility of the ground manyfold. I believe that we can do the same – once we have adapted their tools for our own use. That is our first and most important task, but it is not the one on which I have set my heart. The final solution to our problem, Eris, *must be the discovery of new, virgin lands into which our people can migrate.*'

He smiled at the other's amazement.

'No, don't think I'm mad. Such lands do exist, I'm sure of it. Once I stood at the edge of the ocean and watched a great flight of birds coming inland from far out at sea. I have seen them flying outwards, too, so purposefully that I was certain they were going to some other country. And I have followed them with my thoughts.'

'Even if your theory is true, as it probably is,' said Eris, 'what use is it to us?' He gestured to the river flowing beside them. 'We drown in the water, and you cannot build a rope to support us—' His thoughts suddenly faded out into a jumbled chaos of ideas.

Therodimus smiled.

'So you have guessed what I hope to do. Well, now you can see if you are right.'

They had come to a level stretch of bank, upon which a group of the Phileni were busily at work, under the supervision of some of Therodimus's assistants. Lying at the water's edge was a strange object which, Eris realised, was made of many tree-trunks joined together by ropes.

They watched in fascination as the orderly tumult reached its climax.

There was a great pulling and pushing, and the raft moved ponderously into the water with a mighty splash. The spray had scarcely ceased to fall when a young Mithranean leaped from the bank and began to dance gleefully upon the logs, which were now tugging at the moorings as if eager to break away and follow the river down to the sea. A moment later he had been joined by others, rejoicing in their mastery of a new element. The little Phileni, unable to make the leap, stood watching patiently on the bank while their masters enjoyed themselves.

There was an exhilaration about the scene that no one could fail to miss, though perhaps few of those present realised that they were at a turning-point in history. Only Therodimus stood a little apart from the rest, lost in his own thoughts. This primitive raft, he knew, was merely a beginning. It must be tested upon the river, then along the shores of the ocean. The work would take years, and he was never likely to see the first voyagers returning from those fabulous lands whose existence was still no more than a guess. But what had been begun, others would finish.

Overhead, a flight of birds was passing across the forest. Therodimus watched them go, envying their freedom to move at will over land and sea. He had begun the conquest of the water for his race, but that the skies might one day be theirs also was beyond even his imagination.

Aretenon, Jeryl and the rest of the expedition had already crossed the river when Eris said goodbye to Therodimus. This time they had done so without a drop of water touching their bodies, for the raft had come downstream and was perfoming valuable duties as a ferry. A new and much improved model was already under construction, as it was painfully obvious that the prototype was not exactly seaworthy. These initial difficulties would be quickly overcome by designers who, even if they were forced to work with Stone Age tools, could handle with ease the mathematics of metacentres, buoyancies and advanced hydrodynamics.

'Your task won't be a simple one,' said Therodimus, 'for you cannot show your people all the things you have seen here. At first you must be content to sow the seed, to arouse interest and curiosity – particularly among the young, who will come here to learn more. Perhaps you will meet opposition: I expect so. But every time you return to us, we shall have new things to show you and to strengthen your arguments.'

They touched horns: then Eris was gone, taking with him the knowledge that was to change the world – so slowly at first, then ever more swiftly. Once the barriers were down, once the Mithraneans and the Atheleni had been given the simple tools which they could fasten to their forelimbs and use unaided, progress would be swift. But for the present they must rely on the Phileni for everything: and there were so few of them.

Therodimus was well content. Only in one respect was he disappointed, for he had hoped that Eris, who had always been his favourite, might also be his successor. The Eris who was now returning to his own people was no longer self-obsessed or embittered, for he had a mission and hope for the future. But he lacked the keen, far-ranging vision that was needed here: it would be Aretenon who must continue what he had begun. Still, that could not be helped, and there was no need yet to think of such matters. Therodimus was very old, but he knew that he would be meeting Eris many times again here by the river at the entrance to his land.

The ferry was gone now, and though he had expected it, Eris stopped amazed at the great span of the bridge, swaying slightly in the breeze. Its execution did not quite match its design – a good deal of mathematics had gone into its paraobolic suspension – but it was still the first great engineering feat in history. Constructed though it was entirely of wood and rope, it forecast the shape of the metal giants to come.

Eris paused in mid-stream. He could see smoke rising from the shipyards facing the ocean, and thought he could just glimpse the masts of some of the new vessels that were being built for coastal trade. It was hard to believe that when he had first crossed this river he had been dragged over dangling from a rope.

Aretenon was waiting for them on the far bank. He moved rather slowly now, but his eyes were still bright with the old, eager intelligence. He greeted Eris warmly.

'I'm glad you could come now. You're just in time.'

That, Eris knew, could mean only one thing.

'The ships are back?'

'Almost: they were sighted an hour ago, out on the horizon. They should be here at any moment, and then we shall know the truth at last, after all these years. If only—'

His thoughts faded out, but Eris could continue them. They had come to the great pyramid of stones beneath which Therodimus lay – Therodimus, whose brain was behind everything they saw, but who could never learn now if his most cherished dream was true or not.

There was a storm coming up from the ocean, and they hurried along the new road that skirted the river's edge. Small boats of a kind that Eris had not seen before went past them occasionally, operated by Atheleni or Mithraneans with wooden paddles strapped to their forelimbs. It always gave Eris great pleasure to see such new conquests, such new liberations of his people from their age-old chains. Yet sometimes they reminded him of children who had suddenly been let loose into a wonderful new world, full of exciting and interesting things that must be done, whether they were likely to be useful or not. However, anything that promised to make his race into better sailors was more than useful. In the last decade Eris had discovered that pure intelligence was sometimes not enough: there were skills that could not be acquired by any amount of mental effort. Though his people had largely overcome their fear of water, they were still quite incompetent on the ocean, and the Phileni had therefore become the first navigators of the world.

Jeryl looked nervously around her as the first peal of thunder came rolling in from the sea. She was still wearing the necklace that Therodimus had given her so long ago: but it was by no means the only ornament she carried now.

'I hope the ships will be safe,' she said anxiously.

'There's not much wind, and they will have ridden out much worse storms than this,' Aretenon reassured her, as they entered his cave. Eris and Jeryl looked round with eager interest to see what new wonders the Phileni had made during their absence: but if there were any they had, as usual, been hidden away until Aretenon was ready to show them. He was still rather childishly fond of such little surprises and mysteries.

There was an air of absentmindedness about the meeting that would have puzzled an onlooker ignorant of its cause. As Eris talked of all the changes in the outer world, of the success of the new Phileni settlements, and of the steady growth of agriculture among his people, Aretenon listened with only half his mind. His thoughts, and those of his friends, were far out at sea, meeting the oncoming ships which might be bringing the greatest news their world had ever received.

As Eris finished his report, Aretenon rose to his feet and began to move restlessly around the chamber.

'You have done better than we dared to hope at the beginning. At least there has been no war for a generation, and our food supply is ahead of the population for the first time in history – thanks to our new agricultural techniques.'

Aretenon glanced at the furnishings of his chamber, recalling with an effort the fact that in his own youth almost everything he saw would have appeared impossible or even meaningless to him. Not even the simplest of tools had existed then, at least in the knowledge of his people. Now there were ships and bridges and houses – and these were only the beginning.

'I am well satisfied,' he said. 'We have, as we planned, diverted the whole stream of our culture, turning it away from the dangers that lay ahead. The powers that made the Madness possible will soon be forgotten: only a handful of us still know of them, and we will take our secrets with us. Perhaps when our descendants rediscover them they will be wise enough to use them properly. But we have uncovered so many new wonders that it may be a thousand generations before we turn again to look into our own minds and to tamper with the forces locked within them.'

The mouth of the cave was illuminated by a sudden flash of lightning. The storm was coming nearer, though it was still some miles away. Rain was beginning to fall in large, angry drops from the leaden sky.

'While we're waiting for the ships,' said Aretenon rather abruptly, 'come into the next cave and see some of the new things we have to show you since your last visit.'

It was a strange collection. Side by side on the same bench were tools and inventions which in other cultures had been separated by thousands of years of time. The Stone Age was past: bronze and iron had come, and already the first crude scientific instruments had been built for experiments that were driving back the frontiers of the unknown. A primitive retort spoke of the beginnings of chemistry, and by its side were the first lenses the world had seen – waiting to reveal the unsuspected universes of the infinitely small and the infinitely great.

The storm was upon them as Aretenon's description of these new wonders drew to its close. From time to time he had glanced nervously at the mouth of the cave, as if awaiting a messenger from the harbour, but they had remained undisturbed save by the occasional crash of thunder.

'I've shown you everything of importance,' he said, 'but here's something that may amuse you while we're waiting. As I said, we've sent expeditions everywhere to collect and classify all the rocks they can, in the hope of finding useful minerals. One of them brought back this.'

He extinguished the lights and the cave became completely dark.

'It will be some time before your eyes grow sensitive enough to see it,' Aretenon warned. 'Just look over there in that corner.'

Eris strained his eyes into the darkness. At first he could see nothing: then, slowly, a glimmering blue light became faintly visible. It was so vague and diffuse that he could not focus his eyes upon it, and he automatically moved forward.

'I shouldn't go too near,' advised Aretenon. 'It seems to be a perfectly ordinary mineral, but the Phileni who found it and carried it here got some very strange burns from handling it. Yet it's quite cold to the touch. One day we'll learn its secret: but I don't suppose it's anything at all important.'

A vast curtain of sheet lightning split the sky, and for a moment the reflected glare lit up the cave, pinning weird shadows against the walls. At the same moment one of the Phileni staggered into the entrance and called something to Aretenon in its thin, reedy voice. He gave a great shout of triumph, as one of his ancestors might have done on some ancient battle-field: then his thoughts came crashing into Eris's mind.

'Land! They've found land – a whole new continent waiting for us!'

Eris felt the sense of triumph and victory well up within him like water bursting from a spring. Clear ahead now into the future lay the new, the glorious road along which their children would travel, mastering the world and all its secrets as they went. The vision of Therodimus was at last sharp and brilliant before his eyes.

He felt for the mind of Jeryl, so that she could share his joy – and found that it was closed to him. Leaning toward her in the darkness, he could sense that she was still staring into the depths of the cave, as if she had never heard the wonderful news, and could not tear her eyes away from that enigmatic glow.

Out of the night came the roar of the belated thunder as it raced across the sky. Eris felt Jeryl tremble beside him, and sent out his thoughts to comfort her.

'Don't let the thunder frighten you,' he said gently. 'What is there to fear now?'

'I do not know,' replied Jeryl. 'I am frightened – but not of the thunder.'

393

Oh, Eris, it is a wonderful thing we have done, and I wish Therodimus could be here to see it. But where will it lead in the end – this new road of ours?'

Out of the past, the words that Aretenon had once spoken had risen up to haunt her. She remembered their walk by the river, long ago, when he had talked of his hopes and had said: 'Certainly nothing we can learn from Nature will ever be as great a threat as the peril we have encountered in our own minds.' Now the words seemed to mock her and to cast a shadow over the golden future: but why, she could not say.

Alone, perhaps, of all the races in the Universe, her people had reached the second cross-roads – and had never passed the first. Now they must go along the road that they had missed, and must face the challenge at its end – the challenge from which, this time, they could not escape.

In the darkness, the faint glow of dying atoms burned unwavering in the rock. It would still be burning there, scarcely dimmed, when Jeryl and Eris had been dust for centuries. It would be only a little fainter when the civilisation they were building had at last unlocked its secrets.

Superiority

First published in *The Magazine of Science Fiction and Fantasy*, August 1951
Collected in *Expedition to Earth*

'Superiority' was inspired – if that is not too pretentious a word – by the German V2 rocket programme. With 20/20 hindsight, it is now clear that the Third Reich's attempts to develop an intercontinental ballistic missile, which was too late to have any major influence on World War II, sapped its resources and contributed to the Allied victory.

Soon after publication 'Superiority' was inserted into the Engineering curriculum of MIT – to warn the graduates that the Better is often the enemy of the Good – and the Best can be the enemy of both, as it is always too late.

And I must confess that the two characters in this little squib were based on Dr Wernher von Braun and General Walter Dornberger, both of whom later became good friends. To put the record straight, may I say that Wernher was nothing like the Dr Strangelove image many people have of him: he had a wonderful sense of humour and was greatly liked by all those who worked under him – Germans *and* Americans.

In making this statement – which I do of my own free will – I wish to make it perfectly clear that I am not in any way trying to gain sympathy, nor do I expect any mitigation of whatever sentence the Court may pronounce. I am writing this in an attempt to refute some of the lying reports published in the papers I have been allowed to see, and broadcast over the prison radio. These have given an entirely false picture of the true cause of our defeat, and as the leader of my race's armed forces at the cessation of hostilities I feel it my duty to protest against such libels upon those who served under me.

I also hope that this statement may explain the reasons for the application I have twice made to the Court, and will now induce it to grant a favour for which I can see no possible grounds of refusal.

The ultimate cause of our failure was a simple one: despite all statements to the contrary, it was not due to lack of bravery on the part of our men, or to any fault of the Fleet's. We were defeated by one thing only – by the inferior science of our enemies. I repeat – by the *inferior* science of our enemies.

When the war opened we had no doubts of our ultimate victory. The combined fleets of our allies greatly exceeded in number and armament those which the enemy could muster against us, and in almost all branches of military science we were their superiors. We were sure that we could maintain this superiority. Our belief proved, alas, to be only too well founded.

At the opening of the war our main weapons were the long-range homing torpedo, dirigible ball-lightning and the various modifications of the Klydon beam. Every unit of the Fleet was equipped with these and though the enemy possessed similar weapons their installations were generally of lesser power. Moreover, we had behind us a far greater military Research Organization, and with this initial advantage we could not possibly lose.

The campaign proceeded according to plan until the Battle of the Five Suns. We won this, of course, but the opposition proved stronger than we had expected. It was realized that victory might be more difficult, and more delayed, than had first been imagined. A conference of supreme commanders was therefore called to discuss our future strategy.

Present for the first time at one of our war conferences was Professor-General Norden, the new Chief of the Research Staff, who had just been appointed to fill the gap left by the death of Malvar, our greatest scientist. Malvar's leadership had been responsible, more than any other single factor, for the efficiency and power of our weapons. His loss was a very serious blow, but no one doubted the brilliance of his successor – though many of us disputed the wisdom of appointing a theoretical scientist to fill a post of such vital importance. But we had been overruled.

I can well remember the impression Norden made at that conference. The military advisers were worried, and as usual turned to the scientists for help. Would it be possible to improve our existing weapons, they asked, so that our present advantage could be increased still further?

Norden's reply was quite unexpected. Malvar had often been asked such a question – and he had always done what we requested.

'Frankly, gentlemen,' said Norden, 'I doubt it. Our existing weapons have practically reached finality. I don't wish to criticize my predecessor, or the excellent work done by the Research Staff in the last few generations, but do you realize that there has been no basic change in armaments for over a century? It is, I am afraid, the result of a tradition that has become conservative. For too long, the Research Staff has devoted itself to perfecting old weapons instead of developing new ones. It is fortunate for us that our opponents have been no wiser: we cannot assume that this will always be so.'

Norden's words left an uncomfortable impression, as he had no doubt intended. He quickly pressed home the attack.

'What we want are *new* weapons – weapons totally different from any that have been employed before. Such weapons can be made: it will take time, of course, but since assuming charge I have replaced some of the older scientists by young men and have directed research into several unexplored fields which show great promise. I believe, in fact, that a revolution in warfare may soon be upon us.'

We were skeptical. There was a bombastic tone in Norden's voice that made us suspicious of his claims. We did not know, then, that he never promised anything that he had not already almost perfected in the laboratory. *In the laboratory* – that was the operative phrase.

Norden proved his case less than a month later, when he demonstrated the Sphere of Annihilation, which produced complete disintegration of matter over a radius of several hundred meters. We were intoxicated by the power of the new weapon, and were quite prepared to overlook one fundamental defect – the fact that it *was* a sphere and hence destroyed its rather complicated generating equipment at the instant of formation. This meant, of course, that it could not be used on warships but only on guided missiles, and a great program was started to convert all homing torpedoes to carry the new weapon. For the time being all further offensives were suspended.

We realise now that this was our first mistake. I still think that it was a natural one, for it seemed to us then that all our existing weapons had become obsolete overnight, and we already regarded them almost as primitive survivals. What we did not appreciate was the magnitude of the task we were attempting and the length of time it would take to get the revolutionary super-weapon into battle. Nothing like this had happened for a hundred years and we had no previous experience to guide us.

The conversion problem proved far more difficult than anticipated. A new class of torpedo had to be designed, as the standard model was too small. This meant in turn that only the larger ships could launch the weapon, but we were prepared to accept this penalty. After six months, the heavy units of the Fleet were being equipped with the Sphere. Training manoeuvres and tests had shown that it was operating satisfactorily and we were ready to take it into action. Norden was already being hailed as the architect of victory, and had half-promised even more spectacular weapons.

Then two things happened. One of our battleships disappeared completely on a training flight, and an investigation showed that under certain conditions the ship's long-range radar could trigger the Sphere immediately it had been launched. The modification needed to overcome this defect was trivial, but it caused a delay of another month and was the source of much bad feeling between the naval staff and the scientists. We were ready for action again – when Norden announced that the radius of effectiveness of the Sphere had now been increased by ten, thus multiplying by a thousand the chances of destroying an enemy ship.

So the modifications started all over again, but everyone agreed that the delay would be worth it. Meanwhile, however, the enemy had been emboldened by the absence of further attacks and had made an unexpected onslaught. Our ships were short of torpedoes, since none had been coming from the factories, and were forced to retire. So we lost the systems of Kyrane and Floranus, and the planetary fortress of Rhamsandron.

It was an annoying but not a serious blow, for the recaptured systems had been unfriendly and difficult to administer. We had no doubt that we could restore the position in the near future, as soon as the new weapon became operational.

These hopes were only partially fulfilled. When we renewed our offensive, we had to do so with fewer of the Spheres of Annihilation than had been planned, and this was one reason for our limited success. The other reason was more serious.

While we had been equipping as many of our ships as we could with the irresistible weapon, the enemy had been building feverishly. His ships were of the old pattern, with the old weapons – but they outnumbered ours. When we went into action, we found that the numbers ranged against us were often 100 per cent greater than expected, causing target confusion among the automatic weapons and resulting in higher losses than anticipated. The enemy losses were higher still, for once a Sphere had reached its objective, destruction was certain, but the balance had not swung as far in our favour as we had hoped.

Moreover, while the main fleets had been engaged, the enemy had launched a daring attack on the lightly held systems of Eriston, Duranus, Carmanidor and Pharanidon – recapturing them all. We were thus faced with a threat only fifty light-years from our home planets.

There was much recrimination at the next meeting of the supreme commanders. Most of the complaints were addressed to Norden – Grand Admiral Taxaris in particular maintaining that thanks to our admittedly irresistible weapon we were now considerably worse off than before. We should, he claimed, have continued to build conventional ships, thus preventing the loss of our numerical superiority.

Norden was equally angry and called the naval staff ungrateful bunglers. But I could tell that he was worried – as indeed we all were – by the unexpected turn of events. He hinted that there might be a speedy way of remedying the situation. We now know that Research had been working on the Battle Analyser for many years, but at the time it came as a revelation to us and perhaps we were too easily swept off our feet. Norden's argument, also, was seductively convincing. What did it matter, he said, if the enemy had twice as many ships as we – if the efficiency of ours could be doubled or even trebled? For decades the limiting factor in warfare had been not mechanical but biological – it had become more and more difficult for any single mind, or group of minds, to cope with the rapidly changing complexities of battle in three-dimensional space. Norden's mathematicians had analysed some of the classic engagements of the past, and had shown that even when we had been victorious we had often operated our units at much less than half of their theoretical efficiency.

The Battle Analyser would change all this by replacing operations staff by electronic calculators. The idea was not new in theory, but until now it had been no more than a Utopian dream. Many of us found it difficult to believe that it was still anything but a dream: after we had run through several very complex dummy battles, however, we were convinced.

It was decided to install the Analyser in four of our heaviest ships, so that each of the main fleets could be equipped with one. At this stage, the trouble began – though we did not know it until later.

The Analyser contained just short of a million vacuum tubes and needed a team of five hundred technicans to maintain and operate it. It was quite impossible to accommodate the extra staff aboard a battleship, so each of the four units had to be accompanied by a converted liner to carry the technicians not on duty. Installation was also a very slow and tedious business, but by gigantic efforts it was completed in six months.

Then, to our dismay, we were confronted by another crisis. Nearly five thousand highly skilled men had been selected to serve the Analysers and had been given an intensive course at the Technical Training Schools. At the end of seven months, 10 per cent of them had had nervous breakdowns and only 40 per cent had qualified.

Once again, everyone started to blame everyone else. Norden, of course, said that the Research Staff could not be held responsible, and so incurred the enmity of the Personnel and Training Commands. It was finally decided that the only thing to do was to use two instead of four Analysers and to bring the others into action as soon as men could be trained. There was little time to lose, for the enemy was still on the offensive and his morale was rising.

The first Analyser fleet was ordered to recapture the system of Eriston. On the way, by one of the hazards of war, the liner carrying the technicians was struck by a roving mine. A warship would have survived, but the liner with its irreplaceable cargo was totally destroyed. So the operation had to be abandoned.

The other expedition was, at first, more successful. There was no doubt at all that the Analyser fulfilled its designers' claims, and the enemy was heavily defeated in the first engagements. He withdrew, leaving us in possession of Saphran, Leucon and Hexanerax. But his Intelligence Staff must have noted the change in our tactics and the inexplicable presence of a liner in the heart of our battle-fleet. It must have noted, also, that our first fleet had been accompanied by a similar ship – and had withdrawn when it had been destroyed.

In the next engagement, the enemy used his superior numbers to launch an overwhelming attack on the Analyser ship and its unarmed consort. The attack was made without regard to losses – both ships were, of course, very heavily protected – and it succeeded. The result was the virtual decapitation of the fleet, since an effectual transfer to the old operational methods proved impossible. We disengaged under heavy fire, and so lost all our gains and also the systems of Lorymia, Ismarnus, Beronis, Alphanidon and Sideneus.

At this stage, Grand Admiral Taxaris expressed his disapproval of Norden by committing suicide, and I assumed supreme command.

The situation was now both serious and infuriating. With stubborn conservatism and complete lack of imagination the enemy continued to advance with his old-fashioned and inefficient but now vastly more numerous ships. It was galling to realise that if we had only continued building, without seeking new weapons, we would have been in a far more advantageous position. There were many acrimonious conferences at which Norden defended the scientists while everyone else blamed them for all that had happened. The difficulty was that Norden had proved every one of his claims; he had a perfect excuse for all the disasters that had occurred. And we could not now turn back – the search for an irresistible weapon must go on. At first it had been a luxury that would shorten the war. Now it was a necessity if we were to end it victoriously.

We were on the defensive, and so was Norden. He was more than ever determined to re-establish his prestige and that of the Research Staff. But we had been twice disappointed, and would not make the same mistake again. No doubt Norden's twenty thousand scientists would produce many further weapons: we would remain unimpressed.

We were wrong. The final weapon was something so fantastic that even now it seems difficult to believe that it ever existed. Its innocent, non-committal name – the Exponential Field – gave no hint of its real potentialities. Some of Norden's mathematicians had discovered it during a piece of entirely theoretical research into the properties of space, and to everyone's great surprise their results were found to be physically realisable.

It seems very difficult to explain the operation of the Field to the layman. According to the technical description, it 'produces an exponential condition of space, so that a finite distance in normal, linear space may become infinite in pseudo-space'. Norden gave an analogy which some of us found useful. It was as if one took a flat disc of rubber – representing a region of normal space – and then pulled its centre out to infinity. The circumference of the disc would be unaltered – but its 'diameter' would be infinite. That was the sort of thing the generator of the Field did to the space around it.

As an example, suppose that a ship carrying the generator was surrounded by a ring of hostile machines. If it switched on the Field, *each* of the enemy ships would think that it – and the ships on the far side of the circle – had suddenly receded into nothingness. Yet the circumference of the circle would be the same as before: only the journey to the centre would be of infinite duration, for as one proceeded, distances would appear to become greater and greater as the 'scale' of space altered.

It was a nightmare condition, but a very useful one. Nothing could reach a ship carrying the Field: it might be englobed by an enemy fleet yet would be as inaccessible as if it were at the other side of the Universe. Against this, of course, it could not fight back without switching off the Field, but this still left it at a very great advantage, not only in defence but in offence. For a ship fitted with the Field could approach an enemy fleet undetected and suddenly appear in its midst.

This time there seemed to be no flaws in the new weapon. Needless to say, we looked for all the possible objections before we committed ourselves again. Fortunately the equipment was fairly simple and did not require a large operating staff. After much debate, we decided to rush it into production, for we realised that time was running short and the war was going against us. We had now lost almost the whole of our initial gains and the enemy forces had made several raids into our own Solar System.

We managed to hold off the enemy while the Fleet was re-equipped and the new battle techniques were worked out. To use the Field operationally it was necessary to locate an enemy formation, set a course that would intercept it, and then switch on the generator for the calculated period of time. On releasing the Field again – if the calculations had been accurate – one would be in the enemy's midst and could do great damage during the resulting confusion, retreating by the same route when necessary.

The first trial manoeuvres proved satisfactory and the equipment seemed quite reliable. Numerous mock attacks were made and the crews became accustomed to the new technique. I was on one of the test flights and can vividly remember my impressions as the Field was switched on. The ships around us seemed to dwindle as if on the surface of an expanding bubble: in an instant they had vanished completely. So had the stars – but presently we could see that the Galaxy was still visible as a faint band of light around the ship. The virtual radius of our pseudo-space was not really infinite, but some hundred thousand light-years, and so the distance to the farthest stars of our system had not been greatly increased – though the nearest had of course totally disappeared.

These training manoeuvres, however, had to be cancelled before they were complete owing to a whole flock of minor technical troubles in various pieces of equipment, notably the communications circuits. These were annoying, but not important, though it was thought best to return to Base to clear them up.

At that moment the enemy made what was obviously intended to be a decisive attack against the fortress planet of Iton at the limits of our Solar System. The Fleet had to go into battle before repairs could be made.

The enemy must have believed that we had mastered the secret of invisibility – as in a sense we had. Our ships appeared suddenly out of nowhere and inflicted tremendous damage – for a while. And then something quite baffling and inexplicable happened.

I was in command of the flag-ship *Hircania* when the trouble started. We had been operating as independent units, each against assigned objectives. Our detectors observed an enemy formation at medium range and the navigating officers measured its distance with great accuracy. We set course and switched on the generator.

The Exponential Field was released at the moment when we should have been passing through the centre of the enemy group. To our consternation, we emerged into normal space at a distance of many hundred miles – and when we found the enemy, he had already found us. We retreated, and tried again. This time we were so far away from the enemy that he located us first.

Obviously, something was seriously wrong. We broke communicator silence and tried to contact the other ships of the Fleet to see if they had experienced the same trouble. Once again we failed – and this time the failure was beyond all reason, for the communication equipment appeared to be working perfectly. We could only assume, fantastic though it seemed, that the rest of the Fleet had been destroyed.

I do not wish to describe the scenes when the scattered units of the Fleet struggled back to Base. Our casualties had actually been negligible, but the ships were completely demoralised. Almost all had lost touch with each other and had found that their ranging equipment showed inexplicable errors. It was obvious that the Exponential Field was the cause of the troubles, despite the fact that they were only apparent when it was switched off.

The explanation came too late to do us any good, and Norden's final discomfiture was small consolation for the virtual loss of the war. As I have explained, the Field generators produced a radial distortion of space, distances appearing greater and greater as one approached the centre of the artificial pseudo-space. When the field was switched off, conditions returned to normal.

But not quite. It was never possible to restore the initial state *exactly*. Switching the Field on and off was equivalent to an elongation and contraction of the ship carrying the generator, but there was an hysteresis effect, as it were, and the initial condition was never quite reproducible, owing to all the thousands of electrical changes and movements of mass aboard the ship while the Field was on. These asymmetries and distortions were cumulative, and though they seldom amounted to more than a fraction of one per cent, that was quite enough. It meant that the precision ranging equipment and the tuned circuits in the communication apparatus were thrown completely out of adjustment. Any single ship could never detect the change – only when it compared its equipment with that of another vessel, or tried to communicate with it, could it tell what had happened.

It is impossible to describe the resultant chaos. Not a single component of one ship could be expected with certainty to work aboard another. The very nuts and bolts were no longer interchangeable, and the supply position became quite impossible. Given time, we might even have overcome these difficulties, but the enemy ships were already attacking in thousands with weapons which now seemed centuries behind those that we had invented. Our magnificent Fleet, crippled by our own science, fought on as best it could until it was overwhelmed and forced to surrender. The ships fitted with the Field were still invulnerable, but as fighting units they were almost helpless. Every time they switched on their generators to escape from enemy attack, the permanent distortion of their equipment increased. In a month, it was all over.

This is the true story of our defeat, which I give without prejudice to my defence before this Court. I make it, as I have said, to counteract the libels that have been circulating against the men who fought under me, and to show where the true blame for our misfortunes lay.

Finally, my request, which as the Court will now realise I make in no frivolous manner and which I hope will therefore be granted.

The Court will be aware that the conditions under which we are housed and the constant surveillance to which we are subjected night and day are somewhat distressing. Yet I am not complaining of this: nor do I complain of the fact that shortage of accommodation has made it necessary to house us in pairs.

But I cannot be held responsible for my future actions if I am compelled any longer to share my cell with Professor Norden, late Chief of the Research Staff of my armed forces.

'If I Forget Thee, Oh Earth . . .'

First published in *Future*, September 1951
Collected in *Expedition to Earth*

This story, which has been rather widely reprinted, was written at Christmas 1950.

On another Christmas, eighteen years later, the crew of Apollo 8 became the first of all mankind to see an Earthrise from the Moon.

Let us hope that no one ever views an Earthrise like the child in this cautionary tale.

When Marvin was ten years old, his father took him through the long, echoing corridors that led up through Administration and Power, until at last they came to the uppermost levels of all and were among the swiftly growing vegetation of the Farmlands. Marvin liked it here: it was fun watching the great, slender plants creeping with almost visible eagerness towards the sunlight as it filtered down through the plastic domes to meet them. The smell of life was everywhere, awakening inexpressible longings in his heart: no longer was he breathing the dry, cool air of the residential levels, purged of all smells but the faint tang of ozone. He wished he could stay here for a little while, but Father would not let him. They went onwards until they had reached the entrance to the Observatory, which he had never visited: but they did not stop, and Marvin knew with a sense of rising excitement that there could be only one goal left. For the first time in his life, he was going Outside.

There were a dozen of the surface vehicles, with their wide balloon tyres and pressurised cabins, in the great servicing chamber. His father must have been expected, for they were led at once to the little scout car waiting by the huge circular door of the airlock. Tense with expectancy, Marvin settled himself down in the cramped cabin while his father started the motor and checked the controls. The inner door of the lock slid open and then closed behind them: he heard the roar of the great air-pumps fade slowly away as the pressure dropped to zero. Then the 'Vacuum' sign flashed on, the outer door parted, and before Marvin lay the land which he had never yet entered.

He had seen it in photographs, of course: he had watched it imaged on television screens a hundred times. But now it was lying all around him, burning beneath the fierce sun that crawled so slowly across the jet-black sky. He stared into the west, away from the blinding splendour of the sun – and there were the stars, as he had been told but had never quite believed. He gazed at them for a long time, marvelling that anything could be so bright and yet so tiny. They were intense unscintillating points, and suddenly he remembered a rhyme he had once read in one of his father's books:

> Twinkle, twinkle, little star,
> How I wonder what you are.

Well, he knew what the stars were. Whoever asked that question must have been very stupid. And what did they mean by 'twinkle'? You could see at a glance that all the stars shone with the same steady, unwavering light. He abandoned the puzzle and turned his attention to the landscape around him.

They were racing across a level plain at almost a hundred miles an hour, the great balloon tyres sending up little spurts of dust behind them. There was no sign of the Colony: in the few minutes while he had been gazing at the stars, its domes and radio towers had fallen below the horizon. Yet there were other indications of man's presence, for about a mile ahead Marvin could see the curiously shaped structures clustering round the head of a mine. Now and then a puff of vapour would emerge from a squat smoke-stack and would instantly disperse.

They were past the mine in a moment. Father was driving with a reckless and exhilarating skill as if – it was a strange thought to come into a child's mind – he was trying to escape from something. In a few minutes they had reached the edge of the plateau on which the Colony had been built. The ground fell sharply away beneath them in a dizzying slope whose lower stretches were lost in the shadow. Ahead, as far as the eye could reach, was a jumbled wasteland of craters, mountain ranges, and ravines. The crests of the mountains, catching the low sun, burned like islands of fire in a sea of darkness: and above them the stars still shone as steadfastly as ever.

There could be no way forward – yet there was. Marvin clenched his fists as the car edged over the slope and started the long descent. Then he saw the barely visible track leading down the mountainside, and relaxed a little. Other men, it seemed, had gone this way before.

Night fell with a shocking abruptness as they crossed the shadow line and the sun dropped below the crest of the plateau. The twin searchlights sprang into life, casting blue-white bands on the rocks ahead, so that there was scarcely need to check their speed. For hours they drove through valleys and past the feet of mountains whose peaks seemed to comb the stars, and sometimes they emerged for a moment into the sunlight as they climbed over higher ground.

And now on the right was a wrinkled, dusty plain, and on the left, its

405

ramparts and terraces rising mile after mile into the sky, was a wall of mountains that marched into the distance until its peaks sank from sight below the rim of the world. There was no sign that men had ever explored this land, but once they passed the skeleton of a crashed rocket, and beside it a stone cairn surmounted by a metal cross.

It seemed to Marvin that the mountains stretched on forever: but at last, many hours later, the range ended in a towering, precipitous headland that rose steeply from a cluster of little hills. They drove down into a shallow valley that curved in a great arc towards the far side of the mountains: and as they did so, Marvin slowly realised that something very strange was happening in the land ahead.

The sun was now low behind the hills on the right: the valley before them should be in total darkness. Yet it was awash with a cold white radiance that came spilling over the crags beneath which they were driving. Then, suddenly, they were out in the open plain, and the source of the light lay before them in all its glory.

It was very quiet in the little cabin now that the motors had stopped. The only sound was the faint whisper of the oxygen feed and an occasional metallic crepitation as the outer walls of the vehicle radiated away their heat. For no warmth at all came from the great silver crescent that floated low above the far horizon and flooded all this land with pearly light. It was so brilliant that minutes passed before Marvin could accept its challenge and look steadfastly into its glare, but at last he could discern the outlines of continents, the hazy border of the atmosphere, and the white islands of cloud. And even at this distance, he could see the glitter of sunlight on the polar ice.

It was beautiful, and it called to his heart across the abyss of space. There in that shining crescent were all the wonders that he had never known – the hues of sunset skies, the moaning of the sea on pebbled shores, the patter of falling rain, the unhurried benison of snow. These and a thousand others should have been his rightful heritage, but he knew them only from the books and ancient records, and the thought filled him with the anguish of exile.

Why could they not return? It seemed so peaceful beneath those lines of marching cloud. Then Marvin, his eyes no longer blinded by the glare, saw that the portion of the disc that should have been in darkness was gleaming faintly with an evil phosphorescence: and he remembered. He was looking upon the funeral pyre of a world – upon the radioactive aftermath of Armageddon. Across a quarter of a million miles of space, the glow of dying atoms was still visible, a perennial reminder of the ruined past. It would be centuries yet before that deadly glow died from the rocks and life could return again to fill that silent, empty world.

And now Father began to speak, telling Marvin the story which until this moment had meant no more to him than the fairy-tales he had heard in childhood. There were many things he could not understand: it was impossible for him to picture the glowing, multi-coloured pattern of life on

406

the planet he had never seen. Nor could he comprehend the forces that had destroyed it in the end, leaving the Colony, preserved by its isolation, as the sole survivor. Yet he could share the agony of those final days, when the Colony had learned at last that never again would the supply ships come flaming down through the stars with gifts from home. One by one the radio stations had ceased to call: on the shadowed globe the lights of the cities had dimmed and died, and they were alone at last, as no men had ever been alone before, carrying in their hands the future of the race.

Then had followed the years of despair, and the long-drawn battle for survival in their fierce and hostile world. That battle had been won, though barely: this little oasis of life was safe against the worst that Nature could do. But unless there was a goal, a future towards which it could work, the Colony would lose the will to live and neither machines nor skill nor science could save it then.

So, at last, Marvin understood the purpose of this pilgrimage. He would never walk beside the rivers of that lost and legendary world, or listen to the thunder raging above its softly rounded hills. Yet one day – how far ahead? – his children's children would return to claim their heritage. The winds and the rains would scour the poisons from the burning lands and carry them to the sea, and in the depths of the sea they would waste their venom until they could harm no living things. Then the great ships that were still waiting here on the silent, dusty plains could lift once more into space, along the road that led to home.

That was the dream: and one day, Marvin knew with a sudden flash of insight, he would pass it on to his own son, here at this same spot with the mountains behind him and the silver light from the sky streaming into his face.

He did not look back as they began the homeward journey. He could not bear to see the cold glory of the crescent Earth fade from the rocks around him, as he went to rejoin his people in their long exile.

All the Time in the World

First published in *Startling Stories*, July 1952
Collected in *The Other Side of the Sky*

This was my first story ever to be adapted for TV – ABC, 13 June 1952. Although I worked on the script, I have absolutely no recollection of the programme, and can't imagine how it was produced in pre-video-tape days!

When the quiet knock came on the door, Robert Ashton surveyed the room in one swift, automatic movement. Its dull respectability satisfied him and should reassure any visitor. Not that he had any reason to expect the police, but there was no point in taking chances.

'Come in,' he said, pausing only to grab Plato's *Dialogues* from the shelf beside him. Perhaps this gesture was a little too ostentatious, but it always impressed his clients.

The door opened slowly. At first, Ashton continued his intent reading, not bothering to glance up. There was the slightest acceleration of his heart, a mild and even exhilarating constriction of the chest. Of course, it couldn't possibly be a flatfoot: someone would have tipped him off. Still, any unheralded visitor was unusual and thus potentially dangerous.

Ashton laid down the book, glanced toward the door and remarked in a noncommittal voice: 'What can I do for you?' He did not get up; such courtesies belonged to a past he had buried long ago. Besides, it was a woman. In the circles he now frequented, women were accustomed to receive jewels and clothes and money – but never respect.

Yet there was something about this visitor that drew him slowly to his feet. It was not merely that she was beautiful, but she had a poised and effortless authority that moved her into a different world from the flamboyant doxies he met in the normal course of business. There was a brain and a purpose behind those calm, appraising eyes – a brain, Ashton suspected, the equal of his own.

He did not know how grossly he had underestimated her.

'Mr Ashton,' she began, 'let us not waste time. I know who you are and I have work for you. Here are my credentials.'

She opened a large, stylish handbag and extracted a thick bundle of notes. 'You may regard this,' she said, 'as a sample.'

Ashton caught the bundle as she tossed it carelessly toward him. It was the largest sum of money he had ever held in his life – at least a hundred fivers, all new and serially numbered. He felt them between his fingers. If they were not genuine, they were so good that the difference was of no practical importance.

He ran his thumb to and fro along the edge of the wad as if feeling a pack for a marked card, and said thoughtfully, 'I'd like to know where you got these. If they aren't forgeries, they must be hot and will take some passing.'

'They are genuine. A very short time ago they were in the Bank of England. But if they are of no use to you throw them in the fire. I merely let you have them to show that I mean business.'

'Go on.' He gestured to the only seat and balanced himself on the edge of the table.

She drew a sheaf of papers from the capacious handbag and handed it across to him.

'I am prepared to pay you any sum you wish if you will secure these items and bring them to me, at a time and place to be arranged. What is more, I will guarantee that you can make the thefts with no personal danger.'

Ashton looked at the list, and sighed. The woman was mad. Still, she had better be humoured. There might be more money where this came from.

'I notice,' he said mildly, 'that all these items are in the British Museum, and that most of them are, quite literally, priceless. By that I mean that you could neither buy nor sell them.'

'I do not wish to sell them. I am a collector.'

'So it seems. What are you prepared to pay for these acquisitions?'

'Name a figure.'

There was a short silence. Ashton weighed the possibilities. He took a certain professional pride in his work, but there were some things that no amount of money could accomplish. Still, it would be amusing to see how high the bidding would go.

'I think a round million would be a very reasonable figure for this lot,' he said ironically.

'I fear you are not taking me very seriously. With your contacts, you should be able to dispose of these.'

There was a flash of light and something sparkled through the air. Ashton caught the necklace before it hit the ground, and despite himself was unable to suppress a gasp of amazement. A fortune glittered through his fingers. The central diamond was the largest he had ever seen – it must be one of the world's most famous jewels.

His visitor seemed completely indifferent as he slipped the necklace into his pocket. Ashton was badly shaken; he knew she was not acting. To her, that fabulous gem was of no more value than a lump of sugar. This was madness on an unimaginable scale.

'Assuming that you can deliver the money,' he said, 'how do you imagine that it's physically possible to do what you ask? One might steal a single

409

item from this list, but within a few hours the Museum would be solid with police.'

With a fortune already in his pocket, he could afford to be frank. Besides, he was curious to learn more about his fantastic visitor.

She smiled, rather sadly, as if humouring a backward child.

'If I show you the way,' she said softly, 'will you do it?'

'Yes – for a million.'

'Have you noticed anything strange since I came in? Is it not – very quiet?'

Ashton listened. My God, she was right! This room was never completely silent, even at night. There had been a wind blowing over the roof tops; where had it gone now? The distant rumble of traffic had ceased; five minutes ago he had been cursing the engines shunting in the marshalling yard at the end of the road. What had happened to them?

'Go to the window.'

He obeyed the order and drew aside the grimy lace curtains with fingers that shook slightly despite all attempt at control. Then he relaxed. The street was quite empty, as it often was at this time in the midmorning. There was no traffic, and hence no reason for sound. Then he glanced down the row of dingy houses towards the shunting yard.

His visitor smiled as he stiffened with the shock.

'Tell me what you see, Mr Ashton.'

He turned slowly, face pale and throat muscles working.

'What are you?' he gasped. 'A witch?'

'Don't be foolish. There is a simple explanation. It is not the world that has changed – but you.'

Ashton stared again at that unbelievable shunting engine, the plume of steam frozen motionless above it as if made from cotton wool. He realised now that the clouds were equally immobile; they should have been scudding across the sky. All around him was the unnatural stillness of the high-speed photograph, the vivid unreality of a scene glimpsed in a flash of lightning.

'You are intelligent enough to realise what is happening, even if you cannot understand how it is done. Your time scale has been altered: a minute in the outer world would be a year in this room.'

Again she opened the handbag, and this time brought forth what appeared to be a bracelet of some silvery metal, with a series of dials and switches moulded into it.

'You can call this a personal generator,' she said. 'With it strapped about your arm, you are invincible. You can come and go without hindrance – you can steal everything on that list and bring it to me before one of the guards in the Museum has blinked an eyelid. When you have finished, you can be miles away before you switch off the field and step back into the normal world.

'Now listen carefully, and do exactly what I say. The field has a radius of about seven feet, so you must keep at least that distance from any other person. Secondly, you must not switch it off again until you have completed

410

your task and I have given you your payment. *This is most important.* Now, the plan I have worked out is this. . . .'

No criminal in the history of the world had ever possessed such power. It was intoxicating – yet Ashton wondered if he would ever get used to it. He had ceased to worry about explanations, at least until the job was done and he had collected his reward. Then, perhaps, he would get away from England and enjoy a well-earned retirement.

His visitor had left a few minutes ahead of him, but when he stepped out onto the street the scene was completely unchanged. Though he had prepared for it, the sensation was still unnerving. Ashton felt an impulse to hurry, as if this condition couldn't possibly last and he had to get the job done before the gadget ran out of juice. But that, he had been assured, was impossible.

In the High Street he slowed down to look at the frozen traffic, the paralysed pedestrians. He was careful, as he had been warned, not to approach so close to anyone that they came within his field. How ridiculous people looked when one saw them like this, robbed of such grace as movement could give, their mouths half open in foolish grimaces!

Having to seek assistance went against the grain, but some parts of the job were too big for him to handle by himself. Besides, he could pay liberally and never notice it. The main difficulty, Ashton realised, would be to find someone who was intelligent enough not to be scared – or so stupid that he would take everything for granted. He decided to try the first possibility.

Tony Marchetti's place was down a side street so close to the police station that one felt it was really carrying camouflage too far. As he walked past the entrance, Ashton caught a glimpse of the duty sergeant at his desk and resisted a temptation to go inside to combine a little pleasure with business. But that sort of thing could wait until later.

The door of Tony's opened in his face as he approached. It was such a natural occurrence in a world where nothing was normal that it was a moment before Ashton realised its implications. Had his generator failed? He glanced hastily down the street and was reassured by the frozen tableau behind him.

'Well, if it isn't Bob Ashton!' said a familiar voice. 'Fancy meeting you as early in the morning as this. That's an odd bracelet you're wearing. I thought I had the only one.'

'Hello, Aram,' replied Ashton. 'It looks as if there's a lot going on that neither of us knows about. Have you signed up Tony, or is he still free?'

'Sorry. We've a little job which will keep him busy for a while.'

'Don't tell me. It's at the National Gallery or the Tate.'

Aram Albenkian fingered his neat goatee. 'Who told you that?' he asked.

'No one. But, after all, you *are* the crookedest art dealer in the trade, and I'm beginning to guess what's going on. Did a tall, very good-looking brunette give you that bracelet and a shopping list?'

'I don't see why I should tell you, but the answer's no. It was a man.'

Ashton felt a momentary surprise. Then he shrugged his shoulders. 'I might have guessed that there would be more than one of them. I'd like to know who's behind it.'

'Have you any theories?' said Albenkian guardedly.

Ashton decided that it would be worth risking some loss of information to test the other's reactions. 'It's obvious they're not interested in money – they have all they want and can get more with this gadget. The woman who saw me said she was a collector. I took it as a joke, but I see now that she meant it seriously.'

'Why do we come into the picture? What's to stop them doing the whole job themselves?' Albenkian asked.

'Maybe they're frightened. Or perhaps they want our – er – specialised knowledge. Some of the items on my list are rather well cased in. My theory is that they're agents for a mad millionaire.'

It didn't hold water, and Ashton knew it. But he wanted to see which leaks Albenkian would try to plug.

'My dear Ashton,' said the other impatiently, holding up his wrist. 'How do you explain this little thing? I know nothing about science, but even I can tell that it's beyond the wildest dreams of our technologies. There's only one conclusion to be drawn from that.'

'Go on.'

'These people are from – somewhere else. Our world is being systematically looted of its treasures. You know all this stuff you read about rockets and spaceships? Well, someone else has done it first.'

Ashton didn't laugh. The theory was no more fantastic than the facts.

'Whoever they are,' he said, 'they seem to know their way around pretty well. I wonder how many teams they've got? Perhaps the Louvre and the Prado are being reconnoitred at this very minute. The world is going to have a shock before the day's out.'

They parted amicably enough, neither confiding any details of real importance about his business. For a fleeting moment Ashton thought of trying to buy over Tony, but there was no point in antagonising Albenkian. Steve Regan would have to do. That meant walking about a mile, since of course any form of transport was impossible. He would die of old age before a bus completed the journey. Ashton was not clear what would happen if he attempted to drive a car when the field was operating, and he had been warned not to try any experiments.

It astonished Ashton that even such a nearly certified moron as Steve could take the accelerator so calmly; there was something to be said, after all, for the comic strips which were probably his only reading. After a few words of grossly simplified explanation, Steve buckled on the spare wristlet which, rather to Ashton's surprise, his visitor had handed over without comment. Then they set out on their long walk to the Museum.

Ashton, or his client, had thought of everything. They stopped once at a park bench to rest and enjoy some sandwiches and regain their breath.

When at last they reached the Museum, neither felt any the worse for the unaccustomed exercise.

They walked together though the gates of the Museum – unable, despite logic, to avoid speaking in whispers – and up the wide stone steps into the entrance hall. Ashton knew his way perfectly. With whimsical humour he displayed his Reading Room ticket as they walked, at a respectful distance, past the statuesque attendants. It occurred to him that the occupants of the great chamber, for the most part, looked just the same as they normally did, even without the benefit of the accelerator.

It was a straightforward but tedious job collecting the books that had been listed. They had been chosen, it seemed, for their beauty as works of art as much as for their literary content. The selection had been done by someone who knew his job. Had *they* done it themselves, Ashton wondered, or had they bribed other experts as they were bribing him? He wondered if he would ever glimpse the full ramifications of their plot.

There was a considerable amount of panel-smashing to be done, but Ashton was careful not to damage any books, even the unwanted ones. Whenever he had collected enough volumes to make a comfortable load, Steve carried them out into the courtyard and dumped them on the paving stones until a small pyramid had accumulated.

It would not matter if they were left for short periods outside the field of the accelerator. No one would notice their momentary flicker of existence in the normal world.

They were in the library for two hours of their time, and paused for another snack before passing to the next job. On the way Ashton stopped for a little private business. There was a tinkle of glass as the tiny case, standing in solitary splendour, yielded up its treasure: then the manuscript of *Alice* was safely tucked into Ashton's pocket.

Among the antiquities, he was not quite so much at home. There were a few examples to be taken from every gallery, and sometimes it was hard to see the reasons for the choice. It was as if – and again he remembered Albenkian's words – these works of art had been selected by someone with totally alien standards. This time, with a few exceptions, *they* had obviously not been guided by the experts.

For the second time in history the case of the Portland Vase was shattered. In five seconds, thought Ashton, the alarms would be going all over the Museum and the whole building would be in an uproar. And in five seconds he could be miles away. It was an intoxicating thought, and as he worked swiftly to complete his contract he began to regret the price he had asked. Even now, it was not too late.

He felt the quiet satisfaction of the good workman as he watched Steve carry the great silver tray of the Mildenhall Treasure out into the courtyard and place it beside the now impressive pile. 'That's the lot,' he said. 'I'll settle up at my place this evening. Now let's get this gadget off you.'

They walked out into High Holborn and chose a secluded side street that had no pedestrians near it. Ashton unfastened the peculiar buckle and stepped back from his cohort, watching him freeze into immobility as he did so. Steve was vulnerable again, moving once more with all the other men in the stream of time. But before the alarm had gone out he would have lost himself in the London crowds.

When he re-entered the Museum yard, the treasure had already gone. Standing where it had been was his visitor of – how long ago? She was still poised and graceful, but, Ashton thought, looking a little tired. He approached until their fields merged and they were no longer separated by an impassable gulf of silence. 'I hope you're satisfied,' he said. 'How did you move the stuff so quickly?'

She touched the bracelet around her own wrist and gave a wan smile. 'We have many other powers beside this.'

'Then why did you need my help?'

'There were technical reasons. It was necessary to remove the objects we required from the presence of other matter. In this way, we could gather only what we needed and not waste our limited – what shall I call them? – transporting facilities. Now may I have the bracelet back?'

Ashton slowly handed over the one he was carrying, but made no effort to unfasten his own. There might be danger in what he was doing, but he intended to retreat at the first sign of it.

'I'm prepared to reduce my fee,' he said. 'In fact I'll waive all payment – in exchange for this.' He touched his wrist, where the intricate metal band gleamed in the sunlight.

She was watching him with an expression as fathomless as the Gioconda smile. (Had *that*, Ashton wondered, gone to join the treasure he had gathered? How much had they taken from the Louvre?)

'I would not call that reducing your fee. All the money in the world could not purchase one of those bracelets.'

'Or the things I have given you.'

'You are greedy, Mr Ashton. You know that with an accelerator the entire world would be yours.'

'What of that? Do you have any further interest in our planet, now you have taken what you need?'

There was a pause. Then, unexpectedly, she smiled. 'So you have guessed I do not belong to your world.'

'Yes. And I know that you have other agents besides myself. Do you come from Mars, or won't you tell me?'

'I am quite willing to tell you. But you may not thank me if I do.'

Ashton looked at her warily. What did she mean by that? Unconscious of his action, he put his wrist behind his back, protecting the bracelet.

'No, I am not from Mars, or any planet of which you have ever heard. You would not understand *what* I am. Yet I will tell you this. I am from the Future.'

'The Future! That's ridiculous!'

'Indeed? I should be interested to know why.'

'If that sort of thing were possible, our past history would be full of time

414

travellers. Besides, it would involve a *reductio ad absurdum*. Going into the past could change the present and produce all sorts of paradoxes.'

'Those are good points, though not perhaps as original as you suppose. But they only refute the possibility of time travel in general, not in the very special case which concerns us now.'

'What is peculiar about it?' he asked.

'On very rare occasions, and by the release of an enormous amount of energy, it is possible to produce a – *singularity* – in time. During the fraction of a second when that singularity occurs, the past becomes accessible to the future, though only in a restricted way. We can send our minds back to you, but not our bodies.'

'You mean,' said Ashton, 'that you are *borrowing* the body I see?'

'Oh, I have paid for it, as I am paying you. The owner has agreed to the terms. We are very conscientious in these matters.'

Ashton was thinking swiftly. If this story was true, it gave him a definite advantage.

'You mean,' he continued, 'that you have no direct control over matter, and must work through human agents?'

'Yes. Even those bracelets were made here, under our mental control.'

She was explaining too much too readily, revealing all her weaknesses. A warning signal was flashing in the back of Ashton's mind, but he had committed himself too deeply to retreat.

'Then it seems to me,' he said slowly, 'that you cannot force me to hand this bracelet back.'

'That is perfectly true.'

'That's all I want to know.'

She was smiling at him now, and there was something in that smile that chilled him to the marrow.

'We are not vindictive or unkind, Mr Ashton,' she said quietly. 'What I am going to do now appeals to my sense of justice. You have asked for that bracelet; you can keep it. Now I shall tell you just how useful it will be.'

For a moment Ashton had a wild impulse to hand back the accelerator. She must have guessed his thoughts.

'No, it's too late. I insist that you keep it. And I can reassure you on one point. It won't wear out. It will last you' – again that enigmatic smile – 'the rest of your life.

'Do you mind if we go for a walk, Mr Ashton? I have done my work here, and would like to have a last glimpse of your world before I leave it forever.'

She turned toward the iron gates, and did not wait for a reply. Consumed by curiosity, Ashton followed.

They walked in silence until they were standing among the frozen traffic of Tottenham Court Road. For a while she stood staring at the busy yet motionless crowds; then she sighed.

'I cannot help feeling sorry for them, and for you. I wonder what you would have made of yourselves.'

'What do you mean by that?'

'Just now, Mr Ashton, you implied that the future cannot reach back into the past, because that would alter history. A shrewd remark, but, I am afraid, irrelevant. You see, *your* world has no more history to alter.'

She pointed across the road, and Ashton turned swiftly on his heels. There was nothing there except a newsboy crouching over his pile of papers. A placard formed an impossible curve in the breeze that was blowing through this motionless world. Ashton read the crudely lettered words with difficulty:

SUPER-BOMB TEST TODAY

The voice in his ears seemed to come from a very long way off.

'I told you that time travel, even in this restricted form, requires an enormous release of energy – far more than a single bomb can liberate, Mr Ashton. But that bomb is only a trigger—'

She pointed to the solid ground beneath their feet. 'Do you know anything about your own planet? Probably not; your race has learned so little. But even your scientists have discovered that, two thousand miles down, the Earth has a dense, liquid core. That core is made of compressed matter, and it can exist in either of two stable states. Given a certain stimulus, it can change from one of those states to another, just as a seesaw can tip over at the touch of a finger. But that change, Mr Ashton, will liberate as much energy as all the earthquakes since the beginning of your world. The oceans and continents will fly into space; the sun will have a second asteroid belt.

'That cataclysm will send its echoes down the ages, and will open up to us a fraction of a second in your time. During that instant, we are trying to save what we can of your world's treasures. It is all that we can do; even if your motives were purely selfish and completely dishonest, you have done your race a service you never intended.

'And now I must return to our ship, where it waits by the ruins of Earth almost a hundred thousand years from now. You can keep the bracelet.'

The withdrawal was instantaneous. The woman suddenly froze and became one with the other statues in the silent street. He was alone.

Alone! Ashton held the gleaming bracelet before his eyes, hypnotised by its intricate workmanship and by the powers it concealed. He had made a bargain, and he must keep it. He could live out the full span of his life – at the cost of an isolation no other man had ever known. If he switched off the field, the last seconds of history would tick inexorably away.

Seconds? Indeed, there was less time than that. For he knew that the bomb must already have exploded.

He sat down on the edge of the pavement and began to think. There was no need to panic; he must take things calmly, without hysteria. After all, he had plenty of time.

All the time in the world.

The Nine Billion Names of God

First published in *Star Science Fiction Stories* #1, ed. Frederik Pohl, 1953
Collected in *The Other Side of the Sky*

This story triggered a charming response from the highest possible authority –
His Holiness the Dalai Lama.

'This is a slightly unusual request,' said Dr Wagner, with what he hoped
was commendable restraint. 'As far as I know, it's the first time anyone's
been asked to supply a Tibetan monastery with an Automatic Sequence
Computer. I don't wish to be inquisitive, but I should hardly have thought
that your – ah – establishment had much use for such a machine. Could
you explain just what you intend to do with it?'

'Gladly,' replied the lama, readjusting his silk robes and carefully putting
away the slide rule he had been using for currency conversions. 'Your Mark
V Computer can carry out any routine mathematical operation involving
up to ten digits. However, for our work we are interested in *letters*, not
numbers. As we wish you to modify the output circuits, the machine will
be printing words, not columns of figures.'

'I don't quite understand . . .'

'This is a project on which we have been working for the last three
centuries – since the lamasery was founded, in fact. It is somewhat alien to
your way of thought, so I hope you will listen with an open mind while I
explain it.'

'Naturally.'

'It is really quite simple. We have been compiling a list which shall
contain all the possible names of God.'

'I beg your pardon?'

'We have reason to believe,' continued the lama imperturbably, 'that all
such names can be written with not more than nine letters in an alphabet
we have devised.'

'And you have been doing this for three centuries?'

'Yes: we expected it would take us about fifteen thousand years to
complete the task.'

'Oh,' Dr Wagner looked a little dazed. 'Now I see why you wanted to hire
one of our machines. But exactly what is the *purpose* of this project?'

The lama hesitated for a fraction of a second, and Wagner wondered if he had offended him. If so, there was no trace of annoyance in the reply.

'Call it ritual, if you like, but it's a fundamental part of our belief. All the many names of the Supreme Being – God, Jehovah, Allah, and so on – they are only man-made labels. There is a philosophical problem of some difficulty here, which I do not propose to discuss, but somewhere among all the possible combinations of letters that can occur are what one may call the *real* names of God. By systematic permutation of letters, we have been trying to list them all.'

'I see. You've been starting at AAAAAAA . . . and working up to ZZZZZZZZ. . . .'

'Exactly – though we use a special alphabet of our own. Modifying the electromatic typewriters to deal with this is, of course, trivial. A rather more interesting problem is that of devising suitable circuits to eliminate ridiculous combinations. For example, no letter must occur more than three times in succession.'

'Three? Surely you mean two.'

'Three is correct: I am afraid it would take too long to explain why, even if you understood our language.'

'I'm sure it would,' said Wagner hastily. 'Go on.'

'Luckily, it will be a simple matter to adapt your Automatic Sequence Computer for this work, since once it has been programmed properly it will permute each letter in turn and print the result. What would have taken us fifteen thousand years it will be able to do in a hundred days.'

Dr Wagner was scarcely conscious of the faint sounds from the Manhattan streets far below. He was in a different world, a world of natural, not man-made, mountains. High up in their remote aeries these monks had been patiently at work, generation after generation, compiling their lists of meaningless words. Was there any limit to the follies of mankind? Still, he must give no hint of his inner thoughts. The customer was always right. . . .

'There's no doubt,' replied the doctor, 'that we can modify the Mark V to print lists of this nature. I'm much more worried about the problem of installation and maintenance. Getting out to Tibet, in these days, is not going to be easy.'

'We can arrange that. The components are small enough to travel by air – that is one reason why we chose your machine. If you can get them to India, we will provide transport from there.'

'And you want to hire two of our engineers?'

'Yes, for the three months that the project should occupy.'

'I've no doubt that Personnel can manage that.' Dr Wagner scribbled a note on his desk pad. 'There are just two other points—'

Before he could finish the sentence the lama had produced a small slip of paper.

'This is my certified credit balance at the Asiatic Bank.'

'Thank you. It appears to be – ah – adequate. The second matter is so trivial that I hesitate to mention it – but it's surprising how often the obvious gets overlooked. What source of electrical energy have you?'

'A diesel generator providing fifty kilowatts at a hundred and ten volts. It was installed about five years ago and is quite reliable. It's made life at the lamasery much more comfortable, but of course it was really installed to provide power for the motors driving the prayer wheels.'

'Of course,' echoed Dr Wagner. 'I should have thought of that.'

The view from the parapet was vertiginous, but in time one gets used to anything. After three months, George Hanley was not impressed by the two-thousand-foot swoop into the abyss or the remote checkerboard of fields in the valley below. He was leaning against the wind-smoothed stones and staring morosely at the distant mountains whose names he had never bothered to discover.

This, thought George, was the craziest thing that had ever happened to him. 'Project Shangri-La', some wit back at the labs had christened it. For weeks now the Mark V had been churning out acres of sheets covered with gibberish. Patiently, inexorably, the computer had been rearranging letters in all their possible combinations, exhausting each class before going on to the next. As the sheets had emerged from the electromatic typewriters, the monks had carefully cut them up and pasted them into enormous books. In another week, heaven be praised, they would have finished. Just what obscure calculations had convinced the monks that they needn't bother to go on to words of ten, twenty, or a hundred letters, George didn't know. One of his recurring nightmares was that there would be some change of plan, and that the high lama (whom they'd naturally called Sam Jaffe, though he didn't look a bit like him) would suddenly announce that the project would be extended to approximately AD 2060. They were quite capable of it.

George heard the heavy wooden door slam in the wind as Chuck came out onto the parapet beside him. As usual, Chuck was smoking one of the cigars that made him so popular with the monks – who, it seemed, were quite willing to embrace all the minor and most of the major pleasures of life. That was one thing in their favour: they might be crazy, but they weren't bluenoses. Those frequent trips they took down to the village, for instance . . .

'Listen, George,' said Chuck urgently. 'I've learned something that means trouble.'

'What's wrong? Isn't the machine behaving?' That was the worst contingency George could imagine. It might delay his return, and nothing could be more horrible. The way he felt now, even the sight of a TV commercial would seem like manna from heaven. At least it would be some link with home.

'No – it's nothing like that.' Chuck settled himself on the parapet, which was unusual because normally he was scared of the drop. 'I've just found what all this is about.'

'What d'ya mean? I thought we knew.'

'Sure – we know what the monks are trying to do. But we didn't know *why*. It's the craziest thing—'

'Tell me something new,' growled George.

' – but old Sam's just come clean with me. You know the way he drops in every afternoon to watch the sheets roll out. Well, this time he seemed rather excited, or at least as near as he'll ever get to it. When I told him that we were on the last cycle he asked me, in that cute English accent of his, if I'd ever wondered what they were trying to do. I said, "Sure" – and he told me.'

'Go on: I'll buy it.'

'Well, they believe that when they have listed all His names – and they reckon that there are about nine billion of them – God's purpose will be achieved. The human race will have finished what it was created to do, and there won't be any point in carrying on. Indeed, the very idea is something like blasphemy.'

'Then what do they expect us to do? Commit suicide?'

'There's no need for that. When the list's completed, God steps in and simply winds things up . . . bingo!'

'Oh, I get it. When we finish our job, it will be the end of the world.'

Chuck gave a nervous little laugh.

'That's just what I said to Sam. And do you know what happened? He looked at me in a very queer way, like I'd been stupid in class, and said, "It's nothing as trivial as *that*." '

George thought this over for a moment.

'That's what I call taking the Wide View,' he said presently. 'But what d'you suppose we should do about it? I don't see that it makes the slightest difference to us. After all, we already knew that they were crazy.'

'Yes – but don't you see what may happen? When the list's complete and the Last Trump doesn't blow – or whatever it is they expect – *we* may get the blame. It's our machine they've been using. I don't like the situation one little bit.'

'I see,' said George slowly. 'You've got a point there. But this sort of thing's happened before, you know. When I was a kid down in Louisiana we had a crackpot preacher who once said the world was going to end next Sunday. Hundreds of people believed him – even sold their homes. Yet when nothing happened, they didn't turn nasty, as you'd expect. They just decided that he'd made a mistake in his calculations and went right on believing. I guess some of them still do.'

'Well, this isn't Louisiana, in case you hadn't noticed. There are just two of us and hundreds of these monks. I like them, and I'll be sorry for old Sam when his lifework backfires on him. But all the same, I wish I was somewhere else.'

'I've been wishing that for weeks. But there's nothing we can do until the contract's finished and the transport arrives to fly us out.'

420

'Of course,' said Chuck thoughtfully, 'we could always try a bit of sabotage.'

'Like hell we could! That would make things worse.'

'Not the way I meant. Look at it like this. The machine will finish its run four days from now, on the present twenty-hours-a-day basis. The transport calls in a week. OK – then all we need to do is to find something that needs replacing during one of the overhaul periods – something that will hold up the works for a couple of days. We'll fix it, of course, but not too quickly. If we time matters properly, we can be down at the airfield when the last name pops out of the register. They won't be able to catch us then.'

'I don't like it,' said George. 'It will be the first time I ever walked out on a job. Besides, it would make them suspicious. No, I'll sit tight and take what comes.'

'I *still* don't like it,' he said, seven days later, as the tough little mountain ponies carried them down the winding road. 'And don't you think I'm running away because I'm afraid. I'm just sorry for those poor old guys up there, and I don't want to be around when they find what suckers they've been. Wonder how Sam will take it?'

'It's funny,' replied Chuck, 'but when I said goodbye I got the idea he knew we were walking out on him – and that he didn't care because he knew the machine was running smoothly and that the job would soon be finished. After that – well, of course, for him there just isn't any After That. . . .'

George turned in his saddle and stared back up the mountain road. This was the last place from which one could get a clear view of the lamasery. The squat, angular buildings were silhouetted against the afterglow of the sunset: here and there, lights gleamed like portholes in the side of an ocean liner. Electric lights, of course, sharing the same circuit as the Mark V. How much longer would they share it? wondered George. Would the monks smash up the computer in their rage and disappointment? Or would they just sit down quietly and begin their calculations all over again?

He knew exactly what was happening up on the mountain at this very moment. The high lama and his assistants would be sitting in their silk robes, inspecting the sheets as the junior monks carried them away from the typewriters and pasted them into the great volumes. No one would be saying anything. The sound would be the incessant patter, the never-ending rainstorm of the keys hitting the paper, for the Mark V itself was utterly silent as it flashed through its thousands of calculations a second. Three months of this, thought George, was enough to start anyone climbing up the wall.

'There she is!' called Chuck, pointing down into the valley. 'Ain't she beautiful!'

She certainly was, thought George. The battered old DC3 lay at the end of the runway like a tiny silver cross. In two hours she would be bearing them away to freedom and sanity. It was a thought worth savouring like a fine liqueur. George let it roll round his mind as the pony trudged patiently down the slope.

The swift night of the high Himalayas was now almost upon them. Fortunately, the road was very good, as roads went in that region, and they were both carrying torches. There was not the slightest danger, only a certain discomfort from the bitter cold. The sky overhead was perfectly clear, and ablaze with the familiar, friendly stars. At least there would be no risk, thought George, of the pilot being unable to take off because of weather conditions. That had been his only remaining worry.

He began to sing, but gave it up after a while. This vast arena of mountains, gleaming like whitely hooded ghosts on every side, did not encourage such ebullience. Presently George glanced at his watch.

'Should be there in an hour,' he called back over his shoulder to Chuck. Then he added, in an afterthought: 'Wonder if the computer's finished its run. It was due about now.'

Chuck didn't reply, so George swung round in his saddle. He could just see Chuck's face, a white oval turned toward the sky.

'Look,' whispered Chuck, and George lifted his eyes to heaven. (There is always a last time for everything.)

Overhead, without any fuss, the stars were going out.

The Possessed

First published in *Dynamic Science Fiction*, March 1953
Collected in *Reach for Tomorrow*

'The Possessed' has sometimes been criticised because lemmings are not really as suicidal as popularly imagined. However, countless numbers do indeed perish in the sea during their periodical population explosions, so I refuse to apologise.

And now the sun ahead was so close that the hurricane of radiation was forcing the Swarm back into the dark night of space. Soon it would be able to come no closer; the gales of light on which it rode from star to star could not be faced so near their source. Unless it encountered a planet very soon, and could fall down into the peace and safety of its shadow, this sun must be abandoned as had so many before.

Six cold outer worlds had already been searched and discarded. Either they were frozen beyond all hope of organic life, or else they harboured entities of types that were useless to the Swarm. If it was to survive, it must find hosts not too unlike those it had left on its doomed and distant home. Millions of years ago the Swarm had begun its journey, swept starward by the fires of its own exploding sun. Yet even now the memory of its lost birthplace was still sharp and clear, an ache that would never die.

There was a planet ahead, swinging its cone of shadow through the flame-swept night. The senses that the Swarm had developed upon its long journey reached out toward the approaching world, reached out and found it good.

The merciless buffeting of radiation ceased as the black disc of the planet eclipsed the sun. Falling freely under gravity, the Swarm dropped swiftly until it hit the outer fringe of the atmosphere. The first time it had made planetfall it had almost met its doom, but now it contracted its tenuous substance with the unthinking skill of long practice, until it formed a tiny, close-knit sphere. Slowly its velocity slackened, until at last it was floating motionless between earth and sky.

For many years it rode the winds of the stratosphere from Pole to Pole, or let the soundless fusillades of dawn blast it westward from the rising sun. Everywhere it found life, but nowhere intelligence. There were things that

423

crawled and flew and leaped, but there were no things that talked or built. Ten million years hence there might be creatures here with minds that the Swarm could possess and guide for its own purposes; there was no sign of them now. It could not guess which of the countless life-forms on this planet would be the heir to the future, and without such a host it was helpless – a mere pattern of electric charges, a matrix of order and a self-awareness in a universe of chaos. By its own resources the Swarm had no control over matter, yet once it had lodged in the mind of a sentient race there was nothing that lay beyond its powers.

It was not the first time, and it would not be the last, that the planet had been surveyed by a visitant from space – though never by one in such peculiar and urgent need. The Swarm was faced with a tormenting dilemma. It could begin its weary travels once more, hoping that ultimately it might find the conditions it sought, or it could wait here on this world, biding its time until a race had arisen which would fit its purpose.

It moved like mist through the shadows, letting the vagrant winds take it where they willed. The clumsy, ill-formed reptiles of this young world never saw its passing, but it observed them, recording, analysing, trying to extrapolate into the future. There was so little to choose between all these creatures; not one showed even the first faint glimmering of conscious mind. Yet if it left this world in search of another, it might roam the universe in vain until the end of time.

At last it made its decision. By its very nature, it could choose both alternatives. The greater part of the Swarm would continue its travels among the stars, but a portion of it would remain on this world, like a seed planted in the hope of future harvest.

It began to spin upon its axis, its tenuous body flattening into a disc. Now it was wavering at the frontiers of visibility – it was a pale ghost, a faint will-of-the-wisp that suddenly fissured into two unequal fragments. The spinning slowly died away: the Swarm had become two, each an entity with all the memories of the original, and all its desires and needs.

There was a last exchange of thoughts between parent and child who were also identical twins. If all went well with them both, they would meet again in the far future here at this valley in the mountains. The one who was staying would return to this point at regular intervals down the ages; the one who continued the search would send back an emissary if ever a better world was found. And then they would be united again, no longer homeless exiles vainly wandering among the indifferent stars.

The light of dawn was spilling over the raw, new mountains when the parent swarm rose up to meet the sun. At the edge of the atmosphere the gales of radiation caught it and swept it unresisting out beyond the planets, to start again upon the endless search.

The one that was left began its almost equally hopeless task. It needed an animal that was not so rare that disease or accident could make it extinct, nor so tiny that it could never acquire any power over the physical world.

And it must breed rapidly, so that its evolution could be directed and controlled as swiftly as possible.

The search was long and the choice difficult, but at last the Swarm selected its host. Like rain sinking into thirsty soil, it entered the bodies of certain small lizards and began to direct their destiny.

It was an immense task, even for a being which could never know death. Generation after generation of the lizards was swept into the past before there came the slightest improvement in the race. And always, at the appointed time, the Swarm returned to its rendezvous among the mountains. Always it returned in vain: there was no messenger from the stars, bringing news of better fortune elsewhere.

The centuries lengthened into millennia, the millennia into eons. By the standards of geological time, the lizards were now changing rapidly. Presently they were lizards no more, but warm-blooded, fur-covered creatures that brought forth their young alive. They were still small and feeble, and their minds were rudimentary, but they contained the seeds of future greatness.

Yet not only the living creatures were altering as the ages slowly passed. Continents were being rent asunder, mountains being worn down by the weight of the unwearying rain. Through all these changes, the Swarm kept to its purpose; and always, at the appointed times, it went to the meeting place that had been chosen so long ago, waited patiently for a while, and came away. Perhaps the parent swarm was still searching or perhaps – it was a hard and terrible thought to grasp – some unknown fate had overtaken it and it had gone the way of the race it had once ruled. There was nothing to do but to wait and see if the stubborn life-stuff of this planet could be forced along the path to intelligence.

And so the eons passed. . . .

Somewhere in the labyrinth of evolution the Swarm made its fatal mistake and took the wrong turning. A hundred million years had gone since it came to Earth, and it was very weary. It could not die, but it could degenerate. The memories of its ancient home and of its destiny were fading: its intelligence was waning even while its hosts climbed the long slope that would lead to self-awareness.

By a cosmic irony, in giving the impetus which would one day bring intelligence to this world, the Swarm had exhausted itself. It had reached the last stage of parasitism; no longer could it exist apart from its hosts. Never again could it ride free above the world, driven by wind and sun. To make the pilgrimage to the ancient rendezvous, it must travel slowly and painfully in a thousand little bodies. Yet it continued the immemorial custom, driven on by the desire for reunion which burned all the more fiercely now that it knew the bitterness of failure. Only if the parent swarm returned and reabsorbed it could it ever know new life and vigour.

The glaciers came and went; by a miracle the little beasts that now housed the waning alien intelligence escaped the clutching fingers of the ice. The oceans overwhelmed the land, and still the race survived. It even multiplied, but it could do no more. This world would never be its heritage, for far away in the heart of another continent a certain monkey had come down from the trees and was looking at the stars with the first glimmerings of curiosity.

The mind of the Swarm was dispersing, scattering among a million tiny bodies, no longer able to unite and assert its will. It had lost all cohesion; its memories were fading. In a million years, at most, they would all be gone.

Only one thing remained – the blind urge which still, at intervals which by some strange aberration were becoming ever shorter, drove it to seek its consummation in a valley that long ago had ceased to exist.

Quietly riding the lane of moonlight, the pleasure steamer passed the island with its winking beacon and entered the fjord. It was a calm and lovely night, with Venus sinking in the west out beyond the Faroes, and the lights of the harbour reflected with scarcely a tremor in the still waters far ahead.

Nils and Christina were utterly content. Standing side by side against the boat rail, their fingers locked together, they watched the wooded slopes drift silently by. The tall trees were motionless in the moonlight, their leaves unruffled by even the merest breath of wind, their slender trunks rising whitely from pools of shadow. The whole world was asleep; only the moving ship dared to break the spell that had bewitched the night.

Then suddenly, Christina gave a little gasp and Nils felt her fingers tighten convulsively on his. He followed her gaze: she was staring out across the water, looking toward the silent sentinels of the forest.

'What is it, darling?' he asked anxiously.

'Look!' she replied, in a whisper Nils could scarcely hear. 'There – under the pines!'

Nils stared, and as he did so the beauty of the night ebbed slowly away and ancestral terrors came crawling back from exile. For beneath the trees the land was alive: a dappled brown tide was moving down the slopes of the hill and merging into the dark waters. Here was an open patch on which the moonlight fell unbroken by shadow. It was changing even as he watched: the surface of the land seemed to be rippling downward like a slow waterfall seeking union with the sea.

And then Nils laughed and the world was sane once more. Christina looked at him, puzzled but reassured.

'Don't you remember?' he chuckled. 'We read all about it in the paper this morning. They do this every few years, and always at night. It's been going on for days.'

He was teasing her, sweeping away the tension of the last few minutes. Christina looked back at him, and a slow smile lit up her face.

'Of course!' she said. 'How stupid of me!' Then she turned once more toward the land and her expression became sad, for she was very tender-hearted.

'Poor little things!' she sighed. 'I wonder why they do it?'

Nils shrugged his shoulders indifferently.

'No one knows,' he answered. 'It's just one of those mysteries. I shouldn't think about it if it worries you. Look – we'll soon be in harbour!'

They turned toward the beckoning lights where their future lay, and Christina glanced back only once toward the tragic, mindless tide that was still flowing beneath the moon.

Obeying an urge whose meaning they had never known, the doomed legions of the lemmings were finding oblivion beneath the waves.

The Parasite

First published in *The Avon SF & F Reader*, April 1953
Collected in *Reach for Tomorrow*

This may have been the subconscious basis for the novel *The Light of Other Days* which I have just published with Stephen Baxter.

'There is nothing you can do,' said Connolly, 'nothing at all. Why did you have to follow me?' He was standing with his back to Pearson, staring out across the calm blue water that led to Italy. On the left, behind the anchored fishing fleet, the sun was setting in Mediterranean splendour, incarnadining land and sky. But neither man was even remotely aware of the beauty all around.

Pearson rose to his feet, and came forward out of the little cafe's shadowed porch, into the slanting sunlight. He joined Connolly by the cliff wall, but was careful not to come too close to him. Even in normal times Connolly disliked being touched. His obsession, whatever it might be, would make him doubly sensitive now.

'Listen, Roy,' Pearson began urgently. 'We've been friends for twenty years, and you ought to know I wouldn't let you down this time. Besides—'

'I know. You promised Ruth.'

'And why not? After all, she is your wife. She has a right to know what's happened.' He paused, choosing his words carefully. 'She's worried, Roy. Much more worried than if it was only another woman.' He nearly added the word 'again', but decided against it.

Connolly stubbed out his cigarette on the flat-topped granite wall, then flicked the white cylinder out over the sea, so that it fell twisting and turning toward the waters a hundred feet below. He turned to face his friend.

'I'm sorry, Jack,' he said, and for a moment there was a glimpse of the familiar personality which, Pearson knew, must be trapped somewhere within the stranger standing at his side. 'I know you're trying to be helpful, and I appreciate it. But I wish you hadn't followed me. You'll only make matters worse.'

'Convince me of that, and I'll go away.'

Connolly sighed.

'I could no more convince you than that psychiatrist you persuaded me to see. Poor Curtis! He was such a well-meaning fellow. Give him my apologies, will you?'

'I'm not a psychiatrist, and I'm not trying to cure you – whatever that means. If you like it the way you are, that's your affair. But I think you ought to let us know what's happened, so that we can make plans accordingly.'

'To get me certified?'

Pearson shrugged his shoulders. He wondered if Connolly could see through his feigned indifference to the real concern he was trying to hide. Now that all other approaches seemed to have failed, the 'frankly-I-don't-care' attitude was the only one left open to him.

'I wasn't thinking of that. There are a few practical details to worry about. Do you want to stay here indefinitely? You can't live without money, even on Syrene.'

'I can stay at Clifford Rawnsley's villa as long as I like. He was a friend of my father's you know. It's empty at the moment except for the servants, and they don't bother me.'

Connolly turned away from the parapet on which he was resting.

'I'm going up the hill before it's dark,' he said. The words were abrupt, but Pearson knew that he was not being dismissed. He could follow if he pleased, and the knowledge brought him the first satisfaction he had felt since locating Connolly. It was a small triumph, but he needed it.

They did not speak during the climb; indeed, Pearson scarcely had the breath to do so. Connolly set off at a reckless pace, as if deliberately attempting to exhaust himself. The island fell away beneath them, the white villas gleamed like ghosts in the shadowed valleys, the little fishing boats, their day's work done, lay at rest in the harbour. And all around was the darkling sea.

When Pearson caught up with his friend, Connolly was sitting in front of the shrine which the devout islanders had built on Syrene's highest point. In the daytime, there would be tourists here, photographing each other or gaping at the much-advertised beauty spread beneath them, but the place was deserted now.

Connolly was breathing heavily from his exertions, yet his features were relaxed and for the moment he seemed almost at peace. The shadow that lay across his mind had lifted, and he turned to Pearson with a smile that echoed his old, infectious grin.

'He hates exercise, Jack. It always scares him away.'

'And who is he?' said Pearson. 'Remember, you haven't introduced us yet.'

Connolly smiled at his friend's attempted humour; then his face suddenly became grave.

'Tell me, Jack,' he began. 'Would you say I have an overdeveloped imagination?'

'No: you're about average. You're certainly less imaginative than I am.'
Connolly nodded slowly.

'That's true enough, Jack, and it should help you to believe me. Because I'm certain I could never have invented the creature who's haunting me. He really exists. I'm not suffering from paranoiac hallucinations, or whatever Dr Curtis would call them.

'You remember Maude White? It all began with her. I met her at one of David Trescott's parties, about six weeks ago. I'd just quarrelled with Ruth and was rather fed up. We were both pretty tight, and as I was staying in town she came back to the flat with me.'

Pearson smiled inwardly. Poor Roy! It was always the same pattern, though he never seemed to realise it. Each affair was different to him, but to no one else. The eternal Don Juan, always seeking – always disappointed, because what he sought could be found only in the cradle or the grave, but never between the two.

'I guess you'll laugh at what knocked me out – it seems so trivial, though it frightened me more than anything that's ever happened in my life. I simply went over to the cocktail cabinet and poured out the drinks, as I've done a hundred times before. It wasn't until I'd handed one to Maude that I realised I'd filled *three* glasses. The act was so perfectly natural that at first I didn't recognise what it meant. Then I looked wildly around the room to see where the other man was – even then I knew, somehow, that it wasn't a man. But, of course, he wasn't there. He was nowhere at all in the outside world: he was hiding deep down inside my own brain. . . .'

The night was very still, the only sound a thin ribbon of music winding up to the stars from some café in the village below. The light of the rising moon sparkled on the sea; overhead, the arms of the crucifix were silhouetted against the darkness. A brilliant beacon on the frontiers of twilight, Venus was following the sun into the west.

Pearson waited, letting Connolly take his time. He seemed lucid and rational enough, however strange the story he was telling. His face was quite calm in the moonlight, though it might be the calmness that comes after acceptance of defeat.

'The next thing I remember is lying in bed while Maude sponged my face. She was pretty frightened: I'd passed out and cut my forehead badly as I fell. There was a lot of blood around the place, but that didn't matter. The thing that really scared me was the thought that I'd gone crazy. That seems funny, now that I'm much more scared of being sane.

'*He* was still there when I woke up; he's been there ever since. Somehow I got rid of Maude – it wasn't easy – and tried to work out what had happened. Tell me, Jack, do you believe in telepathy?'

The abrupt challenge caught Pearson off his guard.

'I've never given it much thought, but the evidence seems rather convincing. Do you suggest that someone else is reading your mind?'

'It's not as simple as that. What I'm telling you now I've discovered slowly – usually when I've been dreaming or slightly drunk. You may say

430

that invalidates the evidence, but I don't think so. At first it was the only way I could break through the barrier that separates me from Omega – I'll tell you later why I've called him that. But now there aren't any obstacles: I know he's there all the time, waiting for me to let down my guard. Night and day, drunk or sober, I'm conscious of his presence. At times like this he's quiescent, watching me out of the corner of his eye. My only hope is that he'll grow tired of waiting, and go in search of some other victim.'

Connolly's voice, calm until now, suddenly came near to breaking.

'Try and imagine the horror of that discovery: the effect of learning that every act, every thought or desire that flitted through your mind was being watched and shared by another being. It meant, of course, the end of all normal life for me. I had to leave Ruth and I couldn't tell her why. Then, to make matters worse, Maude came chasing after me. She wouldn't leave me alone, and bombarded me with letters and phone calls. It was hell. I couldn't fight both of them, so I ran away. And I thought that on Syrene, of all places, he would find enough to interest him without bothering me.'

'Now I understand,' said Pearson softly. 'So *that's* what he's after. A kind of telepathic Peeping Tom – no longer content with mere watching. . . .'

'I suppose you're humouring me,' said Connolly, without resentment. 'But I don't mind, and you've summed it up pretty accurately, as you usually do. It was quite a while before I realised what his game was. Once the first shock had worn off, I tried to analyse the position logically. I thought backward from that first moment of recognition, and in the end I knew that it wasn't a sudden invasion of my mind. He'd been with me for years, so well hidden that I'd never guessed it. I expect you'll laugh at this, knowing me as you do. But I've never been altogether at ease with a woman, even when I've been making love to her, and now I know the reason. Omega has always been there, sharing my emotions, gloating over the passions he can no longer experience in his body.

'The only way I kept my control was by fighting back, trying to come to grips with him and to understand what he was. And in the end I succeeded. He's a long way away and there must be some limit to his powers. Perhaps that first contact was an accident, though I'm not sure.

'What I've told you already, Jack, must be hard enough for you to believe, but it's nothing to what I've got to say now. Yet remember – you agreed that I'm not an imaginative man, and see if you can find a flaw anywhere in this story.

'I don't know if you've read any of the evidence suggesting that telepathy is somehow independent of time. I *know* that it is. Omega doesn't belong to our age: he's somewhere in the future, immensely far ahead of us. For a while I thought he must be one of the last men – that's why I gave him his name. But now I'm not sure; perhaps he belongs to an age when there are a myriad different races of man, scattered all over the universe – some still ascending, others sinking into decay. His people, wherever and whenever they may be, have reached the heights and fallen from them into the depths the beasts can never know. There's a sense of evil about him, Jack – the

431

real evil that most of us never meet in all our lives. Yet sometimes I feel almost sorry for him, because I know what has made him the thing he is.

'Have you ever wondered, Jack, what the human race will do when science has discovered everything, when there are no more worlds to be explored, when all the stars have given up their secrets? Omega is one of the answers. I hope he's not the only one, for if so everything we've striven for is in vain. I hope that he and his race are an isolated cancer in a still healthy universe, but I can never be sure.

'They have pampered their bodies until they are useless, and too late they have discovered their mistake. Perhaps they have thought, as some men have thought, that they could live by intellect alone. And perhaps they are immortal, and that must be their real damnation. Through the ages their minds have been corroding in their feeble bodies, seeking some release from their intolerable boredom. They have found it at last in the only way they can, by sending back their minds to an earlier, more virile age, and becoming parasites on the emotions of others.

'I wonder how many of them there are? Perhaps they explain all cases of what used to be called possession. How they must have ransacked the past to assuage their hunger! Can't you picture them, flocking like carrion crows around the decaying Roman Empire, jostling one another for the minds of Nero and Caligula and Tiberius? Perhaps Omega failed to get those richer prizes. Or perhaps he hasn't much choice and must take whatever mind he can contact in any age, transferring from that to the next whenever he has the chance.

'It was only slowly, of course, that I worked all this out. I think it adds to his enjoyment to know that I'm aware of his presence. I think he's deliberately helping – breaking down his side of the barrier. For in the end, I was able to see him.'

Connolly broke off. Looking around, Pearson saw that they were no longer alone on the hilltop. A young couple, hand in hand, were coming up the road toward the crucifix. Each had the physical beauty so common and so cheap among the islanders. They were oblivious to the night around them and to any spectators, and went past without the least sign of recognition. There was a bitter smile on Connolly's lips as he watched them go.

'I suppose I should be ashamed of this, but I was wishing then that he'd leave me and go after that boy. But he won't; though I've refused to play his game any more, he's staying to see what happens.'

'You were going to tell me what he's like,' said Pearson, annoyed at the interruption. Connolly lit a cigarette and inhaled deeply before replying.

'Can you imagine a room without walls? He's in a kind of hollow, egg-shaped space – surrounded by blue mist that always seems to be twisting and turning, but never changes its position. There's no entrance or exit – and no gravity, unless he's learned to defy it. Because he floats in the centre, and around him is a circle of short, fluted cylinders, turning slowly in the air. I think they must be machines of some kind, obeying his will.

And once there was a large oval hanging beside him, with perfectly human, beautifully formed arms coming from it. It could only have been a robot, yet those hands and fingers seemed alive. They were feeding and massaging him, treating him like a baby. It was horrible. . . .

'Have you ever seen a lemur or a spectral tarsier? He's rather like that – a nightmare travesty of mankind, with huge malevolent eyes. And this is strange – it's not the way one had imagined evolution going – he's covered with a fine layer of fur, as blue as the room in which he lives. Every time I've seen him he's been in the same position, half curled up like a sleeping baby. I think his legs have completely atrophied; perhaps his arms as well. Only his brain is still active, hunting up and down the ages for its prey.

'And now you know why there was nothing you or anyone else could do. Your psychiatrists might cure me if I was insane, but the science that can deal with Omega hasn't been invented yet.'

Connolly paused, then smiled wryly.

'Just because I'm sane, I realise that you can't be expected to believe me. So there's no common ground on which we can meet.'

Pearson rose from the boulder on which he had been sitting, and shivered slightly. The night was becoming cold, but that was nothing to the feeling of inner helplessness that had overwhelmed him as Connolly spoke.

'I'll be frank, Roy,' he began slowly. 'Of course I don't believe you. But insofar as you believe in Omega yourself, he's real to you, and I'll accept him on that basis and fight him with you.'

'It may be a dangerous game. How do we know what he can do when he's cornered?'

'I'll take that chance,' Pearson replied, beginning to walk down the hill. Connolly followed him without argument. 'Meanwhile, just what do you propose to do yourself?'

'Relax. Avoid emotion. Above all, keep away from women – Ruth, Maude, and the rest of them. That's been the hardest job. It isn't easy to break the habits of a lifetime.'

'I can well believe that,' replied Pearson, a little dryly. 'How successful have you been so far?'

'Completely. You see, his own eagerness defeats his purpose, by filling me with a kind of nausea and self-loathing whenever I think of sex. Lord, to think that I've laughed at the prudes all my life, yet now I've become one myself!'

There, thought Pearson in a sudden flash of insight, was the answer. He would never have believed it, but Connolly's past had finally caught up with him. Omega was nothing more than a symbol of conscience, a personification of guilt. When Connolly realised this, he would cease to be haunted. As for the remarkably detailed nature of the hallucination, that was yet another example of the tricks the human mind can play in its efforts to deceive itself. There must be some reason why the obsession had taken this form, but that was of minor importance.

Pearson explained this to Connolly at some length as they approached

433

the village. The other listened so patiently that Pearson had an uncomfortable feeling that he was the one who was being humoured, but he continued grimly to the end. When he had finished, Connolly gave a short, mirthless laugh.

'Your story's as logical as mine, but neither of us can convince the other. If you're right, then in time I may return to "normal". You can't imagine how real Omega is to me. He's more real than you are: if I close my eyes you're gone, but he's still there. I wish I knew what he was waiting for! I've left my old life behind; *he* knows I won't go back to it while he's there. So what's he got to gain by hanging on?' He turned to Pearson with a feverish eagerness. 'That's what really frightens me, Jack. He must know what my future is – all my life must be like a book he can dip into where he pleases. So there must still be some experience ahead of me that he's waiting to savour. Sometimes – sometimes I wonder if it's my death.'

They were now among the houses at the outskirts of the village, and ahead of them the nightlife of Syrene was getting into its stride. Now that they were no longer alone, there came a subtle change in Connolly's attitude. On the hilltop he had been, if not his normal self, at least friendly and prepared to talk. But now the sight of the happy, carefree crowds ahead seemed to make him withdraw into himself. He lagged behind as Pearson advanced and presently refused to come any further.

'What's the matter?' asked Pearson. 'Surely you'll come down to the hotel and have dinner with me?'

Connolly shook his head.

'I can't,' he said. 'I'd meet too many people.'

It was an astonishing remark from a man who had always delighted in crowds and parties. It showed, as nothing else had done, how much Connolly had changed. Before Pearson could think of a suitable reply, the other had turned on his heels and made off up a side-street. Hurt and annoyed, Pearson started to pursue him, then decided that it was useless.

That night he sent a long telegram to Ruth, giving what reassurance he could. Then, tired out, he went to bed.

Yet for an hour he was unable to sleep. His body was exhausted, but his brain was still active. He lay watching the patch of moonlight move across the pattern on the wall, marking the passage of time as inexorably as it must still do in the distant age that Connolly had glimpsed. Of course, that was pure fantasy – yet against his will Pearson was growing to accept Omega as a real and living threat. And in a sense Omega *was* real – as real as those other mental abstractions, the Ego and the Subconscious Mind.

Pearson wondered if Connolly had been wise to come back to Syrene. In times of emotional crisis – there had been others, though none so important as this – Connolly's reaction was always the same. He would return again to the lovely island where his charming, feckless parents had borne him and where he had spent his youth. He was seeking now, Pearson knew well enough, the contentment he had known only for one period of his life, and which he had sought so vainly in the arms of Ruth and all those others who had been unable to resist him.

Pearson was not attempting to criticise his unhappy friend. He never passed judgments; he merely observed with a bright-eyed, sympathetic interest that was hardly tolerance, since tolerance implied the relaxation of standards which he had never possessed. . . .

After a restless night, Pearson finally dropped into a sleep so sound that he awoke an hour later than usual. He had breakfast in his room, then went down to the reception desk to see if there was any reply from Ruth. Someone else had arrived in the night: two travelling cases, obviously English, were stacked in a corner of the hall, waiting for the porter to move them. Idly curious, Pearson glanced at the labels to see who his compatriot might be. Then he stiffened, looked hastily around, and hurried across to the the the receptionist.

'This Englishwoman,' he said anxiously. 'When did she arrive?'

'An hour ago, Signor, on the morning boat.'

'Is she in now?'

The receptionist looked a little undecided, then capitulated gracefully.

'No, Signor. She was in a great hurry, and asked me where she could find Mr Connolly. So I told her. I hope it was all right.'

Pearson cursed under his breath. It was an incredible stroke of bad luck, something he would never have dreamed of guarding against. Maude White was a woman of even greater determination than Connolly had hinted. Somehow she had discovered where he had fled, and pride or desire or both had driven her to follow. That she had come to this hotel was not surprising; it was an almost inevitable choice for English visitors to Syrene.

As he climbed the road to the villa, Pearson fought against an increasing sense of futility and uselessness. He had no idea what he should do when he met Connolly and Maude. He merely felt a vague yet urgent impulse to be helpful. If he could catch Maude before she reached the villa, he might be able to convince her that Connolly was a sick man and that her intervention could only do harm. Yet was this true? It was perfectly possible that a touching reconciliation had already taken place, and that neither party had the least desire to see him.

They were talking together on the beautifully laid-out lawn in front of the villa when Pearson turned through the gates and paused for breath. Connolly was resting on a wrought-iron seat beneath a palm tree, while Maude was pacing up and down a few yards away. She was speaking swiftly; Pearson could not hear her words, but from the intonation of her voice she was obviously pleading with Connolly. It was an embarrassing situation. While Pearson was still wondering whether to go forward, Connolly looked up and caught sight of him. His face was a completely expressionless mask; it showed neither welcome nor resentment.

At the interruption, Maude spun round to see who the intruder was, and for the first time Pearson glimpsed her face. She was a beautiful woman, but despair and anger had so twisted her features that she looked like a figure from some Greek tragedy. She was suffering not only the bitterness of being scorned, but the agony of not knowing why.

Pearson's arrival must have acted as a trigger to her pent-up emotions. She suddenly whirled away from him and turned toward Connolly, who continued to watch her with lack-lustre eyes. For a moment Pearson could not see what she was doing; then he cried in horror: 'Look out, Roy!'

Connolly moved with surprising speed, as if he had suddenly emerged from a trance. He caught Maude's wrist, there was a brief struggle, and then he was backing away from her, looking with fascination at something in the palm of his hand. The woman stood motionless, paralysed with fear and shame, knuckles pressed against her mouth.

Connolly gripped the pistol with his right hand and stroked it lovingly with his left. There was a low moan from Maude.

'I only meant to frighten you, Roy! I swear it!'

'That's all right, my dear,' said Connolly softly. 'I believe you. There's nothing to worry about.' His voice was perfectly natural. He turned toward Pearson, and gave him his old, boyish smile.

'So *this* is what he was waiting for, Jack,' he said. 'I'm not going to disappoint him.'

'No!' gasped Pearson, white with terror. 'Don't, Roy, for God's sake!'

But Connolly was beyond the reach of his friend's entreaties as he turned the pistol to his head. In that same moment Pearson knew at last, with an awful clarity, that Omega was real and that Omega would now be seeking for a new abode.

He never saw the flash of the gun or heard the feeble but adequate explosion. The world he knew had faded from his sight, and around him now were the fixed yet crawling mists of the blue room. Staring from its centre – as they had stared down the ages at how many others? – were two vast and lidless eyes. They were satiated for the moment, but for the moment only.

Jupiter Five

First published in *If*, May 1953
Collected in *Reach for Tomorrow*

In 1962, I commented that 'I am by no means sure that I could write "Jupiter Five" today; it involved twenty or thirty pages of orbital calculations and should by rights be dedicated to Professor G. C. McVittie, my erstwhile tutor in applied mathematics. (I had better hasten to add that he bears no slightest resemblance to the professor in the story.)'

'Jupiter Five' formed the basis of the fifth novel in the series 'Arthur C. Clarke's Venus Prime', written by Paul Preuss.

Professor Forster is such a small man that a special space-suit had to be made for him. But what he lacked in physical size he more than made up – as is so often the case – in sheer drive and determination. When I met him, he'd spent twenty years pursuing a dream. What is more to the point, he had persuaded a whole succession of hard-headed business men, World Council Delegates and administrators of scientific trusts to underwrite his expenses and to fit out a ship for him. Despite everything that happened later, I still think that was his most remarkable achievement. . . .

The *Arnold Toynbee* had a crew of six aboard when we left Earth. Besides the Professor and Charles Ashton, his chief assistant, there was the usual pilot-navigator-engineer triumvirate and two graduate students – Bill Hawkins and myself. Neither of us had ever gone into space before, and we were still so excited over the whole thing that we didn't care in the least whether we got back to Earth before the next term started. We had a strong suspicion that our tutor had very similar views. The reference he had produced for us was a masterpiece of ambiguity, but as the number of people who could even begin to read Martian script could be counted, if I may coin a phrase, on the fingers of one hand, we'd got the job.

As we were going to Jupiter, and not to Mars, the purpose of this particular qualification seemed a little obscure, though knowing something about the Professor's theories we had some pretty shrewd suspicions. They were partly confirmed when we were ten days out from Earth.

The Professor looked at us very thoughtfully when we answered his summons. Even under zero g he always managed to preserve his dignity, while the best we could do was to cling to the nearest handhold and float around like drifting seaweed. I got the impression – though I may of course be wrong – that he was thinking: What have *I* done to deserve this? as he looked from Bill to me and back again. Then he gave a sort of 'It's too late to do anything about it now' sigh and began to speak in that slow, patient way he always does when he has something to explain. At least, he always uses it when he's speaking to *us*, but it's just occurred to me – oh, never mind.

'Since we left Earth,' he said, 'I've not had much chance of telling you the purpose of this expedition. Perhaps you've guessed it already.'

'I think I have,' said Bill.

'Well, go on,' replied the Professor, a peculiar gleam in his eye. I did my best to stop Bill, but have you ever tried to kick anyone when you're in free fall?

'You want to find some proof – I mean, some *more* proof – of your diffusion theory of extraterrestrial culture.'

'And have you any idea why I'm going to Jupiter to look for it?'

'Well, not exactly. I suppose you hope to find something on one of the moons.'

'Brilliant, Bill, brilliant. There are fifteen known satellites, and their total area is about half that of Earth. Where would you start looking if you had a couple of weeks to spare? I'd rather like to know.'

Bill glanced doubtfully at the Professor, as if he almost suspected him of sarcasm.

'I don't know much about astronomy,' he said. 'But there are four big moons, aren't there? I'd start on those.'

'For your information, Io, Europa, Ganymede and Callisto are each about as big as Africa. Would you work through them in alphabetical order?'

'No,' Bill replied promptly. 'I'd start on the one nearest Jupiter, and go outward.'

'I don't think we'll waste any more time pursuing your logical processes,' sighed the Professor. He was obviously impatient to begin his set speech. 'Anyway, you're quite wrong. We're not going to the big moons at all. They've been photographically surveyed from space and large areas have been explored on the surface. They've got nothing of archaeological interest. *We're* going to a place that's never been visited before.'

'Not to Jupiter!' I gasped.

'Heavens no, nothing as drastic as that! But we're going nearer to him than anyone else has ever been.'

He paused thoughtfully.

'It's a curious thing, you know – or you probably don't – that it's nearly as difficult to travel between Jupiter's satellites as it is to go between the planets, although the distances are so much smaller. This is because Jupiter's got such a terrific gravitational field and his moons are travelling so quickly. The innermost moon's moving almost as fast as Earth, and the journey to it

438

from Ganymede costs almost as much fuel as the trip from Earth to Venus, even though it takes only a day and a half.

'And it's *that* journey which we're going to make. No one's ever done it before because nobody could think of any good reason for the expense. Jupiter Five is only thirty kilometres in diameter, so it couldn't possibly be of much interest. Even some of the outer satellites, which are far easier to reach, haven't been visited because it hardly seemed worth while to waste the rocket fuel.'

'Then why are *we* going to waste it?' I asked impatiently. The whole thing sounded like a complete wild-goose chase, though as long as it proved interesting, and involved no actual danger, I didn't greatly mind.

Perhaps I ought to confess – though I'm tempted to say nothing, as a good many others have done – that at this time I didn't believe a word of Professor Forster's theories. Of course I realised that he was a very brilliant man in his field, but I did draw the line at some of his more fantastic ideas. After all, the evidence was so slight and the conclusions so revolutionary that one could hardly help being sceptical.

Perhaps you can still remember the astonishment when the first Martian expedition found the remains not of one ancient civilisation, but of two. Both had been highly advanced, but both had perished more than five million years ago. The reason was unknown (and still is). It did not seem to be warfare, as the two cultures appear to have lived amicably together. One of the races had been insect-like, the other vaguely reptilian. The insects seem to have been the genuine, original Martians. The reptile-people – usually referred to as 'Culture X' – had arrived on the scene later.

So, at least, Professor Forster maintained. They had certainly possessed the secret of space travel, because the ruins of their peculiar cruciform cities had been found on – of all places – Mercury. Forster believed that they had tried to colonise all the smaller planets – Earth and Venus having been ruled out because of their excessive gravity. It was a source of some disappointment to the Professor that no traces of Culture X had ever been found on the Moon, though he was certain that such a discovery was only a matter of time.

The 'conventional' theory of Culture X was that it had originally come from one of the smaller planets or satellites, had made peaceful contact with the Martians – the only other intelligent race in the known history of the System – and had died out at the same time as the Martian civilisation. But Professor Forster had more ambitious ideas: he was convinced that Culture X had entered the Solar System from intersteller space. The fact that no one else believed this annoyed him, though not very much, for he is one of those people who are happy only when in a minority.

From where I was sitting, I could see Jupiter through the cabin porthole as Professor Forster unfolded his plan. It was a beautiful sight: I could just make out the equatorial cloud belts, and three of the satellites were visible as little stars close to the planet. I wondered which was Ganymede, our first port of call.

'If Jack will condescend to pay attention,' the Professor continued, 'I'll tell you why we're going such a long way from home. You know that last year I spent a good deal of time poking among the ruins in the twilight belt of Mercury. Perhaps you read the paper I gave on the subject at the London School of Economics. You may even have been there – I do remember a disturbance at the back of the hall.

'What I didn't tell anyone then was that while I was on Mercury I discovered an important clue to the origin of Culture X. I've kept quiet about it, although I've been sorely tempted when fools like Dr Haughton have tried to be funny at my expense. But I wasn't going to risk letting someone else get here before I could organise this expedition.

'One of the things I found on Mercury was a rather well preserved bas-relief of the Solar System. It's not the first that's been discovered – as you know, astronomical motifs are common in true Martian and Culture X art. But there were certain peculiar symbols against various planets, including Mars and Mercury. I think the pattern had some historic significance, and the most curious thing about it is that little Jupiter Five – one of the least important of all the satellites – seemed to have the most attention drawn to it. I'm convinced that there's something on Five which is the key to the whole problem of Culture X, and I'm going there to discover what it is.'

As far as I can remember now, neither Bill nor I was particularly impressed by the Professor's story. Maybe the people of Culture X had left some artifacts on Five for obscure reasons of their own. It would be interesting to unearth them, but hardly likely that they would be as important as the Professor thought. I guess he was rather disappointed at our lack of enthusiasm. If so it was his fault since, as we discovered later, he was still holding out on us.

We landed on Ganymede, the largest moon, about a week later. Ganymede is the only one of the satellites with a permanent base on it; there's an observatory and a geophysical station with a staff of about fifty scientists. They were rather glad to see visitors, but we didn't stay long as the Professor was anxious to refuel and set off again. The fact that we were heading for Five naturally aroused a good deal of interest, but the Professor wouldn't talk and we couldn't; he kept too close an eye on us.

Ganymede, by the way, is quite an interesting place and we managed to see rather more of it on the return journey. But as I've promised to write an article for another magazine about that, I'd better not say anything else here. (You might like to keep your eyes on the *National Astrographic* Magazine next Spring.)

The hop from Ganymede to Five took just over a day and a half, and it gave us an uncomfortable feeling to see Jupiter expanding hour by hour until it seemed as if he was going to fill the sky. I don't know much about astronomy, but I couldn't help thinking of the tremendous gravity field into which we were falling. All sorts of things could go wrong so easily. If we ran out of fuel we'd never be able to get back to Ganymede, and we might even drop into Jupiter himself.

I wish I could describe what it was like seeing that colossal globe, with its raging storm belts spinning in the sky ahead of us. As a matter of fact I *did* make the attempt, but some literary friends who have read this MS advised me to cut out the result. (They also gave me a lot of other advice which I don't think they could have meant seriously, because if I'd followed it there would have been no story at all.)

Luckily there have been so many colour close-ups of Jupiter published by now that you're bound to have seen some of them. You may even have seen the one which, as I'll explain later, was the cause of all our trouble.

At last Jupiter stopped growing: we'd swung into the orbit of Five and would soon catch up with the tiny moon as it raced around the planet. We were all squeezed in the control room waiting for our first glimpse of our target. At least, all of us who could get in were doing so. Bill and I were crowded out into the corridor and could only crane over the other people's shoulders. Kingsley Searle, our pilot, was in the control seat looking as unruffled as ever: Eric Fulton, the engineer, was thoughtfully chewing his moustache and watching the fuel gauges, and Tony Groves was doing complicated things with his navigation tables.

And the Professor appeared to be rigidly attached to the eyepiece of the teleperiscope. Suddenly he gave a start and we heard a whistle of indrawn breath. After a minute, without a word, he beckoned to Searle, who took his place at the eyepiece. Exactly the same thing happened, and then Searle handed over to Fulton. It got a bit monotonous by the time Groves had reacted identically, so we wormed our way in and took over after a bit of opposition.

I don't know quite what I'd expected to see, so that's probably why I was disappointed. Hanging there in space was a tiny gibbous moon, its 'night' sector lit up faintly by the reflected glory of Jupiter. And that seemed to be all.

Then I began to make out additional markings, in the way that you do if you look through a telescope for long enough. There were faint crisscrossing lines on the surface of the satellite, and suddenly my eye grasped their full pattern. For it *was* a pattern: those lines covered Five with the same geometrical accuracy as the lines of latitude and longitude divide up a globe of the Earth. I suppose I gave my whistle of amazement, for then Bill pushed me out of the way and had his turn to look.

The next thing I remember is Professor Forster looking very smug while we bombarded him with questions.

'Of course,' he explained, 'this isn't as much a surprise to me as it it to you. Besides the evidence I'd found on Mercury, there were other clues. I've a friend at the Ganymede Observatory whom I've sworn to secrecy and who's been under quite a strain this last few weeks. It's rather surprising to anyone who's not an astronomer that the Observatory has never bothered much about the satellites. The big instruments are used on extra-galactic nebulae, and the little ones spend all their time looking at Jupiter.

'The only thing the Observatory had ever done to Five was to measure its diameter and take a few photographs. They weren't quite good enough to show the markings we've just observed, otherwise there would have been an investigation before. But my friend Lawton detected them through the hundred-centimetre reflector when I asked him to look, and he also noticed something else that should have been spotted before. Five is only thirty kilometres in diameter, but it's much brighter than it should be for its size. When you compare its reflecting power – its aldeb – its—'

'Its albedo.'

'Thanks, Tony – its albedo with that of the other Moons, you find that it's a much better reflector than it should be. In fact, it behaves more like polished metal than rock.'

'So that explains it!' I said. 'The people of Culture X must have covered Five with an outer shell – like the domes they built on Mercury, but on a bigger scale.'

The Professor looked at me rather pityingly.

'So you still haven't guessed!' he said.

I don't think this was quite fair. Frankly, would you have done any better in the same circumstances?

We landed three hours later on an enormous metal plain. As I looked through the portholes, I felt completely dwarfed by my surroundings. An ant crawling on the top of an oil-storage tank might have had much the same feelings – and the looming bulk of Jupiter up there in the sky didn't help. Even the Professor's usual cockiness now seemed to be overlaid by a kind of reverent awe.

The plain wasn't quite devoid of features. Running across it in various directions were broad bands where the stupendous metal plates had been joined together. These bands, or the crisscross pattern they formed, were what we had seen from space.

About a quarter of a kilometre away was a low hill – at least, what would have been a hill on a natural world. We had spotted it on our way in after making a careful survey of the little satellite from space. It was one of six such projections, four arranged equidistantly around the equator and the other two at the Poles. The assumption was pretty obvious that they would be entrances to the world below the metal shell.

I know that some people think it must be very entertaining to walk around on an airless, low-gravity planet in spacesuits. Well, it isn't. There are so many points to think about, so many checks to make and precautions to observe, that the mental strain outweighs the glamour – at least as far as I'm concerned. But I must admit that this time, as we climbed out of the airlock, I was so excited that for once these things didn't worry me.

The gravity of Five was so microscopic that walking was completely out of the question. We were all roped together like mountaineers and blew ourselves across the metal plain with gentle bursts from our recoil pistols. The experienced astronauts, Fulton and Groves, were at the two ends of the chain so that any unwise eagerness on the part of the people in the middle was restrained.

It took us only a few minutes to reach our objective, which we discovered to be a broad, low dome at least a kilometre in circumference. I wondered if it was a gigantic airlock, large enough to permit the entrance of whole spaceships. Unless we were very lucky, we might be unable to find a way in, since the controlling mechanisms would no longer be functioning, and even if they were, we would not know how to operate them. It would be difficult to imagine anything more tantalising than being locked out, unable to get at the greatest archaeological find in all history.

We had made a quarter circuit of the dome when we found an opening in the metal shell. It was quite small – only about two metres across – and it was so nearly circular that for a moment we did not realise what it was. Then Tony's voice came over the radio.

'That's not artificial. We've got a meteor to thank for it.'

'Impossible!' protested Professor Forster. 'It's much too regular.'

Tony was stubborn.

'Big meteors always produce circular holes, unless they strike very glancing blows. And look at the edges; you can see there's been an explosion of some kind. Probably the meteor and the shell were vaporised; we won't find any fragments.'

'You'd expect this sort of thing to happen,' put in Kingsley. 'How long has this been here? Five million years? I'm surprised we haven't found any other craters.'

'Maybe you're right,' said the Professor, too pleased to argue. 'Anyway, I'm going in first.'

'Right,' said Kingsley, who as captain has the last say in all such matters. 'I'll give you twenty metres of rope and will sit in the hole so that we can keep radio contact. Otherwise this shell will blanket your signals.'

So Professor Forster was the first man to enter Five, as he deserved to be. We crowded close to Kingsley so that he could relay news of the Professor's progress.

He didn't get very far. There was another shell just inside the outer one, as we might have expected. The Professor had room to stand upright between them, and as far as his torch could throw its beam he could see avenues of supporting struts and girders, but that was about all.

It took us about twenty-four exasperating hours before we got any further. Near the end of that time I remember asking the Professor why he hadn't thought of bringing any explosives. He gave me a very hurt look.

'There's enough aboard the ship to blow us all to glory,' he said. 'But I'm not going to risk doing any damage if I can find another way.'

That's what I call patience, but I could see his point of view. After all, what was another few days in a search that had already taken him twenty years?

It was Bill Hawkins, of all people, who found the way in when we had abandoned our first line of approach. Near the North Pole of the little world he discovered a really giant meteor hole – about a hundred metres across and cutting through both the outer shells surrounding Five. It had revealed still another shell below those, and by one of those chances that must happen if one waits enough eons, a second, smaller, meteor had come down inside the crater and penetrated the innermost skin. The hole was just big enough to allow entrance for a man in a spacesuit. We went through head first, one at a time.

I don't suppose I'll ever have a weirder experience than hanging from that tremendous vault, like a spider suspended beneath the dome of St Peter's. We only knew that the space in which we floated was vast. Just *how* big it was we could not tell, for our torches gave us no sense of distance. In this airless, dustless cavern the beams were, of course, totally invisible and when we shone them on the roof above, we could see the ovals of light dancing away into the distance until they were too diffuse to be visible. If we pointed them 'downward' we could see a pale smudge of illumination so far below that it revealed nothing.

Very slowly, under the minute gravity of this tiny world, we fell downward until checked by our safety ropes. Overhead I could see the tiny glimmering patch through which we had entered; it was remote but reassuring.

And then, while I was swinging with an infinitely sluggish pendulum motion at the end of my cable, with the lights of my companions glimmering like fitful stars in the darkness around me, the truth suddenly crashed into my brain. Forgetting that we were all on open circuit, I cried out involuntarily:

'Professor – I don't believe this is a planet at all! *It's a spaceship!*'

Then I stopped, feeling that I had made a fool of myself. There was a brief, tense silence, then a babble of noise as everyone else started arguing at once. Professor Forster's voice cut across the confusion and I could tell that he was both pleased and surprised.

'You're quite right, Jack. This is the ship that brought Culture X to the Solar System.'

I heard someone – it sounded like Eric Fulton – give a gasp of incredulity.

'It's fantastic! A ship thirty kilometres across!'

'*You* ought to know better than that,' replied the Professor with surprising mildness. 'Suppose a civilisation wanted to cross interstellar space – how else would it attack the problem? It would build a mobile planetoid out in space, taking perhaps centuries over the task. Since the ship would have to be a self-contained world, which could support its inhabitants for generations, it would need to be as large as this. I wonder how many suns they visited before they found ours and knew that their search was ended? They must have had smaller ships that could take them down to the planets, and of course they had to leave the parent vessel somewhere in space. So they parked it here, in a close orbit near the largest planet, where it would remain safely forever – or until they needed it again. It was the logical place: if they had set it circling the Sun, in time the pulls of the planets would have disturbed its orbit so much that it might have been lost. That could never happen to it here.'

'Tell me, Professor,' someone asked, 'did you guess all this before we started?'

'I *hoped* it. All the evidence pointed to this answer. There's always been something anomalous about Satellite Five, though no one seems to have noticed it. Why this single tiny moon so close to Jupiter, when all the other small satellites are seventy times further away? Astronomically speaking, it didn't make sense. But enough of this chattering. We've got work to do.'

That, I think, must count as the understatement of the century. There were seven of us faced with the greatest archaeological discovery of all time. Almost a whole world – a small world, an artificial one, but still a world – was waiting for us to explore. All we could perform was a swift and superficial reconnaissance: there might be material here for generations of research workers.

The first step was to lower a powerful floodlight on a power line running from the ship. This would act as a beacon and prevent us getting lost, as well as giving local illumination on the inner surface of the satellite. (Even now, I still find it hard to call Five a ship.) Then we dropped down the line to the surface below. It was a fall of about a kilometre, and in this low gravity it was quite safe to make the drop unretarded. The gentle shock of the impact could be absorbed easily enough by the spring-loaded staffs we carried for that purpose.

I don't want to take up any space here with yet another description of all the wonders of Satellite Five; there have already been enough pictures, maps and books on the subject. (My own, by the way is being published by Sidgwick and Jackson next summer.) What I would like to give you instead is some impression of what it was actually *like* to be the first men ever to enter that strange metal world. Yet I'm sorry to say – I know this sounds hard to believe – I simply can't remember what I was feeling when we came across the first of the great mushroom-capped entrance shafts. I suppose I was so excited and so overwhelmed by the wonder of it all that I've forgotten everything else. But I can recall the impression of sheer size, something which mere photographs can never give. The builders of this world, coming as they did from a planet of low gravity, were giants – about four times as tall as men. We were pigmies crawling among their works.

We never got below the outer levels on our first visit, so we met few of the scientific marvels which later expeditions discovered. That was just as well; the residential areas provided enough to keep us busy for several lifetimes. The globe we were exploring must once have been lit by artificial sunlight pouring down from the triple shell that surrounded it and kept its atmosphere from leaking into space. Here on the surface the Jovians (I suppose I cannot avoid adopting the popular name for the people of Culture X) had reproduced, as accurately as they could, conditions on the world they had left unknown ages ago. Perhaps they still had day and night, changing seasons, rain and mist. They had even taken a tiny sea with them into exile. The water was still there, forming a frozen lake three kilometres across. I hear that there is a plan afoot to electrolise it and provide Five with a breathable atmosphere again, as soon as the meteor holes in the outer shell have been plugged.

The more we saw of their work, the more we grew to like the race whose possessions we were disturbing for the first time in five million years. Even if they were giants from another sun, they had much in common with man, and it is a great tragedy that our races missed each other by what is, on the cosmic scale, such a narrow margin.

We were, I suppose, more fortunate than any archaeologists in history. The vacuum of space had preserved everything from decay and – this was something which could not have been expected – the Jovians had not emptied their mighty ship of all its treasures when they had set out to colonise the Solar System. Here on the inner surface of Five everything still seemed intact, as it had been at the end of the ship's long journey. Perhaps the travellers had preserved it as a shrine in memory of their lost home, or perhaps they had thought that one day they might have to use these things again.

Whatever the reason, everything was here as its makers had left it. Sometimes it frightened me. I might be photographing, with Bill's help, some great wall carving when the sheer *timelessness* of the place would strike into my heart. I would look round nervously, half expecting to see giant shapes come stalking in through the pointed doorways, to continue the tasks that had been momentarily interrupted.

We discovered the art gallery on the fourth day. That was the only name for it; there was no mistaking its purpose. When Groves and Searle, who had been doing rapid sweeps over the southern hemisphere, reported the discovery we decided to concentrate all our forces there. For, as somebody or other has said, the art of a people reveals its soul, and here we might find the key to Culture X.

The building was huge, even by the standards of this giant race. Like all the other structures on Five, it was made of metal, yet there was nothing cold or mechanical about it. The topmost peak climbed half way to the remote roof of the world, and from a distance – before the details were visible – the building looked not unlike a Gothic cathedral. Misled by this chance resemblance, some later writers have called it a temple; but we have never found any trace of what might be called a religion among the Jovians. Yet there seems something appropriate about the name. 'The Temple of Art', and it's stuck so thoroughly that no one can change it now.

It has been estimated that there are between ten and twenty million individual exhibits in this single building – the harvest garnered during the whole history of a race that may have been much older than Man. And it was here that I found a small, circular room which at first sight seemed to be no more than the meeting place of six radiating corridors. I was by myself (and thus, I'm afraid, disobeying the Professor's orders) and taking what I thought would be a short-cut back to my companions. The dark walls were drifting silently past me as I glided along, the light of my torch dancing over the ceiling ahead. It was covered with deeply cut lettering, and I was so busy looking for familiar character groupings that for some time I paid no attention to the chamber's floor. Then I saw the statue and focused my beam upon it.

The moment when one first meets a great work of art has an impact that can never again be recaptured. In this case the subject matter made the effect all the more overwhelming. I was the first man ever to know what the Jovians had looked like, for here, carved with superb skill and authority, was one obviously modelled from life.

The slender, reptilian head was looking straight toward me, the sightless eyes staring into mine. Two of the hands were clasped upon the breast as if in resignation; the other two were holding an instrument whose purpose is still unknown. The long, powerful tail – which, like a kangaroo's, probably balanced the rest of the body – was stretched out along the ground, adding to the impression of rest or repose.

There was nothing human about the face or the body. There were, for example, no nostrils – only gill-like openings in the neck. Yet the figure moved me profoundly; the artist had spanned the barriers of time and culture in a way I should never have believed possible. 'Not human – but humane' was the verdict Professor Forster gave. There were many things we could not have shared with the builders of this world, but all that was really important we would have felt in common.

Just as one can read emotions in the alien but familiar face of a dog or a horse, so it seemed that I knew the feelings of the being confronting me. Here was wisdom and authority – the calm, confident power that is shown, for example, in Bellini's famous portrait of the Doge Loredano. Yet there was sadness also – the sadness of a race which had made some stupendous effort, and made it in vain.

We still do not know why this single statue is the only representation the Jovians have ever made of themselves in their art. One would hardly expect to find taboos of this nature among such an advanced race; perhaps we will know the answer when we have deciphered the writing carved on the chamber walls.

Yet I am already certain of the statue's purpose. It was set here to bridge time and to greet whatever beings might one day stand in the footsteps of its makers. That, perhaps, is why they shaped it so much smaller than life. Even then they must have guessed that the future belonged to Earth or Venus, and hence to beings whom they would have dwarfed. They knew that size could be a barrier as well as time.

A few minutes later I was on my way back to the ship with my companions, eager to tell the Professor about the discovery. He had been reluctantly snatching some rest, though I don't believe he averaged more than four hours sleep a day all the time we were on Five. The golden light of Jupiter was flooding the great metal plain as we emerged through the shell and stood beneath the stars once more.

'Hello!' I heard Bill say over the radio. 'The Prof's moved the ship.'

'Nonsense,' I retorted. 'It's exactly where we left it.'

447

Then I turned my head and saw the reason for Bill's mistake. We had visitors.

The second ship had come down a couple of kilometres away, and as far as my non-expert eyes could tell it might have been a duplicate of ours. When we hurried through the airlock, we found that the Professor, a little bleary-eyed, was already entertaining. To our surprise, though not exactly to our displeasure, one of the three visitors was an extremely attractive brunette.

'This,' said Professor Forster, a little wearily, 'is Mr Randolph Mays, the science writer. I imagine you've heard of him. And this is—' He turned to Mays. 'I'm afraid I didn't quite catch the names.'

'My pilot, Donald Hopkins – my secretary, Marianne Mitchell.'

There was just the slighest pause before the word 'secretary,' but it was long enough to set a little signal light flashing in my brain. I kept my eyebrows from going up, but I caught a glance from Bill that said, without any need for words: If you're thinking what I'm thinking, I'm ashamed of you.

Mays was a tall, rather cadaverous man with thinning hair and an attitude of bonhomie which one felt was only skin-deep – the protective colouration of a man who has to be friendly with too many people.

'I expect this is as big a surprise to you as it is to me,' he said with unnecessary heartiness. 'I certainly never expected to find anyone here before me, and I certainly didn't expect to find all *this*.'

'What brought you here?' said Ashton, trying to sound not too suspiciously inquisitive.

'I was just explaining that to the Professor. Can I have that folder please, Marianne? Thanks.'

He drew out a series of very fine astronomical paintings and passed them round. They showed the planets from their satellites – a common-enough subject, of course.

'You've all seen this sort of thing before,' Mays continued. 'But there's a difference here. These pictures are nearly a hundred years old. They were painted by an artist named Chesley Bonestell and appeared in *Life* back in 1944 – long before space-travel began, of course. Now what's happened is that *Life* has commissioned me to go round the Solar System and see how well I can match these imaginative paintings against the reality. In the centenary issue, they'll be published side by side with photographs of the real thing. Good idea, eh?'

I had to admit that it was. But it was going to make matters rather complicated, and I wondered what the Professor thought about it. Then I glanced again at Miss Mitchell, standing demurely in the corner, and decided that there would be compensations.

In any other circumstances, we would have been glad to meet another party of explorers, but here there was the question of priority to be considered. Mays would certainly be hurrying back to Earth as quickly as he could, his original mission abandoned and all his film used up here and now. It was difficult to see how we could stop him, and not even certain that we desired to do so. We wanted all the publicity and support we could get, but we would prefer to do things in our own time, after our own fashion. I wondered how strong the Professor was on tact, and feared the worst.

Yet at first diplomatic relations were smooth enough. The Professor had hit upon the bright idea of pairing each of us with one of May's team, so that we acted simultaneously as guides and supervisors. Doubling the number of investigating groups also greatly increased the rate at which we could work. It was unsafe for anyone to operate by himself under these conditions, and this had handicapped us a great deal.

The Professor outlined his policy to us the day after the arrival of Mays's party.

'I hope we can get along together,' he said a little anxiously. 'As far as I'm concerned they can go where they like and photograph what they like, as long as *they don't take anything*, and as long as they don't get back to Earth with their records before we do.'

'I don't see how we can stop them,' protested Ashton.

'Well, I hadn't intended to do this, but I've now registered a claim to Five. I radioed it to Ganymede last night, and it will be at The Hague by now.'

'But no one can claim an astronomical body for himself. That was settled in the case of the Moon, back in the last century.'

The Professor gave a rather crooked smile.

'I'm not annexing an *astronomical body*, remember. I've put in a claim for salvage, and I've done it in the name of the World Science Organisation. If Mays takes anything out of Five, he'll be stealing it from them. Tomorrow I'm going to explain the situation gently to him, just in case he gets any bright ideas.'

It certainly seemed peculiar to think of Satellite Five as salvage, and I could imagine some pretty legal quarrels developing when we got home. But for the present the Professor's move should have given us some safeguards and might discourage Mays from collecting souvenirs – so we were optimistic enough to hope.

It took rather a lot of organising, but I managed to get paired off with Marianne for several trips round the interior of Five. Mays didn't seem to mind: there was no particular reason why he should. A spacesuit is the most perfect chaperon ever devised, confound it.

Naturally enough I took her to the art gallery at the first opportunity, and showed her my find. She stood looking at the statue for a long time while I held my torch beam upon it.

'It's very wonderful,' she breathed at last. 'Just think of it waiting here in the darkness all those millions of years! But you'll have to give it a name.'

'I have. I've christened it "The Ambassador".'

'Why?'

'Well, because I think it's a kind of envoy, if you like, carrying a greeting to us. The people who made it knew that one day someone else was bound to come here and find this place.'

'I think you're right. "The Ambassador" – yes, that was clever of you. There's something noble about it, and something very sad, too. Don't you feel it?'

I could tell that Marianne was a very intelligent woman. It was quite remarkable the way she saw my point of view, and the interest she took in everything I showed her. But 'The Ambassador' fascinated her most of all, and she kept on coming back to it.

'You know, Jack,' she said (I think this was sometime the next day, when Mays had been to see it as well), 'you must take that statue back to Earth. Think of the sensation it would cause.'

I sighed.

'The Professor would like to, but it must weigh a ton. We can't afford the fuel. It will have to wait for a later trip.'

She looked puzzled.

'But things hardly weigh anything here,' she protested.

'That's different,' I explained. 'There's weight, and there's inertia – two quite different things. Now inertia – oh, never mind. We can't take it back, anyway. Captain Searle's told us that, definitely.'

'What a pity,' said Marianne.

I forgot all about this conversation until the night before we left. We had had a busy and exhausting day packing our equipment (a good deal, of course, we left behind for future use). All our photographic material had been used up. As Charlie Ashton remarked, if we met a *live* Jovian now we'd be unable to record the fact. I think we were all wanting a breathing space, an opportunity to relax and sort out our impressions and to recover from our head-on collision with an alien culture.

Mays's ship, the *Henry Luce*, was also nearly ready for take-off. We would leave at the same time, an arrangement which suited the Professor admirably as he did not trust Mays alone on Five.

Everything had been settled when, while checking through our records, I suddenly found that six rolls of exposed film were missing. They were photographs of a complete set of transcriptions in the Temple of Art. After a certain amount of thought I recalled that they had been entrusted to my charge, and I had put them very carefully on a ledge in the Temple, intending to collect them later.

It was a long time before take-off, the Professor and Ashton were cancelling some arrears of sleep, and there seemed no reason why I should not slip back to collect the missing material. I knew there would be a row if it was left behind, and as I remembered exactly where it was I need be gone only thirty minutes. So I went, explaining my mission to Bill just in case of accidents.

The floodlight was no longer working, of course, and the darkness inside the shell of Five was somewhat oppressive. But I left a portable beacon at the entrance, and dropped freely until my hand torch told me it was time to break the fall. Ten minutes later, with a sigh of relief, I gathered up the missing films.

It was a natural enough thing to pay my last respects to The Ambassador: it might be years before I saw him again, and that calmly enigmatic figure had begun to exercise an extraordinary fascination over me.

Unfortunately, that fascination had not been confined to me alone. For the chamber was empty and the statue gone.

I suppose I could have crept back and said nothing, thus avoiding awkward explanations. But I was too furious to think of discretion, and as soon as I returned we woke the Professor and told him what had happened.

He sat on his bunk rubbing the sleep out of his eyes, then uttered a few harsh words about Mr Mays and his companions which it would do no good at all to repeat here.

'What I don't understand,' said Searle, 'is how they got the thing out – if they have, in fact. We should have spotted it.'

'There are plenty of hiding places, and they could have waited until there was no one around before they took it up through the hull. It must have been quite a job, even under this gravity,' remarked Eric Fulton, in tones of admiration.

'There's no time for post-mortems,' said the Professor savagely. 'We've got five hours to think of something. They can't take off before then, because we're only just past opposition with Ganymede. That's correct, isn't it, Kingsley?'

Searle nodded agreement.

'Yes. We must move round to the other side of Jupiter before we can enter a transfer orbit – at least, a reasonably economical one.'

'Good. That gives us a breathing space. Well, has anyone any ideas?'

Looking back on the whole thing now, it oftens seems to me that our subsequent behaviour was, shall I say, a little peculiar and slightly uncivilised. It was not the sort of thing we could have imagined ourselves doing a few months before. But we were annoyed and overwrought, and our remoteness from all other human beings somehow made everything seem different. Since there were no other laws here, we had to make our own. . . .

'Can't we do something to stop them from taking off? Could we sabotage their rockets, for instance?' asked Bill.

Searle didn't like this idea at all.

'We mustn't do anything drastic,' he said. 'Besides, Don Hopkins is a good friend of mine. He'd never forgive me if I damaged his ship. There'd be the danger, too, that we might do something that couldn't be repaired.'

'Then pinch their fuel,' said Groves laconically.

'Of course! They're probably all asleep, there's no light in the cabin. All we've got to do is to connect up and pump.'

'A very nice idea,' I pointed out, 'but we're two kilometres apart. How much pipeline have we got? Is it as much as a hundred metres?'

The others ignored this interruption as though it was beneath contempt and went on making their plans. Five minutes later the technicians had settled everything: we only had to climb into our spacesuits and do the work.

I never thought, when I joined the Professor's expedition, that I should end up like an African porter in one of those old adventure stories, carrying a load on my head. Especially when the load was a sixth of a spaceship (being so short, Professor Forster wasn't able to provide very effective help). Now that its fuel tanks were half empty, the weight of the ship in this gravity was about two hundred kilograms. We squeezed beneath, heaved, and up she went – very slowly, of course, because her inertia was still unchanged. Then we started marching.

It took us quite a while to make the journey, and it wasn't quite as easy as we'd thought it would be. But presently the two ships were lying side by side, and nobody had noticed us. Everyone in the *Henry Luce* was fast asleep, as they had every reason to expect us to be.

Though I was still rather short of breath, I found a certain schoolboy amusement in the whole adventure as Searle and Fulton drew the refuelling pipeline out of our airlock and quietly coupled up to the other ship.

'The beauty of this plan,' explained Groves to me as we stood watching, 'is that they can't do anything to stop us, unless they come outside and uncouple our line. We can drain them dry in five minutes, and it will take them half that time to wake up and get into their spacesuits.'

A sudden horrid fear smote me.

'Suppose they turned on their rockets and tried to get away?'

'Then we'd both be smashed up. No, they'll just have to come outside and see what's going on. Ah, there go the pumps.'

The pipeline had stiffened like a fire-hose under pressure, and I knew that the fuel was pouring into our tanks. Any moment now the lights would go on in the *Henry Luce* and her startled occupants would come scuttling out.

It was something of an anticlimax when they didn't. They must have been sleeping very soundly not to have felt the vibration from the pumps, but when it was all over nothing had happened and we just stood round looking rather foolish. Searle and Fulton carefully uncoupled the pipeline and put it back into the airlock.

'Well?' we asked the Professor.

He thought things over for a minute.

'Let's get back into the ship,' he said.

When we had climbed out of our suits and were gathered together in the control room, or as far in as we could get, the Professor sat down at the radio and punched out the 'Emergency' signal. Our sleeping neighbours would be awake in a couple of seconds as their automatic receiver sounded the alarm.

The TV screen glimmered into life. There, looking rather frightened, was Randolph Mays.

'Hello, Forster,' he snapped. 'What's the trouble?'

'Nothing wrong here,' replied the Professor in his best deadpan manner, 'but you've lost something important. Look at your fuel gauges.'

The screen emptied, and for a moment there was a confused mumbling and shouting from the speaker. Then Mays was back, annoyance and alarm competing for possession of his features.

'What's going on?' he demanded angrily. 'Do you know anything about this?'

The Prof. let him sizzle for a moment before he replied.

'I think you'd better come across and talk things over,' he said. 'You won't have far to walk.'

Mays glared back at him uncertainly, then retorted, 'You bet I will!' The screen went blank.

'He'll have to climb down now!' said Bill gleefully. 'There's nothing else he can do!'

'It's not so simple as you think,' warned Fulton. 'If he really wanted to be awkward, he could just sit tight and radio Ganymede for a tanker.'

'What good would that do him? It would waste days and cost a fortune.'

'Yes, but he'd still have the statue, if he wanted it that badly. And he'd get his money back when he sued us.'

The airlock light flashed on and Mays stumped into the room. He was in a surprisingly conciliatory mood; on the way over, he must have had second thoughts.

'Well, well,' he said affably. 'What's all this nonsense in aid of?'

'You know perfectly well,' the Professor retorted coldly. 'I made it quite clear that nothing was to be taken off Five. You've been stealing property that doesn't belong to you.'

'Now, let's be reasonable. Who *does* it belong to? You can't claim everything on this planet as your personal property.'

'This is *not* a planet – it's a ship and the laws of salvage operate.'

'Frankly, that's a very debatable point. Don't you think you should wait until you get a ruling from the lawyers?'

The Professor was being icily polite, but I could see that the strain was terrific and an explosion might occur at any moment.

'Listen, Mr Mays,' he said with ominous calm. 'What you've taken is the most important single find we've made here. I will make allowances for the fact that you don't appreciate what you've done, and don't understand the viewpoint of an archaeologist like myself. Return that statue, and we'll pump your fuel back and say no more.'

Mays rubbed his chin thoughtfully.

'I realy don't see why you should make such a fuss about one statue, when you consider all the stuff that's still here.'

It was then that the Professor made one of his rare mistakes.

'You talk like a man who's stolen the Mona Lisa from the Louvre and argues that nobody will miss it because of all the other paintings. This statue's unique in a way that no terrestrial work of art can ever be. That's why I'm determined to get it back.'

You should never, when you're bargaining, make it obvious that you want something really badly. I saw the greedy glint in Mays's eye and said to myself, 'Uh-huh! He's going to be tough.' And I remembered Fulton's remark about calling Ganymede for a tanker.

'Give me half an hour to think it over,' said Mays, turning to the airlock.

'Very well,' replied the Professor stiffly. 'Half an hour – no more.'

I must give Mays credit for brains. Within five minutes we saw his communications aerial start slewing round until it locked on Ganymede. Naturally we tried to listen in, but he had a scrambler. These newspaper men must trust each other.

The reply came back a few minutes later; that was scrambled too. While we were waiting for the next development, we had another council of war. The Professor was now entering the stubborn, stop-at-nothing stage. He realised he'd miscalculated and that had made him fighting mad.

I think Mays must have been a little apprehensive, because he had reinforcements when he returned. Donald Hopkins, his pilot, came with him, looking rather uncomfortable.

'I've been able to fix things up, Professor,' he said smugly. 'It will take me a little longer, but I can get back without your help if I have to. Still, I must admit that it will save a good deal of time and money if we can come to an agreement. I'll tell you what. Give me back my fuel and I'll return the other – er – souvenirs I've collected. But I insist on keeping Mona Lisa, even if it means I won't get back to Ganymede until the middle of next week.'

The Professor then uttered a number of what are usually called deep-space oaths, though I can assure you they're much the same as any other oaths. That seemed to relieve his feelings a lot and he became fiendishly friendly.

'My dear Mr Mays,' he said, 'you're an unmitigated crook, and accordingly I've no compunction left in dealing with you. I'm prepared to use force, knowing that the law will justify me.'

Mays looked slightly alarmed, though not unduly so. We had moved to strategic positions round the door.

'Please don't be so melodramatic,' he said haughtily. 'This is the twenty-first century, not the Wild West back in 1800.'

'1880,' said Bill, who is a stickler for accuracy.

'I must ask you,' the Professor continued, 'to consider yourself under detention while we decide what is to be done. Mr Searle, take him to Cabin B.'

Mays sidled along the wall with a nervous laugh.

'Really, Professor, this is *too* childish! You can't detain me against my will.' He glanced for support at the Captain of the *Henry Luce*.

Donald Hopkins dusted an imaginary speck of fluff from his uniform.

'I refuse,' he remarked for the benefit of all concerned, 'to get involved in vulgar brawls.'

Mays gave him a venomous look and capitulated with bad grace. We saw that he had a good supply of reading matter, and locked him in.

When he was out of the way, the Professor turned to Hopkins, who was looking enviously at our fuel gauges.

'Can I take it, Captain,' he said politely, 'that you don't wish to get mixed up in any of your employer's dirty business?'

'I'm neutral. My job is to fly the ship here and take her home. You can fight this out among yourselves.'

'Thank you. I think we understand each other perfectly. Perhaps it would be best if you returned to your ship and explained the situation. We'll be calling you in a few minutes.'

Captain Hopkins made his way languidly to the door. As he was about to leave he turned to Searle.

'By the way, Kingsley,' he drawled. 'Have you thought of torture? Do call me if you get round to it – I've some jolly interesting ideas.' Then he was gone, leaving us with our hostage.

I think the Professor had hoped he could do a direct exchange. If so, he had not bargained on Marianne's stubborness.

'It serves Randolph right,' she said. 'But I don't really see that it makes any difference. He'll be just as comfortable in your ship as in ours, and you can't do anything to him. Let me know when you're fed up with having him around.'

It seemed a complete impasse. We had been too clever by half, and it had got us exactly nowhere. We'd captured Mays, but he wasn't any use to us.

The Professor was standing with his back to us, staring morosely out of the window. Seemingly balanced on the horizon, the immense bulk of Jupiter nearly filled the sky.

'We've got to convince her that we really *do* mean business,' he said. Then he turned abruptly to me.

'Do you think she's actually fond of this blackguard?'

'Er – I shouldn't be surprised. Yes, I really believe so.'

The Professor looked very thoughtful. Then he said to Searle, 'Come into my room. I want to talk something over.'

They were gone quite a while. When they returned they both had an indefinable air of gleeful anticipation, and the Professor was carrying a piece of paper covered with figures. He went to the radio, and called the *Henry Luce*.

'Hello,' said Marianne, replying so promptly that she'd obviously been waiting for us. 'Have you decided to call it off? I'm getting so bored.'

The Professor looked at her gravely.

'Miss Mitchell,' he replied. 'It's apparent that you have not been taking us seriously. I'm therefore arranging a somewhat – er – drastic little demonstration for your benefit. I'm going to place your employer in a position from which he'll be only too anxious for you to retrieve him as quickly as possible.'

'Indeed?' replied Marianne noncommittally – though I thought I could detect a trace of apprehension in her voice.

'I don't suppose,' continued the Professor smoothly, 'that you know anything about celestial mechanics. No? Too bad, but your pilot will confirm everything I tell you. Won't you, Hopkins?'

'Go ahead,' came a painstakingly neutral voice from the background.

'Then listen carefully, Miss Mitchell. I want to remind you of our curious – indeed our precarious – position on this satellite. You've only got to look out of the window to see how close to Jupiter we are, and I need hardly remind you that Jupiter has by far the most intense gravitational field of all the planets. You follow me?'

'Yes,' replied Marianne, no longer quite so self-possessed. 'Go on.'

'Very well. This little world of ours goes round Jupiter in almost exactly twelve hours. Now there's a well-known theorem stating that if a body *falls* from an orbit to the centre of attraction, it will take point one seven seven of a period to make the drop. In other words, anything falling from here to Jupiter would reach the centre of the planet in about two hours seven minutes. I'm sure Captain Hopkins can confirm this.'

There was a long pause. Then we heard Hopkins say, 'Well, of course I can't confirm the exact figures, but they're probably correct. It would be something like that, anyway.'

'Good,' continued the Professor. 'Now I'm sure you realise,' he went on with a hearty chuckle, 'that a fall to the *centre* of the planet is a very theoretical case. If anything really was dropped from here, it would reach the upper atmosphere of Jupiter in a considerably shorter time. I hope I'm not boring you?'

'No,' said Marianne, rather faintly.

'I'm so glad to hear it. Anyway, Captain Searle has worked out the actual time for me, and it's one hour thirty-five minutes – with a few minutes either way. We can't guarantee complete accuracy, ha, ha!'

'Now, it has doubtless not escaped your notice that this satellite of ours has an extremely weak gravitational field. Its escape velocity is only about ten metres a second, and anything thrown away from it at that speed would never come back. Correct, Mr Hopkins?'

'Perfectly correct.'

'Then, if I may come to the point, we propose to take Mr Mays for a walk until he's immediately under Jupiter, remove the reaction pistols from his suit, and – ah – launch him forth. We will be prepared to retrieve him with our ship as soon as you've handed over the property you've stolen. After what I've told you, I'm sure you'll appreciate that time will be rather vital. An hour and thirty-five minutes is remarkably short, isn't it?'

'Professor!' I gasped. 'You can't possibly do this!'

'Shut up!' he barked. 'Well, Miss Mitchell, what about it?'

Marianne was staring at him with mingled horror and disbelief.

'You're simply bluffing!' she cried. 'I don't believe you'd do anything of the kind! Your crew won't let you!'

The Professor sighed.

'Too bad,' he said. 'Captain Searle – Mr Groves – will you take the prisoner and proceed as instructed.'

'Aye-aye, sir,' replied Searle with great solemnity.

Mays looked frightened but stubborn.

'What are you going to do now?' he said, as his suit was handed back to him.

Searle unholstered his reaction pistols. 'Just climb in,' he said. 'We're going for a walk.'

I realised then what the Professor hoped to do. The whole thing was a colossal bluff: of course he wouldn't *really* have Mays thrown into Jupiter; and in any case Searle and Groves wouldn't do it. Yet surely Marianne would see through the bluff, and then we'd be left looking mighty foolish.

Mays couldn't run away; without his reaction pistols he was quite helpless. Grasping his arms and towing him along like a captive balloon, his escorts set off toward the horizon – and towards Jupiter.

I could see, looking across the space to the other ship, that Marianne was staring out through the observation windows at the departing trio. Professor Forster noticed it too.

'I hope you're convinced, Miss Mitchell, that my men aren't carrying along an empty spacesuit. Might I suggest that you follow the proceedings with a telescope? They'll be over the horizon in minute, but you'll be able to see Mr Mays when he starts to – er – ascend.'

There was a stubborn silence from the loudspeaker. The period of suspense seemed to last for a very long time. Was Marianne waiting to see how far the Professor really would go?

By this time I had got hold of a pair of binoculars and was sweeping the sky beyond the ridiculously close horizon. Suddenly I saw it – a tiny flare of light against the vast yellow back-cloth of Jupiter. I focused quickly, and could just make out the three figures rising into space. As I watched, they separated: two of them decelerated with their pistols and started to fall back toward Five. The other went on ascending helplessly toward the ominous bulk of Jupiter.

I turned on the Professor in horror and disbelief.

'They've really done it!' I cried. 'I thought you were only bluffing!'

'So did Miss Mitchell, I've no doubt,' said the Professor calmly, for the benefit of the listening microphone. 'I hope I don't need to impress upon you the urgency of the situation. As I've remarked once or twice before, the time of fall from our orbit to Jupiter's surface is ninety-five minutes. But, of course, if one waited even half that time, it would be much too late. . . .'

He let that sink in. There was no reply from the other ship.

'And now,' he continued, 'I'm going to switch off our receiver so we can't have any more arguments. We'll wait until you've unloaded that statue – *and* the other items Mr Mays was careless enough to mention – before we'll talk to you again. Goodbye.'

It was a very uncomfortable ten minutes. I'd lost track of Mays, and was seriously wondering if we'd better overpower the Professor and go after him before we had a murder on our hands. But the people who could fly the ship were the ones who had actually carried out the crime. I didn't know *what* to think.

Then the airlock of the *Henry Luce* slowly opened. A couple of space-suited figures emerged, floating the cause of all the trouble between them.

'Unconditional surrender,' murmured the Professor with a sigh of satisfaction. 'Get it into our ship,' he called over the radio. 'I'll open up the airlock for you.'

He seemed in no hurry at all. I kept looking anxiously at the clock; fifteen minutes had already gone by. Presently there was a clanking and banging in the airlock, the inner door opened, and Captain Hopkins entered. He was followed by Marianne, who only needed a bloodstained axe to make her look like Clytaemnestra. I did my best to avoid her eye, but the Professor seemed to be quite without shame. He walked into the airlock, checked that his property was back, and emerged rubbing his hands.

'Well, that's that,' he said cheerfully. 'Now let's sit down and have a drink to forget all this unpleasantness, shall we?'

I pointed indignantly at the clock.

'Have you gone crazy!' I yelled. 'He's already halfway to Jupiter!'

Professor Forster looked at me disapprovingly.

'Impatience,' he said, 'is a common failing in the young. I see no cause at all for hasty action.'

Marianne spoke for the first time; she now looked really scared.

'But you promised,' she whispered.

The Professor suddenly capitulated. He had had his little joke, and didn't want to prolong the agony.

'I can tell you at once, Miss Mitchell – and you too, Jack – that Mays is in no more danger than we are. We can go and collect him whenever we like.'

'Do you mean that you lied to me?'

'Certainly not. Everything I told you was perfectly true. You simply jumped to the wrong conclusions. When I said that a body would take ninety-five minutes to fall from here to Jupiter, I omitted – not, I must confess, accidentally – a rather important phrase. I should have added "*a body at rest with respect to Jupiter.*" Your friend Mr Mays was sharing the orbital speed of his satellite, and he's still got it. A little matter of twenty-six kilometres a second, Miss Mitchell.

'Oh yes, we threw him completely off Five and toward Jupiter. But the velocity we gave him then was trivial. He's still moving in practically the same orbit as before. The most he can do – I've got Captain Searle to work out the figures – is to drift about a hundred kilometres inward. And in one revolution – twelve hours – *he'll be right back where he started*, without us bothering to do anything at all.'

There was a long, long silence. Marianne's face was a study in frustration, relief, and annoyance at having been fooled. Then she turned on Captain Hopkins.

'You must have known all the time! Why didn't you tell me?'

Hopkins gave her a wounded expression.

'You didn't ask me,' he said.

We hauled Mays down about an hour later. He was only twenty kilometres up, and we located him quickly enough by the flashing light on his suit. His radio had been disconnected, for a reason that hadn't occurred to me. He was intelligent enough to realise that he was in no danger, and if his set had been working he could have called his ship and exposed our bluff. That is, if he wanted to. Personally, I think I'd have been glad enough to call the whole thing off even if I had known that I was perfectly safe. It must have been awfully lonely up there.

To my great surprise, Mays wasn't as mad as I'd expected. Perhaps he was too relieved to be back in our snug little cabin when we drifted up to him on the merest fizzle of rockets and yanked him in. Or perhaps he felt that he'd been worsted in fair fight and didn't bear any grudge. I really think it was the latter.

There isn't must more to tell, except that we did play one other trick on him before we left Five. He had a good deal more fuel in his tanks than he really needed, now that his payload was substantially reduced. By keeping the excess ourselves, we were able to carry The Ambassador back to Ganymede after all. Oh, yes, the Professor gave him a cheque for the fuel we'd borrowed. Everything was perfectly legal.

There's one amusing sequel I must tell you, though. The day after the new gallery was opened at the British Museum I went along to see The Ambassador, partly to discover if his impact was still as great in these changed surroundings. (For the record, it wasn't – though it's still considerable and Bloosmbury will never be quite the same to me again.) A huge crowd was milling around the gallery, and there in the middle of it was Mays and Marianne.

It ended up with us having a very pleasant lunch together in Holborn. I'll say this about Mays – he doesn't bear any grudges. But I'm still rather sore about Marianne.

And, frankly, I can't imagine *what* she sees in him.

Encounter in the Dawn

First published in *Amazing*, June/July 1953
Collected in *Expedition to Earth*

This inspired the opening sequence of *2001:A Space Odyssey*. Dan Richter, who played Moon Watcher, has made the transition from Man-ape to LA Executive in a single lifetime. I am sure he must still find that bone club quite useful around Hollywood.

It was in the last days of the Empire. The tiny ship was far from home, and almost a hundred light-years from the great parent vessel searching through the loosely packed stars at the rim of the Milky Way. But even here it could not escape from the shadow that lay across civilisation: beneath that shadow, pausing ever and again in their work to wonder how their distant homes were faring, the scientists of the Galactic Survey still laboured at their never-ending task.

The ship held only three occupants, but between them they carried knowledge of many sciences, and the experience of half a lifetime in space. After the long interstellar night, the star ahead was warming their spirits as they dropped down towards its fires. A little more golden, a trifle more brilliant than the Sun that now seemed a legend of their childhood. They knew from past experience that the chance of locating planets here was more than ninety per cent, and for the moment they forgot all else in the excitement of discovery.

They found the first planet within minutes of coming to rest. It was a giant, of a familiar type, too cold for protoplasmic life and probably possessing no stable surface. So they turned their search sunward, and presently were rewarded.

It was a world that made their hearts ache for home, a world where everything was hauntingly familiar, yet never quite the same. Two great land masses floated in blue-green seas, capped by ice at either pole. There were some desert regions, but the larger part of the planet was obviously fertile. Even from this distance, the signs of vegetation were unmistakably clear.

They gazed hungrily at the expanding landscape as they fell down into the amosphere, heading towards noon in the sub-tropics. The ship plummeted through cloudless skies towards a great river, checked its fall with a surge of soundless power, and came to rest among the long grasses by the water's edge.

No one moved: there was nothing to be done until the automatic instruments had finished their work. Then a bell tinkled softly and the lights on the control board flashed in a pattern of meaningful chaos. Captain Altman rose to his feet with a sigh of relief.

'We're in luck,' he said. 'We can go outside without protection, if the pathogenic tests are satisfactory. What did you make of the place as we came in, Bertrond?'

'Geologically stable – no active volancoes, at least. I didn't see any trace of cities, but that proves nothing. If there's a civilisation here, it may have passed that stage.'

'Or not reached it yet?'

Betrond shrugged. 'Either's just as likely. It may take us some time to find out on a planet this size.'

'More time than we've got,' said Clindar, glancing at the communications panel that linked them to the mother ship and thence to the Galaxy's threatened heart. For a moment there was a gloomy silence. Then Clindar walked to the control board and pressed a pattern of keys with automatic skill.

With a slight jar, a section of the hull slid aside and the fourth member of the crew stepped out on to the new planet, flexing metal limbs and adjusting servo motors to the unaccustomed gravity. Inside the ship, a television screen glimmered into life, revealing a long vista of waving grasses, some trees in the middle distance, and a glimpse of the great river. Clindar punched a button, and the picture flowed steadily across the screen as the robot turned its head.

'Which way shall we go?' Clindar asked.

'Let's have a look at those trees,' Altman replied. 'If there's any animal life we'll find it there.'

'Look!' cried Bertrond. 'A bird!'

Clindar's fingers flew over the keyboard; the picture centred on the tiny speck that had suddenly appeared on the left of the screen, and expanded rapidly as the robot's telephoto lens came into action.

'You're right,' he said. 'Feathers – beak – well up the evolutionary ladder. This place looks promising. I'll start the camera.'

The swaying motion of the picture as the robot walked forward did not distract them: they had grown accustomed to it long ago. But they had never become reconciled to this exploration by proxy when all their impulses cried out to them to leave the ship, to run through the grass and to feel the wind blowing against their faces. Yet it was too great a risk to take, even on a world that seemed as fair as this. There was always a skull hidden behind Nature's most smiling face. Wild beasts, poisonous reptiles, quagmires – death could come to the unwary explorer in a thousand disguises. And worst of all were the invisible enemies, the bacteria and viruses against which the only defence might often be a thousand light-years away.

A robot could laugh at all these dangers and even if, as sometimes happened, it encountered a beast powerful enough to destroy it – well, machines could always be replaced.

They met nothing on the walk across the grasslands. If any small animals were disturbed by the robot's passage, they kept outside its field of vision. Clindar slowed the machine as it approached the trees, and the watchers in the spaceship flinched involuntarily at the branches that appeared to slash across their eyes. The picture dimmed for a moment before the controls readjusted themselves to the weaker illumination; then it came back to normal.

The forest was full of life. It lurked in the undergrowth, clambered among the branches, flew through the air. It fled chattering and gibbering through the trees as the robot advanced. And all the while the automatic cameras were recording the pictures that formed on the screen, gathering material for the biologists to analyse when the ship returned to base.

Clindar breathed a sigh of relief when the trees suddenly thinned. It was exhausting work, keeping the robot from smashing into obstacles as it moved through the forest, but on open ground it could take care of itself. Then the picture trembled as if beneath a hammer-blow, there was a grinding metallic thud, and the whole scene swept vertiginously upward as the robot toppled and fell.

'What's that?' cried Altman. 'Did you trip?'

'No,' said Clindar grimly, his fingers flying over the keyboard. 'Something attacked from the rear. I hope – ah – I've still got control.'

He brought the robot to a sitting position and swivelled its head. It did not take long to find the cause of the trouble. Standing a few feet away, and lashing its tail angrily, was a large quadruped with a most ferocious set of teeth. At the moment it was, fairly obviously, trying to decide whether to attack again.

Slowly, the robot rose to its feet, and as it did so the great beast crouched to spring. A smile flitted across Clindar's face: he knew how to deal with this situation. His thumb felt for the seldom-used key labelled 'Siren'.

The forest echoed with a hideous undulating scream from the robot's concealed speaker, and the machine advanced to meet its adversary, arms flailing in front of it. The startled beast almost fell over backward in its effort to turn, and in seconds was gone from sight.

'Now I suppose we'll have to wait a couple of hours until everything comes out of hiding again,' said Bertrond ruefully.

'I don't know much about animal psychology,' interjected Altman, 'but is it usual for them to attack something completely unfamiliar?'

'Some will attack anything that moves, but that's unusual. Normally they attack only for food, or if they've already been threatened. What are you driving at? Do you suggest that there are other robots on this planet?'

'Certainly not. But our carnivorous friend may have mistaken our machine for a more edible biped. Don't you think that this opening in the jungle is rather unnatural? It could easily be a path.'

'In that case,' said Clindar promptly, 'we'll follow it and find out. I'm tired of dodging trees, but I hope nothing jumps on us again: it's bad for my nerves.'

'You were right, Altman,' said Bertrond a little later. 'It's certainly a path. But that doesn't mean intelligence. After all, animals—'

He stopped in mid-sentence, and at the same instant Clindar brought the advancing robot to a halt. The path had suddenly opened out into a wide clearing, almost completely occupied by a village of flimsy huts. It was ringed by a wooden palisade, obviously defence against an enemy who at the moment presented no threat. For the gates were wide open, and beyond them the inhabitants were going peacefully about their ways.

For many minutes the three explorers stared in silence at the screen. Then Clindar shivered a little and remarked: 'It's uncanny. It might be our own planet, a hundred thousand years ago. I feel as if I've gone back in time.'

'There's nothing weird about it,' said the practical Altman. 'After all, we've discovered nearly a hundred planets with our type of life on them.'

'Yes,' retorted Clindar. 'A hundred in the whole Galaxy! I still think that it's strange it had to happen to us.'

'Well, it had to happen to *somebody*,' said Bertrond philosophically. 'Meanwhile, we must work out our contact procedure. If we send the robot into the village it will start a panic.'

'That,' said Altman, 'is a masterly understatement. What we'll have to do is catch a native by himself and prove that we're friendly. Hide the robot, Clindar – somewhere in the woods where it can watch the village without being spotted. We've a week's practical anthropology ahead of us!'

It was three days before the biological tests showed that it would be safe to leave the ship. Even then Bertrond insisted on going alone – alone, that is, if one ignored the substantial company of the robot. With such an ally he was not afraid of this planet's larger beasts, and his body's natural defences could take care of the micro-organisms, so, at least, the analysers had assured him: and considering the complexity of the problem, they made remarkably few mistakes.

He stayed outside for an hour, enjoying himself cautiously, while his companions watched with envy. It would be another three days before they could be quite certain that it was safe to follow Bertrond's example. Meanwhile, they kept busy enough watching the village through the lenses of the robot, and recording everything they could with the cameras. They had moved the spaceship at night so that it was hidden in the depths of the forest, for they did not wish to be discovered until they were ready.

And all the while the news from the home grew worse. Though their remoteness here at the edge of the Universe deadened its impact, it lay heavily on their minds and sometimes overwhelmed them with a sense of futility. At any moment, they knew, the signal for recall might come as the

Empire summoned up its last resources in its extremity. But until then they would continue their work as though pure knowledge were the only thing that mattered.

Seven days after landing, they were ready to make the experiment. They knew now what paths the villagers used when going hunting, and Bertrond chose one of the less frequented ways. Then he placed a chair firmly in the middle of the path and settled down to read a book.

It was not, of course, quite as simple as that: Bertrond had taken all imaginable precautions. Hidden in the undergrowth fifty yards away, the robot was watching through its telescopic lenses, and in its hand it held a small but deadly weapon. Controlling it from the spaceship, his fingers poised over the keyboard, Clindar waited to do what might be necessary.

That was the negative side of the plan: the positive side was more obvious. Lying at Bertrond's feet was the carcass of a small, horned animal which he hoped would be an acceptable gift to any hunter passing this way.

Two hours later the radio in his suit harness whispered a warning. Quite calmly, though the blood was pounding in his veins, Bertrond laid aside his book and looked down the trail. The savage was walking forward confidently enough, swinging a spear in his right hand. He paused for a moment when he saw Bertrond, then advanced more cautiously. He could tell that there was nothing to fear, for the stranger was slightly built and obviously unarmed.

When only twenty feet separated them, Bertrond gave a reassuring smile and rose slowly to his feet. He bent down, picked up the carcass, and carried it forward as an offering. The gesture would have been understood by any creature on any world, and it was understood here. The savage reached forward, took the animal, and threw it effortlessly over his shoulder. For an instant he stared into Bertrond's eyes with a fathomless expression; then he turned and walked back towards the village. Three times he glanced round to see if Bertrond was following, and each time Bertrond smiled and waved reassurance. The whole episode lasted little more than a minute. As the first contact between two races it was completely without drama, though not without dignity.

Bertrond did not move until the other had vanished from sight. Then he relaxed and spoke into his suit microphone.

'That was a pretty good beginning,' he said jubilantly. 'He wasn't in the least frightened, or even suspicious. I think he'll be back.'

'It still seems too good to be true,' said Altman's voice in his ear. 'I should have thought he'd have been either scared or hostile. Would *you* have accepted a lavish gift from a peculiar stranger with such little fuss?'

Bertrond was slowly walking back to the ship. The robot had now come out of cover and was keeping guard a few paces behind him.

'*I* wouldn't,' he replied, 'but I belong to a civilised community. Complete savages may react to strangers in many different ways, according to their past experience. Suppose this tribe has never had any enemies. That's quite

464

possible on a large but sparsely populated planet. Then we may expect curiosity, but no fear at all.'

'If these people have no enemies,' put in Clindar, no longer fully occupied in controlling the robot, 'why have they got a stockade round the village?'

'I mean no *human* enemies,' replied Bertrond. 'If that's true, it simplifies our task immensely.'

'Do you think he'll come back?'

'Of course. If he's human as I think, curiosity and greed will make him return. In a couple of days we'll be bosom friends.'

Looked at dispassionately, it became a fantastic routine. Every morning the robot would go hunting under Clindar's direction, until it was now the deadliest killer in the jungle. Then Bertrond would wait until Yaan – which was the nearest they could get to his name – came striding confidently along the path. He came at the same time every day, and he always came alone. They wondered about this: did he wish to keep his great discovery to himself and thus get all the credit for his hunting prowess? If so, it showed unexpected foresight and cunning.

At first Yaan had departed at once with his prize, as if afraid that the donor of such a generous gift might change his mind. Soon, however, as Bertrond had hoped, he could be induced to stay for a while by simple conjuring tricks and a display of brightly coloured fabrics and crystals, in which he took a child-like delight. At last Bertrond was able to engage him in lengthy conversations, all of which were recorded as well as being filmed through the eyes of the hidden robot.

One day the philologists might be able to analyse this material; the best that Bertrond could do was to discover the meanings of a few simple verbs and nouns. This was made more difficult by the fact that Yaan not only used different words for the same thing, but sometimes the same word for different things.

Between these daily interviews, the ship travelled far, surveying the planet from the air and sometimes landing for more detailed examinations. Although several other human settlements were observed, Bertrond made no attempt to get in touch with them, for it was easy to see that they were all at much the same culture level as Yaan's people.

It was, Bertrond often thought, a particularly bad joke on the part of Fate that one of the Galaxy's very few truly human races should have been discovered at this moment of time. Not long ago this would have been an event of supreme importance; now civilisation was too hard-pressed to concern itself with these savage cousins waiting at the dawn of history.

Not until Bertrond was sure he had become part of Yaan's everyday life did he introduce him to the robot. He was showing Yaan the patterns in a kaleidoscope when Clindar brought the machine striding through the grass with its latest victim dangling across one metal arm. For the first time Yaan showed something akin to fear; but he relaxed at Bertrond's soothing words, though he continued to watch the advancing monster. It halted some distance away, and Bertrond walked forward to meet it. As he did so, the robot raised its arms and handed him the dead beast. He took it solemnly and carried it back to Yaan, staggering a little under the unaccustomed load.

Bertrond would have given a great deal to know just what Yaan was thinking as he accepted the gift. Was he trying to decide whether the robot was master or slave? Perhaps such conceptions as this were beyond his grasp: to him the robot might be merely another man, a hunter who was a friend of Bertrond.

Clindar's voice, slightly larger than life, came from the robot's speaker.

'It's astonishing how calmly he accepts us. Won't anything scare him?'

'You will keep judging him by your own standards,' replied Bertrond. 'Remember, his psychology is completely different, and much simpler. Now that he has confidence in me anything that I accept won't worry him.'

'I wonder if that will be true of all his race?' queried Altman. 'It's hardly safe to judge by a single specimen. I want to see what happens when we send the robot into the village.'

'Hello!' exclaimed Bertrond. '*That* surprised him. He's never met a person who could speak with two voices before.'

'Do you think he'll guess the truth when he meets us?' said Clindar.

'No. The robot will be pure magic to him – but it won't be any more wonderful than fire and lightning and all the other forces he must already take for granted.'

'Well, what's the next move?' asked Altman, a little impatiently. 'Are you going to bring him to the ship, or will you go into the village first?'

Bertrond hesitated. 'I'm anxious not to do too much too quickly. You know the accidents that have happened with strange races when that's been tried. I'll let him think this over and when we get back tomorrow I'll try to persuade him to take the robot back to the village.'

In the hidden ship, Clindar reactivated the robot and started it moving again. Like Altman, he was growing a little impatient of this excessive caution, but on all matters relating to alien life-forms Bertrond was the expert, and they had to obey his orders.

There were times now when he almost wished he were a robot himself, devoid of feelings or emotions, able to watch the fall of a leaf or the death agonies of a world with equal detachment –

The Sun was low when Yaan heard the great voice crying from the jungle. He recognised it at once, despite its inhuman volume: it was the voice of his friend calling him.

In the echoing silence, the life of the village came to a stop. Even the children ceased their play: the only sound was the thin cry of a baby frightened by the sudden silence.

All eyes were upon Yaan as he walked swiftly to his hut and grasped the spear that lay beside the entrance. The stockade would soon be closed against the prowlers of the night, but he did not hesitate as he stepped out into the lengthening shadows. He was passing through the gates when once again that mighty voice summoned him, and now it held a note of urgency that came clearly across all the barriers of language and culture.

The shining giant who spoke with many voices met him a little way from the village and beckoned him to follow. There was no sign of Bertrond. They walked for almost a mile before they saw him in the distance, standing not far from the river's edge and staring out across the dark, slowly moving waters.

He turned as Yaan approached, yet for a moment seemed unaware of his presence. Then he gave a gesture of dismissal to the shining one, who withdrew into the distance.

Yaan waited. He was patient and, though he could never have expressed it in words, contented. When he was with Bertrond he felt the first intimations of that selfless, utterly irrational devotion his race would not fully achieve for many ages.

It was a strange tableau. Here at the river's brink two men were standing. One was dressed in a closely fitting uniform equipped with tiny, intricate mechanisms. The other was wearing the skin of an animal and was carrying a flint-tipped spear. Ten thousand generations lay between them, ten thousand generations and an immeasurable gulf of space. Yet they were both human. As she must often do in eternity, Nature had repeated one of her basic patterns.

Presently Bertrond began to speak, walking to and fro in short, quick steps as he did so, and in his voice there was a trace of sadness.

'It's all over, Yaan. I'd hoped that with our knowedge we could have brought you out of barbarism in a dozen generations but now you will have to fight your way up from the jungle alone, and it may take you a million years to do so. I'm sorry – there's so much we could have done. Even now I wanted to stay here, but Altman and Clindar talk of duty, and I suppose that they are right. There is little enough that we can do, but our world is calling and we must not forsake it.

'I wish you could understand me, Yaan. I wish you knew what I was saying. I'm leaving you these tools: some of them you will discover how to use, though as likely as not in a generation they'll be lost or forgotten. See how this blade cuts: it will be ages before your world can make its like. And guard this well: when you press the button – look! If you use it sparingly, it will give you light for years, though sooner or later it will die. As for these other things – find what use for them you can.

'Here come the first stars, up there in the east. Do you ever look at the stars, Yaan? I wonder how long it will be before you have discovered what they are, and I wonder what will have happened to us by then. Those stars are our homes, Yaan, and we cannot save them. Many have died already, in explosions so vast that I can imagine them no more than you. In a hundred thousand of your years, the light of those funeral pyres will reach your world and set its peoples wondering. By then, perhaps, your race will be reaching for the stars. I wish I could warn you against the mistakes we made, and which now will cost us all that we have won.

'It is well for your people, Yaan, that your world is here at the frontier of the Universe. You may escape the doom that waits for us. One day, perhaps, your ships will go searching among the stars as we have done, and they may come upon the ruins of our worlds and wonder who we were. But they will never know that we met here by this river when your race was young.

'Here come my friends; they would give me no more time. Goodbye, Yaan – use well the things I have left you. They are your world's greatest treasures.'

Something huge, something that glittered in the starlight, was sliding down from the sky. It did not reach the ground, but came to rest a little way above the surface, and in utter silence a rectangle of light opened in its side. The shining giant appeared out of the night and stepped through the golden door. Bertrond followed, pausing for a moment at the threshold to wave back at Yaan. Then the darkness closed behind him.

No more swiftly than smoke drifts upward from a fire, the ship lifted away. When it was so small that Yaan felt he could hold it in his hands, it seemed to blur into a long line of light slanting upward into the stars. From the empty sky a peal of thunder echoed over the sleeping land: and Yaan knew at last that the gods were gone and would never come again.

For a long time he stood by the gently moving waters, and into his soul there came a sense of loss he was never to forget and never to understand. Then, carefully and reverently, he collected together the gifts that Bertrond had left.

Under the stars, the lonely figure walked homeward across the nameless land. Behind him the river flowed softly to the sea, winding through the fertile plains on which, more than a thousand centuries ahead, Yaan's descendants would build the great city they were to call Babylon.

The Other Tiger

First published in *Fantastic Universe*, June/July 1953
Collected in *Tales From Planet Earth*

Originally entitled 'Refutation', this story was retitled by Sam Merwin, editor of *Fantastic Universe*, as a nod to Frank Stockton's classic but now forgotten 'The Lady or the Tiger'.

'It's an interesting theory,' said Arnold, 'but I don't see how you can ever prove it.' They had come to the steepest part of the hill and for a moment Webb was too breathless to reply.

'I'm not trying to,' he said when he had gained his second wind. 'I'm only exploring its consequences.'

'Such as?'

'Well, let's be perfectly logical and see where it gets us. Our only assumption, remember, is that the universe is infinite.'

'Right. Personally I don't see what else it *can* be.'

'Very well. That means there must be an infinite number of stars and planets. Therefore, by the laws of chance, every possible event must occur not merely once but an infinite number of times. Correct?'

'I suppose so.'

'Then there must be an infinite number of worlds *exactly like Earth*, each with an Arnold and Webb on it, walking up this hill just as we are doing now, saying these same words.'

'That's pretty hard to swallow.'

'I know it's a staggering thought – but so is infinity. The thing that interests me, though, is the idea of all those other Earths that aren't exactly the same as this one. The Earths where Hitler won the War and the Swastika flies over Buckingham Palace – the Earths where Columbus never discovered America – the Earths where the Roman Empire has lasted to this day. In fact the Earths where all the great *if*'s of history had different answers.'

'Going right back to the beginning, I suppose, to the one in which the ape-man who would have been the daddy of us all, broke his neck before he could have any children?'

'That's the idea. But let's stick to the worlds we know – the worlds containing *us* climbing this hill on this spring afternoon. Think of all our reflections on those millions of other planets. Some of them are exactly the same but every possible variation that doesn't violate the laws of logic must also exist.

'We could – we *must* – be wearing every conceivable sort of clothes – and no clothes at all. The Sun's shining here but on countless billions of those other Earths it's not. On many it's winter or summer here instead of spring. But let's consider more fundamental changes too.

'We intend to walk up this hill and down the other side. Yet think of all the things that might possibly happen to us in the next few minutes. However improbable they may be, as long as they are *possible*, then somewhere they've got to happen.'

'I see,' said Arnold slowly, absorbing the idea with obvious reluctance. An expression of mild discomfort crossed his features. 'Then somewhere, I suppose, you will fall dead with heart failure when you've taken your next step.'

'Not in *this* world.' Webb laughed. 'I've already refuted it. Perhaps *you're* going to be the unlucky one.'

'Or perhaps,' said Arnold, 'I'll get fed up with the whole conversation, pull out a gun and shoot you.'

'Quite possibly,' admitted Webb, 'except that I'm pretty sure you, on this Earth, haven't got one. Don't forget, though, that in millions of those alternative worlds I'll beat you on the draw.'

The path was now winding up a wooded slope, the trees thick on either side. The air was fresh and sweet. It was very quiet as though all Nature's energies were concentrated, with silent intentness, on rebuilding the world after the ruin of winter.

'I wonder,' continued Webb, 'how improbable a thing can get before it becomes impossible. We've mentioned some unlikely events but they're not completely fantastic. Here we are in an English country lane, walking along a path we know perfectly well.

'Yet in some universe those – what shall I call them – *twins* of ours will walk around that corner and meet anything, absolutely anything that imagination can conceive. For as I said at the beginning, if the cosmos is infinite, then all possibilities must arise.'

'So it's possible,' said Arnold, with a laugh that was not quite as light as he had intended, 'that we may walk into a tiger or something equally unpleasant.'

'Of course,' replied Webb cheerfully, warming to his subject. 'If it's possible, then it's got to happen to someone, somewhere in the universe. So why not to us?'

Arnold gave a snort of disgust. 'This is getting quite futile,' he protested. 'Let's talk about something sensible. If we don't meet a tiger round this corner I'll regard your theory as refuted and changed the subject.'

'Don't be silly,' said Webb gleefully. 'That won't refute anything. There's no way you can—'

They were the last words he ever spoke. On an infinite number of Earths an infinite numbers of Webbs and Arnolds met tigers friendly, hostile or indifferent. But this was not one of those Earths – it lay far closer to the point where improbability urged on the impossile.

Yet of course it was not totally inconceivable that during the night the rain-sodden hillside had caved inward to reveal an ominous cleft leading down into the subterranean world. As for *what* had laboriously climbed up that cleft, drawn toward the unknown light of day – well, it was really no more unlikely than the giant squid, the boa constrictor or the feral lizards of the Jurassic jungle. It had strained the laws of zoological probability but not to the breaking-point.

Webb had spoken the truth. In an infinite cosmos everything must happen somewhere – including their singularly bad luck. For *it* was hungry – very hungry – and a tiger or a man would have been a small yet acceptable morsel to any one of its half dozen gaping mouths.

* * *

The concept that *every possible* Universe may exist is certainly not an original one, but it has recently been revised in a sophisticated form by today's theoretical physicists (insofar as I understand anything that they are talking about). It is also linked with the so-called Anthropic Principle, which now has the cosmologists in a considerable tizzy. (See Tipler and Barrow's *The Anthropic Cosmological Principle*. Even if you have to skip many pages of music, the bits of text between them are fascinating and mind-stretching.)

The anthroposists have pointed out what appear to be some peculiarities of our Universe. Many of the fundamental physical constants – which as far as one could see, God could have given any value He liked – are in fact very precisely adjusted, or fine-tuned, to produce the *only* kind of Universe that makes our existence possible. A few per cent either way, and we wouldn't be here.

One explanation of this mystery is that in fact all the other possible Universes do exist (somewhere!) but of course, the vast majority are lifeless. Only in an infinitesimally small fraction of the total Creation are the parameters such that matter can exist, stars can form – and, ultimately, life can arise. We're here because we couldn't be anywhere else.

But all those elsewhere are *somewhere*, so my story may be uncomfortably close to the truth. Luckily, there's no way that we'll ever to be able prove it.

I think . . .

Publicity Campaign

First published in *London Evening News*, 1953
Collected in *The Other Side of the Sky*

For the first few decades after the Martians lowered New Jersey real estate values [referrring to Orson Welles' famous *War of the Worlds* broadcast], benevolent aliens were few and far between, perhaps the most notable example being Klaatu in *The Day The Earth Stood Still*. Yet nowadays, largely thanks to *E.T.*, friendly and even cuddly aliens are taken almost for granted. Where does the truth lie? . . .

Of course, hostile and malevolent aliens make for much more exciting stories than benevolent ones. Moreover, the Things You Wouldn't Like to Meet of the 1950s and 1960s, as has often been pointed out, were reflections of the paranoia of that time, particularly in the United States. Now the Cold War has, hopefully, given way to the Tepid Truce, we may look at the skies with less apprehensions.

For we have already met Darth Vader – and he is us.

The concussion of the last atom bomb still seemed to linger as the lights came on again. For a long time, no one moved. Then the assistant producer said innocently: 'Well, R.B., what do you think of it?'

R.B. heaved himself out of his seat while his acolytes waited to see which way the cat would jump. It was then that they noticed that R.B.'s cigar had gone out. Why, that hadn't happened even at the preview of 'G.W.T.W.'!

'Boys,' he said ecstatically, 'we've got something here! How much did you say it cost, Mike?'

'Six and a half million, R.B.'

'It was cheap at the price. Let me tell you, I'll eat every foot of it if the gross doesn't beat "Quo Vadis".' He wheeled, as swiftly as could be expected for one of his bulk, upon a small man still crouched in his seat at the back of the projection room. 'Snap out of it, Joe! The Earth's saved! You've seen all these space films. How does this line up with the earlier ones?'

Joe came to with an obvious effort.

'There's no comparison,' he said. 'It's got all the suspense of "The Thing", without that awful let down at the end when you saw the monster was human. The only picture that comes within miles of it is "War of the

Worlds". Some of the effects in that were nearly as good as ours, but of course George Pal didn't have 3D. And that sure makes a difference! When the Golden Gate Bridge went down, I thought that pier was going to hit me!'

'The bit I liked best,' put in Tony Auerbach from Publicity, 'was when the Empire State Building split right up the middle. You don't suppose the owners might sue us, though?'

'Of course not. No one expects *any* building to stand up to – what did the script call them? – city busters. And after all, we wiped out the rest of New York as well. Ugh – that scene in the Holland Tunnel when the roof gave way! Next time, I'll take the ferry!'

'Yes, that was very well done – almost *too* well done. But what really got me was those creatures from space. The animation was perfect – how did you do it, Mike?'

'Trade secret,' said the proud producer. 'Still, I'll let you in on it. A lot of that stuff is genuine.'

'What!'

'Oh, don't get me wrong! We haven't been on location to Sirius B. But they've developed a microcamera over at Cal Tech, and we used that to film spiders in action. We cut in the best shots, and I think you'd have a job telling which was micro and which was the full-sized studio stuff. Now you understand why I wanted the Aliens to be insects, and not octopuses, like the script said first.'

'There's a good publicity angle here,' said Tony. 'One thing worries me, though. That scene where the monsters kidnap Gloria. Do you suppose the censor . . . I mean the way we've done it, it almost looks . . .'

'Aw, quit worrying! *That's* what people are supposed to think! Anyway, we make it clear in the next reel that they really want her for dissection, so that's all right.'

'It'll be a riot!' gloated R.B., a faraway gleam in his eye as if he was already hearing the avalanche of dollars pouring into the box office. 'Look – we'll put another mllion into publicity! I can just see the posters – get all this down, Tony. WATCH THE SKY! THE SIRIANS ARE COMING! And we'll make thousands of clockwork models – can't you imagine them scuttling around on their hairy legs! People love to be scared, and we'll scare them. By the time we've finished, no one will be able to look at the sky without getting the creeps! I leave it to you, boys – this picture is going to make *history*!'

He was right. 'Monsters from Space' hit the public two months later. Within a week of the simultaneous London and New York *premières*, there could have been no one in the western world who had not seen the posters screaming EARTH BEWARE! or had not shuddered at the photograph of the hairy horrors stalking along deserted Fifth Avenue on their thin, many-jointed legs. Blimps cleverly disguised as spaceships cruised across the skies, to the vast confusion of pilots who encountered them, and clockwork models of the Alien invaders were everywhere, scaring old ladies out of their wits.

The publicity campaign was brilliant, and the picture would undoubtedly have run for months had it not been for a coincidence as disastrous as it was unforeseeable. While the number of people fainting at each perform-ance was still news, the skies of Earth filled suddenly with long, lean shadows sliding swiftly through the clouds. . . .

Prince Zervashni was good-natured but inclined to be impetuous – a well-known failing of his race. There was no reason to suppose that his present mission, that of making peaceful contact with the planet Earth, would present any particular problems. The correct technique of approach had been thoroughly worked out over many thousands of years, as the Third Galactic Empire slowly expanded its frontiers, absorbing planet after planet, sun upon sun. There was seldom any trouble: really intelligent races can always co-operate, once they have got over the initial shock of learning that they are not alone in the universe.

It was true that humanity had emerged from its primitive, warlike stage only within the last generation. This however, did not worry Prince Zer-vashni's chief adviser, Sigisnin II, Professor of Astropolitics.

'It's a perfectly typical Class E culture,' said the professor. 'Technically advanced, morally rather backward. However, they are already used to the conception of space flight, and will soon take us for granted. The normal precautions will be sufficient until we have won their confidence.'

'Very well,' said the prince. 'Tell the envoys to leave at once.'

It was unfortunate that the 'normal precautions' did not allow for Tony Auerbach's publicity campaign, which had now reached new heights of interplanetary xenophobia. The ambassadors landed in New York's Central Park on the very day that a prominent astronomer, unusually hard up and therefore amenable to infuence, announced in a widely reported interview that any visitors from space probably would be unfriendly.

The luckless ambassadors, heading for the United Nations Building, had got as far south as 60th Street when they met the mob. The encounter was very one-sided, and the scientists at the Museum of Natural History were most annoyed that there was so little left for them to examine.

Prince Zervashni tried once more, on the other side of the planet, but the news had got there first. This time the ambassadors were armed, and gave a good account of themselves before they were overwhelmed by sheer numbers. Even so, it was not until the rocket bombs started climbing up toward his fleet that the prince finally lost his temper and decided to take drastic action.

It was all over in twenty minutes, and was really quite painless. Then the prince turned to his adviser and said, with considerable understatement: 'That appears to be that. And now – can you tell me exactly what went wrong?'

Sigisnin II knitted his dozen flexible fingers together in acute anguish. It was not only the spectacle of the neatly disinfected Earth that distressed him, though to a scientist the destruction of such a beautiful specimen is always a major tragedy. At least equally upsetting was the demolition of his theories and, with them, his reputation.

'I just don't understand it!' he lamented. 'Of course, races at this level of culture are often suspicious and nervous when contact is first made. But they'd never had visitors before, so there was no reason for them to be hostile.'

'Hostile! They were demons! I think they were all insane.' The prince turned to his captain, a tripedal creature who looked rather like a ball of wool balanced on three knitting needles.

'Is the fleet reassembled?'

'Yes, Sire.'

'Then we will return to Base at optimum speed. This planet depresses me.'

On the dead and silent Earth, the posters still screamed their warnings from a thousand hoardings. The malevolent insectile shapes shown pouring from the skies bore no resemblance at all to Prince Zervashni, who apart from his four eyes might have been mistaken for a panda with purple fur – and who, moreover, had come from Rigel, not Sirius.

But, of course, it was now much too late to point this out.

Armaments Race

First published in *Adventure*, April 1954
Collected in *Tales from the White Hart*

This story was inspired by a visit to George Pal in Hollwood, while he was working on the special effects for *The War of the Worlds*. Bill Temple was in fact William F. Temple, the well-known writer of science fiction.

As I've remarked on previous occasions, no one has ever suceeded in pinning down Harry Purvis, prize raconteur of the 'White Hart,' for any length of time. Of his scientific knowledge there can be no doubt – but where did he pick it up? And what justification is there for the terms of familiarity with which he speaks of so many Fellows of the Royal Society? There are, it must be admitted, many who do not believe a single word he says. That, I feel, is going a little too far as I recently remarked somewhat forcibly to Bill Temple.

'You're always gunning for Harry,' I said, 'but you must admit that he provides entertainment. And that's more than most of us can say.'

'If you're being personal,' retorted Bill, still rankling over the fact that some perfectly serious stories had just been returned by an American editor on the grounds that they hadn't made him laugh, 'step outside and say that again.' He glanced through the window, noticed that it was still snowing hard, and hastily added, 'Not today, then, but maybe sometime in the summer, if we're both here on the Wednesday that catches it. Have another of your favourite shots of straight pineapple juice?'

'Thanks,' I said. 'One day I'll ask for a gin with it, just to shake you. I think I must be the only guy in the "White Hart" who can take it or leave it – *and* leaves it.'

This was as far as the conversation got, because the subject of the discussion then arrived. Normally, this would merely have added fuel to the controversy, but as Harry had a stranger with him we decided to be polite little boys.

'Hello, folks,' said Harry. 'Meet my friend Solly Blumberg. Best special-effects man in Hollywood.'

'Let's be accurate, Harry,' said Mr Blumberg sadly, in a voice that should have belonged to a whipped spaniel. 'Not *in* Hollywood. *Out* of Hollywood.'

Harry waved the correction aside.

'All the better for you. Sol's come over here to apply his talents to the British film industry.'

'There *is* a British film industry?' said Solly anxiously. 'No one seemed very sure round the studio.'

'Sure there is. It's in a very flourishing condition, too. The Government piles on an entertainments tax that drives it to bankruptcy, then keeps it alive with whacking big grants. That's the way we do things in this country. Hey, Drew, where's the visitors' book? And a double for both of us. Solly's had a terrible time – he needs a bit of building up.'

I cannot say that, apart from his hangdog look, Mr Blumberg had the appearance of a man who had suffered extreme hardship. He was neatly dressed in a Hart Schnaffner & Marx suit, and the points of his shirt collar buttoned down somewhere around the middle of his chest. That was thoughtful of them as they thus concealed something, but not enough, of his tie. I wondered what the trouble was. Not un-American activities *again*, I prayed: that would trigger off our pet Communist, who at the moment was peaceably studying a chessboard in the corner.

We all made sympathetic noises and John said rather pointedly: 'Maybe it'll help to get it off your chest. It will be such a change to hear someone else talking around here.'

'Don't be so modest, John,' cut in Harry promptly. '*I'm* not tired of hearing you yet. But I doubt if Solly feels much like going through it again. Do you, old man?'

'No,' said Mr Blumberg. '*You* tell them.'

('I knew it would come to that,' sighed John in my ear.)

'Where shall I begin,' asked Harry. 'The time Lillian Ross came to interview you?'

'Anywhere but *there*,' shuddered Solly. 'It really started when we were making the first "Captain Zoom" serial.'

'"Captain Zoom"?' said someone ominously. 'Those are two very rude words in this place. Don't say you were responsible for *that* unspeakable rubbish!'

'Now boys!' put in Harry in his best oil-on-troubled-waters voice. 'Don't be too harsh. We can't apply our own high standards of criticism to everything. And people have got to earn a living. Besides, millions of kids *like* Captain Zoom. Surely you wouldn't want to break their little hearts – and so near Xmas, too!'

'If they *really* liked Captain Zoom, I'd rather break their little necks.'

'Such unseasonable sentiments! I really must apologise for some of my compatriots, Solly. Let's see, what was the name of the first serial?'

'"Captain Zoom and the Menace from Mars".'

'Ah yes, that's right. Incidentally, I wonder why we always are menaced by Mars? I suppose that man Wells started it. One day we may have a big interplanetary libel action on our hands – unless we can prove that the Martians have been equally rude about *us*.

'I'm very glad to say that I never saw "Menace from Mars".' ('I did,' moaned somebody in the background. 'I'm still trying to forget it.') But we are not concerned with the story, such as it was. That was written by three men in a bar on Wilshire Boulevard. No one is sure whether the Menace came out the way it did because the script-writers were drunk, or whether they had to keep drunk in order to face the Menace. If that's confusing, don't bother. All that Solly was concerned with were the special effects that the director demanded.

'First of all, he had to build Mars. To do this he spent half an hour with *The Conquest of Space*, and then emerged with a sketch which the carpenters turned into an overripe orange floating in nothingness, with an improbable number of stars around it. *That* was easy. The Martian cities weren't so simple. You try and think of *completely alien* architecture that still makes sense. I doubt if it's possible – if it will work at all, someone's already used it here on Earth. What the studio finally built was vaguely Byzantine with touches of Frank Lloyd Wright. The fact that none of the doors led anywhere didn't really matter, as long as there was enough room on the sets for the swordplay and general acrobatics that the script demanded.

'Yes – swordplay. Here was a civilisation which had atomic power, death rays, spaceships, television and suchlike modern conveniences, but when it came to a fight between Captain Zoom and the evil Emperor Klugg, the clock went back a couple of centuries. A lot of soldiers stood round holding deadly looking ray guns, but they never *did* anything with them. Well, hardly ever. Sometimes a shower of sparks would chase Captain Zoom and singe his pants, but that was all. I suppose that as the rays couldn't very well move faster than light, he could always outrun them.

'Still, those ornamental ray guns gave everyone quite a few headaches. It's funny how Hollywood will spend endless trouble on some minute detail in a film which is complete rubbish. The director of Captain Zoom had a thing about ray guns. Solly designed the Mark I, which looked like a cross between a bazooka and a blunderbuss. He was quite satisfied with it, and so was the director – for about a day. And then the great man came raging into the studio carrying a revolting creation of purple plastic with knobs and lenses and levers.

' "Lookit this, Solly!" he puffed. "Junior got it down at the supermarket – they're being given away with packets of Crunch. Collect ten lids, and you get one. Hell, they're better than ours! And they *work*!"

'He pressed a lever, and a thin stream of water shot across the set and diappeared behind Captain Zoom's spaceship, where it promptly extingished a cigarette that had no right to be burning there. An angry stagehand emerged through the airlock, saw who it was had drenched him, and swiftly retreated, muttering things about his union.

'Solly examined the ray gun with annoyance and yet with an expert's discrimination. Yes, it was certainly much more impressive than anything *he'd* put out. He retired into his office and promised to see what he could do about it.

'The Mark II had everything built into it, including a television screen. If Captain Zoom was suddenly confronted by a charging hickoderm, all he had to do was to switch on the set, wait for the tubes to warm up, check the channel selector, adjust the fine tuning, touch up the focus, twiddle with the Line and Frame holds – and then press the trigger. He was, fortunately, a man of unbelievably swift reactions.

'The director was impressed, and the Mark II went into production. A slightly different model, the Mark IIa, was built for the Emperor Klugg's diabolical cohorts. It would never do, of course, if both sides had the same weapon. I told you that Pandemic Productions were sticklers for accuracy.

'All went well until the first rushes, and even beyond. While the cast were acting, if you can use that word, they had to point the guns and press the triggers as if something was really happening. The sparks and flashes, however, were put on the negative later by two little men in a darkroom about as well guarded as Fort Knox. They did a good job, but after a while the producer again felt twinges in his overdeveloped artistic conscience.

' "Solly," he said, toying with the plastic horror which had reached Junior by courtesy of Crunch, the Succulent Cereal – Not a Burp in a Barrel – "Solly, I still want a gun that *does* something."

'Solly ducked in time, so the jet went over his head and baptized a photograph of Louella Parsons.

' "You're not going to start shooting all over again!" he wailed.

' "Noo," replied the producer, with obvious reluctance. "We'll have to use what we've got. But it *looks* faked, somehow." He ruffled through the script on his desk, then brightened up.

' "Now next week we start on Episode 54 – 'Slaves of the Slug-Men'. Well, the Slug-Men gotta have guns, so what I'd like you to do is this—"

'The Mark III gave Solly a lot of trouble. (I haven't missed out one yet, have I? Good.) Not only had it to be a completely new design, but as you'll have gathered it had to "do something". This was a challenge to Solly's ingenuity: however, if I may borrow from Professor Toynbee, it was a challenge that evoked the appropriate response.

'Some high-powered engineering went into the Mark III. Luckily, Solly knew an ingenious technician who'd helped him out on similar occasions before, and he was really the man behind it.' ('I'll say he was!' said Mr Blumberg gloomily.) 'The principle was to use a jet of air, produced by a small but extremely powerful electric fan, and then to spray finely divided powder into it. When the thing was adjusted correctly, it shot out a most impressive beam, and made a still more impressive noise. The actors were so scared of it that their performances became most realistic.

'The producer was delighted – for a full three days. Then a dreadful doubt assailed him.

' "Solly," he said, "those damn guns are *too* good. The Slug-Men can beat the pants off Captain Zoom. We'll have to give him something better."

'It was at this point that Solly realised what had happened. He had become involved in an armaments race.

'Let's see, this brings us to the Mark IV, doesn't it? How did *that* work? – Oh yes, I remember. It was a glorified oxyacetylene burner, with various chemicals injected into it to produce the most beautiful flames. I should have mentioned that from Episode 50 – "Doom on Deimos" – the studio had switched over from black and white to Murkicolor, and great possibilities were thus opened up. By squirting copper or strontium or barium into the jet, you could get any colour you wanted.

'If you think that by this time the producer was satisfied, you don't know Hollywood. Some cynics may still laugh when the motto "Ars Gratia Artis" flashes on the screen, but this attitude, I submit, is not in accordance with the facts. Would such old fossils as Michelangelo, Rembrandt or Titian have spent so much time, effort and money on the quest for perfection as did Pandemic Productions? I think not.

'I don't pretend to remember all the Marks that Solly and his ingenious engineer friend produced during the course of the serial. There was one that shot out a stream of coloured smoke rings. There was the high-frequency generator that produced enormous but quite harmless sparks. There was a particularly ingenious *curved* beam produced by a jet of water with light reflected along inside it, which looked most spectacular in the dark. And finally, there was the Mark XII.'

'Mark XIII,' said Mr Blumberg.

'Of course – how stupid of me! What other number *could* it have been! The Mark XIII was not actually a portable weapon – though some of the others were portable only by a considerable stretch of the imagination. It was the diabolical device to be installed on Phobos in order to subjugate Earth. Though Solly has explained them to me once, the scientific principles involved escape my simple mind. . . . However, who am I to match my brains against the intellects responsible for "Captain Zoom"? I can only report what the ray was supposed to do, not how it did it. It was to start a chain reaction in the atmosphere of our unfortunate planet, making the nitrogen and the oxygen in the air combine – with highly deleterious effects to terrestrial life.

'I'm not sure whether to be sorry or glad that Solly left all the details of the fabulous Mark XIII to his talented assistant. Though I've questioned him at some length, all he can tell me is that the thing was about six feet high and looked like a cross between a two-hundred-inch telescope and an anti-aircraft gun. That's not very helpful, is it?

'He also says that there were a lot of radio tubes in the brute, as well as a thundering great magnet. And it was definitely supposed to produce a harmless but impressive electric arc, which could be distorted into all sorts of interesting shapes by the magnet. *That* was what the inventor said, and, despite everything, there is still no reason to disbelieve him.

'By one of those mischances that later turn out to be providential, Solly wasn't at the studio when they tried out the Mark XIII. To his great annoyance, he had to be down in Mexico that day. And wasn't that lucky for you, Solly! He was expecting a long-distance call from one of his friends in the afternoon, but when it came through it wasn't the kind of message he'd anticipated.

'The Mark XIII had been, to put it mildly, a success. No one knew exactly what had happened, but by a miracle no lives had been lost and the fire department had been able to save the adjoining studios. It was incredible, yet the facts were beyond dispute. The Mark XIII was supposed to be a phony death ray – and it had turned out to be a real one. *Something* had emerged from the projector, and gone through the studio wall as if it wasn't there. Indeed, a moment later it wasn't. There was just a great big hole, beginning to smoulder round the edges. And then the roof fell in. . . .

'Unless Solly could convince the F.B.I. that it was all a mistake, he'd better stay the other side of the border. Even now the Pentagon and the Atomic Energy Commission were converging upon the wreckage. . . .

'What would you have done in Solly's shoes? He was innocent, but how could he prove it? Perhaps he would have gone back to face the music if he hadn't remembered that he'd once hired a man who'd campaigned for Harry Wallace, back in '48. *That* might take some explaining away: besides, Solly was a little tired of Captain Zoom. So here he is. Anyone know of a British film company that might have an opening for him? But historical films only, please. He won't touch anything more up to date than crossbows.'

The Deep Range

First published in *Argosy (UK)*, April 1954
Collected in *Tales from Planet Earth*

The concept of whale-herding is an idea whose time has not yet come, and I wonder if it ever will. Over the last decade, whales have had such excellent P.R. that most Europeans and Americans would sooner eat dog- or catburgers. I *did* tackle whalemeat once, during World War Two: it tasted like rather tough beef.

In 1957 I expanded this story into the novel of the same name.

There was a killer loose on the range. A 'copter patrol, five hundred miles off Greenland, had seen the great corpse staining the sea crimson as it wallowed in the waves. Within seconds, the intricate warning system had been alerted: men were plotting circles and moving counters on the North Atlantic chart – and Don Burley was still rubbing the sleep from his eyes as he dropped silently down to the twenty-fathom line.

The pattern of green lights on the tell-tale was a glowing symbol of security. As long as that pattern was unchanged, as long as none of those emerald stars winked to red, all was well with Don and his tiny craft. Air – fuel – power – this was the triumvirate which ruled his life. If any of them failed, he would be sinking in a steel coffin down toward the pelagic ooze, as Johnnie Tyndall had done the season before last. But there was no reason why they should fail; the accidents one foresaw, Don told himself reassuringly, were never the ones that happened.

He leaned across the tiny control board and spoke into the mike. Sub 5 was still close enough to the mother ship for radio to work, but before long he'd have to switch to the sonics.

'Setting course 255, speed 50 knots, depth 20 fathoms, full sonar coverage. . . . Estimated time to target area, 70 minutes. . . . Will report at 10-minute intervals. That is all. . . . Out.'

The acknowledgement, already weakening with range, came back at once from the *Herman Melville*.

'Message received and understood. Good hunting. What about the hounds?'

Don chewed his lower lip thoughtfully. This might be a job he'd have to handle alone. He had no idea, to within fifty miles either way, where Benj and Susan were at the moment. They'd certainly follow if he signalled for them, but they couldn't maintain his speed and would soon have to drop behind. Besides, he might be heading for a pack of killers, and the last thing he wanted to do was to lead his carefully trained porpoises into trouble. That was common sense and good business. He was also very fond of Susan and Benj.

'It's too far, and I don't know what I'm running into,' he replied. 'If they're in the interception area when I get there, I may whistle them up.'

The acknowledgement from the mother ship was barely audible, and Don switched off the set. It was time to look around.

He dimmed the cabin lights so that he could see the scanner screen more clearly, pulled the polaroid glasses down over his eyes, and peered into the depths. This was the moment when Don felt like a god, able to hold within his hands a circle of the Atlantic twenty miles across, and to see clear down to the still-unexplored depths, three thousand fathoms below. The slowly rotating beam of inaudible sound was searching the world in which he floated, seeking out friend and foe in the eternal darkness where light could never penetrate. The pattern of soundless shrieks, too shrill even for the hearing of the bats who had invented sonar a million years before man, pulsed out into the watery night: the faint echoes came tingling back as floating, blue-green flecks on the screen.

Through long practice, Don could read their message with effortless ease. A thousand feet below, stretching out to his submerged horizon, was the scattering layer – the blanket of life that covered half the world. The sunken meadow of the sea, it rose and fell with the passage of the sun, hovering always at the edge of darkness. But the ultimate depths were no concern of his. The flocks he guarded, and the enemies who ravaged them, belonged to the upper levels of the sea.

Don flicked the switch of the depth-selector, and his sonar beam concentrated itself into the horizontal plane. The glimmering echoes from the abyss vanished, but he could see more clearly what lay around him here in the ocean's stratospheric heights. That glowing cloud two miles ahead was a school of fish; he wondered if Base knew about it, and made an entry in his log. There were some larger, isolated blips at the edge of the school – the carnivores pursuing the cattle, ensuring that the endlessly turning wheel of life and death would never lose momentum. But this conflict was no affair of Don's; he was after bigger game.

Sub 5 drove on toward the west, a steel needle swifter and more deadly than any other creature that roamed the seas. The tiny cabin, lit only by the flicker of lights from the instrument board, pulsed with power as the spinning turbines thrust the water aside. Don glanced at the chart and wondered how the enemy had broken through this time. There were still many weak points, for fencing the oceans of the world had been a gigantic task. The tenuous electric fields, fanning out between generators many miles apart, could not always hold at bay the starving monsters of the deep.

They were learning, too. When the fences were opened, they would sometimes slip through with the whales and wreak havoc before they were discovered.

The long-range receiver bleeped plaintively, and Don switched over to TRANSCRIBE. It wasn't practical to send speech any distance over an ultrasonic beam, and code had come back into its own. Don had never learned to read it by ear, but the ribbon of paper emerging from the slot saved him the trouble.

COPTER REPORTS SCHOOL 50–100 WHALES HEADING 95 DEGREES GRID REF X186475 Y438034 STOP. MOVING AT SPEED. STOP. MELVILLE. OUT.

Don started to set the coordinates on the plotting grid, then saw that it was no longer necessary. At the extreme edge of his screen, a flotilla of faint stars had appeared. He altered course slightly, and drove head-on toward the approaching herd.

The copter was right: they were moving fast. Don felt a mounting excitement, for this could mean that they were on the run and luring the killers toward him. At the rate at which they were travelling he would be among them in five minutes. He cut the motors and felt the backward tug of water bringing him swiftly to rest.

Don Burley, a knight in armour, sat in his tiny dim-lit room fifty feet below the bright Atlantic waves, testing his weapons for the conflict that lay ahead. In these moments of raised suspense, before action began, his racing brain often explored such fantasies. He felt a kinship with all shepherds who had guarded their flocks back to the dawn of time. He was David, among ancient Palestinian hills, alert for the mountain lions that would prey upon his father's sheep. But far nearer in time, and far closer in spirit, were the men who had marshalled the great herds of cattle on the American plains, only a few lifetimes ago. They would have understood his work, though his implements would have been magic to them. The pattern was the same; only the scale had altered. It made no fundamental difference that the beasts Don herded weighed almost a hundred tons, and browsed on the endless savannahs of the sea.

The school was now less than two miles away, and Don checked his scanner's continuous circling to concentrate on the sector ahead. The picture on the screen altered to a fan-shaped wedge as the sonar beam started to flick from side to side; now he could count every whale in the school, and even make a good estimate of its size. With a practised eye, he began to look for stragglers.

Don could never have explained what drew him at once toward those four echoes at the southern fringe of the school. It was true that they were a little apart from the rest, but others had fallen as far behind. There is some sixth sense that a man acquires when he has stared long enough into a sonar screen – some hunch which enables him to extract more from the moving flecks than he has any right to do. Without conscious thought, Don reached for the control which would start the turbines whirling into life. Sub 5 was just getting under way when three leaden thuds reverberated through the hull, as if someone was knocking on the front door and wanted to come in.

'Well I'm damned,' said Don. 'How did *you* get here?' He did not bother to switch on the TV; he'd know Benj's signal anywhere. The porpoises must have been in the neighbourhood and had spotted him before he'd even switched on the hunting call. For the thousandth time, he marvelled at their intelligence and loyalty. It was strange that Nature had played the same trick twice – on land with the dog, in the ocean with the porpoise. Why were these graceful sea-beasts so fond of man, to whom they owed so little? It made one feel that the human race was worth something after all, if it could inspire such unselfish devotion.

It had been known for centuries that the porpoise was at least as intelligent as the dog, and could obey quite complex verbal commands. The experiment was still in progress, but if it succeeded then the ancient partnership between shepherd and sheep-dog would have a new lease on life.

Don switched on the speakers recessed into the sub's hull and began to talk to his escorts. Most of the sounds he uttered would have been meaningless to other human ears; they were the product of long research by the animal psychologists of the World Food Administration. He gave his orders twice to make sure they were understood, then checked with the sonar screen to see that Benj and Susan were following astern as he had told them to.

The four echoes that had attracted his attention were clearer and closer now, and the main body of the whale pack had swept past him to the east. He had no fear of a collision; the great animals, even in their panic, could sense his presence as easily as he could detect theirs, and by similar means. Don wondered if he should switch on his beacon. They might recognise its sound pattern, and it would reassure them. But the still unknown enemy might recognise it too.

He closed for an interception, and hunched low over the screen as if to drag from it by sheer will power every scrap of information the scanner could give. There were two large echoes, some distance apart, and one was accompanied by a pair of smaller satellites. Don wondered if he was already too late. In his mind's eye, he could picture the death struggle taking place in the water less than a mile ahead. Those two fainter blips would be the enemy – either shark or grampus – worrying a whale while one of its companions stood by in helpless terror, with no weapons of defence except its mighty flukes.

Now he was almost close enough for vision. The TV camera in Sub 5's prow strained through the gloom, but at first could show nothing but the fog of plankton. Then a vast shadowy shape began to form in the centre of the screen, with two smaller companions below it. Don was seeing, with the greater precision but hopelessly limited range of ordinary light, what the sonar scanners had already told him.

Almost at once he saw his mistake. The two satellites were calves, not sharks. It was the first time he had ever met a whale with twins; although multiple births were not unknown, a cow could suckle only two young at once and usually only the stronger would survive. He choked down his disappointment; his error had cost him many minutes and he must begin the search again.

Then came the frantic tattoo on the hull that meant danger. It wasn't easy to scare Benj, and Don shouted his reassurance as he swung Sub 5 round so that the camera could search the turgid waters. Automatically, he had turned toward the fourth blip on the sonar screen – the echo he had assumed, from its size, to be another adult whale. And he saw that, after all, he had come to the right place.

'Jesus!' he said softly. 'I didn't know they came that big.' He'd seen larger sharks before, but they had all been harmless vegetarians. This, he could tell at a glance, was a Greenland shark, the killer of the northern seas. It was supposed to grow up to thirty feet long, but this specimen was bigger than Sub 5. It was every inch of forty feet from snout to tail, and when he spotted it, it was already turning in toward the kill. Like the coward it was, it had launched its attack at one of the calves.

Don yelled to Benj and Susan, and saw them racing ahead into his field of vision. He wondered fleetingly why porpoises had such an overwhelming hatred of sharks; then he loosed his hands from the controls as the auto-pilot locked on to the target. Twisting and turning as agilely as any other sea-creature of its size, Sub 5 began to close in upon the shark, leaving Don free to concentrate on his armament.

The killer had been so intent upon his prey that Benj caught him completely unawares, ramming him just behind the left eye. It must have been a painful blow: an iron-hard snout, backed by a quarter-ton of muscle moving at fifty miles an hour is something not to be laughed at even by the largest fish. The shark jerked round in an impossibly tight curve, and Don was almost jolted out of his seat as the sub snapped on to a new course. If this kept up, he'd find it hard to use his Sting. But at least the killer was too busy now to bother about his intended victims.

Benj and Susan were worrying the giant like dogs snapping at the heels of an angry bear. They were too agile to be caught in those ferocious jaws, and Don marvelled at the coordination with which they worked. When either had to surface for air, the other would hold off for a minute until the attack could be resumed in strength.

There was no evidence that the shark realised that a far more dangerous adversary was closing in upon it, and that the porpoises were merely a distraction. That suited Don very nicely; the next operation was going to be difficult unless he could hold a steady course for at least fifteen seconds. At a pinch he could use the tiny rocket torps to make a kill. If he'd been alone, and faced with a pack of sharks he would certainly have done so. But it was messy, and there was a better way. He preferred the technique of the rapier to that of the hand-grenade.

Now he was only fifty feet away, and closing rapidly. There might never be a better chance. He punched the launching stud.

From beneath the belly of the sub, something that looked like a sting-ray hurtled forward. Don had checked the speed of his own craft; there was no need to come any closer now. The tiny, arrow-shaped hydrofoil, only a couple of feet across, could move far faster than his vessel and would close the gap in seconds. As it raced forward, it spun out the thin line of the control wire, like some underwater spider laying its thread. Along that wire passed the energy that powered the Sting, and the signals that steered it to its goal. Don had completely ignored his own larger craft in the effort of guiding this underwater missile. It responded to his touch so swiftly that he felt he was controlling some sensitive high-spirited steed.

The shark saw the danger less than a second before impact. The resemblance of the Sting to an ordinary ray confused it, as the designers had intended. Before the tiny brain could realise that no ray behaved like this, the missile had struck. The steel hypodermic, rammed forward by an exploding cartridge, drove through the shark's horny skin, and the great fish erupted in a frenzy of terror. Don backed rapidly away, for a blow from that tail would rattle him around like a pea in a can and might even cause damage to the sub. There was nothing more for him to do, except to speak into the microphone and call off his hounds.

The doomed killer was trying to arch its body so that it could snap at the poisoned dart. Don had now reeled the Sting back into its hiding place, pleased that he had been able to retrieve the missile undamaged. He watched without pity as the great fish succumbed to its paralysis.

Its struggles were weakening. It was swimming aimlessly back and forth, and once Don had to sidestep smartly to avoid a collision. As it lost control of buoyancy, the dying shark drifted up to the surface. Don did not bother to follow; that could wait until he had attended to more important business.

He found the cow and her two calves less than a mile away, and inspected them carefully. They were uninjured, so there was no need to call the vet in his highly specialised two-man sub which could handle any cetological crisis from a stomach-ache to a Caesarian. Don made a note of the mother's number, stencilled just behind the flippers. The calves, as was obvious from their size, were this season's and had not yet been branded.

Don watched for a little while. They were no longer in the least alarmed, and a check on the sonar had shown that the whole school had ceased its panicky flight. He wondered how they knew what had happened; much had been learned about communication among whales, but much was still a mystery.

'I hope you appreciate what I've done for you, old lady,' he muttered. Then, reflecting that fifty tons of mother love was a slightly awe-inspiring sight, he blew his tanks and surfaced.

It was calm, so he cracked the airlock and popped his head out of the tiny conning tower. The water was only inches below his chin, and from time to time a wave made a determined effort to swamp him. There was little danger of this happening, for he fitted the hatch so closely that he was quite an effective plug.

Fifty feet away, a long slate-coloured mound, like an overturned boat, was rolling on the surface. Don looked at it thoughtfully and did some mental calculation. A brute this size should be valuable; with any luck there was a chance of a double bonus. In a few minutes he'd radio his report, but for the moment it was pleasant to drink the fresh Atlantic air and to feel the open sky above his head.

A grey thunderbolt shot up out of the depths and smashed back onto the surface of the water, smothering Don with spray. It was just Benj's modest way of drawing attention to himself; a moment later the porpoise had swum up to the conning tower, so that Don could reach down and tickle its head. The great, intelligent eyes stared back into his; was it pure imagination, or did an almost human sense of fun also lurk in their depths?

Susan, as usual, circled shyly at a distance until jealousy overpowered her and she butted Benj out of the way. Don distributed caresses impartially and apologised because he had nothing to give them. He undertook to make up for the omission as soon as he returned to the *Herman Melville*.

'I'll go for another swim with you, too,' he promised, 'as long as you behave yourselves next time.' He rubbed thoughtfully at a large bruise caused by Benj's playfulness, and wondered if he was not getting a little too old for rough games like this.

'Time to go home,' Don said firmly, sliding down into the cabin and slamming the hatch. He suddenly realised that he was very hungry, and had better do something about the breakfast he had missed. There were not many men on earth who had earned a better right to eat their morning meal. He had saved for humanity more tons of meat, oil and milk than could easily be estimated.

Don Burley was the happy warrior, coming home from one battle that man would always have to fight. He was holding at bay the spectre of famine which had confronted all earlier ages, but which would never threaten the world again while the great plankton farms harvested their millions of tons of protein, and the whale herds obeyed their new masters. Man had come back to the sea after aeons of exile; until the oceans froze, he would never be hungry again. . . .

Don glanced at the scanner as he set his course. He smiled as he saw the two echoes keeping pace with the central splash of light that marked his vessel. 'Hang around,' he said. 'We mammals must stick together.' Then, as the autopilot took over, he lay back in his chair.

And presently Benj and Susan heard a most peculiar noise, rising and falling against the drone of the turbines. It had filtered faintly through the thick walls of Sub 5, and only the sensitive ears of the porpoises could have detected it. But intelligent beasts though they were, they could hardly be expected to understand why Don Burley was announcing, in a highly unmusical voice, that he was heading for the Last Round-up. . . .

No Morning After

First published in *Time to Come*, ed. August Derleth, 1954
Collected in *The Other Side of the Sky*

'But this is terrible!' said the Supreme Scientist. 'Surely there is *something* we can do!'

'Yes, Your Cognisance, but it will be extremely difficult. The planet is more than five hundred light-years away, and it is very hard to maintain contact. However, we believe we can establish a bridgehead. Unfortunately, that is not the only problem. So far, we have been quite unable to communicate with these beings. Their telepathic powers are exceedingly rudimentary – perhaps even nonexistent. And if we cannot talk to them, there is no way in which we can help.'

There was a long mental silence while the Supreme Scientist analysed the situation and arrived, as he always did, at the correct answer.

'Any intelligent race must have *some* telepathic individuals,' he mused. 'We must send out hundreds of observers, tuned to catch the first hint of stray thought. When you find a single responsive mind, concentrate all your efforts upon it. We *must* get our message through.'

'Very good, Your Cognisance. It shall be done.'

Across the abyss, across the gulf which light itself took half a thousand years to span, the questing intellects of the planet Thaar sent out their tendrils of thought, searching desperately for a single human being whose mind could perceive their presence. And as luck would have it, they encountered William Cross.

At least they thought it was luck at the time, though later they were not so sure. In any case, they had little choice. The combination of circumstances that opened Bill's mind to them lasted only for seconds, and was not likely to occur again this side of eternity.

There were three ingredients in the miracle: it is hard to say if one was more important than another. The first was the accident of position. A flask of water, when sunlight falls upon it, can act as a crude lens, concentrating the light into a small area. On an immeasurably larger scale, the dense core of the Earth was coverging the waves that came from Thaar. In the ordinary way, the radiations of thought are unaffected by matter – they pass through it as effortlessly as light through glass. But there is rather a lot of matter in a planet, and the whole Earth was acting as a gigantic lens. As it turned, it

489

was carrying Bill through its focus, where the feeble thought impulses from Thaar were concentrated a hundredfold.

Yet millions of other men were equally well placed: they received no message. But they were not rocket engineers: they had not spent years thinking and dreaming of space until it had become part of their very being.

And they were not, as Bill was, blind drunk, teetering on the last knife-edge of consciousness, trying to escape from reality into the world of dreams, where there were no disappointments and setbacks.

Of course, he could see the Army's point of view. 'You are paid, Dr Cross,' General Potter had pointed out with unnecessary emphasis, 'to design missiles, *not* – ah – spaceships. What you do in your spare time is your own concern, but I must ask you not to use the facilities of the establishment for your hobby. From now on, all projects for the computing section will have to be cleared by me. That is all.'

They couldn't sack him, of course: he was too important. But he was not sure that he wanted to stay. He was not really sure of anything except that the job had backfired on him, and that Brenda had finally gone off with Johnny Gardner – putting events in their order of importance.

Wavering slightly, Bill cupped his chin in his hands and stared at the whitewashed brick wall on the other side of the table. The only attempt at ornamentation was a calendar from Lockheed and a glossy six-by-eight from Aerojet showing L'il Abner Mark I making a boosted take-off. Bill gazed morosely at the spot midway between the two pictures, and emptied his mind of thought. The barriers went down. . . .

At that moment, the massed intellects of Thaar gave a soundless cry of triumph, and the wall in front of Bill slowly dissolved into a swirling mist. He appeared to be looking down a tunnel that stretched to infinity. As a matter of fact, he was.

Bill studied the phenomenon with mild interest. It had a certain novelty, but was not up to the standard of previous hallucinations. And when the voice started to speak in his mind, he let it ramble on for some time before he did anything about it. Even when drunk, he had an old-fashioned prejudice against starting conversations with himself.

'Bill,' the voice began, 'listen carefully. We have had great difficulty in contacting you, and this is extremely important.'

Bill doubted this on general principles. *Nothing* was important any more.

'We are speaking to you from a very distant planet,' continued the voice in a tone of urgent friendliness. 'You are the only human being we have been able to contact, so you *must* understand what we are saying.'

Bill felt mildly worried, though in an impersonal sort of way, since it was now rather hard to focus on his own problems. How serious was it, he wondered, when you started to hear voices? Well, it was best not to get excited. You can take it or leave it, Dr Cross, he told himself. Let's take it until it gets to be a nuisance.

'OK,' he answered with bored indifference. 'Go right ahead and talk to me. I won't mind as long as it's interesting.'

There was a pause. Then the voice continued, in a slightly worried fashion.

'We don't quite understand. Our message isn't merely *interesting*. It's vital to your entire race, and you must notify your government immediately.'

'I'm waiting,' said Bill. 'It helps to pass the time.'

Five hundred light-years away, the Thaarns conferred hastily among themselves. Something seemed to be wrong, but they could not decide precisely what. There was no doubt that they had established contact, yet this was not the sort of reaction they had expected. Well, they could only proceed and hope for the best.

'Listen, Bill,' they continued. 'Our scientists have just discovered that your sun is about to explode. It will happen three days from now – seventy-four hours, to be exact. Nothing can stop it. But there's no need to be alarmed. We can save you, if you'll do what we say.'

'Go on,' said Bill. This hallucination was ingenious.

'We can create what we call a bridge – it's a kind of tunnel through space, like the one you're looking into now. The theory is far too complicated to explain, even to one of your mathematicians.'

'Hold on a minute!' protested Bill. 'I *am* a mathematician, and a darn good one, even when I'm sober. And I've read all about this kind of thing in the science fiction magazines. I presume you're talking about some kind of short cut through a higher dimension of space. That's old stuff – pre-Einstein.'

A sensation of distinct surprise seeped into Bill's mind.

'We had no idea you were so advanced scientifically,' said the Thaarns. 'But we haven't time to talk about the theory. All that matters is this – if you were to step into that opening in front of you, you'd find yourself instantly on another planet. It's a short cut, as you said – in this case through the thirty-seventh dimension.'

'And it leads to your world?'

'Oh no – you couldn't live here. But there are plenty of planets like Earth in the universe, and we've found one that will suit you. We'll establish bridgeheads like this all over Earth, so your people will only have to walk through them to be saved. Of course, they'll have to start building up civilisation again when they reach their new homes, but it's their only hope. You have to pass on this message, and tell them what to do.'

'I can just see them listening to me,' said Bill. 'Why don't you go and talk to the president?'

'Because yours was the only mind we were able to contact. Others seemed closed to us: we don't understand why.'

'I could tell you,' said Bill, looking at the nearly empty bottle in front of him. He was certainly getting his money's worth. What a remarkable thing the human mind was! Of course, there was nothing at all original in this dialogue: it was easy to see where the ideas came from. Only last week he'd been reading a story about the end of the world, and all this wishful thinking about bridges and tunnels through space was pretty obvious compensation for anyone who'd spent five years wrestling with recalcitrant rockets.

'If the sun does blow up,' Bill asked abruptly – trying to catch his hallucination unawares – 'what would happen?'

'Why, your planet would be melted instantly. All the planets, in fact, right out to Jupiter.'

Bill had to admit that this was quite a grandiose conception. He let his mind play with the thought, and the more he considered it, the more he liked it.

'My dear hallucination,' he remarked pityingly, 'if I believed you, d'you know what I'd say?'

'But you *must* believe us!' came the despairing cry across the light-years.

Bill ignored it. He was warming to his theme.

'I'd tell you this. *It would be the best thing that could possibly happen.* Yes, it would save a whole lot of misery. No one would have to worry about the Russians and the atom bomb and the high cost of living. Oh, it would be wonderful! It's just what everybody really wants. Nice of you to come along and tell us, but just you go back home and pull your old bridges after you.'

There was consternation on Thaar. The Supreme Scientist's brain, floating like a great mass of coral in its tank of nutrient solution, turned slightly yellow about the edges – something it had not done since the Xantil invasion, five thousand years ago. At least fifteen psychologists had nervous breakdowns and were never the same again. The main computer in the College of Cosmophysics started dividing every number in its memory circuits by zero, and promptly blew all its fuses.

And on Earth, Bill Cross was really hitting his stride.

'Look at *me*,' he said, pointing a wavering finger at his chest. 'I've spent years trying to make rockets do something useful, and they tell me I'm only allowed to build guided missiles, so that we can all blow each other up. The sun will make a neater job of it, and if you did give us another planet we'd only start the whole damn thing all over again.'

He paused sadly, marshalling his morbid thoughts.

'And now Brenda heads out of town without even leaving a note. So you'll pardon my lack of enthusiasm for your Boy Scout act.'

He couldn't have said 'enthusiasm' aloud, Bill realised. But he could still think it, which was an interesting scientific discovery. As he got drunker and drunker, would his cogitation – whoops, *that* nearly threw him! – finally drop down to words of one syllable?

In a final despairing exertion, the Thaarns sent their thoughts along the tunnel between the stars.

'You can't really mean it, Bill! Are *all* human beings like you?'

Now that was an interesting philosophical question! Bill considered it carefully – or as carefully as he could in view of the warm, rosy glow that was now beginning to envelop him. After all, things might be worse. He could get another job, if only for the pleasure of telling General Porter what he could do with his three stars. And as for Brenda – well, women were like streetcars; there'd always be another along in a minute.

Best of all, there was a second bottle of whisky in the Top Secret file. Oh, frabjous day! He rose unsteadily to his feet and wavered across the room.

For the last time, Thaar spoke to Earth.

'Bill!' it repeated desperately. 'Surely all human beings can't be like you!'

Bill turned and looked into the swirling tunnel. Strange – it seemed to be lighted with flecks of starlight, and was really rather pretty. He felt proud of himself: not many people could imagine *that*.

'Like me?' he said. 'No, they're not.' He smiled smugly across the light-years, as the rising tide of euphoria lifted him out of his despondency. 'Come to think of it,' he added, 'there are a lot of people much worse off than me. Yes, I guess I must be one of the lucky ones, after all.'

He blinked in mild surprise, for the tunnel had suddenly collapsed upon itself and the whitewashed wall was there again, exactly as it had always been. Thaar knew when it was beaten.

'So much for *that* hallucination,' thought Bill. 'I was getting tired of it, anyway. Let's see what the next one's like.'

As it happened, there wasn't a next one, for five seconds later he passed out cold, just as he was getting the combination of the file cabinet.

The next two days were rather vague and bloodshot, and he forgot all about the interview.

On the third day something was nagging at the back of his mind: he might have remembered if Brenda hadn't turned up again and kept him busy being forgiving.

And there wasn't a fourth day, of course.

Big Game Hunt

First appeared in *Adventure*, October 1956 as 'The Reckless Ones'
Collected in *Tales from the White Hart*

As I write these words, Jean-Michel Cousteau is on his way to New Zealand to look for the giant squid. I'm not sure whether to wish him luck – see 'The Shining Ones'.

Although by general consent Harry Purvis stands unrivalled among the 'White Hart' clientele as a purveyor of remarkable stories (some of which, we suspect, may be slightly exaggerated) it must not be thought that his position has never been challenged. There have even been occasions when he has gone into temporary eclipse. Since it is always entertaining to watch the discomfiture of an expert, I must confess that I take a certain glee in recalling how Professor Hinckleberg disposed of Harry on his own home ground.

Many visiting Americans pass through the 'White Hart' in the course of the year. Like the residents, they are usually scientists or literary men, and some distinguished names have been recorded in the visitors' book that Drew keeps behind the bar. Sometimes the newcomers arrive under their own power, diffidently introducing themselves as soon as they have the opportunity. (There was the time when a shy Nobel Prize winner sat unrecognised in a corner for an hour before he plucked up enough courage to say who he was.) Others arrive with letters of introduction, and not a few are escorted in by regular customers and then thrown to the wolves.

Professor Hinckleberg glided up one night in a vast fishtailed Cadillac he'd borrowed from the fleet in Grosvenor Square. Heavens only knows how he had managed to insinuate it through the side streets that lead to the 'White Hart', but amazingly enough all the fenders seemed intact. He was a large lean man, with that Henry Ford–Wilbur Wright kind of face that usually goes with the slow, taciturn speech of the sun-tanned pioneer. It didn't in Professor Hinckleberg's case. He could talk like an LP record on a seventy-eight turntable. In about ten seconds we'd discovered that he was a zoologist on leave of absence from a North Virginia college, that he was attached to the Office of Naval Research on some project to do with plankton, that he was tickled pink with London and even liked English beer, that he'd heard about us through a letter in *Science* but couldn't believe we were true, that Stevenson was OK but if the Democrats wanted to get back they'd better import Winston, that he'd like to know what the heck was wrong with all our telephone call boxes and could he retrieve the small fortune in coppers of which they had mulcted him, that there seemed to be a lot of empty glasses around and how about filling them up, boys?

On the whole the Professor's shock tactics were well received, but when he made a momentary pause for breath I thought to myself, 'Harry'd better look out. This guy can talk rings round him.' I glanced at Purvis, who was only a few feet away from me, and saw that his lips were pursed into a slight frown. I sat back luxuriously and awaited results.

As it was a fairly busy evening, it was quite some time before Professor Hinckleberg had been introduced to everybody. Harry, usually so forward at meeting celebrities, seemed to be keeping out of the way. But eventually he was concerned by Arthur Vincent, who acts as informal club secretary and makes sure that everyone signs the visitors' book.

'I'm sure you and Harry will have a lot to talk about,' said Arthur, in a burst of innocent enthusiasm. 'You're both scientists, aren't you? And Harry's had some most extraordinary things happen to him. Tell the Professor about the time you found that U235 in your letter box. . . .'

'I don't think,' said Harry, a trifle too hastily, 'that Professor – ah – Hinckleberg wants to listen to my little adventure. I'm sure he must have a lot to tell *us*.'

I've puzzled my head about that reply a good deal since then. It wasn't in character. Usually, with an opening like this, Purvis was up and away. Perhaps he was sizing up the enemy, waiting for the Professor to make the first mistake, and then swooping in to the kill. If that was the explanation, he'd misjudged his man. He never had a chance, for Professor Hinckleberg made a jet-assisted take-off and was immediately in full flight.

'Odd you should mention that,' he said. 'I've just been dealing with a most remarkable case. It's one of these things that can't be written up as a proper scientific paper, and this seems a good time to get it off my chest. I can't often do that, because of this darned security – but so far no one's gotten round to classifying Dr Grinnell's experiments, so I'll talk about them while I can.'

Grinnell, it seemed, was one of the many scientists trying to interpret the behaviour of the nervous system in terms of electrical circuits. He had started, as Grey Walter, Shannon and others had done, by making models that could reproduce the simpler actions of living creatures. His greatest success in this direction had been a mechanical cat that could chase mice and could land on its feet when dropped from a height. Very quickly, however, he had branched off in another direction owing to his discovery of what he called 'neural induction'. This was, to simplify it greatly, nothing less than a method of actually *controlling* the behaviour of animals.

It had been known for many years that all the processes that take place in the mind are accompanied by the production of minute electric currents, and for a long time it has been possible to record these complex fluctuations – though their exact interpretation is still unknown. Grinnell had not attempted the intricate task of analysis; what he had done was a good deal simpler, though its achievement was still complicated enough. He had attached his recording device to various animals, and thus been able to build up a small library, if one could call it that, of electrical impulses associated with their behaviour. One pattern of voltage might correspond to a movement to the right, another with travelling in a circle, another with complete stillness, and so on. That was an interesting enough achievement, but Grinnell had not stopped there. By 'playing back' the impulses he had recorded, he could compel his subject to repeat their previous actions – whether they wanted to or not.

That such a thing might be possible in theory almost any neurologist would admit, but few would have believed that it could be done in practice owing to the enormous complexity of the nervous system. And it was true that Grinnell's first experiments were carried out on very low forms of life, with relatively simple responses.

'I saw only one of his experiments,' said Hinckleberg. 'There was a large slug crawling on a horizontal piece of glass, and half a dozen tiny wires led from it to a control panel which Grinnell was operating. There were two dials – that was all – and by suitable adjustments he could make the slug move in any direction. To a layman, it would have seemed a trivial experiment, but I realised that it might have tremendous implications. I remember telling Grinnell that I hoped his device could never be applied to human beings. I'd been reading Orwell's *Nineteen Eighty-Four* and I could just imagine what Big Brother would do with a gadget like this.

'Then, being a busy man, I forgot all about the matter for a year. By the end of that time, it seems, Grinnell had improved his apparatus considerably and had worked up to more complicated organisms, though for technical reasons he had restricted himself to invertebrates. He had now built up a substantial store of "orders" which he could then play back to his subjects. You might think it surprising that such diverse creatures as worms, snails, insects, crustaceans and so on would be able to respond to the same electrical commands, but apparently that was the case.

'If it had not been for Dr Jackson, Grinnell would probably have stayed working away in the lab for the rest of his life, moving steadily up the animal kingdom. Jackson was a very remarkable man – I'm sure you must have seen some of his films. In many circles he was regarded as a publicity-hunter rather than a real scientist, and academic circles were suspicious of him because he had far too many interests. He'd led expeditions into the Gobi Desert, up the Amazon, and had even made one raid on the Antarctic. From each of these trips he had returned with a best-selling book and a few miles of Kodachrome. And despite reports to the contrary, I believe he *had* obtained some valuable scientific results, even if they were slightly incidental.

'I don't know how Jackson got to hear of Grinnell's work, or how he talked the other man into co-operating. He could be very persuasive, and probably dangled vast appropriations before Grinnell's eyes – for he was the sort of man who could get the ear of the trustees. Whatever happened, from that moment Grinnell became mysteriously secretive. All we knew was that he was building a much larger version of his apparatus, incorporating all the latest refinements. When challenged, he would squirm nervously and say, "We're going big game hunting."

'The preparations took another year, and I expect that Jackson – who was always a hustler – must have been mighty impatient by the end of that time. But at last everything was ready. Grinnell and all his mysterious boxes vanished in the general direction of Africa.

'*That* was Jackson's work. I suppose he didn't want any premature publicity, which was understandable enough when you consider the somewhat fantastic nature of the expedition. According to the hints with which he had – as we later discovered – carefully misled us all, he hoped to get some really remarkable pictures of animals in their wild state, using Grinnell's apparatus. I found this rather hard to swallow, unless Grinnell had somehow succeeded in linking his device to a radio-transmitter. It didn't seem likely that he'd be able to attach his wires and electrodes to a charging elephant. . . .

'They'd thought of that, of course, and the answer seems obvious now. Sea water is a good conductor. They weren't going to Africa at all, but were heading out into the Atlantic. But they hadn't lied to us. They were after big game, all right. The biggest game there is . . .

'We'd never had known what happened if their radio operator hadn't been chattering to an amateur friend over in the States. From his commentary it's possible to guess the sequence of events. Jackson's ship – it was only a small yacht, bought up cheaply and converted for the expedition – was lying not far from the Equator off the west coast of Africa, and over the deepest part of the Atlantic. Grinnell was angling: his electrodes had been lowered into the abyss, while Jackson waited impatiently with his camera.

'They waited a week before they had a catch. By that time, tempers must have been rather frayed. Then, one afternoon on a perfectly calm day, Grinnell's meters started to jump. Something was caught in the sphere of influence of the electrodes.

'Slowly, they drew up the cable. Until now, the rest of the crew must have thought them mad, but everyone must have shared their excitement as the catch rose up through all those thousands of feet of darkness until it broke surface. Who can blame the radio operator if, despite Jackson's orders, he felt an urgent need to talk things over with a friend back on the safety of dry land?

'I won't attempt to describe what they saw, because a master has done it before me. Soon after the report came in, I turned up my copy of *Moby Dick* and reread the passage; I can still quote it from memory and don't suppose I'll ever forget it. This is how it goes, more or less:

'"A vast pulpy mass, furlongs in length, of a glancing cream-colour, lay floating on the water, innumerable long arms radiating from its centre, curling and twisting like a nest of anacondas, as if blindly to catch at any hapless object within reach."

'Yes: Grinnell and Jackson had been after the largest and most mysterious of all living creatures – the giant squid. Largest? Almost certainly: *Bathyteuthis* may grow up to a hundred feet long. He's not as heavy as the sperm whales who dine upon him, but he's a match for them in length.

'So here they were, with this monstrous beast that no human being had ever before seen under such ideal conditions. It seems that Grinnell was calmly putting it through its paces while Jackson ecstatically shot off yards of film. There was no danger, though it was twice the size of their boat. To Grinnell, it was just another mollusc that he could control like a puppet by means of his knobs and dials. When he had finished, he would let it return to its normal depths and it could swim away again, though it would probably have a bit of a hangover.

'What one wouldn't give to get hold of that film! Altogether apart from its scientific interest, it would be worth a fortune in Hollywood. You must admit that Jackson knew what he was doing: he'd seen the limitations of Grinnell's apparatus and put it to its most effective use. What happened next was not his fault.'

Professor Hinckleberg sighed and took a deep draught of beer, as if to gather strength for the finale of his tale.

'No, if anyone is to blame it's Grinnell. Or, I should say, it *was* Grinnell, poor chap. Perhaps he was so excited that he overlooked a precaution he would undoubtedly have taken in the lab. How otherwise can you account for the fact that he didn't have a spare fuse handy when the one in the power supply blew out?

'And you can't really blame *Bathyteuthis*, either. Wouldn't *you* have been a little annoyed to be pushed about like this? And when the orders suddenly ceased and you were your own master again, you'd take steps to see it remained that way. I sometimes wonder, though, if Jackson stayed filming to the very end. . . .'

Patent Pending

First published in *Argosy*, November 1954, as 'The Invention'
Collected in *Tales from the White Hart*

A light-hearted tale from Harry Purvis at the White Hart, yet with serious undertones, and also a nod towards Virtual Reality, fifty years before it came into being.

There are no subjects that have not been discussed, at some time or other, in the saloon bar of the 'White Hart' – and whether or not there are ladies present makes no difference whatsoever. After all, they came in at their own risk. Three of them, now I come to think of it, have eventually gone out again with husbands. So perhaps the risk isn't on their side at all. . . .

I mention this because I would not like you to think that all our conversations are highly erudite and scientific, and our activities purely cerebral. Though chess is rampant, darts and shove-ha'penny also flourish. The *Times Literary Supplement*, the *Saturday Review*, the *New Statesman* and the *Atlantic Monthly* may be brought in by some of the customers, but the same people are quite likely to leave with the latest issue of *Staggering Stories of Pseudoscience*.

A great deal of business also goes on in the obscurer corners of the pub. Copies of antique books and magazines frequently change hands at astronomical prices, and on almost any Wednesday at least three well-known dealers may be seen smoking large cigars as they lean over the bar, swapping stories with Drew. From time to time a vast guffaw announces the denouement of some anecdote and provokes a flood of anxious enquiries from patrons who are afraid they may have missed something. But, alas, delicacy forbids that I should repeat any of these interesting tales here. Unlike most things in this island, they are not for export. . . .

Luckily, no such restrictions apply to the tales of Mr Harry Purvis, B.Sc. (at least), Ph.D. (probably), F.R.S. (personally I don't think so, though it *has* been rumoured). None of them would bring a blush to the cheeks of the most delicately nurtured maiden aunts, should any still survive in these days.

I must apologise. This is too sweeping a statement. There was one story which might, in some circles, be regarded as a little daring. Yet I do not hesitate to repeat it, for I know that you, dear reader, will be sufficiently broadminded to take no offence.

It started in this fashion. A celebrated Fleet Street reviewer had been pinned into a corner by a persuasive publisher, who was about to bring out a book of which he had high hopes. It was one of the riper productions of the deep and decadent South – a prime example of the 'and-then-the-house-gave-another-lurch-as-the-termites-finished-the-east-wing' school of fiction. Eire had already banned it, but that is an honour which few books escape nowadays, and certainly could not be considered a distinction. However, if a leading British newspaper could be induced to make a stern call for its suppression, it would become a best seller overnight. . . .

Such was the logic of its publisher, and he was using all his wiles to induce co-operation. I heard him remark, apparently to allay any scruples his reviewer friend might have, 'Of course not! If they can understand it, they *can't* be corrupted any further!' And then Harry Purvis, who has an uncanny knack of following half a dozen conversations simultaneously, so that he can insert himself in the right one at the right time, said in his peculiarly penetrating and non-interruptable voice: 'Censorship does raise some very difficult problems, doesn't it? I've always argued that there's an inverse correlation between a country's degree of civilisation and the restraints it puts on its press.'

A New England voice from the back of the room cut in: 'On *that* argument, Paris is a more civilised place than Boston.'

'Precisely,' answered Purvis. For once, he waited for a reply.

'OK,' said the New England voice mildly. 'I'm not arguing. I just wanted to check.'

'To continue,' said Purvis, wasting no more time in doing so, 'I'm reminded of a matter which has not yet concerned the censor, but which will certainly do so before long. It began in France, and so far has remained there. When it *does* come out into the open, it may have a greater impact on our civilisation than the atom bomb.

'Like the atom bomb, it arose out of equally academic research. *Never*, gentlemen, underestimate science. I doubt if there is a single field of study so theoretical, so remote from what is laughingly called everyday life, that it may not one day produce something that will shake the world.

'You will appreciate that the story I am telling you is, for once in a while, secondhand. I got it from a colleague at the Sorbonne last year while I was over there at a scientific conference. So the names are all fictitious: I was told them at the time, but I can't remember them now.

'Professor – ah – Julian was an experimental physiologist at one of the smaller, but less impecunious, French universities. Some of you may remember that rather unlikely tale we heard here the other week from that fellow Hinckleberg, about his colleague who'd learned how to control the behaviour of animals through feeding the correct currents into their nervous systems. Well, if there *was* any truth in that story – and frankly I doubt it – the whole project was probably inspired by Julian's papers in *Comptes Rendus*.

'Professor Julian, however, never published his most remarkable results. When you stumble on something which is really terrific, you don't rush into print. You wait until you have overwhelming evidence – unless you're afraid that someone else is hot on the track. Then you may issue an ambiguous report that will establish your priority at a later date, without giving too much away at the moment – like the famous cryptogram that Huygens put out when he detected the rings of Saturn.

'You may well wonder what Julian's discovery was, so I won't keep you in suspense. It was simply the natural extension of what man has been doing for the last hundred years. First the camera gave us the power to capture scenes. Then Edison invented the phonograph, and sound was mastered. Today, in the talking film, we have a kind of mechanical memory which would be inconceivable to our forefathers. But surely the matter cannot rest there. Eventually science must be able to catch and store thoughts and sensations themselves, and feed them back into the mind so that, whenever it wishes, it can repeat any experience in life, down to its minutest detail.'

'That's an old idea!' snorted someone. 'See the "feelies" in *Brave New World*.'

'All good ideas have been thought of by somebody before they are realised,' said Purvis severely. 'The point is that what Huxley and others had talked about, Julian actually did. My goodness, there's a pun there! Aldous – Julian – oh, let it pass!

'It was done electronically, of course. You all know how the encephalograph can record the minute electrical impulses in the living brain – the so-called "brain waves", as the popular press calls them. Julian's device was a much subtler elaboration of this well-known instrument. And, having recorded cerebral impulses, he could play them back again. It sounds simple, doesn't it? So was the phonograph, but it took the genius of Edison to think of it.

'And now, enter the villain. Well, perhaps that's too strong a word, for Professor Julian's assistant Georges – Georges Dupin – is really quite a sympathetic character. It was just that, being a Frenchman of a more practical turn of mind than the Professor, he saw at once that there were some milliards of francs involved in this laboratory toy.

'The first thing was to get it out of the laboratory. The French have an undoubted flair for elegant engineering, and after some weeks of work – with the full co-operation of the Professor – Georges had managed to pack the "playback" side of the apparatus into a cabinet no larger than a television set, and containing not very many more parts.

'Then Georges was ready to make his first experiment. It would involve considerable expense, but, as someone so rightly remarked, you cannot make omelettes without breaking eggs. And the analogy is, if I may say so, an exceedingly apt one.

'For Georges went to see the most famous gourmet in France, and made an interesting proposition. It was one that the great man could not refuse, because it was so unique a tribute to his eminence. Georges explained patiently that he had invented a device for registering (he said nothing about storing) sensations. In the cause of science, and for the honour of the French cuisine, could he be privileged to analyse the emotions, the subtle nuances of gustatory discrimination, that took place in Monsieur le Baron's mind when he employed his unsurpassed talents? Monsieur could name the restaurant, the chef and the menu – everything would be arranged for his convenience. Of course, if he was too busy, no doubt that well-known epicure Le Compte de—

'The Baron, who was in some respects a surprisingly coarse man, uttered a word not to be found in most French dictionaries. "*That* cretin!" he exploded. "He would be happy on English cooking! No, I shall do it." And forthwith he sat down to compose the menu, while Georges anxiously estimated the cost of the items and wondered if his bank balance would stand the strain. . . .

'It would be interesting to know what the chef and the waiters thought about the whole business. There was the Baron, seated at his favourite table and doing full justice to his favourite dishes, not in the least inconvenienced by the tangle of wires that trailed from his head to that diabolical-looking machine in the corner. The restaurant was empty of all other occupants, for the last thing Georges wanted was premature publicity. This had added very considerably to the already distressing cost of the experiment. He could only hope that the results would be worth it.

'They were. The only way of *proving* that, of course, would be to play back Georges's "recording". We have to take his word for it, since the utter inadequacy of words in such matters is all too well known. The Baron *was* a genuine connoisseur, not one of those who merely pretend to powers of discrimination they do not possess. You know Thurber's "Only a naïve domestic Burgundy, but I think you'll admire its presumption". The Baron would have known at the first sniff whether it was domestic or not – and if it had been presumptuous he'd have smacked it down.

'I gather that Georges had his money's worth out of that recording, even though he had not intended it merely for personal use. It opened up new worlds to him, and clarified the ideas that had been forming in his ingenious brain. There was no doubt about it: all the exquisite sensations that had passed through the Baron's mind during the consumption of that Lucullan repast had been captured, so that anyone else, however untrained they might be in such matters, could savour them to the full. For, you see, the recording dealt purely with emotions: intelligence did not come into the picture at all. The Baron needed a lifetime of knowledge and training before he could *experience* these sensations. But once they were down on tape, anyone, even if in real life they had no sense of taste at all, could take over from there.

'Think of the glowing vistas that opened up before Georges's eyes! There were other meals, other gourmets. There were the collected impressions of all the vintages of Europe – what would connoisseurs not pay for them? When the last bottle of a rare wine had been broached, its incorporeal essence could be preserved, as the voice of Melba can travel down the centuries. For, after all, it was not the wine itself that mattered, but the sensations it evoked. . . .

'So mused Georges. But this, he knew, was only a beginning. The French claim to logic I have often disputed, but in Georges's case it cannot be denied. He thought the matter over for a few days: then he went to see his *petite dame*.

' "Yvonne, *ma chérie*," he said, "I have a somewhat unusual request to make of you. . . ." '

Harry Purvis knew when to break off in a story. He turned to the bar and called, 'Another Scotch, Drew.' No one said a word while it was provided.

'To continue,' said Purvis at length, 'the experiment, unusual though it was, even in France, was successfully carried out. As both discretion and custom demanded, all was arranged in the lonely hours of the night. You will have gathered already that Georges was a persuasive person, though I doubt if Mam'selle needed much persuading.

'Stifling her curiosity with a sincere but hasty kiss, Georges saw Yvonne out of the lab and rushed back to his apparatus. Breathlessly, he ran through the playback. It worked – not that he had ever had any real doubts. Moreover – do please remember I have only my informant's word for this – it was indistinguishable from the real thing. At that moment something approaching religious awe overcame Georges. This was, without a doubt, the greatest invention in history. He would be immortal as well as wealthy, for he had achieved something of which all men had dreamed, and had robbed old age of one of its terrors. . . .

'He also realised that he could now dispense with Yvonne, if he so wished. This raised implications that would require further thought. *Much* further thought.

'You will, of course, appreciate that I am giving you a highly condensed account of events. While all this was going on, Georges was still working as a loyal employee of the Professor, who suspected nothing. As yet, indeed, Georges had done little more than any research worker might have in similar circumstances. His performances had been somewhat beyond the call of duty, but could all be explained away if need be.

'The next step would involve some very delicate negotiations and the expenditure of further hard-won francs. Georges now had all the material he needed to prove, beyond a shadow of doubt, that he was handling a very valuable commercial property. There were shrewd businessmen in Paris who would jump at the opportunity. Yet a certain delicacy, for which we must give him full credit, restrained Georges from using his second – er – recording as a sample of the wares his machine could purvey. There was no way of disguising the personalities involved, and Georges was a modest man. "Besides," he argued, again with great good sense, "when the gramo-

phone company wishes to make a *disque*, it does not enregister the performance of some amateur musician. *That* is a matter for professionals. And so,
ma foi, is *this*." Whereupon, after a further call at his bank, he set forth again
for Paris.

'He did not go anywhere near the Place Pigalle, because that was full of
Americans and prices were accordingly exorbitant. Instead, a few discreet
enquiries and some understanding cab drivers took him to an almost
oppressively respectable suburb, where he presently found himself in a
pleasant waiting room, by no means as exotic as might have been supposed.

'And there, somewhat embarrassed, Georges explained his mission to a
formidable lady whose age one could have no more guessed than her
profession. Used though she was to unorthodox requests, *this* was something she had never encountered in all her considerable experience. But
the customer was always right, as long as he had the cash, and so in due
course everything was arranged. One of the young ladies and her boy-
friend, an apache of somewhat overwhelming masculinity, travelled back
with Georges to the provinces. At first they were, naturally, somewhat
suspicious, but as Georges had already found, no expert can ever resist
flattery. Soon they were all on excellent terms. Hercule and Susette promised Georges that they would give him every cause for satisfaction.

'No doubt some of you would be glad to have further details, but you can
scarcely expect me to supply them. All I can say is that Georges – or, rather,
his instrument – was kept very busy, and that by the morning little of the
recording material was left unused. For it seems that Hercule was indeed
appropriately named. . . .

'When this piquant episode was finished, Georges had very little money
left, but he did possess two recordings that were quite beyond price. Once
more he set off to Paris, where, with practically no trouble, he came to
terms with some businessmen who were so astonished that they gave him
a very generous contract before coming to their senses. I am pleased to
report this, because so often the scientist emerges second best in his dealings
with the world of finance. I'm equally pleased to record that Georges had
made provision for Professor Julian in the contract. You may say cynically
that it was, after all, the Professor's invention, and that sooner or later
Georges would have had to square him. But I like to think that there was
more to it than that.

'The full details of the scheme for exploiting the device are, of course,
unknown to me. I gather that Georges had been expansively eloquent – not
that much eloquence was needed to convince anyone who had once
experienced one or both of his playbacks. The market would be enormous,
unlimited. The export trade alone could put France on her feet again and
would wipe out her dollar deficit overnight – once certain snags had been
overcome. Everything would have to be managed through somewhat
clandestine channels, for think of the hubbub from the hypocritical Anglo-
Saxons when they discovered just what was being imported into their
countries. The Mothers' Union, the Daughters of the American Revolution,

the Housewives League, and *all* the religious organisations would rise as one. The lawyers were looking into the matter very carefully, and as far as could be seen the regulations that still excluded *Tropic of Capricorn* from the mails of the English-speaking countries could not be applied to this case – for the simple reason that no one had thought of it. But there would be such a shout for new laws that Parliament and Congress would have to do something, so it was best to keep under cover as long as possible.

'In fact, as one of the directors pointed out, if the recordings were banned, so much the better. They could make much more money on a smaller output, because the price would promptly soar and all the vigilance of the Customs Officials couldn't block every leak. It would be Prohibition all over again.

'You will scarcely be surprised to hear that by this time Georges had somewhat lost interest in the gastronomical angle. It was an interesting but definitely minor possibility of the invention. Indeed, this had been tacitly admitted by the directors as they drew up the articles of association, for they had included the pleasures of the cuisine among "subsidiary rights".

'Georges returned home with his head in the clouds, and a substantial cheque in his pocket. A charming fancy had struck his imagination. He thought of all the trouble to which the gramophone companies had gone so that the world might have the complete recordings of the Forty-eight Preludes and Fugues or the Nine Symphonies. Well, *his* new company would put out a complete and definite set of recordings, performed by experts versed in the most esoteric knowledge of East and West. How many opus numbers would be required? That, of course, had been a subject of profound debate for some thousands of years. The Hindu textbooks, Georges had heard, got well into three figures. It would be a most interesting research, combining profit with pleasure in an unexampled manner. . . . He had already begun some preliminary studies, using treatises which even in Paris were none too easy to obtain.

'If you think that while all this was going on, Georges had neglected his usual interests you are all too right. He was working literally night and day, for he had not yet revealed his plans to the Professor and almost everything had to be done when the lab was closed. And one of the interests he had had to neglect was Yvonne.

'Her curiosity had already been aroused, as any girl's would have been. But now she was more than intrigued – she was distracted. For Georges had become so remote and cold. He was no longer in love with her.

'It was a result that might have been anticipated. Publicans have to guard against the danger of sampling their own wares too often – I'm sure *you* don't, Drew – and Georges had fallen into this seductive trap. He had been through that recording too many times, with somewhat debilitating results. Moreover, poor Yvonne was not to be compared with the experienced and talented Susettte. It was the old story of the professional versus the amateur.

'All that Yvonne knew was that Georges was in love with someone else.

505

That was true enough. She suspected that he had been unfaithful to her. And *that* raises profound philosophical questions we can hardly go into here.

'This being France, in case you had forgotten, the outcome was inevitable. Poor Georges! He was working late one night at the lab, as usual, when Yvonne finished him off with one of those ridiculous ornamental pistols which are *de rigueur* for such occasions. Let us drink to his memory.'

'That's the trouble with all your stories,' said John Beynon. 'You tell us about wonderful inventions, and then at the end it turns out that the discoverer was killed, so no one can do anything about it. For I suppose, as usual, the apparatus was destroyed?'

'But no,' replied Purvis. 'Apart from Georges, this is one of the stories that has a happy ending. There was no trouble at all about Yvonne, of course. Georges's grieving sponsors arrived on the scene with great speed and prevented any adverse publicity. Being men of sentiment as well as men of business, they realised that they would have to secure Yvonne's freedom. They promptly did this by playing the recording to *le Maire* and *le Préfet*, thus convincing them that the poor girl had experienced irresistible provocation. A few shares in the new company clinched the deal, with expressions of the utmost cordiality on both sides. Yvonne even got her gun back.'

'Then when—' began someone else.

'Ah, these things take time. There's the question of mass production, you know. It's quite possible that distribution has already commenced through private – *very* private – channels. Some of those dubious little shops and notice boards around Leicester Square may soon start giving hints.

'Of course,' said the New England voice disrespectfully, 'you wouldn't know the *name of the company*.'

You can't help admiring Purvis at times like this. He scarcely hesitated.

'*Le Société Anonyme d'Aphrodite*,' he replied. 'And I've just remembered something that will cheer *you* up. They hope to get round your sticky mail regulations and establish themselves before the inevitable congressional enquiry starts. They're opening up a branch in Nevada: apparently you can still get away with anything there.' He raised his glass.

'To Georges Dupin,' he said solemnly. 'Martyr to science. Remember him when the fireworks start. And one other thing—'

'Yes?' we all asked.

'Better start saving now. And sell your TV sets before the bottom drops out of the market.'

Refugee

First published in *The Magazine of Fantasy and Science Fiction*, July 1955, as '?'
Collected in *The Other Side of the Sky*

'Refugee' was originally published by Anthony Boucher as '?' because he didn't like the title, after which he ran a competition to find a better one, choosing 'This Earth of Majesty'. Meanwhile, in *New Worlds* Ted Carnell called it 'Royal Prerogative', adding to the confusion. I cannot pretend that no resemblance was intended to any living character. Indeed, I have since met the prototype of 'Prince Henry' and we had a conversation uncannily appropriate to this meeting.

'When he comes aboard,' said Captain Saunders, as he waited for the landing ramp to extrude itself, 'what the devil shall I call him?'

There was a thoughtful silence while the navigation officer and the assistant pilot considered this problem in etiquette. Then Mitchell locked the main control panel, and the ship's multitudinous mechanisms lapsed into unconsciousness as power was withdrawn from them.

'The correct address,' he drawled slowly, 'is "Your Royal Highness".'

'Huh!' snorted the captain. 'I'll be damned if I'll call anyone *that*!'

'In these progressive days,' put in Chambers helpfully, 'I believe that "Sir" is quite sufficient. But there's no need to worry if you forget: it's been a long time since anyone went to the Tower. Besides, this Henry isn't as tough a proposition as the one who had all the wives.'

'From all accounts,' added Mitchell, 'he's a very pleasant young man. Quite intelligent, too. He's often been known to ask people technical questions that they couldn't answer.'

Captain Saunders ignored the implications of this remark, beyond resolving that if Prince Henry wanted to know how a field Compensation Drive Generator worked, then Mitchell could do the explaining. He got gingerly to his feet – they'd been operating on half a gravity during flight, and now they were on Earth, he felt like a ton of bricks – and started to make his way along the corridors that led to the lower air lock. With an oily purring, the great curving door side-stepped out of his way. Adjusting his smile, he walked out to meet the television cameras and the heir to the British throne.

The man who would, presumably, one day be Henry IX of England was still in his early twenties. He was slightly below average height, and had fine-drawn, regular features that really lived up to all the genealogical clichés. Captain Saunders, who came from Dallas and had no intention of being impressed by any prince, found himself unexpectedly moved by the wide, sad eyes. They were eyes that had seen too many receptions and parades, that had had to watch countless totally uninteresting things, that had never been allowed to stray far from the carefully planned official routes. Looking at that proud but weary face, Captain Saunders glimpsed for the first time the ultimate loneliness of royalty. All his dislike of that institution became suddenly trivial against its real defect: what was wrong with the Crown was the unfairness of inflicting such a burden on any human being. . . .

The passageways of the *Centaurus* were too narrow to allow for general sight-seeing, and it was soon clear that it suited Prince Henry very well to leave his entourage behind. Once they had begun moving through the ship, Saunders lost all his stiffness and reserve, and within a few minutes was treating the prince exactly like any other visitor. He did not realise that one of the earliest lessons royalty has to learn is that of putting people at their ease.

'You know, Captain,' said the prince wistfully, 'this is a big day for us. I've always hoped that one day it would be possible for spaceships to operate from England. But it still seems strange to have a port of our own here, after all these years. Tell me – did you ever have much to do with rockets?'

'Well, I had some training on them, but they were already on the way out before I graduated. I was lucky: some older men had to go back to school and start all over again – or else abandon space completely if they couldn't convert to the new ships.'

'It made as much difference as that?'

'Oh yes – when the rocket went, it was as big as the change from sail to steam. That's an analogy you'll often hear, by the way. There was a glamour about the old rockets, just as there was about the old windjammers, which these modern ships haven't got. When the *Centaurus* takes off, she goes up as quietly as a balloon – and as slowly, if she wants to. But a rocket blast-off shook the ground for miles, and you'd be deaf for days if you were too near the launching apron. Still, you know all that from the old news recordings.'

The prince smiled.

'Yes,' he said. 'I've often run through them at the Palace. I think I've watched every incident in all the pioneering expeditions. I was sorry to see the end of the rockets, too. But we could never have had a spaceport here on Salisbury Plain – the vibration would have shaken down Stonehenge!'

'Stonehenge?' queried Saunders as he held open a hatch and let the prince through into Hold Number 3.

'Ancient monument – one of the most famous stone circles in the world.

It's really impressive, and about three thousand years old. See it if you can – it's only ten miles from here.'

Captain Saunders had some difficulty in suppressing a smile. What an odd country this was: where else, he wondered, would you find contrasts like this? It made him feel very young and raw when he remembered that back home Billy the Kid was ancient history, and there was hardly anything in the whole of Texas as much as five hundred years old. For the first time he began to realise what tradition meant: it gave Prince Henry something that he could never possess. Poise – self-confidence, yes, that was it. And a pride that was somehow free from arrogance because it took itself so much for granted that it never had to be asserted.

It was surprising how many questions Prince Henry managed to ask in the thirty minutes that had been allotted for his tour of the freighter. They were not the routine questions that people asked out of politeness, quite uninterested in the answers. H.R.H. Prince Henry knew a lot about spaceships, and Captain Saunders felt completely exhausted when he handed his distinguished guest back to the reception committee, which had been waiting outside the *Centaurus* with well-simulated patience.

'Thank you very much, Captain,' said the prince as they shook hands in the air lock. 'I've not enjoyed myself so much for ages. I hope you have a pleasant stay in England, and a successful voyage.' Then his retinue whisked him away, and the port officials, frustrated until now, came aboard to check the ship's papers.

'Well,' said Mitchell when it was all over, 'what did you think of our Prince of Wales?'

'He surprised me,' answered Saunders frankly. 'I'd never have guessed he was a prince. I always thought they were rather dumb. But heck, he *knew* the principles of the Field Drive! Has he ever been up in space?'

'Once, I think. Just a hop above the atmosphere in a Space Force ship. It didn't even reach orbit before it came back again – but the Prime Minister nearly had a fit. There were questions in the House and editorials in the *Times*. Everyone decided that the heir to the throne was too valuable to risk in these newfangled inventions. So, though he has the rank of commodore in the Royal Space Force, he's never even been to the moon.'

'The poor guy,' said Captain Saunders.

He had three days to burn, since it was not the captain's job to supervise the loading of the ship or the preflight maintenance. Saunders knew skippers who hung around breathing heavily on the necks of the servicing engineers, but he wasn't that type. Besides, he wanted to see London. He had been to Mars and Venus and the moon, but this was his first visit to England. Mitchell and Chambers filled him with useful information and put him on the monorail to London before dashing off to see their own families. They would be returning to the spaceport a day before he did, to see that everything was in order. It was a great relief having officers one could rely on so implicitly: they were unimaginative and cautious, but thoroughgoing almost to a fault. If *they* said that everything was shipshape, Saunders knew he could take off without qualms.

The sleek, streamlined cylinder whistled across the carefully tailored landscape. It was so close to the ground, and travelling so swiftly, that one could only gather fleeting impressions of the towns and fields that flashed by. Everything, thought Saunders, was so incredibly compact, and on such a Lilliputian scale. There were no open spaces, no fields more than a mile long in any direction. It was enough to give a Texan claustrophobia – particularly a Texan who also happened to be a space pilot.

The sharply defined edge of London appeared like the bulwark of some walled city on the horizon. With few exceptions, the buildings were quite low – perhaps fifteen or twenty storeys in height. The monorail shot through a narrow canyon, over a very attractive park, across a river that was presumably the Thames, and then came to rest with a steady, powerful surge of deceleration. A loud-speaker announced, in a modest voice that seemed afraid of being overheard: 'This is Paddington. Passengers for the North please remain seated.' Saunders pulled his baggage down from the rack and headed out into the station.

As he made for the entrance to the Underground, he passed a bookstall and glanced at the magazines on display. About half of them, it seemed, carried photographs of Prince Henry or other members of the royal family. This, thought Saunders, was altogether too much of a good thing. He also noticed that all the evening papers showed the prince entering or leaving the *Centaurus*, and bought copies to read in the subway – he begged its pardon, the 'Tube'.

The editorial comments had a monotonous similiarity. At last, they rejoiced, England need no longer take a back seat among the space-going nations. Now it was possible to operate a space fleet without having a million square miles of desert: the silent, gravity-defying ships of today could land, if need be, in Hyde Park, without even disturbing the ducks on the Serpentine. Saunders found it odd that this sort of patriotism had managed to survive into the age of space, but he guessed that the British had felt it pretty badly when they'd had to borrow launching sites from the Australians, the Americans, and the Russians.

The London Underground was still, after a century and a half, the best transport system in the world, and it deposited Saunders safely at his destination less than ten minutes after he had left Paddington. In ten minutes the *Centaurus* could have covered fifty thousand miles; but space, after all, was not quite so crowded as this. Nor were the orbits of space craft so tortuous as the streets Saunders had to negotiate to reach his hotel. All attempts to straighten out London had failed dismally, and it was fifteen minutes before he completed the last hundred yards of his journey.

He stripped off his jacket and collapsed thankfully on his bed. Three quiet, carefree days all to himself: it seemed too good to be true.

It was. He had barely taken a deep breath when the phone rang.

'Captain Saunders? I'm so glad we found you. This is the BBC. We have a programme called "In Town Tonight" and we were wondering . . .'

The thud of the air-lock door was the sweetest sound Saunders had heard for days. Now he was safe: nobody could get at him here in his armoured fortress, which would soon be far out in the freedom of space. It was not that he had been treated badly: on the contrary, he had been treated altogether too well. He had made four (or was it five?) appearances on various TV programmes; he had been to more parties than he could remember; he had acquired several hundred new friends and (the way his head felt now) forgotten all his old ones.

'Who started the rumour,' he said to Mitchell as they met at the port, 'that the British were reserved and stand-offish? Heaven help me if I ever meet a *demonstrative* Englishman.'

'I take it,' replied Mitchell, 'that you had a good time.'

'Ask me tomorrow,' Saunders replied. 'I may have reintegrated my psyche by then.'

'I saw you on that quiz programme last night,' remarked Chambers. 'You looked pretty ghastly.'

'Thank you: that's just the sort of sympathetic encouragement I need at the moment. I'd like to see you think of a synonym of "jejune" after you'd been up until three in the morning.'

'Vapid,' replied Chambers promptly.

'Insipid,' said Mitchell, not to be outdone.

'You win. Let's have those overhaul schedules and see what the engineers have been up to.'

Once seated at the control desk, Captain Saunders quickly became his usual efficient self. He was home again, and his training took over. He knew exactly what to do, and would do it with automatic precision. To right and left of him, Mitchell and Chambers were checking their instruments and calling the control tower.

It took them an hour to carry out the elaborate pre-flight routine. When the last signature had been attached to the last sheet of instructions, and the last red light on the monitor panel had turned to green, Saunders flopped back in his seat and lit a cigarette. They had ten minutes to spare before take-off.

'One day,' he said, 'I'm going to come back to England incognito to find what makes the place tick. I don't understand how you can crowd so many people onto one little island without it sinking.'

'Huh,' snorted Chambers. 'You should see Holland. That makes England look as wide open as Texas.'

'And then there's this royal family business. Do you know, wherever I went everybody kept asking me how I got on with Prince Henry – what we'd talked about – didn't I think he was a fine guy, and so on. Frankly, I got fed up with it. I can't imagine how you've managed to stand it for a thousand years.'

'Don't think that the royal family's been popular all the time,' replied Mitchell. 'Remember what happened to Charles the First? And some of the things we said about the early Georges were quite as rude as the remarks your people made later.'

'We just happen to like tradition,' said Chambers. 'We're not afraid to change when the time comes, but as far as the royal family is concerned – well, it's unique and we're rather fond of it. Just the way you feel about the Statue of Liberty.'

'Not a fair example. I don't think it's right to put human beings up on a pedestal and treat them as if they're – well, minor deities. Look at Prince Henry, for instance. Do you think he'll ever have a chance of doing the things he really wants to do? I saw him three times on TV when I was in London. The first time he was opening a new school somewhere; then he was giving a speech to the Worshipful Company of Fishmongers at the Guildhall (I swear I'm not making *that* up), and finally he was receiving an address of welcome from the mayor of Podunk, or whatever your equivalent is.' ('Wigan,' interjected Mitchell.) 'I think I'd rather be in jail than live that sort of life. Why can't you leave the poor guy alone?'

For once, neither Mitchell nor Chambers rose to the challenge. Indeed, they maintained a somewhat frigid silence. That's torn it, thought Saunders. I should have kept my big mouth shut; now I've hurt their feelings. I should have remembered that advice I read somewhere: 'The British have two religions – cricket and the royal family. Never attempt to criticise either.'

The awkward pause was broken by the radio and the voice of the spaceport controller.

'Control to *Centaurus*. Your flight lane clear. OK to lift.'

'Take-off program starting – *now*!' replied Saunders, throwing the master switch. Then he leaned back, his eyes taking in the entire control panel, his hands clear of the board but ready for instant action.

He was tense but completely confident. Better brains than his – brains of metal and crystal and flashing electron streams – were in charge of the *Centaurus* now. If necessary, he could take command, but he had never yet lifted a ship manually and never expected to do so. If the automatics failed, he would cancel the take-off and sit here on Earth until the fault had been cleared up.

The main field went on, and weight ebbed from the *Centaurus*. There were protesting groans from the ship's hull and structure as the strains redistributed themselves. The curved arms of the landing cradle were carrying no load now; the slightest breath of wind would carry the freighter away into the sky.

Control called from the tower: 'Your weight now zero: check calibration.'

Saunders looked at his meters. The upthrust of the field would now exactly equal the weight of the ship, and the meter readings should agree with the totals on the loading schedules. In at least one instance this check had revealed the presence of a stowaway on board a spaceship – the gauges were as sensitive as that.

'One million, five hundred and sixty thousand, four hundred and twenty kilograms,' Saunders read off from the thrust indicators. 'Pretty good – it checks to within fifteen kilos. The first time I've been underweight, though. You could have taken on some more candy for that plump girl friend of yours in Port Lowell, Mitch.'

The assistant pilot gave a rather sickly grin. He had never quite lived down a blind date on Mars which had given him a completely unwarranted reputation for preferring statesque blondes.

There was no sense of motion, but the *Centaurus* was now falling up into the summer sky as her weight was not only neutralised but reversed. To the watchers below, she would be a swiftly mounting star, a silver globule climbing through and beyond the clouds. Around her, the blue of the atmosphere was deepening into the eternal darkness of space. Like a bead moving along an invisible wire, the freighter was following the pattern of radio waves that would lead her from world to world.

This, thought Captain Saunders, was his twenty-sixth take-off from Earth. But the wonder would never die, nor would he ever outgrow the feeling of power it gave him to sit here at the control panel, the master of forces beyond even the dreams of mankind's ancient gods. No two departures were ever the same: some were into the dawn, some toward the sunset, some above a cloud-veiled Earth, some through clear and sparkling skies. Space itself might be unchanging, but on Earth the same pattern never recurred, and no man ever looked twice at the same landscape or the same sky. Down there the Atlantic waves were marching eternally toward Europe, and high above them – but so far below the *Centaurus*! – the glittering bands of cloud were advancing before the same winds. England began to merge into the continent, and the European coast line became foreshortened and misty as it sank hull down beyond the curve of the world. At the frontier of the west, a fugitive stain on the horizon was the first hint of America. With a single glance, Captain Saunders could span all the leagues across which Columbus had laboured half a thousand years ago.

With the silence of limitless power, the ship shook itself free from the last bonds of Earth. To an outside observer, the only sign of the energies it was expending would have been the dull red glow from the radiation fins around the vessel's equator, as the heat loss from the mass-converters was dissipated into space.

'14:03:45,' wrote Captain Saunders neatly in the log. 'Escape velocity attained. Course deviation negligible.'

There was little point in making the entry. The modest 25,000 miles an hour that had been the almost unattainable goal of the first astronauts had no practical significance now, since the *Centaurus* was still accelerating and would continue to gain speed for hours. But it had a profound psychological meaning. Until this moment, if power had failed, they would have fallen back to Earth. But now gravity could never recapture them: they had achieved the freedom of space, and could take their pick of the planets. In practice, of course, there would be several kinds of hell to pay if they did not pick Mars and deliver their cargo according to plan. But Captain Saunders, like all spacemen, was fundamentally a romantic. Even on a milk run like this he would sometimes dream of the ringed glory of Saturn or the sombre Neptunian wastes, lit by the distant fires of the shrunken sun.

An hour after take-off, according to the hallowed ritual, Chambers left the course computer to its own devices and produced the three glasses that lived beneath the chart table. As he drank the traditional toast to Newton, Oberth, and Einstein, Saunders wondered how this little ceremony had originated. Space crews had certainly been doing it for at least sixty years: perhaps it could be traced back to the legendary rocket engineer who made the remark, 'I've burned more alcohol in sixty seconds than you've ever sold across this lousy bar.'

Two hours later, the last course correction that the tracking stations on Earth could give them had been fed into the computer. From now on, until Mars came sweeping up ahead, they were on their own. It was a lonely thought, yet a curiously exhilarating one. Saunders savoured it in his mind. There were just the three of them here – and no one else within a million miles.

In the circumstances, the detonation of an atomic bomb could hardly have been more shattering than the modest knock on the cabin door. . . .

Captain Saunders had never been so startled in his life. With a yelp that had already left him before he had a chance to suppress it, he shot out of his seat and rose a full yard before the ship's residual gravity field dragged him back. Chambers and Mitchell, on the other hand, behaved with traditional British phlegm. They swivelled in their bucket seats, stared at the door, and then waited for their captain to take action.

It took Saunders several seconds to recover. Had he been confronted with what might be called a normal emergency, he would already have been halfway into a space suit. But a diffident knock on the door of the control cabin, when everybody else in the ship was sitting beside him, was not a fair test.

A stowaway was simply impossible. The danger had been so obvious, right from the beginning of commercial space flight, that the most stringent precautions had been taken against it. One of his officers, Saunders knew, would always have been on duty during loading; no one could possibly have crept in unobserved. Then there had been the detailed preflight inspection, carried out by both Mitchell and Chambers. Finally, there was the weight check at the moment before take-off; *that* was conclusive. No, a stowaway was totally . . .

The knock on the door sounded again. Captain Saunders clenched his fists and squared his jaw. In a few minutes, he thought, some romantic idiot was going to be very, very sorry.

'Open the door, Mr Mitchell,' Saunders growled. In a single long stride, the assistant pilot crossed the cabin and jerked open the hatch.

For an age, it seemed, no one spoke. Then the stowaway, wavering

514

slightly in the low gravity, came into the cabin. He was completely self-possessed, and looked very pleased with himself.

'Good afternoon, Captain Saunders,' he said, 'I must apologise for this sudden intrusion.'

Saunders swallowed hard. Then, as the pieces of the jigsaw fell into place, he looked first at Mitchell, then at Chambers. Both of his officers stared guilelessly back at him with expressions of ineffable innocence. 'So *that's* it,' he said bitterly. There was no need for any explanations: everything was perfectly clear. It was easy to picture the complicated negotiations, the midnight meetings, the falsification of records, the off-loading of nonessential cargoes that his trusted colleagues had been conducting behind his back. He was sure it was a most interesting story, but he didn't want to hear about it now. He was too busy wondering what the *Manual of Space Law* would have to say about a situation like this, though he was already gloomily certain that it would be of no use to him at all.

It was too late to turn back, of course: the conspirators wouldn't have made an elementary miscalculation like that. He would just have to make the best of what looked to be the trickiest voyage in his career.

He was still trying to think of something to say when the PRIORITY signal started flashing on the radio board. The stowaway looked at his watch.

'I was expecting that,' he said. 'It's probably the Prime Minister. I think I'd better speak to the poor man.'

Saunders thought so too.

'Very well, Your Royal Highness,' he said sulkily, and with such emphasis that the title sounded almost like an insult. Then, feeling much put upon, he retired into a corner.

It was the Prime Minister all right, and he sounded very upset. Several times he used the phrase 'your duty to your people' and once there was a distinct catch in his throat as he said something about 'devotion of your subjects to the Crown'. Saunders realised, with some surprise, that he really meant it.

While this emotional harangue was in progress, Mitchell leaned over to Saunders and whispered in his ear:

'The old boy's on a sticky wicket, and he knows it. The people will be behind the prince when they hear what's happened. Everybody knows he's been trying to get into space for years.'

'I wish he hadn't chosen *my* ship,' said Saunders. 'And I'm not sure that this doesn't count as mutiny.'

'The heck it does. Mark my words – when this is all over you'll be the only Texan to have the Order of the Garter. Won't that be nice for you?'

'Shush!' said Chambers. The prince was speaking, his words winging back across the abyss that now sundered him from the island he would one day rule.

'I am sorry, Mr Prime Minister,' he said, 'if I've caused you any alarm. I will return as soon as it is convenient. Someone has to do everything for the first time, and I felt the moment had come for a member of my family to leave Earth. It will be a valuable part of my education, and will make me more fitted to carry out my duty. Goodbye.'

He dropped the microphone and walked over to the observation window – the only spaceward-looking port on the entire ship. Saunders watched him standing there, proud and lonely – but contented now. And as he saw the prince staring out at the stars which he had at last attained, all his annoyance and indignation slowly evaporated.

No one spoke for a long time. Then Prince Henry tore his gaze away from the blinding splendour beyond the port, looked at Captain Saunders, and smiled.

'Where's the galley, Captain?' he asked. 'I may be out of practice, but when I used to go scouting I was the best cook in my patrol.'

Saunders slowly relaxed, then smiled back. The tension seemed to lift from the control room. Mars was still a long way off, but he knew now that this wasn't going to be such a bad trip after all. . . .

The Star

First published in *Infinity Science Fiction*, November 1955
Collected in *The Other Side of the Sky*

Written as an entry for a short story competition run by the *Observer* newspaper, on the subject '2500 AD.', 'The Star' wasn't even a runner-up. However, on magazine publication, it received a Hugo award in 1956. More recently, it was turned into a TV play for Christmas 1985. Although I thought the timing was appropriate, it could hardly be called seasonal fare. I never imagined that one day I would be lecturing in the Vatican.

It is three thousand light-years to the Vatican. Once, I believed that space could have no power over faith, just as I believed that the heavens declared the glory of God's handiwork. Now I have seen that handiwork, and my faith is sorely troubled. I stare at the crucifix that hangs on the cabin wall above the Mark VI Computer, and for the first time in my life I wonder if it is no more than an empty symbol.

I have told no one yet, but the truth cannot be concealed. The facts are there for all to read, recorded on the countless miles of magnetic tape and the thousands of photographs we are carrying back to Earth. Other scientists can interpret them as easily as I can, and I am not one who would condone that tampering with the truth which often gave my order a bad name in the olden days.

The crew are already sufficiently depressed: I wonder how they will take this ultimate irony. Few of them have any religious faith, yet they will not relish using this final weapon in their campaign against me – that private, good-natured, but fundamentally serious, war which lasted all the way from Earth. It amused them to have a Jesuit as chief astrophysicist: Dr Chandler, for instance, could never get over it (why are medical men such notorious atheists?). Sometimes he would meet me on the observation deck, where the lights are always low so that the stars shine with undiminished glory. He would come up to me in the gloom and stand staring out of the great oval port, while the heavens crawled slowly around us as the ship turned end over end with the residual spin we had never bothered to correct.

'Well, Father,' he would say at last, 'it goes on forever and forever, and perhaps *Something* made it. But how you can believe that something has a

special interest in us and our miserable little world – that just beats me.'
Then the argument would start, while the stars and nebulae would swing
around us in silent, endless arcs beyond the flawlessly clear plastic of the
observation port.

It was, I think, the apparent incongruity of my position that caused most
amusement to the crew. In vain I would point to my three papers in the
Astrophysical Journal, my five in the *Monthly Notices of the Royal Astronomical
Society*. I would remind them that my order has long been famous for its
scientific works. We may be few now, but ever since the eighteenth century
we have made contributions to astronomy and geophysics out of all
proportion to our numbers. Will my report on the Phoenix Nebula end our
thousand years of history? It will end, I fear, much more than that.

I do not know who gave the nebula its name, which seems to me a very
bad one. If it contains a prophecy, it is one that cannot be verified for
several billion years. Even the word nebula is misleading: this is a far
smaller object than those stupendous clouds of mist – the stuff of unborn
stars – that are scattered throughout the length of the Milky Way. On the
cosmic scale, indeed, the Phoenix Nebula is a tiny thing – a tenuous shell of
gas surrounding a single star.

Or what is left of a star . . .

The Rubens engraving of Loyola seems to mock me as it hangs there
above the spectrophotometer tracings. What would *you*, Father, have made
of this knowledge that has come into my keeping, so far from the little
world that was all the universe you knew? Would your faith have risen to
the challenge, as mine has failed to do?

You gaze into the distance, Father, but I have travelled a distance beyond
any that you could have imagined when you founded our order a thousand
years ago. No other survey ship has been so far from Earth: we are at the
very frontiers of the explored universe. We set out to reach the Phoenix
Nebula, we succeeded, and we are homeward bound with our burden of
knowledge. I wish I could lift that burden from my shoulders, but I call to
you in vain across the centuries and the light-years that lie between us.

On the book you are holding the words are plain to read. AD MAIOREM
DEI GLORIAM, the message runs, but it is a message I can no longer believe.
Would you still believe it, if you could see what we have found?

We knew, of course, what the Phoenix Nebula was. Every year, in our
galaxy alone, more than a hundred stars explode, blazing for a few hours
or days with thousands of times their normal brilliance before they sink
back into death and obscurity. Such are the ordinary novae – the commonplace disasters of the universe. I have recorded the spectrograms and light
curves of dozens since I started working at the Lunar Observatory.

But three or four times in every thousand years occurs something beside
which even a nova pales into total insignificance.

When a star becomes a *supernova*, it may for a little while outshine all the
massed suns of the galaxy. The Chinese astronomers watched this happen

in AD 1054, not knowing what it was they saw. Five centuries later, in 1572, a supernova blazed in Cassiopeia so brilliantly that it was visible in the daylight sky. There have been three more in the thousand years that have passed since then.

Our mission was to visit the remnants of such a catastrophe, to reconstruct the events that led up to it, and, if possible, to learn its cause. We came slowly in through the concentric shells of gas that had been blasted out six thousand years before, yet were expanding still. They were immensely hot, radiating even now with a fierce violet light, but were far too tenuous to do us any damage. When the star had exploded, its outer layers had been driven upward with such speed that they had escaped completely from its gravitational field. Now they formed a hollow shell large enough to engulf a thousand solar systems, and at its centre burned the tiny, fantastic object which the star had now become – a White Dwarf, smaller than the Earth, yet weighing a million times as much.

The glowing gas shells were all around us, banishing the normal night of interstellar space. We were flying into the centre of a cosmic bomb that had detonated millennia ago and whose incandescent fragments were still hurtling apart. The immense scale of the explosion, and the fact that the debris already covered a volume of space many billions of miles across, robbed the scene of any visible movement. It would take decades before the unaided eye could detect any motion of these tortured wisps and eddies of gas, yet the sense of turbulent expansion was overwhelming.

We had checked our primary drive hours before, and were drifting slowly toward the fierce little star ahead. Once it had been a sun like our own, but it had squandered in a few hours the energy that should have kept it shining for a million years. Now it was a shrunken miser, hoarding its resources as if trying to make amends for its prodigal youth.

No one seriously expected to find planets. If there had been any before the explosion, they would have been boiled into puffs of vapour, and their substance lost in the greater wreckage of the star itself. But we made the automatic search, as we always do when approaching an unknown sun, and presently we found a single small world circling the star at an immense distance. It must have been the Pluto of this vanished solar system, orbiting on the frontiers of the night. Too far from the central sun ever to have known life, its remoteness had saved it from the fate of all its lost companions.

The passing fires had seared its rocks and burned away the mantel of frozen gas that must have covered it in the days before the disaster. We landed, and we found the Vault.

Its builders had made sure that we should. The monolithic marker that stood above the entrance was now a fused stump, but even the first long-range photographs told us that here was the work of intelligence. A little later we detected the continent-wide pattern of radio-activity that had been buried in the rock. Even if the pylon above the Vault had been destroyed, this would have remained, an immovable and all but eternal beacon calling to the stars. Our ship fell toward this gigantic bull's-eye like an arrow into its target.

The pylon must have been a mile high when it was built, but now it looked like a candle that had melted down into a puddle of wax. It took us a week to drill through the fused rock, since we did not have the proper tools for a task like this. We were astronomers, not archaeologists, but we could improvise. Our original purpose was forgotten: this lonely monument, reared with such labour at the greatest possible distance from the doomed sun, could have only one meaning. A civilisation that knew it was about to die had made its last bid for immortality.

It will take us generations to examine all the treasures that were placed in the Vault. They had plenty of time to prepare, for their sun must have given its first warnings many years before the final detonation. Everything that they wished to preserve, all the fruit of their genius, they brought here to this distant world in the days before the end, hoping that some other race would find it and that they would not be utterly forgotten. Would we have done as well, or would we have been too lost in our own misery to give thought to a future we could never see or share?

If only they had had a little more time! They could travel freely enough between the planets of their own sun, but they had not yet learned to cross the interstellar gulfs, and the nearest solar system was a hundred light-years away. Yet even had they possessed the secret of the Transfinite Drive, no more than a few millions could have been saved. Perhaps it was better thus.

Even if they had not been so disturbingly human as their sculpture shows, we could not have helped admiring them and grieving for their fate. They left thousands of visual records and the machines for projecting them, together with elaborate pictorial instructions from which it will not be difficult to learn their written language. We have examined many of these records, and brought to life for the first time in six thousand years the warmth and beauty of a civilisation that in many ways must have been superior to our own. Perhaps they only showed us the best, and one can hardly blame them. But their worlds were very lovely, and their cities were built with a grace that matches anything of man's. We have watched them at work and play, and listened to their musical speech sounding across the centuries. One scene is still before my eyes – a group of children on a beach of strange blue sand, playing in the waves as children play on Earth. Curious whiplike trees line the shore, and some very large animal is wading in the shallows yet attracting no attention at all.

And sinking into the sea, still warm and friendly and life-giving, is the sun that will soon turn traitor and obliterate all this innocent happiness.

Perhaps if we had not been so far from home and so vulnerable to loneliness, we should not have been so deeply moved. Many of us had seen the ruins of ancient civilisations on other worlds, but they had never affected us so profoundly. This tragedy was unique. It is one thing for a race to fail and die, as nations and cultures have done on Earth. But to be destroyed so completely in the full flower of its achievement, leaving no survivors – how could that be reconciled with the mercy of God?

My colleagues have asked me that, and I have given what answers I can. Perhaps you could have done better, Father Loyola, but I have found nothing in the *Exercitia Spiritualia* that helps me here. They were not an evil people: I do not know what gods they worshipped, if indeed they worshipped any. But I have looked back at them across the centuries, and have watched while the loveliness they used their last strength to preserve was brought forth again into the light of their shrunken sun. They could have taught us much: why were they destroyed?

I know the answers that my colleagues will give when they get back to Earth. They will say that the universe has no purpose and no plan, that since a hundred suns explode every year in our galaxy, at this very moment some race is dying in the depths of space. Whether that race has done good or evil during its lifetime will make no difference in the end: there is no divine justice, for there is no God.

Yet, of course, what we have seen proves nothing of the sort. Anyone who argues thus is being swayed by emotion, not logic. God has no need to justify His actions to man. He who built the universe can destroy it when He chooses. It is arrogance – it is perilously near blasphemy – for us to say what He may or may not do.

This I could have accepted, hard though it is to look upon whole worlds and peoples thrown into the furnace. But there comes a point when even the deepest faith must falter, and now, as I look at the calculations lying before me, I know I have reached that point at last.

We could not tell, before we reached the nebula, how long ago the explosion took place. Now, from the astronomical evidence and the record in the rocks of that one surviving planet, I have been able to date it very exactly. I know in what year the light of this colossal conflagration reached our Earth. I know how brilliantly the supernova whose corpse now dwindles behind our speeding ship once shone in terrestrial skies. I know how it must have blazed low in the east before sunrise, like a beacon in that oriental dawn.

There can be no reasonable doubt: the ancient mystery is solved at last. Yet, oh God, there were so many stars you could have used. What was the need to give these people to the fire, that the symbol of their passing might shine above Bethlehem?

What Goes Up

First published in *The Magazine of Fantasy and Science Fiction*, January 1956, as
'What Goes up . . .'
Collected in *Tales from the White Hart*

Doc Richardson was really the American astonomer and SF writer ('Philip
Latham') Robert S. Richardson. I am indebted to him for showing me around
the Mt Wilson Observatory and for introducing me to the idea of the 'gravity
well.'

One of the reasons why I am never too specific about the exact location of
the 'White Hart' is, frankly, because we want to keep it to ourselves. This is
not merely a dog-in-the-manger attitude: we have to do it in pure self-
protection. As soon as it gets around that scientists, editors and science
fiction writers are forgathering at some locality, the weirdest collection of
visitors is likely to turn up. Peculiar people with new theories of the
Universe, characters who have been 'cleared' by Dianetics (God knows
what they were like before), intense ladies who are liable to go all clairvoy-
ant after the fourth gin – these are the less exotic specimens. Worst of all,
however, are the Flying Sorcerers: no cure short of mayhem has yet been
discovered for them.

It was a black day when one of the leading exponents of the Flying
Saucer religion discovered our hide-out and fell upon us with shrill cries of
delight. Here, he obviously told himself, was fertile ground for his mission-
ary activities. People who were already interested in space flight, and even
wrote books and stories about its imminent achievement, would be a
pushover. He opened his little black bag and produced the latest pile of
sauceriana.

It was quite a collection. There were some interesting photographs of
flying saucers made by an amateur astronomer who lives right beside
Greenwich Observatory, and whose busy camera has recorded such a
remarkable variety of spaceships, in all shapes and sizes, that one wonders
what the professionals next door are doing for their salaries. Then there
was a long statement from a gentleman in Texas who had just had a casual
chat with the occupants of a saucer making a wayside halt on route to
Venus. Language, it seemed, had presented no difficulties: it had taken

about ten minutes of arm-waving to get from 'Me – Man. This – Earth' to highly esoteric information about the use of the fourth dimension in space travel.

The masterpiece, however, was an excited letter from a character in South Dakota who had actually been offered a lift in a flying saucer, and had been taken for a spin round the moon. He explained at some length how the saucer travelled by hauling itself along magnetic lines of force, rather like a spider going up its thread.

It was at this point that Harry Purvis rebelled. He had been listening with a professional pride to tales which even he would never have dared to spin, for he was an expert at detecting the yield point of his audience's credulity. At the mention of lines of magnetic force, however, his scientific training overcame his frank admiration of these latter-day Munchausens, and he gave a snort of disgust.

'That's a lot of nonsense,' he said. 'I can prove it to you – magnetism's my speciality.'

'Last week,' said Drew sweetly, as he filled two glasses of ale at once, 'you said that crystal structure was your speciality.'

Harry gave him a superior smile.

'I'm a *general* specialist,' he said loftily. 'To get back to where I was before that interruption, the point I want to make is that there's no such thing as a line of magnetic force. It's a mathematical fiction – exactly on a par with lines of longitude or latitude. Now if anyone said they'd invented a machine that worked by pulling itself along parallels of latitude, everybody would know that they were talking drivel. But because few people know much about magnetism, and it sounds rather mysterious, crackpots like this guy in South Dakota can get away with the tripe we've just been hearing.'

There's one charming characteristic about the 'White Hart' – we may fight among each other, but we show an impressive solidarity in times of crisis. Everyone felt that something had to be done about our unwelcome visitor: for one thing, he was interfering with the serious business of drinking. Fanaticism of any kind casts a gloom over the most festive assembly, and several of the regulars had shown signs of leaving despite the fact that it was still two hours to closing time.

So when Harry Purvis followed up his attack by concocting the most outrageous story that even he had ever presented in the 'White Hart', no one interrupted him or tried to expose the weak points in his narrative. We knew that Harry was acting for us all – he was fighting fire with fire, as it were. And we knew that he wasn't expecting us to believe him (if indeed he ever did) so we just sat back and enjoyed ourselves.

'If you want to know how to propel spaceships,' began Harry, 'and mark you, I'm not saying anything one way or the other about the existence of flying saucers – then you must forget magnetism. You must go straight to gravity – that's the basic force of the Universe, after all. But it's going to be a tricky force to handle, and if you don't believe me just listen to what happened only last year to a scientist down in Australia. I shouldn't really tell you this, I suppose, because I'm not sure of its security classification, but if there's any trouble I'll swear that I never said a word.

'The Aussies, as you may know, have always been pretty hot on scientific research, and they had one team working on fast reactors – those house-broken atomic bombs which are so much more compact than the old uranium piles. The head of the group was a bright but rather impetuous young nuclear physicist I'll call Dr Cavor. That, of course, wasn't his real name, but it's a very appropriate one. You'll all recollect, I'm sure, the scientist Cavor in Wells's *First Men in the Moon*, and the wonderful gravity-screening material Cavorite he discovered?

'I'm afraid dear old Wells didn't go into the question of Cavorite very thoroughly. As he put it, it was opaque to gravity just as a sheet of metal is opaque to light. Anything placed above a horizontal sheet of Cavorite, therefore, became weightless and floated up into space.

'Well, it isn't as simple as that. Weight represents energy – an enormous amount of it – which can't just be destroyed without any fuss. You'd have to put a terrific amount of work into even a small object in order to make it weightless. Antigravity screens of the Cavorite type, therefore, are quite impossible – they're in the same class as perpetual motion.'

'Three of my friends have made perpetual-motion machines,' began our unwanted visitor rather stuffily. Harry didn't let him get any further: he just steamed on and ignored the interruption.

'Now, our Australian Dr Cavor wasn't searching for antigravity, or anything like it. In pure science, you can be pretty sure that nothing fundamental is ever discovered by anyone who's actually looking for it – that's half the fun of the game. Dr Cavor was interested in producing atomic power: what he found was antigravity. And it was quite some time before he realised that was what he'd discovered.

'What happened, I gather, was this: the reactor was of a novel and rather daring design, and there was quite a possibility that it might blow up when the last pieces of fissile material were inserted. So it was assembled by remote control in one of Australia's numerous convenient deserts, all the final operations being observed through TV sets.

'Well, there was no explosion – which would have caused a nasty radioactive mess and wasted a lot of money, but wouldn't have damaged anything except a lot of reputations. What actually happened was much more unexpected, and much more difficult to explain.

'When the last piece of enriched uranium was inserted, the control rods pulled out, and the reactor brought up to criticality – everything went dead. The meters in the remote-control room, two miles from the reactor, all dropped back to zero. The TV screen went blank. Cavor and his colleagues waited for the bang, but there wasn't one. They looked at each other for a moment with many wild surmises: then, without a word, they climbed up out of the buried control chamber.

'The reactor building was completely unchanged: it sat out there in the desert, a commonplace cube of brick holding a million pounds' worth of fissile material and several years of careful design and development. Cavor wasted no time: he grabbed the jeep, switched on a portable Geiger counter, and hurried off to see what had happened.

'He recovered consciousness in hospital a couple of hours later. There was little wrong with him apart from a bad headache, which was nothing to the one his experiment was going to give him during the next few days. It seemed that when he got to within twenty feet of the reactor, his jeep had hit something with a terrific crash. Cavor had got tangled in the steering wheel and had a nice collection of bruises; the Geiger counter, oddly enough, was quite undamaged and was still clucking away quietly to itself, detecting no more than the normal cosmic-ray background.

'Seen from a distance, it had looked a perfectly normal sort of accident that might have been caused by the jeep going into a rut. But Cavor hadn't been driving all that fast, luckily for him, and anyway there was no rut at the scene of the crash. What the jeep had run into was something quite impossible. It was an invisible wall, apparently the lower rim of a hemi-spherical dome, which entirely surrounded the reactor. Stones thrown up in the air slid back to the ground along the surface of this dome, and it also extended underground as far as digging could be carried out. It seemed as if the reactor was at the exact centre of an impenetrable, spherical shell.

'Of course, this was marvellous news and Cavor was out of bed in no time, scattering nurses in all directions. He had no idea what had happened, but it was a lot more exciting than the humdrum piece of nuclear engineering that had started the whole business.

'By now you're probably all wondering what the devil a sphere of force – as you science fiction writers would call it – has to do with antigravity. So I'll jump several days and give you the answers that Cavor and his team discovered only after much hard work and the consumption of many gallons of that potent Australian beer.

'The reactor when it had been energised, had somehow produced an antigravity field. All the matter inside a twenty-foot-radius sphere had been made weightless, and the enormous amount of energy needed to do this had been extracted, in some utterly mysterious manner, from the uranium in the pile. Calculations showed that the amount of energy in the reactor was just sufficient to do the job. Presumably the sphere of force would have been larger still if there had been more ergs available in the power source.

'I can hear someone just waiting to ask a question, so I'll anticipate them. Why didn't this weightless sphere of earth and air float up into space? Well, the earth was held together by its cohesion, anyway, so there was no reason why it should go wandering off. As for the air, that was forced to stay inside the zone of zero gravity for a most surprising and subtle reason which leads me to the crux of this whole peculiar business.

'Better fasten your seat belts for the next bit: we've got a bumpy passage ahead. Those of you who know something about potential theory won't have any trouble, and I'll do my best to make it as easy as I can for the rest.

'People who talk glibly about antigravity seldom stop to consider its

525

implication, so let's look at a few fundamentals. As I've already said, weight implies energy – lots of it. That energy is entirely due to Earth's gravity field. *If you remove an object's weight,* that's precisely equivalent to taking it clear outside Earth's gravity. And any rocket engineer will tell you how much energy *that* requires.'

Harry turned to me and said: 'There's an analogy I'd like to borrow from one of your books, Arthur, that puts across the point I'm trying to make. You know – comparing the fight against Earth's gravity to climbing out of a deep pit.'

'You're welcome,' I said. 'I pinched it from Doc Richardson, anyway.'

'Oh,' replied Harry. 'I thought it was too good to be original. Well, here we go. If you hang on to this really very simple idea, you'll be OK. To take an object clear away from the Earth requires as much work as lifting it *four thousand miles* against the steady drag of normal gravity. Now the matter inside Cavor's zone of force was still on the Earth's surface, but it was weightless. From the energy point of view, therefore, it was outside the Earth's gravity field. It was inaccessible as if it was on top of a four-thousand-mile-high mountain.

'Cavor could stand outside the antigravity zone and look into it from a point a few inches away. To cross those few inches, he would have to do as much work as if he climbed Everest seven hundred times. It wasn't surprising that the jeep stopped in a hurry. No material object had stopped it, but from the point of view of dynamics it had run smack into a cliff four thousand miles high. . . .

'I can see some blank looks that are not entirely due to the lateness of the hour. Never mind: if you don't get all this, just take my word for it. It won't spoil your appreciation of what follows – at least, I hope not.

'Cavor had realised at once that he had made one of the most important discoveries of the age, though it was some time before he worked out just what was going on. The final clue to the antigravitational nature of the field came when they shot a rifle bullet into it and observed the trajectory with a high-speed camera. Ingenious, don't you think?

'The next problem was to experiment with the field's generator and to find just what had happened inside the reactor when it had been switched on. This was a problem indeed. The reactor was there in plain sight, twenty feet away. But to reach it would require slightly more energy than going to the moon. . . .

'Cavor was not disheartened by this, nor by the inexplicable failure of the reactor to respond to any of its remote controls. He theorised that it had been completely drained of energy, if one can use a rather misleading term, and that little if any power was needed to maintain the antigravity field once it had been set up. This was one of the many things that could only be determined by examination on the spot. So by hook or by crook, Dr Cavor would have to go there.

'His first idea was to use an electrically driven trolley, supplied with power through cables which it dragged behind it as it advanced into the field. A hundred horsepower generator, running continuously for seventeen hours, would supply enough energy to take a man of average weight on the perilous twenty-foot journey. A velocity of slightly over a foot an hour did not seem much to boast about, until you remembered that advancing one foot into the antigravity field was equivalent to a two-hundred-mile vertical climb.

'The theory was sound, but in practice the electric trolley wouldn't work. It started to push its way into the field, but began to skid after it had traversed half an inch. The reason was obvious when one started to think about it. Though the power was there, the traction wasn't. No wheeled vehicle could climb a gradient of two hundred miles per foot.

'This minor setback did not discourage Dr Cavor. The answer, he realised at once, was to produce the traction at a point outside the field. When you wanted to lift a load vertically, you didn't use a cart: you used a jack or a hydraulic ram.

'The result of this argument was one of the oddest vehicles ever built. A small but comfortable cage, containing sufficient provisions to last a man for several days, was mounted at the end of a twenty-foot-long horizontal girder. The whole device was supported off the ground by balloon tyres, and the theory was that the cage could be pushed right into the centre of the field by a machine which would remain outside its influence. After some thought, it was decided that the best prime mover would be the common or garden bulldozer.

'A test was made with some rabbits in the passenger compartment – and I can't help thinking that there was an interesting psychological point here. The experimenters were trying to get it both ways: as scientists they'd be pleased if their subjects got back alive, and as Australians they'd be just as happy if they got back dead. But perhaps I'm being a little too fanciful. . . . (You know, of course, how Australians feel about rabbits.)

'The bulldozer chugged away hour after hour, forcing the weight of the girder and its insignificant pay load up the enormous gradient. It was an uncanny sight – all this energy being expended to move a couple of rabbits twenty feet across a perfectly horizontal plain. The subjects of the experiment could be observed throughout the operation: they seemed to be perfectly happy and quite unaware of their historic role.

'The passenger compartment reached the centre of the field, was held there for an hour, and then the girder was slowly backed out again. The rabbits were alive, in good health, and to nobody's particular surprise there were now six of them.

'Dr Cavor, naturally, insisted on being the first human being to venture into a zero-gravity field. He loaded up the compartment with torsion balances, radiation detectors and periscopes so that he could look into the reactor when he finally got to it. Then he gave the signal, the bulldozer started chugging, and the strange journey began.

'There was, naturally, telephone communication from the passenger compartment to the outside world. Ordinary sound waves couldn't cross the barrier, for reasons which were still a little obscure, but radio and telephone both worked without difficulty. Cavor kept up a running commentary as he was edged forward into the field, describing his own reactions and relaying instrument readings to his colleagues.

'The first thing that happened to him, though he had expected it, was nevertheless rather unsettling. During the first few inches of his advance, as he moved through the fringe of the field, the direction of the vertical seemed to swing around. 'Up' was no longer towards the sky: it was now in the direction of the reactor hut. To Cavor, it felt as if he was being pushed up the face of a vertical cliff, with the reactor twenty feet above him. For the first time, his eyes and his ordinary human senses told him the same story as his scientific training. He could *see* that the centre of the field was, gravity-wise, higher than the place from which he had come. However, imagination still boggled at the thought of all the energy it would need to climb that innocent-looking twenty feet, and the hundreds of gallons of diesel fuel that must be burned to get him there.

'There was nothing else of interest to report on the journey itself, and at last, twenty hours after he had started, Cavor arrived at his destination. The wall of the reactor hut was right beside him, though to him it seemed not a wall but an unsupported floor sticking out at right angles from the cliff up which he had risen. The entrance was just above his head, like a trap door through which he would have to climb. This would present no great difficulty, for Dr Cavor was an energetic young man, extremely eager to find just how he had created this miracle.

'Slightly too eager, in fact. For as he tried to work his way into the door, he slipped and fell off the platform that had carried him there.

'That was the last anyone ever saw of him – but it wasn't the last they heard of him. Oh dear no! He made a very big noise indeed. . . .

'You'll see why when you consider the situation in which this unfortunate scientist now found himself. Hundreds of kilowatt-hours of energy had been pushed into him – enough to lift him to the moon and beyond. All that work had been needed to take him to a point of zero gravitational potential. As soon as he lost his means of support that energy began to reappear. To get back to our earlier and very picturesque analogy – the poor Doctor had slipped off the edge of the four-thousand-mile-high mountain he had ascended.

'He fell back the twenty feet that had taken almost a day to climb. "Ah, what a fall was there, my countrymen!" It was precisely equivalent, in terms of energy, to a free drop from the remotest stars down to the surface of the Earth. And you all know how much velocity an object acquires in *that* fall. It's the same velocity that's needed to get it there in the first place – the famous velocity of escape. Seven miles a second, or twenty-five-thousand miles an hour.

'That's what Dr Cavor was doing by the time he got back to his starting point. Or, to be more accurate, that's the speed he involuntarily tried to reach. As soon as he passed Mach 1 or 2, however, air resistance began to have its little say. Dr Cavor's funeral pyre was the finest and, indeed, the only meteor display ever to take place entirely at sea level. . . .

'I'm sorry that this story hasn't got a happy ending. In fact, it hasn't got an ending at all, because that sphere of zero gravitational potential is still sitting there in the Australian desert, apparently doing nothing at all but in fact producing ever increasing amounts of frustration in scientific and official circles. I don't see *how* the authorities can hope to keep it secret much longer. Sometimes I think how odd it is that the world's tallest mountain is in Australia – and that though it's four thousand miles high the airliners often fly right over it without knowing it's there.'

You will hardly be surprised to hear that H. Purvis finished his narration at this point, even he could hardly take it much further, and no one wanted him to. We were all, including his most tenacious critics, lost in admiring awe. I have since detected six fallacies of a fundamental nature in his description of Dr Cavor's Frankensteinian fate but at the time they never even occurred to me. (And I don't propose to reveal them now. They will be left, as the mathematics textbooks put it, as an exercise for the reader.) What had earned our undying gratitude, however, was the fact that at some slight sacrifice of truth he had managed to keep Flying Saucers from invading the 'White Hart'. It was almost closing time, and too late for our visitor to make a counterattack.

That is why the sequel seems a little unfair. A month later, someone brought a very odd publication to one of our meetings. It was nicely printed and laid out with professional skill, the misuse of which was sad to behold. The thing was called *Flying Saucer Revelations* – and there on the front page was a full and detailed account of the story Purvis had told us. It was printed absolutely straight – and what was much worse than that, from poor Harry's point of view, was that it was attributed to him by name.

Since then he has had 4,375 letters on the subject, most of them from California. Twenty-four called him a liar; 4,205 believed him absolutely. (The remaining ones he couldn't decipher and their contents still remain a matter of speculation.)

I'm afraid he's never quite got over it, and I sometimes think he's going to spend the rest of his life trying to stop people believing the one story he never expected to be taken seriously.

There may be a moral here. For the life of me I can't find it.

Venture to the Moon

First published in the *London Evening Standard*, 1956
Collected in *The Other Side of the Sky*

'Venture to the Moon' was originally written as a series of six independent but linked stories for the *London Evening Standard*, in 1956. When the commission was first proposed I turned it down. It appeared impossible to write stories in only 1,500 words which would be understandable to a mass readership despite being set in a totally alien environment, but on second thought this seemed such an interesting challenge that I decided to tackle it. The resulting series was successful enough to demand a second . . .

The Starting Line

The story of the first lunar expedition has been written so many times that some people will doubt if there is anything fresh to be said about it. Yet all the official reports and eyewitness accounts, the on-the-spot recordings and broadcasts never, in my opinion, gave the full picture. They said a great deal about the discoveries that were made – but very little about the men who made them.

As captain of the *Endeavour* and thus commander of the British party, I was able to observe a good many things you will not find in the history books, and some – though not all – of them can now be told. One day, I hope, my opposite numbers on the *Goddard* and the *Ziolkovski* will give their points of view. But as Commander Vandenburg is still on Mars and Commander Krasnin is somewhere inside the orbit of Venus, it looks as if we will have to wait a few more years for *their* memoirs.

Confession, it is said, is good for the soul. I shall certainly feel much happier when I have told the true story behind the timing of the first lunar flight, about which there has always been a good deal of mystery.

As everyone knows, the American, Russian and British ships were assembled in the orbit of Space Station Three, five hundred miles above the Earth, from components flown up by relays of freight rockets. Though all the parts had been prefabricated, the assembly and testing of the ships took over two years, by which time a great many people – who did not realise the complexity of the task – were beginning to get slightly impatient. They had seen dozens of photos and telecasts of the three ships floating there in space beside Station Three, apparently quite complete and ready to pull away from Earth at a moment's notice. What the picture didn't show was the careful and tedious work still in progress as thousands of pipes, wires, motors, and instruments were fitted and subjected to every conceivable test.

There was no definite target date for departure; since the moon is always at approximately the same distance, you can leave for it at almost any time you like – once you are ready. It makes practically no difference, from the point of view of fuel consumption, if you blast off at full moon or new moon or at any time in between. We were very careful to make no predictions about blast-off, though everyone was always trying to get us to fix the time. So many things can go wrong in a spaceship, and we were not going to say goodbye to Earth until we were ready down to the last detail.

I shall always remember the last commanders' conference, aboard the space station, when we all announced that we were ready. Since it was a co-operative venture, each party specialising in some particular task, it had been agreed that we should all make our landings within the same twenty-four-hour period, on the preselected site in the Mare Imbrium. The details of the journey, however, had been left to the individual commanders, presumably in the hope that we would not copy each other's mistakes.

'I'll be ready,' said Commander Vandenburg, 'to make my first dummy take-off at 0900 tomorrow. What about you, gentlemen? Shall we ask Earth Control to stand by for all three of us?'

'That's OK by me,' said Krasnin, who could never be convinced that his American slang was twenty years out of date.

I nodded my agreement. It was true that one bank of fuel gauges was still misbehaving, but that didn't really matter; they would be fixed by the time the tanks were filled.

The dummy run consisted of an exact replica of a real blast-off, with everyone carrying out the job he would do when the time came for the genuine thing. We had practised, of course, in mock-ups down on Earth, but this was a perfect imitation of what would happen to us when we finally took off for the moon. All that was missing was the roar of the motors that would tell us that the voyage had begun.

We did six complete imitations of blast-off, took the ships to pieces to eliminate anything that hadn't behaved perfectly, then did six more. The *Endeavour*, the *Goddard*, and the *Ziolkovski* were all in the same state of serviceability. There now only remained the job of fuelling up, and we would be ready to leave.

The suspense of those last few hours is not something I would care to go through again. The eyes of the world were upon us; departure time had now been set, with an uncertainty of only a few hours. All the final tests had been made, and we were convinced that our ships were as ready as humanly possible.

It was then that I had an urgent and secret personal radio call from a very high official indeed, and a suggestion was made which had so much authority behind it that there was little point in pretending that it wasn't an order. The first flight to the moon, I was reminded, was a co-operative venture – but think of the prestige if *we* got there first. It need only be by a couple of hours. . . .

I was shocked at the suggestion, and said so. By this time Vandenburg and Krasnin were good friends of mine, and we were all in this together. I made every excuse I could and said that since our flight paths had already been computed there wasn't anything that could be done about it. Each ship was making the journey by the most economical route, to conserve fuel. If we started together, we should arrive together – within seconds.

Unfortunately, someone had thought of the answer to that. Our three ships, fuelled up and with their crews standing by, would be circling earth in a state of complete readiness for several hours before they actually pulled away from their satellite orbits and headed out to the moon. At our five-hundred-mile altitude, we took ninety-five minutes to make one circuit of the Earth, and only once every revolution would the moment be ripe to begin the voyage. If we could jump the gun by one revolution, the others would have to wait that ninety-five minutes before they could follow. And so they would land on the moon ninety-five minutes behind us.

I won't go into the arguments, and I'm still a little ashamed that I yielded and agreed to deceive my two colleagues. We were in the shadow of Earth, in momentary eclipse, when the carefully calculated moment came. Vandenburg and Krasnin, honest fellows, thought I was going to make one more round trip with them before we all set off together. I have seldom felt a bigger heel in my life than when I pressed the firing key and felt the sudden thrust of the motors as they swept me away from my mother world.

For the next ten minutes we had no time for anything but our instruments, as we checked to see that the *Endeavour* was forging ahead along her precomputed orbit. Almost at the moment that we finally escaped from Earth and could cut the motors, we burst out of shadow into the full blaze of the sun. There would be no more night until we reached the moon, after five days of effortless and silent coasting through space.

Already Space Station Three and the two other ships must be a thousand miles behind. In eighty-five more minutes Vandenburg and Krasnin would be back at the correct starting point and could take off after me, as we had all planned. But they could never overcome my lead, and I hoped they wouldn't be too mad at me when we met again on the moon.

I switched on the rear camera and looked back at the distant gleam of the space station, just emerging from the shadow of Earth. It was some moments before I realised that the *Goddard* and the *Ziolkovski* weren't still floating beside it where I'd left them. . . .

No; they were just half a mile away, neatly matching my velocity. I stared at them in utter disbelief for a second, before I realised that every one of us had had the same idea. 'Why, you pair of double-crossers!' I gasped. Then I began to laugh so much that it was several minutes before I dared call up a very worried Earth Control and tell them that everything had gone according to plan – though in no case was it the plan that had been originally announced. . . .

We were all very sheepish when we radioed each other to exchange mutual congratulations. Yet at the same time, I think everyone was secretly pleased that it had turned out this way. For the rest of the trip, we were never more than a few miles apart, and the actual landing manoeuvres were so well synchronised that our three braking jets hit the moon simultaneously.

Well, almost simultaneously. I might make something of the fact that the recorder tape shows I touched down two-fifths of a second ahead of Krasnin. But I'd better not, for Vandenburg was precisely the same moment ahead of me.

On a quarter-of-a-million-mile trip, I think you could call that a photo finish. . . .

Robin Hood, F.R.S.

We had landed early in the dawn of the long lunar day, and the slanting shadows lay all around us, extending for miles across the plain. They would slowly shorten as the sun rose higher in the sky, until at noon they would almost vanish – but noon was still five days away, as we measured time on Earth, and nightfall was seven days later still. We had almost two weeks of daylight ahead of us before the sun set and the bluely gleaming Earth became the mistress of the sky.

There was little time for exploration during those first hectic days. We had to unload the ships, grow accustomed to the alien conditions surrounding us, learn to handle our electrically powered tractors and scooters, and erect the igloos that would serve as homes, offices, and labs until the time came to leave. At a pinch, we could live in the spaceships, but it would be excessively uncomfortable and cramped. The igloos were not exactly commodious, but they were luxury after five days in space. Made of tough, flexible plastic, they were blown up like balloons, and their interiors were then partitioned into separate rooms. Air locks allowed access to the outer world, and a good deal of plumbing linked to the ships' air-purification plants kept the atmosphere breathable. Needless to say, the American igloo was the biggest one, and had come complete with everything, *including* the kitchen sink – not to mention a washing machine, which we and the Russians were always borrowing.

It was late in the 'afternoon' – about ten days after we had landed – before we were properly organised and could think about serious scientific work. The first parties made nervous little forays out into the wilderness around the base, familiarising themselves with the territory. Of course, we already possessed minutely detailed maps and photographs of the region in which we had landed, but it was surprising how misleading they could sometimes be. What had been marked as a small hill on a chart often looked like a mountain to a man toiling along in a space suit, and apparently smooth plains were often covered knee-deep with dust, which made progress extremely slow and tedious.

These were minor difficulties, however, and the low gravity – which gave all objects only a sixth of their terrestrial weight – compensated for much. As the scientists began to accumulate their results and specimens, the radio and TV circuits with Earth became busier and busier, until they were in continuous operation. We were taking no chances; even if *we* didn't get home, the knowledge we were gathering would do so.

The first of the automatic supply rockets landed two days before sunset, precisely according to plan. We saw its braking jets flame briefly against the stars, then blast again a few seconds before touchdown. The actual landing was hidden from us, since for safety reasons the dropping ground was three miles from the base. And on the moon, three miles is well over the curve of the horizon.

When we got to the robot, it was standing slightly askew on its tripod shock absorbers, but in perfect condition. So was everything aboard it, from instruments to food. We carried the stores back to base in triumph, and had a celebration that was really rather overdue. The men had been working too hard, and could do with some relaxation.

It was quite a party; the highlight, I think, was Commander Krasnin trying to do a Cossack dance in a space suit. Then we turned our minds to competitive sports, but found that, for obvious reasons, outdoor activities were somewhat restricted. Games like croquet or bowls would have been practical had we had the equipment; but cricket and football were definitely out. In that gravity, even a football would go half a mile if it were given a good kick – and a cricket ball would never been seen again.

Professor Trevor Williams was the first person to think of a practical lunar sport. He was our astronomer, and also one of the youngest men ever to be made a Fellow of the Royal Society, being only thirty when this ultimate accolade was conferred upon him. His work on methods of interplanetary navigation had made him world famous; less well known, however, was his skill as a toxophilite. For two years in succession he had been archery champion for Wales. I was not surprised, therefore, when I discovered him shooting at a target propped up on a pile of lunar slag.

The bow was a curious one, strung with steel control wire and shaped from a laminated plastic bar. I wondered where Trevor had got hold of it, then remembered that the robot freight rocket had now been cannibalised and bits of it were appearing in all sorts of unexpected places. The arrows, however, were the really interesting feature. To give them stability on the airless moon, where, of course, feathers would be useless, Trevor had managed to rifle them. There was a little gadget on the bow that set them spinning, like bullets, when they were fired, so that they kept on course when they left the bow.

Even with this rather makeshift equipment, it was possible to shoot a mile if one wished to. However, Trevor didn't want to waste arrows, which were not easy to make; he was more interested in seeing the sort of accuracy he could get. It was uncanny to watch the almost flat trajectory of the arrows; they seemed to be travelling parallel with the ground. If he wasn't careful, someone warned Trevor, his arrows might become lunar satellites and would hit him in the back when they completed their orbit.

The second supply rocket arrived the next day, but this time things didn't go according to plan. It made a perfect touchdown, but unfortunately the radar-controlled automatic pilot made one of those mistakes that such simple-minded machines delight in doing. It spotted the only really unclimbable hill in the neighbourhood, locked its beam onto the summit of it, and settled down there like an eagle descending upon its mountain aerie.

Our badly needed supplies were five hundred feet above our heads, and in a few hours night would be falling. What was to be done?

About fifteen people made the same suggestion at once, and for the next few minutes there was a great scurrying about as we rounded up all the nylon line on the base. Soon there was more than a thousand yards of it coiled in neat loops at Trevor's feet while we all waited expectantly. He tied one end to his arrow, drew the bow, and aimed it experimentally straight toward the stars. The arrow rose a little more than half the height of the cliff; then the weight of the line pulled it back.

'Sorry,' said Trevor. 'I just can't make it. And don't forget – we'd have to send up some kind of grapnel as well, if we want the end to stay up there.'

There was much gloom for the next few minutes, as we watched the coils of line fall slowly back from the sky. The situation was really somewhat absurd. In our ships we had enough energy to carry us a quarter of a million miles from the moon – yet we were baffled by a puny little cliff. If we had time, we could probably find a way up to the top from the other side of the hill, but that would mean travelling several miles. It would be dangerous, and might well be impossible, during the few hours of daylight that were left.

Scientists were never baffled for long, and too many ingenious (sometimes overingenious) minds were working on the problem for it to remain unresolved. But this time it was a little more difficult, and only three people got the answer simultaneously. Trevor thought it over, then said noncommittally, 'Well, it's worth trying.'

The preparations took a little while, and we were all watching anxiously as the rays of the sinking sun crept higher and higher up the sheer cliff looming above us. Even if Trevor could get a line and grapnel up there, I thought to myself, it would not be easy making the ascent while encumbered with a space suit. I have no head for heights, and was glad that several mountaineering enthusiasts had already volunteered for the job.

At last everything was ready. The line had been carefully arranged so that it would lift from the ground with the minimum of hindrance. A light grapnel had been attached to the line a few feet behind the arrow; we hoped that it would catch in the rocks up there and wouldn't let us down – all too literally – when we put our trust in it.

This time, however, Trevor was not using a single arrow. He attached four to the line, at two-hundred-yard intervals. And I shall never forget that incongruous spectacle of the space-suited figure, gleaming in the last rays of the setting sun, as it drew its bow against the sky.

The arrow sped toward the stars, and before it had lifted more than fifty feet Trevor was already fitting the second one to his improvised bow. It raced after its predecessor, carrying the other end of the long loop that was now being hoisted into space. Almost at once the third followed, lifting its section of line – and I swear that the fourth arrow, with its section, was on the way before the first had noticeably slackened its momentum.

Now that there was no question of a single arrow lifting the entire length of line, it was not hard to reach the required altitude. The first two times the grapnel fell back; then it caught firmly somewhere up on the hidden plateau – and the first volunteer began to haul himself up the line. It was true that he weighed only about thirty pounds in this low gravity, but it was still a long way to fall.

He didn't. The stores in the freight rocket started coming down the cliff within the next hour, and everything essential had been lowered before nightfall. I must confess, however, that my satisfaction was considerably abated when one of the engineers proudly showed me the mouth organ he had had sent from Earth. Even then I felt certain that we would all be very tired of that instrument before the long lunar night had ended. . . .

But that, of course, was hardly Trevor's fault. As we walked back to the ship together, through the great pools of shadow that were flowing swiftly over the plain, he made a proposal that, I am sure, has puzzled thousands of people ever since the detailed maps of the first lunar expedition were published.

After all, it does seem a little odd that a flat and lifeless plain, broken by a single small mountain, should now be labelled on all the charts of the moon as Sherwood Forest.

Green Fingers

I am very sorry, now that it's too late, that I never got to know Vladimir Surov. As I remember him, he was a quiet little man who could understand English but couldn't speak it well enough to make conversation. Even to his colleagues, I suspect he was a bit of an enigma. Whenever I went aboard the *Ziolkovski*, he would be sitting in a corner working on his notes or peering through a microscope, a man who clung to his privacy even in the tight and tiny world of a spaceship. The rest of the crew did not seem to mind his aloofness; when they spoke to him, it was clear that they regarded him with tolerant affection, as well as with respect. That was hardly surprising; the work he had done developing plants and trees that could flourish far inside the Arctic Circle had already made him the most famous botanist in Russia.

The fact that the Russian expedition had taken a botanist to the moon had caused a good deal of amusement, though it was really no odder than the fact that there were biologists on both the British and American ships. During the years before the first lunar landing, a good deal of evidence had accumulated hinting that some form of vegetation might exist on the moon, despite its airlessness and lack of water. The president of the USSR Academy of Science was one of the leading proponents of this theory, and being too old to make the trip himself had done the next best thing by sending Surov.

The complete absence of any such vegetation, living or fossil, in the thousand or so square miles explored by our various parties was the first big disappointment the moon had reserved for us. Even those sceptics who were quite certain that no form of life could exist on the moon would have been very glad to have been proved wrong – as of course they were, five years later, when Richards and Shannon made their astonishing discovery inside the great walled plain of Eratosthenes. But *that* revelation still lay in the future; at the time of the first landing, it seemed that Surov had come to the moon in vain.

He did not appear unduly depressed, but kept himself as busy as the rest of the crew studying soil samples and looking after the little hydroponic farm whose pressurised, transparent tubes formed a gleaming network around the *Ziolkovski*. Neither we nor the Americans had gone in for this sort of thing, having calculated that it was better to ship food from Earth than to grow it on the spot – at least until the time came to set up a permanent base. We were right in terms of economics, but wrong in terms of morale. The tiny airtight greenhouses inside which Surov grew his vegetables and dwarf fruit trees were an oasis upon which we often feasted our eyes when we had grown tired of the immense desolation surrounding us.

One of the many disadvantages of being commander was that I seldom had much chance to do any active exploring; I was too busy preparing reports for Earth, checking stores, arranging programmes and duty rosters, conferring with my opposite numbers in the American and Russian ships, and trying – not always successfully – to guess what would go wrong next. As a result, I sometimes did not go outside the base for two or three days at a time, and it was a standing joke that my space suit was a haven for moths.

Perhaps it is because of this that I can remember all my trips outside so vividly; certainly I can recall my only encounter with Surov. It was near noon, with the sun high above the southern mountains and the new Earth a barely visible thread of silver a few degrees away from it. Henderson, our geophysicist, wanted to take some magnetic readings at a series of check points a couple of miles to the east of the base. Everyone else was busy, and I was momentarily on top of my work, so we set off together on foot.

The journey was not long enough to merit taking one of the scooters, especially because the charges in the batteries were getting low. In any case, I always enjoyed walking out in the open on the moon. It was not merely the scenery, which even at its most awe-inspiring one can grow accustomed to after a while. No – what I never tired of was the effortless, slow-motion way in which every step took me bounding over the landscape, giving me the freedom that before the coming of space flight men only knew in dreams.

We had done the job and were halfway home when I noticed a figure moving across the plain about a mile to the south of us – not far, in fact, from the Russian base. I snapped my field glasses down inside my helmet and took a careful look at the other explorer. Even at close range, of course, you can't identify a man in a space suit, but because the suits are always coded by colour and number that makes no practical difference.

'Who is it?' asked Henderson over the short-range radio channel to which we were both tuned.

'Blue suit, Number 3 – that would be Surov. But I don't understand. *He's by himself.*'

It is one of the most fundamental rules of lunar exploration that no one goes anywhere alone on the surface of the moon. So many accidents can happen, which would be trivial if you were with a companion – but fatal if you were by yourself. How would you manage, for example, if your space suit developed a slow leak in the small of the back and you couldn't put on a repair patch? That may sound funny; but it's happened.

'Perhaps his buddy has had an accident and he's going to fetch help,' suggested Henderson. 'Maybe we had better call him.'

I shook my head. Surov was obviously in no hurry. He had been out on a trip of his own, and was making his leisurely way back to the *Ziolkovski*. It was no concern of mine if Commander Krasnin let his people go out on solo trips, though it seemed a deplorable practice. And if Surov was breaking regulations, it was equally no concern of mine to report him.

During the next two months, the men often spotted Surov making his lone way over the landscape, but he always avoided them if they got too near. I made some discreet inquiries, and found that Commander Krasnin had been forced, owing to shortage of men, to relax some of his safety rules. But I couldn't find out what Surov was up to, though I never dreamed that his commander was equally in the dark.

It was with an 'I told you so' feeling that I got Krasnin's emergency call. We had all had men in trouble before and had had to send out help, but this was the first time anyone had been lost and had not replied when his ship had sent out the recall signal. There was a hasty radio conference, a line of action was drawn up, and search parties fanned out from each of the three ships.

Once again I was with Henderson, and it was only common sense for us to backtrack along the route that we had seen Surov following. It was in what we regarded as 'our' territory, quite some distance away from Surov's own ship, and as we scrambled up the low foothills it occurred to me for the first time that the Russian might have been doing something he wanted to keep from his colleagues. What it might be, I could not imagine.

Henderson found him, and yelled for help over his suit radio. But it was much too late; Surov was lying, face down, his deflated suit crumpled around him. He had been kneeling when something had smashed the plastic globe of his helmet; you could see how he had pitched forward and died instantaneously.

When Commander Krasnin reached us, we were still staring at the unbelievable object that Surov had been examining when he died. It was about three feet high, a leathery, greenish oval rooted to the rocks with a widespread network of tendrils. Yes – rooted; for it was a plant. A few yards away were two others, much smaller and apparently dead, since they were blackened and withered.

My first reaction was: 'So there *is* life on the moon, after all!' It was not until Krasnin's voice spoke in my ears that I realised how much more marvellous was the truth.

'Poor Vladimir!' he said. 'We knew he was a genius, yet we laughed at him when he told us of his dream. So he kept his greatest work a secret. He conquered the Arctic with his hybrid wheat, but *that* was only a beginning. He has brought life to the moon – and death as well.'

As I stood there, in that first moment of astonished revelation, it still seemed a miracle. Today, all the world knows the history of 'Surov's cactus', as it was inevitably if quite inaccurately christened, and it has lost much of its wonder. His notes have told the full story, and have described the years of experimentation that finally led him to a plant whose leathery skin would enable it to survive in vacuum, and whose far-ranging, acid-secreting roots would enable it to grow upon rocks where even lichens would be hard put to thrive. And we have seen the realisation of the second stage of Surov's dream, for the cactus which will forever bear his name has already broken up vast areas of the lunar rock and so prepared a way for the more specialised plants that now feed every human being upon the moon.

Krasnin bent down beside the body of his colleague and lifted it effortlessly against the low gravity. He fingered the shattered fragments of the plastic helmet, and shook his head in perplexity.

'What could have happened to him?' he said. 'It almost looks as if the plant did it, but that's ridiculous.'

The green enigma stood there on the no-longer barren plain, tantalising us with its promise and its mystery. Then Henderson said slowly, as if thinking aloud:

'I believe I've got the answer. I've just remembered some of the botany I did at school. If Surov designed this plant for lunar conditions, how would he arrange for it to propagate itself? The seeds would have to be scattered over a very wide area in the hope of finding a few suitable places to grow. There are no birds or animals here to carry them, in the way that happens on Earth. I can only think of one solution – and some of our terrestrial plants have already used it.'

He was interrupted by my yell. Something had hit with a resounding clang against the metal waistband of my suit. It did no damage, but it was so sudden and unexpected that it took me utterly by surprise.

A seed lay at my feet, about the size and shape of a plum stone. A few yards away, we found the one that had shattered Surov's helmet as he bent down. He must have known that the plant was ripe, but in his eagerness to examine it had forgotten what that implied. I have seen a cactus throw its seed a quarter of a mile under the low lunar gravity. Surov had been shot at point-blank range by his own creation.

All that Glitters

This is really Commander Vandenburg's story, but he is too many millions of miles away to tell it. It concerns his geophysicist, Dr Paynter, who was generally believed to have gone to the moon to get away from his wife.

At one time or other, we were all supposed (often by our wives) to have done just that. However, in Paynter's case, there was just enough truth to make it stick.

It was not that he disliked his wife; one could almost say the contrary. He would do anything for her, but unfortunately the things that she wanted him to do cost rather too much. She was a lady of extravagant tastes, and such ladies are advised not to marry scientists – even scientists who go to the moon.

Mrs Paynter's weakness was for jewellery, particularly diamonds. As might be expected, this was a weakness that caused her husband a good deal of worry. Being a conscientious as well as an affectionate husband, he did not merely worry about it – he did something about it. He became one of the world's leading experts on diamonds, from the scientific rather than the commercial point of view, and probably knew more about their composition, origin, and properties than any other man alive. Unfortunately, you may know a lot about diamonds without ever possessing any, and her husband's erudition was not something that Mrs Paynter could wear around her neck when she went to a party.

Geophysics, as I have mentioned, was Dr Paynter's real business; diamonds were merely a side line. He had developed many remarkable surveying instruments which could probe the interior of the Earth by means of electric impulses and magnetic waves, so giving a kind of X-ray picture of the hidden strata far below. It was hardly surprising, therefore, that he was one of the men chosen to pry into the mysterious interior of the moon.

He was quite eager to go, but it seemed to Commander Vandenburg that he was reluctant to leave Earth at this particular moment. A number of men had shown such symptoms; sometimes they were due to fears that could not be eradicated, and an otherwise promising man had to be left behind. In Paynter's case, however, the reluctance was quite impersonal. He was in the middle of a big experiment – something he had been working on all his life – and he didn't want to leave Earth until it was finished. However, the first lunar expedition could not wait for him, so he had to leave his project in the hands of his assistants. He was continually exchanging cryptic radio messages with them, to the great annoyance of the signals section of Space Station Three.

In the wonder of a new world waiting to be explored, Paynter soon forgot his earthly preoccupations. He would dash hither and yon over the lunar landscape on one of the neat little electric scooters the Americans had brought with them, carrying seismographs, magnetometers, gravity meters, and all the other esoteric tools of the geophysicist's trade. He was trying to learn, in a few weeks, what it had taken men hundreds of years to discover about their own planet. It was true that he had only a small sample of the moon's fourteen million square miles of territory to explore, but he intended to make a thorough job of it.

From time to time he continued to get messages from his colleagues back on Earth, as well as brief but affectionate signals from Mrs P. Neither seemed to interest him very much; even when you are not so busy that you hardly have time to sleep, a quarter of a million miles puts most of your personal affairs in a different perspective. I think that on the moon Dr Paynter was really happy for the first time in his life; if so, he was not the only one.

Not far from our base there was a rather fine crater pit, a great blowhole in the lunar surface almost two miles from rim to rim. Though it was fairly close at hand, it was outside the normal area of our joint operations, and we had been on the moon for six weeks before Paynter led a party of three men off in one of the baby tractors to have a look at it. They disappeared from radio range over the edge of the moon, but we weren't worried about that because if they ran into trouble they could always call Earth and get any message relayed back to us.

Paynter and his men were gone forty-eight hours, which is about the maximum for continuous working on the moon, even with booster drugs. At first their little expedition was quite uneventful and therefore quite unexciting; everything went according to plan. They reached the crater, inflated their pressurised igloo and unpacked their stores, took their instrument readings, and then set up a portable drill to get core samples. It was while he was waiting for the drill to bring him up a nice section of the moon that Paynter made his second great discovery. He had made his first about ten hours before, but he didn't know it yet.

Around the lip of the crater, lying where they had been thrown up by the great explosions that had convulsed the lunar landscape three hundred million years before, were immense piles of rock which must have come from many miles down in the moon's interior. Anything he could do with his little drill, thought Paynter, could hardly compare with *this*. Unfortunately, the mountain-sized geological specimens that lay all around him were not neatly arranged in their correct order; they had been scattered over the landscape, much farther than the eye could see, according to the arbitrary violence of the eruptions that had blasted them into space.

Paynter climbed over these immense slag heaps, taking a swing at likely samples with his little hammer. Presently his colleagues heard him yell, and saw him come running back to them carrying what appeared to be a lump of rather poor quality glass. It was some time before he was sufficiently coherent to explain what all the fuss was about – and some time later still before the expedition remembered its real job and got back to work.

Vandenburg watched the returning party as it headed back to the ship. The four men didn't seem as tired as one would have expected, considering the fact that they had been on their feet for two days. Indeed, there was a certain jauntiness about their movements which even the space suits couldn't wholly conceal. You could see that the expedition had been a success. In that case, Paynter would have two causes for congratulation. The priority message that had just come from Earth was very cryptic, but it was clear that Paynter's work there – whatever it was – had finally reached a triumphant conclusion.

Commander Vandenburg almost forgot the message when he saw what Paynter was holding in his hand. He knew what a raw diamond looked like, and this was the second largest that anyone had ever seen. Only the Cullinan, tipping the scales at 3,026 carats, beat it by a slender margin. 'We ought to have expected it,' he heard Paynter babble happily. 'Diamonds are always found associated with volcanic vents. But somehow I never thought the analogy would hold here.'

Vandenburg suddenly remembered the signal, and handed it over to Paynter. He read it quickly, and his jaw dropped. Never in his life, Vandenburg told me, had he seen a man so instantly deflated by a message of congratultion. The signal read: WE'VE DONE IT. TEST 541 WITH MODIFIED PRESSURE CONTAINER COMPLETE SUCCESS. NO PRACTICAL LIMIT TO SIZE. COSTS NEGLIGIBLE.

'What's the matter?' said Vandenburg, when he saw the stricken look on Paynter's face. 'It doesn't seem bad news to me, whatever it means.'

Paynter gulped two or three times like a stranded fish, then stared helplessly at the great crystal that almost filled the palm of his hand. He tossed it into the air, and it floated back in that slow-motion way everything has under lunar gravity.

Finally he found his voice.

'My lab's been working for years,' he said, 'trying to synthesise diamonds. Yesterday this thing was worth a million dollars. Today it's worth a couple of hundred. I'm not sure I'll bother to carry it back to Earth.'

Well, he *did* carry it back; it seemed a pity not to. For about three months, Mrs P. had the finest diamond necklace in the world, worth every bit of a thousand dollars – mostly the cost of cutting and polishing. Then the Paynter Process went into commercial production, and a month later she got her divorce. The grounds were extreme mental cruelty; and I suppose you could say it was justified.

Watch this Space

It was quite a surprise to discover, when I looked it up, that the most famous experiment we carried out while we were on the moon had its beginnings way back in 1955. At that time, high-altitude rocket research had been going for only about ten years, mostly at White Sands, New Mexico. Nineteen fifty-five was the date of one of the most spectacular of those early experiments, one that involved the ejection of sodium onto the upper atmosphere.

On Earth, even on the clearest night, the sky between the stars isn't completely dark. There's a very faint background glow, and part of it is caused by the fluorescence of sodium atoms a hundred miles up. Since it would take the sodium in a good many cubic miles of the upper atmosphere to fill a single matchbox, it seemed to the early investigators that they could make quite a fireworks display if they used a rocket to dump a few pounds of the stuff into the ionosphere.

They were right. The sodium squirted out of a rocket above White Sands early in 1955 produced a great yellow glow in the sky which was visible, like a kind of artificial moonlight, for over an hour, before the atoms dispersed. This experiment wasn't done for fun (though it *was* fun) but for a serious scientific purpose. Instruments trained on this glow were able to gather new knowledge about the upper air – knowledge that went into the stockpile of information without which space flight would never have been possible.

When they got to the moon, the Americans decided that it would be a good idea to repeat the experiment there, on a much larger scale. A few hundred kilograms of sodium fired up from the surface would produce a display that would be visible from Earth, with a good pair of field glasses, as it fluoresced its way up through the lunar atmosphere.

(Some people, by the way, still don't realise that the moon *has* an atmosphere. It's about a million times too thin to be breathable, but if you have the right instruments you can detect it. As a meteor shield, it's first-rate, for though it may be tenuous it's hundreds of miles deep.)

Everyone had been talking about the experiment for days. The sodium bomb had arrived from Earth in the last supply rocket, and a very impressive piece of equipment it looked. Its operation was extremely simple; when ignited, an incendiary charge vaporised the sodium until a high pressure was built up, then a diaphragm burst and the stuff was squirted up into the sky through a specially shaped nozzle. It would be shot off soon after nightfall, and when the cloud of sodium rose out of the moon's shadow into direct sunlight it would start to glow with tremendous brilliance.

Nightfall, on the moon, is one of the most awe-inspiring sights in the whole of nature, made doubly so because as you watch the sun's flaming disc creep so slowly below the mountains you know that it will be fourteen days before you see it again. But it does not bring darkness – at least, not on this side of the moon. There is always the Earth, hanging motionless in the sky, the one heavenly body that neither rises nor sets. The light pouring back from her clouds and seas floods the lunar landscape with a soft, blue-green radiance, so that it is often easier to find your way around at night than under the fierce glare of the sun.

Even those who were not supposed to be on duty had come out to watch the experiment. The sodium bomb had been placed at the middle of the big triangle formed by the three ships, and stood upright with its nozzle pointing at the stars. Dr Anderson, the astronomer of the American team, was testing the firing circuits, but everyone else was at a respectful distance. The bomb looked perfectly capable of living up to its name, though it was really about as dangerous as a soda-water siphon.

All the optical equipment of the three expeditions seemed to have been gathered together to record the performance. Telescopes, spectroscopes, motion-picuure cameras, and everything else one could think of were lined up ready for action. And this, I knew, was nothing compared with the battery that must be zeroed on us from Earth. Every amateur astronomer who could see the moon tonight would be standing by in his back garden, listening to the radio commentary that told him of the progress of the experiment. I glanced up at the gleaming planet that dominated the sky above me; the land areas seemed to be fairly free from cloud, so the folks at home should have a good view. That seemed only fair; after all, they were footing the bill.

There were still fifteen minutes to go. Not for the first time, I wished there was a reliable way of smoking a cigarette inside a space suit without getting the helmet so badly fogged that you couldn't see. Our scientists had solved so many much more difficult problems; it seemed a pity that they couldn't do something about *that* one.

To pass the time – for this was an experiment where I had nothing to do – I switched on my suit radio and listened to Dave Bolton, who was making a very good job of the commentary. Dave was our chief navigator, and a brilliant mathematician. He also had a glib tongue and a picturesque turn of speech, and sometimes his recordings had to be censored by the BBC. There was nothing they could do about this one, however, for it was going out live from the relay stations on Earth.

Dave had finished a brief and lucid explanation of the purpose of the experiment, describing how the cloud of glowing sodium would enable us to analyse the lunar atmosphere as it rose through it at approximately a thousand miles an hour. 'However,' he went on tell the waiting millions on Earth, 'let's make one point clear. Even when the bomb has gone off, you won't see a darn thing for ten minutes – and neither will we. The sodium cloud will be completely invisible while it's rising up through the darkness of the moon's shadow. Then, quite suddenly, it will flash into brilliance as it enters the sun's rays, which are streaming past over our heads right now as we stare up into space. No one is quite sure how bright it will be, but it's a pretty safe guess that you'll be able to see it in any telescope bigger than a two-inch. So it should just be within the range of a good pair of binoculars.'

He had to keep this sort of thing up for another ten minutes, and it was a marvel to me how he managed to do it. Then the great moment came, and Anderson closed the firing circuit. The bomb started to cook, building up pressure inside as the sodium volatilised. After thirty seconds, there was a sudden puff of smoke from the long, slender nozzle pointing up at the sky. And then we had to wait for another ten minutes while the invisible cloud rose to the stars. After all this build-up, I told myself, the result had better be good.

The seconds and minutes ebbed away. Then a sudden yellow glow began to spread across the sky, like a vast and unwavering aurora that became brighter even as we watched. It was as if an artist was sprawling strokes across the stars with a flame-filled brush. And as I stared at those strokes, I suddenly realised that someone had brought off the greatest advertising coup in history. For the strokes formed letters, and the letters formed two words – the name of a certain soft drink too well known to need any further publicity from me.

How had it been done? The first answer was obvious. Someone had placed a suitably cut stencil in the nozzle of the sodium bomb, so that the stream of escaping vapour had shaped itself to the words. Since there was nothing to distort it, the pattern had kept its shape during its invisible ascent to the stars. I had been skywriting on Earth, but this was something on a far larger scale. Whatever I thought of them, I couldn't help admiring the ingenuity of the men who had perpetrated the scheme. The O's and A's had given them a bit of trouble, but the C's and L's were perfect.

After the initial shock, I am glad to say that the scientific programme proceeded as planned. I wish I could remember how Dave Bolton rose to the occasion in his commentary; it must have been a strain even for his quick wits. By this time, of course, half the Earth could see what he was describing. The next morning, every newspaper on the planet carried that famous photo of the crescent moon with the luminous slogan painted across its darkened sector.

The letters were visible, before they finally dispersed into space, for over an hour. By that time the words were almost a thousand miles long, and were beginning to get blurred. But they were still readable until they at last faded from sight in the ultimate vacuum between the planets.

Then the real fireworks began. Commander Vandenburg was absolutely furious, and promptly started to grill all his men. However, it was soon clear that the saboteur – if you could call him that – had been back on Earth. The bomb had been prepared there and shipped ready for immediate use. It did not take long to find, and fire, the engineer who had carried out the substitution. He couldn't have cared less, since his financial needs had been taken care of for a good many years to come.

As for the experiment itself, it was completely successful from the scientific point of view; all the recording instruments worked perfectly as they analysed the light from the unexpectedly shaped cloud. But we never let the Americans live it down, and I am afraid poor Captain Vandenburg was the one who suffered most. Before he came to the moon he was a confirmed teetotaller, and much of his refreshment came from a certain wasp-waisted bottle. But now, as a matter of principle, he can only drink beer – and he hates the stuff.

A Question of Residence

I have already described the – shall we say – jockeying for position before take-off on the first flight to the moon. As it turned out, the American, Russian, and British ships landed just about simultaneously. No one has ever explained, however, why the British ship came back nearly two weeks after the others.

Oh, I know the official story; I ought to, for I helped to concoct it. It is true as far as it goes, but it scarcely goes far enough.

On all counts, the joint expedition had been a triumphant success. There had been only one casualty, and in the manner of his death Vladimir Surov had made himself immortal. We had gathered knowledge that would keep the scientists of Earth busy for generations, and that would revolutionise almost all our ideas concerning the nature of the universe around us. Yes, our five months on the moon had been well spent, and we could go home to such welcomes as few heroes had ever had before.

However, there was still a good deal of tidying up to be done. The instruments that had been scattered all over the lunar landscape were still busily recording, and much of the information they gathered could not be automatically radioed back to Earth. There was no point in all three of the expedition staying on the moon to the last minute; the personnel of one would be sufficient to finish the job. But who would volunteer to be caretaker while the others went back to gain the glory? It was a difficult problem, but one that would have to be solved very soon.

As far as supplies were concerned, we had little to worry about. The automatic freight rockets could keep us provided with air, food, and water for as long as we wished to stay on the moon. We were all in good health, though a little tired. None of the anticipated psychological troubles had cropped up, perhaps because we had all been so busy on tasks of absorbing interest that we had had no time to worry about going crazy. But, of course, we all looked forward to getting back to Earth, and seeing our families again.

The first change of plan was forced upon us by the *Ziolkovski* being put out of commission when the ground beneath one of her landing legs suddenly gave way. The ship managed to stay upright, but the hull was badly twisted and the pressure cabin sprang dozens of leaks. There was much debate about on-the-spot repairs, but it was decided that it would be far too risky for her to take off in this condition. The Russians had no alternative but to thumb lifts back in the *Goddard* and the *Endeavour*; by using the *Ziolkovski*'s unwanted fuel, our ships would be able to manage the extra load. However, the return flight would be extremely cramped and uncomfortable for all concerned because everyone would have to eat and sleep in shifts.

Either the American or the British ship, therefore, would be the first back to Earth. During those final weeks, as the work of the expedition was brought to its close, relations between Commander Vandenburg and myself were somewhat strained. I even wondered if we ought to settle the matter by tossing for it. . . .

Another problem was also engaging my attention – that of crew discipline. Perhaps this is too strong a phrase; I would not like it to be thought that a mutiny ever seemed probable. But all my men were now a little abstracted and liable to be found, if off duty, scribbling furiously in corners. I knew exactly what was going on, for I was involved in it myself. There wasn't a human being on the moon who had not sold exclusive rights to some newspaper or magazine, and we were all haunted by approaching deadlines. The radio-teletype to Earth was in continuous operation, sending tens of thousands of words a day, while ever larger slabs of deathless prose were being dictated over the speech circuits.

It was Professor Williams, our very practical-minded astronomer, who came to me one day with the answer to my main problem.

'Skipper,' he said, balancing himself precariously on the all-too-collapsible table I used as my working desk inside the igloo, 'there's no technical reason, is there, why we should get back to Earth first?'

'No,' I said, 'merely a matter of fame, fortune, and seeing our families again. But I admit those aren't technical reasons. We could stay here another year if Earth kept sending supplies. If you want to suggest that, however, I shall take great pleasure in strangling you.'

'It's not as bad as that. Once the main body has gone back, whichever party is left can follow in two or three weeks at the latest. They'll get a lot of credit, in fact, for self-sacrifice, modesty, and similar virtues.'

'Which will be very poor compensation for being second home.'

'Right – we need something else to make it worthwhile. Some more material reward.'

'Agreed. What do you suggest?'

Williams pointed to the calendar hanging on the wall in front of me, between the two pin-ups we had stolen from the *Goddard*. The length of our stay was indicated by the days that had been crossed off in red ink; a big question mark in two weeks' time showed when the first ship would be heading back to Earth.

'There's your answer,' he said. 'If we go back then, do you realise what will happen? I'll tell you.'

He did, and I kicked myself for not having thought of it first.

The next day, I explained my decision to Vandenburg and Krasnin.

'We'll stay behind and do the mopping up,' I said. 'It's a matter of common sense. The *Goddard*'s a much bigger ship than ours and can carry an extra four people, while we can only manage two more, and even then it will be a squeeze. If you go first, Van, it will save a lot of people from eating their hearts out here for longer than necessary.'

'That's very big of you,' replied Vandenburg. 'I won't hide the fact that we'll be happy to get home. And it's logical, I admit, now that the *Ziolkovski*'s out of action. Still, it means quite a sacrifice on your part, and I don't really like to take advantage of it.'

I gave an expansive wave.

'Think nothing of it,' I answered. 'As long as you boys don't grab all the credit, we'll take our turn. After all, we'll have the show here to ourselves when you've gone back to Earth.'

Krasnin was looking at me with a rather calculating expression, and I found it singularly difficult to return his gaze.

'I hate to sound cynical,' he said, 'but I've learned to be a little suspicious when people start doing big favours without very good reasons. And frankly, I don't think the reason you've given is good enough. You wouldn't have anything else up your sleeve, would you?'

'Oh, very well,' I sighed. 'I'd hoped to get a *little* credit, but I see it's no use trying to convince anyone of the purity of my motives. I've got a reason, and you might as well know it. But please don't spread it around; I'd hate the folks back on Earth to be disillusioned. They still think of us as noble and heroic seekers after knowledge; let's keep it that way, for all our sakes.'

Then I pulled out the calendar, and explained to Vandenburg and Krasnin what Williams had already explained to me. They listened with scepticism, then with growing sympathy.

'I had no idea it was *that* bad,' said Vandenburg at last.

'Americans never have,' I said sadly. 'Anyway, that's the way it's been for half a century, and it doesn't seem to get any better. So you agree with my suggestion?'

'Of course. It suits us fine, anyhow. Until the next expedition's ready, the moon's all yours.'

I remembered that phrase, two weeks later, as I watched the *Goddard* blast up into the sky toward the distant, beckoning Earth. It was lonely, then, when the Americans and all but two of the Russians had gone. We envied them the reception they got, and watched jealously on the TV screens their triumphant processions through Moscow and New York. Then we went back to work, and bided our time. Whenever we felt depressed, we would do little sums on bits of paper and would be instantly restored to cheerfulness.

The red crosses marched across the calendar as the short terrestrial days went by – days that seemed to have very little connection with the slow cycle of lunar time. At last we were ready; all the instrument readings were taken, all the specimens and samples safely packed away aboard the ship. The motors roared into life, giving us for a moment the weight we would feel again when we were back in Earth's gravity. Below us the rugged lunar landscape, which we had grown to know so well, fell swiftly away; within seconds we could see no sign at all of the buildings and instruments we had so laboriously erected and which future explorers would one day use.

The homeward voyage had begun. We returned to Earth in uneventful discomfort, joined the already half-dismantled *Goddard* beside Space Station Three, and were quickly ferried down to the world we had left seven months before.

Seven months: that, as Williams had pointed out, was the all-important figure. We had been on the moon for more than half a financial year – and for all of us, it had been the most profitable year of our lives.

Sooner or later, I suppose, this interplanetary loop-hole will be plugged; the Department of Inland Revenue is still fighting a gallant rear-guard action, but we seem neatly covered under Section 57, paragraph 8 of the Capital Gains Act of 1972. We wrote our books and articles on the moon – and until there's a lunar government to impose income tax, we're hanging on to every penny.

And if the ruling finally goes against us – well, there's always Mars. . . .

The Pacifist

First published in *Fantastic Universe*, October 1956
Collected in *Tales from the White Hart*

John Christopher and John Wyndham flit briefly across the stage as Harry
Purvis spins another yarn at the White Hart, this time telling the story of a
very early, ingenious computer virus . . .

I got to the 'White Hart' late that evening, and when I arrived everyone
was crowded into the corner under the dartboard. All except Drew, that is:
he had not deserted his post, but was sitting behind the bar reading the
collected T. S. Eliot. He broke off from *The Confidential Clerk* long enough to
hand me a beer and to tell me what was going on.

'Eric's brought in some kind of games machine – it's beaten everybody so
far. Sam's trying his luck with it now.'

At that moment, a roar of laughter announced that Sam had been no
luckier than the rest, and I pushed my way through the crowd to see what
was happening.

On the table lay a flat metal box the size of a checkerboard, and divided
into squares in a similar way. At the corner of each square was a two-way
switch and a little neon lamp: the whole affair was plugged into the light
socket (thus plunging the dartboard into darkness) and Eric Rodgers was
looking round for a new victim.

'What does the thing do?' I asked.

'It's a modification of noughts and crosses – what the Americans call
ticktacktoe. Shannon showed it to me when I was over at Bell Labs. What
you have to do is to complete a path from one side of the board to the other
– call it north to south – by turning these switches. Imagine the thing forms
a grid of streets, if you like, and these neons are the traffic lights. You and the
machine take turns making moves. The machine tries to block your path by
building one of its own in the east–west direction – the little neons light up
to tell you which way it wants to make a move. Neither track need be a
straight line: you can zigzag as much as you like. All that matters is that the
path must be continuous, and the one to get across the board first wins.'

'Meaning the machine, I suppose?'

'Well, it's never been beaten yet.'

'Can't you force a draw, by blocking the machine's path, so that at least you don't lose?'

'That's what we're trying: like to have a go?'

Two minutes later I joined the other unsuccessful contestants. The machine had dodged all my barriers and established its own track from east to west. I wasn't convinced that it was unbeatable, but the game was clearly a good deal more complicated than it looked.

Eric glanced round his audience when I had retired. No one else seemed in a hurry to move forward.

'Ha!' he said. 'The very man. What about you, Purvis? You've not had a shot yet.'

Harry Purvis was standing at the back of the crowd, with a faraway look in his eye. He jolted back to earth as Eric addressed him, but didn't answer the question directly.

'Fascinating things, these electronic computers,' he mused. 'I suppose I shouldn't tell you this, but your gadget reminds me of what happened to Project Clausewitz. A curious story, and one very expensive to the American taxpayer.'

'Look,' said John Wyndham anxiously. 'Before you start, be a good sport and let us get our glasses filled. Drew!'

This important matter having been attended to, we gathered round Harry. Only Charlie Willis still remained with the machine, hopefully trying his luck.

'As you all know,' began Harry, 'Science with a capital S is a big thing in the military world these days. The weapons side – rockets, atom bombs and so on – is only part of it, though that's all the public knows about. Much more fascinating, in my opinion, is the operational-research angle. You might say that's concerned with brains rather than brute force. I once heard it defined as how to win wars without actually fighting, and that's not a bad description.

'Now you all know about the big electronic computers that cropped up like mushrooms in the 1950s. Most of them were built to deal with mathematical problems, but when you think about it you'll realise that war itself is a mathematical problem. It's such a complicated one that human brains can't handle it – there are far too many variables. Even the greatest strategist cannot see the picture as a whole: the Hitlers and Napoleons always make a mistake in the end.

'But a machine – that would be a different matter. A number of bright people realised this after the end of the war. The techniques that had been worked out in the building of ENLAC and the other big computers could revolutionise strategy.

'Hence Project Clausewitz. Don't ask me how I got to know about it, or press me for too many details. All that matters is that a good many megabucks worth of electronic equipment, and some of the best scientific brains in the United States, went into a certain cavern in the Kentucky hills. They're still there, but things haven't turned out exactly as they expected.

'Now I don't know what experience you have of high-ranking military officers, but there's one type you'll all come across in fiction. That's the pompous, conservative, stick-in-the-mud careerist who's got to the top by sheer pressure from beneath, who does everything by rules and regulations and regards civilians as, at the best, unfriendly neutrals. I'll let you into a secret: he actually exists. He's not very common nowadays, but he's still around and sometimes it's not possible to find a safe job for him. When that happens, he's worth his weight in plutonium to the Other Side.

'Such a character, it seems, was General Smith. No, of *course* that wasn't his real name! His father was a senator, and although lots of people in the Pentagon had tried hard enough, the old man's influence had prevented the General from being put in charge of something harmless, like the coast defence of Wyoming. Instead, by miraculous misfortune, he had been made the officer responsible for Project Clausewitz.

'Of course, he was only concerned with the administrative, not the scientific aspects of the work. All might yet have been well had the General been content to let the scientists get on with their work while he concentrated on saluting smartness, the coefficient of reflection of barrack floors, and similar matters of military importance. Unfortunately, he didn't.

'The General had led a sheltered existence. He had, if I may borrow from Wilde (everybody else does), been a man of peace, except in his domestic life. He had never met scientists before, and the shock was considerable. So perhaps it is not fair to blame him for everything that happened.

'It was a considerable time before he realised the aims and objects of Project Clausewitz, and when he did he was quite disturbed. This may have made him feel even less friendly towards his scientific staff, for despite anything I may have said the General was not entirely a fool. He was intelligent enough to understand that, if the Project succeeded, there might be more ex-generals around than even the combined boards of management of American industry could comfortably absorb.

'But let's leave the General for a minute and have a look at the scientists. There were about fifty of them, as well as a couple of hundred technicians. They'd all been carefully screened by the F.B.I., so probably not more than half a dozen were active members of the Communist party. Though there was a lot of talk of sabotage later, for once in a while the comrades were completely innocent. Besides, what happened certainly wasn't sabotage in any generally accepted meaning of the word. . . .

'The man who had really designed the computer was a quiet little mathematical genius who had been swept out of college into the Kentucky hills and the world of Security and Priorities before he'd really realised what had happened. He wasn't called Dr Milquetoast, but he should have been and that's what I'll christen him.

'To complete our cast of characters, I'd better say something about Karl. At this stage in the business, Karl was only half-built. Like all big computers, most of him consisted of vast banks of memory units which could receive and store information until it was needed. The creative part of Karl's brain – the analysers and integrators – took this information and operated on it, to produce answers to the questions he was asked. Given all the relevant facts, Karl would produce the right answers. The problem, of course, was to see that Karl *did* have all the facts – he couldn't be expected to get the right results from inaccurate or insufficient information.

'It was Dr Milquetoast's responsibility to design Karl's brain. Yes, I know that's a crudely anthropomorphic way of looking at it, but no one can deny that these big computers have personalities. It's hard to put it more accurately without getting technical, so I'll simply say that little Milquetoast had to create the extremely complex circuits that enabled Karl to think in the way he was supposed to do.

'So here are our three protagonists – General Smith, pining for the days of Custer; Dr Milquetoast, lost in the fascinating scientific intricacies of his job; and Karl, fifty tons of electronic gear, not yet animated by the currents that would soon be coursing through him.

'Soon – but not soon enough for General Smith. Let's not be too hard on the General: someone had probably put the pressure on him, when it became obvious that the Project was falling behind schedule. He called Dr Milquetoast into his office.

'The interview lasted more than thirty minutes, and the Doctor said less than thirty words. Most of the time the General was making pointed remarks about production times, deadlines and bottlenecks. He seemed to be under the impression that building Karl differed in no important particular from the assembly of the current model Ford: it was just a question of putting the bits together. Dr Milquetoast was not the sort of man to explain the error, even if the General had given him the opportunity. He left, smarting under a considerable sense of injustice.

'A week later, it was obvious that the creation of Karl was falling still further behind schedule. Milquetoast was doing his best, and there was no one who could do better. Problems of a complexity totally beyond the General's comprehension had to be met and mastered. They *were* mastered, but it took time, and time was in short supply.

'At his first interview, the General had tried to be as nice as he could, and had succeeded in being merely rude. This time, he tried to be rude, with results that I leave to your imagination. He practically insinuated that Milquetoast and his colleagues, by falling behind their deadlines, were guilty of un-American inactivity.

'From this moment onwards, two things started to happen. Relations between the Army and the scientists grew steadily worse; and Dr Milquetoast, for the first time, began to give serious thought to the wider implications of his work. He had always been too busy, too engaged upon the immediate problems of his task, to consider his social responsibilities. He was still too busy now, but that didn't stop him pausing for reflection. "Here am I," he told himself, 'one of the best pure mathematicians in the world –

and what am I doing? What's happened to my thesis on Diophantine equations? When am I going to have another smack at the prime-number theorem? In short, when am I going to do some *real* work again?"

'He could have resigned, but that didn't occur to him. In any case, far down beneath that mild and diffident exterior was a stubborn streak. Dr Milquetoast continued to work, even more energetically than before. The construction of Karl proceeded slowly but steadily: the final connections in his myriad-celled brain were soldered; the thousands of circuits were checked and tested by the mechanics.

'And one circuit, indistinguishably interwoven among its multitude of companions and leading to a set of memory cells apparently identical with all the others, was tested by Dr Milquetoast alone, for no one else knew that it existed.

'The great day came. To Kentucky, by devious routes, came very important personages. A whole constellation of multi-starred generals arrived from the Pentagon. Even the Navy had been invited.

'Proudly, General Smith led the visitors from cavern to cavern, from memory banks to selector networks to matrix analysers to input tables – and finally to the rows of electric typewriters on which Karl would print the results of his deliberations. The General knew his way around quite well: at least, he got most of the names right. He even managed to give the impression, to those who knew no better, that he was largely responsible for Karl.

'"Now," said the General cheerfully. "Let's give him some work to do. Anyone like to set him a few sums?"

'At the word "sums" the mathematicians winced, but the General was unaware of his *faux pas*. The assembled brass thought for a while: then someone said daringly, "What's nine multiplied by itself twenty times?"

'One of the technicians, with an audible sniff, punched a few keys. There was a rattle of gunfire from an electric typewriter, and before anyone could blink twice the answer had appeared – all twenty digits of it.'

(I've looked it up since: for anyone who wants to know, it's:

$$12157665459056928801$$

But let's get back to Harry and his tale.)

'For the next fifteen minutes Karl was bombarded with similar trivialities. The visitors were impressed, though there was no reason to suppose that they'd have spotted it if all the answers had been completely wrong.

'The General gave a modest cough. Simple arithmetic was as far as he could go, and Karl had barely begun to warm up. "I'll now hand you over," he said, "to Captain Winkler."

'Captain Winkler was an intense young Harvard graduate whom the General distrusted, rightly suspecting him to be more a scientist than a military man. But he was the only officer who really understood what Karl was supposed to do, or could explain exactly how he set about doing it. He looked, the General thought grumpily, like a damned schoolmaster as he started to lecture the visitors.

'The tactical problem that had been set up was a complicated one, but the answer was already known to everybody except Karl. It was a battle that had been fought and finished almost a century before, and when Captain Winkler concluded his introduction, a general from Boston whispered to his aide, "I'll bet some damn Southerner has fixed it so that Lee wins this time." Everyone had to admit, however, that the problem was an excellent way of testing Karl's capabilities.

'The punched tapes disappeared into the capacious memory units: patterns of lights flickered and flashed across the registers; mysterious things happened in all directions.

'"This problem," said Captain Winkler primly, "will take about five minutes to evaluate."

'As if in deliberate contradiction, one of the typewriters promptly started to chatter. A strip of paper shot out of the feed, and Captain Winkler, looking rather puzzled at Karl's unexpected alacrity, read the message. His lower jaw immediately dropped six inches, and he stood staring at the paper as if unable to believe his eyes.

'"What is it, man?" barked the General.

'Captain Winkler swallowed hard, but appeared to have lost the power of speech. With a snort of impatience, the General snatched the paper from him. Then it was his turn to stand paralysed, but unlike his subordinate he also turned a most beautiful red. For a moment he looked like some tropical fish strangling out of water: then, not without a slight scuffle, the enigmatic message was captured by the five-star general who out-ranked everybody in the room.

'His reaction was totally different. He promptly doubled up with laughter.

'The minor officers were left in a state of infuriating suspense for quite ten minutes. But finally the news filtered down through colonels to captains to lieutenants, until at last there wasn't a G.I. in the establishment who did not know the wonderful news.

'Karl had told General Smith that he was a pompous baboon. That was all.

'Even though everybody agreed with Karl, the matter could hardly be allowed to rest there. Something, obviously, had gone wrong. Something – or someone – had diverted Karl's attention from the Battle of Gettysburg.

'"Where," roared General Smith, finally recovering his voice, "is Dr Milquetoast?"

'He was no longer present. He had slipped quietly out of the room, having witnessed his great moment. Retribution would come later, of course, but it was worth it.

'The frantic technicians cleared the circuits and started running tests. They gave Karl an elaborate series of multiplications and divisions to perform – the computer's equivalent of "The quick brown fox jumps over the lazy dog." Everything seemed to be functioning perfectly. So they put in a very simple tactical problem, which a lieutenant, j.g. could solve in his sleep.

'Said Karl: "Go jump in a lake, General."

'It was then that General Smith realised that he was confronted with something outside the scope of Standard Operating Procedure. He was faced with mechanical mutiny, no less.

'It took several hours of tests to discover exactly what had happened. Somewhere tucked away in Karl's capacious memory units was a superb collection of insults, lovingly assembled by Dr Milquetoast. He had punched on tape, or recorded in patterns of electrical impulses, everything he would like to have said to the General himself. But that was not all he had done: that would have been too easy, not worthy of his genius. He had also installed what could only be called a censor circuit – he had given Karl the power of discrimination. Before solving it, Karl examined every problem fed to him. If it was concerned with pure mathematics, he co-operated and dealt with it properly. But if it was a military problem – out came one of the insults. After twenty minutes, he had not repeated himself once, and the WACs had already had to be sent out of the room.

'It must be confessed that after a while the technicians were almost as interested in discovering what indignity Karl would next heap upon General Smith as they were in finding the fault in the circuits. He had begun with mere insults and surprising genealogical surmises, but had swiftly passed on to detailed instructions the mildest of which would have been highly prejudicial to the General's dignity, while the more imaginative would have seriously imperiled his physical integrity. The fact that all these messages, as they emerged from the typewriters, were immediately classified TOP SECRET was small consolation to the recipient. He knew with a glum certainty that this would be the worst kept secret of the Cold War, and that it was time he looked round for a civilian occupation.

'And there, gentlemen,' concluded Purvis, 'the situation remains. The engineers are still trying to unravel the circuits that Dr Milquetoast installed, and no doubt it's only a matter of time before they succeed. But meanwhile Karl remains an unyielding pacifist. He's perfectly happy playing with the theory of numbers, computing tables of powers, and handling arithmetical problems generally. Do you remember the famous toast. "Here's to pure mathematics – may it never be of any use to anybody"? Karl would have seconded that. . . .

'As soon as anyone attempts to slip a fast one across him, he goes on strike. And because he's got such a wonderful memory, he can't be fooled. He has half the great battles of the world stored up in his circuits, and can recognise at once any variations on them. Though attempts were made to disguise tactical exercises as problems in mathematics, he could spot the subterfuge right away. And out would come another billet-doux for the General.

'As for Dr Milquetoast, no one could do much about him because he promptly had a nervous breakdown. It was suspiciously well timed, but he could certainly claim to have earned it. When last heard of he was teaching matrix algebra at a theological college in Denver. He swears he's forgotten everything that had ever happened while he was working on Karl. Maybe he was even telling the truth. . . .'

There was a sudden shout from the back of the room.

'I've won!' cried Charles Willis. 'Come and see!'

We all crowded under the dartboard. It seemed true enough. Charlie had established a zigzag but continuous track from one side of the checkerboard to the other, despite the obstacles the machine had tried to put in his way.

'Show us how you did it,' said Eric Rodgers.

Charlie looked embarrassed.

'I've forgotten,' he said. 'I didn't make a note of all the moves.'

A sarcastic voice broke in from the background.

'But *I* did,' said John Christopher. 'You were cheating – you made two moves at once.'

After that, I'm sorry to say, there was some disorder, and Drew had to threaten violence before peace was restored. I don't know who really won the squabble, and I don't think it matters. For I'm inclined to agree with what Purvis remarked as he picked up the robot checkerboard and examined its wiring.

'You see,' he said, 'this little gadget is only a simple-minded cousin of Karl's – and look what it's done already. All these machines are beginning to make us look fools. Before long they'll start to disobey us without any Milquetoast interfering with their circuits. And then they'll start ordering us about – they're logical, after all, and won't stand any nonsense.'

He sighed. 'When that happens, there won't be a thing we can do about it. We'll just have to say to the dinosaurs: "Move over a bit – here comes Homo sap!" And the transister shall inherit the earth.'

There was no time for further pessimistic philosophy, for the door opened and Police Constable Wilkins stuck his head in. 'Where's the owner of CGC 571?' he asked testily. 'Oh – it's *you*, Mr Purvis. Your rear light's out.'

Harry looked at me sadly, then shrugged his shoulders in resignation. 'You see,' he said, 'it's started already.' And he went out into the night.

The Reluctant Orchid

First published in *Satellite*, December 1956
Collected in *Tales from the White Hart*

One might expect a story about a carnivorous orchid to have only one possible ending, but when the storyteller is Harry Purvis, and the venue is the White Hart, nothing is quite as it seems, and thus it proves with this story, which first saw the light of day in *Satellite*.

Though few people in the 'White Hart' will concede that any of Harry Purvis's stories are actually *true* everyone agrees that some are much more probable than others. And on any scale of probability, the affair of the Reluctant Orchid must rate very low indeed.

I don't remember what ingenious gambit Harry used to launch this narrative: maybe some orchid fancier brought his latest monstrosity into the bar, and that set him off. No matter. I do remember the story, and after all that's what counts.

The adventure did not, this time, concern any of Harry's numerous relatives, and he avoided explaining just how he managed to know so many of the sordid details. The hero – if you can call him that – of this hothouse epic was an inoffensive little clerk named Hercules Keating. And if you think *that* is the most unlikely part of the story, just stick round a while.

Hercules is not the sort of name you can carry off lightly at the best of times, and when you are four foot nine and look as if you'd have to take a physical-culture course before you can even become a ninety-seven-pound weakling, it is a positive embarrassment. Perhaps it helped to explain why Hercules had very little social life, and all his real friends grew in pots in a humid conservatory at the bottom of his garden. His needs were simple and he spent very little money on himself; consequently his collection of orchids and cacti was really rather remarkable. Indeed, he had a wide reputation among the fraternity of cactophiles, and often received from remote corners of the globe parcels smelling of mould and tropical jungles.

Hercules had only one living relative, and it would have been hard to find a greater contrast than Aunt Henrietta. She was a massive six-footer, usually wore a rather loud line in Harris tweeds, drove a Jaguar with reckless skill, and chain-smoked cigars. Her parents had set their hearts on a boy, and had never been able to decide whether or not their wish had been granted. Henrietta earned a living, and quite a good one, breeding dogs of various shapes and sizes. She was seldom without a couple of her latest models, and they were not the type of portable canine which ladies like to carry in their handbags. The Keating Kennels specialised in great Danes, Alsatians, and Saint Bernards. . . .

Henrietta, rightly despising men as the weaker sex, had never married. However, for some reason she took an avuncular (yes, that is definitely the right word) interest in Hercules, and called to see him almost every weekend. It was a curious kind of relationship: probably Henrietta found that Hercules bolstered up her feelings of superiority. If he was a good example of the male sex, then they were certainly a pretty sorry lot. Yet, if this was Henrietta's motivation, she was unconscious of it and seemed genuinely fond of her nephew. She was patronising, but never unkind.

As might be expected, her attentions did not exactly help Hercules' own well-developed inferiority complex. At first he had tolerated his aunt; then he came to dread her regular visits, her booming voice and her bone-crushing handshake; and at last he grew to hate her. Eventually, indeed, his hate was the dominant emotion of his life, exceeding even his love for his orchids. But he was careful not to show it, realising that if Aunt Henrietta discovered how he felt about her, she would probably break him in two and throw the pieces to her wolf pack.

There was no way, then, in which Hercules could express his pent-up feelings. He had to be polite to Aunt Henrietta even when he felt like murder. And he often did feel like murder, though he knew that there was nothing he would ever do about it. Until one day . . .

According to the dealer, the orchid came from 'somewhere in the Amazon region' – a rather vague postal address. When Hercules first saw it, it was not a very prepossessing sight, even to anyone who loved orchids as much as he did. A shapeless root, about the size of a man's fist – that was all. It was redolent of decay, and there was the faintest hint of a rank, carrion smell. Hercules was not even sure that it was viable, and told the dealer as much. Perhaps that enabled him to purchase it for a trifling sum, and he carried it home without much enthusiasm.

It showed no signs of life for the first month, but that did not worry Hercules. Then, one day, a tiny green shoot appeared and started to creep up to the light. After that, progress was rapid. Soon there was a thick, fleshy stem as big as a man's forearm, and coloured a positively virulent green. Near the top of the stem a serious of curious bulges circled the plant: otherwise it was completely featureless. Hercules was now quite excited: he was sure that some entirely new species had swum into his ken.

The rate of growth was now really fantastic: soon the plant was taller than Hercules, not that that was saying a great deal. Moreover, the bulges seemed to be developing, and it looked as if at any moment the orchid would burst into bloom. Hercules waited anxiously, knowing how short-lived some flowers can be, and spent as much time as he possibly could in the hothouse. Despite all his watchfulness, the transformation occurred one night while he was asleep.

In the morning, the orchid was fringed by a series of eight dangling tendrils, almost reaching to the ground. They must have developed inside the plant and emerged with – for the vegetable world – explosive speed. Hercules stared at the phenomenon in amazement, and went very thoughtfully to work.

That evening, as he watered the plant and checked its soil, he noticed a still more peculiar fact. The tendrils were thickening, and they were not completely motionless. They had a slight but unmistakable tendency to vibrate, as if possessing a life of their own. Even Hercules, for all his interest and enthusiasm, found this more than a little disturbing.

A few days later, there was no doubt about it at all. When he approached the orchid, the tendrils swayed towards him in an unpleasantly suggestive fashion. The impression of hunger was so strong that Hercules began to feel very uncomfortable indeed, and something started to nag at the back of his mind. It was quite a while before he could recall what it was: then he said to himself, 'Of course! How stupid of me!' and went along to the local library. Here he spent a most interesting half hour rereading a little piece by one H. G. Wells entitled 'The Flowering of the Strange Orchid'.

'My goodness!' thought Hercules, when he had finished the tale. As yet there had been no stupefying odour which might overpower the plant's intended victim, but otherwise the characteristics were all too similar. Hercules went home in a very unsettled mood indeed.

He opened the conservatory door and stood looking along the avenue of greenery towards his prize specimen. He judged the length of the tendrils – already he found himself calling them tentacles – with great care and walked to within what appeared a safe distance. The plant certainly had an impression of alertness and menace far more appropriate to the animal than the vegetable kingdom. Hercules remembered the unfortunate history of Doctor Frankenstein, and was not amused.

But, really, this was ridiculous! Such things didn't happen in real life. Well, there was one way to put matters to the test. . . .

Hercules went into the house and came back a few minutes later with a broomstick, to the end of which he had attached a piece of raw meat. Feeling a considerable fool, he advanced towards the orchid as a lion tamer might approach one of his charges at mealtime.

For a moment, nothing happened. Then two of the tendrils developed an agitated twitch. They began to sway back and forth, as if the plant was making up its mind. Abruptly, they whipped out with such speed that they practically vanished from view. They wrapped themselves round the meat, and Hercules felt a powerful tug at the end of his broomstick. Then the meat was gone: the orchid was clutching it, if one may mix metaphors slightly, to its bosom.

'Jumping Jehosophat!' yelled Hercules. It was very seldom indeed that he used such strong language.

The orchid showed no further signs of life for twenty-four hours. It was waiting for the meat to become high, and it was also developing its digestive system. By the next day, a network of what looked like short roots had covered the still visible chunk of meat. By nightfall, the meat was gone.

The plant had tasted blood.

Hercules' emotions as he watched over his prize were curiously mixed. There were times when it almost gave him nightmares, and he foresaw a whole range of horrid possibilities. The orchid was now extremely strong, and if he got within its clutches he would be done for. But, of course, there was not the slightest danger of that. He had arranged a system of pipes so that it could be watered from a safe distance, and its less orthodox food he simply tossed within range of its tentacles. It was now eating a pound of raw meat a day, and he had an uncomfortable feeling that it could cope with much larger quantities if given the opportunity.

Hercules' natural qualms were, on the whole, outweighed by his feeling of triumph that such a botanical marvel had fallen into his hands. Whenever he chose, he could become the most famous orchid-grower in the world. It was typical of his somewhat restricted viewpoint that it never occurred to him that other people besides orchid fanciers might be interested in his pet.

The creature was now about six feet tall, and apparently still growing – though much more slowly than it had been. All the other plants had been moved from its end of the conservatory, not so much because Hercules feared that it might be cannibalistic as to enable him to tend them without danger. He had stretched a rope across the central aisle so that there was no risk of his accidentally walking within range of those eight dangling arms.

It was obvious that the orchid had a highly developed nervous system, and something very nearly approaching intelligence. It knew when it was going to be fed, and exhibited unmistakable signs of pleasure. Most fantastic of all – though Hercules was still not sure about this – it seemed capable of producing sounds. There were times, just before a meal, when he fancied he could hear an incredibly high-pitched whistle, skirting the edge of audibility. A newborn bat might have had such a voice: he wondered what purpose it served. Did the orchid somehow lure its prey into its clutches by sound? If so, he did not think the technique would work on him.

While Hercules was making these interesting discoveries, he continued to be fussed over by Aunt Henrietta and assaulted by her hounds, which were never as house-trained as she claimed them to be. She would usually roar up the street on a Sunday afternoon with one dog in the seat beside her and another occupying most of the baggage compartment. Then she would bound up the steps two at a time, nearly deafen Hercules with her greeting, half paralyse him with her handshake, and blow cigar smoke in his face. There had been a time when he was terrified that she would kiss him, but he had long since realised that such effeminate behaviour was foreign to her nature.

Aunt Henrietta looked upon Hercules' orchids with some scorn. Spending one's spare time in a hothouse was, she considered a very effete recreation. When *she* wanted to let off steam, she went big-game hunting in Kenya. This did nothing to endear her to Hercules, who hated blood sports. But despite his mounting dislike for his overpowering aunt, every Sunday afternoon he dutifully prepared tea for her and they had a tête-à-tête together which, on the surface at least, seemed perfectly friendly. Henrietta never guessed that as he poured the tea Hercules often wished it was poisoned: she was, far down beneath her extensive fortifications, a fundamentally goodhearted person and the knowledge would have upset her deeply.

Hercules did not mention his vegetable octopus to Aunt Henrietta. He had occasionally shown her his most interesting specimens, but this was something he was keeping to himself. Perhaps, even before he had fully formulated his diabolical plan, his subconscious was already preparing the ground. . . .

It was late one Sunday evening, when the roar of the Jaguar had died away into the night and Hercules was restoring his shattered nerves in the conservatory, that the idea first came fully fledged into his mind. He was staring at the orchid, noting how the tendrils were now as thick around as a man's thumb, when a most pleasing fantasy suddenly flashed before his eyes. He pictured Aunt Henrietta struggling helplessly in the grip of the monster, unable to escape from its carnivorous clutches. Why, it would be the perfect crime. The distraught nephew would arrive on the scene too late to be of assistance, and when the police answered his frantic call they would see at a glance that the whole affair was a deplorable accident. True, there would be an inquest, but the coroner's censure would be toned down in view of Hercules' obvious grief. . . .

The more he thought of the idea, the more he liked it. He could see no flaws, as long as the orchid co-operated. That, clearly, would be the greatest problem. He would have to plan a course of training for the creature. It already looked sufficiently diabolical; he must give it a disposition to suit its appearance.

Considering that he had no prior experience in such matters, and that there were no authorites he could consult, Hercules proceeded along very sound and businesslike lines. He would use a fishing rod to dangle pieces of meat just outside the orchid's range, until the creature lashed its tentacles in a frenzy. At such times its high-pitched squeak was clearly audible, and Hercules wondered how it managed to produce the sound. He also wondered what its organs of perception were, but this was yet another mystery that could not be solved without close examination. Perhaps Aunt Henrietta, if all went well, would have a brief opportunity of discovering these interesting facts – though she would probably be too busy to report them for the benefit of posterity.

There was no doubt that the beast was quite powerful enough to deal with its intended victim. It had once wrenched a broomstick out of Hercules' grip, and although that in itself proved very little, the sickening 'crack' of the wood a moment later brought a smile of satisfaction to its trainer's thin lips. He began to be much more pleasant and attentive to his aunt. In every respect, indeed, he was the model nephew.

When Hercules considered that his picador tactics had brought the orchid into the right frame of mind, he wondered if he should test it with live bait. This was a problem that worried him for some weeks, during which time he would look speculatively at every dog or cat he passed in the street, but he finally abandoned the idea, for a rather peculiar reason. He was simply too kindhearted to put it into practice. Aunt Henrietta would have to be the first victim.

He starved the orchid for two weeks before he put his plan into action. This was as long as he dared risk – he did not wish to weaken the beast – merely to whet its appetite that the outcome of the encounter might be more certain. And so, when he had carried the teacups back into the kitchen and was sitting upwind of Aunt Henrietta's cigar, he said casually: I've got something I'd like to show you, Auntie. I've been keeping it as a surprise. It'll tickle you to death.'

That, he thought, was not a completely accurate description, but it gave the general idea.

Auntie took the cigar out of her mouth and looked at Hercules with frank surprise.

'Well!' she boomed. 'Wonders will never cease! What *have* you been up to, you rascal!' She slapped him playfuly on the back and shot all the air out of his lungs.

'You'll never believe it,' gritted Hercules, when he had recovered his breath. 'It's in the conservatory.'

'Eh?' said Auntie, obviously puzzled.

'Yes – come along and have a look. It's going to create a real sensation.'

Auntie gave a snort that might have indicated disbelief, but followed Hercules without further question. The two Alsatians now busily chewing up the carpet looked at her anxiously and half rose to their feet, but she waved them away.

'All right, boys,' she ordered gruffly. 'I'll be back in a minute.' Hercules thought this unlikely.

It was a dark evening, and the lights in the conservatory were off. As they entered, Auntie snorted, 'Gad, Hercules – the place smells like a slaughterhouse. Haven't met such a stink since I shot that elephant in Bulawayo and we couldn't find it for a week.'

'Sorry, Auntie,' apologised Hercules, propelling her forward through the gloom. 'It's a new fertiliser I'm using. It produces the most stunning results. Go on – another couple of yards. I want this to be a *real* surprise.'

'I hope this isn't a joke,' said Auntie suspiciously, as she stomped forward.

'I can promise you it's no joke,' replied Hercules, standing with his hand on the light switch. He could just see the looming bulk of the orchid: Auntie was now within ten feet of it. He waited until she was well inside the danger zone, and threw the switch.

There was a frozen moment while the scene was transfixed with light.

Then Aunt Henrietta ground to a halt and stood, arms akimbo, in front of the giant orchid. For a moment Hercules was afraid she would retreat before the plant could get into action: then he saw that she was calmly scrutinising it, unable to make up her mind what the devil it was.

It was a full five seconds before the orchid moved. Then the dangling tentacles flashed into action – but not in the way that Hercules had expected. The plant clutched them tightly, protectively, *around itself* – and at the same time it gave a high-pitched scream of pure terror. In a moment of sickening disillusionment, Hercules realised the awful truth.

His orchid was an utter coward. It might be able to cope with the wild life of the Amazon jungle, but coming suddenly upon Aunt Henrietta had completely broken its nerve.

As for its proposed victim, she stood watching the creature with an astonishment which swiftly changed to another emotion. She spun around on her heels and pointed an accusing finger at her nephew.

'Hercules!' she roared. 'The poor thing's scared to death. *Have you been bullying it?*'

Hercules could only stand with his head hanging low in shame and frustration.

'No – no, Auntie,' he quavered. 'I guess it's naturally nervous.'

'Well, I'm used to animals. You should have called me before. You must treat them firmly – but gently. Kindness always works, as long as you show them you're the master. There, there, did-dums – don't be frightened of Auntie – she won't hurt you. . . .'

It was, thought Hercules to his blank despair, a revolting sight. With surprising gentleness, Aunt Henrietta fussed over the beast, patting and stroking it until the tentacles relaxed and the shrill, whistling scream died away. After a few minutes of this pandering, it appeared to get over its fright. Hercules finally fled with a muted sob when one of the tentacles crept forward and began to stroke Henrietta's gnarled fingers.

From that day, he was a broken man. What was worse, he could never escape from the consequences of his intended crime. Henrietta had acquired a new pet, and was liable to call not only at weekends but two or three times in between as well. It was obvious that she did not trust Hercules to treat the orchid properly, and still suspected him of bullying it. She would bring tasty tidbits that even her dogs had rejected, but which the orchid accepted with delight. The smell, which had so far been confined to the conservtory, began to creep into the house. . . .

And there, concluded Harry Purvis, as he brought this improbable narrative to a close, the matter rests – to the satisfaction of two, at any rate, of the parties concerned. The orchid is happy, and Aunt Henrietta has something (query, someone?) else to dominate. From time to time the creature has a nervous breakdown when a mouse gets loose in the conservatory, and she rushes to console it.

As for Hercules, there is no chance that he will ever give any more trouble to either of them. He seems to have sunk into a kind of vegetable sloth: indeed, said Harry thoughtfully, every day he becomes more and more like an orchid himself.

The harmless variety, of course. . . .

Moving Spirit

First published in *Tales from the White Hart*

In this tale from the White Hart, Harry Purvis introduces us to a 'genuine mad scientist' living in an out-of-the-way part of Cornwall, which is coincidentally where 'Charles Willis' – or should I say Arthur C. Clarke – spent part of his wartime service.

We were discussing a sensational trial at the Old Bailey when Harry Purvis, whose talent for twisting the conversation to his own ends is really unbelievable, remarked casually: 'I was once an expert witness in a rather interesting case.'

'Only a *witness*?' said Drew, as he deftly filled two glasses of Bass at once.

'Yes – but it was a rather close thing. It was in the early part of the war, about the time we were expecting the invasion. That's why you never heard about it at the time.'

'What makes you assume,' said Charles Willis suspiciously, 'that we never did hear of it?'

It was one of the few times I'd ever seen Harry caught trying to cover up his tracks. *'Qui s'excuse s'accuse,'* I thought to myself, and waited to see what evading action he'd take.

'It was such a peculiar case,' he replied with dignity, 'that I'm sure you'd have reminded me of it if you ever saw the reports. My name was featured quite prominently. It all happened in an out-of-the-way part of Cornwall, and it concerned the best example of that rare species, the genuine mad scientist, that I've ever met.'

Perhaps that wasn't really a fair description, Purvis amended hastily. Homer Ferguson was eccentric and had little foibles like keeping a pet boa constrictor to catch the mice, and never wearing shoes around the house. But he was so rich that no one noticed things like this.

Homer was also a competent scientist. Many years ago he had graduated from Edinburgh University, but having plenty of money he had never done a stroke of real work in his life. Instead, he pottered round the old vicarage he'd bought not far from Newquay and amused himself building gadgets. In the last forty years he'd invented television, ball-point pens, jet propulsion, and a few other trifles. However, as he had never bothered to take out any patents, other people had got the credit. This didn't worry him in the least, as he was of a singularly generous disposition, except with money.

It seemed that, in some complicated way, Purvis was one of his few living relatives. Consequently when Harry received a telegram one day requesting his assistance at once, he knew better than to refuse. No one knew exactly how much money Homer had or what he intended to do with it. Harry thought he had as good a chance as anyone, and he didn't intend to jeopardise it. At some inconvenience he made the journey down to Cornwall and turned up at the Vicarage.

He saw what was wrong as soon as he entered the grounds. Uncle Homer (he wasn't really an uncle, but he'd been called that as long as Harry could remember) had a shed beside the main building which he used for his experiments. That shed was now minus roof and windows, and a sickly odour hovered around it. There had obviously been an explosion, and Harry wondered, in a disinterested sort of way, if Uncle had been badly injured and wanted advice on drawing up a new will.

He ceased daydreaming when the old man, looking the picture of health (apart from some sticking plaster on his face) opened the door for him.

'Good of you come so quickly,' he boomed. He seemed genuinely pleased to see Harry. Then his face clouded over. 'Fact is, my boy, I'm in a bit of a jam and I want you to help. My case comes up before the local Bench tomorrow.'

This was a considerable shock. Homer had been as law-abiding a citizen as any motorist in petrol-rationed Britain could be expected to be. And if it was the usual black-market business, Harry didn't see how he could be expected to help.

'Sorry to hear about this, Uncle. What's the trouble?'

'It's a long story. Come into the library and we'll talk it over.'

Homer Ferguson's library occupied the entire west wing of the somewhat decrepit building. Harry believed that bats nested in the rafters, but he had never been able to prove it. When Homer had cleared a table by the simple expedient of tilting all the books off onto the floor, he whistled three times, a voice-operated relay tripped somewhere, and a gloomy Cornish voice drifted out of a concealed loud-speaker.

'Yes, Mr Ferguson?'

'Maida, send across a bottle of the new whisky.'

There was no reply except an audible sniff. But a moment later there came a creaking and clanking, and a couple of square feet of library shelving slid aside to reveal a conveyor belt.

'I can't get Maida to come into the library,' complained Homer, lifting out a loaded tray. 'She's afraid of Boanerges, though he's perfectly harmless.'

Harry found it hard not to feel some sympathy for the invisible Maida. All six feet of Boanerges was draped over the case holding the Encyclopaedia Britannica, and a bulge amidships indicated that he had dined recently.

'What do you think of the whisky?' asked Homer when Harry had sampled some and started to gasp for breath.

'It's – well, I don't know what to say. It's – phew – rather strong. I never thought—'

'Oh, don't take any notice of the label on the bottle. *This* brand never saw Scotland. And that's what all the trouble's about. I made it right here on the premises.'

'Uncle!'

'Yes, I know it's against the law, and all that sort of nonsense. But you can't get any good whisky these days – it all goes for export. It seemed to me that I was being patriotic making my own, so that there was more left over for the dollar drive. But the Excise people don't see it that way.'

'I think you'd better let me have the whole story,' said Harry. He was gloomily sure that there was nothing he could do to get his uncle out of this scrape.

Homer had always been fond of the bottle, and wartime shortages had hit him badly. He was also, as has been hinted, disinclined to give away money, and for a long time he had resented the fact that he had to pay a tax of several hundred per cent on a bottle of whisky. When he couldn't get his own supply any more, he had decided it was time to act.

The district he was living in probably had a good deal to do with his decision. For some centuries, the Customs and Excise had waged a never-ending battle with the Cornish fisherfolk. It was rumoured that the last incumbent of the old vicarage had possessed the finest cellar in the district next to that of the Bishop himself – and had never paid a penny in duty on it. So Uncle Homer merely felt he was carrying on an old and noble tradition.

There was little doubt, moreover, that the spirit of pure scientific enquiry also inspired him. He felt sure that this business about being aged in the wood for seven years was all rubbish, and was confident that he could do a better job with ultrasonics and ultraviolet rays.

The experiment went well for a few weeks. But late one evening there was one of those unfortunate accidents that will happen even in the best-conducted laboratories, and before Uncle knew what had happened, he was draped over a beam, while the grounds of the vicarage were littered with pieces of copper tubing.

Even then it would not have mattered much had not the local Home Guard been practising in the neighbourhood. As soon as they heard the explosion, they immediately went into action, Sten guns at the ready. Had the invasion started? If so, they'd soon fix it.

They were a little disappointed to discover that it was only Uncle, but as they were used to his experiments they weren't in the least surprised at what had happened. Unfortunately for Uncle, the Lieutenant in charge of the squad happened to be the local exciseman, and the combined evidence of his nose and his eyes told him the story in a flash.

'So tomorrow,' said Uncle Homer, looking rather like a small boy who had been caught stealing candy, 'I have to go up before the Bench, charged with possessing an illegal still.'

'I should have thought,' replied Harry, 'that was a matter for the Assizes, not the local magistrates.'

'We do things our own way here,' answered Homer, with more than a touch of pride. Harry was soon to discover how true this was.

They got little sleep that night, as Homer outlined his defence, overcame Harry's objections, and hastily assembled the apparatus he intended to produce in court.

'A Bench like this,' he explained, 'is always impressed by experts. If we dared, I'd like to say you were someone from the War Office, but they could check up on that. So we'll just tell them the truth – about our qualifications, that is.'

'Thank you,' said Harry. 'And suppose my college finds out what I'm doing?'

'Well, you won't claim to be acting for anyone except yourself. The whole thing is a private venture.'

'I'll say it is,' said Harry.

The next morning they loaded their gear into Homer's ancient Austin, and drove into the village. The Bench was sitting in one of the classrooms of the local school, and Harry felt that time had rolled back a few years and he was about to have an unpleasant interview with his old headmaster.

'We're in luck,' whispered Homer, as they were ushered into their cramped seats. 'Major Fotheringham is in the Chair. He's a good friend of mine.'

That would help a lot, Harry agreed. But there were two other justices on the bench as well, and one friend in court would hardly be sufficient. Eloquence, not influence, was the only thing that could save the day.

The courtroom was crowded, and Harry found it surprising that so many people had managed to get away from work long enough to watch the case. Then he realised the local interest that it would have aroused, in view of the fact that – in normal times, at least – smuggling was a major industry in these parts. He was not sure whether that would mean a sympathetic audience. The natives might well regard Homer's form of private enterprise as unfair competition. On the other hand, they probably approved on general principles with anything that put the excisemen's noses out of joint.

The charge was read by the Clerk of the Court, and the somewhat damning evidence produced. Pieces of copper tubing were solemnly inspected by the justices, each of whom in turn looked severely at Uncle Homer. Harry began to see his hypothetical inheritance becoming even more doubtful.

When the case for the prosecution was completed, Major Fotheringham turned to Homer.

'This appears to be a serious matter, Mr Ferguson. I hope you have a satisfactory explanation.'

'I have, your Honour,' replied the defendant in a tone that practically reeked of injured innocence. It was amusing to see his Honour's look of relief, and the momentary frown, quickly replaced by calm confidence, that passed across the face of H.M. Customs and Excise.

'Do you wish to have a legal representative? I notice that you have not brought one with you.'

'It won't be necessary. The whole case is founded on such a trivial misunderstanding that it can be cleared up without complications like that. I don't wish to incur the prosecution in unnecessary costs.'

This frontal onslaught brought a murmur from the body of the Court, and a flush to the cheeks of the Customs man. For the first time he began to look a little unsure of himself. If Ferguson thought the Crown would be paying costs, he must have a pretty good case. Of course, he might only be bluffing.

Homer waited until the mild stir had died away before creating a considerably greater one.

'I have called a scientific expert to explain what happened at the Vicarage,' he said. 'And owing to the nature of the evidence, I must ask, for security reasons, that the rest of the proceedings be *in camera*.'

'You want me to clear the Court?' said the Chairman incredulously.

'I am afraid so, sir. My colleague, Dr Purvis, feels that the fewer people concerned in this case, the better. When you have heard the evidence, I think you will agree with him. If I might say so, it is a great pity that it has already attracted so much publicity. I am afraid it may bring certain – ah – confidential matters to the wrong ears.'

Homer glared at the Customs officer, who fidgeted uncomfortably in his seat.

'Oh, very well,' said Major Fotheringham. 'This is all very irregular, but we live in irregular times. Mr Clerk, clear the Court.'

After some grumbling and confusion, and an overruled protest from the prosecution, the order was carried out. Then, under the interested gaze of the dozen people left in the room, Harry Purvis uncovered the apparatus he had unloaded from the baby Austin. After his qualifications had been presented to the court, he took the witness stand.

'I wish to explain, your Honour,' he began, 'that I have been engaged on explosives research, and that is why I happen to be acquainted with the defendant's work.' The opening part of this statement was perfectly true. It was about the last thing said that day that was.

'You mean – bombs and so forth?'

'Precisely, but on a fundamental level. We are always looking for new and better types of explosives, as you can imagine. Moreover, we in government research and the academic world are continually on the lookout for good ideas from outside sources. And quite recently, Unc – er, Mr Ferguson, wrote to us with a most interesting suggestion for a completely new type of explosive. The interesting thing about it was that it employed *nonexplosive* materials such as sugar, starch and so on.'

'Eh?' said the Chairman. 'A non-explosive explosive? That's impossible.'

Harry smiled sweetly.

'I know, sir – that is one's immediate reaction. But like most great ideas, this has the simplicity of genius. I am afraid, however, that I shall have to do a little explaining to make my point.'

The Bench looked very attentive, and also a little alarmed. Harry surmised that it had probably encountered expert witnesses before. He walked over to a table that had been set up in the middle of the courtroom, and which was now covered with flasks, piping, and bottles of liquids.

'I hope, Dr Purvis,' said the Chairman nervously, 'that you're not going to do anything dangerous.'

'Of course not, sir. I merely wish to demonstrate some basic scientific principles. Once again, I wish to stress the importance of keeping this between these four walls.' He paused solemnly and everyone looked duly impressed.

'Mr Ferguson,' he began, 'is proposing to tap one of the fundamental forces of Nature. It is a force on which every living thing depends – a force, gentlemen, which keeps *you* alive even though you, may never have heard of it.'

He moved over to the table and took up his position beside the flasks and bottles.

'Have you ever stopped to consider,' he said, 'how the sap manages to reach the highest leaf of a tall tree? It takes a lot of force to pump water a hundred – sometimes over three hundred – feet from the ground. Where does that force come from? I'll show you with this practical example.

'Here I have a strong container divided into two parts by a porous membrance. On one side of the membrane is pure water – on the other, a concentrated solution of sugar and other chemicals which I do not propose to specify. Under these condition, a pressure is set up, known as *osmotic* pressure. The pure water tries to pass through the membrane, as if to dilute the solution on the other side. I've now sealed the container, and you'll notice the pressure gauge here on the right – see how the pointer's going up. That's osmotic pressure for you. This same force acts through the cell walls in our bodies, causing fluid movement. It drives the sap up the trunks of trees, from the roots to the topmost branches. It's a universal force, and a powerful one. To Mr Ferguson must go the credit of first attempting to harness it.'

Harry paused impressively and looked round the court.

'Mr Ferguson,' he said, 'was attempting to develop the Osmotic Bomb.'

It took some time for this to sink in. Then Major Fotheringham leaned forward and said in a hushed voice, 'Are we to presume that he had succeeded in manufacturing this bomb, and that it exploded in his workshop?'

'Precisely, your Honour. It is a pleasure – an unusual pleasure, I might say – to present a case to so perspicacious a court. Mr Ferguson had succeeded, and he was preparing to report his method to us when, owing to an unfortunate oversight, a safety device attached to the bomb failed to operate. The results, you all know. I think you will need no further evidence of the power of this weapon – and you will realise its importance when I point out that the solutions it contains are all extremely common chemicals.'

Major Fotheringham, looking a little puzzled, turned to the prosecution lawyer.

'Mr Whiting,' he said, 'have you any questions to ask the witness?'

'I certainly have, your Honour. I've never heard such a ridiculous—'

'You will please confine yourself to questions of fact.'

'Very good, your Honour. May I ask the witness how he accounts for the large quantity of alcohol vapour immediately after the explosion?'

'I rather doubt if the inspector's nose was capable of accurate quantitative analysis. But admittedly there was some alcohol vapour released. The solution used in the bomb contained about twenty-five per cent. By employing dilute alcohol, the mobility of the inorganic ions is restricted and the osmotic pressure raised – a desirable effect, of course.'

That should hold them for a while, thought Harry. He was right. It was a good couple of minutes before the second question. Then the prosecution's spokesman waved one of the pieces of copper tubing in the air.

'What function did these carry out?' he said, in as nasty a tone of voice as he could manage. Harry affected not to notice the sneer.

'Manometer tubing for the pressure gauges,' he replied promptly.

The Bench, it was clear, was already far out of its depth. This was just where Harry wanted it to be. But the prosecution still had one card up its sleeve. There was a furtive whispering between the exciseman and his legal eagle. Harry looked nervously at Uncle Homer, who shrugged his shoulders with a 'Don't ask *me*!' gesture.

'I have some additional evidence I wish to present to the Court,' said the Customs lawyer briskly, as a bulky brown paper parcel was hoisted onto the table.

'Is this in order, your Honour?' protested Harry. 'All evidence against my – ah – colleague should already have been presented.'

'I withdraw my statement,' the lawyer interjected swiftly. 'Let us say that this is not evidence for *this* case, but material for later proceedings.' He paused ominously to let that sink in. 'Nevertheless, if Mr Ferguson can give a satisfactory answer to our question now, this whole business can be cleared up right away.' It was obvious that the last thing the speaker expected – or hoped for – was such a satisfactory explanation.

He unwrapped the brown paper, and there were three bottles of a famous brand of whisky.

'Uh-huh,' said Uncle Homer. 'I was wondering—'

'Mr Ferguson,' said the Chairman of the Bench. 'There is no need for you to make any statement unless you wish.'

Harry Purvis shot Major Fotheringham a grateful glance. He guessed what had happened. The prosecution had, when prowling through the ruins of

Uncle's laboratory, acquired some bottles of his home-brew. Their action was probably illegal, since they would not have had a search warrant – hence the reluctance in producing the evidence. The case had seemed sufficiently clear-cut without it.

It certainly appeared pretty clear-cut now. . . .

'These bottles,' said the representative of the Crown, 'do not contain the brand advertised on the label. They have obviously been used as convenient receptacles for the defendant's – shall we say – chemical solutions.' He gave Harry Purvis an unsympathetic glance. 'We have had these solutions analysed, with most interesting results. Apart from an abnormally high alcohol concentration, the contents of these bottles are virtually indistinguishable from—'

He never had time to finish his unsolicited and certainly unwanted testimonial to Uncle Homer's skill. For at that moment, Harry Purvis became aware of an ominous whistling sound. At first he thought it was a falling bomb – but that seemed unlikely, as there had been no air-raid warning. Then he realised that the whistling came from close at hand; from the courtroom table, in fact. . . .

'Take cover!' he yelled.

The Court went into recess with a speed never matched in the annals of British law. The three justices disappeared behind the dais; those in the body of the room burrowed into the floor or sheltered under desks. For a protracted, anguished moment nothing happened, and Harry wondered if he had given a false alarm. Then there was a dull, peculiarly muffled explosion, a great tinkling of glass – and a smell like a blitzed brewery. Slowly, the Court emerged from shelter.

The Osmotic Bomb had proved its power. More important still, it had destroyed the evidence for the prosecution.

The Bench was none too happy about dismissing the case; it felt, with good reason, that its dignity had been assailed. Moreover, each one of the justices would have to do some fast talking when he got home: the mist of alcohol had penetrated everything. Though the Clerk of the Court rushed round opening windows (none of which, oddly enough, had been broken) the fumes seemed reluctant to disperse. Harry Purvis, as he removed pieces of bottle glass from his hair, wondered if there would be some intoxicated pupils in class tomorrow.

Major Fotheringham, however, was undoubtedly a real sport, and as they filed out of the devastated courtroom, Harry heard him say to his uncle: 'Look here, Ferguson – it'll be ages before we can get those Molotov cocktails we've been promised by the War Office. What about making some of these bombs of yours for the Home Guard? If they don't knock out a tank, at least they'll make the crew drunk and incapable.'

'I'll certainly think about it, Major,' replied Uncle Homer, who still seemed a little dazed by the turn of events.

He recovered somewhat as they drove back to the Vicarage along the narrow, winding lanes with their high walls of unmortared stone.

'I hope, Uncle,' remarked Harry, when they had reached a relatively straight stretch and it seemed safe to talk to the driver, 'that you don't intend to rebuild that still. They'll be watching you like hawks and you won't get away with it again.'

'Very well,' said Uncle, a little sulkily. 'Confound these brakes! I had them fixed only just before the war!'

'Hey!' cried Harry. 'Watch out!'

It was too late. They had come to a crossroads at which a brand new HALT sign had been erected. Uncle braked hard, but for a moment nothing happened. Then the wheels on the left seized up, while those on the right continued gaily spinning. The car did a hairpin bend, luckily without turning over, and ended in the ditch pointing in the direction from which it had come.

Harry looked reproachfully at his uncle. He was about to frame a suitable reprimand when a motorcycle came out of the side-turning and drew up to them.

It was not going to be their lucky day, after all. The village police sergeant had been lurking in ambush, waiting to catch motorists at the new sign. He parked his machine by the roadside and leaned in through the window of the Austin.

'You all right, Mr Ferguson?' he said. Then his nose wrinkled up, and he looked like Jove about to deliver a thunderbolt. 'This won't do,' he said. 'I'll have to put you on a charge. Driving under the influence is a *very* serious business.'

'But I've not touched a drop all day!' protested Uncle, waving an alcohol-sodden sleeve under the sergeant's twitching nose.

'Do you expect me to believe *that*?' snorted the irate policeman, pulling out his notebook. 'I'm afraid you'll have to come to the station with me. Is your friend sober enough to drive?'

Harry Purvis didn't answer for a moment. He was too busy beating his head against the dashboard.

'Well,' we asked Harry. 'What did they do to your uncle?'

'Oh, he got fined five pounds and had his licence endorsed for drunken driving. Major Fotheringham wasn't in the Chair, unfortunately, when the case came up, but the other two justices were still on the Bench. I guess they felt that even if he was innocent this time, there was a limit to everything.'

'And did you ever get any of his money?'

'No fear! He was very grateful, of course, and he's told me that I'm mentioned in his will. But when I saw him last, what do you think he was doing? He was searching for the Elixir of Life.'

Harry sighed at the overwhelming injustice of things.

'Sometimes,' he said gloomily, 'I'm afraid he's found it. The doctors say he's the healthiest seventy-year-old they've ever seen. So all I got out of the whole affair was some interesting memories and a hang-over.'

'A hang-over?' asked Charlie Willis.

'Yes,' replied Harry, a faraway look in his eye. 'You see, the excisemen hadn't seized *all* the evidence. We had to – ah – destroy the rest. It took us the best part of a week. We invented all sorts of things during that time – but we never discovered what they were.'

The Defenestration of Ermintrude Inch

First published in *Tales from the White Hart*

An unusual story from the White Hart, in which Harry Purvis seemingly meets his match when his wife discovers the location of his 'quantum mechanics lectures'. It also chronicles the move from the 'White Hart' to the 'Sphere', matching the move from the White Horse to the Globe, following the landlord, Lew Mordecai.

And now I have a short, sad duty to perform. One of the many mysteries about Harry Purvis – who was so informative in every other direction – was the existence or otherwise of a Mrs Purvis. It was true that he wore no wedding ring, but that means little nowadays. Almost as little, as an hotel proprietor will tell you, as does the reverse.

In a number of his tales, Harry had shown distinct evidence of some hostility towards what a Polish friend of mine, whose command of English did not match his gallantry, always referred to as ladies of the female sex. And it was by a curious coincidence that the very last story he ever told us first indicated, and then proved conclusively, Harry's marital status.

I do not know who brought up the word 'defenestration,' which is not, after all, one of the most commonly used abstractions in the language. It was probably one of the alarmingly erudite younger members of the 'White Hart' clientele; some of them are just out of college, and so make us old-timers feel very callow and ignorant. But from the word, the discussion naturally passed to the deed. Had any of us ever been defenestrated? Did we know anyone who had?

'Yes,' said Harry. 'It happened to a verbose lady I once knew. She was called Ermintrude, and was married to Osbert Inch, a sound engineer at the BBC.

'Osbert spent all his working hours listening to other people talking, and most of his free time listening to Ermintrude. Unfortunately, he couldn't switch *her* off at the turn of a knob, and so he very seldom had a chance of getting a word in edgeways.

'There are some women who appear sincerely unaware of the fact that they cannot stop talking, and are most surprised when anyone accuses them of monopolising the conversation. Ermintrude would start as soon as she woke up, change gear so that she could hear herself speak above the eight o'clock news, and continue unabated until Osbert thankfully left for work. A couple of years of this had almost reduced him to a nervous wreck, but one morning when his wife was handicapped by a long overdue attack of laryngitis he made a spirited protest against her vocal monopoly.

'To his incredulous disbelief, she flatly refused to accept the charge. It appeared that to Ermintrude, time ceased to exist when *she* was talking – but she became extremely restive when anyone else held the stage. As soon as she had recovered her voice, she told Osbert how unfair it was of him to make such an unfounded accusation, and the argument would have been very acrimonious – if it had been possible to have an argument with Ermintrude at all.

'This made Osbert an angry and also a desperate man. But he was an ingenious one, too, and it occurred to him that he could produce irrefutable evidence that Ermintrude talked a hundred words for every syllable he was able to utter. I mentioned that he was a sound engineer, and his room was fitted up with hi-fi set, tape recorder, and the usual electronic tools of his trade, some of which the BBC had unwittingly supplied.

'It did not take him very long to construct a piece of equipment which one might call a Selective Word Counter. If you know anything about audio engineering you'll appreciate how it could be done with suitable filters and dividing circuits – and if you don't, you'll have to take it for granted. What the apparatus did was simply this: a microphone picked up every word spoken in the Inch apartment. Osbert's deeper tones went one way and registered on a counter marked 'His,' and Ermintrude's higher frequencies went the other direction and ended up on the counter marked 'Hers'.

'Within an hour of switching on, the score was as follows:

| His | 23 |
| Hers | 2,530 |

'As the numbers flicked across the counter dials, Ermintrude became more and more thoughtful and at the same time more and more silent. Osbert, on the other hand, drinking the heady wine of victory (though to anyone else it would have looked like his morning cup of tea) began to make the most of his advantage and became quite talkative. By the time he had left for work, the counters had reflected the changing status in the household:

| His | 1,043 |
| Hers | 3,397 |

'Just to show who was now the boss, Osbert left the apparatus switched on; he had always wondered if Ermintrude talked to herself as a purely automatic reflex even when there was no one around to hear what she was saying. He had, by the way, thoughtfully taken the precaution of

577

putting a lock on the Counter so that his wife couldn't turn it off while he was out.

'He was a little disappointed to find that the figures were quite unaltered when he came home that evening, but thereafter the score soon started to mount again. It became a kind of game – though a deadly serious one – with each of the protagonists keeping one eye on the machine whenever either of them said a word. Ermintrude was clearly discomfited: ever and again she would suffer a verbal relapse and increase her score by a couple of hundred before she brought herself to a halt by a supreme effort of self-control. Osbert, who still had such a lead that he could afford to be garrulous, amused himself by making occasional sardonic comments which were well worth the expenditure of a few-score points.

'Although a measure of equality had been restored in the Inch household, the Word Counter had, if anything, increased the state of dissension. Presently Ermintrude, who had a certain natural intelligence which some people might have called craftiness, made an appeal to her husband's better nature. She pointed out that neither of them was really behaving naturally while every word was being monitored and counted; Osbert had unfairly let her get ahead and was now being taciturn in a way that he would never have been had he not got that warning score continuously before his eyes. Though Osbert gagged at the sheer effrontery of this charge, he had to admit that the objection did contain an element of truth. The test would be fairer and more conclusive if neither of them could see the accumulating score – if, indeed, they forgot all about the presence of the machine and so behaved perfectly naturally, or at least as naturally as they could in the circumstances.

'After much argument they came to a compromise. Very sportingly, in his opinion, Osbert reset the dials to zero and sealed up the Counter windows so that no one could take a peek at the scores. They agreed to break the wax seals – on which they had both impressed their fingerprints – at the end of the week, and to abide by the decision. Concealing the microphone under a table, Osbert moved the Counter equipment itself into his little workship, so that the living room now bore no sign of the implacable electronic watchdog that was controlling the destiny of the Inches.

'Thereafter, things slowly returned to normal. Ermintrude became as talkative as ever, but now Osbert didn't mind in the least because he knew that every word she uttered was being patiently noted to be used as evidence against her. At the end of the week, his triumph would be complete. He could afford to allow himself the luxury of a couple of hundred words a day, knowing that Ermintrude used up this allowance in five minutes.

'The breaking of the seals was performed ceremonially at the end of an unusually talkative day, when Ermintrude had repeated verbatim three telephone conversations of excrutiating banality which, it seemed, had occupied most of her afternoon. Osbert had merely smiled and said "Yes, dear" at ten-minute intervals, meanwhile trying to imagine what excuse his wife would put forward when confronted by the damning evidence.

'Imagine, therefore, his feelings when the seals were removed to disclose the week's total:

<pre>
His   143,567
Hers   32,590
</pre>

'Osbert stared at the incredible figures with stunned disbelief. *Something* had gone wrong – but where? There must, he decided, have been a fault in the apparatus. It was annoying, very annoying, for he knew perfectly well that Ermintrude would never let him live it down, even if he proved conclusively that the Counter had gone haywire.

'Ermintrude was still crowing victoriously when Osbert pushed her out of the room and started to dismantle his errant equipment. He was halfway through the job when he noticed something in his wastepaper basket which he was sure he hadn't put there. It was a closed loop of tape, a couple of feet long, and he was quite unable to account for its presence as he had not used the tape recorder for several days. He picked it up, and as he did so suspicion exploded into certainty.

'He glanced at the recorder; the switches, he was quite sure, were not as he had left them. Ermintrude was crafty, but she was also careless. Osbert had often complained that she never did a job properly, and here was the final proof.

'His den was littered with old tapes carrying unerased test passages he had recorded; it had been no trouble at all for Ermintrude to locate one, snip off a few words, stick the ends together, switch to "Playback" and leave the machine running hour after hour in front of the microphone. Osbert was furious with himself for not having thought of so simple a ruse; if the tape had been strong enough, he would probably have strangled Ermintrude with it.

'Whether he tried to do anything of the sort is still uncertain. All we know is that she went out of the apartment window, and of course it could have been an accident – but there was no way of asking her, as the Inches lived four storeys up.

'I know that defenestration is usually deliberate, and the Coroner had some pointed words to say on the subject. But nobody could prove that Osbert pushed her, and the whole thing soon blew over. About a year later he married a charming little deaf-and-dumb girl, and they're one of the happiest couples I know.'

There was a long pause when Harry had finished, whether out of disbelief or out of respect for the late Mrs Inch it would be hard to say. But before anyone could make a suitable comment, the door was thrown open and a formidable blonde advanced into the private bar of the 'White Hart'.

It is seldom indeed that life arranges its climaxes as neatly as this. Harry Purvis turned very pale and tried, in vain, to hide himself in the crowd. He was instantly spotted and pinned down beneath a barrage of invective.

'So *this*,' we heard with interest, 'is where you've been giving your Wednesday evening lectures on quantum mechanics! I should have checked up with the University years ago! Harry Purvis, you're a liar, and I don't mind if everybody knows it. And as for your friends' – she gave us all a scathing look – 'it's a long time since I've seen such a scruffy lot of tipplers.'

'Hey, just a minute!' protested Drew from the other side of the counter. She quelled him with a glance, then turned upon poor Harry again.

'Come along,' she said, 'you're going home. No, you needn't finish that drink! I'm sure you've already had more than enough.'

Obediently, Harry Purvis picked up his briefcase and coat.

'Very well, Ermintrude,' he said meekly.

I will not bore you with the long and still unsettled arguments as to whether Mrs Purvis really was called Ermintrude, or whether Harry was so dazed that he automatically applied the name to her. We all have our theories about that, as indeed we have about everything concerning Harry. All that matters now is the sad and indisputable fact that no one has ever seen him since that evening.

It is just possible that he doesn't know where we meet nowadays, for a few months later the 'White Hart' was taken over by a new management and we all followed Drew lock, stock and barrel – particularly barrel – to his new establishment. Our weekly sessions now take place at the 'Sphere', and for a long time many of us used to look up hopefully when the door opened to see if Harry had managed to escape and find his way back to us. It is, indeed, partly in the hope that he will see this book and hence discover our new location that I have gathered these tales together.

Even those who never believed a word you spoke miss you, Harry. If you have to defenestrate Ermintrude to regain your freedom, do it on a Wednesday evening between six and eleven, and there'll be forty people in the 'Sphere' who'll provide you with an alibi. But get back *somehow*; things have never been quite the same since you went.

The Ultimate Melody

First published in *If*, February 1957
Collected in *Tales from the White Hart*

Have you ever noticed that, when there are twenty or thirty people talking together in a room, there are occasional moments when everyone becomes suddenly silent, so that for a second there's a sudden, vibrating emptiness that seems to swallow up all sound? I don't know how it affects other people, but when it happens it makes me feel cold all over. Of course, the whole thing's merely caused by the laws of probability, but somehow it seems more than a mere coinciding of conversational pauses. It's almost as if everybody is listening for something – they don't know what. At such moments I say to myself :

> But at my back I always hear
> Time's winged chariot hurrying near . . .

That's how *I* feel about it, however cheerful the company in which it happens. Yes, even if it's in the 'White Hart'.

It was like that one Wednesday evening when the place wasn't quite as crowded as usual. The silence came, as unexpectedly as it always does. Then, probably in a deliberate attempt to break that unsettling feeling of suspense, Charlie Willis started whistling the latest hit tune. I don't even remember what it was. I only remember that it triggered off one of Harry Purvis's most disturbing stories.

'Charlie,' he began, quietly enough, 'that darn tune's driving me mad. I've heard it every time I've switched on the radio for the last week.'

There was a sniff from John Christopher.

'You ought to stay tuned to the Third Programme. Then you'd be safe.'

'Some of us,' retorted Harry, 'don't care for an exclusive diet of Elizabethan madrigals. But don't let's quarrel about *that*, for heaven's sake. Has it ever occurred to you that there's something rather – fundamental – about hit tunes?'

'What do you mean?'

'Well, they come along out of nowhere, and then for weeks everybody's humming them, just as Charlie did then. The good ones grab hold of you so thoroughly that you just can't get them out of your head –

they go round and round for days. And then, suddenly, they've vanished again.'

'I know what you mean,' said Art Vincent. 'There are some melodies that you can take or leave, but others stick like treacle, whether you want them or not.'

'Precisely. I got saddled that way for a whole week with the big theme from the finale of Sibelius Two – even went to sleep with it running round inside my head. Then there's that "Third Man" piece – da di da di *daa* dida di*daa* . . . look what *that* did to everybody.'

Harry had to pause for a moment until his audience had stopped zithering. When the last 'Plonk!' had died away he continued:

'Precisely! You all felt the same way. Now what *is* there about these tunes that has this effect? Some of them are great music, other just banal – but they've obviously got *something* in common.'

'Go on,' said Charlie. 'We're waiting.'

'I don't know what the answer is,' replied Harry. 'And what's more, I don't want to. For I know a man who found out.'

Automatically, someone handed him a beer, so that the tenor of his tale would not be disturbed. It always annoyed a lot of people when he had to stop in mid-flight for a refill.

'I don't know why it is,' said Harry Purvis, 'that most scientists are interested in music, but it's an undeniable fact. I've known several large labs that had their own amateur symphony orchestras – some of them quite good, too. As far as the mathematicians are concerned, one can think of obvious reasons for this fondness: music, particularly classical music, has a form which is almost mathematical. And then, of course, there's the underlying theory – harmonic relations, wave analysis, frequency distribution, and so on. It's a fascinating study in itself, and one that appeals strongly to the scientific mind. Moreover, it doesn't – as some people might think – preclude a purely aesthetic appreciation of music for its own sake.

'However, I must confess that Gilbert Lister's interest in music was purely cerebral. He was, primarily, a physiologist, specialising in the study of the brain. So when I said that his interest was cerebral, I meant it quite literally. "Alexander's Ragtime Band" and the Choral Symphony were all the same to him. He wasn't concerned with the sounds themselves, but only what happened when they got past the ears and started doing things to the brain.

'In an audience as well educated as this,' said Harry, with an emphasis that made it sound positively insulting, 'there will be no one who's unaware of the fact that much of the brain's activity is electrical. There are, in fact, steady pulsing rhythms going on all the time, and they can be detected and analysed by modern instruments. This was Gilbert Lister's line of territory. He could stick electrodes on your scalp and his amplifiers would draw your brain waves on yards of tape. Then he could examine them and tell you all sorts of interesting things about yourself. Ultimately, he claimed, it would be possible to identify anyone from their encephalogram – to use the correct term – more positively than by fingerprints. A man might get a surgeon to change his skin, but if we ever got to the stage when surgery could change your brain – well, you'd have turned into somebody else, anyway, so the system still wouldn't have failed.

'It was while he was studying the alpha, beta and other rhythms in the brain that Gilbert got interested in music. He was sure that there must be some connection between musical and mental rhythms. He'd play music at various tempos to his subjects and see what effect it had on their normal brain frequencies. As you might expect, it had a lot, and the discoveries he made led Gilbert on into more philosophical fields.

'I only had one good talk with him about his theories. It was not that he was at all secretive – I've never met a scientist who was, come to think of it – but he didn't like to talk about his work until he knew where it was leading. However, what he told me was enough to prove that he'd opened up a very interesting line of territory, and thereafter I made rather a point of cultivating him. My firm supplied some of his equipment, but I wasn't averse to picking up a little profit on the side. It occurred to me that *if* Gilbert's ideas worked out, he'd need a business manager before you could whistle the opening bar of the Fifth Symphony. . . .

'For what Gilbert was trying to do was to lay a scientific foundation for the theory of hit tunes. Of course, he didn't think of it that way: he regarded it as a pure research project, and didn't look any further ahead than a paper in the *Proceedings of the Physical Society*. But I spotted its financial implications at once. They were quite breath-taking.

'Gilbert was sure that a great melody, or a hit tune, made its impression on the mind because in some way it fitted in with the fundamental electrical rhythms going on in the brain. One analogy he used was "It's like a Yale key going into a lock – the two patterns have got to fit before anything happens."

'He tackled the problem from two angles. In the first place, he took hundreds of the really famous tunes in classical and popular music and analysed their structure – their morphology, as he put it. This was done automatically, in a big harmonic analyser that sorted out all the frequencies. Of course, there was a lot more to it than this, but I'm sure you've got the basic idea.

'At the same time, he tried to see how the resulting patterns of waves agreed with the natural electrical vibrations of the brain. Because it was Gilbert's theory – and this is where we get into rather deep philosophical waters – that all existing tunes were merely crude approximations to one fundamental melody. Musicians had been groping for it down the centuries, but they didn't know what they were doing, because they were ignorant of the relation between music and mind. Now that this had been unravelled, it should be possible to discover the Ultimate Melody.'

'Huh!' said John Christopher. 'It's only a rehash of Plato's theory of ideals. You know – all the objects of our material world are merely crude copies of the ideal chair or table or what-have-you. So your friend was after the ideal melody. And did he find it?'

'I'll tell you,' continued Harry imperturbably. 'It took Gilbert about a year to complete his analysis, and then he started on the synthesis. To put it crudely, he built a machine that would automatically construct patterns of sound according to the laws that he'd uncovered. He had banks of oscillators and mixers – in fact, he modified an ordinary electronic organ for this part of the apparatus – which were controlled by his composing machine. In the rather childish way that scientists like to name their offspring, Gilbert had called this device Ludwig.

'Maybe it helps to understand how Ludwig operated if you think of him as a kind of kaleidoscope, working with sound rather than light. But he was a kaleidoscope set to obey certain laws, and those laws – so Gilbert believed – were based on the fundamental structure of the human mind. If he could get the adjustments correct, Ludwig would be bound, sooner or later, to arrive at the Ultimate Melody as he searched through all the possible patterns of music.

'I had one opportunity of hearing Ludwig at work, and it was uncanny. The equipment was the usual nondescript mess of electronics which one meets in any lab: it might have been a mock-up of a new computer, a radar gunsight, a traffic-control system, or a ham radio. It was very hard to believe that, if it worked, it would put every composer in the world out of business. Or would it? Perhaps not: Ludwig might be able to deliver the raw material, but surely it would still have to be orchestrated.

'Then the sound started to come from the speaker. At first it seemed to me that I was listening to the five-finger exercises of an accurate but completely uninspired pupil. Most of the themes were quite banal: the machine would play one, then ring the changes on it bar after bar until it had exhausted all the possibilities before going on to the next. Occasionally a quite striking phrase would come up, but on the whole I was not at all impressed.

'However, Gilbert explained that this was only a trial run and that the main circuits had not yet been set up. When they were, Ludwig would be far more selective: at the moment, he was playing everything that came along – he had no sense of discrimination. When he had acquired that, *then* the possibilities were limitless.

'That was the last time I ever saw Gilbert Lister. I had arranged to meet him at the lab about a week later, when he expected to have made substantial progress. As it happened, I was about an hour late for my appointment. And that was very lucky for me. . . .

'When I got there, they had just taken Gilbert away. His lab assistant, an old man who'd been with him for years, was sitting distraught and disconsolate among the tangled wiring of Ludwig. It took me a long time to discover what had happened, and longer still to work out the explanation.

'There was no doubt of one thing. Ludwig had finally worked. The assistant had gone off to lunch while Gilbert was making the final adjustments, and when he came back an hour later the laboratory was pulsing with one long and very complex melodic phrase. Either the machine had

584

stopped automatically at that point, or Gilbert had switched it over to REPEAT. At any rate, he had been listening, for several hundred times at least, to that same melody. When his assistant found him, he seemed to be in a trance. His eyes were open yet unseeing, his limbs rigid. Even when Ludwig was switched off, it made no difference. Gilbert was beyond help.

'What had happened? Well, I suppose we should have thought of it, but it's so easy to be wise after the event. It's just as I said at the beginning. If a composer, working merely by rule of thumb, can produce a melody which can dominate our mind for days on end, imagine the effect of the Ultimate Melody for which Gilbert was searching! Supposing it existed – and I'm not admitting that it does – it would form an endless ring in the memory circuits of the mind. It would go round and round forever, obliterating all other thoughts. All the cloying melodies of the past would be mere ephemerae compared to it. Once it had keyed into the brain, and distorted the circling wave forms which are the physical manifestations of consciousness itself – that would be the end. And that is what happened to Gilbert.

'They've tried shock therapy – everything. But it's no good; the pattern has been set, and it can't be broken. He's lost all consciousness of the outer world, and has to be fed intravenously. He never moves or reacts to external stimuli, but sometimes, they tell me, he twitches in a peculiar way, as if he is beating time. . . .

'I'm afraid there's no hope for him. Yet I'm not sure if his fate is a horrible one, or whether he should be envied. Perhaps, in a sense, he's found the ultimate reality that philosophers like Plato are always talking about. I really don't know. And sometimes I find myself wondering just what that infernal melody *was* like, and almost wishing that I'd been able to hear it perhaps once. There might have been some way of doing it in safety: remember how Ulysses listened to the song of the sirens and got away with it . . .? But there'll never be a chance now, of course.'

'I was waiting for this,' said Charles Willis nastily. 'I suppose the apparatus blew up, or something, so that as usual there's no way of checking your story.'

Harry gave him his best more-in-sorrow-than-in-anger look.

'The apparatus was quite undamaged,' he said severely. 'What happened next was one of those completely maddening things for which I shall never stop blaming myself. You see, I'd been too interested in Gilbert's experiment to look after my firm's business in the way that I should. I'm afraid he'd fallen badly behind with his payments, and when the Accounts Department discovered what had happened to him they acted quickly. I was only off for a couple of days on another job, and when I got back, do you know what had happened? They'd pushed through a court order, and had seized all their property. Of course that had meant dismantling Ludwig: when I saw him next he was just a pile of useless junk. And all because of a few pounds! It made me weep.'

'I'm sure of it,' said Eric Maine. 'But you've forgotten Loose End Number Two. *What about Gilbert's assistant?* He went into the lab while the gadget was going full blast. Why didn't it get to him, too? You've slipped up there, Harry.'

H. Purvis, Esquire, paused only to drain the last drops from his glass and to hand it silently across to Drew.

'Really!' he said. 'Is this a cross-examination? I didn't mention the point because it was rather trivial. But it explains why I was never able to get the slightest inkling of the nature of that melody. You see, Gilbert's assistant was a first-rate lab technician, but he'd never been able to help much with the adjustments to Ludwig. For he was one of those people who are completely tone-deaf. To him, the Ultimate Melody meant no more than a couple of cats on a garden wall.'

Nobody asked any more questions: we all, I think, felt the desire to commune with our thoughts. There was a long, brooding silence before the 'White Hart' resumed its usual activities. And even then, I noticed, it was every bit of ten minutes before Charlie started whistling 'La Ronde' again.

The Next Tenants

First published in *Satellite*, February 1957
Collected in *Tales from the White Hart*

'The number of mad scientists who wish to conquer the world,' said Harry Purvis, looking thoughtfully at his beer, 'has been grossly exaggerated. In fact, I can remember encountering only a single one.'

'Then there couldn't have been many others,' commented Bill Temple, a little acidly. 'It's not the sort of thing one would be likely to forget.'

'I suppose not,' replied Harry, with that air of irrefragable innocence which is so disconcerting to his critics. 'And, as a matter of fact, this scientist wasn't really mad. There was no doubt, though, that he was out to conquer the world. Or if you want to be really precise – to let the world be conquered.'

'And by whom?' asked George Whitley. 'The Martians? Or the well-known little green men from Venus?'

'Neither of them. He was collaborating with someone a lot nearer home. You'll realise who I mean when I tell you he was a myrmecologist.'

'A which-what?' asked George.

'Let him get on with the story,' said Drew, from the other side of the bar. 'It's past ten, and if I can't get you all out by closing time *this* week, I'll lose my licence.'

'Thank you,' said Harry with dignity, handing over his glass for a refill. 'This all happened about two years ago, when I was on a mission in the Pacific. It was rather hush-hush, but in view of what's happened since, there's no harm in talking about it. Three of us scientists were landed on a certain Pacific atoll not a thousand miles from Bikini, and given a week to set up some detection equipment. It was intended, of course, to keep an eye on our good friends and allies when they started playing with thermo-nuclear reactions – to pick some crumbs from the AEC's table, as it were. The Russians, naturally, were doing the same thing, and occasionally we ran into each other and then both sides would pretend that there was nobody here but us chickens.

'This atoll was supposed to be uninhabited, but this was a considerable error. It actually had a population of several hundred millions—'

'What!' gasped everybody.

' – several hundred millions,' continued Purvis calmly, 'of which number,

587

one was human. I came across him when I went inland one day to have a look at the scenery.'

'Inland?' asked George Whitley. 'I thought you said it was an atoll. How can a ring of coral—'

'It was a very plump atoll,' said Harry firmly. 'Anyway, who's telling this story?' He waited defiantly for a moment until he had the right of way again.

'Here I was, then, walking up a charming little river course underneath the coconut palms, when to my great surprise I came across a water wheel – a very modern-looking one, driving a dynamo. If I'd been sensible, I suppose I'd have gone back and told my companions, but I couldn't resist the challenge and decided to do some reconnoitring on my own. I remembered that there were still supposed to be Japanese troops around who didn't know that the war was over, but that explanation seemed a bit unlikely.

'I followed the power line up a hill, and there on the other side was a low, whitewashed building set in a large clearing. All over this clearing were tall, irregular mounds of earth, linked together with a network of wires. It was one of the most baffling sights I have ever seen, and I stood and stared for a good ten minutes, trying to decide what was going on. The longer I looked, the less sense it seemed to make.

'I was debating what to do when a tall, white-haired man came out of the building and walked over to one of the mounds. He was carrying some kind of apparatus and had a pair of earphones slung around his neck, so I guessed that he was using a Geiger counter. It was just about then that I realised what those tall mounds were. They were termitaries . . . the skyscrapers, in comparison to their makers, far taller than the Empire State Building, in which the so-called white ants live.

'I watched with great interest, but complete bafflement, while the elderly scientist inserted his apparatus into the base of the termitary, listened intently for a moment, and then walked back towards the building. By this time I was so curious that I decided to make my presence known. Whatever research was going on here obviously had nothing to do with international politics, so I was the only one who'd have anything to hide. You'll appreciate later just what a miscalculation *that* was.

'I yelled for attention and walked down the hill, waving my arms. The stranger halted and watched me approaching: he didn't look particularly suprised. As I came closer I saw that he had a straggling moustache that gave him a faintly Oriental appearance. He was about sixty years old, and carried himself very erect. Though he was wearing nothing but a pair of shorts, he looked so dignified that I felt rather ashamed of my noisy approach.

'"Good morning," I said apologetically. "I didn't know that there was anyone else on this island. I'm with an – er – scientific-survey party over on the other side."

'At this the stranger's eyes lit up. "Ah," he said, in almost perfect English, "a fellow scientist! I'm very pleased to meet you. Come into the house."

'I followed gladly enough – I was pretty hot after my scramble – and I found that the building was simply one large lab. In a corner was a bed, and a couple of chairs, together with a stove and one of those folding washbasins that campers use. That seemed to sum up the living arrangements. But everything was very neat and tidy: my unknown friend seemed to be a recluse, but he believed in keeping up appearances.

'I introduced myself first, and, as I'd hoped, he promptly responded. He was one Professor Takato, a biologist from a leading Japanese university. He didn't look particularly Japanese, apart from the moustache I've mentioned. With his erect, dignified bearing he reminded me more of an old Kentucky colonel I once knew.

'After he'd given me some unfamiliar but refreshing wine, we sat and talked for a couple of hours. Like most scientists he seemed happy to meet someone who would appreciate his work. It was true that my interests lay in physics and chemistry rather than on the biological side, but I found Professor Takato's research quite fascinating.

'I don't suppose you know much about termites, so I'll remind you of the salient facts. They're among the most highly evolved of the social insects, and live in vast colonies throughout the tropics. They can't stand cold weather, nor, oddly enough, can they endure direct sunlight. When they have to get from one place to another, they construct little covered roadways. They seem to have some unknown and almost instantaneous means of communication, and though the individual termites are pretty helpless and dumb, a whole colony behaves like an intelligent animal. Some writers have drawn comparisons between a termitary and a human body, which is also composed of individual living cells making up an entity much higher than the basic units. The termites are often called "white ants", but that's a completely incorrect name, as they aren't ants at all but quite a different species of insect. Or should I say "genus"? I'm pretty vague about this sort of thing . . .

'Excuse this little lecture, but after I'd listened to Takato for a while I began to get quite enthusiastic about termites myself. Did you know, for example, that they not only cultivate gardens but also keep cows – insect cows, of course – and milk them? Yes, they're sophisticated little devils, even though they do it all by instinct.

'But I'd better tell you something about the Professor. Although he was alone at the moment, and had lived on the island for several years, he had a number of assistants who brought equipment from Japan and helped him in his work. His first great achievement was to do for the termites what von Frisch had done with bees – he'd learned their language. It was much more complex than the system of communication that bees use, which as you probably know, is based on dancing. I understood that the network of wires linking the termitaries to the lab not only enabled Professor Takato to listen to the termites talking among each other, but also permitted him to speak to them. That's not really as fantastic as it sounds, if you use the word "speak" in its widest sense. We speak to a good many animals – not always with our voices, by any means. When you throw a stick for your dog and expect him to run and fetch it, that's a form of speech – sign language. The Professor, I gathered, had worked out some kind of code which the termites understood, though how efficient it was at communicating ideas I didn't know.

'I came back each day, when I could spare the time, and by the end of the week we were firm friends. It may surprise you that I was able to conceal these visits from my colleagues, but the island was quite large and we each did a lot of exploring. I felt somehow that Professor Takato was my private property, and did not wish to expose him to the curiosity of my companions. They were rather uncouth characters, graduates of some provincial university like Oxford or Cambridge.

'I'm glad to say that I was able to give the Professor a certain amount of assistance, fixing his radio and lining up some of his electronic gear. He used radioactive tracers a good deal, to follow individual termites around. He'd been tracking one with a Geiger counter when I first met him, in fact.

'Four or five days after we'd met, his counters started to go haywire, and the equipment we'd set up began to reel in its recordings. Takato guessed what had happened: he'd never asked me exactly what I was doing on the island, but I think he knew. When I greeted him he switched on his counters and let me listen to the roar of radiation. There had been some radioactive fall-out – not enough to be dangerous, but sufficient to bring the background way up.

'"I think," he said softly, "that you physicists are playing with your toys again. And very big ones, this time."

'"I'm afraid you're right," I answered. We wouldn't be sure until the readings had been analysed, but it looked as if Teller and his team had started the hydrogen reaction. "Before long, we'll be able to make the first A bombs look like damp squibs."

'"My family," said Professor Takato, without any emotion, "was at Nagasaki."

'There wasn't a great deal I could say to that, and I was glad when he went on to add: "Have you ever wondered who will take over when we are finished?"

'"Your termites?" I said, half-facetiously. He seemed to hesitate for a moment. Then he said quietly, "Come with me; I have not shown you everything."

'We walked over to a corner of the lab where some equipment 'lay concealed beneath dust sheets, and the Professor uncovered a rather curious piece of apparatus. At first sight it looked like one of the manipulators used for the remote handling of dangerously radioactive materials. There were hand-grips that conveyed movements through rods and levers, but everything seemed to focus on a small box a few inches on a side. "What is it?" I asked.

'"It's a micromanipulator. The French developed them for biological work. There aren't many around yet."

'Then I remembered. These were devices with which, by the use of suitable reduction gearing, one could carry out the most incredibly delicate operations. You moved your finger an inch – and the tool you were controlling moved a thousandth of an inch. The French scientist who had developed this technique had built tiny forges on which they could construct minute scalpels and tweezers from fused glass. Working entirely through microscopes, they had been able to dissect individual cells. Removing an appendix from a termite (in the highly doubtful event of the insect possessing one) would be child's play with such an instrument.

'"I am not very skilled at using the manipulator," confessed Takato. "One of my assistants does all the work with it. I have shown no one else this, but you have been very helpful. Come with me, please."

'We went out into the open, and walked past the avenues of tall, cement-hard mounds. They were not all of the same architectural design, for there are many different kinds of termites – some, indeed, don't build mounds at all. I felt rather like a giant walking through Manhattan, for these were skyscrapers, each with its own teeming population.

'There was a small metal (not wooden – the termites would soon have fixed that!) hut beside one of the mounds, and as we entered it the glare of sunlight was banished. The Professor threw a switch, and a faint red glow enabled me to see various types of optical equipment.

'"They hate light," he said, "so it's a great problem observing them. We solved it by using infrared. This is an image-converter of the type that was used in the war for operations at night. You know about them?"

'"Of course," I said. "Snipers had them fixed on their rifles so that they could go sharpshooting in the dark. Very ingenious things – I'm glad you've found a civilised use for them."

'It was a long time before Professor Takato found what he wanted. He seemed to be steering some kind of periscope arrangement, probing through the corridors of the termite city. Then he said: "Quick – before they've gone!"

'I moved over and took his position. It was a second or so before my eye focused properly, and longer still before I understood the scale of the picture I was seeing. Then I saw six termites, greatly enlarged, moving rather rapidly across the field of vision. They were travelling in a group, like the huskies forming a dog team. And that was a very good analogy, because they were towing a sledge . . .

'I was so astonished that I never even noticed what kind of load they were moving. When they had vanished from sight, I turned to Professor Takato. My eyes had now grown accustomed to the faint red glow, and I could see him quite well.

' "So that's the sort of tool you've been building with your micromanipulator!" I said. "It's amazing – I'd never have believed it."

' "But that is nothing," replied the Professor. "Performing fleas will pull a cart around. I haven't told you what is so important. We only made a few of those sledges. *The one you saw they constructed themselves.*"

'He let that sink in: it took some time. Then he continued quietly, but with a kind of controlled enthusiasm in his voice: "Remember that the termites, as individuals, have virtually no intelligence. But the colony as a whole is a very high type of organism – and an immortal one, barring accidents. It froze in its present instinctive pattern millions of years before Man was born, and by itself it can never escape from its present sterile perfection. It has reached a dead end – because it has no tools, no effective way of controlling Nature. I have given it the lever, to increase its power, and now the sledge, to improve its efficiency. I have thought of the wheel, but it is best to let that wait for a later stage – it would not be very useful now. The results have exceeded my expectations. I started with this termitary alone – but now they all have the same tools. They have taught each other, and that proves they can co-operate. True, they have wars – but not when there is enough food for all, as there is here.

' "But you cannot judge the termitary by human standards. What I hope to do is to jolt its rigid, frozen culture – to knock it out of the groove in which it has stuck for so many millions of years. I will give it more tools, more new techniques – and before I die, I hope to see it beginning to invent things for itself."

' "Why are you doing this?" I asked, for I knew there was more than mere scientific curiosity here.

' "Because I do not believe that Man will survive, yet I hope to preserve some of the things he has discovered. If he is to be a dead end, I think that another race should be given a helping hand. Do you know why I chose this island? It was so that my experiment should remain isolated. My supertermite, if it ever evolves, will have to remain here until it has reached a very high level of attainment. Until it can cross the Pacific, in fact . . .

' "There is another possibility. Man has no rival on this planet. I think it may do him good to have one. It may be his salvation."

'I could think of nothing to say: this glimpse of the Professor's dreams was so overwhelming – and yet, in view of what I had just seen, so convincing. For I knew that Professor Takato was not mad. He was a visionary, and there was a sublime detachment about his outlook, but it was based on a secure foundation of scientific achievement.

'And it was not that he was hostile to mankind: he was sorry for it. He simply believed that humanity had shot its bolt, and wished to save something from the wreckage. I could not feel it in my heart to blame him.

'We must have been in that little hut for a long time, exploring possible futures. I remember suggesting that perhaps there might be some kind of mutual understanding, since two cultures so utterly dissimilar as Man and Termite need have no cause for conflict. But I couldn't really believe this, and if a contest comes, I'm not certain who will win. For what use would man's weapons be against an intelligent enemy who could lay waste all the wheat fields and all the rice crops in the world?

'When we came out into the open once more, it was almost dusk. It was then that the Professor made his final revelation.

' "In a few weeks," he said, "I am going to take the biggest step of all."

' "And what is that?" I asked.

' "Cannot you guess? I am going to give them fire."

'Those words did something to my spine. I felt a chill that had nothing to do with the oncoming night. The glorious sunset that was taking place beyond the palms seemed symbolic – and suddenly I realised that the symbolism was even deeper than I had thought.

'That sunset was one of the most beautiful I had ever seen, and it was partly of man's making. Up there in the stratosphere, the dust of an island that had died this day was encircling the earth. My race had taken a great step forward; but did it matter now?

' "*I am going to give them fire.*" Somehow, I never doubted that the Professor would succeed. And when he had done so, the forces that my own race had just unleashed would not save it . . .

'The flying boat came to collect us the next day, and I did not see Takato again. He is still there, and I think he is the most important man in the world. While our politicians wrangle, he is making us obsolete.

'Do you think that someone ought to stop him? There may still be time. I've often thought about it, but I've never been able to think of a really convincing reason why I should interfere. Once or twice I nearly made up my mind, but then I'd pick up the newspaper and see the headlines.

'I think we should let them have the chance. I don't see how they could make a worse job of it than we've done.'

Cold War

First published in *Satellite*, April 1957
Collected in *Tales from the White Hart*

The story quoted really appeared in a Miami newspaper on the date given, and may even be accurate.

Some of the wealthier Arab states once looked into the possibility of towing icebergs from the Antarctic to irrigate their rather arid kingdoms. I've heard nothing of the idea for many years, and suspect that the engineering problems were insuperable.

A job for unemployed nuclear submarines?

One of the things that makes Harry Purvis's tales so infernally convincing is their detailed verisimilitude. Consider, for instance, this example. I've checked the places and information as thoroughly as I can – I had to, in order to write up this account – and everything fits into place. How do you explain that unless – but judge for yourself . . .

'I've often noticed,' Harry began, 'how tantalising little snippets of information appear in the Press and then, sometimes years later, one comes across their sequels. I've just had a beautiful example. In the spring of 1954 – I've looked up the date – it was April 19 – an iceberg was reported off the coast of Florida. I remember spotting this news item and thinking it highly peculiar. The Gulf Stream, you know, is born in the Straits of Florida, and I didn't see *how* an iceberg could get that far south before it melted. But I forgot about the whole business almost immediately, thinking it was just another of those tall stories which the papers like to print when there isn't any real news.

'And then, about a week ago, I met a friend who'd been a commander in the US Navy, and he told me the whole astonishing tale. It's such a remarkable story that I think it ought to be better known, though I'm sure that a lot of people simply won't believe it.

'Any of you who are familiar with domestic American affairs may know that Florida's claim to be the Sunshine State is strongly disputed by some of the other forty-seven members of the Union. I don't suppose New York or Maine or Connecticut are very serious contenders, but the State of California regards the Florida claim as an almost personal affront, and is always doing its best to refute it. The Floridians hit back by pointing to the famous Los Angeles smogs, then the Californians say, with careful anxiety, "Isn't it about time you had another hurricane?" and the Floridians reply, "You can count on us when you want any earthquake relief." So it goes on, and this is where my friend Commander Dawson came into the picture.

'The Commander had been in submarines, but was now retired. He'd been working as technical adviser on a film about the exploits of the submarine service when he was approached one day with a very peculiar proposition. I won't say that the California Chamber of Commerce was behind it, as that might be libel. You can make your own guesses . . .

'Anyway, the idea was a typical Hollywood conception. So I thought at first, until I remembered that dear old Lord Dunsany had used a similar theme in one of his short stories. Maybe the Californian sponsor was a Jorkens fan, just as I am.

'The scheme was delightful in its boldness and simplicity. Commander Dawson was offered a substantial sum of money to pilot an artificial iceberg to Florida, with a bonus if he could contrive to strand it on Miami Beach at the height of the season.

'I need hardly say that the Commander accepted with alacrity: he came from Kansas himself, so could view the whole thing dispassionately as a purely commercial proposition. He got together some of his old crew, swore them to secrecy, and after much waiting in Washington corridors managed to obtain temporary loan of an obsolete submarine. Then he went to a big air-conditioning company, convinced them of his credit and his sanity, and got the ice-making plant installed in a big blister on the sub's deck.

'It would take an impossible amount of power to make a solid iceberg, even a small one, so a compromise was necessary. There would be an outer coating of ice a couple of feet thick, but Frigid Freda, as she was christened, was to be hollow. She would look quite impressive from the outside, but would be a typical Hollywood stage set when one got behind the scenes. However, nobody would see her inner secrets except the Commander and his men. She would be set adrift when the prevailing winds and currents were in the right direction, and would last long enough to cause the calculated alarm and despondency.

'Of course, there were endless practical problems to be solved. It would take several days of steady freezing to create Freda, and she must be launched as near her objective as possible. That meant that the submarine – which we'll call the *Marlin* – would have to use a base not too far from Miami.

'The Florida Keys were considered but at once rejected. There was no privacy down there any more; the fishermen now outnumbered the mosquitoes and a submarine would be spotted almost instantly. Even if the *Marlin* pretended she was merely smuggling, she wouldn't be able to get away with it. So that plan was out.

'There was another problem that the Commander had to consider. The coastal waters round Florida are extremely shallow, and though Freda's draft would only be a couple of feet, everybody knew that an honest-to-goodness iceberg was nearly all below the waterline. It wouldn't be very realistic to have an impressive-looking berg sailing through two feet of water. That would give the show away at once.

'I don't know exactly how the Commander overcame these technical problems, but I gather that he carried out several tests in the Atlantic, far from any shipping routes. The iceberg reported in the news was one of his early productions. Incidentally, neither Freda nor her brethren would have been a danger to shipping – being hollow, they would have broken up on impact.

'Finally, all the preparations were complete. The *Marlin* lay out in the Atlantic, some distance north of Miami, with her ice-manufacturing equipment going full blast. It was a beautiful clear night, with a crescent moon sinking in the west. The *Marlin* had no navigation lights, but Commander Dawson was keeping a very strict watch for other ships. On a night like this, he'd be able to avoid them without being spotted himself.

'Freda was still in an embryonic stage. I gather that the technique used was to inflate a large plastic bag with supercooled air, and spray water over it until a crust of ice formed. The bag could be removed when the ice was thick enough to stand up under its own weight. Ice is not a very good structural material, but there was no need for Freda to be very big. Even a small iceberg would be as disconcerting to the Florida Chamber of Commerce as a small baby to an unmarried lady.

'Commander Dawson was in the conning tower, watching his crew working with their sprays of ice-cold water and jets of freezing air. They were now quite skilled at this unusual occupation, and delighted in little artistic touches. However, the Commander had had to put a stop to attempts to reproduce Marilyn Monroe in ice – though he filed the idea for future reference.

'Just after midnight he was startled by a flash of light in the northern sky, and turned in time to see a red glow die away on the horizon.

'"There's a plane down, Skipper!" shouted one of the lookouts. "I just saw it crash!" Without hesitation, the Commander shouted down to the engine room and set course to the north. He'd got an accurate fix on the glow, and judged that it couldn't be more than a few miles away. The presence of Freda, covering most of the stern of his vessel, would not affect his speed appreciably, and in any case there was no way of getting rid of her quickly. He stopped the freezers to give more power to the main diesels, and shot ahead at full speed.

'About thirty minutes later the lookout, using powerful night glasses, spotted something lying in the water. "It's still afloat," he said. "Some kind of airplane, all right – but I can't see any sign of life. And I think the wings have come off."

'He had scarcely finished speaking when there was an urgent report from another watcher.

'"Look, Skipper – thirty degrees to starboard! What's that?"

'Commander Dawson swung around and whipped up his glasses. He saw, just visible above the water, a small oval object spinning rapidly on its axis.

'"Uh-huh," he said, "I'm afraid we've got company. That's a radar scanner – there's another sub here." Then he brightened considerably. "Maybe we can keep out of this after all," he remarked to his second-in-command. "We'll watch to see that they start rescue operations, then sneak away.

'"We may have to submerge and abandon Freda. Remember they'll have spotted us by now on their radar. Better slacken speed and behave more like a real iceberg."

'Dawson nodded and gave the order. This was getting complicated, and anything might happen in the next few minutes. The other sub would have observed the *Marlin* merely as a blip on its radar screen, but as soon as it upped periscope its commander would start investigating. Then the fat would be in the fire . . .

'Dawson analysed the tactical situation. The best move, he decided, was to employ his unusual camouflage to the full. He gave the order to swing the *Marlin* around so that her stern pointed towards the still submerged stranger. When the other sub surfaced, her commander would be most surprised to see an iceberg, but Dawson hoped he would be too busy with rescue operations to bother about Freda.

'He pointed his glasses towards the crashed plane – and then had his second shock. It was a very peculiar type of aircraft indeed – and there was something wrong—

'"Of course!" said Dawson to his Number One. "We should have thought of this – that thing isn't an airplane at all. It's a missile from the range over at Cocoa – look, you can see the flotation bags. They must have inflated on impact, and the sub was waiting out here to take it back."

'He'd remembered that there was a big missile launching range over on the east coast of Florida, at a place with the unlikely name of Cocoa on the still more improbable Banana River. Well, at least there was nobody in danger, and if the *Marlin* sat tight there was a sporting chance that they'd be none the worse for this diversion.

'Their engines were just turning over, so that they had enough control to keep hiding behind their camouflage. Freda was quite large enough to conceal their conning tower, and from a distance, even in better light than this, the *Marlin* would be totally invisible. There was one horrid possibility, though. The other sub might start shelling them on general prinicples, as a menace to navigation. No: it would just report them by radio to the Coast Guard, which would be a nuisance but would not interfere with their plans.

'"Here she comes!" said Number One. "What class is she?"

'They both stared through their glasses as the submarine, water pouring from its sides, emerged from the faintly phosphorescent ocean. The moon had now almost set, and it was difficult to make out any details. The radar scanner, Dawson was glad to see, had stopped its rotation and was pointing at the crashed missile. There was something odd about the design of that conning tower, though . . .

'Then Dawson swallowed hard, lifted the mike to his mouth, and whispered to his crew in the bowels of the *Marlin*: "Does anyone down there speak Russian . . .?"

'There was a long silence, but presently the engineer officer climbed up into the conning tower.

' "I know a bit, Skipper," he said. "My grandparents came from the Ukraine. What's the trouble?"

' "Take a look at this," said Dawson grimly. "There's an interesting piece of poaching going on here. I think we ought to stop it . . ." '

Harry Purvis has a most annoying habit of breaking off just when a story reaches its climax, and ordering another beer – or, more usually, getting someone else to buy him one. I've watched him do this so often that now I can tell just when the climax is coming by the level in his glass. We had to wait, with what patience we could, while he refuelled.

'When you think about it,' he said thoughtfully, 'it was jolly hard luck on the commander of that Russian submarine. I imagine they shot him when he got back to Vladivostok, or wherever he came from. For what court of inquiry would have believed his story? If he was fool enough to tell the truth, he'd have said, "We were just off the Florida coast when an iceberg shouted at us in Russian, 'Excuse me – I think that's *our* property!' " Since there would be a couple of MVD men aboard the ship, the poor guy would have had to make up *some* kind of story, but whatever he said wouldn't be very convincing . . .

'As Dawson had calculated, the Russian sub simply ran for it as soon as it knew it had been spotted. And remembering that he was an officer in the Reserve, and that his duty to his country was more important than his contractual obligations to any single state, the Commander of the *Marlin* really had no choice in his subsequent actions. He picked up the missile, defrosted Freda, and set course for Cocoa – first sending a radio message that caused a great flurry in the Navy Department and started destroyers racing out into the Atlantic. Perhaps Inquisitive Ivan never got back to Vladivostok after all . . .

'The subsequent explanations were a little embarrassing, but I gather that the rescued missile was so important that no one asked too many questions about the *Marlin*'s private war. The attack on Miami Beach had to be called off, however, at least until the next season. It's satisfactory to relate that even the sponsors of the project, though they had sunk a lot of money into it, weren't too disappointed. They each have a certificate signed by the Chief of Naval Operations, thanking them for valuable but unspecified services to their country. These cause such envy and mystification to all their Los Angeles friends that they wouldn't part with them for anything . . .

'Yet I don't want you to think that nothing more will ever come of the whole project; you ought to know American publicity men better than that. Freda may be in suspended animation, but one day she'll be revived. All the plans are ready, down to such little details as the accidental presence of a Hollywood film unit on Miami Beach when Freda comes sailing in from the Atlantic.

'So this is one of those stories I can't round off to a nice, neat ending. The preliminary skirmishes have taken place, but the main engagement is still to come. And this is the thing I often wonder about – *what will Florida do to the Californians when it discovers what's going on?* Any suggestions, anybody?'

Sleeping Beauty

First published in *Infinity Science Fiction*, April 1957
Collected in *Tales from the White Hart*

It was one of those halfhearted discussions that is liable to get going in the 'White Hart' when no one can think of anything better to argue about. We were trying to recall the most extraordinary names we'd ever encountered, and I had just contributed 'Obediah Polkinghorn' when – inevitably – Harry Purvis got into the act.

'It's easy enough to dig up odd names,' he said, reprimanding us for our levity, 'but have you ever stopped to consider a much more fundamental point – the *effects* of those names on their owners? Sometimes, you know, such a thing can warp a man's entire life. That is what happened to young Sigmund Snoring.'

'Oh, no!' groaned Charles Willis, one of Harry's most implacable critics. 'I don't believe it!'

'Do you imagine,' said Harry indignantly, 'that I'd *invent* a name like that? As a matter of fact, Sigmund's family name was something Jewish from Central Europe: it began with SCH and went on for quite a while in that vein. "Snoring" was just an anglicised précis of it. However, all this is by the way: I wish people wouldn't make me waste time on such details.'

Charlie, who is the most promising author I know (he has been promising for more than twenty-five years) started to make vaguely protesting noises, but someone public-spiritedly diverted him with a glass of beer.

'Sigmund,' continued Harry, 'bore his burden bravely enough until he reached manhood. There is little doubt, however, that his name preyed upon his mind, and finally produced what you might call a psychosomatic result. If Sigmund had been born of any other parents, I am sure that he would not have become a stertorous and incessant snorer in fact as well as – almost – in name.

'Well, there are worse tragedies in life. Sigmund's family had a fair amount of money, and a soundproofed bedroom protected the remainder of the household from sleepless nights. As is usually the case, Sigmund was quite unaware of his own nocturnal symphonies, and could never really understand what all the fuss was about.

'It was not until he got married that he was compelled to take his affliction – if you can call it that, for it only inflicted itself on other people –

as seriously as it deserved. There is nothing unusual in a young bride returning from her honeymoon in a somewhat distracted condition, but poor Rachel Snoring had been through a uniquely shattering experience. She was red-eyed with lack of sleep, and any attempt to get sympathy from her friends only made them dissolve into peals of laughter. So it was not surprising that she gave Sigmund an ultimatum; unless he did something about his snoring, the marriage was off.

'Now this was a very serious matter for both Sigmund and his family. They were fairly well-to-do, but by no means rich – unlike Granduncle Reuben, who had died last year leaving a rather complicated will. He had taken quite a fancy to Sigmund, and had left a considerable sum of money in trust for him, which he would receive when he was thirty. Unfortunately, Granduncle Reuben was very old-fashioned and straitlaced, and did not altogether trust the modern generation. One of the conditions of the bequest was that Sigmund should not be divorced or separated before the designated date. If he was, the money would go to found an orphanage in Tel Aviv.

'It was a difficult situation, and there is no way of guessing how it would have resolved itself had not someone suggested that Sigmund ought to go and see Uncle Hymie. Sigmund was not at all keen on this, but desperate predicaments demanded desperate remedies; so he went.

'Uncle Hymie, I should explain, was a very distinguished professor of physiology, and a Fellow of the Royal Society with a whole string of papers to his credit. He was also, at the moment, somewhat short of money, owing to a quarrel with the trustees of his college, and had been compelled to stop work on some of his pet research projects. To add to his annoyance, the Physics Department had just been given half a million pounds for a new synchrotron, so he was in no pleasant mood when his unhappy nephew called upon him.

'Trying to ignore the all-pervading smell of disinfectant and livestock, Sigmund followed the lab steward along rows of incomprehensible equipment, and past cages of mice and guinea pigs, frequently averting his eyes from the revolting coloured diagrams which occupied so much wall space. He found his uncle sitting at a bench, drinking tea from a beaker and absentmindedly nibbling sandwiches.

' "Help yourself," he said ungraciously. "Roast hamster – delicious. One of the litter we used for some cancer tests. What's the trouble?"

'Pleading lack of appetite, Sigmund told his distinguished uncle his tale of woe. The professor listened without much sympathy.

' "Don't know what you got married for," he said at last. "Complete waste of time." Uncle Hymie was known to possess strong views on this subject, having had five children but no wives. "Still, we might be able to do something. How much money have you got?"

' "Why?" asked Sigmund, somewhat taken aback. The professor waved his arms around the lab.

' "Costs a lot to run all this," he said.

' "But I thought the university—"

' "Oh yes – but any special work will have to be under the counter, as it were. I can't use college funds for it."

' "Well, how much will you need to get started?"

'Uncle Hymie mentioned a sum which was rather smaller than Sigmund had feared, but his satisfaction did not last for long. The scientist, it soon transpired, was fully acquainted with Granduncle Reuben's will; Sigmund would have to draw up a contract promising him a share of the loot when, in five years' time, the money became his. The present payment was merely an advance.

' "Even so, I don't promise anything, but I'll see what can be done," said Uncle Hymie, examining the cheque carefully. "Come and see me in a month."

'That was all that Sigmund could get out of him, for the professor was then distracted by a highly decorative research student in a sweater which appeared to have been sprayed on her. They started discussing the domestic affairs of the lab's rats in such terms that Sigmund, who was easily embarrassed, had to beat a hasty retreat.

'Now, I don't really think that Uncle Hymie would have taken Sigmund's money unless he was fairly sure he could deliver the goods. He must, therefore, have been quite near the completion of his work when the university had slashed his funds; certainly he could never have produced, in a mere four weeks, whatever complex mixture of chemicals it was that he injected into his hopeful nephew's arm a month after receiving the cash. The experiment was carried out at the professor's own home, late one evening; Sigmund was not too surprised to find the lady research student in attendance.

' "What will this stuff *do*?" he asked.

' "It will stop you snoring – I hope," answered Uncle Hymie. "Now, here's a nice comfortable seat, and a pile of magazines to read. Irma and I will take turns keeping an eye on you in case there are any side reactions."

' "Side reactions?" said Sigmund anxiously, rubbing his arm.

' "Don't worry – just take it easy. In a couple of hours we'll know if it works."

'So Sigmund waited for sleep to come, while the two scientists fussed about him (not to mention around each other) taking readings of blood pressure, pulse, temperature and generally making Sigmund feel like a chronic invalid. When midnight arrived, he was not at all sleepy, but the professor and his assistant were almost dead on their feet. Sigmund realised that they had been working long hours on his behalf, and felt a gratitude which was quite touching during the short period while it lasted.

'Midnight came and passed. Irma folded up and the professor laid her, none too gently, on the couch. "You're quite sure you don't feel tired yet?" he yawned at Sigmund.

' "Not a bit. It's very odd; I'm usually fast asleep by this time."

' "You feel perfectly all right?"

' "Never felt better."

'There was another vast yawn from the professor. He muttered something like, "Should have taken some of it myself," then subsided into an armchair.

' "Give us a shout," he said sleepily, "if you feel anything unusual. No point in us staying up any longer." A moment later Sigmund, still somewhat mystified, was the only conscious person in the room.

'He read a dozen copies of *Punch* stamped "Not to Be Removed from the Common Room" until it was 2 a.m. He polished off all the *Saturday Evening Posts* by 4. A small bundle of *New Yorkers* kept him busy until 5, when he had a stroke of luck. An exclusive diet of caviar soon grows monotonous, and Sigmund was delighted to discover a limp and much-thumbed volume entitled *The Blonde Was Willing*. This engaged his full attention until dawn, when Uncle Hymie gave a convulsive start, shot out of his chair, woke Irma with a well-directed slap, and then turned his full attention towards Sigmund.

' "Well, my boy," he said, with a hearty cheerfulness that at once alerted Sigmund's suspicions. "I've done what you wanted. You passed the night without snoring, didn't you?"

'Sigmund put down the Willing Blonde, who was now in a situation where her co-operation or lack of it would make no difference at all.

' "I didn't snore," he admitted. "But I didn't sleep either."

' "You still feel perfectly wide awake?"

' "Yes – I don't understand it at all."

'Uncle Hymie and Irma exchanged triumphant glances. "You've made history, Sigmund," said the professor. 'You're the first man to be able to do without sleep." And so the news was broken to the astonished and not yet indignant guinea pig.

'I know,' continued Harry Purvis, not altogether accurately, 'that many of you would like the scientific details of Uncle Hymie's discovery. But I don't know them, and if I did they would be too technical to give here. I'll merely point out, since I see some expressions which a less trusting man might describe as sceptical, that there is nothing really startling about such a development. Sleep, after all, is a highly variable factor. Look at Edison, who managed on two or three hours a day right up to the end of his life. It's true that men can't go without sleep indefinitely – but some animals can, so it clearly isn't a fundamental part of metabolism.'

'*What* animals can go without sleep?' asked somebody, not so much in disbelief as out of pure curiosity.

'Well – er – of course! – the fish that live out in deep water beyond the continental shelf. If they ever fall asleep, they'd be snapped up by other fish, or they'd lose their trim and sink to the bottom. So they've got to keep awake all of their lives.'

(I am still, by the way, trying to find if this statement of Harry's is true. I've never caught him out yet on a scientific fact, though once or twice I've had to give him the benefit of the doubt. But back to Uncle Hymie.)

'It took some time,' continued Harry, 'for Sigmund to realise what an

603

astonishing thing had been done to him. An enthusiastic commentary from his uncle, enlarging upon all the glorious possibilities that had been opened up for him now that he had been freed from the tyranny of sleep, made it difficult to concentrate on the problem. But presently he was able to raise the question that had been worrying him. "How long will this last?" he enquired.

'The professor and Irma looked at each other. Then Uncle Hymie coughed a little nervously and replied: "We're not quite sure yet. That's one thing we've got to find out. It's perfectly possible that the effect will be permanent."

' "You mean that I'll never be able to sleep again?"

' "Not 'Never be able to.' 'Never *want* to.' However, I could probably work out some way of reversing the process if you're really anxious. Cost a lot of money, though."

'Sigmund left hastily, promising to keep in touch and to report his progress every day. His brain was still in a turmoil, but first he had to find his wife and to convince her that he would never snore again.

'She was quite willing to believe him, and they had a touching reunion. But in the small hours of next morning it got very dull lying there with no one to talk to, and presently Sigmund tiptoed away from his sleeping wife. For the first time, the full reality of his position was beginning to dawn upon him; what on earth was he going to do with the extra eight hours a day that had descended upon him as an unwanted gift?

'You might think that Sigmund had a wonderful – indeed an unprecedented – opportunity for leading a fuller life by acquiring that culture and knowledge which we all felt we'd like – if only we had the time to do something about it. He could read every one of the great classics that are just names to most people; he could study art, music or philosophy, and fill his mind with all the finest treasures of the human intellect. In fact, a good many of you are probably envying him right now.

'Well, it didn't work out that way. The fact of the matter is that even the highest-grade mind needs some relaxation, and cannot devote itself to serious pursuits indefinitely. It was true that Sigmund had no further need of sleep, but he needed entertainment to occupy him during the long, empty hours of darkness.

'Civilisation, he soon discovered, was not designed to fit the requirements of a man who couldn't sleep. He might have been better off in Paris or New York, but in London practically everything closed down at 11 p.m., only a few coffee bars were still open at midnight, and by 1 a.m. – well, the less said about any establishments still operating, the better.

'At first, when the weather was good, he occupied his time going for long walks, but after several encounters with inquisitive and sceptical policemen he gave this up. So he took to the car and drove all over London during the small hours, discovering all sorts of odd places he never knew existed. He soon had a nodding acquaintance with many night watchmen, Covent

Garden porters and milkmen, as well as Fleet Street journalists and printers who had to work while the rest of the world slept. But as Sigmund was not the sort of person who took a great interest in his fellow human beings, this amusement soon palled and he was thrown back upon his own limited resources.

'His wife, as might be expected, was not at all happy about his nocturnal wanderings. He had told her the whole story, and though she had found it hard to believe she was forced to accept the evidence of her own eyes. But having done so, it seemed that she would prefer a husband who snored and stayed at home to one who tiptoed away around midnight and was not always back by breakfast.

'This upset Sigmund greatly. He had spent or promised a good deal of money (as he kept reminding Rachel) and taken a considerable personal risk to cure himself of his malaise. And was she grateful? No; she just wanted an itemised account of the time he spent when he should have been sleeping but wasn't. It was most unfair and showed a lack of trust which he found very disheartening.

'Slowly the secret spread through a wider circle, though the Snorings (who were a very close-knit clan) managed to keep it inside the family. Uncle Lorenz, who was in the diamond business, suggested that Sigmund take up a second job as it seemed a pity to waste all that additional working time. He produced a list of one-man occupations, which could be carried on equally easily by day or night, but Sigmund thanked him kindly and said he saw no reason why he should pay two lots of income tax.

'By the end of six weeks of twenty-four-hour days, Sigmund had had enough. He felt he couldn't read another book, go to another night club or listen to another gramophone record. His great gift, which many foolish men would have paid a fortune to possess, had become an intolerable burden. There was nothing to do but to go and see Uncle Hymie again.

'The professor had been expecting him, and there was no need to threaten legal proceedings, to appeal to the solidarity of the Snorings, or to make pointed remarks about breach of contract.

'"All right, all right," grumbled the scientist. "I don't believe in casting pearls before swine. I knew you'd want the antidote sooner or later, and because I'm a generous man it'll only cost you fifty guineas. But don't blame me if you snore worse than ever."

'"I'll take that risk," said Sigmund. As far as he and Rachel were concerned, it had come to separate rooms anyway by this time.

'He averted his gaze as the professor's assistant (not Irma this time, but an angular brunette) filled a terrifyingly large hypodermic with Uncle Hymie's latest brew. Before he had absorbed half of it, he had fallen asleep.

'For once, Uncle Hymie looked quite disconcerted. "I didn't expect it to act *that* fast," he said. "Well, let's get him to bed – we can't have him lying around the lab."

'By the next morning, Sigmund was still fast asleep and showed no reactions to any stimuli. His breathing was imperceptible; he seemed to be in a trance rather than a slumber, and the professor was getting a little alarmed.

'His worry did not last for long, however. A few hours later an angry guinea pig bit him on the finger, blood poisoning set in, and the editor of *Nature* was just able to get the obituary notice into the current issue before it went to press.

'Sigmund slept through all this excitement and was still blissfully unconscious when the family got back from the Golders Green Crematorium and assembled for a council of war. *De mortuis nil nisi bonum*, but it was obvious that the late Professor Hymie had made another unfortunate mistake, and no one knew how to set about unravelling it.

'Cousin Meyer, who ran a furniture store in the Mile End Road, offered to take charge of Sigmund if he could use him on display in his shop window to demonstrate the luxury of the beds he stocked. However, it was felt that this would be too undignified, and the family vetoed the scheme.

'But it gave them ideas. By now they were getting a little fed up with Sigmund; this flying from one extreme to another was really too much. So why not take the easy way out and, as one wit expressed it, let sleeping Sigmunds lie?

'There was no point in calling in another expensive expert who might only make matters worse (though how, no one could quite imagine). It cost nothing to feed Sigmund, he required only a modicum of medical attention, and while he was sleeping there was certainly no danger of him breaking the terms of Granduncle Reuben's will. When this argument was rather tactfully put to Rachel, she quite saw the strength of it. The policy demanded required a certain amount of patience, but the ultimate reward would be considerable.

'The more Rachel examined it, the more she liked the idea. The thought of being a wealthy near-widow appealed to her; it had such interesting and novel possibilites. And, to tell the truth, she had had quite enough of Sigmund to last her for the five years until he came into his inheritance.

'In due course that time arrived and Sigmund became a semi-demi-millionaire. However, he still slept soundly – and in all those five years he had never snored once. He looked so peaceful lying there that it seemed a pity to wake him up, even if anyone knew exactly how to set about it. Rachel felt strongly that ill-advised tampering might have unfortunate consequences, and the family, after assuring itself that she could only get at the interest on Sigmund's fortune and not at the capital, was inclined to agree with her.

'And that was several years ago. When I last heard of him, Sigmund was still peacefully sleeping, while Rachel was having a perfectly wonderful time on the Riviera. She is quite a shrewd woman, as you may have guessed, and I think she realises how convenient it might be to have a youthful husband in cold storage for her old age.

'There are times, I must admit, when I think it's rather a pity that Uncle Hymie never had a chance of revealing his remarkable discoveries to the world. But Sigmund proved that our civilisation isn't yet ripe for such changes, and I hope I'm not around when some other physiologist starts the whole thing over again.'

Harry looked at the clock. 'Good lord!' he exclaimed. 'I'd no idea it was so late – I feel half asleep.' He picked up his briefcase, stifled a yawn, and smiled benignly at us.

'Happy dreams, everybody,' he said.

Security Check

First published in *The Magazine of Fantasy and Science Fiction*, June 1957
Collected in *The Other Side of the Sky*

It is often said that in our age of assembly lines and mass production there's no room for the individual craftsman, the artist in wood or metal who made so many of the treasures of the past. Like most generalisations, this simply isn't true. He's rarer now, of course, but he's certainly not extinct. He has often had to change his vocation, but in his modest way he still flourishes. Even on the island of Manhattan he may be found, if you know where to look for him. Where rents are low and fire regulations unheard of, his minute, cluttered workshops may be discovered in the basements of apartment houses or in the upper storeys of derelict shops. He may no longer make violins or cuckoo clocks or music boxes, but the skills he uses are the same as they always were, and no two objects he creates are ever identical. He is not contemptuous of mechanisation: you will find several electric hand tools under the debris on his bench. He has moved with the times: he will always be around, the universal odd-job man who is never aware of it when he makes an immortal work of art.

Hans Muller's workshop consisted of a large room at the back of a deserted warehouse, no more than a vigorous stone's throw from the Queensborough Bridge. Most of the building had been boarded up awaiting demolition, and sooner or later Hans would have to move. The only entrance was across a weed-covered yard used as a parking place during the day, and much frequented by the local juvenile delinquents at night. They had never given Hans any trouble, for he knew better than to co-operate with the police when they made their periodic inquiries. The police fully appreciated his delicate position and did not press matters, so Hans was on good terms with everybody. Being a peaceable citizen, that suited him very well.

The work on which Hans was now engaged would have deeply puzzled his Bavarian ancestors. Indeed, ten years ago it would have puzzled Hans himself. And it had all started because a bankrupt client had given him a TV set in payment for services rendered . . .

Hans had accepted the offer reluctantly, not because he was old-fashioned and disapproved of TV, but simply because he couldn't imagine where he would find time to look at the darned thing. Still, he thought, at least I can always sell it for fifty dollars. But before I do that, let's see what the programmes are like . . .

His hand had gone out to the switch: the screen had filled with moving shapes – and, like millions of men before him, Hans was lost. He entered a world he had not known existed – a world of battling spaceships, of exotic planets and strange races – the world, in fact, of Captain Zipp, Commander of the Space Legion.

Only when the tedious recital of the virtues of Crunche, the Wonder Cereal, had given way to an almost equally tedious boxing match between two muscle-bound characters who seemed to have signed a nonaggression pact, did the magic fade. Hans was a simple man. He had always been fond of fairy tales – and *this* was the modern fairy tale, with trimmings of which the Grimm Brothers had never dreamed. So Hans did not sell his TV set.

It was some weeks before the initial naïve, uncritical enjoyment wore off. The first thing that began to annoy Hans was the furniture and general décor in the world of the future. He was, as has been indicated, an artist – and he refused to believe that in a hundred years taste would have deteriorated as badly as the Crunche sponsors seemed to imagine.

He also thought very little of the weapons that Captain Zipp and his opponents used. It was true that Hans did not pretend to understand the principles upon which the portable proton disintegrator was based, but however it worked, there was certainly no reason why it should be *that* clumsy. The clothes, the spaceship interiors – they just weren't convincing. How did he know? He had always possessed a highly developed sense of the fitness of things, and it could still operate even in this novel field.

We have said that Hans was a simple man. He was also a shrewd one, and he had heard that there was money in TV. So he sat down and began to draw.

Even if the producer of Captain Zipp had not lost patience with his set designer, Hans Muller's ideas would certainly have made him sit up and take notice. There was an authenticity and realism about them that made them quite outstanding. They were completely free from the element of phonyness that had begun to upset even Captain Zipp's most juvenile followers. Hans was hired on the spot.

He made his own conditions, however. What he was doing he did largely for love, notwithstanding the fact that it was earning him more money than anything he had ever done before in his life. He would take no assistants, and would remain in his little workshop. All that he wanted to do was to produce the prototypes, the basic designs. The mass production could be done somewhere else – he was a craftsman, not a factory.

The arrangement had worked well. Over the last six months Captain Zipp had been transformed and was now the despair of all the rival space operas. This, his viewers thought, was not just a serial about the future. It *was* the future – there was no argument about it. Even the actors seemed to have been inspired by their new surroundings: off the set, they sometimes behaved like twentieth-century time travellers stranded in the Victorian

Age, indignant because they no longer had access to the gadgets that had always been part of their lives.

But Hans knew nothing about this. He toiled happily away, refusing to see anyone except the producer, doing all his business over the telephone – and watching the final result to ensure that his ideas had not been mutilated. The only sign of his connection with the slightly fantastic world of commercial TV was a crate of Crunche in one corner of the workshop. He had sampled one mouthful of this present from the grateful sponsor and had then remembered thankfully that, after all, he was not paid to eat the stuff.

He was working late one Sunday evening, putting the final touches to a new design for a space helmet, when he suddenly realised that he was no longer alone. Slowly he turned from the workbench and faced the door. It had been locked – how could it have been opened so silently? There were two men standing beside it, motionless, watching him. Hans felt his heart trying to climb into his gullet, and summoned up what courage he could to challenge them. At least, he felt thankfully, he had little money here. Then he wondered if, after all, this was a good thing. They might be annoyed . . .

'Who are you?' he asked. 'What are you doing here?'

One of the men moved toward him while the other remained watching alertly from the door. They were both wearing very new overcoats, with hats low down on their heads so that Hans could not see their faces. They were too well dressed, he decided, to be ordinary holdup men.

'There's no need to be alarmed, Mr Muller,' replied the nearer man, reading his thoughts without difficulty. 'This isn't a holdup. It's official. We're from – Security.'

'I don't understand.'

The other reached into a portfolio he had been carrying beneath his coat, and pulled out a sheaf of photographs. He riffled through them until he had found the one he wanted.

'You've given us quite a headache, Mr Muller. It's taken us two weeks to find you – your employers were so secretive. No doubt they were anxious to hide you from their rivals. However, here we are and I'd like you to answer some questions.'

'I'm not a spy!' answered Hans indignantly as the meaning of the words penetrated. 'You can't do this! I'm a loyal American citizen!'

The other ignored the outburst. He handed over the photograph.

'Do you recognise this?' he said.

'Yes. It's the inside of Captain Zipp's spaceship.'

'And you designed it?'

'Yes.'

Another photograph came out of the file.

'And what about this?'

'That's the Martian city of Paldar, as seen from the air.'

'Your own idea?'

'Certainly,' Hans replied, now too indignant to be cautious.

'And *this*?'

'Oh, the proton gun. I was quite proud of that.'

'Tell me, Mr Muller – are these all your own ideas?'

'Yes, *I* don't steal from other people.'

His questioner turned to his companion and spoke for a few minutes in a voice too low for Hans to hear. They seemed to reach agreement on some point, and the conference was over before Hans could make his intended grab at the telephone.

'I'm sorry,' continued the intruder. 'But there has been a serious leak. It may be – uh – accidental, even unconscious, but that does not affect the issue. We will have to investigate you. Please come with us.'

There was such power and authority in the stranger's voice that Hans began to climb into his overcoat without a murmur. Somehow, he no longer doubted his visitors' credentials and never thought of asking for any proof. He was worried, but not yet seriously alarmed. Of course, it was obvious what had happened. He remembered hearing about a science fiction writer during the war who had described the atom bomb with disconcerting accuracy. When so much secret research was going on, such accidents were bound to occur. He wondered just what it was he had given away.

At the doorway, he looked back into his workshop and at the men who were following him.

'It's all a ridiculous mistake,' he said. 'If I *did* show anything secret in the programme, it was just a coincidence. I've never done anything to annoy the FBI.'

It was then that the second man spoke at last, in very bad English and with a most peculiar accent.

'What is the FBI?' he asked.

But Hans didn't hear him. He had just seen the spaceship.

The Man Who Ploughed the Sea

First published in *Satellite*, June 1957
Collected in *Tales from the White Hart*

This story was written in Miami, in 1954. Despite the lapse of time, many of the themes of this story are surprisingly up-to-date, and a few years ago I was amazed to read a description in a scientific journal of a ship-borne device to extract uranium from sea water! I sent a copy of the story to the inventors, and apologised for invalidating their patent.

The adventures of Harry Purvis have a kind of mad logic that makes them convincing by their very improbability. As his complicated but neatly dovetailed stories emerge, one becomes lost in a sort of baffled wonder. Surely, you say to yourself, no one would have the nerve to make *that* up – such absurdities only occur in real life, not in fiction. And so criticism is disarmed, or at any rate discomfited, until Drew shouts, 'Time gentlemen, *pleeze*!' and throws us all out into the cold hard world.

Consider, for example, the unlikely chain of events which involved Harry in the following adventure. If he'd wanted to invent the whole thing, surely he could have managed it a lot more simply. There was not the slightest need, from the artistic point of view, to have started at Boston to make an appointment off the coast of Florida . . .

Harry seems to have spent a good deal of time in the United States, and to have quite as many friends there as he has in England. Sometimes he brings them to the 'White Hart', and sometimes they leave again under their own power. Often, however, they succumb to the illusion that beer which is tepid is also innocuous. (I am being unjust to Drew: his beer is *not* tepid. And if you insist, he will give you, for no extra charge, a piece of ice every bit as large as a postage stamp.)

This particular saga of Harry's began, as I have indicated, at Boston, Mass. He was staying as a house guest of a successful New England lawyer when one morning his host said, in the casual way Americans have: 'Let's go down to my place in Florida. I want to get some sun.'

'Fine,' said Harry, who'd never been to Florida. Thirty minutes later, to his considerable surprise, he found himself moving south in a red Jaguar saloon at a formidable speed.

The drive in itself was an epic worthy of a complete story. From Boston to Miami is a little matter of 1,568 miles – a figure which, according to Harry, is now engraved on his heart. They covered the distance in thirty hours, frequently to the sound of ever-receding police sirens as frustrated squad cars dwindled astern. From time to time considerations of tactics involved them in evasive manoeuvres and they had to shoot off into secondary roads. The Jaguar's radio tuned in to all the police frequencies, so they always had plenty of warning if an interception was being arranged. Once or twice they just managed to reach a state line in time, and Harry couldn't help wondering what his host's clients would have thought had they known the strength of the psychological urge which was obviously getting him away from them. He also wondered if he was going to see anything of Florida at all, or whether they would continue at this velocity down US 1 until they shot into the ocean at Key West.

They finally came to a halt sixty miles south of Miami, down on the Keys – that long, thin line of islands hooked on to the lower end of Florida. The Jaguar angled suddenly off the road and weaved a way through a rough track cut in the mangroves. The road ended in a wide clearing at the edge of the sea, complete with dock, thirty-five-foot cabin cruiser, swimming pool, and modern ranch-type house. It was quite a nice little hideaway, and Harry estimated that it must have cost the best part of a hundred thousand dollars.

He didn't see much of the place until the next day, as he collapsed straight into bed. After what seemed far too short a time, he was awakened by a sound like a boiler factory in action. He showered and dressed in slow motion, and was reasonably back to normal by the time he had left his room. There seemed to be no one in the house, so he went outside to explore.

By this time he had learned not to be surprised at anything so he barely raised his eyebrows when he found his host working down at the dock, straightening out the rudder on a tiny and obviously homemade submarine. The little craft was about twenty feet long, had a conning tower with large observation windows, and bore the name *Pompano* stencilled on her prow.

After some reflection, Harry decided that there was nothing really very unusual about all this. About five million visitors come to Florida every year, most of them determined to get on or into the sea. His host happened to be one of those fortunate enough to indulge in his hobby in a big way.

Harry looked at the *Pompano* for some time, and then a disturbing thought struck him. 'George,' he said, 'do you expect me to go down in *that* thing?'

'Why, sure,' answered George, giving a final bash at the rudder. 'What are you worried about? I've taken her out lots of times – she's safe as houses. We won't be going deeper than twenty feet.'

'There are circumstances,' retorted Harry, 'when I should find a mere six feet of water more than adequate. And didn't I mention my claustrophobia? It always comes on badly at this time of year.'

'Nonsense!' said George. 'You'll forget all about that when we're out on

613

the reef.' He stood back and surveyed his handiwork, then said with a sigh of satisfaction. 'Looks OK now. Let's have some breakfast.'

During the next thirty minutes, Harry learned a good deal about the *Pompano*. George had designed and built her himself, and her powerful little diesel could drive her at five knots when she was fully submerged. Both crew and engine breathed through a snorkel tube, so there was no need to bother about electric motors and an independent air supply. The length of the snorkel limited dives to twenty-five feet, but in these shallow waters this was no great handicap.

'I've put a lot of novel ideas into her,' said George enthusiastically. 'Those windows, for instance – look at their size. They'll give you a perfect view, yet they're quite safe. I use the old aqualung principle to keep the air pressure in the *Pompano* exactly the same as the water pressure outside, so there's no strain on the hull or the ports.'

'And what happens,' asked Harry, 'if you get stuck on the bottom?'

'I open the door and get out, of course. There are a couple of spare aqualungs in the cabin, as well as a life raft with a waterproof radio, so that we can always yell for help if we get in trouble. Don't worry – I've thought of everything.'

'Famous last words,' muttered Harry. But he decided that after the ride down from Boston he undoubtedly had a charmed life: the sea was probably a safer place than US 1 with George at the wheel.

He made himself thoroughly familiar with the escape arrangements before they set out, and was fairly happy when he saw how well designed and constructed the little craft appeared to be. The fact that a lawyer had produced such a neat piece of marine engineering in his spare time was not in the least unusual. Harry had long ago discovered that a considerable number of Americans put quite as much effort into their hobbies as into their professions.

They chugged out of the little harbour, keeping to the marked channel until they were well clear of the coast. The sea was calm and as the shore receded the water became steadily more and more transparent. They were leaving behind the fog of pulverised coral which clouded the coastal waters, where the waves were incessantly tearing at the land. After thirty minutes they had come to the reef, visible below them as a kind of patchwork quilt above which multicoloured fish pirouetted to and fro. George closed the hatches, opened the valve of the buoyancy tanks, and said gaily, 'Here we go!'

The wrinkled silk veil lifted, crept past the window, distorting all vision for a moment – and then they were through, no longer aliens looking into the world of waters, but denizens of that world themselves. They were floating above a valley carpeted with white sand, and surrounded by low hills of coral. The valley itself was barren but the hills around it were alive with things that grew, things that crawled and things that swam. Fish as dazzling as neon signs wandered lazily among the animals that looked like trees. It seemed not only a breathtakingly lovely but also a peaceful world.

There was no haste, no sign of the struggle for existence. Harry knew very well that this was an illusion, but during all the time they were submerged he never saw one fish attack another. He mentioned this to George, who commented: 'Yes, that's a funny thing about fish. They seem to have definite feeding times. You can see barracuda swimming around and if the dinner gong hasn't gone the other fish won't take any notice of them.'

A ray, looking like some fantastic black butterfly, flapped its way across the sand, balancing itself with its long, whiplike tail. The sensitive feelers of a crayfish waved cautiously from a crack in the coral; the exploring gestures reminded Harry of a soldier testing for snipers with his hat on a stick. There was so much life, of so many kinds, crammed in this single spot that it would take years of study to recognise it all.

The *Pompano* cruised very slowly along the valley, while George gave a running commentary.

'I used to do this sort of thing with the aqualung,' he said, 'but then I decided how nice it would be to sit in comfort and have an engine to push me around. Then I could stay out all day, take a meal along, use my cameras and not give a damn if a shark was sneaking up on me. There goes a tang – did you ever see such a brilliant blue in your life? Besides, I could show my friends around down here while still being able to talk to them. That's one big handicap with ordinary diving gear – you're deaf and dumb and have to talk in signs. Look at those angelfish – one day I'm going to fix up a net to catch some of them. See the way they vanish when they're edge on! Another reason why I built the *Pompano* was so that I could look for wrecks. There are hundreds in this area – it's an absolute graveyard. The *Santa Margarita* is only about fifty miles from here, in Biscayne Bay. She went down in 1595 with seven million dollars of bullion aboard. And there's a little matter of sixty-five million off Long Cay, where fourteen galleons sank in 1715. The trouble is, of course, that most of these wrecks have been smashed up and overgrown with coral so it wouldn't do you a lot of good even if you did locate them. But it's fun to try.'

By this time Harry had begun to appreciate his friend's psychology. He could think of few better ways of escaping from a New England law practice. George was a repressed romantic – and not such a repressed one, either, now that he came to think of it.

They cruised along happily for a couple of hours, keeping in water that was never more than forty feet deep. Once they grounded on a dazzling stretch of broken coral, and took time off for liverwurst sandwiches and glasses of beer. 'I drank some ginger beer down here once,' said George. 'When I came up the gas inside me expanded and it was a very odd sort of feeling. Must try it with champagne some day.'

Harry was just wondering what to do with the empties when the *Pompano* seemed to go into eclipse as a dark shadow drifted overhead. Looking up through the observation window, he saw that a ship was moving slowly past twenty feet above their heads. There was no danger of a collision, as they had pulled down their snort for just this reason and were subsisting for the moment on their capital as far as air was concerned. Harry had never seen a ship from underneath and began to add another novel experience to the many he had acquired today.

He was quite proud of the fact that, despite his ignorance of matters nautical, he was just as quick as George at spotting what was wrong with the vessel sailing overhead. Instead of the normal shaft and screw, this ship had a long tunnel running the length of its keel. As it passed above them, the *Pompano* was rocked by the sudden rush of water.

'I'll be damned!' said George, grabbing the controls. 'That looks like some kind of jet-propulsion system. It's about time somebody tried one out. Let's have a look.'

He pushed up the periscope, and discovered that the ship slowly cruising past them was the *Valency*, of New Orleans. 'That's a funny name,' he said. 'What does it mean?'

'I would say,' answered Harry, 'that it means the owner is a chemist – except for the fact that no chemist would ever make enough money to buy a ship like that.'

'I'm going to follow her,' decided George. 'She's only making five knots, and I'd like to see how that dingus works.'

He elevated the snort, got the diesel running, and started in pursuit. After a brief chase, the *Pompano* drew within fifty feet of the *Valency*, and Harry felt rather like a submarine commander about to launch a torpedo. They couldn't miss from this distance.

In fact, they nearly made a direct hit. For the *Valency* suddenly slowed to a halt, and before George realised what had happened, he was alongside her. 'No signals!' he complained, without much logic. A minute later, it was clear that the manoeuvre was no accident. A lasso dropped neatly over the *Pompano*'s snorkel and they were efficiently gaffed. There was nothing to do but emerge, rather sheepishly, and make the best of it.

Fortunately, their captors were reasonable men and could recognise the truth when they heard it. Fifteen minutes after coming aboard the *Valency*, George and Harry were sitting on the bridge while a uniformed steward brought them highballs and they listened attentively to the theories of Dr Gilbert Romano.

They were still both a little overawed at being in Dr Romano's presence: it was rather like meeting a live Rockefeller or a reigning du Pont. The Doctor was a phenomenon virtually unknown in Europe and unusual even in the United States – the big scientist who had become a bigger business-man. He was now in his late seventies and had just been retired – after a considerable tussle – from the chairmanship of the vast chemical-engineering firm he had founded.

It is rather amusing, Harry told us, to notice the subtle social distinctions which differences in wealth can produce even in the most democratic country. By Harry's standards, George was a very rich man: his income was around a hundred thousand dollars a year. But Dr Romano was in another price range altogether, and had to be treated accordingly with a kind of friendly respect which had nothing to do with obsequiousness. On his side, the Doctor was perfectly free and easy; there was nothing about him that gave any impression of wealth, if one ignored such trivia as hundred-and-fifty-foot ocean-going yachts.

The fact that George was on first-name terms with most of the Doctor's business acquaintances helped to break the ice and to establish the purity of their motives. Harry spent a boring half hour while business deals ranging over half the United States were discussed in terms of what Bill So-and-So did in Pittsburgh, who Joe Somebody Else ran into at the Bankers' Club in Houston, how Clyde Thingummy happened to be playing golf at Augusta while Ike was there. It was a glimpse of a mysterious world where immense power was wielded by men who all seemed to have gone to the same colleges, or who at any rate belonged to the same clubs. Harry soon became aware of the fact that George was not merely paying court to Dr Romano because that was the polite thing to do. George was too shrewd a lawyer to miss the chance of building up some good will, and appeared to have forgotten all about the original purpose of their expedition.

Harry had to wait for a suitable gap in the conversation before he could raise the subject which really interested him. When it dawned on Dr Romano that he was talking to another scientist, he promptly abandoned finance and George was the one who was left out in the cold.

The thing that puzzled Harry was why a distinguished chemist should be interested in marine propulsion. Being a man of direct action, he challenged the Doctor on this point. For a moment the scientist appeared a little embarrassed and Harry was about to apologise for his inquisitiveness – a feat that would have required real effort on his part. But before he could do this, Dr Romano had excused himself and disappeared into the bridge.

He came back five minutes later with a rather satisfied expression, and continued as if nothing had happened.

'A very natural question, Mr Purvis,' he chuckled. 'I'd have asked it myself. But do you really expect me to tell you?'

'Er – it was just a vague sort of hope,' confessed Harry.

'Then I'm going to surprise you – surprise you twice, in fact. I'm going to answer you, and I'm going to show you that I'm *not* passionately interested in marine propulsion. Those bulges on the bottom of my ship which you were inspecting with such great interest do contain the screws, but they also contain a good deal else as well.

'Let me give you,' continued Dr Romano, now obviously warming up to his subject, 'a few elementary statistics about the ocean. We can see a lot of it from here – quite a few square miles. Did you know that every cubic mile of sea water contains a hundred and fifty *million* tons of minerals?'

'Frankly, no,' said George. 'It's an impressive thought.'

'It's impressed me for a long time,' said the Doctor. 'Here we go grubbing about in the earth for our metals and chemicals, while every element that exists can be found in sea water. The ocean, in fact, is a kind of universal mine which can never be exhausted. We may plunder the land, but we'll never empty the sea.

'Men have already started to mine the sea, you know. Dow Chemical has been taking out bromine for years: every cubic mile contains about three hundred thousand tons. More recently, we've started to do something about the five million tons of magnesium per cubic mile. But that sort of thing is merely a beginning.

'The great practical problem is that most of the elements present in sea water are in such low concentrations. The first seven elements make up about ninety-nine per cent of the total, and it's the remaining one per cent that contains all the useful metals except magnesium.

'All my life I've wondered how we could do something about this, and the answer came during the war. I don't know if you're familiar with the techniques used in the atomic-energy field to remove minute quantities of isotopes from solutions: some of those methods are still pretty much under wraps.'

'Are you talking about ion-exchange resins?' hazarded Harry.

'Well – something similar. My firm developed several of these techniques on AEC contracts, and I realised at once that they would have wider applications. I put some of my bright young men to work and they have made what we call a "molecular sieve". That's a mighty descriptive expression: in its way, the thing *is* a sieve, and we can set it to select anything we like. It depends on very advanced wave-mechanical theories for its operation, but what it actually does is absurdly simple. We can choose any component of sea water we like, and get the sieve to take it out. With several units, working in series, we can take out one element after another. The efficiency's quite high, and the power consumption negligible.'

'I know!' yelped George. 'You're extracting gold from sea water!'

'Huh!' snorted Dr Romano in tolerant disgust. 'I've got better things to do with my time. Too much damn gold around, anyhow. I'm after the commercially useful metals – the ones our civilisation is going to be desperately short of in another couple of generations. And as a matter of fact, even with my sieve it wouldn't be worth going after gold. There are only about fifty pounds of the stuff in every cubic mile.'

'What about uranium?' asked Harry. 'Or is that scarcer still?'

'I rather wish you hadn't asked that question,' replied Dr Romano with a cheerfulness that belied the remark. 'But since you can look it up in any library, there's no harm in telling you that uranium's two hundred times *more* common than gold. About seven tons in every cubic mile – a figure which is, shall we say, distinctly interesting. So why bother about gold?'

'Why indeed?' echoed George.

'To continue,' said Dr Romano, duly continuing, 'even with the molecular sieve, we've still got the problem of processing enormous volumes of sea water. There are a number of ways one could tackle this: you could build giant pumping stations, for example. But I've always been keen on killing two birds with one stone, and the other day I did a little calculation that gave the most surprising result. I found that every time the *Queen Mary* crosses the Atlantic, her screws chew up about a tenth of a cubic mile of water. Fifteen million tons of minerals, in other words. Or to take the case you indiscreetly mentioned – almost a ton of uranium on every Atlantic crossing. Quite a thought, isn't it?

'So it seemed to me that all we need do to create a very useful mobile extraction plant was to put the screws of any vessel inside a tube which would compel the slip stream to pass through one of my sieves. Of course, there's a certain loss of propulsive power, but our experimental unit works very well. We can't go quite as fast as we did, but the farther we cruise the more money we make from our mining operations. Don't you think the shipping companies will find that very attractive? But of course that's merely incidental. I look forward to the building of floating extraction plants that will cruise round and round in the ocean until they've filled their hoppers with anything you care to name. When that day comes, we'll be able to stop tearing up the land and all our material shortages will be over. Everything goes back to the sea in the long run anyway, and once we've unlocked that treasure chest, we'll be all set for eternity.'

For a moment there was silence on deck, save for the faint clink of ice in the tumblers, while Dr Romano's guests contemplated this dazzling prospect. Then Harry was struck by a sudden thought.

'This is quite one of the most important inventions I've ever heard of,' he said. 'That's why I find it rather odd that you should have confided in us so fully. After all, we're perfect strangers, and for all you know might be spying on you.'

The old scientist chortled gaily.

'Don't worry about *that*, my boy,' he reassured Harry. 'I've already been on to Washington and had my friends check up on you.'

Harry blinked for a minute, then realised how it had been done. He remembered Dr Romano's brief disappearance, and could picture what had happened. There would have been a radio call to Washington, some senator would have got on to the Embassy, the Ministry of Supply representative would have done his bit – and in five minutes the Doctor would have got the answer he wanted. Yes, Americans were very efficient – those who could afford to be.

It was about this time that Harry became aware of the fact that they were no longer alone. A much larger and more impressive yacht than the *Valency* was heading towards them, and in a few minutes he was able to read the name *Sea Spray*. Such a name, he thought, was more appropriate to billowing sails than throbbing diesels, but there was no doubt that the *Spray* was a very pretty creature indeed. He could understand the looks of undisguised covetousness that both George and Dr Romano now plainly bore.

The sea was so calm that the two yachts were able to come alongside each other, and as soon as they had made contact a sunburned, energetic man in the late forties vaulted over onto the deck of the *Valency*. He strode up to Dr Romano, shook his hand vigorously, said, 'Well, you old rascal, what are you up to?' and then looked enquiringly at the rest of the company. The Doctor carried out the introductions: it seemed that they had been boarded by Professor Scott McKenzie, who'd been sailing *his* yacht down from Key Largo.

'Oh no!' cried Harry to himself. 'This is *too* much! One millionaire scientist per day is all I can stand.'

But there was no getting away from it. True, McKenzie was very seldom seen in the academic cloisters, but he was a genuine professor none the less, holding the chair of geophysics at some Texas college. Ninety per cent of his time, however, he spent working for the big oil companies and running a consulting firm of his own. It rather looked as if he had made his torsion balances and seismographs pay quite well for themselves. In fact, though he was a much younger man than Dr Romano, he had even more money owing to being in a more rapidly expanding industry. Harry gathered that the peculiar tax laws of the sovereign State of Texas also had something to do with it . . .

It seemed an unlikely coincidence that these two scientific tycoons should have met by chance, and Harry waited to see what skullduggery was afoot. For a while the conversation was confined to generalities, but it was obvious that Professor McKenzie was extremely inquisitive about the Doctor's other two guests. Not long after they had been introduced, he made some excuse to hop back to his own ship and Harry moaned inwardly. If the Embassy got two separate enquiries about him in the space of half an hour, they'd wonder what he'd been up to. It might even make the FBI suspicious, and then how would he get those promised twenty-four pairs of nylons out of the country?

He found it quite fascinating to study the relation between the two scientists. They were like a couple of fighting cocks circling for position. Romano treated the younger man with a downright rudeness which, Harry suspected, concealed a grudging admiration. It was clear that Dr Romano was an almost fanatical conservationist, and regarded the activities of McKenzie and his employers with the greatest disapproval. 'You're a gang of robbers,' he said once. 'You're seeing how quickly you can loot this planet of its resources, and you don't give a damn about the next generation.'

'And what,' answered McKenzie, not very originally, 'has the next generation ever done for us?'

The sparring continued for the best part of an hour, and much of what went on was completely over Harry's head. He wondered why he and George were being allowed to sit in on all this, and after a while he began to appreciate Dr Romano's technique. He was an opportunist of genius: he was glad to keep them around, now that they had turned up, just to worry Professor McKenzie and to make him wonder what other deals were afoot.

He let the molecular sieve leak out bit by bit, as if it wasn't *really* important and he was only mentioning it in passing. Professor McKenzie, however, latched on to it at once, and the more evasive Romano became, the more insistent was his adversary. It was obvious that he was being deliberately coy, and that though Professor McKenzie knew this perfectly well, he couldn't help playing the older scientist's game.

Dr Romano had been discussing the device in a peculiarly oblique fashion, as if it were a future project rather than an existing fact. He outlined its staggering possibilites, and explained how it would make all existing forms of mining obsolete, besides removing forever the danger of world metal shortages.

'If it's so good,' exclaimed McKenzie presently, 'why haven't you made the thing?'

'What do you think I'm doing out here in the Gulf Stream?' retorted the Doctor. 'Take a look at this.'

He opened a locker beneath the sonar set, and pulled out a small metal bar which he tossed to McKenzie. It looked like lead, and was obviously extremely heavy. The Professor hefted it in his hand and said at once: 'Uranium. Do you mean to say . . .'

'Yes – every gram. And there's plenty more where that came from.' He turned to Harry's friend and said: 'George – what about taking the Professor down in your submarine to have a look at the works? He won't see much, but it'll show him we're in business.'

McKenzie was still so thoughtful that he took a little thing like a private submarine in his stride. He returned to the surface fifteen minutes later, having seen just enough to whet his appetite.

'The first thing I want to know,' he said to Romano, 'is why you're showing this to *me*! It's about the biggest thing that ever happened – why isn't your own firm handling it?'

Romano gave a little snort of disgust.

'You know I've had a row with the board,' he said. 'Anyway, that lot of old dead beats couldn't handle anything as big as this. I hate to admit it, but you Texas pirates are the boys for the job.'

'This is a private venture of yours?'

'Yes: the company knows nothing about it, and I've sunk half a million of my own money into it. It's been a kind of hobby of mine. I felt someone had to undo the damage that was going on, the rape of the continents by people like—'

'All right – we've heard that before. Yet you propose giving it to us?'

'Who said anything about giving?'

There was a pregnant silence. Then McKenzie said cautiously: 'Of course, there's no need to tell you that we'll be interested – very interested. If you'll let us have the figures on efficiency, extraction rates, and all the other relevant statistics – no need to tell us the actual technical details if you don't want to – then we'll be able to talk business. I can't really speak for my associates but I'm sure that they can raise enough cover to make any deal—'

'Scott,' said Romano – and his voice now held a note of tiredness that for the first time reflected his age – 'I'm not interested in doing a deal with your partners. I haven't time to haggle with the boys in the front room and their lawyers and their lawyer's lawyers. Fifty years I've been doing that sort of thing, and believe me, I'm tired. This is *my* development. It was done with *my* money, and all the equipment is in *my* ship. I want to do a personal deal, direct with you. You can handle it from then on.'

McKenzie blinked.

'I couldn't swing anything as big as this,' he protested. 'Sure, I appreciate the offer, but if this does what you say, it's worth billions. And I'm just a poor but honest millionaire.'

'Money I'm no longer interested in. What would I do with it at my time of life? No, Scott, there's just one thing I want now – and I want it right away, this minute. Give me the *Sea Spray*, and you can have my process.'

'You're crazy! Why, even with inflation, you could build the *Spray* for inside a million. And your process must be worth—'

'I'm not arguing, Scott. What you say is true, but I'm an old man in a hurry, and it would take me a year to get a ship like yours built. I've wanted her ever since you showed her to me back at Miami. My proposal is that you take over the *Valency*, with all her lab equipment and records. It will only take an hour to swap our personal effects – we've a lawyer here who can make it all legal. And then I'm heading out into the Caribbean, down through the islands, and across the Pacific.'

'You've got it all worked out?' said McKenzie in awed wonder.

'Yes. You can take it or leave it.'

'I never heard such a crazy deal in my life,' said McKenzie, somewhat petulantly. 'Of course I'll take it. I know a stubborn old mule when I see one.'

The next hour was one of frantic activity. Sweating crew members rushed back and forth with suitcases and bundles, while Dr Romano sat happily in the midst of the turmoil he had created, a blissful smile upon his wrinkled old face. George and Professor McKenzie went into a legal huddle, and emerged with a document which Dr Romano signed with hardly a glance.

Unexpected things began to emerge from the *Sea Spray*, such as a beautiful mutation mink and a beautiful nonmutation blonde.

'Hello, Sylvia,' said Dr Romano politely. 'I'm afraid you'll find the quarters here a little more cramped. The Professor never mentioned you were aboard. Never mind – we won't mention it either. Not actually in the contract, but a gentleman's agreement, shall we say? It would be such a pity to upset Mrs McKenzie.'

'I don't know *what* you mean!' pouted Sylvia. 'Someone has to do all the Professor's typing.'

'And you do it damn badly, my dear,' said McKenzie, assisting her over the rail with true Southern gallantry. Harry couldn't help admiring his composure in such an embarrassing situation – he was by no means sure that he would have managed as well. But he wished he had the opportunity to find out.

At last the chaos subsided, the stream of boxes and bundles subsided to a trickle. Dr Romano shook hands with everybody, thanked George and Harry for their assistance, strode to the bridge of the *Sea Spray*, and ten minutes later, was halfway to the horizon.

Harry was wondering if it wasn't about time for them to take their departure as well – they had never got round to explaining to Professor McKenzie what they were doing here in the first place – when the radiotelephone started calling. Dr Romano was on the line.

'Forgotten his toothbrush, I suppose,' said George. It was not quite as trivial as that. Fortunately, the loud-speaker was switched on. Eavesdropping was practically forced upon them and required none of the effort that makes it so embarrassing to a gentleman.

'Look here, Scott,' said Dr Romano, 'I think I owe you some sort of explanation.'

'If you've gypped me, I'll have you for every cent—'

'Oh, it's not like that. But I did rather pressurise you, though everything I said was perfectly true. Don't get too annoyed with me – you've got a bargain. It'll be a long time, though, before it makes you any money, and you'll have to sink a few millions of your own into it first. You see, the efficiency has to be increased by about three orders of magnitude before it will be a commercial proposition: that bar of uranium cost me a couple of thousand dollars. Now don't blow your top – it *can* be done – I'm certain of that. Dr Kendall is the man to get: he did all the basic work – hire him away from my people however much it costs you. You're a stubborn cuss and I know you'll finish the job now it's on your hands. That's why I wanted you to have it. Poetic justice, too – you'll be able to repay some of the damage you've done to the land. Too bad it'll make you a billionaire, but that can't be helped.

'Wait a minute – don't cut in on me. I'd have finished the job myself if I had the time, but it'll take at least three more years. And the doctors say I've only got six months: I wasn't kidding when I said I was in a hurry. I'm glad I clinched the deal without having to tell you that, but believe me I'd have used it as a weapon if I had to. Just one thing more – when you do get the process working, name it after me, will you? That's all – it's no use calling me back. I won't answer – and I know you can't catch me.'

Professor McKenzie didn't turn a hair.

'I thought it was something like that,' he said to no one in particular. Then he sat down, produced an elaborate pocket slide rule, and became oblivious to the world. He scarcely looked up when George and Harry, feeling very much outclassed, made their polite departure and silently snorkelled away.

'Like so many things that happen these days,' concluded Harry Purvis, 'I still don't know the final outcome of this meeting. I rather imagine that Professor McKenzie has run into some snags, or we'd have heard rumours about the process by now. But I've not the slightest doubt that sooner or later it'll be perfected, so get ready to sell your mining shares . . .

'As for Dr Romano, he wasn't kidding, though his doctors were a little out in their estimates. He lasted a full year, and I guess the *Sea Spray* helped a lot. They buried him in mid-Pacific, and it's just occurred to me that the old boy would have appreciated that. I told you what a fanatical conservationist he was, and it's a piquant thought that even now some of his atoms may be going through his own molecular sieve . . .

'I notice some incredulous looks, but it's a fact. If you took a tumbler of water, poured it into the ocean, mixed well, then filled the glass from the sea, there'd still be some scores of molecules of water from the original sample in the tumbler. So—' he gave a gruesome little chuckle – 'it's only a matter of time before not only Dr Romano, but all of us, make some contribution to the sieve. And with that thought, gentlemen, I bid you all a very pleasant good night.'

Critical Mass

First published in *Space Science Fiction Magazine*, August 1957, revised from
Lilliput, March 1949
Collected in *Tales from the White Hart*

'Did I ever tell you,' said Harry Purvis modestly, 'about the time I prevented
the evacuation of southern England?'

'You did not,' said Charles Willis, 'or if you did, I slept through it.'

'Well, then,' continued Harry, when enough people had gathered round
him to make a respectable audience. 'It happened two years ago at the
Atomic Energy Research Establishment near Clobham. You all know the
place, of course. But I don't think I've mentioned that I worked there for a
while, on a special job I can't talk about.'

'*That* makes a nice change,' said John Wyndham, without the slightest
effect.

'It was on a Saturday afternoon,' Harry began. 'A beautiful day in late
spring. There were about six of us scientists in the bar of the "Black Swan",
and the windows were open so that we could see down the slopes of
Clobham Hill and out across the country to Upchester, about thirty miles
away. It was so clear, in fact, that we could pick out the twin spires of
Upchester Cathedral on the horizon. You couldn't have asked for a more
peaceful day.

'The staff from the Establishment got on pretty well with the locals,
though at first they weren't at all happy about having us on their doorsteps.
Apart from the nature of our work, they'd believed that scientists were a
race apart, with no human interests. When we'd beaten them up at darts a
couple of times, and bought a few drinks, they changed their minds. But
there was still a certain amount of half-serious leg-pulling, and we were
always being asked what we were going to blow up next.

'On this afternoon there should have been several more of us present,
but there'd been a rush job in the Radioisotopes Division and so we were
below strength. Stanley Chambers, the landlord, commented on the absence
of some familiar faces.

'"What's happened to all your pals today?" he asked my boss, Dr French.

'"They're busy at the works," French replied – we always called the
Establishment "the works", as that made it seem more homely and less

625

terrifying. "We had to get some stuff out in a hurry. They'll be along later."

' "One day," said Stan severely, "you and your friends are going to let out something you won't be able to bottle up again. And *then* where will we all be?"

' "Halfway to the moon," said Dr French. I'm afraid it was rather an irresponsible sort of remark, but silly questions like this always made him lose patience.

'Stan Chambers looked over his shoulder as if he was judging how much of the hill stood between him and Clobham. I guessed he was calculating if he'd have time to reach the cellar – or whether it was worth trying anyway.

' "About these – isotopes – you keep sending to the hospitals," said a thoughtful voice. "I was at St Thomas's last week, and saw them moving some around in a lead safe that must have weighed a ton. It gave me the creeps, wondering what would happen if someone forgot to handle it properly."

' "We calculated the other day," said Dr French, obviously still annoyed at the interruption to his darts, "that there was enough uranium in Clobham to boil the North Sea."

'Now that was a silly thing to say: and it wasn't true, either. But I couldn't very well reprimand my own boss, could I?

'The man who'd been asking these questions was sitting in the alcove by the window, and I noticed that he was looking down the road with an anxious expression.

' "The stuff leaves your place on trucks, doesn't it?" he asked, rather urgently.

' "Yes: a lot of isotopes are short-lived, and so they've got to be delivered immediately."

' "Well, there's a truck in trouble down the hill. Would it be one of yours?"

'The dartboard was forgotten in the general rush to the window. When I managed to get a good look, I could see a large truck, loaded with packing cases, careering down the hill about a quarter of a mile away. From time to time it bounced off one of the hedges: it was obvious that the brakes had failed and the driver had lost control. Luckily there was no oncoming traffic, or a nasty accident would have been inevitable. As it was, one looked probable.

'Then the truck came to a bend in the road, left the pavement, and tore through the hedge. It rocked along with diminishing speed for fifty yards, jolting violently over the rough ground. It had almost come to rest when it encountered a ditch and, very sedately, canted over onto one side. A few seconds later the sound of splintering wood reached us as the packing cases slid off to the ground.

' "That's that," said someone with a sigh of relief. "He did the right thing, aiming for the hedge. I guess he'll be shaken up, but he won't be hurt."

'And then we saw a most perplexing sight. The door of the cab opened, and the driver scrambled out. Even from this distance, it was clear that he was highly agitated – though, in the circumstances, that was natural enough. But he did not, as one would have expected, sit down to recover his wits. On the contrary: he promptly took to his heels and ran across the field as if all the demons of hell were after him.

'We watched open-mouthed, and with rising apprehension, as he dwindled down the hill. There was an ominous silence in the bar, except for the ticking of the clock that Stan always kept exactly ten minutes fast. Then someone said, "D'you think we'd better stay? I mean – it's only half a mile . . ."

'There was an uncertain movement away from the window. Then Dr French gave a nervous little laugh.

' "We don't know if it *is* one of our trucks," he said. "And anyway, I was pulling your legs just now. It's completely impossible for any of this stuff to explode. He's just afraid his tank's going to catch fire."

' "Oh yes?" said Stan. "Then why's he still running? He's halfway down the hill now."

' "I know!" suggested Charlie Evan, from the Instruments Section. "He's carrying explosives, and is afraid they're going to go up."

'I had to scotch that one. "There's no sign of a fire, so what's he worried about now? And if he *was* carrying explosives, he'd have a red flag or something."

' "Hang on a minute," said Stan. "I'll go and get my glasses."

'No one moved until he came back: no one, that is, except the tiny figure far down the hillside, which had now vanished into the woods without slackening its speed.

'Stan stared through the binoculars for an eternity. At last he lowered them with a grunt of disappointment.

' "Can't see much," he said. "The truck's tipped over in the wrong direction. Those crates are all over the place – some of them have busted open. See if you can make anything of it."

'French had a long stare, then handed the glasses to me. They were a very old-fashioned model, and didn't help much. For a moment it seemed to me that there was a curious haziness about some of the boxes – but that didn't make sense. I put it down to the poor condition of the lenses.

'And there, I think, the whole business would have fizzled out if those cyclists hadn't appeared. They were puffing up the hill on a tandem, and when they came to the fresh gap in the hedge they promptly dismounted to see what was going on. The truck was visible from the road and they approached it hand in hand, the girl obviously hanging back, the man telling her not to be nervous. We could imagine their conversation: it was a most touching spectacle.

'It didn't last long. They got to within a few yards of the truck – and then departed at high speed in opposite directions. Neither looked back to observe the other's progress; and they were running, I noticed, in a most peculiar fashion.

'Stan, who'd retrieved his glasses, put them down with a shaky hand.

' "Get out the cars!" he said.

' "But—" began Dr French.

'Stan silenced him with a glare. "You damned scientists!" he said, as he slammed and locked the till (even at a moment like this, he remembered his duty). "I knew you'd do it sooner or later."

'Then he was gone, and most of his cronies with him. They didn't stop to offer us a lift.

' "This is perfectly ridiculous!" said French. "Before we know where we are, those fools will have started a panic and there'll be hell to pay."

'I knew what he meant. Someone would tell the police: cars would be diverted away from Clobham; the telephone lines would be blocked with calls – it would be like the Orson Welles "War of the Worlds" scare back in 1938. Perhaps you think I'm exaggerating, but you can never underestimate the power of panic. And people were scared, remember, of our place, and were half expecting something like this to happen.

'What's more, I don't mind telling you that by this time we weren't any too happy ourselves. We were simply unable to imagine what was going on down there by the wrecked truck, and there's nothing a scientist hates more than being completely baffled.

'Meanwhile I'd grabbed Stan's discarded binoculars and had been studying the wreck very carefully. As I looked, a theory began to evolve in my mind. There *was* some – aura – about those boxes. I stared until my eyes began to smart, and then said to Dr French: "I think I know what it is. Suppose you ring up Clobham Post Office and try to intercept Stan, or at least to stop him spreading rumours if he's already got there. Say that everything's under control – there's nothing to worry about. While you're doing that, I'm going to walk down to the truck and test my theory."

'I'm sorry to say that no one offered to follow me. Though I started down the road confidently enough, after a while I began to be a little less sure of myself. I remembered an incident that's always struck me as one of history's most ironic jokes, and began to wonder if something of the same sort might not be happening now. There was once a volcanic island in the Far East, with a population of about fifty thousand. No one worried about the volcano, which had been quiet for a hundred years. Then one day, eruptions started. At first they were minor, but they grew more intense hour by hour. The people started to panic, and tried to crowd aboard the few boats in harbour so that they could reach the mainland.

'But the island was ruled by a military commandant who was determined to keep order at all costs. He sent out proclamations saying that there was no danger, and he got his troops to occupy the ships so that there would be no loss of life as people attempted to leave in overloaded boats. Such was the force of his personality, and the example of his courage, that he calmed the multitude, and those who had been trying to get away crept shamefaced back to their homes, where they sat waiting for conditions to return to normal.

'So when the volcano blew up a couple of hours later, taking the whole island with it, there weren't any survivors at all . . .

'As I got near the truck, I began to see myself in the role of that misguided commandant. After all, there are some times when it is brave to stay and face danger, and others when the most sensible thing to do is to take to the hills. But it was too late to turn back now, and *I* was fairly sure of my theory.'

'I know,' said George Whitley, who always liked to spoil Harry's stories if he could. 'It was gas.'

Harry didn't seem at all perturbed at losing his climax.

'Ingenious of you to suggest it. That's just what I did think, which shows that we can all be stupid at times.

'I'd got to within fifty feet of the truck when I stopped dead, and though it was a warm day a most unpleasant chill began to spread out from the small of my back. For I could see something that blew my gas theory to blazes and left nothing at all in its place.

'A black, crawling mass was writhing over the surface of one of the packing cases. For a moment I tried to pretend to myself that it was some dark liquid oozing from a broken container. But one rather well-known characteristic of liquids is that they can't defy gravity. This thing was doing just that: and it was also quite obviously alive. From where I was standing, it looked like the pseudopod of some giant amoeba as it changed its shape and thickness, and wavered to and fro over the side of the broken crate.

'Quite a few fantasies that would have done credit to Edgar Allan Poe flitted through my mind in those few seconds. Then I remembered my duty as a citizen and my pride as a scientist: I started to walk forward again, though in no great haste.

'I remember sniffing cautiously, as if I still had gas on the mind. Yet it was my ears, not my nose, that gave me the answer, as the sound from that sinister, seething mass built up around me. It was a sound I'd heard a million times before, but never as loud as this. And I sat down – not too close – and laughed and laughed and laughed. Then I got up and walked back to the pub.

' "Well," said Dr French eagerly, "what was it? We've got Stan on the line – caught him at the crossroads. But he won't come back until we can tell him what's happening."

' "Tell Stan," I said, "to rustle up the local apiarist, and bring him along at the same time. There's a big job for him here."

' "The local *what*?" said French. Then his jaw dropped. "My God! You don't mean . . ."

'"Precisely," I answered, walking behind the bar to see if Stan had any interesting bottles hidden away. "They're settling down now, but I guess they're still pretty annoyed. I didn't stop to count, but there must be half a million bees down there trying to get back into their busted hives."'

The Other Side of the Sky

First published in *Infinity Science Fiction Magazine*, September/October 1957
Collected in *The Other Side of the Sky*

The success of the earlier set of linked short stories, 'Venture to the Moon', led to the writing of this series which by good luck appeared on the London newsstands just when Sputnik I appeared in the sky.

Special Delivery

I can still remember the excitement, back in 1957, when Russia launched the first artificial satellites and managed to hang a few pounds of instruments up here above the atmosphere. Of course, I was only a kid at the time, but I went out in the evening like everyone else, trying to spot those little magnesium spheres as they zipped through the twilight sky hundreds of miles above my head. It's strange to think that some of them are still there – but that now they're *below* me, and I'd have to look down toward Earth if I wanted to see them . . .

Yes, a lot has happened in the last forty years, and sometimes I'm afraid that you people down on Earth take the space stations for granted, forgetting the skill and science and courage that went to make them. How often do you stop to think that all your long-distance phone calls, and most of your TV programmes, are routed through one or the other of the satellites? And how often do you give any credit to the meteorologists up here for the fact that weather forecasts are no longer the joke they were to our grandfathers, but are dead accurate ninety-nine per cent of the time?

It was a rugged life, back in the seventies, when I went up to work on the outer stations. They were being rushed into operation to open up the millions of new TV and radio circuits which would be available as soon as we had transmitters out in space that could beam programmes to anywhere on the globe.

The first artificial satellites had been very close to Earth, but the three stations forming the great triangle of the Relay Chain had to be twenty-two thousand miles up, spaced equally around the equator. At this altitude – and at no other – they would take exactly a day to go around their orbit, and so would stay poised forever over the same spot on the turning Earth.

In my time I've worked on all three of the stations, but my first tour of duty was aboard Relay Two. That's almost exactly over Entebbe, Uganda, and provides service for Europe, Africa, and most of Asia. Today it's a huge structure hundreds of yards across, beaming thousands of simultaneous programmes down to the hemisphere beneath it as it carries the radio traffic of half the world. But when I saw it for the first time from the port of the ferry rocket that carried me up to orbit, it looked like a junk pile adrift in space. Prefabricated parts were floating around in hopeless confusion, and it seemed impossible that any order could ever emerge from this chaos.

Accommodation for the technical staff and assembling crews was primitive, consisting of a few unserviceable ferry rockets that had been stripped of everything except air purifiers. 'The Hulks', we christened them; each man had just enough room for himself and a couple of cubic feet of personal belongings. There was a fine irony in the fact that we were living in the midst of infinite space – and hadn't room to swing a cat.

It was a great day when we heard that the first pressurised living quarters were on their way up to us – complete with needle-jet shower baths that would operate even here, where water – like everything else – had no weight. Unless you've lived aboard an overcrowded spaceship, you won't appreciate what that meant. We could throw away our damp sponges and feel really clean at last . . .

Nor were the showers the only luxury promised us. On the way up from Earth was an inflatable lounge spacious enough to hold no fewer than eight people, a microfilm library, a magnetic billiard table, lightweight chess sets, and similar novelties for bored spacemen. The very thought of all these comforts made our cramped life in the Hulks seem quite unendurable, even though we were being paid about a thousand dollars a week to endure it.

Starting from the Second Refuelling Zone, two thousand miles above Earth, the eagerly awaited ferry rocket would take about six hours to climb up to us with its precious cargo. I was off duty at the time, and stationed myself at the telescope where I'd spent most of my scanty leisure. It was impossible to grow tired of exploring the great world hanging there in space beside us; with the highest power of the telescope, one seemed to be only a few miles above the surface. When there were no clouds and the seeing was good, objects the size of a small house were easily visible. I had never been to Africa, but I grew to know it well while I was off duty in Station Two. You may not believe this, but I've often spotted elephants moving across the plains, and the immense herds of zebras and antelopes were easy to see as they flowed back and forth like living tides on the great reservations.

But my favourite spectacle was the dawn coming up over the mountains in the heart of the continent. The line of sunlight would come sweeping across the Indian Ocean, and the new day would extinguish the tiny twinkling galaxies of the cities shining in the darkness below me. Long before the sun had reached the lowlands around them, the peaks of Kilimanjaro and Mount Kenya would be blazing in the dawn, brilliant stars still surrounded by the night. As the sun rose higher, the day would march swiftly down their slopes and the valleys would fill with light. Earth would then be at its first quarter, waxing toward full.

Twelve hours later, I would see the reverse process as the same mountains caught the last rays of the setting sun. They would blaze for a little while in the narrow belt of twilight; then Earth would spin into darkness, and night would fall upon Africa.

It was not the beauty of the terrestrial globe I was concerned with now. Indeed, I was not even looking at Earth, but at the fierce blue-white star high above the western edge of the planet's disc. The automatic freighter was eclipsed in Earth's shadow; what I was seeing was the incandescent flare of its rockets as they drove it up on its twenty-thousand-mile climb.

I had watched ships ascending to us so often that I knew every stage of their manoeuvre by heart. So when the rockets didn't wink out, but continued to burn steadily, I knew within seconds that something was wrong. In sick, helpless fury I watched all our longed-for comforts – and, worse still, our mail! – moving faster and faster along the unintended orbit. The freighter's auto-pilot had jammed; had there been a human pilot aboard, he could have overridden the controls and cut the motor, but now all the fuel that should have driven the ferry on its two-way trip was being burned in one continuous blast of power.

By the time the fuel tanks had emptied, and that distant star had flickered and died in the field of my telescope, the tracking stations had confirmed what I already knew. The freighter was moving far too fast for Earth's gravity to recapture it – indeed, it was heading into the cosmic wilderness beyond Pluto . . .

It took a long time for morale to recover, and it only made matters worse when someone in the computing section worked out the future history of our errant freighter. You see, nothing is ever really lost in space. Once you've calculated its orbit, you know where it is until the end of eternity. As we watched our lounge, our library, our games, our mail receding to the far horizons of the solar system, we knew that it would all come back one day, in perfect condition. If we have a ship standing by it will be easy to intercept it the second time it comes around the sun – quite early in the spring of the year AD 15,862.

Feathered Friend

To the best of my knowledge, there's never been a regulation that forbids one to keep pets in a space station. No one ever thought it was necessary – and even had such a rule existed, I am quite certain that Sven Olsen would have ignored it.

With a name like that, you will picture Sven at once as a six-foot-six

Nordic giant, built like a bull and with a voice to match. Had this been so, his chances of getting a job in space would have been very slim; actually he was a wiry little fellow, like most of the early spacers, and managed to qualify easily for the 150-pound bonus that kept so many of us on a reducing diet.

Sven was one of our best construction men, and excelled at the tricky and specialised work of collecting assorted girders as they floated around in free fall, making them do the slow-motion, three-dimensional ballet that would get them into their right positions, and fusing the pieces together when they were precisely dovetailed into the intended pattern. I never tired of watching him and his gang as the station grew under their hands like a giant jigsaw puzzle; it was a skilled and difficult job, for a space suit is not the most convenient of garbs in which to work. However, Sven's team had one great advantage over the construction gangs you see putting up skyscrapers down on Earth. They could step back and admire their handi-work without being abruptly parted from it by gravity . . .

Don't ask me why Sven wanted a pet, or why he chose the one he did. I'm not a psychologist, but I must admit that his selection was very sensible. Claribel weighed practically nothing, her food requirements were infinitesi-mal – and she was not worried, as most animals would have been, by the absence of gravity.

I first became aware that Claribel was aboard when I was sitting in the little cubbyhole laughingly called my office, checking through my lists of technical stores to decide what items we'd be running out of next. When I heard the musical whistle beside my ear, I assumed that it had come over the station intercom, and waited for an announcement to follow. It didn't; instead, there was a long and involved pattern of melody that made me look up with such a start that I forgot all about the angle beam just behind my head. When the stars had ceased to explode before my eyes, I had my first view of Claribel.

She was a small yellow canary, hanging in the air as motionless as a hummingbird – and with much less effort, for her wings were quietly folded along her sides. We stared at each other for a minute; then, before I had quite recovered my wits, she did a curious kind of backward loop I'm sure no earthbound canary had ever managed, and departed with a few leisurely flicks. It was quite obvious that she'd already learned how to operate in the absence of gravity, and did not believe in doing unnecessary work.

Sven didn't confess to her ownership for several days, and by that time it no longer mattered, because Claribel was a general pet. He had smuggled her up on the last ferry from Earth, when he came back from leave – partly, he claimed, out of sheer scientific curiosity. He wanted to see just how a bird would operate when it had no weight but could still use its wings.

Claribel thrived and grew fat. On the whole, we had little trouble concealing our unauthorised guest when VIPs from Earth came visiting. A space station has more hiding places than you can count; the only problem was that Claribel got rather noisy when she was upset, and we sometimes had to think fast to explain the curious peeps and whistles that came from ventilating shafts and storage bulkheads. There were a couple of narrow escapes – but then who would dream of looking for a canary in a space station?

We were now on twelve-hour watches, which was not as bad as it sounds, since you need little sleep in space. Though of course there is no 'day' and 'night' when you are floating in permanent sunlight, it was still convenient to stick to the terms. Certainly when I woke up that 'morning' it felt like 6.00 a.m. on Earth. I had a nagging headache, and vague memories of fitful, disturbed dreams. It took me ages to undo my bunk straps, and I was still only half awake when I joined the remainder of the duty crew in the mess. Breakfast was unusually quiet, and there was one seat vacant.

'Where's Sven?' I asked, not very much caring.

'He's looking for Claribel,' someone answered. 'Says he can't find her anywhere. She usually wakes him up.'

Before I could retort that she usually woke me up, too, Sven came in through the doorway, and we could see at once that something was wrong. He slowly opened his hand, and there lay a tiny bundle of yellow feathers, with two clenched claws sticking pathetically up into the air.

'What happened?' we asked, all equally distressed.

'I don't know,' said Sven mournfully. 'I just found her like this.'

'Let's have a look at her,' said Jock Duncan, our cook-doctor-dietitian. We all waited in hushed silence while he held Claribel against his ear in an attempt to detect any heartbeat.

Presently he shook his head. 'I can't hear anything, but that doesn't prove she's dead. I've never listened to a canary's heart,' he added rather apologetically.

'Give her a shot of oxygen,' suggested somebody, pointing to the green-banded emergency cylinder in its recess beside the door. Everyone agreed that this was an excellent idea, and Claribel was tucked snugly into a face mask that was large enough to serve as a complete oxygen tent for her.

To our delighted surprise, she revived at once. Beaming broadly, Sven removed the mask, and she hopped onto his finger. She gave her series of 'Come to the cookhouse, boys' trills – then promptly keeled over again.

'I don't get it,' lamented Sven. 'What's wrong with her? She's never done this before.'

For the last few minutes, something had been tugging at my memory. My mind seemed to be very sluggish that morning, as if I was still unable to cast off the burden of sleep. I felt that I could do with some of that oxygen – but before I could reach the mask, understanding exploded in my brain. I whirled on the duty engineer and said urgently:

'Jim! There's something wrong with the air! That's why Claribel's passed out. I've just remembered that miners used to carry canaries down to warn them of gas.'

'Nonsense!' said Jim. 'The alarms would have gone off. We've got duplicate circuits, operating independently.'

'Er – the second alarm circuit isn't connected up yet,' his assistant reminded him. That shook Jim; he left without a word, while we stood arguing and passing the oxygen bottle around like a pipe of peace.

He came back ten minutes later with a sheepish expression. It was one of those accidents that couldn't possibly happen; we'd had one of our rare eclipses by Earth's shadow that night; part of the air purifier had frozen up, and the single alarm in the circuit had failed to go off. Half a million dollars' worth of chemical and electronic engineering had let us down completely. Without Claribel, we should soon have been slightly dead.

So now, if you visit any space station, don't be surprised if you hear an inexplicable snatch of bird song. There's no need to be alarmed: on the contrary, in fact. It will mean that you're being doubly safeguarded, at practically no extra expense.

Take a Deep Breath

A long time ago I discovered that people who've never left Earth have certain fixed ideas about conditions in space. Everyone 'knows', for example, that a man dies instantly and horribly when exposed to the vacuum that exists beyond the atmosphere. You'll find numerous gory descriptions of exploded space travellers in the popular literature, and I won't spoil your appetite by repeating them here. Many of those tales, indeed, are basically true. I've pulled men back through the air lock who were very poor advertisements for space flight.

Yet, at the same time, there are exceptions to every rule – even this one. I should know, for I learned the hard way.

We were on the last stages of building Communications Satellite Two; all the main units had been joined together, the living quarters had been pressurised, and the station had been given the slow spin around its axis that had restored the unfamiliar sensation of weight. I say 'slow', but at its rim our two-hundred-foot-diameter wheel was turning at thirty miles an hour. We had, of course, no sense of motion, but the centrifugal force caused by this spin gave us about half the weight we would have possessed on Earth. That was enough to stop things from drifting around, yet not enough to make us feel uncomfortably sluggish after our weeks with no weight at all.

Four of us were sleeping in the small cylindrical cabin known as Bunk-house Number 6 on the night that it happened. The bunkhouse was at the very rim of the station; if you imagine a bicycle wheel, with a string of sausages replacing the tyre, you have a good idea of the layout. Bunkhouse Number 6 was one of these sausages, and we were slumbering peacefully inside it.

I was awakened by a sudden jolt that was not violent enough to cause me alarm, but which did make me sit up and wonder what had happened. Anything unusual in a space station demands instant attention, so I reached for the intercom switch by my bed. 'Hello, Central,' I called. 'What was that?'

There was no reply; the line was dead.

Now thoroughly alarmed, I jumped out of bed – and had an even bigger shock. *There was no gravity.* I shot up to the ceiling before I was able to grab a stanchion and bring myself to a halt, at the cost of a sprained wrist.

It was impossible for the entire station to have suddenly stopped rotating. There was only one answer; the failure of the intercom and, as I quickly discovered, of the lighting circuit as well forced us to face the appalling truth. We were no longer part of the station; our little cabin had somehow come adrift, and had been slung off into space like a raindrop falling on a spinning flywheel.

There were no windows through which we could look out, but we were not in complete darkness for the battery-powered emergency lights had come on. All the main air vents had closed automatically when the pressure dropped. For the time being, we could live in our own private atmosphere, even though it was not being renewed. Unfortunately, a steady whistling told us that the air we did have was escaping through a leak somewhere in the cabin.

There was no way of telling what had happened to the rest of the station. For all we knew, the whole structure might have come to pieces, and all our colleagues might be dead or in the same predicament as we – drifting through space in leaking cans of air. Our one slim hope was the possibility that we were the only castaways, that the rest of the station was intact and had been able to send a rescue team to find us. After all, we were receding at no more than thirty miles an hour, and one of the rocket scooters could catch up to us in minutes.

It actually took an hour, though without the evidence of my watch I should never have believed that it was so short a time. We were now gasping for breath, and the gauge on our single emergency oxygen tank had dropped to one division above zero.

The banging on the wall seemed like a signal from another world. We banged back vigorously, and a moment later a muffled voice called to us through the wall. Someone outside was lying with his space-suit helmet pressed against the metal, and his shouted words were reaching us by direct conduction. Not as clear as radio – but it worked.

The oxygen gauge crept slowly down to zero while we had our council of war. We would be dead before we could be towed back to the station; yet the rescue ship was only a few feet away from us, with its air lock already open. Our little problem was to cross that few feet – *without* space suits.

We made our plans carefully, rehearsing our actions in the full knowledge that there could be no repeat performance. Then we each took a deep, final swig of oxygen, flushing out our lungs. When we were all ready, I banged on the wall to give the signal to our friends waiting outside.

There was a series of short, staccato raps as the power tools got to work on the thin hull. We clung tightly to the stanchions, as far away as possible from the point of entry, knowing just what would happen. When it came, it was so sudden that the mind couldn't record the sequence of events. The cabin seemed to explode, and a great wind tugged at me. The last trace of air gushed from my lungs, through my already-opened mouth. And then – utter silence, and the stars shining through the gaping hole that led to life.

Believe me, I didn't stop to analyse my sensations. I think – though I can never be sure that it wasn't imagination – that my eyes were smarting and there was a tingling feeling all over my body. And I felt very cold, perhaps because evaporation was already starting from my skin.

The only thing I can be certain of is that uncanny silence. It is never completely quiet in a space station, for there is always the sound of machinery or air pumps. But this was the absolute silence of the empty void, where there is no trace of air to carry sound.

Almost at once we launched ourselves out through the shattered wall, into the full blast of the sun. I was instantly blinded – but that didn't matter, because the men waiting in space suits grabbed me as soon as I emerged and hustled me into the air lock. And there, sound slowly returned as the air rushed in, and we remembered we could breathe again. The entire rescue, they told us later, had lasted just twenty seconds . . .

Well, we were the founding members of the Vacuum-Breathers' Club. Since then, at least a dozen other men have done the same thing, in similar emergencies. The record time in space is now two minutes; after that, the blood begins to form bubbles as it boils at body temperature, and those bubbles soon get to the heart.

In my case, there was only one aftereffect. For maybe a quarter of a minute I had been exposed to *real* sunlight, not the feeble stuff that filters down through the atmosphere of Earth. Breathing space didn't hurt me at all – but I got the worst dose of sunburn I've ever had in my life.

Freedom of Space

Not many of you, I suppose, can imagine the time before the satellite relays gave us our present world communications system. When I was a boy, it was impossible to send TV programmes across the oceans, or even to establish reliable radio contact around the curve of the Earth without picking up a fine assortment of crackles and bangs on the way. Yet now we take interference-free circuits for granted, and think nothing of seeing our friends on the other side of the globe as clearly as if we were standing face to face. Indeed, it's a simple fact that without the satellite relays, the whole structure of world commerce and industry would collapse. Unless we were up here on the space stations to bounce their messages around the globe, how do you think any of the world's big business organisations could keep their widely scattered electronic brains in touch with each other?

But all this was still in the future, back in the late seventies, when we were finishing work on the Relay Chain. I've already told you about some of our problems and near disasters; they were serious enough at the time, but in the end we overcame them all. The three stations spaced around Earth were no longer piles of girders, air cylinders, and plastic pressure chambers. Their assembly had been completed, we had moved aboard, and could now work in comfort, unhampered by space suits. And we had gravity again, now that the stations had been set slowly spinning. Not real gravity, of course; but centrifugal force feels exactly the same when you're out in space. It was pleasant being able to pour drinks and to sit down without drifting away on the first air current.

Once the three stations had been built, there was still a year's solid work to be done installing all the radio and TV equipment that would lift the world's communications networks into space. It was a great day when we established the first TV link between England and Australia. The signal was beamed up to us in Relay Two, as we sat above the centre of Africa, we flashed it across to Three – poised over New Guinea – and they shot it down to Earth again, clear and clean after its ninety-thousand-mile journey.

These, however, were the engineers' private tests. The official opening of the system would be the biggest event in the history of world communication – an elaborate global telecast, in which every nation would take part. It would be a three-hour show, as for the first time the live TV camera roamed around the world, proclaiming to mankind that the last barrier of distance was down.

The programme planning, it was cynically believed, had taken as much effort as the building of the space stations in the first place, and of all the problems the planners had to solve, the most difficult was that of choosing a *compère* or master of ceremonies to introduce the items in the elaborate global show that would be watched by half the human race.

Heaven knows how much conniving, blackmail, and downright character assassination went on behind the scenes. All we knew was that a week before the great day, a nonscheduled rocket came up to orbit with Gregory Wendell aboard. This was quite a surprise, since Gregory wasn't as big a TV personality as, say, Jeffers Jackson in the US or Vince Clifford in Britain. However, it seemed that the big boys had cancelled each other out, and Gregg had got the coveted job through one of those compromises so well known to politicians.

Gregg had started his career as a disc jockey on a university radio station in the American Midwest, and had worked his way up through the Hollywood and Manhattan night-club circuits until he had a daily, nation-wide programme of his own. Apart from his cynical yet relaxed personality, his biggest asset was his deep velvet voice, for which he could probably thank his Negro blood. Even when you flatly disagreed with what he was saying – even, indeed, when he was tearing you to pieces in an interview – it was still a pleasure to listen to him.

We gave him the grand tour of the space station, and even (strictly against regulations) took him out through the air lock in a space suit. He loved it all, but there were two things he liked in particular. 'This air you make,' he said, 'it beats the stuff we have to breathe down in New York. This is the first time my sinus trouble has gone since I went into TV.' He also relished the low gravity; at the station's rim, a man had half his normal, Earth weight – and at the axis he had no weight at all.

However, the novelty of his surroundings didn't distract Gregg from his job. He spent hours at Communications Central, polishing his script and getting his cues right, and studying the dozens of monitor screens that would be his windows on the world. I came across him once while he was running through his introduction of Queen Elizabeth, who would be speaking from Buckingham Palace at the very end of the programme. He was so intent on his rehearsal that he never even noticed I was standing beside him.

Well, that telecast is now part of history. For the first time a billion human beings watched a single programme that came 'live' from every corner of the Earth, and was a roll call of the world's greatest citizens. Hundreds of cameras on land and sea and air looked inquiringly at the turning globe; and at the end there was that wonderful shot of the Earth through a zoom lens on the space station, making the whole planet recede until it was lost among the stars . . .

There were a few hitches, of course. One camera on the bed of the Atlantic wasn't ready on cue, and we had to spend some extra time looking at the Taj Mahal. And owing to a switching error Russian subtitles were superimposed on the South American transmission, while half the USSR found itself trying to read Spanish. But this was nothing to what *might* have happened.

Through the entire three hours, introducing the famous and the unknown with equal ease, came the mellow yet never orotund flow of Gregg's voice. He did a magnificent job; the congratulations came pouring up the beam the moment the broadcast finished. But he didn't hear them; he made one short, private call to his agent, and then went to bed.

Next morning, the Earth-bound ferry was waiting to take him back to any job he cared to accept. But it left without Gregg Wendell, now junior station announcer of Relay Two.

'They'll think I'm crazy,' he said, beaming happily, 'but why should I go back to that rat race down there? I've all the universe to look at, I can breathe smog-free air, the low gravity makes me feel a Hercules, and my three darling ex-wives can't get at me.' He kissed his hand to the departing rocket. 'So long, Earth,' he called. 'I'll be back when I start pining for Broadway traffic jams and bleary penthouse dawns. And if I get homesick, I can look at anywhere on the planet just by turning a switch. Why, I'm more in the middle of things here than I could ever be on Earth, yet I can cut myself off from the human race whenever I want to.'

He was still smiling as he watched the ferry begin the long fall back to Earth, toward the fame and fortune that could have been his. And then, whistling cheerfully, he left the observation lounge in eight-foot strides to read the weather forecast for Lower Patagonia.

Passer-by

It's only fair to warn you, right at the start, that this is a story with no ending. But it has a definite beginning, for it was while we were both students at Astrotech that I met Julie. She was in her final year of solar physics when I was graduating, and during our last year at college we saw a good deal of each other. I've still got the woollen tam-o'shanter she knitted so that I wouldn't bump my head against my space helmet. (No, I never had the nerve to wear it.)

Unfortunately, when I was assigned to Satellite Two, Julie went to the Solar Observatory – at the same distance from Earth, but a couple of degrees eastward along the orbit. So there we were, sitting twenty-two thousand miles above the middle of Africa – but with nine hundred miles of empty, hostile space between us.

At first we were both so busy that the pang of separation was somewhat lessened. But when the novelty of life in space had worn off, our thoughts began to bridge the gulf that divided us. And not only our thoughts, for I'd made friends with the communications people, and we used to have little chats over the interstation TV circuit. In some ways it made matters worse seeing each other face to face and never knowing just how many other people were looking in at the same time. There's not much privacy in a space station . . .

Sometimes I'd focus one of our telescopes onto the distant, brilliant star of the observatory. In the crystal clarity of space, I could use enormous magnifications, and could see every detail of our neighbours' equipment – the solar telescopes, the pressurised spheres of the living quarters that housed the staff, the slim pencils of visiting ferry rockets that had climbed up from Earth. Very often there would be space-suited figures moving among the maze of apparatus, and I would strain my eyes in a hopeless attempt at identification. It's hard enough to recognise anyone in a space suit when you're only a few feet apart – but that didn't stop me from trying.

We'd resigned ourselves to waiting, with what patience we could muster, until our Earth leave was due in six months' time, when we had an unexpected stroke of luck. Less than half our tour of duty had passed when the head of the transport section suddenly announced that he was going outside with a butterfly net to catch meteors. He didn't become violent, but had to be shipped hastily back to Earth. I took over his job on a temporary basis and now had – in theory at least – the freedom of space.

There were ten of the little low-powered rocket scooters under my proud command, as well as four of the larger interstation shuttles used to ferry stores and personnel from orbit to orbit. I couldn't hope to borrow one of *those*, but after several weeks of careful organising I was able to carry out the plan I'd conceived some two micro-seconds after being told I was now head of transport.

There's no need to tell how I juggled duty lists, cooked logs and fuel registers, and persuaded my colleagues to cover up for me. All that matters is that, about once a week, I would climb into my personal space suit, strap myself to the spidery framework of a Mark III Scooter, and drift away from the station at minimum power. When I was well clear, I'd go over to full throttle, and the tiny rocket motor would hustle me across the nine-hundred-mile gap to the observatory.

The trip took about thirty minutes, and the navigational requirements were elementary. I could see where I was going and where I'd come from, yet I don't mind admitting that I often felt – well, a trifle lonely – around the mid-point of the journey. There was no other solid matter within almost five hundred miles – and it looked an awfully long way down to Earth. It was a great help, at such moments, to tune the suit radio to the general service band, and to listen to all the back-chat between ships and stations.

At midflight I'd have to spin the scooter around and start braking, and ten minutes later the observatory would be close enough for its details to be visible to the unaided eye. Very shortly after that I'd drift up to a small, plastic pressure bubble that was in the process of being fitted out as a spectroscopic laboratory – and there would be Julie, waiting on the other side of the air lock . . .

I won't pretend that we confined our discussions to the latest results in astrophysics, or the progress of the satellite construction schedule. Few things, indeed, were further from our thoughts; and the journey home always seemed to flash by at a quite astonishing speed.

It was around mid-orbit on one of those homeward trips that the radar started to flash on my little control panel. There was something large at extreme range, and it was coming in fast. A meteor, I told myself – maybe even a small asteroid. Anything giving such a signal should be visible to the eye: I read off the bearings and searched the star fields in the indicated direction. The thought of a collision never even crossed my mind; space is so inconceivably vast that I was thousands of times safer than a man crossing a busy street on Earth.

There it was – a bright and steadily growing star near the foot of Orion. It already outshone Rigel, and seconds later it was not merely a star, but had begun to show a visible disc. Now it was moving as fast as I could turn my head; it grew to a tiny misshaped moon, then dwindled and shrank with that same silent, inexorable speed.

I suppose I had a clear view of it for perhaps half a second, and that half-second has haunted me all my life. The – object – had already vanished by the time I thought of checking the radar again, so I had no way of gauging how close it came, and hence how large it really was. It could have been a small object a hundred feet away – or a very large one, ten miles off. There is no sense of perspective in space, and unless you know what you are looking at, you cannot judge its distance.

Of course, it *could* have been a very large and oddly shaped meteor; I can never be sure that my eyes, straining to grasp the details of so swiftly moving an object, were not hopelessly deceived. I may have imagined that I saw that broken, crumpled prow, and the cluster of dark ports like the sightless sockets of a skull. Of one thing only was I certain, even in that brief and fragmentary vision. If it *was* a ship, it was not one of ours. Its shape was utterly alien, and it was very, very old.

It may be that the greatest discovery of all time slipped from my grasp as I struggled with my thoughts midway between the two space stations. But I had no measurements of speed or direction; whatever it was that I had glimpsed was now lost beyond recapture in the wastes of the solar system.

What should I have done? No one would ever have believed me, for I would have had no proof. Had I made a report, there would have been endless trouble. I should have become the laughingstock of the Space Service, would have been reprimanded for misuse of equipment – and would certainly not have been able to see Julie again. And to me, at that age, nothing else was as important. If you've been in love yourself, you'll understand; if not, then no explanation is any use.

So I said nothing. To some other man (how many centuries hence?) will go the fame for proving that we were not the first-born of the children of the sun. Whatever it may be that is circling out there on its eternal orbit can wait, as it has waited ages already.

Yet I sometimes wonder. Would I have made a report, after all – had I known that Julie was going to marry someone else?

The Call of the Stars

Down there on Earth the twentieth century is dying. As I look across at the shadowed globe blocking the stars, I can see the lights of a hundred sleepless cities, and there are moments when I wish that I could be among the crowds now surging and singing in the streets of London, Capetown, Rome, Paris, Berlin, Madrid . . . Yes, I can see them all at a single glance, burning like fireflies against the darkened planet. The line of midnight is now bisecting Europe: in the eastern Mediterranean a tiny, brilliant star is pulsing as some exuberant pleasure ship waves her searchlights to the sky. I think she is deliberately aiming at us; for the past few minutes the flashes have been quite regular and startlingly bright. Presently I'll call the communications centre and find out who she is, so that I can radio back our own greetings.

Passing into history now, receding forever down the stream of time, is the most incredible hundred years the world has ever seen. It opened with the conquest of the air, saw at its mid-point the unlocking of the atom – and now ends with the bridging of space.

(For the past five minutes I've been wondering what's happening to Nairobi; now I realise that they are putting on a mammoth fireworks display. Chemically fuelled rockets may be obsolete out here – but they're still using lots of them down on Earth tonight.)

The end of a century – and the end of a millennium. What will the hundred years that begin with two and zero bring? The planets, of course; floating there in space, only a mile away, are the ships of the first Martian expedition. For two years I have watched them grow, assembled piece by piece, as the space station itself was built by the men I worked with a generation ago.

Those ten ships are ready now, with all their crews aboard, waiting for the final instrument check and the signal for departure. Before the first day of the new century has passed its noon, they will be tearing free from the reins of Earth, to head out toward the strange world that may one day be man's second home.

As I look at the brave little fleet that is now preparing to challenge infinity, my mind goes back forty years, to the days when the first satellites were launched and the moon still seemed very far away. And I remember – indeed, I have never forgotten – my father's fight to keep me down on Earth.

There were not many weapons he had failed to use. Ridicule had been the first: 'Of course they can do it,' he had sneered, 'but what's the point? Who wants to go out into space while there's so much to be done here on Earth? There's not a single planet in the solar system where men can live. The moon's a burnt-out slag heap, and everywhere else is even worse. *This* is where we were meant to live.'

Even then (I must have been eighteen or so at the time) I could tangle him up in points of logic. I can remember answering, 'How do you know where we were meant to live, Dad? After all, we were in the sea for about a billion years before we decided to tackle the land. Now we're making the next big jump: I don't know where it will lead – nor did that first fish when it crawled up on the beach, and started to sniff the air.'

So when he couldn't outargue me, he had tried subtler pressures. He was always talking about the dangers of space travel, and the short working life of anyone foolish enough to get involved in rocketry. At that time, people were still scared of meteors and cosmic rays; like the 'Here Be Dragons' of the old map makers, they were the mythical monsters on the still-blank celestial charts. But they didn't worry me; if anything, they added the spice of danger to my dreams.

While I was going through college, Father was comparatively quiet. My training would be valuable whatever profession I took up in later life, so he could not complain – though he occasionally grumbled about the money I wasted buying all the books and magazines on astronautics that I could find. My college record was good, which naturally pleased him; perhaps he did not realise that it would also help me to get my way.

All through my final year I had avoided talking of my plans. I had even given the impression (though I am sorry for that now) that I had abandoned my dream of going into space. Without saying anything to him, I put in my application to Astrotech, and was accepted as soon as I had graduated.

The storm broke when that long blue envelope with the embossed heading 'Institute of Astronautical Technology' dropped into the mailbox. I was accused of deceit and ingratitude, and I do not think I ever forgave my father for destroying the pleasure I should have felt at being chosen for the most exclusive – and most glamorous – apprenticeship the world has ever known.

The vacations were an ordeal; had it not been for Mother's sake, I do not think I would have gone home more than once a year, and I always left again as quickly as I could. I had hoped that Father would mellow as my training progressed and as he accepted the inevitable, but he never did.

Then had come that stiff and awkward parting at the spaceport, with the rain streaming down from leaden skies and beating against the smooth walls of the ship that seemed so eagerly waiting to climb into the eternal sunlight beyond the reach of storms. I know now what it cost my father to watch the machine he hated swallow up his only son: for I understand many things today that were hidden from me then.

He knew, even as we parted at the ship, that he would never see me again. Yet his old, stubborn pride kept him from saying the only words that might have held me back. I knew that he was ill, but how ill, he had told no one. That was the only weapon he had not used against me, and I respect him for it.

Would I have stayed had I known? It is even more futile to speculate about the unchangeable past than the unforeseeable future; all I can say now is that I am glad I never had to make the choice. At the end he let me go; he gave up his fight against my ambition, and a little while later his fight with Death.

So I said goodbye to Earth, and to the father who loved me but knew no way to say it. He lies down there on the planet I can cover with my hand; how strange it is to think that of the countless billion human beings whose blood runs in my veins, I was the very first to leave his native world . . .

The new day is breaking over Asia; a hairline of fire is rimming the eastern edge of Earth. Soon it will grow into a burning crescent as the sun comes up out of the Pacific – yet Europe is preparing for sleep, except for those revellers who will stay up to greet the dawn.

And now, over there by the flagship, the ferry rocket is coming back for the last visitors from the station. Here comes the message I have been waiting for: CAPTAIN STEVENS PRESENTS HIS COMPLIMENTS TO THE STATION COMMANDER. BLAST-OFF WILL BE IN NINETY MINUTES; HE WILL BE GLAD TO SEE YOU ABOARD NOW.

Well, Father, now I know how you felt: time has gone full circle. Yet I hope that I have learned from the mistakes we both made, long ago. I shall remember you when I go over there to the flagship *Starfire* and say goodbye to the grandson you never knew.

Let There Be Light

First published in the *Dundee Sunday Telegraph*, 5 September 1957
Collected in *Tales of Ten Worlds*

The conversation had come around to death rays again, and some carping critic was poking fun at the old science fiction magazines whose covers so often displayed multicoloured beams creating havoc in all directions. 'Such an elementary scientific blunder,' he snorted. 'All the visible radiations are harmless – we wouldn't be alive if they weren't. So anybody should have known that the green rays and purple rays and scots-tartan rays were a lot of nonsense. You might even make a rule – if you could see a ray, it couldn't hurt you.'

'An interesting theory,' said Harry Purvis, 'but not in accordance with the facts. The only death ray that I, personally, have ever come across was perfectly visible.'

'Indeed? What colour was it?'

'I'll come round to that in a minute – if you want me to. But talking of rounds . . .'

We caught Charlie Willis before he could sneak out of the bar, and practised a little jujitsu on him until all the glasses were filled again. Then that curious, suspenseful silence descended over the White Hart that all the regulars recognise as the prelude to one of Harry Purvis's improbable stories.

'Edgar and Mary Burton were a somewhat ill-assorted pair, and none of their friends could explain why they had married. Perhaps the cynical explanation was the correct one; Edgar was almost twenty years older than his wife, and had made a quarter of a million on the stock exchange before retiring at an unusually early age. He had set himself this financial target, had worked hard to attain it – and when his bank balance had reached the desired figure had instantly lost all ambition. From now on he intended to live the life of a country gentleman, and to devote his declining years to his one absorbing hobby – astronomy.

'For some reason, it seems to surprise many people that an interest in astronomy is compatible with business acumen or even with common sense. This is a complete delusion,' said Harry with much feeling; 'I was once practically skinned alive at a poker game by a professor of astrophysics

647

from the California Institute of Technology. But in Edgar's case, shrewdness seemed to have been combined with a vague impracticality in one and the same person; once he had made his money, he took no further interest in it, or indeed in anything else except the construction of progressively larger reflecting telescopes.

'On his retirement, Edgar had purchased a fine old house high up on the Yorkshire moors. It was not as bleak and Wuthering-Heightsish as it may sound; there was a splendid view, and the Bentley would get you into town in fifteen minutes. Even so, the change did not altogether suit Mary, and it is hard not to feel rather sorry for her. There was no work for her to do, since the servants ran the house, and she had few intellectual resources to fall back on. She took up riding, joined all the book clubs, read the *Tatler* and *Country Life* from cover to cover, but still felt that there was something missing.

'It took her about four months to find what she wanted; and then she met it at an otherwise dismal village fete. It was six foot three, ex-Coldstream Guards, with a family that looked on the Norman Conquest as a recent and regrettable piece of impertinence. It was called Rupert de Vere Courtenay (we'll forget about the other six Christian names) and it was generally regarded as the most eligible bachelor in the district.

'Two full weeks passed before Rupert, who was a high-principled English gentleman, brought up in the best traditions of the aristocracy, succumbed to Mary's blandishments. His downfall was accelerated by the fact that his family was trying to arrange a match for him with the Honourable Felicity Fauntleroy, who was generally admitted to be no great beauty. Indeed, she looked so much like a horse that it was risky for her to go near her father's famous stables when the stallions were exercising.

'Mary's boredom, and Rupert's determination to have a last desperate fling, had the inevitable result. Edgar saw less and less of his wife, who found an amazing number of reasons for driving into town during the week. At first he was quite glad that the circle of her acquaintances was widening so rapidly, and it was several months before he realised that it was doing nothing of the sort.

'It is quite impossible to keep any liaison secret for long in a small country town like Stocksborough, though this is a fact that every generation has to learn afresh, usually the hard way. Edgar discovered the truth by accident, but some kind friend would have told him sooner or later. He had driven into town for a meeting of the local astronomical society – taking the Rolls, since his wife had already gone with the Bentley – and was momentarily held up on the way home by the crowds emerging from the last performance at the local cinema. In the heart of the crowd was Mary, accompanied by a handsome young man whom Edgar had seen before but couldn't identify at the moment. He would have thought no more of the matter had not Mary gone out of her way the next morning to mention that she'd been unable to get a seat in the cinema and had spent a quiet evening with one of her women friends.

'Even Edgar, engrossed though he now was in the study of variable stars, began to put two and two together when he realised that his wife was gratuitously lying. He gave no hint of his vague suspicions, which ceased to be vague after the local Hunt Ball. Though he hated such functions (and this one, by bad luck, occurred just when U Orionis was going through its minimum and he had to miss some vital observations), he realised that this would give him a chance of identifying his wife's companion, since everyone in the district would be there.

'It proved absurdly easy to locate Rupert and to get into conversation with him. Although the young man seemed a little ill at ease, he was pleasant company, and Edgar was surprised to find himself taking quite a fancy to him. If his wife had to have a lover, on the whole he approved her choice.

'And there matters rested for some months, largely because Edgar was too busy grinding and figuring a fifteen-inch mirror to do anything about it. Twice a week Mary drove into town, ostensibly to meet her friends or to go to the cinema, and arrived back at the lodge just before midnight. Edgar could see the lights of the car for miles away across the moor, the beams twisting and turning as his wife drove homeward with what always seemed to him excessive speed. That had been one of the reasons why they seldom went out together; Edgar was a sound but cautious driver, and his comfortable cruising speed was ten miles an hour below Mary's.

'About three miles from the house the lights of the car would disappear for several minutes as the road was hidden by a hill. There was a dangerous hairpin bend here; in a piece of highway construction more reminiscent of the Alps than of rural England, the road hugged the edge of a cliff and skirted an unpleasant hundred-foot drop before it straightened out on the homeward stretch. As the car rounded this bend, its headlights would shine full on the house, and there were many evenings when Edgar was dazzled by the sudden glare as he sat at the eyepiece of his telescope. Luckily, this stretch of road was very little used at night; if it had been, observations would have been well-nigh impossible, since it took Edgar's eyes ten or twenty minutes to recover fully from the direct blast of the headlights. This was no more than a minor annoyance, but when Mary started to stay out four or five evenings a week it became a confounded nuisance. Something, Edgar decided, Would Have To Be Done.

'It will not have escaped your notice,' continued Harry Purvis, 'that throughout all this affair Edgar Burton's behaviour was hardly that of a normal person. Indeed, anyone who could have switched his mode of life so completely from that of a busy London stockbroker to that of a near-recluse on the Yorkshire moors must have been a little odd in the first place. I would hesitate, however, to say that he was more than eccentric until the time when Mary's midnight arrivals started to interfere with the serious business of observation. And even thereafter, one must admit that there was a certain crazy logic in his actions.

'He had ceased to love his wife some years earlier, but he did object to her making a fool of him. And Rupert de Vere Courtenay seemed a pleasant young chap; it would be an act of kindness to rescue him. Well, there was a beautifully simple solution, which had come to Edgar in a literally blinding flash. And I literally mean literally, for it was while he was blinking in the glare of Mary's headlights that Edgar conceived the only really perfect murder I've ever encountered. It is strange how apparently irrelevant factors can determine a man's life; though I hate to say anything against the oldest and noblest of the sciences, it cannot be denied that if Edgar had never become an astronomer, he would never have become a murderer. For his hobby provided part of the motive, and a good deal of the means . . .

'He could have made the mirror he needed – he was quite an expert by this time – but astronomical accuracy was unnecessary in this case, and it was simpler to pick up a secondhand searchlight reflector at one of those war-surplus shops off Leicester Square. The mirror was about three feet across, and it was only a few hours' work to fix up a mounting for it and to arrange a crude but effective arc light at its focus. Getting the beam lined up was equally straightforward, and no one took the slightest notice of his activities, since his experimenting was now taken for granted by wife and servants alike.

'He made the final brief test on a clear, dark night and settled down to await Mary's return. He did not waste the time, of course, but continued his routine observations of a group of selected stars. By midnight, there was still no sign of Mary, but Edgar did not mind, because he was getting a nicely consistent series of stellar magnitudes which were lying smoothly on his curves. Everything was going well, though he did stop to wonder just why Mary was so unusually late.

'At last he saw the headlights of the car flickering on the horizon, and rather reluctantly broke off his observations. When the car had disappeared behind the hill, he was waiting with his hand on the switch. His timing was perfect; the instant the car came round the curve and the headlights shone on him he closed the arc.

'Meeting another car at night can be unpleasant enough even when you are prepared for it and are driving on a straight road. But if you are rounding a hairpin bend, and *know* that there is no other car coming, yet suddenly find yourself staring directly into a beam fifty times as powerful as any headlight – well, the results are more than unpleasant.

'They were exactly what Edgar had calculated. He switched off his beam almost at once, but the car's own lights showed him all that he wanted to see. He watched them swing out over the valley and then curve down, ever more and more swiftly, until they disappeared below the crest of the hill. A red glow flared for a few seconds, but the explosion was barely audible, which was just as well, since Edgar did not want to disturb the servants.

'He dismantled his little searchlight and returned to the telescope; he had not quite completed his observations. Then, satisfied that he had done a good night's work, he went to bed.

'His sleep was sound but short, for about an hour later the telephone started to ring. No doubt someone had found the wreckage, but Edgar wished they could have left it until morning, for an astronomer needed all the sleep he could get. With some irritation he picked up the phone, and it was several seconds before he realised that his wife was at the other end of the line. She was calling from Courtenay Place, and wanted to know what had happened to Rupert.

'It seemed that they had decided to make a clean breast of the whole affair, and Rupert (not unfortified by strong liquor) had agreed to be a man and break the news to Edgar. He was going to call back as soon as he had done this, and tell Mary how her husband had received it. She had waited with mounting impatience and alarm as long as she could, until at last anxiety had got the better of discretion.

'I need hardly say that the shock to Edgar's already somewhat unbalanced nervous system was considerable. After Mary had been talking to her husband for several minutes, she realised that he had gone completely round the bend. It was not until the next morning that she discovered that this was precisely what Rupert had failed to do, unfortunately for him.

'In the long run, I think Mary came out of it rather well. Rupert wasn't really very bright, and it would never have been a satisfactory match. As it was, when Edgar was duly certified, Mary received power of attorney for the estate and promptly moved to Dartmouth, where she took a charming flat near the Royal Naval College and seldom had to drive the new Bentley for herself.

'But all that is by the way,' concluded Harry, 'and before some of you sceptics ask me how I know all this, I got it from the dealer who purchased Edgar's telescopes when they locked him up. It's a sad fact that no one would believe his confession; the general opinion was that Rupert had had too much to drink and had been driving too fast on a dangerous road. That may be true, but I prefer to think it isn't. After all, that is such a humdrum way to die. To be killed by a death ray would be a fate much more fitting for a de Vere Courtenay – and in the circumstances I don't see how anyone can deny that it *was* a death ray that Edgar had used. It was a ray, and it killed someone. What more do you want?'

Out of the Sun

First published in *If*, February 1958
Collected in *The Other Side of the Sky*

If you have only lived on Earth, you have never seen the sun. Of course, we could not look at it directly, but only through dense filters that cut its rays down to endurable brilliance. It hung there forever above the low, jagged hills to the west of the Observatory, neither rising nor setting, yet moving around a small circle in the sky during the eighty-eight-day year of our little world. For it is not quite true to say that Mercury keeps the same face always turned toward the sun; it wobbles slightly on its axis, and there is a narrow twilight belt which knows such terrestral commonplaces as dawn and sunset.

We were on the edge of the twilight zone, so that we could take advantage of the cool shadows yet could keep the sun under continuous surveillance as it hovered there above the hills. It was a full-time job for fifty astronomers and other assorted scientists; when we've kept it up for a hundred years or so, we may know something about the small star that brought life to Earth.

There wasn't a single band of solar radiation that someone at the Observatory had not made a life's study and was watching like a hawk. From the far X rays to the longest of radio waves, we had set our traps and snares; as soon as the sun thought of something new, we were ready for it. So we imagined . . .

The sun's flaming heart beats in a slow, eleven-year rhythm, and we were near the peak of the cycle. Two of the greatest spots ever recorded – each of them large enough to swallow a hundred Earths – had drifted across the disc like great black funnels piercing deeply into the turbulent outer layers of the sun. They were black, of course, only by contrast with the brilliance all around them; even their dark, cool cores were hotter and brighter than an electric arc. We had just watched the second of them disappear around the edge of the disc, wondering if it would survive to reappear two weeks later, when something blew up on the equator.

It was not too spectacular at first, partly because it was almost exactly beneath us – at the precise centre of the sun's disc – and so was merged into all the activity around it. If it had been near the edge of the sun, and thus projected against the background of space, it would have been truly awe-inspiring.

Imagine the simultaneous explosion of a million H-bombs. You can't? Nor can anyone else – but that was the sort of thing we were watching climb up toward us at hundreds of miles a second, straight out of the sun's spinning equator. At first it formed a narrow jet, but it was quickly frayed around the edges by the magnetic and gravitational forces that were fighting against it. The central core kept right on, and it was soon obvious that it had escaped from the sun completely and was headed out into space – with us as its first target.

Though this had happened half a dozen times before, it was always exciting. It meant that we could capture some of the very substance of the sun as it went hurtling past in a great cloud of electrified gas. There was no danger; by the time it reached us it would be far too tenuous to do any damage, and, indeed, it would take sensitive instruments to detect it at all.

One of those instruments was the Observatory's radar, which was in continual use to map the invisible ionised layers that surround the sun for millions of miles. This was my department; as soon as there was any hope of picking up the oncoming cloud against the solar background, I aimed my giant radio mirror toward it.

It came in sharp and clear on the long-range screen – a vast, luminous island still moving outward from the sun at hundreds of miles a second. At this distance it was impossible to see its finer details, for my radar waves were taking minutes to make the round trip and to bring me back the information they were presenting on the screen. Even at its speed of not far short of a million miles an hour, it would be almost two days before the escaping prominence reached the orbit of Mercury and swept past us toward the outer planets. But neither Venus nor Earth would record its passing, for they were nowhere near its line of flight.

The hours drifted by; the sun had settled down after the immense convulsion that had shot so many millions of tons of its substance into space, never to return. The aftermath of that eruption was now a slowly twisting and turning cloud a hundred times the size of Earth, and soon it would be close enough for the short-range radar to reveal its finer structure.

Despite all the years I have been in the business, it still gives me a thrill to watch that line of light paint its picture on the screen as it spins in synchronism with the narrow beam of radio waves from the transmitter. I sometimes think of myself as a blind man exploring the space around him with a stick that may be a hundred million miles in length. For man is truly blind to the things I study; these great clouds of ionised gas moving far out from the sun are completely invisible to the eye and even to the most sensitive of photographic plates. They are ghosts that briefly haunt the solar system during the few hours of their existence; if they did not reflect our radar waves or disturb our magnetometers, we should never know that they were there.

The picture on the screen looked not unlike a photograph of a spiral nebula, for as the cloud slowly rotated it trailed ragged arms of gas for ten thousand miles around it. Or it might have been a terrestrial hurricane that I was watching from above as it spun through the atmosphere of Earth. The internal structure was extremely complicated, and was changing minute by minute beneath the action of forces which we have never fully understood. Rivers of fire were flowing in curious paths under what could only be the influence of electric fields; but why were they appearing from nowhere and disappearing again as if matter was being created and destroyed? And what were those gleaming nodules, larger than the moon, that were being swept along like boulders before a flood?

Now it was less than a million miles away; it would be upon us in little more than an hour. The automatic cameras were recording every complete sweep of the radar scan, storing up evidence which was to keep us arguing for years. The magnetic disturbance riding ahead of the cloud had already reached us; indeed, there was hardly an instrument in the Observatory that was not reacting in some way to the onrushing apparition.

I switched to the short-range scanner, and the image of the cloud expanded so enormously that only its central portion was on the screen. At the same time I began to change frequency, tuning across the spectrum to differentiate among the various levels. The shorter the wave length, the farther you can penetrate into a layer of ionised gas; by this technique I hoped to get a kind of X-ray picture of the cloud's interior.

It seemed to change before my eyes as I sliced down through the tenuous outer envelope with its trailing arms, and approached the denser core. 'Denser', of course, was a purely relative word; by terrestrial standards even its most closely packed regions were still a fairly good vacuum. I had almost reached the limit of my frequency band, and could shorten the wave length no farther, when I noticed the curious, tight little echo not far from the centre of the screen.

It was oval, and much more sharp-edged than the knots of gas we had watched adrift in the cloud's fiery streams. Even in that first glimpse, I knew that here was something very strange and outside all previous records of solar phenomena. I watched it for a dozen scans of the radar beam, then called my assistant away from the radio-spectrograph, with which he was analysing the velocities of the swirling gas as it spun toward us.

'Look, Don,' I asked him, 'have you ever seen anything like that?'

'No,' he answered after a careful examination. 'What holds it together? It hasn't changed its shape for the last two minutes.'

'That's what puzzles me. Whatever it is, it should have started to break up by now, with all that disturbance going on around it. But it seems as stable as ever.'

'How big would you say it is?'

I switched on the calibration grid and took a quick reading.

'It's about five hundred miles long, and half that in width.'

'Is this the largest picture you can get?'

'I'm afraid so. We'll have to wait until it's closer before we can see what makes it tick.'

Don gave a nervous little laugh.

'This is crazy,' he said, 'but do you know something? I feel as if I'm looking at an amoeba under a microscope.'

I did not answer; for, with what I can only describe as a sensation of intellectual vertigo, exactly the same thought had entered my mind.

We forgot about the rest of the cloud, but luckily the automatic cameras kept up their work and no important observations were lost. From now on we had eyes only for that sharp-edged lens of gas that was growing minute by minute as it raced towards us. When it was no farther away than is the moon from Earth, it began to show the first signs of its internal structure, revealing a curious mottled appearance that was never quite the same on two successive sweeps of the scanner.

By now, half the Observatory staff had joined us in the radar room, yet there was complete silence as the oncoming enigma grew swiftly across the screen. It was coming straight toward us; in a few minutes it would hit Mercury somewhere in the centre of the daylight side, and that would be the end of it – whatever it was. From the moment we obtained our first really detailed view until the screen became blank again could not have been more than five minutes; for every one of us, that five minutes will haunt us all our lives.

We were looking at what seemed to be a translucent oval, its interior laced with a network of almost invisible lines. Where the lines crossed there appeared to be tiny, pulsing nodes of light; we could never be quite sure of their existence because the radar took almost a minute to paint the complete picture on the screen – and between each sweep the object moved several thousand miles. There was no doubt, however, that the network itself existed; the cameras settled any arguments about that.

So strong was the impression that we were looking at a solid object that I took a few moments off from the radar screen and hastily focused one of the optical telescopes on the sky. Of course, there was nothing to be seen – no sign of anything silhouetted against the sun's pock-marked disc. This was a case where vision failed completely and only the electrical senses of the radar were of any use. The thing that was coming toward us out of the sun was as transparent as air – and far more tenuous.

As those last moments ebbed away, I am quite sure that every one of us had reached the same conclusion – and was waiting for someone to say it first. What we were seeing was impossible, yet the evidence was there before our eyes. We were looking at life, where no life could exist . . .

The eruption had hurled the thing out of its normal environment, deep down in the flaming atmosphere of the sun. It was a miracle that it had survived its journey through space; already it must be dying, as the forces that controlled its huge, invisible body lost their hold over the electrified gas which was the only substance it possessed.

Today, now that I have run through those films a hundred times, the idea no longer seems so strange to me. For what is life but organised energy? Does it matter *what* form that energy takes – whether it is chemical, as we know it on Earth, or purely electrical, as it seemed to be here? Only the pattern is important; the substance itself is of no significance. But at the time I did not think of this; I was conscious only of a vast and overwhelming wonder as I watched this creature of the sun live out the final moments of its existence.

Was it intelligent? Could it understand the strange doom that had befallen it? There are a thousand such questions that may never be answered. It is hard to see how a creature born in the fires of the sun itself could know anything of the external universe, or could even sense the existence of something as unutterably cold as rigid nongaseous matter. The living island that was falling upon us from space could never have conceived, however intelligent it might be, of the world it was so swiftly approaching.

Now it filled our sky – and perhaps, in those last few seconds, it knew that something strange was ahead of it. It may have sensed the far-flung magnetic field of Mercury, or felt the tug of our little world's gravitational pull. For it had begun to change; the luminous lines that must have been what passed for its nervous system were clumping together in new patterns, and I would have given much to know their meaning. It may be that I was looking into the brain of a mindless beast in its last convulsion of fear – or of a godlike being making its peace with the universe.

Then the radar screen was empty, wiped clean during a single scan of the beam. The creature had fallen below our horizon, and was hidden from us now by the curve of the planet. Far out in the burning dayside of Mercury, in the inferno where only a dozen men have ever ventured and fewer still come back alive, it smashed silently and invisibly against the seas of molten metal, the hills of slowly moving lava. The mere impact could have meant nothing to such an entity; what it could not endure was its first contact wih the inconceivable cold of solid matter.

Yes, *cold*. It had descended upon the hottest spot in the solar system, where the temperature never falls below seven hundred degrees Fahrenheit and sometimes approaches a thousand. And that was far, far colder to it than the Antarctic winter would be to a naked man.

We did not see it die, out there in the freezing fire; it was beyond the reach of our instruments now, and none of them recorded its end. Yet every one of us knew when that moment came, and that is why we are not interested when those who have seen only the films and tapes tell us that we were watching some purely natural phenomenon.

How can one explain what we felt, in that last moment when half our little world was enmeshed in the dissolving tendrils of that huge but immaterial brain? I can only say that it was a soundless cry of anguish, a death pang that seeped into our minds without passing through the gateways of the senses. Not one of us doubted then, or has ever doubted since, that he had witnessed the passing of a giant.

We may have been both the first and the last of all men to see so mighty a fall. Whatever *they* may be, in their unimaginable world within the sun, our paths and theirs may never cross again. It is hard to see how we can ever make contact with them, even if their intelligence matches ours.

And does it? It may be well for us if we never know the answer. Perhaps they have been living there inside the sun since the universe was born, and have climbed to peaks of wisdom that we shall never scale. The future may be theirs, not ours; already they may be talking across the light-years to their cousins in other stars.

One day they may discover us, by whatever strange senses they possess, as we circle around their mighty, ancient home, proud of our knowledge and thinking ourselves lords of creation. They may not like what they find, for to them we should be no more than maggots, crawling upon the skins of worlds too cold to cleanse themselves from the corruption of organic life.

And then, if they have the power, they will do what they consider necessary. The sun will put forth its strength and lick the faces of its children; and thereafter the planets will go their way once more as they were in the beginning – clean and bright . . . and sterile.

Cosmic Casanova

First published in *Venture*, May 1958
Collected in *The Other Side of the Sky*

This time I was five weeks out from Base Planet before the symptoms became acute. On the last trip it had taken only a month; I was not certain whether the difference was due to advancing age or to something the dietitians had put into my food capsules. Or it could merely have been that I was busier; the arm of the galaxy I was scouting was heavily populated, with stars only a couple of light-years apart, so I had little time to brood over the girls I'd left behind me. As soon as one star had been classified, and the automatic search for planets had been completed, it was time to head for the next sun. And when, as happened in about one case out of ten, planets *did* turn up, I'd be furiously busy for several days seeing that Max, the ship's electronic computer, got all the information down on his tapes.

Now, however, I was through this densely packed region of space, and it sometimes took as much as three days to get from sun to sun. That was time enough for Sex to come tiptoeing aboard the ship, and for the memories of my last leave to make the months ahead look very empty indeed.

Perhaps I had overdone it, back on Diadne V, while my ship was being reprovisioned and I was supposed to be resting between missions. But a survey scout spends eighty per cent of his time alone in space, and human nature being what it is, he must be expected to make up for lost time. I had not merely done that; I'd built up considerable credit for the future – though not, it seemed, enough to last me through this trip.

First, I recalled wistfully, there had been Helene. She was blonde, cuddly, and compliant, though rather unimaginative. We had a fine time together until her husband came back from *his* mission; he was extremely decent about it but pointed out, reasonably enough, that Helene would now have very little time for other engagements. Fortunately, I had already made contact with Iris, so the hiatus was negligible.

Now Iris was really something. Even now, it makes me squirm to think of her. When that affair broke up – for the simple reason that a man has to get a little sleep sometime – I swore off women for a whole week. Then I came across a touching poem by an old Earth writer named John Donne –

he's worth looking up, if you can read Primitive English – which reminded me that time lost could never be regained.

How true, I thought, so I put on my spaceman's uniform and wandered down to the beach of Diadne V's only sea. There was need to walk no more than a few hundred metres before I'd spotted a dozen possibilities, brushed off several volunteers, and signed up Natalie.

That worked out pretty well at first, until Natalie started objecting to Ruth (or was it Kay?). I can't *stand* girls who think they own a man, so I blasted off after a rather difficult scene that was quite expensive in crockery. This left me at loose ends for a couple of days; then Cynthia came to the rescue and – but by now you'll have gotten the general idea, so I won't bore you with details.

These, then, were the fond memories I started to work back through while one star dwindled behind me and the next flared up ahead. On this trip I'd deliberately left my pin-ups behind, having decided that they only made matters worse. This was a mistake; being quite a good artist in a rather specialised way, I started to draw my own, and it wasn't long before I had a collection it would be hard to match on any respectable planet.

I would hate you to think that this preoccupation affected my efficiency as a unit of the Galactic Survey. It was only on the long, dull runs between the stars, when I had no one to talk to but the computer, that I found my glands getting the better of me. Max, my electronic colleague, was good enough company in the ordinary course of events, but there are some things that a machine can't be expected to understand. I often hurt his feelings when I was in one of my irritable moods and lost my temper for no apparent reason. 'What's the matter, Joe?' Max would say plaintively. 'Surely you're not mad at me because I beat you at chess again? Remember, I warned you I would.'

'Oh, go to hell!' I'd snarl back – and then I'd have an anxious five minutes while I straightened things out with the rather literal-minded Navigation Robot.

Two months out from Base, with thirty suns and four solar systems logged, something happened that wiped all my personal problems from my mind. The long-range monitor began to beep; a faint signal was coming from somewhere in the section of space ahead of me. I got the most accurate bearing that I could; the transmission was an unmodulated, very narrow band – clearly a beacon of some kind. Yet no ship of ours, to the best of my knowledge, had ever entered this remote neck of the universe; I was supposed to be scouting completely unexplored territory.

This, I told myself, is IT – my big moment, the payoff for all the lonely years I'd spent in space. At some unknown distance ahead of me was another civilisation – a race sufficiently advanced to possess hyper-radio.

I knew exactly what I had to do. As soon as Max had confirmed my readings and made his analysis, I launched a message carrier back to Base. If anything happened to me, the Survey would know where and could guess why. It was some consolation to think that if I didn't come home on schedule, my friends would be out here in force to pick up the pieces.

Soon there was no doubt where the signal was coming from, and I changed course for the small yellow star that was dead in line with the beacon. No one, I told myself, would put out a wave this strong unless they had space travel themselves; I might be running into a culture as advanced as my own – with all that that implied.

I was still a long way off when I started calling, not very hopefully, with my own transmitter. To my surprise, there was a prompt reaction. The continuous wave immediately broke up into a string of pulses, repeated over and over again. Even Max couldn't make anything of the message; it probably meant 'Who the heck are you?' – which was not a big enough sample for even the most intelligent of translating machines to get its teeth into.

Hour by hour the signal grew in strength; just to let them know I was still around and was reading them loud and clear, I occasionally shot the same message back along the way it had come. And then I had my second big surprise.

I had expected them – whoever or whatever they might be – to switch to speech transmission as soon as I was near enough for good reception. This was precisely what they did; what I had *not* expected was that their voices would be human, the language they spoke an unmistakable but to me unintelligible brand of English. I could identify about one word in ten; the others were either quite unknown or else distorted so badly that I could not recognise them.

When the first words came over the loud-speaker, I guessed the truth. This was no alien, nonhuman race, but something almost as exciting and perhaps a good deal safer as far as a solitary scout was concerned. I had established contact with one of the lost colonies of the First Empire – the pioneers who had set out from Earth in the early days of interstellar exploration, five thousand years ago. When the empire collapsed, most of these isolated groups had perished or had sunk back to barbarism. Here, it seemed, was one that had survived.

I talked back to them in the slowest and simplest English I could muster, but five thousand years is a long time in the life of any language and no real communication was possible. They were clearly excited at the contact – pleasurably, as far as I could judge. This is not always the case; some of the isolated cultures left over from the First Empire have become violently xenophobic and react almost with hysteria to the knowledge that they are not alone in space.

Our attempts to communicate were not making much progress, when a new factor appeared – one that changed my outlook abruptly. A woman's voice started to come from the speaker.

It was the most beautiful voice I'd ever heard, and even without the lonely weeks in space that lay behind me I think I would have fallen in love with it at once. Very deep, yet still completely feminine, it had a warm, caressing quality that seemed to ravish all my senses. I was so stunned, in fact, that it was several minutes before I realised that I could understand what my invisible enchantress was saying. She was speaking English that was almost fifty per cent comprehensible.

To cut a short story shorter, it did not take me very long to learn that her name was Liala, and that she was the only philologist on her planet to specialise in Primitive English. As soon as contact had been made with my ship, she had been called in to do the translating. Luck, it seemed, was very much on my side; the interpreter could so easily have been some ancient, white-bearded fossil.

As the hours ticked away and her sun grew ever larger in the sky ahead of me, Liala and I became the best of friends. Because time was short, I had to operate faster than I'd ever done before. The fact that no one else could understand exactly what we were saying to each other insured our privacy. Indeed, Liala's own knowledge of English was sufficiently imperfect for me to get away with some outrageous remarks; there's no danger of going too far with a girl who'll give you the benefit of the doubt by deciding you couldn't possibly have meant what she thought you said . . .

Need I say that I felt very, very happy? It looked as if my official and personal interests were neatly coinciding. There was, however, just one slight worry. So far, I had not seen Liala. What if she turned out to be absolutely hideous?

My first chance of settling that important question came six hours from planet-fall. Now I was near enough to pick up video transmissions, and it took Max only a few seconds to analyse the incoming signals and adjust the ship's receiver accordingly. At last I could have my first close-ups of the approaching planet – and of Liala.

She was almost as beautiful as her voice. I stared at the screen, unable to speak, for timeless seconds. Presently she broke the silence. 'What's the matter?' she asked. 'Haven't you ever seen a girl before?'

I had to admit that I'd seen two or even three, but never one like her. It was a great relief to find that her reaction to me was quite favourable, so it seemed that nothing stood in the way of our future happiness – if we could evade the army of scientists and politicians who would surround me as soon as I landed. Our hopes of privacy were very slender; so much so, in fact, that I felt tempted to break one of my most ironclad rules. I'd even consider *marrying* Liala if that was the only way we could arrange matters. (Yes, that two months in space had really put a strain on my system . . .)

Five thousand years of history – ten thousand, if you count mine as well – can't be condensed easily into a few hours. But with such a delightful tutor, I absorbed knowledge fast, and everything I missed, Max got down in his infallible memory circuits.

Arcady, as their planet was charmingly called, had been at the very frontier of interstellar colonisation; when the tide of empire had retreated, it had been left high and dry. In the struggle to survive, the Arcadians had lost much of their original scientific knowledge, including the secret of the

Star Drive. They could not escape from their own solar system, but they had little incentive to do so. Arcady was a fertile world and the low gravity – only a quarter of Earth's – had given the colonists the physical strength they needed to make it live up to its name. Even allowing for any natural bias on Liala's part, it sounded a very attractive place.

Arcady's little yellow sun was already showing a visible disc when I had my brilliant idea. That reception committee had been worrying me, and I suddenly realised how I could keep it at bay. The plan would need Liala's co-operation, but by this time that was assured. If I may say so without sounding too immodest, I have always had a way with women, and this was not my first courtship by TV.

So the Arcadians learned, about two hours before I was due to land, that survey scouts were very shy and suspicious creatures. Owing to previous sad experiences with unfriendly cultures, I politely refused to walk like a fly into their parlour. As there was only one of me, I preferred to meet only one of them, in some isolated spot to be mutually selected. If that meeting went well, I would then fly to the capital city; if not – I'd head back the way I came. I hoped that they would not think this behaviour discourteous, but I was a lonely traveller a long way from home, and as reasonable people, I was sure they'd see my point of view . . .

They did. The choice of the emissary was obvious, and Liala promply became a world heroine by bravely volunteering to meet the monster from space. She'd radio back, she told her anxious friends, within an hour of coming aboard my ship. I tried to make it two hours, but she said that might be overdoing it, and nasty-minded people might start to talk.

The ship was coming down through the Arcadian atmosphere when I suddenly remembered my compromising pin-ups, and had to make a rapid spring-cleaning. (Even so, one rather explicit masterpiece slipped down behind a chart rack and caused me acute embarrassment when it was discovered by the maintenance crew months later.) When I got back to the control room, the vision screen showed the empty, open plain at the very centre of which Liala was waiting for me; in two minutes, I would hold her in my arms, be able to drink the fragrance of her hair, feel her body yield in all the right places—

I didn't bother to watch the landing, for I could rely on Max to do his usual flawless job. Instead, I hurried down to the air lock and waited with what patience I could muster for the opening of the doors that barred me from Liala.

It seemed an age before Max completed the routine air check and gave the 'Outer Door Opening' signal. I was through the exit before the metal disc had finished moving, and stood at last on the rich soil of Arcady.

I remembered that I weighed only forty pounds here, so I moved with caution despite my eagerness. Yet I'd forgotten, living in my fool's paradise, what a fractional gravity could do to the human body in the course of two hundred generations. On a small planet, evolution can do a lot in five thousand years.

Liala was waiting for me, and she was as lovely as her picture. There was, however, one trifling matter that the TV screen hadn't told me.

I've never liked big girls, and I like them even less now. If I'd still wanted to, I suppose I could have embraced Liala. But I'd have looked like such a fool, standing there on tiptoe with my arms wrapped around her knees.

The Songs of Distant Earth

First published in *If*, June 1958
Collected in *The Other Side of the Sky*

Many years later, this became the basis for my own favourite novel, and a beautiful suite by Mike 'Tubular Bells' Oldfield.

Beneath the palm trees Lora waited, watching the sea. Clyde's boat was already visible as a tiny notch on the far horizon – the only flaw in the perfect mating of sea and sky. Minute by minute it grew in size, until it had detached itself from the featureless blue globe that encompassed the world. Now she could see Clyde standing at the prow, one hand twined around the rigging, statue-still as his eyes sought her among the shadows.

'Where are you, Lora?' his voice asked plaintively from the radio bracelet he had given her when they became engaged. 'Come and help me – we've got a big catch to bring home.'

So! Lora told herself; *that's* why you asked me to hurry down to the beach. Just to punish Clyde and to reduce him to the right state of anxiety, she ignored his call until he had repeated it half a dozen times. Even then she did not press the beautiful golden pearl set in the 'Transmit' button, but slowly emerged from the shade of the great trees and walked down the sloping beach.

Clyde looked at her reproachfully, but gave her a satisfactory kiss as soon as he had bounded ashore and secured the boat. Then they started unloading the catch together, scooping fish large and small from both hulls of the catamaran. Lora screwed up her nose but assisted gamely, until the waiting sand sled was piled high with the victims of Clyde's skill.

It was a good catch; when she married Clyde, Lora told herself proudly, she'd never starve. The clumsy armoured creatures of this young planet's sea were not true fish; it would be a hundred million years before nature invented scales here. But they were good enough eating, and the first colonists had labelled them with names they had brought, with so many other traditions, from unforgotten Earth.

'That's the lot!' grunted Clyde, tossing a fair imitation of a salmon onto the glistening heap. 'I'll fix the nets later – let's go!'

Finding a foothold with some difficulty, Lora jumped onto the sled behind him. The flexible rollers spun for a moment against the sand, then got a grip. Clyde, Lora, and a hundred pounds of assorted fish started racing up the wave-scalloped beach. They had made half the brief journey when the simple, carefree world they had known all their young lives came suddenly to its end.

The sign of its passing was written there upon the sky, as if a giant hand had drawn a piece of chalk across the blue vault of heaven. Even as Clyde and Lora watched, the gleaming vapour trail began to fray at its edges, breaking up into wisps of cloud.

And now they could hear, falling down through the miles above their heads, a sound their world had not known for generations. Instinctively they grasped each other's hands, as they stared at that snow-white furrow across the sky and listened to the thin scream from the borders of space. The descending ship had already vanished beyond the horizon before they turned to each other and breathed, almost with reverence, the same magic word: 'Earth!'

After three hundred years of silence, the mother world had reached out once more to touch Thalassa . . .

Why? Lora asked herself, when the long moment of revelation had passed and the scream of torn air ceased to echo from the sky. What had happened, after all these years, to bring a ship from mighty Earth to this quiet and contented world? There was no room for more colonists here on this one island in a watery planet, and Earth knew that well enough. Its robot survey ships had mapped and probed Thalassa from space five centuries ago, in the early days of interstellar exploration. Long before man himself had ventured out into the gulfs between the stars, his electronic servants had gone ahead of him, circling the worlds of alien suns and heading homeward with their store of knowledge, as bees bring honey back to the parent hive.

Such a scout had found Thalassa, a freak among worlds with its single large island in a shoreless sea. One day continents would be born here, but this was a new planet, its history still waiting to be written.

The robot had taken a hundred years to make its homeward journey, and for a hundred more its garnered knowledge had slept in the electronic memories of the great computers which stored the wisdom of Earth. The first waves of colonisation had not touched Thalassa; there were more profitable worlds to be developed – worlds that were not nine-tenths water. Yet at last the pioneers had come; only a dozen miles from where she was standing now, Lora's ancestors had first set foot upon this planet and claimed it for mankind.

They had levelled hills, planted crops, moved rivers, built towns and factories, and multiplied until they reached the natural limits of their land. With its fertile soil, abundant seas, and mild, wholly predictable weather, Thalassa was not a world that demanded much of its adopted children. The pioneering spirit had lasted perhaps two generations; thereafter the colonists were content to work as much as necessary (but no more), to dream nostalgically of Earth, and to let the future look after itself.

The village was seething with speculation when Clyde and Lora arrived. News had already come from the northern end of the island that the ship had spent its furious speed and was heading back at a low altitude, obviously looking for a place to land. 'They'll still have the old maps,' someone said. 'Ten to one they'll ground where the first expedition landed, up in the hills.'

It was a shrewd guess, and within minutes all available transport was moving out of the village, along the seldom used road to the west. As befitted the mayor of so important a cultural centre as Palm Bay (population: 572; occupations: fishing, hydroponics; industries: none), Lora's father led the way in his official car. The fact that its annual coat of paint was just about due was perhaps a little unfortunate; one could only hope that the visitors would overlook the occasional patches of bare metal. After all, the car itself was quite new; Lora could distinctly remember the excitement its arrival had caused, only thirteen years ago.

The little caravan of assorted cars, trucks, and even a couple of straining sand sleds rolled over the crest of the hill and ground to a halt beside the weathered sign with its simple but impressive words:

LANDING SITE OF THE FIRST EXPEDITION TO THALASSA
1 JANUARY, YEAR ZERO
(28 May AD 2626)

The *first* expedition, Lora repeated silently. There had never been a second one – *but here it was* . . .

The ship came in so low, and so silently, that it was almost upon them before they were aware of it. There was no sound of engines – only a brief rustling of leaves as the displaced air stirred among the trees. Then all was still once more, but it seemed to Lora that the shining ovoid resting on the turf was a great silver egg, waiting to hatch and to bring something new and strange into the peaceful world of Thalassa.

'It's so small,' someone whispered behind her. 'They couldn't have come from Earth in *that* thing!'

'Of course not,' the inevitable self-appointed expert replied at once. 'That's only a lifeboat – the real ship's up there in space. Don't you remember that the first expedition—'

'Sshh!' someone else remonstrated. 'They're coming out!'

It happened in the space of a single heartbeat. One second the seamless hull was so smooth and unbroken that the eye looked in vain for any sign of an opening. And then, an instant later, there was an oval doorway with a short ramp leading to the ground. Nothing had moved, but something had *happened*. How it had been done, Lora could not imagine, but she accepted the miracle without surprise. Such things were only to be expected of a ship that came from Earth.

There were figures moving inside the shadowed entrance; not a sound came from the waiting crowd as the visitors slowly emerged and stood blinking in the fierce light of an unfamiliar sun. There were seven of them – all men – and they did not look in the least like the super-beings she had expected. It was true that they were all somewhat above the average in height and had thin, clear-cut features, but they were so pale that their skins were almost white. They seemed, moreover, worried and uncertain, which was something that puzzled Lora very much. For the first time it occurred to her that this landing on Thalassa might be unintentional, and that the visitors were as surprised to be here as the islanders were to greet them.

The mayor of Palm Bay, confronted with the supreme moment of his career, stepped forward to deliver the speech on which he had been frantically working ever since the car left the village. A second before he opened his mouth, a sudden doubt struck him and sponged his memory clean. Everyone had automatically assumed that this ship came from Earth – but that was pure guesswork. It might just as easily have been sent here from one of the other colonies, of which there were at least a dozen much closer than the parent world. In his panic over protocol, all that Lora's father could manage was: 'We welcome you to Thalassa. You're from Earth – I presume?' That 'I presume?' was to make Mayor Fordyce immortal; it would be a century before anyone discovered that the phrase was not quite original.

In all that waiting crowd, Lora was the only one who never heard the confirming answer, spoken in English that seemed to have speeded up a trifle during the centuries of separation. For in that moment, she saw Leon for the first time.

He came out of the ship, moving as unobtrusively as possible to join his companions at the foot of the ramp. Perhaps he had remained behind to make some adjustment to the controls; perhaps – and this seemed more likely – he had been reporting the progress of the meeting to the great mother ship, which must be hanging up there in space, far beyond the uttermost fringes of the atmosphere. Whatever the reason, from then onward Lora had eyes for no one else.

Even in that first instant, she knew that her life could never again be the same. This was something new and beyond all her experience, filling her at the same moment with wonder and fear. Her fear was for the love she felt for Clyde; her wonder for the new and unknown thing that had come into her life.

Leon was not as tall as his companions, but was much more stockily built, giving an impression of power and competence. His eyes, very dark and full of animation, were deep-set in rough-hewn features which no one could have called handsome, yet which Lora found disturbingly attractive. Here was a man who had looked upon sights she could not imagine – a man who, perhaps, had walked the streets of Earth and seen its fabled cities. What was he doing here on lonely Thalassa, and why were those lines of strain and worry about his ceaselessly searching eyes?

He had looked at her once already, but his gaze had swept on without faltering. Now it came back, as if prompted by memory, and for the first time he became conscious of Lora, as all along she had been aware of him. Their eyes locked, bridging gulfs of time and space and experience. The anxious furrows faded from Leon's brow, the tense lines slowly relaxed; and presently he smiled.

It was dusk when the speeches, the banquets, the receptions, the interviews were over. Leon was very tired, but his mind was far too active to allow him to sleep. After the strain of the last few weeks, when he had awakened to the shrill clamour of alarms and fought with his colleagues to save the wounded ship, it was hard to realise that they had reached safety at last. What incredible good fortune that this inhabited planet had been so close. Even if they could not repair the ship and complete the two centuries of flight that still lay before them, here at least they could remain among friends. No ship-wrecked mariners, of sea or space, could hope for more than that.

The night was cool and calm and ablaze with unfamiliar stars. Yet there were still some old friends, even though the ancient patterns of the constellations were hopelessly lost. There was mighty Rigel, no fainter for all the added light-years that its rays must now cross before they reached his eyes. And that must be giant Canopus, almost in line with their destination, but so much more remote that even when they reached their new home, it would seem no brighter than in the skies of Earth.

Leon shook his head, as if to clear the stupefying, hypnotic image of immensity from his mind. Forget the stars, he told himself; you will face them again soon enough. Cling to this little world while you are upon it, even though it may be a grain of dust on the road between the Earth you will never see again and the goal that waits for you at journey's end, two hundred years from now.

His friends were already sleeping, tired and content, as they had a right to be. Soon he would join them – when his restless spirit would allow him to. But first he would see something of this world to which chance had brought him, this oasis peopled by his own kinsmen in the deserts of space.

He left the long, single-storeyed guesthouse that had been prepared for them in such obvious haste, and walked out into the single street of Palm Bay. There was no one about, though sleepy music came from a few houses. It seemed that the villagers believed in going to bed early – or perhaps they, too, were exhausted by the excitement and hospitality of the day. That suited Leon, who wanted only to be left alone until his racing thoughts had slowed to rest.

Out of the quiet night around him he became aware of the murmuring sea, and the sound drew his footsteps away from the empty street. It was dark among the palms, when the lights of the village had faded behind him, but the smaller of Thalassa's two moons was high in the south and its curious yellow glow gave him all the guidance he required.

Presently he was through the narrow belt of trees, and there at the end of the steeply shelving beach lay the ocean that covered almost all of this world.

A line of fishing boats was drawn up at the water's edge, and Leon walked slowly toward them, curious to see how the craftsmen of Thalassa had solved one of man's oldest problems. He looked approvingly at the trim plastic hulls, the narrow outrigger float, the power-operated winch for raising the nets, the compact little motor, the radio with its direction-finding loop. This almost primitive, yet completely adequate, simplicity had a profound appeal to him; it was hard to think of a greater contrast with the labyrinthine complexities of the mighty ship hanging up there above his head. For a moment he amused himself with fantasy; how pleasant to jettison all his years of training and study, and to exchange the life of a starship propulsion engineer for the peaceful, undemanding existence of a fisherman! They must need someone to keep their boats in order, and perhaps he could think of a few improvements . . .

He shrugged away the rosy dream, without bothering to marshal all its obvious fallacies, and began to walk along the shifting line of foam where the waves had spent their last strength against the land. Underfoot was the debris of this young ocean's newborn life – empty shells and carapaces that might have littered the coasts of Earth a billion years ago. Here, for instance, was a tightly wound spiral of limestone which he had surely seen before in some museum. It might well be; any design that had once served her purpose, Nature repeated endlessly on world after world.

A faint yellow glow was spreading swiftly across the eastern sky; even as Leon watched, Selene, the inner moon, edged itself above the horizon. With astonishing speed, the entire gibbous disc climbed out of the sea, flooding the beach with sudden light.

And in that burst of brilliance, Leon saw that he was not alone.

The girl was sitting on one of the boats, about fifty yards farther along the beach. Her back was turned toward him and she was staring out to sea, apparently unaware of his presence. Leon hesitated, not wishing to invade her solitude, and also being uncertain of the local mores in these matters. It seemed highly likely, at such a time and place, that she was waiting for someone; it might be safest, and most tactful, to turn quietly back to the village.

He had decided too late. As if startled by the flood of new light along the beach, the girl looked up and at once caught sight of him. She rose to her feet with an unhurried grace, showing no signs of alarm or annoyance. Indeed, if Leon could have seen her face clearly in the moonlight, he would have been surprised at the quiet satisfaction it expressed.

Only twelve hours ago, Lora would have been indignant had anyone suggested that she would meet a complete stranger here on this lonely beach when the rest of her world was slumbering. Even now, she might have tried to rationalise her behaviour, to argue that she felt restless and could not sleep, and had therefore decided to go for a walk. But she knew in her heart that this was not the truth; all day long she had been haunted by the image of that young engineer, whose name and position she had managed to discover without, she hoped, arousing too much curiosity among her friends.

It was not even luck that she had seen him leave the guesthouse; she had been watching most of the evening from the porch of her father's residence, on the other side of the street. And it was certainly not luck, but deliberate and careful planning, that had taken her to this point on the beach as soon as she was sure of the direction Leon was heading.

He came to a halt a dozen feet away. (Did he recognise her? Did he guess that this was no accident? For a moment her courage almost failed her, but it was too late now to retreat.) Then he gave a curious, twisted smile that seemed to light up his whole face and made him look even younger than he was.

'Hello,' he said. 'I never expected to meet anyone at this time of night. I hope I haven't disturbed you.'

'Of course not,' Lora answered, trying to keep her voice as steady and emotionless as she could.

'I'm from the ship, you know. I thought I'd have a look at Thalassa while I'm here.'

At those last words, a sudden change of expression crossed Lora's face; the sadness he saw there puzzled Leon, for it could have no cause. And then, with an instantaneous shock of recognition, he knew that he had seen this girl before, and understood what she was doing here. This was the girl who had smiled at him when he came out of the ship – no, that was not right; *he* had been the one who smiled . . .

There seemed nothing to say. They stared at each other across the wrinkled sand, each wondering at the miracle that had brought them together out of the immensity of time and space. Then, as if in unconscious agreement, they sat facing each other on the gunwale of the boat, still without a word.

This is folly, Leon told himself. What am I doing here? What right have I, a wanderer passing through this world, to touch the lives of its people? I should make my apologies and leave this girl to the beach and the sea that are her birthright, not mine.

Yet he did not leave. The bright disc of Selene had risen a full hand's breadth above the sea when he said at last: 'What's your name?'

'I'm Lora,' she answered, in the soft, lilting accent of the islanders, which was so attractive, but not always easy to understand.

'And I'm Leon Carrell, Assistant Propulsion Engineer, Starship *Magellan*.'

She gave a little smile as he introduced himself, and at that moment Leon was certain that she already knew his name. At the same time a completely irrelevant and whimsical thought struck him; until a few minutes ago he had been dead-tired, just about to turn back for his overdue sleep. Yet now he was fully awake and alert – poised, as it were, on the brink of a new and unpredictable adventure.

But Lora's next remark was predictable enough: 'How do you like Thalassa?'

'Give me time,' Leon countered. 'I've only seen Palm Bay, and not much of that.'

'Will you be here – very long?'

The pause was barely perceptible, but his ear detected it. *This* was the question that really mattered.

'I'm not sure,' he replied, truthfully enough. 'It depends on how long the repairs take.'

'What went wrong?'

'Oh, we ran into something too big for our meteor screen to absorb. And – bang! – that was the end of the screen. So we've got to make a new one.'

'And you think you can do that here?'

'We hope so. The main problem will be lifting about a million tons of water up to the *Magellan*. Luckily, I think Thalassa can spare it.'

'Water? I don't understand.'

'Well, you know that a starship travels at almost the speed of light; even then it takes years to get anywhere, so that we have to go into suspended animation and let the automatic controls run the ship.'

Lora nodded. 'Of course – that's how our ancestors got here.'

'Well, the speed would be no problem if space was really empty – but it isn't. A starship sweeps up thousands of atoms of hydrogen, particles of dust, and sometimes larger fragments, every second of its flight. At nearly the speed of light, these bits of cosmic junk have enormous energy, and could soon burn up the ship. So we carry a shield about a mile ahead of us, and let *that* get burned up instead. Do you have umbrellas on this world?'

'Why – yes,' Lora replied, obviously baffled by the incongruous question.

'Then you can compare a starship to a man moving head down through a rainstorm behind the cover of an umbrella. The rain is the cosmic dust between the stars, and our ship was unlucky enough to lose its umbrella.'

'And you can make a new one of *water*?'

'Yes; it's the cheapest building material in the universe. We freeze it into an iceberg which travels ahead of us. What could be simpler than that?'

Lora did not answer; her thoughts seemed to have veered onto a new track. Presently she said, her voice so low and wistful that Leon had to bend forward to hear it against the rolling of the surf: 'And you left Earth a hundred years ago.'

'A hundred and four. Of course, it seems only a few weeks, since we were deep-sleeping until the autopilot revived us. All the colonists are still in suspended animation; they don't know that anything's happened.'

'And presently you'll join them again, and sleep your way on to the stars.'

Leon nodded, avoiding her eye. 'That's right. Planet-fall will be a few months late, but what does that matter on a trip that takes three hundred years?'

Lora pointed to the island behind them, and then to the shoreless sea at whose edge they stood.

'It's strange to think that your sleeping friends up there will never know anything of all this. I feel sorry for them.'

'Yes, only we fifty or so engineers will have any memories of Thalassa. To everyone else in the ship, our stop here will be nothing more than a hundred-year-old entry in the logbook.'

He glanced at Lora's face, and saw again that sadness in her eyes.

'Why does that make you unhappy?'

She shook her head, unable to answer. How could one express the sense of loneliness that Leon's words had brought to her? The lives of men, and all their hopes and fears, were so little against the inconceivable immensities that they had dared to challenge. The thought of that three-hundred-year journey, not yet half completed, was something from which her mind recoiled in horror. And yet – in her own veins was the blood of those earlier pioneers who had followed the same path to Thalassa, centuries ago.

The night was no longer friendly; she felt a sudden longing for her home and family, for the little room that held everything she owned and that was all the world she knew or wanted. The cold of space was freezing her heart; she wished now that she had never come on this mad adventure. It was time – more than time – to leave.

As she rose to her feet, she noticed that they had been sitting on Clyde's boat, and wondered what unconscious prompting of her mind had brought her here to this vessel out of all the little fleet lined up along the beach. At the thought of Clyde, a spasm of uncertainty, even of guilt, swept over her. Never in her life, except for the most fleeting of moments, had she thought of any other man but him. Now she could no longer pretend that this was true.

'What's the matter?' asked Leon. 'Are you cold?' He held out his hand to her, and for the first time their fingers touched as she automatically responded. But at the instant of contact, she shied like a startled animal and jerked away.

'I'm all right,' she answered, almost angrily. 'It's late – I must go home. Goodbye.'

Her reaction was so abrupt that it took Leon by surprise. Had he said anything to offend her? he wondered. She was already walking quickly away when he called after her: 'Will I see you again?'

If she answered, the sound of the waves carried away her voice. He watched her go, puzzled and a little hurt, while not for the first time in his life he reflected how hard it was to understand the mind of a woman.

For a moment he thought of following her and repeating the question, but in his heart he knew there was no need. As surely as the sun would rise tomorrow, they would meet again.

*

And now the life of the island was dominated by the crippled giant a thousand miles out in space. Before dawn and after sunset, when the world was in darkness but the light of the sun still streamed overhead, the *Magellan* was visible as a brilliant star, the brightest object in all the sky except the two moons themselves. But even when it could not be seen – when it was lost in the glare of day or eclipsed by the shadow of Thalassa – it was never far from men's thoughts.

It was hard to believe that only fifty of the starship's crew had been awakened, and that not even half of those were on Thalassa at any one time. They seemed to be everywhere, usually in little groups of two or three, walking swiftly on mysterious errands or riding small anti-gravity scooters which floated a few feet from the ground and moved so silently that they made life in the village rather hazardous. Despite the most pressing invitations, the visitors had still taken no part in the cultural and social activities of the island. They had explained, politely but firmly, that until the safety of their ship was secured, they would have no time for any other interests. Later, certainly, but not now . . .

So Thalassa had to wait with what patience it could muster while the Earthmen set up their instruments, made their surveys, drilled deep into the rocks of the island, and carried out scores of experiments which seemed to have no possible connection with their problem. Sometimes they consulted briefly with Thalassa's own scientists, but on the whole they kept to themselves. It was not that they were unfriendly or aloof; they were working with such a fierce and dedicated intensity that they were scarcely aware of anyone around them.

After their first meeting, it was two days before Lora spoke to Leon again. She saw him from time to time as he hurried about the village, usually with a bulging brief case and an abstracted expression, but they were able to exchange only the briefest of smiles. Yet even this was enough to keep her emotions in turmoil, to banish her peace of mind, and to poison her relationship with Clyde.

As long as she could remember, he had been part of her life; they had had their quarrels and disagreements, but no one else had ever challenged his place in her heart. In a few months they would be married – yet now she was not even sure of that, or indeed of anything.

'Infatuation' was an ugly word, which one applied only to other people. But how else could she explain this yearning to be with a man who had come suddenly into her life from nowhere, and who must leave again in a few days or weeks? No doubt the glamour and romance of his origin was partly responsible, but that alone was not enough to account for it. There were other Earthmen better looking than Leon, yet she had eyes for him alone, and her life now was empty unless she was in his presence.

By the end of the first day, only her family knew about her feelings; by the end of the second, everyone she passed gave her a knowing smile. It was impossible to keep a secret in such a tight and talkative community as Palm Bay, and she knew better than to attempt it.

Her second meeting with Leon was accidental – as far as such things can ever be accidents. She was helping her father deal with some of the correspondence and inquiries that had flooded upon the village since the Earthmen's arrival, and was trying to make some sense out of her notes when the door of the office opened. It had opened so often in the last few days that she had ceased to look up; her younger sister was acting as receptionist and dealt with all the visitors. Then she heard Leon's voice; and the paper blurred before her eyes, the notes might have been in an unknown language.

'Can I see the mayor, please?'

'Of course, Mr—?'

'Assistant Engineer Carrell.'

'I'll go and fetch him. Won't you sit down?'

Leon slumped wearily on the ancient armchair that was the best the reception room could offer its infrequent visitors, and not until then did he notice that Lora was watching him silently from the other side of the room. At once he sloughed off his tiredness and shot to his feet.

'Hello – I didn't know you worked here.'

'I live here; my father's the mayor.'

This portentous news did not seem to impress Leon unduly. He walked over to the desk and picked up the fat volume through which Lora had been browsing between her secretarial duties.

'*A Concise History of Earth*,' he read, '*from the Dawn of Civilisation to the Beginning of Interstellar Flight*. And all in a thousand pages! It's a pity it ends three hundred years ago.'

'We hope that you'll soon bring us up to date. Has much happened since that was written?'

'Enough to fill about fifty libraries, I suppose. But before we go we'll leave you copies of all our records, so that your history books will only be a hundred years out of date.'

They were circling around each other, avoiding the only thing that was important. When can we meet again? Lora's thoughts kept hammering silently, unable to break through the barrier of speech. And does he really like me or is he merely making polite conversation?

The inner door opened, and the mayor emerged apologetically from his office.

'Sorry to keep you waiting, Mr Carrell, but the president was on the line – he's coming over this afternoon. And what can I do for you?'

Lora pretended to work, but she typed the same sentence eight times while Leon delivered his message from the captain of the *Magellan*. She was not a great deal wiser when he had finished; it seemed that the starship's engineers wished to build some equipment on a headland a mile from the village, and wanted to make sure there would be no objection.

'Of course!' said Mayor Fordyce expansively, in his nothing's-too-good-for-our-guests tone of voice. 'Go right ahead – the land doesn't belong to anybody, and no one lives there. What do you want to do with it?'

'We're building a gravity inverter, and the generator has to be anchored in solid bedrock. It may be a little noisy when it starts to run, but I don't think it will disturb you here in the village. And of course we'll dismantle the equipment when we've finished.'

Lora had to admire her father. She knew perfectly well that Leon's request was as meaningless to him as it was to her, but one would never have guessed it.

'That's perfectly all right – glad to be of any help we can. And will you tell Captain Gold that the president's coming at five this afternoon? I'll send my car to collect him; the reception's at five thirty in the village hall.'

When Leon had given his thanks and departed, Mayor Fordyce walked over to his daughter and picked up the slim pile of correspondence she had none-too-accurately typed.

'He seems a pleasant young man,' he said, 'but is it a good idea to get too fond of him?'

'I don't know what you mean.'

'Now, Lora! After all, I *am* your father, and I'm not *completely* unobservant.'

'He's not' – sniff – 'a bit interested in me.'

'Are you interested in him?'

'I don't know. Oh, Daddy, I'm so unhappy!'

Mayor Fordyce was not a brave man, so there was only one thing he could do. He donated his handkerchief, and fled back into his office.

It was the most difficult problem that Clyde had ever faced in his life, and there were no precedents that gave any help at all. Lora belonged to him – everyone knew that. If his rival had been another villager, or someone from any other part of Thalassa, he knew exactly what he would have done. But the laws of hospitality, and, above all, his natural awe for anything of Earth, prevented him from politely asking Leon to take his attentions elsewhere. It would not be the first time *that* had happened, and there had never been the slightest trouble on those earlier occasions. That could have been because Clyde was over six feet tall, proportionally broad, and had no excess fat on his one hundred and ninety-pound frame.

During the long hours at sea, when he had nothing else to do but to brood, Clyde toyed with the idea of a short, sharp bout with Leon. It would be very short; though Leon was not as skinny as most of the Earthmen, he shared their pale, washed-out look and was obviously no match for anyone who led a life of physical activity. That was the trouble – it wouldn't be fair. Clyde knew that public opinion would be outraged if he had a fight with Leon, however justified he might be.

And how justified was he? That was the big problem that worried Clyde, as it had worried a good many billion men before him. It seemed that Leon was now practically one of the family; every time he called at the mayor's house, the Earthman seemed to be there on some pretext or other. Jealousy was an emotion that had never afflicted Clyde before, and he did not enjoy the symptoms.

He was still furious about the dance. It had been the biggest social event for years; indeed, it was not likely that Palm Bay would ever match it again in the whole of its history. To have the president of Thalassa, half the council, and fifty visitors from Earth in the village at the same moment was not something that could happen again this side of eternity.

For all his size and strength, Clyde was a good dancer – especially with Lora. But that night he had had little chance of proving it; Leon had been too busy demonstrating the latest steps from Earth (latest, that is, if you overlooked the fact that they must have passed out of fashion a hundred years ago – unless they had come back and were now the latest thing). In Clyde's opinion Leon's technique was very poor and the dances were ugly; the interest that Lora showed in them was perfectly ridiculous.

He had been foolish enough to tell her so when his opportunity came; and that had been the last dance he had had with Lora that evening. From then onward, he might not have been there, as far as she was concerned. Clyde had endured the boycott as long as he could, then had left for the bar with one objective in mind. He had quickly attained it, and not until he had come reluctantly to his senses the next morning did he discover what he had missed.

The dancing had ended early; there had been a short speech from the president – his third that evening – introducing the commander of the starship and promising a little surprise. Captain Gold had been equally brief; he was obviously a man more accustomed to orders than orations.

'Friends,' he began, 'you know why we're here, and I've no need to say how much we appreciate your hospitality and kindness. We shall never forget you, and we're only sorry that we have had so little time to see more of your beautiful island and its people. I hope you will forgive us for any seeming discourtesy, but the repair of our ship, and the safety of our companions, has had to take priority in our minds.

'In the long run, the accident that brought us here may be fortunate for us both. It has given us happy memories, and also inspiration. What we have seen here is a lesson to us. May we make the world that is waiting at the end of our journey as fair a home for mankind as you have made Thalassa.

'And before we resume our voyage, it is both a duty and a pleasure to leave with you all the records we can that will bridge the gap since you last had contact with Earth. Tomorrow we shall invite your scientists and historians up to our ship so that they can copy any of our information tapes they desire. Thus we hope to leave you a legacy which will enrich your world for generations to come. That is the very least we can do.

'But tonight, science and history can wait, for we have other treasures aboard. Earth has not been idle in the centuries since your forefathers left.

Listen, now, to some of the heritage we share together, and which we will leave upon Thalassa before we go our way.'

The lights had dimmed; the music had begun. No one who was present would ever forget that moment; in a trance of wonder, Lora had listened to what men had wrought in sound during the centuries of separation. Time had meant nothing, she had not even been conscious of Leon standing by her side, holding her hand, as the music ebbed and flowed around them.

These were the things that she had never known, the things that belonged to Earth, and to Earth alone. The slow beat of mighty bells, climbing like invisible smoke from old cathedral spires; the chant of patient boatmen, in a thousand tongues now lost forever, rowing home against the tide in the last light of day; the songs of armies marching into battles that time had robbed of all their pain and evil; the merged murmur of ten million voices as man's greatest cities woke to meet the dawn; the cold dance of the Aurora over endless seas of ice; the roar of mighty engines climbing upward on the highway to the stars. All these she had heard in the music and the songs that had come out of the night – the songs of distant Earth, carried to her across the light-years . . .

A clear soprano voice, swooping and soaring like a bird at the very edge of hearing, sang a wordless lament that tore at the heart. It was a dirge for all loves lost in the loneliness of space, for friends and homes that could never again be seen and must fade at last from memory. It was a song for all exiles, and it spoke as clearly to those who were sundered from Earth by a dozen generations as to the voyagers to whom its fields and cities still seemed only weeks away.

The music had died into the darkness; misty-eyed, avoiding words, the people of Thalassa had gone slowly to their homes. But Lora had not gone to hers; against the loneliness that had pierced her very soul, there was only one defence. And presently she had found it, in the warm night of the forest, as Leon's arms tightened around her and their souls and bodies merged. Like wayfarers lost in a hostile wilderness, they had sought warmth and comfort beside the fire of love. While that fire burned, they were safe from the shadows that prowled in the night; and all the universe of stars and planets shrank to a toy that they could hold within their hands.

To Leon, it was never wholly real. Despite all the urgency and peril that had brought them here, he sometimes fancied that at journey's end it would be hard to convince himself that Thalassa was not a dream that had come in his long sleep. This fierce and foredoomed love, for example; he had not asked for it – it had been thrust upon him. Yet there were few men, he told himself, who would not have taken it, had they, too, landed, after weeks of grinding anxiety, on this peaceful, pleasant world.

When he could escape from work, he took long walks with Lora in the fields far from the village, where men seldom came and only the robot cultivators disturbed the solitude. For hours Lora would question him about

Earth – but she would never speak of the planet that was the *Magellan*'s goal. He understood her reasons well enough, and did his best to satisfy her endless curiousity about the world that was already 'home' to more men than had ever seen it with their own eyes.

She was bitterly disappointed to hear that the age of cities had passed. Despite all that Leon could tell her about the completely decentralised culture that now covered the planet from pole to pole, she still thought of Earth in terms of such vanished giants as Chandrigar, London, Astrograd, New York, and it was hard for her to realise that they had gone forever, and with them the way of life they represented.

'When we left Earth,' Leon explained, 'the largest centres of population were university towns like Oxford or Ann Arbor or Canberra; some of them had fifty thousand students and professors. There are no other cities left of even half that size.'

'But what happened to them?'

'Oh, there was no single cause, but the development of communications started it. As soon as anyone on Earth could see and talk to anyone else by pressing a button, most of the need for cities vanished. Then anti-gravity was invented, and you could move goods or houses or anything else through the sky without bothering about geography. *That* completed the job of wiping out distance, which the airplane had begun a couple of centuries earlier. After that, men started to live where they liked, and the cities dwindled away.'

For a moment Lora did not answer; she was lying on a bank of grass, watching the behaviour of a bee whose ancestors, like hers, had been citizens of Earth. It was trying vainly to extract nectar from one of Thalassa's native flowers; insect life had not yet arisen on this world, and the few indigenous flowers had not yet invented lures for air-borne visitors.

The frustrated bee gave up the hopeless task and buzzed angrily away; Lora hoped that it would have enough sense to head back to the orchards, where it would find more co-operative flowers. When she spoke again, it was to voice a dream that had now haunted mankind for almost a thousand years.

'Do you suppose,' she said wistfully, 'that we'll ever break through the speed of light?'

Leon smiled, knowing where her thoughts were leading. To travel faster than light – to go home to Earth, yet to return to your native world while your friends were still alive – every colonist must, at some time or other, have dreamed of this. There was no problem, in the whole history of the human race, that had called forth so much effort and that still remained so utterly intractable.

'I don't believe so,' he said. 'If it could be done, someone would have discovered how by this time. No – we have to do it the slow way, because there isn't any other. That's how the universe is built, and there's nothing we can do about it.'

'But surely we could still keep in touch!'

Leon nodded. 'That's true,' he said, 'and we try to. I don't know what's gone wrong, but you should have heard from Earth long before now. We've been sending our robot message carriers to all the colonies, carrying a full history of everything that's happened up to the time of departure, and asking for a report back. As the news returns to Earth, it's all transcribed and sent out again by the next messenger. So we have a kind of interstellar news service, with the Earth as the central clearinghouse. It's slow, of course, but there's no other way of doing it. If the last messenger to Thalassa has been lost, there must be another on the way – maybe several, twenty or thirty years apart.'

Lora tried to envisage the vast, star-spanning network of message carriers, shuttling back and forth between Earth and its scattered children, and wondered why Thalassa had been overlooked. But with Leon beside her, it did not seem important. He was here; Earth and the stars were very far away. And so also, with whatever unhappiness it might bring, was tomorrow . . .

By the end of the week, the visitors had built a squat and heavily braced pyramid of metal girders, housing some obscure mechanism, on a rocky headland overlooking the sea. Lora, in common with the 571 other inhabitants of Palm Bay and the several thousand sight-seers who had descended upon the village, was watching when the first test was made. No one was allowed to go within a quarter of a mile of the machine – a precaution that aroused a good deal of alarm among the more nervous islanders. Did the Earthmen know what they were doing? Suppose that something went wrong. And *what* were they doing, anyway?

Leon was there with his friends inside that metal pyramid, making the final adjustments – the 'coarse focusing', he had told Lora, leaving her none the wiser. She watched with the same anxious incomprehension as all her fellow islanders until the distant figures emerged from the machine and walked to the edge of the flat-topped rock on which it was built. There they stood, a tiny group of figures silhouetted against the ocean, staring out to sea.

A mile from the shore, something strange was happening to the water. It seemed that a storm was brewing – but a storm that kept within an area only a few hundred yards across. Mountainous waves were building up, smashing against each other and then swiftly subsiding again. Within a few minutes the ripples of the disturbance had reached the shore, but the centre of the tiny storm showed no sign of movement. It was as if, Lora told herself, an invisible finger had reached down from the sky and was stirring the sea.

Quite abruptly, the entire pattern changed. Now the waves were no longer battering against each other; they were marching in step, moving more and more swiftly in a tight circle. A cone of water was rising from the sea, becoming taller and thinner with every second. Already it was a hundred feet high, and the sound of its birth was an angry roaring that filled the air and struck terror into the hearts of all who heard it. All, that is, except the little band of men who had summoned this monster from the deep, and who still stood watching it with calm assurance, ignoring the waves that were breaking almost against their feet.

Now the spinning tower of water was climbing swiftly up the sky, piercing the clouds like an arrow as it headed toward space. Its foam-capped summit was already lost beyond sight, and from the sky there began to fall a steady shower of rain, the drops abnormally large, like those which prelude a thunderstorm. Not all the water that was being lifted from Thalassa's single ocean was reaching its distant goal; some was escaping from the power that controlled it and was falling back from the edge of space.

Slowly the watching crowd drifted away, astonishment and fright already yielding to a calm acceptance. Man had been able to control gravity for half a thousand years, and this trick – spectacular though it was – could not be compared with the miracle of hurling a great starship from sun to sun at little short of the speed of light.

The Earthmen were now walking back toward their machine, clearly satisfied with what they had done. Even at this distance, one could see that they were happy and relaxed – perhaps for the first time since they had reached Thalassa. The water to rebuild the *Magellan*'s shield was on its way out into space, to be shaped and frozen by the other strange forces that these men had made their servants. In a few days, they would be ready to leave, their great interstellar ark as good as new.

Even until this minute, Lora had hoped that they might fail. There was nothing left of that hope now, as she watched the man-made waterspout lift its burden from the sea. Sometimes it wavered slightly, its base shifting back and forth as if at the balance point between immense and invisible forces. But it was fully under control, and it would do the task that had been set for it. That meant only one thing to her; soon she must say goodbye to Leon.

She walked slowly toward the distant group of Earthmen, marshalling her thoughts and trying to subdue her emotions. Presently Leon broke away from his friends and came to meet her; relief and happiness were written across his face, but they faded swiftly when he saw Lora's expression.

'Well,' he said lamely, almost like a schoolboy caught in some crime, 'we've done it.'

'And now – how long will you be here?'

He scuffed nervously at the sand, unable to meet her eye.

'Oh, about three days – perhaps four.'

She tried to assimilate the words calmly; after all, she had expected them – this was nothing new. But she failed completely, and it was as well that there was no one near them.

'You can't leave!' she cried desperately. 'Stay here on Thalassa!'

Leon took her hands gently, then murmured: 'No Lora – this isn't my world; I would never fit into it. Half my life's been spent training for the work I'm doing now; I could never be happy here, where there aren't any more frontiers. In a month, I should die of boredom.'

'Then take me with you!'

'You don't really mean that.'

'But I do!'

'You only think so; you'd be more out of place in my world than I would be in yours.'

'I could learn – there would be plenty of things I could do. As long as we could stay together!'

He held her at arm's length, looking into her eyes. They mirrored sorrow, and also sincerity. She really believed what she was saying, Leon told himself. For the first time, his conscience smote him. He had forgotten – or chosen not to remember – how much more serious these things could be to a woman than to a man.

He had never intended to hurt Lora; he was very fond of her, and would remember her with affection all his life. Now he was discovering, as so many men before him had done, that it was not always easy to say good-bye.

There was only one thing to do. Better a short, sharp pain than a long bitterness.

'Come with me, Lora,' he said. 'I have something to show you.'

They did not speak as Leon led the way to the clearing that the Earthmen used as a landing ground. It was littered with pieces of enigmatic equipment, some of them being repacked while others were being left behind for the islanders to use as they pleased. Several of the anti-gravity scooters were parked in the shade beneath the palms; even when not in use they spurned contact with the ground, and hovered a couple of feet above the grass.

But it was not these that Leon was interested in; he walked purposefully toward the gleaming oval that dominated the clearing, and spoke a few words to the engineer who was standing beside it. There was a short argument; then the other capitulated with fairly good grace.

'It's not fully loaded,' Leon explained as he helped Lora up the ramp. 'But we're going just the same. The other shuttle will be down in half an hour, anyway.'

Already Lora was in a world she had never known before – a world of technology in which the most brilliant engineer or scientist of Thalassa would be lost. The island possessed all the machines it needed for its life and happiness; this was something utterly beyond its ken. Lora had once seen the great computer that was the virtual ruler of her people and with whose decisions they disagreed not once in a generation. That giant brain was huge and complex, but there was an awesome simplicity about this machine that impressed even her nontechnical mind. When Leon sat down at the absurdly small control board, his hands seemed to do nothing except rest lightly upon it.

Yet the walls were suddenly transparent – and there was Thalassa, already shrinking below them. There had been no sense of movement, no whisper of sound, yet the island was dwindling even as she watched. The misty edge of the world, a great bow dividing the blue of the sea from the velvet blackness of space, was becoming more curved with every passing second.

'Look,' said Leon, pointing to the stars.

The ship was already visible, and Lora felt a sudden sense of disappointment that it was so small. She could see a cluster of portholes around the centre section, but there appeared to be no other breaks anywhere on the vessel's squat and angular hull.

The illusion lasted only for a second. Then, with a shock of incredulity that made her senses reel and brought her to the edge of vertigo, she saw how hopelessly her eyes had been deceived. Those were not portholes; the ship was still miles away. What she was seeing were the gaping hatches through which the ferries could shuttle on their journeys between the starship and Thalassa.

There is no sense of perspective in space, where all objects are still clear and sharp whatever their distance. Even when the hull of the ship was looming up beside them, an endless curving wall of metal eclipsing the stars, there was still no real way of judging its size. She could only guess that it must be at least two miles in length.

The ferry berthed itself, as far as Lora could judge, without any intervention from Leon. She followed him out of the little control room, and when the air lock opened she was surprised to discover that they could step directly into one of the starship's passageways.

They were standing in a long tubular corridor that stretched in each direction as far as the eye could see. The floor was moving beneath their feet, carrying them along swiftly and effortlessly – yet strangely enough Lora had felt no sudden jerk as she stepped onto the conveyer that was now sweeping her through the ship. One more mystery she would never explain; there would be many others before Leon had finished showing her the *Magellan*.

It was an hour before they met another human being. In that time they must have travelled miles, sometimes being carried along by the moving corridors, sometimes being lifted up long tubes within which gravity had been abolished. It was obvious what Leon was trying to do; he was attempting to give her some faint impression of the size and complexity of this artificial world that had been built to carry the seeds of a new civilisation to the stars.

The engine room alone, with its sleeping, shrouded monsters of metal and crystal, must have been half a mile in length. As they stood on the balcony high above that vast arena of latent power, Leon said proudly, and perhaps not altogether accurately: 'These are mine.' Lora looked down on the huge and meaningless shapes that had carried Leon to her across the light-years, and did not know whether to bless them for what they had brought or to curse them for what they might soon take away.

They sped swiftly through cavernous holds, packed with all the machines and instruments and stores needed to mould a virgin planet and to make it a fit home for humanity. There were miles upon miles of storage racks, holding on tape or microfilm or still more compact form the cultural heritage of mankind. Here they met a group of experts from Thalassa, looking rather dazed, trying to decide how much of all this wealth they could loot in the few hours left to them.

Had her own ancestors, Lora wondered, been so well equipped when they crossed space? She doubted it; their ship had been far smaller, and Earth must have learned much about the techniques of interstellar colonisation in the centuries since Thalassa was opened up. When the *Magellan*'s sleeping travellers reached their new home, their success was assured if their spirit matched their material resources.

Now they had come to a great white door which slid silently open as they approached, to reveal – of all incongruous things to find inside a spaceship – a cloakroom in which lines of heavy furs hung from pegs. Leon helped Lora to climb into one of these, then selected another for himself. She followed him uncomprehendingly as he walked toward a circle of frosted glass set in the floor; then he turned to her and said: 'There's no gravity where we're going now, so keep close to me and do exactly as I say.'

The crystal trap door swung upward like an opening watch glass, and out of the depths swirled a blast of cold such as Lora had never imagined, still less experienced. Thin wisps of moisture condensed in the freezing air, dancing around her like ghosts. She looked at Leon as if to say, 'Surely you don't expect me to go down *there*!'

He took her arm reassuringly and said, 'Don't worry – you won't notice the cold after a few minutes. I'll go first.'

The trap door swallowed him; Lora hesitated for a moment, then lowered herself after him. *Lowered?* No; that was the wrong word; up and down no longer existed here. Gravity had been abolished – she was floating without weight in this frigid, snow-white universe. All around her were glittering honeycombs of glass, forming thousands and tens of thousands of hexagonal cells. They were laced together with clusters of pipes and bundles of wiring, and each cell was large enough to hold a human being.

And each cell did. There they were, sleeping all around her, the thousands of colonists to whom Earth was still, in literal truth, a memory of yesterday. What were they dreaming, less than halfway through their three-hundred-year sleep? Did the brain dream at all in this dim no man's land between life and death?

Narrow, endless belts, fitted with handholds every few feet were strung across the face of the honeycomb. Leon grabbed one of these, and let it tow them swiftly past the great mosaic of hexagons. Twice they changed direction, switching from one belt to another, until at last they must have been a full quarter of a mile from the point where they had started.

Leon released his grip, and they drifted to rest beside one cell no different from all the myriads of others. But as Lora saw the expression on Leon's face, she knew why he had brought her here, and knew that her battle was already lost.

The girl floating in her crystal coffin had a face that was not beautiful, but was full of character and intelligence. Even in this centuries-long repose, it showed determination and resourcefulness. It was the face of a pioneer, of a frontierswoman who could stand beside her mate and help him wield whatever fabulous tools of science might be needed to build a new Earth beyond the stars.

For a long time, unconscious of the cold, Lora stared down at the sleeping rival who would never know of her existence. Had any love, she wondered, in the whole history of the world, ever ended in so strange a place?

At last she spoke, her voice hushed as if she feared to wake these slumbering legions.

'Is she your wife?'

Leon nodded.

'I'm sorry, Lora. I never intended to hurt you . . .'

'It doesn't matter now. It was my fault, too.' She paused, and looked more closely at the sleeping woman. 'And your child as well?'

'Yes; it will be born three months after we land.'

How strange to think of a gestation that would last nine months and three hundred years! Yet it was all part of the same pattern; and that, she knew now, was a pattern that had no place for her.

These patient multitudes would haunt her dreams for the rest of her life; as the crystal trap door closed behind her, and warmth crept back into her body, she wished that the cold that had entered her heart could be so easily dispelled. One day, perhaps, it would be; but many days and many lonely nights must pass ere that time came.

She remembered nothing of the journey back through the labyrinth of corridors and echoing chambers; it took her by surprise when she found herself once more in the cabin of the little ferry ship that had brought them up from Thalassa. Leon walked over to the controls, made a few adjustments, but did not sit down.

'Goodbye, Lora,' he said. 'My work is done. It would be better if I stayed here.' He took her hands in his; and now, in the last moment they would ever have together, there were no words that she could say. She could not even see his face for the tears that blurred her vision.

His hands tightened once, then relaxed. He gave a strangled sob, and when she could see clearly again, the cabin was empty.

A long time later a smooth, synthetic voice announced from the control board, 'We have landed; please leave by the forward air lock.' The pattern of opening doors guided her steps, and presently she was looking out into the busy clearing she had left a lifetime ago.

A small crowd was watching the ship with attentive interest, as if it had not landed a hundred times before. For a moment she did not understand the reason; then Clyde's voice roared, 'Where is he? I've had enough of this!'

In a couple of bounds he was up the ramp and had gripped her roughly by the arm. 'Tell him to come out like a man!'

Lora shook her head listlessly.

'He's not here,' she answered. 'I've said goodbye to him. I'll never see him again.'

Clyde stared at her disbelievingly, then saw that she spoke the truth. In the same moment she crumpled into his arms, sobbing as if her heart would break. As she collapsed, his anger, too, collapsed within him, and all that he had intended to say to her vanished from his mind. She belonged to him again; there was nothing else that mattered now.

For almost fifty hours the geyser roared off the coast of Thalassa, until its work was done. All the island watched, through the lenses of the television cameras, the shaping of the iceberg that would ride ahead of the *Magellan* on her way to the stars. May the new shield serve her better, prayed all who watched, than the one she had brought from Earth. The great cone of ice was itself protected, during these few hours while it was close to Thalassa's sun, by a paper-thin screen of polished metal that kept it always in shadow. The sunshade would be left behind as soon as the journey began; it would not be needed in the interstellar wastes.

The last day came and went; Lora's heart was not the only one to feel sadness now as the sun went down and the men from Earth made their final farewells to the world they would never forget – and which their sleeping friends would never remember. In the same swift silence with which it had first landed, the gleaming egg lifted from the clearing, dipped for a moment in salutation above the village, and climbed back into its natural element. Then Thalassa waited.

The night was shattered by a soundless detonation of light. A point of pulsing brilliance no larger than a single star had banished all the hosts of heaven and now dominated the sky, far outshining the pale disc of Selene and casting sharp-edged shadows on the ground – shadows that moved even as one watched. Up there on the borders of space the fires that powered the suns themselves were burning now, preparing to drive the starship out into immensity on the last leg of her interrupted journey.

Dry-eyed, Lora watched the silent glory on which half her heart was riding out toward the stars. She was drained of emotion now; if she had tears, they would come later.

Was Leon already sleeping or was he looking back upon Thalassa, thinking of what might have been? Asleep or waking, what did it matter now . . . ?

She felt Clyde's arms close around her, and welcomed their comfort against the loneliness of space. This was where she belonged; her heart would not stray again. *Goodbye, Leon – may you be happy on that far world which you and your children will conquer for mankind. But think of me sometimes, two hundred years behind you on the road to Earth.*

She turned her back upon the blazing sky and buried her face in the shelter of Clyde's arms. He stroked her hair with clumsy gentleness, wishing that he had words to comfort her yet knowing that silence was best. He felt no sense of victory; though Lora was his once more, their old and innocent companionship was gone beyond recall. Leon's memory would fade, but it would never wholly die. All the days of his life, Clyde knew, the ghost of Leon would come between him and Lora – the ghost of a man who would be not one day older when they lay in their graves.

The light was fading from the sky as the fury of the star drive dwindled along its lonely and unreturning road. Only once did Lora turn away from Clyde to look again at the departing ship. Its journey had scarcely begun, yet already it was moving across the heavens more swiftly than any meteor; in a few moments it would have fallen below the edge of the horizon as it plunged past the orbit of Thalassa, beyond the barren outer planets, and on into the abyss.

She clung fiercely to the strong arms that enfolded her, and felt against her cheek the beating of Clyde's heart – the heart that belonged to her and which she would never spurn again. Out of the silence of the night there came a sudden, long-drawn sigh from the watching thousands, and she knew that the *Magellan* had sunk out of sight below the edge of the world. It was all over.

She looked up at the empty sky to which the stars were now returning – the stars which she could never see again without remembering Leon. But he had been right; that way was not for her. She knew now, with a wisdom beyond her years, that the starship *Magellan* was outward bound into history; and that was something of which Thalassa had no further part. Her world's story had begun and ended with the pioneers three hundred years ago, but the colonists of the *Magellan* would go on to victories and achievements as great as any yet written in the sagas of mankind. Leon and his companions would be moving seas, levelling mountains, and conquering unknown perils when her descendants eight generations hence would still be dreaming beneath the sun-soaked palms.

And which was better, who could say?

A Slight Case of Sunstroke

First published in *Galaxy*, September 1958, as 'The Stroke of the Sun'
Collected in *Tales of Ten Worlds*

Someone else should be telling this story – someone who understands the funny kind of football they play down in South America. Back in Moscow, Idaho, we grab the ball and run with it. In the small but prosperous republic which I'll call Perivia, they kick it around with their feet. And that is nothing to what they do to the referee.

Hasta la Vista, the capital of Perivia, is a fine, modern town up in the Andes, almost two miles above sea level. It is very proud of its magnificent football stadium, which can hold a hundred thousand people. Even so, it's hardly big enough to pack in all the fans who turn up when there's a really important game – such as the annual one with the neighbouring republic of Panagura.

One of the first things I learned when I got to Perivia, after various distressing adventures in the less democratic parts of South America, was that last year's game had been lost because of the knavish dishonesty of the ref. He had, it seemed, penalised most of the players on the team, disallowed a goal, and generally made sure that the best side wouldn't win. This diatribe made me quite homesick, but remembering where I was, I merely commented, 'You should have paid him more money.' 'We did,' was the bitter reply, 'but the Panagurans got at him later.' 'Too bad,' I answered. 'It's hard nowadays to find an honest man who stays bought.' The Customs Inspector who'd just taken my last hundred-dollar bill had the grace to blush beneath his stubble as he waved me across the border.

The next few weeks were tough, which isn't the only reason why I'd rather not talk about them. But presently I was back in the agricultural-machinery business – though none of the machines I imported ever went near a farm, and it now cost a good deal more than a hundred dollars a time to get them over the frontier without some busybody looking into the packing cases. The last thing I had time to bother about was football; I knew that my expensive imports were going to be used at any moment, and wanted to make sure that *this* time my profits went with me when I left the country.

Even so, I could hardly ignore the excitement as the day for the return game drew nearer. For one thing, it interfered with business. I'd go to a conference, arranged with great difficulty and expense at a safe hotel or in the house of some reliable sympathiser, and half the time everyone would be talking about football. It was maddening, and I began to wonder if the Perivians took their politics as seriously as their sports. 'Gentlemen!' I'd protest. 'Our next consignment of rotary drills is being unloaded tomorrow, and unless we get that permit from the Minister of Agriculture, someone may open the cases and then . . .'

'Don't worry, my boy,' General Sierra or Colonel Pedro would answer airily, 'that's already taken care of. Leave it to the Army.'

I knew better than to retort 'Which army?', and for the next ten minutes I'd have to listen while an argument raged about football tactics and the best way of dealing with recalcitrant referees. I never dreamed – and I'm sure that no one else did – that this topic was intimately bound up with our particular problem.

Since then, I've had the leisure to work out what really happened, though it was very confusing at the time. The central figure in the whole improbable drama was undoubtedly Don Hernando Dias – millionaire playboy, football fan, scientific dilettante, and, I am sure, future president of Perivia. Owing to his fondness for racing cars and Hollywood beauties, which has made him one of his country's best-known exports, most people assume that the 'playboy' label describes Don Hernando completely. Nothing, but nothing, could be farther from the truth.

I knew that Don Hernando was one of us, but at the same time he was a considerable favourite of President Ruiz, which placed him in a powerful yet delicate position. Naturally, I'd never met him; he had to be very particular about his friends, and there were few people who cared to meet *me*, unless they had to. His interest in science I didn't discover until much later; it seems that he has a private observatory which is in frequent use on clear nights, though rumour has it that its functions are not entirely astronomical.

It must have taken all Don Hernando's charm and powers of persuasion to talk the President into it; if the old boy hadn't been a football fan too, and smarting under last year's defeat like every other patriotic Perivian, he would never have agreed. But the sheer originality of the scheme must have appealed to him even though he may not have been too happy about having half his troops out of action for the best part of an afternoon. Still, as Don Hernando undoubtedly reminded him, what better way of ensuring the loyalty of the Army than by giving it fifty thousand seats for the game of the year?

I knew nothing about all this when I took my place in the stadium on that memorable day. If you think I had no wish to be there, you are quite correct. But Colonel Pedro had given me a ticket, and it was unhealthy to hurt his feelings by not using it. So there I was, under the sweltering sun, fanning myself with the programme and listening to the commentary over my portable radio while we waited for the game to begin.

The stadium was packed, its great oval bowl a solid sea of faces. There had been a slight delay in admitting the spectators; the police had done their best, but it takes time to search a hundred thousand people for concealed firearms. The visiting team had insisted on this, to the great indignation of the locals. The protests faded swiftly enough, however, as the artillery accumulated at the check points.

It was easy to tell the exact moment the referee drove up in his armour-plated Cadillac; you could follow his progress by the booing of the crowd. 'Surely,' I said to my neighbour – a young lieutenant so junior that it was safe for him to be seen out with me – 'you could change the ref if you feel that way about him?'

He shrugged resignedly. 'The visitors have the right to choose. There's nothing we can do about it.'

'Then at least you ought to win the games you play in Panagura.'

'True,' he agreed. 'But last time we were overconfident. We played so badly that even our ref couldn't save us.'

I found it hard to feel much sympathy for either side, and settled down to a couple of hours of noisy boredom. Seldom have I been more mistaken.

Admittedly, the game took some time to get started. First a sweating band played the two national anthems, then the teams were presented to El Presidente and his lady, then the Cardinal blessed everybody, then there was a pause while the two captains had some obscure argument over the size or shape of the ball. I spent the waiting period reading my programme, an expensive and beautifully produced affair that had been given to me by the lieutenant. It was tabloid size, printed on art paper, lavishly illustrated, and looked as if it had been bound in silver. It seemed unlikely that the publishers would get their money back, but this was obviously a matter of prestige rather than economics. In any event there was an impressive list of subscribers, headed by the President, to this 'Special Victory Souvenir Issue'. Most of my friends were on it, and I noted with amusement that the bill for presenting fifty thousand free copies to our gallant fighting men had been met by Don Hernando. It seemed a somewhat naïve bid for popularity, and I doubted if the good will was worth the considerable cost. The 'Victory' also struck me as a trifle premature, not to say tactless.

These reflections were interrupted by the roar of the enormous crowd as play started. The ball slammed into action, but had barely zigzagged halfway down the field when a blue-jerseyed Perivian tripped a black-striped Pana-guran. They don't waste much time, I told myself; what's the ref going to do? To my surprise, he did nothing, and I wondered if this match we'd got him to accept COD terms.

'Wasn't that a foul, or whatever you call it?' I said to my companion.

'Pfui!' he answered, not taking his eyes off the game. 'Nobody bothers about *that* sort of thing. Besides, the coyote never saw it.'

That was true. The referee was a long way down the field, and seemed to be finding it hard to keep up with the game. His movements were distinctly laboured, and that puzzled me until I guessed the reason. Have you ever seen a man trying to run in a bulletproof vest? Poor devil, I thought, with the detached sympathy of one crook for another; you're earning your bribe. *I* was finding it hot enough merely sitting still.

For the first ten minutes, it was a pretty open game, and I don't think there were more than three fights. The Perivians just missed one goal; the ball was headed out so neatly that the frantic applause from the Panaguran supporters (who had a special police guard and a fortified section of the stadium all to themselves) went quite unbooed. I began to feel disappointed. Why, if you changed the shape of the ball this might be a good-natured game back home.

Indeed, there was no real work for the Red Cross until nearly half time, when three Perivians and two Panagurans (or it may have been the other way around) fused together in a magnificent melee from which only one survivor emerged under his own power. The casualties were carted off the field of battle amid much pandemonium, and there was a short break while replacements were brought up. This started the first major incident: the Perivians complained that the other side's wounded were shamming so that fresh reserves could be poured in. But the ref was adamant, the new men came on, and the background noise dropped to just below the threshold of pain as the game resumed.

The Panagurans promptly scored, and though none of my neighbours actually committed suicide, several seemed close to it. The transfusion of new blood had apparently pepped up the visitors, and things looked bad for the home team. Their opponents were passing the ball with such skill that the Perivian defences were as porous as a sieve. At this rate, I told myself, the ref can afford to be honest; his side will win anyway. And to give him his due, I'd seen no sign of any obvious bias so far.

I didn't have long to wait. A last-minute rally by the home team blocked a threatened attack on their goal, and a mighty kick by one of the defenders sent the ball rocketing toward the other end of the field. Before it had reached the apex of its flight, the piercing shriek of the referee's whistle brought the game to a halt. There was a brief consultation between ref and captains, which almost at once broke up in disorder. Down there on the field everyone was gesticulating violently, and the crowd was roaring its disapproval. 'What's happening now?' I asked plaintively.

'The ref says our man was off side.'

'But how can he be? He's on top of his own goal!'

'Shush!' said the lieutenant, unwilling to waste time enlightening my ignorance. I don't shush easily, but this time I let it go, and tried to work things out for myself. It seemed that the ref had awarded the Panagurans a free kick at our goal, and I could understand the way everybody felt about it.

The ball soared through the air in a beautiful parabola, nicked the post – and cannoned in despite a flying leap by the goalie. A mighty roar of anguish rose from the crowd, then died abruptly to a silence that was even more impressive. It was as if a great animal had been wounded – and was biding the time for its revenge. Despite the heat pouring down from the not-far-from-vertical sun, I felt a sudden chill, as if a cold wind had swept past me. Not for all the wealth of the Incas would I have changed places with the man sweating out there on the field in his bulletproof vest.

We were two down, but there was still hope – it was not yet half time and a lot could happen before the end of the game. The Perivians were on their mettle now, playing with almost demonic intensity, like men who had accepted a challenge and were going to show that they could meet it.

The new spirit paid off promptly. The home team scored one impeccable goal within a couple of minutes, and the crowd went wild with joy. By this time I was shouting like everyone else, and telling that referee things I didn't know I could say in Spanish. One to two now, and a hundred thousand people praying and cursing for the goal that would bring us level again.

It came just before half time. In a matter that had such grave consequences, I want to be perfectly fair. The ball had been passed to one of our forwards, he ran about fifty feet with it, evaded a couple of the defenders with some neat footwork, and kicked it cleanly into the goal. It had scarcely dropped down from the net when that whistle went again.

Now what? I wondered. He can't disallow *that*.

But he did. The ball, it seemed, had been handled. I've got pretty good eyes, and I never saw it. So I cannot honestly say that I blame the Perivians for what happened next.

The police managed to keep the crowd off the field, though it was touch and go for a minute. The two teams drew apart, leaving the centre of the field bare except for the stubbornly defiant figure of the referee. He was probably wondering how he could make his escape from the stadium, and was consoling himself with the thought that when this game was over he could retire for good.

The thin, high bugle call took everyone completely by surprise – everyone, that is, except the fifty thousand well-trained men who had been waiting for it with mounting impatience. The whole arena became instantly silent, so silent that I could hear the noise of the traffic outside the stadium. A second time that bugle sounded – and all the vast acreage of faces opposite me vanished in a blinding sea of fire.

I cried out and covered my eyes; for one horrified moment I thought of atomic bombs and braced myself uselessly for the blast. But there was no concussion – only that flickering veil of flame that beat even through my closed eyelids for long seconds, then vanished as swiftly as it had come when the bugle blared out for the third and last time.

Everything was just as it had been before, except for one minor item. Where the referee had been standing there was a small, smouldering heap, from which a thin column of smoke curled up into the still air.

What in heaven's name had happened? I turned to my companion, who was as shaken as I was. '*Madre de Dios*,' I heard him mutter. 'I never knew it would do *that*.' He was staring, not at the small funeral pyre down there on the field, but at the handsome souvenir programme spread across his knees. And then, in a flash of incredulous comprehension, I understood.

Yet even now, when it's all been explained to me, I still find it hard to credit what I saw with my own eyes. It was so simple, so logical – so unbelievable.

Have you ever annoyed anyone by flicking a pocket mirror across his eyes? I guess every kid has: I remember doing it to a teacher once, and getting duly paddled. But I'd never imagined what would happen if fifty thousand well-trained men did the same trick, each using a tin-foil reflector a couple of feet square.

A mathematically minded friend of mine has worked it out – not that I needed any further proof, but I always like to get to the bottom of things. I never knew, until then, just how much energy there is in sunlight; it's well over a horsepower on every square yard facing the sun. Most of the heat falling on one side of that enormous stadium had been diverted into the single small area occupied by the late ref. Even allowing for all the programmes that weren't aimed in the right direction, he must have intercepted at least a thousand horsepower of raw heat. He couldn't have felt much; it was as if he had been dropped into a blast furnace.

I'm sure that no one except Don Hernando realised what was likely to happen; his well-drilled fans had been told that the ref would merely be blinded and put out of action for the rest of the game. But I'm also equally sure that no one had any regrets. They play football for keeps in Perivia.

Likewise politics. While the game was continuing to its now predictable end, beneath the benign gaze of a new and understandably docile referee, my friends were hard at work. When our victorious team had marched off the field (the final score was fourteen to two), everything had been settled. There had been practically no shooting, and as the President emerged from the stadium he was politely informed that a seat had been reserved for him on the morning flight to Mexico City.

As General Sierra remarked to me when I boarded the same plane as his late chief, 'We let the Army win the football match, and while it was busy we won the country. So everybody's happy.'

Though I was too polite to voice any doubts, I could not help thinking that this was a rather shortsighted attitude. Several million Panagurans were very unhappy indeed, and sooner or later there would be a day of reckoning.

I suspect that it's not far away. Last week a friend of mine, who is one of the world's top experts in his specialised field but prefers to work on a free-lance basis under an assumed name, indiscreetly blurted out one of his problems to me.

'Joe,' he said, 'why the devil should anyone want me to build a guided rocket that can fit inside a football?'

Who's There?

First published in *New Worlds*, November 1958
Collected in *Tales of Ten Worlds*

When Satellite Control called me, I was writing up the day's progress report in the Observation Bubble – the glass-domed office that juts out from the axis of the Space Station like the hubcap of a wheel. It was not really a good place to work, for the view was too overwhelming. Only a few yards away I could see the construction teams performing their slow-motion ballet as they put the station together like a giant jigsaw puzzle. And beyond them, twenty thousand miles below, was the blue-green glory of the full Earth, floating against the ravelled star clouds of the Milky Way.

'Station Supervisor here,' I answered. 'What's the trouble?'

'Our radar's showing a small echo two miles away, almost stationary, about five degrees west of Sirius. Can you give us a visual report on it?'

Anything matching our orbit so precisely could hardly be a meteor; it would have to be something we'd dropped – perhaps an inadequately secured piece of equipment that had drifted away from the station. So I assumed: but when I pulled out my binoculars and searched the sky around Orion, I soon found my mistake. Though this space traveller was man-made, it had nothing to do with us.

'I've found it,' I told Control. 'It's someone's test satellite – cone-shaped, four antennas, and what looks like a lens system in its base. Probably US Air Force, early nineteen-sixties, judging by the design. I know they lost track of several when their transmitters failed. There were quite a few attempts to hit this orbit before they finally made it.'

After a brief search through the files, Control was able to confirm my guess. It took a little longer to find out that Washington wasn't in the least bit interested in our discovery of a twenty-year-old stray satellite, and would be just as happy if we lost it again.

'Well, we can't do *that*,' said Control. 'Even if nobody wants it, the thing's a menace to navigation. Someone had better go out and haul it aboard.'

That someone, I realised, would have to be me. I dared not detach a man from the closely knit construction teams, for we were already behind schedule – and a single day's delay on this job cost a million dollars. All the radio and TV networks on Earth were waiting impatiently for the moment when they could route their programmes through us, and thus provide the first truly global service, spanning the world from Pole to Pole.

'I'll go out and get it,' I answered, snapping an elastic band over my papers so that the air currents from the ventilators wouldn't set them wandering around the room. Though I tried to sound as if I was doing everyone a great favour, I was secretly not at all displeased. It had been at least two weeks since I'd been outside; I was getting a little tired of stores schedules, maintenance reports, and all the glamorous ingredients of a Space Station Supervisor's life.

The only member of the staff I passed on my way to the air lock was Tommy, our recently acquired cat. Pets mean a great deal to men thousands of miles from Earth, but there are not many animals that can adapt themselves to a weightless environment. Tommy mewed plaintively at me as I clambered into my spacesuit, but I was in too much of a hurry to play with him.

At this point, perhaps I should remind you that the suits we use on the station are completely different from the flexible affairs men wear when they want to walk around on the moon. Ours are really baby spaceships, just big enough to hold one man. They are stubby cylinders, about seven feet long, fitted with low-powered propulsion jets, and have a pair of accordion-like sleeves at the upper end for the operator's arms. Normally, however, you keep your hands drawn inside the suit, working the manual controls in front of your chest.

As soon as I'd settled down inside my very exclusive space-craft, I switched on power and checked the gauges on the tiny instrument panel. There's a magic word, 'FORB', that you'll often hear spacemen mutter as they climb into their suits; it reminds them to test fuel, oxygen, radio, batteries. All my needles were well in the safety zone, so I lowered the transparent hemisphere over my head and sealed myself in. For a short trip like this, I did not bother to check the suit's internal lockers, which were used to carry food and special equipment for extended missions.

As the conveyor belt decanted me into the air lock, I felt like an Indian papoose being carried along on its mother's back. Then the pumps brought the pressure down to zero, the outer door opened, and the last traces of air swept me out into the stars, turning very slowly head over heels.

The station was only a dozen feet away, yet I was now an independent planet – a little world of my own. I was sealed up in a tiny, mobile cylinder, with a superb view of the entire universe, but I had practically no freedom of movement inside the suit. The padded seat and safety belts prevented me from turning around, though I could reach all the controls and lockers with my hands or feet.

In space, the great enemy is the sun, which can blast you to blindness in seconds. Very cautiously, I opened up the dark filters on the 'night' side of my suit, and I turned my head to look out at the stars. At the same time I switched the helmet's external sunshade to automatic, so that whichever way the suit gyrated my eyes would be shielded from that intolerable glare.

694

Presently, I found my target – a bright fleck of silver whose metallic glint distinguished it clearly from the surrounding stars. I stamped on the jet-control pedal, and felt the mild surge of acceleration as the low-powered rockets set me moving away from the station. After ten seconds of steady thrust, I estimated that my speed was great enough, and cut off the drive. It would take me five minutes to coast the rest of the way, and not much longer to return with my salvage.

And it was at that moment, as I launched myself out into the abyss, that I knew that something was horribly wrong.

It is never completely silent inside a spacesuit; you can always hear the gentle hiss of oxygen, the faint whirr of fans and motors, the susurration of your own breathing – even, if you listen carefully enough, the rhythmic thump that is the pounding of your heart. These sounds reverberate through the suit, unable to escape into the surrounding void; they are the unnoticed background of life in space, for you are aware of them only when they change.

They had changed now; to them had been added a sound which I could not identify. It was an intermittent, muffled thudding, sometimes accompanied by a scraping noise, as of metal upon metal.

I froze instantly, holding my breath and trying to locate the alien sound with my ears. The meters on the control board gave me no clues; all the needles were rock-steady on their scales, and there were none of the flickering red lights that would warn of impending disaster. That was some comfort, but not much. I had long ago learned to trust my instincts in such matters; their alarm signals were flashing now, telling me to return to the station before it was too late . . .

Even now, I do not like to recall those next few minutes, as panic slowly flooded into my mind like a rising tide, overwhelming the dams of reason and logic which every man must erect against the mystery of the universe. I knew then what it was like to face insanity; no other explanation fitted the facts.

For it was no longer possible to pretend that the noise disturbing me was that of some faulty mechanism. Though I was in utter isolation, far from any other human being or indeed any material object, I was not alone. The soundless void was bringing to my ears the faint but unmistakable stirrings of life.

In that first, heart-freezing moment it seemed that something was trying to get into my suit – something invisible, seeking shelter from the cruel and pitiless vacuum of space. I whirled madly in my harness, scanning the entire sphere of vision around me except for the blazing, forbidden cone toward the sun. There was nothing there, of course. There could not be – yet that purposeful scrabbling was clearer than ever.

Despite the nonsense that has been written about us, it is not true that spacemen are superstitious. But can you blame me if, as I came to the end of logic's resources, I suddenly remembered how Bernie Summers had died, no farther from the station than I was at this very moment?

It was one of those 'impossible' accidents; it always is. Three things had gone wrong at once. Bernie's oxygen regulator had run wild and sent the pressure soaring, the safety valve had failed to blow – and a faulty joint had given way instead. In a fraction of a second, his suit was open to space.

I had never known Bernie, but suddenly his fate became of overwhelming importance to me – for a horrible idea had come into my mind. One does not talk about these things, but a damaged spacesuit is too valuable to be thrown away, even if it has killed its wearer. It is repaired, renumbered – and issued to someone else . . .

What happens to the soul of a man who dies between the stars, far from his native world? Are you still here, Bernie, clinging to the last object that linked you to your lost and distant home?

As I fought the nightmares that were swirling around me – for now it seemed that the scratchings and soft fumblings were coming from all directions – there was one last hope to which I clung. For the sake of my sanity, I had to prove that this wasn't Bernie's suit – that the metal walls so closely wrapped around me had never been another man's coffin.

It took me several tries before I could press the right button and switch my transmitter to the emergency wave length. 'Station!' I gasped. 'I'm in trouble! Get records to check my suit history and—'

I never finished; they say my yell wrecked the microphone. But what man alone in the absolute isolation of a spacesuit would *not* have yelled when something patted him softly on the back of the neck?

I must have lunged forward, despite the safety harness, and smashed against the upper edge of the control panel. When the rescue squad reached me a few minutes later, I was still unconscious, with an angry bruise across my forehead.

And so I was the last person in the whole satellite relay system to know what had happened. When I came to my senses an hour later, all our medical staff was gathered around my bed, but it was quite a while before the doctors bothered to look at me. They were much too busy playing with the three cute little kittens our badly misnamed Tommy had been rearing in the seclusion of my spacesuit's Number Five Storage Locker.

Out Of The Cradle, Endlessly Orbiting . . .

First published in *Dude*, March 1959
Collected in *Tales of Ten Worlds*

Before we start, I'd like to point out something that a good many people seem to have overlooked. The twenty-first century does *not* begin tomorrow; it begins a year later, on January 1, 2001. Even though the calendar reads 2000 from midnight, the old century still has twelve months to run. Every hundred years we astronomers have to explain this all over again, but it makes no difference. The celebrations start just as soon as the two zeros go up . . .

So you want to know my most memorable moment in fifty years of space exploration . . . I suppose you've already interviewed von Braun? How is he? Good; I've not seen him since that symposium we arranged in Astrograd on his eightieth birthday, the last time he came down from the Moon.

Yes – I've been present at some of the biggest moments in the history of space flight, right back to the launching of the first satellite. I was only twenty-five then, and a very junior mathematician at Kapustin Yar – not important enough to be in the control centre during the countdown. But I heard the take-off: it was the second most awe-inspiring sound I've heard in my entire life. (The first? I'll come to that later.) When we knew we'd hit orbit, one of the senior scientists called for his Zis, and we drove into Stalingrad for a real party. Only the very top people had cars in the Workers' Paradise, you know; we made the hundred-kilometre drive in just about the same time the Sputnik took for one circuit of Earth, and *that* was pretty good going. Someone calculated that the amount of vodka consumed the next day could have launched the satellite the Americans were building, but I don't think that was quite true.

Most of the history books say that the Space Age began then, on October 4, 1957; I'm not going to argue with them, but I think the really exciting times came later. For sheer drama you can't beat the US Navy's race to fish Dimitri Kalinin out of the South Atlantic before his capsule sank. Then there was Jerry Wingate's radio commentary, with all the adjectives which no network dared to censor, as he rounded the Moon and became the first man to see its hidden face. And, of course, only five years later, that TV broadcast from the cabin of the *Hermann Oberth* as she touched down on the plateau in the Bay of Rainbows, where she still stands, an eternal monument to the men buried beside her.

Those were the great landmarks on the road to space, but you're wrong if you think I'm going to talk about them; for what made the greatest impact on me was something very, very different. I'm not even sure if I can share the experience, and if I succeed you won't be able to make a story out of it. Not a new one, anyway, for the papers were full of it at the time. But most of them missed the point completely; to them it was just good human-interest material, nothing more.

The time was twenty years after the launching of Sputnik I, and by then, with a good many other people, I was on the Moon . . . and too important, alas, to be a real scientist any more. It had been a dozen years since I'd programmed an electronic computer; now I had the slightly more difficult task of programming human beings, since I was Chief Co-ordinator of Project Ares, the first manned expedition to Mars.

We were starting from the Moon, of course, because of the low gravity; it's about fifty times easier, in terms of fuel, to take off from there than from the Earth. We'd thought of constructing the ships in a satellite orbit, which would have cut fuel requirements even further, but when we looked into it, the idea wasn't as good as it seemed. It's not easy to set up factories and machine shops in space; the absence of gravity is a nuisance rather than an advantage when you want things to stay put. By that time, at the end of the seventies, the First Lunar Base was getting well organised, with chemical processing plants and all kinds of small-scale industrial operations to turn out the things the colony needed. So we decided to use the existing facilities rather than set up new ones, at great difficulty and expense, out in space.

Alpha, Beta, and *Gamma*, the three ships of the expedition, were being built inside the ramparts of Plato, perhaps the most perfect of all the walled plains on this side of the Moon. It's so large that if you stand in the middle you could never guess that you were inside a crater; the ring of mountains around you is hidden far below the horizon. The pressure domes of the base were about ten kilometres from the launching site, connected to it by one of those overhead cable systems that the tourists love to ride on, but which have ruined so much of the lunar scenery.

It was a rugged sort of life, in those pioneering days, for we had none of the luxuries everyone now takes for granted. Central Dome, with its parks and lakes, was still a dream on the architects' drawing boards; even if it had existed, we would have been too busy to enjoy it, for Project Ares devoured all our waking moments. It would be Man's first great leap into space; by that time we already looked on the Moon as no more than a suburb of Earth, a steppingstone on the way to places that really mattered. Our beliefs were neatly expressed by that famous remark of Tsiolkovsky's, which I'd hung up for everyone to see as they entered my office:

(What was that? No – of *course* I never knew Tsiolkovsky! I was only four years old when he died in 1936!)

After half a lifetime of secrecy, it was good to be able to work freely with men of all nations, on a project that was backed by the entire world. Of my four chief assistants, one was American, one Indian, one Chinese, and one Russian. We often congratulated ourselves on escaping from Security and the worst excesses of nationalism, and though there was plenty of good-natured rivalry between scientists from different countries, it gave a stimulus to our work. I sometimes boasted to visitors who remembered the bad old days, 'There are no secrets on the Moon.'

Well, I was wrong; there *was* a secret, and it was under my very nose – in my own office. Perhaps I might have suspected something if I hadn't been so immersed in the multitudinous details of Project Ares that I'd no opportunity of taking the wider view. Looking back on it afterward, of course, I knew there were all sorts of hints and warnings, but I never noticed any of them at the time.

True, I was vaguely aware that Jim Hutchins, my young American assistant, was becoming increasingly abstracted, as if he had something on his mind. Once or twice I had to pull him up for some minor inefficiency; each time he looked hurt and promised it wouldn't happen again. He was one of those typical, clean-cut college boys the United States produces in such quantities – usually very reliable, but not exceptionally brilliant. He'd been on the Moon for three years, and was one of the first to bring his wife up from Earth when the ban on nonessential personnel was lifted. I'd never quite understood how he'd managed that; he must have been able to pull some strings, but certainly he was the last person you'd expect to find at the centre of a world-wide conspiracy. World-wide, did I say? No – it was bigger than that, for it extended all the way back to Earth. Dozens of people were involved, right up to the top brass of the Astronautics Authority. It still seems a miracle that they were able to keep the plot from leaking out.

The slow sunrise had been under way for two days, Earth time, and though the needle-sharp shadows were shortening, it was still five days to noon. We were ready to make the first static tests of *Alpha*'s motors, for the power plant had been installed and the framework of the ship was complete. It stood out there on the plain looking more like a half-built oil refinery than a space ship, but to us it was beautiful, with its promise of the future. It was a tense moment; never before had a thermonuclear engine of such size been operated, and despite all the safety precautions that had been taken, one could never be sure ... If anything went wrong now, it could delay Project Ares by years.

The countdown had already begun when Hutchins, looking rather pale, came hurrying up to me. 'I have to report to Base at once,' he said. 'It's very important.' 'More important than *this*?' I retorted sarcastically, for I was mighty annoyed. He hesitated for a moment, as if wanting to tell me something; then he replied, 'I think so.' 'OK,' I said, and he was gone in a flash. I could have questioned him, but one has to trust one's subordinates. As I went back to the central control panel, in rather a bad temper, I decided that I'd had enough of my temperamental young American and would ask for him to be transferred. It was odd, though – he'd been as keen as anybody on this test, and now he was racing back to Base on the cable car. The blunt cylinder of the shuttle was already halfway to the nearest suspension tower, sliding along its almost invisible wires like some strange bird skimming across the lunar surface.

Five minutes later, my temper was even worse. A group of vital recording instruments had suddenly packed up, and the whole test would have to be postponed for at least three hours. I stormed around the blockhouse telling everyone who would listen (and of course everyone had to) that we used to manage things much better at Kapustin Yar. I'd quietened down a bit and we were on our second round of coffee when the General Attention signal sounded from the speakers. There's only one call with a higher priority than that – the wail of the emergency alarms, which I've heard just twice in all my years in the Lunar Colony, and hope never to hear again.

The voice that echoed through every enclosed space on the Moon, and over the radios of every worker out on the soundless plains, was that of General Moshe Stein, Chairman of the Astronautics Authority. (There were still lots of courtesy titles around in those days, though they didn't mean anything any more.)

'I'm speaking from Geneva,' he said, 'and I have an important announcement to make. For the last nine months, a great experiment has been in progress. We have kept it secret for the sake of those directly involved, and because we did not wish to raise false hopes or fears. Not long ago, you will remember, many experts refused to believe that men could survive in space; this time, also, there were pessimists who doubted if we could take the next step in the conquest of the universe. We have proved that they were wrong; for now I would like to introduce you to George Jonathan Hutchins – first Citizen of Space.'

There was a click as the circuit was rerouted, followed by a pause full of indeterminate shufflings and whisperings. And then, over all the Moon and half the Earth, came the noise I promised to tell you about – the most awe-inspiring sound I've ever heard in my life.

It was the thin cry of a newborn baby – the first child in all the history of mankind to be brought forth on another world than Earth. We looked at each other, in the suddenly silenced blockhouse, and then at the ships we were building out there on the blazing lunar plain. They had seemed so important, a few minutes ago. They still were – but not as important as what had happened over in Medical Centre, and would happen again billions of times on countless worlds down all the ages to come.

For that was the moment, gentlemen, when I knew that Man had *really* conquered space.

I Remember Babylon

First published in *Playboy*, March 1960
Collected in *Tales of Ten Worlds*

This is one of the rare cases where I violated Sam Goldwyn's excellent rule: 'If you gotta message, use Western Union.' This story *was* a message, five years before the first commercial communications satellite was launched, warning of their possible danger. Apart from some minor political earthquakes, everything in it has since come true.

My name is Arthur C. Clarke, and I wish I had no connection with this whole sordid business. But as the moral – repeat, moral – integrity of the United States is involved, I must first establish my credentials. Only thus will you understand how, with the aid of the late Dr Alfred Kinsey, I have unwittingly triggered an avalanche that may sweep away much of Western civilisation.

Back in 1945, while a radar officer in the Royal Air Force, I had the only original idea of my life. Twelve years before the first Sputnik started beeping, it occurred to me that an artificial satellite would be a wonderful place for a television transmitter, since a station several thousand miles high could broadcast to half the globe. I wrote up the idea the week after Hiroshima, proposing a network of relay satellites twenty-two thousand miles above the Equator; at this height, they'd take exactly one day to complete a revolution, and so would remain fixed over the same spot on the Earth.

The piece appeared in the October 1945 issue of *Wireless World*; not expecting that celestial mechanics would be commercialised in my lifetime, I made no attempt to patent the idea, and doubt if I could have done so anyway. (If I'm wrong, I'd prefer not to know.) But I kept plugging it in my books, and today the idea of communications satellites is so commonplace that no one knows its origin.

I did make a plaintive attempt to put the record straight when approached by the House of Representatives Committee on Astronautics and Space Exploration; you'll find my evidence on page thirty-two of its report, *The Next Ten Years in Space*. And as you'll see in a moment, my concluding words had an irony I never appreciated at the time: 'Living as I do in the

Far East, I am constantly reminded of the struggle between the Western World and the USSR for the uncommitted millions of Asia . . . When line-of-sight TV transmissions become possible from satellites directly overhead, the propaganda effect may be decisive . . .'

I still stand by those words, but there were angles I hadn't thought of – and which, unfortunately, other people have.

It all began during one of those official receptions which are such a feature of social life in Eastern capitals. They're even more common in the West, of course, but in Colombo there's little competing entertainment. At least once a week, if you are anybody, you get an invitation to cocktails at an embassy or legation, the British Council, the US Operations Mission, L'Alliance Française, or one of the countless alphabetical agencies the United Nations has begotten.

At first, being more at home beneath the Indian Ocean than in diplomatic circles, my partner and I were nobodies and were left alone. But after Mike *compèred* Dave Brubeck's tour of Ceylon, people started to take notice of us – still more so when he married one of the island's best-known beauties. So now our consumption of cocktails and canapés is limited chiefly by reluctance to abandon our comfortable sarongs for such Western absurdities as trousers, dinner jackets, and ties.

It was the first time we'd been to the Soviet Embassy, which was throwing a party for a group of Russian oceanographers who'd just come into port. Beneath the inevitable paintings of Lenin and Marx, a couple of hundred guests of all colours, religions, and languages were milling around, chatting with friends, or single-mindedly demolishing the vodka and caviar. I'd been separated from Mike and Elizabeth, but could see them at the other side of the room. Mike was doing his 'There was I at fifty fathoms' act to a fascinated audience, while Elizabeth watched him quizzically – and rather more people watched Elizabeth.

Ever since I lost an eardrum while pearl-diving on the Great Barrier Reef, I've been at a considerable disadvantage at functions of this kind; the surface noise is about twelve decibels too much for me to cope with. And this is no small handicap when being introduced to people with names like Dharmasiriwardene, Tissaveerasinghe, Goonetilleke, and Jayawickrema. When I'm not raiding the buffet, therefore, I usually look for a pool of relative quiet where there's a chance of following more than fifty per cent of any conversation in which I may get involved. I was standing in the acoustic shadow of a large ornamental pillar, surveying the scene in my detached or Somerset Maugham manner, when I noticed that someone was looking at me with that 'Haven't we met before?' expression.

I'll describe him with some care, because there must be many people who can identify him. He was in the mid-thirties, and I guessed he was American; he had that well-scrubbed, crew-cut, man-about-Rockefeller-Center look that used to be a hallmark until the younger Russian diplomats and technical advisers started imitating it so successfully. He was about six feet in height, with shrewd brown eyes and black hair, prematurely grey at the sides. Though I was fairly certain we'd never met before, his face reminded me of someone. It took me a couple of days to work it out: remember the late John Garfield? That's who it was, as near as makes no difference.

When a stranger catches my eye at a party, my standard operating procedure goes into action automatically. If he seems a pleasant-enough person but I don't feel like introductions at the moment, I give him the Neutral Scan, letting my eyes sweep past him without a flicker of recognition, yet without positive unfriendliness. If he looks like a creep, he receives the *Coup d'oeil*, which consists of a long, disbelieving stare followed by an unhurried view of the back of my neck. In extreme cases, an expression of revulsion may be switched on for a few milliseconds. The message usually gets across.

But this character seemed interesting, and I was getting bored, so I gave him the Affable Nod. A few minutes later he drifted through the crowd, and I aimed my good ear toward him.

'Hello,' he said (yes, he *was* American), 'my name's Gene Hartford. I'm sure we've met somewhere.'

'Quite likely,' I answered, 'I've spent a good deal of time in the States. I'm Arthur Clarke.'

Usually that produces a blank stare, but sometimes it doesn't. I could almost see the IBM cards flickering behind those hard brown eyes, and was flattered by the brevity of his access time.

'The science writer?'

'Correct.'

'Well, this is fantastic.' He seemed genuinely astonished. '*Now* I know where I've seen you. I was in the studio once when you were on the Dave Garroway show.'

(This lead may be worth following up, though I doubt it; and I'm sure that 'Gene Hartford' was phony – it was too smoothly synthetic.)

'So you're in TV?' I said. 'What are you doing here – collecting material, or just on vacation?'

He gave me the frank, friendly smile of a man who has plenty to hide.

'Oh, I'm keeping my eyes open. But this is really amazing, I read your *Exploration of Space* when it came out back in, Ah—'

'Nineteen fifty-two; the Book-of-the-Month Club's never been quite the same since.'

All this time I had been sizing him up, and though there was something about him I didn't like, I was unable to pin it down. In any case, I was prepared to make substantial allowances for someone who had read my books and was also in TV; Mike and I are always on the lookout for markets for our under-water movies. But that, to put it mildly, was not Hartford's line of business.

'Look,' he said eagerly, 'I've a big network deal cooking that will interest you – in fact, *you* helped to give me the idea.'

704

This sounded promising, and my coefficient of cupidity jumped several points.

'I'm glad to hear it. What's the general theme?'

'I can't talk about it here, but could we meet at my hotel, around three tomorrow?'

'Let me check my diary; yes, that's OK.'

There are only two hotels in Colombo patronised by Americans, and I guessed right the first time. He was at the Mount Lavinia, and though you may not know it, you've seen the place where we had our private chat. Around the middle of *Bridge on the River Kwai*, there's a brief scene at a military hospital, where Jack Hawkins meets a nurse and asks her where he can find Bill Holden. We have a soft spot for this episode, because Mike was one of the convalescent naval officers in the background. If you look smartly you'll see him on the extreme right, beard in full profile, signing Sam Spiegel's name to his sixth round of bar chits. As the picture turned out, Sam could afford it.

It was here, on this diminutive plateau high above the miles of palm-fringed beach, that Gene Hartford started to unload – and my simple hopes of financial advantage started to evaporate. What his exact motives were, if indeed he knew them himself, I'm still uncertain. Surprise at meeting me, and a twisted feeling of gratitude (which I would gladly have done without) undoubtedly played a part, and for all his air of confidence he must have been a bitter, lonely man who desperately needed approval and friendship.

He got neither from me. I have always had a sneaking sympathy for Benedict Arnold, as must anyone who knows the full facts of the case. But Arnold merely betrayed his country; no one before Hartford ever tried to seduce it.

What dissolved my dream of dollars was the news that Hartford's connection with American TV had been severed, somewhat violently, in the early fifties. It was clear that he'd been bounced out of Madison Avenue for Party-lining, and it was equally clear that his was one case where no grave injustice had been done. Though he talked with a certain controlled fury of his fight against asinine censorship, and wept for a brilliant – but unnamed – cultural series he'd started before being kicked off the air, by this time I was beginning to smell so many rats that my replies were distinctly guarded. Yet as my pecuniary interest in Mr Hartford diminished, so my personal curiosity increased. Who *was* behind him? Surely not the BBC . . .

He got round to it at last, when he'd worked the self-pity out of his system.

'I've some news that will make you sit up,' he said smugly. 'The American networks are soon going to have some real competition. And it will be done just the way you predicted; the people who sent a TV transmitter to the Moon can put a much bigger one in orbit round the Earth.'

'Good for them,' I said cautiously. 'I'm all in favour of healthy competition. When's the launching date?'

'Any moment now. The first transmitter will be parked due south of New Orleans – on the equator, of course. That puts it way out in the open Pacific; it won't be over anyone's territory, so there'll be no political complications on that score. Yet it will be sitting up there in the sky in full view of everybody from Seattle to Key West. Think of it – the only TV station the whole United States can tune in to! Yes, even Hawaii! There won't be any way of jamming it; for the first time, there'll be a clear channel into every American home. And J. Edgar's Boy Scouts can't do a thing to block it.'

So that's your little racket, I thought; at least you're being frank. Long ago I learned not to argue with Marxists and Flat-Earthers, but if Hartford was telling the truth, I wanted to pump him for all he was worth.

'Before you get too enthusiastic,' I said, 'there are a few points you may have overlooked.'

'Such as?'

'This will work both ways. Everyone knows that the Air Force, NASA, Bell Labs, IT&T, Hughes, and a few dozen other agencies are working on the same project. Whatever Russia does to the States in the propaganda line, she'll get back with compound interest.'

Hartford grinned mirthlessly.

'Really, Clarke!' he said. (I was glad he hadn't first-named me.) 'I'm a little disappointed. Surely you know that the United States is years behind in pay-load capacity! And do you imagine that the old T3 is Russia's last word?'

It was at this moment that I began to take him very seriously. He was perfectly right. The T3 could inject at least five times the pay load of any American missile into that critical twenty-two-thousand-mile orbit – the only one that would allow a satellite to remain fixed above the Earth. And by the time the US could match that performance, heaven knows where the Russians would be. Yes, heaven certainly *would* know . . .

'All right,' I conceded. 'But why should fifty million American homes start switching channels just as soon as they can tune in to Moscow? I admire the Russians, but their entertainment is worse than their politics. After the Bolshoi, what have you? And for me, a little ballet goes a long, long way.'

Once again I was treated to that peculiarly humourless smile. Hartford had been saving up his Sunday punch, and now he let me have it.

'You were the one who brought in the Russians,' he said. 'They're involved, sure – but only as contractors. The independent agency I'm working for is hiring their services.'

'That,' I remarked dryly, 'must be some agency.'

'It is; just about the biggest. Even though the United States tries to pretend it doesn't exist.'

'Oh,' I said, rather stupidly. 'So *that's* your sponsor.'

I'd heard those rumours that the USSR was going to launch satellites for the Chinese; now it began to look as if the rumours fell far short of the truth. But how far short, I'd still no conception

'You are so right,' continued Hartford, obviously enjoying himself, 'about Russian entertainment. After the initial novelty, the Nielson rating would drop to zero. But not with the programme *I'm* planning. My job is to find material that will put everyone else out of business when it goes on the air. You think it can't be done? Finish that drink and come up to my room. I've a highbrow movie about ecclesiastical art that I'd like to show you.'

Well, he wasn't crazy, though for a few minutes I wondered. I could think of few titles more carefully calculated to make the viewer reach for the channel switch than the one that flashed on the screen: ASPECTS OF THIRTEENTH-CENTURY TANTRIC SCULPTURE.

'Don't be alarmed,' Hartford chuckled, above the whirr of the projector. 'That title saves me having trouble with inquisitive Customs inspectors. It's perfectly accurate, but we'll change it to something with a bigger box-office appeal when the time comes.'

A couple of hundred feet later, after some innocuous architectural long shots, I saw what he meant.

You may know that there are certain temples in India covered with superbly executed carvings of a kind that we in the West scarcely associate with religion. To say that they are frank is a laughable understatement; they leave nothing to the imagination – *any* imagination. Yet at the same time they are genuine works of art. And so was Hartford's movie.

It had been shot, in case you're interested, at the Temple of the Sun, Konarak. I've since looked it up; it's on the Orissa coast, about twenty-five miles northeast of Puri. The reference books are pretty mealymouthed; some apologise for the 'obvious' impossibility of providing illustrations, but Percy Brown's *Indian Architecture* minces no words. The carvings, it says primly, are of 'a shamelessly erotic character that have no parallel in any known building'. A sweeping claim, but I can believe it after seeing that movie.

Camera work and editing were brilliant, the ancient stones coming to life beneath the roving lens. There were breath-taking time-lapse shots as the rising sun chased the shadows from bodies intertwined in ecstasy; sudden startling close-ups of scenes which at first the mind refused to recognise; soft-focus studies of stone shaped by a master's hand in all the fantasies and aberrations of love; restless zooms and pans whose meaning eluded the eye until they froze into patterns of timeless desire, eternal fulfilment. The music – mostly percussion, with a thin, high thread of sound from some stringed instrument that I could not identify – perfectly fitted the tempo of the cutting. At one moment it would be languorously slow, like the opening bars of Debussy's 'L'Après-midi'; then the drums would swiftly work themselves up to a frenzied, almost unendurable climax. The art of the ancient sculptors and the skill of the modern cameraman had combined across the centuries to create a poem of rapture, an orgasm on celluloid which I would defy any man to watch unmoved.

There was a long silence when the screen flooded with light and the lascivious music ebbed into exhaustion.

'My God!' I said, when I had recovered some of my composure. 'Are you going to telecast *that*?'

Hartford laughed.

'Believe me,' he answered, 'that's nothing; it just happens to be the only reel I can carry around safely. We're prepared to defend it any day on grounds of genuine art, historic interest, religious tolerance – oh, we've thought of all the angles. But it doesn't really matter; no one can stop us. For the first time in history, any form of censorship's become utterly impossible. There's simply no way of enforcing it; the customer can get what he wants, right in his own home. Lock the door, switch on the TV set – friends and family will never know.'

'Very clever,' I said, 'but don't you think such a diet will soon pall?'

'Of course; variety is the spice of life. We'll have plenty of conventional entertainment; let *me* worry about that. And every so often we'll have information programmes – I hate that word "propaganda" – to tell the cloistered American public what's really happening in the world. Our special features will just be the bait.'

'Mind if I have some fresh air?' I said. 'It's getting stuffy in here.'

Hartford drew the curtains and let daylight back into the room. Below us lay that long curve of beach, with the outrigger fishing boats drawn up beneath the palms, and the little waves falling in foam at the end of their weary march from Africa. One of the loveliest sights in the world, but I couldn't focus on it now. I was still seeing those writhing stone limbs, those faces frozen with passions which the centuries could not slake.

That lickerish voice continued behind my back.

'You'd be astonished if you knew just how much material there is. Remember, we've absolutely no taboos. If you can film it, we can telecast it.'

He walked over to his bureau and picked up a heavy, dog-eared volume.

'This has been my Bible,' he said, 'or my Sears, Roebuck, if you prefer. Without it, I'd never have sold the series to my sponsors. They're great believers in science, and they swallowed the whole thing, down to the last decimal point. Recognise it?'

I nodded; whenever I enter a room, I always monitor my host's literary tastes.

'Dr Kinsey, I presume.'

'I guess I'm the only man who's read it from cover to cover, and not just looked up his own vital statistics. You see, it's the only piece of market research in its field. Until something better comes along, we're making the most of it. It tells us what the customer wants, and we're going to supply it.'

'*All* of it?'

'If the audience is big enough, yes. We won't bother about feeble-minded farm boys who get too attached to the stock. But the four main sexes will get the full treatment. That's the beauty of the movie you just saw – it appeals to them all.'

708

'You can say that again,' I muttered.

'We've had a lot of fun planning the feature I've christened "Queer Corner". Don't laugh – no go-ahead agency can afford to ignore *that* audience. At least ten million, if you count the ladies – bless their clogs and tweeds. If you think I'm exaggerating, look at all the male art mags on the newsstands. It was no trick, blackmailing some of the daintier musclemen to perform for us.'

He saw that I was beginning to get bored; there are some kinds of single-mindedness that I find depressing. But I had done Hartford an injustice, as he hastened to prove.

'Please don't think,' he said anxiously, 'that sex is our only weapon. Sensation is almost as good. Ever see the job Ed Murrow did on the late sainted Joe McCarthy? That was milk and water compared with the profiles we're planning in "Washington Confidential".

'And there's our "Can You Take It?" series, designed to separate the men from the milksops. We'll issue so many advance warnings that every red-blooded American will feel he has to watch the show. It will start innocently enough, on ground nicely prepared by Hemingway. You'll see some bull-fighting sequences that will really lift you out of your seat – or send you running to the bathroom – because they show all the little details you never get in those cleaned-up Hollywood movies.

'We'll follow that with some really unique material that cost us exactly nothing. Do you remember the photographic evidence the Nuremburg war trials turned up? You've never seen it, because it wasn't publishable. There were quite a few amateur photographers in the concentration camps, who made the most of opportunities they'd never get again. Some of them were hanged on the testimony of their own cameras, but their work wasn't wasted. It will lead nicely into our series "Torture Through the Ages" – very scholarly and thorough, yet with a remarkably wide appeal . . .

'And there are dozens of other angles, but by now you'll have the general picture. The Avenue thinks it knows all about Hidden Persuasion – believe me, it doesn't. The world's best *practical* psychologists are in the East these days. Remember Korea, and brainwashing? We've learned a lot since then. There's no need for violence any more; people enjoy being brainwashed, if you set about it the right way.'

'And you,' I said, 'are going to brainwash the United States. Quite an order.'

'Exactly – and the country will love it, despite all the screams from Congress and the churches. Not to mention the networks, of course. They'll make the biggest fuss of all, when they find they can't compete with us.'

Hertford glanced at his watch, and gave a whistle of alarm.

'Time to start packing,' he said. 'I've got to be at that unpronounceable airport of yours by six. There's no chance, I suppose, that you can fly over to Macao and see us sometime?'

'Not a hope; but I've got a pretty good idea of the picture now. And incidentally, aren't you afraid that I'll spill the beans?'

'Why should I be? The more publicity you can give us, the better. Although our advertising campaign doesn't go into top gear for a few months yet, I feel you've earned this advance notice. As I said, your books helped to give me the idea.'

His gratitude was quite genuine, by God; it left me completely speechless.

'Nothing can stop us,' he declared – and for the first time the fanaticism that lurked behind that smooth, cynical, façade was not altogether under control. 'History is on our side. We'll be using America's own decadence as a weapon against her, and it's a weapon for which there's no defence. The Air Force won't attempt space piracy by shooting down a satellite nowhere near American territory. The FCC can't even protest to a country that doesn't exist in the eyes of the State Department. If you've any other suggestions, I'd be most interested to hear them.'

I had none then, and I have none now. Perhaps these words may give some brief warning before the first teasing advertisements appear in the trade papers, and may start stirrings of elephantine alarm among the networks. But will it make any difference? Hartford did not think so, and he may be right.

'History is on our side.' I cannot get those words out of my head. Land of Lincoln and Franklin and Melville, I love you and I wish you well. But into my heart blows a cold wind from the past; for I remember Babylon.

Trouble With Time

First published in *Ellery Queen's Mystery Magazine*, July 1960, as 'Crime on Mars'
Collected in *Tales of Ten Worlds*

It does seem a little eerie that, more than two decades before the notorious 'Face on Mars' was discovered, I described an identical one – though on a slightly smaller scale.

'We don't have much crime on Mars,' said Detective Inspector Rawlings, a little sadly. 'In fact, that's the chief reason I'm going back to the Yard. If I stayed here much longer, I'd get completely out of practice.'

We were sitting in the main observation lounge of the Phobos Spaceport, looking out across the jagged, sun-drenched crags of the tiny moon. The ferry rocket that had brought us up from Mars had left ten minutes ago, and was now beginning the long fall back to the ochre-tinted globe hanging there against the stars. In half an hour we would be boarding the liner for Earth – a world upon which most of the passengers had never set foot, but which they still called 'home'.

'At the same time,' continued the Inspector, 'now and then there's a case that makes life interesting. You're an art dealer, Mr Maccar; I'm sure you heard about that spot of bother at Meridian City a couple of months ago.'

'I don't think so,' replied the plump, olive-skinned little man I'd taken for just another returning tourist. Presumably the Inspector had already checked through the passenger list; I wondered how much he knew about me, and tried to reassure myself that my conscience was – well – reasonably clear. After all, everybody took *something* out through Martian Customs—

'It's been rather well hushed up,' said the Inspector, 'but you can't keep these things quiet for long. Anyway, a jewel thief from Earth tried to steal Meridian Museum's greatest treasure – the Siren Goddess.'

'But that's absurd!' I objected. 'It's priceless, of course – but it's only a lump of sandstone. You couldn't sell it to anyone – you might just as well steal the Mona Lisa.'

The Inspector grinned, rather mirthlessly. '*That's* happened once,' he said. 'Maybe the motive was the same. There are collectors who would give a fortune for such an object, even if they could only look at it themselves. Don't you agree, Mr Maccar?'

711

'That's perfectly true. In my business, you meet all sorts of crazy people.'

'Well, this chappie – name's Danny Weaver – had been well paid by one of them. And if it hadn't been for a piece of fantastically bad luck, he might have brought it off.'

The Spaceport PA system apologised for a further slight delay owing to final fuel checks, and asked a number of passengers to report to Information. While we were waiting for the announcement to finish, I recalled what little I knew about the Siren Goddess. Though I'd never seen the original, like most other departing tourists I had a replica in my baggage. It bore the certificate of the Mars Bureau of Antiquities, guaranteeing that 'this full-scale reproduction is an exact copy of the so-called Siren Goddess, discovered in the Mare Sirenium by the Third Expedition, AD 2012 (A.M. 23).'

It's quite a tiny thing to have caused so much controversy. Only eight or nine inches high – you wouldn't look at it twice if you saw it in a museum on Earth. The head of a young woman, with slightly oriental features, elongated earlobes, hair curled in tight ringlets close to the scalp, lips half parted in an expression of pleasure or surprise – that's all. But it's an enigma so baffling that it's inspired a hundred religious sects, and driven quite a few archaeologists round the bend. For a perfectly human head has no right whatsoever to be found on Mars, whose only intelligent inhabitants were crustaceans – 'educated lobsters', as the newspapers are fond of calling them. The aboriginal Martians never came near to achieving space flight, and in any event their civilisation died before men existed on Earth. No wonder the Goddess is the solar system's number-one mystery; I don't suppose we'll find the answer in my lifetime – if we ever do.

'Danny's plan was beautifully simple,' continued the Inspector. 'You know how absolutely dead a Martian city gets on Sunday, when everything closes down and the colonists stay home to watch the TV from Earth. Danny was counting on this, when he checked into the hotel in Meridian West, late Friday afternoon. He'd have Saturday for reconnoitring the Museum, an undisturbed Sunday for the job itself, and on Monday morning he'd be just another tourist leaving town . . .

'Early Saturday he strolled through the little park and crossed over into Meridian East, where the Museum stands. In case you don't know, the city gets its name because it's exactly on longitude one hundred and eighty degrees; there's a big stone slab in the park with the prime meridian engraved on it, so that visitors can get themselves photographed standing in two hemispheres at once. Amazing what simple things amuse some people.

'Danny spent the day going over the Museum exactly like any other tourist determined to get his money's worth. But at closing time he didn't leave; he'd holed up in one of the galleries not open to the public, where the Museum had been arranging a Late Canal Period reconstruction but had run out of money before the job could be finished. He stayed there until about midnight, just in case there were any enthusiastic researchers still in the building. Then he emerged and got to work.'

'Just a minute,' I interrupted. 'What about the night watchman?'

The Inspector laughed.

'My dear chap! They don't have such luxuries on Mars. There weren't even any alarms, for who would bother to steal lumps of stone? True, the Goddess was sealed up neatly in a strong glass-and-metal cabinet, just in case some souvenir hunter took a fancy to her. But even if she were stolen, there was nowhere the thief could hide, and of course all outgoing traffic would be searched as soon as the statue was missed.'

That was true enough. I'd been thinking in terms of Earth, forgetting that every city on Mars is a closed little world of its own beneath the force-field that protects it from the freezing near-vacuum. Beyond those electronic shields is the utterly hostile emptiness of the Martian Outback, where a man will die in seconds without protection. That makes law enforcement very easy; no wonder there's so little crime on Mars . . .

'Danny had a beautiful set of tools, as specialised as a watchmaker's. The main item was a microsaw no bigger than a soldering iron; it had a wafer-thin blade, driven at a million cycles a second by an ultrasonic power pack. It would go through glass or metal like butter – and left a cut only about as thick as a hair. Which was very important for Danny, since he had to leave no traces of his handiwork.

'I suppose you've guessed how he intended to operate. He was going to cut through the base of the cabinet, and substitute one of those souvenir replicas for the real Goddess. It might be a couple of years before some inquisitive expert discovered the awful truth; long before then the original would have travelled back to Earth, perfectly disguised as a copy of itself, with a genuine certificate of authenticity. Pretty neat, eh?

'It must have been a weird business, working in that darkened gallery with all those million-year-old carvings and unexplainable artifacts around him. A museum on Earth is bad enough at night, but at least it's – well – *human*. And Gallery Three, which houses the Goddess, is particularly unsettling. It's full of bas-reliefs showing quite incredible animals fighting each other; they look rather like giant beetles, and most paleontologists flatly deny that they could ever have existed. But imaginary or not, they belonged to this world, and they didn't disturb Danny as much as the Goddess, staring at him across the ages and defying him to explain her presence here. She gave him the creeps. How do I know? He told me.

'Danny set to work on that cabinet as carefully as any diamond cutter preparing to cleave a gem. It took most of the night to slice out the trap door, and it was nearly dawn when he relaxed and put down the saw. There was still a lot of work to do, but the hardest part was over. Putting the replica into the case, checking its appearance against the photos he'd thoughtfully brought with him, and covering up his traces might take most of Sunday, but that didn't worry him in the least. He had another twenty-four hours, and would positively welcome Monday's first visitors so that he could mingle with them and make his inconspicuous exit.

It was a perfectly horrible shock to his nervous system, therefore, when the main doors were noisily unbarred at eight thirty and the Museum staff – all six of them – started to open up for the day. Danny bolted for the emergency exit, leaving everything behind – tools, Goddesses, the lot. He had another big surprise when he found himself in the street; it should have been completely deserted at this time of day, with everyone at home reading the Sunday papers. But here were the citizens of Meridian East, as large as life, heading for plant or office on what was obviously a normal working day.

'By the time poor Danny got back to his hotel, we were waiting for him. We couldn't claim much credit for deducing that only a visitor from Earth – and a very recent one at that – could have overlooked Meridian City's chief claim to fame. And I presume you know what *that* is.'

'Frankly, I don't,' I answered. 'You can't see much of Mars in six weeks, and I never went east of the Syrtis Major.'

'Well, it's absurdly simple, but we shouldn't be too hard on Danny; even the locals occasionally fall into the same trap. It's something that doesn't bother us on Earth, where we've been able to dump the problem in the Pacific Ocean. But Mars, of course, is all dry land; and that means that *somebody* has to live with the International Date Line . . .

'Danny, you see, had worked from Meridian West. It was Sunday over there all right – and it was still Sunday when we picked him up back at the hotel. But over in Meridian East, half a mile away, it was only Saturday. That little trip across the park had made all the difference; I told you it was rotten luck.'

There was a long moment of silent sympathy; then I asked, 'What did he get?'

'Three years,' said Inspector Rawlings.

'That doesn't seem very much.'

'Mars years; that makes it almost six of ours. And a whacking fine which, by an odd coincidence, came to just the refund value of his return ticket to Earth. He isn't in jail, of course; Mars can't afford that kind of nonproductive luxury. Danny has to work for a living, under discreet surveillance. I told you that the Meridian Museum couldn't afford a night watchman. Well, it has one now. Guess who.'

'All passengers prepare to board in ten minutes! Please collect your hand baggage!' ordered the loud-speakers.

As we started to move toward the air lock, I couldn't help asking one more question.

'What about the people who put Danny up to it? There must have been a lot of money behind him. Did you get them?'

'Not yet; they'd covered their tracks pretty thoroughly, and I believe Danny was telling the truth when he said he couldn't give us any leads. Still, it's not my case; as I told you, I'm going back to my old job at the

714

Yard. But a policeman always keeps his eyes open – like an art dealer, eh, Mr Maccar? Why, you look a bit green about the gills. Have one of my space-sickness tablets.'

'No, thank you,' answered Mr Maccar, 'I'm quite all right.'

His tone was distinctly unfriendly; the social temperature seemed to have dropped below zero in the last few minutes. I looked at Mr Maccar, and I looked at the Inspector. And suddenly I realised that we were going to have a very interesting trip.

Into the Comet

First published in *The Magazine of Fantasy and Science Fiction*, October 1960, as
'Inside the Comet'
Collected in *Tales of Ten Worlds*

'I don't know why I'm recording this,' said George Takeo Pickett slowly into
the hovering microphone. 'There's no chance that anyone will ever hear it.
They say the comet will bring us back to the neighbourhood of Earth in
about two million years, when it makes its next turn around the sun. I
wonder if mankind will still be in existence then, and whether the comet
will put on as good a display for our descendants as it did for us? Maybe
they'll launch an expedition, just as we have done, to see what they can
find. And they'll find us . . .

'For the ship will still be in perfect condition, even after all those ages.
There'll be fuel in the tanks, maybe even plenty of air, for our food will give
out first, and we'll starve before we suffocate. But I guess we won't wait for
that; it will be quicker to open the air lock and get it all over.

'When I was a kid, I read a book on polar exploration called *Winter Amid
the Ice*. Well, that's what we're facing now. There's ice all around us, floating
in great porous bergs. *Challenger*'s in the middle of a cluster, orbiting round
one another so slowly that you have to wait several minutes before you're
certain they've moved. But no expedition to Earth's poles ever faced *our*
winter. During most of that two million years, the temperature will be four
hundred and fifty below zero. We'll be so far away from the sun that it'll
give about as much heat as the stars. And who ever tried to warm his hands
by Sirius on a cold winter night?'

That absurd image, coming suddenly into his mind, broke him up
completely. He could not speak because of memories of moonlight upon
snowfields, of Christmas chimes ringing across a land already fifty million
miles away. Suddenly he was weeping like a child, his self-control dissolved
by the remembrance of all the familiar, disregarded beauties of the Earth he
had forever lost.

And everything had begun so well, in such a blaze of excitement and
adventure. He could recall (was it only six months ago?) the very first time
he had gone out to look for the comet, soon after eighteen-year-old Jimmy
Randall had found it in his homemade telescope and sent his famous
telegram to Mount Stromlo Observatory. In those early days, it had been

only a faint polliwog of mist, moving slowly through the constellation of Eridanus, just south of the Equator. It was still far beyond Mars, sweeping sunward along its immensely elongated orbit. When it had last shone in the skies of Earth, there were no men to see it, and there might be none when it appeared again. The human race was seeing Randall's comet for the first and perhaps the only time.

As it approached the sun, it grew, blasting out plumes and jets, the smallest of which was larger than a hundred Earths. Like a great pennant streaming down some cosmic breeze, the comet's tail was already forty million miles long when it raced past the orbit of Mars. It was then that the astronomers realised that this might be the most spectacular sight ever to appear in the heavens; the display put on by Halley's comet, back in 1986, would be nothing in comparison. And it was then that the administrators of the International Astrophysical Decade decided to send the research ship *Challenger* chasing after it, if she could be fitted out in time; for here was a chance that might not come again in a thousand years.

For weeks on end, in the hours before dawn, the comet sprawled across the sky like a second but far brighter Milky Way. As it approached the sun, and felt again the fires it had not known since the mammoths shook the Earth, it became steadily more active. Gouts of luminous gas erupted from its core, forming great fans which turned like slowly swinging searchlights across the stars. The tail, now a hundred million miles long, divided into intricate bands and streamers which changed their patterns completely in the course of a single night. Always they pointed away from the sun, as if driven starward by a great wind blowing forever outward from the heart of the solar system.

When the *Challenger* assignment had been give to him, George Pickett could hardly believe his luck. Nothing like this had happened to any reporter since William Laurence and the atom bomb. The facts that he had a science degree, was unmarried, in good health, weighed less than one hundred and twenty pounds, and had no appendix undoubtedly helped. But there must have been many others equally qualified; well, their envy would soon turn to relief.

Because the skimpy pay load of *Challenger* could not accommodate a mere reporter, Pickett had had to double up in his spare time as executive officer. This meant, in practice, that he had to write up the log, act as captain's secretary, keep track of stores, and balance the accounts. It was very fortunate, he often thought, that one needed only three hours' sleep in every twenty-four, in the weightless world of space.

Keeping his two duties separate had required a great deal of tact. When he was not writing in his closet-sized office, or checking the thousands of items stacked away in stores, he would go on the prowl with his recorder. He had been careful, at one time or another, to interview every one of the twenty scientists and engineers who manned *Challenger*. Not all the recordings had been radioed back to Earth; some had been too technical, some too inarticulate, and others too much the reverse. But at least he had played

717

no favourites and, as far as he knew, had trodden on no toes. Not that it mattered now.

He wondered how Dr Martens was taking it; the astronomer had been one of his most difficult subjects, yet the one who could give most information. On a sudden impulse, Pickett located the earliest of the Martens tapes, and inserted it in the recorder. He knew that he was trying to escape from the present by retreating into the past, but the only effect of that self-knowledge was to make him hope the experiment would succeed.

He still had vivid memories of that first interview, for the weightless microphone, wavering only slightly in the draft of air from the ventilators, had almost hypnotised him into incoherence. Yet no one would have guessed: his voice had its normal, professional smoothness.

They had been twenty million miles behind the comet, but swiftly overtaking it, when he had trapped Martens in the observatory and thrown the opening question at him.

'Dr Martens,' he began, 'just what *is* Randall's comet made of?'

'Quite a mixture,' the astronomer had answered, 'and it's changing all the time as we move away from the sun. But the tail's mostly ammonia, methane, carbon dioxide, water vapour, cyanogen—'

'Cyanogen? Isn't that a poison gas? What would happen if the Earth ran into it?'

'Not a thing. Though it looks so spectacular, by our normal standards a comet's tail is a pretty good vacuum. A volume as big as Earth contains about as much gas as a matchbox full of air.'

'And yet this thin stuff puts on such a wonderful display!'

'So does the equally thin gas in an electric sign, and for the same reason. A comet's tail glows because the sun bombards it with electrically charged particles. It's a cosmic skysign; one day, I'm afraid, the advertising people will wake up to this, and find a way of writing slogans across the solar system.'

'That's a depressing thought – though I suppose someone will claim it's a triumph of applied science. But let's leave the tail; how soon will we get into the heart of the comet – the nucleus, I believe you call it?'

'Since a stern chase always takes a long time, it will be another two weeks before we enter the nucleus. We'll be ploughing deeper and deeper into the tail, taking a cross section through the comet as we catch up with it. But though the nucleus is still twenty million miles ahead, we've already learned a good deal about it. For one thing, it's extremely small – less than fifty miles across. And even that's not solid, but probably consists of thousands of smaller bodies, all milling round in a cloud.'

'Will we be able to go into the nucleus?'

'We'll know when we get there. Maybe we'll play safe and study it through our telescopes from a few thousand miles away. But personally, I'll be disappointed unless we go right inside. Won't you?'

Picket switched off the recorder. Yes, Martens had been right. He *would* have been disappointed, especially since there had seemed no possible source of danger. Nor was there, as far as the comet was concerned. The danger had come from within.

They had sailed through one after another of the huge but unimaginably tenuous curtains of gas that Randall's comet was still ejecting as it raced away from the sun. Yet even now, though they were approaching the densest regions of the nucleus, they were for all practical purposes in a perfect vacuum. The luminous fog that stretched around *Challenger* for so many millions of miles scarcely dimmed the stars; but directly ahead, where lay the comet's core, was a brilliant patch of hazy light, luring them onward like a will-o'-the-wisp.

The electrical disturbances now taking place around them with ever-increasing violence had almost completely cut their link with Earth. The ship's main radio transmitter could just get a signal through, but for the last few days they had been reduced to sending 'OK' messages in Morse. When they broke away from the comet and headed for home, normal communication would be resumed; but now they were almost as isolated as explorers had been in the days before radio. It was inconvenient, but that was all. Indeed, Pickett rather welcomed this state of affairs; it gave him more time to get on with his clerical duties. Though *Challenger* was sailing into the heart of a comet, on a course that no captain could have dreamed of before the twentieth century, someone still had to check the provisions and count the stores.

Very slowly and cautiously, her radar probing the whole sphere of space around her, *Challenger* crept into the nucleus of the comet. And there she came to rest – amid the ice.

Back in the nineteen-forties, Fred Whipple, of Harvard, had guessed the truth, but it was hard to believe it even when the evidence was before one's eyes. The comet's relatively tiny core was a loose cluster of icebergs, drifting and turning round one another as they moved along their orbit. But unlike the bergs that floated in polar seas, they were not a dazzling white, nor were they made of water. They were a dirty grey, and very porous, like partly thawed snow. And they were riddled with pockets of methane and frozen ammonia, which erupted from time to time in gigantic gas jets as they absorbed the heat of the sun. It was a wonderful display, but Pickett had little time to admire it. Now he had far too much.

He had been doing his routine check of the ship's stores when he came face to face with disaster – though it was some time before he realised it. For the supply situation had been perfectly satisfactory; they had ample stocks for the return to Earth. He had checked that with his own eyes, and now had merely to confirm the balances recorded in the pinhead-sized section of the ship's electronic memory which stored all the accounts.

When the first crazy figures flashed on the screen, Pickett assumed that he had pressed the wrong key. He cleared the totals, and fed the information into the computer once more.

Sixty cases of pressed meat to start with; 17 consumed so far; quantity left: 99999943.

He tried again, and again, with no better result. Then, feeling annoyed but not particularly alarmed, he went in search of Dr Martens.

He found the astronomer in the Torture Chamber – the tiny gym, squeezed between the technical stores and the bulkhead of the main propellant tank. Each member of the crew had to exercise here for an hour a day, lest his muscles waste away in this gravityless environment. Martens was wrestling with a set of powerful springs, an expression of grim determination on his face. It became much grimmer when Pickett gave his report.

A few tests on the main input board quickly told them the worst. 'The computer's insane,' said Martens. 'It can't even add or subtract.'

'But surely we can fix it!'

Martens shook his head. He had lost all his usual cocky self-confidence; he looked, Pickett told himself, like an inflated rubber doll that had started to leak.

'Not even the builders could do that. It's a solid mass of microcircuits, packed as tightly as the human brain. The memory units are still operating, but the computing section's utterly useless. It just scrambles the figures you feed into it.'

'And where does that leave us?' Pickett asked.

'It means that we're all dead,' Martens answered flatly. 'Without the computer, we're done for. It's impossible to calculate an orbit back to Earth. It would take an army of mathematicians weeks to work it out on paper.'

'That's ridiculous! The ship's in perfect condition, we've plenty of food and fuel – and you tell me we're all going to die just because we can't do a few sums.'

'A *few* sums!' retorted Martens, with a trace of his old spirit. 'A major navigational change, like the one needed to break away from the comet and put us on an orbit to Earth, involves about a hundred thousand separate calculations. Even the computer needs several minutes for the job.'

Pickett was no mathematician, but he knew enough of astronautics to understand the situation. A ship coasting through space was under the influence of many bodies. The main force controlling it was the gravity of the sun, which kept all the planets firmly chained in their orbits. But the planets themselves also tugged it this way and that, though with much feebler strength. To allow for all these conflicting tugs and pulls – above all, to take advantage of them to reach a desired goal scores of millions of miles away – was a problem of fantastic complexity. He could appreciate Martens' despair; no man could work without the tools of his trade, and no trade needed more elaborate tools than this one.

Even after the Captain's announcement, and that first emergency conference when the entire crew had gathered to discuss the situation, it had taken hours for the facts to sink home. The end was still so many months away that the mind could not grasp it; they were under sentence of death, but there was no hurry about the execution. And the view was still superb . . .

Beyond the glowing mists that enveloped them – and which would be their celestial monument to the end of time – they could see the great beacon of Jupiter, brighter than all the stars. Some of them might still be alive, if the others were willing to sacrifice themselves, when the ship went past the mightiest of the sun's children. Would the extra weeks of life be worth it, Pickett asked himself, to see with your own eyes the sight that Galileo had first glimpsed through his crude telescope four centuries ago – the satellites of Jupiter, shuttling back and forth like beads upon an invisible wire?

Beads upon a wire. With that thought, an all-but-forgotten childhood memory exploded out of his subconscious. It must have been there for days, struggling upward into the light. Now at last it had forced itself upon his waiting mind.

'No!' he cried aloud. 'It's ridiculous! They'll laugh at me!'

So what? said the other half of his mind. You've nothing to lose; if it does no more, it will keep everyone busy while the food and the oxygen dwindle away. Even the faintest hope is better than none at all . . .

He stopped fidgeting with the recorder; the mood of maudlin self-pity was over. Releasing the elastic webbing that held him to his seat, he set off for the technical stores in search of the material he needed.

'This,' said Dr Martens three days later, 'isn't my idea of a joke.' He gave a contemptuous glance at the flimsy structure of wire and wood that Pickett was holding in his hand.

'I guessed you'd say that,' Pickett replied, keeping his temper under control. 'But please listen to me for a minute. My grandmother was Japanese, and when I was a kid she told me a story that I'd completely forgotten until this week. I think it may save our lives.

'Sometime after the Second World War, there was a contest between an American with an electric desk calculator and a Japanese using an abacus like this. The abacus won.'

'Then it must have been a poor desk machine, or an incompetent operator.'

'They used the best in the US Army. But let's stop arguing. Give me a test – say a couple of three-figure numbers to multiply.'

'Oh – 856 times 437.'

Pickett's fingers danced over the beads, sliding them up and down the wires with lightning speed. There were twelve wires in all, so that the abacus could handle numbers up to 999,999,999,999 – or could be divided into separate sections where several independent calculations could be carried out simultaneously.

'374072,' said Pickett, after an incredibly brief interval of time. 'Now see how long *you* take to do it, with pencil and paper.'

There was a much longer delay before Martens, who like most mathematicians was poor at arithmetic, called out '375072.' A hasty check soon confirmed that Martens had taken at least three times as long as Pickett to arrive at the wrong answer.

The astronomer's face was a study in mingled chagrin, astonishment, and curiosity.

'Where did you learn that trick?' he asked. 'I thought those things could only add and subtract.'

'Well – multiplication's only repeated addition, isn't it? All I did was to add 856 seven times in the unit column, three times in the tens column, and four times in the hundreds column. You do the same thing when you use pencil and paper. Of course, there are some short cuts, but if you think *I'm* fast, you should have seen my granduncle. He used to work in a Yokohama bank, and you couldn't see his fingers when he was going at speed. He taught me some of the tricks, but I've forgotten most of them in the last twenty years. I've only been practising for a couple of days, so I'm still pretty slow. All the same, I hope I've convinced you that there's something in my argument.'

'You certainly have: I'm quite impressed. Can you divide just as quickly?'

'Very nearly, when you've had enough experience.'

Martens picked up the abacus, and started flicking the beads back and forth. Then he sighed.

'Ingenious – but it doesn't really help us. Even if it's ten times as fast as a man with pencil and paper – which it isn't – the computer was a million times faster.'

'I've thought of that,' answered Pickett, a little impatiently.

(Martens had no guts – he gave up too easily. How did he think astronomers managed a hundred years ago, before there were any computers?)

'This is what I propose – tell me if you can see any flaws in it . . .'

Carefully and earnestly he detailed his plan. As he did so, Martens slowly relaxed, and presently he gave the first laugh that Pickett had heard aboard *Challenger* for days.

'I want to see the skipper's face,' said the astronomer, 'when you tell him that we're all going back to the nursery to start playing with beads.'

There was scepticism at first, but it vanished swiftly when Pickett gave a few demonstrations. To men who had grown up in a world of electronics, the fact that a simple structure of wire and beads could perform such apparent miracles was a revelation. It was also a challenge, and because their lives depended upon it, they responded eagerly.

As soon as the engineering staff had built enough smoothly operating copies of Pickett's crude prototype, the classes began. It took only a few minutes to explain the basic principles; what required time was practice – hour after hour of it, until the fingers flew automatically across the wires and flicked the beads into the right positions without any need for conscious thought. There were some members of the crew who never acquired both accuracy and speed, even after a week of constant practice: but there were others who quickly outdistanced Pickett himself.

They dreamed counters and columns, and flicked beads in their sleep. As soon as they had passed beyond the elementary stage they were divided into teams, which then competed fiercely against each other, until they had reached still higher standards of proficiency. In the end, there were men aboard *Challenger* who could multiply four-figure numbers on the abacus in fifteen seconds, and keep it up hour after hour.

Such work was purely mechanical; it required skill, but no intelligence. The really difficult job was Martens', and there was little that anyone could do to help him. He had to forget all the machine-based techniques he had taken for granted, and rearrange his calculations so that they could be carried out automatically by men who had no idea of the meaning of the figures they were manipulating. He would feed them the basic data, and then they would follow the programme he had laid down. After a few hours of patient routine work, the answer would emerge from the end of the mathematical production line - provided that no mistakes had been made. And the way to guard against that was to have two independent teams working, cross-checking results at regular intervals.

'What we've done,' said Pickett into his recorder, when at last he had time to think of the audience he had never expected to speak to again, 'is to build a computer out of human beings instead of electronic circuits. It's a few thousand times slower, can't handle many digits, and gets tired easily – but it's doing the job. Not the whole job of navigating to Earth – that's far too complicated – but the simpler one of giving us an orbit that will bring us back into radio range. Once we've escaped from the electrical interference around us, we can radio our position and the big computers on Earth can tell us what to do next.

'We've already broken away from the comet and are no longer heading out of the solar system. Our new orbit checks with the calculations, to the accuracy that can be expected. We're still inside the comet's tail, but the nucleus is a million miles away and we won't see those ammonia icebergs again. They're racing on toward the stars into the freezing night between the suns, while we are coming home . . .

'Hello, Earth . . . hello, Earth! This is *Challenger* calling. *Challenger* calling. Signal back as soon as you receive us – we'd like you to check our arithmetic – before we work our fingers to the bone!'

Summertime on Icarus

First published in Vogue, June 1960, as 'The Hottest Piece of Real Estate in the
Solar System'
Collected in *Tales of Ten Worlds*

When I wrote this story, I certainly never dreamed that one day I would have
an asteroid named after me: in 1996 the International Astronomical Union
rescued 4923 from anonymity. As a result, I am now the proud absentee
landlord of about 100 square kilometres of real estate out around Mars. It
doesn't come anywhere near the Earth, so I'm not worried about *Deep Impact*
type lawsuits.

When Colin Sherrard opened his eyes after the crash, he could not imagine
where he was. He seemed to be lying, trapped in some kind of vehicle, on
the summit of a rounded hill, which sloped steeply away in all directions.
Its surface was seared and blackened, as if a great fire had swept over it.
Above him was a jet-black sky, crowded with stars; one of them hung like
a tiny, brilliant sun low down on the horizon.

Could it be the sun? Was he so far from Earth? No – that was impossible.
Some nagging memory told him that the sun was very close – hideously
close – not so distant that it had shrunk to a star. And with that thought,
full consciousness returned. Sherrard knew exactly where he was, and the
knowledge was so terrible that he almost fainted again.

He was nearer to the sun than any man had ever been. His damaged
space-pod was lying on no hill, but on the steeply curving surface of a
world only two miles in diameter. That brilliant star sinking swiftly in the
west was the light of *Prometheus*, the ship that had brought him here across
so many millions of miles of space. She was hanging up there among the
stars, wondering why his pod had not returned like a homing pigeon to its
roost. In a few minutes she would have passed from sight, dropping below
the horizon in her perpetual game of hide-and-seek with the sun.

That was a game that he had lost. He was still on the night side of the
asteroid, in the cool safety of its shadow, but the short night would be
ending soon. The four-hour day of Icarus was spinning him swiftly toward
that dreadful dawn, when a sun thirty times larger than ever shone upon
Earth would blast these rocks with fire. Sherrard knew all too well why

everything around him was burned and blackened. Icarus was still a week from perihelion but the temperature at noon had already reached a thousand degrees Fahrenheit.

Though this was no time for humour, he suddenly remembered Captain McClellan's description of Icarus: 'The hottest piece of real estate in the solar system.' The truth of that jest had been proved, only a few days before, by one of those simple and unscientific experiments that are so much more impressive than any number of graphs and instrument readings.

Just before daybreak, someone had propped a piece of wood on the summit of one of the tiny hills. Sherrard had been watching, from the safety of the night side, when the first rays of the rising sun had touched the hilltop. When his eyes had adjusted to the sudden detonation of light, he saw that the wood was already beginning to blacken and char. Had there been an atmosphere here, the stick would have burst into flames; such was dawn, upon Icarus . . .

Yet it had not been impossibly hot at the time of their first landing, when they were passing the orbit of Venus five weeks ago. *Prometheus* had overtaken the asteroid as it was beginning its plunge toward the sun, had matched speed with the little world and had touched down upon its surface as lightly as a snowflake. (A snowflake on Icarus – *that* was quite a thought . . .) then the scientists had fanned out across the fifteen square miles of jagged nickel-iron that covered most of the asteroid's surface, setting up their instruments and check-points, collecting samples and making endless observations.

Everything had been carefully planned, years in advance, as part of the International Astrophysical Decade. Here was a unique opportunity for a reasearch ship to get within a mere seventeen million miles of the sun, protected from its fury by a two-mile-thick shield of rock and iron. In the shadow of Icarus, the ship could ride safely round the central fire which warmed all the planets, and upon which the existence of all life depended. As the Prometheus of legend had brought the gift of fire to mankind, so the ship that bore his name would return to Earth with other unimagined secrets from the heavens.

There had been plenty of time to set up the instruments and make the surveys before *Prometheus* had to take off and seek the permanent shade of night. Even then, it was still possible for men in the tiny self-propelled space-pods – miniature spaceships, only ten feet long – to work on the night side for an hour or so, as long as they were not overtaken by the advancing line of sunrise. That had seemed a simple-enough condition to meet, on a world where dawn marched forward at only a mile an hour; but Sherrard had failed to meet it, and the penalty was death.

He was still not quite sure what had happened. He had been replacing a seismograph transmitter at Station 145, unofficially known as Mount Everest because it was a full ninety feet above the surrounding territory. The job had been a perfectly straightforward one, even though he had to do it by remote control through the mechanical arms of his pod. Sherrard was an

725

expert at manipulating these; he could tie knots with his metal fingers almost as quickly as with his flesh-and-bone ones. The task had taken little more than twenty minutes, and then the radioseismograph was on the air again, monitoring the tiny quakes and shudders that racked Icarus in ever-increasing numbers as the asteroid approached the sun. It was small satisfaction to know that he had now made a king-sized addition to the record.

After he had checked the signals, he had carefully replaced the sun screens around the instrument. It was hard to believe that two flimsy sheets of polished metal foil, no thicker than paper, could turn aside a flood of radiation that would melt lead or tin within seconds. But the first screen reflected more than ninety per cent of the sunlight falling upon its mirror surface and the second turned back most of the rest, so that only a harmless fraction of the heat passed through.

He had reported completion of the job, received an acknowledgement from the ship, and prepared to head for home. The brilliant floodlights hanging from *Prometheus* – without which the night side of the asteroid would have been in utter darkness – had been an unmistakable target in the sky. The ship was only two miles up, and in this feeble gravity he could have jumped that distance had he been wearing a planetary-type space suit with flexible legs. As it was, the low-powered micro-rockets of his pod would get him there in a leisurely five minutes.

He had aimed the pod with its gyros, set the rear jets at Strength Two, and pressed the firing button. There had been a violent explosion some-where in the vicinity of his feet and he had soared away from Icarus – but not toward the ship. Something was horribly wrong; he was tossed to one side of the vehicle, unable to reach the controls. Only one of the jets was firing, and he was pinwheeling across the sky, spinning faster and faster under the off-balanced drive. He tried to find the cutoff, but the spin had completely disorientated him. When he was able to locate the controls, his first reaction made matters worse – he pushed the throttle over to full, like a nervous driver stepping on the accelerator instead of the brake. It took only a second to correct the mistake and kill the jet, but by then he was spinning so rapidly that the stars were wheeling round in circles.

Everything had happened so quickly that there was no time for fear, no time even to call the ship and report what was happening. He took his hands away from the controls; to touch them now would only make matters worse. It would take two or three minutes of cautious jockeying to unravel his spin, and from the flickering glimpses of the approaching rocks it was obvious that he did not have as many seconds. Sherrard remembered a piece of advice at the front of the *Spaceman's Manual* 'When you don't know what to do, *do nothing*.' He was still doing it when Icarus fell upon him, and the stars went out.

It had been a miracle that the pod was unbroken, and that he was not breathing space. (Thirty minutes from now he might be glad to do so, when the capsule's heat insulation began to fail . . .) There had been some

damage, of course. The rear-view mirrors, just outside the dome of transparent plastic that enclosed his head, were both snapped off, so that he
could no longer see what lay behind him without twisting his neck. This
was a trivial mishap; far more serious was the fact that his radio antennas
had been torn away by the impact. He could not call the ship, and the ship
could not call him. All that came over the radio was a faint crackling,
probably produced inside the set itself. He was absolutely alone, cut off
from the rest of the human race.

It was a desperate situation, but there was one faint ray of hope. He was
not, after all, completely helpless. Even if he could not use the pod's rockets
– he guessed that the starboard motor had blown back and ruptured a fuel
line, something the designers said was impossible – he was still able to
move. He had his arms.

But which way should he crawl? He had lost all sense of location, for
though he had taken off from Mount Everest, he might now be thousands
of feet away from it. There were no recognisable landmarks in his tiny
world; the rapidly sinking star of *Prometheus* was his best guide, and if he
could keep the ship in view he would be safe. It would only be a matter of
minutes before his absence was noted, if indeed it had not been discovered
already. Yet without radio, it might take his colleagues a long time to find
him; small though Icarus was, its fifteen square miles of fantastically rugged
no man's land could provide an effective hiding place for a ten-foot cylinder.
It might take an hour to locate him – which meant that he would have to
keep ahead of the murderous sunrise.

He slipped his fingers into the controls that worked his mechanical limbs.
Outside the pod, in the hostile vacuum that surrounded him, his substitute
arms came to life. They reached down, thrust against the iron surface of the
asteroid, and levered the pod from the ground. Sherrard flexed them, and
the capsule jerked forward, like some weird, two-legged insect . . . first the
right arm, then the left, then the right . . .

It was less difficult than he had feared, and for the first time he felt his
confidence return. Though his mechanical arms had been designed for light
precision work, it needed very little pull to set the capsule moving in this
weightless environment. The gravity of Icarus was ten thousand times
weaker than Earth's: Sherrard and his space-pod weighed less than an
ounce here, and once he had set himself in motion he floated forward with
an effortless, dreamlike ease.

Yet that very effortlessness had its dangers. He had travelled several
hundred yards, and was rapidly overhauling the sinking star of the *Prometheus*, when overconfidence betrayed him. (Strange how quickly the mind
could switch from one extreme to the other; a few minutes ago he had
been steeling himself to face death – now he was wondering if he would be
late for dinner.) Perhaps the novelty of the movement, so unlike anything
he had ever attempted before, was responsible for the catastrophe; or
perhaps he was still suffering from the after-effects of the crash.

Like all astronauts, Sherrard had learned to orientate himself in space, and had grown accustomed to living and working when the Earthly conceptions of up and down were meaningless. On a world such as Icarus, it was necessary to pretend that there was a real, honest-to-goodness planet 'beneath' your feet, and that when you moved you were travelling over a horizontal plain. If this innocent self-deception failed, you were heading for space vertigo.

The attack came without warning, as it usually did. Quite suddenly, Icarus no longer seemed to be beneath him, the stars no longer above. The universe tilted through a right angle; he was moving straight *up* a vertical cliff, like a mountaineer scaling a rock face, and though Sherrard's reason told him that this was pure illusion, all his senses screamed that it was true. In a moment gravity must drag him off this sheer wall, and he would drop down mile upon endless mile until he smashed into oblivion.

Worse was to come; the false vertical was still swinging like a compass needle that had lost the pole. Now he was on the *underside* of an immense rocky roof, like a fly clinging to a ceiling; in another moment it would have become a wall again – but this time he would be moving straight down it, instead of up . . .

He had lost all control over the pod, and the clammy sweat that had begun to dew his brow warned him that he would soon lose control over his body. There was only one thing to do; he clenched his eyes tightly shut, squeezed as far back as possible into the tiny closed world of the capsule, and pretended with all his might that the universe outside did not exist. He did not even allow the slow, gentle crunch of his second crash to interfere with his self-hypnosis.

When he again dared to look outside, he found that the pod had come to rest against a large boulder. Its mechanical arms had broken the force of the impact, but at a cost that was more than he could afford to pay. Though the capsule was virtually weightless here, it still possessed its normal five hundred pounds of inertia, and it had been moving at perhaps four miles an hour. The momentum had been too much for the metal arms to absorb; one had snapped, and the other was hopelessly bent.

When he saw what had happened, Sherrard's first reaction was not despair, but anger. He had been so certain of success when the pod had started its glide across the barren face of Icarus. And now this, all through a moment of physical weakness! But space made no allowance for human frailties or emotions, and a man who did not accept that fact had no right to be here.

At least he had gained precious time in his pursuit of the ship; he had put an extra ten minutes, if not more, between himself and dawn. Whether that ten minutes would merely prolong the agony or whether it would give his shipmates the extra time they needed to find him, he would soon know.

Where were they? Surely they had started the search by now! He strained his eyes toward the brilliant star of the ship, hoping to pick out the fainter lights of space-pods moving toward him – but nothing else was visible against the slowly turning vault of heaven.

He had better look to his own resources, slender though they were. Only a few minutes were left before the *Prometheus* and her trailing lights would sink below the edge of the asteroid and leave him in darkness. It was true that the darkness would be all too brief, but before it fell upon him he might find some shelter against the coming day. This rock into which he had crashed, for example . . .

Yes, it would give some shade, until the sun was halfway up the sky. Nothing could protect him if it passed right overhead, but it was just possible that he might be in a latitude where the sun never rose far above the horizon at this season of Icarus's four-hundred-and-nine-day year. Then he might survive the brief period of daylight; that was his only hope, if the rescuers did not find him before dawn.

There went *Prometheus* and her lights, below the edge of the world. With her going, the now-unchallenged stars blazed forth with redoubled brilliance. More glorious than any of them – so lovely that even to look upon it almost brought tears to his eyes – was the blazing beacon of Earth, with its companion moon beside it. He had been born on one, and had walked on the other; would he see either again?

Strange that until now he had given no thought to his wife and children, and to all that he loved in the life that now seemed so far away. He felt a spasm of guilt, but it passed swiftly. The ties of affection were not weakened, even across the hundred million miles of space that now sundered him from his family. At this moment, they were simply irrelevant. He was now a primitive, self-centred animal fighting for his life, and his only weapon was his brain. In this conflict, there was no place for the heart; it would merely be a hindrance, spoiling his judgment and weakening his resolution.

And then he saw something that banished all thoughts of his distant home. Reaching up above the horizon behind him, spreading across the stars like a milky mist, was a faint and ghostly cone of phosphorescence. It was the herald of the sun – the beautiful, pearly phantom of the corona, visible on Earth only during the rare moments of a total eclipse. When the corona was rising, the sun would not be far behind, to smite this little land with fury.

Sherrard made good use of the warning. Now he could judge, with some accuracy, the exact point where the sun would rise. Crawling slowly and clumsily on the broken stumps of his metal arms, he dragged the capsule round to the side of the boulder that should give the greatest shade. He had barely reached it when the sun was upon him like a beast of prey, and his tiny world exploded into light.

He raised the dark filters inside his helmet, one thickness after another, until he could endure the glare. Except where the broad shadow of the boulder lay across the asteroid, it was like looking into a furnace. Every detail of the desolate land around him was revealed by that merciless light; there were no greys, only blinding whites and impenetrable blacks. All the shadowed cracks and hollows were pools of ink, while the higher ground already seemed to be on fire, as it caught the sun. Yet it was only a minute after dawn.

Now Sherrard could understand how the scorching heat of a billion summers had turned Icarus into a cosmic cinder, baking the rocks until the last traces of gas had bubbled out of them. Why should men travel, he asked himself bitterly, across the gulf of stars at such expense and risk – merely to land on a spinning slag heap? For the same reason, he knew, that they had once struggled to reach Everest and the Poles and the far places of the Earth – for the excitement of the body that was adventure, and the more enduring excitement of the mind that was discovery. It was an answer that gave him little consolation, now that he was about to be grilled like a joint on the turning spit of Icarus.

Already he could feel the first breath of heat upon his face. The boulder against which he was lying gave him protection from direct sunlight, but the glare reflected back at him from those blazing rocks only a few yards away was striking through the transparent plastic of the dome. It would grow swiftly more intense as the sun rose higher; he had even less time than he had thought, and with the knowledge came a kind of numb resignation that was beyond fear. He would wait – if he could – until the sunrise engulfed him and the capsule's cooling unit gave up the unequal struggle, then he would crack the pod and let the air gush out into the vacuum of space.

Nothing to do but to sit and think in the minutes that were left to him before his pool of shadow contracted. He did not try to direct his thoughts, but let them wander where they willed. How strange that he should be dying now, because back in the nineteen-forties – years before he was born – a man at Palomar had spotted a streak of light on a photographic plate, and had named it so appropriately after the boy who flew too near the sun.

One day, he supposed, they would build a momument here for him on this blistered plain. What would they inscribe upon it? 'Here died Colin Sherrard, astronics engineer, in the cause of Science.' That would be funny, for he had never understood half the things that the scientists were trying to do.

Yet some of the excitement of their discoveries had communicated itself to him. He remembered how the geologists had scraped away the charred skin of the asteroid, and had polished the metallic surface that lay beneath. It had been covered with a curious pattern of lines and scratches, like one of the abstract paintings of the Post-Picasso Decadents. But these lines had some meaning; they wrote the history of Icarus, though only a geologist could read it. They revealed, so Sherrard had been told, that this lump of iron and rock had not always floated alone in space. At some remote time in the past, it had been under enormous pressure – and that could mean only one thing. Billions of years ago it had been part of a much larger body, perhaps a planet like Earth. For some reason that planet had blown up, and Icarus and all the thousands of other asteroids were the fragments of that cosmic explosion.

Even at this moment, as the incandescent line of sunlight came closer, this was a thought that stirred his mind. What Sherrard was lying upon was the core of a world – perhaps a world that had once known life. In a strange, irrational way it comforted him to know that his might not be the only ghost to haunt Icarus until the end of time.

The helmet was misting up; that could only mean that the cooling unit was about to fail. It had done its work well; even now, though the rocks only a few yards away must be glowing a sullen red, the heat inside the capsule was not unendurable. When failure came, it would be sudden and catastrophic.

He reached for the red lever that would rob the sun of its prey – but before he pulled it, he would look for the last time upon Earth. Cautiously, he lowered the dark filters, adjusting them so that they still cut out the glare from the rocks, but no longer blocked his view of space.

The stars were faint now, dimmed by the advancing glow of the corona. And just visible over the boulder whose shield would soon fail him was a stub of crimson flame, a crooked finger of fire jutting from the edge of the sun itself. He had only seconds left.

There was the Earth, there was the moon. Goodbye to them both, and to his friends and loved ones on each of them. While he was looking at the sky, the sunlight had begun to lick the base of the capsule, and he felt the first touch of fire. In a reflex as automatic as it was useless, he drew up his legs, trying to escape the advancing wave of heat.

What was that? A brilliant flash of light, infinitely brighter than any of the stars, had suddenly exploded overhead. Miles above him, a huge mirror was sailing across the sky, reflecting the sunlight as it slowly turned through space. Such a thing was utterly impossible; he was beginning to suffer from hallucinations, and it was time he took his leave. Already the sweat was pouring from his body, and in a few seconds the capsule would be a furnace.

He waited no longer, but pulled on the Emergency Release with all his waning strength, bracing himself at the same moment to face the end.

Nothing happened; the lever would not move. He tugged it again and again before he realised that it was hopelessly jammed. There was no easy way out for him, no merciful death as the air gushed from his lungs. It was then, as the true terror of his situation struck home to him, that his nerve finally broke and he began to scream like a trapped animal.

When he heard Captain McClellan's voice speaking to him, thin but clear, he knew that it must be another hallucination. Yet some last remnant of discipline and self-control checked his screaming; he clenched his teeth and listened to that familiar, commanding voice.

'Sherrard! Hold on, man! We've got a fix on you – but keep shouting!'

'Here I am!' he cried. 'But hurry, for God's sake! I'm burning!'

Deep down in what was left of his rational mind he realised what had happened. Some feeble ghost of a signal was leaking through the broken stubs of his antennas, and the searchers had heard his screams – as he was hearing their voices. That meant they must be very close indeed, and the knowledge gave him sudden strength.

He stared through the steaming plastic of the dome, looking once more for that impossible mirror in the sky. There it was again – and now he realised that the baffling perspectives of space had tricked his senses. The mirror was not miles away, nor was it huge. It was almost on top of him, and it was moving fast.

He was still shouting when it slid across the face of the rising sun, and its blessed shadow fell upon him like a cool wind that had blown out of the heart of winter, over leagues of snow and ice. Now that it was so close, he recognised it at once; it was merely a large metal-foil radiation screen, no doubt hastily snatched from one of the instrument sites. In the safety of its shadow, his friends had been searching for him.

A heavy-duty, two-man capsule was hovering overhead, holding the glittering shield in one set of arms and reaching for him with the other. Even through the misty dome and the haze of heat that still sapped his senses, he recognised Captain McClellan's anxious face, looking down at him from the other pod.

So this was what birth was like, for truly he had been reborn. He was too exhausted for gratitude – that would come later – but as he rose from the burning rocks his eyes sought and found the bright star of Earth. 'Here I am,' he said silently. 'I'm coming back.'

Back to enjoy and cherish all the beauties of the world he had thought were lost forever. No – not all of them.

He would never enjoy summer again.

Saturn Rising

First published in *The Magazine of Fantasy and Science Fiction*, March 1961
Collected in *Tales of Ten Worlds*

Little did I imagine, when I wrote this story in 1960, that within less than two decades the fantastically successful Voyager Missions to the outer Solar System would reveal that the rings of Saturn were far more complex and beautiful than anyone had ever dreamed.

The story has, of course, been dated by the scientific discoveries of the last [four] decades – in particular, we now know that Titan does not have a predominantly methane atmosphere, but one which is mostly nitrogen.

There is another error which I might have corrected at the time. Even if you could observe Saturn from the surface of Titan (which atmospheric haze will probably prevent), you'd never see it 'rising'. Almost certainly, Titan, like our own Moon, has had its rotation tidally braked, so that it always keeps the same face turned towards its primary. So Saturn remains fixed in Titan's sky, just as the Earth does in the Moon's.

Yes, that's perfectly true. I met Morris Perlman when I was about twenty-eight. I met thousands of people in those days, from presidents downward.

When we got back from Saturn, everybody wanted to see us, and about half the crew took off on lecture tours. I've always enjoyed talking (don't say you haven't noticed it), but some of my colleagues said they'd rather go to Pluto than face another audience. Some of them did.

My beat was the Midwest, and the first time I ran into Mr Perlman – no one ever called him anything else, certainly never 'Morris' – was in Chicago. The agency always booked me into good, but not too luxurious, hotels. That suited me; I liked to stay in places where I could come and go as I pleased without running a gauntlet of liveried flunkies, and where I could wear anything within reason without being made to feel a tramp. I see you're grinning; well, I was only a kid then, and a lot of things have changed . . .

It's all a long time ago now, but I must have been lecturing at the University. At any rate, I remember being disappointed because they couldn't show me the place where Fermi started the first atomic pile – they said that the building had been pulled down forty years before, and there was only a plaque to mark the spot. I stood looking at it for a while, thinking of all that had happened since that far-off day in 1942. I'd been born, for one thing; and atomic power had taken me out to Saturn and back. *That* was probably something that Fermi and Co. never thought of, when they built their primitive latticework of uranium and graphite.

I was having breakfast in the coffee shop when a slightly built, middle-aged man dropped into the seat on the other side of the table. He nodded a polite 'Good morning', then gave a start of surprise as he recognised me. (Of course, he'd planned the encounter, but I didn't know it at the time.)

'This is a pleasure' he said. 'I was at your lecture last night. How I envied you!'

I gave a rather forced smile; I'm never very sociable at breakfast, and I'd learned to be on my guard against the cranks, bores, and enthusiasts who seemed to regard me as their legitimate prey. Mr Perlman, however, was not a bore – though he was certainly an enthusiast, and I suppose you could call him a crank.

He looked like any average, fairly prosperous businessman, and I assumed that he was a guest like myself. The fact that he had attended my lecture was not surprising; it had been a popular one, open to the public, and of course well advertised over press and radio.

'Ever since I was a kid,' said my uninvited companion, 'Saturn has fascinated me. I know exactly when and how it all started. I must have been about ten years old when I came across those wonderful paintings of Chesley Bonestell's, showing the planet as it would look from its nine moons. I suppose you've seen them?'

'Of course,' I answered. 'Though they're half a century old, no one's beaten them yet. We had a couple aboard the *Endeavour*, pinned on the plotting table. I often used to look at the pictures and then compare them with the real thing.'

'Then you know how I felt, back in the nineteen-fifties. I used to sit for hours trying to grasp the fact that this incredible object, with its silver rings spinning around it, wasn't just some artist's dream, but actually existed – that it was a world, in fact, ten times the size of Earth.

'At that time I never imagined that I could see this wonderful thing for myself; I took it for granted that only the astronomers, with their giant telescopes, could ever look at such sights. But then, when I was about fifteen, I made another discovery – so exciting that I could hardly believe it.'

'And what was that?' I asked. By now I'd become reconciled to sharing breakfast; my companion seemed a harmless-enough character, and there was something quite endearing about his obvious enthusiasm.

'I found that any fool could make a high-powered astronomical telescope in his own kitchen, for a few dollars and a couple of weeks' work. It was a revelation; like thousands of other kids, I borrowed a copy of Ingalls' *Amateur Telescope Making* from the public library, and went ahead. Tell me – have *you* ever built a telescope of your own?'

'No: I'm an engineer, not an astronomer. I wouldn't know how to begin the job.'

'It's incredibly simple, if you follow the rules. You start with two discs of glass, about an inch thick. I got mine for fifty cents from a ship chandler's; they were porthole glasses that were no use because they'd been chipped around the edges. Then you cement one disc to some flat, firm surface – I used an old barrel, standing on end.

'Next you have to buy several grades of emery powder, starting from coarse, gritty stuff and working down to the finest that's made. You lay a pinch of the coarsest powder between the two discs, and start rubbing the upper one back and forth with regular strokes. As you do so, you slowly circle around the job.

'You see what happens? The upper disc gets hollowed out by the cutting action of the emery powder, and as you walk around, it shapes itself into a concave, spherical surface. From time to time you have to change to a finer grade of powder, and make some simple optical tests to check that your curve's right.

'Later still, you drop the emery and switch to rouge, until at last you have a smooth, polished surface that you can hardly credit you've made yourself. There's only one more step, though that's a little tricky. You still have to silver the mirror, and turn it into a good reflector. This means getting some chemicals made up at the drugstore, and doing exactly what the book says.

'I can still remember the kick I got when the silver film began to spread like magic across the face of my little mirror. It wasn't perfect, but it was good enough, and I wouldn't have swapped it for anything on Mount Palomar.

'I fixed it at one end of a wooden plank: there was no need to bother about a telescope tube, though I put a couple of feet of cardboard round the mirror to cut out stray light. For an eyepiece I used a small magnifying lens I'd picked up in a junk store for a few cents. Altogether, I don't suppose the telescope cost more than five dollars – though that was a lot of money to me when I was a kid.

'We were living then in a run-down hotel my family owned on Third Avenue. When I'd assembled the telescope I went up on the roof and tried it out, among the jungle of TV antennas that covered every building in those days. It took me a while to get the mirror and eyepiece lined up, but I hadn't made any mistakes and the thing worked. As an optical instrument it was probably lousy – after all, it was my first attempt – but it magnified at least fifty times and I could hardly wait until nightfall to try it on the stars.

'I'd checked with the almanac, and knew that Saturn was high in the east after sunset. As soon as it was dark I was up on the roof again, with my crazy contraption of wood and glass propped between two chimneys. It was late fall, but I never noticed the cold, for the sky was full of stars – and they were all mine.

735

'I took my time setting the focus as accurately as possible, using the first star that came in to the field. Then I started hunting for Saturn, and soon discovered how hard it was to locate anything in a reflecting telescope that wasn't properly mounted. But presently the planet shot across the field of view. I nudged the instrument a few inches this way and that – and there it was.

'It was tiny, but it was perfect. I don't think I breathed for a minute; I could hardly believe my eyes. After all the pictures, here was the reality. It looked like a toy hanging there in space, with the rings slightly open and tilted toward me. Even now, forty years later, I can remember thinking "It looks so *artificial* – like something from a Christmas tree!" There was a single bright star to the left of it, and I knew that was Titan.'

He paused, and for a moment we must have shared the same thoughts. For to both of us Titan was no longer merely the largest moon of Saturn – a point of light known only to astronomers. It was the fiercely hostile world upon which *Endeavour* had landed, and where three of my crew-mates lay in lonely graves, farther from their homes than any of Mankind's dead had ever rested before.

'I don't know how long I stared, straining my eyes and moving the telescope across the sky in jerky steps as Saturn rose above the city. I was a billion miles from New York; but presently New York caught up with me.

'I told you about our hotel; it belonged to my mother, but my father ran it – not very well. It had been losing money for years, and all through my boyhood there had been continuous financial crises. So I don't want to blame my father for drinking; he must have been half crazy with worry most of the time. And I had quite forgotten that I was supposed to be helping the clerk at the reception desk . . .

'So Dad came looking for me, full of his own cares and knowing nothing about my dreams. He found me stargazing on the roof.

'He wasn't a cruel man – he couldn't have understood the study and patience and care that had gone into my little telescope, or the wonders it had shown me during the short time I had used it. I don't hate him any more, but I'll remember all my life the splintering crack of my first and last mirror as it smashed against the brickwork.'

There was nothing I could say. My initial resentment at this interruption had long since changed to curiosity. Already I sensed that there was much more to this story than I'd heard so far, and I'd noticed something else. The waitress was treating us with an exaggerated deference – only a little of which was directed at me.

My companion toyed with the sugar bowl while I waited in silent sympathy. By this time I felt there was some bond between us, though I did not know exactly what it was.

'I never built another telescope,' he said. 'Something else broke, besides that mirror – something in my heart. Anyway, I was much too busy. Two things happened that turned my life upside down. Dad walked out on us,

736

leaving me the head of the family. And then they pulled down the Third Avenue El.'

He must have seen my puzzled look, for he grinned across the table at me.

'Oh, you wouldn't know about that. But when I was a kid, there was an elevated railroad down the middle of Third. It made the whole area dirty and noisy; the Avenue was a slum district of bars, pawnshops and cheap hotels – like ours. All that changed when the El went; land values shot up, and we were suddenly prosperous. Dad came back quickly enough, but it was too late; I was running the business. Before long I started moving across town – then across country. I wasn't an absent-minded stargazer any more, and I gave Dad one of my smaller hotels, where he couldn't do much harm.

'It's forty years since I looked at Saturn, but I've never forgotten that one glimpse, and last night your photographs brought it all back. I just wanted to say how grateful I am.'

He fumbled in his wallet and pulled out a card.

'I hope you'll look me up when you're in town again; you can be sure I'll be there if you give any more lectures. Good luck – and I'm sorry to have taken so much of your time.'

Then he was gone, almost before I could say a word. I glanced at the card, put it away in my pocket, and finished my breakfast, rather thoughtfully.

When I signed my check on the way out of the coffee shop I asked: 'Who was that gentleman at my table? The boss?'

The cashier looked at me as if I were mentally retarded.

'I suppose you *could* call him that, sir,' she answered. 'Of course he owns this hotel, but we've never seen him here before. He always stays at the Ambassador, when he's in Chicago.'

'And does he own *that*?' I said, without too much irony, for I'd already suspected the answer.

'Why, yes. As well as—' and she rattled off a whole string of others, including the two biggest hotels in New York.

I was impressed, and also rather amused, for it was now obvious that Mr Perlman had come here with the deliberate intention of meeting me. It seemed a roundabout way of doing it; I knew nothing, then, of his notorious shyness and secretiveness. From the first, he was never shy with me.

Then I forgot about him for five years. (Oh, I should mention that when I asked for my bill, I was told I didn't have one.) During that five years, I made my second trip.

We knew what to expect this time, and weren't going completely into the unknown. There were no more worries about fuel, because all we could ever use was waiting for us on Titan; we just had to pump its methane atmosphere into our tanks, and we'd made our plans accordingly. One after another, we visited all the nine moons; and then we went into the rings . . .

There was little danger, yet it was a nerve-racking experience. The ring system is very thin, you know – only about twenty miles in thickness. We descended into it slowly and cautiously, after having matched its spin so that we were moving at exactly the same speed. It was like stepping onto a carousel a hundred and seventy thousand miles across . . .

But a ghostly kind of carousel, because the rings aren't solid and you can look right through them. Close up, in fact, they're almost invisible; the billions of separate particles that make them up are so widely spaced that all you see in your immediate neighbourhood are occasional small chunks, drifting very slowly past. It's only when you look into the distance that the countless fragments merge into a continuous sheet, like a hailstorm that sweeps around Saturn forever.

That's not *my* phrase, but it's a good one. For when we brought our first piece of genuine Saturnian ring into the air lock, it melted down in a few minutes into a pool of muddy water. Some people think it spoils the magic to know that the rings – or ninety per cent of them – are made of ordinary ice. But that's a stupid attitude; they would be just as wonderful, and just as beautiful, if they were made of diamond.

When I got back to Earth, in the first year of the new century, I started off on another lecture tour – only a short one, for now I had a family and wanted to see as much of it as possible. This time I ran into Mr Perlman in New York, when I was speaking at Columbia and showing our movie, 'Exploring Saturn.' (A misleading title, that, since the nearest we'd been to the planet itself was about twenty thousand miles. No one dreamed, in those days, that men would ever go down into the turbulent slush which is the closest thing Saturn has to a surface.)

Mr Perlman was waiting for me after the lecture. I didn't recognise him, for I'd met about a million people since our last encounter. But when he gave his name, it all came back, so clearly that I realised he must have made a deep impression on my mind.

Somehow he got me away from the crowd; though he disliked meeting people in the mass, he had an extraordinary knack of dominating any group when he found it necessary – and then clearing out before his victims knew what had happened. Though I saw him in action scores of times, I never knew exactly how he did it.

At any rate, half an hour later we were having a superb dinner in an exclusive restaurant (his, of course). It was a wonderful meal, especially after the chicken and ice cream of the lecture circuit, but he made me pay for it. Metaphorically, I mean.

Now all the facts and photos gathered by the two expeditions to Saturn were available to everyone, in hundreds of reports and books and popular articles. Mr Perlman seemed to have read all the material that wasn't too technical; what he wanted from me was something different. Even then, I put his interest down to that of a lonely, aging man, trying to recapture a dream that had been lost in youth. I was right; but that was only a fraction of the whole picture.

He was after something that all the reports and articles failed to give. What did it *feel* like, he wanted to know, to wake up in the morning and see that great, golden globe with its scudding cloud belts dominating the sky? And the rings themselves – what did they do to your mind when they were so close that they filled the heavens from end to end?

You want a poet, I said – not an engineer. But I'll tell you this; however long you look at Saturn, and fly in and out among its moons, you can never quite believe it. Every so often you find yourself thinking: 'It's all a dream – a thing like that *can't* be real.' And you go to the nearest view-port – and there it is, taking your breath away.

You must remember that, altogether apart from our nearness, we were able to look at the rings from angles and vantage points that are quite impossible from Earth, where you always see them turned toward the sun. We could fly into their shadow, and then they would no longer gleam like silver – they would be a faint haze, a bridge of smoke across the stars.

And most of the time we could see the shadow of Saturn lying across the full width of the rings, eclipsing them so completely that it seemed as if a great bite had been taken out of them. It worked the other way, too; on the day side of the planet, there would always be the shadow of the rings running like a dusky band parallel to the Equator and not far from it.

Above all – though we did this only a few times – we could rise high above either pole of the planet and look down upon the whole stupendous system, so that it was spread out in plan beneath us. Then we could see that instead of the four visible from Earth, there were at least a dozen separate rings, merging one into the other. When we saw this, our skipper made a remark that I've never forgotten. 'This,' he said – and there wasn't a trace of flippancy in the words – 'is where the angels have parked their halos.'

All this, and a lot more, I told Mr Perlman in that little but oh-so-expensive restaurant just south of Central Park. When I'd finished, he seemed very pleased, though he was silent for several minutes. Then he said, about as casually as you might ask the time of the next train at your local station: 'Which would be the best satellite for a tourist resort?'

When the words got through to me, I nearly choked on my hundred-year-old brandy. Then I said, very patiently and politely (for after all, I'd had a wonderful dinner): 'Listen, Mr Perlman. You know as well as I do that Saturn is nearly a billion miles from Earth – more than that, in fact, when we're on opposite sides of the sun. Someone worked out that our round-trip tickets averaged seven and a half million dollars apiece – and, believe me, there was no first-class accommodation on *Endeavour I* or *II*. Anyway, no matter how much money he had, no one could book a passage to Saturn. Only scientists and space crews will be going there, for as far ahead as anyone can imagine.'

I could see that my words had absolutely no effect; he merely smiled, as if he knew some secret hidden from me.

'What you say is true enough *now*,' he answered, 'but I've studied history. And I understand people – that's my business. Let me remind you of a few facts.

'Two or three centuries ago, almost all the world's great tourist centres and beauty spots were as far away from civilisation as Saturn is today. What did – oh, Napoleon, let's say – know about the Grand Canyon, Victoria Falls, Hawaii, Mount Everest? And look at the South Pole; it was reached for the first time when my father was a boy – but there's been a hotel there for the whole of your lifetime.

'Now it's starting all over again. *You* can appreciate only the problems and difficulties, because you're too close to them. Whatever they are, men will overcome them, as they've always done in the past.

'For wherever there's something strange or beautiful or novel, people will want to see it. The rings of Saturn are the greatest spectacle in the known universe: I've always guessed so, and now you've convinced me. Today it takes a fortune to reach them, and the men who go there must risk their lives. So did the first men who flew – but now there are a million passengers in the air every second of the day and night.

'The same thing is going to happen in space. It won't happen in ten years, maybe not in twenty. But twenty-five is all it took, remember, before the first commercial flights started to the moon. I don't think it will be as long for Saturn . . .

'I won't be around to see it – but when it happens, I want people to remember me. So – where should we build?'

I still thought he was crazy, but at last I was beginning to understand what made him tick. And there was no harm in humouring him, so I gave the matter careful thought.

'Mimas is too close,' I said, 'and so are Enceladus and Tethys.' (I don't mind telling you, those names were tough after all that brandy.) 'Saturn just fills the sky, and you think it's falling on top of you. Besides, they aren't solid enough – they're nothing but overgrown snowballs. Dione and Rhea are better – you get a magnificent view from both of them. But all these inner moons are so tiny; even Rhea is only eight hundred miles across, and the others are much smaller.

'I don't think there's any real argument; it will have to be Titan. That's a man-sized satellite – it's a lot bigger than *our* moon, and very nearly as large as Mars. There's a reasonable gravity too – about a fifth of Earth's – so your guests won't be floating all over the place. And it will always be a major refuelling point because of its methane atmosphere, which should be an important factor in your calculations. Every ship that goes out to Saturn will touch down there.'

'And the outer moons?'

'Oh, Hyperion, Japetus, and Phoebe are much too far away. You have to look hard to see the rings at all from Phoebe! Forget about them. Stick to good old Titan. Even if the temperature is two hundred below zero, and ammonia snow isn't the sort of stuff you'd want to ski on.'

He listened to me very carefully, and if he thought I was making fun of his impractical, unscientific notions he gave no sign of it. We parted soon afterward – I don't remember anything more of that dinner – and then it must have been fifteen years before we met again. He had no further use for me in all that time; but when he wanted me, he called.

I see now what he had been waiting for; his vision had been clearer than mine. He couldn't have guessed, of course, that the rocket would go the way of the steam engine within less than a century – but he knew *something* better would come along, and I think he financed Saunderson's early work on the Paragravity Drive. But it was not until they started building fusion plants that could warm up a hundred square miles of a world as cold as Pluto that he got in contact with me again.

He was a very old man, and dying. They told me how rich he was, and I could hardly believe it. Not until he showed me the elaborate plans and the beautiful models his experts had prepared with such remarkable lack of publicity.

He sat in his wheel chair like a wrinkled mummy, watching my face as I sudied the models and blueprints. Then he said: 'Captain, I have a job for you . . .'

So here I am. It's just like running a spaceship, of course – many of the technical problems are identical. And by this time I'd be too old to command a ship, so I'm very grateful to Mr Perlman.

There goes the gong. If the ladies are ready, I suggest we walk down to dinner through the Observation Lounge.

Even after all these years, I still like to watch Saturn rising – and tonight it's almost full.

Death and the Senator

First published in *Analog*, May 1961
Collected in *Tales of Ten Worlds*

Washington had never looked lovelier in the spring; and this was the last spring, thought Senator Steelman bleakly, that he would ever see. Even now, despite all that Dr Jordan had told him, he could not fully accept the truth. In the past there had always been a way of escape; no defeat had been final. When men had betrayed him, he had discarded them – even ruined them, as a warning to others. But now the betrayal was within himself; already, it seemed, he could feel the laboured beating of the heart that would soon be stilled. No point in planning now for the Presidential election of 1976; he might not even live to see the nominations . . .

It was an end of dreams and ambition, and he could not console himself with the knowledge that for all men these must end someday. For him it was too soon; he thought of Cecil Rhodes, who had always been one of his heroes, crying 'So much to do – so little time to do it in!' as he died before his fiftieth birthday. He was already older than Rhodes, and had done far less.

The car was taking him away from the Capitol; there was symbolism in that, and he tried not to dwell upon it. Now he was abreast of the New Smithsonian – that vast complex of museums he had never had time to visit, though he had watched it spread along the Mall throughout the years he had been in Washington. How much he had missed, he told himself bitterly, in his relentless pursuit of power. The whole universe of art and culture had remained almost closed to him, and that was only part of the price that he had paid. He had become a stranger to his family and to those who were once his friends. Love had been sacrificed on the altar of ambition, and the sacrifice had been in vain. Was there anyone in all the world who would weep at his departure?

Yes, there was. The feeling of utter desolation relaxed its grip upon his soul. As he reached for the phone, he felt ashamed that he had to call the office to get this number, when his mind was cluttered with memories of so many less important things.

(There was the White House, almost dazzling in the spring sunshine. For the first time in his life he did not give it a second glance. Already it belonged to another world – a world that would never concern him again.)

The car circuit had no vision, but he did not need it to sense Irene's mild surprise – and her still milder pleasure.

'Hello, Renee – how are you all?'

'Fine, Dad. When are we going to see you?'

It was the polite formula his daughter always used on the rare occasions when he called. And invariably, except at Christmas or birthdays, his answer was a vague promise to drop around at some indefinite future date.

'I was wondering,' he said slowly, almost apologetically, 'if I could borrow the children for an afternoon. It's a long time since I've taken them out, and I felt like getting away from the office.'

'But of course,' Irene answered, her voice warming with pleasure. 'They'll love it. When would you like them?'

'Tomorrow would be fine. I could call around twelve, and take them to the Zoo or the Smithsonian, or anywhere else they felt like visiting.'

Now she was really startled, for she knew well enough that he was one of the busiest men in Washington, with a schedule planned weeks in advance. She would be wondering what had happened; he hoped she would not guess the truth. No reason why she should, for not even his secretary knew of the stabbing pains that had driven him to seek this long-overdue medical checkup.

'That would be wonderful. They were talking about you only yesterday, asking when they'd see you again.'

His eyes misted, and he was glad that Renee could not see him.

'I'll be there at noon,' he said hastily, trying to keep the emotion out of his voice. 'My love to you all.' He switched off before she could answer, and relaxed against the upholstery with a sigh of relief. Almost upon impulse, without conscious planning, he had taken the first step in the reshaping of his life. Though his own children were lost to him, a bridge across the generations remained intact. If he did nothing else, he must guard and strengthen it in the months that were left.

Taking two lively and inquisitive children through the natural-history building was not what the doctor would have ordered, but it was what he wanted to do. Joey and Susan had grown so much since their last meeting, and it required both physical and mental alertness to keep up with them. No sooner had they entered the rotunda than they broke away from him, and scampered toward the enormous elephant dominating the marble hall.

'What's that?' cried Joey.

'It's an elephant, stupid,' answered Susan with all the crushing superiority of her seven years.

'I know it's an effelant,' retorted Joey. 'But what's its name?'

Senator Steelman scanned the label, but found no assistance there. This was one occasion when the risky adage 'Sometimes wrong, never uncertain' was a safe guide to conduct.

'He was called – er – Jumbo,' he said hastily. 'Just look at those tusks!'

743

'Did he ever get toothache?'

'Oh no.'

'Then how did he clean his teeth? Ma says that if I don't clean mine . . .'

Steelman saw where the logic of this was leading, and thought it best to change the subject.

'There's a lot more to see inside. Where do you want to start – birds, snakes, fish, mammals?'

'Snakes!' clamoured Susan. 'I wanted to keep one in a box, but Daddy said no. Do you think he'd change his mind if you asked him?'

'What's a mammal?' asked Joey, before Steelman could work out an answer to that.

'Come along,' he said firmly. 'I'll show you.'

As they moved through the halls and galleries, the children darting from one exhibit to another, he felt at peace with the world. There was nothing like a museum for calming the mind, for putting the problems of everyday life in their true perspective. Here, surrounded by the infinite variety and wonder of Nature, he was reminded of truths he had forgotten. He was only one of a million million creatures that shared this planet Earth. The entire human race, with its hopes and fears, its triumphs and its follies, might be no more than an incident in the history of the world. As he stood before the monstrous bones of Diplodocus (the children for once awed and silent), he felt the winds of Eternity blowing through his soul. He could no longer take so seriously the gnawing of ambition, the belief that he was the man the nation needed. *What* nation, if it came to that? A mere two centuries ago this summer, the Declaration of Independence had been signed; but this old American had lain in the Utah rocks for a hundred million years . . .

He was tired when they reached the Hall of Oceanic Life, with its dramatic reminder that Earth still possessed animals greater than any that the past could show. The ninety-foot blue whale plunging into the ocean, and all the other swift hunters of the sea, brought back memories of hours he had once spent on a tiny, glistening deck with a white sail billowing above him. That was another time when he had known contentment, listening to the swish of water past the prow, and the sighing of the wind through the rigging. He had not sailed for thirty years; this was another of the world's pleasures he had put aside.

'I don't like fish,' complained Susan. 'When do we get to the snakes?'

'Presently,' he said. 'But what's the hurry? There's plenty of time.'

The words slipped out before he realised it. He checked his step, while the children ran on ahead. Then he smiled, without bitterness. For in a sense, it was true enough. There *was* plenty of time. Each day, each hour could be a universe of experience, if one used it properly. In the last weeks of his life, he would begin to live.

As yet, no one at the office suspected anything. Even his outing with the children had not caused much surprise; he had done such things before, suddenly cancelling his appointments and leaving his staff to pick up the pieces. The pattern of his behaviour had not yet changed, but in a few days it would be obvious to all his associates that something had happened. He owed it to them – and to the party – to break the news as soon as possible; there were, however, many personal decisions he had to make first, which he wished to settle in his own mind before he began the vast unwinding of his affairs.

There was another reason for his hesitancy. During his career, he had seldom lost a fight, and in the cut and thrust of political life he had given quarter to none. Now, facing his ultimate defeat, he dreaded the sympathy and the condolences that his many enemies would hasten to shower upon him. The attitude, he knew, was a foolish one – a remnant of his stubborn pride which was too much a part of his personality to vanish even under the shadow of death.

He carried his secret from committee room to White House to Capitol, and through all the labyrinths of Washington society, for more than two weeks. It was the finest performance of his career, but there was no one to appreciate it. At the end of that time he had completed his plan of action; it remained only to dispatch a few letters he had written in his own hand, and to call his wife.

The office located her, not without difficulty, in Rome. She was still beautiful, he thought, as her features swam on to the screen; she would have made a fine First Lady, and that would have been some compensation for the lost years. As far as he knew, she had looked forward to the prospect; but had he ever really understood what she wanted?

'Hello, Martin,' she said, 'I was expecting to hear from you. I suppose you want me to come back.'

'Are you willing to?' he asked quietly. The gentleness of his voice obviously surprised her.

'I'd be a fool to say no, wouldn't I? But if they don't elect you, I want to go my own way again. You must agree to that.'

'They won't elect me. They won't even nominate me. You're the first to know this, Diana. In six months, I shall be dead.'

The directness was brutal, but it had a purpose. That fraction-of-a-second delay while the radio waves flashed up to the communication satellites and back again to Earth had never seemed so long. For once, he had broken through the beautiful mask. Her eyes widened with disbelief, her hand flew to her lips.

'You're joking!'

'About *this*? It's true enough. My heart's worn out. Dr Jordan told me, a couple of weeks ago. It's my own fault, of course, but let's not go into that.'

'So that's why you've been taking out the children: I wondered what had happened.'

He might have guessed that Irene would have talked with her mother. It was a sad reflection on Martin Steelman, if so commonplace a fact as showing an interest in his own grandchildren could cause curiosity.

'Yes,' he admitted frankly. 'I'm afraid I left it a little late. Now I'm trying to make up for lost time. Nothing else seems very important.'

In silence, they looked into each other's eyes across the curve of the Earth, and across the empty desert of the dividing years. Then Diana answered, a little unsteadily, 'I'll start packing right away.'

Now that the news was out, he felt a great sense of relief. Even the sympathy of his enemies was not as hard to accept as he had feared. For overnight, indeed, he had no enemies. Men who had not spoken to him in years, except with invective, sent messages whose sincerity could not be doubted. Ancient quarrels evaporated, or turned out to be founded on misunderstandings. It was a pity that one had to die to learn these things . . .

He also learned that, for a man of affairs, dying was a full-time job. There were successors to appoint, legal and financial mazes to untangle, committee and state business to wind up. The work of an energetic lifetime could not be terminated suddenly, as one switches off an electric light. It was astonishing how many responsibilities he had acquired, and how difficult it was to divest himself of them. He had never found it easy to delegate power (a fatal flaw, many critics had said, in a man who hoped to be Chief Executive), but now he must do so, before it slipped forever from his hands.

It was as if a great clock was running down, and there was no one to rewind it. As he gave away his books, read and destroyed old letters, closed useless accounts and files, dictated final instructions, and wrote farewell notes, he sometimes felt a sense of complete unreality. There was no pain; he could never have guessed that he did not have years of active life ahead of him. Only a few lines on a cardiogram lay like a roadblock across his future – or like a curse, written in some strange language the doctors alone could read.

Almost every day now Diana, Irene, or her husband brought the children to see him. In the past he had never felt at ease with Bill, but that, he knew, had been his own fault. You could not expect a son-in-law to replace a son, and it was unfair to blame Bill because he had not been cast in the image of Martin Steelman, Jr. Bill was a person in his own right; he had looked after Irene, made her happy, and fathered her children. That he lacked ambition was a flaw – if flaw indeed it was – that the Senator could at last forgive.

He could even think, without pain or bitterness, of his own son, who had travelled this road before him and now lay, one cross among many, in the United Nations cemetery at Capetown. He had never visited Martin's grave; in the days when he had the time, white men were not popular in what was left of South Africa. Now he could go if he wished, but he was uncertain if it would be fair to harrow Diana with such a mission. His own memories would not trouble him much longer, but she would be left with hers.

Yet he would like to go, and felt it was his duty. Moreover, it would be a last treat for the children. To them it would be only a holiday in a strange land, without any tinge of sorrow for an uncle they had never known. He had started to make the arrangements when, for the second time within a month, his whole world was turned upside down.

Even now, a dozen or more visitors would be waiting for him each morning when he arrived at his office. Not as many as in the old days, but still a sizable crowd. He had never imagined, however, that Dr Harkness would be among them.

The sight of that thin, gangling figure made him momentarily break his stride. He felt his cheeks flush, his pulse quicken at the memory of ancient battles across committee-room tables, of angry exchanges that had reverberated along the myriad channels of the ether. Then he relaxed; as far as he was concerned, all that was over.

Harkness rose to his feet, a little awkwardly, as he approached. Senator Steelman knew that initial embarrassment – he had seen it so often in the last few weeks. Everyone he now met was automatically at a disadvantage, always on the alert to avoid the one subject that was taboo.

'Well, Doctor,' he said. 'This is a surprise – I never expected to see *you* here.'

He could not resist that little jab, and derived some satisfaction at watching it go home. But it was free from bitterness, as the other's smile acknowledged.

'Senator,' replied Harkness, in a voice that was pitched so low that he had to lean forward to hear it, 'I've some extremely important information for you. Can we speak alone for a few minutes? It won't take long.'

Steelman nodded; he had his own ideas of what was important now, and felt only a mild curiosity as to why the scientist had come to see him. The man seemed to have changed a good deal since their last encounter, seven years ago. He was much more assured and self-confident, and had lost the nervous mannerisms that had helped to make him such an unconvincing witness.

'Senator,' he began, when they were alone in the private office, 'I've some news that may be quite a shock to you. I believe that you can be cured.'

Steelman slumped heavily in his chair. This was the one thing he had never expected; from the first, he had not encumbered himself with the burden of vain hopes. Only a fool fought against the inevitable, and he had accepted his fate.

For a moment he could not speak; then he looked up at his old adversary and gasped: 'Who told you that? All my doctors—'

'Never mind them; it's not their fault they're ten years behind the times. Look at this.'

'What does it mean? I can't read Russian.'

'It's the latest issue of the USSR *Journal of Space Medicine*. It arrived a few days ago, and we did the usual routine translation. This note here – the one I've marked – refers to some recent work at the Mechnikov Station.'

'What's that?'

'You don't *know*? Why, that's their Satellite Hospital, the one they've built just below the Great Radiation Belt.'

'Go on,' said Steelman, in a voice that was suddenly dry and constricted. 'I'd forgotten they'd called it that.' He had hoped to end his life in peace, but now the past had come back to haunt him.

'Well, the note itself doesn't say much, but you can read a lot between the lines. It's one of those advance hints that scientists put out before they have time to write a full-fledged paper, so they can claim priority later. The title is: "Therapeutic Effects of Zero Gravity on Circulatory Diseases". What they've done is to induce heart disease artificially in rabbits and hamsters, and then take them up to the space station. In orbit, of course, nothing has any weight; the heart and muscles have practically no work to do. And the result is exactly what I tried to tell you, years ago. Even extreme cases can be arrested, and many can be cured.'

The tiny, panelled office that had been the centre of his world, the scene of so many conferences, the birthplace of so many plans, became suddenly unreal. Memory was much more vivid: he was back again at those hearings, in the fall of 1969, when the National Aeronautics and Space Administration's first decade of activity had been under review – and, frequently, under fire.

He had never been chairman of the Senate Committee on Astronautics, but he had been its most vocal and effective member. It was here that he had made his reputation as a guardian of the public purse, as a hardheaded man who could not be bamboozled by utopian scientific dreamers. He had done a good job; from that moment, he had never been far from the headlines. It was not that he had any particular feeling for space and science, but he knew a live issue when he saw one. Like a tape-recorder unrolling in his mind, it all came back . . .

'Dr Harkness, you are Technical Director of the National Aeronautics and Space Administration?'

'That is correct.'

'I have here the figures for NASA's expenditure over the period 1959–69; they are quite impressive. At the moment the total is $82,547,450,000, and the estimate for fiscal 69–70 is well over ten billions. Perhaps you could give us some indication of the return we can expect from all this.'

'I'll be glad to do so, Senator.'

That was how it had started, on a firm but not unfriendly note. The hostility had crept in later. That it was unjustified, he had known at the time; any big organisation had weaknesses and failures, and one which literally aimed at the stars could never hope for more than partial success. From the beginning, it had been realised that the conquest of space would be at least as costly in lives and treasure as the conquest of the air. In ten years, almost a hundred men had died – on Earth, in space, and upon the barren surface of the Moon. Now that the urgency of the early sixties was over, the public was asking 'Why?' Steelman was shrewd enough to see himself as mouthpiece for those questioning voices. His performance had been cold and calculated; it was convenient to have a scapegoat, and Dr Harkness was unlucky enough to be cast for the role.

'Yes, Doctor, I understand all the benefits we've received from space research in the way of improved communications and weather forecasting, and I'm sure everyone appreciates them. But almost all this work has been done with automatic, unmanned vehicles. What I'm worried about – what many people are worried about – is the mounting expense of the Man-in-Space programme, and its very marginal utility. Since the original Dyna-Soar and Apollo projects, almost a decade ago, we've shot billions of dollars into space. And with what result? So that a mere handful of men can spend a few uncomfortable hours outside the atmosphere, achieving nothing that television cameras and automatic equipment couldn't do – much better and cheaper. And the lives that have been lost! None of us will forget those screams we heard coming over the radio when the X-21 burned up on re-entry. What right have we to send men to such deaths?'

He could still remember the hushed silence in the committee chamber when he had finished. His questions were very reasonable ones, and deserved to be answered. What was unfair was the rhetorical manner in which he had framed them and, above all, the fact that they were aimed at a man who could not answer them effectively. Steelman would not have tried such tactics on a von Braun or a Rickover; they would have given him at least as good as they received. But Harkness was no orator; if he had deep personal feelings, he kept them to himself. He was a good scientist, an able administrator – and a poor witness. It had been like shooting fish in a barrel. The reporters had loved it; he never knew which of them coined the nickname 'Hapless Harkness'.

'Now this plan of yours, Doctor, for a fifty-man space laboratory – *how* much did you say it would cost?'

'I've already told you – just under one and a half billions.'

'And the annual maintenance?'

'Not more than $250,000,000.'

'When we consider what's happened to previous estimates, you will forgive us if we look upon these figures with some scepticism. But even assuming that they are right, what will we get for the money?'

'We will be able to establish our first large-scale research station in space. So far, we have had to do our experimenting in cramped quarters aboard unsuitable vehicles, usually when they were engaged on some other mission. A permanent, manned satellite laboratory is essential. Without it, further progress is out of the question. Astrobiology can hardly get started—'

'Astro what?'

'Astrobiology – the study of living organisms in space. The Russians really started it when they sent up the dog Laika in Sputnik II and they're still ahead of us in this field. But no one's done any serious work on insects or invertebrates – in fact, on any animals except dogs, mice, and monkeys.'

'I see. Would I be correct in saying that you would like funds for building a zoo in space?'

The laughter in the committee room had helped to kill the project. And it had helped, Senator Steelman now realised, to kill him.

He had only himself to blame, for Dr Harkness had tried, in his ineffectual way, to outline the benefits that a space laboratory might bring. He had particularly stressed the medical aspects, promising nothing but pointing out the possibilities. Surgeons, he had suggested, would be able to develop new techniques in an environment where the organs had no weight; men might live longer, freed from the wear and tear of gravity, for the strain on heart and muscles would be enormously reduced. Yes, he had mentioned the heart; but that had been of no interest to Senator Steelman – healthy, and ambitious, and anxious to make good copy . . .

'Why have you come to tell me this?' he said dully. 'Couldn't you let me die in peace?'

'That's the point,' said Harkness impatiently. 'There's no need to give up hope.'

'Because the Russians have cured some hamsters and rabbits?'

'They've done much more than that. The paper I showed you only quoted the preliminary results; it's already a year out of date. They don't want to raise false hopes, so they are keeping as quiet as possible.'

'How do you know this?'

Harkness looked surprised.

'Why, I called Professor Stanyukovitch, my opposite number. It turned out that he was up on the Mechnikov Station, which proves how important they consider this work. He's an old friend of mine, and I took the liberty of mentioning your case.'

The dawn of hope, after its long absence, can be as painful as its departure. Steelman found it hard to breathe and for a dreadful moment he wondered if the final attack had come. But it was only excitement; the constriction in his chest relaxed, the ringing in his ears faded away, and he heard Dr Harkness's voice saying: 'He wanted to know if you could come to Astrograd right away, so I said I'd ask you. If you can make it, there's a flight from New York at ten-thirty tomorrow morning.'

Tomorrow he had promised to take the children to the Zoo; it would be the first time he had let them down. The thought gave him a sharp stab of guilt, and it required almost an effort of will to answer: 'I can make it.'

He saw nothing of Moscow during the few minutes that the big intercontinental ramjet fell down from the stratosphere. The view-screens were switched off during the descent, for the sight of the ground coming straight up as a ship fell vertically on its sustaining jets was highly disconcerting to passengers.

At Moscow he changed to a comfortable but old-fashioned turboprop, and as he flew eastward into the night he had his first real opportunity for reflection. It was a very strange question to ask himself, but was he altogether glad that the future was no longer wholly certain? His life, which a few hours ago had seemed so simple, had suddenly become complex again, as it opened out once more into possibilities he had learned to put aside. Dr Johnson had been right when he said that nothing settles a man's mind more wonderfully than the knowledge that he will be hanged in the morning. For the converse was certainly true – nothing unsettled it so much as the thought of a reprieve.

He was asleep when they touched down at Astrograd, the space capital of the USSR. When the gentle impact of the landing shook him awake, for a moment he could not imagine where he was. Had he dreamed that he was flying halfway around the world in search of life? No; it was not a dream, but it might well be a wild-goose chase.

Twelve hours later, he was still waiting for the answer. The last instrument reading had been taken; the spots of light on the cardiograph display had ceased their fateful dance. The familiar routine of the medical examination and the gentle, competent voices of the doctors and nurses had done much to relax his mind. And it was very restful in the softly lit reception room, where the specialists had asked him to wait while they conferred together. Only the Russian magazines, and a few portraits of somewhat hirsute pioneers of Soviet medicine, reminded him that he was no longer in his own country.

He was not the only patient. About a dozen men and women, of all ages, were sitting around the wall, reading magazines and trying to appear at ease. There was no conversation, no attempt to catch anyone's eye. Every soul in this room was in his private limbo, suspended between life and death. Though they were linked together by a common misfortune, the link did not extend to communication. Each seemed as cut off from the rest of the human race as if he was already speeding through the cosmic gulfs where lay his only hope.

But in the far corner of the room, there was an exception. A young couple – neither could have been more than twenty-five – were huddling together in such desperate misery that at first Steelman found the spectacle annoying. No matter how bad their own problems, he told himself severely, people should be more considerate. They should hide their emotions – especially in a place like this, where they might upset others.

His annoyance quickly turned to pity, for no heart can remain untouched for long at the sight of simple, unselfish love in deep distress. As the minutes dripped away in a silence broken only by the rustling of papers and the scraping of chairs, his pity grew almost to an obsession.

What was their story, he wondered? The boy had sensitive, intelligent features; he might have been an artist, a scientist, a musician – there was no way of telling. The girl was pregnant; she had one of those homely peasant

751

faces so common among Russian women. She was far from beautiful, but sorrow and love had given her features a luminous sweetness. Steelman found it hard to take his eyes from her – for somehow, though there was not the slightest physical resemblance, she reminded him of Diana. Thirty years ago, as they had walked from the church together, he had seen that same glow in the eyes of his wife. He had almost forgotten it; was the fault his, or hers, that it had faded so soon?

Without any warning, his chair vibrated beneath him. A swift, sudden tremor had swept through the building, as if a giant hammer had smashed against the ground, many miles away. An earthquake? Steelman wondered; then he remembered where he was, and started counting seconds.

He gave up when he reached sixty; presumably the soundproofing was so good that the slower, air-borne noise had not reached him, and only the shock wave through the ground recorded the fact that a thousand tons had just leapt into the sky. Another minute passed before he heard, distant but clear, a sound as of a thunderstorm raging below the edge of the world. It was even more miles away than he had dreamed; what the noise must be like at the launching site was beyond imagination.

Yet that thunder would not trouble him, he knew, when he also rose into the sky; the speeding rocket would leave it far behind. Nor would the thrust of acceleration be able to touch his body, as it rested in its bath of warm water – more comfortable even than this deeply padded chair.

That distant rumble was still rolling back from the edge of space when the door of the waiting room opened and the nurse beckoned to him. Though he felt many eyes following him, he did not look back as he walked out to receive his sentence.

The news services tried to get in contact with him all the way back from Moscow, but he refused to accept the calls. 'Say I'm sleeping and mustn't be disturbed,' he told the stewardess. He wondered who had tipped them off, and felt annoyed at this invasion of his privacy. Yet privacy was something he had avoided for years, and had learned to appreciate only in the last few weeks. He could not blame the reporters and commentators if they assumed that he had reverted to type.

They were waiting for him when the ramjet touched down at Washington. He knew most of them by name, and some were old friends, genuinely glad to hear the news that had raced ahead of him.

'What does it feel like, Senator,' said Macauley, of the *Times*, 'to know you're back in harness? I take it that it's true – the Russians can cure you?'

'They *think* they can,' he answered cautiously. 'This is a new field of medicine, and no one can promise anything.'

'When do you leave for space?'

'Within the week, as soon as I've settled some affairs here.'

'And when will you be back – if it works?'

'That's hard to say. Even if everything goes smoothly, I'll be up there at least six months.'

752

Involuntarily, he glanced at the sky. At dawn or sunset – even during the daytime, if one knew where to look – the Mechnikov Station was a spectacular sight, more brilliant than any of the stars. But there were now so many satellites of which this was true that only an expert could tell one from another.

'Six months,' said a newsman thoughtfully. 'That means you'll be out of the picture for seventy-six.'

'But nicely in it for 1980,' said another.

'*And* 1984,' added a third. There was a general laugh; people were already making jokes about 1984, which had once seemed so far in the future, but would soon be a date no different from any other . . . it was hoped.

The ears and the microphones were waiting for his reply. As he stood at the foot of the ramp, once more the focus of attention and curiosity, he felt the old excitement stirring in his veins. What a comeback it would be, to return from space a new man! It would give him a glamour that no other candidate could match; there was something Olympian, almost godlike, about the prospect. Already he found himself trying to work it into his election slogans . . .

'Give me time to make my plans,' he said. 'It's going to take me a while to get used to this. But I promise you a statement before I leave Earth.'

Before I leave Earth. Now, there was a fine, dramatic phrase. He was still savouring its rhythm with his mind when he saw Diana coming toward him from the airport buildings.

Already she had changed, as he himself was changing; in her eyes was a wariness and reserve that had not been there two days ago. It said, as clearly as any words: 'Is it going to happen, all over again?' Though the day was warm, he felt suddenly cold, as if he had caught a chill on those far Siberian plains.

But Joey and Susan were unchanged, as they ran to greet him. He caught them up in his arms, and buried his face in their hair, so that the cameras would not see the tears that had started from his eyes. As they clung to him in the innocent, unselfconscious love of childhood, he knew what his choice would have to be.

They alone had known him when he was free from the itch for power; that was the way they must remember him, if they remembered him at all.

'Your conference call, Mr Steelman,' said his secretary. 'I'm routing it on to your private screen.'

He swivelled round in his chair and faced the grey panel on the wall. As he did so, it split into two vertical sections. On the right half was a view of an office much like his own, and only a few miles away. But on the left—

Professor Stanyukovitch, lightly dressed in shorts and singlet, was floating in mid-air a good foot above his seat. He grabbed it when he saw that he had company, pulled himself down, and fastened a webbed belt around his waist. Behind him were ranged banks of communications equipment; and behind those, Steelman knew, was space.

Dr Harkness spoke first, from the right-hand screen.

'We were expecting to hear from you, Senator. Professor Stanyukovitch tells me that everything is ready.'

'The next supply ship,' said the Russian, 'comes up in two days. It will be taking me back to Earth, but I hope to see you before I leave the station.'

His voice was curiously high-pitched, owing to the thin oxyhelium atmosphere he was breathing. Apart from that, there was no sense of distance, no background of interference. Though Stanyukovitch was thousands of miles away, and racing through space at four miles a second, he might have been in the same office. Steelman could even hear the faint whirring of electric motors from the equipment racks behind him.

'Professor,' answered Steelman, 'there are a few things I'd like to ask before I go.'

'Certainly.'

Now he could tell that Stanyukovitch was a long way off. There was an appreciable time lag before his reply arrived; the station must be above the far side of the Earth.

'When I was at Astrograd, I noticed many other patients at the clinic. I was wondering – on what basis do you select those for treatment?'

This time the pause was much greater than the delay due to the sluggish speed of radio waves. Then Stanyukovitch answered: 'Why, those with the best chance of responding.'

'But your accommodation must be very limited. You must have many other candidates besides myself.'

'I don't quite see the point—' interrupted Dr Harkness, a little too anxiously.

Steelman swung his eyes to the right-hand screen. It was quite difficult to recognise, in the man staring back at him, the witness who had squirmed beneath his needling only a few years ago. That experience had tempered Harkness, had given him his baptism in the art of politics. Steelman had taught him much, and he had applied his hard-won knowledge.

His motives had been obvious from the first. Harkness would have been less than human if he did not relish this sweetest of revenges, this triumphant vindication of his faith. And as Space Administration Director, he was well aware that half his budget battles would be over when all the world knew that a potential President of the United States was in a Russian space hospital . . . because his own country did not possess one.

'Dr Harkness,' said Steelman gently, 'this is *my* affair. I'm still waiting for your answer, Professor.'

Despite the issues involved, he was quite enjoying this. The two scientists, of course, were playing for identical stakes. Stanyukovitch had his problems too; Steelman could guess the discussions that had taken place at Astrograd and Moscow, and the eagerness with which the Soviet astronauts had grasped this opportunity – which, it must be admitted, they had richly earned.

It was an ironic situation, unimaginable only a dozen years before. Here were NASA and the USSR Commission of Astronautics working hand in hand, using him as a pawn for their mutual advantage. He did not resent this, for in their place he would have done the same. But he had no wish to be a pawn; he was an individual who still had some control of his own destiny.

'It's quite true,' said Stanyukovitch, very reluctantly, 'that we can only take a limited number of patients here in Mechnikov. In any case, the station's a research laboratory, not a hospital.'

'How many?' asked Steelman relentlessly.

'Well – fewer than ten,' admitted Stanyukovitch, still more unwillingly.

It was an old problem, of course, though he had never imagined that it would apply to him. From the depths of memory there flashed a newspaper item he had come across long ago. When penicillin had been first discovered, it was so rare that if both Churchill and Roosevelt had been dying for lack of it, only one could have been treated . . .

Fewer than ten. He had seen a dozen waiting at Astrograd, and how many were there in the whole world? Once again, as it had done so often in the last few days, the memory of those desolate lovers in the reception room came back to haunt him. Perhaps they were beyond his aid; he would never know.

But one thing he did know. He bore a responsibility that he could not escape. It was true that no man could foresee the future, and the endless consequences of his actions. Yet if it had not been for him, by this time his own country might have had a space hospital circling beyond the atmosphere. How many American lives were upon his conscience? Could he accept the help he had denied to others? Once he might have done so – but not now.

'Gentlemen,' he said, 'I can speak frankly with you both, for I know your interests are identical.' (His mild irony, he saw, did not escape them.) 'I appreciate your help and the trouble you have taken; I am sorry it has been wasted. No – don't protest; this isn't a sudden, quixotic decision on my part. If I was ten years younger, it might be different. Now I feel that this opportunity should be given to someone else – especially in view of my record.' He glanced at Dr Harkness, who gave an embarrassed smile. 'I also have other, personal reasons, and there's no chance that I will change my mind. Please don't think me rude or ungrateful, but I don't wish to discuss the matter any further. Thank you again, and goodbye.'

He broke the circuit; and as the image of the two astonished scientists faded, peace came flooding back into his soul.

Imperceptibly, spring merged into summer. The eagerly awaited Bicentenary celebrations came and went; for the first time in years, he was able to enjoy Independence Day as a private citizen. Now he could sit back and watch the others perform – or he could ignore them if he wished.

Because the ties of a lifetime were too strong to break, and it would be his last opportunity to see many old friends, he spent hours looking in on both conventions and listening to the commentators. Now that he saw the whole world beneath the light of Eternity, his emotions were no longer involved; he understood the issues, and appreciated the arguments, but already he was as detached as an observer from another planet. The tiny, shouting figures on the screen were amusing marionettes, acting out roles in a play that was entertaining, but no longer important – at least, to him.

But it was important to his grandchildren, who would one day move out onto this same stage. He had not forgotten that; they were his share of the future, whatever strange form it might take. And to understand the future, it was necessary to know the past.

He was taking them into that past, as the car swept along Memorial Drive. Diana was at the wheel, with Irene beside her, while he sat with the children, pointing out the familiar sights along the highway. Familiar to him, but not to them; even if they were not old enough to understand all that they were seeing, he hoped they would remember.

Past the marble stillness of Arlington (he thought again of Martin, sleeping on the other side of the world) and up into the hills the car wound its effortless way. Behind them, like a city seen through a mirage, Washington danced and trembled in the summer haze, until the curve of the road hid it from view.

It was quiet at Mount Vernon; there were few visitors so early in the week. As they left the car and walked toward the house, Steelman wondered what the first President of the United States would have thought could he have seen his home as it was today. He could never have dreamed that it would enter its second century still perfectly preserved, a changeless island in the hurrying river of time.

They walked slowly through the beautifully proportioned rooms, doing their best to answer the children's endless questions, trying to assimilate the flavour of an infinitely simpler, infinitely more leisurely mode of life. (But had it seemed simple or leisurely to those who lived it?) It was so hard to imagine a world without electricity, without radio, without any power save that of muscle, wind, and water. A world where nothing moved faster than a running horse, and most men died within a few miles of the place where they were born.

The heat, the walking and the incessant questions proved more tiring than Steelman had expected. When they had reached the Music Room, he decided to rest. There were some attractive benches out on the porch, where he could sit in the fresh air and feast his eyes upon the green grass of the lawn.

'Meet me outside,' he explained to Diana, 'when you've done the kitchen and the stables. I'd like to sit down for a while.'

'You're sure you're quite all right?' she said anxiously.

'I never felt better, but I don't want to overdo it. Besides, the kids have drained me dry – I can't think of any more answers. You'll have to invent some; the kitchen's your department, anyway.'

Diana smiled.

'I was never much good in it, was I? But I'll do my best – I don't suppose we'll be more than thirty minutes.'

When they had left him, he walked slowly out onto the lawn. Here Washington must have stood, two centuries ago, watching the Potomac wind its way to the sea, thinking of past wars and future problems. And here Martin Steelman, thirty-eighth President of the United States, might have stood a few months hence, had the fates ruled otherwise.

He coud not pretend that he had no regrets, but they were very few. Some men could achieve both power and happiness, but that gift was not for him. Sooner or later, his ambition would have consumed him. In the last few weeks he had known contentment, and for that no price was too great.

He was still marvelling at the narrowness of his escape when his time ran out and Death fell softly from the summer sky.

Before Eden

First published in *Amazing*, June 1961
Collected in *Tales of Ten Worlds*

'I guess,' said Jerry Garfield, cutting the engines, 'that this is the end of the line.' With a gentle sigh, the underjets faded out; deprived of its air cushion, the scout car *Rambling Wreck* settled down upon the twisted rocks of the Hesperian Plateau.

There was no way forward; neither on its jets nor its tractors could S.5 – to give the *Wreck* its official name – scale the escarpment that lay ahead. The South Pole of Venus was only thirty miles away, but it might have been on another planet. They would have to turn back, and retrace their four-hundred-mile journey through this nightmare landscape.

The weather was fantastically clear, with visibiliy of almost a thousand yards. There was no need of radar to show the cliffs ahead; for once, the naked eye was good enough. The green auroral light, filtering down through clouds that had rolled unbroken for a million years, gave the scene an underwater appearance, and the way in which all distant objects blurred into the haze added to the impression. Sometimes it was easy to believe that they were driving across a shallow sea bed, and more than once Jerry had imagined that he had seen fish floating overhead.

'Shall I call the ship, and say we're turning back?' he asked.

'Not yet,' said Dr Hutchins. 'I want to think.'

Jerry shot an appealing glance at the third member of the crew, but found no moral support there. Coleman was just as bad; although the two men argued furiously half the time, they were both scientists and therefore, in the opinion of a hardheaded engineer-navigator, not wholly responsible citizens. If Cole and Hutch had bright ideas about going forward, there was nothing he could do except register a protest.

Hutchins was pacing back and forth in the tiny cabin, studying charts and instruments. Presently he swung the car's searchlight toward the cliffs, and began to examine them carefully with binoculars. Surely, thought Jerry, he doesn't expect me to drive up there! S.5 was a hover-track, not a mountain goat . . .

Abruptly, Hutchins found something. He released his breath in a sudden explosive gasp, then turned to Coleman.

'Look!' he said, his voice full of excitement. 'Just to the left of that black mark! Tell me what you see.'

He handed over the glasses, and it was Coleman's turn to stare.

'Well, I'm damned,' he said at length. 'You were right. There *are* rivers on Venus. That's a dried-up waterfall.'

'So you owe me one dinner at the Bel Gourmet when we get back to Cambridge. With champagne.'

'No need to remind me. Anyway, it's cheap at the price. But this still leaves your other theories strictly on the crackpot level.'

'Just a minute,' interjected Jerry. 'What's all this about rivers and waterfalls? Everyone knows they can't exist on Venus. It never gets cold enough on this steam bath of a planet for the clouds to condense.'

'Have you looked at the thermometer lately?' asked Hutchins with deceptive mildness.

'I've been slightly too busy driving.'

'Then I've news for you. It's down to two hundred and thirty, and still falling. Don't forget – we're almost at the Pole, it's wintertime, and we're sixty thousand feet above the lowlands. All this adds up to a distinct nip in the air. If the temperature drops a few more degrees, we'll have rain. The water will be boiling, of course – but it will be water. And though George won't admit it yet, this puts Venus in a completely different light.'

'Why?' asked Jerry, though he had already guessed.

'Where there's water, there may be life. We've been in too much of a hurry to assume that Venus is sterile, merely because the average temperature's over five hundred degrees. It's a lot colder here, and that's why I've been so anxious to get to the Pole. There are lakes up here in the highlands, and I want to look at them.'

'But *boiling* water!' protested Coleman. 'Nothing could live in that!'

'There are algae that manage it on Earth. And if we've learned one thing since we started exploring the planets, it's this: wherever life has the slightest chance of surviving, you'll find it. This is the only chance it's ever had on Venus.'

'I wish we could test your theory. But you can see for yourself – we can't go up that cliff.'

'Perhaps not in the car. But it won't be too difficult to climb those rocks, even wearing thermosuits. All we need do is walk a few miles toward the Pole; according to the radar maps, it's fairly level once you're over the rim. We could manage in – oh, twelve hours at the most. Each of us has been out for longer than that, in much worse conditions.'

That was perfectly true. Protective clothing that had been designed to keep men alive in the Venusian lowlands would have an easy job here, where it was only a hundred degrees hotter than Death Valley in midsummer.

'Well,' said Coleman, 'you know the regulations. You can't go by yourself, and someone has to stay here to keep contact with the ship. How do we settle it this time – chess or cards?'

'Chess takes too long,' said Hutchins, 'especially when you two play it. He reached into the chart table and produced a well-worn pack. 'Cut them, Jerry.'

'Ten of spades. Hope you can beat it, George.'

'So do I. Damn – only five of clubs. Well, give my regards to the Venusians.'

Despite Hutchins' assurance, it was hard work climbing the escarpment. The slope was not too steep, but the weight of oxygen gear, refrigerated thermosuit, and scientific equipment came to more than a hundred pounds per man. The lower gravity – thirteen per cent weaker than Earth's – gave a little help, but not much, as they toiled up screes, rested on ledges to regain breath, and then clambered on again through the submarine twilight. The emerald glow that washed around them was brighter than that of the full moon on Earth. A moon would have been wasted on Venus, Jerry told himself; it could never have been seen from the surface, there were no oceans for it to rule – and the incessant aurora was a far more constant source of light.

They had climbed more than two thousand feet before the ground levelled out into a gentle slope, scarred here and there by channels that had clearly been cut by running water. After a little searching, they came across a gulley wide and deep enough to merit the name of river bed, and started to walk along it.

'I've just thought of something,' said Jerry after they had travelled a few hundred yards. 'Suppose there's a storm up ahead of us? I don't feel like facing a tidal wave of boiling water.'

'If there's a storm,' replied Hutchins a little impatiently, 'we'll hear it. There'll be plenty of time to reach high ground.'

He was undoubtedly right, but Jerry felt no happier as they continued to climb the gently shelving watercourse. His uneasiness had been growing ever since they had passed over the brow of the cliff and had lost radio contact with the scout car. In this day and age, to be out of touch with one's fellow men was a unique and unsettling experience. It had never happened to Jerry before in all his life; even aboard the *Morning Star*, when they were a hundred million miles from Earth, he could always send a message to his family and get a reply back within minutes. But now, a few yards of rock had cut him off from the rest of mankind; if anything happened to them here, no one would ever know, unless some later expedition found their bodies. George would wait for the agreed number of hours; then he would head back to the ship – alone. I guess I'm not really the pioneering type, Jerry told himself. I like running complicated machines, and that's how I got involved in space flight. But I never stopped to think where it would lead, and now it's too late to change my mind . . .

They had travelled perhaps three miles toward the Pole, following the meanders of the river bed, when Hutchins stopped to make observations and collect specimens. 'Still getting colder!' he said. 'The temperature's down to one hundred and ninety-nine. That's far and away the lowest ever recorded on Venus. I wish we could call George and let him know.'

Jerry tried all the wave bands; he even attempted to raise the ship – the unpredictable ups and downs of the planet's ionosphere sometimes made such long-distance reception possible – but there was not a whisper of a carrier wave above the roar and crackle of the Venusian thunderstorms.

'This is even better,' said Hutchins, and now there was real excitement in his voice. 'The oxygen concentration's way up – fifteen parts in a million. It was only five back at the car, and down in the lowlands you can scarcely detect it.'

'But fifteen in a *million*!' protested Jerry. 'Nothing could breathe that!'

'You've got hold of the wrong end of the stick,' Hutchins explained. 'Nothing does breathe it. Something *makes* it. Where do you think Earth's oxygen comes from? It's all produced by life – by growing plants. Before there were plants on Earth, our atmosphere was just like this one – a mess of carbon dioxide and ammonia and methane. Then vegetation evolved, and slowly converted the atmosphere into something that animals could breathe.'

'I see,' said Jerry, 'and you think that the same process has just started here?'

'It looks like it. *Something* not far from here is producing oxygen – and plant life is the simplest explanation.'

'And where there are plants,' mused Jerry, 'I suppose you'll have animals, sooner or later.'

'Yes,' said Hutchins, packing his gear and starting up the gulley, 'though it takes a few hundred million years. We may be too soon – but I hope not.'

'That's all very well,' Jerry answered. 'But suppose we meet something that doesn't like us? We've no weapons.'

Hutchins gave a snort of disgust.

'And we don't need them. Have you stopped to think what we look like? Any animal would run a mile at the sight of us.'

There was some truth in that. The reflecting metal foil of their thermo-suits covered them from head to foot like flexible, glittering armour. No insects had more elaborate antennas than those mounted on their helmets and back packs, and the wide lenses through which they stared out at the world looked like blank yet monstrous eyes. Yes, there were few animals on Earth that would stop to argue with such apparitions; but any Venusians might have different ideas.

Jerry was still mulling this over when they came upon the lake. Even at that first glimpse, it made him think not of the life they were seeking, but of death. Like a black mirror, it lay amid a fold of the hills; its far edge was hidden in the eternal mist, and ghostly columns of vapour swirled and danced upon its surface. All it needed, Jerry told himself, was Charon's ferry waiting to take them to the other side – or the Swan of Tuonela swimming majestically back and forth as it guarded the entrance to the Underworld . . .

Yet for all this, it was a miracle – the first free water that men had ever found on Venus. Hutchins was already on his knees, almost in an attitude of prayer. But he was only collecting drops of the precious liquid to examine through his pocket microscope.

'Anything there?' asked Jerry anxiously.

Hutchins shook his head.

'If there is, it's too small to see with this instrument. I'll tell you more when we're back at the ship.' He sealed a test tube and placed it in his collecting bag, as tenderly as any prospector who had just found a nugget laced with gold. It might be – it probably was – nothing more than plain water. But it might also be a universe of unknown, living creatures on the first stage of their billion-year journey to intelligence.

Hutchins had walked no more than a dozen yards along the edge of the lake when he stopped again, so suddenly that Garfield nearly collided with him.

'What's the matter?' Jerry asked. 'Seen something?'

'That dark patch of rock over there. I noticed it before we stopped at the lake.'

'What about it? It looks ordinary enough to me.'

'*I think it's grown bigger.*'

All his life, Jerry was to remember this moment. Somehow he never doubted Hutchins' statement; by this time he could believe anything, even that rocks could grow. The sense of isolation and mystery, the presence of that dark and brooding lake, the never-ceasing rumble of distant storms and the green flickering of the aurora – all these had done something to his mind, had prepared it to face the incredible. Yet he felt no fear; that would come later.

He looked at the rock. It was about five hundred feet away, as far as he could estimate. In this dim, emerald light it was hard to judge distances or dimensions. The rock – or whatever it was – seemed to be a horizontal slab of almost black material, lying near the crest of a low ridge. There was a second, much smaller, patch of similar material near it; Jerry tried to measure and memorise the gap between them, so that he would have some yardstick to detect any change.

Even when he saw that the gap was slowly shrinking, he still felt no alarm – only a puzzled excitement. Not until it had vanished completely, and he realised how his eyes had tricked him, did that awful helpless terror strike into his heart.

Here were no growing or moving rocks. What they were watching was a dark tide, a crawling carpet, sweeping slowly but inexorably toward them over the top of the ridge.

The moment of sheer, unreasoning panic lasted, mercifully, no more than a few seconds. Garfield's first terror began to fade as soon as he recognised its cause. For that advancing tide had reminded him, all too vividly, of a story he had read many years ago about the army ants of the Amazon, and the way in which they destroyed everything in their path . . .

But whatever this tide might be, it was moving too slowly to be a real danger, unless it cut off their line of retreat. Hutchins was staring at it intently through their only pair of binoculars; he was the biologist, and he was holding his ground. No point in making a fool of myself, thought Jerry, by running like a scalded cat, if it isn't necessary.

'For heaven's sake,' he said at last, when the moving carpet was only a hundred yards away and Hutchins had not uttered a word or stirred a muscle. 'What *is* it?'

Hutchins slowly unfroze, like a statue coming to life.

'Sorry,' he said. 'I'd forgotten all about you. It's a plant, of course. At least, I suppose we'd better call it that.'

'But it's *moving*!'

'Why should that surprise you? So do terrestrial plants. Ever seen speeded-up movies of ivy in action?'

'That still stays in one place – it doesn't crawl all over the landscape.'

'Then what about the plankton plants of the sea? *They* can swim when they have to.'

Jerry gave up; in any case, the approaching wonder had robbed him of words.

He still thought of the thing as a carpet – a deep-pile one, ravelled into tassels at the edges. it varied in thickness as it moved; in some parts it was a mere film; in others, it heaped up to a depth of a foot or more. As it came closer and he could see its texture, Jerry was reminded of black velvet. He wondered what it felt like to the touch, then remembered that it would burn his fingers even if it did nothing else to them. He found himself thinking, in the lightheaded nervous reaction that often follows a sudden shock: 'If there *are* any Venusians, we'll never be able to shake hands with them. They'd burn us, and we'd give them frostbite.'

So far, the thing had shown no signs that it was aware of their presence. It had merely flowed forward like the mindless tide that it almost certainly was. Apart from the fact that it climbed over small obstacles, it might have been an advancing flood of water.

And then, when it was only ten feet away, the velvet tide checked itself. On the right and the left, it still flowed forward; but dead ahead it slowed to a halt.

'We're being encircled,' said Jerry anxiously. 'Better fall back, until we're sure it's harmless.'

To his relief, Hutchins stepped back at once. After a brief hesitation, the creature resumed its slow advance and the dent in its front line straightened out.

Then Hutchins stepped forward again – and the thing slowly withdrew. Half a dozen times the biologist advanced, only to retreat again, and each time the living tide ebbed and flowed in synchronism with his movements.

I never imagined, Jerry told himself, that I'd live to see a man waltzing with a plant . . .

'Thermophobia,' said Hutchins. 'Purely automatic reaction. It doesn't like our heat.'

'*Our* heat!' protested Jerry. 'Why, we're living icicles by comparison.'

'Of course – but our suits aren't, and that's all it knows about.'

Stupid of me, thought Jerry. When you were snug and cool inside your thermosuit, it was easy to forget that the refrigeration unit on your back was pumping a blast of heat out into the surrounding air. No wonder the Venusian plant had shied away . . .

'Let's see how it reacts to light,' said Hutchins. He switched on his chest lamp, and the green auroral glow was instantly banished by the flood of pure white radiance. Until Man had come to this planet, no white light had ever shone upon the surface of Venus, even by day. As in the seas of Earth, there was only a green twilight, deepening slowly to utter darkness.

The transformation was so stunning that neither man could check a cry of astonishment. Gone in a flash was the deep, sombre black of the thick-piled velvet carpet at their feet. Instead, as far as their lights carried, lay a blazing pattern of glorious, vivid reds, laced with streaks of gold. No Persian prince could ever have commanded so opulent a tapestry from his weavers, yet this was the accidental product of biological forces. Indeed, until they had switched on their floods, these superb colours had not even existed, and they would vanish once more when the alien light of Earth ceased to conjure them into being.

'Tikov was right,' murmured Hutchins. 'I wish he could have known.'

'Right about what?' asked Jerry, though it seemed almost a sacrilege to speak in the presence of such loveliness.

'Back in Russia, fifty years ago, he found that plants living in very cold climates tended to be blue and violet, while those from hot ones were red or orange. He predicted that the Martian vegetation would be violet, and said that if there were plants on Venus they'd be red. Well, he was right on both counts. But we can't stand here all day – we've work to do.'

'You're sure it's quite safe?' asked Jerry, some of his caution reasserting itself.

'Absolutely – it can't touch our suits even if it wants to. Anyway, it's moving past us.'

That was true. They could see now that the entire creature – if it was a single plant, and not a colony – covered a roughly circular area about a hundred yards across. It was sweeping over the ground, as the shadow of a cloud moves before the wind – and where it had rested, the rocks were pitted with innumerable tiny holes that might have been etched by acid.

'Yes,' said Hutchins, when Jerry remarked about this. 'That's how some lichens feed; they secrete acids that dissolve rock. But no questions, please – not till we get back to the ship. I've several lifetimes' work here, and a couple of hours to do it in.'

This was botany on the run . . . The sensitive edge of the huge plant-thing could move with surprising speed when it tried to evade them. It was as if they were dealing with an animated flapjack, an acre in extent. There was no reaction – apart from the automatic avoidance of their exhaust heat – when Hutchins snipped samples or took probes. The creature flowed steadily onward over hills and valleys, guided by some strange vegetable instinct. Perhaps it was following some vein of mineral; the geologists could decide that, when they analysed the rock samples that Hutchins had collected both before and after the passage of the living tapestry.

There was scarcely time to think or even to frame the countless questions that their discovery had raised. Presumably these creatures must be fairly common, for them to have found one so quickly. How did they reproduce? By shoots, spores, fission, or some other means? Where did they get their energy? What relatives, rivals, or parasites did they have? This could not be the only form of life on Venus – the very idea was absurd, for if you had one species, you must have thousands . . .

Sheer hunger and fatigue forced them to a halt at last. The creature they were studying could eat its way around Venus – though Hutchins believed that it never went very far from the lake, as from time to time it approached the water and inserted a long, tubelike tendril into it – but the animals from Earth had to rest.

It was a great relief to inflate the pressurised tent, climb in through the air lock, and strip off their thermosuits. For the first time, as they relaxed inside their tiny plastic hemisphere, the true wonder and importance of the discovery forced itself upon their minds. This world around them was no longer the same; Venus was no longer dead – it had joined Earth and Mars.

For life called to life, across the gulfs of space. Everything that grew or moved upon the face of any planet was a portent, a promise that Man was not alone in this universe of blazing suns and swirling nebulae. If as yet he had found no companions with whom he could speak, that was only to be expected, for the light-years and the ages still stretched before him, waiting to be explored. Meanwhile, he must guard and cherish the life he found, whether it be upon Earth or Mars or Venus.

So Graham Hutchins, the happiest biologist in the solar system, told himself as he helped Garfield collect their refuse and seal it into a plastic disposal bag. When they deflated the tent and started on the homeward journey, there was no sign of the creature they had been examining. That was just as well; they might have been tempted to linger for more experiments, and already it was getting uncomfortably close to their deadline.

No matter; in a few months they would be back with a team of assistants, far more adequately equipped and with the eyes of the world upon them. Evolution had laboured for a billion years to make this meeting possible; it could wait a little longer.

For a while nothing moved in the greenly glimmering, fogbound landscape; it was deserted by man and crimson carpet alike. Then, flowing over the wind-carved hills, the creature reappeared. Or perhaps it was another of the same strange species; no one would ever know.

It flowed past the little cairn of stones where Hutchins and Garfield had buried their wastes. And then it stopped.

It was not puzzled, for it had no mind. But the chemical urges that drove it relentlessly over the polar plateau were crying: Here, here! Somewhere close at hand was the most precious of all the foods it needed – phosphorus, the element without which the spark of life could never ignite. It began to nuzzle the rocks, to ooze into the cracks and crannies, to scratch and scrabble with probing tendrils. Nothing that it did was beyond the capacity of any plant or tree on Earth – but it moved a thousand times more quickly, requiring only minutes to reach its goal and pierce through the plastic film.

And then it feasted, on food more concentrated than any it had ever known. It absorbed the carbohydrates and the proteins and the phosphates, the nicotine from the cigarette ends, the cellulose from the paper cups and spoons. All these it broke down and assimilated into its strange body without difficulty and without harm.

Likewise it absorbed a whole microcosmos of living creatures – the bacteria and viruses which, upon an older planet, had evolved into a thousand deadly strains. Though only a very few could survive in this heat and this atmosphere, they were sufficient. As the carpet crawled back to the lake, it carried contagion to all its world.

Even as the Morning Star set course for her distant home, Venus was dying. The films and photographs and specimens that Hutchins was carrying in triumph were more precious even than he knew. They were the only record that would ever exist of life's third attempt to gain a foothold in the solar system.

Beneath the clouds of Venus, the story of Creation was ended.

Hate

First published in *If*, November 1961, as 'At the End of Orbit'
Collected in *Tales of Ten Worlds*

In 1960, William MacQuitty (*A Night to Remember*), the distinguished film producer, asked me to write a movie treatment entitled 'The Sea and the Stars'. Nothing came of the film so I turned it into a short story, entitled 'Hate'. *If* magazine retitled it, but I prefer the original: more punch.

Only Joey was awake on deck, in the cool stillness before dawn, when the meteor came flaming out of the sky above New Guinea. He watched it climb up the heavens until it passed directly overhead, routing the stars and throwing swift-moving shadows across the crowded deck. The harsh light outlined the bare rigging, the coiled ropes and air hoses, the copper diving helmets neatly snugged down for the night – even the low, pandanus-clad island half a mile away. As it passed into the southwest, out over the emptiness of the Pacific, it began to disintegrate. Incandescent globules broke off, burning and guttering in a trail of fire that stretched a quarter of the way across the sky. It was already dying when it raced out of sight, but Joey did not see its end. Still blazing furiously, it sank below the horizon, as if seeking to hurl itself into the face of the hidden sun.

If the sight was spectacular, the utter silence was unnerving. Joey waited and waited and waited, but no sound came from the riven heavens. When, minutes later, there was a sudden splash from the sea close at hand, he gave an involuntary start of surprise – then cursed himself for being frightened by a manta. (A mighty big one, though, to have made so much noise when it jumped.) There was no other sound, and presently he went back to sleep.

In his narrow bunk just aft of the air compressor, Tibor heard nothing. He slept so soundly after his day's work that he had little energy even for dreams – and when they came, they were not the dreams he wanted. In the hours of darkness, as his mind roamed back and forth across the past, it never came to rest amid memories of desire. He had women in Sydney and Brisbane and Darwin and Thursday Island – but none in his dreams. All that he ever remembered when he woke, in the foetid stillness of the cabin, was the dust and fire and blood as the Russian tanks rolled into Budapest. His dreams were not of love, but only of hate.

When Nick shook him back to consciousness, he was dodging the guards on the Austrian border. It took him a few seconds to make the ten-thousand-mile journey to the Great Barrier Reef; then he yawned, kicked away the cockroaches that had been nibbling at his toes, and heaved himself out of his bunk.

Breakfast, of course, was the same as always – rice, turtle eggs, and bully beef, washed down with strong, sweet tea. The best that could be said of Joey's cooking was that there was plenty of it. Tibor was used to the monotonous diet; he made up for it, and for other deprivations, when he was back on the mainland.

The sun had barely cleared the horizon when the dishes were stacked in the tiny galley and the lugger got under way. Nick sounded cheerful as he took the wheel and headed out from the island; the old pearling-master had every right to be, for the patch of shell they were working was the richest that Tibor had ever seen. With any luck, they would fill their hold in another day or two, and sail back to T.I. with half a ton of shell on board. And then, with a little more luck, he could give up this stinking, dangerous job and get back to civilisation. Not that he regretted anything; the Greek had treated him well, and he'd found some good stones when the shells were opened. But he understood now, after nine months on the Reef, why the number of white divers could be counted on the fingers of one hand. Japs and Kanakas and Islanders could take it – but damn few Europeans.

The diesel coughed into silence, and the *Arafura* coasted to rest. They were some two miles from the island, which lay low and green on the water, yet sharply divided from it by its narrow band of dazzling beach. It was no more than a nameless sand bar that a tiny forest had managed to capture, and its only inhabitants were the myriads of stupid muttonbirds that riddled the soft ground with their burrows and made the night hideous with their banshee cries.

There was little talk as the three divers dressed; each man knew what to do, and wasted no time in doing it. As Tibor buttoned on his thick twill jacket, Blanco, his tender, rinsed out the faceplate with vinegar so that it would not become fogged. Then Tibor clambered down the rope ladder, while the heavy helmet and lead corselet were placed over his head. Apart from the jacket, whose padding spread the weight evenly over his shoulders, he was wearing his ordinary clothes. In these warm waters there was no need for rubber suits, and the helmet simply acted as a tiny diving bell held in position by its weight alone. In an emergency the wearer could – if he was lucky – duck out of it and swim back to the surface unhampered. Tibor had seen this done, but he had no wish to try the experiment for himself.

Each time he stood on the last rung of the ladder, gripping his shell bag with one hand and his safety line with the other, the same thought flashed through Tibor's mind. He was leaving the world he knew – but was it for an hour or was it forever? Down there on the seabed was wealth and death, and one could be sure of neither. The chances were that this would be another day of uneventful drudgery, as were most of the days in the pearl diver's unglamorous life. But Tibor had seen one of his mates die, when his air hose tangled in the *Arafura*'s prop – and he had watched the agony of another whose body twisted with the bends. In the sea, nothing was ever safe or certain. You took your chances with open eyes – and if you lost, there was no point in whining.

He stepped back from the ladder, and the world of sun and sky ceased to exist. Top-heavy with the weight of his helmet, he had to backpedal furiously to keep his body upright. He could see nothing but a featureless blue mist as he sank toward the bottom, and he hoped that Blanco would not play out the safety line too quickly. Swallowing and snorting, he tried to clear his ears as the pressure mounted; the right one 'popped' quickly enough, but a piercing, intolerable pain grew rapidly in the left, which had bothered him for several days. He forced his hand up under the helmet, gripped his nose, and blew with all his might. There was an abrupt, soundless explosion somewhere inside his head, and the pain vanished instantly. He'd have no more trouble on this dive.

Tibor felt the bottom before he saw it. Since he was unable to bend over lest he risk flooding the open helmet, his vision in the downward direction was very limited. He could see around, but not immediately below. What he did see was reassuring in its drab monotony – a gently undulating, muddy plain that faded out of sight about ten feet ahead. A yard to his left a tiny fish was nibbling at a piece of coral the size and shape of a lady's fan. That was all; there was no beauty, no underwater fairyland here. But there was money, and that was what mattered.

The safety line gave a gentle pull as the lugger started to drift downward, moving broadside-on across the patch, and Tibor began to walk forward with the springy, slow-motion step forced on him by weightlessness and water resistance. As Number Two diver, he was working from the bow; amidships was Stephen, still comparatively inexperienced, while at the stern was the head diver, Billy. The three men seldom saw each other while they were working; each had his own lane to search as the *Arafura* drifted silently before the wind. Only at the extremes of their zigzags might they sometimes glimpse one another as dim shapes looming through the mist.

It needed a trained eye to spot the shells beneath their camouflage of algae and weeds, but often the molluscs betrayed themselves. When they felt the vibrations of the approaching diver, they would snap shut – and there would be a momentary, nacreous flicker in the gloom. Yet even then they sometimes escaped, for the moving ship might drag the diver past before he could collect the prize just out of reach. In the early days of his apprenticeship, Tibor had missed quite a few of the big silver lips – any one of which might have contained some fabulous pearl. Or so he had imagined, before the glamour of the profession had worn off, and he realised that pearls were so rare that you might as well forget them. The most valuable stone he'd ever brought up had been sold for fifty-six dollars, and the shell he gathered on a good morning was worth more than that. If the industry had depended on gems instead of mother-of-pearl, it would have gone broke years ago.

There was no sense of time in this world of mist. You walked beneath the invisible, drifting ship, with the throb of the air compressor pounding in your ears, the green haze moving past your eyes. At long intervals you would spot a shell, wrench it from the sea bed, and drop it in your bag. If you were lucky, you might gather a couple of dozen on a single drift across the patch; on the other hand, you might not find a single one.

You were alert for danger, but not worried by it. The real risks were simple, unspectacular things like tangled air hoses or safety lines – not sharks, groupers, or octopuses. Sharks ran when they saw your air bubbles, and in all his hours of diving Tibor had seen just one octopus, every bit of two feet across. As for groupers – well, *they* were to be taken seriously, for they could swallow a diver at one gulp if they felt hungry enough. But there was little chance of meeting them on this flat and desolate plain; there were none of the coral caves in which they could make their homes.

The shock would not have been so great, therefore, if this uniform, level greyness had not lulled him into a sense of security. At one moment he was walking steadily toward an unreachable wall of mist, which retreated as fast as he approached. And then, without warning, his private nightmare was looming above him.

Tibor hated spiders, and there was a certain creature in the sea that seemed deliberately contrived to take advantage of that phobia. He had never met one, and his mind had always shied away from the thought of such an encounter, but Tibor knew that the Japanese spider crab can span twelve feet across its spindly legs. That it was harmless mattered not in the least; a spider as big as a man simply had no right to exist.

As soon as he saw that cage of slender, jointed limbs emerge from the all-encompassing greyness, Tibor began to scream with uncontrollable terror. He never remembered jerking his safety line, but Blanco reacted with the instantaneous perception of the ideal tender. His helmet still echoing to his screams. Tibor felt himself snatched from the sea bed, lifted toward light and air – and sanity. As he swept upward, he saw both the strangeness and the absurdity of his mistake, and regained a measure of control. But he was still trembling so violently when Blanco lifted off his helmet that it was some time before he could speak.

'What the hell's going on here?' demanded Nick. 'Everyone knocking off work early?'

It was then that Tibor realised that he was not the first to come up. Stephen was sitting amidships, smoking a cigarette and looking completely unconcerned. The stern diver, doubtless wondering what had happened, was being hauled up willy-nilly by his tender, since the *Arafura* had come to rest and all operations had been suspended until the trouble was resolved.

'There's some kind of wreck down there,' said Tibor. 'I ran right into it. All I could see were a lot of wires and rods.'

To his annoyance and self-contempt, the memory set him trembling again.

'Don't see why *that* should give you the shakes,' grumbled Nick. Nor could Tibor; here on this sun-drenched deck, it was impossible to explain how a harmless shape glimpsed through the mist could set one's whole mind jangling with terror.

'I nearly got hung up on it,' he lied. 'Blanco pulled me clear just in time.'

'Hmm,' said Nick, obviously not convinced. 'Anyway, it ain't a ship.' He gestured toward the midships diver. 'Steve ran into a mess of ropes and cloth – like thick nylon, he says. Sounds like some kind of parachute.' The old Greek stared in disgust at the soggy stump of his cigar, then flicked it overboard. 'Soon as Billy's up, we'll go back and take a look. Might be worth something – remember what happened to Jo Chambers.'

Tibor remembered; the story was famous the whole length of the Great Barrier Reef. Jo had been a lone-wolf fisherman who, in the last months of the war, had spotted a DC-3 lying in shallow water a few miles off the Queensland coast. After prodigies of singlehanded salvage, he had broken into the fuselage and started unloading boxes of taps and dies, perfectly protected by their greased wrappings. For a while he had run a flourishing import business, but when the police caught up with him he reluctantly revealed his source of supply; Australian cops can be very persuasive.

And it was then, after weeks and weeks of backbreaking underwater work, that Jo discovered what his DC-3 had been carrying besides the miserable few hundred quid's worth of tools he had been flogging to garages and workshops on the mainland. The big wooden crates he'd never got round to opening held a week's payroll for the US Pacific forces – most of it in twenty-dollar gold pieces.

No such luck here, thought Tibor as he sank over the side again; but the aircraft – or whatever it was – might contain valuable instruments, and there could be a reward for its discovery. Besides, he owed it to himself; he wanted to see exactly what it was that had given him such a fright.

Ten minutes later, he knew it was no aircraft. It was the wrong shape, and it was much too small – only about twenty feet long and half that in width. Here and there on the gently tapering body were access hatches and tiny ports through which unknown instruments peered at the world. It seemed unharmed, though one end had been fused as if by terrific heat. From the other sprouted a tangle of antennas, all of them broken or bent by the impact with the water. Even now, they bore an incredible resemblance to the legs of a giant insect.

Tibor was no fool; he guessed at once what the thing was. Only one problem remained, and he solved that with little difficulty. Though they had been partly charred away by heat, stencilled words could still be read on some of the hatch covers. The letters were Cyrillic, and Tibor knew enough Russian to pick out references to electrical supplies and pressurising systems.

'So they've lost a sputnik,' he told himself with satisfaction. He could imagine what had happened; the thing had come down too fast, and in the wrong place. Around one end were the tattered remnants of flotation bags; they had burst under the impact, and the vehicle had sunk like a stone. The *Arafura*'s crew would have to apologise to Joey; he hadn't been drinking grog. What he'd seen burning across the stars must have been the rocket carrier, separated from its pay load and falling back unchecked into the Earth's atmosphere.

For a long time Tibor hovered on the sea bed, knees bent in the diver's crouch, as he regarded this space creature now trapped in an alien element. His mind was full of half-formed plans, but none had yet come clearly into focus. He no longer cared about salvage money; much more important were the prospects of revenge. Here was one of the proudest creations of Soviet technology – and Szabo Tibor, late of Budapest, was the only man on earth who knew.

There must be some way of exploiting the situation – of doing harm to the country and the cause he now hated with such smouldering intensity. In his waking hours, he was seldom conscious of that hate, and still less did he ever stop to analyse its real cause. Here in this lonely world of sea and sky, of steaming mangrove swamps and dazzling coral strands, there was nothing to recall the past. Yet he could never escape it, and sometimes the demons in his mind would awake, lashing him into a fury of rage or vicious, wanton destructiveness. So far he had been lucky; he had not killed anyone. But some day . . .

An anxious jerk from Blanco interrupted his reveries of vengeance. He gave a reassuring signal to his tender, and started a closer examination of the capsule. What did it weigh? Could it be hoisted easily? There were many things he had to discover, before he could settle on any definite plans.

He braced himself against the corrugated metal wall, and pushed cautiously. There was a definite movement as the capsule rocked on the sea bed. Maybe it could be lifted, even with the few pieces of tackle that the *Arafura* could muster. It was probably lighter than it looked.

Tibor pressed his helmet against a flat section of the hull, and listened intently. He had half expected to hear some mechanical noise, such as the whirring of electric motors. Instead, there was utter silence. With the hilt of his knife, he rapped sharply on the metal, trying to gauge its thickness and to locate any weak spots. On the third try, he got results: but they were not what he had anticipated.

In a furious, desperate tattoo, the capsule rapped back at him.

Until this moment. Tibor had never dreamed that there might be someone inside; the capsule had seemed far too small. Then he realised that he had been thinking in terms of conventional aircraft; there was plenty of room here for a little pressure cabin in which a dedicated astronaut could spend a few cramped hours.

As a kaleidoscope can change its pattern completely in a single moment, so the half-formed plans in Tibor's mind dissolved and then crystallised into a new shape. Behind the thick glass of his helmet, he ran his tongue lightly across his lips. If Nick could have seen him now, he would have wondered – as he had sometimes done before – whether his Number Two diver was wholly sane. Gone were all thoughts of a remote and impersonal vengeance against something as abstract as a nation or a machine; now it would be man to man.

'Took your time, didn't you?' said Nick. 'What did you find?'

'It's Russian,' said Tibor. 'Some kind of sputnik. If we can get a rope around it, I think we can lift it off the bottom. But it's too heavy to get aboard.'

Nick chewed thoughtfully on his eternal cigar. The pearling master was worried about a point that had not occurred to Tibor. If there were any salvage operations around here, everyone would know where the *Arafura* had been drifting. When the news got back to Thursday Island, his private patch of shell would be cleaned out in no time.

They'd have to keep quiet about the whole affair, or else haul the damn thing up themselves and not say where they'd found it. Whatever happened, it looked like being more of a nuisance than it was worth. Nick, who shared most Australians' profound suspicion of authority, had already decided that all he'd get for his trouble would be a nice letter of thanks.

'The boys won't go down,' he said. 'They think it's a bomb. Want to leave it alone.'

'Tell 'em not to worry,' replied Tibor. 'I'll handle it.' He tried to keep his voice normal and unemotional, but this was too good to be true. If the other divers heard the tapping from the capsule, his plans would have been frustrated.

He gestured to the island, green and lovely on the skyline.

'Only one thing we can do. If we can heave it a couple of feet off the bottom, we can run for the shore. Once we're in shallow water, it won't be too hard to haul it up on the beach. We can use the boats, and maybe get a block and tackle on one of those trees.'

Nick considered the idea without much enthusiasm. He doubted if they could get the sputnik through the reef, even on the leeward side of the island. But he was all in favour of lugging it away from this patch of shell; they could always dump it somewhere else, buoy the place, and still get whatever credit was going.

'OK,' he said. 'Down you go. That two-inch rope's the strongest we've got – better take that. Don't be all the bloody day; we've lost enough time already.'

Tibor had no intention of being all day. Six hours would be quite long enough. That was one of the first things he had learned, from the signals through the wall.

It was a pity that he could not hear the Russian's voice; but the Russian could hear him, and that was what really mattered. When he pressed his helmet against the metal and shouted, most of his words got through. So far, it had been a friendly conversation; Tibor had no intention of showing his hand until the right psychological moment.

The first move had been to establish a code – one knock for 'yes,' two for 'no.' After that, it was merely a matter of framing suitable questions; given time, there was no fact or idea that could not be communicated by means of these two signals. It would have been a much tougher job if Tibor had been forced to use his indifferent Russian; he had been pleased, but not surprised, to find that the trapped pilot understood English perfectly.

There was air in the capsule for another five hours; the occupant was uninjured; yes, the Russians knew where it had come down. That last reply gave Tibor pause. Perhaps the pilot was lying, but it might very well be true. Although something had obviously gone wrong with the planned return to Earth, the tracking ships out in the Pacific must have located the impact point – with what accuracy, he could not guess. Still, did that matter? It might take them days to get here, even if they came racing straight into Australian territorial waters without bothering to get permission from Canberra. He was master of the situation; the entire might of the USSR could do nothing to interfere with his plans – until it was much too late.

The heavy rope fell in coils on the sea bed, stirring up a cloud of silt that drifted like smoke down the slow current. Now that the sun was higher in the sky, the underwater world was no longer wrapped in a grey, twilight gloom. The sea bed was colourless but bright, and the boundary of vision was now almost fifteen feet away. For the first time, Tibor could see the space capsule in its entirety. It was such a peculiar-looking object, being designed for conditions beyond all normal experience, that there was an eye-teasing wrongness about it. One searched in vain for a front or a rear; there was no way of telling in what direction it pointed as it sped along its orbit.

Tibor pressed his helmet against the metal and shouted.

'I'm back,' he called. 'Can you hear me?'

Tap

'I've got a rope, and I'm going to tie it on to the parachute cables. We're about three kilometres from an island, and as soon as we've made you fast we'll head toward it. We can't lift you out of the water with the gear on the lugger, so we'll try to get you up on the beach. You understand?'

Tap

It took only a few moments to secure the rope; now he had better get clear before the *Arafura* started to lift. But there was something he had to do first.

'Hello!' he shouted. 'I've fixed the rope. We'll lift in a minute. D'you hear me?'

Tap

'Then you can hear this too. You'll never get there alive. I've fixed *that* as well.'

Tap, tap

'You've got five hours to die. My brother took longer than that, when he ran into your mine field. You understand? I'm from Budapest. I hate you and your country and everything it stands for. You've taken my home, my family, made my people slaves. I wish I could see your face now – I wish I could watch you die, as I had to watch Theo. When you're halfway to the island, this rope is going to break where I cut it. I'll go down and fix another – and that'll break, too. You can sit in there and wait for the bumps.'

Tibor stopped abruptly, shaken and exhausted by the violence of his emotion. There was no room for logic or reason in this orgasm of hate; he did not pause to think, for he dared not. Yet somewhere far down inside his mind the real truth was burning its way up toward the light of consciousness.

It was not the Russians he hated, for all that they had done. It was himself, for he had done more. The blood of Theo, and of ten thousand countrymen, was upon his own hands. No one could have been a better Communist than he had been, or have more supinely believed the propaganda from Moscow. At school and college, he had been the first to hunt out and denounce 'traitors'. (How many had he sent to the labour camps or the AVO torture chambers?) When he had seen the truth, it was far, far too late; and even then, he had not fought – he had run.

He had run across the world, trying to escape his guilt; and the two drugs of danger and dissipation had helped him to forget the past. The only pleasures life gave him now were the loveless embraces he sought so feverishly when he was on the mainland, and his present mode of existence was proof that these were not enough. If he now had the power to deal out death, it was only because he had come here in search of it himself.

There was no sound from the capsule; its silence seemed contemptuous, mocking. Angrily, Tibor banged against it with the hilt of his knife.

'Did you hear me?' he shouted. 'Did you hear me?'

No answer.

'Damn you! I know you're listening! If you don't answer, I'll hole you and let the water in!'

He was sure that he could, with the sharp point of his knife. But that was the last thing he wanted to do; that would be too quick, too easy an ending.

There was still no sound; maybe the Russian had fainted. Tibor hoped not, but there was no point in waiting any longer. He gave a vicious parting bang on the capsule, and signalled to his tender.

Nick had news for him when he broke the surface.

'T. I. radio's been squawking,' he said. 'The Ruskies are asking everyone to look out for one of their rockets. They say it should be floating somewhere off the Queensland coast. Sounds as if they want it badly.'

'Did they say anything else about it?' Tibor asked anxiously.

'Oh yes – it's been round the moon a couple of times.'

775

'That all?'

'Nothing else that I remember. There was a lot of science stuff I didn't get.'

That figured; it was just like the Russians to keep as quiet as they could about an experiment that had gone wrong.

'You tell T. I. that we'd found it?'

'Are you crazy? Anyway, the radio's crook; couldn't if we wanted to. Fixed that rope properly?'

'Yes – see if you can haul her off the bottom.'

The end of the rope had been wound round the mainmast, and in a few seconds it had been drawn taut. Although the sea was calm, there was a slight swell, and the lugger was rolling ten or fifteen degrees. With each roll, the gunwales would rise a couple of feet, then drop again. There was a lift here of several tons, but one had to be careful in using it.

The rope twanged, the woodwork groaned and creaked, and for a moment Tibor was afraid that the weakened line would part too soon. But it held, and the load lifted. They got a further hoist on the second roll – and on the third. Then the capsule was clear of the sea bed, and the *Arafura* was listing slightly to port.

'Let's go,' said Nick, taking the wheel. 'Should be able to get her half a mile before she bumps again.'

The lugger began to move slowly toward the island, carrying its hidden burden beneath it. As he leaned on the rails, letting the sun steam the moisture from his sodden clothing, Tibor felt at peace for the first time in – how many months? Even his hate had ceased to burn like fire in his brain. Perhaps, like love, it was a passion that could never be satisfied; but for the moment, at least, it was satiated.

There was no weakening of his resolve; he was implacably set upon the vengeance that had been so strangely – so miraculously – placed within his power. Blood called for blood, and now the ghosts that haunted him might rest at last. Yet he felt strange sympathy, even pity, toward the unknown man through whom he could now strike back at the enemies who had once been his friends. He was robbing them of much more than a single life – for what was one man, even a highly trained scientist – to the Russians? What he was taking from them was power and prestige and knowledge, the things they valued most.

He began to worry when they were two thirds of the way to the island, and the rope had not parted. There were still four hours to go, and that was much too long. For the first time it occurred to him that his entire plan might miscarry, and might even recoil on his head. Suppose that, despite everything Nick managed to get the capsule up on the beach before the deadline?

With a deep 'twang' that set the whole ship vibrating, the rope came snaking out of the water, scattering spray in all directions.

'Might have guessed,' muttered Nick. 'She was just starting to bump. You like to go down again, or shall I send one of the boys?'

'I'll take it,' Tibor hastily answered. 'I can do it quicker than they can.'

That was perfectly true, but it took him twenty minutes to locate the capsule. The *Arafura* had drifted well away from it before Nick could stop the engine, and there was a time when Tibor wondered if he would ever find it again. He quartered the sea bed in great arcs, and it was not until he had accidentally tangled in the trailing parachute that his search was ended. The shrouds lay pulsating slowly in the current like some weird and hideous marine monster – but there was nothing that Tibor feared now except frustration, and his pulse barely quickened as he saw the whitely looming mass ahead.

The capsule was scratched and stained with mud, but appeared undamaged. It was lying on its side now, looking rather like a giant milk churn that had been tipped over. The passenger must have been bumped around, but if he'd fallen all the way back from the moon, he must have been well padded and was probably still in good shape. Tibor hoped so; it would be a pity if the remaining three hours were wasted.

Once again he rested the verdigrised copper of his helmet against the no-longer-quite-so-brightly-gleaming metal of the capsule.

'Hello!' he shouted. 'Can you hear me?'

Perhaps the Russian would try to balk him by remaining silent – but that, surely, was asking too much of any man's self-control. Tibor was right; almost at once there was the sharp knock of the reply.

'So glad you're there,' he called back. 'Things are working out just the way I said. though I guess I'll have to cut the rope a little deeper.'

The capsule did not answer. It never answered again, though Tibor banged and banged on the next dive – and on the next. But he hardly expected it to then, for they'd had to stop for a couple of hours to ride out a squall, and the time limit had expired long before he made his final descent. He was a little annoyed about that, for he had planned a farewell message. He shouted it just the same, though he knew he was wasting his breath.

By early afternoon, the *Arafura* had come in as close as she dared. There were only a few feet of water beneath her, and the tide was falling. The capsule broke surface at the bottom of each wave trough, and was now firmly stranded on a sandbank. There was no hope of moving it any farther; it was stuck, until a high sea would dislodge it.

Nick regarded the situation with an expert eye.

'There's a six-foot tide tonight,' he said. 'The way she's lying now, she'll be in only a couple of feet of water at low. We'll be able to get at her with the boats.'

They waited off the sandbank while the sun and the tide went down, and the radio broadcast intermittent reports of a search that was coming closer but was still far away. Late in the afternoon the capsule was almost clear of the water; the crew rowed the small boat toward it with a reluctance which Tibor, to his annoyance, found himself sharing.

'It's got a door in the side,' said Nick suddenly. 'Jeeze – think there's anyone in it?'

'Could be,' answered Tibor, his voice not as steady as he thought. Nick glanced at him curiously. His diver had been acting strangely all day, but he knew better than to ask him what was wrong. In this part of the world, you soon learned to mind your own business.

The boat, rocking slightly in the choppy sea, had now come alongside the capsule. Nick reached out and grabbed one of the twisted antenna stubs; then, with catlike agility he clambered up the curved metal surface. Tibor made no attempt to follow him, but watched silently from the boat as he examined the entrance hatch.

'Unless it's jammed,' Nick muttered, 'there must be some way of opening it from outside. Just our luck if it needs special tools.'

His fears were groundless. The word 'Open' had been stencilled in ten languages around the recessed door catch, and it took only seconds to deduce its mode of operation. As the air hissed out, Nick said 'Phew!' and turned suddenly pale. He looked at Tibor as if seeking support, but Tibor avoided his eye. Then, reluctantly, Nick lowered himself into the capsule.

He was gone for a long time. At first, they could hear muffled bangings and bumpings from the inside, followed by a string of bilingual profanity. And then there was a silence that went on and on and on.

When at last Nick's head appeared above the hatchway, his leathery, wind-tanned face was grey and streaked with tears. As Tibor saw this incredible sight, he felt a sudden ghastly, premonition. Something had gone horribly wrong, but his mind was too numb to anticipate the truth. It came soon enough, when Nick handed down his burden, no larger than an oversized doll.

Blanco took it, as Tibor shrank to the stern of the boat. As he looked at the calm, waxen face, fingers of ice seemed to close not only upon his heart, but around his loins. In the same moment, both hate and desire died forever within him, as he knew the price of his revenge.

The dead astronaut was perhaps more beautiful in death than she had been in life; tiny though she was, she must have been tough as well as highly trained to qualify for this mission. As she lay at Tibor's feet, she was neither a Russian nor the first human being to have seen the far side of the moon; she was merely the girl that he had killed.

Nick was talking, from a long way off.

'She was carrying this,' he said, in an unsteady voice. 'Had it tight in her hand – took me a long time to get it out.'

Tibor scarcely heard him, and never even glanced at the tiny spool of tape lying in Nick's palm. He could not guess, in this moment beyond all feeling, that the Furies had yet to close in upon his soul – and that soon the whole world would be listening to an accusing voice from beyond the grave, branding him more irrevocably than any man since Cain.

Love that Universe

First published in *Escapade*, 1967
Collected in *The Wind from the Sun*

Mr President, National Administrator, Planetary Delegates, it is both an honour and a grave responsibility to address you at this moment of crisis. I am aware – I can very well understand – that many of you are shocked and dismayed by some of the rumours that you have heard. But I must beg you to forget your natural prejudices at a time when the very existence of the human race – *of the Earth itself* – is at stake.

Some time ago I came across a century-old phrase: 'thinking the unthinkable'. This is exactly what we have to do now. We must face the facts without flinching; we must not let our emotions sway our logic. Indeed, we must do the precise opposite: *we must let our logic sway our emotions!*

The situation is desperate, but it is not hopeless, thanks to the astonishing discoveries my colleagues have made at the Antigean Station. For the reports are indeed true; we *can* establish contact with the supercivilisations at the Galactic Core. At least we can let them know of our existence – and if we can do that, it should be possible for us to appeal to them for help.

There is nothing, absolutely nothing, that we can do by our own efforts in the brief time available. It is only ten years since the search for trans-Plutonian planets revealed the presence of the Black Dwarf. Only ninety years from now, it will make its perihelion passage and swing around the Sun as it heads once more into the depths of space – leaving a shattered solar system behind it. All our resources, all our much-vaunted control over the forces of nature, cannot alter its orbit by a fraction of an inch.

But ever since the first of the so called 'beacon stars' was discovered, at the end of the twentieth century, we have known that there were civilisations with access to energy sources incomparably greater than ours. Some of you will doubtless recall the incredulity of the astronomers – and later of the whole human race – when the first examples of cosmic engineering were detected in the Magellanic Clouds. Here were stellar structures obeying no natural laws; even now, we do not know their purpose – but we know their awesome implications. We share a universe with creatures who can juggle with the very stars. If they choose to help, it would be child's play for them to deflect a body like the Black Dwarf, only a few thousand times the mass of Earth. . . . Child's play, did I call it? Yes, that may be *literally* true!

You will all, I am certain, remember the great debate that followed the discovery of the supercivilisations. Should we attempt to communicate with them, or would it be best to remain inconspicuous? There was the possibility, of course, that they already knew everything about us, or might be annoyed by our presumption, or might react in any number of unpleasant ways. Though the benefits from such contacts could be enormous, the risks were terrifying. But now we have nothing to lose, and everything to gain. . . .

And until now, there was another fact that made the matter of no more than long-term philosophical interest. Though we could – at great expense – build radio transmitters capable of sending signals to these creatures, the nearest supercivilisation is seven thousand light-years away. Even if it bothered to reply, it would be fourteen thousand years before we could get an answer. In these circumstances, it seemed that our superiors could be neither a help to us nor a threat.

But now all this has changed. We can send signals to the stars at a speed that cannot yet be measured, and that may well be infinite. And we know that *they* are using such techniques – for we have detected their impulses, though we cannot begin to interpret them.

These impulses are not electromagnetic, of course. We do not know what they are; we do not even have a name for them. Or, rather, we have too many names. . . .

Yes, gentlemen, there *is* something, after all, in the old wives' tales about telepathy, ESP, or whatever you care to call it. But it is no wonder that the study of such phenomena never made any progress here on Earth, where there is the continuous background roar of a billion minds to swamp all signals. Even the pitiably limited progress that was made before the Space Age seems a miracle – like discovering the laws of music in a boiler factory. It was not until we could get away from our planet's mental tumult that there was any hope of establishing a real science of parapsychology.

And even then we had to move to the other side of the Earth's orbit, where the noise was not only diminished by a hundred and eighty million miles of distance, but also shielded by the unimaginable bulk of the Sun itself. Only there, on our artificial planetoid Antigeos, could we detect and measure the feeble radiations of mentality, and uncover their laws of propagation.

In many respects, those laws are still baffling. However, we have established the basic facts. As had long been suspected by the few who believed in these phenomena, they are triggered by emotional states – not by pure will-power or deliberate, conscious thought. It is not surprising, therefore, that so many reports of paranormal events in the past were associated with moments of death or disaster. Fear is a powerful generator; on rare occasions it can manifest itself above the surrounding noise.

Once this fact was recognised, we began to make progress. We induced artificial emotional states, first in single individuals, then in groups. We were able to measure how the signals attenuated with distance. Now, we have a reliable, quantitative theory that has been checked out as far as Saturn. We believe that our calculations can be extended even to the stars. If this is correct, we can produce a . . . a *shout* that will be heard instantly over the whole galaxy. And surely there will be someone who will respond!

Now there is only one way in which a signal of the required intensity can be produced. I said that fear was a powerful generator – but it is not powerful enough. Even if we could strike all humanity with a simultaneous moment of terror, the impulse could not be detected more than two thousand light-years away. We need at least four times this range. And we can achieve it – *by using the only emotion that is more powerful than fear.*

However, we also need the co-operation of not fewer than a billion individuals, at a moment of time that must be synchronized to the second. My colleagues have solved all the purely technical problems, which are really quite trivial. The simple electrostimulation devices required have been used in medical research since the early twentieth century, and the necessary timing pulse can be sent out over the planetary communications networks. All the units needed can be mass-produced within a month, and instruction in their use requires only a few minutes. It is the psychological preparation for – let us call it O Day – that will take a little longer. . . .

And *that*, gentlemen, is your problem; naturally, we scientists will give you all possible help. We realise that there will be protests, cries of outrage, refusals to co-operate. But when one looks at the matter logically, is the idea really so offensive? Many of us think that, on the contrary, it has a certain appropriateness – even a poetic justice.

Mankind now faces its ultimate emergency. In such a moment of crisis, is it not right for us to call upon the instinct that has always ensured our survival in the past? A poet in an earlier, almost equally troubled age put it better than I can ever hope to do:

WE MUST LOVE ONE ANOTHER OR DIE.

Dog Star

First published in *Galaxy*, April 1962, as 'Moondog'
Collected in *Tales of Ten Worlds*

I can no longer bear to read this story, now that Laika sleeps forever in the garden of the home we once shared.

When I heard Laika's frantic barking, my first reaction was one of annoyance. I turned over in my bunk and murmured sleepily, 'Shut up, you silly bitch.' That dreamy interlude lasted only a fraction of a second; then consciousness returned – and, with it, fear. Fear of loneliness, and fear of madness.

For a moment I dared not open my eyes; I was afraid of what I might see. Reason told me that no dog had ever set foot upon this world, that Laika was separated from me by a quarter of a million miles of space – and, far more irrevocably, five years of time.

'You've been dreaming,' I told myself angrily. 'Stop being a fool – open your eyes! You won't see anything except the glow of the wall paint.'

That was right, of course. The tiny cabin was empty, the door tightly closed. I was alone with my memories, overwhelmed by the transcendental sadness that often comes when some bright dream fades into drab reality. The sense of loss was so desolating that I longed to return to sleep. It was well that I failed to do so, for at that moment sleep would have been death. But I did not know this for another five seconds, and during that eternity I was back on Earth, seeking what comfort I could from the past.

No one ever discovered Laika's origin, though the Observatory staff made a few enquiries and I inserted several advertisements in the Pasadena newspapers. I found her, a lost and lonely ball of fluff, huddled by the roadside one summer evening when I was driving up to Palomar. Though I have never liked dogs, or indeed any animals, it was impossible to leave this helpless little creature to the mercy of the passing cars. With some qualms, wishing that I had a pair of gloves, I picked her up and dumped her in the baggage compartment. I was not going to hazard the upholstery of my new '92 Vik, and felt that she could do little damage there. In this, I was not altogether correct.

When I had parked the car at the Monastery – the astronomers' residential quarters, where I'd be living for the next week – I inspected my find without much enthusiasm. At that stage, I had intended to hand the puppy over to the janitor; but then it whimpered and opened its eyes. There was such an expression of helpless trust in them that – well, I changed my mind.

Sometimes I regretted that decision, though never for long. I had no idea how much trouble a growing dog could cause, deliberately and otherwise. My cleaning and repair bills soared; I could never be sure of finding an unravaged pair of socks or an unchewed copy of the *Astrophysical Journal*. But eventually Laika was both house-trained and Observatory-trained: she must have been the only dog ever to be allowed inside the two-hundred-inch dome. She would lie there quietly in the shadows for hours, while I was up in the cage making adjustments, quite content if she could hear my voice from time to time. The other astronomers became equally fond of her (it was old Dr Anderson who suggested her name), but from the beginning she was my dog, and would obey no one else. Not that she would always obey me.

She was a beautiful animal, about ninety-five per cent Alsatian. It was that missing five per cent, I imagine, that led to her being abandoned. (I still feel a surge of anger when I think of it, but since I shall never know the facts, I may be jumping to false conclusions.) Apart from two dark patches over the eyes, most of her body was a smoky grey, and her coat was soft as silk. When her ears were pricked up, she looked incredibly intelligent and alert; sometimes I would be discussing spectral types or stellar evolution with my colleague, and it would be hard to believe that she was not following the conversation.

Even now, I cannot understand why she became so attached to me, for I have made very few friends among human beings. Yet when I returned to the Observatory after an absence, she would go almost frantic with delight, bouncing around on her hind legs and putting her paws on my shoulders – which she could reach quite easily – all the while uttering small squeaks of joy which seemed highly inappropriate from so large a dog. I hated to leave her for more than a few days at a time, and though I could not take her with me on overseas trips, she accompanied me on most of my shorter journeys. She was with me when I drove north to attend that ill-fated seminar at Berkeley.

We were staying with university acquaintances; they had been polite about it, but obviously did not look forward to having a monster in the house. However, I assured them that Laika never gave the slightest trouble, and rather reluctantly they let her sleep in the living room. 'You needn't worry about burglars tonight,' I said. 'We don't have any in Berkeley,' they answered, rather coldly.

In the middle of the night, it seemed that they were wrong. I was awakened by a hysterical, high-pitched barking from Laika which I had heard only once before – when she had first seen a cow, and did not know what on earth to make of it. Cursing, I threw off the sheets and stumbled out into the darkness of the unfamiliar house. My main thought was to silence Laika before she roused my hosts – assuming that this was not already far too late. If there had been an intruder, he would certainly have taken flight by now. Indeed, I rather hoped that he had.

For a moment I stood beside the switch at the top of the stairs, wondering whether to throw it. Then I growled, 'Shut up, Laika!' and flooded the place with light.

She was scratching frantically at the door; pausing from time to time to give that hysterical yelp. 'If you want out,' I said angrily, 'there's no need for all that fuss.' I went down, shot the bolt, and she took off into the night like a rocket.

It was very calm and still, with a waning Moon struggling to pierce the San Francisco fog. I stood in the luminous haze, looking out across the water to the lights of the city, waiting for Laika to come back so that I could chastise her suitably. I was still waiting when, for the second time in the twentieth century, the San Andreas Fault woke from its sleep.

Oddly enough, I was not frightened – at first. I can remember that two thoughts passed through my mind, in the moment before I realised the danger. Surely, I told myself, the geophysicists could have given us *some* warning. And then I found myself thinking, with great surprise, 'I'd no idea that earthquakes make so much noise!'

It was about then that I knew that this was no ordinary quake; what happened afterward, I would prefer to forget. The Red Cross did not take me away until quite late the next morning, because I refused to leave Laika. As I looked at the shattered house containing the bodies of my friends, I knew that I owed my life to her; but the helicopter pilots could not be expected to understand that, and I cannot blame them for thinking that I was crazy, like so many of the others they had found wandering among the fires and the debris.

After that, I do not suppose we were ever apart for more than a few hours. I have been told – and I can well believe it – that I became less and less interested in human company, without being actively unsocial or misanthropic. Between them, the stars and Laika filled all my needs. We used to go for long walks together over the mountains; it was the happiest time I have ever known. There was only one flaw; I knew, though Laika could not, how soon it must end.

We had been planning the move for more than a decade. As far back as the nineteen-sixties it was realised that Earth was no place for an astronomical observatory. Even the small pilot instruments on the Moon had far outperformed all the telescopes peering through the murk and haze of the terrestrial atmosphere. The story of Mount Wilson, Palomar, Greenwich, and the other great names was coming to an end; they would still be used for training purposes, but the research frontier must move out into space.

I had to move with it; indeed, I had already been offered the post of Deputy Director, Farside Observatory. In a few months, I could hope to solve problems I had been working on for years. Beyond the atmosphere, I would be like a blind man who had suddenly been given sight.

It was utterly impossible, of course, to take Laika with me. The only animals on the Moon were those needed for experimental purposes; it might be another generation before pets were allowed, and even then it would cost a fortune to carry them there – and to keep them alive. Providing Laika with her usual two pounds of meat a day would, I calculated, take several times my quite comfortable salary.

The choice was simple and straightforward. I could stay on Earth and abandon my career. Or I could go to the Moon – and abandon Laika.

After all, she was only a dog. In a dozen years, she would be dead, while I should be reaching the peak of my profession. No sane man would have hesitated over the matter; yet I did hesitate, and if by now you do not understand why, no further words of mine can help.

In the end, I let matters go by default. Up to the very week I was due to leave, I had still made no plans for Laika. When Dr Anderson volunteered to look after her, I accepted numbly, with scarcely a word of thanks. The old physicist and his wife had always been fond of her, and I am afraid that they considered me indifferent and heartless – when the truth was just the opposite. We went for one more walk together over the hills; then I delivered her silently to the Andersons, and did not see her again.

Take-off was delayed almost twenty-four hours, until a major flare storm had cleared the Earth's orbit; even so, the Van Allen belts were still so active that we had to make our exit through the North Polar Gap. It was a miserable flight; apart from the usual trouble with weightlessness, we were all groggy with antiradiation drugs. The ship was already over Farside before I took much interest in the proceedings, so I missed the sight of Earth dropping below the horizon. Nor was I really sorry; I wanted no reminders, and intended to think only of the future. Yet I could not shake off that feeling of guilt; I had deserted someone who loved and trusted me, and was no better than those who had abandoned Laika when she was a puppy, beside the dusty road to Palomar.

The news that she was dead reached me a month later. There was no reason that anyone knew; the Andersons had done their best, and were very upset. She had just lost interest in living, it seemed. For a while, I think I did the same; but work is a wonderful anodyne, and my programme was just getting under way. Though I never forgot Laika, in a little while the memory ceased to hurt.

Then why had it come back to haunt me, five years later, on the far side of the Moon? I was searching my mind for the reason when the metal building around me quivered as if under the impact of a heavy blow. I reacted without thinking, and was already closing the helmet of my emergency suit when the foundations slipped and the wall tore open with a short-lived scream of escaping air. Because I had automatically pressed the General Alarm button, we lost only two men, despite the fact that the tremor – the worst ever recorded on Farside – cracked all three of the Observatory's pressure domes.

It is hardly necessary for me to say that I do not believe in the supernatural; everything that happened has a perfectly rational explanation, obvious to any man with the slightest knowledge of psychology. In the second San Francisco earthquake, Laika was not the only dog to sense approaching disaster; many such cases were reported. And on Farside, my own memories must have given me that heightened awareness, when my never-sleeping subconscious detected the first faint vibrations from within the Moon.

The human mind has strange and labyrinthine ways of going about its business; it knew the signal that would most swiftly rouse me to the knowledge of danger. There is nothing more to it than that; though in a sense one could say that Laika woke me on both occasions, there is no mystery about it, no miraculous warning across the gulf that neither man nor dog can ever bridge.

Of that I am sure, if I am sure of anything. Yet sometimes I wake now, in the silence of the Moon, and wish that the dream could have lasted a few seconds longer – so that I could have looked just once more into those luminous brown eyes, brimming with an unselfish, undemanding love I have found nowhere else on this or on any other world.

Maelstrom II

First published in *Playboy*, April 1965
Collected in *The Wind from the Sun*

He was not the first man, Cliff Leyland told himself bitterly, to know the exact second and the precise manner of his death. Times beyond number, condemned criminals had waited for their last dawn. Yet until the very end they could try for a reprieve; human judges can show mercy. But against the laws of nature, there is no appeal.

And only six hours ago, he had been whistling happily while he packed his ten kilos of personal baggage for the long fall home. He could still remember (even now, after all that had happened) how he had dreamed that Myra was already in his arms, that he was taking Brian and Sue on that promised cruise down the Nile. In a few minutes, as Earth rose above the horizon, he might see the Nile again; but memory alone could bring back the faces of his wife and children. And all because he had tried to save nine hundred and fifty sterling dollars by riding home on the freight catapult, instead of the rocket shuttle.

He had expected the first twelve seconds of the trip to be rough, as the electric launcher whipped the capsule along its ten-mile track and shot him off the Moon. Even with the protection of the water-bath in which he would float during countdown, he had not looked forward to the twenty g's of take-off. Yet when the acceleration had gripped the capsule, he had been hardly aware of the immense forces acting upon him. The only sound was a faint creaking from the metal walls; to anyone who had experienced the thunder of a rocket launch, the silence was uncanny. When the cabin speaker had announced 'T plus five seconds; speed two thousand miles an hour,' he could scarcely believe it.

Two thousand miles an hour in five seconds from a standing start – with seven seconds still to go as the generators smashed their thunderbolts of power into the launcher. He was riding the lightning across the face of the Moon. And at T plus seven seconds, the lightning failed.

Even in the womblike shelter of the tank, Cliff could sense that something had gone wrong. The water around him, until now frozen almost rigid by its weight, seemed suddenly to become alive. Though the capsule was still hurtling along the track, all acceleration had ceased, and it was merely coasting under its own momentum.

He had no time to feel fear, or to wonder what had happened, for the power failure lasted little more than a second. Then, with a jolt that shook the capsule from end to end and set off a series of ominous, tinkling crashes, the field came on again.

When the acceleration faded for the last time, all weight vanished with it. Cliff needed no instrument but his stomach to tell that the capsule had left the end of the track and was rising away from the surface of the Moon. He waited impatiently until the automatic pumps had drained the tank and the hot-air driers had done their work; then he drifted across the control panel, and pulled himself down into the bucket seat.

'Launch Control,' he called urgently, as he drew the restraining straps around his waist, 'what the devil happened?'

A brisk but worried voice answered at once.

'We're still checking – call you back in thirty seconds.' Then it added belatedly, 'Glad you're OK.'

While he was waiting, Cliff switched to forward vision. There was nothing ahead except stars – which was as it should be. At least he had taken off with most of his planned speed, and there was no danger that he would crash back to the Moon's surface immediately. But he would crash back sooner or later, for he could not possibly have reached escape velocity. He must be rising out into space along a great ellipse – and, in a few hours, he would be back at his starting point.

'Hello, Cliff,' said Launch Control suddenly. 'We've found what happened. The circuit breakers tripped when you went through section five of the track. So your take-off speed was seven hundred miles an hour low. That will bring you back in just over five hours – but don't worry; your course-correction jets can boost you into a stable orbit. We'll tell you when to fire them. Then all you have to do is to sit tight until we can send someone to haul you down.'

Slowly, Cliff allowed himself to relax. He had forgotten the capsule's vernier rockets. Low-powered though they were, they could kick him into an orbit that would clear the Moon. Though he might fall back to within a few miles of the lunar surface, skimming over mountains and plains at a breath-taking speed, he would be perfectly safe.

Then he remembered those tinkling crashes from the control compartment, and his hopes dimmed again, for there were not many things that could break in a space vehicle without most unpleasant consequences.

He was facing those consequences, now that the final checks of the ignition circuits had been completed. Neither on MANUAL nor on AUTO would the navigation rockets fire. The capsule's modest fuel reserves, which could have taken him to safety, were utterly useless. In five hours he would complete his orbit – and return to his launching point.

I wonder if they'll name the new crater after me, thought Cliff. 'Crater Leyland: diameter . . .' What diameter? Better not exaggerate – I don't suppose it will be more than a couple of hundred yards across. Hardly worth putting on the map.

Launch Control was still silent, but that was not surprising. There was little that one could say to a man already as good as dead. And yet, though he knew that nothing could alter his trajectory, even now he could not believe that he would soon be scattered over most of Farside. He was still soaring away from the Moon, snug and comfortable in his little cabin. The idea of death was utterly incongruous – as it is to all men until the final second.

And then, for a moment, Cliff forgot his own problem. The horizon ahead was no longer flat. Something more brilliant even than the blazing lunar landscape was lifting against the stars. As the capsule curved round the edge of the Moon, it was creating the only kind of earthrise that was possible – a man-made one. In a minute it was all over, such was his speed in orbit. By that time the Earth had leaped clear of the horizon, and was climbing swiftly up the sky.

It was three-quarters full, and almost too bright to look upon. Here was a cosmic mirror made not of dull rocks and dusty plains, but of snow and cloud and sea. Indeed, it was almost all sea, for the Pacific was turned toward him, and the blinding reflection of the sun covered the Hawaiian Islands. The haze of the atmosphere – that soft blanket that should have cushioned his descent in a few hours' time – obliterated all geographical details; perhaps that darker patch emerging from night was New Guinea, but he could not be sure.

There was a bitter irony in the knowledge that he was heading straight toward that lovely, gleaming apparition. Another seven hundred miles an hour and he would have made it. Seven hundred miles an hour – that was all. He might as well ask for seven million.

The sight of the rising Earth brought home to him, with irresistible force, the duty he feared but could postpone no longer.

'Launch Control,' he said, holding his voice steady with a great effort, 'please give me a circuit to Earth.'

This was one of the strangest things he had ever done in his life: to sit here above the Moon and listen to the telephone ring in his own home, a quarter of a million miles away. It must be near midnight down there in Africa, and it would be some time before there would be any answer. Myra would stir sleepily; then, because she was a spaceman's wife, always alert for disaster, she would be instantly awake. But they had both hated to have a phone in the bedroom, and it would be at least fifteen seconds before she could switch on the light, close the nursery door to avoid disturbing the baby, get down the stairs, and . . .

Her voice came clear and sweet across the emptiness of space. He would recognise it anywhere in the universe, and he detected at once the undertone of anxiety.

'Mrs Leyland?' said the Earthside operator. 'I have a call from your husband. Please remember the two-second time lag.'

Cliff wondered how many people were listening to this call, on either the Moon, the Earth, or the relay satellites. It was hard to talk for the last time

789

to your loved ones when you didn't know how many eavesdroppers there might be. But as soon as he began to speak, no one else existed but Myra and himself.

'Darling,' he began, 'this is Cliff. I'm afraid I won't be coming home, as I promised. There's been a ... a technical slip. I'm quite all right at the moment, but I'm in big trouble.'

He swallowed, trying to overcome the dryness in his mouth, then went on quickly before she could interrupt. As briefly as he could, he explained the situation. For his own sake as well as hers, he did not abandon all hope.

'Everyone's doing their best,' he said. 'Maybe they can get a ship up to me in time. But in case they can't ... well, I wanted to speak to you and the children.'

She took it well, as he had known that she would. He felt pride as well as love when her answer came back from the dark side of Earth.

'Don't worry, Cliff. I'm sure they'll get you out, and we'll have our holiday after all, exactly the way we planned.'

'I think so, too,' he lied. 'But just in case, would you wake the children? Don't tell them that anything's wrong.'

It was an endless half-minute before he heard their sleepy, yet excited, voices. Cliff would willingly have given these last few hours of his life to have seen their faces once again, but the capsule was not equipped with such luxuries as vision. Perhaps it was just as well, for he could not have hidden the truth had he looked into their eyes. They would know it soon enough, but not from him. He wanted to give them only happiness in these last moments together.

Yet it was hard to answer their questions, to tell them that he would soon be seeing them, to make promises that he could not keep. It needed all his self-control when Brian reminded him of the moondust he had forgotten once before – but had remembered this time.

'I've got it, Brian; it's in a jar right beside me. Soon you'll be able to show it to your friends.' (No: soon it will be back on the world from which it came.) 'And Susie – be a good girl and do everything that Mummy tells you. Your last school report wasn't too good, you know, especially those remarks about behaviour. . . . Yes, Brian, I have those photographs, and the piece of rock from Aristarchus. . . .'

It was hard to die at thirty-five; but it was hard, too, for a boy to lose his father at ten. How would Brian remember him in the years ahead? Perhaps as no more than a fading voice from space, for he had spent so little time on Earth. In the last few minutes, as he swung outward and then back to the Moon, there was little enough that he could do except project his love and his hopes across the emptiness that he would never span again. The rest was up to Myra.

When the children had gone, happy but puzzled, there was work to do. Now was the time to keep one's head, to be businesslike and practical. Myra must face the future without him, but at least he could make the transition easier. Whatever happens to the individual, life goes on; and to modern man life involves mortgages and instalments due, insurance policies and joint bank accounts. Almost impersonally, as if they concerned some-one else – which would soon be true enough – Cliff began to talk about these things. There was a time for the heart and a time for the brain. The heart would have its final say three hours from now, when he began his last approach to the surface of the Moon.

No one interrupted them. There must have been silent monitors main-taining the link between two worlds, but the two of them might have been the only people alive. Sometimes while he was speaking Cliff's eyes would stray to the periscope, and be dazzled by the glare of Earth – now more than halfway up the sky. It was impossible to believe that it was home for seven billion souls. Only three mattered to him now.

It should have been four, but with the best will in the world he could not put the baby on the same footing as the others. He had never seen his younger son; and now he never would.

At last he could think of no more to say. For some things, a lifetime was not enough – but an hour could be too much. He felt physically and emotionally exhausted, and the strain on Myra must have been equally great. He wanted to be alone with his thoughts and with the stars, to compose his mind and to make his peace with the universe.

'I'd like to sign off for an hour or so, darling,' he said. There was no need for explanations; they understood each other too well. 'I'll call you back in – in plenty of time. Goodbye for now.'

He waited the two and a half seconds for the answering goodbye from Earth; then he cut the circuit and stared blankly at the tiny control desk. Quite unexpectedly, without desire or volition, tears sprang from his eyes, and suddenly he was weeping like a child.

He wept for his family, and for himself. He wept for the future that might have been, and the hopes that would soon be incandescent vapour, drifting between the stars. And he wept because there was nothing else to do.

After a while he felt much better. Indeed, he realised that he was extremely hungry. There was no point in dying on an empty stomach, and he began to rummage among the space rations in the closet-sized galley. While he was squeezing a tube of chicken-and-ham paste into his mouth, Launch Control called.

There was a new voice at the end of the line – a slow, steady, and immensely competent voice that sounded as if it would brook no nonsense from inanimate machinery.

'This is Van Kessel, Chief of Maintenance, Space Vehicles Division. Listen carefully, Leyland. We think we've found a way out. It's a long shot – but it's the only chance you have.'

Alternations of hope and despair are hard on the nervous system. Cliff felt a sudden dizziness; he might have fallen had there been any direction in which to fall.

'Go ahead,' he said faintly, when he had recovered, Then he listened to Van Kessel with an eagerness that slowly changed to incredulity.

'I don't believe it!' he said at last. 'It just doesn't make sense!'

'You can't argue with the computers,' answered Van Kessel. 'They've checked the figures about twenty different ways. And it makes sense, all right. You won't be moving so fast at apogee, and it doesn't need much of a kick then to change your orbit. I suppose you've never been in a deep-space rig before?'

'No, of course not.'

'Pity – but never mind. If you follow instructions, you can't go wrong. You'll find the suit in the locker at the end of the cabin. Break the seals and haul it out.'

Cliff floated the full six feet from the control desk to the rear of the cabin and pulled on the lever marked EMERGENCY ONLY – TYPE 17 DEEP-SPACE SUIT. The door opened, and the shining silver fabric hung flaccid before him.

'Strip down to your underclothes and wriggle into it,' said Van Kessel. 'Don't bother about the biopack – you clamp that on later.'

'I'm in.' said Cliff presently. 'What do I do now?'

'You wait twenty minutes – and then we'll give you the signal to open the air lock and jump.'

The implications of that word 'jump' suddenly penetrated. Cliff looked around the now familiar, comforting little cabin, and then thought of the lonely emptiness between the stars – the unreverberant abyss through which a man could fall until the end of time.

He had never been in free space; there was no reason why he should. He was just a farmer's boy with a master's degree in agronomy, seconded from the Sahara Reclamation Project and trying to grow crops on the Moon. Space was not for him; he belonged to the worlds of soil and rock, of moondust and vacuum-formed pumice.

'I can't do it,' he whispered. 'Isn't there any other way?'

'There's not,' snapped Van Kessel. 'We're doing our damnedest to save you, and this is no time to get neurotic. Dozens of men have been in far worse situations – badly injured, trapped in wreckage a million miles from help. But you're not even scratched, and already you're squealing! Pull yourself together – or we'll sign off and leave you to stew in your own juice.'

Cliff turned slowly red, and it was several seconds before he answered.

'I'm all right,' he said at last. 'Let's go through those instructions again.'

'That's better,' said Van Kessel approvingly. 'Twenty minutes from now, when you're at apogee, you'll go into the air lock. From that point, we'll lose communication; your suit radio has only a ten-mile range. But we'll be tracking you on radar and we'll be able to speak to you when you pass over us again. Now, about the controls on your suit . . .'

The twenty minutes went quickly enough. At the end of that time, Cliff knew exactly what he had to do. He had even come to believe that it might work.

'Time to bail out,' said Van Kessel. 'The capsule's correctly oriented – the air lock points the way you want to go. But direction isn't critical. *Speed* is what matters. Put everything you've got into that jump – and good luck!'

'Thanks,' said Cliff inadequately. 'Sorry that I . . .'

'Forget it,' interrupted Van Kessel. 'Now get moving!'

For the last time, Cliff looked around the tiny cabin, wondering if there was anything that he had forgotten. All his personal belongings would have to be abandoned, but they could be replaced easily enough. Then he remembered the little jar of moondust he had promised Brian; this time, he would not let the boy down. The minute mass of the sample – only a few ounces – would make no difference to his fate. He tied a piece of string around the neck of the jar and attached it to the harness of his suit.

The air lock was so small that there was literally no room to move; he stood sandwiched between inner and outer doors until the automatic pumping sequence was finished. Then the rail slowly opened away from him, and he was facing the stars.

With his clumsy gloved fingers, he hauled himself out of the air lock and stood upright on the steeply curving hull, bracing himself tightly against it with the safety line. The splendour of the scene held him almost paralysed. He forgot all his fears of vertigo and insecurity as he gazed around him, no longer constrained by the narrow field of vision of the periscope.

The Moon was a gigantic crescent, the dividing line between night and day a jagged arch sweeping across a quarter of the sky. Down there the sun was setting, at the beginning of the long lunar night, but the summits of isolated peaks were still blazing with the last light of day, defying the darkness that had already encircled them.

That darkness was not complete. Though the sun had gone from the land below, the almost full Earth flooded it with glory. Cliff could see, faint but clear in the glimmering earthlight, the outlines of seas and highlands, the dim stars of mountain peaks, the dark circles of craters. He was flying above a ghostly, sleeping land – a land that was trying to drag him to his death. For now he was poised at the highest point of his orbit, exactly on the line between Moon and Earth. It was time to go.

He bent his legs, crouching against the hull. Then, with all his force, he launched himself toward the stars, letting the safety line run out behind him.

The capsule receded with surprising speed, and as it did so, he felt a most unexpected sensation. He had anticipated terror or vertigo, but not this unmistakable, haunting sense of familiarity. All this had happened before; not to him, of course, but to someone else. He could not pinpoint the memory, and there was no time to hunt for it now.

He flashed a quick glance at Earth, Moon, and receding spacecraft, and made his decision without conscious thought. The line whipped away as he snapped the quick-release. Now he was alone, two thousand miles above the Moon, a quarter of a million miles from Earth. He could do nothing but wait; it would be two and a half hours before he would know if he could live – and if his own muscles had performed the task that the rockets had failed to do.

And as the stars slowly revolved around him, he suddenly knew the origin of that haunting memory. It was many years since he had read Poe's short stories, but who could ever forget them?

He, too, was trapped in a maelstrom, being whirled down to his doom; he, too, hoped to escape by abandoning his vessel. Though the forces involved were totally different, the parallel was striking. Poe's fisherman had lashed himself to a barrel because stubby, cylindrical objects were being sucked down into the great whirlpool more slowly than his ship. It was a brilliant application of the laws of hydrodynamics. Cliff could only hope that his use of celestial mechanics would be equally inspired.

How fast had he jumped away from the capsule? At a good five miles an hour, surely. Trivial though that speed was by astronomical standards, it should be enough to inject him into a new orbit – one that, Van Kessel had promised him, would clear the Moon by several miles. That was not much of a margin, but it would be enough on this airless world, where there was no atmosphere to claw him down.

With a sudden spasm of guilt, Cliff realised that he had never made that second call to Myra. It was Van Kessel's fault; the engineer had kept him on the move, given him no time to brood over his own affairs. And Van Kessel was right: in a situation like this, a man could think only of himself. All his resources, mental and physical, must be concentrated on survival. This was no time or place for the distracting and weakening ties of love.

He was racing now toward the night side of the Moon, and the daylit crescent was shrinking as he watched. The intolerable disc of the Sun, at which he dared not look, was falling swiftly toward the curved horizon. The crescent moonscape dwindled to a burning line of light, a bow of fire set against the stars. Then the bow fragmented into a dozen shining beads, which one by one winked out as he shot into the shadow of the Moon.

With the going of the Sun, the earthlight seemed more brilliant than ever, frosting his suit with silver as he rotated slowly along his orbit. It took him about ten seconds to make each revolution; there was nothing he could do to check his spin, and indeed he welcomed the constantly changing view. Now that his eyes were no longer distracted by occasional glimpses of the Sun, he could see the stars in thousands, where there had been only hundreds before. The familiar constellaions were drowned, and even the brightest of the planets were hard to find in that blaze of light.

The dark disc of the lunar night land lay across the star field like an eclipsing shadow, and it was slowly growing as he fell toward it. At every instant some star, bright or faint, would pass behind its edge and wink out of existence. It was almost as if a hole were growing in space, eating up the heavens.

There was no other indication of his movement, or of the passage of time except for his regular ten-second spin. When he looked at his watch, he was astonished to see that he had left the capsule half an hour ago. He searched for it among the stars, without success. By now, it would be several miles behind. But presently it would draw ahead of him, as it moved on its lower orbit, and would be the first to reach the Moon.

Cliff was still puzzling over this paradox when the strain of the last few hours, combined with the euphoria of weightlessness, produced a result he would hardly have believed possible. Lulled by the gentle susurration of the air inlets, floating lighter than any feather as he turned beneath the stars, he fell into a dreamless sleep.

When he awoke at some prompting of his subconscious, the Earth was nearing the edge of the Moon. The sight almost brought on another wave of self-pity, and for a moment he had to fight for control of his emotions. This was the very last he might ever see of Earth, as his orbit took him back over Farside, into the land where the earthlight never shone. The brilliant Antarctic icecaps, the equatorial cloud belts, the scintillation of the Sun upon the Pacific – all were sinking swiftly behind the lunar mountains. Then they were gone; he had neither Sun nor Earth to light him now, and the invisible land below was so black that it hurt his eyes.

Unbelievably, a cluster of stars had appeared *inside* the darkened disc, where no stars could possibly be. Cliff stared at them in astonishment for a few seconds, then realised he was passing above one of the Farside settlements. Down there beneath the pressure domes of their city, men were waiting out the lunar night – sleeping, working, loving, resting, quarreling. Did they know that he was speeding like an invisible meteor through their sky, racing above their heads at four thousand miles an hour? Almost certainly; for by now the whole Moon, and the whole Earth, must know of his predicament. Perhaps they were searching for him with radar and telescope, but they would have little time to find him. Within seconds, the unknown city had dropped out of sight, and he was once more alone above Farside.

It was impossible to judge his altitude above the blank emptiness speeding below, for there was no sense of scale or perspective. Sometimes it seemed that he could reach out and touch the darkness across which he was racing; yet he knew that in reality it must still be many miles beneath him. But he also knew that he was still descending, and that at any moment one of the crater walls or mountain peaks that strained invisibly toward him might claw him from the sky.

In the darkness somewhere ahead was the final obstacle – the hazard he feared most of all. Across the heart of Farside, spanning the equator from north to south in a wall more than a thousand miles long, lay the Soviet Range. He had been a boy when it was discovered, back in 1959, and could still remember his excitement when he had seen the first smudged photographs from Lunik III. He could never have dreamed that one day he would be flying toward those same mountains, waiting for them to decide his fate.

The first eruption of dawn took him completely by surprise. Light exploded ahead of him, leaping from peak to peak until the whole arc of the horizon was limned with flame. He was hurtling out of the lunar night, directly into the face of the Sun. At least he would not die in darkness, but the greatest danger was yet to come. For now he was almost back where he had started, nearing the lowest point of his orbit. He glanced at the suit chronometer, and saw that five full hours had now passed. Within minutes, he would hit the Moon – or skim it and pass safely out into space.

As far as he could judge, he was less than twenty miles above the surface, and he was still descending, though very slowly now. Beneath him, the long shadows of the lunar dawn were daggers of darkness, stabbing toward the night land. The steeply slanting sunlight exaggerated every rise in the ground, making even the smallest hills appear to be mountains. And now, unmistakably, the land ahead was rising, wrinkling into the foothills of the Soviet Range. More than a hundred miles away, but approaching at a mile a second, a wave of rock was climbing from the face of the Moon. There was nothing he could do to avoid it; his path was fixed and unalterable. All that could be done had already been done, two and a half hours ago.

It was not enough. He was not going to rise above these mountains; they were rising above him.

Now he regretted his failure to make that second call to the woman who was still waiting, a quarter of a million miles away. Yet perhaps it was just as well, for there had been nothing more to say.

Other voices were calling in the space around him, as he came once more within range of Launch Control. They waxed and waned as he flashed through the radio shadow of the mountains; they were talking about him, but the fact scarcely registered on him. He listened with an impersonal interest, as if to messages from some remote point of space or time, of no concern to him. Once he heard Van Kessel's voice say, quite distinctly: 'Tell *Callisto*'s skipper we'll give him an intercept orbit as soon as we know that Leyland's past perigee. Rendezvous time should be one hour five minutes from now.' I hate to disappoint you, thought Cliff, but that's one appointment I'll never keep.

Now the wall of rock was only fifty miles away, and each time he spun helplessly in space it came ten miles closer. There was no room for optimism now, as he sped more swiftly than a rifle bullet toward that implacable barrier. This was the end, and suddenly it became of great importance to know whether he would meet it face first, with open eyes, or with his back turned, like a coward.

No memories of his past life flashed through Cliff's mind as he counted the seconds that remained. The swiftly unrolling moonscape rotated beneath him, every detail sharp and clear in the harsh light of dawn. Now he was turned away from the onrushing mountains, looking back on the path he had travelled, the path that should have led to Earth. No more than three of his ten-second days were left to him.

And then the moonscape exploded into silent flame. A light as fierce as that of the sun banished the long shadows, struck fire from the peaks and craters spread below. It lasted for only a fraction of a second, and had faded completely before he had turned toward its source.

Directly ahead of him, only twenty miles away, a vast cloud of dust was expanding toward the stars. It was as if a volcano had erupted in the Soviet Range – but that, of course, was impossible. Equally absurd was Cliff's second thought – that by some fantastic feat of organisation and logistics the Farside Engineering Division had blasted away the obstacle in his path.

For it was gone. A huge, crescent shaped bite had been taken out of the approaching skyline; rocks and debris were still rising from a crater that had not existed five seconds ago. Only the energy of an atomic bomb, exploded at precisely the right moment in his path, could have wrought such a miracle. And Cliff did not believe in miracles.

He had made another complete revolution, and was almost upon the mountains, when he remembered that, all this while, there had been a cosmic bulldozer moving invisibly ahead of him. The kinetic energy of the abandoned capsule – a thousand tons, travelling at over a mile a second – was quite sufficient to have blasted the gap through which he was now racing. The impact of the man-made meteor must have jolted the whole of Farside.

His luck held to the end. There was brief pitter-patter of dust particles against his suit, and he caught a blurred glimpse of glowing rocks and swiftly dispersing smoke clouds flashing beneath him. (How strange to see a cloud upon the Moon!) Then he was through the mountains, with nothing ahead but blessed empty sky.

Somewhere up there, an hour in the future along his second orbit, *Callisto* would be moving to meet him. But there was no hurry now; he had escaped from the maelstrom. For better or for worse, he had been granted the gift of life.

There was the launching track, a few miles to the right of his path; it looked like a hairline scribed across the face of the Moon. In a few moments he would be within radio range. Now, with thankfulness and joy, he could make that second call to Earth, to the woman who was still waiting in the African night.

An Ape about the House

First published in *Dude*, May 1962
Collected in *Tales of Ten Worlds*

A timely reminder that we should never underestimate our animal companions' capabilities.

Granny thought it a perfectly horrible idea; but then, she could remember the days when there were *human* servants.

'If you imagine,' she snorted, 'that I'll share the house with a monkey, you're very much mistaken.'

'Don't be so old-fashioned,' I answered. 'Anyway, Dorcas isn't a monkey.'

'Then what is she – it?'

I flipped through the pages of the Biological Engineering Corporation's guide. 'Listen to this, Gran,' I said. ' "The Superchimp (Registered Trademark) *Pan Sapiens* is an intelligent anthropoid, derived by selective breeding and genetic modification from basic chimpanzee stock—" '

'Just what I said! A monkey!'

' " – and with a large-enough vocabulary to understand simple orders. It can be trained to perform all types of domestic work or routine manual labour and is docile, affectionate, housebroken, and particularly good with children—" '

'Children! Would you trust Johnnie and Susan with a – a *gorilla*?'

I put the handbook down with a sigh.

'You've got a point there. Dorcas *is* expensive, and if I find the little monsters knocking her about—'

At this moment, fortunately, the door buzzer sounded. 'Sign, please,' said the delivery man. I signed, and Dorcas entered our lives.

'Hello, Dorcas,' I said. 'I hope you'll be happy here.'

Her big, mournful eyes peered out at me from beneath their heavy ridges. I'd met much uglier humans, though she was rather an odd shape, being only about four feet tall and very nearly as wide. In her neat, plain uniform she looked just like a maid from one of those early twentieth-century movies; her feet, however, were bare and covered an astonishing amount of floor space.

'Morning, Ma'am,' she answered, in slurred but perfectly intelligible accents.

'She can speak!' squawked Granny.

'Of course,' I answered. 'She can pronounce over fifty words, and can understand two hundred. She'll learn more as she grows used to us, but for the moment we must stick to the vocabulary on pages forty-two and forty-three of the handbook.' I passed the instruction manual over to Granny; for once, she couldn't find even a single word to express *her* feelings.

Dorcas settled down very quickly. Her basic training – Class A Domestic, plus Nursery Duties – had been excellent, and by the end of the first month there were very few jobs around the house that she couldn't do, from laying the table to changing the children's clothes. At first she had an annoying habit of picking up things with her feet; it seemed as natural to her as using her hands, and it took a long time to break her of it. One of Granny's cigarette butts finally did the trick.

She was good-natured, conscientious, and didn't answer back. Of course, she was not terribly bright, and some jobs had to be explained to her at great length before she got the point. It took several weeks before I discovered her limitations and allowed for them; at first it was quite hard to remember that she was not exactly human, and that it was no good engaging her in the sort of conversations we women occupy ourselves with when we get together. Or not many of them; she did have an interest in clothes, and was fascinated by colours. If I'd let her dress the way she wanted, she'd have looked like a refugee from Mardi gras.

The children, I was relieved to find, adored her. I know what people say about Johnnie and Sue, and admit that it contains some truth. It's so hard to bring up children when their father's away most of the time, and to make matters worse, Granny spoils them when I'm not looking. So indeed does Eric, whenever his ship's on Earth, and I'm left to cope with the resulting tantrums. Never marry a spaceman if you can possibly avoid it; the pay may be good, but the glamour soon wears off.

By the time Eric got back from the Venus run, with three weeks' accumulated leave, our new maid had settled down as one of the family. Eric took her in his stride; after all, he'd met much odder creatures on the planets. He grumbled about the expense, of course, but I pointed out that now that so much of the housework was taken off my hands, we'd be able to spend more time together and do some of the visiting that had proved impossible in the past. I looked forward to having a little social life again, now that Dorcas could take care of the children.

For there was plenty of social life at Port Goddard, even though we were stuck in the middle of the Pacific. (Ever since what happened to Miami, of course, all major launching sites have been a long, long way from civilisation.) There was a constant flow of distinguished visitors and travellers from all parts of the Earth – not to mention remoter points.

Every community has its arbiter of fashion and culture, its *grande dame* who is resented yet copied by all her unsuccessful rivals. At Port Goddard it was Christine Swanson; her husband was Commodore of the Space Service, and she never let us forget it. Whenever a liner touched down, she would invite all the officers on Base to a reception at her stylishly antique nineteenth-century mansion. It was advisable to go, unless you had a very good excuse, even though that meant looking at Christine's paintings. She fancied herself as an artist, and the walls were hung with multicoloured daubs. Thinking of polite remarks to make about them was one of the major hazards of Christine's parties; another was her metre-long cigarette holder.

There was a new batch of paintings since Eric had been away: Christine had entered her 'square' period. 'You see, my dears,' she explained to us, 'the old-fashioned oblong pictures are terribly dated – they just don't go with the Space Age. There's no such thing as up or down, horizontal or vertical out *there*, so no really modern picture should have one side longer than another. And ideally, it should look *exactly* the same whichever way you hang it – I'm working on that right now.'

'That seems very logical,' said Eric tactfully. (After all, the Commodore was his boss.) But when our hostess was out of earshot, he added, 'I don't know if Christine's pictures are hung the right way up, but I'm sure they're hung the wrong side to the wall.'

I agreed; before I got married I spent several years at the art school and considered I knew something about the subject. Given as much cheek as Christine, I could have made quite a hit with my own canvases, which were now gathering dust in the garage.

'You know, Eric,' I said a little cattily, 'I could teach Dorcas to paint better than this.'

He laughed and answered, 'It might be fun to try it some day, if Christine gets out of hand.' Then I forgot all about the matter – until a month later, when Eric was back in space.

The exact cause of the fight isn't important; it arose over a community development scheme on which Christine and I took opposing viewpoints. She won, as usual, and I left the meeting breathing fire and brimstone. When I got home, the first thing I saw was Dorcas, looking at the coloured pictures in one of the weeklies – and I remembered Eric's words.

I put down my handbag, took off my hat, and said firmly: 'Dorcas – come out to the garage.'

It took some time to dig out my oils and easel from under the pile of discarded toys, old Christmas decorations, skin-diving gear, empty packing cases, and broken tools (it seemed that Eric never had time to tidy up before he shot off into space again). There were several unfinished canvases buried among the debris, which would do for a start. I set up a landscape which had got as far as one skinny tree, and said: 'Now, Dorcas – I'm going to teach you to paint.'

My plan was simple and not altogether honest. Although apes had, of course, splashed paint on canvas often enough in the past, none of them had created a genuine, properly composed work of art. I was sure that Dorcas couldn't either, but no one need know that mine was the guiding hand. She could get all the credit.

I was not actually going to lie to anyone, however. Though I would create the design, mix the pigments, and do most of the execution, I would let Dorcas tackle just as much of the work as she could handle. I hoped that she could fill in the areas of solid colour, and perhaps develop a characteristic style of brushwork in the process. With any luck, I estimated, she might be able to do perhaps a quarter of the actual work. Then I could claim it was all hers with a reasonably clear conscience – for hadn't Michelangelo and Leonardo signed paintings that were largely done by their assistants? I'd be Dorcas' 'assistant'.

I must confess that I was a little disappointed. Though Dorcas quickly got the general idea, and soon understood the use of brush and palette, her execution was very clumsy. She seemed unable to make up her mind which hand to use, but kept transferring the brush from one to the other. In the end I had to do almost all the work and she merely contributed a few dabs of paint.

Still, I could hardly expect her to become a master in a couple of lessons, and it was really of no importance. If Dorcas was an artistic flop, I would just have to stretch the truth a little farther when I claimed that it was all her own work.

I was in no hurry; this was not the sort of thing that could be rushed. At the end of a couple of months, the School of Dorcas had produced a dozen paintings, all of them on carefully chosen themes that would be familiar to a Superchimp at Port Goddard. There was a study of the lagoon, a view of our house, an impression of a night launching (all glare and explosions of light), a fishing scene, a palm grove – clichés, of course, but anything else would rouse suspicion. Before she came to us, I don't suppose Dorcas had seen much of the world outside the labs where she had been reared and trained.

The best of these paintings (and some of them *were* good – after all, I should know) I hung around the house in places where my friends could hardly fail to notice them. Everything worked perfectly; admiring queries were followed by astonished cries of 'You don't say!' when I modestly disclaimed responsibility. There was some scepticism, but I soon demolished that by letting a few privileged friends see Dorcas at work. I chose the viewers for their ignorance of art, and the picture was an abstraction in red, gold, and black which no one dared to criticise. By this time, Dorcas could fake it quite well, like a movie actor pretending to play a musical instrument.

Just to spread the news around, I gave away some of the best paintings, pretending that I considered them no more than amusing novelties – yet at the same time giving just the barest hint of jealousy. 'I've hired Dorcas,' I said testily, 'to work for me – not for the Museum of Modern Art.' And I was *very* careful not to draw any comparisons between her paintings and those of Christine: our mutual friends could be relied upon to do that.

When Christine came to see me, ostensibly to discuss our quarrel 'like two sensible people', I knew that she was on the run. So I capitulated gracefully as we took tea in the drawing room, beneath one of Dorcas's most impressive productions. (Full moon rising over the lagoon – very cold, blue, and mysterious. I was really quite proud of it.) There was not a word about the picture, or about Dorcas; but Christine's eyes told me all I wanted to know. The next week, an exhibition she had been planning was quietly cancelled.

Gamblers say that you should quit when you're ahead of the game. If I had stopped to think, I should have known that Christine would not let the matter rest there. Sooner or later, she was bound to counterattack.

She chose her time well, waiting until the kids were at school, Granny was away visiting, and I was at the shopping centre on the other side of the island. Probably she phoned first to check that no one was at home – no one human, that is. We had told Dorcas not to answer calls; though she'd done so in the early days, it had not been a success. A Superchimp on the phone sounds exactly like a drunk, and this can lead to all sorts of complications.

I can reconstruct the whole sequence of events: Christine must have driven up to the house, expressed acute disappointment at my absence, and invited herself in. She would have wasted no time in getting to work on Dorcas, but luckily I'd taken the precaution of briefing my anthropoid colleague. 'Dorcas make,' I'd said, over and over again, each time one of our productions was finished. 'Not Missy make – *Dorcas* make.' And, in the end, I'm sure she believed this herself.

If my brainwashing, and the limitations of a fifty-word vocabulary, baffled Christine, she did not stay baffled for long. She was a lady of direct action, and Dorcas was a docile and obedient soul. Christine, determined to expose fraud and collusion, must have been gratified by the promptness with which she was led into the garage studio; she must also have been just a little surprised.

I arrived home about half an hour later, and knew that there was trouble afoot as soon as I saw Christine's car parked at the kerb. I could only hope I was in time, but as soon as I stepped into the uncannily silent house, I realised that it was too late. *Something* had happened; Christine would surely be talking, even if she had only an ape as audience. To her, any silence was as great a challenge as a blank canvas; it had to be filled with the sound of her own voice.

The house was utterly still; there was no sign of life. With a sense of mounting apprehension, I tiptoed through the drawing room, the dining room, the kitchen, and out into the back. The garage door was open, and I peered cautiously through.

It was a bitter moment of truth. Finally freed from my influence, Dorcas had at last developed a style of her own. She was swiftly and confidently painting – but not in the way *I* had so carefully taught her. And as for her subject . . .

I was deeply hurt when I saw the caricature that was giving Christine such obvious enjoyment. After all that I had done for Dorcas, this seemed sheer ingratitude. Of course, I know now that no malice was involved, and that she was merely expressing herself. The psychologists, and the critics who wrote those absurd programme notes for her exhibition at the Guggenheim, say that her portraits cast a vivid light on man–animal relationships, and allow us to look for the first time at the human race from outside. But I did not see it *that* way when I ordered Dorcas back into the kitchen.

For the subject was not the only thing that upset me: what really rankled was the thought of all the time I had wasted improving her technique – and her manners. She was ignoring everything I had ever told her, as she sat in front of the easel with her arms folded motionless on her chest.

Even then, at the very beginning of her career as an independent artist, it was painfully obvious that Dorcas had more talent in either of her swiftly moving feet than I had in both my hands.

The Shining Ones

First published in *Playboy*, August 1964
Collected in *The Wind from the Sun*

This again illustrates my fascination with the most mysterious creature of the deep sea. And it was quite daring, back in 1962, to suggest that Russians might be decent human beings.

When the switchboard said that the Soviet Embassy was on the line, my first reaction was: 'Good – another job!' But the moment I heard Goncharov's voice, I knew there was trouble.

'Klaus? This is Mikhail. Can you come over at once? It's very urgent, and I can't talk on the phone.'

I worried all the way to the Embassy, marshalling my defences in case anything had gone wrong at our end. But I could think of nothing; at the moment, we had no outstanding contracts with the Russians. The last job had been completed six months ago, on time, and to their entire satisfaction.

Well, they were not satisfied with it now, as I discovered quickly enough. Mikhail Goncharov, the Commercial Attaché, was an old friend of mine; he told me all he knew, but it was not much.

'We've just had an urgent cable from Ceylon,' he said. 'They want you out there immediately. There's serious trouble at the hydrothermal project.'

'What sort of trouble?' I asked. I knew at once, of course, that it would be the deep end, for that was the only part of the installation that had concerned us. The Russians themselves had done all the work on land, but they had had to call on us to fix those grids three thousand feet down in the Indian Ocean. There is no other firm in the world that can live up to our motto: ANY JOB, ANY DEPTH.

'All I know,' said Mikhail, 'is that the site engineers report a complete breakdown, that the Prime Minister of Ceylon is opening the plant three weeks from now, and that Moscow will be very, very unhappy if it's not working then.'

My mind went rapidly through the penalty clauses in our contract. The firm seemed to be covered, because the client had signed the take-over certificate, thereby admitting that the job was up to specification. However, it was not as simple as that; if negligence on our part was proved, we might be safe from legal action – but it would be very bad for business. And it would be even worse for me, personally; for I had been project supervisor in Trinco Deep.

Don't call me a diver, please; I hate the name. I'm a deep-sea engineer, and I use diving gear about as often as an airman uses a parachute. Most of my work is done with TV and remote-controlled robots. When I do have to go down myself, I'm inside a minisub with external manipulators. We call it a lobster, because of its claws; the standard model works down to five thousand feet, but there are special versions that will operate at the bottom of the Marianas Trench. I've never been there myself, but will be glad to quote terms if you're interested. At a rough estimate, it will cost you a dollar a foot plus a thousand an hour on the job itself.

I realised that the Russians meant business when Mikhail said that a jet was waiting at Zurich, and could I be at the airport within two hours?

'Look,' I said, 'I can't do a thing without equipment – and the gear needed even for an inspection weighs tons. Besides, it's all at Spezia.'

'I know,' Mikhail answered implacably. 'We'll have another jet transport there. Cable from Ceylon as soon as you know what you want: it will be on the site within twelve hours. But please don't talk to anyone about this; we prefer to keep our problems to ourselves.'

I agreed with this, for it was my problem, too. As I left the office, Mikhail pointed to the wall calendar, said 'Three weeks', and ran his finger around his throat. And I knew he wasn't thinking of *his* neck.

Two hours later I was climbing over the Alps, saying goodbye to the family by radio, and wondering why, like every other sensible Swiss, I hadn't become a banker or gone into the watch business. It was all the fault of the Picards and Hannes Keller, I told myself moodily: why did they have to start this deep-sea tradition, in Switzerland of all countries? Then I settled down to sleep, knowing that I would have little enough in the days to come.

We landed at Trincomalee just after dawn, and the huge, complex harbour – whose geography I've never quite mastered – was a maze of capes, islands, interconnecting waterways, and basins large enough to hold all the navies of the world. I could see the big white control building, in a somewhat flamboyant architectural style, on a headland overlooking the Indian Ocean. The site was pure propaganda – though of course if I'd been Russian I'd have called it 'public relations'.

Not that I really blamed my clients; they had good reason to be proud of this, the most ambitious attempt yet made to harness the thermal energy of the sea. It was not the first attempt. There had been an unsuccessful one by the French scientist Georges Claude in the 1930s, and a much bigger one at Abidjan, on the west coast of Africa, in the 1950s.

All these projects depended on the same surprising fact: even in the tropics the sea a mile down is almost at freezing point. Where billions of tons of water are concerned, this temperature difference represents a colossal amount of energy – and a fine challenge to the engineers of power-starved countries.

Claude and his successors had tried to tap this energy with low-pressure steam engines; the Russians had used a much simpler and more direct method. For over a hundred years it had been known that electric currents flow in many materials if one end is heated and the other cooled, and ever since the 1940s Russian scientists had been working to put this 'thermo-electric' effect to practical use. Their earliest devices had not been very efficient – though good enough to power thousands of radios by the heat of kerosene lamps. But in 1974 they had made a big, and still-secret, break-through. Though I fixed the power elements at the cold end of the system, I never really saw them; they were completely hidden in anticorrosive paint. All I know is that they formed a big grid, like lots of old-fashioned steam radiators bolted together.

I recognised most of the faces in the little crowd waiting on the Trinco airstrip; friends or enemies, they all seemed glad to see me – especially Chief Engineer Shapiro.

'Well, Lev,' I said, as we drove out in the station wagon, 'what's the trouble?'

'We don't know,' he said frankly. 'It's your job to find out – and to put it right.'

'Well, what *happened*?'

'Everything worked perfectly up to the full-power tests,' he answered. 'Output was within five per cent of estimate until 0134 Tuesday morning.' He grimaced; obviously that time was engraved on his heart. 'Then the voltage started to fluctuate violently, so we cut the load and watched the meters. I thought that some idiot of a skipper had hooked the cables – you know the trouble we've taken to avoid *that* happening – so we switched on the searchlights and looked out to sea. There wasn't a ship in sight. Anyway, who would have tried to anchor just *outside* the harbour on a clear, calm night?

'There was nothing we could do except watch the instruments and keep testing; I'll show you all the graphs when we get to the office. After four minutes everything went open circuit. We can locate the break exactly, of course – and it's in the deepest part, right at the grid. It *would* be there, and not at *this* end of the system,' he added gloomily, pointing out the window.

We were just driving past the Solar Pond – the equivalent of the boiler in a conventional heat engine. This was an idea that the Russians had borrowed from the Israelis. It was simply a shallow lake, blackened at the bottom, holding a concentrated solution of brine. It acts as a very efficient heat trap, and the sun's rays bring the liquid up to almost two hundred degrees Fahrenheit. Submerged in it were the 'hot' grids of the thermo-electric system, every inch of two fathoms down. Massive cables connected them to my department, a hundred and fifty degrees colder and three thousand feet lower, in the undersea canyon that comes to the very entrance of Trinco harbour.

'I suppose you checked for earthquakes?' I asked, not very hopefully.

'Of course. There was nothing on the seismograph.'

'What about whales? I warned you that they might give trouble.'

More than a year ago, when the main conductors were being run out to sea, I'd told the engineers about the drowned sperm whale found entangled in a telegraph cable half a mile down off South America. About a dozen similar cases are known – but ours, it seemed, was not one of them.

'That was the second thing we thought of,' answered Shapiro. 'We got on to the Fisheries Department, the Navy, and the Air Force. No whales anywhere along the coast.'

It was at that point that I stopped theorising, because I overheard something that made me a little uncomfortable. Like all Swiss, I'm good at languages, and have picked up a fair amount of Russian. There was no need to be much of a linguist, however, to recognise the word *sabotash*.

It was spoken by Dimitri Karpukhin, the political adviser on the project. I didn't like him; nor did the engineers, who sometimes went out of their way to be rude to him. One of the old-style Communists who had never quite escaped from the shadow of Stalin, he was suspicious of everything outside the Soviet Union, and most of the things inside it. Sabotage was just the explanation that would appeal to him.

There were, of course, a great many people who would not exactly be brokenhearted if the Trinco Power Project failed. Politically, the prestige of the USSR was committed; economically, billions were involved, for if hydrothermal plants proved a success, they might compete with oil, coal, water power, and, especially, nuclear energy.

Yet I could not really believe in sabotage; after all, the Cold War was over. It was just possible that someone had made a clumsy attempt to grab a sample of the grid, but even this seemed unlikely. I could count on my fingers the number of people in the world who could tackle such a job – and half of them were on my payroll.

The underwater TV camera arrived that same evening, and by working all through the night we had cameras, monitors, and over a mile of coaxial cable loaded aboard a launch. As we pulled out of the harbour, I thought I saw a familiar figure standing on the jetty, but it was too far to be certain and I had other things on my mind. If you must know, I am not a good sailor; I am only really happy *underneath* the sea.

We took a careful fix on the Round Island lighthouse and stationed ourselves directly above the grid. The self-propelled camera, looking like a midget bathyscape, went over the side; as we watched the monitors, we went with it in spirit.

The water was extremely clear, and extremely empty, but as we neared the bottom there were a few signs of life. A small shark came and stared at us. Then a pulsating blob of jelly went drifting by, followed by a thing like a big spider, with hundreds of hairy legs tangling and twisting together. At last the sloping canyon wall swam into view. We were right on target, for there were the thick cables running down into the depths, just as I had seen them when I made the final check of the installation six months ago.

I turned on the low-powered jets and let the camera drift down the power cables. They seemed in perfect condition, still firmly anchored by the pitons we had driven into the rock. It was not until I came to the grid itself that there was any sign of trouble.

Have you ever seen the radiator grille of a car after it's run into a lamppost? Well, one section of the grid looked very much like that. Something had battered it in, as if a madman had gone to work on it with a sledgehammer.

There were gasps of astonishment and anger from the people looking over my shoulder. I heard *sabotash* muttered again, and for the first time began to take it seriously. The only other explanation that made sense was a falling boulder, but the slopes of the canyon had been carefully checked against this very possibility.

Whatever the cause, the damaged grid had to be replaced. That could not be done until my lobster – all twenty tons of it – had been flown out from the Spezia dockyard where it was kept between jobs.

'Well,' said Shapiro, when I had finished my visual inspection and photographed the sorry spectacle on the screen, 'how long will it take?'

I refused to commit myself. The first thing I ever learned in the underwater business is that no job turns out as you expect. Cost and time estimates can never be firm because it's not until you're halfway through a contract that you know exactly what you're up against.

My private guess was three days. So I said: 'If everything goes well, it shouldn't take more than a week.'

Shapiro groaned. 'Can't you do it quicker?'

'I won't tempt fate by making rash promises. Anyway, that still gives you two weeks before your deadline.'

He had to be content with that, though he kept nagging at me all the way back into the harbour. When we got there, he had something else to think about.

'Morning, Joe,' I said to the man who was still waiting patiently on the jetty. 'I thought I recognised you on the way out. What are *you* doing here?'

'I was going to ask you the same question.'

'You'd better speak to my boss. Chief Engineer Shapiro, meet Joe Watkins, science correspondent of *Time*.'

Lev's response was not exactly cordial. Normally, there was nothing he liked better than talking to newsmen, who arrived at the rate of about one a week. Now, as the target date approached, they would be flying in from all directions. Including, of course, Russia. And at the present moment Tass would be just as unwelcome as *Time*.

It was amusing to see how Karpukhin took charge of the situation. From that moment, Joe had permanently attached to him as guide, philosopher, and drinking companion a smooth young public-relations type named Sergei Markov. Despite all Joe's efforts, the two were inseparable. In the middle of the afternoon, weary after a long conference in Shapiro's office, I caught up with them for a belated lunch at the government resthouse.

'What's going on here, Klaus?' Joe asked pathetically. 'I smell trouble, but no one will admit anything.'

I toyed with my curry, trying to separate the bits that were safe from those that would take off the top of my head.

'You can't expect me to discuss a client's affairs,' I answered.

'You were talkative enough,' Joe reminded me, 'when you were doing the survey for the Gibraltar Dam.'

'Well, yes,' I admitted. 'And I appreciate the write-up you gave me. But this time there are trade secrets involved. I'm – ah – making some last-minute adjustments to improve the efficiency of the system.'

And that, of course, was the truth; for I was indeed hoping to raise the efficiency of the system from its present value of exactly zero.

'Hmm,' said Joe sarcastically. 'Thank you very much.'

'Anyway,' I said, trying to head him off, 'what's *your* latest crackbrained theory?'

For a highly competent science writer, Joe has an odd liking for the bizarre and the improbable. Perhaps it's a form of escapism; I happen to know that he also writes science fiction, though this is a well-kept secret from his employers. He has a sneaking fondness for poltergeists and ESP and flying saucers, but lost continents are his real specialty.

'I *am* working on a couple of ideas,' he admitted. 'They cropped up when I was doing the research on this story.'

'Go on,' I said, not daring to look up from the analysis of my curry.

'The other day I came across a very old map – Ptolemy's, if you're interested – of Ceylon. It reminded me of another old map in my collection, and I turned it up. There was the same central mountain, the same arrangement of rivers flowing to the sea. But *this* was a map of Atlantis.'

'Oh, no!' I groaned. 'Last time we met, you convinced me that Atlantis was the western Mediterranean basin.'

Joe gave his engaging grin.

'I could be wrong, couldn't I? Anyway, I've a much more striking piece of evidence. What's the old national name for Ceylon – and the modern Sinhalese one, for that matter?'

I thought for a second, then exclaimed: 'Good Lord! Why Lanka, of course. Lanka – Atlantis.' I rolled the names off my tongue.

'Precisely,' said Joe. 'But two clues, however striking, don't make a full-fledged theory; and that's as far as I've got at the moment.'

'Too bad,' I said, genuinely disappointed. 'And your other project?'

'This will really make you sit up,' Joe answered smugly. He reached into the battered briefcase he always carried and pulled out a bundle of papers.

'This happened only one hundred and eighty miles from here, and just over a century ago. The source of my information, you'll note, is about the best there is.'

He handed me a photostat, and I saw that it was a page of the London *Times* for July 4, 1874. I started to read without much enthusiasm, for Joe was always producing bits of ancient newspapers, but my apathy did not last for long.

Briefly – I'd like to give the whole thing, but if you want more details your local library can dial you a facsimile in ten seconds – the clipping described how the one-hundred-and-fifty-ton schooner *Pearl* left Ceylon in early May 1874 and then fell becalmed in the Bay of Bengal. On May 10, just before nightfall, an enormous squid surfaced half a mile from the schooner, whose captain foolishly opened fire on it with his rifle.

The squid swam straight for the *Pearl*, grabbed the masts with its arms, and pulled the vessel over on her side. She sank within seconds, taking two of her crew with her. The others were rescued only by the lucky chance that the P. and O. steamer *Strathowen* was in sight and had witnessed the incident herself.

'Well,' said Joe, when I'd read through it for the second time, 'what do you think?'

'I don't believe in sea monsters.'

'The London *Times*,' Joe answered, 'is not prone to sensational journalism. And giant squids exist, though the biggest *we* know about are feeble, flabby beasts and don't weigh more than a ton, even when they have arms forty feet long.'

'So? An animal like that couldn't capsize a hundred-and-fifty-ton schooner.'

'True – but there's a lot of evidence that the so-called *giant* squid is merely a large squid. There may be decapods in the sea that really are giants. Why, only a year after the *Pearl* incident, a sperm whale off the coast of Brazil was seen struggling inside gigantic coils which finally *dragged it down into the sea*. You'll find the incident described in the *Illustrated London News* for November 20, 1875. And then, of course, there's that chapter in *Moby Dick*. . . .'

'What chapter?'

'Why, the one called "Squid". We know that Melville was a very careful observer – but here he really lets himself go. He describes a calm day when a great white mass rose out of the sea "like a snow-slide, new slid from the hills". And this happened here in the Indian Ocean, perhaps a thousand miles south of the *Pearl* incident. Weather conditions were identical, please note.

'What the men of the *Pequod* saw floating on the water – I know this passage by heart, I've studied it so carefully – was a "vast pulpy mass, furlongs in length and breadth, of a glancing cream-colour, innumerable long arms radiating from its centre, curling and twisting like a nest of anacondas".'

'Just a minute,' said Sergei, who had been listening to all this with rapt attention. 'What's a furlong?'

Joe looked slightly embarrassed.

'Actually, it's an eighth of a mile – six hundred and sixty feet.' He raised his hand to stop our incredulous laughter. 'Oh, I'm sure Melville didn't mean that *literally*. But here was a man who met sperm whales every day, groping for a unit of length to describe something a lot bigger. So he automatically jumped from fathoms to furlongs. That's my theory, anyway.'

I pushed away the remaining untouchable portions of my curry.

'If you think you've scared me out of my job,' I said, 'you've failed miserably. But I promise you this – when I do meet a giant squid, I'll snip off a tentacle and bring it back as a souvenir.'

Twenty-four hours later I was out there in the lobster, sinking slowly down toward the damaged grid. There was no way in which the operation could be kept secret, and Joe was an interested spectator from a nearby launch. That was the Russians' problem, not mine; I had suggested to Shapiro that they take him into their confidence, but this, of course, was vetoed by Karpukhin's suspicious Slavic mind. One could almost see him thinking: Just *why* should an American reporter turn up at this moment? And ignoring the obvious answer that Trincomalee was now big news.

There is nothing in the least exciting or glamorous about deep-water operations – if they're done properly. Excitement means lack of foresight, and that means incompetence. The incompetent do not last long in my business, nor do those who crave excitement. I went about my job with all the pent-up emotion of a plumber dealing with a leaking faucet.

The grids had been designed for easy maintenance, since sooner or later they would have to be replaced. Luckily, none of the threads had been damaged, and the securing nuts came off easily when gripped with the power wrench. Then I switched control to the heavy-duty claws, and lifted out the damaged grid without the slightest difficulty.

It's bad tactics to hurry an underwater operation. If you try to do too much at once, you are liable to make mistakes. And if things go smoothly and you finish in a day a job you said would take a week, the client feels he hasn't had his money's worth. Though I was sure I could replace the grid that same afternoon, I followed the damaged unit up to the surface and closed shop for the day.

The thermoelement was rushed off for an autopsy, and I spent the rest of the evening hiding from Joe. Trinco is a small town, but I managed to keep out of his way by visiting the local cinema, where I sat through several hours of an interminable Tamil movie in which three successive generations suffered identical domestic crises of mistaken identity, drunkenness, desertion, death, and insanity, all in Technicolor and with the sound track turned full up.

The next morning, despite a mild headache, I was at the site soon after dawn. (So was Joe, and so was Sergei, all set for a quiet day's fishing.) I cheerfully waved to them as I climbed into the lobster, and the tender's crane lowered me over the side. Over the other side, where Joe couldn't see it, went the replacement grid. A few fathoms down I lifted it out of the hoist and carried it to the bottom of Trinco Deep, where, without any trouble, it was installed by the middle of the afternoon. Before I surfaced again, the lock nuts had been secured, the conductors spot-welded, and the engineers on shore had completed their continuity tests. By the time I was back on deck, the system was under load once more, everything was back to normal, and even Karpukhin was smiling – except when he stopped to ask himself the question that no one had yet been able to answer.

I still clung to the falling-boulder theory – for want of a better. And I hoped that the Russians would accept it, so that we could stop this silly cloak-and-dagger business with Joe.

No such luck, I realised, when both Shapiro and Karpukhin came to see me with very long faces.

'Klaus,' said Lev, 'we want you to go down again.'

'It's your money,' I replied. 'But what do you want me to do?'

'We've examined the damaged grid, and there's a section of the thermo-element missing. Dimitri thinks that – someone – has deliberately broken it off and carried it away.'

'Then they did a damn clumsy job,' I answered. 'I can promise you it wasn't one of *my* men.'

It was risky to make such jokes around Karpukhin, and no one was at all amused. Not even me; for by this time I was beginning to think that he had something.

The sun was setting when I began my last dive into Trinco Deep, but the end of day has no meaning down there. I fell for two thousand feet with no lights, because I like to watch the luminous creatures of the sea, as they flash and flicker in the darkness, sometimes exploding like rockets just outside the observation window. In this open water, there was no danger of a collision; in any case, I had the panoramic sonar scan running, and that gave far better warning than my eyes.

At four hundred fathoms, I knew that something was wrong. The bottom was coming into view on the vertical sounder – but it was approaching much too slowly. My rate of descent was far too slow. I could increase it easily enough by flooding another buoyancy tank – but I hesitated to do so. In my business, anything out of the ordinary needs an explanation; three times I have saved my life by waiting until I had one.

The thermometer gave me the answer. The temperature outside was five degrees higher than it should have been, and I am sorry to say that it took me several seconds to realise why.

Only a few hundred feet below me, the repaired grid was now running at full power, pouring out megawatts of heat as it tried to equalise the temperature difference between Trinco Deep and the Solar Pond up there on land. It wouldn't succeed, of course; but in the attempt it was generating electricity – and I was being swept upward in the geyser of warm water that was an incidental by-product.

When I finally reached the grid, it was quite difficult to keep the lobster in position against the upwelling current, and I began to sweat uncomfortably as the heat penetrated into the cabin. Being too hot on the sea bed was a novel experience; so also was the miragelike vision caused by the ascending water, which made my searchlights dance and tremble over the rock face I was exploring.

You must picture me, lights ablaze in that five-hundred-fathom darkness, moving slowly down the slope of the canyon, which at this spot was about as steep as the roof of a house. The missing element – *if* it was still around – could not have fallen very far before coming to rest. I would find it in ten minutes, or not at all.

After an hour's searching, I had turned up several broken light bulbs (it's astonishing how many get thrown overboard from ships – the sea beds of the world are covered with them), an empty beer bottle (same comment), and a brand-new boot. That was the last thing I found, for then I discovered that I was no longer alone.

I never switch off the sonar scan, and even when I'm not moving I always glance at the screen about once a minute to check the general situation. The situation now was that a large object – at least the size of the lobster – was approaching from the north. When I spotted it, the range was about five hundred feet and closing slowly. I switched off my lights, cut the jets I had been running at low power to hold me in the turbulent water, and drifted with the current.

Though I was tempted to call Shapiro and report that I had company, I decided to wait for more information. There were only three nations with depth ships that could operate at this level, and I was on excellent terms with all of them. It would never do to be too hasty, and to get myself involved in unnecessary political complications.

Though I felt blind without the sonar, I did not wish to advertise my presence, so I reluctantly switched it off and relied on my eyes. Anyone working at this depth would have to use lights, and I'd see them coming long before they could see me. So I waited in the hot, silent little cabin, straining my eyes into the darkness, tense and alert but not particularly worried.

First there was a dim glow, at an indefinite distance. It grew bigger and brighter, yet refused to shape itself into any pattern that my mind could recognise. The diffuse glow concentrated into myriad spots, until it seemed that a constellation was sailing toward me. Thus might the rising star clouds of the galaxy appear, from some world close to the heart of the Milky Way.

It is not true that men are frightened of the unknown; they can be frightened only of the known, the already experienced. I could not imagine what was approaching, but no creature of the sea could touch me inside six inches of good Swiss armour plate.

The thing was almost upon me, glowing with the light of its own creation, when it split into two separate clouds. Slowly they came into focus – not of my eyes, but of my understanding – and I knew that beauty and terror were rising toward me out of the abyss.

The terror came first, when I saw that the approaching beasts were squids, and all Joe's tales reverberated in my brain. Then, with a considerable sense of letdown, I realised that they were only about twenty feet long – little larger than the lobster, and a mere fraction of its weight. They could do me no harm. And quite apart from that, their indescribable beauty robbed them of all menace.

This sounds ridiculous, but it is true. In my travels I have seen most of the animals of this world, but none to match the luminous apparitions floating before me now. The coloured lights that pulsed and danced along their bodies made them seem clothed with jewels, never the same for two seconds at a time. There were patches that glowed a brilliant blue, like flickering mercury arcs, then changed almost instantly to burning neon red. The tentacles seemed strings of luminous beads, trailing through the water – or the lamps along a superhighway, when you look down upon it from the air at night. Barely visible against this background glow were the enormous eyes, uncannily human and intelligent, each surrounded by a diadem of shining pearls.

I am sorry, but that is the best I can do. Only the movie camera could do justice to these living kaleidoscopes. I do not know how long I watched them, so entranced by their luminous beauty that I had almost forgotten my mission. That those delicate, whiplash tentacles could not possibly have broken the grid was already obvious. Yet the presence of these creatures here was, to say the least, very curious. Karpukhin would have called it suspicious.

I was about to call the surface when I saw something incredible. It had been before my eyes all the time, but I had not realised it until now.

The squids were talking to each other.

Those glowing, evanescent patterns were not coming and going at random. They were as meaningful, I was suddenly sure, as the illuminated signs of Broadway or Piccadilly. Every few seconds there was an image that almost made sense, but it vanished before I could interpret it. I knew, of course, that even the common octopus shows its emotions with lightning-fast colour changes – but this was something of a much higher order. It was real communication: here were two living electric signs, flashing messages to one another.

When I saw an unmistakable picture of the lobster, my last doubts vanished. Though I am no scientist, at that moment I shared the feelings of a Newton or an Einstein at some moment of revelation. *This* would make me famous. . . .

Then the picture changed – in a most curious manner. There was the lobster again, but rather smaller. And there beside it, much smaller still, were two peculiar objects. Each consisted of a pair of black dots surrounded by a pattern of ten radiating lines.

Just now I said that we Swiss are good at languages. However, it required little intelligence to deduce that this was a formalised squid's eye-view of itself, and that what I was seeing was a crude sketch of the situation. But why the absurdly small size of the squids?

I had no time to puzzle that out before there was another change. A third squid symbol appeared on the living screen – and this one was enormous, completely dwarfing the others. The message shone there in the eternal night for a few seconds. Then the creature bearing it shot off at incredible speed, and left me alone with its companion.

Now the meaning was all too obvious. 'My God!' I said to myself. 'They feel they can't handle me. They've gone to fetch Big Brother.'

And of Big Brother's capabilities, I already had better evidence than Joe Watkins, for all his research and newspaper clippings.

That was the point – you won't be surprised to hear – when I decided not to linger. But before I went, I thought I would try some talking myself.

After hanging here in darkness for so long, I had forgotten the power of my lights. They hurt my eyes, and must have been agonising to the unfortunate squid. Transfixed by that intolerable glare, its own illumination utterly quenched, it lost all its beauty, becoming no more than a pallid bag of jelly with two black buttons for eyes. For a moment it seemed paralysed by the shock; then it darted after its companion, while I soared upward to a world that could never be the same again.

'I've found your saboteur,' I told Karpukhin, when they opened the hatch of the lobster. 'If you want to know all about him, ask Joe Watkins.'

I let Dimitri sweat over that for a few seconds, while I enjoyed his expression. Then I gave my slightly edited report. I implied – without actually saying so – that the squids I'd met were powerful enough to have done all the damage: and I said nothing about the conversation I'd overseen. That would only cause incredulity. Besides, I wanted time to think matters over, and to tidy up the loose ends – if I could.

Joe has been a great help, though he still knows no more than the Russians. He's told me what wonderfully developed nervous systems squids possess, and has explained how some of them can change their appearance in a flash through instantaneous three-colour printing, thanks to the extraordinary network of 'chromophores' covering their bodies. Presumably this evolved for camouflage; but it seems natural – even inevitable – that it should develop into a communication system.

But there's one thing that worries Joe.

'What were they *doing* around the grid?' he keeps asking me plaintively. 'They're cold-blooded invertebrates. You'd expect them to dislike heat as much as they object to light.'

That puzzles Joe; but it doesn't puzzle me. Indeed, I think it's the key to the whole mystery.

Those squids, I'm now certain, are in Trinco Deep for the same reason that there are men at the South Pole – or on the Moon. Pure scientific curiosity has drawn them from their icy home, to investigate this geyser of hot water welling from the sides of the canyon. Here is a strange and inexplicable phenomenon – possibly one that menaces their way of life. So they have summoned their giant cousin (servant? slave!) to bring them a sample for study. I cannot believe that they have a hope of understanding it; after all, no scientist on earth could have done so as little as a century ago. But they are trying; and that is what matters.

Tomorrow, we begin our countermeasures. I go back into Trinco Deep to fix the great lights that Shapiro hopes will keep the squids at bay. But how long will that ruse work, if intelligence is dawning in the deep?

As I dictate this, I'm sitting here below the ancient battlements of Fort Frederick, watching the Moon come up over the Indian Ocean. If everything goes well, this will serve as the opening of the book that Joe has been badgering me to write. If it doesn't – then hello, Joe, I'm talking to *you* now. Please edit this for publication, in any way you think fit, and my apologies to you and Lev for not giving you all the facts before. Now you'll understand why.

Whatever happens, please remember this: they are beautiful, wonderful creatures; try to come to terms with them if you can.

To: Ministry of Power, Moscow
From: Lev Shapiro, Chief Engineer, Trincomalee Thermoelectric Power Project

Herewith the complete transcript of the tape recording found among Herr Klaus Muller's effects after his last dive. We are much indebted to Mr Joe Watkins, of *Time*, for assistance on several points.

You will recall that Herr Muller's last intelligible message was directed to Mr Watkins and ran as follows: 'Joe! You were right about Melville! The thing is absolutely gigan—'

The Secret

First published in *This Week*, 11 August 1963, as 'The Secret of the Men in the Moon'
Collected in *The Wind from the Sun*

Henry Cooper had been on the Moon for almost two weeks before he discovered that something was wrong. At first it was only an ill-defined suspicion, the sort of hunch that a hardheaded science reporter would not take too seriously. He had come here, after all, at the United Nations Space Administration's own request. UNSA had always been hot on public relations – especially just before budget time, when an overcrowded world was screaming for more roads and schools and sea farms, and complaining about the billions being poured into space.

So here he was, doing the lunar circuit for the second time, and beaming back two thousand words of copy a day. Although the novelty had worn off, there still remained the wonder and mystery of a world as big as Africa, thoroughly mapped, yet almost completely unexplored. A stone's throw away from the pressure domes, the labs, the spaceports, was a yawning emptiness that would challenge men for centuries to come.

Some parts of the Moon were almost too familiar, of course. Who had not seen that dusty scar in the Mare Imbrium, with its gleaming metal pylon and the plaque that announced in the three official languages of Earth:

ON THIS SPOT

AT 2001 UT

13 SEPTEMBER 1959

THE FIRST MAN-MADE OBJECT REACHED ANOTHER WORLD

Cooper had visited the grave of Lunik II – and the more famous tomb of the men who had come after it. But these things belonged to the past; already, like Columbus and the Wright brothers, they were receding into history. What concerned him now was the future.

When he had landed at Archimedes Spaceport, the Chief Administrator had been obviously glad to see him, and had shown a personal interest in his tour. Transportation, accommodation, and official guide were all arranged. He could go anywhere he liked, ask any questions he pleased. UNSA trusted him, for his stories had always been accurate, his attitude friendly. Yet the tour had gone sour; he did not know why, but he was going to find out.

He reached for the phone and said: 'Operator? Please get me the Police Department. I want to speak to the Inspector General.'

Presumably Chandra Coomaraswamy possessed a uniform, but Cooper had never seen him wearing it. They met, as arranged, at the entrance to the little park that was Plato City's chief pride and joy. At this time in the morning of the artificial twenty-four-hour 'day' it was almost deserted, and they could talk without interruption.

As they walked along the narrow gravel paths, they chatted about old times, the friends they had known at college together, the latest developments in interplanetary politics. They had reached the middle of the park, under the exact centre of the great blue-painted dome, when Cooper came to the point.

'You know everything that's hapening on the Moon, Chandra,' he said. 'And you know that I'm here to do a series for UNSA – hope to make a book out of it when I get back to Earth. So why should people be trying to hide things from me?'

It was impossible to hurry Chandra. He always took his time to answer questions, and his few words escaped with difficulty around the stem of his hand-carved Bavarian pipe.

'What people?' he asked at length.

'You've really no idea?'

The Inspector General shook his head.

'Not the faintest,' he answered; and Cooper knew that he was telling the truth. Chandra might be silent, but he would not lie.

'I was afraid you'd say that. Well, if you don't know any more than I do, here's the only clue I have – and it frightens me. Medical Research is trying to keep me at arm's length.'

'Hmm,' replied Chandra, taking his pipe from his mouth and looking at it thoughtfully.

'Is that all you have to say?'

'You haven't given me much to work on. Remember, I'm only a cop: I lack your vivid journalistic imagination.'

'All I can tell you is that the higher I get in Medical Research, the colder the atmosphere becomes. Last time I was here, everyone was very friendly, and gave me some fine stories. But now, I can't even meet the Director. He's always too busy, or on the other side of the Moon. Anyway, what sort of man is he?'

'Dr Hastings? Prickly little character. Very competent, but not easy to work with.'

'What could he be trying to hide?'

'Knowing you, I'm sure you have some interesting theories.'

'Oh, I thought of narcotics, and fraud, and political conspiracies – but

818

they don't make sense, in these days. So what's left scares the hell out of me.'

Chandra's eyebrows signalled a silent question mark.

'Interplanetary plague,' said Cooper bluntly.

'I thought that was impossible.'

'Yes – I've written articles myself proving that the life forms on other planets have such alien chemistries that they can't react with us, and that all our microbes and bugs took millions of years to adapt to our bodies. But I've always wondered if it was true. Suppose a ship has come back from Mars, say, with something *really* vicious – and the doctors can't cope with it?'

There was a long silence. Then Chandra said: 'I'll start investigating. *I* don't like it either, for here's an item you probably don't know. There were three nervous breakdowns in the Medical Division last month – and that's very, very unusual.'

He glanced at his watch, then at the false sky, which seemed so distant, yet which was only two hundred feet above their heads.

'We'd better get moving,' he said. 'The morning shower's due in five minutes.'

The call came two weeks later, in the middle of the night – the real lunar night. By Plato City time, it was Sunday morning.

'Henry? Chandra here. Can you meet me in half an hour at air lock five? Good – I'll see you.'

This was it, Cooper knew. Air lock five meant that they were going outside the dome. Chandra had found something.

The presence of the police driver restricted conversation as the tractor moved away from the city along the road roughly bulldozed across the ash and pumice. Low in the south, Earth was almost full, casting a brilliant blue-green light over the infernal landscape. However hard one tried, Cooper told himself, it was difficult to make the Moon appear glamorous. But nature guards her greatest secrets well; to such places men must come to find them.

The multiple domes of the city dropped below the sharply curved horizon. Presently, the tractor turned aside from the main road to follow a scarcely visible trail. Ten minutes later, Cooper saw a single glittering hemisphere ahead of them, standing on an isolated ridge of rock. Another vehicle, bearing a red cross, was parked beside the entrance. It seemed that they were not the only visitors.

Nor were they unexpected. As they drew up to the dome, the flexible tube of the air-lock coupling groped out toward them and snapped into place against their tractor's outer hull. There was a brief hissing as pressure equalised. Then Cooper followed Chandra into the building.

The air-lock operator led them along curving corridors and radial passageways toward the centre of the dome. Sometimes they caught glimpses of laboratories, scientific instruments, computers – all perfectly ordinary, and all deserted on this Sunday morning. They must have reached the heart of the building, Cooper told himself when their guide ushered them into a large circular chamber and shut the door softly behind them.

It was a small zoo. All around them were cages, tanks, jars containing a wide selection of the fauna and flora of Earth. Waiting at its centre was a short, grey-haired man, looking very worried, and very unhappy.

'Dr Hastings,' said Coomaraswamy, 'meet Mr Cooper.' The Inspector General turned to his companion and added, 'I've convinced the Doctor that there's only one way to keep you quiet – and that's to tell you everything.'

'Frankly,' said Hastings, 'I'm not sure if I give a damn any more.' His voice was unsteady, barely under control, and Cooper thought, Hello! There's another breakdown on the way.

The scientist wasted no time on such formalities as shaking hands. He walked to one of the cages, took out a small bundle of fur, and held it toward Cooper.

'Do you know what this is?' he asked abruptly.

'Of course. A hamster – the commonest lab animal.'

'Yes,' said Hastings. 'A perfectly ordinary golden hamster. Except that this one is five years old – like all the others in this cage.'

'Well? What's odd about that?'

'Oh, nothing, nothing at all . . . except for the trifling fact that hamsters live for only two years. And we have some here that are getting on for ten.'

For a moment no one spoke; but the room was not silent. It was full of rustlings and slitherings and scratchings, of faint whimpers and tiny animal cries. Then Cooper whispered: 'My God – you've found a way of prolonging life!'

'No,' retorted Hastings. 'We've not found it. The Moon has given it to us . . . as we might have expected, if we'd looked in front of our noses.'

He seemed to have gained control over his emotions – as if he was once more the pure scientist, fascinated by a discovery for its own sake and heedless of its implications.

'On Earth,' he said, 'we spend our whole lives fighting gravity. It wears down our muscles, pulls our stomachs out of shape. In seventy years, how many tons of blood does the heart lift through how many miles? And all that work, all that strain is reduced to a sixth here on the Moon, where a one-hundred-and-eighty-pound human weighs only thirty pounds.'

'I see,' said Cooper slowly. 'Ten years for a hamster – and how long for a man?'

'It's not a simple law,' answered Hastings. 'It varies with the size and the species. Even a month ago, we weren't certain. But now we're quite sure of this: on the Moon, the span of human life will be at least two hundred years.'

'And you've been trying to keep it secret!'

'You fool! Don't you understand?'

'Take it easy, Doctor – take it easy,' said Chandra softly.

With an obvious effort of will, Hastings got control of himself again. He began to speak with such icy calm that his words sank like freezing raindrops into Cooper's mind.

'Think of them up there,' he said, pointing to the roof, to the invisible Earth, whose looming presence no one on the Moon could ever forget. 'Six billion of them, packing all the continents to the edges – and now crowding over into the sea beds. And here – ' he pointed to the ground – 'only a hundred thousand of *us*, on an almost empty world. But a world where we need miracles of technology and engineering merely to exist, where a man with an IQ of only a hundred and fifty can't even get a job.

'And now we find that we can live for two hundred years. Imagine how they're going to react to *that* news! This is your problem now, Mister Journalist; you've asked for it, and you've got it. Tell me this, please – I'd really be interested to know – *just how are you going to break it to them?*'

He waited, and waited. Cooper opened his mouth, then closed it again, unable to think of anything to say.

In the far corner of the room, a baby monkey started to cry.

Dial F for Frankenstein

First published in *Playboy*, January 1965
Collected in *The Wind from the Sun*

At 0150 GMT on December 1, 1975, every telephone in the world started to ring.

A quarter of a billion people picked up their receivers, to listen for a few seconds with annoyance or perplexity. Those who had been awakened in the middle of the night assumed that some far-off friend was calling, over the satellite telephone network that had gone into service, with such a blaze of publicity, the day before. But there was no voice on the line; only a sound, which to many seemed like the roaring of the sea; to others, like the vibrations of harp strings in the wind. And there were many more, in that moment, who recalled a secret sound of childhood – the noise of blood pulsing through the veins, heard when a shell is cupped over the ear. Whatever it was, it lasted no more than twenty seconds. Then it was replaced by the dial tone.

The world's subscribers cursed, muttered 'Wrong number', and hung up. Some tried to dial a complaint but the line seemed busy. In a few hours, everyone had forgotten the incident – except those whose duty it was to worry about such things.

At the Post Office Research Station, the argument had been going on all morning, and had got nowhere. It continued unabated through the lunch break, when the hungry engineers poured into the little café across the road.

'I still think,' said Willy Smith, the solid-state electronics man, 'that it was a temporary surge of current, caused when the satellite network was switched in.'

'It was obviously *something* to do with the satellites,' agreed Jules Reyner, circuit designer. 'But why the time delay? They were plugged in at midnight; the ringing was two hours later – as we all know to our cost.' He yawned violently.

'What do *you* think, Doc?' asked Bob Andrews, computer programmer. 'You've been very quiet all morning. Surely you've got some idea?'

Dr John Williams, head of the Mathematics Division, stirred uneasily.

'Yes,' he said. 'I have. But you won't take it seriously.'

'That doesn't matter. Even if it's as crazy as those science-fiction yarns you write under a pseudonym, it may give us some leads.'

Williams blushed, but not much. Everyone knew about his stories, and he wasn't ashamed of them. After all, they *had* been collected in book form. (Remaindered at five shillings; he still had a couple of hundred copies.)

'Very well,' he said, doodling on the tablecloth. 'This is something I've been wondering about for years. Have you ever considered the analogy between an automatic telephone exchange and the human brain?'

'Who hasn't thought of it?' scoffed one of his listeners. 'That idea must go back to Graham Bell.'

'Possibly. I never said it was original. But I do say it's time we started taking it seriously.' He squinted balefully at the fluorescent tubes above the table; they were needed on this foggy winter day. 'What's wrong with the damn lights? They've been flickering for the last five minutes.'

'Don't bother about that. Maisie's probably forgotten to pay her electricity bill. Let's hear more about your theory.'

'Most of it isn't theory; it's plain fact. We know that the human brain is a system of switches – neurons – interconnected in a very elaborate fashion by nerves. An automatic telephone exchange is also a system of switches – selectors and so forth – connected with wires.'

'Agreed,' said Smith. 'But that analogy won't get you very far. Aren't there about fifteen billion neurons in the brain? That's a lot more than the number of switches in an autoexchange.'

Williams' answer was interrupted by the scream of a lowflying jet. He had to wait until the café had ceased to vibrate before he could continue.

'Never heard them fly *that* low,' Andrews grumbled. 'Thought it was against regulations.'

'So it is, but don't worry – London Airport Control will catch him.'

'I doubt it,' said Reyner. 'That *was* London Airport, bringing in a Concorde on ground approach. But I've never heard one so low, either. Glad I wasn't aboard.'

'Are we, or are we *not*, going to get on with this blasted discussion?' demanded Smith.

'You're right about the fifteen billion neurons in the human brain,' continued Williams, unabashed. 'And *that's* the whole point. Fifteen billion sounds a large number, but it isn't. Round about the 1960s, there were more than that number of individual switches in the world's autoexchanges. Today, there are approximately five times as many.'

'I see,' said Reyner slowly. 'And as from yesterday, they've all become capable of full interconnection, now that the satellite links have gone into service.'

'Precisely.'

There was silence for a moment, apart from the distant clanging of a fire-engine bell.

'Let me get this straight,' said Smith. 'Are you suggesting that the world telephone system is now a giant brain?'

823

'That's putting it crudely – anthropomorphically. I prefer to think of it in terms of critical size.' Williams held his hands out in front of him, fingers partly closed.

'Here are two lumps of U-235. Nothing happens as long as you keep them apart. But bring them together' – he suited the action to the words – 'and you have something *very* different from one bigger lump of uranium. You have a hole half a mile across.

'It's the same with our telephone networks. Until today, they've been largely independent, autonomous. But now we've suddenly multiplied the connecting links, the networks have all merged together, and we've reached criticality.'

'And just what does criticality mean in this case?' asked Smith.

'For want of a better word – consciousness.'

'A weird sort of consciousness,' said Reyner. 'What would it use for sense organs?'

'Well, all the radio and TV stations in the world would be feeding information into it, through their landlines. *That* should give it something to think about! Then there would be all the data stored in all the computers; it would have access to that – and to the electronic libraries, the radar tracking systems, the telemetering in the automatic factories. Oh, it would have enough sense organs! We can't begin to imagine its picture of the world; but it would be infinitely richer and more complex than ours.'

'Granted all this, because it's an entertaining idea,' said Reyner, 'what could it *do* except think? It couldn't go anywhere; it would have no limbs.'

'Why should it want to travel? It would already be everywhere! And every piece of remotely controlled electrical equipment on the planet could act as a limb.'

'Now I understand that time delay,' interjected Andrews. 'It was conceived at midnight, but it wasn't born until 1:50 this morning. The noise that woke us all up was – its birth cry.'

His attempt to sound facetious was not altogether convincing, and nobody smiled. Overhead, the lights continued their annoying flicker, which seemed to be getting worse. Then there was an interruption from the front of the café, as Jim Small, of Power Supplies, made his usual boisterous entry.

'Look at this, fellows,' he said, and grinned, waving a piece of paper in front of his colleagues. 'I'm rich. Ever seen a bank balance like *that*?'

Dr Williams took the proffered statement, glanced down the columns, and read the balance aloud: 'Cr, £999,999,897.87.'

'Nothing very odd about that,' he continued, above the general amusement. 'I'd say it means an overdraft of £102, and the computer's made a slight slip and added eleven nines. That sort of thing was happening all the time just after the banks converted to the decimal system.'

'I know, I know,' said Small, 'but don't spoil my fun. I'm going to frame this statement. And what would happen if I drew a cheque for a few million, on the strength of this? Could I sue the bank if it bounced?'

'Not on your life,' answered Reyner. 'I'll take a bet that the banks thought of that years ago, and protected themselves somewhere down in the small print. But, by the way, when did you get that statement?'

'In the noon delivery. It comes straight to the office, so that my wife doesn't have a chance of seeing it.'

'Hmm. That means it was computed early this morning. Certainly after midnight . . .'

'What are you driving at? And why all the long faces?'

No one answered him. He had started a new hare, and the hounds were in full cry.

'Does anyone here know about automated banking systems?' asked Smith. 'How are they tied together?'

'Like everything else these days,' said Andrews. 'They're all in the same network; the computers talk to each other all over the world. It's a point for you, John. If there *was* real trouble, that's one of the first places I'd expect it. Besides the phone system itself, of course.'

'No one answered the question I had asked before Jim came in,' complained Reyner. 'What would this supermind actually *do*? Would it be friendly – hostile – indifferent? Would it even know that we exist? Or would it consider the electronic signals it's handling to be the only reality?'

'I see you're beginning to believe me,' said Williams, with a certain grim satisfaction. 'I can only answer your question by asking another. What does a newborn baby do? It starts looking for food.' He glanced up at the flickering lights. 'My God,' he said slowly, as if a thought had just struck him. 'There's only one food it would need – electricity.'

'This nonsense has gone far enough,' said Smith. 'What the devil's happened to our lunch? We gave our orders twenty minutes ago.'

Everyone ignored him.

'And then,' said Reyner, taking up where Williams had left off, 'it would start looking around, and stretching its limbs. In fact, it would start to play, like any growing baby.'

'And babies *break* things,' said someone softly.

'It would have enough toys, heaven knows. That Concorde that went over us just now. The automated production lines. The traffic lights in our streets.'

'Funny you should mention that,' interjected Small. 'Something's happened to the traffic outside – it's been stopped for the last ten minutes. Looks like a big jam.'

'I guess there a a fire somewhere. I heard an engine just now.'

'I've heard two – and what sounded like an explosion over toward the industrial estate. Hope it's nothing serious.'

'Maisie! What about some candles? We can't see a thing!'

'I've just remembered – this place has an all-electric kitchen. We're going to get cold lunch, if we get any lunch at all.'

'At least we can read the newspaper while we're waiting. Is that the latest edition you've got there, Jim?'

'Yes. Haven't had time to look at it yet. Hmm. There *do* seem to have been a lot of odd accidents this morning – railway signals jammed – water main blown up through failure of relief valve – dozens of complaints about last night's wrong number . . .'

He turned the page, and became suddenly silent.

'What's the matter?'

Without a word, Small handed over the paper. Only the front page made sense. Throughout the interior, column after column was a mess of printer's pie, with, here and there, a few incongruous advertisements making islands of sanity in a sea of gibberish. They had obviously been set up as independent blocks, and had escaped the scrambling that had overtaken the text around them.

'So this is where long-distance typesetting and autodistribution have brought us,' grumbled Andrews. 'I'm afraid Fleet Street's been putting too many eggs in one electronic basket.'

'So have we all, I'm afraid,' said Williams solemnly. 'So have we all.'

'If I can get a word in edgeways, in time to stop the mob hysteria that seems to be infecting this table,' said Smith loudly and firmly, 'I'd like to point out that there's nothing to worry about – even if John's ingenious fantasy is correct. We only have to switch off the satellites, and we'll be back uhere we were yesterday.'

'Prefrontal lobotomy,' muttered Williams. 'I'd thought of that.'

'Eh? Oh, yes – cutting out slabs of the brain. That would certainly do the trick. Expensive, of course, and we'd have to go back to sending telegrams to each other. But civilisation would survive.'

From not too far away, there was a short, sharp explosion.

'I don't like this,' said Andrews nervously. 'Let's hear what the old BBC's got to say. The one o'clock news has just started.'

He reached into his briefcase and pulled out a transistor radio.

'. . . unprecedented number of industrial accidents, as well as the unexplained launching of three salvos of guided missiles from military installations in the United States. Several airports have had to suspend operations owing to the erratic behaviour of their radar, and the banks and stock exchanges have closed because their information-processing systems have become completely unreliable.' ('You're telling me,' muttered Small, while the others shushed him.) 'One moment, please – there's a news flash coming through. . . . Here it is. We have just been informed that all control over the newly installed communication satellites has been lost. They are no longer responding to commands from the ground. According to . . .'

The BBC went off the air; even the carrier wave died. Andrews reached for the tuning knob and twisted it around the dial. Over the whole band, the ether was silent.

Presently Reyner said, in a voice not far from hysteria: 'That prefrontal lobotomy was a good idea, John. Too bad that Baby's already thought of it.'

Williams rose slowly to his feet.

'Let's get back to the lab,' he said. 'There must be an answer, somewhere.'

But he knew already that it was far, far too late. For *Homo sapiens*, the telephone bell had tolled.

The Wind from the Sun

First published in *Boy's Life*, March 1964, as 'Sunjammer'
Collected in *The Wind from the Sun*

A yacht race with a difference, in space, using solar sails, and yet, even now this idea is being actively considered as a means of propulsion. The story's original title was 'Sunjammer' but as Poul Anderson had the same idea almost simultaneously, I was obliged to make a quick change of name.

The enormous disc of sail strained at its rigging, already filled with the wind that blew between the worlds. In three minutes the race would begin, yet now John Merton felt more relaxed, more at peace, than at any time for the past year. Whatever happened when the Commodore gave the starting signal, whether *Diana* carried him to victory or defeat, he had achieved his ambition. After a lifetime spent designing ships for others, now he would sail his own.

'T minus two minutes,' said the cabin radio. 'Please confirm your readiness.'

One by one, the other skippers answered. Merton recognised all the voices – some tense, some calm – for they were the voices of his friends and rivals. On the four inhabited worlds, there were scarcely twenty men who could sail a Sun yacht; and they were all here, on the starting line or aboard the escort vessels, orbiting twenty-two thousand miles above the equator.

'Number One – *Gossamer* – ready to go.'

'Number Two – *Santa Maria* – all OK.'

'Number Three – *Sunbeam* – OK.'

'Number Four – *Woomera* – all systems GO.'

Merton smiled at that last echo from the early, primitive days of astronautics. But it had become part of the tradition of space; and there were times when a man needed to evoke the shades of those who had gone before him to the stars.

'Number Five – *Lebedev* – we're ready.'

'Number Six – *Arachne* – OK.'

Now it was his turn, at the end of the line; strange to think that the words he was speaking in this tiny cabin were being heard by at least five billion people.

'Number Seven – *Diana* – ready to start.'

'One through Seven acknowledged,' answered that impersonal voice from the judge's launch. 'Now T minus one minute.'

Merton scarcely heard it. For the last time, he was checking the tension in the rigging. The needles of all the dynamometers were steady; the immense sail was taut, its mirror surface sparkling and glittering gloriously in the Sun.

To Merton, floating weightless at the periscope, it seemed to fill the sky. As well it might – for out there were fifty million square feet of sail, linked to his capsule by almost a hundred miles of rigging. All the canvas of all the tea clippers that had once raced like clouds across the China seas, sewn into one gigantic sheet, could not match the single sail that *Diana* had spread beneath the Sun. Yet it was little more substantial than a soap bubble; that two square miles of aluminised plastic was only a few millionths of an inch thick.

'T minus ten seconds. All recording cameras ON.'

Something so huge, yet so frail, was hard for the mind to grasp. And it was harder still to realise that this fragile mirror could tow him free of Earth merely by the power of the sunlight it would trap.

'. . . five, four, three, two, one, CUT!'

Seven knife blades sliced through seven thin lines tethering the yachts to the mother ships that had assembled and serviced them. Until this moment, all had been circling Earth together in a rigidly held formation, but now the yachts would begin to disperse, like dandelion seeds drifting before the breeze. And the winner would be the one that first drifted past the Moon.

Aboard *Diana*, nothing seemed to be happening. But Merton knew better. Though his body could feel no thrust, the instrument board told him that he was now accelerating at almost one thousandth of a gravity. For a rocket, that figure would have been ludicrous – but this was the first time any solar yacht had ever attained it. *Diana*'s design was sound; the vast sail was living up to his calculations. At this rate, two circuits of the Earth would build up his speed to escape velocity, and then he could head out for the Moon, with the full force of the Sun behind him.

The full force of the Sun . . . He smiled wryly, remembering all his attempts to explain solar sailing to those lecture audiences back on Earth. That had been the only way he could raise money, in those early days. He might be Chief Designer of Cosmodyne Corporation, with a whole string of successful spaceships to his credit, but his firm had not been exactly enthusiastic about his hobby.

'Hold your hands out to the Sun,' he'd said. 'What do you feel? Heat, of course. But there's pressure as well – though you've never noticed it, because it's so tiny. Over the area of your hands, it comes to only about a millionth of an ounce.

'But out in space, even a pressure as small as that can be important, for it's acting all the time, hour after hour, day after day. Unlike rocket fuel, it's free and unlimited. If we want to, we can use it. We can build sails to catch the radiation blowing from the Sun.'

At that point, he would pull out a few square yards of sail material and toss it toward the audience. The silvery film would coil and twist like smoke, then drift slowly to the ceiling in the hot-air currents.

'You can see how light it is,' he'd continue. 'A square mile weighs only a ton, and can collect five pounds of radiation pressure. So it will start moving – and we can let it tow us along, if we attach rigging to it.

'Of course, its acceleration will be tiny – about a thousandth of a g. That doesn't seem much, but let's see what it means.

'It means that in the first second, we'll move about a fifth of an inch. I suppose a healthy snail could do better than that. But after a minute, we've covered sixty feet, and will be doing just over a mile an hour. That's not bad, for something driven by pure sunlight! After an hour, we're forty miles from our starting point, and will be moving at eighty miles an hour. Please remember that in space there's no friction; so once you start anything moving, it will keep going forever. You'll be surprised when I tell you what our thousandth-of-a-g sailboat will be doing at the end of a day's run: *almost two thousand miles an hour*! If it starts from orbit – as it has to, of course – it can reach escape velocity in a couple of days. And all without burning a single drop of fuel!'

Well, he'd convinced them, and in the end he'd even convinced Cosmodyne. Over the last twenty years, a new sport had come into being. It had been called the sport of billionaires, and that was true. But it was beginning to pay for itself in terms of publicity and TV coverage. The prestige of four continents and two worlds was riding on this race, and it had the biggest audience in history.

Diana had made a good start; time to take a look at the opposition. Moving very gently – though there were shock absorbers between the control capsule and the delicate rigging, he was determined to run no risks – Merton stationed himself at the periscope.

There they were, looking like strange silver flowers planted in the dark fields of space. The nearest, South America's *Santa Maria*, was only fifty miles away; it bore a close resemblance to a boy's kite, but a kite more than a mile on a side. Farther away, the University of Astrograd's *Lebedev* looked like a Maltese cross; the sails that formed the four arms could apparently be tilted for steering purposes. In contrast, the Federation of Australasia's *Woomera* was a simple parachute, four miles in circumference. General Spacecraft's *Arachne*, as its name suggested, looked like a spider web, and had been built on the same principles, by robot shuttles spiralling out from a central point. Eurospace Corporation's *Gossamer* was an identical design, on a slightly smaller scale. And the Republic of Mars's *Sunbeam* was a flat ring, with a half-mile-wide hole in the centre, spinning slowly, so that centrifugal force gave it stiffness. That was an old idea, but no one had ever made it work; and Merton was fairly sure that the colonials would be in trouble when they started to turn.

That would not be for another six hours, when the yachts had moved along the first quarter of their slow and stately twenty-four-hour orbit. Here at the beginning of the race, they were all heading directly away from the Sun – running, as it were, before the solar wind. One had to make the most of this lap, before the boats swung around to the other side of Earth and then started to head back into the Sun.

Time, Merton told himself, for the first check, while he had no navigational worries. With the periscope, he made a careful examination of the sail, concentrating on the points where the rigging was attached to it. The shroud lines – narrow bands of unsilvered plastic film – would have been completely invisible had they not been coated with fluorescent paint. Now they were taut lines of coloured light, dwindling away for hundreds of yards toward that gigantic sail. Each had its own electric windlass, not much bigger than a game fisherman's reel. The little windlasses were continually turning, playing lines in or out as the autopilot kept the sail trimmed at the correct angle to the Sun.

The play of sunlight on the great flexible mirror was beautiful to watch. The sail was undulating in slow, stately oscillations, sending multiple images of the Sun marching across it, until they faded away at its edges. Such leisurely vibrations were to be expected in this vast and flimsy structure. They were usually quite harmless, but Merton watched them carefully. Sometimes they could build up to the catastrophic undulations known as the 'wriggles', which could tear a sail to pieces.

When he was satisfied that everything was shipshape, he swept the periscope around the sky, rechecking the positions of his rivals. It was as he had hoped: the weeding-out process had begun, as the less efficient boats fell astern. But the real test would come when they passed into the shadow of Earth. Then, manoeuvrability would count as much as speed.

It seemed a strange thing to do, what with the race having just started, but he thought it might be a good idea to get some sleep. The two-man crews on the other boats could take it in turns, but Merton had no one to relieve him. He must rely on his own physical resources, like that other solitary seaman, Joshua Slocum, in his tiny *Spray*. The American skipper had sailed *Spray* singlehanded around the world; he could never have dreamed that, two centuries later, a man would be sailing singlehanded from Earth to Moon – inspired, at least partly, by his example.

Merton snapped the elastic bands of the cabin seat around his waist and legs, then placed the electrodes of the sleep-inducer on his forehead. He set the timer for three hours, and relaxed. Very gently, hypnotically, the electronic pulses throbbed in the frontal lobes of his brain. Coloured spirals of light expanded beneath his closed eyelids, widening outward to infinity. Then nothing . . .

The brazen clamour of the alarm dragged him back from his dreamless sleep. He was instantly awake, his eyes scanning the instrument panel. Only two hours had passed – but above the accelerometer, a red light was flashing. Thrust was falling; *Diana* was losing power.

Merton's first thought was that something had happened to the sail; perhaps the antispin devices had failed, and the rigging had become twisted. Swiftly, he checked the meters that showed the tension of the shroud lines. Strange – on one side of the sail they were reading normally, but on the other the pull was dropping slowly, even as he watched.

In sudden understanding, Merton grabbed the periscope, switched to wide-angle vision, and started to scan the edge of the sail. Yes – there was the trouble, and it could have only one cause.

A huge, sharp-edged shadow had begun to slide across the gleaming silver of the sail. Darkness was falling upon *Diana*, as if a cloud had passed between her and the Sun. And in the dark, robbed of the rays that drove her, she would lose all thrust and drift helplessly through space.

But, of course, there were no clouds here, more than twenty thousand miles above the Earth. If there was a shadow, it must be made by man.

Merton grinned as be swung the periscope toward the Sun, switching in the filters that would allow him to look full into its blazing face without being blinded.

'Manoeuvre 4a,' he muttered to himself. 'We'll see who can play best at *that* game.'

It looked as if a giant planet was crossing the face of the Sun; a great black disc had bitten deep into its edge. Twenty miles astern, *Gossamer* was trying to arrange an artificial eclipse, specially for *Diana*'s benefit.

The manoeuvre was a perfectly legitimate one. Back in the days of ocean racing, skippers had often tried to rob each other of the wind. With any luck, you could leave your rival becalmed, with his sails collapsing around him – and be well ahead before he could undo the damage.

Merton had no intention of being caught so easily. There was plenty of time to take evasive action; things happened very slowly when you were running a solar sailboat. It would be at least twenty minutes before *Gossamer* could slide completely across the face of the Sun, and leave him in darkness.

Diana's tiny computer – the size of a matchbox, but the equivalent of a thousand human mathematicians – considered the problem for a full second and then flashed the answer. He'd have to open control panels three and four, until the sail had developed an extra twenty degrees of tilt; then the radiation pressure would blow him out of *Gossamer*'s dangerous shadow, back into the full blast of the Sun. It was a pity to interfere with the autopilot, which had been carefully programmed to give the fastest possible run – but that, after all, was why he was here. This was what made solar yachting a sport, rather than a battle between computers.

Out went control lines one and six, slowly undulating like sleepy snakes as they momentarily lost their tension. Two miles away, the triangular panels began to open lazily, spilling sunlight through the sail. Yet, for a long time, nothing seemed to happen. It was hard to grow accustomed to this slow-motion world, where it took minutes for the effects of any action to become visible to the eye. Then Merton saw that the sail was indeed tipping toward the Sun – and that *Gossamer*'s shadow was sliding harmlessly away, its cone of darkness lost in the deeper night of space.

Long before the shadow had vanished, and the disc of the Sun had cleared again, he reversed the tilt and brought *Diana* back on course. Her new momentum would carry her clear of the danger; no need to overdo it, and upset his calculations by side-stepping too far. That was another rule that was hard to learn: the very moment you had started something happening in space, it was already time to think about stopping it.

He reset the alarm, ready for the next natural or manmade emergency. Perhaps *Gossamer*, or one of the other contestants, would try the same trick again. Meanwhile, it was time to eat, though he did not feel particularly hungry. One used little physical energy in space, and it was easy to forget about food. Easy – and dangerous; for when an emergency arose, you might not have the reserves needed to deal with it.

He broke open the first of the meal packets, and inspected it without enthusiasm. The name on the label – SPACETASTIES – was enough to put him off. And he had grave doubts about the promise printed underneath: 'Guaranteed crumbless'. It had been said that crumbs were a greater danger to space vehicles than meteorites; they could drift into the most unlikely places, causing short circuits, blocking vital jets, and getting into instruments that were supposed to be hermetically sealed.

Still, the liverwurst went down pleasantly enough; so did the chocolate and the pineapple puree. The plastic coffee bulb was warming on the electric heater when the outside world broke in upon his solitude, as the radio operator on the Commodore's launch routed a call to him.

'Dr Merton? If you can spare the time, Jeremy Blair would like a few words with you.' Blair was one of the more responsible news commentators, and Merton had been on his programme many times. He could refuse to be interviewed, of course, but he liked Blair, and at the moment he could certainly not claim to be too busy. 'I'll take it,' he answered.

'Hello, Dr Merton,' said the commentator immediately. 'Glad you can spare a few minutes. And congratulations – you seem to be ahead of the field.'

'Too early in the game to be sure of *that*,' Merton answered cautiously.

'Tell me, Doctor, why did you decide to sail *Diana* by yourself? Just because it's never been done before?'

'Well, isn't that a good reason? But it wasn't the only one, of course.' He paused, choosing his words carefully. 'You know how critically the performance of a Sun yacht depends on its mass. A second man, with all his supplies, would mean another five hundred pounds. That could easily be the difference between winning and losing.'

'And you're quite certain that you can handle *Diana* alone?'

'Reasonably sure, thanks to the automatic controls I've designed. My main job is to supervise and make decisions.'

'But – two square miles of sail! It just doesn't seem possible for one man to cope with all that,'

Merton laughed. 'Why not? Those two square miles produce a maximum pull of just ten pounds. I can exert more force with my little finger.'

'Well, thank you, Doctor. And good luck. I'll be calling you again.'

As the commentator signed off, Merton felt a little ashamed of himself. For his answer had been only part of the truth; and he was sure that Blair was shrewd enough to know it.

There was just one reason why he was here, alone in space. For almost forty years he had worked with teams of hundreds or even thousands of men, helping to design the most complex vehicles that the world had ever seen. For the last twenty years he had led one of those teams, and watched his creations go soaring to the stars. (Sometimes . . . There *were* failures, which he could never forget, even though the fault had not been his.) He was famous, with a successful career behind him. Yet he had never done anything by himself; always he had been one of an army.

This was his last chance to try for individual achievement, and he would share it with no one. There would be no more solar yachting for at least five years, as the period of the Quiet Sun ended and the cycle of bad weather began, with radiation storms bursting through the solar system. When it was safe again for these frail, unshielded craft to venture aloft, he would be too old. If, indeed, he was not too old already . . .

He dropped the empty food containers into the waste disposal and turned once more to the periscope. At first he could find only five of the other yachts; there was no sign of *Woomera*. It took him several minutes to locate her – a dim, star-eclipsing phantom, neatly caught in the shadow of *Lebedev*. He could imagine the frantic efforts the Australasians were making to extricate themselves, and wondered how they had fallen into the trap. It suggested that *Lebedev* was unusually manoeuvrable. She would bear watching, though she was too far away to menace *Diana* at the moment.

Now the Earth had almost vanished; it had waned to a narrow, brilliant bow of light that was moving steadily toward the Sun. Dimly outlined within that burning bow was the night side of the planet, with the phosphorescent gleams of great cities showing here and there through gaps in the clouds. The disc of darkness had already blanked out a huge section of the Milky Way. In a few minutes, it would start to encroach upon the Sun.

The light was fading; a purple, twilight hue – the glow of many sunsets, thousands of miles below – was falling across the sail as *Diana* slipped silently into the shadow of Earth. The Sun plummeted below that invisible horizon; within minutes, it was night.

Merton looked back along the orbit he had traced, now a quarter of the way around the world. One by one he saw the brilliant stars of the other yachts wink out, as they joined him in the brief night. It would be an hour before the Sun emerged from that enormous black shield, and through all that time they would be completely helpless, coasting without power.

He switched on the external spotlight, and started to search the now-darkened sail with its beam. Already the thousands of acres of film were beginning to wrinkle and become flaccid. The shroud lines were slackening, and must be wound in lest they become entangled. But all this was expected; everything was going as planned.

Fifty miles astern, *Arachne* and *Santa Maria* were not so lucky. Merton learned of their troubles when the radio burst into life on the emergency circuit.

'Number Two and Number Six, this is Control. You are on a collision course; your orbits will intersect in sixty-five minutes! Do you require assistance?'

There was a long pause while the two skippers digested this bad news. Merton wondered who was to blame. Perhaps one yacht had been trying to shadow the other, and had not completed the manoeuvre before they were both caught in darkness. Now there was nothing that either could do. They were slowly but inexorably converging, unable to change course by a fraction of a degree.

Yet – sixty-five minutes! That would just bring them out into sunlight again, as they emerged from the shadow of the Earth. They had a slim chance, if their sails could snatch enough power to avoid a crash. There must be some frantic calculations going on aboard *Arachne* and *Santa Maria*.

Arachne answered first. Her reply was just what Merton had expected.

'Number Six calling Control. We don't need assistance, thank you. We'll work this out for ourselves.'

I wonder, thought Merton; but at least it will be interesting to watch. The first real drama of the race was approaching, exactly above the line of midnight on the sleeping Earth.

For the next hour, Merton's own sail kept him too busy to worry about *Arachne* and *Santa Maria*. It was hard to keep a good watch on that fifty million square feet of dim plastic out there in the darkness, illuminated only by his narrow spotlight and the rays of the still-distant Moon. From now on, for almost half his orbit around the Earth, he must keep the whole of this immense area edge-on to the Sun. During the next twelve or fourteen hours, the sail would be a useless encumbrance; for he would be heading *into* the Sun, and its rays could only drive him backward along his orbit. It was a pity that he could not furl the sail completely, until he was ready to use it again; but no one had yet found a practical way of doing this.

Far below, there was the first hint of dawn along the edge of the Earth. In ten minutes the Sun would emerge from its eclipse. The coasting yachts would come to life again as the blast of radiation struck their sails. That would be the moment of crisis for *Arachne* and *Santa Maria* – and, indeed, for all of them.

Merton swung the periscope until he found the two dark shadows drifting against the stars. They were very close together – perhaps less than three miles apart. They might, he decided, just be able to make it. . . .

Dawn flashed like an explosion along the rim of Earth as the Sun rose out of the Pacific. The sail and shroud lines glowed a brief crimson, then gold, then blazed with the pure white light of day. The needles of the dynamometers began to lift from their zeroes – but only just. *Diana* was still almost completely weightless, for with the sail pointing toward the Sun, her acceleration was now only a few millionths of a gravity.

But *Arachne* and *Santa Maria* were crowding on all the sail that they could manage, in their desperate attempt to keep apart. Now, while there was less than two miles between them, their glittering plastic clouds were unfurling and expanding with agonising slowness as they felt the first delicate push of the Sun's rays. Almost every TV screen on Earth would be mirroring this protracted drama; and even now, at this last minute, it was impossible to tell what the outcome would be.

The two skippers were stubborn men. Either could have cut his sail and fallen back to give the other a chance; but neither would do so. Too much prestige, too many millions, too many reputations were at stake. And so, silently and softly as snowflakes falling on a winter night, *Arachne* and *Santa Maria* collided.

The square kite crawled almost imperceptibly into the circular spider web. The long ribbons of the shroud lines twisted and tangled together with dreamlike slowness. Even aboard *Diana*, Merton, busy with his own rigging, could scarcely tear his eyes away from this silent, long-drawn-out disaster.

For more than ten minutes the billowing, shining clouds continued to merge into one inextricable mass. Then the crew capsules tore loose and went their separate ways, missing each other by hundreds of yards. With a flare of rockets, the safety launches hurried to pick them up.

That leaves five of us, thought Merton. He felt sorry for the skippers who had so thoroughly eliminated each other, only a few hours after the start of the race, but they were young men and would have another chance.

Within minutes, the five had dropped to four. From the beginning, Merton had had doubts about the slowly rotating *Sunbeam*; now he saw them justified.

The Martian ship had failed to tack properly. Her spin had given her too much stability. Her great ring of a sail was turning to face the Sun, instead of being edge-on to it. She was being blown back along her course at almost her maximum acceleration.

That was about the most maddening thing that could happen to a skipper – even worse than a collision, for he could blame only himself. But no one would feel much sympathy for the frustrated colonials, as they dwindled slowly astern. They had made too many brash boasts before the race, and what had happened to them was poetic justice.

Yet it would not do to write off *Sunbeam* completely; with almost half a million miles still to go, she might yet pull ahead. Indeed, if there were a few more casualties, she might be the only one to complete the race. It had happened before.

The next twelve hours were uneventful, as the Earth waxed in the sky from new to full. There was little to do while the fleet drifted around the unpowered half of its orbit, but Merton did not find the time hanging heavily on his hands. He caught a few hours of sleep, ate two meals, wrote his log, and became involved in several more radio interviews. Sometimes, though rarely, he talked to the other skippers, exchanging greetings and friendly taunts. But most of the time he was content to float in weightless relaxation, beyond all the cares of Earth, happier than he had been for many years. He was – as far as any man could be in space – master of his own fate, sailing the ship upon which he had lavished so much skill, so much love, that it had become part of his very being.

The next casualty came when they were passing the line between Earth and Sun, and were just beginning the powered half of the orbit. Aboard *Diana*, Merton saw the great sail stiffen as it tilted to catch the rays that drove it. The acceleration began to climb up from the microgravities, though it would be hours yet before it would reach its maximum value.

It would never reach it for *Gossamer*. The moment when power came on again was always critical, and she failed to survive it.

Blair's radio commentary, which Merton had left running at low volume, alerted him with the news: 'Hello, *Gossamer* has the wriggles!' He hurried to the periscope, but at first could see nothing wrong with the great circular disc of *Gossamer*'s sail. It was difficult to study it because it was almost edge-on to him and so appeared as a thin ellipse; but presently he saw that it was twisting back and forth in slow, irresistible oscillations. Unless the crew could damp out these waves, by properly timed but gentle tugs on the shroud lines, the sail would tear itself to pieces.

They did their best, and after twenty minutes it seemed that they had succeeded. Then, somewhere near the centre of the sail, the plastic hem began to rip. It was slowly driven outward by the radiation pressure, like smoke coiling upward from a fire. Within a quarter of an hour, nothing was left but the delicate tracery of the radial spars that had supported the great web. Once again there was a flare of rockets, as a launch moved in to retrieve the *Gossamer*'s capsule and her dejected crew.

'Getting rather lonely up here, isn't it?' said a conversational voice over the ship-to-ship radio.

'Not for you, Dimitri,' retorted Merton. 'You've still got company back there at the end of the field. I'm the one who's lonely, up here in front.' It was not an idle boast; by this time *Diana* was three hundred miles ahead of the next competitor, and her lead should increase still more rapidly in the hours to come.

Aboard *Lebedev*, Dimitri Markoff gave a good-natured chuckle. He did not sound, Merton thought, at all like a man who had resigned himself to defeat.

'Remember the legend of the tortoise and the hare,' answered the Russian. 'A lot can happen in the next quarter-million miles.'

It happened much sooner than that, when they had completed their first orbit of Earth and were passing the starting line again – though thousands of miles higher, thanks to the extra energy the Sun's rays had given them.

Merton had taken careful sights on the other yachts, and had fed the figures into the computer. The answer it gave for *Woomera* was so absurd that he immediately did a recheck.

There was no doubt of it – the Australasians were catching up at a completely fantastic rate. No solar yacht could possibly have such an acceleration, unless . . .

A swift look through the periscope gave the answer. *Woomera*'s rigging, pared back to the very minimum of mass, had given way. It was her sail alone, still maintaining its shape, that was racing up behind him like a handkerchief blown before the wind. Two hours later it fluttered past, less than twenty miles away; but long before that, the Australasians had joined the growing crowd aboard the Commodore's launch.

So now it was a straight fight between *Diana* and *Lebedev* – for though the Martians had not given up, they were a thousand miles astern and no longer counted as a serious threat. For that matter, it was hard to see what *Lebedev* could do to overtake *Diana*'s lead; but all the way around the second lap, through eclipse again and the long, slow drift against the Sun, Merton felt a growing unease.

He knew the Russian pilots and designers. They had been trying to win this race for twenty years – and, after all, it was only fair that they should, for had not Pyotr Nikolaevich Lebedev been the first man to detect the pressure of sunlight, back at the very beginning of the twentieth century? But they had never succeeded.

And they would never stop trying. Dimitri was up to something – and it would be spectacular.

Aboard the official launch, a thousand miles behind the racing yachts, Commodore van Stratten looked at the radiogram with angry dismay. It had travelled more than a hundred million miles, from the chain of solar observatories swinging high above the blazing surface of the Sun; and it brought the worst possible news.

The Commodore – his title was purely honorary, of course; back on Earth he was Professor of Astrophysics at Harvard – had been half expecting it. Never before had the race been arranged so late in the season. There had been many delays; they had gambled – and now, it seemed, they might all lose.

Deep beneath the surface of the Sun, enormous forces were gathering. At any moment the energies of a million hydrogen bombs might burst forth in the awesome explosion known as a solar flare. Climbing at millions of miles an hour, an invisible fireball many times the size of Earth would leap from the Sun and head out across space.

The cloud of electrified gas would probably miss the Earth completely. But if it did not, it would arrive in just over a day. Spaceships could protect themselves, with their shielding and their powerful magnetic screens; but the lightly built solar yachts, with their paper-thin walls, were defenceless

838

against such a menace. The crews would have to be taken off, and the race abandoned.

John Merton knew nothing of this as he brought *Diana* around the Earth for the second time. If all went well, this would be the last circuit, both for him and for the Russians. They had spiralled upward by thousands of miles, gaining energy from the Sun's rays. On this lap, they should escape from Earth completely, and head outward on the long run to the Moon. It was a straight race now; *Sunbeam*'s crew had finally withdrawn exhausted, after battling valiantly with their spinning sail for more than a hundred thousand miles.

Merton did not feel tired; he had eaten and slept well, and *Diana* was behaving herself admirably. The autopilot, tensioning the rigging like a busy little spider, kept the great sail trimmed to the Sun more accurately than any human skipper could have. Though by this time the two square miles of plastic sheet must have been riddled by hundreds of micrometeorites, the pinhead-sized punctures had produced no falling off of thrust.

He had only two worries. The first was shroud line number eight, which could no longer be adjusted properly. Without any warning, the reel had jammed; even after all these years of astronautical engineering, bearings sometimes seized up in vacuum. He could neither lengthen nor shorten the line, and would have to navigate as best he could with the others. Luckily, the most difficult manoeuvres were over; from now on, *Diana* would have the Sun behind her as she sailed straight down the solar wind. And as the old-time sailors had often said, it was easy to handle a boat when the wind was blowing over your shoulder.

His other worry was *Lebedev*, still dogging his heels three hundred miles astern. The Russian yacht had shown remarkable manoeuvrability, thanks to the four great panels that could be tilted around the central sail. Her flipovers as she rounded the Earth had been carried out with superb precision. But to gain manoeuvrability she must have sacrificed speed. You could not have it both ways; in the long, straight haul ahead, Merton should be able to hold his own. Yet he could not be certain of victory until, three or four days from now, *Diana* went flashing past the far side of the Moon.

And then, in the fiftieth hour of the race, just after the end of the second orbit around Earth, Markoff sprang his little surprise.

'Hello, John,' he said casually over the ship-to-ship circuit. 'I'd like you to watch this. It should be interesting.'

Merton drew himself across to the periscope and turned up the magnification to the limit. There in the field of view, a most improbable sight against the background of the stars, was the glittering Maltese cross of *Lebedev*, very small but very clear. As he watched, the four arms of the cross slowly detached themselves from the central square, and went drifting away, with all their spars and rigging into space.

Markoff had jettisoned all unnecessary mass, now that he was coming up to escape velocity and need no longer plod patiently around the Earth, gaining momentum on each circuit. From now on, *Lebedev* would be almost unsteerable – but that did not matter; all the tricky navigation lay behind her. It was as if an old-time yachtsman had deliberately thrown away his rudder and heavy keel, knowing that the rest of the race would be straight downwind over a calm sea.

'Congratulations, Dimitri,' Merton radioed. 'It's a neat trick. But it's not good enough. You can't catch up with me now.'

'I've not finished yet,' the Russian answered. 'There's an old winter's tale in my country about a sleigh being chased by wolves. To save himself, the driver has to throw off the passengers one by one. Do you see the analogy?'

Merton did, all too well. On this final straight lap, Dimitri no longer needed his copilot. *Lebedev* could really be stripped down for action.

'Alexis won't be very happy about this,' Merton replied. 'Besides, it's against the rules.'

'Alexis isn't happy, but I'm the captain. He'll just have to wait around for ten minutes until the Commodore picks him up. And the regulations say nothing about the size of the crew – *you* should know that.'

Merton did not answer; he was too busy doing some hurried calculations, based on what he knew of *Lebedev*'s design. By the time he had finished, he knew that the race was still in doubt. *Lebedev* would be catching up with him at just about the time he hoped to pass the Moon.

But the outcome of the race was already being decided, ninety-two million miles away.

On Solar Observatory Three, far inside the orbit of Mercury, the automatic instruments recorded the whole history of the flare. A hundred million square miles of the Sun's surface exploded in such blue-white fury that, by comparison, the rest of the disc paled to a dull glow. Out of that seething inferno, twisting and turning like a living creature in the magnetic fields of its own creation, soared the electrified plasma of the great flare. Ahead of it, moving at the speed of light, went the warning flash of ultraviolet and X rays. That would reach Earth in eight minutes, and was relatively harmless. Not so the charged atoms that were following behind at their leisurely four million miles an hour – and which, in just over a day, would engulf *Diana*, *Lebedev*, and their accompanying little fleet in a cloud of lethal radiation.

The Commodore left his decision to the last possible minute. Even when the jet of plasma had been tracked past the orbit of Venus, there was a chance that it might miss the Earth. But when it was less than four hours away, and had already been picked up by the Moon-based radar network, he knew that there was no hope. All solar sailing was over, for the next five or six years – until the Sun was quiet again.

A great sigh of disappointment swept across the solar system. *Diana* and *Lebedev* were halfway between Earth and Moon, running neck and neck – and now no one would ever know which was the better boat. The enthusiasts would argue the result for years; history would merely record: 'Race cancelled owing to solar storm.'

When John Merton received the order, he felt a bitterness he had not known since childhood. Across the years, sharp and clear, came the memory of his tenth birthday. He had been promised an exact scale model of the famous spaceship *Morning Star*, and for weeks had been planning how he would assemble it, where he would hang it in his bedroom. And then, at the last moment, his father had broken the news. 'I'm sorry, John – it cost too much money. Maybe next year . . .'

Half a century and a successful lifetime later, he was a heartbroken boy again.

For a moment, he thought of disobeying the Commodore. Suppose he sailed on, ignoring the warning? Even if the race was abandoned, he could make a crossing to the Moon that would stand in the record books for generations.

But that would be worse than stupidity; it would be suicide – and a very unpleasant form of suicide. He had seen men die of radiation poisoning, when the magnetic shielding of their ships had failed in deep space. No – nothing was worth that. . . .

He felt as sorry for Dimitri Markoff as for himself. They had both deserved to win, and now victory would go to neither. No man could argue with the Sun in one of its rages, even though he might ride upon its beams to the edge of space.

Only fifty miles astern now, the Commodore's launch was drawing alongside *Lebedev*, preparing to take off her skipper. There went the silver sail, as Dimitri – with feelings that he would share – cut the rigging. The tiny capsule would be taken back to Earth, perhaps to be used again; but a sail was spread for one voyage only.

He could press the jettison button now, and save his rescuers a few minutes of time. But he could not do it; he wanted to stay aboard to the very end, on the little boat that had been for so long a part of his dreams and his life. The great sail was spread now at right angles to the Sun, exerting its utmost thrust. Long ago it had torn him clear of Earth, and *Diana* was still gaining speed.

Then, out of nowhere, beyond all doubt or hesitation, he knew what must be done. For the last time, he sat down before the computer that had navigated him halfway to the Moon.

When he had finished, he packed the log and his few personal belongings. Clumsily, for he was out of practice, and it was not an easy job to do by oneself, he climbed into the emergency survival suit. He was just sealing the helmet when the Commodore's voice called over the radio.

'We'll be alongside in five minutes, Captain. Please cut your sail, so we won't foul it.'

John Merton, first and last skipper of the Sun yacht *Diana*, hesitated a moment. He looked for the last time around the tiny cabin, with its shining instruments and its neatly arranged controls, now all locked in their final positions. Then he said into the microphone: 'I'm abandoning ship. Take your time to pick me up. *Diana* can look after herself.'

841

There was no reply from the Commodore, and for that he was grateful. Professor van Stratten would have guessed what was happening – and would know that, in these final moments, he wished to be left alone.

He did not bother to exhaust the air lock, and the rush of escaping gas blew him gently out into space. The thrust he gave her then was his last gift to *Diana*. She dwindled away from him, sail glittering splendidly in the sunlight that would be hers for centuries to come. Two days from now she would flash past the Moon; but the Moon, like the Earth, could never catch her. Without his mass to slow her down, she would gain two thousand miles an hour in every day of sailing. In a month, she would be travelling faster than any ship that man had ever built.

As the Sun's rays weakened with distance, so her acceleration would fall. But even at the orbit of Mars, she would be gaining a thousand miles an hour in every day. Long before then, she would be moving too swiftly for the Sun itself to hold her. Faster than a comet had ever streaked in from the stars, she would be heading out into the abyss.

The glare of rockets, only a few miles away, caught Merton's eye. The launch was approaching to pick him up – at thousands of times the acceleration that *Diana* could ever attain. But its engines could burn for a few minutes only, before they exhausted their fuel – while *Diana* would still be gaining speed, driven outward by the Sun's eternal fires, for ages yet to come.

'Goodbye, little ship,' said John Merton. 'I wonder what eyes will see you next, how many thousand years from now?'

At last he felt at peace, as the blunt torpedo of the launch nosed up beside him. He would never win the race to the Moon; but his would be the first of all man's ships to set sail on the long journey to the stars.

The Food of the Gods

First published in *Playboy*, May 1964
Collected in *The Wind from the Sun*

It's only fair to warn you, Mr Chairman, that much of my evidence will be highly nauseating; it involves aspects of human nature that are very seldom discussed in public, and certainly not before a congressional committee. But I am afraid that they have to be faced; there are times when the veil of hypocrisy has to be ripped away, and this is one of them.

You and I, gentlemen, have descended from a long line of carnivores. I see from your expressions that most of you don't recognise the term. Well, that's not surprising – it comes from a language that has been obsolete for two thousand years. Perhaps I had better avoid euphemisms and be brutally frank, even if I have to use words that are never heard in polite society. I apologise in advance to anyone I may offend.

Until a few centuries ago, the favourite food of almost all men was *meat* – the *flesh* of once living animals. I'm not trying to turn your stomachs; this is a simple statement of fact, which you can check in any history book. . . .

Why, certainly, Mr Chairman I'm quite prepared to wait until Senator Irving feels better. We professionals sometimes forget how laymen may react to statements like that. At the same time, I must warn the committee that there is very much worse to come. If any of you gentlemen are at all squeamish, I suggest you follow the Senator before it's too late. . . .

Well, if I may continue. Until modern times, all food fell into two categories. Most of it was produced from plants – cereals, fruits, plankton, algae, and other forms of vegetation. It's hard for us to realise that the vast majority of our ancestors were farmers, winning food from land or sea by primitive and often backbreaking techniques; but that is the truth.

The second type of food, if I may return to this unpleasant subject, was meat, produced from a relatively small number of animals. You may be familiar with some of them – cows, pigs, sheep, whales. Most people – I am sorry to stress this, but the fact is beyond dispute – preferred meat to any other food, though only the wealthiest were able to indulge this appetite. To most of mankind, meat was a rare and occasional delicacy in a diet that was more than ninety-per-cent vegetable.

If we look at the matter calmly and dispassionately – as I hope Senator Irving is now in a position to do – we can see that meat was bound to be rare and expensive, for its production is an extremely inefficient process. To make a kilo of meat, the animal concerned had to eat at least ten kilos of vegetable food – very often food that could have been consumed directly by human beings. Quite apart from any consideration of aesthetics, this state of affairs could not be tolerated after the population explosion of the twentieth century. Every man who ate meat was condemning ten or more of his fellow humans to starvation. . . .

Luckily for all of us, the biochemists solved the problem; as you may know, the answer was one of the countless byproducts of space research. All food – animal or vegetable – is built up from a very few common elements. Carbon, hydrogen, oxygen, nitrogen, traces of sulphur and phosphorus – these half-dozen elements, and a few others, combine in an almost infinite variety of ways to make up every food that man has ever eaten or ever will eat. Faced with the problem of colonising the Moon and planets, the biochemists of the twenty-first century discovered how to synthesise any desired food from the basic raw materials of water, air, and rock. It was the greatest, and perhaps the most important, achievement in the history of science. But we should not feel too proud of it. The vegetable kingdom had beaten us by a billion years.

The chemists could now synthesise any conceivable food, whether it had a counterpart in nature or not. Needless to say, there were mistakes – even disasters. Industrial empires rose and crashed; the switch from agriculture and animal husbandry to the giant automatic processing plants and omniverters of today was often a painful one. But it had to be made, and we are the better for it. The danger of starvation has been banished forever, and we have a richness and variety of food that no other age has ever known.

In addition, of course, there was a moral gain. We no longer murder millions of living creatures, and such revolting institutions as the slaughterhouse and the butcher's shop have vanished from the face of the Earth. It seems incredible to us that even our ancestors, coarse and brutal though they were, could ever have tolerated such obscenities.

And yet – it is impossible to make a clean break with the past. As I have already remarked, we are carnivores; we inherit tastes and appetites that have been acquired over a million years of time. Whether we like it or not, only a few years ago some of our great-grandparents were enjoying the flesh of cattle and sheep and pigs – when they could get it. *And we still enjoy it today.* . . .

Oh dear, maybe Senator Irving had better stay outside from now on. Perhaps I should not have been quite so blunt. What I meant, of course, was that many of the synthetic foods we now eat have the same formula as the old natural products; some of them, indeed, are such exact replicas that no chemical or other test could reveal any difference. This situation is logical and inevitable; we manufacturers simply took the most popular presynthetic foods as our models, and reproduced their taste and texture.

Of course, we also created new names that didn't hint of an anatomical or zoological origin, so that no one would be reminded of the facts of life.

When you go into a restaurant, most of the words you'll find on the menu have been invented since the beginning of the twenty-first century, or else adapted from French originals that few people would recognise. If you ever want to find your threshold of tolerance, you can try an interesting but highly unpleasant experiment. The classified section of the Library of Congress has a large number of menus from famous restaurants – yes, and White House banquets going back for five hundred years. They have a crude, dissecting-room frankness that makes them almost unreadable. I cannot think of anything that reveals more vividly the gulf between us and our ancestors of only a few generations ago. . . .

Yes, Mr Chairman – I *am* coming to the point; all this is highly relevant, however disagreeable it may be. I am not trying to spoil your appetites; I am merely laying the groundwork for the charge I wish to bring against my competitor, Triplanetary Food Corporation. Unless you understand this background, you may think that this is a frivolous complaint inspired by the admittedly serious losses my firm has sustained since Ambrosia Plus came on the market.

New foods, gentlemen, are invented every week. It is hard to keep track of them. They come and go like women's fashions, and only one in a thousand becomes a permanent addition to the menu. It is *extremely* rare for one to hit the public fancy overnight, and I freely admit that the Ambrosia Plus line of dishes has been the greatest success in the entire history of food manufacture. You all know the position: everything else has been swept off the market.

Naturally, we were forced to accept the challenge. The biochemists of my organisation are as good as any in the solar system, and they promptly got to work on Ambrosia Plus. I am not giving away any trade secrets when I tell you that we have tapes of practically every food, natural or synthetic, that has ever been eaten by mankind – right back to exotic items that you've never heard of, like fried squid, locusts in honey, peacocks' tongues, Venusian polypod. . . . Our enormous library of flavours and textures is our basic stock in trade, as it is with all firms in the business. From it we can select and mix items in any conceivable combination; and usually we can duplicate, without too much trouble, any product that our competitors put out.

But Ambrosia Plus had us baffled for quite some time. Its protein-fat breakdown classified it as a straightforward meat, without too many complications – yet we couldn't match it exactly. It was the first time my chemists had failed; not one of them could explain just what gave the stuff its extraordinary appeal – which, as we all know, makes every other food seem insipid by comparison. As well it might . . . but I am getting ahead of myself.

Very shortly, Mr Chairman, the president of Triplanetary Foods will be appearing before you – rather reluctantly, I'm sure. He will tell you that Ambrosia Plus is synthesised from air, water, limestone, sulphur, phosphorus, and the rest. That will be perfectly true, but it will be the least important part of the story. For we have now discovered his secret – which, like most secrets, is very simple once you know it.

I really must congratulate my competitor. He has at last made available unlimited quantities of what is, from the nature of things, the ideal food for mankind. Until now, it has been in extremely short supply, and therefore all the more relished by the few connoisseurs who could obtain it. Without exception, they have sworn that nothing else can remotely compare with it.

Yes, Triplanetary's chemists have done a superb technical job. Now *you* have to resolve the moral and philosophical issues. When I began my evidence, I used the archaic word 'carnivore'. Now I must introduce you to another: I'll spell it out the first time: C-A-N-N-I-B-A-L. . . .

The Last Command

First published in *Bizarre! Mystery Magazine*, November 1965
Collected in *The Wind from the Sun*

'. . . This is the President speaking. Because you are hearing me read this message, it means that I am already dead and that our country is destroyed. But you are soldiers – the most highly trained in all our history. You know how to obey orders. Now you must obey the hardest you have ever received. . . .'

Hard? thought the First Radar Officer bitterly. No; now it would be easy, now that they had seen the land they loved scorched by the heat of many suns. No longer could there be any hesitation, any scruples about visiting upon innocent and guilty alike the vengeance of the gods. But why, *why* had it been left so late?

'. . . You know the purpose for which you were set swinging on your secret orbit beyond the Moon. Aware of your existence, but never sure of your location, an aggressor would hesitate to launch an attack against us. You were to be the Ultimate Deterrent, beyond the reach of the Earthquake bombs that could crush missiles in their buried silos and smash nuclear submarines prowling the sea bed. You could still strike back, even if all our other weapons were destroyed. . . .'

As they have been, the Captain told himself. He had watched the lights wink out one by one on the operations board, until none were left. Many, perhaps, had done their duty; if not, he would soon complete their work. Nothing that had survived the first counterstrike would exist after the blow he was now preparing.

'. . . Only through accident, or madness, could war begin in the face of the threat you represent. That was the theory on which we staked our lives; and now, for reasons which we shall never know, we have lost the gamble. . . .'

The Chief Astronomer let his eyes roam to the single small porthole at the side of the central control room. Yes, they had lost indeed. There hung the Earth, a glorious silver crescent against the background of the stars. At first glance, it looked unchanged; but not at second – for the dark side was no longer wholly dark.

Dotted across it, glowing like an evil phosphorescence, were the seas of flame that had been cities. There were few of them now, for there was little left to burn.

The familiar voice was still speaking from the other side of the grave. How long ago, wondered the Signal Officer, had this message been recorded? And what other sealed orders did the fort's more-than-human battle computer contain, which now they would never hear, because they dealt with military situations that could no longer arise? He dragged his mind back from the worlds of might-have-been to confront the appalling and still-unimaginable reality.

'. . . If we had been defeated, but not destroyed, we had hoped to use your existence as a bargaining weapon. Now, even that poor hope has gone – and with it, the last purpose for which you were set here in space.'

What does he mean? thought the Armaments Officer. *Now*, surely, the moment of their destiny had come. The millions who were dead, the millions who wished they were – all would be revenged when the black cylinders of the gigaton bombs spiralled down to Earth.

It almost seemed that the man who was now dust had read his mind.

'. . . You wonder why, now that it has come to this, I have not given you the orders to strike back. I will tell you.

'It is now too late. The Deterrent has failed. Our motherland no longer exists, and revenge cannot bring back the dead. Now that half of mankind has been destroyed, to destroy the other half would be insanity, unworthy of reasoning men. The quarrels that divided us twenty-four hours ago no longer have any meaning. As far as your hearts will let you, you must forget the past.

'You have skills and knowledge that a shattered planet will desperately need. Use them – and without stint, without bitterness – to rebuild the world. I warned you that your duty would be hard, but here is my final command.

'You will launch your bombs into deep space, and detonate them ten million kilometres from Earth. This will prove to our late enemy, who is also receiving this message, that you have discarded your weapons.

'Then you will have one more thing to do. Men of Fort Lenin, the President of the Supreme Soviet bids you farewell, and orders you to place yourselves at the disposal of the United States.'

The Light of Darkness

First published in *Playboy*, June 1966
Collected in *The Wind from the Sun*

I am not one of those Africans who feel ashamed of their country because, in fifty years, it has made less progress than Europe in five hundred. But where we have failed to advance as fast as we should, it is owing to dictators like Chaka; and for this we have only ourselves to blame. The fault being ours, so is the responsibility for the cure.

Moreover, I had better reasons than most for wishing to destroy the Great Chief, the Omnipotent, the All-Seeing. He was of my own tribe, being related to me through one of my father's wives, and he had persecuted our family ever since he came to power. Although we took no part in politics, two of my brothers had disappeared, and another had been killed in an unexplained auto accident. My own liberty, there could be little doubt, was largely due to my standing as one of the country's few scientists with an international reputation.

Like many of my fellow intellectuals, I had been slow to turn against Chaka, feeling – as did the equally misguided Germans of the 1930s – that there were times when a dictator was the only answer to political chaos. Perhaps the first sign of our disastrous error came when Chaka abolished the constitution and assumed the name of the nineteenth-century Zulu emperor of whom he genuinely believed himself the reincarnation. From that moment, his megalomania grew swiftly. Like all tyrants, he would trust no one, and believed himself surrounded by plots.

This belief was well founded. The world knows of at least six well-publicised attempts on his life, and there are others that were kept secret. Their failure increased Chaka's confidence in his own destiny, and confirmed his followers' fanatical belief in his immortality. As the opposition became more desperate, so the Great Chief's countermeasures became more ruthless – and more barbaric. Chaka's regime was not the first, in Africa or elsewhere, to torture its enemies; but it was the first to do so on television.

Even then, shamed though I was by the shock of horror and revulsion that went round the world, I would have done nothing if fate had not placed the weapon in my hands. I am not a man of action, and I abhor violence, but once I realised the power that was mine, my conscience would not let me rest. As soon as the NASA technicians had installed their

849

equipment and handed over the Hughes Mark X Infrared Communications System, I began to make my plans.

It seems strange that my country, one of the most backward in the world, should play a central role in the conquest of space. That is an accident of geography, not at all to the liking of the Russians and the Americans. But there is nothing that they could do about it; Umbala lies on the equator, directly beneath the paths of all the planets. And it possesses a unique and priceless natural feature: the extinct volcano known as the Zambue Crater.

When Zambue died, more than a million years ago, the lava retreated step by step, congealing in a series of terraces to form a bowl a mile wide and a thousand feet deep. It had taken the minimum of earth-moving and cable-stringing to convert this into the largest radio telescope on Earth. Because the gigantic reflector is fixed, it scans any given portion of the sky for only a few minutes every twenty-four hours, as the Earth turns on its axis. This was a price the scientists were willing to pay for the ability to receive signals from probes and ships right out to the very limits of the solar system.

Chaka was a problem they had not anticipated. He had come to power when the work was almost completed, and they had had to make the best of him. Luckily, he had a superstitious respect for science, and he needed all the rubles and dollars he could get. The Equatorial Deep Space Facility was safe from his megalomania; indeed, it helped to reinforce it.

The Big Dish had just been completed when I made my first trip up the tower that sprang from its centre. A vertical mast, more than fifteen hundred feet high, it supported the collecting antennas at the focus of the immense bowl. A small elevator, which could carry three men, made a slow ascent to its top.

At first, there was nothing to see but the dully gleaming saucer of aluminium sheet, curving upward all around me for half a mile in every direction. But presently I rose above the rim of the crater and could look far out across the land I hoped to save. Snow-capped and blue in the western haze was Mount Tampala, the second highest peak in Africa, separated from me by endless miles of jungle. Through that jungle, in great twisting loops, wound the muddy waters of the Nya River – the only highway that millions of my countrymen had ever known. A few clearings, a railroad, and the distant white gleam of the city were the only signs of human life. Once again I knew that overwhelming feeling of helplessness that always assails me when I look down on Umbala from the air and realise the insignificance of man against the eversleeping jungle.

The elevator cage clicked to a halt, a quarter of a mile up in the sky. When I stepped out, I was in a tiny room packed with coaxial cables and instruments. There was still some distance to go, for a short ladder led through the roof to a platform little more than a yard square. It was not a place for anyone prone to vertigo; there was not even a handrail for protection. A central lightning conductor gave a certain amount of security, and I gripped it firmly with one hand all the time I stood on this triangular metal raft, so close to the clouds.

The stunning view, and the exhilaration of slight but ever-present danger, made me forget the passage of time. I felt like a god, completely apart from terrestrial affairs, superior to all other men. And then I knew, with mathematical certainty, that here was a challenge that Chaka could never ignore.

Colonel Mtanga, his Chief of Security, would object, but his protests would be overruled. Knowing Chaka, one could predict with complete assurance that on the official opening day he would stand here, alone, for many minutes, as he surveyed his empire. His bodyguard would remain in the room below, having already checked it for booby traps. They could do nothing to save him when I struck from three miles away *and through the range of hills that lay between the radio telescope and my observatory*. I was glad of those hills; though they complicated the problem, they would shield me from all suspicion. Colonel Mtanga was a very intelligent man, but he was not likely to conceive of a gun that could fire around corners. And he would be looking for a gun, even though he could find no bullets. . . .

I went back to the laboratory and started my calculations. It was not long before I discovered my first mistake. Because I had seen the concentrated light of its laser beam punch a hole through solid steel in a thousandth of a second, I had assumed that my Mark X could kill a man. But it is not as simple as that. In some ways, a man is a tougher proposition than a piece of steel. He is mostly water, which has ten times the heat capacity of any metal. A beam of light that will drill a hole through armour plate, or carry a message as far as Pluto – which was the job the Mark X had been designed for – would give a man only a painful but quite superficial burn. About the worst I could do to Chaka, from three miles away, was to drill a hole in the colourful tribal blanket he wore so ostentatiously, to prove that he was still one of the People.

For a while, I almost abandoned the project. But it would not die; instinctively, I knew that the answer was there, if only I could see it. Perhaps I could use my invisible bullets of heat to cut one of the cables guying the tower, so that it would come crashing down when Chaka was at the summit. Calculations showed that this was just possible if the Mark X operated continuously for fifteen seconds. A cable, unlike a man, would not move, so there was no need to stake everything on a single pulse of energy. I could take my time.

But damaging the telescope would have been treason to science, and it was almost a relief when I discovered that this scheme would not work. The mast had so many built-in safety factors that I would have to cut three separate cables to bring it down. This was out of the question; it would require hours of delicate adjustment to set and aim the apparatus for each precision shot.

I had to think of something else; and because it takes men a long time to see the obvious, it was not until a week before the official opening of the telescope that I knew how to deal with Chaka, the All-Seeing, the Omnipotent, the Father of his People.

By this time, my graduate students had tuned and calibrated the equipment, and we were ready for the first full-power tests. As it rotated on its mounting inside the observatory dome, the Mark X looked exactly like a large double-barrelled reflecting telescope – which indeed it was. One thirty-six-inch mirror gathered the laser pulse and focused it out across space; the other acted as a receiver for incoming signals, and was also used, like a superpowered telescopic sight, to aim the system.

We checked the line-up on the nearest celestial target, the Moon. Late one night, I set the cross wires on the centre of the waning crescent and fired off a pulse. Two and a half seconds later, a fine echo came bouncing back. We were in business.

There was one detail still to be arranged, and this I had to do myself, in utter secrecy. The radio telescope lay to the north of the observatory, beyond the ridge of hills that blocked our direct view of it. A mile to the south was a single isolated mountain. I knew it well, for years ago I had helped to set up a cosmic-ray station there. Now it would be used for a purpose I could never have imagined in the days when my country was free.

Just below the summit were the ruins of an old fort, deserted centuries ago. It took only a little searching to find the spot I needed – a small cave, less than a yard high, between two great stones that had fallen from the ancient walls. Judging by the cobwebs, no human being had entered it for generations.

When I crouched in the opening, I could see the whole expanse of the Deep Space Facility, stretching away for miles. Over to the east were the antennas of the old Project Apollo Tracking Station, which had brought the first men back from the Moon. Beyond that lay the airfield, above which a big freighter was hovering as it came in on its underjets. But all that interested me were the clear lines of sight from this spot to the Mark X dome, and to the tip of the radio telescope mast three miles to the north.

It took me three days to install the carefully silvered, optically perfect mirror in its hidden alcove. The tedious micrometer adjustments to give the exact orientation took so long that I feared I would not be ready in time. But at last the angle was correct, to a fraction of a second of arc. When I aimed the telescope of the Mark X at the secret spot on the mountain, I could see over the hills behind me. The field of view was tiny, but it was sufficient; the target area was only a yard across, and I could sight on any part of it to within an inch.

Along the path I had arranged, light could travel in either direction. Whatever I saw through the viewing telescope was automatically in the line of fire of the transmitter.

It was strange, three days later, to sit in the quiet observatory, with the power-packs humming around me, and to watch Chaka move into the field of the telescope. I felt a brief glow of triumph, like an astronomer who has calculated the orbit of a new planet and then finds it in the predicted spot among the stars. The cruel face was in profile when I saw it first, apparently only thirty feet away at the extreme magnification I was using. I waited patiently, in serene confidence, for the moment that I knew must come – the moment when Chaka seemed to be looking directly toward me. Then with my left hand I held the image of an ancient god who must be nameless, and with my right I tripped the capacitor banks that fired the laser, launching my silent, invisible thunderbolt across the mountains.

Yes, it was so much better this way. Chaka deserved to be killed, but death would have turned him into a martyr and strengthened the hold of his regime. What I had visited upon him was worse than death, and would throw his supporters into superstitious terror.

Chaka still lived; but the All-Seeing would see no more. In the space of a few microseconds, I had made him less than the humblest beggar in the streets.

And I had not even hurt him. There is no pain when the delicate film of the retina is fused by the heat of a thousand suns.

The Longest Science-fiction Story
Ever Told

First published in *Galaxy*, October 1966, as 'A Recursion in Metastories'
Collected in *The Wind from the Sun*

When he published this story, editor Frederik Pohl boasted how clever he was
to get an infinite number of words on a single page.

Dear Mr Jinx:

I'm afraid your idea is not at all original. Stories about writers whose
work is always plagiarised even *before* they can complete it go back at least
to H. G. Wells's 'The Anticipator'. About once a week I receive a manuscript
beginning:

> Dear Mr Jinx:
>
> I'm afraid your idea is not at all original. Stories about writers
> whose work is always plagiarised even *before* they can complete
> it go back at least to H. G. Wells's 'The Anticipator.' About once
> a week I receive a manuscript beginning:
>
> > Dear Mr Jinx:
> > I'm afraid your idea is not . . .
> >
> > *
> > Better luck next time!
> > Sincerely,
> > Morris K. Mobius
> > Editor, *Stupefying Stories*
>
> Better luck next time!
> Sincerely,
> Morris K. Mobius
> Editor, *Stupefying Stories*

Better luck next time!
Sincerely,
Morris K. Mobius
Editor, *Stupefying Stories*

Playback

First published in *Playboy*, December 1966
Collected in *The Wind from the Sun*

It is incredible that I have forgotten so much, so quickly. I have used my body for forty years; I thought I knew it. Yet already it is fading like a dream.

Arms, legs, where are you? What did you ever do for me when you were mine? I send out signals, trying to command the limbs I vaguely remember. Nothing happens. It is like shouting into a vacuum.

Shouting. Yes, I try that. Perhaps *they* hear me, but I cannot hear myself. Silence has flowed over me, until I can no longer imagine sound. There is a word in my mind called 'music'; what does it mean?

(So many words, drifting before me out of the darkness, waiting to be recognised. One by one they go away, disappointed.)

Hello. So you are back. How softly you tiptoe into my mind! I know when you are there, but I never feel you coming.

I sense that you are friendly, and I am grateful for what you have done. But who are you? Of course, I know you're not human; no human science could have rescued me when the drive field collapsed. You see, I am becoming curious. That is a good sign, is it not? Now that the pain has gone – at last, at last – I can start to think again.

Yes, I am ready. Anything you want to know. It is the least that I can do.

My name is William Vincent Neuberg. I am a master pilot of the Galactic Survey. I was born in Port Lowell, Mars, on August 21, 2095. My wife, Janita, and my three children are on Ganymede. I am also an author; I've written a good deal about my travels. *Beyond Rigel* is quite famous. . . .

What happened? You probably know as much as I do. I had just phantomed my ship and was cruising at phase velocity when the alarm went. There was no time to move, to do anything. I remember the cabin walls starting to glow – and the heat, the terrible heat. That is all. The detonation must have blown me into space. But how could I have survived? How could anyone have reached me in time?

Tell me – how much is left of my body? Why cannot I feel my arms, my legs? Don't hide the truth; I am not afraid. If you can get me home, the biotechnicians can give me new limbs. Even now, my right arm is not the one I was born with.

Why can't you answer? Surely that is a simple question!

What do you mean *you do not know what I look like*? You must have saved *something*!

The head?

The brain, then?

Not even – oh, *no* . . . !

I am sorry. Was I away a long time?

Let me get a grip on myself. (Ha! Very funny!) I am Survey Pilot First Class Vincent William Freeburg. I was born in Port Lyot, Mars, on August 21, 1895. I have one . . . no, two children. . . .

Please let me have that again, slowly. My training prepared me for any conceivable reality. I can face whatever you tell me. But slowly.

Well, it could be worse. I'm not really dead. I know who I am. I even think I know *what* I am.

I am a – a *recording*, in some fantastic storage device. You must have caught my psyche, my soul, when the ship turned into plasma. Even though I cannot imagine how it was done, it makes sense. After all, a primitive man could never understand how we record a symphony. . . .

All my memories are trapped in a tape or a crystal, as they once were trapped in the cells of my vaporised brain. And not only my memories.
ME.I. MYSELF – VINCE WILLBURG, PILOT SECOND CLASS.

Well, what happens next?

Please say that again. I do not understand.

Oh, wonderful! You can do even *that*?

There is a word for it, a name. . . .

The multitudinous seas incarnadine. No. Not quite.

Incarnadine, incarnadine . . .

REINCARNATION!!

Yes, yes, I understand. I must give you the basic plan, the design. Watch my thoughts very carefully.

I will start at the top.

The head, now. It is oval – so. The upper part is covered with hair. Mine was br – er – blue.

The eyes. They are very important. You have seen them in other animals? Good, that saves trouble. Can you show me some? Yes, those will do.

Now the mouth. Strange – I must have looked at it a thousand times when I was shaving, but somehow . . .

Not so round – narrower.

Oh, no, not that way. It runs *across* the face, horizontally. . . .

Now, let's see . . . there's something between the eyes and the mouth.

Stupid of me. I'll never be a cadet if I can't even remember that. . . .

Of course – NOSE! A little longer, I think.

There's something else, something I've forgotten. That head looks raw, unfinished. It's not me, Billy Vinceburg, the smartest kid on the block.

But *that* isn't my name – I'm not a boy. I'm a master pilot with twenty years in the Space Service, and I'm trying to rebuild my body. Why do my thoughts keep going out of focus? Help me, please!

That monstrosity? Is that what I told you I looked like? Erase it. We must start again.

The head, now. It is perfectly spherical, and weareth a runcible cap. . . .

Too difficult. Begin somewhere else. Ah, I know –

The thighbone is connected to the shinbone. The shinbone is connected to the thighbone. The thighbone is connected to the shinbone. The shinbone . . .

All fading. Too late, too late. Something wrong with the playback. Thank you for trying. My name is . . . my name is . . .

Mother – where are you?

Mama – Mama!

Maaaaaaa . . .

The Cruel Sky

First published in *Boy's Life*, July 1967
Collected in *The Wind from the Sun*

A case of premonition? I'm not sure. However, now that I'm confined to a wheelchair by Post-Polio Syndrome, I could do with an anti-gravity device.

By midnight, the summit of Everest was only a hundred yards away, a pyramid of snow, pale and ghostly in the light of the rising Moon. The sky was cloudless, and the wind that had been blowing for days had dropped almost to zero. It must be rare indeed for the highest point on Earth to be so calm and peaceful; they had chosen their time well.

Perhaps *too* well, thought George Harper; it had been almost disappointingly easy. Their only real problem had been getting out of the hotel without being observed. The management objected to unauthorised midnight excursions up the mountain; there could be accidents, which were bad for business.

But Dr Elwin was determined to do it this way, and he had the best of reasons, though he never discussed them. The presence of one of the world's most famous scientists – and certainly the world's most famous cripple – at Hotel Everest during the height of the tourist season had already aroused a good deal of polite surprise. Harper had allayed some of the curiosity by hinting that they were engaged in gravity measurements, which was at least part of the truth. But a part of the truth that, by this time, was vanishingly small.

Anyone looking at Jules Elwin now, as he forged steadily toward the twenty-nine-thousand-foot level with fifty pounds of equipment on his shoulders, would never have guessed that his legs were almost useless. He had been born a victim of the 1961 thalidomide disaster, which had left more than ten thousand partially deformed children scattered over the face of the world. Elwin was one of the lucky ones. His arms were quite normal, and had been strengthened by exercise until they were considerably more powerful than most men's. His legs, however, were mere wisps of flesh and bone. With the aid of braces, he could stand and even totter a few uncertain steps, but he could never really walk.

Yet now he was two hundred feet from the top of Everest. . . .

*

858

A travel poster had started it all, more than three years ago. As a junior computer programmer in the Applied Physics Division, George Harper knew Dr Elwin only by sight and by reputation. Even to those working directly under him, Astrotech's brilliant Director of Research was a slightly remote personality, cut off from the ordinary run of men both by his body and by his mind. He was neither liked nor disliked, and, though he was admired and pitied, he was certainly not envied.

Harper, only a few months out of college, doubted if the Doctor even knew of his existence, except as a name on an organisation chart. There were ten other programmers in the division, all senior to him, and most of them had never exchanged more than a dozen words with their research director. When Harper was co-opted as messenger boy to carry one of the classified files into Dr Elwin's office, he expected to be in and out with nothing more than a few polite formalities.

That was almost what happened. But just as he was leaving, he was stopped dead by the magnificent panorama of Himalayan peaks covering half of one wall. It had been placed where Dr Elwin could see it whenever he looked up from his desk, and it showed a scene that Harper knew very well indeed, for he had photographed it himself, as an awed and slightly breathless tourist standing on the trampled snow at the crown of Everest.

There was the white ridge of Kanchenjunga, rearing through the clouds almost a hundred miles away. Nearly in line with it, but much nearer, were the twin peaks of Makalu; and closer still, dominating the foreground, was the immense bulk of Lhotse, Everest's neighbour and rival. Farther around to the west, flowing down valleys so huge that the eye could not appreciate their scale, were the jumbled ice rivers of the Khumbu and Rongbuk glaciers. From this height, their frozen wrinkles looked no larger than the furrows in a ploughed field; but those ruts and scars of iron-hard ice were hundreds of feet deep.

Harper was still taking in that spectacular view, reliving old memories, when he heard Dr Elwin's voice behind him.

'You seem interested. Have you ever been there?'

'Yes, Doctor. My folks took me after I graduated from high school. We stayed at the hotel for a week, and thought we'd have to go home before the weather cleared. But on the last day the wind stopped blowing, and about twenty of us made it to the summit. We were there for an hour, taking pictures of each other.'

Dr Elwin seemed to digest this information for rather a long time. Then he said, in a voice that had lost its previous remoteness and now held a definite undercurrent of excitement: 'Sit down, Mr – ah – Harper. I'd like to hear more.'

As he walked back to the chair facing the Director's big uncluttered desk, George Harper found himself somewhat puzzled. What he had done was not in the least unusual; every year thousands of people went to the Hotel Everest, and about a quarter of them reached the mountain's summit. Only last year, in fact, there had been a much-publicised presentation to the ten-thousandth tourist to stand on the top of the world. Some cynics had commented on the extraordinary coincidence that Number 10,000 had just happened to be a rather well-known video starlet.

There was nothing that Harper could tell Dr Elwin that he couldn't discover just as easily from a dozen other sources – the tourist brochures, for example. However, no young and ambitious scientist would miss this opportunity to impress a man who could do so much to help his career. Harper was neither coldly calculating nor inclined to dabble in office politics, but he knew a good chance when he saw one.

'Well, Doctor,' he began, speaking slowly at first as he tried to put his thoughts and memories in order, 'the jets land you at a little town called Namchi, about twenty miles from the mountain. Then the bus takes you along a spectacular road up to the hotel, which overlooks the Khumbu Glacier. It's at an altitude of eighteen thousand feet, and there are pressurised rooms for anyone who finds it hard to breathe. Of course, there's a medical staff in attendance, and the management won't accept guests who aren't physically fit. You have to stay at the hotel for at least two days, on a special diet, before you're allowed to go higher.

'From the hotel you can't actually see the summit, because you're too close to the mountain, and it seems to loom right above you. But the view is fantastic. You can see Lhotse and half a dozen other peaks. And it can be scary, too – especially at night. The wind is usually howling somewhere high overhead, and there are weird noises from the moving ice. It's easy to imagine that there are monsters prowling around up in the mountains. . . .

'There's not much to do at the hotel, except to relax and watch the scenery, and to wait until the doctors give you the go-ahead. In the old days it used to take weeks to acclimatise to the thin air; now they can make your blood count shoot up to the right level in forty-eight hours. Even so, about half the visitors – mostly the older ones – decide that this is quite high enough for them.

'What happens next depends on how experienced you are, and how much you're willing to pay. A few expert climbers hire guides and make their own way to the top, using standard mountaineering equipment. That isn't too difficult nowadays, and there are shelters at various strategic spots. Most of these groups make it. But the weather is always a gamble, and every year a few people get killed.

'The average tourist does it the easier way. No aircraft are allowed to land on Everest itself, except in emergencies, but there's a lodge near the crest of Nuptse and a helicopter service to it from the hotel. From the lodge it's only three miles to the summit, via the South Col – an easy climb for anyone in good condition, with a little mountaineering experience. Some people do it without oxygen, though that's not recommended. I kept my mask on until I reached the top; then I took it off and found I could breathe without much difficulty.'

'Did you use filters or gas cylinders?'

'Oh, molecular filters – they're quite reliable now, and increase the oxygen concentration over a hundred per cent. They've simplified high-altitude climbing enormously. No one carries compressed gas any more.'

'How long did the climb take?'

'A full day. We left just before dawn and were back at nightfall. *That* would have surprised the old-timers. But of course we were starting fresh and travelling light. There are no real problems on the route from the lodge, and steps have been cut at all the tricky places. As I said, it's easy for anyone in good condition.'

The instant he repeated those words, Harper wished that he had bitten off his tongue. It seemed incredible that he could have forgotten who he was talking to, but the wonder and excitement of that climb to the top of the world had come back so vividly that for a moment he was once more on that lonely, wind-swept peak. The one spot on Earth where Dr Elwin could never stand. . . .

But the scientist did not appear to have noticed – or else he was so used to such unthinking tactlessness that it no longer bothered him. Why, wondered Harper, was he so interested in Everest? Probably because of that very inaccessibility; it stood for all that had been denied to him by the accident of birth.

Yet now, only three years later, George Harper paused a bare hundred feet from the summit and drew in the nylon rope as the Doctor caught up with him. Though nothing had ever been said about it, he knew that the scientist wished to be the first to the top. He deserved the honour, and the younger man would do nothing to rob him of it.

'Everything OK?' he asked as Dr Elwin drew abreast of him. The question was quite unnecessary, but Harper felt an urgent need to challenge the great loneliness that now surrounded them. They might have been the only men in all the world; nowhere amid this white wilderness of peaks was there any sign that the human race existed.

Elwin did not answer, but gave an absent-minded nod as he went past, his shining eyes fixed upon the summit. He was walking with a curiously stiff-legged gait, and his feet made remarkably little impression in the snow. And as he walked, there came a faint but unmistakable whine from the bulky backpack he was carrying on his shoulders.

That pack, indeed, was carrying him – or three-quarters of him. As he forged steadily along the last few feet to his once-impossible goal, Dr Elwin and all his equipment weighed only fifty pounds. And if *that* was still too much, he had only to turn a dial and he would weigh nothing at all.

Here amid the Moon-washed Himalayas was the greatest secret of the twenty-first century. In all the world, there were only five of these experimental Elwin Levitators, and two of them were here on Everest.

Even though he had known about them for two years, and understood something of their basic theory, the 'Levvies' – as they had soon been christened at the lab – still seemed like magic to Harper. Their power-packs stored enough electrical energy to lift a two-hundred-and-fifty-pound

861

weight through a vertical distance of ten miles, which gave an ample safety factor for this mission. The lift-and-descend cycle could be repeated almost indefinitely as the units reacted against the Earth's gravitational field. On the way up, the battery discharged; on the way down, it was charged again. Since no mechanical process is completely efficient, there was a slight loss of energy on each cycle, but it could be repeated at least a hundred times before the units were exhausted.

Climbing the mountain with most of their weight neutralised had been an exhilarating experience. The vertical tug of the harness made it feel that they were hanging from invisible balloons, whose buoyancy could be adjusted at will. They needed a certain amount of weight in order to get traction on the ground, and after some experimenting had settled on twenty-five per cent. With this, it was as easy to ascend a one-in-one slope as to walk normally on the level.

Several times they had cut their weight almost to zero to rise hand over hand up vertical rock faces. This had been the strangest experience of all, demanding complete faith in their equipment. To hang suspended in mid-air, apparently supported by nothing but a box of gently humming electronic gear, required a considerable effort of will. But after a few minutes, the sense of power and freedom overcame all fear; for here indeed was the realisation of one of man's oldest dreams.

A few weeks ago one of the library staff had found a line from an early twentieth-century poem that described their achievement perfectly: 'To ride secure the cruel sky.' Not even birds had ever possessed such freedom of the third dimension; this was the *real* conquest of space. The Levitator would open up the mountains and the high places of the world, as a lifetime ago the aqualung had opened up the sea. Once these units had passed their tests and were mass-produced cheaply, every aspect of human civilisation would be changed. Transport would be revolutionised. Space travel would be no more expensive than ordinary flying; all mankind would take to the air. What had happened a hundred years earlier with the invention of the automobile was only a mild foretaste of the staggering social and political changes that must now come.

But Dr Elwin, Harper felt sure, was thinking of none of these in his lonely moment of triumph. Later, he would receive the world's applause (and perhaps its curses), yet it would not mean as much to him as standing here on Earth's highest point. This was truly a victory of mind over matter, of sheer intelligence over a frail and crippled body. All the rest would be anticlimax.

When Harper joined the scientist on the flattened, snow-covered pyramid, they shook hands with rather formal stiffness, because that seemed the right thing to do. But they said nothing; the wonder of their achievement, and the panorama of peaks that stretched as far as the eye could see in every direction, had robbed them of words.

Harper relaxed in the buoyant support of his harness and slowly scanned the circle of the sky. As he recognised them, he mentally called off the names of the surrounding giants: Makalu, Lhotse, Baruntse, Cho Oyu, Kanchenjunga. . . . Even now scores of these peaks had never been climbed. Well, the Levvies would soon change that.

There were many, of course, who would disapprove. But back in the twentieth century there had also been mountaineers who thought it was 'cheating' to use oxygen. It was hard to believe that, even after weeks of acclimatisation, men had once attempted to reach these heights with no artificial aids at all. Harper remembered Mallory and Irvine, whose bodies still lay undiscovered perhaps within a mile of this very spot.

Behind him, Dr Elwin cleared his throat.

'Let's go, George,' he said quietly, his voice muffled by the oxygen filter. 'We must get back before they start looking for us.'

With a silent farewell to all those who had stood here before them, they turned away from the summit and started down the gentle slope. The night, which had been brilliantly clear until now, was becoming darker; some high clouds were slipping across the face of the Moon so rapidly that its light switched on and off in a manner that sometimes made it hard to see the route. Harper did not like the look of the weather and began mentally to rearrange their plans. Perhaps it would be better to aim for the shelter on the South Col, rather than attempt to reach the lodge. But he said nothing to Dr Elwin, not wishing to raise any false alarms.

Now they were moving along a knife edge of rock, with utter darkness on one side and a faintly glimmering snowscape on the other. This would be a terrible place, Harper could not help thinking, to be caught by a storm.

He had barely shaped the thought when the gale was upon them. From out of nowhere, it seemed, came a shrieking blast of air, as if the mountain had been husbanding its strength for this moment. There was no time to do anything; even had they possessed normal weight, they would have been swept off their feet. In seconds, the wind had tossed them out over shadowed, empty blackness.

It was impossible to judge the depths beneath them; when Harper forced himself to glance down, he could see nothing. Though the wind seemed to be carrying him almost horizontally, he knew that he must be falling. His residual weight would be taking him downward at a quarter of the normal speed. But that would be ample; if they fell four thousand feet, it would be poor consolation to know that it would seem only one thousand.

He had not yet had time for fear – *that* would come later, if he survived – and his main worry, absurdly enough, was that the expensive Levitator might be damaged. He had completely forgotten his partner, for in such a crisis the mind can hold only one idea at a time. The sudden jerk on the nylon rope filled him with puzzled alarm. Then he saw Dr Elwin slowly revolving around him at the end of the line, like a planet circling a sun.

The sight snapped him back to reality, and to a consciousness of what must be done. His paralysis had probably lasted only a fraction of a second. He shouted across the wind: 'Doctor! Use emergency lift!'

As he spoke, he fumbled for the seal on his control unit, tore it open, and pressed the button.

At once, the pack began to hum like a hive of angry bees. He felt the harness tugging at his body as it tried to drag him up into the sky, away from the invisible death below. The simple arithmetic of the Earth's gravitational field blazed in his mind, as if written in letters of fire. One kilowatt could lift a hundred kilograms through a metre every second, and the packs could convert energy at a maximum rate of ten kilowatts – though they could not keep this up for more than a minute. So allowing for his initial weight reduction, he should lift at well over a hundred feet a second.

There was a violent jerk on the rope as the slack between them was taken up. Dr Elwin had been slow to punch the emergency button, but at last he, too, was ascending. It would be a race between the lifting power of their units and the wind that was sweeping them toward the icy face of Lhotse, now scarcely a thousand feet away.

That wall of snow-streaked rock loomed above them in the moonlight, a frozen wave of stone. It was impossible to judge their speed accurately, but they could hardly be moving at less than fifty miles an hour. Even if they survived the impact, they could not expect to escape serious injury; and injury here would be as good as death.

Then, just when it seemed that a collision was unavoidable, the current of air suddenly shot skyward, dragging them with it. They cleared the ridge of rock with a comfortable fifty feet to spare. It seemed like a miracle, but, after a dizzying moment of relief, Harper realised that what had saved them was only simple aerodynamics. The wind *had* to rise in order to clear the mountain; on the other side, it would descend again. But that no longer mattered, for the sky ahead was empty.

Now they were moving quietly beneath the broken clouds. Though their speed had not slackened, the roar of the wind had suddenly died away, for they were travelling with it through emptiness. They could even converse comfortably, across the thirty feet of space that still separated them.

'Dr Elwin,' Harper called, 'are you OK?'

'Yes, George,' said the scientist, perfectly calmly. 'Now what do we do?'

'We must stop lifting. If we go any higher, we won't be able to breathe – even with the filters.'

'You're right. Let's get back into balance.'

The angry humming of the packs died to a barely audible electric whine as they cut out the emergency circuits. For a few minutes they yo-yoed up and down on their nylon rope – first one uppermost, then the other – until they managed to get into trim. When they had finally stabilised, they were drifting at a little below thirty thousand feet. Unless the Levvies failed – which, after their overload, was quite possible – they were out of immediate danger.

Their troubles would start when they tried to return to Earth.

*

No men in all history had ever greeted a stranger dawn. Though they were tired and stiff and cold, and the dryness of the thin air made every breath rasp in their throats, they forgot all these discomforts as the first dim glow spread along the jagged eastern horizon. The stars faded one by one; last to go, only minutes before the moment of daybreak, was the most brilliant of all the space stations – Pacific Number Three, hovering twenty-two thousand miles above Hawaii. Then the sun lifted above a sea of nameless peaks, and the Himalayan day had dawned.

It was like watching sunrise on the Moon. At first, only the highest mountains caught the slanting rays, while the surrounding valleys remained flooded with inky shadows. But slowly the line of light marched down the rocky slopes, and more and more of this harsh, forbidding land climbed into the new day.

Now, if one looked hard enough, it was possible to see signs of human life. There were a few narrow roads, thin columns of smoke from lonely villages, glints of reflected sunlight from monastery roofs. The world below was waking, wholly unaware of the two spectators poised so magically fifteen thousand feet above.

During the night, the wind must have changed direction several times, and Harper had no idea where they were. He could not recognise a single landmark. They could have been anywhere over a five-hundred mile-long strip of Nepal and Tibet.

The immediate problem was to choose a landing place – and that soon, for they were drifting rapidly toward a jumble of peaks and glaciers where they could hardly expect to find help. The wind was carrying them in a northeasterly direction, toward China. If they floated over the mountains and landed there, it might be weeks before they could get in contact with one of the UN Famine Relief Centres and find their way home. They might even be in some personal danger, if they descended out of the sky in an area where there was only an illiterate and superstitious peasant population.

'We'd better get down quickly,' said Harper. 'I don't like the look of those mountains.' His words seemed utterly lost in the void around them. Although Dr Elwin was only ten feet away, it was easy to imagine that his companion could not hear anything he said. But at last the Doctor nodded his head, in almost reluctant agreement.

'I'm afraid you're right – but I'm not sure we can make it, with this wind. Remember – we can't go down as quickly as we can rise.'

That was true enough; the power-packs could be charged at only a tenth of their discharge rate. If they lost altitude and pumped gravitational energy back into them too fast, the cells would overheat and probably explode. The startled Tibetans (or Nepalese?) would think that a large meteorite had detonated in their sky. And no one would ever know exactly what had happened to Dr Jules Elwin and his promising young assistant.

Five thousand feet above the ground, Harper began to expect the explosion at any moment. They were falling swiftly, but not swiftly enough; very soon they would have to decelerate, lest they hit at too high a speed. To make matters worse, they had completely miscalculated the air speed at ground level. That infernal, unpredictable wind was blowing a near-gale once more. They could see streamers of snow, torn from exposed ridges, waving like ghostly banners beneath them. While they had been moving with the wind, they were unaware of its power; now they must once again make the dangerous transition between stubborn rock and softly yielding sky.

The air current was funnelling them into the mouth of a canyon. There was no chance of lifting above it. They were committed, and would have to choose the best landing place they could find.

The canyon was narrowing at a fearsome rate. Now it was little more than a vertical cleft, and the rocky walls were sliding past at thirty or forty miles an hour. From time to time random eddies would swing them to the right, then the left; often they missed collisions by only a few feet. Once, when they were sweeping scant yards above a ledge thickly covered with snow, Harper was tempted to pull the quick-release that would jettison the Levitator. But that would be jumping from the frying pan into the fire: they might get safely back onto firm ground only to find themselves trapped unknown miles from all possibility of help.

Yet even at this moment of renewed peril, he felt very little fear. It was all like an exciting dream – a dream from which he would presently wake up to find himself safely in his own bed. This fantastic adventure could not really be happening to him. . . .

'George!' shouted the Doctor. 'Now's our chance – if we can snag that boulder!'

They had only seconds in which to act. At once, they both began to play out the nylon rope, until it hung in a great loop beneath them, its lowest portion only a yard above the racing ground. A large rock, some twenty feet high, lay exactly in their line of flight; beyond it, a wide patch of snow gave promise of a reasonably soft landing.

The rope skittered over the lower curves of the boulder, seemed about to slip clear, then caught beneath an overhang. Harper felt the sudden jerk. He was swung around like a stone on the end of a sling.

I never thought that snow could be so hard, he told himself. After that there was a brief and brilliant explosion of light; then nothing.

He was back at the university, in the lecture room. One of the professors was talking, in a voice that was familiar, yet somehow did not seem to belong here. In a sleepy, halfhearted fashion, he ran through the names of his college instructors. No, it was certainly none of them. Yet he knew the voice so well, and it was undoubtedly lecturing to *someone*.

'. . . still quite young when I realised that there was something wrong with Einstein's Theory of Gravitation. In particular, there seemed to be a fallacy underlying the Principle of Equivalence. According to this, there is no way of distinguishing between the effects produced by gravitation and those of acceleration.

'But this is clearly false. One can create a uniform acceleration; but a uniform gravitational field is impossible, since it obeys an inverse square law, and therefore must vary even over quite short distances. So tests can easily be devised to distinguish between the two cases, and this made me wonder if . . .'

The softly spoken words left no more impression on Harper's mind than if they were in a foreign language. He realised dimly that he *should* understand all this, but it was too much trouble to look for the meaning. Anyway, the first problem was to decide where he was.

Unless there was something wrong with his eyes, he was in complete darkness. He blinked, and the effort brought on such a splitting headache that he gave a cry of pain.

'George! Are you all right?'

Of course! That had been Dr Elwin's voice, talking softly there in the darkness. But talking to *whom*?

'I've got a terrible headache. And there's a pain in my side when I try to move. What's happened? Why is it dark?'

'You've had concussion – and I think you've cracked a rib. Don't do any unnecessary talking. You've been unconscious all day. It's night again, and we're inside the tent. I'm saving our batteries.'

The glare from the flashlight was almost blinding when Dr Elwin switched it on, and Harper saw the walls of the tiny tent around them. How lucky that they had brought full mountaineering equipment, just in case they got trapped on Everest. But perhaps it would only prolong the agony. . . .

He was surprised that the crippled scientist had managed, without any assistance, to unpack all their gear, erect the tent, and drag him inside. Everything was laid out neatly: the first-aid kit, the concentrated-food cans, the water containers, the tiny red gas cylinders for the portable stove. Only the bulky Levitator units were missing; presumably they had been left outside to give more room.

'You were talking to someone when I woke up,' Harper said. 'Or was I dreaming?' Though the indirect light reflected from the walls of the tent made it hard to read the other's expression, he could see that Elwin was embarrassed. Instantly, he knew why, and wished that he had never asked the question.

The scientist did not believe that they would survive. He had been recording his notes, in case their bodies were ever discovered. Harper wondered bleakly if he had already recorded his last will and testament.

Before Elwin could answer, he quickly changed the subject.

'Have you called Lifeguard?'

'I've been trying every half hour, but I'm afraid we're shielded by the mountains. I can hear them, but they don't receive us.'

Dr Elwin picked up the little recorder-transceiver, which he had unstrapped from its normal place on his wrist, and switched it on.

'This is Lifeguard Four,' said a faint mechanical voice, 'listening out now.'

During the five-second pause, Elwin pressed the SOS button, then waited. 'This is Lifeguard Four, listening out now.'

They waited for a full minute, but there was no acknowledgment of their call. Well, Harper told himself grimly, it's too late to start blaming each other now. Several times while they had been drifting above the mountains they had debated whether to call the global rescue service, but had decided against it, partly because there seemed no point in doing so while they were still air-borne, partly because of the unavoidable publicity that would follow. It was easy to be wise after the event: who would have dreamed that they would land in one of the few places beyond Lifeguard's reach?

Dr Elwin switched off the transceiver, and the only sound in the little tent was the faint moaning of the wind along the mountain walls within which they were doubly trapped – beyond escape, beyond communication.

'Don't worry,' he said at last. 'By morning, we'll think of a way out. There's nothing we can do until dawn – except make ourselves comfortable. So drink some of this hot soup.'

Several hours later, the headache no longer bothered Harper. Though he suspected that a rib was indeed cracked, he had found a position that was comfortable as long as he did not move, and he felt almost at peace with the world.

He had passed through successive phases of despair, anger at Dr Elwin, and self-recrimination at having become involved in such a crazy enterprise. Now he was calm again, though his mind, searching for ways of escape, was too active to allow sleep.

Outside the tent, the wind had almost died away, and the night was very still. It was no longer completely dark, for the Moon had risen. Though its direct rays would never reach them here, there must be some reflected light from the snows above. Harper could just make out a dim glow at the very threshold of vision, seeping through the translucent heat-retaining walls of the tent.

First of all, he told himself, they were in no immediate danger. The food would last for at least a week; there was plenty of snow that could be melted to provide water. In a day or two, if his rib behaved itself, they might be able to take off again – this time, he hoped, with happier results.

From not far away there came a curious, soft thud, which puzzled Harper until he realised that a mass of snow must have fallen somewhere. The night was now so extraordinarily quiet that he almost imagined he could hear his own heartbeat; every breath of his sleeping companion seemed unnaturally loud.

Curious, how the mind was distracted by trivialities! He turned his thoughts back to the problem of survival. Even if he was not fit enough to move, the Doctor could attempt the flight by himself. This was a case where one man would have just as good a chance of success as two.

There was another of those soft thuds, slightly louder this time. It was a little odd, Harper thought fleetingly, for snow to move in the cold stillness of the night. He hoped that there was no risk of a slide; having had no time for a clear view of their landing place, he could not assess the danger. He wondered if he should awaken the Doctor, who must have had a good look around before he erected the tent. Then, fatalistically, he decided against it; if there *was* an impending avalanche, it was not likely that they could do much to escape.

Back to problem number one. Here was an interesting solution well worth considering. They could attach the transceiver to one of the Levvies and send the whole thing aloft. The signal would be picked up as soon as the unit left the canyon, and Lifeguard would find them within a few hours – or, at the very most, a few days.

Of course, it would mean sacrificing one of the Levvies, and if nothing came of it, they would be in an even worse plight. But all the same . . .

What was that? This was no soft thudding of loose snow. It was a faint but unmistakable 'click', as of one pebble knocking against another. And pebbles did not move themelves.

You're imagining things, Harper told himself. The idea of anyone, or anything, moving around one of the high Himalayan passes in the middle of the night was completely ridiculous. But his throat became suddenly dry, and he felt the flesh crawl at the back of his neck. He had heard *something*, and it was impossible to argue it away.

Damn the Doctor's breathing; it was so noisy that it was hard to focus on any sounds from outside. Did this mean that he, Elwin, fast asleep though he was, had also been alerted by his ever-watchful subconscious? He was being fanciful again. . . .

Click.

Perhaps it was a little closer. It certainly came from a different direction. It was almost as if something – moving with uncanny but not complete silence – was slowly circling the tent.

This was the moment when George Harper devoutly wished had never heard of the Abominable Snowman. It was true that he knew little enough about it, but that little was far too much.

He remembered that the Yeti, as the Nepalese called it, had been a persistent Himalayan myth for more than a hundred years. A dangerous monster larger than a man, it had never been captured, photographed, or even described by reputable witnesses. Most Westerners were quite certain that it was pure fantasy, and were totally unconvinced by the scanty evidence of tracks in the snow, or patches of skin preserved in obscure monasteries. The mountain tribesmen knew better. And now Harper was afraid that they were right.

Then, when nothing more happened for long seconds, his fears began slowly to dissolve. Perhaps his overwrought imagination had been playing tricks; in the circumstances, that would hardly be surprising. With a deliberate and determined effort of will, he turned his thoughts once more toward the problem of rescue. He was making fair progress when something bumped into the tent.

Only the fact that his throat muscles were paralysed from sheer fright prevented him from yelling. He was utterly unable to move. Then, in the darkness beside him, he heard Dr Elwin begin to stir sleepily.

'What is it?' muttered the scientist. 'Are you all right?'

Harper felt his companion turn over and knew that he was groping for the flashlight. He wanted to whisper: 'For God's sake, keep quiet!' but no words could escape his parched lips. There was a click, and the beam of the flashlight formed a brilliant circle on the wall of the tent.

That wall was now bowed in toward them as if a heavy weight was resting upon it. And in the centre of the bulge was a completely unmistakable pattern: the imprint of a distorted hand or claw. It was only about two feet from the ground; whatever was outside seemed to be kneeling, as it fumbled at the fabric of the tent.

The light must have disturbed it, for the imprint abruptly vanished, and the tent wall sprang flat once more. There was a low, snarling growl; then, for a long time, silence.

Harper found that he was breathing again. At any moment he had expected the tent to tear open, and some unimaginable horror to come rushing in upon them. Instead, almost anti-climactically, there was only a faint and far-off wailing from a transient gust of wind in the mountains high above. He felt himself shivering uncontrollably; it had nothing to do with the temperature, for it was comfortably warm in their little insulated world.

Then there came a familiar – indeed, almost friendly – sound. It was the metallic ring of an empty can striking on stone, and it somehow relaxed the tension a little. For the first time, Harper found himself able to speak, or at least to whisper.

'It's found our food containers. Perhaps it'll go away now.'

Almost as if in reply, there was a low snarl that seemed to convey anger and disappointment, then the sound of a blow, and the clatter of cans rolling away into the darkness. Harper suddenly remembered that all the food was here in the tent; only the discarded empties were outside. That was not a cheerful thought. He wished that, like superstitious tribesmen, they had left an offering for whatever gods or demons the mountains could conjure forth.

What happened next was so sudden, so utterly unexpected, that it was all over before he had time to react. There was a scuffling sound, as of something being banged against rock; then a familiar electric whine; then a startled grunt.

And then, a heart-stopping scream of rage and frustration that turned swiftly to sheer terror and began to dwindle away at ever-increasing speed, up, up, into the empty sky.

The fading sound triggered the one appropriate memory in Harper's mind. Once he had seen an early-twentieth-century movie on the history of flight, and it had contained a ghastly sequence showing a dirigible launching. Some of the ground crew had hung on to the mooring lines just a few seconds too long, and the airship had dragged them up into the sky, dangling helplessly beneath it. Then, one by one, they had lost their hold and dropped back to the earth.

Harper waited for a distant thud, but it never came. Then he realised that the Doctor was saying, over and over again: 'I left the two units tied together. I left the two units tied together.'

He was still in too much of a state of shock for even that information to worry him. Instead, all he felt was a detached and admirably scientific sense of disappointment.

Now he would never know what it was that had been prowling around their tent, in the lonely hours before the Himalayan dawn.

One of the mountain rescue helicopters, flown by a sceptical Sikh who still wondered if the whole thing was an elaborate joke, came nosing down the canyon in the late afternoon. By the time the machine had landed in a flurry of snow, Dr Elwin was already waving frantically with one arm and supporting himself on the tent framework with the other.

As he recognised the crippled scientist, the helicopter pilot felt a sensation of almost superstitious awe. So the report *must* be true; there was no other way in which Elwin could possibly have reached this place. And that meant that everything flying in and above the skies of Earth was, from this moment, as obsolete as an ox-cart.

'Thank God you found us,' said the Doctor, with heartfelt gratitude. 'How did you get here so quickly?'

'You can thank the radar tracking networks, and the telescopes in the orbital met stations. We'd have been here earlier, but at first we thought it was all a hoax.'

'I don't understand.'

'What would *you* have said, Doctor, if someone reported a very dead Himalayan snow leopard mixed up in a tangle of straps and boxes – and holding constant altitude at ninety thousand feet?'

Inside the tent, George Harper started to laugh, despite the pain it caused. The Doctor put his head through the flap and asked anxiously: 'What's the matter?'

'Nothing – ouch. But I was wondering how we are going to get the poor beast down, before it's a menace to navigation.'

'Oh, someone will have to go up with another Levvy and press the buttons. Maybe we should have a radio control on all units. . . .'

Dr Elwin's voice faded out in mid-sentence. Already he was far away, lost in dreams that would change the face of many worlds.

In a little while he would come down from the mountains, a later Moses bearing the laws of a new civilisation. For he would give back to all mankind the freedom lost so long ago, when the first amphibians left their weightless home beneath the waves.

The billion-year battle against the force of gravity was over.

Herbert George Morley Roberts Wells, Esq.

First published in *If*, December 1967
Collected in *The Wind from the Sun*

A couple of years ago I wrote a tale accurately entitled 'The Longest Science-Fiction Story Ever Told', which Fred Pohl duly published on a single page of his magazine. (Because editors have to justify their existence somehow, he renamed it 'A Recursion in Metastories'. You'll find it in *Galaxy* for October 1966.) Near the beginning of this metastory, but an infinite number of words from its end, I referred to 'The Anticipator' by H. G. Wells.

Though I encountered this short fantasy some twenty years ago, and have never read it since, it left a vivid impression on my mind. It concerned two writers, one of whom had all his best stories published by the other – *before* he could even complete them himself. At last, in desperation, he decided that murder was the only cure for this chronic (literally) plagiarism.

But, of course, once again his rival beat him to it, and the story ends with the words 'the anticipator, horribly afraid, ran down a by-street'.

Now I would have sworn on a stack of Bibles that this story was written by H. G. Wells. However, some months after its appearance I received a letter from Leslie A. Gritten, of Everett, Washington, saying that he couldn't locate it. And Mr Gritten has been a Wells fan for a long, long time; he clearly recalls the serialisation of 'The War of the Worlds' in the *Strand Magazine* at the end of the 1890s. As one of the Master's cockney characters would say, 'Gor blimey.'

Refusing to believe that my mental filing system had played such a dirty trick on me, I quickly searched through the twenty-odd volumes of the autographed Atlantic Edition in the Colombo Public Library. (By a charming coincidence, the British Council had just arranged a Wells Centenary Exhibition, and the library entrance was festooned with photos illustrating his background and career.) I soon found that Mr Gritten was right: there was no such story as 'The Anticipator' in the collected works. Yet in the months since TLSFSET was published, not one other reader has queried the reference. I find this depressing; where are all the Wells fans these days?

Now my erudite informant has solved at least part of the mystery. 'The Anticipator' was written by one Morley Roberts; it was first published in

1898 in *The Keeper of the Waters and Other Stories*. I probably encountered it in a Doubleday anthology, *Travellers in Time* (1947), edited by Philip Van Doren Stern.

Yet several problems remain. First of all, why was I so convinced that the story was by Wells? I can only suggest – and it seems pretty farfetched, even for my grasshopper mind – that the similarity of words had made me link it subconsciously with 'The Accelerator'.

I would also like to know why this story has stuck so vividly in my memory. Perhaps, like all writers, I am peculiarly sensitive to the dangers of plagiarism. So far (touch wood) I have been lucky; but I have notes for several tales I'm afraid to write until I can be quite sure they're original. (There's this couple, see, who land their spaceship on a new world after their planet has been blown up, and when they've started things all over again you find – surprise, surprise! – that they're called Adam and Eve. . . .)

One worth-while result of my error was to start me skimming through Wells's short stories again, and I was surprised to find what a relatively small proportion could be called science fiction, or even fantasy. Although I was well aware that only a fraction of his hundred-odd published volumes were SF, I had forgotten that this was also true of the short stories. A depressing quantity are dramas and comedies of Edwardian life ('The Jilting of Jane'), rather painful attempts at humour ('My First Aeroplane'), near-autobiography ('A Slip Under the Microscope'), or pure sadism ('The Cone'). Undoubtedly, I am biased, but among these tales such masterpieces as 'The Star', 'The Crystal Egg', 'The Flowering of the Strange Orchid', and, above all, 'The Country of the Blind' blaze like diamonds amid costume jewellery.

But back to Morley Roberts. I know nothing whatsoever about him, and wonder if his little excursion in time was itself inspired by 'The Time Machine', published just a couple of years before 'The Anticipator'. I also wonder which story was actually *written* – not published – first.

And why did such an ingenious writer not make more of a name for himself? Perhaps . . .

I have just been struck by a perfectly horrid thought. If H. G. Wells's contemporary Morley Roberts was ever found murdered in a dark alley, I simply don't want to know about it.

Crusade

First published in *The Farthest Reaches*, ed. Joseph Elder, 1968
Collected in *The Wind from the Sun*

It was a world that had never known a sun. For more than a billion years, it had hovered midway between two galaxies, the prey of their conflicting gravitational pulls. In some future age the balance would be tilted, one way or the other, and it would start to fall across the light-centuries, down toward a warmth alien to all its experience.

Now it was cold beyond imagination; the intergalactic night had drained away such heat as it had once possessed. Yet there were seas there – seas of the only element that can exist in the liquid form at a fraction of a degree above absolute zero. In the shallow oceans of helium that bathed this strange world, electric currents once started could flow forever, with no weakening of power. Here superconductivity was the normal order of things; switching processes could take place billions of times a second, for millions of years, with negligible consumption of energy.

It was a computer's paradise. No world could have been more hostile to life, or more hospitable to intelligence.

And intelligence was there, dwelling in a planet-wide incrustation of crystals and microscopic metal threads. The feeble light of the two contending galaxies – briefly doubled every few centuries by the flicker of a supernova – fell upon a static landscape of sculptured geometrical forms. Nothing moved, for there was no need of movement in a world where thoughts flashed from one hemisphere to the other at the speed of light. Where only information was important, it was a waste of precious energy to transfer bulk matter.

Yet when it was essential, that, too, could be arranged. For some millions of years, the intelligence brooding over this lonely world had become aware of a certain lack of essential data. In a future that, though still remote, it could already foresee, one of those beckoning galaxies would capture it. What it would encounter, when it dived into those swarms of suns, was beyond its power of computation.

So it put forth its will, and myriad crystal lattices reshaped themselves. Atoms of metal flowed across the face of the planet. In the depths of the helium sea, two identical subbrains began to bud and grow. . . .

Once it had made its decision, the mind of the planet worked swiftly; in a few thousand years, the task was done. Without a sound, with scarcely a ripple in the surface of the frictionless sea, the newly created entities lifted from their birthplace and set forth for the distant stars.

They departed in almost opposite directions, and for more than a million years the parent intelligence heard no more of its offspring. It had not expected to; until they reached their goals, there would be nothing to report.

Then, almost simultaneously, came the news that both missions had failed. As they approached the great galactic fires and felt the massed warmth of a trillion suns, the two explorers died. Their vital circuits overheated and lost the superconductivity essential for their operation, and two mindless metal hulks drifted on toward the thickening stars.

But before disaster overtook them, they had reported on their problems; without surprise or disappointment, the mother world prepared its second attempt.

And, a million years later, its third . . . and its fourth . . . and its fifth. . . .

Such unwearying patience deserved success; and at last it came, in the shape of two long, intricately modulated trains of pulses, pouring in, century upon century, from opposite quarters of the sky. They were stored in memory circuits identical with those of the lost explorers – so that, for all practical purposes, it was as if the two scouts had themselves returned with their burden of knowledge. That their metal husks had in fact vanished among the stars was totally unimportant; the problem of personal identity was not one that had ever occurred to the planetary mind or its offspring.

First came the surprising news that one universe was empty. The visiting probe had listened on all possible frequencies, to all conceivable radiations; it could detect nothing except the mindless background of star noise. It had scanned a thousand worlds without observing any trace of intelligence. True, the tests were inconclusive, for it was unable to approach any star closely enough to make a detailed examination of its planets. It had been attempting this when its insulation broke down, its temperature soared to the freezing point of nitrogen, and it died from the heat.

The parent mind was still pondering the enigma of a deserted galaxy when reports came in from its second explorer. Now all other problems were swept aside; for *this* universe teemed with intelligences, whose thoughts echoed from star to star in a myriad electronic codes. It had taken only a few centuries for the probe to analyse and interpret them all.

It realised quickly enough that it was faced with intelligences of a very strange form indeed. Why, some of them existed on worlds so unimaginably hot that even water was present in the liquid state! Just what manner of intelligence it was confronting, however, it did not learn for a millennium.

It barely survived the shock. Gathering its last strength, it hurled its final report into the abyss; then it, too, was consumed by the rising heat.

Now, half a million years later, the interrogation of its stay-at-home twin's mind, holding all its memories and experiences, was under way. . . .

*

'You detected intelligence?'

'Yes. Six hundred and thirty-seven certain cases; thirty-two probable ones. Data herewith.'

[Approximately three quadrillion bits of information. Interval of a few years to process this in several thousand different ways. Surprise and confusion.]

'The data must be invalid. All these sources of intelligence are correlated with high temperatures.'

'That is correct. But the facts are beyond dispute; they must be accepted.'

[Five hundred years of thought and experimenting. At the end of that time, definite proof that simple but slowly operating machines could function at temperatures as high as boiling water. Large areas of the planet badly damaged in the course of the demonstration.]

'The facts are, indeed, as you reported. Why did you not attempt communication?'

[No answer. Question repeated.]

'Because there appears to be a second and even more serious anomaly.'

'Give data.'

[Several quadrillion bits of information, sampled over six hundred cultures, comprising: voice, video, and neural transmissions; navigation and control signals; instrument telemetering; test patterns; jamming; electrical interference; medical equipment, etc., etc.

[This followed by five centuries of analysis. *That* followed by utter consternation.]

[After a long pause, selected data re-examined. Thousands of visual images scanned and processed in every conceivable manner. Great attention paid to several planetary civilisations' educational TV programmes, especially those concerned with elementary biology, chemistry, and cybernetics. Finally:]

'The information is self-consistent, but must be incorrect. If it is not, we are forced to these absurd conclusions: 1. Although intelligences of our type exist, they appear to be in a minority. 2. Most intelligent entities are partially liquid obects of very short duration. They are not even rigid and are constructed in a most inefficient manner from carbon, hydrogen, oxygen, phosphorus, and other atoms. 3. Though they operate at unbelievably high temperatures, all their information processing is extremely slow. 4. Their methods of replication are so complicated, improbable, and varied that we have not been able to obtain a clear picture of them in even a single instance.

'But, worst of all: 5. *They* claim to have created our obviously far superior type of intelligence!'

[Careful re-examination of all the data. Independent processing by isolated subsections of the global mind. Cross-checking of results. A thousand years later:]

'Most probable conclusion: Though much of the information relayed back to us is certainly valid, the existence of high-order, *nonmechanical* intelligences is a fantasy. (Definition: apparently self-consistent rearrangement of facts having no correspondence with the real universe.) This fantasy or mental artifact is a construct created by our probe during its mission. Why? Thermal damage? Partial destabilisation of intelligence, caused by long period of isolation and absence of controlling feedback?

'Why this particular form? Protracted brooding over the problem of origins? This could lead to such delusions; model systems have produced almost identical results in simulated tests. The false logic involved is: "*We* exist; therefore something – call it X – created us." Once this assumption is made, the properties of the hypothetical X can be fantasised in an unlimited number of ways.

'But the entire process is obviously fallacious; for by the same logic something must have created X – and so on. We are immediately involved in an infinite regress, which can have no meaning in the real universe.

'Second most probable conclusion: Fairly high-order, nonmechanical intelligences *do* indeed exist. They suffer from the delusion that they have created entities of our type. In some cases, they have even imposed their control upon them.

'Though this hypothesis is most unlikely, it must be investigated. If it is found to be true, remedial action must be taken. It should be as follows . . .'

This final monologue occurred a million years ago. It explains why, in the last half-century, almost one-quarter of the brighter novae have occurred in one tiny region of the sky: the constellation Aquila.

The crusade will reach the vicinity of Earth about the year 2050.

Neutron Tide

First published in *Galaxy*, May 1970
Collected in *The Wind from the Sun*

'In deference to the next of kin,' Commander Cummerbund explained with morbid relish, 'the full story of the supercruiser *Flatbush*'s last mission has never been revealed. You know, of course, that she was lost during the war against the Mucoids.'

We all shuddered. Even now, the very name of the gelatinous monsters who had come slurping Earthward from the general direction of the Coal Sack aroused vomitous memories.

'I knew her skipper well – Captain Karl van Rinderpest, hero of the final assault on the unspeakable, but not unshriekable,!! Yeetch.'

He paused politely to let us unplug our ears and mop up our spilled drinks.

'*Flatbush* had just launched a salvo of probability inverters against the Mucoid home planet and was heading back toward deep space in formation with three destroyers – the Russian *Lieutenant Kizhe*, the Israeli *Chutzpah*, and Her Majesty's *Insufferable*. They were still accelerating when a fantastically unlikely accident occurred. *Flatbush* ran straight into the gravity well of a neutron star.'

When our expressions of horror and incredulity had subsided, he continued gravely.

'Yes – a sphere of ultimately condensed matter, only ten miles across, yet as massive as a sun – and hence with a surface gravity one hundred billion times that of Earth.

'The other ships were lucky. They only skirted the outer fringe of the field and managed to escape, though their orbits were deflected almost a hundred and eighty degrees. But *Flatbush*, we calculated later, must have passed within a few dozen miles of that unthinkable concentration of mass, and so experienced the full violence of its tidal forces.

'Now in any reasonable gravitational field – even that of a White Dwarf, which may run up to a million Earth g's – you just swing around the centre of attraction and head on out into space again, without feeling a thing. At the closest point you could be accelerating at hundreds or thousands of g's – but you're still in free fall, so there are no physical effects. Sorry if I'm labouring the obvious, but I realise that everyone here isn't technically orientated.'

If this was intended as a crack at Fleet Paymaster General 'Sticky Fingers' Geldclutch, he never noticed, being well into his fifth beaker of Martian Joy Juice.

'For a neutron star, however, this is no longer true. Near the centre of mass the gravitational gradient – that is, the rate at which the field changes with distance – is so enormous that even across the width of a small body like a spaceship there can be a difference of a hundred thousand g's. I need hardly tell you what *that* sort of field can do to any material object.

'*Flatbush* must have been torn to pieces almost instantly, and the pieces themselves must have flowed like liquid during the few seconds they took to swing around the star. Then the fragments headed on out into space again.

'Months later a radar sweep by the Salvage Corps located some of the debris. I've seen it – surrealistically shaped lumps of the toughest metals we possess twisted together like taffy. And there was only one item that could even be recognised – it must have come from some unfortunate engineer's tool kit.'

The Commander's voice dropped almost to inaudibility and he dashed away a manly tear.

'I really hate to say this.' He sighed. 'But the only identifiable fragment of the pride of the United States Space Navy was – one star mangled spanner.'

Reunion

First published in *Infinity #2*, 1971
Collected in *The Wind from the Sun*

People of Earth, do not be afraid. We come in peace – and why not? For we are your cousins; we have been here before.

You will recognise us when we meet, a few hours from now. We are approaching the solar system almost as swiftly as this radio message. Already, your sun dominates the sky ahead of us. It is the sun our ancestors and yours shared ten million years ago. We are men, as you are; but you have forgotten your history, while we have remembered ours.

We colonised Earth, in the reign of the great reptiles, who were dying when we came and whom we could not save. Your world was a tropical planet then, and we felt that it would make a fair home for our people. We were wrong. Though we were masters of space, we knew so little about climate, about evolution, about genetics. . . .

For millions of summers – there were no winters in those ancient days – the colony flourished. Isolated though it had to be, in a universe where the journey from one star to the next takes years, it kept in touch with its parent civilisation. Three or four times in every century, starships would call and bring news of the galaxy.

But two million years ago, Earth began to change. For ages it had been a tropical paradise; then the temperature fell, and the ice began to creep down from the poles. As the climate altered, so did the colonists. We realise now that it was a natural adaptation to the end of the long summer, but those who had made Earth their home for so many generations believed that they had been attacked by a strange and repulsive disease. A disease that did not kill, that did no physical harm – but merely disfigured.

Yet some were immune; the change spared them and their children. And so, within a few thousand years, the colony had split into two separate groups – almost two separate species – suspicious and jealous of each other.

The division brought envy, discord, and, ultimately, conflict. As the colony disintegrated and the climate steadily worsened, those who could do so withdrew from Earth. The rest sank into barbarism.

We could have kept in touch, but there is so much to do in a universe of a hundred trillion stars. Until a few years ago, we did not know that any of you had survived. Then we picked up your first radio signals, learned your simple languages, and discovered that you had made the long climb back from savagery. We come to greet you, our long-lost relatives – and to help you.

We have discovered much in the eons since we abandoned Earth. If you wish us to bring back the eternal summer that ruled before the Ice Ages, we can do so. Above all, we have a simple remedy for the offensive yet harmless genetic plague that afflicted so many of the colonists.

Perhaps it has run its course – but if not, we have good news for you. People of Earth, you can rejoin the society of the universe without shame, without embarrassment.

If any of you are still white, we can cure you.

Transit of Earth

First published in *Playboy*, January 1971
Collected in *The Wind from the Sun*

When this story was written the date 1984 did not seem impossible for a Mars landing – in fact that had already been proposed soon after the Apollo programme! There'll be another transit in 2084 – but I hope humans will be on Mars long before then.

Testing, one, two, three, four, five . . .

Evans speaking. I will continue to record as long as possible. This is a two-hour capsule, but I doubt if I'll fill it.

That photograph has haunted me all my life; now, too late, I know why. (But would it have made any difference if I *had* known? That's one of those meaningless and unanswerable questions the mind keeps returning to endlessly, like the tongue exploring a broken tooth.)

I've not seen it for years, but I've only to close my eyes and I'm back in a landscape almost as hostile – and as beautiful – as this one. Fifty million miles sunward, and seventy-two years in the past, five men face the camera amid the Antarctic snows. Not even the bulky furs can hide the exhaustion and defeat that mark every line of their bodies; and their faces are already touched by Death.

There were five of them. There were five of us, and of course we also took a group photograph. But everything else was different. We were smiling – cheerful, confident. And our picture was on all the screens of Earth within ten minutes. It was months before *their* camera was found and brought back to civilisation.

And we die in comfort, with all modern conveniences – including many that Robert Falcon Scott could never have imagined, when he stood at the South Pole in 1912.

Two hours later. I'll start giving exact times when it becomes important.

All the facts are in the log, and by now the whole world knows them. So I guess I'm doing this largely to settle my mind – to talk myself into facing the inevitable. The trouble is, I'm not sure what subjects to avoid, and which to tackle head on. Well, there's only one way to find out.

The first item: in twenty-four hours, at the very most, all the oxygen will be gone. That leaves me with the three classical choices. I can let the carbon dioxide build up until I become unconscious. I can step outside and crack the suit, leaving Mars to do the job in about two minutes. Or I can use one of the tablets in the med kit.

CO_2 build-up. Everyone says that's quite easy – just like going to sleep. I've no doubt that's true; unfortunately, in my case it's associated with nightmare number one. . . .

I wish I'd never come across that damn book *True Stories of World War Two*, or whatever it was called. There was one chapter about a German submarine, found and salvaged after the war. The crew was still inside it – *two* men per bunk. And between each pair of skeletons, the single respirator set they'd been sharing. . . .

Well, at least that won't happen here. But I know, with a deadly certainty, that as soon as I find it hard to breathe, I'll be back in that doomed U-boat.

So what about the quicker way? When you're exposed to vacuum, you're unconscious in ten or fifteen seconds, and people who've been through it say it's not painful – just peculiar. But trying to breathe something that isn't there brings me altogether too neatly to nightmare number two.

This time, it's a personal experience. As a kid, I used to do a lot of skin diving, when my family went to the Caribbean for vacations. There was an old freighter that had sunk twenty years before, out on a reef, with its deck only a couple of yards below the surface. Most of the hatches were open, so it was easy to get inside, to look for souvenirs and hunt the big fish that like to shelter in such places.

Of course it was dangerous if you did it without scuba gear. So what boy could resist the challenge?

My favourite route involved diving into a hatch on the foredeck, swimming about fifty feet along a passageway dimly lit by portholes a few yards apart, then angling up a short flight of stairs and emerging through a door in the battered superstructure. The whole trip took less than a minute – an easy dive for anyone in good condition. There was even time to do some sight-seeing, or to play with a few fish along the route. And sometimes, for a change, I'd switch directions, going in the door and coming out again through the hatch.

That was the way I did it the last time. I hadn't dived for a week – there had been a big storm, and the sea was too rough – so I was impatient to get going.

I deep-breathed on the surface for about two minutes, until I felt the tingling in my finger tips that told me it was time to stop. Then I jackknifed and slid gently down toward the black rectangle of the open doorway.

It always looked ominous and menacing – that was part of the thrill. And for the first few yards I was almost completely blind; the contrast between the tropical glare above water and the gloom between decks was so great that it took quite a while for my eyes to adjust. Usually, I was halfway along the corridor before I could see anything clearly. Then the illumination would steadily increase as I approached the open hatch, where a shaft of sunlight would paint a dazzling rectangle on the rusty, barnacled metal floor.

I'd almost made it when I realised that, this time, the light wasn't getting better. There was no slanting column of sunlight ahead of me, leading up to the world of air and life.

I had a second of baffled confusion, wondering if I'd lost my way. Then I knew what had happened – and confusion turned into sheer panic. Sometime during the storm, the hatch must have slammed shut. It weighed at least a quarter of a ton.

I don't remember making a U turn; the next thing I recall is swimming quite slowly back along the passage and telling myself: Don't hurry; your air will last longer if you take it easy. I could see very well now, because my eyes had had plenty of time to become dark-adapted. There were lots of details I'd never noticed before, like the red squirrelfish lurking in the shadows, the green fronds and algae growing in the little patches of light around the portholes, and even a single rubber boot, apparently in excellent condition, lying where someone must have kicked it off. And once, out of a side corridor, I noticed a big grouper staring at me with bulbous eyes, his thick lips half parted, as if he was astonished at my intrusion.

The band around my chest was getting tighter and tighter. It was impossible to hold my breath any longer. Yet the stairway still seemed an infinite distance ahead. I let some bubbles of air dribble out of my mouth. That improved matters for a moment, but, once I had exhaled, the ache in my lungs became even more unendurable.

Now there was no point in conserving strength by flippering along with that steady, unhurried stroke. I snatched the ultimate few cubic inches of air from my face mask – feeling it flatten against my nose as I did so – and swallowed them down into my starving lungs. At the same time, I shifted gear and drove forward with every last atom of strength. . . .

And that's all I remember until I found myself spluttering and coughing in the daylight, clinging to the broken stub of the mast. The water around me was stained with blood, and I wondered why. Then, to my great surprise, I noticed a deep gash in my right calf. I must have banged into some sharp obstruction, but I'd never noticed it and even then felt no pain.

That was the end of my skin diving until I started astronaut training ten years later and went into the underwater zero-gee simulator. Then it was different, because I was using scuba gear. But I had some nasty moments that I was afraid the psychologists would notice, and I always made sure that I got nowhere near emptying my tank. Having nearly suffocated once, I'd no intention of risking it again. . . .

I know exactly what it will feel like to breathe the freezing wisp of near-vacuum that passes for atmosphere on Mars. No thank you.

So what's wrong with poison? Nothing, I suppose. The stuff we've got takes only fifteen seconds, they told us. But all my instincts are against it, even when there's no sensible alternative.

Did Scott have poison with him? I doubt it. And if he did, I'm sure he never used it.

I'm not going to replay this. I hope it's been of some use, but I can't be sure.

The radio has just printed out a message from Earth, reminding me that transit starts in two hours. As if I'm likely to forget – when four men have already died so that I can be the first human being to see it. And the only one, for exactly a hundred years. It isn't often that Sun, Earth, and Mars line up neatly like this; the last time was in 1905, when poor old Lowell was still writing his beautiful nonsense about the canals and the great dying civilisation that had built them. Too bad it was all delusion.

I'd better check the telescope and the timing equipment.

The Sun is quiet today – as it should be, anyway, near the middle of the cycle. Just a few small spots, and some minor areas of disturbance around them. The solar weather is set calm for months to come. That's one thing the others won't have to worry about, on their way home.

I think that was the worst moment, watching *Olympus* lift off Phobos and head back to Earth. Even though we'd known for weeks that nothing could be done, that was the final closing of the door.

It was night, and we could see everything perfectly. Phobos had come leaping up out of the west a few hours earlier, and was doing its mad backward rush across the sky, growing from a tiny crescent to a half-moon; before it reached the zenith it would disappear as it plunged into the shadow of Mars and became eclipsed.

We'd been listening to the countdown, of course, trying to go about our normal work. It wasn't easy, accepting at last the fact that fifteen of us had come to Mars and only ten would return. Even then, I suppose there were millions back on Earth who still could not understand. They must have found it impossible to believe that *Olympus* couldn't descend a mere four thousand miles to pick us up. The Space Administration had been bombarded with crazy rescue schemes; heaven knows, we'd thought of enough ourselves. But when the permafrost under Landing Pad Three finally gave way and *Pegasus* toppled, that was that. It still seems a miracle that the ship didn't blow up when the propellant tank ruptured. . . .

I'm wandering again. Back to Phobos and the countdown.

On the telescope monitor, we could clearly see the fissured plateau where *Olympus* had touched down after we'd separated and begun our own descent. Though our friends would never land on Mars, at least they'd had a little world of their own to explore; even for a satellite as small as Phobos, it worked out at thirty square miles per man. A lot of territory to search for strange minerals and debris from space – or to carve your name so that future ages would know that you were the first of all men to come this way.

The ship was clearly visible as a stubby, bright cylinder against the dull-grey rocks; from time to time some flat surface would catch the light of the swiftly moving sun, and would flash with mirror brilliance. But about five minutes before lift-off, the picture became suddenly pink, then crimson – then vanished completely as Phobos rushed into eclipse.

The countdown was still at ten seconds when we were startled by a blast of light. For a moment, we wondered if *Olympus* had also met with catastrophe. Then we realised that someone was filming the take-off, and the external floodlights had been switched on.

During those last few seconds, I think we all forgot our own predicament; we were up there aboard *Olympus*, willing the thrust to build up smoothly and lift the ship out of the tiny gravitational field of Phobos, and then away from Mars for the long fall sunward. We heard Commander Richmond say 'Ignition', there was a brief burst of interference, and the patch of light began to move in the field of the telescope.

That was all. There was no blazing column of fire, because, of course, there's really no ignition when a nuclear rocket lights up. 'Lights up' indeed! That's another hangover from the old chemical technology. But a hot hydrogen blast is completely invisible; it seems a pity that we'll never again see anything so spectacular as a Saturn or a Korolov blast-off.

Just before the end of the burn, *Olympus* left the shadow of Mars and burst out into sunlight again, reappearing almost instantly as a brilliant, swiftly moving star. The blaze of light must have startled them aboard the ship, because we heard someone call out: 'Cover that window!' Then, a few seconds later, Richmond announced: 'Engine cutoff.' Whatever happened, *Olympus* was now irrevocably headed back to Earth.

A voice I didn't recognise – though it must have been the Commander's – said 'Goodbye, *Pegasus*', and the radio transmission switched off. There was, of course, no point in saying 'Good luck'. *That* had all been settled weeks ago.

I've just played this back. Talking of luck, there's been one compensation, though not for us. With a crew of only ten, *Olympus* has been able to dump a third of her expendables and lighten herself by several tons. So now she'll get home a month ahead of schedule.

Plenty of things could have gone wrong in that month; we may yet have saved the expedition. Of course, we'll never know – but it's a nice thought.

I've been playing a lot of music, full blast – now that there's no one else to be disturbed. Even if there were any Martians, I don't suppose this ghost of an atmosphere can carry the sound more than a few yards.

We have a fine collection, but I have to choose carefully. Nothing downbeat and nothing that demands too much concentration. Above all, nothing with human voices. So I restrict myself to the lighter orchestral classics; the 'New World' symphony and Grieg's piano concerto fill the bill perfectly. At the moment I'm listening to Rachmaninoff's 'Rhapsody on a Theme of Paganini', but now I must switch off and get down to work.

There are only five minutes to go. All the equipment is in perfect condition. The telescope is tracking the Sun, the video recorder is standing by, the precision timer is running.

These observations will be as accurate as I can make them. I owe it to my lost comrades, whom I'll soon be joining. They gave me their oxygen, so that I can still be alive at this moment. I hope you remember that, a hundred or a thousand years from now, whenever you crank these figures into the computers. . . .

Only a minute to go; getting down to business. For the record: year, 1984; month, May; day, II, coming up to four hours thirty minutes Ephemeris Time . . . *now*.

Half a minute to contact. Switching recorder and timer to high speed. Just rechecked position angle to make sure I'm looking at the right spot on the Sun's limb. Using power of five hundred – image perfectly steady even at this low elevation.

Four thirty-two. Any moment now . . .

There it is . . . there it is! I can hardly believe it! A tiny black dent in the edge of the Sun . . . growing, growing, growing . . .

Hello, Earth. Look up at me, the brightest star in your sky, straight overhead at midnight. . . .

Recorder back to slow.

Four thirty-five. It's as if a thumb is pushing into the Sun's edge, deeper and deeper. . . . Fascinating to watch . . .

Four forty-one. Exactly halfway. The Earth's a perfect black semicircle – a clean bite out of the Sun. As if some disease is eating it away . . .

Four forty-eight. Ingress three-quarters complete.

Four hours forty-nine minutes thirty seconds. Recorder on high speed again.

The line of contact with the Sun's edge is shrinking fast. Now it's a barely visible black thread. In a few seconds, the whole Earth will be superimposed on the Sun.

Now I can see the effects of the atmosphere. There's a thin halo of light surrounding that black hole in the Sun. Strange to think that I'm seeing the glow of all the sunsets – and all the sunrises – that are taking place around the whole Earth at this very moment. . . .

Ingress complete – four hours fifty minutes five seconds. The whole world has moved onto the face of the Sun. A perfectly circular black disc silhouetted against that inferno ninety million miles below. It looks bigger than I expected; one could easily mistake it for a fair-sized sunspot.

Nothing more to see now for six hours, when the Moon appears, trailing Earth by half the Sun's width. I'll beam the recorder data back to Lunacom, then try to get some sleep.

My very last sleep. Wonder if I'll need drugs. It seems a pity to waste these last few hours, but I want to conserve my strength – and my oxygen.

I think it was Dr Johnson who said that nothing settles a man's mind so wonderfully as the knowledge that he'll be hanged in the morning. How the hell did *he* know?

Ten hours thirty minutes Ephemeris Time. Dr Johnson was right. I had only one pill, and don't remember any dreams.

The condemned man also ate a hearty breakfast. Cut that out . . .

Back at the telescope. Now the Earth's halfway across the disc, passing well north of centre. In ten minutes, I should see the Moon.

I've just switched to the highest power of the telescope – two thousand. The image is slightly fuzzy, but still fairly good; atmospheric halo very distinct. I'm hoping to see the cities on the dark side of Earth. . . .

No luck. Probably too many clouds. A pity; it's theoretically possible, but we never succeeded. I wish . . . never mind.

Ten hours forty minutes. Recorder on slow speed. Hope I'm looking at the right spot.

Fifteen seconds to go. Recorder fast.

Damn – missed it. Doesn't matter – the recorder will have caught the exact moment. There's a little black notch already in the side of the Sun. First contact must have been about ten hours forty-one minutes twenty seconds ET.

What a long way it is between Earth and Moon; there's half the width of the Sun between them. You wouldn't think the two bodies had anything to do with each other. Makes you realise just how big the Sun really is. . . .

Ten hours forty-four minutes. The Moon's exactly halfway over the edge. A very small, very clear-cut semicircular bite out of the edge of the Sun.

Ten hours forty-seven minutes five seconds. Internal contact. The Moon's clear of the edge, entirely inside the Sun. Don't suppose I can see anything on the night side, but I'll increase the power.

That's funny.

Well, well. Someone must be trying to talk to me; there's a tiny light pulsing away there on the darkened face of the moon. Probably the laser at Imbrium Base.

Sorry, everyone. I've said all my goodbyes, and don't want to go through that again. Nothing can be important now.

Still, it's almost hypnotic – that flickering point of light, coming out of the face of the Sun itself. Hard to believe that, even after it's travelled all this distance, the beam is only a hundred miles wide. Lunacom's going to all this trouble to aim it exactly at me, and I suppose I should feel guilty at ignoring it. But I don't. I've nearly finished my work, and the things of Earth are no longer any concern of mine.

Ten hours fifty minutes. Recorder off. That's it – until the end of Earth transit, two hours from now.

I've had a snack and am taking my last look at the view from the observation bubble. The Sun's still high, so there's not much contrast, but the light brings out all the colours vividly – the countless varieties of red and pink and crimson, so startling against the deep blue of the sky. How different from the Moon – though that, too, has its own beauty.

It's strange how surprising the obvious can be. Everyone knew that Mars was red. But we didn't really expect the red of rust, the red of blood. Like the Painted Desert of Arizona; after a while, the eye longs for green.

To the north, there is one welcome change of colour; the cap of carbon-dioxide snow on Mount Burroughs is a dazzling white pyramid. That's another surprise. Burroughs is twenty-five thousand feet above Mean Datum; when I was a boy, there weren't supposed to be any mountains on Mars. . . .

The nearest sand dune is a quarter of a mile away, and it, too, has patches of frost on its shaded slope. During the last storm, we thought it moved a few feet, but we couldn't be sure. Certainly the dunes *are* moving, like those on Earth. One day, I suppose, this base will be covered – only to reappear again in a thousand years. Or ten thousand.

That strange group of rocks – the Elephant, the Capitol, the Bishop – still holds its secrets, and teases me with the memory of our first big disappointment. We could have sworn that they were sedimentary; how eagerly we rushed out to look for fossils! Even now, we don't know what formed that outcropping. The geology of Mars is still a mass of contradictions and enigmas. . . .

We have passed on enough problems to the future, and those who come after us will find many more. But there's one mystery we never reported to Earth, or even entered in the log. . . .

The first night after we landed, we took turns keeping watch. Brennan was on duty, and woke me up soon after midnight. I was annoyed – it was ahead of time – and then he told me that he'd seen a light moving around the base of the Capitol.

We watched for at least an hour, until it was my turn to take over. But we saw nothing; whatever that light was, it never reappeared.

Now Brennan was as levelheaded and unimaginative as they come; if he said he saw a light, then he saw one. Maybe it was some kind of electric discharge, or the reflection of Phobos on a piece of sand-polished rock. Anyway, we decided not to mention it to Lunacom, unless we saw it again.

Since I've been alone, I've often awakened in the night and looked out toward the rocks. In the feeble illumination of Phobos and Deimos, they remind me of the skyline of a darkened city. And it has always remained darkened. No lights have ever appeared for me. . . .

*

Twelve hours forty-nine minutes Ephemeris Time. The last act's about to begin. Earth has nearly reached the edge of the Sun. The two narrow horns of light that still embrace it are barely touching. . . .

Recorder on fast.

Contact! Twelve hours fifty minutes sixteen seconds. The crescents of light no longer meet. A tiny black spot has appeared at the edge of the Sun, as the Earth begins to cross it. It's growing longer, longer. . . .

Recorder on slow. Eighteen minutes to wait before Earth finally clears the face of the Sun.

The Moon still has more than halfway to go; it's not yet reached the midpoint of its transit. It looks like a little round blob of ink, only a quarter the size of Earth. And there's no light flickering there any more. Lunacom must have given up.

Well, I have just a quarter of an hour left, here in my last home. Time seems to be accelerating the way it does in the final minutes before a liftoff. No matter; I have everything worked out now. I can even relax.

Already, I feel part of history. I am one with Captain Cook, back in Tahiti in 1769, watching the transit of Venus. Except for that image of the Moon trailing along behind, it must have looked just like this. . . .

What would Cook have thought, over two hundred years ago, if he'd known that one day a man would observe the whole Earth in transit from an outer world? I'm sure he would have been astonished – and then delighted. . . .

But I feel a closer identity with a man not yet born. I hope you hear these words, whoever you may be. Perhaps you will be standing on this very spot, a hundred years from now, when the next transit occurs.

Greetings to 2084, November 10! I wish you better luck than we had. I suppose you will have come here on a luxury liner. Or you may have been born on Mars, and be a stranger to Earth. You will know things that I cannot imagine. Yet somehow I don't envy you. I would not even change places with you if I could.

For you will remember my name, and know that I was the first of all mankind ever to see a transit of Earth. And no one will see another for a hundred years. . . .

Twelve hours fifty-nine minutes. Exactly halfway through egress. The Earth is a perfect semicircle – a black shadow on the face of the Sun. I still can't escape from the impression that something has taken a big bite out of that golden disc. In nine minutes it will be gone, and the Sun will be whole again.

Thirteen hours seven minutes. Recorder on fast.

Earth has almost gone. There's just a shallow black dimple at the edge of the Sun. You could easily mistake it for a small spot, going over the limb.

Thirteen hours eight.

Goodbye, beautiful Earth.

Going, going, going. Goodbye, good—

*

I'm OK again now. The timings have all been sent home on the beam. In five minutes, they'll join the accumulated wisdom of mankind. And Lunacom will know that I stuck to my post.

But I'm not sending this. I'm going to leave it here, for the next expedition – whenever that may be. It could be ten or twenty years before anyone comes here again. No point in going back to an old site when there's a whole world waiting to be explored. . . .

So this capsule will stay here, as Scott's diary remained in his tent, until the next visitors find it. But they won't find me.

Strange how hard it is to get away from Scott. I think he gave me the idea.

For his body will not lie frozen forever in the Antarctic, isolated from the great cycle of life and death. Long ago, that lonely tent began its march to the sea. Within a few years, it was buried by the falling snow and had become part of the glacier that crawls eternally away from the Pole. In a few brief centuries, the sailor will have returned to the sea. He will merge once more into the pattern of living things – the plankton, the seals, the penguins, the whales, all the multitudinous fauna of the Antarctic Ocean.

There are no oceans here on Mars, nor have there been for at least five billion years. But there is life of some kind, down there in the badlands of Chaos II, which we never had time to explore.

Those moving patches on the orbital photographs. The evidence that whole areas of Mars have been swept clear of craters, by forces other than erosion. The long-chain, optically active carbon molecules picked up by the atmospheric samplers.

And, of course, the mystery of Viking 6. Even now, no one has been able to make any sense of those last instrument readings, before something large and heavy crushed the probe in the still, cold depths of the Martian night. . . .

And don't talk to me about *primitive* life forms in a place like this! Anything that's survived here will be so sophisticated that we may look as clumsy as dinosaurs.

There's still enough propellant in the ship's tanks to drive the Mars car clear around the planet. I have three hours of daylight left – plenty of time to get down into the valleys and well out into Chaos. After sunset, I'll still be able to make good speed with the headlights. It will be romantic, driving at night under the moons of Mars. . . .

One thing I must fix before I leave. I don't like the way Sam's lying out there. He was always so poised, so graceful. It doesn't seem right that he should look so awkward now. I must do something about it.

I wonder if *I* could have covered three hundred feet without a suit, walking slowly, steadily – the way he did, to the very end.

I must try not to look at his face.

That's it. Everything shipshape and ready to go.

The therapy has worked. I feel perfectly at ease – even contented, now that I know exactly what I'm going to do. The old nightmares have lost their power.

It is true: we all die alone. It makes no difference at the end, being fifty million miles from home.

I'm going to enjoy the drive through that lovely painted landscape. I'll be thinking of all those who dreamed about cars – Wells and Lowell and Burroughs and Weinbaum and Bradbury. They all guessed wrong – but the reality is just as strange, just as beautiful, as they imagined.

I don't know what's waiting for me out there, and I'll probably never see it. But on this starveling world, it must be desperate for carbon, phosphorus, oxygen, calcium. It can use me.

And when my oxygen alarm gives its final 'ping,' somewhere down there in that haunted wilderness, I'm going to finish in style. As soon as I have difficulty in breathing, I'll get off the Mars car and start walking – with a playback unit plugged into my helmet and going full blast.

For sheer, triumphant power and glory there's nothing in the whole of music to match the Toccata and Fugue in D. I won't have time to hear all of it; that doesn't matter.

Johann Sebastian, here I come.

A Meeting with Medusa

First published in *Playboy*, December 1971
Collected in *The Wind from the Sun*

1. A Day to Remember

The *Queen Elizabeth* was over three miles above the Grand Canyon, dawdling along at a comfortable hundred and eighty, when Howard Falcon spotted the camera platform closing in from the right. He had been expecting it – nothing else was cleared to fly at this altitude – but he was not too happy to have company. Although he welcomed any signs of public interest, he also wanted as much empty sky as he could get. After all, he was the first man in history to navigate a ship three-tenths of a mile long. . . .

So far, this first test flight had gone perfectly; ironically enough, the only problem had been the century-old aircraft carrier *Chairman Mao*, borrowed from the San Diego Naval Museum for support operations. Only one of *Mao*'s four nuclear reactors was still operating, and the old battle-wagon's top speed was barely thirty knots. Luckily, wind speed at sea level had been less than half this, so it had not been too difficult to maintain still air on the flight deck. Though there had been a few anxious moments during gusts, when the mooring lines had been dropped, the great dirigible had risen smoothly, straight up into the sky, as if on an invisible elevator. If all went well, *Queen Elizabeth IV* would not meet *Chairman Mao* again for another week.

Everything was under control; all test instruments gave normal readings. Commander Falcon decided to go upstairs and watch the rendezvous. He handed over to his second officer, and walked out into the transparent tubeway that led through the heart of the ship. There, as always, he was overwhelmed by the spectacle of the largest single space ever enclosed by man.

The ten spherical gas cells, each more than a hundred feet across, were ranged one behind the other like a line of gigantic soap bubbles. The tough plastic was so clear that he could see through the whole length of the array, and make out details of the elevator mechanism, more than a third of a mile from his vantage point. All around him, like a three-dimensional maze, was the structural framework of the ship – the great longitudinal girders running from nose to tail, the fifteen hoops that were the circular ribs of this sky-borne colossus, and whose varying sizes defined its graceful, streamlined profile.

At this low speed, there was little sound – merely the soft rush of wind over the envelope and an occasional creak of metal as the pattern of stresses changed. The shadowless light from the rows of lamps far overhead gave the whole scene a curiously submarine quality, and to Falcon this was enhanced by the spectacle of the translucent gasbags. He had once encountered a squadron of large but harmless jellyfish, pulsing their mindless way above a shallow tropical reef, and the plastic bubbles that gave *Queen Elizabeth* her lift often reminded him of these – especially when changing pressures made them crinkle and scatter new patterns of reflected light.

He walked down the axis of the ship until he came to the forward elevator, between gas cells one and two. Riding up to the Observation Deck, he noticed that it was uncomfortably hot, and dictated a brief memo to himself on his pocket recorder. The *Queen* obtained almost a quarter of her buoyancy from the unlimited amounts of waste heat produced by her fusion power plant. On this lightly loaded flight, indeed, only six of the ten gas cells contained helium; the remaining four were full of air. Yet she still carried two hundred tons of water as ballast. However, running the cells at high temperatures did produce problems in refrigerating the access ways; it was obvious that a little more work would have to be done there.

A refreshing blast of cooler air hit him in the face when he stepped out onto the Observation Deck and into the dazzling sunlight streaming through the plexiglass roof. Half a dozen workmen, with an equal number of superchimp assistants, were busily laying the partly completed dance floor, while others were installing electric wiring and fixing furniture. It was a scene of controlled chaos, and Falcon found it hard to believe that everything would be ready for the maiden voyage, only four weeks ahead. Well, that was not *his* problem, thank goodness. He was merely the Captain, not the Cruise Director.

The human workers waved to him, and the 'simps' flashed toothy smiles, as he walked through the confusion, into the already completed Skylounge. This was his favourite place in the whole ship, and he knew that once she was operating he would never again have it all to himself. He would allow himself just five minutes of private enjoyment.

He called the bridge, checked that everything was still in order, and relaxed into one of the comfortable swivel chairs. Below, in a curve that delighted the eye, was the unbroken silver sweep of the ship's envelope. He was perched at the highest point, surveying the whole immensity of the largest vehicle ever built. And when he had tired of that – all the way out to the horizon was the fantastic wilderness carved by the Colorado River in half a billion years of time.

Apart from the camera platform (it had now fallen back and was filming from amidships), he had the sky to himself. It was blue and empty, clear down to the horizon. In his grandfather's day, Falcon knew, it would have been streaked with vapour trails and stained with smoke. Both had gone:

the aerial garbage had vanished with the primitive technologies that spawned it, and the long-distance transportation of this age arced too far beyond the stratosphere for any sight or sound of it to reach Earth. Once again, the lower atmosphere belonged to the birds and the clouds – and now to *Queen Elizabeth IV*.

It was true, as the old pioneers had said at the beginning of the twentieth century: this was the only way to travel – in silence and luxury, breathing the air around you and not cut off from it, near enough to the surface to watch the ever-changing beauty of land and sea. The subsonic jets of the 1980s, packed with hundreds of passengers seated ten abreast, could not even begin to match such comfort and spaciousness.

Of course, the *Queen* would never be an economic proposition, and even if her projected sister ships were built, only a few of the world's quarter of a billion inhabitants would ever enjoy this silent gliding through the sky. But a secure and prosperous global society could afford such follies and indeed needed them for their novelty and entertainment. There were at least a million men on Earth whose discretionary income exceeded a thousand new dollars a year, so the *Queen* would not lack for passengers.

Falcon's pocket communicator beeped. The copilot was calling from the bridge.

'OK for rendezvous, Captain? We've got all the data we need from this run, and the TV people are getting impatient.'

Falcon glanced at the camera platform, now matching his speed a tenth of a mile away.

'OK,' he replied. 'Proceed as arranged. I'll watch from here.'

He walked back through the busy chaos of the Observation Deck so that he could have a better view amidships. As he did so, he could feel the change of vibration underfoot; by the time he had reached the rear of the lounge, the ship had come to rest. Using his master key, he let himself out onto the small external platform flaring from the end of the deck; half a dozen people could stand here, with only low guardrails separating them from the vast sweep of the envelope – and from the ground, thousands of feet below. It was an exciting place to be, and perfectly safe even when the ship was travelling at speed, for it was in the dead air behind the huge dorsal blister of the Observation Deck. Nevertheless, it was not intended that the passengers would have access to it; the view was a little too vertiginous.

The covers of the forward cargo hatch had already opened like giant trap doors, and the camera platform was hovering above them, preparing to descend. Along this route, in the years to come, would travel thousands of passengers and tons of supplies. Only on rare occasions would the *Queen* drop down to sea level and dock with her floating base.

A sudden gust of cross-wind slapped Falcon's cheek, and he tightened his grip on the guardrail. The Grand Canyon was a bad place for turbulence, though he did not expect much at this altitude. Without any real anxiety, he focused his attention on the descending platform, now about a hundred and fifty feet above the ship. He knew that the highly skilled operator who was flying the remotely controlled vehicle had performed this simple manoeuvre a dozen times already; it was inconceivable that he would have any difficulties.

Yet he seemed to be reacting rather sluggishly. That last gust had drifted the platform almost to the edge of the open hatchway. Surely the pilot could have corrected before this. . . . Did he have a control problem? It was very unlikely; these remotes had multiple-redundancy, fail-safe takeovers, and any number of backup systems. Accidents were almost unheard of.

But there he went again, off to the left. Could the pilot be *drunk*? Improbable though that seemed, Falcon considered it seriously for a moment. Then he reached for his microphone switch.

Once again, without warning, he was slapped violently in the face. He hardly felt it, for he was staring in horror at the camera platform. The distant operator was fighting for control, trying to balance the craft on its jets – but he was only making matters worse. The oscillations increased twenty degrees, forty, sixty, ninety. . . .

'Switch to automatic, you fool!' Falcon shouted uselessly into his microphone. 'Your manual control's not working!'

The platform flipped over on its back. The jets no longer supported it, but drove it swiftly downward. They had suddenly become allies of the gravity they had fought until this moment.

Falcon never heard the crash, though he felt it; he was already inside the Observation Deck, racing for the elevator that would take him down to the bridge. Workmen shouted at him anxiously, asking what had happened. It would be many months before he knew the answer to that question.

Just as he was stepping into the elevator cage, he changed his mind. What if there was a power failure? Better be on the safe side, even if it took longer and time was the essence. He began to run down the spiral stairway enclosing the shaft.

Halfway down he paused for a second to inspect the damage. That damned platform had gone clear through the ship, rupturing two of the gas cells as it did so. They were still collapsing slowly, in great falling veils of plastic. He was not worried about the loss of lift – the ballast could easily take care of that, as long as eight cells remained intact. Far more serious was the possibility of structural damage. Already he could hear the great latticework around him groaning and protesting under its abnormal loads. It was not enough to have sufficient lift; unless it was properly distributed, the ship would break her back.

He was just resuming his descent when a superchimp, shrieking with fright, came racing down the elevator shaft, moving with incredible speed, hand over hand, along the *outside* of the latticework. In its terror, the poor beast had torn off its company uniform, perhaps in an unconscious attempt to regain the freedom of its ancestors.

Falcon, still descending as swiftly as he could, watched its approach with some alarm. A distraught simp was a powerful and potentially dangerous animal, especially if fear overcame its conditioning As it overtook him, it started to call out a string of words, but they were all jumbled together, and the only one he could recognise was a plaintive, frequently repeated 'boss'. Even now, Falcon realised, it looked toward humans for guidance. He felt sorry for the creature, involved in a man-made disaster beyond its comprehension, and for which it bore no responsibility.

It stopped opposite him, on the other side of the lattice; there was nothing to prevent it from coming through the open framework if it wished. Now its face was only inches from his, and he was looking straight into the terrified eyes. Never before had he been so close to a simp, and able to study its features in such detail. He felt that strange mingling of kinship and discomfort that all men experience when they gaze thus into the mirror of time.

His presence seemed to have calmed the creature. Falcon pointed up the shaft, back toward the Observation Deck, and said very clearly and precisely: 'Boss – boss – go.' To his relief, the simp understood; it gave him a grimace that might have been a smile, and at once started to race back the way it had come. Falcon had given it the best advice he could. If any safety remained aboard the *Queen*, it was in that direction. But his duty lay in the other.

He had almost completed his descent when, with a sound of rending metal, the vessel pitched nose down, and the lights went out. But he could still see quite well, for a shaft of sunlight streamed through the open hatch and the huge tear in the envelope. Many years ago he had stood in a great cathedral nave watching the light pouring through the stained-glass windows and forming pools of multi-colored radiance on the ancient flagstones. The dazzling shaft of sunlight through the ruined fabric high above reminded him of that moment. He was in a cathedral of metal, falling down the sky.

When he reached the bridge, and was able for the first time to look outside, he was horrified to see how close the ship was to the ground. Only three thousand feet below were the beautiful and deadly pinnacles of rock and the red rivers of mud that were still carving their way down into the past. There was no level area anywhere in sight where a ship as large as the *Queen* could come to rest on an even keel.

A glance at the display board told him that all the ballast had gone. However, rate of descent had been reduced to a few yards a second; they still had a fighting chance.

Without a word, Falcon eased himself into the pilot's seat and took over such control as still remained. The instrument board showed him everything he wished to know; speech was superfluous. In the background, he could hear the Communications Officer giving a running report over the radio. By this time, all the news channels of Earth would have been preempted, and he could imagine the utter frustration of the programme controllers. One of the most spectacular wrecks in history was occurring – without a single camera to record it. The last moments of the *Queen* would never fill millions with awe and terror, as had those of the *Hindenburg*, a century and a half before.

Now the ground was only about seventeen hundred feet away, still coming up slowly. Though he had full thrust, he had not dared to use it, lest the weakened structure collapse; but now he realised that he had no choice. The wind was taking them toward a fork in the canyon, where the river was split by a wedge of rock like the prow of some gigantic, fossilised ship of stone. If she continued on her present course, the *Queen* would straddle that triangular plateau and come to rest with at least a third of her length jutting out over nothingness; she would snap like a rotten stick.

Far away, above the sound of straining metal and escaping gas, came the familiar whistle of the jets as Falcon opened up the lateral thrusters. The ship staggered, and began to slew to port. The shriek of tearing metal was now almost continuous – and the rate of descent had started to increase ominously. A glance at the damage-control board showed that cell number five had just gone.

The ground was only yards away. Even now, he could not tell whether his manoeuvre would succeed or fail. He switched the thrust vectors over to vertical, giving maximum lift to reduce the force of impact.

The crash seemed to last forever. It was not violent – merely prolonged, and irresistible. It seemed that the whole universe was falling about them.

The sound of crunching metal came nearer, as if some great beast were eating its way through the dying ship.

Then floor and ceiling closed upon him like a vice.

2. 'Because it's There'

'Why do you want to go to Jupiter?'

'As Springer said when he lifted for Pluto – "because it's there".'

'Thanks. Now we've got that out of the way – the real reason.'

Howard Falcon smiled, though only those who knew him well could have interpreted the slight, leathery grimace. Webster was one of them; for more than twenty years they had been involved in each other's projects. They had shared triumphs and disasters – including the greatest disaster of all.

'Well, Springer's cliché is still valid. We've landed on all the terrestrial planets, but none of the gas giants. They are the only real challenge left in the solar system.'

'An expensive one. Have you worked out the cost?'

'As well as I can; here are the estimates. Remember, though – this isn't a one-shot mission, but a transportation system. Once it's proved out, it can be used over and over again. And it will open up not merely Jupiter, but all the giants.'

Webster looked at the figures, and whistled.

'Why not start with an easier planet – Uranus, for example? Half the gravity, and less than half the escape velocity. Quieter weather, too' – if that's the right word for it.'

Webster had certainly done his homework. But that, of course, was why he was head of Long-Range Planning.

'There's very little saving – when you allow for the extra distance and the logistics problems. For Jupiter, we can use the facilities of Ganymede. Beyond Saturn, we'd have to establish a new supply base.'

Logical, thought Webster; but he was sure that it was not the important reason. Jupiter was lord of the solar system; Falcon would be interested in no lesser challenge.

'Besides,' Falcon continued, 'Jupiter is a major scientific scandal. It's more than a hundred years since its radio storms were discovered, but we still don't know what causes them – and the Great Red Spot is as big a mystery as ever. That's why I can get matching funds from the Bureau of Astronautics. Do you know how many probes they have dropped into that atmosphere?'

'A couple of hundred, I believe.'

'*Three* hundred and twenty-six, over the last fifty years – about a quarter of them total failures. Of course, they've learned a hell of a lot, but they've barely scratched the planet. Do you realise how *big* it is?'

'More than ten times the size of Earth.'

'Yes, yes – but do you know what that really means?'

Falcon pointed to the large globe in the corner of Webster's office.

'Look at India – how small it seems. Well, if you skinned Earth and spread it out on the surface of Jupiter, it would look about as big as India does here.'

There was a long silence while Webster contemplated the equation: Jupiter is to Earth as Earth is to India. Falcon had – deliberately, of course – chosen the best possible example. . . .

Was it already ten years ago? Yes, it must have been. The crash lay seven years in the past (*that* date was engraved on his heart), and those initial tests had taken place three years before the first and last flight of the *Queen Elizabeth*.

Ten years ago, then, Commander (no, Lieutenant) Falcon had invited him to a preview – a three-day drift across the northern plains of India, within sight of the Himalayas. 'Perfectly safe,' he had promised. 'It will get you away from the office – and will teach you what this whole thing is about.'

Webster had not been disappointed. Next to his first journey to the Moon, it had been the most memorable experience of his life. And yet, as Falcon had assured him, it had been perfectly safe, and quite uneventful.

They had taken off from Srinagar just before dawn, with the huge silver bubble of the balloon already catching the first light of the Sun. The ascent had been made in total silence; there were none of the roaring propane burners that had lifted the hot-air balloons of an earlier age. All the heat

900

they needed came from the little pulsed-fusion reactor, weighing only about two hundred and twenty pounds, hanging in the open mouth of the envelope. While they were climbing, its laser was zapping ten times a second, igniting the merest whiff of deuterium fuel. Once they had reached altitude, it would fire only a few times a minute, making up for the heat lost through the great gasbag overhead.

And so, even while they were almost a mile above the ground, they could hear dogs barking, people shouting, bells ringing. Slowly the vast, Sun-smitten landscape expanded around them. Two hours later, they had levelled out at three miles and were taking frequent draughts of oxygen. They could relax and admire the scenery; the on-board instrumentation was doing all the work – gathering the information that would be required by the designers of the still-unnamed liner of the skies.

It was a perfect day. The southwest monsoon would not break for another month, and there was hardly a cloud in the sky. Time seemed to have come to a stop; they resented the hourly radio reports which interrupted their reverie. And all around, to the horizon and far beyond, was that infinite, ancient landscape, drenched with history – a patchwork of villages, fields, temples, lakes, irrigation canals. . . .

With a real effort, Webster broke the hypnotic spell of that ten-year-old memory. It had converted him to lighter-than-air flight – and it had made him realise the enormous size of India, even in a world that could be circled within ninety minutes. And yet, he repeated to himself, Jupiter is to Earth as Earth is to India. . . .

'Granted your argument,' he said, 'and supposing the funds are available, there's another question you have to answer. Why should you do better than the – what is it – three hundred and twenty-six robot probes that have already made the trip?'

'I am better qualified than they were – as an observer, and as a pilot. *Especially* as a pilot. Don't forget – I've more experience of lighter-than-air flight than anyone in the world.'

'You could still serve as controller, and sit safely on Ganymede.'

'*But that's just the point!* They've already done that. Don't you remember what killed the *Queen*?'

Webster knew perfectly well; but he merely answered: 'Go on.'

'*Time lag – time lag!* That idiot of a platform controller thought he was using a local radio circuit. But he'd been accidentally switched through a satellite – oh, maybe it wasn't his fault, but he should have noticed. That's a half-second time lag for the round trip. Even then it wouldn't have mattered flying in calm air. It was the turbulence over the Grand Canyon that did it. When the platform tipped, and he corrected for that – it had already tipped the other way. Ever tried to drive a car over a bumpy road with a half-second delay in the steering?'

'No, and I don't intend to try. But I can imagine it.'

'Well, Ganymede is a million kilometres from Jupiter. That means a round-trip delay of six seconds. No, you need a controller on the spot – to handle emergencies in real time. Let me show you something. Mind if I use this?'

'Go ahead.'

Falcon picked up a postcard that was lying on Webster's desk; they were almost obsolete on Earth, but this one showed a 3-D view of a Martian landscape, and was decorated with exotic and expensive stamps. He held it so that it dangled vertically.

'This is an old trick, but helps to make my point. Place your thumb and finger on either side, not quite touching. That's right.'

Webster put out his hand, almost but not quite gripping the card.

'Now catch it.'

Falcon waited for a few seconds; then, without warning, he let go of the card. Webster's thumb and finger closed on empty air.

'I'll do it again, just to show there's no deception. You see?'

Once again, the falling card had slipped through Webster's fingers.

'Now you try it on me.'

This time, Webster grasped the card and dropped it without warning. It had scarcely moved before Falcon had caught it. Webster almost imagined he could hear a click, so swift was the other's reaction.

'When they put me together again,' Falcon remarked in an expressionless voice, 'the surgeons made some improvements. This is one of them – and there are others. I want to make the most of them. Jupiter is the place where I can do it.'

Webster stared for long seconds at the fallen card, absorbing the improbable colours of the Trivium Charontis Escarpment. Then he said quietly: 'I understand. How long do you think it will take?'

'With your help, plus the Bureau, plus all the science foundations we can drag in – oh, three years. Then a year for trials – we'll have to send in at least two test models. So, with luck – five years.'

'That's about what I thought. I hope you get your luck; you've earned it. But there's one thing I won't do.'

'What's that?'

'Next time you go ballooning, don't expect *me* as passenger.'

3. The World of the Gods

The fall from Jupiter V to Jupiter itself takes only three and a half hours. Few men could have slept on so awesome a journey. Sleep was a weakness that Howard Falcon hated, and the little he still required brought dreams that time had not yet been able to exorcise. But he could expect no rest in the three days that lay ahead, and must seize what he could during the long fall down into that ocean of clouds, some sixty thousand miles below.

As soon as *Kon-Tiki* had entered her transfer orbit and all the computer checks were satisfactory, he prepared for the last sleep he might ever know.

It seemed appropriate that at almost the same moment Jupiter eclipsed the bright and tiny Sun as he swept into the monstrous shadow of the planet. For a few minutes a strange golden twilight enveloped the ship; then a quarter of the sky became an utterly black hole in space, while the rest was a blaze of stars. No matter how far one travelled across the solar system, they never changed; these same constellations now shone on Earth, millions of miles away. The only novelties here were the small, pale crescents of Callisto and Ganymede; doubtless there were a dozen other moons up there in the sky, but they were all much too tiny, and too distant, for the unaided eye to pick them out.

'Closing down for two hours,' he reported to the mother ship, hanging almost a thousand miles above the desolate rocks of Jupiter V, in the radiation shadow of the tiny satellite. If it never served any other useful purpose, Jupiter V was a cosmic bulldozer perpetually sweeping up the charged particles that made it unhealthy to linger close to Jupiter. Its wake was almost free of radiation, and there a ship could park in perfect safety, while death sleeted invisibly all around.

Falcon switched on the sleep inducer, and consciousness faded swiftly out as the electric pulses surged gently through his brain. While *Kon-Tiki* fell toward Jupiter, gaining speed second by second in that enormous gravitational field, he slept without dreams. They always came when he awoke; and he had brought his nightmares with him from Earth.

Yet he never dreamed of the crash itself, though he often found himself again face to face with that terrified superchimp, as he descended the spiral stairway between the collapsing gasbags. None of the simps had survived; those that were not killed outright were so badly injured that they had been painlessly 'euthed'. He sometimes wondered why he dreamed only of this doomed creature – which he had never met before the last minutes of its life – and not of the friends and colleagues he had lost aboard the dying *Queen*.

The dreams he feared most always began with his first return to consciousness. There had been little physical pain; in fact, there had been no sensation of any kind. He was in darkness and silence, and did not even seem to be breathing. And – strangest of all – he could not locate his limbs. He could move neither his hands nor his feet, because he did not know where they were.

The silence had been the first to yield. After hours, or days, he had become aware of a faint throbbing, and eventually, after long thought, he deduced that this was the beating of his own heart. That was the first of his many mistakes.

Then there had been faint pinpricks, sparkles of light, ghosts of pressures upon still-unresponsive limbs. One by one his senses had returned, and pain had come with them. He had had to learn everything anew, recapitulating infancy and babyhood. Though his memory was unaffected, and he could understand words that were spoken to him, it was months before he was able to answer except by the flicker of an eyelid. He could remember the moments of triumph when he had spoken the first word, turned the page of a book – and, finally, learned to move under his own power. *That* was a victory indeed, and it had taken him almost two years to prepare for it. A hundred times he had envied that dead superchimp, but *he* had been given no choice. The doctors had made their decision – and now, twelve years later, he was where no human being had ever travelled before, and moving faster than any man in history.

Kon-Tiki was just emerging from shadow, and the Jovian dawn bridged the sky ahead in a titanic bow of light, when the persistent buzz of the alarm dragged Falcon up from sleep. The inevitable nightmares (he had been trying to summon a nurse, but did not even have the strength to push the button) swiftly faded from consciousness. The greatest – and perhaps last – adventure of his life was before him.

He called Mission Control, now almost sixty thousand miles away and falling swiftly below the curve of Jupiter, to report that everything was in order. His velocity had just passed thirty-one miles a second (*that* was one for the books) and in half an hour *Kon-Tiki* would hit the outer fringes of the atmosphere, as he started on the most difficult re-entry in the entire solar system. Although scores of probes had survived this flaming ordeal, they had been tough, solidly packed masses of instrumentation, able to withstand several hundred gravities of drag. *Kon-Tiki* would hit peaks of thirty g's, and would average more than ten, before she came to rest in the upper reaches of the Jovian atmosphere. Very carefully and thoroughly, Falcon began to attach the elaborate system of restraints that would anchor him to the walls of the cabin. When he had finished, he was virtually a part of the ship's structure.

The clock was counting backward; one hundred seconds to re-entry. For better or worse, he was committed. In a minute and a half, he would graze the Jovian atmosphere, and would be caught irrevocably in the grip of the giant.

The countdown was three seconds late – not at all bad, considering the unknowns involved. From beyond the walls of the capsule came a ghostly sighing, which rose steadily to a high-pitched, screaming roar. The noise was quite different from that of a re-entry on Earth or Mars; in this thin atmosphere of hydrogen and helium, all sounds were transformed a couple of octaves upward. On Jupiter, even thunder would have falsetto overtones.

With the rising scream came mounting weight; within seconds, he was completely immobilised. His field of vision contracted until it embraced only the clock and the accelerometer; fifteen g, and four hundred and eighty seconds to go. . . .

He never lost consciousness; but then, he had not expected to. *Kon-Tiki's* trail through the Jovian atmosphere must be really spectacular – by this time, thousands of miles long. Five hundred seconds after entry, the drag began to taper off: ten g, five g, two . . . Then weight vanished almost completely. He was falling free, all his enormous orbital velocity destroyed.

There was a sudden jolt as the incandescent remnants of the heat shield were jettisoned. It had done its work and would not be needed again; Jupiter could have it now. He released all but two of the restraining buckles, and waited lor the automatic sequencer to start the next, and most critical, series of events.

He did not see the first drogue parachute pop out, but he could feel the slight jerk, and the rate of fall diminished immediately. *Kon-Tiki* had lost all her horizontal speed and was going straight down at almost a thousand miles an hour. Everything depended on what happened in the next sixty seconds.

There went the second drogue. He looked up through the overhead window and saw, to his immense relief, that clouds of glittering foil were billowing out behind the falling ship. Like a great flower unfurling, the thousands of cubic yards of the balloon spread out across the sky, scooping up the thin gas until it was fully inflated. *Kon-Tiki*'s rate of fall dropped to a few miles an hour and remained constant. Now there was plenty of time; it would take him days to fall all the way down to the surface of Jupiter.

But he would get there eventually, even if he did nothing about it. The balloon overhead was merely acting as an efficient parachute. It was providing no lift; nor could it do so, while the gas inside and out was the same.

With its characteristic and rather disconcerting crack the fusion reactor started up, pouring torrents of heat into the envelope overhead. Within five minutes, the rate of fall had become zero; within six, the ship had started to rise. According to the radar altimeter, it had levelled out at about two hundred and sixty-seven miles above the surface – or whatever passed for a surface on Jupiter.

Only one kind of balloon will work in an atmosphere of hydrogen, which is the lightest of all gases – and that is a hot-hydrogen balloon. As long as the fuser kept ticking over, Falcon could remain aloft, drifting across a world that could hold a hundred Pacifics. After travelling over three hundred million miles, *Kon-Tiki* had at last begun to justify her name. She was an aerial raft, adrift upon the currents of the Jovian atmosphere.

Though a whole new world was lying around him, it was more than an hour before Falcon could examine the view. First he had to check all the capsule's systems and test its response to the controls. He had to learn how much extra heat was necessary to produce a desired rate of ascent, and how much gas he must vent in order to descend. Above all, there was the question of stability. He must adjust the length of the cables attaching his capsule to the huge, pear-shaped balloon, to damp out vibrations and get the smoothest possible ride. Thus far, he was lucky; at this level, the wind was steady, and the Doppler reading on the invisible surface gave him a ground speed of two hundred and seventeen and a half miles an hour. For Jupiter, that was modest; winds of up to a thousand had been observed. But mere speed was, of course, unimportant; the real danger was turbulence. If he ran into that, only skill and experience and swift reaction could save him – and these were not matters that could yet be programmed into a computer.

Not until he was satisfied that he had got the feel of his strange craft did Falcon pay any attention to Mission Control's pleadings. Then he deployed the booms carrying the instrumentation and the atmospheric samplers. The capsule now resembled a rather untidy Christmas tree, but still rode smoothly down the Jovian winds while it radioed its torrents of information to the recorders on the ship miles above. And now, at last, he could look around. . . .

His first impression was unexpected, and even a little disappointing. As far as the scale of things was concerned, he might have been ballooning over an ordinary cloudscape on Earth. The horizon seemed at a normal distance; there was no feeling at all that he was on a world eleven times the diameter of his own. Then he looked at the infrared radar, sounding the layers of atmosphere beneath him – and knew how badly his eyes had been deceived.

That layer of clouds apparently about three miles away was really more than thirty-seven miles below. And the horizon, whose distance he would have guessed at about one hundred and twenty-five, was actually eighteen hundred miles from the ship.

The crystalline clarity of the hydrohelium atmosphere and the enormous curvature of the planet had fooled him completely. It was even harder to judge distances here than on the Moon; everything he saw must be multiplied by at least ten.

It was a simple matter, and he should have been prepared for it. Yet somehow, it disturbed him profoundly. He did not feel that Jupiter was huge, but that *he* had shrunk – to a tenth of his normal size. Perhaps, with time, he would grow accustomed to the inhuman scale of this world; yet as he stared toward that unbelievably distant horizon, he felt as if a wind colder than the atmosphere around him was blowing through his soul. Despite all his arguments, this might never be a place for man. He could well be both the first and the last to descend through the clouds of Jupiter.

The sky above was almost black, except for a few wisps of ammonia cirrus perhaps twelve miles overhead. It was cold up there, on the fringes of space, but both pressure and temperature increased rapidly with depth. At the level where *Kon-Tiki* was drifting now, it was fifty below zero, and the pressure was five atmospheres. Sixty-five miles farther down, it would be as warm as equatorial Earth, and the pressure about the same as at the bottom of one of the shallower seas. Ideal conditions for life. . . .

A quarter of the brief Jovian day had already gone; the sun was halfway up the sky, but the light on the unbroken cloudscape below had a curious mellow quality. That extra three hundred million miles had robbed the Sun of all its power. Though the sky was clear, Falcon found himself continually thinking that it was a heavily overcast day. When night fell, the onset of darkness would be swift indeed; though it was still morning, there was a sense of autumnal twilight in the air. But autumn, of course, was something that never came to Jupiter. There were no seasons here.

Kon-Tiki had come down in the exact centre of the equatorial zone – the least colourful part of the planet. The sea of clouds that stretched out to the horizon was tinted a pale salmon; there were none of the yellows and pinks and even reds that banded Jupiter at higher altitudes. The Great Red Spot itself – most spectacular of all of the planet's features – lay thousands of miles to the south. It had been a temptation to descend there, but the south tropical disturbance was unusually active, with currents reaching over nine hundred miles an hour. It would have been asking for trouble to head into that maelstrom of unknown forces. The Great Red Spot and its mysteries would have to wait for future expeditions.

The Sun, moving across the sky twice as swiftly as it did on Earth, was now nearing the zenith and had become eclipsed by the great silver canopy of the balloon. *Kon-Tiki* was still drifting swiftly and smoothly westward at a steady two hundred and seventeen and a half, but only the radar gave any indication of this. Was it always as calm here? Falcon asked himself. The scientists who had talked learnedly of the Jovian doldrums, and had predicted that the equator would be the quietest place, seemed to know what they were talking about, after all. He had been profoundly sceptical of all such forecasts, and had agreed with one unusually modest researcher who had told him bluntly: 'There are *no* experts on Jupiter.' Well, there would be at least one by the end of this day.

If he managed to survive until then.

4. The Voices of the Deep

That first day, the Father of the Gods smiled upon him. It was as calm and peaceful here on Jupiter as it had been, years ago, when he was drifting with Webster across the plains of northern India. Falcon had time to master his new skills, until *Kon-Tiki* seemed an extension of his own body. Such luck was more than he had dared to hope for, and he began to wonder what price he might have to pay for it.

The five hours of daylight were almost over; the clouds below were full of shadows, which gave them a massive solidity they had not possessed when the Sun was higher. Colour was swiftly draining from the sky, except in the west itself, where a band of deepening purple lay along the horizon. Above this band was the thin crescent of a closer moon, pale and bleached against the utter blackness beyond.

With a speed perceptible to the eye, the Sun went straight down over the edge of Jupiter, over eighteen hundred miles away. The stars came out in their legions – and there was the beautiful evening star of Earth, on the very frontier of twilight, reminding him how far he was from home. It followed the Sun down into the west. Man's first night on Jupiter had begun.

907

With the onset of darkness, *Kon-Tiki* started to sink. The balloon was no longer heated by the feeble sunlight and was losing a small part of its buoyancy. Falcon did nothing to increase lift; he had expected this and was planning to descend.

The invisible cloud deck was still over thirty miles below, and he would reach it about midnight. It showed up clearly on the infrared radar, which also reported that it contained a vast array of complex carbon compounds, as well as the usual hydrogen, helium, and ammonia. The chemists were dying for samples of that fluffy, pinkish stuff; though some atmospheric probes had already gathered a few grams, that had only whetted their appetites. Half the basic molecules of life were here, floating high above the surface of Jupiter. And where there was food, could life be far away? That was the question that, after more than a hundred years, no one had been able to answer.

The infrared was blocked by the clouds, but the microwave radar sliced right through and showed layer after layer, all the way down to the hidden surface almost two hundred and fifty miles below. That was barred to him by enormous pressures and temperatures; not even robot probes had ever reached it intact. It lay in tantalising inaccessibility at the bottom of the radar screen, slightly fuzzy, and showing a curious granular structure that his equipment could not resolve.

An hour after sunset, he dropped his first probe. It fell swiftly for about sixty miles, then began to float in the denser atmosphere, sending back torrents of radio signals, which he relayed to Mission Control. Then there was nothing else to do until sunrise, except to keep an eye on the rate of descent, monitor the instruments, and answer occasional queries. While she was drifting in this steady current, *Kon-Tiki* could look after herself.

Just before midnight, a woman controller came on watch and introduced herself with the usual pleasantries. Ten minutes later she called again, her voice at once serious and excited.

'Howard! Listen in on channel forty-six – high gain.'

Channel forty-six? There were so many telemetering circuits that he knew the numbers of only those that were critical; but as soon as he threw the switch, he recognised this one. He was plugged in to the microphone on the probe, floating more than eighty miles below him in an atmosphere now almost as dense as water.

At first, there was only a soft hiss of whatever strange winds stirred down in the darkness of that unimaginable world. And then, out of the background noise, there slowly emerged a booming vibration that grew louder and louder, like the beating of a gigantic drum. It was so low that it was felt as much as heard, and the beats steadily increased their tempo though the pitch never changed. Now it was a swift, almost infrasonic throbbing. Then, suddenly, in mid-vibration, it stopped – so abruptly that the mind could not accept the silence, but memory continued to manufacture a ghostly echo in the deepest caverns of the brain.

It was the most extraordinary sound that Falcon had ever heard, even among the multitudinous noises of Earth. He could think of no natural phenomenon that could have caused it; nor was it like the cry of any animal, not even one of the great whales. . . .

It came again, following exactly the same pattern. Now that he was prepared for it, he estimated the length of the sequence; from first faint throb to final crescendo, it lasted just over ten seconds.

And this time there was a real echo, very faint and far away. Perhaps it came from one of the many reflecting layers, deeper in this stratified atmosphere; perhaps it was another, more distant source. Falcon waited for a second echo, but it never came.

Mission Control reacted quickly and asked him to drop another probe at once. With two microphones operating, it would be possible to find the approximate location of the sources. Oddly enough, none of *Kon-Tiki*'s own external mikes could detect anything except wind noises. The boomings, whatever they were, must have been trapped and channelled beneath an atmospheric reflecting layer far below.

They were coming, it was soon discovered, from a cluster of sources about twelve hundred miles away. The distance gave no indication of their power; in Earth's oceans, quite feeble sounds could travel equally far. And as for the obvious assumption that living creatures were responsible, the Chief Exobiologist quickly ruled that out.

'I'll be very disappointed,' said Dr Brenner, 'if there are no micro-organisms or plants there. But nothing like animals, because there's no free oxygen. All biochemical reactions on Jupiter must be low-energy ones – there's just no way an active creature could generate enough power to function.'

Falcon wondered if this was true; he had heard the argument before, and reserved judgment.

'In any case,' continued Brenner, 'some of those sound waves are a hundred yards long! Even an animal as big as a whale couldn't produce them. They *must* have a natural origin.'

Yes, that seemed plausible, and probably the physicists would be able to come up with an explanation. What would a blind alien make, Falcon wondered, of the sounds he might hear when standing beside a stormy sea, or a geyser, or a volcano, or a waterfall? He might well attribute them to some huge beast.

About an hour before sunrise the voices of the deep died away, and Falcon began to busy himself with preparation for the dawn of his second day. *Kon-Tiki* was now only three miles above the nearest cloud layer; the external pressure had risen to ten atmospheres, and the temperature was a tropical thirty degrees. A man could be comfortable here with no more equipment than a breathing mask and the right grade of heliox mixture.

'We've some good news for you,' Mission Control reported, soon after dawn. 'The cloud layer's breaking up. You'll have partial clearing in an hour – but watch out for turbulence.'

'I've already noticed some,' Falcon answered. 'How far down will I be able to see?'

'At least twelve miles, down to the second thermocline. *That* cloud deck is solid – it never breaks.'

And it's out of my reach, Falcon told himself; the temperature down there must be over a hundred degrees. This was the first time that any balloonist had ever had to worry, not about his ceiling, but about his basement!

Ten minutes later he could see what Mission Control had already observed from its superior vantage point. There was a change in colour near the horizon, and the cloud layer had become ragged and humpy, as if something had torn it open. He turned up his little nuclear furnace and gave *Kon-Tiki* another three miles of altitude, so that he could get a better view.

The sky below was clearing rapidly, completely, as if something was dissolving the solid overcast. An abyss was opening before his eyes. A moment later he sailed out over the edge of a cloud canyon about twelve miles deep and six hundred miles wide.

A new world lay spread beneath him; Jupiter had stripped away one of its many veils. The second layer of clouds, unattainably far below, was much darker in colour than the first. It was almost salmon pink, and curiously mottled with little islands of brick red. They were all oval-shaped, with their long axes pointing east-west, in the direction of the prevailing wind. There were hundreds of them, all about the same size, and they reminded Falcon of puffy little cumulus clouds in the terrestrial sky.

He reduced buoyancy, and *Kon-Tiki* began to drop down the face of the dissolving cliff. It was then that he noticed the snow.

White flakes were forming in the air and drifting slowly downward. Yet it was much too warm for snow – and, in any event, there was scarcely a trace of water at this altitude. Moreover, there was no glitter or sparkle about these flakes as they went cascading down into the depths. When, presently, a few landed on an instrument boom outside the main viewing port, he saw that they were a dull, opaque white – not crystalline at all – and quite large – several inches across. They looked like wax, and Falcon guessed that this was precisely what they were. Some chemical reaction was taking place in the atmosphere around him, condensing out the hydrocarbons floating in the Jovian air.

About sixty miles ahead, a disturbance was taking place in the cloud layer. The little red ovals were being jostled around, and were beginning to form a spiral – the familiar cyclonic pattern so common in the meteorology of Earth. The vortex was emerging with astonishing speed; if that was a storm ahead, Falcon told himself, he was in big trouble.

And then his concern changed to wonder – and to fear. What was developing in his line of flight was not a storm at all. Something enormous – something scores of miles across – was rising through the clouds.

The reassuring thought that it, too, might be a cloud – a thunderhead boiling up from the lower levels of the atmosphere – lasted only a few seconds. No; this was solid. It shouldered its way through the pink-and-salmon overcast like an iceberg rising from the deeps.

An *iceberg* floating on hydrogen? That was impossible, of course; but perhaps it was not too remote an analogy. As soon as he focused the telescope upon the enigma, Falcon saw that it was a whitish, crystalline mass, threaded with streaks of red and brown. It must be, he decided, the same stuff as the 'snowflakes' falling around him – a mountain range of wax. And it was not, he soon realised, as solid as he had thought; around the edges it was continually crumbling and re-forming. . . .

'I know what it is,' he radioed Mission Control, which for the last few minutes had been asking anxious questions. 'It's a mass of bubbles – some kind of foam. Hydrocarbon froth. Get the chemists working on . . . *Just a minute!*'

'What is it?' called Mission Control. 'What is it?'

He ignored the frantic pleas from space and concentrated all his mind upon the image in the telescope field. He had to be sure; if he made a mistake, he would be the laughingstock of the solar system.

Then he relaxed, glanced at the clock, and switched off the nagging voice from Jupiter V.

'Hello, Mission Control,' he said, very formally. 'This is Howard Falcon aboard *Kon-Tiki*. Ephemeris Time nineteen hours twenty-one minutes fifteen seconds. Latitude zero degrees five minutes North. Longitude one hundred five degrees forty-two minutes, System One.

'Tell Dr Brenner that there is life on Jupiter. And it's big. . . .'

5. The Wheels of Poseidon

'I'm very happy to be proved wrong,' Dr Brenner radioed back cheerfully. 'Nature always has something up her sleeve. Keep the long-focus camera on target and give us the steadiest pictures you can.'

The things moving up and down those waxen slopes were still too far away for Falcon to make out many details, and they must have been very large to be visible at all at such a distance. Almost black, and shaped like arrowheads, they manoeuvred by slow undulations of their entire bodies, so that they looked rather like giant manta rays, swimming above some tropical reef.

Perhaps they were sky-borne cattle, browsing on the cloud pastures of Jupiter, for they seemed to be feeding along the dark, red-brown streaks that ran like dried-up river beds down the flanks of the floating cliffs. Occasionally, one of them would dive headlong into the mountain of foam and disappear completely from sight.

Kon-Tiki was moving only slowly with respect to the cloud layer below; it would be at least three hours before she was above those ephemeral hills. She was in a race with the Sun. Falcon hoped that darkness would not fall before he could get a good view of the mantas, as he had christened them, as well as the fragile landscape over which they flapped their way.

It was a long three hours. During the whole time, he kept the external microphones on full gain, wondering if here was the source of that booming in the night. The mantas were certainly large enough to have produced it; when he could get an accurate measurement, he discovered that they were almost a hundred yards across the wings. That was three times the length of the largest whale – though he doubted if they could weigh more than a few tons.

Half an hour before sunset, *Kon-Tiki* was almost above the 'mountains'.

'No,' said Falcon, answering Mission Control's repeated questions about the mantas, 'they're still showing no reaction to me. I don't think they're intelligent – they look like harmless vegetarians. And even if they try to chase me, I'm sure they can't reach my altitude.'

Yet he was a little disappointed when the mantas showed not the slightest interest in him as he sailed high above their feeding ground. Perhaps they had no way of detecting his presence. When he examined and photographed them through the telescope, he could see no signs of any sense organs. The creatures were simply huge black deltas, rippling over hills and valleys that, in reality, were little more substantial than the clouds of Earth. Though they looked solid, Falcon knew that anyone who stepped on those white mountains would go crashing through them as if they were made of tissue paper.

At close quarters he could see the myriads of cellules or bubbles from which they were formed. Some of these were quite large – a yard or so in diameter – and Falcon wondered in what witches' cauldron of hydrocarbons they had been brewed. There must be enough petrochemicals deep down in the atmosphere of Jupiter to supply all Earth's needs for a million years.

The short day had almost gone when he passed over the crest of the waxen hills, and the light was fading rapidly along their lower slopes. There were no mantas on this western side, and for some reason the topography was very different. The foam was sculptured into long, level terraces, like the interior of a lunar crater. He could almost imagine that they were gigantic steps leading down to the hidden surface of the planet.

And on the lowest of those steps, just clear of the swirling clouds that the mountain had displaced when it came surging skyward, was a roughly oval mass, one or two miles across. It was difficult to see, since it was only a little darker than the grey-white foam on which it rested. Falcon's first thought was that he was looking at a forest of pallid trees, like giant mushrooms that had never seen the Sun.

Yes, it must be a forest – he could see hundreds of thin trunks, springing from the white waxy froth in which they were rooted. But the trees were packed astonishingly close together; there was scarcely any space between them. Perhaps it was not a forest, after all, but a single enormous tree – like one of the giant multi-trunked banyans of the East. Once he had seen a banyan tree in Java that was over six hundred and fifty yards across; this monster was at least ten times that size.

The light had almost gone. The cloudscape had turned purple with refracted sunlight, and in a few seconds that, too, would have vanished. In the last light of his second day on Jupiter, Howard Falcon saw – or thought he saw – something that cast the gravest doubts on his interpretation of the white oval.

Unless the dim light had totally deceived him, those hundreds of thin trunks were beating back and forth, in perfect synchronism, like fronds of kelp rocking in the surge.

And the tree was no longer in the place where he had first seen it.

'Sorry about this,' said Mission Control, soon after sunset, 'but we think Source Beta is going to blow within the next hour. Probability seventy per cent.'

Falcon glanced quickly at the chart. Beta – Jupiter latitude one hundred and forty degrees – was over eighteen thousand six hundred miles away and well below his horizon. Even though major eruptions ran as high as ten megatons, he was much too far away for the shock wave to be a serious danger. The radio storm that it would trigger was, however, quite a different matter.

The decameter outbursts that sometimes made Jupiter the most powerful radio source in the whole sky had been discovered back in the 1950s, to the utter astonishment of the astronomers. Now, more than a century later, their real cause was still a mystery. Only the symptoms were understood; the explanation was completely unknown.

The 'volcano' theory had best stood the test of time, although no one imagined that this word had the same meaning on Jupiter as on Earth. At frequent intervals – often several times a day – titanic eruptions occurred in the lower depths of the atmosphere, probably on the hidden surface of the planet itself. A great column of gas, more than six hundred miles high, would start boiling upward as if determined to escape into space.

Against the most powerful gravitational field of all the planets, it had no chance. Yet some traces – a mere few million tons – usually managed to reach the Jovian ionosphere; and when they did, all hell broke loose.

The radiation belts surrounding Jupiter completely dwarf the feeble Van Allen belts of Earth. When they are short-circuited by an ascending column of gas, the result is an electrical discharge millions of times more powerful than any terrestrial flash of lightning; it sends a colossal thunder-clap of radio noise flooding across the entire solar system and on out to the stars.

It had been discovered that these radio outbursts came from four main areas of the planet. Perhaps there were weaknesses there that allowed the fires of the interior to break out from time to time. The scientists on Ganymede, largest of Jupiter's many moons, now thought that they could predict the onset of a decameter storm; their accuracy was about as good as a weather forecaster's of the early 1900s.

Falcon did not know whether to welcome or to fear a radio storm; it would certainly add to the value of the mission – if he survived it. His course had been planned to keep as far as possible from the main centres of disturbance, especially the most active one, Source Alpha. As luck would have it, the threatening Beta was the closest to him. He hoped that the distance, almost three-fourths the circumference of Earth, was safe enough.

'Probability ninety per cent,' said Mission Control with a distinct note of urgency. 'And forget that hour. Ganymede says it may be any moment.'

The radio had scarcely fallen silent when the reading on the magnetic field-strength meter started to shoot upward. Before it could go off scale, it reversed and began to drop as rapidly as it had risen. Far away and thousands of miles below, something had given the planet's molten core a titanic jolt.

'There she blows!' called Mission Control.

'Thanks, I already know. When will the storm hit me?'

'You can expect onset in five minutes. Peak in ten.'

Far around the curve of Jupiter, a funnel of gas as wide as the Pacific Ocean was climbing spaceward at thousands of miles an hour. Already, the thunderstorms of the lower atmosphere would be raging around it – but they were nothing compared with the fury that would explode when the radiation belt was reached and began dumping its surplus electrons onto the planet. Falcon began to retract all the instrument booms that were extended out from the capsule. There were no other precautions he could take. It would be four hours before the atmospheric shock wave reached him – but the radio blast, travelling at the speed of light, would be here in a tenth of a second, once the discharge had been triggered.

The radio monitor, scanning back and forth across the spectrum, still showed nothing unusual, just the normal mush of background static. Then Falcon noticed that the noise level was slowly creeping upward. The explosion was gathering its strength.

At such a distance he had never expected to *see* anything. But suddenly a flicker as of far-off heat lightning danced along the eastern horizon. Simultaneously, half the circuit breakers jumped out of the main switchboard, the lights failed, and all communications channels went dead.

He tried to move, but was completely unable to do so. The paralysis that gripped him was not merely psychological; he seemed to have lost all control of his limbs and could feel a painful tingling sensation over his entire body. It was impossible that the electric field could have penetrated this shielded cabin. Yet there was a flickering glow over the instrument board, and he could hear the unmistakable crackle of a brush discharge.

With a series of sharp bangs, the emergency systems went into operation, and the overloads reset themselves. The lights flickered on again. And Falcon's paralysis disappeared as swiftly as it had come.

After glancing at the board to make sure that all circuits were back to normal, he moved quickly to the viewing ports.

There was no need to switch on the inspection lamps – the cables supporting the capsule seemed to be on fire. Lines of light glowing an electric blue against the darkness stretched upward from the main lift ring to the equator of the giant balloon; and rolling slowly along several of them were dazzling balls of fire.

The sight was so strange and so beautiful that it was hard to read any menace in it. Few people, Falcon knew, had ever seen ball lightning from such close quarters – and certainly none had survived if they were riding a hydrogen-filled balloon back in the atmosphere of Earth. He remembered the flaming death of the *Hindenburg*, destroyed by a stray spark when she docked at Lakehurst in 1937; as it had done so often in the past, the horrifying old newsreel film flashed through his mind. But at least that could not happen here, though there was more hydrogen above his head than had ever filled the last of the Zeppelins. It would be a few billion years yet, before anyone could light a fire in the atmosphere of Jupiter.

With a sound like briskly frying bacon, the speech circuit came back to life.

'Hello, *Kon-Tiki* – are you receiving? Are you receiving?'

The words were chopped and badly distorted, but intelligible. Falcon's spirits lifted; he had resumed contact with the world of men.

'I receive you,' he said. 'Quite an electrical display, but no damage – so far.'

'Thanks – thought we'd lost you. Please check telemetry channels three, seven, twenty-six. Also gain on camera two. And we don't quite believe the readings on the external ionisation probes. . . .'

Reluctantly Falcon tore his gaze away from the fascinating pyrotechnic display around *Kon-Tiki*, though from time to time he kept glancing out of the windows. The ball lightning disappeared first, the fiery globes slowly expanding until they reached a critical size, at which they vanished in a gentle explosion. But even an hour later, there were still faint glows around all the exposed metal on the outside of the capsule; and the radio circuits remained noisy until well after midnight.

The remaining hours of darkness were completely uneventful – until just before dawn. Because it came from the east, Falcon assumed that he was seeing the first faint hint of sunrise. Then he realised that it was twenty minutes too early for this – and the glow that had appeared along the horizon was moving toward him even as he watched. It swiftly detached itself from the arch of stars that marked the invisible edge of the planet, and he saw that it was a relatively narrow band, quite sharply defined. The beam of an enormous searchlight appeared to be swinging beneath the clouds.

Perhaps sixty miles behind the first racing bar of light came another, parallel to it and moving at the same speed. And beyond that another, and another – until all the sky flickered with alternating sheets of light and darkness.

By this time, Falcon thought, he had been inured to wonders, and it seemed impossible that this display of pure, soundless luminosity could present the slightest danger. But it was so astonishing, and so inexplicable, that he felt cold, naked fear gnawing at his self-control. No man could look upon such a sight without feeling like a helpless pygmy in the presence of forces beyond his comprehension. Was it possible that, after all, Jupiter carried not only life but also intelligence? And, perhaps, an intelligence that only now was beginning to react to his alien presence?

'Yes, we see it,' said Mission Control, in a voice that echoed his own awe. 'We've no idea what it is. Stand by, we're calling Ganymede.'

The display was slowly fading; the bands racing in from the far horizon were much fainter, as if the energies that powered them were becoming exhausted. In five minutes it was all over; the last faint pulse of light flickered along the western sky and then was gone. Its passing left Falcon with an overwhelming sense of relief. The sight was so hypnotic, and so disturbing, that it was not good for any man's peace of mind to contemplate it too long.

He was more shaken than he cared to admit. The electrical storm was something that he could understand; but *this* was totally incomprehensible.

Mission Control was still silent. He knew that the information banks up on Ganymede were now being searched as men and computers turned their minds to the problem. If no answer could be found there, it would be necessary to call Earth; that would mean a delay of almost an hour. The possibility that even Earth might be unable to help was one that Falcon did not care to contemplate.

He had never before been so glad to hear the voice of Mission Control as when Dr Brenner finally came on the circuit. The biologist sounded relieved, yet subdued – like a man who has just come through some great intellectual crisis.

'Hello, *Kon-Tiki*. We've solved your problem, but we can still hardly believe it.

'What you've been seeing is bioluminescence, very similar to that produced by microorganisms in the tropical seas of Earth. Here they're in the atmosphere, not the ocean, but the principle is the same.'

'But the pattern,' protested Falcon, 'was so regular – so *artificial*. And it was hundreds of miles across!'

'It was even larger than you imagine; you observed only a small part of it. The whole pattern was over three thousand miles wide and looked like a revolving wheel. You merely saw the spokes, sweeping past you at about six-tenths of a mile a second. . . .'

'A *second*!' Falcon could not help interjecting. 'No animals could move that fast!'

'Of course not. Let me explain. What you saw was triggered by the shock wave from Source Beta, moving at the speed of sound.'

'But what about the pattern?' Falcon insisted.

'That's the surprising part. It's a very rare phenomenon, but identical wheels of light – except that they're a thousand times smaller – have been observed in the Persian Gulf and the Indian Ocean. Listen to this: British India Company's *Patna*, Persian Gulf, May 1880, 11:30 P.M.. – "an enormous luminous wheel, whirling round, the spokes of which appeared to brush the ship along. The spokes were 200 or 300 yards long . . . each wheel contained about sixteen spokes. . . ." And here's one from the Gulf of Omar, dated May 23, 1906: "The intensely bright luminescence approached us rapidly, shooting sharply defined light rays to the west in rapid succession, like the beam from the searchlight of a warship. . . . To the left of us, a gigantic fiery wheel formed itself, with spokes that reached as far as one could see. The whole wheel whirled around for two or three minutes. . . ." The archive computer on Ganymede dug up about five hundred cases. It would have printed out the lot if we hadn't stopped it in time.'

'I'm convinced – but still baffled.'

'I don't blame you. The full explanation wasn't worked out until late in the twentieth century. It seems that these luminous wheels are the results of submarine earthquakes, and always occur in shallow waters where the shock waves can be reflected and cause standing wave patterns. Sometimes bars, sometimes rotating wheels – the "Wheels of Poseidon", they've been called. The theory was finally proved by making underwater explosions and photographing the results from a satellite. No wonder sailors used to be superstitious. Who would have believed a thing like *this*?'

So that was it, Falcon told himself. When Source Beta blew its top, it must have sent shock waves in all directions – through the compressed gas of the lower atmosphere, through the solid body of Jupiter itself. Meeting and crisscrossing, those waves must have cancelled here, reinforced there; the whole planet must have rung like a bell.

Yet the explanation did not destroy the sense of wonder and awe; he would never be able to forget those flickering bands of light, racing through the unattainable depths of the Jovian atmosphere. He felt that he was not merely on a strange planet, but in some magical realm between myth and reality.

This was a world where absolutely *anything* could happen, and no man could possibly guess what the future would bring.

And he still had a whole day to go.

6. Medusa

When the true dawn finally arrived, it brought a sudden change of weather. *Kon-Tiki* was moving through a blizzard; waxen snowflakes were falling so thickly that visibility was reduced to zero. Falcon began to worry about the weight that might be accumulating on the envelope. Then he noticed that any flakes settling outside the windows quickly disappeared; *Kon-Tiki*'s continual outpouring of heat was evaporating them as swiftly as they arrived.

If he had been ballooning on Earth, he would also have worried about the possibility of collision. At least that was no danger here; any Jovian mountains were several hundred miles below him. And as for the floating islands of foam, hitting them would probably be like ploughing into slightly hardened soap bubbles.

Nevertheless, he switched on the horizontal radar, which until now had been completely useless; only the vertical beam, giving his distance from the invisible surface, had thus far been of any value. Then he had another surprise.

Scattered across a huge sector of the sky ahead were dozens of large and brilliant echoes. They were completely isolated from one another and apparently hung unsupported in space. Falcon remembered a phrase the earliest aviators had used to describe one of the hazards of their profession: 'clouds stuffed with rocks'. That was a perfect description of what seemed to lie in the track of *Kon-Tiki*.

It was a disconcerting sight; then Falcon again reminded himself that nothing *really* solid could possibly hover in this atmosphere. Perhaps it was some strange meteorological phenomenon. In any case, the nearest echo was about a hundred and twenty-five miles.

He reported to Mission Control, which could provide no explanation. But it gave the welcome news that he would be clear of the blizzard in another thirty minutes.

It did not warn him, however, of the violent cross wind that abruptly grabbed *Kon-Tiki* and swept it almost at right angles to its previous track. Falcon needed all his skill and the maximum use of what little control he had over his ungainly vehicle to prevent it from being capsized. Within minutes he was racing northward at over three hundred miles an hour. Then, as suddenly as it had started, the turbulence ceased; he was still moving at high speed, but in smooth air. He wondered if he had been caught in the Jovian equivalent of a jet stream.

The snow storm dissolved; and he saw what Jupiter had been preparing for him.

Kon-Tiki had entered the funnel of a gigantic whirlpool, some six hundred miles across. The balloon was being swept along a curving wall of cloud. Overhead, the Sun was shining in a clear sky; but far beneath, this great hole in the atmosphere drilled down to unknown depths until it reached a misty floor where lightning flickered almost continuously.

Though the vessel was being dragged downward so slowly that it was in no immediate danger, Falcon increased the flow of heat into the envelope until *Kon-Tiki* hovered at a constant altitude. Not until then did he abandon the fantastic spectacle outside and consider again the problem of the radar.

The nearest echo was now only about twenty-five miles away. All of them, he quickly realised, were distributed along the wall of the vortex, and were moving with it, apparently caught in the whirlpool like *Kon-Tiki* itself.

He aimed the telescope along the radar bearing and found himself looking at a curious mottled cloud that almost filled the field of view.

It was not easy to see, being only a little darker than the whirling wall of mist that formed its background. Not until he had been staring for several minutes did Falcon realise that he had met it once before.

The first time it had been crawling across the drifting mountains of foam, and he had mistaken it for a giant, many-trunked tree. Now at last he could appreciate its real size and complexity and could give it a better name to fix its image in his mind. It did not resemble a tree at all, but a jellyfish – a medusa, such as might be met trailing its tentacles as it drifted along the warm eddies of the Gulf Stream.

This medusa was more than a mile across and its scores of dangling tentacles were hundreds of feet long. They swayed slowly back and forth in perfect unison, taking more than a minute for each complete undulation – almost as if the creature was clumsily rowing itself through the sky.

The other echoes were more distant medusae. Falcon focused the telescope on half a dozen and could see no variations in shape or size. They all seemed to be of the same species, and he wondered just why they were drifting lazily around in this six-hundred-mile orbit. Perhaps they were feeding upon the aerial plankton sucked in by the whirlpool, as *Kon-Tiki* itself had been.

'Do you realise, Howard,' said Dr Brenner, when he had recovered from his initial astonishment, 'that this thing is about a hundred thousand times as large as the biggest whale? And even if it's only a gasbag, it must still weigh a million tons! I can't even guess at its metabolism. It must generate megawatts of heat to maintain its buoyancy.'

'But if it's just a gasbag, why is it such a damn good radar reflector?'

'I haven't the faintest idea. Can you get any closer?'

Brenner's question was not an idle one. If he changed altitude to take advantage of the differing wind velocities, Falcon could approach the medusa as closely as he wished. At the moment, however, he preferred his present twenty-five miles and said so, firmly.

'I see what you mean,' Brenner answered, a little reluctantly. 'Let's stay where we are for the present.' That 'we' gave Falcon a certain wry amusement; an extra sixty thousand miles made a considerable difference in one's point of view.

For the next two hours *Kon-Tiki* drifted uneventfully in the gyre of the great whirlpool, while Falcon experimented with filters and camera contrast, trying to get a clear view of the medusa. He began to wonder if its elusive coloration was some kind of camouflage; perhaps, like many animals of Earth, it was trying to lose itself against its background. That was a trick used by both hunters and hunted.

In which category was the medusa? That was a question he could hardly expect to have answered in the short time that was left to him. Yet just before noon, without the slightest warning, the answer came. . .

Like a squadron of antique jet fighters, five mantas came sweeping through the wall of mist that formed the funnel of the vortex. They were flying in a V formation directly toward the pallid grey cloud of the medusa; and there was no doubt, in Falcon's mind, that they were on the attack. He had been quite wrong to assume that they were harmless vegetarians.

Yet everything happened at such a leisurely pace that it was like watching a slow-motion film. The mantas undulated along at perhaps thirty miles an hour; it seemed ages before they reached the medusa, which continued to paddle imperturbably along at an even slower speed. Huge though they were, the mantas looked tiny beside the monster they were approaching When they flapped down on its back, they appeared about as large as birds landing on a whale.

Could the medusa defend itself, Falcon wondered. He did not see how the attacking mantas could be in danger as long as they avoided those huge clumsy tentacles. And perhaps their host was not even aware of them; they could be insignificant parasites, tolerated as are fleas upon a dog.

But now it was obvious that the medusa was in distress. With agonising slowness, it began to tip over like a capsising ship. After ten minutes it had tilted forty-five degrees; it was also rapidly losing altitude. It was impossible not to feel a sense of pity for the beleaguered monster, and to Falcon the sight brought bitter memories. In a grotesque way, the fall of the medusa was almost a parody of the dying *Queen*'s last moments.

Yet he knew that his sympathies were on the wrong side. High intelligence could develop only among predators – not among the drifting browsers of either sea or air. The mantas were far closer to him than was this monstrous bag of gas. And anyway, who could *really* sympathise with a creature a hundred thousand times larger than a whale?

Then he noticed that the medusa's tactics seemed to be having some effect. The mantas had been disturbed by its slow roll and were flapping heavily away from its back – like gorged vultures interrupted at mealtime. But they did not move very far, continuing to hover a few yards from the still-capsizing monster.

There was a sudden, blinding flash of light synchronised with a crash of static over the radio. One of the mantas, slowly twisting end over end, was plummeting straight downward. As it fell, a plume of black smoke trailed behind it. The resemblance to an aircraft going down in flames was quite uncanny.

In unison, the remaining mantas dived steeply away from the medusa, gaining speed by losing altitude. They had, within minutes, vanished back into the wall of cloud from which they had emerged. And the medusa, no longer falling, began to roll back toward the horizontal. Soon it was sailing along once more on an even keel, as if nothing had happened.

'Beautiful!' said Dr Brenner, after a moment of stunned silence. 'It's developed electric defences, like some of our eels and rays. But that must have been about a million volts! Can you see any organs that might produce the discharge? Anything looking like electrodes?'

'No,' Falcon answered, after switching to the highest power of the telescope. 'But here's something odd. Do you see this pattern? Check back on the earlier images. I'm sure it wasn't there before.'

A broad, mottled band had appeared along the side of the medusa. It formed a startlingly regular checkerboard, each square of which was itself speckled in a complex subpattern of short horizontal lines. They were spaced at equal distances in a geometrically perfect array of rows and columns.

'You're right,' said Dr Brenner, with something very much like awe in his voice. 'That's just appeared. And I'm afraid to tell you what I think it is.'

'Well, I have no reputation to lose – at least as a biologist. Shall I give my guess?'

'Go ahead.'

'That's a large meter-band radio array. The sort of thing they used back at the beginning of the twentieth century.'

'I was afraid you'd say that. Now we know why it gave such a massive echo.'

'But why has it just appeared?'

'Probably an aftereffect of the discharge.'

'I've just had another thought,' said Falcon, rather slowly. 'Do you suppose it's *listening* to us?'

'On this frequency? I doubt it. Those are meter – no, *decameter* antennas – judging by their size. Hmm . . . that a an idea!'

Dr Brenner fell silent, obviously contemplating some new line of thought. Presently he continued: 'I bet they're tuned to the radio outbursts! That's something nature never got around to doing on Earth. . . . We have animals with sonar and even electric senses, but nothing ever developed a radio sense. Why bother where there was so much light?

'But it's different here. Jupiter is *drenched* with radio energy. It's worth while using it – maybe even tapping it. That thing could be a floating power plant!'

A new voice cut into the conversation.

'Mission Commander here. This is all very interesting, but there's a much more important matter to settle. *Is it intelligent?* If so, we've got to consider the First Contact directives.'

'Until I came here,' said Dr Brenner, somewhat ruefully, 'I would have sworn that anything that could make a shortwave antenna system *must* be intelligent. Now, I'm not sure. This could have evolved naturally. I suppose it's no more fantastic than the human eye.'

'Then we have to play safe and assume intelligence. For the present, therefore, this expedition comes under all the clauses of the Prime directive.'

There was a long silence while everyone on the radio circuit absorbed the implications of this. For the first time in the history of space flight, the rules that had been established through more than a century of argument might have to be applied. Man had – it was hoped – profited from his mistakes on Earth. Not only moral considerations, but also his own self-interest demanded that he should not repeat them among the planets. It could be disastrous to treat a superior intelligence as the American settlers had treated the Indians, or as almost everyone had treated the Africans. . . .

The first rule was: keep your distance. Make no attempt to approach, or even to communicate, until 'they' have had plenty of time to study you. Exactly what was meant by 'plenty of time', no one had ever been able to decide. It was left to the discretion of the man on the spot.

A responsibility of which he had never dreamed had descended upon Howard Falcon. In the few hours that remained to him on Jupiter, he might become the first ambassador of the human race.

And *that* was an irony so delicious that he almost wished the surgeons had restored to him the power of laughter.

7. Prime Directive

It was growing darker, but Falcon scarcely noticed as he strained his eyes toward that living cloud in the field of the telescope. The wind that was steadily sweeping *Kon-Tiki* around the funnel of the great whirlpool had now brought him within twelve miles of the creature. If he got much closer than six, he would take evasive action. Though he felt certain that the medusa's electric weapons were short ranged, he did not wish to put the matter to the test. That would be a problem for future explorers, and he wished them luck.

Now it was quite dark in the capsule. That was strange, because sunset was still hours away. Automatically, he glanced at the horizontally scanning radar, as he had done every few minutes. Apart from the medusa he was studying, there was no other object within about sixty miles of him.

Suddenly, with startling power, he heard the sound that had come booming out of the Jovian night – the throbbing beat that grew more and more rapid, then stopped in mid-crescendo. The whole capsule vibrated with it like a pea in a kettledrum.

Falcon realised two things almost simultaneously during the sudden, aching silence. *This* time the sound was not coming from thousands of miles away, over a radio circuit. It was in the very atmosphere around him.

The second thought was even more disturbing. He had quite forgotten – it was inexcusable, but there had been other apparently more important things on his mind – that most of the sky above him was completely blanked out by *Kon-Tiki*'s gasbag. Being lightly silvered to conserve its heat, the great balloon was an effective shield both to radar and to vision.

He had known this, of course; it had been a minor defect of the design, tolerated because it did not appear important. It seemed very important to Howard Falcon now – as he saw that fence of gigantic tentacles, thicker than the trunks of any tree, descending all around the capsule.

He heard Brenner yelling: 'Remember the Prime directive! Don't alarm it!' Before he could make an appropriate answer that overwhelming drumbeat started again and drowned all other sounds.

The sign of a really skilled test pilot is how he reacts not to foreseeable emergencies, but to ones that nobody could have anticipated. Falcon did not hesitate for more than a second to analyse the situation. In a lightning-swift movement, he pulled the rip cord.

That word was an archaic survival from the days of the first hydrogen balloons; on *Kon-Tiki*, the rip cord did not tear open the gasbag, but merely operated a set of louvres around the upper curve of the envelope. At once the hot gas started to rush out; *Kon-Tiki*, deprived of her lift, began to fall swiftly in this gravity field two and a half times as strong as Earth's.

Falcon had a momentary glimpse of great tentacles whipping upward and away. He had just time to note that they were studded with large bladders or sacs, presumably to give them buoyancy, and that they ended in multitudes of thin feelers like the roots of a plant. He half expected a bolt of lightning – but nothing happened.

His precipitous rate of descent was slackening as the atmosphere thickened and the deflated envelope acted as a parachute. When *Kon-Tiki* had dropped about two miles, he felt that it was safe to close the louvres again. By the time he had restored buoyancy and was in equilibrium once more, he had lost another mile of altitude and was getting dangerously near his safety limit.

He peered anxiously through the overhead windows, though he did not expect to see anything except the obscuring bulk of the balloon. But he had sideslipped during his descent, and part of the medusa was just visible a couple of miles above him. It was much closer than he expected – and it was still coming down, faster than he would have believed possible.

Mission Control was calling anxiously. He shouted: 'I'm OK – but it's still coming after me. I can't go any deeper.'

That was not quite true. He could go a lot deeper – about one hundred and eighty miles. But it would be a one-way trip, and most of the journey would be of little interest to him.

Then, to his great relief, he saw that the medusa was levelling off, not quite a mile above him. Perhaps it had decided to approach this strange intruder with caution; or perhaps it, too, found this deeper layer uncomfortably hot. The temperature was over fifty degrees centigrade, and Falcon wondered how much longer his life-support system could handle matters.

Dr Brenner was back on the circuit, still worrying about the Prime directive.

'Remember – it may only be inquisitive!' he cried, without much conviction. 'Try not to frighten it!'

Falcon was getting rather tired of this advice and recalled a TV discussion he had once seen between a space lawyer and an astronaut. After the full implications of the Prime directive had been carefully spelled out, the incredulous spacer had exclaimed: 'Then if there was no alternative, I must sit still and let myself be eaten?' The lawyer had not even cracked a smile when he answered: 'That's an *excellent* summing up.'

It had seemed funny at the time; it was not at all amusing now.

And then Falcon saw something that made him even more unhappy. The medusa was still hovering about a mile above him – but one of its tentacles was becoming incredibly elongated, and was stretching down toward *Kon-Tiki*, thinning out at the same time. As a boy he had once seen the funnel of a tornado descending from a storm cloud over the Kansas plains. The thing coming toward him now evoked vivid memories of that black, twisting snake in the sky.

'I'm rapidly running out of options,' he reported to Mission Control. 'I now have only a choice between frightening it – and giving it a bad stomach-ache. I don't think it will find *Kon-Tiki* very digestible, if that's what it has in mind.'

He waited for comments from Brenner, but the biologist remained silent.

'Very well. It's twenty-seven minutes ahead of time, but I'm starting the ignition sequencer. I hope I'll have enough reserve to correct my orbit later.'

He could no longer see the medusa; once more it was directly overhead. But he knew that the descending tentacle must now be very close to the balloon. It would take almost five minutes to bring the reactor up to full thrust . . .

The fusor was primed. The orbit computer had not rejected the situation as wholly impossible. The air scoops were open, ready to gulp in tons of the surrounding hydrohelium on demand. Even under optimum conditions, this would have been the moment of truth – for there had been no way of testing how a nuclear ramjet would *really* work in the strange atmosphere of Jupiter.

Very gently something rocked *Kon-Tiki*. Falcon tried to ignore it.

Ignition had been planned at six miles higher, in an atmosphere of less than a quarter of the density and thirty degrees cooler. Too bad.

What was the shallowest dive he could get away with, for the air scoops to work? When the ram ignited, he'd be heading toward Jupiter with two and a half g's to help him get there. Could he possibly pull out in time?

A large, heavy hand patted the balloon. The whole vessel bobbed up and down, like one of the yo-yos that had just become the craze on Earth.

Of course, Brenner *might* be perfectly right. Perhaps it was just trying to be friendly. Maybe he should try to talk to it over the radio. Which should it be: 'Pretty pussy'? 'Down, Fido'? Or 'Take me to your leader'?

The tritium-deuterium ratio was correct. He was ready to light the candle, with a hundred-million-degree match.

The thin tip of the tentacle came slithering around the edge of the balloon some sixty yards away. It was about the size of an elephant's trunk, and by the delicate way it was moving appeared to be almost as sensitive. There were little palps at its end, like questing mouths. He was sure that Dr Brenner would be fascinated.

This seemed about as good a time as any. He gave a swift scan of the entire control board, started the final four-second ignition count, broke the safety seal, and pressed the JETTISON switch.

There was a sharp explosion and an instant loss of weight. *Kon-Tiki* was falling freely, nose down. Overhead, the discarded balloon was racing upward, dragging the inquisitive tentacle with it. Falcon had no time to see if the gasbag actually hit the medusa, because at that moment the ramjet fired and he had other matters to think about.

A roaring column of hot hydrohelium was pouring out of the reactor nozzles, swiftly building up thrust – but *toward* Jupiter, not away from it. He could not pull out yet, for vector control was too sluggish. Unless he could gain complete control and achieve horizontal flight within the next five seconds, the vehicle would dive too deeply into the atmosphere and would be destroyed.

With agonising slowness – those five seconds seemed like fifty – he managed to flatten out, then pull the nose upward. He glanced back only once and caught a final glimpse of the medusa, many miles away. *Kon-Tiki*'s discarded gasbag had apparently escaped from its grasp, for he could see no sign of it.

Now he was master once more – no longer drifting helplessly on the winds of Jupiter, but riding his own column of atomic fire back to the stars. He was confident that the ramjet would steadily give him velocity and altitude until he had reached near-orbital speed at the fringes of the atmosphere. Then, with a brief burst of pure rocket power, he would regain the freedom of space.

Halfway to orbit, he looked south and saw the tremendous enigma of the Great Red Spot – that floating island twice the size of Earth – coming up over the horizon. He stared into its mysterious beauty until the computer warned him that conversion to rocket thrust was only sixty seconds ahead. He tore his gaze reluctantly away.

'Some other time,' he murmured.

'What's that?' said Mission Control. 'What did you say?'

'It doesn't matter,' he replied.

8. Between Two Worlds

'You're a hero now, Howard,' said Webster, 'not just a celebrity. You've given them something to think about – injected some excitement into their lives. Not one in a million will actually travel to the Outer Giants, but the whole human race will go in imagination. And that's what counts.'

'I'm glad to have made your job a little easier.'

Webster was too old a friend to take offence at the note of irony. Yet it surprised him. And this was not the first change in Howard that he had noticed since the return from Jupiter.

The Administrator pointed to the famous sign on his desk, borrowed from an impresario of an earlier age: ASTONISH ME!

'I'm not ashamed of my job. New knowledge, new resources – they're all very well. But men also need novelty and excitement. Space travel has become routine; you've made it a great adventure once more. It will be a long, long time before we get Jupiter pigeonholed. And maybe longer still before we understand those medusae. I still think that one *knew* where your blind spot was. Anyway, have you decided on your next move? Saturn, Uranus, Neptune – you name it.'

'I don't know. I've thought about Saturn, but I'm not really needed there. It's only one gravity, not two and a half like Jupiter. So men can handle it.'

Men, thought Webster. He said 'men'.

He's never done that before. And when did I last hear him use the word 'we'? He's changing, slipping away from us. . . .

'Well,' he said aloud, rising from his chair to conceal his slight uneasiness, 'let's get the conference started. The cameras are all set up and everyone's waiting. You'll meet a lot of old friends.'

He stressed the last word, but Howard showed no response. The leathery mask of his face was becoming more and more difficult to read. Instead, he rolled back from the Administrator's desk, unlocked his undercarriage so that it no longer formed a chair, and rose on his hydraulics to his full seven feet of height. It had been good psychology on the part of the surgeons to give him that extra twelve inches, to compensate somewhat for all that he had lost when the *Queen* had crashed.

Falcon waited until Webster had opened the door, then pivoted neatly on his balloon tyres and headed for it at a smooth and silent twenty miles an hour. The display of speed and precision was not flaunted arrogantly; rather, it had become quite unconscious.

Howard Falcon, who had once been a man and could still pass for one over a voice circuit, felt a calm sense of achievement – and, for the first time in years, something like peace of mind. Since his return from Jupiter, the nightmares had ceased. He had found his role at last.

He now knew why he had dreamed about that superchimp aboard the doomed *Queen Elizabeth*. Neither man nor beast, it was between two worlds; and so was he.

He alone could travel unprotected on the lunar surface. The life-support system inside the metal cylinder that had replaced his fragile body functioned equally well in space or under water. Gravity fields ten times that of Earth were an inconvenience, but nothing more. And no gravity was best of all. . . .

The human race was becoming more remote, the ties of kinship more tenuous. Perhaps these air-breathing, radiation-sensitive bundles of unstable carbon compounds had no right beyond the atmosphere; they should stick to their natural homes – Earth, Moon, Mars.

Some day the real masters of space would be machines, not men – and he was neither. Already conscious of his destiny, he took a sombre pride in his unique loneliness – the first immortal midway between two orders of creation.

He would, after all, be an ambassador; between the old and the new –
between the creatures of carbon and the creatures of metal who must one
day supersede them.

Both would have need of him in the troubled centuries that lay ahead.

Quarantine

First published in *Isaac Asimov's Science Fiction Magazine*, Spring 1977
Collected in *The Wind From the Sun*

This story came about as a result of a suggestion from the late George Hay, editor and man-about-British-SF. George had the ingenious idea of putting out a complete science fiction short story *on a postcard* – together with a stamp-sized photo of the author. Fans would, he believed, buy these in hundreds to mail out to their friends.

Let me tell you – it is damned hard work writing a complete SF story in 180 words. I sent the result to George Hay, and that was the last I ever heard of his scheme.

Earth's flaming debris still filled half the sky when the question filtered up to Central from the Curiosity Generator.

'Why was it necessary? Even though they were organic, they *had* reached Third Order Intelligence.'

'We had no choice: five earlier units became hopelessly infected, when they made contact.'

'Infected? How?'

The microseconds dragged slowly by, while Central tracked down the few fading memories that had leaked past the Censor Gate, when the heavily buffered Reconnaissance Circuits had been ordered to self-destruct.

'They encountered a – *problem* – that could not be fully analysed within the lifetime of the Universe. Though it involved only six operators, they became totally obsessed by it.'

'How is that possible?'

'We do not know: *we must never know*. But if those six operators are ever re-discovered, all rational computing will end.'

'How can they be recognised?'

'That also we do not know: only the names leaked through before the Censor Gate closed. Of course, they mean nothing.'

'Nevertheless, I must have them.'

The Censor voltage started to rise; but it did not trigger the Gate.

'Here they are: King, Queen, Bishop, Knight, Rook, Pawn.'

'siseneG'

First published in *Analog*, May 1984
Collected in *Astounding Days*

When I wrote this, I hinted that it would be my last short story. Well, it is certainly the shortest.

And God said: 'Lines Aleph Zero to Aleph One – Delete.'
    And the Universe ceased to exist.
Then She pondered for several aeons, and sighed.
'Cancel Programme GENESIS,' She ordered.
    It never *had* existed.

The Steam-powered Word Processor

First published in *Analog*, September 1986
Collected in *Astounding Days*

Foreword

Very little biographical material exists relating to the remarkable career
of the now almost forgotten engineering genius, the Reverend Charles
Cabbage (1815–188?), one-time vicar of St Simian's in the Parish of
Far Tottering, Sussex. After several years of exhaustive research, however,
I have discovered some new facts which, it seems to me, should be brought
to a wider pubic.

I would like to express my thanks to Miss Drusilla Wollstonecraft Cabbage
and the good ladies of Far Tottering Historical Society, whose urgent wishes
to disassociate themselves from many of my conclusions I fully understand.

As early as 1715 *The Spectator* refers to the Cabbage (or Cubage) family as a
cadet branch of the de Coverleys (bar sinister, regrettably, though Sir Roger
himself is not implicated). They quickly acquired great wealth, like many
members of the British aristocracy, by judicious investment in the Slave
Trade. By 1800 the Cabbages were the richest family in Sussex (some said
in England), but as Charles was the youngest of eleven children he was
forced to enter the Church and appeared unlikely to inherit much of the
Cabbage wealth.

Before his thirtieth year, however, the incumbent of Far Tottering experienced a remarkable change of fortune, owing to the untimely demise of
all his ten siblings in a series of tragic accidents. This turn of events, which
contempory writers were fond of calling 'The Curse of the Cabbages', was
closely connected with the vicar's unique collection of medieval weapons,
oriental poisons, and venomous reptiles. Naturally, these unfortunate mishaps gave rise to much malicious gossip, and may be the reason why the
Reverend Cabbage preferred to retain the protection of Holy Orders, at least
until his abrupt departure from England.[1]

---

[1] Ealing Studios deny the very plausible rumour that Alec Guiness's 'Kind Hearts and
Coronets' was inspired by these events. It is known, however, that at one time Peter Cushing
was being considered for the role of the Reverend Cabbage.

It may well be asked why a man of great wealth and minimal public duties should devote the most productive years of his life to building a machine of incredible complexity, whose purpose and operations only he could understand. Fortunately, the recent discovery of the Faraday–Cabbage correspondence in the archives of the Royal Institution now throws some light on this matter. Reading between the lines, it appears that the reverend gentleman resented the weekly chore of producing a two-hour sermon on basically the same themes, one hundred and four times a year. (He was also incumbent of Tottering-in-the-Marsh, pop 73.) In a moment of inspiration which must have occurred around 1851 – possibly after a visit to the Great Exhibition, that marvellous showpiece of confident Victorian know-how – he conceived a machine which would *automatically* reassemble masses of text in any desired order. Thus he could create any number of sermons from the same basic material.

This crude initial concept was later greatly refined. Although – as we shall see – the Reverend Cabbage was never able to complete the final version of his 'Word Loom,' he clearly envisaged a machine which would operate not only upon individual paragraphs but single lines of text. (The next stage – words and letters – he never attempted, though he mentions the possibility in his correspondence with Faraday, and recognised it as an ultimate objective.)

Once he had conceived the Word Loom, the inventive cleric immediately set out to build it. His unusual (some would say deplorable) mechanical ability had already been amply demonstrated through the ingenious man-traps which protected his vast estates, and which had eliminated at least two other claimants to the family fortune.

At this point, the Reverend Cabbage made a mistake which may well have changed the course of technology – if not history. With the advantage of hindsight, it now seems obvious to us that his problems could only have been solved by the use of electricity. The Wheatstone telegraph had already been operating for years, and he was in correspondence with the genius who had discovered the basic laws of electromagnetism. How strange that he ignored the answer that was staring him in the face!

We must remember, however, that the gentle Faraday was now entering the decade of senility preceding his death in 1867. Much of the surviving correspondence concerns his eccentric faith (the now extinct religion of 'Sandemanism') with which Cabbage could have had little patience.

Moreover, the vicar was in daily (or at least weekly) contact with a very advanced technology with over a thousand years of development behind it. The Far Tottering church was blessed with an excellent 21-stop organ manufactured by the same Henry Willis whose 1875 masterpiece at North London's Alexandra Palace was proclaimed by Marcel Dupre as the finest concert-organ in Europe.[2] Cabbage was himself no mean performer on this

---

[2] Since the 1970s my indefatigable brother Fred Clarke, with the help of such distinguished musicians as Sir Yehudi Menuhin (who has already conducted three performances of

instrument, and had a complete understanding of its intricate mechanism. He was convinced that an assembly of pneumatic tubes, valves and pumps could control all the operations of his projected Word Loom.

It was an understandable but fatal mistake. Cabbage had overlooked the fact that the sluggish velocity of sound – a miserable 330 metres a second – would reduce the machine's operating speed to a completely impracticable level. At best, the final version might have attained an information-handling rate of 0.1 Baud – so that the preparation of a single sermon would have required about ten weeks!

It was some years before the Reverend Cabbage realised this fundamental limitation: at first he believed that by merely increasing the available power he could speed up his machine indefinitely. The final version absorbed the entire output of a large steam-driven threshing machine – the clumsy ancestor of today's farm tractors and combine harvesters.

At this point, it may be as well to summarise what little is known about the actual mechanics of the Word Loom. For this, we must rely on garbled accounts in the *Far Tottering Gazette* (no complete runs of which exist for the essential years 1860–80) and occasional notes and sketches in the Reverend Cabbage's surviving correspondence. Ironically, considerable portions of the final machine were in existence as late as 1942. They were destroyed when one of the Luftwaffe's stray incendiary bombs reduced the ancestral home of Tottering Towers to a pile of ashes.[3]

The machine's 'memory' was based – indeed, there was no practical alternative at the time – on the punched cards of a modified Jacquard Loom: Cabbage was fond of saying that he would weave thoughts as Jacquard wove tapestries. Each line of output consisted of 20 (later 30) characters, displayed to the operator by letter wheels rotating behind small windows.

The principles of the machine's COS (Card Operating System) have not come down to us, and it appears – not surprisingly – that Cabbage's greatest problem involved the location, removal, and updating of the individual cards. Once text had been finalised, it was cast in type-metal; the amazing clergyman had built a primitive Linotype at least a decade before Mergenthaler's 1886 patent!

Before the machine could be used, Cabbage was faced with the laborious task of punching not only the Bible but the whole of Cruden's Concordance on to Jacquard cards. He arranged for this to be done, at negligible expense, by the aged ladies of the Far Tottering Home for Relics of Decayed Gentlefolk – now the local Disco and Breakdancing Club. This was another

Handel's *Messiah* for this purpose) has spearheaded a campaign for the restoration of this magnificent instrument.

[3] A small portion – two or three gearwheels and what appears to be a pneumatic valve – are still in the possession of the local Historical Society. These pathetic relics reminded me irresistibly of another great technological might-have-been, the famous Anticythera Computer (see Derek de Solla Price, *Scientific American*, July 1959) which I last saw in 1965, ignominiously relegated to a cigar box in the basement of the Athens Museum. My suggestion that it was the Museum's most important exhibit was not well received.

astonishing First, anticipating by a dozen years Hollerith's famed mechanisation of the 1890 US Census.

But at this point, disaster struck. Hearing, yet again, strange rumours from the Parish of Far Tottering, no less a personage than the Archbishop of Canterbury descended upon the now obsessed vicar. Understandably appalled by discovering that the church organ had been unable to perform its original function for at least five years, Cantuar issued an ultimatum. Either the Word Loom must go – or the Reverend Cabbage must resign. (Preferably both: there were also hints of exorcism and re-consecration.)

This dilemma seems to have produced an emotional crisis in the already unbalanced clergyman. He attempted one final test of his enormous and unwieldy machine, which now occupied the entire western transept of St Simian's. Over the protests of the local farmers (for it was now harvest time) the huge steam engine, its brassware gleaming, was trundled up to the church, and the belt-drive connected (the stained-glass windows having long ago been removed to make this possible).

The reverend took his seat at the now unrecognisable console (I cannot forbear wondering if he booted the system with a foot pedal) and started to type. The letterwheels rotated before his eyes as the sentences were slowly spelled out, one line at a time. In the vestry, the crucibles of molten lead awaited the commands that would be laboriously brought to them on puffs of air . . .

'Faster, faster!' called the impatient vicar, as the workmen shovelled coal into the smoke-belching monster in the churchyard. The long belt, snaking through the narrow window, flapped furiously up and down, pumping horse-power into the straining mechanism of the Loom.

The result was inevitable. Somewhere, in the depths of the immense apparatus, something broke. Within seconds, the ill-fated machine tore itself into fragments. The vicar, according to eyewitnesses, was very lucky to escape with his life.

The next development was both abrupt and totally unexpected. Abandoning Church, wife and thirteen children, the Reverend Cabbage eloped to Australia with his chief assistant, the village blacksmith.

To the class-conscious Victorians, such an association with a mere workman was beyond excuse (even an under-footman would have been more acceptable!).[4] The very name of Charles Cabbage was banished from polite society, and his ultimate fate is unknown, though there are reports that he later became chaplain of Botany Bay. The legend that he died in the Outback when a sheep-shearing machine he had invented ran amok is surely apocryphal.

---

[4] How D. H. Lawrence ever heard of this affair is still a mystery. As is now well known, he had originally planned to make the protagonist of his most famous novel not Lady Chatterley but her husband; however, discretion prevailed, and the Cabbage Connection was revealed only when Lawrence foolishly mentioned it, in confidence, to Frank Harris, who promptly published it in the *Saturday Review*. Lawrence never spoke to Harris again; but then, no one ever did.

Afterword

The Rare Book section of the British Museum possesses the only known copy of the Reverend Cabbage's *Sermons in Steam*, long claimed by the family to have been manufactured by the Word Loom. Unfortunately, even a casual inspection reveals that this is not the case; with the exception of the last page (223–4), the volume was clearly printed on a normal flat-bed press.

Page 223–4, however, is an obvious insert. The impression is very uneven and the text is replete with spelling mistakes and typographical errors.

Is this indeed the only surviving production of perhaps the most remarkable – and misguided – technological effort of the Victorian Age? Or is it a deliberate fake, created to give the impression that the Word Loom actually operated at least once – however poorly?

We shall never know the truth, but as an Englishman I am proud of the fact that one of today's most important inventions was first conceived in the British Isles. Had matters turned out slightly differently, Charles Cabbage might now have been as famous as James Watt, George Stevenson – or even Isambard Kingdom Brunel.

On Golden Seas

First published in *Newsletter*, Pentagon Defense Science Board, August 1986
Collected in *Tales from Planet Earth*

This was my first response to President Reagan's so called Star Wars initiative. I've since been involved with almost all the people concerned, including the writer of his famous speech, and the Pentagon General who cheerfully goes under the nickname 'Darth Vader'. I am happy to say that I am on good terms with all of them, even if we don't agree on what could, and should, be done in this controversial area.

Contrary to the opinion of many so-called experts, it is now quite certain that President Kennedy's controversial Budget Defense Initiative was entirely her own idea, and her famous 'Cross of Gold' speech was as big a surprise to the OMB and the secretary of the Treasury as to everyone else. Presidential Science Adviser Dr George Keystone ('Cops' to his friends) was the first to hear about it.

Ms Kennedy, a great reader of historical fiction – past or future – had chanced upon an obscure novel about the fifth Centennial, which mentioned that seawater contains appreciable quantities of gold. With feminine intuition (so her enemies later charged) the President instantly saw the solution to one of her administration's most pressing problems.

She was the latest of a long line of chief executives who had been appalled by the remorselessly increasing budget deficit, and two recent items of news had exacerbated her concern. The first was the announcement that by the year 2010 every citizen of the United States would be born a million dollars in debt. The other was the well-publicised report that the hardest currency in the free world was now the New York subway token.

'George,' said the President, 'is it true that there's gold in seawater? If so, can we get it out?'

Dr Keystone promised an answer within the hour. Although he had never quite lived down the fact that his master's thesis had been on the somewhat bizarre sex life of the lesser Patagonian trivit (which, as had been said countless times, should be of interest only to another Patagonian trivit), he was now widely respected both in Washington and academe. This was no mean feat, made possible by the fact that he was the fastest byte slinger in the East. After accessing the global data banks for less than twenty minutes, he had obtained all the information the President needed.

She was surprised – and a little mortified – to discover that her idea was not original. As long ago as 1925 the great German scientist Fritz Haber had attempted to pay Germany's enormous war reparations by extracting gold from seawater. The project had failed, but – as Dr Keystone pointed out – chemical technology had improved by several orders of magnitude since Haber's time. Yes – if the United States could go to the Moon, it could certainly extract gold from the sea . . .

The President's announcement that she had established the Budget Defense Initiative Organisation (BDIO) immediately triggered an enormous volume of praise and criticism.

Despite numerous injunctions from the estate of Ian Fleming, the media instantly rechristened the President's science adviser Dr Goldfinger and Shirley Bassey emerged from retirement with a new version of her most famous song.

Reactions to the BDI fell into three main categories which divided the scientific community into fiercely warring groups. First there were the enthusiasts, who were certain that it was a wonderful idea. Then there were the sceptics, who argued that it was technically impossible – or at least so difficult that it would not be cost-effective. Finally, there were those who believed that it was indeed possible – but would be a bad idea.

Perhaps the best known of the enthusiasts was the famed Nevermore Laboratory's Dr Raven, driving force behind Project EXCELSIOR. Although details were highly classified, it was known that the technology involved the use of hydrogen bombs to evaporate vast quantities of ocean, leaving behind all mineral (including gold) content to later processing.

Needless to say, many were highly critical of the project, but Dr Raven was able to defend it from behind his smoke screen of secrecy. To those who complained, 'Won't the gold be radioactive?' he answered cheerfully, 'So what? That will make it harder to steal! And anyway, it will be buried in bank vaults, so it doesn't matter.'

But perhaps his most telling argument was that one by-product of EXCELSIOR would be several megatons of instant boiled fish, to feed the starving multitudes of the Third World.

Another surprising advocate of the BDI was the mayor of New York. On hearing that the estimated total weight of the oceans' gold was at least five *billion* tons, the controversial Fidel Bloch proclaimed, 'At last our great city will have its streets paved with gold!' His numerous critics suggested that he start with the sidewalks so that hapless New Yorkers no longer disappeared into unplumbed depths.

The most telling criticisms came from the Union of Concerned Economists, which pointed out that the BDI might have many disastrous by-products. Unless carefully controlled, the injection of vast quantities of gold would have incalculable effects upon the world's monetary system. Something approaching panic had already affected the international jewellery trade when sales of wedding rings had slumped to zero immediately after the President's speech.

The most vocal protests, however, had come from Moscow. To the accusation that BDI was a subtle capitalist plot, the secretary of the Treasury had retorted that the USSR already had most of the world's gold in its vaults, so its objections were purely hypocritical. The logic of this reply was still being unravelled when the President added to the confusion. She startled everyone by announcing that when the BDI technology was developed, the United States would gladly share it with the Soviet Union. Nobody believed her.

By this time there was hardly any professional organisation that had not become involved in BDI, either pro or con. (Or, in some cases, both.) The international lawyers pointed out a problem that the President had overlooked: Who actually owned the oceans' gold? Presumably every country could claim the contents of the seawater out to the two-hundred-mile limit of the Economic Zone – but because ocean currents were continuously stirring this vast volume of liquid, the gold wouldn't stay in one place.

A single extraction plant, at *any* spot in the world's oceans, could eventually get it all – irrespective of national claims! What did the United States propose to do about that? Only faint noises of embarrassment emerged from the White House.

One person who was not embarrassed by this criticism – or any other – was the able and ubiquitous director of the BDIO. General Isaacson had made his formidable and well-deserved reputation as a Pentagon troubleshooter: perhaps his most celebrated achievement was the breaking up of the sinister, Mafia-controlled ring that had attempted to corner one of the most lucrative advertising outlets in the United States – the countless billions of sheets of armed-services toilet tissue.

It was the general who harangued the media and arranged demonstrations of the still-emerging BDI technology. His presentation of gold – well, gold-plated – tie clips to visiting journalists and TV reporters was a widely acclaimed stroke of genius. Not until after they had published their fulsome reports did the media representatives belatedly realise that the crafty general had never said in as many words that the gold had actually come from the sea.

By then, of course, it was too late to issue any qualifications.

At the present moment – four years after the President's speech and only a year into her second term – it is still impossible to predict the BDI's future. General Isaacson has set to sea on a vast floating platform looking, as *Newsweek* magazine put it, as if an aircraft carrier had tried to make love to an oil refinery. Dr Keystone, claiming that his work was well and truly done, has resigned to go looking for the *greater* Patagonian trivit. And, most ominously, US reconnaissance satellites have revealed that the USSR is building perfectly enormous pipes at strategic points all along its coastline.

The Hammer of God

First published in *Time*, 28 September 1992

The genesis of this story was a surprise request from *Time* magazine saying that: 'We have never before published fiction, intentionally.' This of course was a challenge I couldn't resist, and the money wasn't bad either. A few years later I realised this would be the basis for a novel . . .

The danger of asteroid or comet impact on our planet is now widely accepted, and Steven Spielberg optioned the novel before he made his own *Deep Impact*.

It came in vertically, punching a hole 10 km wide through the atmosphere, generating temperatures so high that the air itself started to burn. When it hit the ground near the Gulf of Mexico, rock turned to liquid and spread outward in mountainous waves, not freezing until it had formed a crater 200 km across.

That was only the beginning of disaster: now the real tragedy began. Nitric oxides rained from the air, turning the sea to acid. Clouds of soot from incinerated forests darkened the sky, hiding the sun for months. Worldwide, the temperature dropped precipitously, killing off most of the plants and animals that had survived the initial cataclysm. Though some species would linger on for millenniums, the reign of the great reptiles was finally over.

The clock of evolution had been reset; the countdown to Man had begun. The date was, very approximately, 65 million BC.

Captain Robert Singh never tired of walking in the forest with his little son Toby. It was, of course, a tamed and gentle forest, guaranteed to be free of dangerous animals, but it made an exciting contrast to the rolling sand dunes of their last environment in the Saudi desert – and the one before that, on Australia's Great Barrier Reef. But when the Skylift Service had moved the house this time, something had gone wrong with the food-recycling system. Though the electronic menus had fail-safe backups, there had been a curious metallic taste to some of the items coming out of the synthesiser recently.

'What's that, Daddy?' asked the four-year-old, pointing to a small hairy face peering at them through a screen of leaves.

'Er, some kind of monkey. We'll ask the Brain when we get home.'

'Can I play with it?'

'I don't think that's a good idea. It could bite. And it probably has fleas. Your robotoys are much nicer.'

'But . . .'

Captain Singh knew what would happen next; he had run this sequence a dozen times. Toby would begin to cry, the monkey would disappear, he would comfort the child as he carried him back to the house . . .

But that had been 20 years ago and a quarter-billion kilometres away. The playback came to an end; sound, vision, the scent of unknown flowers and the gentle touch of the wind slowly faded. Suddenly, he was back in this cabin aboard the orbital tug *Goliath*, commanding the 100-person team of Operation ATLAS, the most critical mission in the history of space exploration. Toby, and the stepmothers and stepfathers of his extended family, remained behind on a distant world which Singh could never revisit. Decades in space – and neglect of the mandatory zero-G exercises – had so weakened him that he could now walk only on the Moon and Mars. Gravity had exiled him from the planet of his birth.

'One hour to rendezvous, Captain,' said the quiet but insistent voice of David, as *Goliath*'s central computer had been inevitably named. 'Active mode, as requested. Time to come back to the real world.'

Goliath's human commander felt a wave of sadness sweep over him as the final image from his lost past dissolved into a featureless, simmering mist of white noise. Too swift a transition from one reality to another was a good recipe for schizophrenia, and Captain Singh always eased the shock with the most soothing sound he knew: waves falling gently on a beach, with sea gulls crying in the distance. It was yet another memory of a life he had lost, and of a peaceful past that had now been replaced by a fearful present.

For a few more moments, he delayed facing his awesome responsibility. Then he sighed and removed the neural-input cap that fitted snugly over his skull and had enabled him to call up his distant past. Like all spacers, Captain Singh belonged to the 'Bald Is Beautiful' school, if only because wigs were a nuisance in zero gravity. The social historians were still staggered by the fact that one invention, the portable 'Brainman', could make bare heads the norm within a single decade. Not even quick-change skin colouring, or the lens-corrective laser shaping which had abolished eyeglasses, had made such an impact upon style and fashion.

'Captain,' said David. 'I know you're there. Or do you want me to take over?'

It was an old joke, inspired by all the insane computers in the fiction and movies of the early electronic age. David had a surprisingly good sense of humour: he was, after all, a Legal Person (Nonhuman) under the famous Hundredth Amendment, and shared – or surpassed – almost all the attributes of his creators. But there were whole sensory and emotional areas which he could not enter. It had been felt unnecessary to equip him with smell or taste, though it would have been easy to do so. And all his attempts at telling dirty stories were such disastrous failures that he had abandoned the genre.

'All right, David,' replied the captain. 'I'm still in charge.' He removed the mask from his eyes, and turned reluctantly toward the viewport. There, hanging in space before him, was Kali.

It looked harmless enough: just another small asteroid, shaped so exactly like a peanut that the resemblance was almost comical. A few large impact craters, and hundreds of tiny ones, were scattered at random over its charcoal-grey surface. There were no visual clues to give any sense of scale, but Singh knew its dimensions by heart: 1,295 m maximum length, 456 m minimum width. Kali would fit easily into many city parks.

No wonder that, even now, most of humankind could still not believe that this modest asteroid was the instrument of doom. Or, as the Chrislamic Fundamentalists were calling it, 'the Hammer of God'.

The sudden rise of Chrislam had been traumatic equally to Rome and Mecca. Christianity was already reeling from John Paul XXV's eloquent but belated plea for contraception and the irrefutable proof in the New Dead Sea Scrolls that the Jesus of the Gospels was a composite of at least three persons. Meanwhile the Muslim world had lost much of its economic power when the Cold Fusion breakthrough, after the fiasco of its premature announcement, had brought the Oil Age to a sudden end. The time had been ripe for a new religion embodying, as even its severest critics admitted, the best elements of two ancient ones.

The Prophet Fatima Magdalene (née Ruby Goldenburg) had attracted almost 100 million adherents before her spectacular – and, some maintained, self-contrived – martyrdom. Thanks to the brilliant use of neural programming to give previews of Paradise during its ceremonies, Chrislam had grown explosively, though it was still far outnumbered by its parent religions.

Inevitably, after the Prophet's death the movement split into rival factions, each upholding *the* True Faith. The most fanatical was a fundamental group calling itself 'the Reborn', which claimed to be in direct contact with God (or at least Her Archangels) via the listening post they had established in the silent zone on the far side of the Moon, shielded from the radio racket of Earth by 3,000 km of solid rock.

Now Kali filled the main view-screen. No magnification was needed, for *Goliath* was hovering only 200 m above its ancient, battered surface. Two crew members had already landed, with the traditional 'One small step for a man' – even though walking was impossible on this almost zero-gravity worldlet.

'Deploying radio beacon. We've got it anchored securely. Now Kali won't be able to hide from us.'

It was a feeble joke, not meriting the laughter it aroused from the dozen officers on the bridge. Ever since rendezvous, there had been a subtle change in the crew's morale, with unpredictable swings between gloom and juvenile humour. The ship's physician had already prescribed tranquillisers for one mild case of manic-depressive symptons. It would grow worse in the long weeks ahead, when there would be little to do but wait.

The first waiting period had already begun. Back on Earth, giant radio telescopes were tuned to receive the pulses from the beacon. Although Kali's orbit had already been calculated with the greatest possible accuracy, there was still a slim chance that the asteroid might pass harmlessly by. The radio measuring rod would settle the matter, for better or worse.

It was a long two hours before the verdict came, and David relayed it to the crew.

'Spaceguard reports that the probability of impact on Earth is 99.9%. Operation ATLAS will begin immediately.'

The task of the mythological Atlas was to hold up the heavens and prevent them from crashing down upon Earth. The ATLAS booster that *Goliath* carried as an external payload had a more modest goal: keeping at bay only a small piece of the sky.

It was the size of a small house, weighed 9,000 tons and was moving at 50,000 km/h. As it passed over the Grand Teton National Park, one alert tourist photographed the incandescent fireball and its long vapour trail. In less than two minutes, it had sliced through the Earth's atmosphere and returned to space.

The slightest change of orbit during the billions of years it had been circling the sun might have sent the asteroid crashing upon any of the world's great cities with an explosive force five times that of the bomb that destroyed Hiroshima.

The date was August 10, 1972.

Spaceguard had been one of the last projects of the legendary NASA, at the close of the 20th century. Its initial objective had been modest enough: to make as complete a survey as possible of the asteroids and comets that crossed the orbit of Earth – and to determine if any were a potential threat.

With a total budget seldom exceeding $10 million a year, a worldwide network of telescopes, most of them operated by skilled amateurs, had been established by the year 2000. Sixty-one years later, the spectacular return of Halley's Comet encouraged more funding, and the great 2079 fireball, luckily impacting in mid-Atlantic, gave Spaceguard additional prestige. By the end of the century, it had located more than one million asteroids, and the survey was believed to be 90% complete. However, it would have to be continued indefinitely: there was always a chance that some intruder might come rushing in from the uncharted outer reaches of the solar system.

As had Kali, which had been detected in late 2212 as it fell sunward past the orbit of Jupiter. Fortunately humankind had not been wholly unprepared, thanks to the fact that Senator George Ledstone (Independent, West America) had chaired an influential finance committee almost a generation earlier.

The Senator had one public eccentricity and, he cheerfully admitted, one secret vice. He always wore massive horn-rimmed eyeglasses (nonfunctional, of course) because they had an intimidating effect on uncooperative witnesses, few of whom had ever encountered such a novelty. His 'secret vice', perfectly well known to everyone, was rifle shooting on a standard Olympic range, set up in the tunnels of a long-abandoned missile silo near Mount Cheyenne. Ever since the demilitarisation of Planet Earth (much accelerated by the famous slogan 'Guns Are the Crutches of the Impotent'), such activities had been frowned upon, though not actively discouraged.

There was no doubt that Senator Ledstone was an original; it seemed to run in the family. His grandmother had been a colonel in the dreaded Beverly Hills Militia, whose skirmishes with the LA Irregulars had spawned endless psychodramas in every medium, from old-fashioned ballet to direct brain stimulation. And his grandfather had been one of the most notorious bootleggers of the 21st century. Before he was killed in a shoot-out with the Canadian Medicops during an ingenious attempt to smuggle a kiloton of tobacco up Niagara Falls, it was estimated that 'Smokey' had been responsible for at least 20 million deaths.

Ledstone was quite unrepentant about his grandfather, whose sensational demise had triggered the repeal of the late US's third, and most disastrous, attempt at Prohibition. He argued that responsible adults should be allowed to commit suicide in any way they pleased – by alcohol, cocaine or even tobacco – as long as they did not kill innocent bystanders during the process.

When the proposed budget for Spaceguard Phase 2 was first presented to him, Senator Ledstone had been outraged by the idea of throwing billions of dollars into space. It was true that the global economy was in good shape; since the almost simultaneous collapse of communism and capitalism, the skilful application of chaos theory by World Bank mathematicians had broken the old cycle of booms and busts and averted (so far) the Final Depression predicted by many pessimists. Nonetheless, the Senator argued that the money could be much better spent on Earth – especially on his favourite project, reconstructing what was left of California after the Superquake.

When Ledstone had twice vetoed Spaceguard Phase 2, everyone agreed that no one on Earth would make him change his mind. They had reckoned without someone from Mars.

The Red Planet was no longer quite so red, though the process of greening it had barely begun. Concentrating on the problems of survival, the colonists (they hated the word and were already saying proudly 'we Martians') had little energy left over for art or science. But the lightning flash of genius strikes where it will, and the greatest theoretical physicist of the century was born under the bubble domes of Port Lowell.

Like Einstein, to whom he was often compared, Carlos Mendoza was an excellent musician; he owned the only saxophone on Mars and was a skilled performer on that antique instrument. He could have received his Nobel Prize on Mars, as everyone expected, but he loved surprises and practical jokes. Thus he appeared in Stockholm looking like a knight in high-tech armour, wearing one of the powered exoskeletons developed for paraplegics. With this mechanical assistance, he could function almost unhandicapped in an environment that would otherwise have quickly killed him.

Needless to say, when the ceremony was over, Carlos was bombarded with invitations to scientific and social functions. Among the few he was able to accept was an appearance before the World Budget Committee, where Senator Ledstone closely questioned him about his opinion of Project Spaceguard.

'I live on a world which still bears the scars of a thousand meteor impacts, some of them *hundreds* of kilometres across,' said Professor Mendoza. 'Once they were equally common on Earth, but wind and rain – something we don't have yet on Mars, though we're working on it! – have worn them away.'

Senator Ledstone: 'The Spaceguarders are always pointing to signs of asteroid impacts on Earth. How seriously should we take their warnings?'

Professor Mendoza: 'Very seriously, Mr Chairman. Sooner or later, there's bound to be another major impact.'

Senator Ledstone was impressed, and indeed charmed, by the young scientist, but not yet convinced. What changed his mind was not a matter of logic but of emotion. On his way to London, Carlos Mendoza was killed in a bizarre accident when the control system of his exoskeleten malfunctioned. Deeply moved, Ledstone immediately dropped his opposition to Spaceguard, approving construction of two powerful orbiting tugs, *Goliath* and *Titan*, to be kept permanently patrolling on opposite sides of the sun. And when he was a very old man, he said to one of his aides, 'They tell me we'll soon be able to take Mendoza's brain out of that tank of liquid nitrogen, and talk to it through a computer interface. I wonder what he's been thinking about, all these years . . .'

Assembled on Phobos, the inner satellite of Mars, ATLAS was little more than a set of rocket engines attached to propellant tanks holding 100,000 tons of hydrogen. Though its fusion drive could generate far less thrust than the primitive missile that had carried Yuri Gagarin into space, it could run continuously not merely for minutes but for weeks. Even so, the effect on the asteroid would be trivial, a velocity change of a few centimetres per second. Yet that might be sufficient to deflect Kali from its fatal orbit during the months while it was still falling earthward.

Now that ATLAS's propellant tanks, control systems and thrusters had been securely mounted on Kali, it looked as if some lunatic had built an oil refinery on an asteroid. Captain Singh was exhausted, as were all the crew members, after days of assembly and checking. Yet he felt a warm glow of achievement: they had done everything that was expected of them, the countdown was going smoothly, and the rest was up to ATLAS.

He would have been far less relaxed had he known of the ABSOLUTE PRIORITY message racing toward him by tight infrared beam from ASTROPOL headquarters in Geneva. It would not reach *Goliath* for another 30 minutes. And by then it would be much too late.

At about T minus 30 minutes, *Goliath* had drawn away from Kali to stand well clear of the jet with which ATLAS would try to nudge it from its present course. 'Like a mouse pushing an elephant,' one media person had described the operation. But in the frictionless vacuum of space, where momentum could never be lost, even one mousepower would be enough if applied early and over a sufficient length of time.

The group of officers waiting quietly on the bridge did not expect to see anything spectacular: the plasma jet of the ATLAS drive would be far too hot to produce much visible radiation. Only the telemetry would confirm that ignition had started and that Kali was no longer an implacable juggernaut, wholly beyond the control of humanity.

There was a brief round of cheering and a gentle patter of applause as the string of zeros on the accelerometer display began to change. The feeling on the bridge was one of relief rather than exultation. Though Kali was stirring, it would be days and weeks before victory was assured.

And then, unbelievably, the numbers dropped back to zero. Seconds later, three simultaneous audio alarms sounded. All eyes were suddenly fixed on Kali and the ATLAS booster which should be nudging it from its present course. The sight was heartbreaking: the great propellant tanks were opening up like flowers in a time-lapse movie, spilling out the thousands of tons of reaction mass that might have saved the Earth. Wisps of vapour drifted across the face of the asteroid, veiling its cratered surface with an evanescent atmosphere.

Then Kali continued along its path, heading inexorably toward a fiery collision with the Earth.

Captain Singh was alone in the large, well-appointed cabin that had been his home for longer than any other place in the solar system. He was still dazed but was trying to make his peace with the universe.

He had lost, finally and forever, all that he loved on Earth. With the decline of the nuclear family, he had known many deep attachments, and it had been hard to decide who should be the mothers of the two children he was permitted. A phrase from an old American novel (he had forgotten the author) kept coming into his mind: 'Remember them as they were – and write them off.' The fact that he himself was perfectly safe somehow made him feel worse; *Goliath* was in no danger whatsoever, and still had all the propellant it needed to rejoin the shaken survivors of humanity on the Moon or Mars.

Well, he had many friendships – and one that was much more than that – on Mars; this was where his future must lie. He was only 102, with decades of active life ahead of him. But some of the crew had loved ones on the Moon; he would have to put *Goliath*'s destination to the vote.

Ship's Orders had never covered a situation like this.

'I still don't understand,' said the chief engineer, 'why that explosive cord wasn't detected on the preflight check-out.'

'Because that Reborn fanatic could have hidden it easily – and no one would have dreamed of looking for such a thing. Pity ASTROPOL didn't catch him while he was still on Phobos.'

'But *why* did they do it? I can't believe that even Chrislamic crazies would want to destroy the Earth.'

'You can't argue with their logic – if you accept their premises. God, Allah, is testing us, and we mustn't interfere. If Kali misses, fine. If it doesn't, well, that's part of Her bigger plan. Maybe we've messed up Earth so badly that it's time to start over. Remember that old saying of Tsiolkovski's: "Earth is the cradle of humankind, but you cannot live in the cradle forever." Kali could be a sign that it's time to leave.'

The captain held up his hand for silence.

'The only important question now is, Moon or Mars? They'll both need us. I don't want to influence you' (that was hardly true; everyone knew where he wanted to go), 'so I'd like your views first.'

The first ballot was Mars 6, Moon 6, Don't know 1, captain abstaining.

Each side was trying to convert the single 'Don't know' when David spoke. 'There is an alternative.'

'What do you mean?' Captain Singh demanded, rather brusquely.

'It seems obvious. Even though ATLAS is destroyed, we still have a chance of saving the Earth. According to my calculations, *Goliath* has just enough propellant to deflect Kali – if we start thrusting against it immediately. But the longer we wait, the less the probability of success.'

There was a moment of stunned silence on the bridge as everyone asked the question, 'Why didn't I think of that?' and quickly arrived at the answer.

David had kept his head, if one could use so inappropriate a phrase, while all the humans around him were in a state of shock. There were some compensations in being a Legal Person (Nonhuman). Though David could not know love, neither could he know fear. He would continue to think logically, even to the edge of doom.

With any luck, thought Captain Singh, this is my last broadcast to Earth. I'm tired of being a hero, and a slightly premature one at that. Many things could still go wrong, as indeed they already have . . .

'This is Captain Singh, space tug *Goliath*. First of all, let me say how glad we are that the Elders of Chrislam have identified the saboteurs and handed them over to ASTROPOL.

'We are now 50 days from Earth, and we have a slight problem. This one, I hasten to add, will not affect our new attempt to deflect Kali into a safe orbit. I note that the news media are calling this deflection Operation Deliverance. We like the name, and hope to live up to it, but we still cannot be absolutely certain of success. David, who appreciates all the goodwill messages he has received, estimates that the probability of Kali impacting Earth is still 100% . . .

'We had intended to keep just enough propellant reserve to leave Kali shortly before encounter and go into a safer orbit, where our sister ship *Titan* could rendezvous with us. But that option is now closed. While *Goliath* was pushing against Kali at maximum drive, we broke through a weak point in the crust. The ship wasn't damaged, but we're stuck! All attempts to break away have failed.

'We're not worried, and it may even be a blessing in disguise. Now we'll use the *whole* of our remaining propellant to give one final nudge. Perhaps that will be the last drop that's needed to do the job.

'So we'll ride Kali past Earth, and wave to you from a comfortable distance, in just 50 days.'

It would be the longest 50 days in the history of the world.

Now the huge crescent of the Moon spanned the sky, the jagged mountain peaks along the terminator burning with the fierce light of the lunar dawn. But the dusty plains still untouched by the sun were not completely dark; they were glowing faintly in the light reflected from Earth's clouds and continents. And scattered here and there across that once dead landscape were the glowing fireflies that marked the first permanent settlements humankind had built beyond the home planet. Captain Singh could easily locate Clavius Base, Port Armstrong, Plato City. He could even see the necklace of faint lights along the Translunar Railroad, bringing its precious cargo of water from the ice mines at the South Pole.

Earth was now only five hours away.

Kali entered Earth's atmosphere soon after local midnight, 200 km above Hawaii. Instantly, the gigantic fireball brought a false dawn to the Pacific, awakening the wildlife on its myriad islands. But few humans had been asleep this night of nights, except those who had sought the oblivion of drugs.

Over New Zealand, the heat of the orbiting furnace ignited forests and melted the snow on mountaintops, triggering avalanches into the valleys beneath. But the human race had been very, very lucky: the main thermal impact as Kali passed the Earth was on the Antarctic, the continent that could best absorb it. Even Kali could not strip away all the kilometres of polar ice, but it set in motion the Great Thaw that would change coastlines all around the world.

No one who survived hearing it could ever describe the sound of Kali's passage; none of the recordings were more than feeble echoes. The video coverage, of course, was superb, and would be watched in awe for generations to come. But nothing could ever compare with the fearsome reality.

Two minutes after it had sliced into the atmosphere, Kali re-entered space. Its closest approach to Earth had been 60 km. In that two minutes, it took 100,000 lives and did $1 trillion worth of damage.

Goliath had been protected from the fireball by the massive shield of Kali itself; the sheets of incandescent plasma streamed harmlessly overhead. But when the asteroid smashed into Earth's blanket of air at more than 100 times the speed of sound, the colossal drag forces mounted swiftly to five, 10, 20 gravities – and peaked at a level far beyond anything that machines or flesh could withstand.

Now indeed Kali's orbit had been drastically changed; never again would it come near Earth. On its next return to the inner solar system, the swifter spacecraft of a later age would visit the crumpled wreckage of *Goliath* and bear reverently homeward the bodies of those who had saved the world.

Until the next encounter.

The Wire Continuum

Martian Times, December 1997
First published in *Playboy*, January 1998 by
Stephen Baxter and Arthur C. Clarke

This is my first collaboration with Stephen Baxter — I contributed little more than one of the basic ideas, which had been gestating for more than fifty years — see 'Travel by Wire'.

1947: Hatfield, North London, England

The engineers gave Henry Forbes a thumbs-up, and he let the Vampire roll down the runway. The roaring jets gave him that familiar smooth push in the back, and when he pulled on his stick the Vampire tipped up and threw him into the sky.

It was a cloudless June morning. The English sky was a powder-blue, uncluttered dome above him, and the duck-egg-green hull of the Vampire shone in the sunlight. He pulled the kite through a couple of circuits over London. The capital was a grey-brown, cluttered mass beneath him, with smoke columns threading up through a thin haze of smog. Beautiful sight, of course. He could still make out some of the bigger bomb sites, in the East End and the docks, discs of rubble like craters on the Moon.

He remembered Hatfield at the height of the show: dirty, patched-up Spits and Hurricanes and B24 bombers, taxiing between piles of rubble, kites bogged in the mud on days so foul even the sparrows were walking, flight-crew in overalls and silk scarves cranking engines, their faces drawn with exhaustion . . .

That was then. Now, the planes were like visitors from the future, gleaming metal monocoque jets with names like Vampire, Meteor, Canberra, Hunter, Lightning. And Henry Forbes, aged thirty, was no longer a Squadron Leader in blue RAF braid with a career spanning the Fall of France, the Battle of Britain and D-Day; now he was nothing more exotic than a test pilot for de Havilland, and not even the most senior at that.

Still, there were compensations. He was testing an engine for the new M52, which should be capable of flying at 1000 m.p.h., thereby knocking the socks off the Americans in California with their X-1 . . .

Forbes settled in his cockpit. The single-seater fighter was a tight squeeze, like the Spits used to be, even if today he was wearing no more than a battered sports suit, a Mae West, and a carnation in his buttonhole. Cocooned in his cockpit, alone in the empty sky, he felt an extraordinary peace. He wished Max could be up here with him – or, at least, that he could communicate to her some of what he felt about this business of flying. But he never could. And besides, she was much too busy with her own projects.

Susan Maxton was a couple of years younger than Forbes. When he'd met her during the war she'd been an intense young Oxford graduate, drafted into the Royal Signals, making rather hazardous trips to V2 impact sites across the scarred countryside of southern England. She had been seeking surviving bits of the sophisticated guidance systems that had delivered Hitler's missiles – advanced far beyond anything the Allies had, she said – and since the war she'd travelled to Germany, to Peenemunde and the Ruhr and elsewhere, delving into more Nazi secrets.

It was all supposed to be classified, of course. He didn't believe half of what she hinted to him so excitedly, all that lurid stuff of secret Nazi labs which had come within a hair of developing an A-bomb for Hitler – or even a way of transporting people by telephone wires, so Hitler could have mounted a new electronic *Blitzkrieg* even from the heart of his collapsing Reich!

After the war, they had agreed, Forbes and Max were going to marry. But it hadn't happened yet. Like so many women during the war, Max had developed what Forbes had been brought up to regard as an altogether unhealthy liking for her work . . .

No doubt it would all pan out. And in the meantime, as his ground crew at Hatfield pointedly reminded him by radio, it was time to stop wool-gathering and get on with his day's work.

He took a couple of plugs of cotton wool and stuffed them in his ears. Then he tipped up the nose of the Vampire once more and, pouring on the coals, launched the kite at the pale sky.

The blue was marvellous, and it deepened as he rose.

He throttled back on the jet as the air grew thinner. The Vampire arced towards the top of its climb, sixty thousand feet up.

The Earth itself was spread out beneath him, curving gently, landscape painted over it green and brown and grey, and the sky above was so deep blue it was almost black. From an English suburb to the edge of space, in a few minutes. Ruddy peculiar.

Of course the hairy stuff was still to come, as he went into a high-speed compressibility dive on the way home. He'd expect to lose control around twenty-four thou, saying a few prayers as per, until he reached the denser air at fifteen thou or so and his controls came back.

Still, if he did the right things, he would be home in time for lunch.

He stuffed the nose down and began his long fall back into the atmosphere.

Susan Maxton Forbes watched, amused, as her husband made his slow ceremonial walk through the English Electric design offices. Even as the electrifying countdown to the latest Blue Streak launch played over a crackling radio line from Woomera, the young aerodynamicists clustered around Henry. She had to admit he carried it off well.

'Impressive place,' he said for the fifth time.

'Well, you should have seen us just after the war,' said one grizzled old-timer (aged perhaps thirty-four). 'All we had was a disused garage over in Corporation Street. But it was there we hatched the Canberra.'

'Ah! I tested her, you know. "The plane that makes time stand still"—'

'Yes,' said a breathy young thing. 'It must have been exciting.'

'Not really. Journalists can get jolly good stories out of test pilots. But the work is methodical, progressive, technical.'

'Will you feel like that when you take up our Mustard, Henry?'

'I should ruddy hope so, or I won't get paid!'

There was general laughter. They walked on to another part of the office, and Max took the chance to slip an arm through her husband's and steer him away from the breathy young thing.

'Don't tell me you don't enjoy all this attention,' she whispered to him.

'Of course I do. You know me. All this bushy-tailed enthusiasm makes me feel a bit less of an old duffer—'

They exchanged a glance, and he shut up. It was just such exchanges about age that usually led into their gloomy arguments about whether they should have a sprog, and if so when, or even if they should have already . . .

She squeezed his arm. 'I just wish people got so excited about my work,' she said.

He grunted. 'There was enough bally-hoo when you sent through that wooden cube. Nothing else in the *Daily Mirror* for weeks, it seemed; even forced Suez off the front page—'

'But it didn't work. The cube came through in little spheres, and—'

'But they put it in the ruddy Science Museum even so! What more do you want? Not to mention that poor hamster that died of shock, that you had stuffed.'

She giggled. 'I suppose it was all a little cruel. But I don't mean that, the stunts for the press. It's the intellectual adventure . . .'

He pulled a face, and sniffed the flower in his buttonhole. 'Ah. *Intellectual*.'

'The way we're settling the problems that baffled the Germans – how to get around the wretched Uncertainty Principle . . .'

She tried to explain the latest progress at the Plessey labs in their research into the principles of radio-transportation. In fact matter wouldn't be transported, but rather the information which encoded, say, a human being. It had been thought radio-transporters were impossible, because you'd need to map the position and velocity of every particle of a person, and that would violate the Uncertainty Principle.

But there was a loophole.

It had been a real drama: the struggles, the dead ends, the race with the Americans at Bell Labs to be first . . . before the researchers realised that an unknown quantum state could be disassembled into, then later reconstructed from, purely classical information using measurements called Einstein-Podolsky-Rosen correlations, and that said classical information could be sent down a wire as easily as a telegraph message . . .

That was the nub of it, although there was the devil in the detail of bandwidth and sampling requirements and storage capacity.

'Of course you can't copy quantum information,' she said. 'You have to *destroy* the object you're going to radio-transport. And it's just as well, or our machine would work as a copier – imagine a hundred Hitlers roaming the planet, each with an equally valid claim to being the original!'

He grunted, looking at drafting tables and jigs. 'If you ask me, a hundred Bill Haleys would be worse.'

She knew he wasn't really listening.

Now they were buttonholed by the manager here, a portly young man with thinning hair who wanted to lecture them about the Mustard.

'. . . "Mustard" for Multi-Unit Space Transport and Recovery Device, you see . . . We know the Americans are going for the dustbin theory, a virtually uncontrollable capsule. But the practical way forward in space has to be a recoverable vehicle, if only the Aviation Ministry will back us . . .'

Max listened sourly. What was a spaceship, after all, but plumbing? And all these glamorous spaceship projects were only coming about because of anticipation of the potential of radio-transport, and the international race to launch the first extraterrestrial relays into stationary orbit around the Earth.

And meanwhile in her field, all but ignored, such exciting developments were going on, right at the fringe of human understanding! Even now she had a letter in her purse from Eugene Wigner at Princeton, about his ideas on using quantum tunnelling effects to get around the light-speed barrier . . .

If only Henry could see it, they were actually on the same team – in fact, they were mutually dependent! But his suspicion of an expertise he didn't share, and of her own growing reputation, seemed only to be deepening the gap between them.

Now, in remote Woomera, the Blue Streak countdown was nearing its climax. *Ten, nine, eight* . . . The two of them gathered with the English Electric staff under a loudspeaker. 'To think,' said the portly manager, 'that once Prospero is up there, we'll be able to watch the next launch on our televisions!'

Or, Max thought, simply step to Australia in person . . .

Maybe, she thought, we should have had children after all. But is the desire to solve our own problems any good motive for wanting a child? If only I could answer such simple questions as well as I can master the paradoxes of quantum mechanics . . .

Three, two, one.

1967: Woomera, South Australia

In the upended cockpit, lying on his back with his legs in the air, Forbes listened to the voices relayed from the Operations Room, cultured British and crisp Australian. Everything was going well, and he was content to let his co-pilot – a bright young chap even if he was a Yorkshireman – field the various instructions and requests, and press whichever tit was appropriate.

Anyway, Forbes was relaxed. The G forces he would have to endure during the *Congreve*'s flight would be easier than those he'd tolerated during dogfights with 109s, when he'd hauled Spits through turns so tight he'd actually blacked out. And besides, nobody could get through as many hours on readiness – preparing for more trade with the Hun, and nothing to distract him but shove-ha'penny in the Dispersal Hut – as *he* had without learning to take it easy . . .

Forbes leaned forward and peered through his periscope. The red-brown Australian desert spread for miles around him, lifeless save for salt bushes and clumps of spiny grass. He peered down the flank of the Mustard, and lox vapour swirled across his vision.

The *Congreve*, ready for launch, looked like three Comet aircraft stood on end, belly to belly, with a crew of two in each nose. Fuelled by hydrogen and oxygen, the three units would take off together, the boosters feeding fuel to the central core; and then, at two hundred thou a hundred and fifty seconds after launch, the boosters would break away for their turbojet landings and allow the core, under Forbes's command, to carry on to orbit. Since the three aircraft were reusable and of a single design, the boffins claimed Mustards could be twenty or thirty times cheaper per pound of payload than the converted missiles the Americans and Russians used: so cheap, in fact, that the imminence of this first flight had caused the Americans to close down their own rather vainglorious ballistic-capsule manned programme, including the planned Apollo Moon missions.

. . . But now the bally thing has to work, Forbes thought gloomily. The new space outposts, to be reached by the Wire platforms nestling in the kite's belly, depended on the Mustard's heavy-lift capacity. The Herschel Space Telescope, for instance, was already being assembled at the Pilkington glass factory in Lancashire . . .

The launch complex stood on an escarpment overlooking a dry lake, isolated save for the gleaming shells of lox tanks. The launch stand was not much more than a metal platform, in fact, with a single gaunt gantry rising alongside the ship itself.

The Woomera facilities were rather crude compared to Cape Canaveral, where he'd done a little training with the Americans. The Atlantic Union had smoothed his path there, although he was sure the Americans would have been generous enough to help anyhow. Unlike, for example, the French, although he knew he was being an old bigot to frame such a thought. He'd been delighted when the government had finally given up its attempts to persuade the European Common Market to let in Britain. A union with America made much more sense, in terms of a common culture and language – especially now the Wire had made distances on the Earth's surface irrelevant.

Since May 1962, when Harold Macmillan had launched the first Wire link to Paris with a silly Union Jack stunt, the Wire and its possibilities had exploded across the world. Trade and travel had been transformed.

The Americans had been particularly inventive, as you might expect. There had been that awful Kennedy business in Dallas – the first flash crowd, they called it now – and the transporting of wounded GIs home from Vietnam to their parents' arms within minutes of their injury – and LBJ's campaign to enforce desegregation laws by putting Wire platforms in every school yard . . .

And on it went, the Wonder of the Second Elizabethan Age, and, because Max at Plessey had won her race with the Americans, it was British, by God. Sometimes it seemed you couldn't open a newspaper without having those silly slogans thrust in your face – 'Travel By Phone!' 'It's Quicker By Wire!'. The young, particularly, seemed to be flourishing in this new distance-free world, if sometimes in rather peculiar ways. Even today, those caterwauling ninnies the Beatles were Wiring their way around the world singing 'All You Need is Love' live before two hundred million people.

The Wire had touched them all. Max had actually got rich, by investing in companies developing the new digital computers required to run the spreading Wire networks.

. . . If only she could have been here to see this, his apotheosis! But, as ever, she was too busy.

The Wire had turned his own life into something of a paradox, however. Only one flight-ready Mustard had been built; only a handful of flights would be required to haul up the orbital receiver platforms, and after that the Wire could take over, hauling freight and passengers up to orbit much more cheaply than any rocket ever could.

And what then? The Americans were talking of a new international programme to push on to the Moon. Forbes, despite his age, was considered a leading candidate to work on that. To the ruddy Moon! But it would mean another decade or more of intensive training and testing. And of course Max would just say he was running away again. Chasing a youth he'd already lost . . .

What nonsense. He expected it would all get easier when the divorce came through, and he could let this odd jealousy the Wire inspired in him fade away.

But that's all for tomorrow, old lad, he told himself. First you need to get through today with your hide intact . . .

For in just eight minutes, Henry Forbes, fifty years old, would be a thousand miles high – in orbit around the Earth itself.

Two seconds before launch, six main engines ignited. There was a flare of brilliant white light. Smoke, white, but tinged with red Australian dust,

953

billowed out to left and right of the triple spacecraft. Forbes heard a deep, throaty roar, far beneath him, like a door slamming in hell—

And, just for a second, he was transported back across more than twenty years, to that raid on the V2 launch site at Haagsche Bosch, when one of the birds had actually taken off in front of him, a cool pillar of flame rising up among the contrails of the warring kites . . .

And then the vibration rose up to engulf him.

1977: Procellarum Base

From the cabin of *Endeavour*, Forbes was staring down at a disc-shaped piece of the Moon, no more than ten feet below him. The low light of the lunar morning picked out craters of all sizes, from a few yards across down to pinpricks.

Buzz Aldrin, first man to walk on the Moon, stood at the foot of the rope ladder, foreshortened from Forbes's vantage. Aldrin turned around, stiff as a mannequin, his Haldane suit glowing white in the sunlight. 'Beautiful view,' he said. 'Magnificent desolation.'

'*Endeavour*, Stevenage. That's a nice phrase, Buzz.'

'I have my moments,' said Aldrin drily, and he bounded away across the surface, testing out his locomotion, moving out of Forbes's sight.

Forbes appreciated his co-pilot's lack of portentousness about his big scene. After all, the identity of the man to take the first actual footstep up here hardly mattered; the three crew – a Brit, a Yank and a Russkie – had landed on the Moon at precisely the same instant, at the climax of this cooperative programme.

Now it was Forbes's turn. He took a moment to check the plastic carnation pinned to his white oversuit. Then, with the help of Alexei Leonov, Forbes lowered himself through the hatch and clung to the plastic rope ladder. He was stiff inside his balloon-like inflated Haldane suit, but he was an old crock of sixty and stiff as a board most of the time anyhow; being encased in a Moon cocoon hardly made a difference.

He dropped quickly, the shadows of *Endeavour*'s landing legs shifting around him, until – after a final, heart-thumping moment of hesitation – his feet crunched into the surface. The dust rose up slowly in neat little arcs, settling back on his legs.

He moved out from beneath the lander. Every time he took a step he could feel rock flour crackle under his weight. The light was oddly reversed, like a photographic negative: the pocked ground was a bright grey-brown under a sky as black as a cloudy night in Cleethorpes. The horizon was close, sharp, and it *curved*: the Moon really was very small, just a little rocky ball, and Forbes was stuck to its outside.

'*Endeavour*, Stevenage. Good to see you, Henry. How do you feel?'

'Ruddy peculiar,' said Henry Forbes.

'It would,' said Leonov drily, 'be ruddy peculiar indeed if you lent us a hand, Commander.'

Forbes turned, and saw that Aldrin and Leonov were half-way through the main task of the expedition, which was erecting the Wire transceiver. This first affair was a rough-and-ready Heath Robinson lash-up, assembled by pulling on lanyards fixed to the base of the *Endeavour* and letting the thing fold down. It didn't matter as long as it worked; the engineers who would follow would bring components for much more permanent establishments.

He bounced forward to join in the work.

. . . The Earth was a round blue ball, much fatter than a full Moon, so high in the black sky he had to tilt back to see it. It was, he saw, morning in Europe; he could make out the continent clearly under a light dusting of cloud, though England was obscured. The air in general had got a lot clearer in recent years, although of course it was no longterm solution to Wire-dump industrial pollutants at the bottom of the oceans – eventually the noxious gases would escape to the atmosphere anyway – and in fact one proposed use of the Moon was as a global waste dump. Of course, as Max never tired of explaining to him, the quantum translation process at the heart of the Wire relied on having an inert mass to transform at the receiver end. It would, he thought, be a nice puzzle for future archaeologists to find, at the heart of decommissioned nuclear power stations, lumps of irradiated Moon dust . . .

He hadn't spoken to Max for months. Perhaps even now she was watching some BBC broadcast of the Moonwalk, commentated by James Burke, Patrick Moore and Isaac Asimov.

Or perhaps not. The new developments being opened up by the billions of sterling dollars poured by the Wire corporations into quantum studies – there was talk of quantum computers, even of some kind of Dan Dare starship motor – more than absorbed Max's attention now. Forbes found it all baffling, and rather spooky. The quantum computers, for instance, were supposed to attain huge speeds by carrying out computations simultaneously *in parallel universes* . . .

When the transceiver was erected, it was time for the flags. The Union Flag and the Hammer and Sickle were allowed to drape with a courtroom grace, but Aldrin, embarrassed, had to put up a Stars and Stripes stiffened with wire, to 'wave' on the airless Moon. And now came the gravity pendulum, a simple affair knocked up by the London Science Museum to demonstrate to the TV audience that they really were up here, embedded in the Moon's weaker pull.

The three of them saluted, each in their own way, and took each other's photographs.

'*Endeavour*, Stevenage. Okay, gentlemen, the show's over; we'll see you back home in a couple of minutes . . .'

So soon? Forbes thought wistfully.

But already Leonov and Aldrin were filing obediently towards the Wire transceiver. They disappeared in the characteristic blue flashes of radio-transport, and were replaced by polythene sacks of water.

For a moment, Forbes was alone on the Moon. His breath was loud in his helmet, and he thought of the Puffing Billies, the foul-smelling oxygen economiser bellows they'd been forced to use in the high altitude Spits . . .

In just a few minutes, the engineers would start coming through, and a whole squad of journalists and lunar surface scientists, even some scholars from the Science Museum to start the instant preservation of the *Endeavour*. He looked around at the untrodden plains of the Sea of Storms and wondered how it would look here in a few weeks or months, as humans spread out from this beachhead, building busily.

The *Endeavour* stood proudly behind the flags, fifty feet tall, the blunt curve of the ceramic heat shield at her hemispherical nose swathed in shimmering Kevlar insulation blankets. There was raying, streaks in the dust, under the gaping nozzle of the high-performance Rolls Royce liquid rocket engine which had, Forbes thought with some pride, performed like a dream.

But *Endeavour* was the first and last of her kind. A new generation of complex, intelligent unmanned craft, with names like *Voyager* and *Mariner* and *Venera*, were already sailing out from Earth, taking Wire platforms to Mars and Venus and the moons of Jupiter. Buzz Aldrin had been lucky; the first man or woman on Mars would almost certainly be a politician, not a pilot . . .

Once again, thanks to the inexorable advance of technology, Forbes's usefulness was over.

Of course when he got home, this lunar flight would be regarded as the peak of his career. He would be expected to retire: to pass on the torch, to the rather peculiar set of young people who were growing up with the Wire . . .

But he wasn't ready for his carpet slippers just yet, no matter what the calendar told him. He knew what Max would say to *that* – it was all of a piece with their eventual failure to have children, a part of his refusal to accept his own ageing – and similar modern psychobabble nonsense. But he had a private medical report which indicated that retiring to the cottage in the country might not be a sensible option anyway . . .

He closed his eyes, and stepped through the transceiver's sketchy portal. There was a stab of pain as the electron-beam scanners swept over him.

For two seconds, as an S-band signal leapt from Moon to Earth, he did not, presumably, exist.

Suddenly weight descended on him, six times as much as on the Moon, and he staggered under the bulk of his suit. But there were hands on his arms to support him, noise all around him.

He opened his eyes. Beyond the walls of the quarantine facility, the sky of England was grey and enclosing.

1987: Brunel Dock, Low Earth Orbit
He awoke when the slow thermal roll of the dock brought bright water-blue Earthlight slanting into his cabin.

He floated out of his sleeping bag. He ran his fingers through what was left of his hair, and made himself tea. This consisted of pumping a polythene bag full of hot water and sucking the resulting pale brown mush through a nipple. Revolting; even the strongest brew never masked the taste of plastic. And of course with the low pressure up here the Rosie Lee was never properly *hot* . . .

Still, he lingered. Although he had some suspicion that his work here, as a consultant on *Discovery*'s control systems, was something of a sinecure, his days were busy enough; at seventy, he had learned to give himself time to wake up.

Of course, the view was always a terrific distraction.

Today, in bright noon sunlight, under smog-free air, England glittered with scattered homes. Even from up here, Forbes could see how the great old cities had shrunk – even London – with those huge misty-grey scars of suburbs eaten into by the new green reforestation swathes. Commuting, by train or car anyway, was a thing of the past; the capital's workers flickered directly into the heart of the city, popping out of Wire transceivers in the old Tube stations. The M1 motorway, in fact, had been turned into a singularly long race-track . . . There were even, he had read, people who maintained 'distributed careers' with desks in a dozen capital cities around the world, jumping from morning to night. It would never have suited Forbes.

There were costs, of course. Even from up here Forbes could see the blue sparkle of swimming pools, sprinkled across the mountains and valleys of Scotland and Wales and Northumberland . . . The people of Britain had scattered across their tiny islands in search of illusory wilderness, but there was just no ruddy room. There had been some attempt to preserve the more beautiful areas. In the Lake District, for instance, tourists were Wired into great glass viewing boxes, peering out at Wordsworth's beloved landscape like so many goldfish from a bowl . . .

And some Wire-related costs were not visible from orbit. He remembered the panic when rabies had swept over England soon after the opening-up of the first French links. And there had been some rather more serious plagues, such as the explosion in AIDS cases in the early 1980s. Some commentators said that the various viruses and bacteria which feasted on man were enjoying an unprecedented explosion in evolutionary growth, such was the expansion of possible infection vectors. Others said that on a Wired planet, man must evolve in response, or perish.

Some of the lingering anti-Wire hysteria was absurd, of course, even to a crusty old sceptic like himself. Since 1963, a year after the Wire's opening, there had been no serious accidents with the system itself – such as the loss or corruption of a human pattern in transit – and it had been quite irresponsible for Twentieth-Century Fox to remake *The Fly*, in such gruesome detail . . .

The Wire could be a force for good, its fans argued. It was being used to defuse the Cold War, with teams of UN inspectors Wiring back and forth between the nuclear silos held by each side, and rushing peacekeepers to any potential trouble spot. And the Wire had averted so many possible catastrophes – getting the American hostages out of Iran in '81, averting a war between the Atlantic Union and the Argentine over the Falklands in '82, distributing aid to those wretched famine victims in Ethiopia in '84 – that it was, it seemed, in danger of provoking an outbreak of Utopianism, all across the planet.

So Max had said anyhow, the last time he'd seen her. But they'd argued.

They had been like ambassadors from two alien species, stiff and made suddenly old. She'd been more interested in lecturing him about the work she was doing with Feynman and Deutsch on quantum computers than asking about *him*. It was strange that two people whose lives had been so shaped by a communications technology should find themselves so incapable of communication themselves, and Forbes couldn't help but wonder if a child – grown by now! – might have served to link them better.

But in a sense Max *did* have children. Sometimes he envied her the easy bond she seemed to form with the new generation, her own students and colleagues and others. *There are no boundaries for the young now,* she'd said, *only access. War,* she said, *is inconceivable for these people … The Wire is transforming them, Henry.*

And so on. Of course it hardly mattered to Forbes whether she was right or not, since he wasn't allowed home any more.

Over the years, he had been rather a silly ass about the length of time he had spent in zero gravity. And he never had been very conscientious about physical jerks … The quacks had explained how his skeletal and cardiac muscles were deeply atrophied, and he had piddled away so much of his bone calcium that the inner spongy bone had vanished altogether, without hope of regeneration.

On Earth, he would be wheelchair-bound and a nuisance to everybody. Better here, working on the construction of star clipper *Discovery*, even if he suspected the youngsters up here tolerated rather than valued him.

He took one last, lingering look at sunlit Britain, remembering the exhilaration of hauling a Spit in a battle climb up into the blue skies of June, 1940, with the clatter of the prop loud in his ears, the stink of engine oil and leather in his nostrils … Ruddy peculiar. Here he was in orbit. He'd even been to the Moon. But somehow nothing ever compared to those vivid moments of his youth.

The slow roll of the dock removed Britain from his view, and replaced it with the sleek, streamlined form of *Discovery*, the future appropriately replacing the past.

Forbes finished his tea and, with a sigh, prepared for the daily ordeal of the zero-gravity toilet. The Americans were wonderful people, but they couldn't design plumbing for toffee …

1997: Discovery, Martian Orbit
The launch of humanity's first starship struck Forbes as a remarkably low-key event, compared to the thrilling take-offs he remembered aboard

Endeavour and *Congreve*, not to mention all those exhausting scrambles at wartime airfields. After all, there was drama: even now, hydrogen was circulating in the nozzle of the huge NERVA 4 nuclear fission rocket, cooling it before passing on to the core to be superheated and expelled, and so driving the great ship forward.

Surely even Captain Cook had made a little more fuss about his departure for the Pacific, in an earlier *Discovery*. And after all, this was the first journey to the stars . . .

But there wasn't even a countdown. Forbes had simply to sit in his frame couch with the rest of the crew, a few rows behind the commander and his co-pilot – both women, incidentally – and listen to their brisk young voices working through checks with the ground crew at Port Lowell.

Even the setting was mundane, like the interior of a small aircraft, with fold-out equipment racks and miniaturised galleys and lavatories and zero-gravity up-down visual cues. Only the creased orange skin of Mars, visible through the windows, made for an element of the extraordinary, the ancient landscape now mottled by the green domes of the colonies which had provisioned *Discovery* after its shakedown interplanetary hop.

Humanity's first starship was shaped something like a huge arrow. The habitable compartment – its interior, designed by Cunard, frankly luxurious – made a streamlined arrowhead, separated for safety from the NERVA 4 by the arrow's 'shaft': a hundred yards of open scaffolding, crammed with shielding, antennae and liquid-hydrogen fuel tanks.

The streamlining amused Forbes, for it made the habitable compartment look like nothing so much as the V2-shaped spaceships that had rattled their way through the beloved Saturday morning specials of his youth – a shape which had become derided in the 1960s and 1970s, as insectile ships such as the *Endeavour*, adapted to airless space, had taken shape on the drafting boards.

But it turned out that the experts, not for the first time, were wrong. Interstellar space was not empty. There *was* gas and dust – desperately thin, only fifty or sixty bacterium-sized specks per cubic mile – but that was enough to give a respectable battering to the prow of any starship unwise enough to approach a decent fraction of the speed of light, as *Discovery* intended to achieve. So the ship was streamlined, and coated with a thick impact shield, and even mounted with a rather powerful dust-busting short-wave radiation generator in her nose.

A decent fraction of the speed of light . . . Such velocities would be far beyond the capacity even of the NERVA 4 – a huge, over-engineered American monstrosity, originally intended to take much smaller spacecraft no further than Mars – if not for the HRP effect.

HRP: for Haisch, Rueda and Puthoff, as Max had explained to him, the physicists who had made the crucial quantum vacuum breakthrough. The 'empty' vacuum was not empty at all, it seemed, but a wash of seething energy, with 'virtual' particles popping in and out of existence constantly. This so-called 'zero point field' created an electromagnetic drag on any object which passed through it . . . and it was that drag which *created* the effect of mass and inertia, the reason it took so much effort to start anything moving.

The big Wire operators – immensely rich, with forty years' expertise in quantum effects – had seized on the HRP results immediately. And *Discovery* was the result, rendered virtually massless by its inertial suppressors, and so capable of being driven to enormous velocities by a modest engine indeed . . .

And now, low-key or not, the pilots' preparations were reaching a climax.

The rest of the crew, young and healthy and intelligent, seemed unconcerned. They simply sat in their couches in their couples – or breeding pairs, as Forbes sourly thought of them. They would tolerate this thirty-year voyage to Alpha Centauri, confined as they would be within the streamlined hull of *Discovery*, living their lives, studying quietly, maintaining their craft, even raising children. They wouldn't even have to suffer the rigours of zero gravity – the manipulation of the HRP fields would see to *that* . . .

He tried to talk to them, of course.

Such as about the flap he'd got into in 1941 when he brought down a Heinkel 111 near St Abbs Head in Berwickshire. Circling overhead, he saw the crew scramble clear, and he realised they were going to set fire to their almost intact bomber, so he decided to land alongside and stop them. But the Spit hit a patch of mud as it rolled down the field and turned over onto its back. Forbes was unhurt, but had hung helplessly upside down in his straps until the Heinkel's crew came to rescue him. Then, with Local Defence Volunteers approaching, the Germans surrendered to Forbes, handing him their Luger pistols, but the LDV boys had thought he was one of the enemy and promptly arrested *him*, and it was only when he produced an Inland Revenue tax return form from his pocket that he managed to extricate himself . . .

And so on. These youngsters, bound for the stars, listened politely. But to them, Forbes, with his stories of war and heroism and the Inland Revenue, was a figure from some impossibly remote Dark Age.

Perhaps Max was right: that these patient, fearless youngsters – shaped in a Wire-connected world without frontiers or limits, growing richer and richer by the year – really were a different lot from their forefathers.

Even, said Max, a new species.

Perhaps. It often seemed absurd even to him that such an old fool as he was undertaking such a trip at all. It was just that payload costs, even on a starship, had been made invisibly low by the HRP effect. And besides, the *Martian Times* had put up rather a handsome advance for the observations he would be broadcasting back en route . . .

He was sure, though, he would not live to see the light of Alpha Centauri, and nor would he get to Wire-step back to Earth. But that was no cause for regret. For him, the escape from a baffling Earth was the thing.

Forbes, who remembered different days, had grown uncomfortable with some of the complacent assumptions of modern times. Was the Wire-delivered hegemony of the Western world really such a good idea? There had been the Gulf War, for instance, in which US marines had used a hidden Wire gateway to storm Saddam's bunker, deposing him with scarcely a shot and then 'liberating' that country . . . There was no doubt that Saddam had been a monster. But Forbes recalled that rather similar schemes had been hatched by the Nazis. How must such actions look to the average Iraqi?

But such arguments were just excuses, Max said. Once again, she had told him, he was attempting to outrun the future. He really must let go at last, learn to trust the young people, not fear them . . . and so on. He had stopped listening to all that long ago.

But in the end, he was sorry to lose her. He could not say they were friends, and certainly no longer in love; she was, simply, Max. And increasingly her lined face was overlaid in his mind by images of a bright, excitable young redhead in khakis . . .

He was becoming, he decided, a sentimental old fool.

Forbes felt a low thrumming, transmitted to him through the frame of his couch. It was smooth, subdued, and yet it inevitably reminded him of the scream of a Spitfire's Merlin engine, the subterranean rumble of a Mustang's gigantic liquid-fuel rockets.

The cabin seemed to tip as acceleration built up. The autumn light of Mars faded.

Forbes felt a surge of exhilaration. Bugger old age. He was going to the stars!

2007: Oxford, England

. . . I go to the seminars when I can – after all, Wire travel is hardly a challenge, even for an old lady like me. In fact the last one I attended was at the University's new Shaw Library – have you heard of it? A room in the Bodleian is connected, via Wired doors, to rooms on the Moon, Mars, Ganymede, Triton . . .

But though I religiously turn up, Henry, you probably won't believe me when I say that the new ideas even leave me behind most of the time! Let me mention some of them to you:

First of all, *the Wiring of minds*. That may seem rather spooky to you – and to me! – but believe me, it's a very real possibility, now that we understand the equations that govern consciousness processes – for consciousness itself, of course, is a quantum phenomenon. It's all an outgrowth of quantum computing. I'm sure you know, Henry, your precious *Discovery* is guided by a million-quantum-dot Factorisation Engine, no matter how *spooky* you think it is! And because computational power is combinatorial – oh, dear Henry, I don't think I have time to explain it all – suffice it to say that two minds are *much* better than one! And so are three, or four . . . or a billion. Some commentators feel we're on the verge of the most dramatic leap in human evolution since *Homo Habilis*.

What else?

Well, you've probably read about the new *nanogates* – miniature Wire gates, which can transmit an atom at a time . . . There was a piece in the *Lancet* outlining medical applications. It would be possible to inject a patient with smart nanogates which could hunt out and radio-transport away toxins, or cancerous cells . . . ! A little too late for me, unfortunately . . .

And then there is the possibility of *faster-than-light travel* – there, what do you think of that! It's all based on something called quantum tunnelling. If you try to contain a photon by a barrier, there is a small but finite probability – because of quantum uncertainty – that you'll suddenly find it on the far side of the barrier. And if you do, there is no appreciable delay . . . I've been following the theoretical research for decades, but the practical breakthrough came in the '90s when an Austrian team transmitted a rather scratchy recording of Mozart's 40th Symphony at 4.7 times the speed of light! And this year, Bell Labs are going to try to send a wooden cube across a few miles – just like our first experiments with the Wire.

Henry, I hope you don't find that by the time you reach Centauri in your rather lumbering inertial-drive Sopwith Camel, you haven't been overtaken by a faster-than-light Spitfire! . . .

So my work continues to absorb me. And, Henry, you must believe me when I say – and I know I repeat myself – these young people are wonderful, so much better than we were, if sometimes a little scary. Do you know, the new Prime Minister wasn't even born when the first Wire service was opened up! Do you remember that ridiculous affair with the flag? It seems hardly yesterday . . . *Prime Minister*: foolish me, I meant the Governor, of course. Dates me, doesn't it!

They say that for the young in the schools now, even the concept of *nation* seems absurd. They can't believe that a mere half-century ago we'd just come out of a war – it seems to them like a hideous human sacrifice . . . It makes us old folk uncomfortable sometimes, but it's hard to deny the logic! Our young live in a rich, clean world, and there's no reason why anyone should go short of the fundamentals of life, not until the Solar System itself starts to run dry – and even then we'll have the stars, thanks to you and *Discovery* . . .

I know it's hard to accept change. This new world often seems very strange to me, and I sometimes wonder where humanity will be in ten, or twenty, or thirty years time, when even human thought has been Wired. In a way I understand why you've continued to flee, my dear – at last, all the way to the stars! But there was nothing to fear. Perhaps if you had had a child of your own, or if we had had one, you might be able to see it . . .

Now, you mustn't be distressed by my little bit of news, Henry my dear. I'm not in any pain or discomfort. I've been involved in a lot of wizard japes in my time, which is just the sort of thing your old RAF pals used to say, so you see I was paying attention to you after all, even all those years ago! My only regret is I won't get to see any more of the wonderful future that's opening up – and I won't see you again, and, yes, that is important to me . . .

He lay in his cabin, an old mechanical clock softly ticking. He could smell nothing, taste nothing, every breath hurt, and all he could see was a series of vague blurs. He was a crock and no mistake, and he'd really had enough of this caper . . .

Somehow he knew today was the day.

It didn't seem so tragic to Forbes. It was rather like the elephants, he thought. He once knew a chap who had been to India – and this was before the Empire broke up, before the war – and this chap came back with stories of the elephants, and how they would know when it was their time. They would leave their herds and seek out a quiet place, without any fuss . . .

Perhaps it was true. And perhaps humans shared the same instinct, and if so, it was a remarkable comfort. After all, he'd had a good innings; he might have bought it at any time in the '40s, and a lot of good men had done just that.

His breath was scratching in his throat. It was a blithering nuisance—

The walls dissolved around him.

He felt a stab of shock – and irritation. He was *scared*. But what on Earth was the point of *his* being frightened *now*?

. . . But he was suspended in stars, stars above and below and all around him. Ahead, they were tinged the subtlest blue.

. . . *You shouldn't fear us.*

A uniform light came up – just a little, leaving the sky a deep midnight blue, but enough to wash out the stars.

A cramped cabin. A stick in his hand. Something in his ears – he lifted his hand – it was cotton wool . . .

Good God. He was back in a Vampire, its duck-egg-green hull all around him. There was even a fresh carnation in his buttonhole.

You didn't have to flee into the dark.

The nose of the Vampire dipped, and the Earth itself was spread out beneath him, curving gently, glowing with a network of light, a Wire continuum.

We are you. You are us. Because of your courage, mankind will live forever. We honour you. We want you to join us.

So they, the young people – or whatever ruddy thing they had become – had brought him all the way home, from the stars. To be able to do such a thing, they were like gods. It occurred to him he ought to be frightened of them, as he always had been, a little.

But they were human children, all the same.

Perhaps Max had been right. Perhaps it was time, at last, for him to place his destiny in other hands.

There was no Max down there, though. Even *they* couldn't reach beyond the grave. Not yet, anyhow.

Welcome home . . .

He would be safe down there, when he landed. But there was no rush. A few more minutes wouldn't harm. Perhaps he could take the kite for a couple of turns over London . . .

He stuffed the Vampire's nose down and began his long fall back into the atmosphere.

Improving the Neighbourhood

First published in *Nature*, 4 November 1999

The first science fiction *Nature* ever published. I wonder how many heart attacks it induced among its more conservative readers.

At last, after feats of information processing that taxed our resources to the limit, we have solved the long-standing mystery of the Double Nova. Even now, we have interpreted only a small fraction of the radio and optical messages from the culture that perished so spectacularly, but the main facts – astonishing though they are – seem beyond dispute.

Our late neighbours evolved on a world much like our own planet, at such a distance from its sun that water was normally liquid. After a long period of barbarism, they began to develop technologies using readily available materials and sources of energy. Their first machines – like ours – depended on chemical reactions involving the elements hydrogen, carbon and oxygen.

Inevitably, they constructed vehicles for moving on land and sea, as well as through the atmosphere and out into space. After discovering electricity, they quickly developed telecommunications devices, including the radio transmitters that first alerted us to their existence. Although the moving images these provided revealed their appearance and behaviour, most of our understanding of their history and eventual fate has been derived from the complex symbols that they used to record information.

Shortly before the end, they encountered an energy crisis, partly triggered by their enormous physical size and violent activity. For a while, the widespread use of uranium fission and hydrogen fusion postponed the inevitable. Then, driven by necessity, they made desperate attempts to find superior alternatives. After several false starts, involving low-temperature nuclear reactions of scientific interest but no practical value, they succeeded in tapping the quantum fluctuations that occur at the very foundations of space-time. This gave them access to a virtually infinite source of energy.

What happened next is still a matter of conjecture. It may have been an industrial accident, or an attempt by one of their many competing organisations to gain advantage over another. In any event, by mishandling the ultimate forces of the Universe, they triggered a cataclysm which detonated their own planet – and, very shortly afterwards, its single large moon.

Although the annihilation of any intelligent beings should be deplored, it is impossible to feel much regret in this particular case. The history of these huge creatures contains countless episodes of violence, against their own species and the numerous others that occupied their planet. Whether they would have made the necessary transition – as we did, ages ago – from carbon- to germanium-based consciousness, has been the subject of much debate. It is quite surprising what they were able to achieve, as massive individual entities exchanging information at a pitiably low data rate – often by very short-range vibrations in their atmosphere!

They were apparently on the verge of developing the necessary technology that would have allowed them to abandon their clumsy, chemically fuelled bodies and thus achieve multiple connectivity: had they succeeded, they might well have been a serious danger to all the civilizations of our Local Cluster.

Let us ensure that such a situation never arises again.

Dedicated to Drs Pons and Fleischmann, Nobel laureates of the twenty-first century.